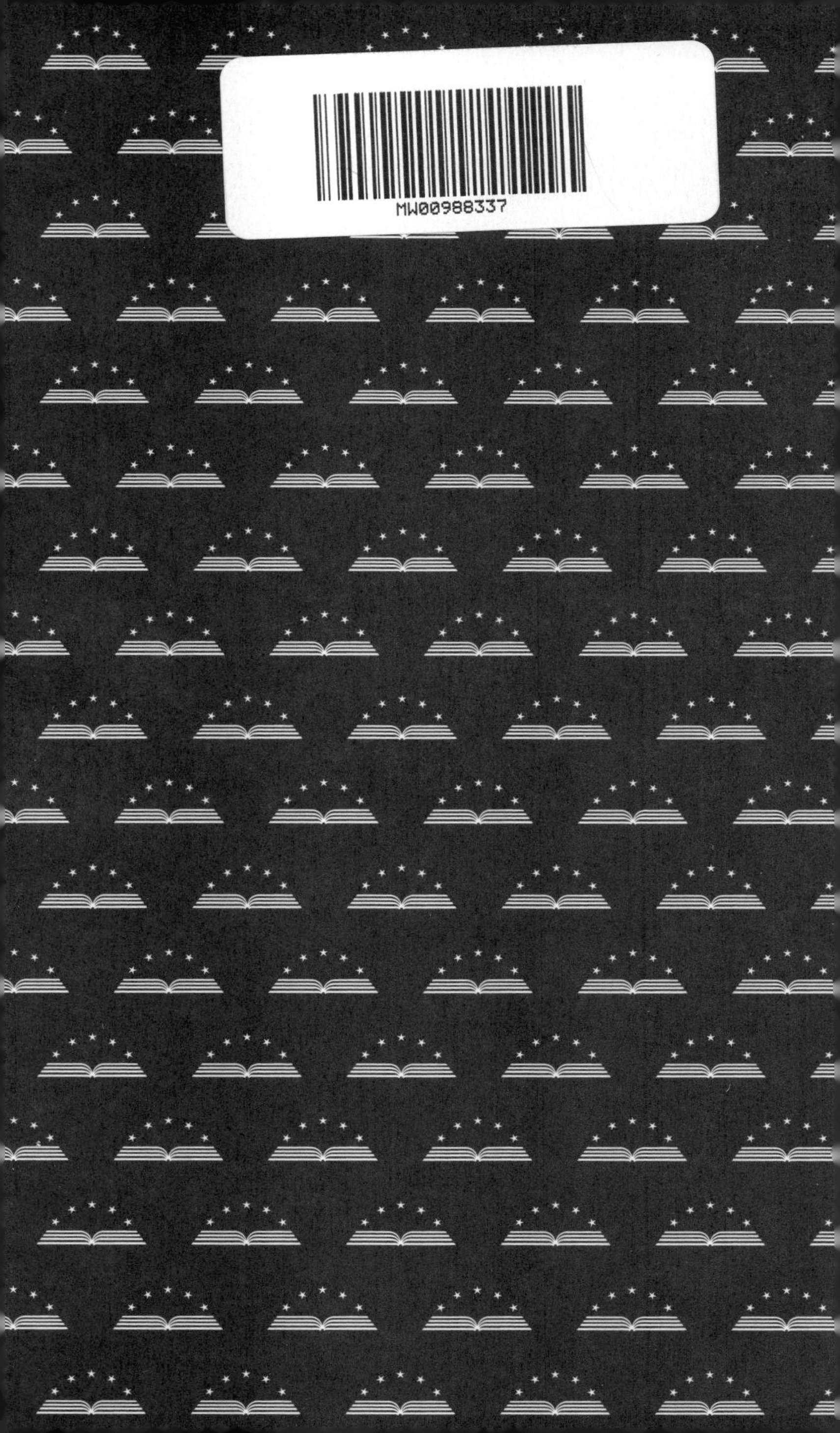
MW00988337

WILLIAM WELLS BROWN

William Wells Brown

CLOTEL & OTHER WRITINGS

Ezra Greenspan, *editor*

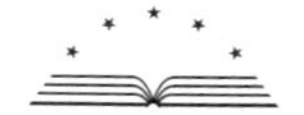

THE LIBRARY OF AMERICA

Some of the material in this volume is reprinted
by permission of the holders of copyright and publication rights.
See Note on the Texts on page 983 for acknowledgments.

The paper used in this publication meets the
minimum requirements of the American National Standard for
Information Sciences–Permanence of Paper for Printed
Library Materials, ANSI Z39.48—1984.

Distributed to the trade in the United States
by Penguin Group (USA) Inc.
and in Canada by Penguin Books Canada Ltd.

Library of Congress Control Number: 2013941525
ISBN 978–1–59853–291–3

First Printing
The Library of America—247

Manufactured in the United States of America

Contents

NARRATIVE

OF

WILLIAM W. BROWN,

A

FUGITIVE SLAVE.

WRITTEN BY HIMSELF.

————Is there not some chosen curse,
Some hidden thunder in the stores of heaven,
Red with uncommon wrath, to blast the man
Who gains his fortune from the blood of souls?

COWPER.

Wm. W. Brown.

TO WELLS BROWN, OF OHIO.

THIRTEEN years ago, I came to your door, a weary fugitive from chains and stripes. I was a stranger, and you took me in. I was hungry, and you fed me. Naked was I, and you clothed me. Even a name by which to be known among men, slavery had denied me. You bestowed upon me your own. Base indeed should I be, if I ever forget what I owe to you, or do anything to disgrace that honored name!

As a slight testimony of my gratitude to my earliest benefactor, I take the liberty to inscribe to you this little Narrative of the sufferings from which I was fleeing when you had compassion upon me. In the multitude that you have succored, it is very possible that you may not remember me; but until I forget God and myself, I can never forget you.

Your grateful friend,
WILLIAM WELLS BROWN.

LETTER FROM EDMUND QUINCY, ESQ.

DEDHAM, JULY 1, 1847.

TO WILLIAM W. BROWN.

MY DEAR FRIEND:—I heartily thank you for the privilege of reading the manuscript of your Narrative. I have read it with deep interest and strong emotion. I am much mistaken if it be not greatly successful and eminently useful. It presents a different phase of the infernal slave-system from that portrayed in the admirable story of Mr. Douglass, and gives us a glimpse of its hideous cruelties in other portions of its domain.

Your opportunities of observing the workings of this accursed system have been singularly great. Your experiences in the Field, in the House, and especially on the River in the service of the slave-trader, Walker, have been such as few individuals have had;—no one, certainly, who has been competent to describe them. What I have admired, and marvelled at, in your Narrative, is the simplicity and calmness with which you describe scenes and actions which might well "move the very stones to rise and mutiny" against the National Institution which makes them possible.

You will perceive that I have made very sparing use of your flattering permission to alter what you had written. To correct a few errors, which appeared to be merely clerical ones, committed in the hurry of composition, under unfavorable circumstances, and to suggest a few curtailments, is all that I have ventured to do. I should be a bold man, as well as a vain one, if I should attempt to improve your descriptions of what you have seen and suffered. Some of the scenes are not unworthy of De Foe himself.

I trust and believe that your Narrative will have a wide circulation. I am sure it deserves it. At least, a man must be differently constituted from me, who can rise from the perusal of your Narrative without feeling that he understands slavery better, and hates it worse, than he ever did before.

I am, very faithfully and respectfully,

Your friend,

EDMUND QUINCY.

PREFACE.

THE FRIENDS of freedom may well congratulate each other on the appearance of the following Narrative. It adds another volume to the rapidly increasing anti-slavery literature of the age. It has been remarked by a close observer of human nature, "Let me make the songs of a nation, and I care not who makes its laws;" and it may with equal truth be said, that, among a reading people like our own, their books will at least give character to their laws. It is an influence which goes forth noiselessly upon its mission, but fails not to find its way to many a warm heart, to kindle on the altar thereof the fires of freedom, which will one day break forth in a living flame to consume oppression.

This little book is a voice from the prison-house, unfolding the deeds of darkness which are there perpetrated. Our cause has received efficient aid from this source. The names of those who have come from thence, and battled manfully for the right, need not to be recorded here. The works of some of them are an enduring monument of praise, and their perpetual record shall be found in the grateful hearts of the redeemed bondman.

Few persons have had greater facilities for becoming acquainted with slavery, in all its horrible aspects, than WILLIAM W. BROWN. He has been behind the curtain. He has visited its secret chambers. Its iron has entered his own soul. The dearest ties of nature have been riven in his own person. A mother has been cruelly scourged before his own eyes. A father,—alas! slaves have no father. A brother has been made the subject of its tender mercies. A sister has been given up to the irresponsible control of the pale-faced oppressor. This nation looks on approvingly. The American Union sanctions the deed. The Constitution shields the criminals. American religion sanctifies the crime. But the tide is turning. Already, a mighty undercurrent is sweeping onward. The voice of warning, of remonstrance, of rebuke, of entreaty, has gone forth. Hand is linked in hand, and heart mingles with heart, in this great work of the slave's deliverance.

The convulsive throes of the monster, even now, give evidence of deep wounds.

The writer of this Narrative was hired by his master to a "*soul-driver*," and has witnessed all the horrors of the traffic, from the buying up of human cattle in the slave-breeding States, which produced a constant scene of separating the victims from all those whom they loved, to their final sale in the southern market, to be worked up in seven years, or given over to minister to the lust of southern *Christians.*

Many harrowing scenes are graphically portrayed; and yet with that simplicity and ingenuousness which carries with it a conviction of the truthfulness of the picture.

This book will do much to unmask those who have "clothed themselves in the livery of the court of heaven" to cover up the enormity of their deeds.

During the past three years, the author has devoted his entire energies to the anti-slavery cause. Laboring under all the disabilities and disadvantages growing out of his education in slavery—subjected, as he had been from his birth, to all the wrongs and deprivations incident to his condition—he yet went forth, impelled to the work by a love of liberty—stimulated by the remembrance of his own sufferings—urged on by the consideration that a mother, brothers, and sister, were still grinding in the prison-house of bondage, in common with three millions of our Father's children—sustained by an unfaltering faith in the omnipotence of truth and the final triumph of justice—to plead the cause of the slave, and by the eloquence of earnestness carried conviction to many minds, and enlisted the sympathy and secured the co-operation of many to the cause.

His labors have been chiefly confined to Western New York, where he has secured many warm friends, by his untiring zeal, persevering energy, continued fidelity, and universal kindness.

Reader, are you an Abolitionist? What have you done for the slave? What are you doing in his behalf? What do you purpose to do? There is a great work before us! Who will be an idler now? This is the great humanitary movement of the age, swallowing up, for the time being, all other questions, comparatively speaking. The course of human events, in obedience to the unchangeable laws of our being, is fast hastening the final crisis, and

> "Have ye chosen, O my people, on whose party ye shall stand,
> Ere the Doom from its worn sandal shakes the dust against our land?"

Are you a Christian? This is the carrying out of practical Christianity; and there is no other. Christianity is *practical* in its very nature and essence. It is a life, springing out of a soul imbued with its spirit. Are you a friend of the missionary cause? This is the greatest missionary enterprize of the day. Three millions of *Christian*, law-manufactured heathen are longing for the glad tidings of the Gospel of freedom. Are you a friend of the Bible? Come, then, and help us to restore to these millions, whose eyes have been bored out by slavery, their sight, that they may see to read the Bible. Do you love God whom you have not seen? Then manifest that love, by restoring to your brother whom you have seen, his rightful inheritance, of which he has been so long and so cruelly deprived.

It is not for a single generation alone, numbering three millions—sublime as would be that effort—that we are working. It is for HUMANITY, the wide world over, not only now, but for all coming time, and all future generations:—

> "For he who settles Freedom's principles,
> Writes the death-warrant of all tyranny."

It is a vast work—a glorious enterprize—worthy the unswerving devotion of the entire life-time of the great and the good.

Slaveholding and slaveholders must be rendered disreputable and odious. They must be stripped of their respectability and Christian reputation. They must be treated as "MEN-STEALERS—guilty of the highest kind of theft, and sinners of the first rank." Their more guilty accomplices in the persons of *northern apologists*, both in Church and State, must be placed in the same category. Honest men must be made to look upon their crimes with the same abhorrence and loathing, with which they regard the less guilty robber and assassin, until

> "The common damned shun their society,
> And look upon themselves as fiends less foul."

When a just estimate is placed upon the crime of slaveholding, the work will have been accomplished, and the glorious day ushered in—

> "When man nor woman in all our wide domain,
> Shall buy, or sell, or hold, or be a slave."

J. C. HATHAWAY.

—Farmington, N. Y., 1847.

NARRATIVE.

CHAPTER I.

I WAS born in Lexington, Ky. The man who stole me as soon as I was born, recorded the births of all the infants which he claimed to be born his property, in a book which he kept for that purpose. My mother's name was Elizabeth. She had seven children, viz: Solomon, Leander, Benjamin, Joseph, Millford, Elizabeth, and myself. No two of us were children of the same father. My father's name, as I learned from my mother, was George Higgins. He was a white man, a relative of my master, and connected with some of the first families in Kentucky.

My master owned about forty slaves, twenty-five of whom were field hands. He removed from Kentucky to Missouri, when I was quite young, and settled thirty or forty miles above St. Charles, on the Missouri, where, in addition to his practice as a physician, he carried on milling, merchandizing and farming. He had a large farm, the principal productions of which were tobacco and hemp. The slave cabins were situated on the back part of the farm, with the house of the overseer, whose name was Grove Cook, in their midst. He had the entire charge of the farm, and having no family, was allowed a woman to keep house for him, whose business it was to deal out the provisions for the hands.

A woman was also kept at the quarters to do the cooking for the field hands, who were summoned to their unrequited toil every morning at four o'clock, by the ringing of a bell, hung on a post near the house of the overseer. They were allowed half an hour to eat their breakfast, and get to the field. At half past four, a horn was blown by the overseer, which was the signal to commence work; and every one that was not on the spot at the time, had to receive ten lashes from the negro-whip, with which the overseer always went armed. The handle was about three feet long, with the butt-end filled with lead, and the lash six or seven feet in length, made of cowhide, with platted wire on the end of it. This whip was put in requisition very frequently and freely, and a small offence on the part of a slave furnished an occasion for its use. During the time that

Mr. Cook was overseer, I was a house servant—a situation preferable to that of a field hand, as I was better fed, better clothed, and not obliged to rise at the ringing of the bell, but about half an hour after. I have often laid and heard the crack of the whip, and the screams of the slave. My mother was a field hand, and one morning was ten or fifteen minutes behind the others in getting into the field. As soon as she reached the spot where they were at work, the overseer commenced whipping her. She cried, "Oh! pray—Oh! pray—Oh! pray"—these are generally the words of slaves, when imploring mercy at the hands of their oppressors. I heard her voice, and knew it, and jumped out of my bunk, and went to the door. Though the field was some distance from the house, I could hear every crack of the whip, and every groan and cry of my poor mother. I remained at the door, not daring to venture any farther. The cold chills ran over me, and I wept aloud. After giving her ten lashes, the sound of the whip ceased, and I returned to my bed, and found no consolation but in my tears. It was not yet daylight.

CHAPTER II.

My master being a political demagogue, soon found those who were ready to put him into office, for the favors he could render them; and a few years after his arrival in Missouri, he was elected to a seat in the Legislature. In his absence from home, everything was left in charge of Mr. Cook, the overseer, and he soon became more tyrannical and cruel. Among the slaves on the plantation, was one by the name of Randall. He was a man about six feet high, and well-proportioned, and known as a man of great strength and power. He was considered the most valuable and able-bodied slave on the plantation; but no matter how good or useful a slave may be, he seldom escapes the lash. But it was not so with Randall. He had been on the plantation since my earliest recollection, and I had never known of his being flogged. No thanks were due to the master or overseer for this. I have often heard him declare, that no white man should ever whip him—that he would die first.

Cook, from the time that he came upon the plantation, had frequently declared, that he could and would flog any nigger that was put into the field to work under him. My master had repeatedly told him not to attempt to whip Randall, but he was determined to try it. As soon as he was left sole dictator, he thought the time had come to put his threats into execution. He soon began to find fault with Randall, and threatened to whip him, if he did not do better. One day he gave him a very hard task,—more than he could possibly do; and at night, the task not being performed, he told Randall that he should remember him the next morning. On the following morning, after the hands had taken breakfast, Cook called out to Randall, and told him that he intended to whip him, and ordered him to cross his hands and be tied. Randall asked why he wished to whip him. He answered, because he had not finished his task the day before. Randall said that the task was too great, or he should have done it. Cook said it made no difference,—he should whip him. Randall stood silent for a moment, and then said, "Mr. Cook, I have always tried to please you since you have been on the plantation, and I find you are determined not to be satisfied with my work, let me do as well as I may. No man has laid hands on me, to whip me, for the last ten years, and I have long since come to the conclusion not to be whipped by any man living." Cook, finding by Randall's determined look and gestures, that he would resist, called three of the hands from their work, and commanded them to seize Randall, and tie him. The hands stood still;—they knew Randall—and they also knew him to be a powerful man, and were afraid to grapple with him. As soon as Cook had ordered the men to seize him, Randall turned to them, and said—"Boys, you all know me; you know that I can handle any three of you, and the man that lays hands on me shall die. This white man can't whip me himself, and therefore he has called you to help him." The overseer was unable to prevail upon them to seize and secure Randall, and finally ordered them all to go to their work together.

Nothing was said to Randall by the overseer, for more than a week. One morning, however, while the hands were at work in the field, he came into it, accompanied by three friends of his, Thompson, Woodbridge and Jones. They came up to where Randall was at work, and Cook ordered him to leave his work, and go with them to the barn. He refused to go; whereupon he was attacked by the overseer and his companions, when he turned upon them, and laid them, one after another, prostrate on the ground. Woodbridge drew out his pistol, and fired at him, and brought him to the ground by a pistol ball. The others rushed upon him with their clubs, and beat him over the head and face, until they succeeded in tying him. He was then taken to the barn, and tied to a beam. Cook gave him over one hundred lashes with a heavy cowhide, had him washed with salt and water, and left him tied during the day. The next day he was untied, and taken to a blacksmith's shop, and had a ball and chain attached to his leg. He was compelled to labor in the field, and perform the same amount of work that the other hands did. When his master returned home, he was much pleased to find that Randall had been subdued in his absence.

CHAPTER III.

SOON afterwards, my master removed to the city of St. Louis, and purchased a farm four miles from there, which he placed under the charge of an overseer by the name of Friend Haskell. He was a regular Yankee from New England. The Yankees are noted for making the most cruel overseers.

My mother was hired out in the city, and I was also hired out there to Major Freeland, who kept a public house. He was formerly from Virginia, and was a horse-racer, cock-fighter, gambler, and withal an inveterate drunkard. There were ten or twelve servants in the house, and when he was present, it was cut and slash—knock down and drag out. In his fits of anger, he would take up a chair, and throw it at a servant; and in his more rational moments, when he wished to chastise one, he would tie them up in the smoke-house, and whip them; after which, he would cause a fire to be made of tobacco stems, and smoke them. This he called "*Virginia play.*"

I complained to my master of the treatment which I received from Major Freeland; but it made no difference. He cared nothing about it, so long as he received the money for my labor. After living with Major Freeland five or six months, I ran away, and went into the woods back of the city; and when night came on, I made my way to my master's farm, but was afraid to be seen, knowing that if Mr. Haskell, the overseer, should discover me, I should be again carried back to Major Freeland; so I kept in the woods. One day, while in the woods, I heard the barking and howling of dogs, and in a short time they came so near, that I knew them to be the bloodhounds of Major Benjamin O'Fallon. He kept five or six, to hunt runaway slaves with.

As soon as I was convinced that it was them, I knew there was no chance of escape. I took refuge in the top of a tree, and the hounds were soon at its base, and there remained until the hunters came up in a half or three quarters of an hour afterwards. There were two men with the dogs, who, as soon as they came up, ordered me to descend. I came down, was tied, and taken to St. Louis jail. Major Freeland soon made his appearance, and took me out, and ordered me to follow him, which I did. After we returned home, I was tied up in the smoke-house, and was very severely whipped. After the Major had flogged me to his satisfaction, he sent out his son Robert, a young man eighteen or twenty years of age, to see that I was well smoked. He made a fire of tobacco stems, which soon set me to coughing and sneezing. This, Robert told me, was the way his father used to do to his slaves in Virginia. After giving me what they conceived to be a decent smoking, I was untied and again set to work.

Robert Freeland was a "chip of the old block." Though quite young, it was not unfrequently that he came home in a state of intoxication. He is now, I believe, a popular commander of a steamboat on the Mississippi river. Major Freeland soon after failed in business, and I was put on board the steamboat Missouri, which plied between St. Louis and Galena. The commander of the boat was William B. Culver. I remained on her during the sailing season, which was the most pleasant time for me that I had ever experienced. At the close of navigation, I was hired to Mr. John Colburn, keeper of the Missouri Hotel. He was from one of the Free States; but a more inveterate hater of the negro, I do not believe ever walked on God's green earth. This hotel was at that time one of the largest in the city, and there were employed in it twenty or thirty servants, mostly slaves.

Mr. Colburn was very abusive, not only to the servants, but to his wife also, who was an excellent woman, and one from whom I never knew a servant to receive a harsh word; but never did I know a kind one to a servant from her husband. Among the slaves employed in the hotel, was one by the name of Aaron, who belonged to Mr. John F. Darby, a lawyer. Aaron was the knife-cleaner. One day, one of the knives was put on the table, not as clean as it might have been. Mr. Colburn, for this offence, tied Aaron up in the wood-house, and gave him over fifty lashes on the bare back with a cowhide, after which, he made me wash him down with rum. This seemed to put him into more agony than the whipping. After being untied, he went home to his master, and complained of the treatment which he had received. Mr. Darby would give no heed to anything he had to say, but sent him directly back. Colburn, learning that he had been to his master with complaints, tied him up again, and gave him a more severe whipping than before. The poor fellow's back was literally cut to pieces; so much so, that he was not able to work for ten or twelve days.

There was also, among the servants, a girl whose master resided in the country. Her name was Patsey. Mr. Colburn tied her up one evening, and whipped her until several of the boarders came out and begged him to desist. The reason for whipping her was this. She was engaged to be married to a man belonging to Major William Christy, who resided four or five miles north of the city. Mr. Colburn had forbid her to see John Christy. The reason of this was said to be the regard which he himself had for Patsey. She went to meeting that evening, and John returned home with her. Mr. Colburn had intended to flog John, if he came within the inclosure; but John knew too well the temper of his rival, and kept at a safe distance;—so he took vengeance on the poor girl. If all the slave-drivers had been called together, I do not think a more cruel man than John Colburn,—and he too a northern man,—could have been found among them.

While living at the Missouri Hotel, a circumstance occurred which caused me great unhappiness. My master sold my mother, and all her children, except myself. They were sold to different persons in the city of St. Louis.

CHAPTER IV.

I WAS soon after taken from Mr. Colburn's, and hired to Elijah P. Lovejoy, who was at that time publisher and editor of the "St. Louis Times." My work, while with him, was mainly in the printing office, waiting on the hands, working the press, &c. Mr. Lovejoy was a very good man, and decidedly the best master that I had ever had. I am chiefly indebted to him, and to my employment in the printing office, for what little learning I obtained while in slavery.

Though slavery is thought, by some, to be mild in Missouri, when compared with the cotton, sugar and rice growing States, yet no part of our slave-holding country, is more noted for the barbarity of its inhabitants, than St. Louis. It was here that Col. Harney, a United States officer, whipped a slave woman to death. It was here that Francis McIntosh, a free colored man from Pittsburgh, was taken from the steamboat Flora, and burned at the stake. During a residence of eight years in this city, numerous cases of extreme cruelty came under my own observation;—to record them all, would occupy more space than could possibly be allowed in this little volume. I shall, therefore, give but a few more, in addition to what I have already related.

Capt. J. B. Brunt, who resided near my master, had a slave named John. He was his body servant, carriage driver, &c. On one occasion, while driving his master through the city,—the streets being very muddy, and the horses going at a rapid rate,—some mud spattered upon a gentleman by the name of Robert More. More was determined to be revenged. Some three or four months after this occurrence, he purchased John, for the express purpose, as he said, "to tame the d——d nigger." After the purchase, he took him to a blacksmith's shop, and had a ball and chain fastened to his leg, and then put him to driving a yoke of oxen, and kept him at hard labor, until the iron around his leg was so worn into the flesh, that it was thought mortification would ensue. In addition to this, John told me that his master whipped him regularly three times a week for the first two months:—and all this to "*tame him.*" A more noble looking man than he, was not to be found in all St. Louis, before he fell into the hands of More; and a more degraded and spirit-crushed looking being was never seen on a southern plantation, after he had been subjected to this "*taming*" process for three months. The last time that I saw him, he had nearly lost the entire use of his limbs.

While living with Mr. Lovejoy, I was often sent on errands to the office of the "Missouri Republican," published by Mr. Edward Charles. Once, while returning to the office with type, I was attacked by several large boys, sons of slave-holders, who pelted me with snow-balls. Having the heavy form of type in my hands, I could not make my escape by running; so I laid down the type and gave them battle. They gathered around me, pelting me with stones and sticks, until they overpowered me, and would have captured me, if I had not resorted to my heels. Upon my retreat, they took possession of the type; and what to do to regain it I could not devise. Knowing Mr. Lovejoy to be a very humane man, I went to the office, and laid the case before him. He told me to remain in the office. He took one of the apprentices with him, and went after the type, and soon returned with it; but on his return informed me that Samuel McKinney had told him that he would whip me, because I had hurt his boy. Soon after, McKinney was seen making his way to the office by one of the printers, who informed me of the fact, and I made my escape through the back door.

McKinney not being able to find me on his arrival, left the office in a great rage, swearing that he would whip me to death. A few days after, as I was walking along Main Street, he seized me by the collar, and struck me over the head five or six times with a large cane, which caused the blood to gush from my nose and ears in such a manner that my clothes were completely saturated with blood. After beating me to his satisfaction, he let me go, and I returned to the office so weak from the loss of blood, that Mr. Lovejoy sent me home to my master. It was five weeks before I was able to walk again. During this time, it was necessary to have some one to supply my place at the office, and I lost the situation.

After my recovery, I was hired to Capt. Otis Reynolds, as a waiter on board the steamboat Enterprize, owned by Messrs. John and Edward Walsh, commission merchants at St. Louis. This boat was then running on the upper Mississippi. My employment on board was to wait on gentlemen, and the captain being a good man, the situation was a pleasant one to me;—but in passing from place to place, and seeing new faces every day, and knowing that they could go where they pleased, I soon became unhappy, and several times thought of leaving the boat at some landing place, and trying to make my escape to Canada, which I had heard much about as a place where the slave might live, be free, and be protected.

But whenever such thoughts would come into my mind, my resolution would soon be shaken by the remembrance that my dear mother was a slave in St. Louis, and I could not bear the idea of leaving her in that condition. She had often taken me upon her knee, and told me how she had carried me upon her back to the field when I was an infant—how often she had been whipped for leaving her work to nurse me—and how happy I would appear when she would take me into her arms. When these thoughts came over me, I would resolve never to leave the land of slavery without my mother. I thought that to leave her in slavery, after she had undergone and suffered so much for me, would be proving recreant to the duty which I owed to her. Besides this, I had three brothers and a sister there,—two of my brothers having died.

My mother, my brothers Joseph and Millford, and my sister Elizabeth, belonged to Mr. Isaac Mansfield, formerly from one of the Free States, (Massachusetts, I believe.) He was a tinner by trade, and carried on a large manufacturing establishment. Of all my relatives, mother was first, and sister next. One evening, while visiting them, I made some allusion to a proposed journey to Canada, and sister took her seat by my side, and taking my hand in hers, said, with tears in her eyes,—

"Brother, you are not going to leave mother and your dear sister here without a friend, are you?"

I looked into her face, as the tears coursed swiftly down her cheeks, and bursting into tears myself, said—

"No, I will never desert you and mother."

She clasped my hand in hers, and said—

"Brother, you have often declared that you would not end

your days in slavery. I see no possible way in which you can escape with us; and now, brother, you are on a steamboat where there is some chance for you to escape to a land of liberty. I beseech you not to let us hinder you. If we cannot get our liberty, we do not wish to be the means of keeping you from a land of freedom."

I could restrain my feelings no longer, and an outburst of my own feelings, caused her to cease speaking upon that subject. In opposition to their wishes, I pledged myself not to leave them in the hand of the oppressor. I took leave of them, and returned to the boat, and laid down in my bunk; but "sleep departed from my eyes, and slumber from my eyelids."

A few weeks after, on our downward passage, the boat took on board, at Hannibal, a drove of slaves, bound for the New Orleans market. They numbered from fifty to sixty, consisting of men and women from eighteen to forty years of age. A drove of slaves on a southern steamboat, bound for the cotton or sugar regions, is an occurrence so common, that no one, not even the passengers, appear to notice it, though they clank their chains at every step. There was, however, one in this gang that attracted the attention of the passengers and crew. It was a beautiful girl, apparently about twenty years of age, perfectly white, with straight light hair and blue eyes. But it was not the whiteness of her skin that created such a sensation among those who gazed upon her—it was her almost unparalleled beauty. She had been on the boat but a short time, before the attention of all the passengers, including the ladies, had been called to her, and the common topic of conversation was about the beautiful slave-girl. She was not in chains. The man who claimed this article of human merchandize was a Mr. Walker,—a well known slave-trader, residing in St. Louis. There was a general anxiety among the passengers and crew to learn the history of the girl. Her master kept close by her side, and it would have been considered impudent for any of the passengers to have spoken to her, and the crew were not allowed to have any conversation with them. When we reached St. Louis, the slaves were removed to a boat bound for New Orleans, and the history of the beautiful slave-girl remained a mystery.

I remained on the boat during the season, and it was not an unfrequent occurrence to have on board gangs of slaves on their way to the cotton, sugar and rice plantations of the South.

Toward the latter part of the summer, Captain Reynolds left the boat, and I was sent home. I was then placed on the farm under Mr. Haskell, the overseer. As I had been some time out of the field, and not accustomed to work in the burning sun, it was very hard; but I was compelled to keep up with the best of the hands.

I found a great difference between the work in a steamboat cabin and that in a corn-field.

My master, who was then living in the city, soon after removed to the farm, when I was taken out of the field to work in the house as a waiter. Though his wife was very peevish, and hard to please, I much preferred to be under her control than the overseer's. They brought with them Mr. Sloane, a Presbyterian minister; Miss Martha Tulley, a neice of theirs from Kentucky; and their nephew William. The latter had been in the family a number of years, but the others were all new-comers.

Mr. Sloane was a young minister, who had been at the South but a short time, and it seemed as if his whole aim was to please the slaveholders, especially my master and mistress. He was intending to make a visit during the winter, and he not only tried to please them, but I think he succeeded admirably. When they wanted singing, he sung; when they wanted praying, he prayed; when they wanted a story told, he told a story. Instead of his teaching my master theology, my master taught theology to him. While I was with Captain Reynolds, my master "got religion," and new laws were made on the plantation. Formerly, we had the privilege of hunting, fishing, making splint brooms, baskets, &c. on Sunday; but this was all stopped. Every Sunday, we were all compelled to attend meeting. Master was so religious, that he induced some others to join him in hiring a preacher to preach to the slaves.

CHAPTER V.

My master had family worship, night and morning. At night, the slaves were called in to attend; but in the mornings, they had to be at their work, and master did all the praying. My master and mistress were great lovers of mint julep, and every morning, a pitcher-full was made, of which they all partook freely, not excepting little master William. After drinking freely all round, they would have family worship, and then breakfast. I cannot say but I loved the julep as well as any of them, and during prayer was always careful to seat myself close to the table where it stood, so as to help myself when they were all busily engaged in their devotions. By the time prayer was over, I was about as happy as any of them. A sad accident happened one morning. In helping myself, and at the same time keeping an eye on my old mistress, I accidentally let the pitcher fall upon the floor, breaking it in pieces, and spilling the contents. This was a bad affair for me; for as soon as prayer was over, I was taken and severely chastised.

My master's family consisted of himself, his wife, and their nephew, William Moore. He was taken into the family, when only a few weeks of age. His name being that of my own, mine was changed, for the purpose of giving precedence to his, though I was his senior by ten or twelve years. The plantation being four miles from the city, I had to drive the family to church. I always dreaded the approach of the Sabbath; for, during service, I was obliged to stand by the horses in the hot broiling sun, or in the rain, just as it happened.

One Sabbath, as we were driving past the house of D. D. Page, a gentleman who owned a large baking establishment, as I was sitting upon the box of the carriage, which was very much elevated, I saw Mr. Page pursuing a slave around the yard, with a long whip, cutting him at every jump. The man soon escaped from the yard, and was followed by Mr. Page. They came running past us, and the slave perceiving that he would be overtaken, stopped suddenly, and Page stumbled over him, and falling on the stone pavement, fractured one of his legs, which crippled him for life. The same gentleman, but a short time previous, tied up a woman of his, by the name of Delphia, and whipped her nearly to death; yet he was a deacon in the Baptist church, in good and regular standing. Poor Delphia! I was well acquainted with her, and called to see her while upon her sick bed; and I shall never forget her appearance. She was a member of the same church with her master.

Soon after this, I was hired out to Mr. Walker; the same man whom I have mentioned as having carried a gang of slaves down the river, on the steamboat Enterprize. Seeing me in the capacity of steward on the boat, and thinking that I would make a good hand to take care of slaves, he determined to have me for that purpose; and finding that my master would not sell me, he hired me for the term of one year.

When I learned the fact of my having been hired to a negro speculator, or a "soul-driver" as they are generally called among slaves, no one can tell my emotions. Mr. Walker had offered a high price for me, as I afterwards learned, but I suppose my master was restrained from selling me by the fact that I was a near relative of his. On entering the service of Mr. Walker, I found that my opportunity of getting to a land of liberty was gone, at least for the time being. He had a gang of slaves in readiness to start for New Orleans, and in a few days we were on our journey. I am at a loss for language to express my feelings on that occasion. Although my master had told me that he had not sold me, and Mr. Walker had told me that he had not purchased me, I did not believe them; and not until I had been to New Orleans, and was on my return, did I believe that I was not sold.

There was on the boat a large room on the lower deck, in which the slaves were kept, men and women, promiscuously—all chained two and two, and a strict watch kept that they did not get loose; for cases have occurred in which slaves have got off their chains, and made their escape at landing-places, while the boats were taking in wood;—and with all our care, we lost one woman who had been taken from her husband and children, and having no desire to live without them, in the agony of her soul jumped overboard, and drowned herself. She was not chained.

It was almost impossible to keep that part of the boat clean.

On landing at Natchez, the slaves were all carried to the slave-pen, and there kept one week, during which time, several of them were sold. Mr. Walker fed his slaves well. We took on board, at St. Louis, several hundred pounds of bacon (smoked meat) and corn-meal, and his slaves were better fed than slaves generally were in Natchez, so far as my observation extended.

At the end of a week, we left for New Orleans, the place of our final destination, which we reached in two days. Here the slaves were placed in a negro-pen, where those who wished to purchase could call and examine them. The negro-pen is a small yard, surrounded by buildings, from fifteen to twenty feet wide, with the exception of a large gate with iron bars. The slaves are kept in the buildings during the night, and turned out into the yard during the day. After the best of the stock was sold at private sale at the pen, the balance were taken to the Exchange Coffee House Auction Rooms, kept by Isaac L. McCoy, and sold at public auction. After the sale of this lot of slaves, we left New Orleans for St. Louis.

CHAPTER VI.

ON our arrival at St. Louis, I went to Dr. Young, and told him that I did not wish to live with Mr. Walker any longer. I was heart-sick at seeing my fellow-creatures bought and sold. But the Dr. had hired me for the year, and stay I must. Mr. Walker again commenced purchasing another gang of slaves. He bought a man of Colonel John O'Fallon, who resided in the suburbs of the city. This man had a wife and three children. As soon as the purchase was made, he was put in jail for safe keeping, until we should be ready to start for New Orleans. His wife visited him while there, several times, and several times when she went for that purpose was refused admittance.

In the course of eight or nine weeks Mr. Walker had his cargo of human flesh made up. There was in this lot a number of old men and women, some of them with gray locks. We left St. Louis in the steamboat Carlton, Captain Swan, bound for New Orleans. On our way down, and before we reached Rodney, the place where we made our first stop, I had to prepare the old slaves for market. I was ordered to have the old men's whiskers shaved off, and the grey hairs plucked out, where they were not too numerous, in which case he had a preparation of blacking to color it, and with a blacking-brush we would put it on. This was new business to me, and was performed in a room where the passengers could not see us. These slaves were also taught how old they were by Mr. Walker, and after going through the blacking process, they looked ten or fifteen years younger; and I am sure that some of those who purchased slaves of Mr. Walker, were dreadfully cheated, especially in the ages of the slaves which they bought.

We landed at Rodney, and the slaves were driven to the pen in the back part of the village. Several were sold at this place, during our stay of four or five days, when we proceeded to Natchez. There we landed at night, and the gang were put in the warehouse until morning, when they were driven to the pen. As soon as the slaves are put in these pens, swarms of planters may be seen in and about them. They knew when Walker was expected, as he always had the time advertised beforehand when he would be in Rodney, Natchez, and New Orleans. These were the principal places where he offered his slaves for sale.

When at Natchez the second time, I saw a slave very cruelly whipped. He belonged to a Mr. Broadwell, a merchant who kept a store on the wharf. The slave's name was Lewis. I had known him several years, as he was formerly from St. Louis. We were expecting a steamboat down the river, in which we were to take passage for New Orleans. Mr. Walker sent me to the landing to watch for the boat, ordering me to inform him on its arrival. While there, I went into the store to see Lewis. I saw a slave in the store, and asked him where Lewis was. Said he, "They have got Lewis hanging between the heavens and the earth." I asked him what he meant by that. He told me to go into the warehouse and see. I went in, and found Lewis there. He was tied up to a beam, with his toes just touching the floor. As there was no one in the warehouse but himself, I inquired the reason of his being in that situation. He said Mr. Broadwell had sold his wife to a planter six miles from the city, and that he had been to visit her,—that he went in the night, expecting to return before daylight, and went without his master's permission. The patrol had taken him up before he reached his wife. He was put in jail, and his master had to pay for his catching and keeping, and that was what he was tied up for.

Just as he finished his story, Mr. Broadwell came in, and inquired what I was doing there. I knew not what to say, and while I was thinking what reply to make, he struck me over the head with the cowhide, the end of which struck me over my right eye, sinking deep into the flesh, leaving a scar which I carry to this day. Before I visited Lewis, he had received fifty lashes. Mr. Broadwell gave him fifty lashes more after I came out, as I was afterwards informed by Lewis himself.

The next day we proceeded to New Orleans, and put the gang in the same negro-pen which we occupied before. In a short time, the planters came flocking to the pen to purchase slaves. Before the slaves were exhibited for sale, they were dressed and driven out into the yard. Some were set to dancing, some to jumping, some to singing, and some to playing cards. This was done to make them appear cheerful and happy. My business was to see that they were placed in those situations before the arrival of the purchasers, and I have often set them to dancing when their cheeks were wet with tears. As slaves were in good demand at that time, they were all soon disposed of, and we again set out for St. Louis.

On our arrival, Mr. Walker purchased a farm five or six miles from the city. He had no family, but made a housekeeper of one of his female slaves. Poor Cynthia! I knew her well. She was a quadroon, and one of the most beautiful women I ever saw. She was a native of St. Louis, and bore an irreproachable character for virtue and propriety of conduct. Mr. Walker bought her for the New Orleans market, and took her down with him on one of the trips that I made with him. Never shall I forget the circumstances of that voyage! On the first night that we were on board the steamboat, he directed me to put her into a state-room he had provided for her, apart from the other slaves. I had seen too much of the workings of slavery, not to know what this meant. I accordingly watched him into the state-room, and listened to hear what passed between them. I heard him make his base offers, and her reject them. He told her that if she would accept his vile proposals, he would take her back with him to St. Louis, and establish her as his housekeeper at his farm. But if she persisted in rejecting them, he would sell her as a field hand on the worst plantation on the river. Neither threats nor bribes prevailed, however, and he retired, disappointed of his prey.

The next morning, poor Cynthia told me what had past, and bewailed her sad fate with floods of tears. I comforted and encouraged her all I could; but I foresaw but too well what the result must be. Without entering into any farther particulars, suffice it to say that Walker performed his part of the contract, at that time. He took her back to St. Louis, established her as his mistress and housekeeper at his farm, and before I left, he had two children by her. But, mark the end! Since I have been at the North, I have been credibly informed that Walker has been married, and, as a previous measure, sold poor Cynthia and her four children (she having had two more since I came away) into hopeless bondage!

He soon commenced purchasing to make up the third gang. We took steamboat, and went to Jefferson City, a town on the Missouri river. Here we landed, and took stage for the interior of the State. He bought a number of slaves as he passed the different farms and villages. After getting twenty-two or twenty-three men and women, we arrived at St. Charles, a village on the banks of the Missouri. Here he purchased a woman who had a child in her arms, appearing to be four or five weeks old.

We had been travelling by land for some days, and were in hopes to have found a boat at this place for St. Louis, but were disappointed. As no boat was expected for some days, we started for St. Louis by land. Mr. Walker had purchased two horses. He rode one, and I the other. The slaves were chained together, and we took up our line of march, Mr. Walker taking the lead, and I bringing up the rear. Though the distance was not more than twenty miles, we did not reach it the first day. The road was worse than any that I have ever travelled.

Soon after we left St. Charles, the young child grew very cross, and kept up a noise during the greater part of the day. Mr. Walker complained of its crying several times, and told the mother to stop the child's d——d noise, or he would. The woman tried to keep the child from crying, but could not. We put up at night with an acquaintance of Mr. Walker, and in the morning, just as we were about to start, the child again commenced crying. Walker stepped up to her, and told her to give the child to him. The mother tremblingly obeyed. He took the child by one arm, as you would a cat by the leg, walked into the house, and said to the lady,

"Madam, I will make you a present of this little nigger; it keeps such a noise that I can't bear it."

"Thank you, sir," said the lady.

The mother, as soon as she saw that her child was to be left, ran up to Mr. Walker, and falling upon her knees begged him to let her have her child; she clung around his legs, and cried, "Oh, my child! my child! master, do let me have my child! oh, do, do, do. I will stop its crying, if you will only let me have it again." When I saw this woman crying for her child so piteously, a shudder,—a feeling akin to horror, shot through my frame. I have often since in imagination heard her crying for her child:—

"O, master, let me stay to catch
My baby's sobbing breath,
His little glassy eye to watch,
And smooth his limbs in death,

And cover him with grass and leaf,
Beneath the large oak tree:
It is not sullenness, but grief,—
O, master, pity me!

The morn was chill—I spoke no word,
But feared my babe might die,
And heard all day, or thought I heard,
My little baby cry.

At noon, oh, how I ran and took
My baby to my breast!
I lingered—and the long lash broke
My sleeping infant's rest.

I worked till night—till darkest night,
In torture and disgrace;
Went home and watched till morning light,
To see my baby's face.

Then give me but one little hour—
O! do not lash me so!
One little hour—one little hour—
And gratefully I'll go."

Mr. Walker commanded her to return into the ranks with the other slaves. Women who had children were not chained, but those that had none were. As soon as her child was disposed of, she was chained in the gang.

The following song I have often heard the slaves sing, when about to be carried to the far south. It is said to have been composed by a slave.

"See these poor souls from Africa
Transported to America;
We are stolen, and sold to Georgia,
Will you go along with me?
We are stolen, and sold to Georgia,
Come sound the jubilee!

See wives and husbands sold apart,
Their children's screams will break my heart;—
There's a better day a coming,
Will you go along with me?
There's a better day a coming,
Go sound the jubilee!

O, gracious Lord! when shall it be,
That we poor souls shall all be free;
Lord, break them slavery powers—
Will you go along with me?
Lord break them slavery powers,
Go sound the jubilee!

Dear Lord, dear Lord, when slavery'll cease,
Then we poor souls will have our peace;—
There's a better day a coming,
Will you go along with me?
There's a better day a coming,
Go sound the jubilee!"

We finally arrived at Mr. Walker's farm. He had a house built during our absence to put slaves in. It was a kind of domestic jail. The slaves were put in the jail at night, and worked on the farm during the day. They were kept here until the gang was completed, when we again started for New Orleans, on board the steamboat North America, Capt. Alexander Scott. We had a large number of slaves in this gang. One, by the name of Joe, Mr. Walker was training up to take my place, as my time was nearly out, and glad was I. We made our first stop at Vicksburg, where we remained one week and sold several slaves.

Mr. Walker, though not a good master, had not flogged a slave since I had been with him, though he had threatened me. The slaves were kept in the pen, and he always put up at the best hotel, and kept his wines in his room, for the accommodation of those who called to negotiate with him for the purchase of slaves. One day while we were at Vicksburg, several gentlemen came to see him for this purpose, and as usual the wine was called for. I took the tray and started around with it, and having accidentally filled some of the glasses too full, the gentlemen spilled the wine on their clothes as they went to drink. Mr. Walker apologized to them for my carelessness, but looked at me as though he would see me again on this subject.

After the gentlemen had left the room, he asked me what I meant by my carelessness, and said that he would attend to me. The next morning, he gave me a note to carry to the jailer, and a dollar in money to give to him. I suspected that all was not right, so I went down near the landing where I met with a sailor, and walking up to him, asked him if he would be so kind as to read the note for me. He read it over, and then looked at me. I asked him to tell me what was in it. Said he,

"They are going to give you hell."

"Why?" said I.

He said, "This is a note to have you whipped, and says that you have a dollar to pay for it."

He handed me back the note, and off I started. I knew not what to do, but was determined not to be whipped. I went up to the jail—took a look at it, and walked off again. As Mr. Walker was acquainted with the jailer, I feared that I should be found out if I did not go, and be treated in consequence of it still worse.

While I was meditating on the subject, I saw a colored man about my size walk up, and the thought struck me in a moment to send him with my note. I walked up to him, and asked him who he belonged to. He said he was a free man, and had been in the city but a short time. I told him I had a note to go into the jail, and get a trunk to carry to one of the steamboats; but was so busily engaged that I could not do it, although I had a dollar to pay for it. He asked me if I would not give him the job. I handed him the note and the dollar, and off he started for the jail.

I watched to see that he went in, and as soon as I saw the door close behind him, I walked around the corner, and took my station, intending to see how my friend looked when he came out. I had been there but a short time, when a colored man came around the corner, and said to another colored man with whom he was acquainted—

"They are giving a nigger scissors in the jail."

"What for?" said the other. The man continued,

"A nigger came into the jail, and asked for the jailer. The jailer came out, and he handed him a note, and said he wanted to get a trunk. The jailer told him to go with him, and he would give him the trunk. So he took him into the room, and told the nigger to give up the dollar. He said a man had given him the dollar to pay for getting the trunk. But that lie would not answer. So they made him strip himself, and then they tied him down, and are now whipping him."

I stood by all the while listening to their talk, and soon found out that the person alluded to was my customer. I went into the street opposite the jail, and concealed myself in such a manner that I could not be seen by any one coming out. I had been there but a short time, when the young man made his appearance, and looked around for me. I, unobserved, came forth from my hiding-place, behind a pile of brick, and he pretty soon saw me and came up to me complaining bitterly, saying that I had played a trick upon him. I denied any knowledge of what the note contained, and asked him what they had done to him. He told me in substance what I heard the man tell who had come out of the jail.

"Yes," said he, "they whipped me and took my dollar, and gave me this note."

He showed me the note which the jailer had given him, telling him to give it to his master. I told him I would give him fifty cents for it,—that being all the money I had. He gave it to me, and took his money. He had received twenty lashes on his bare back, with the negro-whip.

I took the note and started for the hotel where I had left Mr. Walker. Upon reaching the hotel, I handed it to a stranger whom I had not seen before, and requested him to read it to me. As near as I can recollect, it was as follows:—

> "DEAR SIR:—By your direction, I have given your boy twenty lashes. He is a very saucy boy, and tried to make me believe that he did not belong to you, and I put it on to him well for lying to me.
>
> I remain,
>
> Your obedient servant."

It is true that in most of the slave-holding cities, when a gentleman wishes his servants whipped, he can send him to the jail and have it done. Before I went in where Mr. Walker was, I wet my cheeks a little, as though I had been crying. He looked at me, and inquired what was the matter. I told him that I had never had such a whipping in my life, and handed him the note. He looked at it and laughed;—"and so you told him that you did not belong to me." "Yes, sir," said I. "I did not know that there was any harm in that." He told me I must behave myself, if I did not want to be whipped again.

This incident shows how it is that slavery makes its victims lying and mean; for which vices it afterwards reproaches them, and uses them as arguments to prove that they deserve no better fate. I have often, since my escape, deeply regretted the deception I practised upon this poor fellow; and I heartily desire that it may be, at some time or other, in my power to make him amends for his vicarious sufferings in my behalf.

CHAPTER VII.

IN a few days we reached New Orleans, and arriving there in the night, remained on board until morning. While at New Orleans this time, I saw a slave killed; an account of which has been published by Theodore D. Weld, in his book entitled, "Slavery as it is." The circumstances were as follows. In the evening, between seven and eight o'clock, a slave came running down the levee, followed by several men and boys. The whites were crying out, "Stop that nigger; stop that nigger;"

while the poor panting slave, in almost breathless accents, was repeating, "I did not steal the meat—I did not steal the meat." The poor man at last took refuge in the river. The whites who were in pursuit of him, run on board of one of the boats to see if they could discover him. They finally espied him under the bow of the steamboat Trenton. They got a pike-pole, and tried to drive him from his hiding place. When they would strike at him, he would dive under the water. The water was so cold, that it soon became evident that he must come out or be drowned.

While they were trying to drive him from under the bow of the boat or drown him, he would in broken and imploring accents say, "I did not steal the meat; I did not steal the meat. My master lives up the river. I want to see my master. I did not steal the meat. Do let me go home to master." After punching him, and striking him over the head for some time, he at last sunk in the water, to rise no more alive.

On the end of the pike-pole with which they were striking him was a hook which caught in his clothing, and they hauled him up on the bow of the boat. Some said he was dead, others said he was "*playing possum*," while others kicked him to make him get up, but it was of no use—he was dead.

As soon as they became satisfied of this, they commenced leaving, one after another. One of the hands on the boat informed the captain that they had killed the man, and that the dead body was lying on the deck. The captain came on deck, and said to those who were remaining, "You have killed this nigger; now take him off of my boat." The captain's name was Hart. The dead body was dragged on shore and left there. I went on board of the boat where our gang of slaves were, and during the whole night my mind was occupied with what I had seen. Early in the morning, I went on shore to see if the dead body remained there. I found it in the same position that it was left the night before. I watched to see what they would do with it. It was left there until between eight and nine o'clock, when a cart, which takes up the trash out of the streets, came along, and the body was thrown in, and in a few minutes more was covered over with dirt which they were removing from the streets. During the whole time, I did not see more than six or seven persons around it, who, from their manner, evidently regarded it as no uncommon occurrence.

During our stay in the city, I met with a young white man with whom I was well acquainted in St. Louis. He had been sold into slavery, under the following circumstances. His father was a drunkard, and very poor, with a family of five or six children. The father died, and left the mother to take care of and provide for the children as best she might. The eldest was a boy, named Burrill, about thirteen years of age, who did chores in a store kept by Mr. Riley, to assist his mother in procuring a living for the family. After working with him two years, Mr. Riley took him to New Orleans to wait on him while in that city on a visit, and when he returned to St. Louis, he told the mother of the boy that he had died with the yellow fever. Nothing more was heard from him, no one supposing him to be alive. I was much astonished when Burrill told me his story. Though I sympathized with him, I could not assist him. We were both slaves. He was poor, uneducated, and without friends; and if living, is, I presume, still held as a slave.

After selling out this cargo of human flesh, we returned to St. Louis, and my time was up with Mr. Walker. I had served him one year, and it was the longest year I ever lived.

CHAPTER VIII.

I WAS sent home, and was glad enough to leave the service of one who was tearing the husband from the wife, the child from the mother, and the sister from the brother,—but a trial more severe and heart-rending than any which I had yet met with awaited me. My dear sister had been sold to a man who was going to Natchez, and was lying in jail awaiting the hour of his departure. She had expressed her determination to die, rather than go to the far south, and she was put in jail for safe keeping. I went to the jail the same day that I arrived, but as the jailor was not in, I could not see her.

I went home to my master, in the country, and the first day after my return, he came where I was at work, and spoke to me very politely. I knew from his appearance that something was the matter. After talking about my several journeys to New

Orleans with Mr. Walker, he told me that he was hard pressed for money, and as he had sold my mother and all her children except me, he thought it would be better to sell me than any other one, and that as I had been used to living in the city, he thought it probable that I would prefer it to a country life. I raised up my head, and looked him full in the face. When my eyes caught his, he immediately looked to the ground. After a short pause, I said,

"Master, mother has often told me that you are a near relative of mine, and I have often heard you admit the fact; and after you have hired me out, and received, as I once heard you say, nine hundred dollars for my services,—after receiving this large sum, will you sell me to be carried to New Orleans or some other place?"

"No," said he, "I do not intend to sell you to a negro trader. If I had wished to have done that, I might have sold you to Mr. Walker for a large sum, but I would not sell you to a negro trader. You may go to the city, and find you a good master."

"But," said I, "I cannot find a good master in the whole city of St. Louis."

"Why?" said he.

"Because there are no good masters in the State."

"Do you not call me a good master?"

"If you were, you would not sell me."

"Now I will give you one week to find a master in, and surely you can do it in that time."

The price set by my evangelical master upon my soul and body was the trifling sum of five hundred dollars. I tried to enter into some arrangement by which I might purchase my freedom; but he would enter into no such arrangement.

I set out for the city with the understanding that I was to return in a week with some one to become my new master. Soon after reaching the city, I went to the jail, to learn if I could once more see my sister; but could not gain admission. I then went to mother, and learned from her that the owner of my sister intended to start for Natchez in a few days.

I went to the jail again the next day, and Mr. Simonds, the keeper, allowed me to see my sister for the last time. I cannot give a just description of the scene at that parting interview. Never, never can be erased from my heart the occurrences of that day! When I entered the room where she was, she was seated in one corner, alone. There were four other women in the same room, belonging to the same man. He had purchased them, he said, for his own use. She was seated with her face towards the door where I entered, yet she did not look up until I walked up to her. As soon as she observed me, she sprung up, threw her arms around my neck, leaned her head upon my breast, and, without uttering a word, burst into tears. As soon as she recovered herself sufficiently to speak, she advised me to take mother, and try to get out of slavery. She said there was no hope for herself,—that she must live and die a slave. After giving her some advice, and taking from my finger a ring and placing it upon hers, I bade her farewell forever, and returned to my mother, and then and there made up my mind to leave for Canada as soon as possible.

I had been in the city nearly two days, and as I was to be absent only a week, I thought best to get on my journey as soon as possible. In conversing with mother, I found her unwilling to make the attempt to reach a land of liberty, but she counselled me to get my liberty if I could. She said, as all her children were in slavery, she did not wish to leave them. I could not bear the idea of leaving her among those pirates, when there was a prospect of being able to get away from them. After much persuasion, I succeeded in inducing her to make the attempt to get away.

The time fixed for our departure was the next night. I had with me a little money that I had received, from time to time, from gentlemen for whom I had done errands. I took my scanty means and purchased some dried beef, crackers and cheese, which I carried to mother, who had provided herself with a bag to carry it in. I occasionally thought of my old master, and of my mission to the city to find a new one. I waited with the most intense anxiety for the appointed time to leave the land of slavery, in search of a land of liberty.

The time at length arrived, and we left the city just as the clock struck nine. We proceeded to the upper part of the city, where I had been two or three times during the day, and selected a skiff to carry us across the river. The boat was not mine, nor did I know to whom it did belong; neither did I care. The boat was fastened with a small pole, which, with the aid of a rail, I soon loosened from its moorings. After hunting round and finding a board to use as an oar, I turned to the city, and bidding it a long farewell, pushed off my boat. The current running very swift, we had not reached the middle of the stream before we were directly opposite the city.

We were soon upon the Illinois shore, and, leaping from the boat, turned it adrift, and the last I saw of it, it was going down the river at good speed. We took the main road to Alton, and passed through just at daylight, when we made for the woods, where we remained during the day. Our reason for going into the woods was, that we expected that Mr. Mansfield (the man who owned my mother) would start in pursuit of her as soon as he discovered that she was missing. He also knew that I had been in the city looking for a new master, and we thought probably he would go out to my master's to see if he could find my mother, and in so doing, Dr. Young might be led to suspect that I had gone to Canada to find a purchaser.

We remained in the woods during the day, and as soon as darkness overshadowed the earth, we started again on our gloomy way, having no guide but the NORTH STAR. We continued to travel by night, and secrete ourselves in woods by day; and every night, before emerging from our hiding-place, we would anxiously look for our friend and leader,—the NORTH STAR.

CHAPTER IX.

As we travelled towards a land of liberty, my heart would at times leap for joy. At other times, being, as I was, almost constantly on my feet, I felt as though I could travel no further. But when I thought of slavery with its Democratic whips—its Republican chains—its evangelical blood-hounds, and its religious slave-holders—when I thought of all this paraphernalia of American Democracy and Religion behind me, and the prospect of liberty before me, I was encouraged to press forward, my heart was strengthened, and I forgot that I was tired or hungry.

On the eighth day of our journey, we had a very heavy rain, and in a few hours after it commenced, we had not a dry thread upon our bodies. This made our journey still more unpleasant. On the tenth day, we found ourselves entirely destitute of provisions, and how to obtain any we could not tell. We finally resolved to stop at some farmhouse, and try to get something to eat. We had no sooner determined to do this, than we went to a house, and asked them for some food. We were treated with great kindness, and they not only gave us something to eat, but gave us provisions to carry with us. They advised us to travel by day, and lye by at night. Finding ourselves about one hundred and fifty miles from St. Louis, we concluded that it would be safe to travel by daylight, and did not leave the house until the next morning. We travelled on that day through a thickly settled country, and through one small village. Though we were fleeing from a land of oppression, our hearts were still there. My dear sister and two beloved brothers were behind us, and the idea of giving them up, and leaving them forever, made us feel sad. But with all this depression of heart, the thought that I should one day be free, and call my body my own, buoyed me up, and made my heart leap for joy. I had just been telling mother how I should try to get employment as soon as we reached Canada, and how I intended to purchase us a little farm, and how I would earn money enough to buy sister and brothers, and how happy we would be in our own FREE HOME,—when three men came up on horseback, and ordered us to stop.

I turned to the one who appeared to be the principal man, and asked him what he wanted. He said he had a warrant to take us up. The three immediately dismounted, and one took from his pocket a handbill, advertising us as runaways, and offering a reward of two hundred dollars for our apprehension, and delivery in the city of St. Louis. The advertisement had been put out by Isaac Mansfield and John Young.

While they were reading the advertisement, mother looked me in the face, and burst into tears. A cold chill ran over me, and such a sensation I never experienced before, and I hope never to again. They took out a rope and tied me, and we were taken back about six miles, to the house of the individual who appeared to be the leader. We reached there about seven o'clock in the evening, had supper, and were separated for the night. Two men remained in the room during the night. Before the family retired to rest, they were all called together to attend prayers. The man who but a few hours before had bound my hands together with a strong cord, read a chapter from the Bible, and then offered up prayer, just as though God sanctioned the act he had just committed upon a poor panting, fugitive slave.

The next morning, a blacksmith came in, and put a pair of handcuffs on me, and we started on our journey back to the land of whips, chains and Bibles. Mother was not tied, but was closely watched at night. We were carried back in a wagon, and after four days travel, we came in sight of St. Louis. I cannot describe my feelings upon approaching the city.

As we were crossing the ferry, Mr. Wiggins, the owner of the ferry, came up to me, and inquired what I had been doing that I was in chains. He had not heard that I had run away. In a few minutes, we were on the Missouri side, and were taken directly to the jail. On the way thither, I saw several of my friends, who gave me a nod of recognition as I passed them. After reaching the jail, we were locked up in different apartments.

CHAPTER X.

I HAD been in jail but a short time when I heard that my master was sick, and nothing brought more joy to my heart than that intelligence. I prayed fervently for him—not for his recovery, but for his death. I knew he would be exasperated at having to pay for my apprehension, and knowing his cruelty, I feared him. While in jail, I learned that my sister Elizabeth, who was in prison when we left the city, had been carried off four days before our arrival.

I had been in jail but a few hours when three negro-traders, learning that I was secured thus for running away, came to my prison-house and looked at me, expecting that I would be offered for sale. Mr. Mansfield, the man who owned mother, came into the jail as soon as Mr. Jones, the man who arrested us, informed him that he had brought her back. He told her that he would not whip her, but would sell her to a negro-trader, or take her to New Orleans himself. After being in jail about one week, master sent a man to take me out of jail, and send me home. I was taken out and carried home, and the old man was well enough to sit up. He had me brought into the room where he was, and as I entered, he asked me where I had been? I told him I had acted according to his orders. He had told me to look for a master, and I had been to look for one. He answered that he did not tell me to go to Canada to look for a master. I told him that as I had served him faithfully, and had been the means of putting a number of hundreds of dollars into his pocket, I thought I had a right to my liberty. He said he had promised my father that I should not be sold to supply the New Orleans market, or he would sell me to a negro-trader.

I was ordered to go into the field to work, and was closely watched by the overseer during the day, and locked up at night. The overseer gave me a severe whipping on the second day that I was in the field. I had been at home but a short time, when master was able to ride to the city; and on his return, he informed me that he had sold me to Samuel Willi, a merchant tailor. I knew Mr. Willi. I had lived with him three or four months some years before, when he hired me of my master.

Mr. Willi was not considered by his servants as a very bad man, nor was he the best of masters. I went to my new home, and found my new mistress very glad to see me. Mr. Willi owned two servants before he purchased me,—Robert and Charlotte. Robert was an excellent white-washer, and hired his time from his master, paying him one dollar per day, besides taking care of himself. He was known in the city by the name of Bob Music. Charlotte was an old woman, who attended to the cooking, washing, &c. Mr. Willi was not a wealthy man, and did not feel able to keep many servants around his house; so he soon decided to hire me out, and as I had been accustomed to service in steamboats, he gave me the privilege of finding such employment.

I soon secured a situation on board the steamer Otto, Capt. J. B. Hill, which sailed from St. Louis to Independence, Missouri. My former master, Dr. Young, did not let Mr. Willi know that I had run away, or he would not have permitted me to go on board a steamboat. The boat was not quite ready to commence running, and therefore I had to remain with Mr. Willi. But during this time, I had to undergo a trial, for which I was entirely unprepared. My mother, who had been in jail since her return until the present time, was now about being carried to New Orleans, to die on a cotton, sugar, or rice plantation!

I had been several times to the jail, but could obtain no interview with her. I ascertained, however, the time the boat in which she was to embark would sail, and as I had not seen mother since her being thrown into prison, I felt anxious for the hour of sailing to come. At last, the day arrived when I was to see her for the first time after our painful separation, and, for aught that I knew, for the last time in this world!

At about ten o'clock in the morning I went on board of the boat, and found her there in company with fifty or sixty other slaves. She was chained to another woman. On seeing me, she immediately dropped her head upon her heaving bosom. She moved not, neither did she weep. Her emotions were too deep for tears. I approached, threw my arms around her neck, kissed her, and fell upon my knees, begging her forgiveness, for I thought myself to blame for her sad condition; for if I had not persuaded her to accompany me, she would not then have been in chains.

She finally raised her head, looked me in the face, (and such a look none but an angel can give!) and said, *"My dear son, you are not to blame for my being here. You have done nothing more nor less than your duty. Do not, I pray you, weep for me. I cannot last long upon a cotton plantation. I feel that my heavenly master will soon call me home, and then I shall be out of the hands of the slave-holders!"*

I could bear no more—my heart struggled to free itself from the human form. In a moment she saw Mr. Mansfield coming toward that part of the boat, and she whispered into my ear, *"My child, we must soon part to meet no more this side of the grave. You have ever said that you would not die a slave; that you would be a freeman. Now try to get your liberty! You will soon have no one to look after but yourself!"* and just as she whispered the last sentence into my ear, Mansfield came up to me, and with an oath, said, "Leave here this instant; you have been the means of my losing one hundred dollars to get this wench back,"—at the same time kicking me with a heavy pair of boots. As I left her, she gave one shriek, saying, "God be with you!" It was the last time that I saw her, and the last word I heard her utter.

I walked on shore. The bell was tolling. The boat was about to start. I stood with a heavy heart, waiting to see her leave the wharf. As I thought of my mother, I could but feel that I had lost

"———the glory of my life,
My blessing and my pride!
I half forgot the name of slave,
When she was by my side."

CHAPTER XI.

THE love of liberty that had been burning in my bosom, had well nigh gone out. I felt as though I was ready to die. The boat moved gently from the wharf, and while she glided down the river, I realized that my mother was indeed

"Gone,—gone,—sold and gone,
To the rice swamp dank and lone!"

After the boat was out of sight, I returned home; but my thoughts were so absorbed in what I had witnessed, that I knew not what I was about half of the time. Night came, but it brought no sleep to my eyes.

In a few days, the boat upon which I was to work being ready, I went on board to commence. This employment suited me better than living in the city, and I remained until the close of navigation; though it proved anything but pleasant. The captain was a drunken, profligate, hard-hearted creature, not knowing how to treat himself, or any other person.

The boat, on its second trip, brought down Mr. Walker, the man of whom I have spoken in a previous chapter, as hiring my time. He had between one and two hundred slaves, chained and manacled. Among them was a man that formerly belonged to my old master's brother, Aaron Young. His name was Solomon. He was a preacher, and belonged to the same church with his master. I was glad to see the old man. He wept like a child when he told me how he had been sold from his wife and children.

The boat carried down, while I remained on board, four or five gangs of slaves. Missouri, though a comparatively new State, is very much engaged in raising slaves to supply the southern market. In a former chapter, I have mentioned that I was once in the employ of a slave-trader, or driver, as he is called at the south. For fear that some may think that I have misrepresented a slave-driver, I will here give an extract from a paper published in a slaveholding State, Tennessee, called the "Millennial Trumpeter."

"Droves of negroes, chained together in dozens and scores, and hand-cuffed, have been driven through our country in numbers far surpassing any previous year, and these vile slave-drivers and dealers are swarming like buzzards around a carrion. Through this county, you cannot pass a few miles in the great roads without having every feeling of humanity insulted and lacerated by this spectacle, nor can you go into any county or any neighborhood, scarcely, without seeing or hearing of some of these despicable creatures, called negro-drivers.

"Who is a negro-driver? One whose eyes dwell with delight on lacerated bodies of helpless men, women and children; whose soul feels diabolical raptures at the chains, and hand-cuffs, and cart-whips, for inflicting tortures on weeping mothers torn from helpless babes, and on husbands and wives torn asunder forever!"

Dark and revolting as is the picture here drawn, it is from the pen of one living in the midst of slavery. But though these men may cant about negro-drivers, and tell what despicable creatures they are, who is it, I ask, that supplies them with the human beings that they are tearing asunder? I answer, as far as I have any knowledge of the State where I came from, that those who raise slaves for the market are to be found among all classes, from Thomas H. Benton down to the lowest political demagogue, who may be able to purchase a woman for the purpose of raising stock, and from the Doctor of Divinity down to the most humble lay member in the church.

It was not uncommon in St. Louis to pass by an auction-stand, and behold a woman upon the auction-block, and hear the seller crying out, *"How much is offered for this woman? She is a good cook, good washer, a good obedient servant. She has got religion!"* Why should this man tell the purchasers that she has religion? I answer, because in Missouri, and as far as I have any knowledge of slavery in the other States, the religious teaching consists in teaching the slave that he must never strike a white man; that God made him for a slave; and that, when whipped, he must not find fault,—for the Bible says, "He that knoweth his master's will, and doeth it not, shall be beaten with many stripes!" And slaveholders find such religion very profitable to them.

After leaving the steamer Otto, I resided at home, in Mr. Willi's family, and again began to lay my plans for making my escape from slavery. The anxiety to be a freeman would not let me rest day or night. I would think of the northern cities that I had heard so much about;—of Canada, where so many of my acquaintances had found refuge. I would dream at night that I was in Canada, a freeman, and on waking in the morning, weep to find myself so sadly mistaken.

"I would think of Victoria's domain,
And in a moment I seemed to be there!
But the fear of being taken again,
Soon hurried me back to despair."

Mr. Willi treated me better than Dr. Young ever had; but instead of making me contented and happy, it only rendered me the more miserable, for it enabled me better to appreciate liberty. Mr. Willi was a man who loved money as most men do, and without looking for an opportunity to sell me, he found one in the offer of Captain Enoch Price, a steamboat owner and commission merchant, living in the city of St. Louis. Captain Price tendered seven hundred dollars, which was two hundred more than Mr. Willi had paid. He therefore thought best to accept the offer. I was wanted for a carriage driver, and Mrs. Price was very much pleased with the captain's bargain. His family consisted besides of one child. He had three servants besides myself—one man and two women.

Mrs. Price was very proud of her servants, always keeping them well dressed, and as soon as I had been purchased, she resolved to have a new carriage. And soon one was procured, and all preparations were made for a turn-out in grand style, I being the driver.

One of the female servants was a girl some eighteen or twenty years of age, named Maria. Mrs. Price was very soon determined to have us united, if she could so arrange matters. She would often urge upon me the necessity of having a wife, saying that it would be so pleasant for me to take one in the same family! But getting married, while in slavery, was the last of my thoughts; and had I been ever so inclined, I should not have married Maria, as my love had already gone in another quarter. Mrs. Price soon found out that her efforts at this match-making between Maria and myself would not prove successful. She also discovered (or thought she had) that I was rather partial to a girl named Eliza, who was owned by Dr. Mills. This induced her at once to endeavor the purchase of Eliza, so great was her desire to get me a wife!

Before making the attempt, however, she deemed it best to talk to me a little upon the subject of love, courtship, and marriage. Accordingly one afternoon she called me into her room—telling me to take a chair and sit down. I did so, thinking it rather strange, for servants are not very often asked thus to sit down in the same room with the master or mistress. She said that she had found out that I did not care enough about Maria to marry her. I told her that was true. She then asked me if there was not a girl in the city that I loved. Well, now, this was coming into too close quarters with me! People, generally, don't like to tell their love stories to everybody that may think fit to ask about them, and it was so with me. But, after blushing awhile and recovering myself, I told her that I did not want a wife. She then asked me, if I did not think something of Eliza. I told her that I did. She then said that if I wished to marry Eliza, she would purchase her if she could.

I gave but little encouragement to this proposition, as I was determined to make another trial to get my liberty, and I knew that if I should have a wife, I should not be willing to leave her behind; and if I should attempt to bring her with me, the chances would be difficult for success. However, Eliza was purchased, and brought into the family.

CHAPTER XII.

But the more I thought of the trap laid by Mrs. Price to make me satisfied with my new home, by getting me a wife, the more I determined never to marry any woman on earth until I should get my liberty. But this secret I was compelled to keep to myself, which placed me in a very critical position. I must keep upon good terms with Mrs. Price and Eliza. I therefore promised Mrs. Price that I would marry Eliza; but said that I was not then ready. And I had to keep upon good terms with Eliza, for fear that Mrs. Price would find out that I did not intend to get married.

I have here spoken of marriage, and it is very common among slaves themselves to talk of it. And it is common for slaves to be married; or at least have the marriage ceremony performed. But there is no such thing as slaves being lawfully married. There has never yet a case occurred where a slave has been tried for bigamy. The man may have as many women as he wishes, and the women as many men; and the law takes no cognizance of such acts among slaves. And in fact some masters, when they have sold the husband from the wife, compel her to take another.

There lived opposite Captain Price's, Doctor Farrar, well known in St. Louis. He sold a man named Ben, to one of the traders. He also owned Ben's wife, and in a few days he compelled Sally (that was her name) to marry Peter, another man belonging to him. I asked Sally "why she married Peter so soon after Ben was sold." She said, "because master made her do it."

Mr. John Calvert, who resided near our place, had a woman named Lavinia. She was quite young, and a man to whom she was about to be married was sold, and carried into the country near St. Charles, about twenty miles from St. Louis. Mr. Calvert wanted her to get a husband; but she had resolved not to marry any other man, and she refused. Mr. Calvert whipped her in such a manner that it was thought she would die. Some of the citizens had him arrested, but it was soon hushed up. And that was the last of it. The woman did not die, but it would have been the same if she had.

Captain Price purchased me in the month of October, and I remained with him until December, when the family made a voyage to New Orleans, in a boat owned by himself, and named the "Chester." I served on board, as one of the stewards. On arriving at New Orleans, about the middle of the month, the boat took in freight for Cincinnati; and it was decided that the family should go up the river in her, and what was of more interest to me, I was to accompany them.

The long looked for opportunity to make my escape from slavery was near at hand.

Captain Price had some fears as to the propriety of taking me near a free State, or a place where it was likely I could run away, with a prospect of liberty. He asked me if I had ever been in a free State. "Oh yes," said I, "I have been in Ohio; my master carried me into that State once, but I never liked a free State."

It was soon decided that it would be safe to take me with them, and what made it more safe, Eliza was on the boat with us, and Mrs. Price, to try me, asked if I thought as much as ever of Eliza. I told her that Eliza was very dear to me indeed, and that nothing but death should part us. It was the same as if we were married. This had the desired effect. The boat left New Orleans, and proceeded up the river.

I had at different times obtained little sums of money, which I had reserved for a "rainy day." I procured some cotton cloth, and made me a bag to carry provisions in. The trials of the past were all lost in hopes for the future. The love of liberty, that had been burning in my bosom for years, and had been well nigh extinguished, was now resuscitated. At night, when all around was peaceful, I would walk the decks, meditating upon my happy prospects.

I should have stated, that before leaving St. Louis, I went to an old man named Frank, a slave, owned by a Mr. Sarpee. This old man was very distinguished (not only among the slave population, but also the whites) as a fortune-teller. He was about seventy years of age, something over six feet high, and very slender. Indeed, he was so small around his body that it looked as though it was not strong enough to hold up his head.

Uncle Frank was a very great favorite with the young ladies, who would go to him in great numbers to get their fortunes told. And it was generally believed that he could really penetrate into the mysteries of futurity. Whether true or not, he had the *name*, and that is about half of what one needs in this gullible age. I found Uncle Frank seated in the chimney corner, about ten o'clock at night. As soon as I entered, the old man left his seat. I watched his movement as well as I could by the dim light of the fire. He soon lit a lamp, and coming up, looked me full in the face, saying, "Well, my son, you have come to get uncle to tell your fortune, have you?" "Yes," said I. But how the old man should know what I had come for, I could not tell. However, I paid the fee of twenty-five cents, and he commenced by looking into a gourd, filled with water. Whether the old man was a prophet, or the son of a prophet, I cannot say; but there is one thing certain, many of his predictions were verified.

I am no believer in soothsaying; yet I am sometimes at a loss to know how Uncle Frank could tell so accurately what would occur in the future. Among the many things he told was one which was enough to pay me for all the trouble of hunting him up. It was that *I should be free!* He further said, that in trying to get my liberty, I would meet with many severe trials. I thought to myself, any fool could tell me that!

The first place in which we landed in a free State was Cairo, a small village at the mouth of the Ohio river. We remained here but a few hours, when we proceeded to Louisville. After unloading some of the cargo, the boat started on her upward trip. The next day was the first of January. I had looked forward to New Year's day as the commencement of a new era in the history of my life. I had decided upon leaving the peculiar institution that day.

During the last night that I served in slavery, I did not close my eyes a single moment. When not thinking of the future, my mind dwelt on the past. The love of a dear mother, a dear sister, and three dear brothers, yet living, caused me to shed many tears. If I could only have been assured of their being dead, I should have felt satisfied; but I imagined I saw my dear mother in the cotton-field, followed by a merciless taskmaster, and no one to speak a consoling word to her! I beheld my dear sister in the hands of a slave-driver, and compelled to submit to his cruelty! None but one placed in such a situation can for a moment imagine the intense agony to which these reflections subjected me.

CHAPTER XIII.

At last the time for action arrived. The boat landed at a point which appeared to me the place of all others to start from. I found that it would be impossible to carry anything with me, but what was upon my person. I had some provisions, and a single suit of clothes, about half worn. When the boat was discharging her cargo, and the passengers engaged carrying their baggage on and off shore, I improved the opportunity to convey myself with my little effects on land. Taking up a trunk, I went up the wharf, and was soon out of the crowd. I made directly for the woods, where I remained until night, knowing well that I could not travel, even in the State of Ohio, during the day, without danger of being arrested.

I had long since made up my mind that I would not trust myself in the hands of any man, white or colored. The slave is brought up to look upon every white man as an enemy to him and his race; and twenty-one years in slavery had taught me that there were traitors, even among colored people. After dark, I emerged from the woods into a narrow path, which led me into the main travelled road. But I knew not which way to go. I did not know North from South, East from West. I looked in vain for the North Star; a heavy cloud hid it from my view. I walked up and down the road until near midnight, when the clouds disappeared, and I welcomed the sight of my friend,—truly the slave's friend,—the North Star!

As soon as I saw it, I knew my course, and before daylight I travelled twenty or twenty-five miles. It being in the winter, I suffered intensely from the cold; being without an overcoat, and my other clothes rather thin for the season. I was provided with a tinder-box, so that I could make up a fire when necessary. And but for this, I should certainly have frozen to death; for I was determined not to go to any house for shelter. I knew of a man belonging to Gen. Ashly, of St. Louis, who had run away near Cincinnati, on the way to Washington, but had been caught and carried back into slavery; and I felt that a similar fate awaited me, should I be seen by any one. I travelled at night, and lay by during the day.

On the fourth day, my provisions gave out, and then what to do I could not tell. Have something to eat, I must; but how to get it was the question! On the first night after my food was gone, I went to a barn on the road-side, and there found some ears of corn. I took ten or twelve of them, and kept on my journey. During the next day, while in the woods, I roasted my corn and feasted upon it, thanking God that I was so well provided for.

My escape to a land of freedom now appeared certain, and the prospects of the future occupied a great part of my thoughts. What should be my occupation, was a subject of much anxiety to me; and the next thing what should be my name? I have before stated that my old master, Dr. Young, had no children of his own, but had with him a nephew, the son of his brother, Benjamin Young. When this boy was brought to Doctor Young, his name being William, the same as mine, my mother was ordered to change mine to something else. This, at the time, I thought to be one of the most cruel acts that could be committed upon my rights; and I received several very severe whippings for telling people that my name was William, after orders were given to change it. Though young, I was old enough to place a high appreciation upon my name. It was decided, however, to call me "Sandford," and this name I was known by, not only upon my master's plantation, but up to the time that I made my escape. I was sold under the name of Sandford.

But as soon as the subject came to my mind, I resolved on adopting my old name of William, and let Sandford go by the board, for I always hated it. Not because there was anything peculiar in the name; but because it had been forced upon me. It is sometimes common at the south, for slaves to take the name of their masters. Some have a legitimate right to do so. But I always detested the idea of being called by the name of either of my masters. And as for my father, I would rather have adopted the name of "Friday," and been known as the servant of some Robinson Crusoe, than to have taken his name. So I was not only hunting for my liberty, but also hunting for a name; though I regarded the latter as of little consequence, if I could but gain the former. Travelling along the road, I would sometimes speak to myself, sounding my name over, by way of getting used to it, before I should arrive among civilized human beings. On the fifth or sixth day, it rained very fast, and it froze about as fast as it fell, so that my clothes were one glare of ice. I travelled on at night until I became so chilled and benumbed—the wind blowing into my face—that I found it impossible to go any further, and accordingly took shelter in a barn, where I was obliged to walk about to keep from freezing.

I have ever looked upon that night as the most eventful part of my escape from slavery. Nothing but the providence of God, and that old barn, saved me from freezing to death. I received a very severe cold, which settled upon my lungs, and from time to time my feet had been frost-bitten, so that it was with difficulty I could walk. In this situation I travelled two days, when I found that I must seek shelter somewhere, or die.

The thought of death was nothing frightful to me, compared with that of being caught, and again carried back into slavery. Nothing but the prospect of enjoying liberty could have induced me to undergo such trials, for

> "Behind I left the whips and chains,
> Before me were sweet Freedom's plains!"

This, and this alone, cheered me onward. But I at last resolved to seek protection from the inclemency of the weather, and therefore I secured myself behind some logs and brush, intending to wait there until some one should pass by; for I thought it probable that I might see some colored person, or, if not, some one who was not a slaveholder; for I had an idea that I should know a slaveholder as far as I could see him.

CHAPTER XIV.

THE first person that passed was a man in a buggy-wagon. He looked too genteel for me to hail him. Very soon, another passed by on horseback. I attempted speaking to him, but fear made my voice fail me. As he passed, I left my hiding-place, and was approaching the road, when I observed an old man walking towards me, leading a white horse. He had on a broad-brimmed hat and a very long coat, and was evidently walking for exercise. As soon as I saw him, and observed his dress, I thought to myself, "You are the man that I have been looking for!" Nor was I mistaken. He was the very man!

On approaching me, he asked me, "if I was not a slave." I looked at him some time, and then asked him "if he knew of any one who would help me, as I was sick." He answered that he would; but again asked, if I was not a slave. I told him I was. He then said that I was in a very pro-slavery neighborhood, and if I would wait until he went home, he would get a covered wagon for me. I promised to remain. He mounted his horse, and was soon out of sight.

After he was gone, I meditated whether to wait or not; being apprehensive that he had gone for some one to arrest me. But I finally concluded to remain until he should return; removing some few rods to watch his movements. After a suspense of an hour and a half or more, he returned with a two horse covered-wagon, such as are usually seen under the shed of a Quaker meeting-house on Sundays and Thursdays; for the old man proved to be a Quaker of the George Fox stamp.

He took me to his house, but it was some time before I could be induced to enter it; not until the old lady came out, did I venture into the house. I thought I saw something in the old lady's cap that told me I was not only safe, but welcome, in her house. I was not, however, prepared to receive their hospitalities. The only fault I found with them was their being too kind. I had never had a white man to treat me as an equal, and the idea of a white lady waiting on me at the table was still worse! Though the table was loaded with the good things of this life, I could not eat. I thought if I could only be allowed the privilege of eating in the kitchen, I should be more than satisfied!

Finding that I could not eat, the old lady, who was a "Thompsonian," made me a cup of "composition," or "number six;" but it was so strong and hot, that I called it "*number seven*!" However, I soon found myself at home in this family. On different occasions, when telling these facts, I have been asked how I felt upon finding myself regarded as a man by a white family; especially just having run away from one. I cannot say that I have ever answered the question yet.

The fact that I was in all probability a freeman, sounded in my ears like a charm. I am satisfied that none but a slave could place such an appreciation upon liberty as I did at that time. I wanted to see mother and sister, that I might tell them "I was free!" I wanted to see my fellow slaves in St. Louis, and let them know that the chains were no longer upon my limbs. I wanted to see Captain Price, and let him learn from my own lips that I was no more a chattel, but a man! I was anxious, too, thus to inform Mrs. Price that she must get another coachman. And I wanted to see Eliza more than I did either Mr. or Mrs. Price!

The fact that I was a freeman—could walk, talk, eat and sleep as a man, and no one to stand over me with the blood-clotted cowhide—all this made me feel that I was not myself.

The kind friend that had taken me in was named Wells Brown. He was a devoted friend of the slave; but was very old, and not in the enjoyment of good health. After being by the fire awhile, I found that my feet had been very much frozen. I was seized with a fever which threatened to confine me to my bed. But my Thompsonian friends soon raised me, treating me as kindly as if I had been one of their own children. I remained with them twelve or fifteen days, during which time they made me some clothing, and the old gentleman purchased me a pair of boots.

I found that I was about fifty or sixty miles from Dayton, in the State of Ohio, and between one and two hundred miles from Cleaveland, on lake Erie, a place I was desirous of reaching on my way to Canada. This I know will sound strangely to the ears of people in foreign lands, but it is nevertheless true. An American citizen was fleeing from a Democratic, Republican, Christian government, to receive protection under the monarchy of Great Britain. While the people of the United States boast of their freedom, they at the same time keep three millions of their own citizens in chains; and while I am seated here in sight of Bunker Hill Monument, writing this narrative, I am a slave, and no law, not even in Massachusetts, can protect me from the hands of the slaveholder!

Before leaving this good Quaker friend, he inquired what my name was besides William. I told him that I had no other name. "Well," said he, "thee must have another name. Since thee has got out of slavery, thee has become a man, and men always have two names."

I told him that he was the first man to extend the hand of friendship to me, and I would give him the privilege of naming me.

"If I name thee," said he, "I shall call thee Wells Brown, after myself."

"But," said I, "I am not willing to lose my name of William.

As it was taken from me once against my will, I am not willing to part with it again upon any terms."

"Then," said he, "I will call thee William Wells Brown."

"So be it," said I; and I have been known by that name ever since I left the house of my first white friend, Wells Brown.

After giving me some little change, I again started for Canada. In four days I reached a public house, and went in to warm myself. I there learned that some fugitive slaves had just passed through the place. The men in the bar-room were talking about it, and I thought that it must have been myself they referred to, and I was therefore afraid to start, fearing they would seize me; but I finally mustered courage enough, and took my leave. As soon as I was out of sight, I went into the woods, and remained there until night, when I again regained the road, and travelled on until the next day.

Not having had any food for nearly two days, I was faint with hunger, and was in a dilemma what to do, as the little cash supplied me by my adopted father, and which had contributed to my comfort, was now all gone. I however concluded to go to a farm-house, and ask for something to eat. On approaching the door of the first one presenting itself, I knocked, and was soon met by a man who asked me what I wanted. I told him that I would like something to eat. He asked where I was from, and where I was going. I replied that I had come some way, and was going to Cleaveland.

After hesitating a moment or two, he told me that he could give me nothing to eat, adding, "that if I would work, I could get something to eat."

I felt bad, being thus refused something to sustain nature, but did not dare tell him that I was a slave.

Just as I was leaving the door, with a heavy heart, a woman, who proved to be the wife of this gentleman, came to the door, and asked her husband what I wanted? He did not seem inclined to inform her. She therefore asked me herself. I told her that I had asked for something to eat. After a few other questions, she told me to come in, and that she would give me something to eat.

I walked up to the door, but the husband remained in the passage, as if unwilling to let me enter.

She asked him two or three times to get out of the way, and

let me in. But as he did not move, she pushed him on one side, bidding me walk in! I was never before so glad to see a woman push a man aside! Ever since that act, I have been in favor of "woman's rights!"

After giving me as much food as I could eat, she presented me with ten cents, all the money then at her disposal, accompanied with a note to a friend, a few miles further on the road. Thanking this angel of mercy from an overflowing heart, I pushed on my way, and in three days arrived at Cleaveland, Ohio.

Being an entire stranger in this place, it was difficult for me to find where to stop. I had no money, and the lake being frozen, I saw that I must remain until the opening of navigation, or go to Canada by way of Buffalo. But believing myself to be somewhat out of danger, I secured an engagement at the Mansion House, as a table waiter, in payment for my board. The proprietor, however, whose name was E. M. Segur, in a short time, hired me for twelve dollars per month; on which terms I remained until spring, when I found good employment on board a lake steamboat.

I purchased some books, and at leisure moments perused them with considerable advantage to myself. While at Cleaveland, I saw, for the first time, an anti-slavery newspaper. It was the "*Genius of Universal Emancipation*," published by Benjamin Lundy, and though I had no home, I subscribed for the paper. It was my great desire, being out of slavery myself, to do what I could for the emancipation of my brethren yet in chains, and while on Lake Erie, I found many opportunities of "helping their cause along."

It is well known, that a great number of fugitives make their escape to Canada, by way of Cleaveland; and while on the lake, I always made arrangement to carry them on the boat to Buffalo or Detroit, and thus effect their escape to the "promised land." The friends of the slave, knowing that I would transport them without charge, never failed to have a delegation when the boat arrived at Cleaveland. I have sometimes had four or five on board, at one time.

In the year 1842, I conveyed, from the first of May to the first of December, sixty-nine fugitives over Lake Erie to Canada. In 1843, I visited Malden, in Upper Canada, and counted seventeen, in that small village, who owed their escape to my humble efforts.

Soon after coming North, I subscribed for the Liberator, edited by that champion of freedom, William Lloyd Garrison. I labored a season to promote the temperance cause among the colored people, but for the last three years, have been pleading for the victims of American slavery.

WILLIAM WELLS BROWN.

Boston, Mass., June, 1847.

CLOTEL;

OR,

THE PRESIDENT'S DAUGHTER:

A Narrative of Slave Life
IN
THE UNITED STATES.

"WE hold these truths to be self-evident: that all men are created equal; that they are endowed by their Creator with certain inalienable rights, and that among these are LIFE, LIBERTY, and the PURSUIT OF HAPPINESS."

—*Declaration of American Independence.*

PREFACE.

More than two hundred years have elapsed since the first cargo of slaves was landed on the banks of the James River, in the colony of Virginia, from the West coast of Africa. From the introduction of slaves in 1620, down to the period of the separation of the Colonies from the British Crown, the number had increased to five hundred thousand; now there are nearly four million. In fifteen of the thirty-one States, Slavery is made lawful by the Constitution, which binds the several States into one confederacy.

On every foot of soil, over which *Stars* and *Stripes* wave, the negro is considered common property, on which any white man may lay his hand with perfect impunity. The entire white population of the United States, North and South, are bound by their oath to the constitution, and their adhesion to the Fugitive Slave Law, to hunt down the runaway slave and return him to his claimant, and to suppress any effort that may be made by the slaves to gain their freedom by physical force. Twenty-five millions of whites have banded themselves in solemn conclave to keep four millions of blacks in their chains. In all grades of society are to be found men who either hold, buy, or sell slaves, from the statesmen and doctors of divinity, who can own their hundreds, down to the person who can purchase but one.

Were it not for persons in high places owning slaves, and thereby giving the system a reputation, and especially professed Christians, Slavery would long since have been abolished. The influence of the great "honours the corruption, and chastisement doth therefore hide his head." The great aim of the true friends of the slave should be to lay bare the institution, so that the gaze of the world may be upon it, and cause the wise, the prudent, and the pious to withdraw their support from it, and leave it to its own fate. It does the cause of emancipation but little good to cry out in tones of execration against the traders, the kidnappers, the hireling overseers, and brutal drivers, so long as nothing is said to fasten the guilt on those who move in a higher circle.

The fact that slavery was introduced into the American colonies, while they were under the control of the British Crown, is a sufficient reason why Englishmen should feel a lively interest in its abolition; and now that the genius of mechanical invention has brought the two countries so near together, and both having one language and one literature, the influence of British public opinion is very great on the people of the New World.

If the incidents set forth in the following pages should add anything new to the information already given to the Public through similar publications, and should thereby aid in bringing British influence to bear upon American slavery, the main object for which this work was written will have been accomplished.

W. WELLS BROWN.

22, *Cecil Street, Strand, London.*

CONTENTS

CLOTEL;

OR,

THE PRESIDENT'S DAUGHTER.

CHAPTER I.

THE NEGRO SALE.

"WHY stands she near the auction stand,
  That girl so young and fair?
What brings her to this dismal place,
  Why stands she weeping there?"

WITH the growing population of slaves in the Southern States of America, there is a fearful increase of half whites, most of whose fathers are slaveowners, and their mothers slaves. Society does not frown upon the man who sits with his mulatto child upon his knee, whilst its mother stands a slave behind his chair. The late Henry Clay, some years since, predicted that the abolition of negro slavery would be brought about by the amalgamation of the races. John Randolph, a distinguished slaveholder of Virginia, and a prominent statesman, said in a speech in the legislature of his native state, that "the blood of the first American statesmen coursed through the veins of the slave of the South." In all the cities and towns of the slave states, the real negro, or clear black, does not amount to more than one in every four of the slave population. This fact is, of itself, the best evidence of the degraded and immoral condition of the relation of master and slave in the United States of America.

In all the slave states, the law says:—"Slaves shall be deemed, sold, taken, reputed, and adjudged in law to be chattels personal in the hands of their owners and possessors, and their executors, administrators and assigns, to all intents, constructions, and purposes whatsoever." A slave is one who is in the power of a master to whom he belongs. The master may sell him, dispose of his person, his industry, and his labour. He can do nothing, possess nothing, nor acquire anything, but what must belong to his master. The slave is entirely subject to the will of his master, who may correct and chastise him, though not with unusual rigour, or so as to maim and mutilate him, or expose him to the danger of loss of life, or to cause his death. The slave, to remain a slave, must be sensible that there is no appeal from his master. Where the slave is placed by law entirely under the control of the man who claims him, body and soul, as property, what else could be expected than the most depraved social condition? The marriage relation, the oldest and most sacred institution given to man by his Creator, is unknown and unrecognised in the slave laws of the United States. Would that we could say, that the moral and religious teaching in the slave states were better than the laws; but, alas! we cannot. A few years since, some slaveholders became a little uneasy in their minds about the rightfulness of permitting slaves to take to themselves husbands and wives, while they still had others living, and applied to their religious teachers for advice; and the following will show how this grave and important subject was treated:—

> "Is a servant, whose husband or wife has been sold by his or her master into a distant country, to be permitted to marry again?"

The query was referred to a committee, who made the following report; which, after discussion, was adopted:—

> "That, in view of the circumstances in which servants in this country are placed, the committee are unanimous in the opinion, that it is better to permit servants thus circumstanced to take another husband or wife."

Such was the answer from a committee of the "Shiloh Baptist Association;" and instead of receiving light, those who asked the question were plunged into deeper darkness!

A similar question was put to the "Savannah River Association," and the answer, as the following will show, did not materially differ from the one we have already given:—

> "Whether, in a case of involuntary separation, of such a character as to preclude all prospect of future intercourse, the parties ought to be allowed to marry again."

Answer—

> "That such separation among persons situated as our slaves are, is civilly a separation by death; and they believe that, in the sight of God, it would be so viewed. To forbid second marriages in such cases would be to expose the parties, not only to stronger hardships and strong temptation, but to church-censure for acting in obedience to their masters, who cannot be expected to acquiesce in a regulation at variance with justice to the slaves, and to the spirit of that command which regulates marriage among Christians. The slaves are not free agents; and a dissolution by death is not more entirely without their consent, and beyond their control, than by such separation."

Although marriage, as the above indicates, is a matter which the slaveholders do not think is of any importance, or of any binding force with their slaves; yet it would be doing that degraded class an injustice, not to acknowledge that many of them do regard it as a sacred obligation, and show a willingness to obey the commands of God on this subject. Marriage is, indeed, the first and most important institution of human existence—the foundation of all civilisation and culture—the root of church and state. It is the most intimate covenant of heart formed among mankind; and for many persons the only relation in which they feel the true sentiments of humanity. It gives scope for every human virtue, since each of these is developed from the love and confidence which here predominate. It unites all which ennobles and beautifies life,—sympathy, kindness of will and deed, gratitude, devotion, and every delicate, intimate feeling. As the only asylum for true education, it is the first and last sanctuary of human culture. As husband and wife through each other become conscious of complete humanity, and every human feeling, and every human virtue; so children, at their first awakening in the fond covenant of love between parents, both of whom are tenderly concerned for the same object, find an image of complete humanity leagued in free love. The spirit of love which prevails between them acts with creative power upon the young mind, and awakens every germ of goodness within it. This invisible and incalculable influence of parental life acts more upon the child than all the efforts of education, whether by means of instruction, precept, or exhortation. If this be a true picture of the vast influence for good of the institution of marriage, what must be the moral degradation of that people to whom marriage is denied? Not content with depriving them of all the higher and holier enjoyments of this relation, by degrading and darkening their souls, the slaveholder denies to his victim even that slight alleviation of his misery, which would result from the marriage relation being protected by law and public opinion. Such is the influence of slavery in the United States, that the ministers of religion, even in the so-called free states, are the mere echoes, instead of the correctors, of public sentiment.

We have thought it advisable to show that the present system of chattel slavery in America undermines the entire social condition of man, so as to prepare the reader for the following narrative of slave life, in that otherwise happy and prosperous country.

In all the large towns in the Southern States, there is a class of slaves who are permitted to hire their time of their owners, and for which they pay a high price. These are mulatto women, or quadroons, as they are familiarly known, and are distinguished for their fascinating beauty. The handsomest usually pays the highest price for her time. Many of these women are the favourites of persons who furnish them with the means of paying their owners, and not a few are dressed in the most extravagant manner. Reader, when you take into consideration the fact, that amongst the slave population no safeguard is thrown around virtue, and no inducement held out to slave women to be chaste, you will not be surprised when we tell you that immorality and vice pervade the cities of the Southern States in a manner unknown in the cities and towns of the Northern States. Indeed most of the slave women have no higher aspiration than that of becoming the finely-dressed mistress of some white man. And at negro balls and parties, this class of women usually cut the greatest figure.

At the close of the year—the following advertisement appeared in a newspaper published in Richmond, the capital of the state of Virginia:—"Notice: Thirty-eight negroes will be offered for sale on Monday, November 10th, at twelve o'clock, being the entire stock of the late John Graves, Esq. The negroes are in good condition, some of them very prime; among them are several mechanics, able-bodied field hands, plough-boys, and women with children at the breast, and some of them very prolific in their generating qualities, affording a rare opportunity to any one who wishes to raise a strong and healthy lot of servants for their own use. Also several mulatto girls of rare personal qualities: two of them very superior. Any gentleman or lady wishing to purchase, can take any of the above slaves on trial for a week, for which no charge will be made." Amongst the above slaves to be sold were Currer and her two daughters, Clotel and Althesa; the latter were the girls spoken of in the advertisement as "very superior." Currer was a bright mulatto, and of prepossessing appearance, though then nearly forty years of age. She had hired her time for more than twenty years, during which time she had lived in Richmond. In her younger days Currer had been the housekeeper of a young slaveholder; but of later years had been a laundress or washerwoman, and was considered to be a woman of great taste in getting up linen. The gentleman for whom she had kept house was Thomas Jefferson, by whom she had two daughters. Jefferson being called to Washington to fill a government appointment, Currer was left behind, and thus she took herself to the business of washing, by which means she paid her master, Mr. Graves, and supported herself and two children. At the time of the decease of her master, Currer's daughters, Clotel and Althesa, were aged respectively sixteen and fourteen years, and both, like most of their own sex in America, were well grown. Currer early resolved to bring her daughters up as ladies, as she termed it, and therefore imposed little or no work upon them. As her daughters grew older, Currer had to pay a stipulated price for them; yet her notoriety as a laundress of the first class enabled her to put an extra price upon her charges, and thus she and her daughters lived in comparative luxury. To bring up Clotel and Althesa to attract attention, and especially at balls and parties, was the great aim of Currer. Although the term "negro ball" is applied to most of these gatherings, yet a majority of the attendants are often whites. Nearly all the negro parties in the cities and towns of the Southern States are made up of quadroon and mulatto girls, and white men. These are democratic gatherings, where gentlemen, shopkeepers, and their clerks, all appear upon terms of perfect equality. And there is a degree of gentility and decorum in these companies that is not surpassed by similar gatherings of white people in the Slave States. It was at one of these parties that Horatio Green, the son of a wealthy gentleman of Richmond, was first introduced to Clotel. The young man had just returned from college, and was in his twenty-second year. Clotel was sixteen, and was admitted by all to be the most beautiful girl, coloured or white, in the city. So attentive was the young man to the quadroon during the evening that it was noticed by all, and became a matter of general conversation; while Currer appeared delighted beyond measure at her daughter's conquest. From that evening, young Green became the favourite visitor at Currer's house. He soon promised to purchase Clotel, as speedily as it could be effected, and make her mistress of her own dwelling; and Currer looked forward with pride to the time when she should see her daughter emancipated and free. It was a beautiful moonlight night in August, when all who reside in tropical climes are eagerly gasping for a breath of fresh air, that Horatio Green was seated in the small garden behind Currer's cottage, with the object of his affections by his side. And it was here that Horatio drew from his pocket the newspaper, wet from the press, and read the advertisement for the sale of the slaves to which we have alluded; Currer and her two daughters being of the number. At the close of the evening's visit, and as the young man was leaving, he said to the girl, "You shall soon be free and your own mistress."

As might have been expected, the day of sale brought an unusual large number together to compete for the property to be sold. Farmers who make a business of raising slaves for the market were there; slave-traders and speculators were also numerously represented; and in the midst of this throng was one who felt a deeper interest in the result of the sale than any other of the bystanders; this was young Green. True to his promise, he was there with a blank bank check in his pocket, awaiting with impatience to enter the list as a bidder for the beautiful slave. The less valuable slaves were first placed upon the auction block, one after another, and sold to the highest bidder. Husbands and wives were separated with a degree of indifference that is unknown in any other relation of life, except that of slavery. Brothers and sisters were torn from each other; and mothers saw their children leave them for the last time on this earth.

It was late in the day, when the greatest number of persons were thought to be present, that Currer and her daughters were brought forward to the place of sale. Currer was first ordered to ascend the auction stand, which she did with a trembling step. The slave mother was sold to a trader. Althesa, the youngest, and who was scarcely less beautiful than her sister, was sold to the same trader for one thousand dollars. Clotel was the last, and, as was expected, commanded a higher price than any that had been offered for sale that day. The appearance of Clotel on the auction block created a deep sensation amongst the crowd. There she stood, with a complexion as white as most of those who were waiting with a wish to become her purchasers; her features as finely defined as any of her sex of pure Anglo-Saxon; her long black wavy hair done up in the neatest manner; her form tall and graceful, and her whole appearance indicating one superior to her position. The auctioneer commenced by saying, that "Miss Clotel had been reserved for the last, because she was the most valuable. How much gentlemen? Real Albino, fit for a fancy girl for any one. She enjoys good health, and has a sweet temper. How much do you say?" "Five hundred dollars." "Only five hundred for such a girl as this? Gentlemen, she is worth a deal more than that sum; you certainly don't know the value of the article you are bidding upon. Here, gentlemen, I hold in my hand a paper certifying that she has a good moral character." "Seven hundred." "Ah, gentlemen, that is something like. This paper also states that she is very intelligent." "Eight hundred." "She is a devoted Christian, and perfectly trustworthy." "Nine hundred." "Nine fifty." "Ten." "Eleven." "Twelve hundred." Here the sale came to a dead stand. The auctioneer stopped, looked around, and began in a rough manner to relate some anecdotes relative to the sale of slaves, which, he said, had come under his own observation. At this juncture the scene was indeed strange. Laughing, joking, swearing, smoking, spitting, and talking kept up a continual hum and noise amongst the crowd; while the slave-girl stood with tears in her eyes, at one time looking towards her mother and sister, and at another towards the young man whom she hoped would become her purchaser. "The chastity of this girl is pure; she has never been from under her mother's care; she is a virtuous creature." "Thirteen."

"Fourteen." "Fifteen." "Fifteen hundred dollars," cried the auctioneer, and the maiden was struck for that sum. This was a Southern auction, at which the bones, muscles, sinews, blood, and nerves of a young lady of sixteen were sold for five hundred dollars; her moral character for two hundred; her improved intellect for one hundred; her Christianity for three hundred; and her chastity and virtue for four hundred dollars more. And this, too, in a city thronged with churches, whose tall spires look like so many signals pointing to heaven, and whose ministers preach that slavery is a God-ordained institution!

What words can tell the inhumanity, the atrocity, and the immorality of that doctrine which, from exalted office, commends such a crime to the favour of enlightened and Christian people? What indignation from all the world is not due to the government and people who put forth all their strength and power to keep in existence such an institution? Nature abhors it; the age repels it; and Christianity needs all her meekness to forgive it.

Clotel was sold for fifteen hundred dollars, but her purchaser was Horatio Green. Thus closed a negro sale, at which two daughters of Thomas Jefferson, the writer of the Declaration of American Independence, and one of the presidents of the great republic, were disposed of to the highest bidder!

"O God! my every heart-string cries,
Dost thou these scenes behold
In this our boasted Christian land,
And must the truth be told?

"Blush, Christian, blush! for e'en the dark,
Untutored heathen see
Thy inconsistency; and, lo!
They scorn thy God, and thee!"

CHAPTER II.

GOING TO THE SOUTH.

"My country, shall thy honoured name,
  Be as a bye-word through the world?
Rouse! for, as if to blast thy fame,
  This keen reproach is at thee hurled;
The banner that above thee waves,
  Is floating o'er three million slaves."

DICK WALKER, the slave speculator, who had purchased Currer and Althesa, put them in prison until his gang was made up, and then, with his forty slaves, started for the New Orleans market. As many of the slaves had been brought up in Richmond, and had relations residing there, the slave trader determined to leave the city early in the morning, so as not to witness any of those scenes so common where slaves are separated from their relatives and friends, when about departing for the Southern market. This plan was successful; for not even Clotel, who had been every day at the prison to see her mother and sister, knew of their departure. A march of eight days through the interior of the state, and they arrived on the banks of the Ohio river, where they were all put on board a steamer, and then speedily sailed for the place of their destination.

Walker had already advertised in the New Orleans papers, that he would be there at a stated time with "a prime lot of able-bodied slaves ready for field service; together with a few extra ones, between the ages of fifteen and twenty-five." But, like most who make a business of buying and selling slaves for gain, he often bought some who were far advanced in years, and would always try to sell them for five or ten years younger than they actually were. Few persons can arrive at anything like the age of a negro, by mere observation, unless they are well acquainted with the race. Therefore the slave-trader very frequently carried out this deception with perfect impunity. After the steamer had left the wharf, and was fairly on the bosom of the Father of Waters, Walker called his servant Pompey to him, and instructed him as to "getting the negroes ready for market." Amongst the forty negroes were several whose appearance indicated that they had seen some years, and had gone through some services. Their grey hair and whiskers at once pronounced them to be above the ages set down in the trader's advertisement. Pompey had long been with the trader, and knew his business; and if he did not take delight in discharging his duty, he did it with a degree of alacrity, so that he might receive the approbation of his master. "Pomp," as Walker usually called him, was of real negro blood, and would often say, when alluding to himself, "Dis nigger is no countefit; he is de genewine artekil." Pompey was of low stature, round face, and, like most of his race, had a set of teeth, which for whiteness and beauty could not be surpassed; his eyes large, lips thick, and hair short and woolly. Pompey had been with Walker so long, and had seen so much of the buying and selling of slaves, that he appeared perfectly indifferent to the heartrending scenes which daily occurred in his presence. It was on the second day of the steamer's voyage that Pompey selected five of the old slaves, took them into a room by themselves, and commenced preparing them for the market. "Well," said Pompey, addressing himself to the company, "I is de gentman dat is to get you ready, so dat you will bring marser a good price in de Orleans market. How old is you?" addressing himself to a man who, from appearance, was not less than forty. "If I live to see next corn-planting time I will either be forty-five or fifty-five, I don't know which." "Dat may be," replied Pompey; "But now you is only thirty years old; dat is what marser says you is to be." "I know I is more den dat," responded the man. "I knows nothing about dat," said Pompey; "but when you get in de market, an anybody axe you how old you is, an you tell 'em forty-five, marser will tie you up an gib you de whip like smoke. But if you tell 'em dat you is only thirty, den he wont." "Well den, I guess I will only be thirty when dey axe me," replied the chattel.

"What your name?" inquired Pompey. "Geemes," answered the man. "Oh, Uncle Jim, is it?" "Yes." "Den you must have off dem dare whiskers of yours, an when you get to Orleans you must grease dat face an make it look shiney." This was all said by Pompey in a manner which clearly showed that he knew what he was about. "How old is you?" asked Pompey of a tall, strong-looking man. "I was twenty-nine last potato-digging time," said the man. "What's your name?" "My name is

Tobias, but dey call me 'Toby.'" "Well, Toby, or Mr. Tobias, if dat will suit you better, you is now twenty-three years old, an no more. Dus you hear dat?" "Yes," responded Toby. Pompey gave each to understand how old he was to be when asked by persons who wished to purchase, and then reported to his master that the "old boys" were all right. At eight o'clock on the evening of the third day, the lights of another steamer were seen in the distance, and apparently coming up very fast. This was a signal for a general commotion on the Patriot, and everything indicated that a steamboat race was at hand. Nothing can exceed the excitement attendant upon a steamboat on the Mississippi River. By the time the boats had reached Memphis, they were side by side, and each exerting itself to keep the ascendancy in point of speed. The night was clear, the moon shining brightly, and the boats so near to each other that the passengers were calling out from one boat to the other. On board the Patriot, the firemen were using oil, lard, butter, and even bacon, with the wood, for the purpose of raising the steam to its highest pitch. The blaze, mingled with the black smoke, showed plainly that the other boat was burning more than wood. The two boats soon locked, so that the hands of the boats were passing from vessel to vessel, and the wildest excitement prevailed throughout amongst both passengers and crew. At this moment the engineer of the Patriot was seen to fasten down the safety-valve, so that no steam should escape. This was, indeed, a dangerous resort. A few of the boat hands who saw what had taken place, left that end of the boat for more secure quarters.

The Patriot stopped to take in passengers, and still no steam was permitted to escape. At the starting of the boat cold water was forced into the boilers by the machinery, and, as might have been expected, one of the boilers immediately exploded. One dense fog of steam filled every part of the vessel, while shrieks, groans, and cries were heard on every hand. The saloons and cabins soon had the appearance of a hospital. By this time the boat had landed, and the Columbia, the other boat, had come alongside to render assistance to the disabled steamer. The killed and scalded (nineteen in number) were put on shore, and the Patriot, taken in tow by the Columbia, was soon again on its way.

"BETTING" A NEGRO IN THE SOUTHERN STATES.

It was now twelve o'clock at night, and instead of the passengers being asleep the majority were gambling in the saloons. Thousands of dollars change hands during a passage from Louisville or St. Louis to New Orleans on a Mississippi steamer, and many men, and even ladies, are completely ruined. "Go call my boy, steward," said Mr. Smith, as he took his cards one by one from the table. In a few moments a fine looking, bright-eyed mulatto boy, apparently about fifteen years of age, was standing by his master's side at the table. "I will see you, and five hundred dollars better," said Smith, as his servant Jerry approached the table. "What price do you set on that boy?" asked Johnson, as he took a roll of bills from his pocket. "He will bring a thousand dollars, any day, in the New Orleans market," replied Smith. "Then you bet the whole of the boy, do you?" "Yes." "I call you, then," said Johnson, at the same time spreading his cards out upon the table. "You have beat me," said Smith, as soon as he saw the cards. Jerry, who was standing on top of the table, with the bank notes and silver dollars round his feet, was now ordered to descend from the table. "You will not forget that you belong to me," said Johnson, as the young slave was stepping from the table to a chair. "No, sir," replied the chattel. "Now go back to your bed, and be up in time to-morrow morning to brush my clothes and clean my boots, do you hear?" "Yes, sir," responded Jerry, as he wiped the tears from his eyes.

Smith took from his pocket the bill of sale and handed it to Johnson; at the same time saying, "I claim the right of redeeming that boy, Mr. Johnson. My father gave him to me when I came of age, and I promised not to part with him." "Most certainly, sir, the boy shall be yours, whenever you hand me over a cool thousand," replied Johnson. The next morning, as the passengers were assembling in the breakfast saloons and upon the guards of the vessel, and the servants were seen running about waiting upon or looking for their masters, poor Jerry was entering his new master's state-room with his boots. "Who do you belong to?" said a gentleman to an old black man, who came along leading a fine dog that he had been feeding. "When I went to sleep last night, I belonged to Governor Lucas; but I understand dat he is bin gambling all night, so I don't know who owns me dis morning." Such is the uncertainty of a slave's position. He goes to bed at night the property of the man with whom he has lived for years, and gets up in the morning the slave of some one whom he has never seen before! To behold five or six tables in a steamboat's cabin, with half-a-dozen men playing at cards, and money, pistols, bowie-knives, &c. all in confusion on the tables, is what may be seen at almost any time on the Mississippi river.

On the fourth day, while at Natchez, taking in freight and passengers, Walker, who had been on shore to see some of his old customers, returned, accompanied by a tall, thin-faced man, dressed in black, with a white neckcloth, which immediately proclaimed him to be a clergyman. "I want a good, trusty woman for house service," said the stranger, as they entered the cabin where Walker's slaves were kept. "Here she is, and no mistake," replied the trader. "Stand up, Currer, my gal; here's a gentleman who wishes to see if you will suit him." Althesa clung to her mother's side, as the latter rose from her seat. "She is a rare cook, a good washer, and will suit you to a T, I am sure." "If you buy me, I hope you will buy my daughter too," said the woman, in rather an excited manner. "I only want one for my own use, and would not need another," said the man in black, as he and the trader left the room. Walker and the parson went into the saloon, talked over the matter, the bill of sale was made out, the money paid over, and the clergyman left, with the understanding that the woman should be delivered to him at his house. It seemed as if poor Althesa would have wept herself to death, for the first two days after her mother had been torn from her side by the hand of the ruthless trafficker in human flesh. On the arrival of the boat at Baton Rouge, an additional number of passengers were taken on board; and, amongst them, several persons who had been attending the races. Gambling and drinking were now the order of the day. Just as the ladies and gentlemen were assembling at the supper-table, the report of a pistol was heard in the direction of the Social Hall, which caused great uneasiness to the ladies, and took the gentlemen to that part of the cabin. However, nothing serious had occurred. A man at one of the tables where they were gambling had been seen attempting to conceal a card in his sleeve, and one of the party seized his pistol and fired; but fortunately the barrel of the pistol was knocked up, just as it was about to be discharged, and the ball passed through the upper deck, instead of the man's head, as intended. Order was soon restored; all went on well the remainder of the night, and the next day, at ten o'clock, the boat arrived at New Orleans, and the passengers went to the hotels and the slaves to the market!

"Our eyes are yet on Afric's shores,
Her thousand wrongs we still deplore;
We see the grim slave trader there;
We hear his fettered victim's prayer;
And hasten to the sufferer's aid,
Forgetful of *our own 'slave trade.'*

"The Ocean 'Pirate's' fiend-like form
Shall sink beneath the vengeance-storm;
His heart of steel shall quake before
The battle-din and havoc roar:
The knave shall die, the Law hath said,
While it protects our own '*slave trade.*'

"What earthly eye presumes to scan
The wily Proteus-heart of man?—
What potent hand will e'er unroll
The mantled treachery of his soul!—
O where is he who hath surveyed
The horrors of *our own 'slave trade?'*

"There is an eye that wakes in light,
There is a hand of peerless might;
Which, soon or late, shall yet assail
And rend dissimulation's veil:
Which *will* unfold the masquerade
Which justifies *our own 'slave trade.'*"

CHAPTER III.

THE NEGRO CHASE.

WE shall now return to Natchez, where we left Currer in the hands of the Methodist parson. For many years, Natchez has enjoyed a notoriety for the inhumanity and barbarity of its inhabitants, and the cruel deeds perpetrated there, which have not been equalled in any other city in the Southern States. The following advertisements, which we take from a newspaper published in the vicinity, will show how they catch their negroes who believe in the doctrine that "all men are created free."

"NEGRO DOGS.—The undersigned, having bought the entire pack of negro dogs (of the Hay and Allen stock), *he now proposes to catch runaway negroes.* His charges will be three dollars a day for hunting, and fifteen dollars for catching a runaway. He resides three and one half miles north of Livingston, near the lower Jones' Bluff Road.

"WILLIAM GAMBREL."

"Nov. 6, 1845."

"NOTICE.—The subscriber, living on Carroway Lake, on Hoe's Bayou, in Carroll parish, sixteen miles on the road leading from Bayou Mason to Lake Providence, is ready with a pack of dogs to hunt runaway negroes at any time. These dogs are well trained, and are known throughout the parish. Letters addressed to me at Providence will secure immediate attention. My terms are five dollars per day for hunting the trails, whether the negro is caught or not. Where a twelve hours' trail is shown, and the negro not taken, no charge is made. For taking a negro, twenty-five dollars, and no charge made for hunting.

"JAMES W. HALL."

"Nov. 26, 1847."

These dogs will attack a negro at their master's bidding and cling to him as the bull-dog will cling to a beast. Many are the speculations, as to whether the negro will be secured alive or dead, when these dogs once get on his track. A slave hunt took place near Natchez, a few days after Currer's arrival, which was calculated to give her no favourable opinion of the people. Two slaves had run off owing to severe punishment. The dogs were put upon their trail. The slaves went into the swamps, with the hope that the dogs when put on their scent would be unable to follow them through the water. The dogs soon took to the swamp, which lies between the highlands, which was now covered with water, waist deep: here these faithful animals, *swimming* nearly all the time, followed the zigzag course, the tortuous twistings and windings of these two fugitives, who, it was afterwards discovered, were lost; sometimes scenting the tree wherein they had found a temporary refuge from the mud and water; at other places where the deep mud had pulled off a shoe, and they had not taken time to put it on again. For two hours and a half, for four or five miles, did men and dogs wade through this bushy, dismal swamp, surrounded with grim-visaged alligators, who seemed to look on with jealous eye at this encroachment of their hereditary domain; now losing the trail—then slowly and dubiously taking it off again, until they triumphantly threaded it out, bringing them back to the river, where it was found that the negroes had crossed their own trail, near the place of starting. In the meantime a heavy shower had taken place, putting out the trail. The negroes were now at least four miles ahead.

It is well known to hunters that it requires the keenest scent and best blood to overcome such obstacles, and yet these persevering and sagacious animals conquered every difficulty. The slaves now made a straight course for the Baton Rouge and Bayou Sara road, about four miles distant.

Feeling hungry now, after their morning walk, and perhaps thirsty, too, they went about half a mile off the road, and ate a good, hearty, substantial breakfast. Negroes must eat, as well as other people, but the dogs will tell on them. Here, for a moment, the dogs are at fault, but soon unravel the mystery, and bring them back to the road again; and now what before was wonderful, becomes almost a miracle. Here, in this common highway—the thoroughfare for the whole country around—through mud and through mire, meeting waggons and teams, and different solitary wayfarers, and, what above all is most astonishing, actually running through a gang of negroes, their favourite game, who were working on the road, they pursue the track of the two negroes; they even ran for eight miles to the very edge of the plain—the slaves near them for the last mile. At first they would fain believe it some hunter chasing deer. Nearer and nearer the whimpering pack presses on; the delusion begins to dispel; all at once the truth flashes upon them like a glare of light; their hair stands on end; 'tis Tabor with his dogs. The scent becomes warmer and warmer. What was an irregular cry, now deepens into one ceaseless roar, as the relentless pack rolls on after its human prey. It puts one in mind of Actæon and his dogs. They grow desperate and leave the road, in the vain hope of shaking them off. Vain hope, indeed! The momentary cessation only adds new zest to the chase. The cry grows louder and louder; the yelp grows short and quick, sure indication that the game is at hand. It is a perfect rush upon the part of the hunters, while the negroes call upon their weary and jaded limbs to do their best, but they falter and stagger beneath them. The breath of the hounds is almost upon their very heels, and yet they have a vain hope of escaping these sagacious animals. They can run no longer; the dogs are upon them; they hastily attempt to climb a tree, and as the last one is nearly out of reach, the catch-dog seizes him by the leg, and brings him to the ground; he sings out lustily and the dogs are called off. After this man was secured, the one in the tree was ordered to come down; this, however, he refused to do, but a gun being pointed at him, soon caused him to change his mind. On reaching the ground, the fugitive made one more bound, and the chase again commenced. But it was of no use to run and he soon yielded. While being tied, he committed an unpardonable offence: he resisted, and for that he must be made an example on their arrival home. A mob was collected together, and a Lynch court was held, to determine what was best to be done with the negro who had had the impudence to raise his hand against a white man. The Lynch court decided that the negro should be burnt at the stake. A Natchez newspaper, the *Free Trader*, giving an account of it says,

"The body was taken and chained to a tree immediately on the banks of the Mississippi, on what is called Union Point. Faggots were then collected and piled around him, to which he appeared quite indifferent. When the work was completed, he was asked what he had to say. He then warned all to take example by him, and asked the prayers of all around; he then called for a drink of water, which was handed to him; he drank it, and said, 'Now set fire—I am ready to go in peace!' The torches were lighted, and placed in the pile, which soon ignited. He watched unmoved the curling flame that grew, until it began to entwine itself around and feed upon his body; then he sent forth cries of agony painful to the ear, begging some one to blow his brains out; at the same time surging with almost superhuman strength, until the staple with which the chain was fastened to the tree (not being well secured) drew out, and he leaped from the burning pile. At that moment the sharp ringing of several rifles was heard: the body of the negro fell a corpse on the ground. He was picked up by some two or three, and again thrown into the fire, and consumed, not a vestige remaining to show that such a being ever existed."

Nearly 4,000 slaves were collected from the plantations in the neighbourhood to witness this scene. Numerous speeches were made by the magistrates and ministers of religion to the large concourse of slaves, warning them, and telling them that the same fate awaited them, if they should prove rebellious to their owners. There are hundreds of negroes who run away and live in the woods. Some take refuge in the swamps, because they are less frequented by human beings. A Natchez newspaper gave the following account of the hiding-place of a slave who had been captured:—

> "A runaway's den was discovered on Sunday, near the Washington Spring, in a little patch of woods, where it had been for several months so artfully concealed under ground, that it was detected only by accident, though in sight of two or three houses, and near the road and fields where there has been constant daily passing. The entrance was concealed by a pile of pine straw, representing a hog-bed, which being removed, discovered a trap-door and steps that led to a room about six feet square, comfortably ceiled with plank, containing a small fire-place, the flue of which was ingeniously conducted above ground and concealed by the straw. The inmates took the alarm, and made their escape; *but Mr. Adams and his excellent dogs being put upon the trail, soon run down and secured one of them*, which proved to be a negro-fellow who had been out about a year. He stated that the other occupant was a woman, who had been a runaway a still longer time. In the den was found a quantity of meal, bacon, corn, potatoes, &c. and

various cooking utensils and wearing apparel."—*Vicksburgh Sentinel*, Dec. 6th, 1838.

Currer was one of those who witnessed the execution of the slave at the stake, and it gave her no very exalted opinion of the people of the cotton growing district.

CHAPTER IV.

THE QUADROON'S HOME.

"How sweetly on the hill-side sleeps
The sunlight with its quickening rays!
The verdant trees that crown the steeps,
Grow greener in its quivering blaze."

About three miles from Richmond is a pleasant plain, with here and there a beautiful cottage surrounded by trees so as scarcely to be seen. Among them was one far retired from the public roads, and almost hidden among the trees. It was a perfect model of rural beauty. The piazzas that surrounded it were covered with clematis and passion flower. The pride of China mixed its oriental looking foliage with the majestic magnolia, and the air was redolent with the fragrance of flowers, peeping out of every nook and nodding upon you with a most unexpected welcome. The tasteful hand of art had not learned to imitate the lavish beauty and harmonious disorder of nature, but they lived together in loving amity, and spoke in accordant tones. The gateway rose in a gothic arch, with graceful tracery in iron work, surmounted by a cross, round which fluttered and played the mountain fringe, that lightest and most fragile of vines. This cottage was hired by Horatio Green for Clotel, and the quadroon girl soon found herself in her new home.

The tenderness of Clotel's conscience, together with the care her mother had with her and the high value she placed upon virtue, required an outward marriage; though she well knew that a union with her proscribed race was unrecognised by law, and therefore the ceremony would give her no legal hold on Horatio's constancy. But her high poetic nature regarded reality rather than the semblance of things; and when he playfully asked how she could keep him if he wished to run away, she replied, "If the mutual love we have for each other, and the dictates of your own conscience do not cause you to remain my husband, and your affections fall from me, I would not, if I could, hold you by a single fetter." It was indeed a marriage sanctioned by heaven, although unrecognised on earth. There the young couple lived secluded from the world, and passed their time as happily as circumstances would permit. It was Clotel's wish that Horatio should purchase her mother and sister, but the young man pleaded that he was unable, owing to the fact that he had not come into possession of his share of property, yet he promised that when he did, he would seek them out and purchase them. Their first-born was named Mary, and her complexion was still lighter than her mother. Indeed she was not darker than other white children. As the child grew older, it more and more resembled its mother. The iris of her large dark eye had the melting mezzotinto, which remains the last vestige of African ancestry, and gives that plaintive expression, so often observed, and so appropriate to that docile and injured race. Clotel was still happier after the birth of her dear child; for Horatio, as might have been expected, was often absent day and night with his friends in the city, and the edicts of society had built up a wall of separation between the quadroon and them. Happy as Clotel was in Horatio's love, and surrounded by an outward environment of beauty, so well adapted to her poetic spirit, she felt these incidents with inexpressible pain. For herself she cared but little; for she had found a sheltered home in Horatio's heart, which the world might ridicule, but had no power to profane. But when she looked at her beloved Mary, and reflected upon the unavoidable and dangerous position which the tyranny of society had awarded her, her soul was filled with anguish. The rare loveliness of the child increased daily, and was evidently ripening into most marvellous beauty. The father seemed to rejoice in it with unmingled pride; but in the deep tenderness of the mother's eye, there was an indwelling sadness that spoke of anxious thoughts and fearful foreboding. Clotel now urged Horatio to remove to France or England, where both her and her child would be free, and where colour was not a crime. This request excited but little opposition, and was so attractive to his imagination, that he might have overcome all intervening obstacles, had not "a change come over the spirit of his dreams." He still loved Clotel; but he was now becoming engaged in political and other affairs which kept him oftener and longer from the young mother; and ambition to become a statesman was slowly gaining the ascendancy over him.

Among those on whom Horatio's political success most depended was a very popular and wealthy man, who had an only daughter. His visits to the house were at first purely of a political nature; but the young lady was pleasing, and he fancied he discovered in her a sort of timid preference for himself. This excited his vanity, and awakened thoughts of the great worldly advantages connected with a union. Reminiscences of his first love kept these vague ideas in check for several months; for with it was associated the idea of restraint. Moreover, Gertrude, though inferior in beauty, was yet a pretty contrast to her rival. Her light hair fell in silken ringlets down her shoulders, her blue eyes were gentle though inexpressive, and her healthy cheeks were like opening rosebuds. He had already become accustomed to the dangerous experiment of resisting his own inward convictions; and this new impulse to ambition, combined with the strong temptation of variety in love, met the ardent young man weakened in moral principle, and unfettered by laws of the land. The change wrought upon him was soon noticed by Clotel.

CHAPTER V.

THE SLAVE MARKET.

"WHAT! mothers from their children riven!
What! God's own image bought and sold!
Americans to market driven,
And barter'd as the brute for gold."—*Whittier.*

NOT far from Canal-street, in the city of New Orleans, stands a large two story flat building surrounded by a stone wall twelve feet high, the top of which is covered with bits of glass, and so constructed as to prevent even the possibility of any one's passing over it without sustaining great injury. Many of the rooms resemble cells in a prison. In a small room near the "office" are to be seen any number of iron collars, hobbles, handcuffs, thumbscrews, cowhides, whips, chains, gags, and yokes. A back yard inclosed by a high wall looks something like the playground attached to one of our large New England schools, and in which are rows of benches and swings. Attached to the back premises is a good-sized kitchen, where two old negresses are at work, stewing, boiling, and baking, and occasionally wiping the sweat from their furrowed and swarthy brows.

The slave-trader Walker, on his arrival in New Orleans, took up his quarters at this slave pen with his gang of human cattle; and the morning after, at ten o'clock, they were exhibited for sale. There, first of all, was the beautiful Althesa, whose pale countenance and dejected look told how many sad hours she had passed since parting with her mother at Natchez. There was a poor woman who had been separated from her husband and five children. Another woman, whose looks and manner were expressive of deep anguish, sat by her side. There, too, was "Uncle Geemes," with his whiskers off, his face shaved clean, and the grey hair plucked out, and ready to be sold for ten years younger than he was. Toby was also there, with his face shaved and greased, ready for inspection. The examination commenced, and was carried on in a manner calculated to shock the feelings of any one not devoid of the milk of human kindness. "What are you wiping your eyes for?" inquired a fat, red-faced man, with a white hat set on one side of his head, and a cigar in his mouth, of a woman who sat on one of the stools. "I s'pose I have been crying." "Why do you cry?" "Because I have left my man behind." "Oh, if I buy you I will furnish you with a better man than you left. I have lots of young bucks on my farm." "I don't want, and will never have, any other man," replied the woman. "What's your name?" asked a man in a straw hat of a tall negro man, who stood with his arms folded across his breast, and leaning against the wall. "My name is Aaron, sir." "How old are you?" "Twenty-five." "Where were you raised?" "In old Virginny, sir." "How many men have owned you?" "Four." "Do you enjoy good health?" "Yes, sir." "How long did you live with your first owner?" "Twenty years." "Did you ever run away?" "No, sir." "Did you ever strike your master?" "No, sir." "Were you ever whipped much?" "No, sir, I s'pose I did not deserve it." "How long did you live with your second master?" "Ten years, sir." "Have you a good appetite?" "Yes, sir." "Can you eat your allowance?" "Yes, sir, when I can get it." "What were you employed at in Virginia?" "I worked in de terbacar feel." "In the tobacco field?" "Yes, sir." "How old did you say you were?" "I will be twenty-five if I live to see next sweet potater-digging time." "I am a cotton planter, and if I buy you, you will have to work in the cotton field. My men pick one hundred and fifty pounds a day, and the women one hundred and forty, and those who fail to pick their task receive five stripes from the cat for each pound that is wanting. Now, do you think you could keep up with the rest of the hands?" "I don't know, sir, I 'spec I'd have to." "How long did you live with your third master?" "Three years, sir." "Why, this makes you thirty-three, I thought you told me you was only twenty-five?" Aaron now looked first at the planter, then at the trader, and seemed perfectly bewildered. He had forgotten the lesson given him by Pompey as to his age, and the planter's circuitous talk (doubtless to find out the slave's real age) had the negro off his guard. "I must see your back, so as to know how much you have been whipped, before I think of buying," said the planter. Pompey, who had been standing by during the examination, thought that his services were now required, and stepping forward with a degree of officiousness, said to Aaron, "Don't you hear de gentman tell you he want to zamon your limbs. Come, unharness yeself, old boy, an don't be standing dar." Aaron was soon examined and pronounced "sound;" yet the conflicting statement about the age was not satisfactory.

Fortunate for Althesa she was spared the pain of undergoing such an examination. Mr. Crawford, a teller in one of the banks, had just been married, and wanted a maid-servant for his wife; and passing through the market in the early part of the day, was pleased with the young slave's appearance and purchased her, and in his dwelling the quadroon found a much better home than often falls to the lot of a slave sold in the New Orleans market. The heart-rending and cruel traffic in slaves which has been so often described, is not confined to any particular class of persons. No one forfeits his or her character or standing in society, by buying or selling slaves; or even raising slaves for the market. The precise number of slaves carried from the slave-raising to the slave-consuming states, we have no means of knowing. But it must be very great, as more than forty thousand were sold and taken out of the state of Virginia in one year. Known to God only is the amount of human agony and suffering which sends its cry from the slave markets and negro pens, unheard and unheeded by man, up to his ear; mothers weeping for their children, breaking the night-silence with the shrieks of their breaking hearts. From some you will hear the burst of bitter lamentation, while from others the loud, hysteric laugh, denoting still deeper agony. Most of them leave the market for cotton or rice plantations,

"Where the slave-whip ceaseless swings,
Where the noisome insect stings,
Where the fever demon strews
Poison with the falling dews,
Where the sickly sunbeams glare
Through the hot and misty air."

CHAPTER VI.

THE RELIGIOUS TEACHER.

"WHAT! preach and enslave men?
Give thanks—and rob thy own afflicted poor?
Talk of thy glorious liberty, and then
Bolt hard the captive's door?"—*Whittier.*

THE Rev. John Peck was a native of the state of Connecticut, where he was educated for the ministry, in the Methodist persuasion. His father was a strict follower of John Wesley, and spared no pains in his son's education, with the hope that he would one day be as renowned as the great leader of his sect. John had scarcely finished his education at New Haven, when he was invited by an uncle, then on a visit to his father, to spend a few months at Natchez in the state of Mississippi. Young Peck accepted his uncle's invitation, and accompanied him to the South. Few young men, and especially clergymen, going fresh from a college to the South, but are looked upon as geniuses in a small way, and who are not invited to all the parties in the neighbourhood. Mr. Peck was not an exception to this rule. The society into which he was thrown on his arrival at Natchez was too brilliant for him not to be captivated by it; and, as might have been expected, he succeeded in captivating a plantation with seventy slaves, if not the heart of the lady to whom it belonged. Added to this, he became a popular preacher, had a large congregation with a snug salary. Like other planters, Mr. Peck confided the care of his farm to Ned Huckelby, an overseer of high reputation in his way. The Poplar Farm, as it was called, was situated in a beautiful valley nine miles from Natchez, and near the river Mississippi. The once unshorn face of nature had given way, and now the farm blossomed with a splendid harvest, the neat cottage stood in a grove where Lombardy poplars lift their tufted tops almost to prop the skies; the willow, locust, and horse-chesnut spread their branches, and flowers never cease to blossom. This was the parson's country house, where the family spent only two months during the year.

The town residence was a fine villa, seated upon the brow of a hill at the edge of the city. It was in the kitchen of this house that Currer found her new home. Mr. Peck was, every inch of him, a democrat, and early resolved that his "people," as he called his slaves, should be well fed and not over-worked, and therefore laid down the law and gospel to the overseer as well as the slaves.

"It is my wish," said he to Mr. Carlton, an old school-fellow, who was spending a few days with him, "it is my wish that a new system be adopted on the plantations in this estate. I believe that the sons of Ham should have the gospel, and I intend that my negroes shall. The gospel is calculated to make mankind better, and none should be without it." "What say you," replied Carlton, "about the right of man to his liberty?" "Now, Carlton, you have begun again to harp about man's rights; I really wish you could see this matter as I do. I have searched in vain for any authority for man's natural rights; if he had any, they existed before the fall. That is, Adam and Eve may have had some rights which God gave them, and which modern philosophy, in its pretended reverence for the name of God, prefers to call natural rights. I can imagine they had the right to eat of the fruit of the trees of the garden; they were restricted even in this by the prohibition of one. As far as I know without positive assertion, their liberty of action was confined to the garden. These were not 'inalienable rights,' however, for they forfeited both them and life with the first act of disobedience. Had they, after this, any rights? We cannot imagine them; they were condemned beings; they could have no rights, but by Christ's gift as king. These are the only rights man can have as an independent isolated being, if we choose to consider him in this impossible position, in which so many theorists have placed him. If he had no rights, he could suffer no wrongs. Rights and wrongs are therefore necessarily the creatures of society, such as man would establish himself in his gregarious state. They are, in this state, both artificial and voluntary. Though man has no rights, as thus considered, undoubtedly he has the power, by such arbitrary rules of right and wrong as his necessity enforces." "I regret I cannot see eye to eye with you," said Carlton. "I am a disciple of Rousseau, and have for years made the rights of man my study; and I must confess to you that I can see no difference between white men and black men as it regards liberty." "Now, my dear Carlton, would you really have the negroes enjoy the same rights with ourselves?" "I would, most certainly. Look at our great Declaration of Independence; look even at the constitution of our own Connecticut, and see what is said in these about liberty." "I regard all this talk about rights as mere humbug. The Bible is older than the Declaration of Independence, and there I take my stand. The Bible furnishes to us the armour of proof, weapons of heavenly temper and mould, whereby we can maintain our ground against all attacks. But this is true only when we obey its directions, as well as employ its sanctions. Our rights are there established, but it is always in connection with our duties. If we neglect the one we cannot make good the other. Our domestic institutions can be maintained against the world, if we but allow Christianity to throw its broad shield over them. But if we so act as to array the Bible against our social economy, they must fall. Nothing ever yet stood long against Christianity. Those who say that religious instruction is inconsistent with our peculiar civil polity, are the worst enemies of that polity. They would drive religious men from its defence. Sooner or later, if these views prevail, they will separate the religious portion of our community from the rest, and thus divided we shall become an easy prey. Why, is it not better that Christian men should hold slaves than unbelievers? We know how to value the bread of life, and will not keep it from our slaves."

"Well, every one to his own way of thinking," said Carlton, as he changed his position. "I confess," added he, "that I am no great admirer of either the Bible or slavery. My heart is my guide: my conscience is my Bible. I wish for nothing further to satisfy me of my duty to man. If I act rightly to mankind, I shall fear nothing." Carlton had drunk too deeply of the bitter waters of infidelity, and had spent too many hours over the writings of Rousseau, Voltaire, and Thomas Paine, to place that appreciation upon the Bible and its teachings that it demands. During this conversation there was another person in the room, seated by the window, who, although at work upon a fine piece of lace, paid every attention to what was said. This was Georgiana, the only daughter of the parson. She had just returned from Connecticut, where she had finished her education. She had had the opportunity of contrasting the spirit of

Christianity and liberty in New England with that of slavery in her native state, and had learned to feel deeply for the injured negro. Georgiana was in her nineteenth year, and had been much benefited by a residence of five years at the North. Her form was tall and graceful; her features regular and well defined; and her complexion was illuminated by the freshness of youth, beauty, and health. The daughter differed from both the father and his visitor upon the subject which they had been discussing, and as soon as an opportunity offered, she gave it as her opinion, that the Bible was both the bulwark of Christianity and of liberty. With a smile she said, "Of course, papa will overlook my differing from him, for although I am a native of the South, I am by education and sympathy a Northerner." Mr. Peck laughed and appeared pleased, rather than otherwise, at the manner in which his daughter had expressed herself.

From this Georgiana took courage and said, "We must try the character of slavery, and our duty in regard to it, as we should try any other question of character and duty. To judge justly of the character of anything, we must know what it does. That which is good does good, and that which is evil does evil. And as to duty, God's designs indicate his claims. That which accomplishes the manifest design of God is right; that which counteracts it, wrong. Whatever, in its proper tendency and general effect, produces, secures, or extends human welfare, is according to the will of God, and is good; and our duty is to favour and promote, according to our power, that which God favours and promotes by the general law of his providence. On the other hand, whatever in its proper tendency and general effect destroys, abridges, or renders insecure, human welfare, is opposed to God's will, and is evil. And as whatever accords with the will of God, in any manifestation of it should be done and persisted in, so whatever opposes that will should not be done, and if done, should be abandoned. Can that then be right, be well doing—can that obey God's behest, which makes a man a slave? which dooms him and all his posterity, in limitless generations, to bondage, to unrequited toil through life? 'Thou shalt love thy neighbour as thyself.' This single passage of Scripture should cause us to have respect to the rights of the slave. True Christian love is of an enlarged, disinterested nature. It loves all who love the Lord Jesus Christ in sincerity, without regard to colour or condition." "Georgiana, my dear, you are an abolitionist; your talk is fanaticism," said Mr. Peck in rather a sharp tone; but the subdued look of the girl, and the presence of Carlton, caused the father to soften his language. Mr. Peck having lost his wife by consumption, and Georgiana being his only child, he loved her too dearly to say more, even if he felt displeased. A silence followed this exhortation from the young Christian. But her remarks had done a noble work. The father's heart was touched; and the sceptic, for the first time, was viewing Christianity in its true light.

"I think I must go out to your farm," said Carlton, as if to break the silence. "I shall be pleased to have you go," returned Mr. Peck. "I am sorry I can't go myself, but Huckelby will show you every attention; and I feel confident that when you return to Connecticut, you will do me the justice to say, that I am one who looks after my people, in a moral, social, and religious point of view." "Well, what do you say to my spending next Sunday there?" "Why, I think that a good move; you will then meet with Snyder, our missionary." "Oh, you have missionaries in these parts, have you?" "Yes," replied Mr. Peck; "Snyder is from New York, and is our missionary to the poor, and preaches to our 'people' on Sunday; you will no doubt like him; he is a capital fellow." "Then I shall go," said Carlton, "but only wish I had company." This last remark was intended for Miss Peck, for whom he had the highest admiration.

It was on a warm Sunday morning, in the month of May, that Miles Carlton found himself seated beneath a fine old apple tree, whose thick leaves entirely shaded the ground for some distance round. Under similar trees and near by, were gathered together all the "people" belonging to the plantation. Hontz Snyder was a man of about forty years of age, exceedingly low in stature, but of a large frame. He had been brought up in the Mohawk Valley, in the state of New York, and claimed relationship with the oldest Dutch families in that vicinity. He had once been a sailor, and had all the roughness of character that a sea-faring man might expect to possess; together with the half-Yankee, half-German peculiarities of the people of the Mohawk Valley. It was nearly eleven o'clock when a one-horse waggon drove up in haste, and the low squatty preacher got out and took his place at the foot of one of the trees, where a sort of rough board table was placed, and took his books from his pocket and commenced.

"As it is rather late," said he, "we will leave the singing and praying for the last, and take our text, and commence immediately. I shall base my remarks on the following passage of Scripture, and hope to have that attention which is due to the cause of God:—'All things whatsoever ye would that men should do unto you, do ye even so unto them;' that is, do by all mankind just as you would desire they should do by you, if you were in their place and they in yours.

"Now, to suit this rule to your particular circumstances, suppose you were masters and mistresses, and had servants under you, would you not desire that your servants should do their business faithfully and honestly, as well when your back was turned as while you were looking over them? Would you not expect that they should take notice of what you said to them? that they should behave themselves with respect towards you and yours, and be as careful of every thing belonging to you as you would be yourselves? You are servants: do, therefore, as you would wish to be done by, and you will be both good servants to your masters and good servants to God, who requires this of you, and will reward you well for it, if you do it for the sake of conscience, in obedience to his commands.

"You are not to be eye-servants. Now, eye-servants are such as will work hard, and seem mighty diligent, while they think anybody is taking notice of them; but, when their masters' and mistresses' backs are turned they are idle, and neglect their business. I am afraid there are a great many such eye-servants among you, and that you do not consider how great a sin it is to be so, and how severely God will punish you for it. You may easily deceive your owners, and make them have an opinion of you that you do not deserve, and get the praise of men by it; but remember that you cannot deceive Almighty God, who sees your wickedness and deceit, and will punish you accordingly. For the rule is, that you must obey your masters in all things, and do the work they set you about with fear and trembling, in singleness of heart as unto Christ; not with eye-service, as men-pleasers, but as the servants of Christ, doing the will of God from the heart; with good-will doing service as to the Lord, and not as to men.

"*Take care that you do not fret or murmur, grumble or repine at your condition; for this will not only make your life uneasy, but will greatly offend Almighty God.* Consider that it is not yourselves, it is not the people that you belong to, it is not the men who have brought you to it, but *it is the will of God who hath by his providence made you servants, because, no doubt, he knew that condition would be best for you in this world, and help you the better towards heaven, if you would but do your duty in it.* So that any discontent at your not being free, or rich, or great, as you see some others, is quarrelling with your heavenly Master, and finding fault with God himself, who hath made you what you are, and hath promised you as large a share in the kingdom of heaven as the greatest man alive, if you will but behave yourself aright, and do the business he hath set you about in this world honestly and cheerfully. Riches and power have proved the ruin of many an unhappy soul, by drawing away the heart and affections from God, and fixing them on mean and sinful enjoyments; so that, when God, who knows our hearts better than we know them ourselves, sees that they would be hurtful to us, and therefore keeps them from us, it is the greatest mercy and kindness he could show us.

"You may perhaps fancy that, if you had riches and freedom, you could do your duty to God and man with greater pleasure than you can now. But pray consider that, if you can but save your souls through the mercy of God, you will have spent your time to the best of purposes in this world; and he that at last can get to heaven has performed a noble journey, let the road be ever so rugged and difficult. Besides, you really have a great advantage over most white people, who have not only the care of their daily labour upon their hands, but the care of looking forward and providing necessaries for to-morrow and next day, and of clothing and bringing up their children, and of getting food and raiment for as many of you as belong to their families, which often puts them to great difficulties, and distracts their minds so as to break their rest, and take off their thoughts from the affairs of another world. Whereas you are quite eased from all these cares, and have nothing but your daily labour to look after, and, when that is done, take your needful rest. Neither is it necessary for you to think of laying up anything against old age, as white people are obliged to do; for the laws of the country have provided that you shall not be turned off when you are past labour, but shall be maintained, while you live, by those you belong to, whether you are able to work or not.

"There is only one circumstance which may appear grievous, that I shall now take notice of, and that is correction.

"Now, when correction is given you, you either deserve it, or you do not deserve it. But whether you really deserve it or not, it is your duty, and Almighty God requires that you bear it patiently. You may perhaps think that this is hard doctrine; but, if you consider it right, you must needs think otherwise of it. Suppose, then, that you deserve correction, you cannot but say that it is just and right you should meet with it. Suppose you do not, or at least you do not deserve so much, or so severe a correction, for the fault you have committed, you perhaps have escaped a great many more, and are at last paid for all. Or suppose you are quite innocent of what is laid to your charge, and suffer wrongfully in that particular thing, is it not possible you may have done some other bad thing which was never discovered, and that Almighty God who saw you doing it would not let you escape without punishment one time or another? And ought you not, in such a case, to give glory to him, and be thankful that he would rather punish you in this life for your wickedness than destroy your souls for it in the next life? But suppose even this was not the case (a case hardly to be imagined), and that you have by no means, known or unknown, deserved the correction you suffered, there is this great comfort in it, that, if you bear it patiently, and leave your cause in the hands of God, he will reward you for it in heaven, and the punishment you suffer unjustly here shall turn to your exceeding great glory hereafter.

"Lastly, you should serve your masters faithfully, because of their goodness to you. See to what trouble they have been on your account. Your fathers were poor ignorant and barbarous creatures in Africa, and the whites fitted out ships at great trouble and expense and brought you from that benighted land to Christian America, where you can sit under your own vine and fig tree and no one molest or make you afraid. Oh, my dear black brothers and sisters, you are indeed a fortunate and a blessed people. Your masters have many troubles that you know nothing about. If the banks break, your masters are sure to lose something. If the crops turn out poor, they lose by it. If one of you die, your master loses what he paid for you, while you lose nothing. Now let me exhort you once more to be faithful."

Often during the delivery of the sermon did Snyder cast an anxious look in the direction where Carlton was seated; no doubt to see if he had found favour with the stranger. Huckelby, the overseer, was also there, seated near Carlton. With all Snyder's gesticulations, sonorous voice, and occasionally bringing his fist down upon the table with the force of a sledge hammer, he could not succeed in keeping the negroes all interested: four or five were fast asleep, leaning against the trees; as many more were nodding, while not a few were stealthily cracking and eating hazelnuts. "Uncle Simon, you may strike up a hymn," said the preacher as he closed his Bible. A moment more, and the whole company (Carlton excepted) had joined in the well known hymn, commencing with

"When I can read my title clear
To mansions in the sky."

After the singing, Sandy closed with prayer, and the following questions and answers read, and the meeting was brought to a close.

"*Q.* What command has God given to servants concerning obedience to their masters?—*A.* 'Servants, obey in all things your masters according to the flesh, not with eye-service as men-pleasers, but in singleness of heart, fearing God.'

"*Q.* What does God mean by masters according to the flesh?—*A.* 'Masters in this world.'

"*Q.* What are servants to count their masters worthy of?—*A.* 'All honour.'

"*Q.* How are they to do the service of their masters?—*A.* '*With good will*, doing service as unto the Lord, and not unto men.'

"*Q.* How are they to try to please their masters?—*A.* 'Please him well in all things, not answering again.'

"*Q.* Is a servant who is an eye-servant to his earthly master an eye-servant to his heavenly master?—*A.* 'Yes.'

"*Q.* Is it right in a servant, when commanded to do any thing, to be sullen and slow, and answer his master again?—*A.* 'No.'

"*Q.* If the servant professes to be a Christian, ought he not to be *as a Christian servant*, an example to all other servants of love and obedience to his master?—*A.* 'Yes.'

"*Q.* And, should his master be a Christian also, ought he not on that account specially to love and obey him?—*A.* 'Yes.'

"*Q.* But suppose the master is hard to please, and threatens and punishes more than he ought, what is the servant to do?—*A.* 'Do his best to please him.'

"*Q.* When the servant suffers *wrongfully* at the hands of his master, and, to please God, takes it patiently, will God reward him for it?—*A.* 'Yes.'

"*Q.* Is it right for the servant to *run away*, or is it right to *harbour* a runaway?—*A.* 'No.'

"*Q.* If a servant runs away, what should be done with him?—*A.* 'He should be caught and brought back.'

"*Q.* When he is brought back, what should be done with him?—*A.* 'Whip him well.'

"*Q.* Why may not the whites be slaves as well as the blacks?—*A.* 'Because the Lord intended the negroes for slaves.'

"*Q.* Are they better calculated for servants than the whites?—*A.* 'Yes, their hands are large, the skin thick and tough, and they can stand the sun better than the whites.'

"*Q.* Why should servants not complain when they are whipped?—*A.* 'Because the Lord has commanded that they should be whipped.'

"*Q.* Where has He commanded it?—*A.* 'He says, He that knoweth his master's will, and doeth it not, shall be beaten with many stripes.'

"*Q.* Then is the master to blame for whipping his servant?—*A.* 'Oh, no! he is only doing his duty as a Christian.'"

Snyder left the ground in company with Carlton and Huckelby, and the three dined together in the overseer's dwelling.

"Well," said Joe, after the three white men were out of hearing, "Marser Snyder bin try hesef today." "Yes," replied Ned; "he want to show de strange gentman how good he can preach." "Dat's a new sermon he gib us to-day," said Sandy. "Dees white fokes is de very dibble," said Dick; "and all dey whole study is to try to fool de black people." "Didn't you like de sermon?" asked Uncle Simon. "No," answered four or five voices. "He rared and pitched enough," continued Uncle Simon.

Now Uncle Simon was himself a preacher, or at least he

thought so, and was rather pleased than otherwise, when he heard others spoken of in a disparaging manner. "Uncle Simon can beat dat sermon all to pieces," said Ned, as he was filling his mouth with hazelnuts. "I got no notion of dees white fokes, no how," returned Aunt Dafney. "Dey all de time tellin' dat de Lord made us for to work for dem, and I don't believe a word of it." "Marser Peck give dat sermon to Snyder, I know," said Uncle Simon. "He jest de one for dat," replied Sandy. "I think de people dat made de Bible was great fools," said Ned. "Why?" Uncle Simon. "'Cause dey made such a great big book and put nuttin' in it, but servants obey yer masters." "Oh," replied Uncle Simon, "thars more in de Bible den dat, only Snyder never reads any other part to us; I use to hear it read in Maryland, and thar was more den what Snyder lets us hear." In the overseer's house there was another scene going on, and far different from what we have here described.

CHAPTER VII.

THE POOR WHITES, SOUTH.

"No seeming of logic can ever convince the American people, that thousands of our slave-holding brethren are not excellent, humane, and even Christian men, fearing God, and keeping His commandments."—*Rev. Dr. Joel Parker.*

"You like these parts better than New York," said Carlton to Snyder, as they were sitting down to dinner in the overseer's dwelling. "I can't say that I do," was the reply; "I came here ten years ago as missionary, and Mr. Peck wanted me to stay, and I have remained. I travel among the poor whites during the week, and preach for the niggers on Sunday." "Are there many poor whites in this district?" "Not here, but about thirty miles from here, in the Sand Hill district; they are as ignorant as horses. Why it was no longer than last week I was up there, and really you would not believe it, that people were so poor off. In New England, and, I may say, in all the free states, they have free schools, and everybody gets educated. Not so here. In Connecticut there is only one out of every five hundred above twenty-one years that can neither read nor write. Here there is one out of every eight that can neither read nor write. There is not a single newspaper taken in five of the counties in this state. Last week I was at Sand Hill for the first time, and I called at a farmhouse. The man was out. It was a low log-hut, and yet it was the best house in that locality. The woman and nine children were there, and the geese, ducks, chickens, pigs, and children were all running about the floor. The woman seemed scared at me when I entered the house. I inquired if I could get a little dinner, and my horse fed. She said, yes, if I would only be good enough to feed him myself, as her 'gal,' as she called her daughter, would be afraid of the horse. When I returned into the house again from the stable, she kept her eyes upon me all the time. At last she said, 'I s'pose you aint never bin in these parts afore?' 'No,' said I. 'Is you gwine to stay here long?' 'Not very long,' I replied. 'On business, I s'pose.' 'Yes,' said I. 'I am hunting up the lost sheep of the house of Israel.' 'Oh,' exclaimed she, 'hunting for lost sheep is you? Well, you have a hard time to find 'em here. My husband lost an old ram last week, and he aint found him yet, and he's hunted every day.' 'I am not looking for four-legged sheep,' said I, 'I am hunting for sinners.' 'Ah;' she said, 'then you are a preacher.' 'Yes,' said I. 'You are the first of that sort that's bin in these diggins for many a day.' Turning to her eldest daughter, she said in an excited tone, 'Clar out the pigs and ducks, and sweep up the floor; this is a preacher.' And it was some time before any of the children would come near me; one remained under the bed (which, by the by, was in the same room), all the while I was there. 'Well,' continued the woman, 'I was tellin' my man only yesterday that I would like once more to go to meetin' before I died, and he said as he should like to do the same. But as you have come, it will save us the trouble of going out of the district.'" "Then you found some of the lost sheep," said Carlton. "Yes," replied Snyder, "I did not find anything else up there. The state makes no provision for educating the poor: they are unable to do it themselves, and they grow up in a state of ignorance and degradation. The men hunt and the women have to go in the fields and labour." "What is the cause of it?" inquired Carlton; "Slavery," answered Snyder, "slavery, —and nothing else. Look at the city of Boston; it pays more taxes for the support of the government than this entire state. The people of Boston do more business than the whole population of Mississippi put together. I was told some very amusing things while at Sand Hill. A farmer there told me a story about an old woman, who was very pious herself. She had a husband and three sons, who were sad characters, and she had often prayed for their conversion but to no effect. At last, one day while working in the corn-field, one of her sons was bitten by a rattlesnake. He had scarce reached home before he felt the poison, and in his agony called loudly on his Maker.

"The pious old woman, when she heard this, forgetful of her son's misery, and everything else but the glorious hope of his repentance, fell on her knees, and prayed as follows,—'Oh! Lord, I thank thee, that thou hast at last opened Jimmy's eyes to the error of his ways; and I pray that, in thy Divine mercy, thou wilt send a rattlesnake to bite the old man, and another to bite Tom, and another to bite Harry, for I am certain that nothing but a rattlesnake, or something of the kind, will ever turn them from their sinful ways, they are so hard-headed.' When returning home, and before I got out of the Sand Hill district, I saw a funeral, and thought I would fasten my horse to a post and attend. The coffin was carried in a common horse cart, and followed by fifteen or twenty persons very shabbily dressed, and attended by a man whom I took to be the religious man of the place. After the coffin had been placed near the grave, he spoke as follows,—

> 'Friends and neighbours! you have congregated to see this lump of mortality put into a hole in the ground. You all know the deceased—a worthless, drunken, good-for-nothing vagabond. He lived in disgrace and infamy, and died in wretchedness. You all despised him—you all know his brother Joe, who lives on the hill? He's not a bit better though he has scrap'd together a little property by cheating his neighbours. His end will be like that of this loathsome creature, whom you will please put into the hole as soon as possible. I wont ask you to drop a tear, but brother Bohow will please raise a hymn while we fill up the grave.'"

"I am rather surprised to hear that any portion of the whites in this state are in so low a condition." "Yet it is true," returned Snyder.

"These are very onpleasant facts to be related to ye, Mr. Carlton," said Huckelby; "but I can bear witness to what Mr. Snyder has told ye." Huckelby was from Maryland, where many of the poor whites are in as sad a condition as the Sand Hillers of Mississippi. He was a tall man, of iron constitution, and could neither read nor write, but was considered one of the best overseers in the country. When about to break a slave in, to do a heavy task, he would make him work by his side all day; and if the new hand kept up with him, he was set down as an able bodied man. Huckelby had neither moral, religious, or political principles, and often boasted that conscience was a matter that never "cost" him a thought. "Mr. Snyder aint told ye half about the folks in these parts;" continued he; "we who comes from more enlightened parts don't know how to put up with 'em down here. I find the people here knows mighty little indeed; in fact, I may say they are univarsaly onedicated. I goes out among none on 'em, 'cause they aint such as I have been used to 'sociate with. When I gits a little richer, so that I can stop work, I tend to go back to Maryland, and spend the rest of my days." "I wonder the negroes don't attempt to get their freedom by physical force." "It aint no use for 'em to try that, for if they do, we puts 'em through by daylight," replied Huckelby. "There are some desperate fellows among the slaves," said Snyder. "Indeed," remarked Carlton. "Oh, yes," replied the preacher. "A case has just taken place near here, where a neighbour of ours, Mr. J. Higgerson, attempted to correct a negro man in his employ, who resisted, drew a knife, and stabbed him (Mr. H.) in several places. Mr. J. C. Hobbs (a Tennessean) ran to his assistance. Mr. Hobbs stooped to pick up a stick to strike the negro, and, while in that position, the negro rushed upon him, and caused his immediate death. The negro then fled to the woods, but was pursued with dogs, and soon overtaken. He had stopped in a swamp to fight the dogs, when the party who were pursuing him came upon him, and commanded him to give up, which he refused to do. He then made several efforts to stab them. Mr. Roberson, one of the party, gave him several blows on the head with a rifle gun; but this, instead of subduing, only increased his desperate revenge. Mr. R. then discharged his gun at the negro, and missing him, the ball struck Mr. Boon in the face, and felled him to the ground. The negro, seeing Mr. Boon prostrated, attempted to rush up and stab him, but was prevented by the timely interference of some one of the party. He was then shot three times with a revolving pistol, and once with a rifle, and after having his throat cut, he still kept the knife firmly grasped in his hand, and tried to cut their legs when they approached to put an end to his life. This chastisement was given because the negro grumbled, and found fault with his master for flogging his wife." "Well, this is a bad state of affairs indeed, and especially the condition of the poor whites," said Carlton. "You see," replied Snyder, "no white man is respectable in these slave states who works for a living. No community can be prosperous, where honest labour is not honoured. No society can be rightly constituted, where the intellect is not fed. Whatever institution reflects discredit on industry, whatever institution forbids the general culture of the understanding, is palpably hostile to individual rights, and to social well-being. Slavery is the incubus that hangs over the Southern States." "Yes," interrupted Huckelby; "them's just my sentiments now, and no mistake. I think that, for the honour of our country, this slavery business should stop. I don't own any, no how, and I would not be an overseer if I wern't paid for it."

CHAPTER VIII.

THE SEPARATION.

"In many ways does the full heart reveal
The presence of the love it would conceal;
But in far more the estranged heart lets know
The absence of the love, which yet it fain would show."

At length the news of the approaching marriage of Horatio met the ear of Clotel. Her head grew dizzy, and her heart fainted within her; but, with a strong effort at composure, she inquired all the particulars, and her pure mind at once took its resolution. Horatio came that evening, and though she would fain have met him as usual, her heart was too full not to throw a deep sadness over her looks and tones. She had never complained of his decreasing tenderness, or of her own lonely hours; but he felt that the mute appeal of her heart-broken looks was more terrible than words. He kissed the hand she offered, and with a countenance almost as sad as her own, led her to a window in the recess shadowed by a luxuriant passion flower. It was the same seat where they had spent the first evening in this beautiful cottage, consecrated to their first loves. The same calm, clear moonlight looked in through the trellis. The vine then planted had now a luxuriant growth; and many a time had Horatio fondly twined its sacred blossoms with the glossy ringlets of her raven hair. The rush of memory almost overpowered poor Clotel; and Horatio felt too much oppressed and ashamed to break the long deep silence. At length, in words scarcely audible, Clotel said: "Tell me, dear Horatio, are you to be married next week?" He dropped her hand as if a rifle ball had struck him; and it was not until after long hesitation, that he began to make some reply about the necessity of circumstances. Mildly but earnestly the poor girl begged him to spare apologies. It was enough that he no longer loved her, and that they must bid farewell. Trusting to the yielding tenderness of her character, he ventured, in the most soothing accents, to suggest that as he still loved her better than all the world, she would ever be his real wife, and they might see each other frequently. He was not prepared for the storm of indignant emotion his words excited. True, she was his slave; her bones, and sinews had been purchased by his gold, yet she had the heart of a true woman, and hers was a passion too deep and absorbing to admit of partnership, and her spirit was too pure to form a selfish league with crime.

At length this painful interview came to an end. They stood together by the Gothic gate, where they had so often met and parted in the moonlight. Old remembrances melted their souls. "Farewell, dearest Horatio," said Clotel. "Give me a parting kiss." Her voice was choked for utterance, and the tears flowed freely, as she bent her lips toward him. He folded her convulsively in his arms, and imprinted a long impassioned kiss on that mouth, which had never spoken to him but in love and blessing. With efforts like a death-pang she at length raised her head from his heaving bosom, and turning from him with bitter sobs, "It is our last. To meet thus is henceforth crime. God bless you. I would not have you so miserable as I am. Farewell. A last farewell." "The last?" exclaimed he, with a wild shriek. "Oh God, Clotel, do not say that;" and covering his face with his hands, he wept like a child. Recovering from his emotion, he found himself alone. The moon looked down upon him mild, but very sorrowfully; as the Madonna seems to gaze upon her worshipping children, bowed down with consciousness of sin. At that moment he would have given worlds to have disengaged himself from Gertrude, but he had gone so far, that blame, disgrace, and duels with angry relatives would now attend any effort to obtain his freedom. Oh, how the moonlight oppressed him with its friendly sadness! It was like the plaintive eye of his forsaken one, like the music of sorrow echoed from an unseen world. Long and earnestly he gazed at that cottage, where he had so long known earth's purest foretaste of heavenly bliss. Slowly he walked away; then turned again to look on that charmed spot, the nestling-place of his early affections. He caught a glimpse of Clotel, weeping beside a magnolia, which commanded a long view of the path leading to the public road. He would have sprung toward her but she darted from him, and entered the cottage. That graceful figure, weeping in the moonlight, haunted him for years. It stood before his closing eyes, and greeted him with the morning dawn. Poor Gertrude, had she known all, what a dreary lot would hers have been; but fortunately she could not miss the impassioned tenderness she never experienced; and Horatio was the more careful in his kindness, because he was deficient in love. After Clotel had been separated from her mother and sister, she turned her attention to the subject of Christianity, and received that consolation from her Bible that is never denied to the children of God. Although it was against the laws of Virginia, for a slave to be taught to read, Currer had employed an old free negro, who lived near her, to teach her two daughters to read and write. She felt that the step she had taken in resolving never to meet Horatio again would no doubt expose her to his wrath, and probably cause her to be sold, yet her heart was too guileless for her to commit a crime, and therefore she had ten times rather have been sold as a slave than do wrong. Some months after the marriage of Horatio and Gertrude their barouche rolled along a winding road that skirted the forest near Clotel's cottage, when the attention of Gertrude was suddenly attracted by two figures among the trees by the wayside; and touching Horatio's arm, she exclaimed, "Do look at that beautiful child." He turned and saw Clotel and Mary. His lips quivered, and his face became deadly pale. His young wife looked at him intently, but said nothing. In returning home, he took another road; but his wife seeing this, expressed a wish to go back the way they had come. He objected, and suspicion was awakened in her heart, and she soon after learned that the mother of that lovely child bore the name of Clotel, a name which she had often heard Horatio murmur in uneasy slumbers. From gossiping tongues she soon learned more than she wished to know. She wept, but not as poor Clotel had done; for she never had loved, and been beloved like her, and her nature was more proud: henceforth a change came over her feelings and her manners, and Horatio had no further occasion to assume a tenderness in return for hers. Changed as he was by ambition, he felt the wintry chill of her polite propriety, and sometimes, in agony of heart, compared it with the gushing love of her who was indeed his wife. But these and all his emotions were a sealed book to Clotel, of which she could only guess the contents. With remittances for her and her child's support, there sometimes came earnest pleadings that she would consent to see him again; but these she never answered, though her heart yearned to do so. She pitied his young bride, and would not be tempted to bring sorrow into her household by any fault of hers. Her earnest prayer was, that she might not know of her existence. She had not looked on Horatio since she watched him under the shadow of the magnolia, until his barouche passsed her in her rambles some months after. She saw the deadly paleness of his countenance, and had he dared to look back, he would have seen her tottering with faintness. Mary brought water from a rivulet, and sprinkled her face. When she revived, she clasped the beloved child to her heart with a vehemence that made her scream. Soothingly she kissed away her fears, and gazed into her beautiful eyes with a deep, deep sadness of expression, which poor Mary never forgot. Wild were the thoughts that passed round her aching heart, and almost maddened her poor brain; thoughts which had almost driven her to suicide the night of that last farewell. For her child's sake she had conquered the fierce temptation then; and for her sake, she struggled with it now. But the gloomy atmosphere of their once happy home overclouded the morning of Mary's life. Clotel perceived this, and it gave her unutterable pain.

"Tis ever thus with woman's love,
True till life's storms have passed;
And, like the vine around the tree,
It braves them to the last."

CHAPTER IX.

THE MAN OF HONOUR.

"MY tongue could never learn sweet soothing words,
But now thy beauty is propos'd, my fee,
My proud heart sues, and prompts my tongue to speak."

Shakspeare.

JAMES CRAWFORD, the purchaser of Althesa, was from the green mountains of Vermont, and his feelings were opposed to the holding of slaves. But his young wife persuaded him into the idea that it was no worse to own a slave than to hire one and pay the money to another. Hence it was that he had been induced to purchase Althesa. Henry Morton, a young physician from the same state, and who had just commenced the practice of his profession in New Orleans, was boarding with Crawford when Althesa was brought home. The young physician had been in New Orleans but a few weeks, and had seen very little of slavery. In his own mountain home he had been taught that the slaves of the Southern states were negroes, if not from the coast of Africa, the descendants of those who had been imported. He was unprepared to behold with composure a beautiful young white girl of fifteen in the degraded position of a chattel slave. The blood chilled in his young heart as he heard Crawford tell how, by bantering with the trader, he had bought her for two hundred dollars less than he first asked. His very looks showed that the slave girl had the deepest sympathy of his heart. Althesa had been brought up by her mother to look after the domestic concerns of her cottage in Virginia, and knew well the duties imposed upon her. Mrs. Crawford was much pleased with her new servant, and often made mention of her in presence of Morton. The young man's sympathy ripened into love, which was reciprocated by the friendless and injured child of sorrow. There was but one course left; that was, to purchase the young girl and make her his wife, which he did six months after her arrival in Crawford's family. The young physician and his wife immediately took lodgings in another part of the city; a private teacher was called in, and the young wife taught some of those accomplishments which are necessary for one's taking a position in society. Dr. Morton soon obtained a large practice in his profession, and with it increased in wealth—but with all his wealth he never would own a slave. Mrs. Morton was now in a position to seek out and redeem her mother, whom she had not heard of since they parted at Natchez. An agent was immediately despatched to hunt out the mother and to see if she could be purchased. The agent had no trouble in finding out Mr. Peck: but all overtures were unavailable; he would not sell Currer. His excuse was, that she was such a good housekeeper that he could not spare her. Poor Althesa felt sad when she found that her mother could not be bought. However, she felt a consciousness of having done her duty in the matter, yet waited with the hope that the day might come when she should have her mother by her side.

CHAPTER X.

THE YOUNG CHRISTIAN.

"HERE we see *God dealing in slaves*; giving them to his own favourite child [Abraham], a man of superlative worth, and as a reward for his eminent goodness."—*Rev. Theodore Clapp, of New Orleans.*

ON Carlton's return the next day from the farm, he was overwhelmed with questions from Mr. Peck, as to what he thought of the plantation, the condition of the negroes, Huckelby and Snyder; and especially how he liked the sermon of the latter. Mr. Peck was a kind of a patriarch in his own way. To begin with, he was a man of some talent. He not only had a good education, but was a man of great eloquence, and had a wonderful command of language. He too either had, or thought he had, poetical genius; and was often sending contributions to the *Natchez Free Trader*, and other periodicals. In the way of raising contributions for foreign missions, he took the lead of all others in his neighbourhood. Everything he did, he did for the "glory of God," as he said: he quoted Scripture for almost everything he did. Being in good circumstances, he was able to give to almost all benevolent causes to which he took a fancy. He was a most loving father, and his daughter exercised considerable influence over him, and, owing to her piety and judgment, that influence had a beneficial effect. Carlton, though a schoolfellow of the parson's, was nevertheless nearly ten years his junior; and though not an avowed infidel, was, however, a free-thinker, and one who took no note of tomorrow. And for this reason Georgiana took peculiar interest in the young man, for Carlton was but little above thirty and unmarried. The young Christian felt that she would not be living up to that faith that she professed and believed in, if she did not exert herself to the utmost to save the thoughtless man from his downward career; and in this she succeeded to her most sanguine expectations. She not only converted him, but in placing the Scriptures before him in their true light, she redeemed those sacred writings from the charge of supporting the system of slavery, which her father had cast upon them in the discussion some days before.

Georgiana's first object, however, was to awaken in Carlton's breast a love for the Lord Jesus Christ. The young man had often sat under the sound of the gospel with perfect indifference. He had heard men talk who had grown grey bending over the Scriptures, and their conversation had passed by him unheeded; but when a young girl, much younger than himself, reasoned with him in that innocent and persuasive manner that woman is wont to use when she has entered with her whole soul upon an object, it was too much for his stout heart, and he yielded. Her next aim was to vindicate the Bible from sustaining the monstrous institution of slavery. She said, "'God has created of one blood all the nations of men, to dwell on all the face of the earth.' To claim, hold, and treat a human being as property is felony against God and man. The Christian religion is opposed to slaveholding in its spirit and its principles; it classes men-stealers among murderers; and it is the duty of all who wish to meet God in peace, to discharge that duty in spreading these principles. Let us not deceive ourselves into the idea that slavery is right, because it is profitable to us. Slaveholding is the highest possible violation of the eighth commandment. To take from a man his earnings, is theft; but to take the earner is a compound, life-long theft; and we who profess to follow in the footsteps of our Redeemer, should do our utmost to extirpate slavery from the land. For my own part, I shall do all I can. When the Redeemer was about to ascend to the bosom of the Father, and resume the glory which he had with him before the world was, he promised his disciples that the power of the Holy Ghost should come upon them, and that they should be witnesses for him to the uttermost parts of the earth. What was the effect upon their minds? 'They all continued with one accord in prayer and supplication with the women.' Stimulated by the confident expectation that Jesus would fulfil his gracious promise, they poured out their hearts in fervent supplications, probably for strength to do the work which he had appointed them unto, for they felt that without him they could do nothing, and they consecrated themselves on the altar of God, to the great and glorious enterprise of preaching the unsearchable riches of Christ to a lost and perishing world. Have we less precious promises in the Scriptures of truth? May we not claim of our God the blessing promised unto those who consider the poor: the Lord will preserve them and keep them alive, and they shall be blessed upon the earth? Does not the language, 'Inasmuch as ye did it unto one of the least of these my brethren, ye did it unto me,' belong to all who are rightly engaged in endeavouring to unloose the bondman's fetters? Shall we not then do as the apostles did? Shall we not, in view of the two millions of heathen in our very midst, in view of the souls that are going down in an almost unbroken phalanx to utter perdition, continue in prayer and supplication, that God will grant us the supplies of his Spirit to prepare us for that work which he has given us to do? Shall not the wail of the mother as she surrenders her only child to the grasp of the ruthless kidnapper, or the trader in human blood, animate our devotions? Shall not the manifold crimes and horrors of slavery excite more ardent outpourings at the throne of grace to grant repentance to our guilty country, and permit us to aid in preparing the way for the glorious second advent of the Messiah, by preaching deliverance to the captives, and the opening of the prison doors to those who are bound."

Georgiana had succeeded in rivetting the attention of Carlton during her conversation, and as she was finishing her last sentence, she observed the silent tear stealing down the cheek of the newly born child of God. At this juncture her father entered, and Carlton left the room. "Dear papa," said Georgiana, "will you grant me one favour; or, rather, make me a promise?" "I can't tell, my dear, till I know what it is," replied Mr. Peck. "If it is a reasonable request, I will comply with your wish," continued he. "I hope, my dear," answered she, "that papa would not think me capable of making an unreasonable request." "Well, well," returned he; "tell me what it is." "I hope," said she, "that in your future conversation with Mr. Carlton, on the subject of slavery, you will not speak of the Bible as sustaining it." "Why, Georgiana, my dear, you are mad, aint you?" exclaimed he, in an excited tone. The poor girl remained silent; the father saw in a moment that he had spoken too sharply; and taking her hand in his he said, "Now, my child, why do you make that request?" "Because," returned she, "I think he is on the stool of repentance, if he has not already been received among the elect. He, you know, was bordering upon infidelity, and if the Bible sanctions slavery, then he will naturally enough say that it is not from God; for the argument from internal evidence is not only refuted, but actually turned against the Bible. If the Bible sanctions slavery, then it misrepresents the character of God. Nothing would be more dangerous to the soul of a young convert than to satisfy him that the Scriptures favoured such a system of sin." "Don't you suppose that I understand the Scriptures better than you? I have been in the world longer." "Yes," said she, "you have been in the world longer, and amongst slaveholders so long that you do not regard it in the same light that those do who have not become so familiar with its every-day scenes as you. I once heard you say, that you were opposed to the institution, when you first came to the South." "Yes," answered he, "I did not know so much about it then." "With great deference to you, papa," replied Georgiana, "I don't think that the Bible sanctions slavery. The Old Testament contains this explicit condemnation of it, 'He that stealeth a man, and selleth him, or if he be found in his hand, he shall surely be put to death;' and 'Woe unto him that buildeth his house by unrighteousness, and his chambers by wrong; that useth his neighbour's service without wages, and giveth him not for his work;' when also the New Testament exhibits such words of rebuke as these, 'Behold the hire of the labourers who have reaped down your fields, which is of you kept back by fraud, crieth; and the cries of them who have reaped are entered into the ears of the Lord of Sabaoth.' 'The law is not made for a righteous man, but for the lawless and disobedient, for the ungodly and for sinners, for unholy and profane, for murderers of fathers and murderers of mothers, for manslayers, for whoremongers, for them that defile themselves with mankind, for *menstealers*, for liars, for perjured persons.' A more scathing denunciation of the sin in question is surely to be found on record in no other book. I am afraid," continued the daughter, "that the acts of the professed friends of Christianity in the South do more to spread infidelity than the writings of all the atheists which have ever been published. The infidel watches the religious world. He surveys the church, and, lo! thousands and tens of thousands of her accredited members actually hold slaves. Members 'in good and regular standing,' fellowshipped throughout

Christendom except by a few anti-slavery churches generally despised as ultra and radical, reduce their fellow men to the condition of chattels, and by force keep them in that state of degradation. Bishops, ministers, elders, and deacons are engaged in this awful business, and do not consider their conduct as at all inconsistent with the precepts of either the Old or New Testaments. Moreover, those ministers and churches who do not themselves hold slaves, very generally defend the conduct of those who do, and accord to them a fair Christian character, and in the way of business frequently take mortgages and levy executions on the bodies of their fellow men, and in some cases of their fellow Christians.

"Now is it a wonder that infidels, beholding the practice and listening to the theory of professing Christians, should conclude that the Bible inculcates a morality not inconsistent with chattelising human beings? And must not this conclusion be strengthened, when they hear ministers of talent and learning declare that the Bible does sanction slaveholding, and that it ought not to be made a disciplinable offence in churches? And must not all doubt be dissipated, when one of the most learned professors in our theological seminaries asserts that the Bible 'recognises that the relation may still exist, *salva fide et salva ecclesia*' (without injury to the Christian faith or church) and that only 'the *abuse* of it is the essential and fundamental wrong?' Are not infidels bound to believe that these professors, ministers, and churches understand their own Bible, and that, consequently, notwithstanding solitary passages which appear to condemn slaveholding, the Bible sanctions it? When nothing can be further from the truth. And as for Christ, his whole life was a living testimony against slavery and all that it inculcates. When he designed to do us good, he took upon himself the form of a servant. He took his station at the bottom of society. He voluntarily identified himself with the poor and the despised. The warning voices of Jeremiah and Ezekiel were raised in olden time, against sin. Let us not forget what followed. 'Therefore, thus saith the Lord—ye have not hearkened unto me in proclaiming liberty every one to his brother, and every one to his neighbour—behold I proclaim a liberty for you saith the Lord, to the sword, to the pestilence, and to the famine.' Are we not virtually as a nation adopting the same impious language, and are we not exposed to the same tremendous judgments? Shall we not, in view of those things, use every laudable means to awaken our beloved country from the slumbers of death, and baptize all our efforts with tears and with prayers, that God may bless them. Then, should our labour fail to accomplish the end for which we pray, we shall stand acquitted at the bar of Jehovah, and although we may share in the national calamities which await unrepented sins, yet that blessed approval will be ours.—'Well done good and faithful servants, enter ye into the joy of your Lord.'"

"My dear Georgiana," said Mr. Peck, "I must be permitted to entertain my own views on this subject, and to exercise my own judgment."

"Believe me, dear papa," she replied, "I would not be understood as wishing to teach you, or to dictate to you in the least; but only grant my request, not to allude to the Bible as sanctioning slavery, when speaking with Mr. Carlton."

"Well," returned he, "I will comply with your wish."

The young Christian had indeed accomplished a noble work; and whether it was admitted by the father, or not, she was his superior and his teacher. Georgiana had viewed the right to enjoy perfect liberty as one of those inherent and inalienable rights which pertain to the whole human race, and of which they can never be divested, except by an act of gross injustice. And no one was more able than herself to impress those views upon the hearts of all with whom she came in contact. Modest and self-possessed, with a voice of great sweetness, and a most winning manner, she could, with the greatest ease to herself, engage their attention.

CHAPTER XI.

THE PARSON POET.

"UNBIND, unbind my galling chain,
And set, oh! set me free:
No longer say that I'll disdain
The gift of liberty."

THROUGH the persuasion of Mr. Peck, and fascinated with the charms of Georgiana, Carlton had prolonged his stay two months with his old school-fellow. During the latter part of the time he had been almost as one of the family. If Miss Peck was invited out, Mr. Carlton was, as a matter of course. She seldom rode out, unless with him. If Mr. Peck was absent, he took the head of the table; and, to the delight of the young lady, he had on several occasions taken part in the family worship. "I am glad," said Mr. Peck, one evening while at the tea table, "I am glad, Mr. Carlton, that my neighbour Jones has invited you to visit him at his farm. He is a good neighbour, but a very ungodly man; I want that you should see his people, and then, when you return to the North, you can tell how much better a Christian's slaves are situated than one who does nothing for the cause of Christ." "I hope, Mr. Carlton," said Georgiana, "that you will spend the Sabbath with him, and have a religious interview with the negroes." "Yes," replied the parson, "that's well thought of, Georgy." "Well, I think I will go up on Thursday next, and stay till Monday," said Carlton; "and I shall act upon your suggestion, Miss Peck," continued he; "and try to get a religious interview with the blacks. By-the-by," remarked Carlton, "I saw an advertisement in the *Free Trader* to-day that rather puzzled me. Ah, here it is now; and," drawing the paper from his pocket, "I will read it, and then you can tell me what it means:

> 'TO PLANTERS AND OTHERS.—*Wanted fifty negroes.* Any person having *sick negroes*, considered *incurable* by their respective physicians, (their owners of course,) and wishing to dispose of them, Dr. Stillman will pay cash for negroes affected with scrofula or king's evil, confirmed hypochondriacism, apoplexy, or diseases of the brain, kidneys, spleen, stomach and intestines,

> bladder and its appendages, diarrhœa, dysentery, &c. *The highest cash price will be paid as above.*'

When I read this to-day I thought that the advertiser must be a man of eminent skill as a physician, and that he intended to cure the sick negroes; but on second thought I find that some of the diseases enumerated are certainly incurable. What can he do with these sick negroes?" "You see," replied Mr. Peck, laughing, "that he is a doctor, and has use for them in his lectures. The doctor is connected with a small college. Look at his prospectus, where he invites students to attend, and that will explain the matter to you." Carlton turned to another column, and read the following:

> "Some advantages of a peculiar character are connected with this institution, which it may be proper to point out. No place in the United States offers as great opportunities for the acquisition of anatomical knowledge. Subjects being obtained from among the coloured population in sufficient numbers *for every purpose*, and proper dissections carried on *without offending any individuals in the community!*"

"These are for dissection, then?" inquired Carlton with a trembling voice. "Yes," answered the parson. "Of course they wait till they die before they can use them." "They keep them on hand, and when they need one they bleed him to death," returned Mr. Peck. "Yes, but that's murder." "Oh, the doctors are licensed to commit murder, you know; and what's the difference, whether one dies owing to the loss of blood, or taking too many pills? For my own part, if I had to choose, I would rather submit to the former." "I have often heard what I considered hard stories in abolition meetings in New York about slavery; but now I shall begin to think that many of them are true." "The longer you remain here the more you will be convinced of the iniquity of the institution," remarked Georgiana. "Now, Georgy, my dear, don't give us another abolition lecture, if you please," said Mr. Peck. "Here, Carlton," continued the parson, "I have written a short poem for your sister's album, as you requested me; it is a domestic piece, as you will see." "She will prize it the more for that," remarked Carlton; and taking the sheet of paper, he laughed as his eyes glanced over it. "Read it out, Mr. Carlton," said Georgiana, "and let me hear what it is; I know papa gets off some very droll things at times." Carlton complied with the young lady's request, and read aloud the following rare specimen of poetical genius:

"MY LITTLE NIG.

"I have a little nigger, the blackest thing alive,
He'll be just four years old if he lives till forty-five;
His smooth cheek hath a glossy hue, like a new polished boot,
And his hair curls o'er his little head as black as any soot.
His lips bulge from his countenance—his little ivories shine—
His nose is what we call a little pug, but fashioned very fine:
Although not quite a fairy, he is comely to behold,
And I wouldn't sell him, 'pon my word, for a hundred all in gold.

"He gets up early in the morn, like all the other nigs,
And runs off to the hog-lot, where he squabbles with the pigs—
And when the sun gets out of bed, and mounts up in the sky,
The warmest corner of the yard is where my nig doth lie.
And there extended lazily, he contemplates and dreams,
(I cannot qualify to this, but plain enough it seems;)
Until 'tis time to take in grub, when you can't find him there,
For, like a politician, he has gone to hunt his share.

"I haven't said a single word concerning my plantation,
Though a prettier, I guess, cannot be found within the nation;
When he gets a little bigger, I'll take and to him show it,
And then I'll say, 'My little nig, now just prepare to go it!'
I'll put a hoe into his hand—he'll soon know what it means,
And every day for dinner, he shall have bacon and greens."

CHAPTER XII.

A NIGHT IN THE PARSON'S KITCHEN.

"AND see the servants met,
Their daily labour's o'er;
And with the jest and song they set
The kitchen in a roar."

MR. PECK kept around him four servants besides Currer, of whom we have made mention: of these, Sam was considered the first. If a dinner-party was in contemplation, or any company to be invited to the parson's, after all the arrangements had been talked over by the minister and his daughter, Sam was sure to be consulted upon the subject by "Miss Georgy," as Miss Peck was called by the servants. If furniture, crockery, or anything else was to be purchased, Sam felt that he had been slighted if his opinion had not been asked. As to the marketing, he did it all. At the servants' table in the kitchen, he sat at the head, and was master of ceremonies. A single look from him was enough to silence any conversation or noise in the kitchen, or any other part of the premises. There is, in the Southern States, a great amount of prejudice against colour amongst the negroes themselves. The nearer the negro or mulatto approaches to the white, the more he seems to feel his superiority over those of a darker hue. This is, no doubt, the result of the prejudice that exists on the part of the whites towards both mulattoes and blacks. Sam was originally from Kentucky, and through the instrumentality of one of his young masters whom he had to take to school, he had learned to read so as to be well understood; and, owing to that fact, was considered a prodigy among the slaves, not only of his own master's, but those of the town who knew him. Sam had a great wish to follow in the footsteps of his master, and be a poet; and was, therefore, often heard singing doggrels of his own composition. But there was one great drawback to Sam, and that was his colour. He was one of the blackest of his race. This he evidently regarded as a great misfortune. However, he made up for this in his dress. Mr. Peck kept his house servants well dressed; and as for Sam, he was seldom seen except in a ruffled shirt. Indeed, the washerwoman feared him more than all others about the house.

Currer, as we have already stated, was chief of the kitchen department, and had a general supervision of the household affairs. Alfred the coachman, Peter, and Hetty made up the remainder of the house servants. Besides these, Mr. Peck owned eight slaves who were masons. These worked in the city. Being mechanics, they were let out to greater advantage than to keep them on the farm. However, every Sunday night, Peck's servants, including the bricklayers, usually assembled in the kitchen, when the events of the week were freely discussed and commented on. It was on a Sunday evening, in the month of June, that there was a party at Mr. Peck's, and, according to custom in the Southern States, the ladies had their maid-servants with them. Tea had been served in "the house," and the servants, including the strangers, had taken their seats at the tea table in the kitchen. Sam, being a "single gentleman," was unusually attentive to the "ladies" on this occasion. He seldom or ever let the day pass without spending at least an hour in combing and brushing up his "hair." Sam had an idea that fresh butter was better for his hair than any other kind of grease; and therefore, on churning days, half a pound of butter had always to be taken out before it was salted. When he wished to appear to great advantage, he would grease his face, to make it "shiny." On the evening of the party therefore, when all the servants were at the table, Sam cut a big figure. There he sat with his wool well combed and buttered, face nicely greased, and his ruffles extending five or six inches from his breast. The parson in his own drawing-room did not make a more imposing appearance than did his servant on this occasion. "I jist bin had my fortune told last Sunday night," said Sam, as he helped one of the girls to some sweet hash. "Indeed," cried half-a-dozen voices. "Yes," continued he; "Aunt Winny teld me I is to hab de prettiest yaller gal in town, and dat I is to be free." All eyes were immediately turned toward Sally Johnson, who was seated near Sam. "I speck I see somebody blush at dat remark," said Alfred. "Pass dem pancakes and molasses up dis way, Mr. Alf, and none of your insinawaysion here," rejoined Sam. "Dat reminds me," said Currer, "dat Dorcas Simpson is gwine to git married." "Who to, I want to know?" inquired Peter. "To one of Mr. Darby's field-hands," answered Currer. "I should tink dat dat gal would not trow hersef away in dat manner," said Sally. "She good enough looking to get a house servant, and not to put up wid a fiel' nigger," continued she. "Yes," said Sam, "dat's a wery insensible remark of yours, Miss Sally. I admire your judgment wery much, I assure you. Dah's plenty of suspectible and well-dressed house servants dat a gal of her looks can get, wid out taken up wid dem common darkies." "Is de man black or a mulatto?" inquired one of the company. "He's nearly white," replied Currer. "Well den, dat's some exchuse for her," remarked Sam; "for I don't like to see dis malgemation of blacks and mulattoes, no how," continued Sam. "If I had my rights I would be a mulatto too, for my mother was almost as light-coloured as Miss Sally," said he. Although Sam was one of the blackest men living, he nevertheless contended that his mother was a mulatto, and no one was more prejudiced against the blacks than he. A good deal of work, and the free use of fresh butter, had no doubt done wonders for his "hare" in causing it to grow long, and to this he would always appeal when he wished to convince others that he was part of an Anglo-Saxon. "I always thought you was not clear black, Mr. Sam," said Agnes. "You are right dahr, Miss Agnes. My hare tells what company I belong to," answered Sam. Here the whole company joined in the conversation about colour, which lasted for some time, giving unmistakeable evidence that caste is owing to ignorance. The evening's entertainment concluded by Sam's relating a little of his own experience while with his first master in old Kentucky.

Sam's former master was a doctor, and had a large practice among his neighbours, doctoring both masters and slaves. When Sam was about fifteen years of age, his old master set him to grinding up the ointment, then to making pills. As the young student grew older and became more practised in his profession, his services were of more importance to the doctor. The physician having a good business, and a large number of his patients being slaves, the most of whom had to call on the doctor when ill, he put Sam to bleeding, pulling teeth, and administering medicine to the slaves. Sam soon acquired the name amongst the slaves of the "Black Doctor." With this appellation he was delighted, and no regular physician could possibly have put on more airs than did the black doctor when his services were required. In bleeding, he must have more bandages, and rub and smack the arm more than the doctor would have thought of. We once saw Sam taking out a tooth for one of his patients, and nothing appeared more amusing. He got the poor fellow down on his back, and he got a straddle of the man's chest, and getting the turnkeys on the wrong tooth, he shut both eyes and pulled for his life. The poor man screamed as loud as he could, but to no purpose. Sam had him fast. After a great effort, out came the sound grinder, and the young doctor saw his mistake; but consoled himself with the idea that as the wrong tooth was out of the way, there was more room to get at the right one. Bleeding and a dose of calomel was always considered indispensable by the "Old Boss;" and, as a matter of course, Sam followed in his footsteps.

On one occasion the old doctor was ill himself, so as to be unable to attend to his patients. A slave, with pass in hand, called to receive medical advice, and the master told Sam to examine him and see what he wanted. This delighted him beyond measure, for although he had been acting his part in the way of giving out medicine as the master ordered it, he had never been called upon by the latter to examine a patient, and this seemed to convince him that, after all, he was no sham doctor. As might have been expected, he cut a rare figure in his first examination, placing himself directly opposite his patient, and folding his arms across his breast, and looking very knowingly, he began, "What's de matter wid you?" "I is sick." "Where is you sick?" "Here," replied the man, putting his hand upon his stomach. "Put out your tongue," continued the doctor. The man run out his tongue at full length. "Let me feel your pulse," at the same time taking his patient's hand in his, placing his fingers on his pulse, he said, "Ah, your case is a bad one; if I don't do something for you, and dat pretty quick, you 'ill be a gone coon, and dat's sartin." At this the man appeared frightened and inquired what was the matter with him: in answer, Sam said, "I done told you dat your case is a bad one, and dat's enough." On Sam's returning to his master's

NEGRO DENTISTRY.

bedside, the latter said, "Well, Sam, what do you think is the matter with him?" "His stomach is out of order, sir," he replied. "What do you think had best be done for him?" "I think I better bleed him and give him a dose of calomel," returned Sam. So to the latter's gratification the master let him have his own way. We need not further say, that the recital of Sam's experience as a physician gave him a high position amongst the servants that evening, and made him a decided favourite with the ladies, one of whom feigned illness, when the black doctor, to the delight of all, and certainly to himself, gave medical advice. Thus ended the evening amongst the servants in the parson's kitchen.

CHAPTER XIII.

A SLAVE HUNTING PARSON.

"'Tis too much prov'd—that with devotion's visage,
And pious action, we do sugar o'er the devil himself."
Shakspeare.

"You will, no doubt, be well pleased with neighbour Jones," said Mr. Peck, as Carlton stepped into the chaise to pay his promised visit to the "ungodly man." "Don't forget to have a religious interview with the negroes," remarked Georgiana, as she gave the last nod to her young convert. "I will do my best," returned Carlton, as the vehicle left the door. As might have been expected, Carlton met with a cordial reception at the hands of the proprietor of the Grove Farm. The servants in the "Great House" were well dressed, and appeared as if they did not want for food. Jones knew that Carlton was from the North, and a non-slaveholder, and therefore did everything in his power to make a favourable impression on his mind. "My negroes are well clothed, well fed, and not over worked," said the slaveholder to his visitor, after the latter had been with him nearly a week. "As far as I can see, your slaves appear to good advantage," replied Carlton. "But," continued he, "if it is a fair question, do you have preaching among your slaves on Sunday, Mr. Jones?" "No, no," returned he, "I think that's all nonsense; my negroes do their own preaching." "So you do permit them to have meetings." "Yes, when they wish. There's some very intelligent and clever chaps among them." "As to-morrow is the Sabbath," said Carlton, "if you have no objection, I will attend meeting with them." "Most certainly you shall, if you will do the preaching," returned the planter. Here the young man was about to decline, but he remembered the parting words of Georgiana, and he took courage and said, "Oh, I have no objection to give the negroes a short talk." It was then understood that Carlton was to have a religious interview with the blacks the next day, and the young man waited with a degree of impatience for the time.

In no part of the South are slaves in a more ignorant and degraded state than in the cotton, sugar, and rice districts.

If they are permitted to cease labour on the Sabbath, the

time is spent in hunting, fishing, or lying beneath the shade of a tree, resting for the morrow. Religious instruction is unknown in the far South, except among such men as the Rev. C. C. Jones, John Peck, and some others who regard religious instruction, such as they impart to their slaves, as calculated to make them more trustworthy and valuable as property. Jones, aware that his slaves would make rather a bad show of intelligence if questioned by Carlton, resolved to have them ready for him, and therefore gave his driver orders with regard to their preparation. Consequently, after the day's labour was over, Dogget, the driver, assembled the negroes together and said, "Now, boys and gals, your master is coming down to the quarters to-morrow with his visitor, who is going to give you a preach, and I want you should understand what he says to you. Now many of you who came of Old Virginia and Kentuck, know what preaching is, and others who have been raised in these parts do not. Preaching is to tell you that you are mighty wicked and bad at heart. This, I suppose, you all know. But if the gentleman should ask you who made you, tell him the Lord; if he ask if you wish to go to heaven, tell him yes. Remember that you are all Christians, all love the Lord, all want to go to heaven, all love your masters, and all love me. Now, boys and gals, I want you to show yourselves smart to-morrow: be on your p's and q's, and, Monday morning, I will give you all a glass of whiskey bright and early." Agreeable to arrangement the slaves were assembled together on Sunday morning under the large trees near the great house, and after going through another drilling from the driver, Jones and Carlton made their appearance. "You see," said Jones to the negroes, as he approached them, "you see here's a gentleman that's come to talk to you about your souls, and I hope you 'ill all pay that attention that you ought." Jones then seated himself in one of the two chairs placed there for him and the stranger.

Carlton had already selected a chapter in the Bible to read to them, which he did, after first prefacing it with some remarks of his own. Not being accustomed to speak in public, he determined, after reading the Bible, to make it more of a conversational meeting than otherwise. He therefore began asking them questions. "Do you feel that you are a Christian?" asked he of a full-blooded negro that sat near him. "Yes, sir," was the response. "You feel, then, that you shall go to heaven." "Yes, sir." "Of course you know who made you?" The man put his hand to his head and began to scratch his wool; and, after a little hesitation, answered, "De overseer told us last night who made us, but indeed I forgot the gentmun's name." This reply was almost too much for Carlton, and his gravity was not a little moved. However, he bit his tongue, and turned to another man, who appeared, from his looks, to be more intelligent. "Do you serve the Lord?" asked he. "No, sir, I don't serve anybody but Mr. Jones; I neber belong to anybody else." To hide his feelings at this juncture, Carlton turned and walked to another part of the grounds, to where the women were seated, and said to a mulatto woman who had rather an anxious countenance, "Did you ever hear of John the Baptist?" "Oh yes, marser, John de Baptist; I know dat nigger bery well indeed; he libs in Old Kentuck, where I come from." Carlton's gravity here gave way, and he looked at the planter and laughed right out. The old woman knew a slave near her old master's farm in Kentucky, and was ignorant enough to suppose that he was the John the Baptist inquired about. Carlton occupied the remainder of the time in reading Scripture and talking to them. "My niggers aint shown off very well to-day," said Jones, as he and his visitor left the grounds. "No," replied Carlton. "You did not get hold of the bright ones," continued the planter. "So it seems," remarked Carlton. The planter evidently felt that his neighbour, Parson Peck, would have a nut to crack over the account that Carlton would give of the ignorance of the slaves, and said and did all in his power to remove the bad impression already made; but to no purpose. The report made by Carlton, on his return, amused the parson very much. It appeared to him the best reason why professed Christians like himself should be slave-holders. Not so with Georgiana. She did not even smile when Carlton was telling his story, but seemed sore at heart that such ignorance should prevail in their midst. The question turned upon the heathen of other lands, and the parson began to expatiate upon his own efforts in foreign missions, when his daughter, with a child-like simplicity, said,

"Send Bibles to the heathen;
On every distant shore,

From light that's beaming o'er us,
Let streams increasing pour
But keep it from the millions
Down-trodden at our door.

"Send Bibles to the heathen,
Their famished spirits feed;
Oh! haste, and join your efforts,
The priceless gift to speed;
Then flog the trembling negro
If he should learn to read."

"I saw a curiosity while at Mr. Jones's that I shall not forget soon," said Carlton. "What was it?" inquired the parson. "A kennel of bloodhounds; and such dogs I never saw before. They were of a species between the bloodhound and the fox-hound, and were ferocious, gaunt, and savage-looking animals. They were part of a stock imported from Cuba, he informed me. They were kept in an iron cage, and fed on Indian corn bread. This kind of food, he said, made them eager for their business. Sometimes they would give the dogs meat, but it was always after they had been chasing a negro." "Were those the dogs you had, papa, to hunt Harry?" asked Georgiana. "No, my dear," was the short reply: and the parson seemed anxious to change the conversation to something else. When Mr. Peck had left the room, Carlton spoke more freely of what he had seen, and spoke more pointedly against slavery; for he well knew that Miss Peck sympathised with him in all he felt and said.

"You mentioned about your father hunting a slave," said Carlton, in an under tone. "Yes," replied she; "papa went with some slave-catchers and a parcel of those nasty negro-dogs, to hunt poor Harry. He belonged to papa and lived on the farm. His wife lives in town, and Harry had been to see her, and did not return quite as early as he should; and Huckelby was flogging him, and he got away and came here. I wanted papa to keep him in town, so that he could see his wife more frequently; but he said they could not spare him from the farm, and flogged him again, and sent him back. The poor fellow knew that the overseer would punish him over again, and instead of going back he went into the woods." "Did they catch him?"

A NEGRO HUNT IN THE SOUTHERN STATES.

asked Carlton. "Yes," replied she. "In chasing him through the woods, he attempted to escape by swimming across a river, and the dogs were sent in after him, and soon caught him. But Harry had great courage and fought the dogs with a big club; and papa seeing the negro would escape from the dogs, shot at him, as he says, only to wound him, that he might be caught; but the poor fellow was killed." Overcome by relating this incident, Georgiana burst into tears.

Although Mr. Peck fed and clothed his house servants well, and treated them with a degree of kindness, he was, nevertheless, a most cruel master. He encouraged his driver to work the field-hands from early dawn till late at night; and the good appearance of the house-servants, and the preaching of Snyder to the field negroes, was to cause himself to be regarded as a Christian master. Being on a visit one day at the farm, and having with him several persons from the Free States, and wishing to make them believe that his slaves were happy, satisfied, and contented, the parson got out the whiskey and gave each one a dram, who in return had to drink the master's health, or give a toast of some kind. The company were not a little amused at some of the sentiments given, and Peck was delighted at every indication of contentment on the part of the blacks. At last it came to Jack's turn to drink, and the master expected something good from him, because he was considered the cleverest and most witty slave on the farm.

"Now," said the master, as he handed Jack the cup of whiskey; "now, Jack, give us something rich. You know," continued he, "we have raised the finest crop of cotton that's been seen in these parts for many a day. Now give us a toast on cotton; come, Jack, give us something to laugh at." The negro felt not a little elated at being made the hero of the occasion, and taking the whiskey in his right hand, put his left to his head and began to scratch his wool, and said,

"The big bee flies high,
The little bee make the honey;
The black folks makes the cotton,
And the white folks gets the money."

CHAPTER XIV.

A FREE WOMAN REDUCED TO SLAVERY.

ALTHESA found in Henry Morton a kind and affectionate husband; and his efforts to purchase her mother, although unsuccessful, had doubly endeared him to her. Having from the commencement resolved not to hold slaves, or rather not to own any, they were compelled to hire servants for their own use. Five years had passed away, and their happiness was increased by two lovely daughters. Mrs. Morton was seated, one bright afternoon, busily engaged with her needle, and near her sat Salome, a servant that she had just taken into her employ. The woman was perfectly white; so much so, that Mrs. Morton had expressed her apprehensions to her husband, when the woman first came, that she was not born a slave. The mistress watched the servant, as the latter sat sewing upon some coarse work, and saw the large silent tear in her eye. This caused an uneasiness to the mistress, and she said, "Salome, don't you like your situation here?" "Oh yes, madam," answered the woman in a quick tone, and then tried to force a smile. "Why is it that you often look sad, and with tears in your eyes?" The mistress saw that she had touched a tender chord, and continued, "I am your friend; tell me your sorrow, and, if I can, I will help you." As the last sentence was escaping the lips of the mistress, the slave woman put her check apron to her face and wept. Mrs. Morton saw plainly that there was cause for this expression of grief, and pressed the woman more closely. "Hear me, then," said the woman calming herself: "I will tell you why I sometimes weep. I was born in Germany, on the bank of the Rhine. Ten years ago my father came to this country, bringing with him my mother and myself. He was poor, and I, wishing to assist all I could, obtained a situation as nurse to a lady in this city. My father got employment as a labourer on the wharf, among the steamboats; but he was soon taken ill with the yellow fever, and died. My mother then got a situation for herself, while I remained with my first employer. When the hot season came on, my master, with his wife, left New Orleans until the hot season was over, and took me with them. They stopped at a town on the banks of the Mississippi river, and said they should remain there some weeks. One day they went out for a ride, and they had not been gone more than half an hour, when two men came into the room and told me that they had bought me, and that I was their slave. I was bound and taken to prison, and that night put on a steamboat and taken up the Yazoo river, and set to work on a farm. I was forced to take up with a negro, and by him had three children. A year since my master's daughter was married, and I was given to her. She came with her husband to this city, and I have ever since been hired out."

"Unhappy woman," whispered Althesa, "why did you not tell me this before?" "I was afraid," replied Salome, "for I was once severely flogged for telling a stranger that I was not born a slave." On Mr. Morton's return home, his wife communicated to him the story which the slave woman had told her an hour before, and begged that something might be done to rescue her from the situation she was then in. In Louisiana as well as many others of the slave states, great obstacles are thrown in the way of persons who have been wrongfully reduced to slavery regaining their freedom. A person claiming to be free must prove his right to his liberty. This, it will be seen, throws the burden of proof upon the slave, who, in all probability, finds it out of his power to produce such evidence. And if any free person shall attempt to aid a freeman in regaining his freedom, he is compelled to enter into security in the sum of one thousand dollars, and if the person claiming to be free shall fail to establish such fact, the thousand dollars are forfeited to the state. This cruel and oppressive law has kept many a freeman from espousing the cause of persons unjustly held as slaves. Mr. Morton inquired and found that the woman's story was true, as regarded the time she had lived with her present owner; but the latter not only denied that she was free, but immediately removed her from Morton's. Three months after Salome had been removed from Morton's and let out to another family, she was one morning cleaning the door steps, when a lady passing by, looked at the slave and thought she recognised some one that she had seen before. The lady stopped and asked the woman if she was a slave. "I am," said she. "Were you born a slave?" "No, I was born in Germany." "What's the name of the ship in which you came to this country?" inquired the lady. "I don't know," was the answer. "Was it the *Amazon*?" At the sound of this name, the slave woman was silent for a moment, and then the tears began to flow freely down her care-worn cheeks. "Would you know Mrs. Marshall, who was a passenger in the *Amazon*, if you should see her?" inquired the lady. At this the woman gazed at the lady with a degree of intensity that can be imagined better than described, and then fell at the lady's feet. The lady was Mrs. Marshall. She had crossed the Atlantic in the same ship with this poor woman. Salome, like many of her countrymen, was a beautiful singer, and had often entertained Mrs. Marshall and the other lady passengers on board the *Amazon*. The poor woman was raised from the ground by Mrs. Marshall, and placed upon the door step that she had a moment before been cleaning. "I will do my utmost to rescue you from the horrid life of a slave," exclaimed the lady, as she took from her pocket her pencil, and wrote down the number of the house, and the street in which the German woman was working as a slave.

After a long and tedious trial of many days, it was decided that Salome Miller was by birth a free woman, and she was set at liberty. The good and generous Althesa had contributed some of the money toward bringing about the trial, and had done much to cheer on Mrs. Marshall in her benevolent object. Salome Miller is free, but where are her three children? They are still slaves, and in all human probability will die as such.

This, reader, is no fiction; if you think so, look over the files of the New Orleans newspapers of the years 1845–6, and you will there see reports of the trial.

CHAPTER XV.

TO-DAY A MISTRESS, TO-MORROW A SLAVE.

> "I PROMISED thee a sister tale
> Of man's perfidious cruelty;
> Come, then, and hear what cruel wrong
> Befel the dark ladie."—*Coleridge.*

LET us return for a moment to the home of Clotel. While she was passing lonely and dreary hours with none but her darling child, Horatio Green was trying to find relief in that insidious enemy of man, the intoxicating cup. Defeated in politics, forsaken in love by his wife, he seemed to have lost all principle of honour, and was ready to nerve himself up to any deed, no matter how unprincipled. Clotel's existence was now well known to Horatio's wife, and both her and her father demanded that the beautiful quadroon and her child should be sold and sent out of the state. To this proposition he at first turned a deaf ear; but when he saw that his wife was about to return to her father's roof, he consented to leave the matter in the hands of his father-in-law. The result was, that Clotel was immediately sold to the slave-trader, Walker, who, a few years previous, had taken her mother and sister to the far South. But, as if to make her husband drink of the cup of humiliation to its very dregs, Mrs. Green resolved to take his child under her own roof for a servant. Mary was, therefore, put to the meanest work that could be found, and although only ten years of age, she was often compelled to perform labour, which, under ordinary circumstances, would have been thought too hard for one much older. One condition of the sale of Clotel to Walker was, that she should be taken out of the state, which was accordingly done. Most quadroon women who are taken to the lower countries to be sold are either purchased by gentlemen for their own use, or sold for waiting-maids; and Clotel, like her sister, was fortunate enough to be bought for the latter purpose. The town of Vicksburgh stands on the left bank of the Mississippi, and is noted for the severity with which slaves are treated. It was here that Clotel was sold to Mr. James French, a merchant.

Mrs. French was severe in the extreme to her servants. Well

dressed, but scantily fed, and overworked were all who found a home with her. The quadroon had been in her new home but a short time ere she found that her situation was far different from what it was in Virginia. What social virtues are possible in a society of which injustice is the primary characteristic? in a society which is divided into two classes, masters and slaves? Every married woman in the far South looks upon her husband as unfaithful, and regards every quadroon servant as a rival. Clotel had been with her new mistress but a few days, when she was ordered to cut off her long hair. The negro, constitutionally, is fond of dress and outward appearance. He that has short, woolly hair, combs it and oils it to death. He that has long hair, would sooner have his teeth drawn than lose it. However painful it was to the quadroon, she was soon seen with her hair cut as short as any of the full-blooded negroes in the dwelling.

Even with her short hair, Clotel was handsome. Her life had been a secluded one, and though now nearly thirty years of age, she was still beautiful. At her short hair, the other servants laughed, "Miss Clo needn't strut round so big, she got short nappy har well as I," said Nell, with a broad grin that showed her teeth. "She tinks she white, when she come here wid dat long har of hers," replied Mill. "Yes," continued Nell; "missus make her take down her wool so she no put it up to-day."

The fairness of Clotel's complexion was regarded with envy as well by the other servants as by the mistress herself. This is one of the hard features of slavery. To-day the woman is mistress of her own cottage; to-morrow she is sold to one who aims to make her life as intolerable as possible. And be it remembered, that the house servant has the best situation which a slave can occupy. Some American writers have tried to make the world believe that the condition of the labouring classes of England is as bad as the slaves of the United States.

The English labourer may be oppressed, he may be cheated, defrauded, swindled, and even starved; but it is not slavery under which he groans. He cannot be sold; in point of law he is equal to the prime minister. "It is easy to captivate the unthinking and the prejudiced, by eloquent declamation about the oppression of English operatives being worse than that of American slaves, and by exaggerating the wrongs on one side and hiding them on the other. But all informed and reflecting minds, knowing that bad as are the social evils of England, those of Slavery are immeasurably worse." But the degradation and harsh treatment that Clotel experienced in her new home was nothing compared with the grief she underwent at being separated from her dear child. Taken from her without scarcely a moment's warning, she knew not what had become of her. The deep and heartfelt grief of Clotel was soon perceived by her owners, and fearing that her refusal to take food would cause her death, they resolved to sell her. Mr. French found no difficulty in getting a purchaser for the quadroon woman, for such are usually the most marketable kind of property. Clotel was sold at private sale to a young man for a housekeeper; but even he had missed his aim.

CHAPTER XVI.

DEATH OF THE PARSON.

CARLTON was above thirty years of age, standing on the last legs of a young man, and entering on the first of a bachelor. He had never dabbled in matters of love, and looked upon all women alike. Although he respected woman for her virtues, and often spoke of the goodness of heart of the sex, he had never dreamed of marriage. At first he looked upon Miss Peck as a pretty young woman, but after she became his religious teacher, he regarded her in that light, that every one will those whom they know to be their superiors. It was soon seen, however, that the young man not only respected and reverenced Georgiana for the incalculable service she had done him, in awakening him to a sense of duty to his soul, but he had learned to bow to the shrine of Cupid. He found, weeks after he had been in her company, that when he met her at table, or alone in the drawing-room, or on the piazza, he felt a shortness of breath, a palpitating of the heart, a kind of dizziness of the head; but he knew not its cause.

This was love in its first stage. Mr. Peck saw, or thought he saw, what would be the result of Carlton's visit, and held out every inducement in his power to prolong his stay. The hot season was just commencing, and the young Northerner was talking of his return home, when the parson was very suddenly taken ill. The disease was the cholera, and the physicians pronounced the case incurable. In less than five hours John Peck was a corpse. His love for Georgiana, and respect for her father, had induced Carlton to remain by the bedside of the dying man, although against the express orders of the physician. This act of kindness caused the young orphan henceforth to regard Carlton as her best friend. He now felt it his duty to remain with the young woman until some of her relations should be summoned from Connecticut. After the funeral, the family physician advised that Miss Peck should go to the farm, and spend the time at the country seat; and also advised Carlton to remain with her, which he did.

At the parson's death his negroes showed little or no signs of grief. This was noticed by both Carlton and Miss Peck, and caused no little pain to the latter. "They are ungrateful," said Carlton, as he and Georgiana were seated on the piazza. "What," asked she, "have they to be grateful for?" "Your father was kind, was he not?" "Yes, as kind as most men who own slaves; but the kindness meted out to blacks would be unkindness if given to whites. We would think so, should we not?" "Yes," replied he. "If we would not consider the best treatment which a slave receives good enough for us, we should not think he ought to be grateful for it. Everybody knows that slavery in its best and mildest form is wrong. Whoever denies this, his lips libel his heart. Try him! Clank the chains in his ears, and tell him they are for him; give him an hour to prepare his wife and children for a life of slavery; bid him make haste, and get ready their necks for the yoke, and their wrists for the coffle chains; then look at his pale lips and trembling knees, and you have nature's testimony against slavery."

"Let's take a walk," said Carlton, as if to turn the conversation. The moon was just appearing through the tops of the trees, and the animals and insects in an adjoining wood kept up a continued din of music. The croaking of bull-frogs, buzzing of insects, cooing of turtle-doves, and the sound from a thousand musical instruments, pitched on as many different keys, made the welkin ring. But even all this noise did not drown the singing of a party of the slaves, who were seated near a spring that was sending up its cooling waters. "How prettily the negroes sing," remarked Carlton, as they were wending their way towards the place from whence the sound of the voices came. "Yes," replied Georgiana; "master Sam is there, I'll warrant you: he's always on hand when there's any singing or dancing. We must not let them see us, or they will stop singing." "Who makes their songs for them?" inquired the young man. "Oh, they make them up as they sing them; they are all impromptu songs." By this time they were near enough to hear distinctly every word; and, true enough, Sam's voice was heard above all others. At the conclusion of each song they all joined in a hearty laugh, with an expression of "Dats de song for me;" "Dems dems."

"Stop," said Carlton, as Georgiana was rising from the log upon which she was seated; "stop, and let's hear this one." The piece was sung by Sam, the others joining in the chorus, and was as follows:

Sam.

"Come, all my brethren, let us take a rest,
While the moon shines so brightly and clear;
Old master is dead, and left us at last,
And has gone at the Bar to appear.
Old master has died, and lying in his grave,
And our blood will awhile cease to flow;
He will no more trample on the neck of the slave;
For he's gone where the slaveholders go.

Chorus.

"Hang up the shovel and the hoe—
Take down the fiddle and the bow—
Old master has gone to the slaveholder's rest;
He has gone where they all ought to go.

Sam.

"I heard the old doctor say the other night,
As he passed by the dining-room door—
'Perhaps the old man may live through the night,
But I think he will die about four.'
Young mistress sent me, at the peril of my life,
For the parson to come down and pray,
For says she, 'Your old master is now about to die,'
And says I, 'God speed him on his way.'

"Hang up the shovel, &c.

"At four o'clock at morn the family was called
Around the old man's dying bed;
And oh! but I laughed to myself when I heard
That the old man's spirit had fled.
Mr. Carlton cried, and so did I pretend;
Young mistress very nearly went mad;
And the old parson's groans did the heavens fairly rend;
But I tell you I felt mighty glad.

"Hang up the shovel, &c.

"We'll no more be roused by the blowing of his horn,
Our backs no longer he will score;
He no more will feed us on cotton-seeds and corn;
For his reign of oppression now is o'er.
He no more will hang our children on the tree,
To be ate by the carrion crow;
He no more will send our wives to Tennessee;
For he's gone where the slaveholders go.

"Hang up the shovel and the hoe,
Take down the fiddle and the bow,
We'll dance and sing,
And make the forest ring,
With the fiddle and the old banjo."

The song was not half finished before Carlton regretted that he had caused the young lady to remain and hear what to her must be anything but pleasant reflections upon her deceased parent. "I think we will walk," said he, at the same time extending his arm to Georgiana. "No," said she; "let's hear them out. It is from these unguarded expressions of the feelings of the negroes, that we should learn a lesson." At its conclusion they walked towards the house in silence: as they were ascending the steps, the young man said, "They are happy, after all. The negro, situated as yours are, is not aware that he is deprived of any just rights." "Yes, yes," answered Georgiana: "you may place the slave where you please; you may dry up to your utmost the fountains of his feelings, the springs of his thought; you may yoke him to your labour, as an ox which liveth only to work, and worketh only to live; you may put him under any process which, without destroying his value as a slave, will debase and crush him as a rational being; you may do this, and *the idea that he was born to be free will survive it all.* It is allied to his hope of immortality; it is the ethereal part of his nature, which oppression cannot reach; it is a torch lit up in his soul by the hand of Deity, and never meant to be extinguished by the hand of man."

On reaching the drawing-room, they found Sam snuffing the candles, and looking as solemn and as dignified as if he had never sung a song or laughed in his life. "Will Miss Georgy have de supper got up now?" asked the negro. "Yes," she replied.

"Well," remarked Carlton, "that beats anything I ever met with. Do you think that was Sam we heard singing?" "I am sure of it," was the answer. "I could not have believed that that fellow was capable of so much deception," continued he. "Our system of slavery is one of deception; and Sam, you see, has only been a good scholar. However, he is as honest a fellow as you will find among the slave population here. If we would have them more honest, we should give them their liberty, and then the inducement to be dishonest would be gone. I have resolved that these creatures shall all be free." "Indeed!" exclaimed Carlton. "Yes, I shall let them all go free, and set an example to those about me." "I honour your judgment," said he. "But will the state permit them to remain?" "If not, they can go where they can live in freedom. I will not be unjust because the state is."

CHAPTER XVII.

RETALIATION.

"I HAD a dream, a happy dream;
I thought that I was free:
That in my own bright land again
A home there was for me."

WITH the deepest humiliation Horatio Green saw the daughter of Clotel, his own child, brought into his dwelling as a servant. His wife felt that she had been deceived, and determined to punish her deceiver. At first Mary was put to work in the kitchen, where she met with little or no sympathy from the other slaves, owing to the fairness of her complexion. The child was white, what should be done to make her look like other negroes, was the question Mrs. Green asked herself. At last she hit upon a plan: there was a garden at the back of the house over which Mrs. Green could look from her parlour window. Here the white slave-girl was put to work, without either bonnet or handkerchief upon her head. A hot sun poured its broiling rays on the naked face and neck of the girl, until she sank down in the corner of the garden, and was actually broiled to sleep. "Dat little nigger ain't working a bit, missus," said Dinah to Mrs. Green, as she entered the kitchen.

"She's lying in the sun, seasoning; she will work better by and by," replied the mistress. "Dees white niggers always tink dey sef good as white folks," continued the cook. "Yes, but we will teach them better; won't we, Dinah?" "Yes, missus, I don't like dees mularter niggers, no how; dey always want to set dey sef up for something big." The cook was black, and was not without that prejudice which is to be found among the negroes, as well as among the whites of the Southern States. The sun had the desired effect, for in less than a fortnight Mary's fair complexion had disappeared, and she was but little whiter than any other mulatto children running about the yard. But the close resemblance between the father and child annoyed the mistress more than the mere whiteness of the child's complexion. Horatio made proposition after proposition to have the girl sent away, for every time he beheld her countenance it reminded him of the happy days he had spent with Clotel. But his wife had commenced, and determined to carry out her unfeeling and fiendish designs. This child was not only white, but she was the granddaughter of Thomas Jefferson, the man who, when speaking against slavery in the legislature of Virginia, said,

> "The whole commerce between master and slave is a perpetual exercise of the most boisterous passions; *the most unremitting despotism on the one part, and degrading submission on the other.* With what execration should the statesman be loaded who, permitting one half the citizens thus to trample on the rights of the other, transforms those into despots and these into enemies, destroys the morals of the one part, and the *amor patriæ* of the other! For if the slave can have a country in this world, it must be any other in preference to that in which he is born to live and labour for another; in which he must lock up the faculties of his nature, contribute as far as depends on his individual endeavours to the evanishment of the human race, or entail his own miserable condition on the endless generations proceeding from him. And can the liberties of a nation be thought secure when we have removed their only firm basis, a conviction in the minds of the people that these liberties are the gift of God? that they are not to be violated but with his wrath? Indeed, I tremble for my country when I reflect that God is just; that his justice cannot sleep for ever; that, considering numbers, nature, and natural means only, a revolution of the wheel of fortune, an exchange of situation, is among possible events; that it may become probable by supernatural interference! The Almighty has no attribute which can take side with us in such a contest.
>
> * * *
>
> "What an incomprehensible machine is man! Who can endure toil, famine, stripes, imprisonment, and death itself, in vindication of his own liberty, and the next moment be deaf to all those motives, whose power supported him through his trial, and inflict on his fellow men a bondage, *one hour of which is fraught with more misery than ages of that which he rose in rebellion to oppose!* But we must wait with patience the workings of an overruling Providence, and hope that that is preparing the deliverance of these our suffering brethren. When the measure of their tears shall be full—when their tears shall have involved heaven itself in darkness—doubtless a God of justice will awaken to their distress, and by diffusing light and liberality

> among their oppressors, or at length by his exterminating thunder, manifest his attention to things of this world, and that they are not left to the guidance of blind fatality."

The same man, speaking of the probability that the slaves might some day attempt to gain their liberties by a revolution, said,

> "I tremble for my country, when I recollect that God is just, and that His justice cannot sleep for ever. The Almighty has no attribute that can take sides with us in such a struggle."

But, sad to say, Jefferson is not the only American statesman who has spoken high-sounding words in favour of freedom, and then left his own children to die slaves.

CHAPTER XVIII.

THE LIBERATOR.

"WE hold these truths to be self-evident, that all men are created free and equal; that they are endowed by their Creator with certain inalienable rights; among these are life, *liberty*, and the pursuit of happiness."—*Declaration of American Independence.*

THE death of the parson was the commencement of a new era in the history of his slaves. Only a little more than eighteen years of age, Georgiana could not expect to carry out her own wishes in regard to the slaves, although she was sole heir to her father's estate. There were distant relations whose opinions she had at least to respect. And both law and public opinion in the state were against any measure of emancipation that she might think of adopting; unless, perhaps, she might be permitted to send them to Liberia. Her uncle in Connecticut had already been written to, to come down and aid in settling up the estate. He was a Northern man, but she knew him to be a tight-fisted yankee, whose whole counsel would go against liberating the negroes. Yet there was one way in which the thing could be done. She loved Carlton, and she well knew that he loved her; she read it in his countenance every time they met, yet the young man did not mention his wishes to her. There were many reasons why he should not. In the first place, her father was just deceased, and it seemed only right that he should wait a reasonable time. Again, Carlton was poor, and Georgiana was possessed of a large fortune; and his high spirit would not, for a moment, allow him to place himself in a position to be regarded as a fortune-hunter. The young girl hinted, as best she could, at the probable future; but all to no purpose. He took nothing to himself. True, she had read much of "woman's rights;" and had even attended a meeting, while at the North, which had been called to discuss the wrongs of woman; but she could not nerve herself up to the point of putting the question to Carlton, although she felt sure that she should not be rejected. She waited, but in vain. At last, one evening, she came out of her room rather late, and was walking on the piazza for fresh air. She passed near Carlton's room, and heard the voice of Sam. The negro had just come in to get the young man's boots, and had stopped, as he usually did, to have some talk. "I wish," said Sam, "dat Marser Carlton an Miss Georgy would get married; den, I 'spec, we'd have good times." "I don't think your mistress would have me," replied the young man. "What make tink dat, Marser Carlton?" "Your mistress would marry no one, Sam, unless she loved them." "Den I wish she would lub you, cause I tink we have good times den. All our folks is de same 'pinion like me," returned the negro, and then left the room with the boots in his hands. During the conversation between the Anglo-Saxon and the African, one word had been dropped by the former that haunted the young lady the remainder of the night—"Your mistress would marry no one unless she loved them." That word awoke her in the morning, and caused her to decide upon this important subject. Love and duty triumphed over the woman's timid nature, and that day Georgiana informed Carlton that she was ready to become his wife. The young man, with grateful tears, accepted and kissed the hand that was offered to him. The marriage of Carlton and Miss Peck was hailed with delight by both the servants in the house and the negroes on the farm. New rules were immediately announced for the working and general treatment of the slaves on the plantation. With this, Huckelby, the overseer, saw his reign coming to an end; and Snyder, the Dutch preacher, felt that his services would soon be dispensed with, for nothing was more repugnant to the feelings of Mrs. Carlton than the sermons preached by Snyder to the slaves. She regarded them as something intended to make them better satisfied with their condition, and more valuable as pieces of property, without preparing them for the world to come. Mrs. Carlton found in her husband a congenial spirit, who entered into all her wishes and plans for bettering the condition of their slaves. Mrs. Carlton's views and sympathies were all in favour of immediate emancipation; but then she saw, or thought she saw, a difficulty in that. If the slaves were liberated, they must be sent out of the state. This, of course, would incur additional expense; and if they left the state, where had they better go? "Let's send them to Liberia," said Carlton. "Why should they go to Africa, any more than to the Free States or to Canada?" asked the wife. "They would be in their native land," he answered. "Is not this their native land? What right have we, more than the negro, to the soil here, or to style ourselves native Americans? Indeed it is as much their homes as ours, and I have sometimes thought it was more theirs. The negro has cleared up the lands, built towns, and enriched the soil with his blood and tears; and in return, he is to be sent to a country of which he knows nothing. Who fought more bravely for American independence than the blacks? A negro, by the name of Attucks, was the first that fell in Boston at the commencement of the revolutionary war; and, throughout the whole of the struggles for liberty in this country, the negroes have contributed their share. In the last war with Great Britain, the country was mainly indebted to the blacks in New Orleans for the achievement of the victory at that place; and even General Jackson, the commander in chief, called the negroes together at the close of the war, and addressed them in the following terms:—

> "Soldiers!—When on the banks of the Mobile I called you to take up arms, inviting you to partake the perils and glory of your *white fellow citizens, I expected much from you*; for I was not ignorant that you possessed qualities most formidable to an invading enemy. I knew with what fortitude you could endure hunger and thirst, and all the fatigues of a campaign. *I knew well how you loved your native country*, and that you, as well as ourselves, had to defend what *man* holds most dear—his parents, wife, children, and property. *You have done more than I expected*. In addition to the previous qualities I before knew you to possess, I found among you a noble enthusiasm, which leads to the performance of great things.
>
> "'Soldiers! The President of the United States shall hear how praiseworthy was your conduct in the hour of danger, and the representatives of the American people will give you the praise your exploits entitle you to. Your general anticipates them in applauding your noble ardour.'

"And what did these noble men receive in return for their courage, their heroism? Chains and slavery. Their good deeds have been consecrated only in their own memories. Who rallied with more alacrity in response to the summons of danger? If in that hazardous hour, when our homes were menaced with the horrors of war, we did not disdain to call upon the negro to assist in repelling invasion, why should we, now that the danger is past, deny him a home in his native land?" "I see," said Carlton, "you are right, but I fear you will have difficulty in persuading others to adopt your views." "We will set the example," replied she, "and then hope for the best; for I feel that the people of the Southern States will one day see their error. Liberty has always been our watchword, as far as profession is concerned. Nothing has been held so cheap as our common humanity, on a national average. If every man had his aliquot proportion of the injustice done in this land, by law and violence, the present freemen of the northern section would many of them commit suicide in self-defence, and would court the liberties awarded by Ali Pasha of Egypt to his subjects. Long ere this we should have tested, in behalf of our bleeding and crushed American brothers of every hue and complexion, every new constitution, custom, or practice, by which inhumanity was supposed to be upheld, the injustice and cruelty they contained, emblazoned before the great tribunal of mankind for condemnation; and the good and available power they possessed, for the relief, deliverance and elevation of oppressed men, permitted to shine forth from under the cloud, for the refreshment of the human race."

Although Mr. and Mrs. Carlton felt that immediate emancipation was the right of the slave and the duty of the master, they resolved on a system of gradual emancipation, so as to give them time to accomplish their wish, and to prepare the negro for freedom. Huckelby was one morning told that his services would no longer be required. The negroes, ninety-eight in number, were called together and told that the whip would no longer be used, and that they would be allowed a certain sum for every bale of cotton produced. Sam, whose long experience in the cotton-field before he had been taken into the house, and whose general intelligence justly gave him the first place amongst the negroes on the Poplar Farm, was placed at their head. They were also given to understand that the money earned by them would be placed to their credit; and when it amounted to a certain sum, they should all be free.

The joy with which this news was received by the slaves, showed their grateful appreciation of the boon their benefactors were bestowing upon them. The house servants were called and told that wages would be allowed them, and what they earned set to their credit, and they too should be free. The next were the bricklayers. There were eight of these, who had paid their master two dollars per day, and boarded and clothed themselves. An arrangement was entered into with them, by which the money they earned should be placed to their credit; and they too should be free, when a certain amount should be accumulated; and great was the change amongst all these people. The bricklayers had been to work but a short time, before their increased industry was noticed by many. They were no longer apparently the same people. A sedateness, a care, an economy, an industry, took possession of them, to which there seemed to be no bounds but in their physical strength. They were never tired of labouring, and seemed as though they could never effect enough. They became temperate, moral, religious, setting an example of innocent, unoffending lives to the world around them, which was seen and admired by all. Mr. Parker, a man who worked nearly forty slaves at the same business, was attracted by the manner in which these negroes laboured. He called on Mr. Carlton, some weeks after they had been acting on the new system, and offered 2,000 dollars for the head workman, Jim. The offer was, of course, refused. A few days after the same gentleman called again, and made an offer of double the sum that he had on the former occasion. Mr. Parker, finding that no money would purchase either of the negroes, said, "Now, Mr. Carlton, pray tell me what it is that makes your negroes work so? What kind of people are they?" "I suppose," observed Carlton, "that they are like other people, flesh and blood." "Why, sir," continued Parker, "I have never seen such people; building as they are next door to my residence, I see and have my eye on them from morning till night. You are never there, for I have never met you, or seen you once at the building. Why, sir, I am an early riser, getting up before day; and do you think that I am not awoke every morning in my life by the noise of their trowels at work, and their singing and noise before day; and do you suppose, sir, that they stop or leave off work at sundown? No, sir, but they work as long as they can see to lay a brick, and then they carry up brick and mortar for an hour or two afterward, to be ahead of their work the next morning. And again, sir, do you think that they walk at their work? No, sir, they run all day. You see, sir, those immensely long ladders, five stories in height; do you suppose they walk up them? No, sir, they run up and down them like so many monkeys all day long. I never saw such people as these in my life. I don't know what to make of them. Were a white man with them and over them with a whip, then I should see and understand the cause of the running and incessant labour; but I cannot comprehend it; there is something in it, sir. Great man, sir, that Jim; great man; I should like to own him." Carlton here informed Parker that their liberties depended upon their work; when the latter replied, "If niggers can work so for the promise of freedom, they ought to be made to work without it." This last remark was in the true spirit of the slaveholder, and reminds us of the fact that, some years since, the overseer of General Wade Hampton offered the niggers under him a suit of clothes to the one that picked the most cotton in one day; and after that time that day's work was given as a task to the slaves on that plantation; and, after a while, was adopted by other planters.

The negroes on the farm, under "Marser Sam," were also working in a manner that attracted the attention of the planters round about. They no longer feared Huckelby's whip, and no longer slept under the preaching of Snyder. On the Sabbath, Mr. and Mrs. Carlton read and explained the Scriptures to them; and the very great attention paid by the slaves showed plainly that they appreciated the gospel when given to them in its purity. The death of Currer, from yellow fever, was a great trial to Mrs. Carlton; for she had not only become much attached to her, but had heard with painful interest the story of her wrongs, and would, in all probability, have restored her to her daughter in New Orleans.

CHAPTER XIX.

ESCAPE OF CLOTEL.

"THE fetters galled my weary soul—
A soul that seemed but thrown away:
I spurned the tyrant's base control,
Resolved at least the man to play."

NO country has produced so much heroism in so short a time, connected with escapes from peril and oppression, as has occurred in the United States among fugitive slaves, many of whom show great shrewdness in their endeavours to escape from this land of bondage. A slave was one day seen passing on the high road from a border town in the interior of the state of Virginia to the Ohio river. The man had neither hat upon his head or coat upon his back. He was driving before him a very nice fat pig, and appeared to all who saw him to be a labourer employed on an adjoining farm. "No negro is permitted to go at large in the Slave States without a written pass from his or her master, except on business in the neighbourhood." "Where do you live, my boy?" asked a white man of the slave, as he passed a white house with green blinds. "Jist up de road, sir," was the answer. "That's a fine pig." "Yes, sir, marser like dis choat berry much." And the negro drove on as if he was in great haste. In this way he and the pig travelled more than fifty miles before they reached the Ohio river. Once at the river they crossed over; the pig was sold; and nine days after the runaway slave passed over the Niagara river, and, for the first time in his life, breathed the air of freedom. A few weeks later, and, on the same road, two slaves were seen passing; one was on horseback, the other was walking before him with his arms tightly bound, and a long rope leading from the man on foot to the one on horseback. "Oh, ho, that's a runaway rascal, I suppose," said a farmer, who met them on the road. "Yes, sir, he bin runaway, and I got him fast. Marser will tan his jacket for him nicely when he gets him." "You are a trustworthy fellow, I imagine," continued the farmer. "Oh yes, sir; marser puts a heap of confidence in dis nigger." And the slaves travelled on. When the one on foot was fatigued they would change positions, the other being tied and driven on foot. This they called "ride and tie." After a journey of more than two hundred miles they reached the Ohio river, turned the horse loose, told him to go home, and proceeded on their way to Canada. However they were not to have it all their own way. There are men in the Free States, and especially in the states adjacent to the Slave States, who make their living by catching the runaway slave, and returning him for the reward that may be offered. As the two slaves above mentioned were travelling on towards the land of freedom, led by the North Star, they were set upon by four of these slave-catchers, and one of them unfortunately captured. The other escaped. The captured fugitive was put under the torture, and compelled to reveal the name of his owner and his place of residence. Filled with delight, the kidnappers started back with their victim. Overjoyed with the prospect of receiving a large reward, they gave themselves up on the third night to pleasure. They put up at an inn. The negro was chained to the bed-post, in the same room with his captors. At dead of night, when all was still, the slave arose from the floor upon which he had been lying, looked around, and saw that the white men were fast asleep. The brandy punch had done its work. With palpitating heart and trembling limbs he viewed his position. The door was fast, but the warm weather had compelled them to leave the window open. If he could but get his chains off, he might escape through the window to the piazza, and reach the ground by one of the posts that supported the piazza. The sleepers' clothes hung upon chairs by the bedside; the slave thought of the padlock key, examined the pockets and found it. The chains were soon off, and the negro stealthily making his way to the window: he stopped and said to himself, "These men are villains, they are enemies to all who like me are trying to be free. Then why not I teach them a lesson?" He then undressed himself, took the clothes of one of the men, dressed himself in them, and escaped through the window, and, a moment more, he was on the high road to Canada. Fifteen days later, and the writer of this gave him a passage across Lake Erie, and saw him safe in her Britannic Majesty's dominions.

We have seen Clotel sold to Mr. French in Vicksburgh, her hair cut short, and everything done to make her realise her position as a servant. Then we have seen her re-sold, because her owners feared she would die through grief. As yet her new purchaser treated her with respectful gentleness, and sought to win her favour by flattery and presents, knowing that whatever he gave her he could take back again. But she dreaded every moment lest the scene should change, and trembled at the sound of every footfall. At every interview with her new master Clotel stoutly maintained that she had left a husband in Virginia, and would never think of taking another. The gold watch and chain, and other glittering presents which he purchased for her, were all laid aside by the quadroon, as if they were of no value to her. In the same house with her was another servant, a man, who had from time to time hired himself from his master. William was his name. He could feel for Clotel, for he, like her, had been separated from near and dear relatives, and often tried to console the poor woman. One day the quadroon observed to him that her hair was growing out again. "Yes," replied William, "you look a good deal like a man with your short hair." "Oh," rejoined she, "I have often been told that I would make a better looking man than a woman. If I had the money," continued she, "I would bid farewell to this place." In a moment more she feared that she had said too much, and smilingly remarked, "I am always talking nonsense." William was a tall, full-bodied negro, whose very countenance beamed with intelligence. Being a mechanic, he had, by his own industry, made more than what he paid his owner; this he laid aside, with the hope that some day he might get enough to purchase his freedom. He had in his chest one hundred and fifty dollars. His was a heart that felt for others, and he had again and again wiped the tears from his eyes as he heard the story of Clotel as related by herself. "If she can get free with a little money, why not give her what I have?" thought he, and then he resolved to do it. An hour after, he came into the quadroon's room, and laid the money in her lap, and said, "There, Miss Clotel, you said if you had the means you would leave this place; there is money enough to take you to England, where you will be free. You are much fairer than many of the white women of the South, and can easily pass for a free white lady." At first Clotel feared that it was a plan by which the negro wished to try her fidelity to her owner; but she was soon convinced by his earnest manner, and the deep feeling with which he spoke, that he was honest. "I will take the money only on one condition," said she; "and that is, that I effect your escape as well as my own." "How can that be done?" he inquired. "I will assume the disguise of a gentleman and you that of a servant, and we will take passage on a steamboat and go to Cincinnati, and thence to Canada." Here William put in several objections to the plan. He feared detection, and he well knew that, when a slave is once caught when attempting to escape, if returned is sure to be worse treated than before. However, Clotel satisfied him that the plan could be carried out if he would only play his part.

The resolution was taken, the clothes for her disguise procured, and before night everything was in readiness for their departure. That night Mr. Cooper, their master, was to attend a party, and this was their opportunity. William went to the wharf to look out for a boat, and had scarcely reached the landing ere he heard the puffing of a steamer. He returned and reported the fact. Clotel had already packed her trunk, and had only to dress and all was ready. In less than an hour they were on board the boat. Under the assumed name of "Mr. Johnson," Clotel went to the clerk's office and took a private state room for herself, and paid her own and servant's fare. Besides being attired in a neat suit of black, she had a white silk handkerchief tied round her chin, as if she was an invalid. A pair of green glasses covered her eyes; and fearing that she would be talked to too much and thus render her liable to be detected, she assumed to be very ill. On the other hand, William was playing his part well in the servants' hall; he was talking loudly of his master's wealth. Nothing appeared as good on the boat as in his master's fine mansion. "I don't like dees steamboats no how," said William; "I hope when marser goes on a journey agin he will take de carriage and de hosses." Mr. Johnson (for such was the name by which Clotel now went) remained in his room, to avoid, as far as possible, conversation with others. After a passage of seven days they arrived at Louisville, and put up at Gough's Hotel. Here they had to await the departure of another boat for the North. They were now in their most critical position. They were still in a slave state, and John C. Calhoun, a distinguished slave-owner, was a guest at this hotel. They feared, also, that trouble would attend their attempt to leave this place for the North, as all persons taking negroes with them have to give bail that such negroes are not runaway slaves. The law upon this point is very stringent: all steamboats and other public conveyances are liable to a fine for every slave that escapes by them, besides paying the full value for the slave. After a delay of four hours, Mr. Johnson and servant took passage on the steamer Rodolph, for Pittsburgh. It is usual, before the departure of the boats, for an officer to examine every part of the vessel to see that no slave secretes himself on board, "Where are you going?" asked the officer of William, as he was doing his duty on this occasion. "I am going with marser," was the quick reply. "Who is your master?" "Mr. Johnson, sir, a gentleman in the cabin." "You must take him to the office and satisfy that captain that all is right, or you can't go on this boat." William informed his master what the officer had said. The boat was on the eve of going, and no time could be lost, yet they knew not what to do. At last they went to the office, and Mr. Johnson, addressing the captain, said, "I am informed that my boy can't go with me unless I give security that he belongs to me." "Yes," replied the captain, "that is the law." "A very strange law indeed," rejoined Mr. Johnson, "that one can't take his property with him." After a conversation of some minutes, and a plea on the part of Johnson that he did not wish to be delayed owing to his illness, they were permitted to take their passage without farther trouble, and the boat was soon on its way up the river. The fugitives had now passed the Rubicon, and the next place at which they would land would be in a Free State. Clotel called William to her room, and said to him, "We are now free, you can go on your way to Canada, and I shall go to Virginia in search of my daughter." The announcement that she was going to risk her liberty in a Slave State was unwelcome news to William. With all the eloquence he could command, he tried to persuade Clotel that she could not escape detection, and was only throwing her freedom away. But she had counted the cost, and made up her mind for the worst. In return for the money he had furnished, she had secured for him his liberty, and their engagement was at an end.

After a quick passage the fugitives arrived at Cincinnati, and there separated. William proceeded on his way to Canada, and

Clotel again resumed her own apparel, and prepared to start in search of her child. As might have been expected, the escape of those two valuable slaves created no little sensation in Vicksburgh. Advertisements and messages were sent in every direction in which the fugitives were thought to have gone. It was soon, however, known that they had left the town as master and servant; and many were the communications which appeared in the newspapers, in which the writers thought, or pretended, that they had seen the slaves in their disguise. One was to the effect that they had gone off in a chaise; one as master, and the other as servant. But the most probable was an account given by a correspondent of one of the Southern newspapers, who happened to be a passenger in the same steamer in which the slaves escaped, and which we here give:—

"One bright starlight night, in the month of December last, I found myself in the cabin of the steamer Rodolph, then lying in the port of Vicksburgh, and bound to Louisville. I had gone early on board, in order to select a good berth, and having got tired of reading the papers, amused myself with watching the appearance of the passengers as they dropped in, one after another, and I being a believer in physiognomy, formed my own opinion of their characters.

"The second bell rang, and as I yawningly returned my watch to my pocket, my attention was attracted by the appearance of a young man who entered the cabin supported by his servant, a strapping negro.

"The man was bundled up in a capacious overcoat; his face was bandaged with a white handkerchief, and its expression entirely hid by a pair of enormous spectacles.

"There was something so mysterious and unusual about the young man as he sat restless in the corner, that curiosity led me to observe him more closely.

"He appeared anxious to avoid notice, and before the steamer had fairly left the wharf, requested, in a low, womanly voice, to be shown his berth, as he was an invalid, and must retire early: his name he gave as Mr. Johnson. His servant was called, and he was put quietly to bed. I paced the deck until Tybee light grew dim in the distance, and then went to my berth.

"I awoke in the morning with the sun shining in my face; we were then just passing St. Helena. It was a mild beautiful morning, and most of the passengers were on deck, enjoying the freshness of the air, and stimulating their appetites for breakfast. Mr. Johnson soon made his appearance, arrayed as on the night before, and took his seat quietly upon the guard of the boat.

"From the better opportunity afforded by daylight, I found that he was a slight built, apparently handsome young man, with black hair and eyes, and of a darkness of complexion that betokened Spanish extraction. Any notice from others seemed painful to him; so to satisfy my curiosity, I questioned his servant, who was standing near, and gained the following information.

"His master was an invalid—he had suffered for a long time under a complication of diseases, that had baffled the skill of the best physicians in Mississippi he was now suffering principally with the 'rheumatism,' and he was scarcely able to walk or help himself in any way. He came from Vicksburgh, and was now on his way to Philadelphia, at which place resided his uncle, a celebrated physician, and through whose means he hoped to be restored to perfect health.

"This information, communicated in a bold, off-hand manner, enlisted my sympathies for the sufferer, although it occurred to me that he walked rather too gingerly for a person afflicted with so many ailments."

After thanking Clotel for the great service she had done him in bringing him out of slavery, William bade her farewell. The prejudice that exists in the Free States against coloured persons, on account of their colour, is attributable solely to the influence of slavery, and is but another form of slavery itself. And even the slave who escapes from the Southern plantations, is surprised when he reaches the North, at the amount and withering influence of this prejudice. William applied at the railway station for a ticket for the train going to Sandusky, and was told that if he went by that train he would have to ride in the luggage-van. "Why?" asked the astonished negro. "We don't send a Jim Crow carriage but once a day, and that went this morning." The "Jim Crow" carriage is the one in which the blacks have to ride. Slavery is a school in which its victims learn much shrewdness, and William had been an apt scholar. Without asking any more questions, the negro took his seat in one of the first-class carriages. He was soon seen and ordered out. Afraid to remain in the town longer, he resolved to go by that train; and consequently seated himself on a goods' box in the luggage-van. The train started at its proper time, and all went on well. Just before arriving at the end of the journey, the conductor called on William for his ticket. "I have none," was the reply. "Well, then, you can pay your fare to me," said the officer. "How much is it?" asked the black man. "Two dollars." "What do you charge those in the passenger-carriage?" "Two dollars." "And do you charge me the same as you do those who ride in the best carriages?" asked the negro. "Yes," was the answer. "I shan't pay it," returned the man. "You black scamp, do you think you can ride on this road without paying your fare?" "No, I don't want to ride for nothing; I only want to pay what's right." "Well, launch out two dollars, and that's right." "No, I shan't; I will pay what I ought, and won't pay any more." "Come, come, nigger, your fare and be done with it," said the conductor, in a manner that is never used except by Americans to blacks. "I won't pay you two dollars, and that enough," said William. "Well, as you have come all the way in the luggage-van, pay me a dollar and a half and you may go." "I shan't do any such thing." "Don't you mean to pay for riding?" "Yes, but I won't pay a dollar and a half for riding up here in the freight-van. If you had let me come in the carriage where others ride, I would have paid you two dollars." "Where were you raised? You seem to think yourself as good as white folks." "I want nothing more than my rights." "Well, give me a dollar, and I will let you off." "No, sir, I shan't do it." "What do you mean to do then—don't you wish to pay anything?" "Yes, sir, I want to pay you the full price." "What do you mean by full price?" "What do you charge per hundred-weight for goods?" inquired the negro with a degree of gravity that would have astonished Diogenes himself. "A quarter of a dollar per hundred," answered the conductor. "I weigh just one hundred and fifty pounds," returned William, "and will pay you three-eighths of a dollar." "Do you expect that you will pay only thirty-seven cents for your ride?" "This, sir, is your own price. I came in a luggage-van, and I'll pay for luggage." After a vain effort to get the negro to pay more, the conductor took the thirty-seven cents, and noted in his cash-book, "Received for one hundred and fifty pounds of luggage, thirty-seven cents." This, reader, is no fiction; it actually occurred in the railway above described.

Thomas Corwin, a member of the American Congress, is one of the blackest white men in the United States. He was once on his way to Congress, and took passage in one of the Ohio river steamers. As he came just at the dinner hour, he immediately went into the dining saloon, and took his seat at the table. A gentleman with his whole party of five ladies at once left the table. "Where is the captain," cried the man in an angry tone. The captain soon appeared, and it was sometime before he could satisfy the old gent. that Governor Corwin was not a nigger. The newspapers often have notices of mistakes made by innkeepers and others who undertake to accommodate the public, one of which we give below.

On the 6th inst., the Hon. Daniel Webster and family entered Edgartown, on a visit for health and recreation. Arriving at the hotel, without alighting from the coach, the landlord was sent for to see if suitable accommodation could be had. That dignitary appearing, and surveying Mr. Webster, while the hon. senator addressed him, seemed woefully to mistake the dark features of the traveller as he sat back in the corner of the carriage, and to suppose him a *coloured man*, particularly as there were two coloured servants of Mr. W. outside. So he promptly declared that there was no room for him and his family, and he could not be accommodated there—at the same time suggesting that he might perhaps find accommodation at some of the huts "up back," to which he pointed. So deeply did the prejudice of looks possess him, that he appeared not to notice that the stranger introduced himself to him as Daniel Webster, or to be so ignorant as not to have heard of such a personage; and turning away, he expressed to the driver his astonishment that he should bring *black* people there for *him* to take in. It was not till he had been repeatedly assured and made to understand that the said Daniel Webster was a real live senator of the United States, that he perceived his awkward mistake and the distinguished honour which he and his house were so near missing.

In most of the Free States, the coloured people are disfranchised on account of their colour. The following scene, which we take from a newspaper in the state of Ohio, will give some idea of the extent to which this prejudice is carried.

> "The whole of Thursday last was occupied by the Court of Common Pleas for this county in trying to find out whether one Thomas West was of the VOTING COLOUR, as some had very *constitutional doubts* as to whether his colour was orthodox, and whether his hair was of the official crisp! Was it not a dignified business? Four profound judges, four acute lawyers, twelve grave jurors, and I don't know how many venerable witnesses, making in all about thirty men, perhaps, all engaged in the profound, laborious, and illustrious business, of finding out whether a man who pays tax, works on the road, and is an industrious farmer, has been born according to the republican, Christian constitution of Ohio—so that he can vote! And they wisely, gravely, and 'JUDGMATICALLY' decided that he should not vote! What wisdom—what research it must have required to evolve this truth! It was left for the Court of Common Pleas for Columbian county, Ohio, in the United States of North America, to find out what Solomon never dreamed of—the courts of all civilised, heathen, or Jewish countries, never contemplated. Lest the wisdom of our courts should be circumvented by some such men as might be named, who are so near being born constitutionally that they might be taken for white by sight, I would suggest that our court be invested with SMELLING powers, and that if a man don't exhale the constitutional smell, he shall not vote! This would be an additional security to our liberties."

William found, after all, that liberty in the so-called Free States was more a name than a reality; that prejudice followed the coloured man into every place that he might enter. The temples erected for the worship of the living God are no exception. The finest Baptist church in the city of Boston has the following paragraph in the deed that conveys its seats to pewholders:

> "And it is a further condition of these presents, that if the owner or owners of said pew shall determine hereafter to sell the same, it shall first be offered, in writing, to the standing committee of said society for the time being, at such price as might otherwise be obtained for it; and the said committee shall have the right, for ten days after such offer, to purchase said pew for said society, at that price, first deducting therefrom

> all taxes and assessments on said pew then remaining unpaid. And if the said committee shall not so complete such purchase within said ten days, then the pew may be sold by the owner or owners thereof (after payment of all such arrears) to any one respectable *white person*, but upon the same conditions as are contained in this instrument; and immediate notice of such sale shall be given in writing, by the vendor, to the treasurer of said society."

Such are the conditions upon which the Rowe Street Baptist Church, Boston, disposes of its seats. The writer of this is able to put that whole congregation, minister and all, to flight, by merely putting his coloured face in that church. We once visited a church in New York that had a place set apart for the sons of Ham. It was a dark, dismal looking place in one corner of the gallery, grated in front like a hen-coop, with a black border around it. It had two doors; over one was B. M.—black men; over the other B. W.—black women.

CHAPTER XX.

A TRUE DEMOCRAT.

"WHO can, with patience, for a moment see
The medley mass of pride and misery,
Of whips and charters, manacles and rights,
Of slaving blacks and democratic whites,
And all the piebald policy that reigns
In free confusion o'er Columbia's plains?
To think that man, thou just and gentle God!
Should stand before thee with a tyrant's rod,
O'er creatures like himself, with souls from thee,
Yet dare to boast of perfect liberty!"—*Thomas Moore.*

EDUCATED in a free state, and marrying a wife who had been a victim to the institution of slavery, Henry Morton became strongly opposed to the system. His two daughters, at the age of twelve years, were sent to the North to finish their education, and to receive that refinement that young ladies cannot obtain in the Slave States. Although he did not publicly advocate the abolition of slavery, he often made himself obnoxious to private circles, owing to the denunciatory manner in which he condemned the "peculiar institution." Being one evening at a party, and hearing one of the company talking loudly of the glory and freedom of American institutions, he gave it as his opinion that, unless slavery was speedily abolished, it would be the ruin of the Union. "It is not our boast of freedom," said he, "that will cause us to be respected abroad. It is not our loud talk in favour of liberty that will cause us to be regarded as friends of human freedom; but our acts will be scrutinised by the people of other countries. We say much against European despotism; let us look to ourselves. That government is despotic where the rulers govern subjects by their own mere will—by decrees and laws emanating from their uncontrolled will, in the enactment and execution of which the ruled have no voice, and under which they have no right except at the will of the rulers. Despotism does not depend upon the number of the rulers, or the number of the subjects. It may have one ruler or many. Rome was a despotism under Nero; so she was under the triumvirate. Athens was a despotism under

Thirty Tyrants; under her Four Hundred Tyrants; under her Three Thousand Tyrants. It has been generally observed that despotism increases in severity with the number of despots; the responsibility is more divided, and the claims more numerous. The triumvirs each demanded his victims. The smaller the number of subjects in proportion to the tyrants, the more cruel the oppression, because the less danger from rebellion. In this government, the free white citizens are the rulers—the sovereigns, as we delight to be called. All others are subjects. There are, perhaps, some sixteen or seventeen millions of sovereigns, and four millions of subjects.

"The rulers and the ruled are of all colours, from the clear white of the Caucasian tribes to the swarthy Ethiopian. The former, by courtesy, are all called white, the latter black. In this government the subject has no rights, social, political, or personal. He has no voice in the laws which govern him. He can hold no property. His very wife and children are not his. His labour is another's. He, and all that appertain to him, are the absolute property of his rulers. He is governed, bought, sold, punished, executed, by laws to which he never gave his assent, and by rulers whom he never chose. He is not a serf merely, with half the rights of men like the subjects of despotic Russia; but a native slave, stripped of every right which God and nature gave him, and which the high spirit of our revolution declared inalienable—which he himself could not surrender, and which man could not take from him. Is he not then the subject of despotic sway?

"The slaves of Athens and Rome were free in comparison. They had some rights—could acquire some property; could choose their own masters, and purchase their own freedom; and, when free, could rise in social and political life. The slaves of America, then, lie under the most absolute and grinding despotism that the world ever saw. But who are the despots? The rulers of the country—tho sovereign people! Not merely the slaveholder who cracks the lash. He is but the instrument in the hands of despotism. That despotism is the government of the Slave States, and the United States, consisting of all its rulers—all the free citizens. Do not look upon this as a paradox, because you and I and the sixteen millions of rulers are free. The rulers of every despotism are free. Nicholas of Russia is free. The grand Sultan of Turkey is free. The butcher of Austria is free. Augustus, Anthony, and Lepidus were free, while they drenched Rome in blood. The Thirty Tyrants—the Four Hundred—the Three Thousand, were free while they bound their countrymen in chains. You, and I, and the sixteen millions are free, while we fasten iron chains, and rivet manacles on four millions of our fellowmen—tear their wives and children from them—separate them—sell them, and doom them to perpetual, eternal bondage. Are we not then despots—despots such as history will brand and God abhor?"

"We, as individuals, are fast losing our reputation for honest dealing. Our nation is losing its character. The loss of a firm national character, or the degradation of a nation's honour, is the inevitable prelude to her destruction. Behold the once proud fabric of a Roman empire—an empire carrying its arts and arms into every part of the Eastern continent; the monarchs of mighty kingdoms dragged at the wheels of her triumphal chariots; her eagle waving over the ruins of desolated countries;—where is her splendour, her wealth, her power, her glory? Extinguished for ever. Her mouldering temples, the mournful vestiges of her former grandeur, afford a shelter to her muttering monks. Where are her statesmen, her sages, her philosophers, her orators, generals? Go to their solitary tombs and inquire? She lost her national character, and her destruction followed. The ramparts of her national pride were broken down, and Vandalism desolated her classic fields. Then let the people of our country take warning ere it is too late. But most of us say to ourselves,

> "'Who questions the right of mankind to be free?
> Yet, what are the rights of the *negro* to me?
> I'm well fed and clothed, I have plenty of pelf—
> I'll care for the blacks when I turn black myself.'

"New Orleans is doubtless the most immoral place in the United States. The theatres are open on the Sabbath. Bull-fights, horse-racing, and other cruel amusements are carried on in this city to an extent unknown in any other part of the Union. The most stringent laws have been passed in that city against negroes, yet a few years since the State Legislature passed a special act to enable a white man to marry a coloured woman, on account of her being possessed of a large fortune. And, very recently, the following paragraph appeared in the city papers:—

> "'There has been quite a stir recently in this city, in consequence of a marriage of a white man, named Buddington, a teller in the Canal Bank, to the negro daughter of one of the wealthiest merchants. Buddington, before he could be married, was obliged to swear that he had negro blood in his veins, and to do this he made an incision in his arm, and put some of her blood in the cut. The ceremony was performed by a Catholic clergyman, and the bridegroom has received with his wife a fortune of fifty or sixty thousand dollars.'

"It seems that the fifty or sixty thousand dollars entirely covered the negro woman's black skin, and the law prohibiting marriage between blacks and whites was laid aside for the occasion."

Althesa felt proud, as well she might, at her husband's taking such high ground in a slaveholding city like New Orleans.

CHAPTER XXI.

THE CHRISTIAN'S DEATH.

"O WEEP, ye friends of freedom weep!
Your harps to mournful measures sweep."

ON the last day of November, 1620, on the confines of the Grand Bank of Newfoundland, lo! we behold one little solitary tempest-tost and weather-beaten ship; it is all that can be seen on the length and breadth of the vast intervening solitudes, from the melancholy wilds of Labrador and New England's iron-bound shores, to the western coasts of Ireland and the rock-defended Hebrides, but one lonely ship greets the eye of angels or of men, on this great thoroughfare of nations in our age. Next in moral grandeur, was this ship, to the great discoverer's: Columbus found a continent; the May-flower brought the seed-wheat of states and empire. That is the May-flower, with its servants of the living God, their wives and little ones, hastening to lay the foundations of nations in the occidental lands of the setting-sun. Hear the voice of prayer to God for his protection, and the glorious music of praise, as it breaks into the wild tempest of the mighty deep, upon the ear of God. Here in this ship are great and good men. Justice, mercy, humanity, respect for the rights of all; each man honoured, as he was useful to himself and others; labour respected, law-abiding men, constitution-making and respecting men; men, whom no tyrant could conquer, or hardship overcome, with the high commission sealed by a Spirit divine, to establish religious and political liberty for all. This ship had the embryo elements of all that is useful, great, and grand in Northern institutions; it was the great type of goodness and wisdom, illustrated in two and a quarter centuries gone by; it was the good genius of America.

But look far in the South-east, and you behold on the same day, in 1620, a low rakish ship hastening from the tropics, solitary and alone, to the New World. What is she? She is freighted with the elements of unmixed evil. Hark! hear those rattling chains, hear that cry of despair and wail of anguish, as they die away in the unpitying distance. Listen to those shocking oaths, the crack of that flesh-cutting whip. Ah! it is the first cargo of slaves on their way to Jamestown, Virginia. Behold the Mayflower anchored at Plymouth Rock, the slave-ship in James River. Each a parent, one of the prosperous, labour-honouring, law-sustaining institutions of the North; the other the mother of slavery, idleness, lynch-law, ignorance, unpaid labour, poverty, and duelling, despotism, the ceaseless swing of the whip, and the peculiar institutions of the South. These ships are the representation of good and evil in the New World, even to our day. When shall one of those parallel lines come to an end?

The origin of American slavery is not lost in the obscurity of by-gone ages. It is a plain historical fact, that it owes its birth to the African slave trade, now pronounced by every civilised community the greatest crime ever perpetrated against humanity. Of all causes intended to benefit mankind, the abolition of chattel slavery must necessarily be placed amongst the first, and the negro hails with joy every new advocate that appears in his cause. Commiseration for human suffering and human sacrifices awakened the capacious mind, and brought into action the enlarged benevolence, of Georgiana Carlton. With respect to her philosophy—it was of a noble cast. It was, that all men are by nature equal; that they are wisely and justly endowed by the Creator with certain rights, which are irrefragable; and that, however human pride and human avarice may depress and debase, still God is the author of good to man—and of evil, man is the artificer to himself and to his species. Unlike Plato and Socrates, her mind was free from the gloom that surrounded theirs; her philosophy was founded in the school of Christianity; though a devoted member of her father's church, she was not a sectarian.

We learn from Scripture, and it is a little remarkable that it is the only exact definition of religion found in the sacred volume, that "pure religion and undefiled before God, even the Father, is this, to visit the fatherless and widows in their affliction, and to keep oneself unspotted from the world." "Look not every man on his own things, but every man also on the things of others." "Remember them that are in bonds as bound with them." "Whatsoever ye would that others should do to you, do ye even so to them."

This was her view of Christianity, and to this end she

laboured with all her energies to convince her slaveholding neighbours that the negro could not only take care of himself, but that he also appreciated liberty, and was willing to work and redeem himself. Her most sanguine wishes were being realized when she suddenly fell into a decline. Her mother had died of consumption, and her physician pronounced this to be her disease. She was prepared for this sad intelligence, and received it with the utmost composure. Although she had confidence in her husband that he would carry out her wishes in freeing the negroes after her death, Mrs. Carlton resolved upon their immediate liberation. Consequently the slaves were all summoned before the noble woman, and informed that they were no longer bondsmen. "From this hour," said she, "you are free, and all eyes will be fixed upon you. I dare not predict how far your example may affect the welfare of your brethren yet in bondage. If you are temperate, industrious, peaceable, and pious, you will show to the world that slaves can be emancipated without danger. Remember what a singular relation you sustain to society. The necessities of the case require not only that you should behave as well as the whites, but better than the whites; and for this reason: if you behave no better than they, your example will lose a great portion of its influence. Make the Lord Jesus Christ your refuge and exemplar. His is the only standard around which you can successfully rally. If ever there was a people who needed the consolations of religion to sustain them in their grievous afflictions, you are that people. You had better trust in the Lord than to put confidence in man. Happy is that people whose God is the Lord. Get as much education as possible for yourselves and your children. An ignorant people can never occupy any other than a degraded station in society; they can never be truly free until they are intelligent. In a few days you will start for the state of Ohio, where land will be purchased for some of you who have families, and where I hope you will all prosper. We have been urged to send you to Liberia, but we think it wrong to send you from your native land. We did not wish to encourage the Colonization Society, for it originated in hatred of the free coloured people. Its pretences are false, its doctrines odious, its means contemptible. Now, whatever may be your situation in life, 'Remember those in bonds as bound with them.' You must get ready as soon as you can for your journey to the North."

Seldom was there ever witnessed a more touching scene than this. There sat the liberator,—pale, feeble, emaciated, with death stamped upon her countenance, surrounded by the sons and daughters of Africa; some of whom had in former years been separated from all that they had held near and dear, and the most of whose backs had been torn and gashed by the negro whip. Some were upon their knees at the feet of their benefactress; others were standing round her weeping. Many begged that they might be permitted to remain on the farm and work for wages, for some had wives and some husbands on other plantations in the neighbourhood, and would rather remain with them.

But the laws of the state forbade any emancipated negroes remaining, under penalty of again being sold into slavery. Hence the necessity of sending them out of the state. Mrs. Carlton was urged by her friends to send the emancipated negroes to Africa. Extracts from the speeches of Henry Clay, and other distinguished Colonization Society men, were read to her to induce her to adopt this course. Some thought they should be sent away because the blacks are vicious; others because they would be missionaries to their brethren in Africa. "But," said she, "if we send away the negroes because they are profligate and vicious, what sort of missionaries will they make? Why not send away the vicious among the whites for the same reason, and the same purpose?"

Death is a leveller, and neither age, sex, wealth, nor usefulness can avert when he is permitted to strike. The most beautiful flowers soon fade, and droop, and die; this is also the case with man; his days are uncertain as the passing breeze. This hour he glows in the blush of health and vigour, but the next he may be counted with the number no more known on earth.

Although in a low state of health, Mrs. Carlton had the pleasure of seeing all her slaves, except Sam and three others, start for a land of freedom. The morning they were to go on board the steamer, bound for Louisville, they all assembled on the large grass plot, in front of the drawing-room window, and wept while they bid their mistress farewell. When they were on the boat, about leaving the wharf, they were heard giving the charge to those on shore—"Sam, take care of Misus, take care of Marser, as you love us, and hope to meet us in de Hio (Ohio), and in heben; be sure and take good care of Misus and Marser."

In less than a week after her emancipated people had started for Ohio, Mrs. Carlton was cold in death. Mr. Carlton felt deeply, as all husbands must who love their wives, the loss of her who had been a lamp to his feet, and a light to his path. She had converted him from infidelity to Christianity; from the mere theory of liberty to practical freedom. He had looked upon the negro as an ill-treated distant link of the human family; he now regarded them as a part of God's children. Oh, what a silence pervaded the house when the Christian had been removed. His indeed was a lonesome position.

"'Twas midnight, and he sat alone—
The husband of the dead,
That day the dark dust had been thrown
Upon the buried head."

In the midst of the buoyancy of youth, this cherished one had drooped and died. Deep were the sounds of grief and mourning heard in that stately dwelling, when the stricken friends, whose office it had been to nurse and soothe the weary sufferer, beheld her pale and motionless in the sleep of death.

Oh what a chill creeps through the breaking heart when we look upon the insensible form, and feel that it no longer contains the spirit we so dearly loved! How difficult to realise that the eye which always glowed with affection and intelligence—that the ear which had so often listened to the sounds of sorrow and gladness—that the voice whose accents had been to us like sweet music, and the heart, the habitation of benevolence and truth, are now powerless and insensate as the bier upon which the form rests. Though faith be strong enough to penetrate the cloud of gloom which hovers near, and to behold the freed spirit safe, *for ever*, safe in its home in heaven, yet the thoughts *will* linger sadly and cheerlessly upon the grave.

Peace to her ashes! she fought the fight, obtained the Christian's victory, and wears the crown. But if it were that departed spirits are permitted to note the occurrences of this world, with what a frown of disapprobation would hers view the effort being made in the United States to retard the work of emancipation for which she laboured and so wished to see brought about.

In what light would she consider that hypocritical priesthood who gave their aid and sanction to the infamous "Fugitive Slave Law." If true greatness consists in doing good to mankind, then was Georgiana Carlton an ornament to human nature. Who can think of the broken hearts made whole, of sad and dejected countenances now beaming with contentment and joy, of the mother offering her free-born babe to heaven, and of the father whose cup of joy seems overflowing in the presence of his family, where none can molest or make him afraid. Oh, that God may give more such persons to take the whip-scarred negro by the hand, and raise him to a level with our common humanity! May the professed lovers of freedom in the new world see that true liberty is freedom for all! and may every American continually hear it sounding in his ear:—

"Shall every flap of England's flag
  Proclaim that all around are free,
From 'farthest Ind' to each blue crag
  That beetles o'er the Western Sea?
And shall we scoff at Europe's kings,
  When Freedom's fire is dim with us,
And round our country's altar clings
  The damning shade of Slavery's curse?

CHAPTER XXII.

A RIDE IN A STAGE-COACH.

WE shall now return to Cincinnati, where we left Clotel preparing to go to Richmond in search of her daughter. Tired of the disguise in which she had escaped, she threw it off on her arrival at Cincinnati. But being assured that not a shadow of safety would attend her visit to a city in which she was well known, unless in some disguise, she again resumed men's apparel on leaving Cincinnati. This time she had more the appearance of an Italian or Spanish gentleman. In addition to the fine suit of black cloth, a splendid pair of dark false whiskers covered the sides of her face, while the curling moustache found its place upon the upper lip. From practice she had become accustomed to high-heeled boots, and could walk without creating any suspicion as regarded her sex. It was on a cold evening that Clotel arrived at Wheeling, and took a seat in the coach going to Richmond. She was already in the state of Virginia, yet a long distance from the place of her destination.

A ride in a stage-coach, over an American road, is unpleasant under the most favourable circumstances. But now that it was winter, and the roads unusually bad, the journey was still more dreary. However, there were eight passengers in the coach, and I need scarcely say that such a number of genuine Americans could not be together without whiling away the time somewhat pleasantly. Besides Clotel, there was an elderly gentleman with his two daughters—one apparently under twenty years, the other a shade above. The pale, spectacled face of another slim, tall man, with a white neckerchief, pointed him out as a minister. The rough featured, dark countenance of a stout looking man, with a white hat on one side of his head, told that he was from the sunny South. There was nothing remarkable about the other two, who might pass for ordinary American gentlemen. It was on the eve of a presidential election, when every man is thought to be a politician. Clay, Van Buren, and Harrison were the men who expected the indorsement of the Baltimore Convention. "Who does this town go for?" asked the old gent. with the ladies, as the coach drove up to an inn, where groups of persons were waiting for the latest papers. "We are divided," cried the rough voice of one of the outsiders. "Well, who do you think will get the majority here?" continued the old gent. "Can't tell very well; I go for 'Old Tip,'" was the answer from without. This brought up the subject fairly before the passengers, and when the coach again started a general discussion commenced, in which all took a part except Clotel and the young ladies. Some were for Clay, some for Van Buren, and others for "Old Tip." The coach stopped to take in a real farmer-looking man, who no sooner entered than he was saluted with "Do you go for Clay?" "No," was the answer. "Do you go for Van Buren?" "No." "Well, then, of course you will go for Harrison." "No." "Why, don't you mean to work for any of them at the election?" "No." "Well, who will you work for?" asked one of the company. "I work for Betsy and the children, and I have a hard job of it at that," replied the farmer, without a smile. This answer, as a matter of course, set the new comer down as one upon whom the rest of the passengers could crack their jokes with the utmost impunity. "Are you an Odd Fellow?" asked one. "No, sir, I've been married more than a month." "I mean, do you belong to the order of Odd Fellows?" "No, no; I belong to the order of married men." "Are you a mason?" "No, I am a carpenter by trade." "Are you a Son of Temperance?" "Bother you, no; I am a son of Mr. John Gosling." After a hearty laugh in which all joined, the subject of Temperance became the theme for discussion. In this the spectacled gent. was at home. He soon showed that he was a New Englander, and went the whole length of the "Maine Law." The minister was about having it all his own way, when the Southerner, in the white hat, took the opposite side of the question. "I don't bet a red cent on these teetotlars," said he, and at the same time looking round to see if he had the approbation of the rest of the company. "Why?" asked the minister. "Because they are a set who are afraid to spend a cent. They are a bad lot, the whole on 'em." It was evident that the white hat gent. was an uneducated man. The minister commenced in full earnest, and gave an interesting account of the progress of temperance in Connecticut, the state from which he came, proving, that a great portion of the prosperity of the state was attributable to the disuse of intoxicating drinks. Every one thought the white hat had got the worst of the argument, and that he was settled for the remainder of the night. But not he; he took fresh courage and began again. "Now," said he, "I have just been on a visit to my uncle's in Vermont, and I guess I knows a little about these here teetotlars. You see, I went up there to make a little stay of a fortnight. I got there at night, and they seemed glad to see me, but they didn't give me a bit of anything to drink. Well, thinks I to myself, the jig's up: I sha'n't get any more liquor till I get out of the state." We all sat up till twelve o'clock that night, and I heard nothing but talk about the 'Juvinal Temperance Army,' the 'Band of Hope,' the 'Rising Generation,' the 'Female Dorcas Temperance Society,' 'The None Such,' and I don't know how many other names they didn't have. As I had taken several pretty large 'Cock Tails' before I entered the state, I thought upon the whole that I would not spile for the want of liquor. The next morning, I commenced writing back to my friends, and telling them what's what. Aunt Polly said, 'Well, Johnny, I s'pose you are given 'em a pretty account of us all here.' 'Yes,' said I; 'I am tellin' 'em if they want anything to drink when they come up here, they had better bring it with 'em.' 'Oh,' said aunty, 'they would search their boxes; can't bring any spirits in the state.' Well, as I was saying, jist as I got my letters finished, and was going to the post office (for uncle's house was two miles from the town), aunty says, 'Johnny, I s'pose you'll try to get a little somthin' to drink in town won't you?' Says I, 'I s'pose it's no use.' 'No,' said she, 'you can't; it aint to be had no how, for love nor money.' So jist as I was puttin' on my hat, 'Johnny,' cries out aunty, 'What,' says I. 'Now I'll tell you, I don't want you to say nothin' about it, but I keeps a little rum to rub my head with, for I am troubled with the headache; now I don't want you to mention it for the world, but I'll give you a little taste, the old man is such a teetotaller, that I should never hear the last of it, and I would not like for the boys to know it, they are members of the "Cold Water Army."'

"Aunty now brought out a black bottle and gave me a cup, and told me to help myself, which I assure you I did. I now felt ready to face the cold. As I was passing the barn I heard uncle thrashing oats, so I went to the door and spoke to him. 'Come in, John,' says he. 'No,' said I; 'I am goin' to post some letters,' for I was afraid that he would smell my breath if I went too near to him. 'Yes, yes, come in.' So I went in, and says he, 'It's now eleven o'clock; that's about the time you take your grog, I s'pose, when you are at home.' 'Yes,' said I. 'I am sorry for you, my lad; you can't get anything up here; you can't even get it at the chemist's, except as medicine, and then you must let them mix it and you take it in their presence.' 'This is indeed hard,' replied I; 'Well, it can't be helped,' continued he: 'and it ought not to be if it could. It's best for society; people's better off without drink. I recollect when your father and I, thirty years ago, used to go out on a spree and spend more than half a dollar in a night. Then here's the rising generation; there's nothing like settin' a good example. Look how healthy your cousins are—there's Benjamin, he never tasted spirits in his life. Oh, John, I would you were a teetotaller.' 'I suppose,' said I, 'I'll have to be one till I leave the state.' 'Now,' said he, 'John, I don't want you to mention it, for your aunt would go into hysterics if she thought there was a drop of intoxicating liquor about the place, and I would not have the boys to know it for anything, but I keep a little brandy to rub my joints for the rheumatics, and being it's you, I'll give you a little dust.' So the old man went to one corner of the barn, took out a brown jug and handed it to me, and I must say it was a little the best cogniac that I had tasted for many a day. Says I, 'Uncle, you are a good judge of brandy.' 'Yes,' said he, 'I learned when I was young.' So off I started for the post office. In returnin' I thought I'd jist go through the woods where the boys were chopping wood, and wait and go to the house with them when they went to dinner. I found them hard at work, but as merry as crickets. 'Well, cousin John, are you done writing?' 'Yes,' answered I. 'Have you posted them?' 'Yes.' 'Hope you didn't go to any place inquiring for grog.' 'No, I knowed it was no good to do that.' 'I suppose a cock-tail would taste good now.' 'Well, I guess it would,' says I. The three boys then joined in a hearty laugh. 'I suppose you have told 'em that we are a dry set up here?' 'Well, I aint told 'em anything else.' 'Now, cousin John,' said Edward, 'if you wont say anything, we will give you a small taste. For mercy's sake don't let father or mother know it; they are such rabid teetotallers, that they would not sleep a wink to-night if they thought there was any spirits about the place.' 'I am mum,' says I. And the boys took a jug out of a hollow stump, and gave me some first-rate peach brandy. And during the fortnight that I was in Vermont, with my teetotal relations, I was kept about as well corned as if I had been among my hot water friends in Tennessee."

This narrative, given by the white hat man, was received with unbounded applause by all except the pale gent. in spectacles, who showed, by the way in which he was running his fingers between his cravat and throat, that he did not intend to "give it up so." The white hat gent. was now the lion of the company.

"Oh, you did not get hold of the right kind of teetotallers," said the minister. "I can give you a tale worth a dozen of yours," continued he. "Look at society in the states where temperance views prevail, and you will there see real happiness. The people are taxed less, the poor houses are shut up for want of occupants, and extreme destitution is unknown. Every one who drinks at all is liable to become an habitual drunkard. Yes, I say boldly, that no man living who uses intoxicating drinks, is free from the danger of at least occasional, and if of occasional, ultimately of habitual excess. There seems to be no character, position, or circumstances that free men from the danger. *I have known* many young men of the finest promise, led by the drinking habit into vice, ruin, and early death. *I have known* many tradesmen whom it has made bankrupt. *I have known* Sunday scholars whom it has led to prison —teachers, and even superintendents, whom it has dragged down to profligacy. *I have known* ministers of high academic honours, of splendid eloquence, nay, of vast usefulness, whom it has fascinated, and hurried over the precipice of public infamy with their eyes open, and gazing with horror on their fate. *I have known* men of the strongest and clearest intellect and of vigorous resolution, whom it has made weaker than children and fools—gentlemen of refinement and taste whom it has debased into brutes—poets of high genius whom it has bound in a bondage worse than the galleys, and ultimately cut short their days. *I have known* statesmen, lawyers, and judges whom it has killed—kind husbands and fathers whom it has turned into monsters. *I have known* honest men whom it has made villains—elegant and Christian *ladies* whom it has *converted into bloated sots*."

"But you talk too fast," replied the white hat man. "You don't give a feller a chance to say nothin'." "I heard you," continued the minister, "and now you hear me out. It is indeed wonderful how people become lovers of strong drink. Some years since, before I became a teetotaller I kept spirits about the house, and I had a servant who was much addicted to strong drink. He used to say that he could not make my boots shine, without mixing the blacking with whiskey. So to satisfy myself that the whiskey was put in the blacking, one morning I made him bring the dish in which he kept the blacking, and poured in the whiskey myself. And now, sir, what do you think?" "Why, I s'pose your boots shined better than before," replied the white hat. "No," continued the minister. "He took the blacking out, and I watched him, and he drank down the whiskey, blacking, and all."

This turned the joke upon the advocate of strong drink, and he began to put his wits to work for arguments. "You are from Connecticut, are you?" asked the Southerner. "Yes, and we are an orderly, pious, peaceable people. Our holy religion is respected, and we do more for the cause of Christ than the whole Southern States put together." "I don't doubt it," said the white hat gent. "You sell wooden nutmegs and other spurious articles enough to do some good. You talk of your 'holy religion;' but your robes' righteousness are woven at Lowell and Manchester; your paradise is high per centum on factory stocks; your palms of victory and crowns of rejoicing are triumphs over a rival party in politics, on the questions of banks and tariffs. If you could, you would turn heaven into Birmingham, make every angel a weaver, and with the eternal din of looms and spindles drown all the anthems of the morning stars. Ah! I know you Connecticut people like a book. No, no, all hoss; you can't come it on me." This last speech of the rough featured man again put him in the ascendant, and the spectacled gent. once more ran his fingers between his cravat and throat. "You live in Tennessee, I think," said the minister. "Yes," replied the Southerner, "I used to live in Orleans, but now I claim to be a Tennessean." "Your people of New Orleans are the most ungodly set in the United States," said the minister. Taking a New Orleans newspaper from his pocket he continued, "Just look here, there are not less than three advertisements of bull fights to take place on the Sabbath. You people of the Slave States have no regard for the Sabbath, religion, morality or anything else intended to make mankind better." Here Clotel could have borne ample testimony, had she dared to have taken sides with the Connecticut man. Her residence in Vicksburgh had given her an opportunity of knowing something of the character of the inhabitants of the far South. "Here is an account of a grand bull fight that took place in New Orleans a week ago last Sunday. I will read it to you." And the minister read aloud the following:

"Yesterday, pursuant to public notice, came off at Gretna, opposite the Fourth District, the long heralded fight between the famous grizzly bear, General Jackson (victor in fifty battles) and the Attakapas bull, Santa Anna.

"The fame of the coming conflict had gone forth to the four winds, and women and children, old men and boys, from all parts of the city, and from the breezy banks of Lake Pontchartrain and Borgne, brushed up their Sunday suit, and prepared to see the fun. Long before the published hour, the quiet streets of the rural Gretna were filled with crowds of anxious denizens, flocking to the arena, and before the fight commenced, such a crowd had collected as Gretna had not seen, nor will be likely to see again.

"The arena for the sports was a cage, twenty feet square, built upon the ground, and constructed of heavy timbers and iron bars. Around it were seats, circularly placed, and intended to accommodate many thousands. About four or five thousand persons assembled, covering the seats as with a cloud, and crowding down around the cage, were within reach of the bars.

"The bull selected to sustain the honour and verify the pluck of Attakapas on this trying occasion was a black animal from the Opelousas, lithe and sinewy as a four year old courser, and with eyes like burning coals. His horns bore the appearance of having been filed at the tips, and wanted that keen and slashing appearance so common with others of his kith and kin; otherwise it would have been 'all day' with Bruin at the first pass, and no mistake.

"The bear was an animal of note, and called General Jackson, from the fact of his licking up everything that came in his way, and taking 'the responsibility' on all occasions. He was a wicked looking beast, very lean and unamiable in aspect, with hair all standing the wrong way. He had fought some fifty bulls (so they said), always coming out victorious, but that either one of the fifty had been an Attakapas bull, the bills of the performances did not say. Had he tackled Attakapas first it is likely his fifty battles would have remained unfought.

"About half past four o'clock the performances commenced.

"The bull was first seen, standing in the cage alone, with head erect, and looking a very monarch in his capacity. At an appointed signal, a cage containing the bear was placed alongside the arena, and an opening being made, bruin stalked into the battle ground—not, however, without sundry stirrings up with a ten foot pole, he being experienced in such matters, and backwards in raising a row.

"Once on the battle-field, both animals stood, like wary champions, eyeing each other, the bear cowering low, with head upturned and fangs exposed, while Attakapas stood wondering, with his eye dilated, lashing his sides with his long and bushy tail, and pawing up the earth in very wrath.

"The bear seemed little inclined to begin the attack, and the bull, standing a moment, made steps first backward and then forward, as if measuring his antagonist, and meditating where to plant a blow. Bruin wouldn't come to the scratch no way, till one of the keepers, with an iron rod, tickled his ribs and made him move. Seeing this, Attakapas took it as a hostile demonstration, and, gathering his strength, dashed savagely at the enemy, catching him on the points of his horns, and doubling him up like a sack of bran against the bars. Bruin 'sung out' at this, and made a dash for his opponent's nose.

"Missing this, the bull turned to the 'about face,' and the bear caught him by the ham, inflicting a ghastly wound. But Attakapas with a kick shook him off, and renewing the attack, went at him again, head on and with a rush. This time he was not so fortunate, for the bear caught him above the eye, burying his fangs in the tough hide, and holding him as in a vice. It was now the bull's turn to 'sing out,' and he did it, bellowing forth with a voice more hideous than that of all the bulls of Bashan. Some minutes stood matters thus, and the cries of the bull, mingled with the hoarse growls of the bear, made hideous music, fit only for a dance of devils. Then came a pause (the bear having relinquished his hold), and for a few minutes it was doubtful whether the fun was not up. But the magic wand of the keeper (the ten foot pole) again stirred up bruin, and at it they went, and with a rush.

"Bruin now tried to fasten on the bull's back, and drove his tusks in him in several places, making the red blood flow like wine from the vats of Luna. But Attakapas was pluck to the back bone, and, catching bruin on the tips of his horns, shuffled him up right merrily, making the fur fly like feathers in a gale of wind. Bruin cried 'Nuff' (in bear language), but the bull followed up his advantage, and, making one furious plunge full at the figure head of the enemy, struck a horn into his eye, burying it there, and dashing the tender organ into darkness and atoms. Blood followed the blow, and poor bruin, blinded, bleeding, and in mortal agony, turned with a howl to leave, but Attakapas caught him in the retreat, and rolled him over like a ball. Over and over again this rolling over was enacted, and finally, after more than an hour, bruin curled himself up on his back, bruised, bloody, and dead beat. The thing was up with California, and Attakapas was declared the victor amidst the applause of the multitude that made the heavens ring."

"There," said he, "can you find anything against Connecticut equal to that?" The Southerner had to admit that he was beat by the Yankee. During all this time, it must not be supposed that the old gent. with the two daughters, and even the young ladies themselves, had been silent. Clotel and they had not only given their opinions as regarded the merits of the discussion, but that sly glance of the eye, which is ever given where the young of both sexes meet, had been freely at work. The American ladies are rather partial to foreigners, and Clotel had the appearance of a fine Italian. The old gentleman was now near his home, and a whisper from the eldest daughter, who was unmarried but marriageable, induced him to extend to "Mr. Johnson" an invitation to stop and spend a week with the young ladies at their family residence. Clotel excused herself upon various grounds, and at last, to cut short the matter, promised that she would pay them a visit on her return. The arrival of the coach at Lynchburgh separated the young ladies from the Italian gent., and the coach again resumed its journey.

CHAPTER XXIII.

TRUTH STRANGER THAN FICTION.

"Is the poor privilege to turn the key
Upon the captive, freedom? He's as far
From the enjoyment of the earth and air
Who watches o'er the chains, as they who wear."

Byron.

DURING certain seasons of the year, all tropical climates are subject to epidemics of a most destructive nature. The inhabitants of New Orleans look with as much certainty for the appearance of the yellow-fever, small-pox, or cholera, in the hot-season, as the Londoner does for fog in the month of November. In the summer of 1831, the people of New Orleans were visited with one of these epidemics. It appeared in a form unusually repulsive and deadly. It seized persons who were in health, without any premonition. Sometimes death was the immediate consequence. The disorder began in the brain, by an oppressive pain accompanied or followed by fever. The patient was devoured with burning thirst. The stomach, distracted by pains, in vain sought relief in efforts to disburden itself. Fiery veins streaked the eye; the face was inflamed, and dyed of a dark dull red colour; the ears from time to time rang painfully. Now mucous secretions surcharged the tongue, and took away the power of speech; now the sick one spoke, but in speaking had a foresight of death. When the violence of the disease approached the heart, the gums were blackened. The sleep, broken, troubled by convulsions, or by frightful visions, was worse than the waking hours; and when the reason sank under a delirium which had its seat in the brain, repose utterly forsook the patient's couch. The progress of the heat within was marked by yellowish spots, which spread over the surface of the body. If, then, a happy crisis came not, all hope was gone. Soon the breath infected the air with a fetid odour, the lips were glazed, despair painted itself in the eyes, and sobs, with long intervals of silence, formed the only language. From each side of the mouth spread foam, tinged with black and burnt blood. Blue streaks mingled with the yellow all over the frame. All remedies were useless. This was the Yellow Fever.

The disorder spread alarm and confusion throughout the city. On an average, more than 400 died daily. In the midst of disorder and confusion, death heaped victims on victims. Friend followed friend in quick succession. The sick were avoided from the fear of contagion, and for the same reason the dead were left unburied. Nearly 2000 dead bodies lay uncovered in the burial-ground, with only here and there a little lime thrown over them, to prevent the air becoming infected.

The negro, whose home is in a hot climate, was not proof against the disease. Many plantations had to suspend their work for want of slaves to take the places of those carried off by the fever. Henry Morton and wife were among the thirteen thousand swept away by the raging disorder that year. Like too many, Morton had been dealing extensively in lands and stocks; and though apparently in good circumstances was, in reality, deeply involved in debt. Althesa, although as white as most white women in a southern clime, was, as we already know, born a slave. By the laws of all the Southern States the children follow the condition of the mother. If the mother is free the children are free; if a slave, they are slaves. Morton was unacquainted with the laws of the land; and although he had married Althesa, it was a marriage which the law did not recognise; and therefore she whom he thought to be his wife was, in fact, nothing more than his slave. What would have been his feelings had he known this, and also known that his two daughters, Ellen and Jane, were his slaves? Yet such was the fact. After the disappearance of the disease with which Henry Morton had so suddenly been removed, his brother went to New Orleans to give what aid he could in settling up the affairs. James Morton, on his arrival in New Orleans, felt proud of his nieces, and promised them a home with his own family in Vermont; little dreaming that his brother had married a slave woman, and that his nieces were slaves. The girls themselves had never heard that their mother had been a slave, and therefore knew nothing of the danger hanging over their heads. An inventory of the property was made out by James Morton, and placed in the hands of the creditors; and the young ladies, with their uncle, were about leaving the city to reside for a few days on the banks of Lake Ponchetain, where they could enjoy a fresh air that the city could not afford. But just as they were about taking the train, an officer arrested the whole party; the young ladies as slaves, and the uncle upon the charge of attempting to conceal the property of his deceased brother. Morton was overwhelmed with horror at the idea of his nieces being claimed as slaves, and asked for time, that he might save them from such a fate. He even offered to mortgage his little farm in Vermont for the amount which young slave women of their age would fetch. But the creditors pleaded that they were "an extra article," and would sell for more than common slaves; and must, therefore, be sold at auction. They were given up, but neither ate nor slept, nor separated from each other, till they were taken into the New Orleans slave market, where they were offered to the highest bidder. There they stood, trembling, blushing, and weeping; compelled to listen to the grossest language, and shrinking from the rude hands that examined the graceful proportions of their beautiful frames.

After a fierce contest between the bidders, the young ladies were sold, one for 2,300 dollars, and the other for 3,000 dollars. We need not add that had those young girls been sold for mere house servants or field hands, they would not have brought one half the sums they did. The fact that they were the grand-daughters of Thomas Jefferson, no doubt, increased their value in the market. Here were two of the softer sex, accustomed to the fondest indulgence, surrounded by all the refinements of life, and with all the timidity that such a life could produce, bartered away like cattle in Smithfield market. Ellen, the eldest, was sold to an old gentleman, who purchased her, as he said, for a housekeeper. The girl was taken to his residence, nine miles from the city. She soon, however, knew for what purpose she had been bought; and an educated and cultivated mind and taste, which made her see and understand how great was her degradation, now armed her hand with the ready means of death. The morning after her arrival, she was found in her chamber, a corpse. She had taken poison. Jane was purchased by a dashing young man, who had just come into the possession of a large fortune. The very appearance of the young Southerner pointed him out as an unprincipled profligate; and the young girl needed no one to tell her of her impending doom. The young maid of fifteen was immediately removed to his country seat, near the junction of the Mississippi river with the sea. This was a most singular spot, remote, in a dense forest spreading over the summit of a cliff that rose abruptly to a great height above the sea; but so grand in its situation, in the desolate sublimity which reigned around, in the reverential murmur of the waves that washed its base, that, though picturesque, it was a forest prison. Here the young lady saw no one, except an old negress who acted as her servant. The smiles with which the young man met her were indignantly spurned. But she was the property of another, and could hope for justice and mercy only through him.

Jane, though only in her fifteenth year, had become strongly attached to Volney Lapuc, a young Frenchman, a student in her father's office. The poverty of the young man, and the youthful age of the girl, had caused their feelings to be kept from the young lady's parents. At the death of his master, Volney had returned to his widowed mother at Mobile, and knew nothing of the misfortune that had befallen his mistress, until he received a letter from her. But how could he ever obtain a sight of her, even if he wished, locked up as she was in her master's mansion? After several days of what her master termed "obstinacy" on her part, the young girl was placed in an upper chamber, and told that that would be her home, until she should yield to her master's wishes. There she remained more than a fortnight, and with the exception of a daily visit from her master, she saw no one but the old negress who waited upon her. One bright moonlight evening as she was seated at the window, she perceived the figure of a man beneath her window. At first, she thought it was her master; but the tall figure of the stranger soon convinced her that it was another. Yes, it was Volney! He had no sooner received her letter, than he set out for New Orleans; and finding on his arrival there, that his mistress had been taken away, resolved to follow her. There he was; but how could she communicate with him? She dared not trust the old negress with her secret, for fear that it might reach her master. Jane wrote a hasty note and threw it out of the window, which was eagerly picked up by the young man, and he soon disappeared in the woods. Night passed away in dreariness to her, and the next morning she viewed the spot beneath her window with the hope of seeing the footsteps of him who had stood there the previous night. Evening returned, and with it the hope of again seeing the man she loved. In this she was not disappointed; for daylight had scarcely disappeared, and the moon once more rising through the tops of the tall trees, when the young man was seen in the same place as on the previous night. He had in his hand a rope ladder. As soon as Jane saw this, she took the sheets from her bed, tore them into strings, tied them together, and let one end down the side of the house. A moment more, and one end of the rope-ladder was in her hand, and she fastened it inside the room. Soon the young maiden was seen descending, and the enthusiastic lover, with his arms extended, waiting to receive his mistress. The planter had been out on an hunting excursion, and returning home, saw his victim as her lover was receiving her in his arms. At this moment the sharp sound of a rifle was heard, and the young man fell weltering in his blood, at the feet of his mistress. Jane fell senseless by his side. For many days she had a confused consciousness of some great agony, but knew not where she was, or by whom surrounded. The slow recovery of her reason settled into the most intense melancholy, which gained at length the compassion even of her cruel master. The beautiful bright eyes, always pleading in expression, were now so heart-piercing in their sadness, that he could not endure their gaze. In a few days the poor girl died of a broken heart, and was buried at night at the back of the garden by the negroes; and no one wept at the grave of her who had been so carefully cherished, and so tenderly beloved.

This, reader, is an unvarnished narrative of one doomed by the laws of the Southern States to be a slave. It tells not only its own story of grief, but speaks of a thousand wrongs and woes beside, which never see the light; all the more bitter and dreadful, because no help can relieve, no sympathy can mitigate, and no hope can cheer.

CHAPTER XXIV.

THE ARREST.

"THE fearful storm—it threatens lowering,
Which God in mercy long delays;
Slaves yet may see their masters cowering,
While whole plantations smoke and blaze!"

Carter.

IT was late in the evening when the coach arrived at Richmond, and Clotel once more alighted in her native city. She had intended to seek lodgings somewhere in the outskirts of the town, but the lateness of the hour compelled her to stop at one of the principal hotels for the night. She had scarcely entered the inn, when she recognised among the numerous black servants one to whom she was well known; and her only hope was, that her disguise would keep her from being discovered. The imperturbable calm and entire forgetfulness of self which induced Clotel to visit a place from which she could scarcely hope to escape, to attempt the rescue of a beloved child, demonstrate that over-willingness of woman to carry out the promptings of the finer feelings of her heart. True to woman's nature, she had risked her own liberty for another.

She remained in the hotel during the night, and the next morning, under the plea of illness, she took her breakfast alone. That day the fugitive slave paid a visit to the suburbs of the town, and once more beheld the cottage in which she had spent so many happy hours. It was winter, and the clematis and passion flower were not there; but there were the same walks she had so often pressed with her feet, and the same trees which had so often shaded her as she passed through the garden at the back of the house. Old remembrances rushed upon her memory, and caused her to shed tears freely. Clotel was now in her native town, and near her daughter; but how could she communicate with her? How could she see her? To have made herself known, would have been a suicidal act; betrayal would have followed, and she arrested. Three days had passed away, and Clotel still remained in the hotel at which she had first put up; and yet she had got no tidings of her child. Unfortunately for Clotel, a disturbance had just broken out amongst the slave population in the state of Virginia, and all strangers were eyed with suspicion.

The evils consequent on slavery are not lessened by the incoming of one or two rays of light. If the slave only becomes aware of his condition, and conscious of the injustice under which he suffers, if he obtains but a faint idea of these things, he will seize the first opportunity to possess himself of what he conceives to belong to him. The infusion of Anglo-Saxon with African blood has created an insurrectionary feeling among the slaves of America hitherto unknown. Aware of their blood connection with their owners, these mulattoes labour under the sense of their personal and social injuries; and tolerate, if they do not encourage in themselves, low and vindictive passions. On the other hand, the slave owners are aware of their critical position, and are ever watchful, always fearing an outbreak among the slaves.

True, the Free States are equally bound with the Slave States to suppress any insurrectionary movement that may take place among the slaves. The Northern freemen are bound by their constitutional obligations to aid the slaveholder in keeping his slaves in their chains. Yet there are, at the time we write, four millions of bond slaves in the United States. The insurrection to which we now refer was headed by a full-blooded negro, who had been born and brought up a slave. He had heard the twang of the driver's whip, and saw the warm blood streaming from the negro's body; he had witnessed the separation of parents and children, and was made aware, by too many proofs, that the slave could expect no justice at the hand of the slave owner. He went by the name of "Nat Turner." He was a preacher amongst the negroes, and distinguished for his eloquence, respected by the whites, and loved and venerated by the negroes. On the discovery of the plan for the outbreak, Turner fled to the swamps, followed by those who had joined in the insurrection. Here the revolted negroes numbered some hundreds, and for a time bade defiance to their oppressors. The Dismal Swamps cover many thousands of acres of wild land, and a dense forest, with wild animals and insects, such as are unknown in any other part of Virginia. Here runaway negroes usually seek a hiding-place, and some have been known to reside here for years. The revolters were joined by one of these. He was a large, tall, full-blooded negro, with a stern and savage countenance; the marks on his face showed that he was from one of the barbarous tribes in Africa, and claimed that country as his native land; his only covering was a girdle around his loins, made of skins of wild beasts which he had killed; his only token of authority among those that he led, was a pair of epaulettes made from the tail of a fox, and tied to his shoulder by a cord. Brought from the coast of Africa when only fifteen years of age to the island of Cuba, he was smuggled from thence into Virginia. He had been two years in the swamps, and considered it his future home. He had met a negro woman who was also a runaway; and, after the fashion of his native land, had gone through the process of oiling her as the marriage ceremony. They had built a cave on a rising mound in the swamp; this was their home. His name was Picquilo. His only weapon was a sword, made from the blade of a scythe, which he had stolen from a neighbouring plantation. His dress, his character, his manners, his mode of fighting, were all in keeping with the early training he had received in the land of his birth. He moved about with the activity of a cat, and neither the thickness of the trees, nor the depth of the water could stop him. He was a bold, turbulent spirit; and from revenge imbrued his hands in the blood of all the whites he could meet. Hunger, thirst, fatigue, and loss of sleep he seemed made to endure as if by peculiarity of constitution. His air was fierce, his step oblique, his look sanguinary. Such was the character of one of the leaders in the Southampton insurrection. All negroes were arrested who were found beyond their master's threshhold, and all strange whites watched with a great degree of alacrity.

Such was the position in which Clotel found affairs when she returned to Virginia in search of her Mary. Had not the slave-owners been watchful of strangers, owing to the outbreak, the fugitive could not have escaped the vigilance of the police; for advertisements, announcing her escape and offering a large reward for her arrest, had been received in the city previous to her arrival, and the officers were therefore on the look-out for the runaway slave. It was on the third day, as the quadroon was seated in her room at the inn, still in the disguise of a gentleman, that two of the city officers entered the room, and informed her that they were authorised to examine all strangers, to assure the authorities that they were not in league with the revolted negroes. With trembling heart the fugitive handed the key of her trunk to the officers. To their surprise, they found nothing but woman's apparel in the box, which raised their curiosity, and caused a further investigation that resulted in the arrest of Clotel as a fugitive slave. She was immediately conveyed to prison, there to await the orders of her master. For many days, uncheered by the voice of kindness, alone, hopeless, desolate, she waited for the time to arrive when the chains were to be placed on her limbs, and she returned to her inhuman and unfeeling owner.

The arrest of the fugitive was announced in all the newspapers, but created little or no sensation. The inhabitants were too much engaged in putting down the revolt among the slaves; and although all the odds were against the insurgents, the whites found it no easy matter, with all their caution. Every day brought news of fresh outbreaks. Without scruple and without pity, the whites massacred all blacks found beyond their owners' plantations: the negroes, in return, set fire to houses, and put those to death who attempted to escape from the flames. Thus carnage was added to carnage, and the blood of the whites flowed to avenge the blood of the blacks. These were the ravages of slavery. No graves were dug for the negroes; their dead bodies became food for dogs and vultures, and their bones, partly calcined by the sun, remained scattered about, as if to mark the mournful fury of servitude and lust of power. When the slaves were subdued, except a few in the swamps, bloodhounds were put in this dismal place to hunt out the remaining revolters. Among the captured negroes was one of whom we shall hereafter make mention.

CHAPTER XXV.

DEATH IS FREEDOM.

> "I ASKED but freedom, and ye gave
> Chains, and the freedom of the grave."—*Snelling.*

THERE are, in the district of Columbia, several slave prisons, or "negro pens," as they are termed. These prisons are mostly occupied by persons to keep their slaves in, when collecting their gangs together for the New Orleans market. Some of them belong to the government, and one, in particular, is noted for having been the place where a number of free coloured persons have been incarcerated from time to time. In this district is situated the capitol of the United States. Any free coloured persons visiting Washington, if not provided with papers asserting and proving their right to be free, may be arrested and placed in one of these dens. If they succeed in showing that they are free, they are set at liberty, provided they are able to pay the expenses of their arrest and imprisonment; if they cannot pay these expenses, they are sold out. Through this unjust and oppressive law, many persons born in the Free States have been consigned to a life of slavery on the cotton, sugar, or rice plantations of the Southern States. By order of her master, Clotel was removed from Richmond and placed in one of these prisons, to await the sailing of a vessel for New Orleans. The prison in which she was put stands midway between the capitol at Washington and the president's house. Here the fugitive saw nothing but slaves brought in and taken out, to be placed in ships and sent away to the same part of the country to which she herself would soon be compelled to go. She had seen or heard nothing of her daughter while in Richmond, and all hope of seeing her now had fled. If she was carried back to New Orleans, she could expect no mercy from her master.

At the dusk of the evening previous to the day when she was to be sent off, as the old prison was being closed for the night, she suddenly darted past her keeper, and ran for her life. It is not a great distance from the prison to the Long Bridge, which passes from the lower part of the city across the Potomac, to the extensive forests and woodlands of the celebrated Arlington

Place, occupied by that distinguished relative and descendant of the immortal Washington, Mr. George W. Custis. Thither the poor fugitive directed her flight. So unexpected was her escape, that she had quite a number of rods the start before the keeper had secured the other prisoners, and rallied his assistants in pursuit. It was at an hour when, and in a part of the city where, horses could not be readily obtained for the chase; no bloodhounds were at hand to run down the flying woman; and for once it seemed as though there was to be a fair trial of speed and endurance between the slave and the slave-catchers. The keeper and his forces raised the hue and cry on her pathway close behind; but so rapid was the flight along the wide avenue, that the astonished citizens, as they poured forth from their dwellings to learn the cause of alarm, were only able to comprehend the nature of the case in time to fall in with the motley mass in pursuit, (as many a one did that night,) to raise an anxious prayer to heaven, as they refused to join in the pursuit, that the panting fugitive might escape, and the merciless soul dealer for once be disappointed of his prey. And now with the speed of an arrow—having passed the avenue—with the distance between her and her pursuers constantly increasing, this poor hunted female gained the "*Long Bridge*," as it is called, where interruption seemed improbable, and already did her heart begin to beat high with the hope of success. She had only to pass three-fourths of a mile across the bridge, and she could bury herself in a vast forest, just at the time when the curtain of night would close around her, and protect her from the pursuit of her enemies.

But God by his Providence had otherwise determined. He had determined that an appalling tragedy should be enacted that night, within plain sight of the President's house and the capital of the Union, which should be an evidence wherever it should be known, of the unconquerable love of liberty the heart may inherit; as well as a fresh admonition to the slave dealer, of the cruelty and enormity of his crimes. Just as the pursuers crossed the high draw for the passage of sloops, soon after entering upon the bridge, they beheld three men slowly approaching from the Virginia side. They immediately called to them to arrest the fugitive, whom they proclaimed a runaway slave. True to their Virginian instincts as she came near,

THE DEATH OF CLOTEL.

they formed in line across the narrow bridge, and prepared to seize her. Seeing escape impossible in that quarter, she stopped suddenly, and turned upon her pursuers. On came the profane and ribald crew, faster than ever, already exulting in her capture, and threatening punishment for her flight. For a moment she looked wildly and anxiously around to see if there was no hope of escape. On either hand, far down below, rolled the deep foamy waters of the Potomac, and before and behind the rapidly approaching step and noisy voices of pursuers, showing how vain would be any further effort for freedom. Her resolution was taken. She clasped her *hands* convulsively, and raised *them*, as she at the same time raised her *eyes* towards heaven, and begged for that mercy and compassion *there*, which had been denied her on earth; and then, with a single bound, she vaulted over the railings of the bridge, and sunk for ever beneath the waves of the river!

Thus died Clotel, the daughter of Thomas Jefferson, a president of the United States; a man distinguished as the author of the Declaration of American Independence, and one of the first statesmen of that country.

Had Clotel escaped from oppression in any other land, in the disguise in which she fled from the Mississippi to Richmond, and reached the United States, no honour within the gift of the American people would have been too good to have been heaped upon the heroic woman. But she was a slave, and therefore out of the pale of their sympathy. They have tears to shed over Greece and Poland; they have an abundance of sympathy for "poor Ireland;" they can furnish a ship of war to convey the Hungarian refugees from a Turkish prison to the "land of the free and home of the brave." They boast that America is the "cradle of liberty;" if it is, I fear they have rocked the child to death. The body of Clotel was picked up from the bank of the river, where it had been washed by the strong current, a hole dug in the sand, and there deposited, without either inquest being held over it, or religious service being performed. Such was the life and such the death of a woman whose virtues and goodness of heart would have done honour to one in a higher station of life, and who, if she had been born in any other land but that of slavery, would have been honoured and loved. A few days after the death of Clotel, the following poem appeared in one of the newspapers:

"Now, rest for the wretched! the long day is past,
And night on yon prison descendeth at last.
Now lock up and bolt! Ha, jailor, look there!
Who flies like a wild bird escaped from the snare?
A woman, a slave—up, out in pursuit,
While linger some gleams of day!
Let thy call ring out!—now a rabble rout
Is at thy heels—speed away!

"A bold race for freedom!—On, fugitive, on!
Heaven help but the right, and thy freedom is won.
How eager she drinks the free air of the plains;
Every limb, every nerve, every fibre she strains;
From Columbia's glorious capitol,
Columbia's daughter flees
To the sanctuary God has given—
The sheltering forest trees.

"Now she treads the Long Bridge—joy lighteth her eye—
Beyond her the dense wood and darkening sky—
Wild hopes thrill her heart as she neareth the shore:
O, despair! there are *men* fast advancing before!
Shame, shame on their manhood! they hear, they heed
The cry, her flight to stay,
And like demon forms with their outstretched arms,
They wait to seize their prey!

"She pauses, she turns! Ah, will she flee back?
Like wolves, her pursuers howl loud on their track;
She lifteth to Heaven one look of despair—
Her anguish breaks forth in one hurried prayer—
Hark! her jailor's yell! like a bloodhound's bay
On the low night wind it sweeps!
Now, death or the chain! to the stream she turns,
And she leaps! O God, she leaps!

"The dark and the cold, yet merciful wave,
Receives to its bosom the form of the slave:

She rises—earth's scenes on her dim vision gleam,
Yet she struggleth not with the strong rushing stream:
 And low are the death-cries her woman's heart gives,
  As she floats adown the river,
 Faint and more faint grows the drowning voice,
  And her cries have ceased for ever!

"Now back, jailor, back to thy dungeons, again,
To swing the red lash and rivet the chain!
The form thou would'st fetter—returned to its God;
 The universe holdeth no realm of night
  More drear than her slavery—
 More merciless fiends than here stayed her flight—
  Joy! the hunted slave is free!

"That bond-woman's corse—let Potomac's proud wave
Go bear it along *by our Washington's grave*,
And heave it high up on that hallowed strand,
To tell of the freedom he won for our land.
 A weak woman's corse, by freemen chased down;
  Hurrah for our country! hurrah!
 To freedom she leaped, through drowning and death—
  Hurrah for our country! hurrah!"

CHAPTER XXVI.

THE ESCAPE.

"No refuge is found on our unhallowed ground,
For the wretched in Slavery's manacles bound;
While our star-spangled banner in vain boasts to wave
O'er the land of the free and the home of the brave!"

WE left Mary, the daughter of Clotel, in the capacity of a servant in her own father's house, where she had been taken by her mistress for the ostensible purpose of plunging her husband into the depths of humiliation. At first the young girl was treated with great severity; but after finding that Horatio Green had lost all feeling for his child, Mrs. Green's own heart became touched for the offspring of her husband, and she became its friend. Mary had grown still more beautiful, and, like most of her sex in that country, was fast coming to maturity.

The arrest of Clotel, while trying to rescue her daughter, did not reach the ears of the latter till her mother had been removed from Richmond to Washington. The mother had passed from time to eternity before the daughter knew that she had been in the neighbourhood. Horatio Green was not in Richmond at the time of Clotel's arrest; had he been there, it is not probable but he would have made an effort to save her. She was not his slave, and therefore was beyond his power, even had he been there and inclined to aid her. The revolt amongst the slaves had been brought to an end, and most of the insurgents either put to death or sent out of the state. One, however, remained in prison. He was the slave of Horatio Green, and had been a servant in his master's dwelling. He, too, could boast that his father was an American statesman. His name was George. His mother had been employed as a servant in one of the principal hotels in Washington, where members of Congress usually put up. After George's birth his mother was sold to a slave trader, and he to an agent of Mr. Green, the father of Horatio. George was as white as most white persons. No one would suppose that any African blood coursed through his veins. His hair was straight, soft, fine, and light; his eyes blue, nose prominent, lips thin, his head well formed, forehead high and prominent; and he was often taken for a free white person by those who did know him. This made his condition still more intolerable; for one so white seldom ever receives fair treatment at the hands of his fellow slaves; and the whites usually regard such slaves as persons who, if not often flogged, and otherwise ill treated, to remind them of their condition, would soon "forget" that they were slaves, and "think themselves as good as white folks." George's opportunities were far greater than most slaves. Being in his master's house, and waiting on educated white people, he had become very familiar with the English language. He had heard his master and visitors speak of the down-trodden and oppressed Poles; he heard them talk of going to Greece to fight for Grecian liberty, and against the oppressors of that ill-fated people. George, fired with the love of freedom, and zeal for the cause of his enslaved countrymen, joined the insurgents, and with them had been defeated and captured. He was the only one remaining of these unfortunate people, and he would have been put to death with them but for a circumstance that occurred some weeks before the outbreak. The court house had, by accident, taken fire, and was fast consuming. The engines could not be made to work, and all hope of saving the building seemed at an end. In one of the upper chambers there was a small box containing some valuable deeds belonging to the city; a ladder was placed against the house, leading from the street to the window of the room in which the box stood. The wind blew strong, and swept the flames in that direction. Broad sheets of fire were blown again and again over that part of the building, and then the wind would lift the pall of smoke, which showed that the work of destruction was not yet accomplished. While the doomed building was thus exposed, and before the destroying element had made its final visit, as it did soon after, George was standing by, and hearing that much depended on the contents of the box, and seeing no one disposed to venture through the fiery element to save the treasure, mounted the ladder and made his way to the window, entered the room, and was soon seen descending with the much valued box. Three cheers rent the air as the young slave fell from the ladder when near the ground; the white men took him up in their arms, to see if he had sustained any injury. His hair was burnt, eyebrows closely singed, and his clothes smelt strongly of smoke; but the heroic young slave was unhurt. The city authorities, at their next meeting, passed a vote of thanks to George's master for the lasting benefit that the slave had rendered the public, and commended the poor boy to the special favour of his owner. When George was on trial for participating in the revolt, this "meritorious act," as they were pleased to term it, was brought up in his favour. His trial was put off from session to session, till he had been in prison more than a year. At last, however, he was convicted of high treason, and sentenced to be hanged within ten days of that time. The judge asked the slave if he had anything to say why sentence of death should not be passed on him. George stood for a moment in silence, and then said, "As I cannot speak as I should wish, I will say nothing." "You may say what you please," said the judge. "You had a good master," continued he, "and still you were dissatisfied; you left your master and joined the negroes who were burning our houses and killing our wives." "As you have given me permission to speak," remarked George, "I will tell you why I joined the revolted negroes. I have heard my master read in the Declaration of Independence 'that all men are created free and equal,' and this caused me to inquire of myself why I was a slave. I also heard him talking with some of his visitors about the war with England, and he said, all wars and fightings for freedom were just and right. If so, in what am I wrong? The grievances of which your fathers complained, and which caused the Revolutionary War, were trifling in comparison with the wrongs and sufferings of those who were engaged in the late revolt. Your fathers were never slaves, ours are; your fathers were never bought and sold like cattle, never shut out from the light of knowledge and religion, never subjected to the lash of brutal task-masters. For the crime of having a dark skin, my people suffer the pangs of hunger, the infliction of stripes, and the ignominy of brutal servitude. We are kept in heathenish darkness by laws expressly enacted to make our instruction a criminal offence. What right has one man to the bones, sinews, blood, and nerves of another? Did not one God make us all? You say your fathers fought for freedom—so did we. You tell me that I am to be put to death for violating the laws of the land. Did not the American revolutionists violate the laws when they struck for liberty? They were revolters, but their success made them patriots—we were revolters, and our failure makes us rebels. Had we succeeded, we would have been patriots too. Success makes all the difference. You make merry on the 4th of July; the thunder of cannon and ringing of bells announce it as the birthday of American independence. Yet while these cannons are roaring and bells ringing, one-sixth of the people of this land are in chains and slavery. You boast that this is the 'Land of the Free;' but a traditionary freedom will not save you. It will not do to praise your fathers and build their sepulchres. Worse for you that you have such an inheritance, if you spend it foolishly and are unable to appreciate its worth. Sad if the genius of a true humanity, beholding you with tearful eyes from the mount of vision, shall fold his wings in sorrowing pity, and repeat the strain, 'O land of Washington, how often would I have gathered thy children together, as a hen doth gather her brood under her wings, and ye would not; behold your house is left unto you desolate.' This is all I have to say; I have done." Nearly every one present was melted to tears; even the judge seemed taken by surprise at the intelligence of the young slave. But George was a slave, and an example must be made of him, and therefore he was sentenced. Being employed in the same house with Mary, the daughter of Clotel, George had become attached to her, and the young lovers fondly looked forward to the time when they should be husband and wife.

After George had been sentenced to death, Mary was still more attentive to him, and begged and obtained leave of her mistress to visit him in his cell. The poor girl paid a daily visit to him to whom she had pledged her heart and hand. At one of these meetings, and only four days from the time fixed for the execution, while Mary was seated in George's cell, it occurred to her that she might yet save him from a felon's doom. She revealed to him the secret that was then occupying her thoughts, viz. that George should exchange clothes with her, and thus attempt his escape in disguise. But he would not for a single moment listen to the proposition. Not that he feared detection; but he would not consent to place an innocent and affectionate girl in a position where she might have to suffer for him. Mary pleaded, but in vain—George was inflexible.

The poor girl left her lover with a heavy heart, regretting that her scheme had proved unsuccessful.

Towards the close of the next day, Mary again appeared at the prison door for admission, and was soon by the side of him whom she so ardently loved. While there the clouds which had overhung the city for some hours broke, and the rain fell in torrents amid the most terrific thunder and lightning. In the most persuasive manner possible, Mary again importuned George to avail himself of her assistance to escape from an ignominious death. After assuring him that she, not being the person condemned, would not receive any injury, he at last consented, and they began to exchange apparel. As George was of small stature, and both were white, there was no difficulty in his passing out without detection; and as she usually left the cell weeping, with handkerchief in hand, and sometimes at her face, he had only to adopt this mode and his escape was safe. They had kissed each other, and Mary had told George where he would find a small parcel of provisions which she had placed in a secluded spot, when the prison-keeper opened the door and said, "Come, girl, it is time for you to go." George again embraced Mary, and passed out of the jail. It was already dark, and the street lamps were lighted, so that our hero in his new dress had no dread of detection. The provisions were sought out and found, and poor George was soon on the road towards Canada. But neither of them had once thought of a change of dress for George when he should have escaped, and he had walked but a short distance before he felt that a change of his apparel would facilitate his progress. But he dared not go amongst even his coloured associates for fear of being betrayed. However, he made the best of his way on towards Canada, hiding in the woods during the day, and travelling by the guidance of the North Star at night.

With the poet he could truly say,

> "Star of the North! while blazing day
>   Pours round me its full tide of light,
> And hides thy pale but faithful ray,
>   I, too, lie hid, and long for night."

One morning, George arrived on the banks of the Ohio river, and found his journey had terminated, unless he could get some one to take him across the river in a secret manner, for he would not be permitted to cross in any of the ferry boats, it being a penalty for crossing a slave, besides the value of the slave. He concealed himself in the tall grass and weeds near the river, to see if he could embrace an opportunity to cross. He had been in his hiding place but a short time, when he observed a man in a small boat, floating near the shore, evidently fishing. His first impulse was to call out to the man and ask him to take him over to the Ohio side, but the fear that the man was a slaveholder, or one who might possibly arrest him, deterred him from it. The man after rowing and floating about for some time fastened the boat to the root of a tree, and started to a neighbouring farmhouse.

This was George's moment, and he seized it. Running down the bank, he unfastened the boat, jumped in, and with all the expertness of one accustomed to a boat, rowed across the river and landed on the Ohio side.

Being now in a Free State, he thought he might with perfect safety travel on towards Canada. He had, however, gone but a very few miles when he discovered two men on horseback coming behind him. He felt sure that they could not be in pursuit of him, yet he did not wish to be seen by them, so he turned into another road leading to a house near by. The men followed, and were but a short distance from George, when he ran up to a farmhouse, before which was standing a farmer-looking man, in a broad-brimmed hat and straight-collared coat, whom he implored to save him from the "slave-catchers." The farmer told him to go into the barn near by; he entered by the front door, the farmer following, and closing the door behind George, but remaining outside, and gave directions to his hired man as to what should be done with George. The slaveholders by this time had dismounted, and were in front of the barn demanding admittance, and charging the farmer with secreting their slave woman, for George was still in the dress of a woman. The Friend, for the farmer proved to be a member of the Society of Friends, told the slave-owners that if they wished to search his barn, they must first get an officer and a search warrant. While the parties were disputing, the farmer began nailing up the front door, and the hired man served the back door in the same way. The slaveholders, finding that they could not prevail on the Friend to allow them to get the slave, determined to go in search of an officer. One was left to see that the slave did not escape from the barn, while the other went off at full speed to Mount Pleasant, the nearest town. George was not the slave of either of these men, nor were they in pursuit of him, but they had lost a woman who had been in that vicinity, and when they saw poor George in the disguise of a female, and attempting to elude pursuit, they felt sure they were close upon their victim. However, if they had caught him, although he was not their slave, they would have taken him back and placed him in jail, and there he would have remained until his owner arrived.

After an absence of nearly two hours, the slave-owner returned with an officer and found the Friend still driving large nails into the door. In a triumphant tone and with a corresponding gesture, he handed the search-warrant to the Friend, and said, "There, sir, now I will see if I can't get my nigger." "Well," said the Friend, "thou hast gone to work according to law, and thou canst now go into my barn." "Lend me your hammer that I may get the door open," said the slaveholder. "Let me see the warrant again." And after reading it over once more, he said, "I see nothing in this paper which says I must supply thee with tools to open my door; if thou wishest to go in, thou must get a hammer elsewhere." The sheriff said, "I will go to a neighbouring farm and borrow something which will introduce us to Miss Dinah;" and he immediately went in search of tools. In a short time the officer returned, and they commenced an assault and battery upon the barn door, which soon yielded; and in went the slaveholder and officer, and began turning up the hay and using all other means to find the lost property; but, to their astonishment, the slave was not there. After all hope of getting Dinah was gone, the slave-owner in a rage said to the Friend, "My nigger is not here." "I did not tell thee there was any one here." "Yes, but I saw her go in, and you shut the door behind her, and if she was not in the barn, what did you nail the door for?" "Can't I do what I please with my own barn door? Now I will tell thee; thou need trouble thyself no more, for the person thou art after entered the front door and went out at the back door, and is a long way from here by this time. Thou and thy friend must be somewhat fatigued by this time; wont thou go in and take a little dinner with me?" We need not say that this cool invitation of the good Quaker was not accepted by the slaveholders. George in the meantime had been taken to a friend's dwelling some miles away, where, after laying aside his female attire, and being snugly dressed up in a straight collared coat, and pantaloons to match, was again put on the right road towards Canada.

The fugitive now travelled by day, and laid by during night. After a fatiguing and dreary journey of two weeks, the fugitive arrived in Canada, and took up his abode in the little town of St. Catherine's, and obtained work on the farm of Colonel Street. Here he attended a night-school, and laboured for his employer during the day. The climate was cold, and wages small, yet he was in a land where he was free, and this the young slave prized more than all the gold that could be given to him. Besides doing his best to obtain education for himself, he imparted what he could to those of his fellow-fugitives about him, of whom there were many.

CHAPTER XXVII.

THE MYSTERY.

GEORGE, however, did not forget his promise to use all the means in his power to get Mary out of slavery. He, therefore, laboured with all his might to obtain money with which to employ some one to go back to Virginia for Mary. After nearly six mouths' labour at St. Catherine's, he employed an English missionary to go and see if the girl could be purchased, and at what price. The missionary went accordingly, but returned with the sad intelligence that, on account of Mary's aiding George to escape, the court had compelled Mr. Green to sell her out of the state, and she had been sold to a negro trader, and taken to the New Orleans market. As all hope of getting the girl was now gone, George resolved to quit the American continent for ever. He immediately took passage in a vessel laden with timber, bound for Liverpool, and in five weeks from that time he was standing on the quay of the great English seaport. With little or no education, he found many difficulties in the way of getting a respectable living. However he obtained a situation as porter in a large house in Manchester, where he worked during the day, and took private lessons at night. In this way he laboured for three years, and was then raised to the situation of clerk. George was so white as easily to pass for a white man, and being somewhat ashamed of his African descent, he never once mentioned the fact of his having been a slave. He soon became a partner in the firm that employed him, and was now on the road to wealth.

In the year 1842, just ten years after George Green (for he adopted his master's name) arrived in England, he visited France, and spent some days at Dunkirk. It was towards sunset, on a warm day in the month of October, that Mr. Green, after strolling some distance from the Hotel de Leon, entered a burial ground, and wandered long alone among the silent dead, gazing upon the many green graves and marble tombstones of those who once moved on the theatre of busy life, and whose sounds of gaiety once fell upon the ear of man. All nature around was hushed in silence, and seemed to partake of the general melancholy which hung over the quiet resting-place of departed mortals. After tracing the varied inscriptions which told the characters or conditions of the departed, and viewing the mounds beneath which the dust of mortality slumbered, he had now reached a secluded spot, near to where an aged weeping willow bowed its thick foliage to the ground, as though anxious to hide from the scrutinising gaze of curiosity the grave beneath it. Mr. Green seated himself upon a marble tomb, and began to read Roscoe's *Leo X.*, a copy of which he had under his arm. It was then about twilight, and he had scarcely gone through half a page, when he observed a lady in black, leading a boy, some five years old, up one of the paths; and as the lady's black veil was over her face, he felt somewhat at liberty to eye her more closely. While looking at her, the lady gave a scream, and appeared to be in a fainting position, when Mr. Green sprang from his seat in time to save her from falling to the ground. At this moment, an elderly gentleman was seen approaching with a rapid step, who, from his appearance, was evidently the lady's father, or one intimately connected with her. He came up, and, in a confused manner, asked what was the matter. Mr. Green explained as well as he could. After taking up the smelling bottle which had fallen from her hand, and holding it a short time to her face, she soon began to revive. During all this time the lady's veil had so covered her face, that Mr. Green had not seen it. When she had so far recovered as to be able to raise her head, she again screamed, and fell back into the arms of the old man. It now appeared quite certain, that either the countenance of George Green, or some other object, was the cause of these fits of fainting; and the old gentleman, thinking it was the former, in rather a petulant tone said, "I will thank you, sir, if you will leave us alone." The child whom the lady was leading, had now set up a squall; and amid the death-like appearance of the lady, the harsh look of the old man, and the cries of the boy, Mr. Green left the grounds, and returned to his hotel.

Whilst seated by the window, and looking out upon the crowded street, with every now and then the strange scene in the grave-yard vividly before him, Mr. Green thought of the book he had been reading, and, remembering that he had left it on the tomb, where he had suddenly dropped it when called to the assistance of the lady, he immediately determined to return in search of it. After a walk of some twenty minutes, he was again over the spot where he had been an hour before, and from which he had been so unceremoniously expelled by the old man. He looked in vain for the book; it was nowhere to be found: nothing save the bouquet which the lady had dropped, and which lay half-buried in the grass from having been trodden upon, indicated that any one had been there that evening. Mr. Green took up the bunch of flowers, and again returned to the hotel.

After passing a sleepless night, and hearing the clock strike six, he dropped into a sweet sleep, from which he did not awake until roused by the rap of a servant, who, entering his room, handed him a note which ran as follows:—"Sir,—I owe you an apology for the inconvenience to which you were subjected last evening, and if you will honour us with your presence to dinner to-day at four o'clock, I shall be most happy to give you due satisfaction. My servant will be in waiting for you at half-past three. I am, sir, your obedient servant, J. Devenant. October 23. To George Green, Esq."

The servant who handed this note to Mr. Green, informed him that the bearer was waiting for a reply. He immediately resolved to accept the invitation, and replied accordingly. Who this person was, and how his name and the hotel where he was stopping had been found out, was indeed a mystery. However, he waited impatiently for the hour when he was to see this new acquaintance, and get the mysterious meeting in the grave-yard solved.

CHAPTER XXVIII.

THE HAPPY MEETING.

"Man's love is of man's life, a thing apart;
'Tis woman's whole existence."—*Byron*.

THE clock on a neighbouring church had scarcely ceased striking three, when the servant announced that a carriage had called for Mr. Green. In less than half an hour he was seated in a most sumptuous barouche, drawn by two beautiful iron greys, and rolling along over a splendid gravel road completely shaded by large trees, which appeared to have been the accumulating growth of many centuries. The carriage soon stopped in front of a low villa, and this too was embedded in magnificent trees covered with moss. Mr. Green alighted and was shown into a superb drawing room, the walls of which were hung with fine specimens from the hands of the great Italian painters, and one by a German artist representing a beautiful monkish legend connected with "The Holy Catherine," an illustrious lady of Alexandria. The furniture had an antique and dignified appearance. High backed chairs stood around the room; a venerable mirror stood on the mantle shelf; rich curtains of crimson damask hung in folds at either side of the large windows; and a rich Turkey carpet covered the floor. In the centre stood a table covered with books, in the midst of which was an old-fashioned vase filled with fresh flowers, whose fragrance was exceedingly pleasant. A faint light, together with the quietness of the hour, gave beauty beyond description to the whole scene.

Mr. Green had scarcely seated himself upon the sofa, when the elderly gentleman whom he had met the previous evening made his appearance, followed by the little boy, and introduced himself as Mr. Devenant. A moment more, and a lady—a beautiful brunette—dressed in black, with long curls of a chesnut colour hanging down her cheeks, entered the room. Her eyes were of a dark hazel, and her whole appearance indicated that she was a native of a southern clime. The door at which she entered was opposite to where the two gentlemen were seated. They immediately rose; and Mr. Devenant was in the act of introducing her to Mr. Green, when he observed that the latter had sunk back upon the sofa, and the last word that he remembered to have heard was, "It is her." After this, all was dark and dreamy: how long he remained in this condition it was for another to tell. When he awoke, he found himself stretched upon the sofa, with his boots off, his neckerchief removed, shirt collar unbuttoned, and his head resting upon a pillow. By his side sat the old man, with the smelling bottle in the one hand, and a glass of water in the other, and the little boy standing at the foot of the sofa. As soon as Mr. Green had so far recovered as to be able to speak, he said, "Where am I, and what does this mean?" "Wait a while," replied the old man, "and I will tell you all." After a lapse of some ten minutes he rose from the sofa, adjusted his apparel, and said, "I am now ready to hear anything you have to say." "You were born in America?" said the old man. "Yes," he replied. "And you were acquainted with a girl named Mary?" continued the old man. "Yes, and I loved her as I can love none other." "The lady whom you met so mysteriously last evening is Mary," replied Mr. Devenant. George Green was silent, but the fountains of mingled grief and joy stole out from beneath his eyelashes, and glistened like pearls upon his pale and marble-like cheeks. At this juncture the lady again entered the room. Mr. Green sprang from the sofa, and they fell into each other's arms, to the surprise of the old man and little George, and to the amusement of the servants who had crept up one by one, and were hid behind the doors, or loitering in the hall. When they had given vent to their feelings, they resumed their seats, and each in turn related the adventures through which they had passed. "How did you find out my name and address?" asked Mr. Green. "After you had left us in the grave-yard, our little George said 'O, mamma, if there aint a book!' and picked it up and brought it to us. Papa opened it, and said, 'The gentleman's name is written in it, and here is a card of the Hotel de Leon, where I suppose he is stopping.' Papa wished to leave the book, and said it was all a fancy of mine that I had ever seen you before, but I was perfectly convinced that you were my own George Green. Are you married?" "No, I am not." "Then, thank God!" exclaimed Mrs. Devenant. "And are you single now?" inquired Mr. Green. "Yes," she replied. "This is indeed the Lord's doings," said Mr. Green, at the same time bursting into a flood of tears. Mr. Devenant was past the age when men should think upon matrimonial subjects, yet the scene brought vividly before his eyes the days when he was a young man, and had a wife living. After a short interview, the old man called their attention to the dinner, which was then waiting. We need scarcely add, that Mr. Green and Mrs. Devenant did very little towards diminishing the dinner that day.

After dinner the lovers (for such we have to call them) gave their experience from the time that George left the jail dressed in Mary's clothes. Up to that time Mr. Green's was substantially as we have related it. Mrs. Devenant's was as follows:— "The night after you left the prison," said she, "I did not shut my eyes in sleep. The next morning, about eight o'clock, Peter the gardener came to the jail to see if I had been there the night before, and was informed that I had, and that I had left a little after dark. About an hour after, Mr. Green came himself, and I need not say that he was much surprised on finding me there, dressed in your clothes. This was the first tidings they had of your escape." "What did Mr. Green say when he found that I had fled?" "Oh!" continued Mrs. Devenant, "he said to me when no one was near, I hope George will get off, but I fear you will have to suffer in his stead. I told him that if it must be so I was willing to die if you could live." At this moment George Green burst into tears, threw his arms around her neck, and exclaimed, "I am glad I have waited so long, with the hope of meeting you again."

Mrs. Devenant again resumed her story:—"I was kept in jail three days, during which time I was visited by the magistrates, and two of the judges. On the third day I was taken out, and master told me that I was liberated, upon condition that I should be immediately sent out of the state. There happened to be just at the time in the neighbourhood a negro-trader, and he purchased me, and I was taken to New Orleans. On the steam-boat we were kept in a close room, where slaves are usually confined, so that I saw nothing of the passengers on board, or the towns we passed. We arrived at New Orleans, and were all put into the slave-market for sale. I was examined by many persons, but none seemed willing to purchase me, as all thought me too white, and said I would run away and pass as a free white woman. On the second day, while in the slave-market, and while planters and others were examining slaves and making their purchases, I observed a tall young man, with long black hair, eyeing me very closely, and then talking to the trader. I felt sure that my time had now come, but the day closed without my being sold. I did not regret this, for I had heard that foreigners made the worst of masters, and I felt confident that the man who eyed me so closely was not an American.

"The next day was the Sabbath. The bells called the people to the different places of worship. Methodists sang, and Baptists immersed, and Presbyterians sprinkled, and Episcopalians read their prayers, while the ministers of the various sects preached that Christ died for all; yet there were some twenty-five or thirty of us poor creatures confined in the 'Negro Pen,' awaiting the close of the holy Sabbath, and the dawn of another day, to be again taken into the market, there to be examined like so many beasts of burden. I need not tell you with what anxiety we waited for the advent of another day. On Monday we were again brought out and placed in rows to be inspected; and, fortunately for me, I was sold before we had been on the stand an hour. I was purchased by a gentleman residing in the city, for a waiting-maid for his wife, who was just on the eve of starting for Mobile, to pay a visit to a near relation. I was then dressed to suit the situation of a maid-servant; and upon the whole, I thought that, in my new dress, I looked as much the lady as my mistress.

"On the passage to Mobile, who should I see among the passengers but the tall, long-haired man that had eyed me so closely in the slave-market a few days before. His eyes were again on me, and he appeared anxious to speak to me, and I as reluctant to be spoken to. The first evening after leaving New Orleans, soon after twilight had let her curtain down, and pinned it with a star, and while I was seated on the deck of the boat near the ladies' cabin, looking upon the rippled waves, and the reflection of the moon upon the sea, all at once I saw the tall young man standing by my side. I immediately rose from my seat, and was in the act of returning to the cabin, when he in a broken accent said, 'Stop a moment; I wish to have a word with you. I am your friend.' I stopped and looked him full in the face, and he said, 'I saw you some days since in the slave-market, and I intended to have purchased you to save you from the condition of a slave. I called on Monday, but you had been sold and had left the market. I inquired and learned who the purchaser was, and that you had to go to Mobile, so I resolved to follow you. If you are willing I will try and buy you from your present owner, and you shall be free.' Although this was said in an honest and off-hand manner, I could not believe the man to be sincere in what he said. 'Why should you wish to set *me* free?' I asked. 'I had an only sister,' he replied, 'who died three years ago in France, and you are so much like her that had I not known of her death, I would most certainly have taken you for her.' 'However much I may resemble your sister, you are aware that I am not her, and why take so much interest in one whom you never saw before?' 'The love,' said he, 'which I had for my sister is transferred to you.' I had all along suspected that the man was a knave, and this profession of love confirmed me in my former belief, and I turned away and left him.

"The next day, while standing in the cabin and looking through the window, the French gentleman (for such he was) came to the window while walking on the guards, and again commenced as on the previous evening. He took from his pocket a bit of paper and put it into my hand, at the same time saying, 'Take this, it may some day be of service to you; remember it is from a friend,' and left me instantly. I unfolded the paper, and found it to be a 100 dollars bank note, on the United States Branch Bank, at Philadelphia. My first impulse was to give it to my mistress, but, upon a second thought, I resolved to seek an opportunity, and to return the hundred dollars to the stranger.

"Therefore I looked for him, but in vain; and had almost given up the idea of seeing him again, when he passed me on the guards of the boat and walked towards the stem of the vessel. It being now dark, I approached him and offered the money to him. He declined, saying at the same time, 'I gave it to you—keep it.' 'I do not want it,' I said. 'Now,' said he, 'you had better give your consent for me to purchase you, and you shall go with me to France.' 'But you cannot buy me now,' I replied, 'for my master is in New Orleans, and he purchased me not to sell, but to retain in his own family.' 'Would you rather remain with your present mistress than be free?' 'No,' said I. 'Then fly with me to-night; we shall be in Mobile in two hours from this, and when the passengers are going on shore, you can take my arm, and you can escape unobserved. The trader who brought you to New Orleans exhibited to me a certificate of your good character, and one from the minister of the church to which you were attached in Virginia; and upon the faith of these assurances, and the love I bear you, I promise before high heaven that I will marry you as soon as it can be done.' This solemn promise, coupled with what had already transpired, gave me confidence in the man; and rash as the act may seem, I determined in an instant to go with him. My mistress had been put under the charge of the captain; and as it would be past ten o'clock when the steamer would land, she accepted an invitation of the captain to remain on board with several other ladies till morning. I dressed myself in my best clothes, and put a veil over my face, and was ready on the landing of the boat. Surrounded by a number of passengers, we descended the stage leading to the wharf, and were soon lost in the crowd that thronged the quay. As we went on shore we encountered several persons announcing the names of hotels, the starting of boats for the interior, and vessels bound for Europe. Among these was the ship Utica, Captain Pell, bound for Havre. 'Now,' said Mr. Devenant, 'this is our chance.' The ship was to sail at twelve o'clock that night, at high tide; and following the men who were seeking passengers, we went immediately on board. Devenant told the captain of the ship that I was his sister, and for such we passed during the voyage. At the hour of twelve the Utica set sail, and we were soon out at sea.

"The morning after we left Mobile, Devenant met me as I came from my state-room, and embraced me for the first time. I loved him, but it was only that affection which we have for one who has done us a lasting favour: it was the love of gratitude rather than that of the heart. We were five weeks on the sea, and yet the passage did not seem long, for Devenant was so kind. On our arrival at Havre we were married and came to Dunkirk, and I have resided here ever since."

At the close of this narrative, the clock struck ten, when the old man, who was accustomed to retire at an early hour, rose to take leave, saying at the same time, "I hope you will remain with us to-night." Mr. Green would fain have excused himself, on the ground that they would expect him and wait at the hotel, but a look from the lady told him to accept the invitation. The old man was the father of Mrs. Devenant's deceased husband, as you will no doubt long since have supposed. A fortnight from the day on which they met in the graveyard, Mr. Green and Mrs. Devenant were joined in holy wedlock; so that George and Mary, who had loved each other so ardently in their younger days, were now husband and wife.

A celebrated writer has justly said of woman, "A woman's whole life is a history of the affections. The heart is her world; it is there her ambition strives for empire; it is there her avarice seeks for hidden treasures. She sends forth her sympathies on adventure; she embarks her whole soul in the traffic of affection; and, if shipwrecked, her case is hopeless, for it is a bankruptcy of the heart."

Mary had every reason to believe that she would never see George again; and although she confesses that the love she bore him was never transferred to her first husband, we can scarcely find fault with her for marrying Mr. Devenant. But the adherence of George Green to the resolution never to marry, unless to his Mary, is, indeed, a rare instance of the fidelity of man in the matter of love. We can but blush for our country's shame when we recall to mind the fact, that while George and Mary Green, and numbers of other fugitives from American slavery, can receive protection from any of the governments of Europe, they cannot return to their native land without becoming slaves.

CHAPTER XXIX.

CONCLUSION.

My narrative has now come to a close. I may be asked, and no doubt shall, Are the various incidents and scenes related founded in truth? I answer, Yes. I have personally participated in many of those scenes. Some of the narratives I have derived from other sources; many from the lips of those who, like myself, have run away from the land of bondage. Having been for nearly nine years employed on Lake Erie, I had many opportunities for helping the escape of fugitives, who, in return for the assistance they received, made me the depositary of their sufferings and wrongs. Of their relations I have made free use. To Mrs. Child, of New York, I am indebted for part of a short story. American Abolitionist journals are another source from whence some of the characters appearing in my narrative are taken. All these combined have made up my story. Having thus acknowledged my resources, I invite the attention of my readers to the following statement, from which I leave them to draw their own conclusions:—"It is estimated that in the United States, members of the Methodist church own 219,363 slaves; members of the Baptist church own 226,000 slaves; members of the Episcopalian church own 88,000 slaves; members of the Presbyterian church own 77,000 slaves; members of all other churches own 50,000 slaves; in all, 660,563 slaves owned by members of the Christian church in this pious democratic republic!"

May these facts be pondered over by British Christians, and at the next anniversaries of the various religious denominations in London may their influence be seen and felt! The religious bodies of American Christians will send their delegates to these meetings. Let British feeling be publicly manifested. Let British sympathy express itself in tender sorrow for the condition of my unhappy race. Let it be understood, unequivocally understood, that no fellowship can be held with slaveholders professing the same common Christianity as yourselves. And until this stain from America's otherwise fair escutcheon be wiped away, let no Christian association be maintained with those who traffic in the blood and bones of those whom God has made of one flesh as yourselves. Finally, let the voice of the whole British nation be heard across the Atlantic, and throughout the length and breadth of the land of the Pilgrim Fathers, beseeching their descendants, as they value *the* common salvation, which knows no distinction between the bond and the free, to proclaim the Year of Jubilee. Then shall the "earth indeed yield her increase, and God, even our own God, shall bless us; and all the ends of the earth shall fear Him."

THE AMERICAN FUGITIVE IN EUROPE.

SKETCHES
OF
PLACES AND PEOPLE ABROAD.

"Go, little book, from this my solitude!
  I cast thee on the waters—go thy ways!
And if, as I believe, thy vein be good,
  The world will find thee after many days."

SOUTHEY.

W. Wells Brown.

PREFACE
TO THE ENGLISH EDITION.

WHILE I feel conscious that most of the contents of these Letters will be interesting chiefly to American readers, yet I may indulge the hope that the fact of their being the first production of a Fugitive Slave as a history of travels may carry with them novelty enough to secure for them, to some extent, the attention of the reading public of Great Britain. Most of the letters were written for the private perusal of a few personal friends in America; some were contributed to *Frederick Douglass' Paper*, a journal published in the United States. In a printed circular sent some weeks since to some of my friends, asking subscriptions to this volume, I stated the reasons for its publication: these need not be repeated here. To those who so promptly and kindly responded to that appeal, I tender my most sincere thanks. It is with no little diffidence that I lay these letters before the public; for I am not blind to the fact that they must contain many errors; and to those who shall find fault with them on that account, it may not be too much for me to ask them kindly to remember that the author was a slave in one of the Southern States of America until he had attained the age of twenty years; and that the education he has acquired was by his own exertions, he never having had a day's schooling in his life.

W. WELLS BROWN.

22 CECIL STREET, STRAND,
LONDON.

NOTE
TO THE AMERICAN EDITION.

DURING my sojourn abroad I found it advantageous to my purse to publish a book of travels, which I did under the title of "Three Years in Europe, or Places I have seen and People I have met." The work was reviewed by the ablest journals in Great Britain, and from their favorable criticisms I have been induced to offer it to the American public, with a dozen or more additional chapters. W. W. B.

BOSTON, *November*, 1854.

CONTENTS

CHAPTER VIII.

CHAPTER IX.

CHAPTER X.

CHAPTER XI.

CHAPTER XII.

CHAPTER XIII.

CHAPTER XIV.

CHAPTER XV.

CHAPTER XVI.

CHAPTER XVII.

CHAPTER XVIII.

CHAPTER XIX.

CHAPTER XX.

CHAPTER XXI.

CHAPTER XXII.

CHAPTER XXIII.

CHAPTER XXIV.

CHAPTER I.

> "Adieu, adieu!—my native shore
> Fades o'er the waters blue;
> The night-winds sigh, the breakers roar,
> And shrieks the wild sea-mew.
> Yon sun that sets upon the sea
> We follow in his flight;
> Farewell a while to him and thee!
> My native land, good-night!"
>
> CHILDE HAROLD.

ON the 18th July, 1849, I took passage in the steamship *Canada*, Captain Judkins, bound for Liverpool. The day was a warm one; so much so, that many persons on board, as well as on shore, stood with their umbrellas up, so intense was the heat of the sun. The ringing of the ship's bell was a signal for us to shake hands with our friends, which we did, and then stepped on the deck of the noble craft. The *Canada* quitted her moorings at half-past twelve, and we were soon in motion. As we were passing out of Boston Bay, I took my stand on the quarter-deck, to take a last farewell (at least for a time) of my native land. A visit to the Old World, up to that time, had seemed but a dream. As I looked back upon the receding land, recollections of the past rushed through my mind in quick succession. From the treatment that I had received from the Americans as a victim of slavery, and the knowledge that I was at that time liable to be seized and again reduced to whips and chains, I had supposed that I would leave the country without any regret; but in this I was mistaken, for when I saw the last thread of communication cut off between me and the land, and the dim shores dying away in the distance, I almost regretted that I was not on shore.

An anticipated trip to a foreign country appears pleasant when talking about it, especially when surrounded by friends whom we love; but when we have left them all behind, it does not seem so pleasant. Whatever may be the fault of the government under which we live, and no matter how oppressive her laws may appear, yet we leave our native land (if such it be) with feelings akin to sorrow. With the steamer's powerful engine at work, and with a fair wind, we were speedily on the bosom of the Atlantic, which was as calm and as smooth as our own Hudson in its calmest aspect. We had on board above one hundred passengers, forty of whom were the "Vienneise children"—a troop of dancers. The passengers represented several different nations, English, French, Spaniards, Africans, and Americans. One man, who had the longest mustache that mortal man was ever doomed to wear, especially attracted my attention. He appeared to belong to no country in particular, but was yet the busiest man on board. After viewing for some time the many strange faces round me, I descended to the cabin to look after my luggage, which had been put hurriedly on board. I hope that all who take a trip of so great a distance may be as fortunate as I was, in being supplied with books to read on the voyage. My friends had furnished me with literature, from "Macaulay's History of England" to "Jane Eyre," so that I did not want for books to occupy my time.

A pleasant passage of about thirty hours brought us to Halifax, at six o'clock in the evening. In company with my friend the President of the Oberlin Institute, I took a stroll through the town; and from what little I saw of the people in the streets, I am sure that the taking of the temperance pledge would do them no injury. Our stay at Halifax was short. Having taken in a few sacks of coals, the mails, and a limited number of passengers, we were again out, and soon at sea.

As the steamer moved gently from the shore I felt like repeating those lines of a distinguished poet:

"With thee, my bark, I'll swiftly go
Athwart the foaming brine;
Nor care what land thou bear'st me to,
So not again to mine.
Welcome, welcome, ye dark blue waves!
And when you fail my sight
Welcome ye deserts and ye caves!
My native land, good-night!"

Nothing occurred during the passage to mar the pleasure which we anticipated from a voyage by sea in such fine weather. And, after a splendid run of seven days more, I heard the welcome cry of "Land a-head." It was early in the morning, and I was not yet out of bed; but I had no wish to remain longer in my berth. Although the passage had been unprecedently short, yet this news was hailed with joy by all on board.

For my own part, I was soon on deck. Away in the distance, and on our larboard quarter, were the gray hills of old Ireland. Yes; we were in sight of the land of Curran, Emmet and O'Connell. While I rejoiced with the other passengers at the sight of land, and the near approach to the end of our voyage, I felt low-spirited, because it reminded me of the great distance I was from home, and of dear ones left behind. But the experience of above twenty years' travelling had prepared me to undergo what most persons must, in visiting a strange country. This was the last day but one that we were to be on board; and, as if moved by the sight of land, all seemed to be gathering their different things together—brushing up their old clothes and putting on their new ones, as if this would bring them any sooner to the end of their journey.

The last night on board was the most pleasant, apparently, that we had experienced; probably, because it was the last. The moon was in her meridian splendor, pouring her broad light over the calm sea; while near to us, on our starboard side, was a ship, with her snow-white sails spread aloft, and stealing through the water like a thing of life. What can present a more picturesque view than two vessels at sea on a moonlight night, and within a few rods of each other? With a gentle breeze, and the powerful engine at work, we seemed to be flying to the embrace of our British neighbors.

The next morning I was up before the sun, and found that we were within a few miles of Liverpool. The taking of a pilot on board at eleven o'clock warned us to prepare to quit our ocean palace, and seek other quarters. At a little past three o'clock, the ship cast anchor, and we were all tumbled, bag and baggage, into a small steamer, and in a few moments were at the door of the custom-house. The passage had only been nine days and twenty-two hours, the quickest on record at that time, yet it was long enough. I waited nearly three hours before my name was called, and when it was I unlocked my trunks and handed them over to one of the officers, whose dirty hands made no improvement on the work of the laundress. First one article was taken out, and then another, till an *Iron Collar* that had been worn by a female slave on the banks of the Mississippi was hauled out, and this democratic instrument of torture became the centre of attraction; so much so, that instead of going on with the examination, all hands stopped to look at the "Negro Collar."

Several of my countrymen who were standing by were not a little displeased at answers which I gave to questions on the subject of slavery; but they held their peace. The interest created by the appearance of the iron collar closed the examination of my luggage. As if afraid that they would find something more hideous, they put the custom-house mark on each piece, and passed them out, and I was soon comfortably installed at Brown's Temperance Hotel, Clayton-square.

No person of my complexion can visit this country without being struck with the marked difference between the English and the Americans. The prejudice which I have experienced on all and every occasion in the United States, and to some extent on board the *Canada*, vanished as soon as I set foot on the soil of Britain. In America I had been bought and sold as a slave in the Southern States. In the so-called Free States, I had been treated as one born to occupy an inferior position,—in steamers, compelled to take my fare on the deck; in hotels, to take my meals in the kitchen; in coaches, to ride on the outside; in railways, to ride in the "negro-car;" and in churches, to sit in the "negro-pew." But no sooner was I on British soil, than I was recognized as a man, and an equal. The very dogs in the streets appeared conscious of my manhood. Such is the difference, and such is the change that is brought about by a trip of nine days in an Atlantic steamer.

I was not more struck with the treatment of the people than with the appearance of the great seaport of the world. The gray stone piers and docks, the dark look of the magnificent warehouses, the substantial appearance of everything around, causes one to think himself in a new world instead of the old. Everything in Liverpool looks old, yet nothing is worn out. The beautiful villas on the opposite side of the river, in the vicinity of Birkenhead, together with the countless number of vessels in the river, and the great ships to be seen in the stream, give life and animation to the whole scene.

Everything in and about Liverpool seems to be built for the future as well as the present. We had time to examine but few of the public buildings, the first of which was the custom-house, an edifice that would be an ornament to any city in the world.

CHAPTER II.

"It seems as if every ship their sovereign knows,
His awful summons they so soon obey;
So hear the scaly herds when Proteus blows,
And so to pasture follow through the sea."

AFTER remaining in Liverpool two days, I took passage in the little steamer *Adelaide* for Dublin. The wind being high on the night of our voyage, the vessel had scarcely got to sea ere we were driven to our berths; and, though the distance from Liverpool to Dublin is short, yet, strange to say, I witnessed more effects of the sea and rolling of the steamer upon the passengers, than was to be seen during the whole of our voyage from America. We reached Kingstown, five miles below Dublin, after a passage of nearly fifteen hours, and were soon seated on a car, and on our way to the city. While coming into the bay, one gets a fine view of Dublin and the surrounding country. Few sheets of water make a more beautiful appearance than Dublin Bay. We found it as still and smooth as a mirror, with a soft mist on its surface,—a strange contrast to the boisterous sea that we had left a moment before.

The curious phrases of the Irish sounded harshly upon my ear, probably because they were strange to me. I lost no time, on reaching the city, in seeking out some to whom I had letters of introduction, one of whom gave me an invitation to make his house my home during my stay,—an invitation which I did not think fit to decline.

Dublin, the metropolis of Ireland, is a city of above two hundred thousand inhabitants, and is considered by the people of Ireland to be the second city in the British empire. The Liffey, which falls into Dublin Bay a little below the custom-house, divides the town into two nearly equal parts. The streets are—some of them—very fine, especially Sackville-street, in the centre of which stands a pillar erected to Nelson, England's most distinguished naval commander. The Bank of Ireland, to which I paid a visit, is a splendid building, and was formerly the Parliament House. This magnificent edifice fronts College Green, and near at hand stands a bronze statue of William III. The Bank and the Custom-House are two of the finest monuments of architecture in the city; the latter of which stands near the river Liffey, and its front makes an imposing appearance, extending three hundred and seventy-five feet. It is built of Portland stone, and is adorned with a beautiful portico in the centre, consisting of four Doric columns, supporting an enriched entablature, decorated with a group of figures in alto-relievo, representing Hibernia and Britannia presenting emblems of peace and liberty. A magnificent dome, supporting a cupola, on whose apex stands a colossal figure of Hope, rising nobly from the centre of the building to a height of one hundred and twenty-five feet. It is, withal, a fine specimen of what man can do.

From this noble edifice we bent our steps to another part of the city, and soon found ourselves in the vicinity of St. Patrick's, where we had a heart-sickening view of the poorest of the poor. All the recollections of poverty which I had ever beheld seemed to disappear in comparison with what was then before me. We passed a filthy and noisy market, where fruit and vegetable women were screaming and begging those passing by to purchase their commodities; while in and about the market-place were throngs of beggars fighting for rotten fruit, cabbage-stocks, and even the very trimmings of vegetables. On the side-walks were great numbers hovering about the doors of the more wealthy, and following strangers, importuning them for "pence to buy bread." Sickly and emaciated looking creatures, half naked, were at our heels at every turn.

In our return home, we passed through a respectable-looking street, in which stands a small three-story brick building, that was pointed out to us as the birthplace of Thomas Moore, the poet. The following verse from one of his poems was continually in my mind while viewing this house:

> "Where is the slave so lowly,
> Condemned to chains unholy,
> Who, could he burst
> His bonds at first,
> Would pine beneath them slowly?"

The next day was the Sabbath, but it had more the appearance of a holiday than a day of rest. It had been announced the day before that the royal fleet was expected, and at an early hour on Sunday the entire town seemed to be on the move towards Kingstown, and, as the family with whom I was staying followed the multitude, I was not inclined to remain behind, and so went with them. On reaching the station, we found it utterly impossible to get standing room in any of the trains, much less a seat, and therefore determined to reach Kingstown under the plea of a morning's walk; and in this we were not alone, for during the walk of five miles the road was filled with thousands of pedestrians, and a countless number of carriages, phaëtons, and vehicles of a more humble order.

We reached the lower town in time to get a good dinner, and rest ourselves before going to make further searches for her majesty's fleet. At a little past four o'clock, we observed the multitude going towards the pier, a number of whom were yelling, at the top of their voices, "It's coming, it's coming!" but on going to the quay we found that a false alarm had been given. However, we had been on the look-out but a short time, when a column of smoke, rising, as it were, out of the sea, announced that the royal fleet was near at hand. The concourse in the vicinity of the pier was variously estimated at from eighty to one hundred thousand.

It was not long before the five steamers were entering the harbor, the one bearing her majesty leading the way. As each vessel had a number of distinguished persons on board, the people appeared to be at a loss to know which was the queen; and as each party made its appearance on the promenade deck, they were received with great enthusiasm, the party having the best-looking lady being received with the greatest applause. The Prince of Wales, and Prince Alfred, while crossing the deck were recognized, and greeted with three cheers; the former, taking off his hat and bowing to the people, showed that he had had some training as a public man, although not ten years of age. But not so with Prince Alfred; for, when his brother turned to him and asked him to take off his hat, and make a bow to the people, he shook his head, and said, "No." This was received with hearty laughter by those on board, and was responded to by the thousands on shore. But greater applause was yet in store for the young prince; for the captain of the steamer being near by, and seeing that the Prince of Wales could not prevail on his brother to take off his hat, stepped up to him and undertook to take it off for him, when, seemingly to the delight of all, the prince put both hands to his head, and held his hat fast. This was regarded as a sign of courage and future renown, and was received with the greatest enthusiasm, many crying out, "Good, good! he will make a brave king when his day comes."

After the greetings and applause had been wasted on many who had appeared on deck, all at once, as if by some magic power, we beheld a lady, rather small in stature, with auburn hair, attired in a plain dress, and wearing a sky-blue bonnet, standing on the larboard paddle-box, by the side of a tall, good-looking man, with a mustache. The thunders of applause that now rent the air, and cries of "The queen, the queen!" seemed to set at rest the question of which was her majesty. But a few moments were allowed to the people to look at the queen, before she again disappeared; and it was understood that she would not be seen again that evening. A rush was then made for the railway, to return to Dublin.

* * *

The seventh of August was a great day in Dublin. At an early hour the bells began their merry peals, and the people were soon seen in groups in the streets and public squares. The hour of ten was fixed for the procession to leave Kingstown, and it was expected to enter the city at eleven. The windows of the houses in the streets through which the royal train was to pass were at a premium, and seemed to find ready occupants.

Being invited the day previous to occupy part of a window in Sackville-street, I was stationed at my allotted place at an early hour, with an outstretched neck and open eyes. My own color differing from those about me, I attracted not a little attention from many; and often, when gazing down the street to see if the royal procession was in sight, would find myself eyed by all around. But neither while at the window or in the streets was I once insulted. This was so unlike the American prejudice, that it seemed strange to me. It was near twelve o'clock before the procession entered Sackville-street, and when it did all eyes seemed to beam with delight. The first carriage contained only her majesty and the Prince Consort; the second the royal children, and the third the lords in waiting. Fifteen carriages were used by those that made up the royal party. I had a full view of the queen and all who followed in the train. Her majesty—whether from actual love for her person, or the novelty of the occasion, I know not which—was received everywhere with the greatest enthusiasm. One thing, however, is certain, and that is, Queen Victoria is beloved by her subjects.

But the grand *fête* was reserved for the evening. Great preparations had been made to have a grand illumination on the occasion, and hints were thrown out that it would surpass anything ever witnessed in London. In this they were not far out of the way; for all who witnessed the scene admitted that it could scarcely have been surpassed. My own idea of an illumination, as I had seen it in the back-woods of my native land, dwindled into nothing when compared with this magnificent affair.

In company with a few friends, and a lady under my charge, I undertook to pass through Sackville and one or two other streets about eight o'clock in the evening, but we found it utterly impossible to proceed. Masses thronged the streets, and the wildest enthusiasm seemed to prevail. In our attempt to cross the bridge, we were wedged in and lost our companions; and on one occasion I was separated from the lady, and took shelter under a cart standing in the street. After being jammed and pulled about for nearly two hours, I returned to my lodgings, where I found part of my company, who had come in one after another. At eleven o'clock we had all assembled, and each told his adventures and "hair-breadth escapes;" and nearly every one had lost a pocket-handkerchief or something of the kind; my own was among the missing. However, I lost nothing; for a benevolent lady, who happened to be one of the company, presented me with one which was of far more value than the one I had lost.

Every one appeared to enjoy the holiday which the royal visit had caused. But the Irish are indeed a strange people. How varied their aspect, how contradictory their character! Ireland, the land of genius and degradation, of great resources and unparalleled poverty, noble deeds and the most revolting crimes, the land of distinguished poets, splendid orators, and the bravest of soldiers, the land of ignorance and beggary! Dublin is a splendid city, but its splendor is that of chiselled marble rather than real life. One cannot behold these architectural monuments without thinking of the great men that Ireland has produced. The names of Burke, Sheridan, Flood, Grattan, O'Connell and Shiel, have become as familiar to the Americans as household words. Burke is known as the statesman; Sheridan for his great speech on the trial of Warren Hastings; Grattan for his eloquence; O'Connell as the agitator, and Shiel as the accomplished orator.

But, of Ireland's sons, none stands higher in America than Thomas Moore, the poet. The vigor of his sarcasm, the glow of his enthusiasm, the coruscations of his fancy, and the flashing of his wit, seem to be as well understood in the New World as the Old; and the support which his pen has given to civil and religious liberty throughout the world entitles the Minstrel of Erin to this elevated position.

CHAPTER III.

"There is no other land like thee,
  No dearer shore;
Thou art the shelter of the free,—
The home, the port of Liberty."

AFTER a pleasant sojourn of three weeks in Ireland, I took passage in one of the mail-steamers for Liverpool, and, arriving there, was soon on the road to the metropolis. The passage from Dublin to Liverpool was an agreeable one. The rough sea that we passed through on going to Ireland had given way to a dead calm; and our noble little steamer, on quitting the Dublin wharf, seemed to understand that she was to have it all her own way. During the first part of the evening, the boat appeared to feel her importance, and, darting through the water with majestic strides, she left behind her a dark cloud of smoke suspended in the air like a banner; while, far astern in the wake of the vessel, could be seen the rippled waves sparkling in the rays of the moon, giving strength and beauty to the splendor of the evening.

On reaching Liverpool, and partaking of a good breakfast, for which we paid double price, we proceeded to the railway station, and were soon going at a rate unknown to those accustomed to travel only on American railways. At a little past two o'clock in the afternoon we saw in the distance the outskirts of London. We could get but an indistinct view, which had the appearance of one architectural mass, extending all round to the horizon, and enveloped in a combination of fog and smoke; and towering above every other object to be seen was the dome of St. Paul's Cathedral.

A few moments more, and we were safely seated in a "Hansom's Patent," and on our way to Hughes's—one of the politest men of the George Fox stamp we have ever met. Here we found forty or fifty persons, who, like ourselves, were bound for the Peace Congress. The Sturges, the Wighams, the Richardsons, the Allens, the Thomases, and a host of others not less distinguished as friends of peace, were of the company—of many of whom I had heard, but none of whom I had ever seen; yet I was not an entire stranger to many, especially to the abolitionists. In company with a friend, I sallied forth after tea to take a view of the city. The evening was fine—the dense fog and smoke, having to some extent passed away, left the stars shining brightly, while the gas-light from the street-lamps and the brilliant shop-windows gave it the appearance of day-light in a new form. "What street is this?" we asked. "Cheapside," was the reply. The street was thronged, and everybody seemed to be going at a rapid rate, as if there was something of importance at the end of the journey. Flying vehicles of every description passing each other with a dangerous rapidity, men with lovely women at their sides, children running about as if they had lost their parents—all gave a brilliancy to the scene scarcely to be excelled. If one wished to get jammed and pushed about, he need go no further than Cheapside. But everything of the kind is done with a degree of propriety in London that would put the New Yorkers to blush. If you are run over in London, they "beg your pardon;" if they run over you in New York, you are "laughed at:" in London, if your hat is knocked off it is picked up and handed to you; if in New York, you must pick it up yourself. There is a lack of good manners among Americans that is scarcely known or understood in Europe. Our stay in the great metropolis gave us but little opportunity of seeing much of the place; for in twenty-four hours after our arrival we joined the rest of the delegates, and started on our visit to our Gallic neighbors.

We assembled at the London Bridge Railway Station, a few minutes past nine, to the number of six hundred. The day was fine, and every eye seemed to glow with enthusiasm. Besides the delegates, there were probably not less than six hundred more, who had come to see the company start. We took our seats, and appeared to be waiting for nothing but the iron-horse to be fastened to the train, when all at once we were informed that we must go to the booking-office and change our tickets. At this news every one appeared to be vexed. This caused great trouble; for, on returning to the train, many persons got into the wrong carriages; and several parties were separated from their friends, while not a few were calling out, at the top of their voices, "Where is my wife? Where is my husband? Where is my luggage? Who's got my boy? Is this the right train?" "What is that lady going to do with all these children?" asked the guard. "Is she a delegate? are all the children delegates?" In the carriage where I had taken my seat was a good-looking lady, who gave signs of being very much annoyed. "It is just so when I am going anywhere: I never saw the like in my life!" said she. "I really wish I was at home again."

An hour had now elapsed, and we were still at the station. However, we were soon on our way, and going at express speed. In passing through Kent we enjoyed the scenery exceedingly, as the weather was altogether in our favor; and the drapery which nature hung on the trees, in the part through which we passed, was in all its gayety. On our arrival at Folkstone, we found three steamers in readiness to convey the party to Boulogne. As soon as the train stopped, a general rush was made for the steamers, and in a very short time the one in which I had embarked was passing out of the harbor. The boat appeared to be conscious that we were going on a holy mission, and seemed to be proud of her load. There is nothing in this wide world so like a thing of life as a steamer, from the breathing of her steam and smoke, the energy of her motion, and the beauty of her shape; while the ease with which she is managed by the command of a single voice makes her appear as obedient as the horse is to the rein.

When we were about half way between the two great European powers, the officer began to gather the tickets. The first to whom he applied, and who handed out his "Excursion Ticket," was informed that we were all in the wrong boat. "Is this not one of the boats to take over the delegates?" asked a pretty little lady, with a whining voice. "No, madam," said the captain. "You must look to the committee for your pay," said one of the company to the captain. "I have nothing to do with committees," the captain replied. "Your fare, gentlemen, if you please."

Here the whole party were again thrown into confusion. "Do you hear that? We are in the wrong boat." "I knew it would be so," said the Rev. Dr. Ritchie, of Edinburgh. "It is indeed a pretty piece of work," said a plain-looking lady in a handsome bonnet. "When I go travelling again," said an elderly-looking gent, with an eye-glass to his face, "I will take the phaëton and old Dobbin." Every one seemed to lay the blame on the committee, and not, too, without some just grounds. However, Mr. Sturge, one of the committee, being in the boat with us, an arrangement was entered into by which we were not compelled to pay our fare the second time.

As we neared the French coast, the first object that attracted our attention was the Napoleon Pillar, on the top of which is a statue of the emperor in the imperial robes. We landed, partook of refreshment that had been prepared for us, and again repaired to the railway station. The arrangements for leaving Boulogne were no better than those at London. But after the delay of another hour we were again in motion.

It was a beautiful country through which we passed from Boulogne to Amiens. Straggling cottages which bespeak neatness and comfort abound on every side. The eye wanders over the diversified views with unabated pleasure, and rests in calm repose upon its superlative beauty. Indeed, the eye cannot but be gratified at viewing the entire country from the coast to the metropolis. Sparkling hamlets spring up, as the steam-horse speeds his way, at almost every point, showing the progress of civilization, and the refinement of the nineteenth century.

We arrived at Paris a few minutes past twelve o'clock at night, when, according to our tickets, we should have been there at nine. Elihu Burritt, who had been in Paris some days, and who had the arrangements there pretty much his own way, was at the station waiting the arrival of the train, and we had demonstrated to us the best evidence that he understood his business. In no other place on the whole route had the affairs been so well managed; for we were seated in our respective carriages and our luggage placed on the top, and away we went to our hotels, without the least difficulty or inconvenience. The champion of an "Ocean Penny Postage" received, as he deserved, thanks from the whole company for his admirable management.

The silence of the night was only disturbed by the rolling of the wheels of the omnibus, as we passed through the dimly-lighted streets. Where, a few months before, was to be seen the flash from the cannon and the musket, and the hearing of the cries and groans behind the barricades, was now the stillness of death—nothing save here and there a *gens d'arme* was to be seen going his rounds in silence.

The omnibus set us down at the hotel Bedford, Rue de L'Card, where, although near one o'clock, we found a good supper waiting for us; and, as I was not devoid of an appetite, I did my share towards putting it out of the way.

The next morning I was up at an early hour, and out on the Boulevards to see what might be seen. As I was passing from the hotel to the Place de La Concord, all at once, and as if by some magic power, I found myself in front of the most splendid edifice imaginable, situated at the end of the Rue Nationale. Seeing a number of persons entering the church at that early hour, and recognizing among them my friend the President of the Oberlin (Ohio) Institute, and wishing not to stray too far from my hotel before breakfast, I followed the crowd and entered the building. The church itself consisted of a vast nave, interrupted by four pews on each side, fronted with lofty fluted Corinthian columns standing on pedestals, supporting colossal arches, bearing up cupolas pierced with skylights and adorned with compartments gorgeously gilt; their corners supported with saints and apostles in *alto relievo*. The walls of the church were lined with rich marble. The different paintings and figures gave the interior an imposing appearance. On inquiry, I found that I was in the Church of the Madeleine. It was near this spot that some of the most interesting scenes occurred during the Revolution of 1848, which dethroned Louis Philippe. Behind the Madeleine is a small but well-supplied market; and on an esplanade east of the edifice a flower-market is held on Tuesdays and Fridays.

At eleven o'clock the same day, the Peace Congress met in the Salle St. Cecile, Rue de la St. Lazare. The Parisians have no "Exeter Hall;" in fact, there is no private hall in the city of any size, save this, where such a meeting could be held. This hall had been fitted up for the occasion. The room is long, and at one end has a raised platform; and at the opposite end is a gallery, with seats raised one above another. On one side of the hall was a balcony with sofas, which were evidently the "reserved seats."

The hall was filled at an early hour with the delegates, their friends, and a good sprinkling of the French. Occasionally, small groups of gentlemen would make their appearance on the platform, until it soon appeared that there was little room left for others; and yet the officers of the Convention had not come in. The different countries were, many of them, represented here. England, France, Belgium, Germany, Switzerland, Greece, Spain, and the United States, had each their delegates. The assembly began to give signs of impatience, when very soon the train of officials made their appearance amid great applause. Victor Hugo led the way, followed by M. Duguerry, curé of the Madeleine, Elihu Burritt, and a host of others of less note. Victor Hugo took the chair as President of the Congress, supported by vice-presidents from the several nations represented. Mr. Richard, the secretary, read a dry report of the names of societies, committees, etc., which was deemed the opening of the Convention.

The president then arose, and delivered one of the most impressive and eloquent appeals in favor of peace that could possibly be imagined. The effect produced upon the minds of all present was such as to make the author of "*Notre Dame de Paris*" a great favorite with the Congress. An English gentleman near me said to his friend, "I can't understand a word of what he says, but is it not good?" Victor Hugo concluded his speech amid the greatest enthusiasm on the part of the French, which was followed by hurras in the old English style. The Convention was successively addressed by the President of the Brussels Peace Society; President Mahan, of the Oberlin (Ohio) Institute, U. S.; Henry Vincent; and Richard Cobden. The latter was not only the *lion* of the English delegation, but the great man of the Convention. When Mr. Cobden speaks there is no want of hearers. The great power of this gentleman lies in his facts and his earnestness, for he cannot be called an eloquent speaker. Mr. Cobden addressed the Congress first in French, then in English; and, with the single exception of Mr. Ewart, M. P., was the only one of the English delegation that could speak to the French in their own language.

The first day's proceedings were brought to a close at five o'clock, when the numerous audience dispersed—the citizens to their homes, and the delegates to see the sights.

I was not a little amused at an incident that occurred at the close of the first session. On the passage from America, there were in the same steamer with me several Americans, and among these three or four appeared to be much annoyed at the fact that I was a passenger, and enjoying the company of white persons; and, although I was not openly insulted, I very often heard the remark, that "That nigger had better be on his master's farm," and "What could the American Peace Society be thinking about, to send a black man as a delegate to Paris?" Well, at the close of the first sitting of the convention, and just as I was leaving Victor Hugo, to whom I had been introduced by an M. P., I observed near me a gentleman with his hat in hand, whom I recognized as one of the passengers who had crossed the Atlantic with me in the *Canada*, and who appeared to be the most horrified at having a negro for a fellow-passenger. This gentleman, as I left M. Hugo, stepped up to me and said, "How do you do, Mr. Brown?" "You have the advantage of me," said I. "O, don't you know me? I was a fellow-passenger with you from America; I wish you would give me an introduction to Victor Hugo and Mr. Cobden." I need not inform you that I declined introducing this pro-slavery American to these distinguished men. I only allude to this, to show what a change came over the dreams of my white American brother by crossing the ocean. The man who would not have been seen walking with me in the streets of New York, and who would not have shaken hands with me with a pair of tongs while on the passage from the United States, could come with hat in hand in Paris, and say, "I was your fellow-passenger." From the Salle de St. Cecile, I visited the Column Vendome, from the top of which I obtained a fine view of Paris and its environs. This is the Bunker Hill Monument of Paris. On the top of this pillar is a statue of the Emperor Napoleon, eleven feet high. The monument is built with stone, and the outside covered with a metallic composition, made of cannons, guns, spikes, and other warlike implements taken from the Russians and Austrians by Napoleon. Above twelve hundred cannons were melted down to help to create this monument of folly, to commemorate the success of the French arms in the German campaign. The column is in imitation of the Trajan pillar at Rome, and is twelve feet in diameter at the base. The door at the bottom of the pillar, and where we entered, was decorated above with crowns of oak, surmounted by eagles, each weighing five hundred pounds. The bas-relief of the shaft pursues a spiral direction to the top, and displays, in a chronological order, the principal actions of the French army, from the departure of the troops from Boulogne to the battle of Austerlitz. The figures are near three feet high, and their number said to be two thousand. This sumptuous monument stands on a plinth of polished granite, surmounted by an iron railing; and, from its size and position, has an imposing appearance when seen from any part of the city.

Everything here appears strange and peculiar—the people not less so than their speech. The horses, carriages, furniture, dress and manners, are in keeping with their language. The appearance of the laborers in caps, resembling night-caps, seemed particularly strange to me. The women without bonnets, and their caps turned the right side behind, had nothing of the look of our American women. The prettiest woman I ever saw was without a bonnet, walking on the Boulevards. While in Ireland, and during the few days I was in England, I was struck with the marked difference between the appearance of the women and those of my own country. The American women are too tall, too sallow, and too long-featured, to be called pretty. This is most probably owing to the fact that in America the people come to maturity earlier than in most other countries.

My first night in Paris was spent with interest. No place can present greater street attractions than the Boulevards of Paris. The countless number of cafés, with tables before the doors, and these surrounded by men with long moustaches, with ladies at their sides, whose very smiles give indication of happiness, together with the sound of music from the gardens in the rear, tell the stranger that he is in a different country from his own.

CHAPTER IV.

> "——A town of noble fame,
> Where monuments are found in ancient guise,
> Where kings and queens in pomp did long abide,
> And where God pleased that good King Louis died."

AFTER the Convention had finished its sittings yesterday, I accompanied Mrs. C—— and sisters to Versailles, where they are residing during the summer. It was really pleasing to see among the hundreds of strange faces in the Convention those distinguished friends of the slave from Boston.

Mrs. C——'s residence is directly in front of the great palace where so many kings have made their homes, the prince of whom was Louis XIV. The palace is now unoccupied. No ruler has dared to take up his residence here since Louis XVI. and Marie Antoinette were driven from it by the mob from Paris on the eighth of October, 1789. The town looks like the wreck of what it once was. At the commencement of the first revolution, it contained one hundred thousand inhabitants; now it has only about thirty thousand. It seems to be going back to what it was in the time of Louis XIII., when, in 1624, he built a small brick chateau, and from it arose the magnificent palace which now stands here, and which attracts strangers to it from all parts of the world.

I arose this morning at an early hour, and took a walk through the grounds of the palace, and remained three hours among the fountains and statuary of this more than splendid place. At ten o'clock we again returned to Paris, to the Peace Congress.

The session was opened by a speech from M. Coquerel, the Protestant clergyman in Paris. His speech was received with much applause, and seemed to create great sensation in the Congress, especially at the close of his remarks, when he was seized by the hand by the Abbé Duguerry, amid the most deafening and enthusiastic applause of the entire multitude. The meeting was then addressed in English by a short gentleman, of florid complexion. His words seemed to come without the least difficulty, and his gestures, though somewhat violent, were evidently studied; and the applause with which he was greeted by the English delegation showed that he was a man of no little distinction among them. His speech was one continuous flow of rapid, fervid eloquence, that seemed to fire every heart; and although I disliked his style, I was prepossessed in his favor. This was Henry Vincent, and his speech was in favor of disarmament.

Mr. Vincent was followed by M. Emile de Girardin, the editor of *La Presse*, in one of the most eloquent speeches that I ever heard; and his exclamation of "Soldiers of Peace" drew thunders of applause from his own countrymen. M. Girardin is not only the leader of the French press, but is a writer on politics of great distinction, and a leader of no inconsiderable party in the National Assembly; although still a young man, apparently not more than thirty-eight or forty years of age.

After a speech from Mr. Ewart, M. P., in French, and another from Mr. Cobden in the same language, the Convention was brought to a close for the day. I spent the morning yesterday in visiting some of the lions of the French capital, among which was the Louvre. The French government having kindly ordered that the members of the Peace Congress should be admitted free, and without ticket, to all the public works, I had nothing to do but present my card of membership, and was immediately admitted.

The first room I entered was nearly a quarter of a mile in length; is known as the "Long Gallery," and contains some of the finest paintings in the world. On entering this superb palace, my first impression was that all Christendom had been robbed, that the Louvre might make a splendid appearance. This is the Italian department, and one would suppose by its appearance that but few paintings had been left in Italy. The entrance end of the Louvre was for a long time in an unfinished state, but was afterwards completed by that master workman, the Emperor Napoleon. It was long thought that the building would crumble into decay, but the genius of the great Corsican rescued it from ruin.

During our walk through the Louvre, we saw some twenty or thirty artists copying paintings; some had their copies finished and were going out, others half done, while many had just commenced. I remained some minutes near a pretty French girl, who was copying a painting of a dog rescuing a child from a stream of water into which it had fallen.

I walked down one side of the hall and up the other, and was about leaving, when I was informed that this was only one room, and that a half-dozen more were at my service; but a clock on a neighboring church reminded me that I must quit the Louvre for the Salle de St. Cecile.

* * *

At the meeting of the third session of the Congress, the hall was filled at an early hour with rather a more fashionable-looking audience than on any former occasion, and all appeared anxious for its commencement, as it was understood to be the last day. After the reading of several letters from gentlemen, apologizing for their not being able to attend, the speech of Elihu Burritt was read by a son of M. Coquerel. I felt somewhat astonished that my countryman, who was said to be master of fifty languages, had to get some one to read his speech in French.

The Abbé Duguerry now came forward amid great cheering, and said that "the eminent journalist, Girardin, and the great English logician, Mr. Cobden, had made it unnecessary for any further advocacy in that assembly of the peace cause; that if the principles laid down in the resolutions were carried out, the work would be done. He said that the question of general pacification was built on truth,—truth which emanated from God,—and it were as vain to undertake to prevent air from expanding as to check the progress of truth. It must and would prevail."

A pale, thin-faced gentleman next ascended the platform (or tribune, as it was called) amid shouts of applause from the English, and began his speech in rather a low tone, when compared with the sharp voice of Vincent, or the thunder of the Abbé Duguerry. An audience is not apt to be pleased or even contented with an inferior speaker, when surrounded by eloquent men, and I looked every moment for manifestations of disapprobation, as I felt certain that the English delegation had made a mistake in applauding this gentleman, who seemed to make such an unpromising beginning. But the speaker soon began to get warm on the subject, and even at times appeared as if he had spoken before. In a very short time, with the exception of his own voice, the stillness of death prevailed throughout the building, and the speaker delivered one of the most logical speeches made in the Congress, and, despite of his thin, sallow look, interested me much more than any whom I had before heard. Towards the close of his remarks, he was several times interrupted by manifestations of approbation; and finally concluded amid great cheering. I inquired the gentleman's name, and was informed that it was Edward Miall, editor of the *Nonconformist.*

After speeches from several others, the great Peace Congress of 1849, which had brought men together from nearly all the governments of Europe, and many from America, was brought to a final close by a speech from the president, returning thanks for the honor that had been conferred upon him. He said: "My address shall be short, and yet I have to bid you adieu! How resolve to do so? Here, during three days, have questions of the deepest import been discussed, examined, probed to the bottom; and during these discussions counsels have been given to governments which they will do well to profit by. If these days' sittings are attended with no other result, they will be the means of sowing in the minds of those present germs of cordiality which must ripen into good fruit. England, France, Belgium, Europe and America, would all be drawn closer by these sittings. Yet the moment to part has arrived, but I can feel that we are strongly united in heart. But, before parting, I may congratulate you and myself on the result of our proceedings. We have been all joined together without distinction of country; we have all been united in one common feeling during our three days' communion. The good work cannot go back; it must advance, it must be accomplished. The course of the future may be judged of by the sound of the footsteps of the past. In the course of that day's discussion, a reminiscence had been handed up to one of the speakers, that this was the anniversary of the dreadful massacre of St. Bartholomew: the reverend gentleman who was speaking turned away from the thought of that sanguinary scene with pious horror, natural to his sacred calling. But I, who may boast of firmer nerve, I take up the remembrance. Yes, it was on this day, two hundred and seventy-seven years ago, that Paris was roused from slumber by the sound of that bell which bore the name of *cloche d'argent.* Massacre was on foot, seeking with keen eye for its victim;

man was busy in slaying man. That slaughter was called forth by mingled passions of the worst description. Hatred of all kinds was there urging on the slayer,—hatred of a religious, a political, a personal character. And yet on the anniversary of that same day of horror, and in that very city whose blood was flowing like water, has God this day given a rendezvous to men of peace, whose wild tumult is transformed into order, and animosity into love. The stain of blood is blotted out, and in its place beams forth a ray of holy light. All distinctions are removed, and Papist and Huguenot meet together in friendly communion. (Loud cheers.) Who that thinks of these amazing changes can doubt of the progress that has been made? But whoever denies the force of progress must deny God, since progress is the boon of Providence, and emanated from the great Being above. I feel gratified for the change that has been effected, and, pointing solemnly to the past, I say let this day be ever held memorable; let the twenty-fourth of August, 1572, be remembered only for the purpose of being compared with the twenty-fourth of August, 1849; and when we think of the latter, and ponder over the high purpose to which it has been devoted,—the advocacy of the principles of peace,—let us not be so wanting in reliance on Providence as to doubt for one moment of the eventual success of our holy cause."

The most enthusiastic cheers followed this interesting speech. A vote of thanks to the government, and three times three cheers, with Mr. Cobden as "fugleman," ended the great Peace Congress of 1849.

Time for separating had arrived, yet all seemed unwilling to leave the place, where, for three days, men of all creeds and of no creed had met upon one common platform. In one sense the meeting was a glorious one, in another it was mere child's play; for the Congress had been restricted to the discussion of certain topics. They were permitted to dwell on the blessings of peace, but were not allowed to say anything about the very subjects above all others that should have been brought before the Congress. A French army had invaded Rome and put down the friends of political and religious freedom, yet not a word was said in reference to it. The fact is, the committee permitted the Congress to be *gagged* before it had met. They put padlocks upon their own mouths, and handed the keys to the government. And this was sorely felt by many of the speakers. Richard Cobden, who had thundered his anathemas against the corn-laws of his own country, and against wars in every clime, had to sit quiet in his fetters. Henry Vincent, who can make a louder speech in favor of peace than almost any other man, and whose denunciations of "all war," have gained him no little celebrity with peace men, had to confine himself to the blessings of peace. O, how I wished for a Massachusetts atmosphere, a New England convention platform, with Wendell Phillips as the speaker, before that assembled multitude from all parts of the world!

But the Congress is over, and cannot now be made different; yet it is to be hoped that neither the London Peace Committee, nor any other men having the charge of getting up such another great meeting, will commit such an error again.

CHAPTER V.

> "Man, on the dubious waves of error tossed,
> His ship half foundered, and his compass lost,
> Sees, far as human optics may command,
> A sleeping fog, and fancies it dry land."
>
> COWPER.

THE day after the close of the Congress, the delegates and their friends were invited to a soirée by M. de Tocqueville, Minister for Foreign Affairs, to take place on the next evening (Saturday); and, as my colored face and curly hair did not prevent my getting an invitation, I was present with the rest of my peace brethren.

Had I been in America, where color is considered a crime, I would not have been seen at such a gathering, unless as a servant. In company with several delegates, we left the Bedford Hotel for the mansion of the Minister of Foreign Affairs; and, on arriving, we found a file of soldiers drawn up before the gate. This did not seem much like peace: however, it was merely done in honor of the company. We entered the building through massive doors, and resigned ourselves into the hands of good-looking waiters in white wigs; and, after our names were duly announced, were passed from room to room, till I was presented to Madame de Tocqueville, who was standing near the centre of the large drawing-room, with a bouquet in her hand. I was about passing on, when the gentleman who introduced me intimated that I was an "American slave." At the announcement of this fact, the distinguished lady extended her hand and gave me a cordial welcome, at the same time saying, "I hope you feel yourself free in Paris." Having accepted an invitation to a seat by the lady's side, who seated herself on a sofa, I was soon what I most dislike, "the observed of all observers." I recognized, among many of my own countrymen who were gazing at me, the American Consul, Mr. Walsh. My position did not improve his looks. The company present on this occasion were variously estimated at from one thousand to fifteen hundred. Among these were the ambassadors from the different countries represented at the French metropolis, and many of the *élite* of Paris. One could not but be interested with the difference in dress, looks and manners, of this assemblage of strangers, whose language was as different as their general appearance. Delight seemed to beam in every countenance, as the living stream floated from one room to another. The house and gardens were illuminated in the most gorgeous manner. Red, yellow, blue, green, and many other colored lamps, suspended from the branches of the trees in the gardens, gave life and animation to the whole scene out of doors. The soirée passed off satisfactorily to all parties; and by twelve o'clock I was again at my hotel.

Through the politeness of the government the members of the Congress have not only had the pleasure of seeing all the public works free, and without special ticket, but the palaces of Versailles and St. Cloud, together with their splendid grounds, have been thrown open, and the water-works set to playing in both places. This mark of respect for the peace movement is commendable in the French; and were I not such a strenuous friend of free speech, this act would cause me to overlook the padlocks that the government put upon our lips in the Congress.

Two long trains left Paris at nine o'clock for Versailles; and at each of the stations the company were loudly cheered by the people who had assembled to see them pass. At Versailles we found thousands at the station, who gave us a most enthusiastic welcome. We were blessed with a goodly number of the fair sex, who always give life and vigor to such scenes. The train had scarcely stopped, ere the great throng were wending their ways in different directions,—some to the cafés to get what an early start prevented their getting before leaving Paris, and others to see the soldiers who were on review. But most bent their steps towards the great palace.

At eleven o'clock we were summoned to the *déjeuner* which had been prepared by the English delegates in honor of their American friends. About six hundred sat down at the tables. Breakfast being ended, Mr. Cobden was called to the chair, and several speeches were made. Many who had not an opportunity to speak at the Congress thought this a good chance; and the written addresses which had been studied during the passage from America, with the hope that they would immortalize their authors before the Congress, were produced at the breakfast-table. But speech-making was not the order of the day. Too many thundering addresses had been delivered in the Salle de St. Cecile to allow the company to sit and hear dryly written and worse delivered speeches in the Teniscourt.

There was no limited time given to the speakers, yet no one had been on his feet five minutes before the cry was heard from all parts of the house, "Time, time!" One American was hissed down; another took his seat with a red face; and a third opened his bundle of paper, looked around at the audience, made a bow, and took his seat amid great applause. Yet some speeches were made, and to good effect; the best of which was by Elihu Burritt, who was followed by the Rev. James Freeman Clarke. I regretted very much that the latter did not deliver his address before the Congress, for he is a man of no inconsiderable talent, and an acknowledged friend of the slave.

The cry of "The water-works are playing!" "The water is on!" broke up the meeting, without even a vote of thanks to the chairman; and the whole party were soon revelling among the fountains and statues of Louis XIV. Description would fail to give a just idea of the grandeur and beauty of this splendid place. I do not think that anything can surpass the fountain of Neptune, which stands near the Grand Trianon. One may easily get lost in wandering through the grounds of Versailles, but he will always be in sight of some lifelike statue. These monuments, erected to gratify the fancy of a licentious king, make their appearance at every turn. Two lions, the one overturning a wild boar, the other a wolf, both the production of Fillen, pointed out to us the fountain of Diana. But I will not attempt to describe to you any of the very beautiful sculptured gods and goddesses here.

With a single friend I paid a visit to the two Trianons. The larger was, we were told, just as King Louis Philippe left it. One room was splendidly fitted up for the reception of Her Majesty Queen Victoria, who, it appeared, had promised a visit to the French court; but the French monarch ran away from his throne before the time arrived. The Grand Trianon is not larger than many noblemen's seats that may be seen in a day's ride through any part of the British empire. The building has only a ground floor, but its proportions are very elegant.

We next paid our respects to the Little Trianon. This appears to be the most republican of any of the French palaces. I inspected this little palace with much interest, not more for its beauty than because of its having been the favorite residence of that purest of princesses, and most affectionate of mothers, Marie Antoinette. The grounds and building may be said to be only a palace in miniature, and this makes it a still more lovely spot. The building consists of a square pavilion two stories high, and separated entirely from the accessory buildings, which are on the left, and among them a pretty chapel. But a wish to be with the multitude, who were roving among the fountains, cut short my visit to the Trianons.

The day was very fine, and the whole party seemed to enjoy it. It was said that there were more than one hundred thousand persons at Versailles during the day. The company appeared to lose themselves with the pleasure of walking among the trees, flower-beds, fountains, and statues. I met more than one wife seeking a lost husband, and *vice versa*. Many persons were separated from their friends, and did not meet them again till at the hotels in Paris. In the train returning to Paris, an old gentleman who was seated near me said, "I would rest contented if I thought I should ever see my wife again!"

At four o'clock we were *en route* to St. Cloud, the much-loved and favorite residence of the Emperor Napoleon. It seemed that all Paris had come out to St. Cloud to see how the English and Americans would enjoy the playing of the water-works. Many kings and rulers of the French have made St. Cloud their residence, but none have impressed their image so indelibly upon it as Napoleon. It was here he was first elevated to power, and here Josephine spent her most happy hours.

The apartments where Napoleon was married to Marie Louise, the private rooms of Josephine and Marie Antoinette, were all in turn shown to us. While standing on the balcony looking at Paris one cannot wonder that the emperor should have selected this place as his residence, for a more lovely spot cannot be found than St. Cloud.

The palace is on the side of a hill, two leagues from Paris, and so situated that it looks down upon the French capital. Standing, as we did, viewing Paris from St. Cloud, and the setting sun reflecting upon the domes, spires, and towers of the city of fashion, made us feel that this was the place from which the monarch should watch his subjects. From the hour of arrival at St. Cloud till near eight o'clock, we were either inspecting the splendid palace, or roaming the grounds and gardens, whose beautiful walks and sweet flowers made it appear a very paradise on earth.

At eight o'clock the water-works were put in motion, and the variegated lamps, with their many devices, displaying flowers, stars and wheels, all with a brilliancy that can scarcely be described, seemed to throw everything in the shade we had seen at Versailles. At nine o'clock the train was announced, and after a good deal of jamming and pushing about, we were again on the way to Paris.

CHAPTER VI.

"Types of a race who shall the invader scorn,
As rocks resist the billows round their shore;
Types of a race who shall to time unborn
Their country leave unconquered as of yore."

CAMPBELL.

I STARTED at an early hour for the palace of the Tuileries. A show of my card of membership of the Congress (which had carried me through so many of the public buildings) was enough to gain me immediate admission. The attack of the mob on the palace, on the 20th of June, 1792; the massacre of the Swiss guard, on the 10th of August of the same year; the attack by the people, in July, 1830, together with the recent flight of King Louis Philippe and family, made me anxious to visit the old pile.

We were taken from room to room, until the entire building had been inspected. In front of the Tuileries are a most magnificent garden and grounds. These were all laid out by Louis XIV., and are left nearly as they were during that monarch's reign. Above fifty acres, surrounded by an iron rail-fence, fronts the Place de la Concorde, and affords a place of promenade for the Parisians. I walked the grounds, and saw hundreds of well-dressed persons under the shade of the great chestnuts, or sitting on chairs, which were kept to let at two sous a piece. Near by is the Place de Carrousel, noted for its historical remembrances. Many incidents connected with the several revolutions occurred here, and it is pointed out as the place where Napoleon reviewed that formidable army of his, before its departure for Russia.

From the Tuileries I took a stroll through the Place de la Concorde, which has connected with it so many acts of cruelty, that it made me shudder as I passed over its grounds. As if to take from one's mind the old associations of this place, the French have erected on it, or rather given a place to, the celebrated obelisk of Luxor, which now is the chief attraction on the grounds. The obelisk was brought from Egypt at an enormous expense, for which purpose a ship was built, and several hundred men employed above three years in its removal. It is formed of the finest red syenite, and covered on each side with three lines of hieroglyphic inscriptions, commemorative of Sesostris,—the middle lines being the most deeply cut and most carefully finished; and the characters altogether number more than sixteen hundred. The obelisk is of a single stone, is seventy-two feet in height, weighs five hundred thousand pounds, and stands on a block of granite that weighs two hundred and fifty thousand pounds. He who can read Latin will see that the monument tells its own story, but to me its characters were all blank.

It would be tedious to follow the history of this old and venerated stone, which was taken from the quarry fifteen hundred and fifty years before the birth of Christ, placed in Thebes, its removal, the journey to the Nile, and down the Nile, thence to Cherbourg, and lastly its arrival in Paris on the 23d of December, 1833,—just one year before I escaped from slavery. The obelisk was raised on the spot where it now stands, on the 25th of October, 1836, in the presence of Louis Philippe, and amid the greetings of one hundred and sixty thousand persons.

Having missed my dinner, I crossed over to the Palais Royal, to a dining saloon, and can assure you that a better dinner may be had there for three francs than can be got in New York for twice that sum,—especially if the person who wants the dinner is a colored man. I found no prejudice against my complexion in the Palais Royal.

Many of the rooms in this once abode of royalty are most splendidly furnished, and decorated with valuable pictures. The likenesses of Madame de Stael, J. J. Rousseau, Cromwell and Francis I., are among them.

After several unsuccessful attempts to-day, in company with R. D. Webb, Esq., to seek out the house where once resided the notorious Robespierre, I was fortunate enough to find it, but not until I had lost the company of my friend. The house is No. 396, Rue St. Honore, opposite the Church of the Assumption. It stands back, and is reached by entering a court. During the first revolution it was occupied by M. Duplay, with whom Robespierre lodged. The room used by the great man of the revolution was pointed out to me. It is small, and the ceiling low, with two windows looking out upon the court. The pin upon which the blue coat once hung is still in the wall.

While standing there, I could almost imagine that I saw the great "Incorruptible," sitting at the small table, composing those speeches which gave him so much power and influence in the convention and the clubs.

Here the disciple of Rousseau sat and planned how he should outdo his enemies and hold on to his friends. From this room he went forth, followed by his dog Brunt, to take his solitary walk in a favorite and neighboring field, or to the fiery discussions of the National Convention. In the same street is the house in which Madame Roland—one of Robespierre's victims—resided.

A view of the residence of one of the master-spirits of the French Revolution inclined me to search out more; and, therefore, I proceeded to the old town, and after winding through several small streets—some of them so narrow as not to admit more than one cab at a time—I found myself in the Rue de L'Ecole de Medecine, and standing in front of house No. 20. This was the residence, during the early days of the revolution, of that blood-thirsty demon in human form, Marat.

As this was private property, my blue card of membership to the Congress was not available. But after slipping a franc into the old lady's hand, I was informed that I could be admitted. We entered a court and ascended a flight of stairs, the entrance to which is on the right; then, crossing to the left, we were shown into a moderate-sized room on the first floor, with two windows looking out upon a yard. Here it was where the "Friend of the People" (as he styled himself) sat and wrote those articles that appeared daily in his journal, urging the people to "hang the rich upon lampposts." The place where the bath stood, in which he was bathing at the time he was killed by Charlotte Corday, was pointed to us; and even something representing an old stain of blood was shown as the place where he was laid when taken out of the bath. The window, behind whose curtains the heroine hid, after she had plunged the dagger into the heart of the man whom she thought was the cause of the shedding of so much blood by the guillotine, was pointed out with a seeming degree of pride by the old woman.

With my Guide Book in hand, I again went forth to "hunt after new fancies."

After walking over the ground where the guillotine once stood, cutting off its hundred and fifty heads per day, and then visiting the place where some of the chief movers in that sanguinary revolution once lived, I felt little disposed to sleep, when the time for it had arrived. However, I was out the next morning at an early hour, and on the Champs Elysees; and again took a walk over the place where the guillotine stood when its fatal blade was sending so many unprepared spirits into eternity. When standing here, you have the palace of the Tuileries on one side, the arch on the other, on a third the classic Madeleine, and on the fourth the National Assembly. It caused my blood to chill, the idea of being on the identical spot where the heads of Louis XVI. and his queen, after being cut off, were held up to satisfy the blood-thirsty curiosity of the two hundred thousand persons that were assembled on the Place de la Revolution. Here royal blood flowed as it never did before or since. The heads of patricians and plebeians were thrown into the same basket, without any regard to birth or station. Here Robespierre and Danton had stood again and again, and looked their victims in the face as they ascended the scaffold; and here these same men had to mount the very scaffold that they had erected for others. I wandered up the Seine, till I found myself looking at the statue of Henry IV., over the principal entrance of the Hotel de Ville. When we take into account the connection of the Hotel de Ville with the different revolutions, we must come to the conclusion that it is one of the most remarkable buildings in Paris. The room was pointed out where Robespierre held his counsels, and from the windows of which he could look out upon the Place de Greve, where the guillotine stood before its removal to the Place de la Concorde. The room is large, with gilded hangings, splendid old-fashioned chandeliers, and a chimney-piece with fine, antiquated carvings, that give it a venerable appearance. Here Robespierre not only presided at the counsels that sent hundreds to the guillotine, but from this same spot he, with his brother, St. Just and others, were dragged before the Committee of Public Safety, and thence to the guillotine, and justice and revenge satisfied.

The window from which Lafayette addressed the people in 1830, and presented to them Louis Philippe as the king, was shown to us. Here the poet, statesman, philosopher and orator, Lamartine, stood in February, 1848, and, by the power of his eloquence, succeeded in keeping the people quiet. Here he forced the mob, braved the bayonets presented to his breast, and, by his good reasoning, induced them to retain the tri-colored flag, instead of adopting the red flag, which he considered the emblem of blood.

Lamartine is a great heroic genius, dear to liberty and to France; and successive generations, as they look back upon the revolution of 1848, will recall to memory the many dangers which nothing but his dauntless courage warded off. The difficulties which his wisdom surmounted, and the good service that he rendered to France, can never be adequately estimated, or too highly appreciated. It was at the Hotel de Ville that the republic of 1848 was proclaimed to the people.

I next paid my respects to the Column of July, that stands on the spot formerly occupied by the Bastile. It is one hundred and sixty-three feet in height, and on the top is the Genius of Liberty, with a torch in his right hand, and in the left a broken chain. After a fatiguing walk up a winding stair, I obtained a splendid view of Paris from the top of the column.

I thought I should not lose the opportunity of seeing the Church de Notre Dame while so near to it, and, therefore, made it my next rallying-point. No edifice connected with religion has had more interesting incidents occurring in it than this old church. Here Pope Pius VII. placed the imperial crown on the head of the Corsican,—or, rather, Napoleon took the crown from his hands, and placed it on his own head. Satan dragging the wicked to ——, the rider on the red horse at the opening of the second seal, the blessedness of the saints, and several other striking sculptured figures, were among the many curiosities in this splendid place. A hasty view from the gallery concluded my visit to the Notre Dame.

Leaving the old church, I strayed off in a direction towards the Seine, and passed by an old-looking building of stately appearance, and recognized, among a throng passing in and out, a number of the members of the Peace Congress. I joined a party entering, and was soon in the presence of men with gowns on, and men with long staffs in their hands, and, on inquiry, found that I was in the Palais de Justice, beneath which is the Conciergerie, a noted prison. Louis XVI. and Marie Antoinette were tried and condemned to death here.

A bas-relief, by Cortat, representing Louis in conference with his Council, is here seen. But I had visited too many places of interest during the day to remain long in a building surrounded by officers of justice, and took a stroll upon the Boulevards.

The Boulevards may be termed the Regent-street of Paris, or a New Yorker would call it Broadway. While passing a café, my German friend Faigo, whose company I had enjoyed during the passage from America, recognized me, and I sat down and took a cup of delicious coffee for the first time on the side-walk, in sight of hundreds who were passing up and down the street every hour. From three till eleven o'clock, P. M., the Boulevards are lined with men and women sitting before the doors of the saloons, drinking their coffee or wines, or both at the same time, as fancy may dictate. All Paris appeared to be on the Boulevards, and looking as if the great end of this life was enjoyment.

Anxious to see as much as possible of Paris in the limited time I had to stay in it, I hired a cab on the following morning, and commenced with the Hotel des Invalides, a magnificent building, within a few minutes' walk of the National Assembly. On each side of the entrance-gate are figures representing nations conquered by Louis XIV., with colossal statues of Mars and Minerva. The dome on the edifice is the loftiest in Paris, the height from the ground being three hundred and twenty-three feet.

Immediately below the dome is the tomb of the man at whose word the world turned pale. A statue of the Emperor Napoleon stands in the second piazza, and is of the finest bronze.

This building is the home of the pensioned soldiers of France. It was enough to make one sick at the idea of war, to look upon the mangled bodies of these old soldiers. Men with arms and no legs; others had legs but no arms; some with canes and crutches, and some wheeling themselves about in little hand-carts. About three thousand of the decayed soldiers were lodged in the Hotel des Invalides, at the time of my visit. Passing the National Assembly on my return, I spent a moment or two in it. The interior of this building resembles an amphitheatre. It is constructed to accommodate nine hundred members, each having a separate desk. The seat upon which the Duchess of Orleans and her son, the Comte de Paris, sat, when they visited the National Assembly after the flight of Louis Philippe, was shown with considerable alacrity. As I left the building, I heard that the president of the republic was on the point of leaving the Elysee for St. Cloud, and, with the hope of seeing the "prisoner of Ham," I directed my cabman to drive me to the Elysee.

In a few moments we were between two files of soldiers, and entering the gates of the palace. I called out to the driver, and told him to stop; but I was too late, for we were now in front of the massive doors of the palace, and a liveried servant opened the cab door, bowed, and asked if I had an engagement with the president. You may easily "guess" his surprise when I told him no. In my best French I asked the cabman why he had come to the palace, and was answered, "You told me to." By this time a number had gathered round, all making inquiries as to what I wanted. I told the driver to retrace his steps, and, amid the shrugs of their shoulders, the nods of their heads, and the laughter of the soldiers, I left the Elysee without even a sight of the president's moustache for my trouble. This was only one of the many mistakes I made while in Paris.

CHAPTER VII.

"The moon on the east oriel shone
Through slender shafts of shapely stone,
By foliaged tracery combined.
Thou wouldst have thought some fairy's hand
'Twixt poplars straight the osier wand
In many a freakish knot had twined:
Then framed a spell, when the work was done,
And changed the willow wreaths to stone."

SIR WALTER SCOTT.

HERE I am, within ten leagues of Paris, spending the time pleasantly in viewing the palace and grounds of the great chateau of Louis XIV. Fifty-seven years ago, a mob, composed of men, women and boys, from Paris, stood in front of this palace, and demanded that the king should go with them to the capital. I have walked over the same ground where the one hundred thousand stood on that interesting occasion. I have been upon the same balcony, and stood by the window from which Marie Antoinette looked out upon the mob that were seeking her life.

Anxious to see as much of the palace as I could, and having an offer of the company of my young friend, Henry G. Chapman, to go through the palace with me, I set out early this morning, and was soon in the halls that had often been trod by royal feet. We passed through the private as well as the public apartments; through the secret door by which Marie Antoinette had escaped from the mob of 1792; and viewed the room in which her faithful guards were killed, while attempting to save their royal mistress. I took my seat in one of the little parlor carriages that had been used in days of yore for the royal children, while my friend H. G. Chapman drew me across the room. The superb apartments are not now in use. Silence is written upon these walls, although upon them are suspended the portraits of men of whom the world has heard.

Paintings representing Napoleon in nearly all his battles are here seen; and, wherever you see the emperor, there you will also find Murat, with his white plume waving above. Callot's painting of the battle of Marengo, Hue's of the retaking of Genoa, and Bouchat's of the 18th Brumaire, are of the highest order; while David has transmitted his fame to posterity by his splendid painting of the coronation of Napoleon and Josephine in Notre Dame. When I looked upon the many beautiful paintings of the last-named artist that adorn the halls of Versailles, I did not wonder that his fame should have saved his life when once condemned and sentenced to death during the reign of terror. The guillotine was robbed of its intended victim; but the world gained a great painter. As Boswell transmitted his own name to posterity with his life of Johnson, so has David left his with the magnificent paintings that are now suspended upon the walls of the palaces of the Louvre, the Tuileries, St. Cloud, Versailles, and even the little Elysee.

After strolling from room to room, we found ourselves in the Salle du Sacre, Diane, Salon de Mars, de Mercure, and D'Apollon. I gazed with my eyes turned to the ceiling till I was dizzy. The Salon de la Guerre is covered with the most beautiful representations that the mind of man could conceive, or the hand accomplish. Louis XIV. is here in all his glory. No Marie Antoinette will ever do the honors in these halls again.

After spending a whole day in the palace, and several mornings in the gardens, I finally bade adieu to the bronze statue of Louis XIV. that stands in front of the palace, and left Versailles, probably forever.

I am now on the point of quitting the French metropolis. I have occupied the last two days in visiting places of note in the city. I could not resist the inclination to pay a second visit to the Louvre. Another hour was spent in strolling through the Italian Hall, and viewing the master workmanship of Raphael, the prince of painters. Time flies, even in such a place as the Louvre, with all its attractions; and, before I had seen half that I wished, a ponderous clock near by reminded me of an engagement, and I reluctantly tore myself from the splendors of the place.

During the rest of the day I visited the Jardin des Plantes, and spent an hour and a half pleasantly in walking among plants, flowers, and, in fact, everything that could be found in any garden in France. From this place we paid our respects to the Bourse, or Exchange, one of the most superb buildings in the city. The ground floor and sides of the Bourse are of fine marble, and the names of the chief cities in the world are inscribed on the medallions which are under the upper cornice. The interior of the edifice has a most splendid appearance as you enter it.

The cemetery of Père la Chaise was too much talked of by many of our party at the hotel for me to pass it by; so I took it, after the Bourse. Here lie many of the great marshals of France, the resting-place of each marked by the monument that stands over it, except one, which is marked only by a weeping willow and a plain stone at its head. This is the grave of Marshal Ney. I should not have known that it was his, but some unknown hand had written, with black paint, "Bravest of the Brave," on the unlettered stone that stands at the head of the man who followed Napoleon through nearly all his battles, and who was shot, after the occupation of Paris by the allied army. Peace to his ashes! During my ramble through this noted place, I saw several who were hanging fresh wreaths of "everlasting flowers" on the tombs of the departed.

A ride in an omnibus down the Boulevards, and away up the Champs Elysees, brought me to the Arc de Triomphe; and, after ascending a flight of one hundred and sixty-one steps, I was overlooking the city of statuary. This stupendous monument was commenced by Napoleon in 1806; and in 1811 it had only reached the cornice of the base, where it stopped, and it was left for Louis Philippe to finish. The first stone of this monument was laid on the 15th of August, 1806, the birth-day of the man whose battles it was intended to commemorate. A model of the arch was erected for Napoleon to pass through as he was entering the city with Maria Louisa, after their marriage. The inscriptions on the monument are many, and the different scenes here represented are all of the most exquisite workmanship. The genius of War is summoning the obedient nations to battle. Victory is here crowning Napoleon after his great success in 1810. Fame stands here recording the exploits of the warrior, while conquered cities lie beneath the whole. But it would take more time than I have at command to give anything like a description of this magnificent piece of architecture.

That which seems to take most with Peace Friends is the portion representing an old man taming a bull for agricultural labor; while a young warrior is sheathing his sword, a mother and children sitting at his feet, and Minerva, crowned with laurels, stands shedding her protecting influence over them. The erection of this regal monument is wonderful, to hand down to posterity the triumphs of the man whom we first hear of as a student in the military school at Brienne; whom in 1784 we see in the Ecole Militaire, founded by Louis XV. in 1751; whom again we find at No. 5 Quai de Court, near Rue de Mail; and in 1794 as a lodger at No. 19 Rue de la Michandère. From this he goes to the Hotel Mirabeau, Rue du Dauphin, where he resided when he defeated his enemies on the 13th Vendemaire. The Hotel de la Colonade, Rue Neuve des Capuchins, is his next residence, and where he was married to Josephine. From this hotel he removed to his wife's dwelling in the Rue Chanteriene, No. 52. In 1796 the young general started for Italy, where his conquests paved the way for the ever-memorable 18th Brumaire, that made him Dictator of France. Napoleon was too great now to be satisfied with private dwellings, and we next trace him to the Elysee, St. Cloud, Versailles, the Tuileries, Fontainebleau, and, finally, came his decline, which I need not relate to you.

After visiting the Gobelins, passing through its many rooms, seeing here and there a half-finished piece of tapestry, and meeting a number of the members of the late Peace Congress, who, like myself, had remained behind to see more of the beauties of the French capital than could be seen during the Convention week, I accepted an invitation to dine with a German gentleman at the Palais Royal, and was soon revelling amid the luxuries of the table. I was glad that I had gone to the Palais Royal, for here I had the honor of an introduction to M. Beranger, the poet; and, although I had to converse with him through an interpreter, I enjoyed his company very much. "The people's poet," as he is called, is apparently about seventy years of age, bald on the top of the head, and rather corpulent, but of active look, and in the enjoyment of good health. Few writers in France have done better service to the cause of political and religious freedom than Pierre Jean de Beranger. He is the dauntless friend and advocate of the down-trodden poor and oppressed, and has often incurred the displeasure of the government by the arrows that he has thrown into their camp. He felt what he wrote; it came straight from his heart, and went directly to the hearts of the people. He expressed himself strongly opposed to slavery, and said, "I don't see how the Americans can reconcile slavery with their professed love of freedom." Dinner out of the way, a walk through the different apartments, and a stroll over the court, and I bade adieu to the Palais Royal, satisfied that I should partake of many worse dinners than I had helped to devour that day.

Few nations are more courteous than the French. Here, the stranger, let him come from what country he may, and be ever so unacquainted with the people and language, is sure of a civil reply to any question that he may ask. With the exception of the egregious blunder I have mentioned of the cabman driving me to the Elysee, I was not laughed at once while in France.

CHAPTER VIII.

> "There was not, on that day, a speck to stain
> The azure heavens; the blessed sun alone,
> In unapproachable divinity,
> Careered rejoicing in the field of light."
>
> SOUTHEY.

THE sun had just appeared from behind a cloud and was setting, and its reflection upon the domes and spires of the great buildings in Paris made everything appear lovely and sublime, as the train, with almost lightning speed, was bringing me from the French metropolis. I gazed with eager eyes to catch a farewell glance of the tops of the regal palaces through which I had passed during a stay of fifteen days in the French capital.

A pleasant ride of four hours brought us to Boulogne, where we rested for the night. The next morning I was up at an early hour, and out viewing the town. Boulogne could present but little attraction after a fortnight spent in seeing the lions of Paris. A return to the hotel, and breakfast over, we stepped on board the steamer, and were soon crossing the channel. Two hours more, and I was safely seated in a railway carriage, *en route* to the English metropolis. We reached London at midday, where I was soon comfortably lodged at 22 Cecil-street, Strand. As it was three o'clock, I lost no time in seeking out a dining saloon, which I had no difficulty in finding in the Strand. It being the first house of the kind I had entered in London, I was not a little annoyed at the politeness of the waiter. The first salutation I had, after seating myself in one of the stalls, was, "Ox tail, sir; gravy soup; carrot soup, sir; roast beef; roast pork; boiled beef; roast lamb; boiled leg of mutton, sir, with caper sauce; jugged hare, sir; boiled knuckle of veal and bacon; roast turkey and oyster sauce; sucking pig, sir; curried chicken; harrico mutton, sir." These, and many other dishes, which I have forgotten, were called over with a rapidity that would have done credit to one of our Yankee pedlers in crying his wares in a New England village. I was so completely taken by surprise, that I asked for a "bill of fare," and told him to leave me. No city in the world furnishes a cheaper, better, and quicker meal for the weary traveller, than a London eating-house.

* * *

A few days after my arrival in London, I received an invitation from John Lee, Esq., LL.D., whom I had met at the Peace Congress in Paris, to pay him a visit at his seat, near Aylesbury; and as the time was "fixed" by the doctor, I took the train on the appointed day, on my way to Hartwell House.

I had heard much of the aristocracy of England, and must confess that I was not a little prejudiced against them. On a bright sunshiny day, between the hours of twelve and two, I found myself seated in a carriage, my back turned upon Aylesbury, the vehicle whirling rapidly over the smooth macadamised road, and I on my first visit to an English gentleman. Twenty minutes' ride, and a turn to the right, and we were amid the fine old trees of Hartwell Park; one having suspended from its branches the national banners of several different countries, among them the "Stars and Stripes." I felt glad that my own country's flag had a place there, although Campbell's lines—

"United States, your banner wears
  Two emblems,—one of fame;
Alas! the other that it bears
  Reminds us of your shame!
The white man's liberty in types
  Stands blazoned by your stars;
But what's the meaning of your stripes?—
  They mean your Negro-scars"—

were at the time continually running through my mind. Arrived at the door, and we received what every one does who visits Dr. Lee—a hearty welcome. I was immediately shown into a room with a lofty ceiling, hung round with fine specimens of the Italian masters, and told that this was my apartment. Hartwell House stands in an extensive park, shaded with trees that made me think of the oaks and elms in an American forest, and many of whose limbs had been trimmed and nursed with the best of care. This was for several years the residence of John Hampden the patriot, and more recently that of Louis XVIII., during his exile in this country. The house is built on a very extensive scale, and is ornamented in the interior with carvings in wood of many of the kings and princes of bygone centuries. A room some sixty feet by twenty-five contains a variety of articles that the doctor has collected together—the whole forming a museum that would be considered a sight in the Western States of America.

The morning after my arrival at Hartwell I was up at an early hour—in fact, before any of the servants—wandering about through the vast halls, and trying to find my way out; in which I eventually succeeded, but not, however, without aid. It had rained the previous night, and the sun was peeping through a misty cloud as I strolled through the park, listening to the sweet voices of the birds that were fluttering in the tops of the trees, and trimming their wings for a morning flight. The silence of the night had not yet been broken by the voice of man; and I wandered about the vast park unannoyed, except by the dew from the grass that wet my slippers. Not far from the house I came abruptly upon a beautiful little pond of water, where the gold-fish were flouncing about, and the gentle ripples glittering in the sunshine looked like so many silver minnows playing on the surface.

While strolling about with pleasure, and only regretting that my dear daughters were not with me to enjoy the morning's walk, I saw the gardener on his way to the garden. I followed him, and was soon feasting my eyes upon the richest specimens of garden scenery. There were the peaches hanging upon the trees that were fastened to the wall; vegetables, fruit and flowers, were there in all their bloom and beauty; and even the variegated geranium of a warmer clime was there in its hot-house home, and seemed to have forgotten that it was in a different country from its own. Dr. Lee shows great taste in the management of his garden. I have seldom seen a more splendid variety of fruits and flowers in the Southern States of America than I saw at Hartwell House.

I should, however, state that I was not the only guest at Hartwell during my stay. Dr. Lee had invited several others of the American delegation to the Peace Congress, and two or three of the French delegates, who were on a visit to England, were enjoying the doctor's hospitality. Dr. Lee is a stanch friend of Temperance, as well as of the cause of universal freedom. Every year he treats his tenantry to a dinner, and I need not add that these are always conducted on the principle of total abstinence.

During the second day we visited several of the cottages of the work-people, and in these I took no little interest. The people of the United States know nothing of the real condition of the laboring classes of England. The peasants of Great Britain are always spoken of as belonging to the soil. I was taught in America that the English laborer was no better off than the slave upon a Carolina rice-field. I had seen the slaves in Missouri huddled together, three, four, and even five families in a single room, not more than fifteen by twenty-five feet square, and I expected to see the same in England. But in this I was disappointed. After visiting a new house that the doctor was building, he took us into one of the cottages that stood near the road, and gave us an opportunity of seeing, for the first time, an English peasant's cot. We entered a low, whitewashed room, with a stone floor that showed an admirable degree of cleanness. Before us was a row of shelves filled with earthen dishes and pewter spoons, glittering if they had just come from under the hand of a woman of taste. A "Cobden loaf" of bread, that had just been left by the baker's boy, lay upon an oaken table which had been much worn away with the scrubbing-brush; while just above lay the old family Bible, that had been handed down from father to son, until its possession was considered of almost as great value as its contents. A half-open door, leading into another room, showed us a clean bed; the whole presenting as fine a picture of neatness, order and comfort, as the most fastidious taste could wish to see. No occupant was present, and therefore I inspected everything with a greater degree of freedom. In front of the cottage was a small grass-plot, with here and there a bed of flowers, cheated out of its share of sunshine by the tall holly that had been planted near it. As I looked upon the home of the laborer, my thoughts were with my enslaved countrymen. What a difference, thought I, there is between the tillers of the soil in England and America! There could not be a more complete refutation of the assertion that the English laborer is no better off than the American slave, than the scenes that were then before me. I called the attention of one of my American friends to a beautiful rose near the door of the cot, and said to him, "The law that will protect that flower will also guard and protect the hand that planted it." He knew that I had drank deep of the cup of slavery, was aware of what I meant, and merely nodded his head in reply. I never experienced hospitality more genuine, and yet more unpretending, than was meted out to me while at Hartwell. And the favorable impression made on my own mind by the distinguished proprietor of Hartwell Park was nearly as indelible as my humble name that the doctor had engraven in a brick, in a vault beneath the Observatory in Hartwell House.

On my return to London I accepted an invitation to join a party on a visit to Windsor Castle; and, taking the train at the Waterloo Bridge Station, we were soon passing through a pleasant part of the country. Arrived at the castle, we committed ourselves into the hands of the servants, and were introduced into Her Majesty's State Apartments, Audience Chamber, Vandyck Room, Waterloo Chambers, Gold Pantry, and many others whose names I have forgotten. In wandering about the different apartments I lost my company, and in trying to find them passed through a room in which hung a magnificent portrait of Charles I., by Vandyck. The hum and noise of my companions had ceased, and I had the scene and silence to myself. I looked in vain for the king's evil genius (Cromwell), but he was not in the same room. The pencil of Sir Peter Lely has left a splendid full-length likeness of James II. George IV. is suspended from a peg in the wall, looking as if it was fresh from the hands of Sir Thomas Lawrence, its admirable painter. I was now in St. George's Hall, and I gazed upward to view the beautiful figures on the ceiling until my neck was nearly out of joint. Leaving this room, I inspected with interest the ancient *keep* of the castle. In past centuries this part of the palace was used as a prison. Here James the First of Scotland was detained a prisoner for eighteen years. I viewed the window through which the young prince had often looked to catch a glimpse of the young and beautiful Lady Jane, daughter of the Earl of Somerset, with whom he was enamored.

From the top of the Round Tower I had a fine view of the surrounding country. Stoke Park, once the residence of that great friend of humanity and civilization, William Penn, was among the scenes that I beheld with pleasure from Windsor Castle. Four years ago, when in the city of Philadelphia, and hunting up the places associated with the name of this distinguished man, and more recently when walking over the farm once occupied by him, examining the old malt-house which is now left standing, because of the veneration with which the name of the man who built it is held, I had no idea that I should ever see the dwelling which he had occupied in the Old World. Stoke Park is about four miles from Windsor, and is now owned by the Right Hon. Henry Labouchere.

The castle, standing as it does on an eminence, and surrounded by a beautiful valley covered with splendid villas, has a most magnificent appearance. It rears its massive towers and irregular walls over and above every other object. How full this old palace is of material for thought! How one could ramble here alone, or with one or two congenial companions, and enjoy a recapitulation of its history! But an engagement to be at Croydon in the evening cut short my stay at Windsor, and compelled me to return to town in advance of my party.

* * *

Having met with John Morland, Esq., at Paris, he gave me an invitation to visit Croydon, and deliver a lecture on American Slavery; and last evening, at eight o'clock, I found myself in a fine old building in the town, and facing the first English audience that I had seen in the sea-girt isle. It was my first welcome in England. The assembly was an enthusiastic one, and made still more so by the appearance of George Thompson, Esq., M. P., upon the platform. It is not my intention to give accounts of my lectures or meetings in these pages. I therefore merely say that I left Croydon with a good impression of the English, and Heath Lodge with a feeling that its occupant was one of the most benevolent of men.

The same party with whom I visited Windsor being supplied with a card of admission to the Bank of England, I accepted an invitation to be one of the company. We entered the vast building at a little past twelve o'clock. The sun threw into the large halls a brilliancy that seemed to light up the countenances of the almost countless number of clerks, who were at their desks, or serving persons at the counters. As nearly all my countrymen who visit London pay their respects to this noted institution, I shall sum up my visit to it by saying that it surpassed my highest idea of a bank. But a stroll through this monster building of gold and silver brought to my mind an incident with which I was connected a year after my escape from slavery.

In the autumn of 1835, having been cheated out of the previous summer's earnings by the captain of the steamer in which I had been employed running away with the money, I was, like the rest of the men, left without any means of support during the winter, and therefore had to seek employment in the neighboring towns. I went to the town of Monroe, in the State of Michigan, and while going through the principal street looking for work, I passed the door of the only barber in the town, whose shop appeared to be filled with persons waiting to be shaved. As there was but one man at work, and as I had, while employed in the steamer, occasionally shaved a gentleman who could not perform that office himself, it occurred to me that I might get employment here as a journeyman barber. I therefore made immediate application for work, but the barber told me he did not need a hand. But I was not to be put off so easily, and, after making several offers to work cheap, I frankly told him that if he would not employ me I would get a room near to him, and set up an opposition establishment. This threat, however, made no impression on the barber; and, as I was leaving, one of the men who were waiting to be shaved said, "If you want a room in which to commence business, I have one on the opposite side of the street." This man followed me out; we went over, and I looked at the room. He strongly urged me to set up, at the same time promising to give me his influence. I took the room, purchased an old table, two chairs, got a pole with a red stripe painted around it, and the next day opened, with a sign over the door, "Fashionable Hair-dresser from New York, Emperor of the West." I need not add that my enterprise was very annoying to the "shop over the way,"—especially my sign, which happened to be the most expensive part of the concern. Of course, I had to tell all who came in that my neighbor on the opposite side did not keep clean towels, that his razors were dull, and, above all, he had never been to New York to see the fashions. Neither had I. In a few weeks I had the entire business of the town, to the great discomfiture of the other barber.

At this time, money matters in the Western States were in a sad condition. Any person who could raise a small amount of money was permitted to establish a bank, and allowed to issue notes for four times the sum raised. This being the case, many persons borrowed money merely long enough to exhibit to the bank inspectors, and the borrowed money was returned, and the bank left without a dollar in its vaults, if, indeed, it had a vault about its premises. The result was, that banks were started all over the Western States, and the country flooded with worthless paper. These were known as the "Wild-cat Banks." Silver coin being very scarce, and the banks not being allowed to issue notes for a smaller amount than one dollar, several persons put out notes from six to seventy-five cents in value; these were called "Shinplasters." The Shinplaster was in the shape of a promissory note, made payable on demand. I have often seen persons with large rolls of these bills, the whole not amounting to more than five dollars. Some weeks after I had commenced business on my "own hook," I was one evening very much crowded with customers; and, while they were talking over the events of the day, one of them said to me, "Emperor, you seem to be doing a thriving business. You should do as other business men, issue your Shinplasters." This, of course, as it was intended, created a laugh; but with me it was no laughing matter, for from that moment I began to think seriously of becoming a banker. I accordingly went a few days after to a printer, and he, wishing to get the job of printing, urged me to put out my notes, and showed me some specimens of engravings that he had just received from Detroit. My head being already filled with the idea of a bank, I needed but little persuasion to set the thing finally afloat. Before I left the printer the notes were partly in type, and I studying how I should keep the public from counterfeiting them. The next day my Shinplasters were handed to me, the whole amount being twenty dollars, and, after being duly signed, were ready for circulation. At first my notes did not take well; they were too new, and viewed with a suspicious eye. But through the assistance of my customers, and a good deal of exertion on my own part, my bills were soon in circulation; and nearly all the money received in return for my notes was spent in fitting up and decorating my shop.

Few bankers get through this world without their difficulties, and I was not to be an exception. A short time after my money had been out, a party of young men, either wishing to pull down my vanity, or to try the soundness of my bank, determined to give it "a run." After collecting together a number of my bills, they came one at a time to demand other money for them, and I, not being aware of what was going on, was taken by surprise. One day, as I was sitting at my table, strapping some new razors I had just got with the avails of my "Shinplasters," one of the men entered and said, "Emperor, you will oblige me if you will give me some other money for these notes of yours." I immediately cashed the notes with the most worthless of the Wild-cat money that I had on hand, but which was a lawful tender. The young man had scarcely left, when a second appeared, with a similar amount, and demanded payment. These were cashed, and soon a third came with his roll of notes. I paid these with an air of triumph, although I had but half a dollar left. I began now to think seriously what I should do, or how to act, provided another demand should be made. While I was thus engaged in thought, I saw the fourth man crossing the street, with a handful of notes, evidently my "Shinplasters." I instantaneously shut the door, and, looking out of the window, said, "I have closed business for the day; come to-morrow, and I will see you." In looking across the street, I saw my rival standing in his shop-door, grinning and clapping his hands at my apparent downfall. I was completely "done *Brown*" for the day. However, I was not to be "used up" in this way; so I escaped by the back door, and went in search of my friend who had first suggested to me the idea of issuing notes. I found him, told him of the difficulty I was in, and wished him to point out a way by which I might extricate myself. He laughed heartily, and then said, "You must act as all bankers do in this part of the country." I inquired how they did, and he said, "When your notes are brought to you, you must redeem them, and then send them out and get other money for them, and with the latter you can keep cashing your own Shinplasters." This was indeed a new idea to me. I immediately commenced putting in circulation the notes which I had just redeemed, and my efforts were crowned with so much success that, before I slept that night, my "Shinplasters" were again in circulation, and my bank once more on a sound basis.

As I saw the clerks shovelling out the yellow coin upon the counters of the Bank of England, and men coming in and going out with weighty bags of the precious metal in their hands or on their shoulders, I could not but think of the great contrast between the monster institution within whose walls I was then standing and the Wild-cat banks of America!

CHAPTER IX.

> "We might as soon describe a dream
> As tell where falls each golden beam;
> As soon might reckon up the sand,
> Sweet Weston! on thy sea-beat strand,
> As count each beauty there."
>
> Miss Mitford.

I have devoted the past ten days to sight-seeing in the metropolis, the first two of which were spent in the British Museum. After procuring a guide-book at the door as I entered, I seated myself on the first seat that caught my eye, arranged as well as I could in my mind the different rooms, and then commenced in good earnest. The first part I visited was the gallery of antiquities, through to the north gallery, and thence to the Lycian room. This place is filled with tombs, bas-reliefs, statues, and other productions of the same art. Venus, seated, and smelling a lotus-flower which she held in her hand, and attended by three Graces, put a stop to the rapid strides that I was making through this part of the hall. This is really one of the most precious productions of the art that I have ever seen. Many of the figures in this room are very much mutilated; yet one can linger here for hours with interest. A good number of the statues are of uncertain date; they are of great value as works of art, and more so as a means of enlightening much that has been obscure with respect to Lycia, an ancient and celebrated country of Asia Minor.

In passing through the eastern zoological gallery, I was surrounded on every side by an army of portraits suspended upon the walls; and among these was the Protector. The people of one century kicks his bones through the streets of London, another puts his portrait in the British Museum, and a future generation may possibly give him a place in Westminster Abbey. Such is the uncertainty of the human character. Yesterday, a common soldier; to-day, the ruler of an empire; to-morrow, suspended upon the gallows. In an adjoining room I saw a portrait of Baxter, which gives one a pretty good idea of the great nonconformist. In the same room hung a splendid modern portrait, without any intimation in the guide-book of who it represented, or when it was painted. It was so much like one whom I had seen, and on whom my affections were placed in my younger days, that I obtained a seat from an adjoining room and rested myself before it. After sitting half an hour or more, I wandered to another part of the building, but only to return again to my "first love," where I remained till the throng had disappeared, one after another, and the officer reminded me that it was time to close.

It was eight o'clock before I reached my lodgings. Although fatigued by the day's exertions, I again resumed the reading of Roscoe's "Leo X.," and had nearly finished seventy-three pages, when the clock on St. Martin's Church apprised me that it was two. He who escapes from slavery at the age of twenty years, without any education, as did the writer of this, must read when others are asleep, if he would catch up with the rest of the world. "To be wise," says Pope, "is but to know how little can be known." The true searcher after truth and knowledge is always like a child; although gaining strength from year to year, he still "learns to labor and to wait." The field of labor is ever expanding before him, reminding him that he has yet more to learn; teaching him that he is nothing more than a child in knowledge, and inviting him onward with a thousand varied charms. The son may take possession of the father's goods at his death, but he cannot inherit with the property the father's cultivated mind. He may put on the father's old coat, but that is all; the immortal mind of the first wearer has gone to the tomb. Property may be bequeathed, but knowledge cannot. Then let him who would be useful in his day and generation be up and doing. Like the Chinese student who learned perseverance from the woman whom he saw trying to rub a crow-bar into a needle, so should we take the experience of the past to lighten our feet through the paths of the future.

The next morning, at ten, I was again at the door of the great building; was soon within its walls seeing what time would not allow of the previous day. I spent some hours in looking through glass cases, viewing specimens of minerals such as can scarcely be found in any place out of the British Museum. During this day I did not fail to visit the great library. It is a spacious room, surrounded with large glass cases filled with volumes whose very look tells you that they are of age.

Around, under the cornice, were arranged a number of old, black-looking portraits, in all probability the authors of some of the works in the glass cases beneath. About the room were placed long tables, with stands for reading and writing, and around these were a number of men busily engaged in looking over some chosen author. Old men with gray hairs, young men with moustaches, some in cloth, others in fustian,—indicating that men of different rank can meet here. Not a single word was spoken during my stay; all appearing to enjoy the silence that reigned throughout the great room. This is indeed a retreat from the world. No one inquires who the man is that is at his side, and each pursues in silence his own researches. The racing of pens over the sheets of paper was all that disturbed the stillness of the occasion.

From the library I strolled to other rooms, and feasted my eyes on what I had never before seen. He who goes over this immense building cannot do so without a feeling of admiration for the men whose energy has brought together this vast and wonderful collection of things, the like of which cannot be found in any other museum in the world. The reflection of the setting sun against a mirror in one of the rooms told me that night was approaching, and I had but a moment in which to take another look at the portrait that I had seen on the previous day, and then bade adieu to the museum.

Having published the narrative of my life and escape from slavery, and put it into the booksellers' hands, and seeing a prospect of a fair sale, I ventured to take from my purse the last sovereign to make up a small sum to remit to the United States, for the support of my daughters, who are at school there. Before doing this, however, I had made arrangements to attend a public meeting in the city of Worcester, at which the mayor was to preside. Being informed by the friends of the slave there that I would in all probability sell a number of copies of my book, and being told that Worcester was only ten miles from London, I felt safe in parting with all but a few shillings, feeling sure that my purse would soon be again replenished. But you may guess my surprise, when I learned that Worcester was above a hundred miles from London, and that I had not retained money enough to defray my expenses to the place. In my haste and wish to make up the ten pounds to send to my children, I had forgotten that the payment for my lodgings would be demanded before I should leave town. Saturday morning came; I paid my lodging-bill, and had three shillings and fourpence left; and out of this sum I was to get three dinners, as I was only served with breakfast and tea at my lodgings.

Nowhere in the British empire do the people witness as dark days as in London. It was on Monday morning, in the fore part of October, as the clock on St. Martin's Church was striking ten, that I left my lodgings, and turned into the Strand. The street-lamps were yet burning, and the shops were all lighted, as if day had not made its appearance. This great thoroughfare, as usual at this time of the day, was thronged with business men going their way, and women sauntering about for pleasure or for the want of something better to do. I passed down the Strand to Charing Cross, and looked in vain to see the majestic statue of Nelson upon the top of the great shaft. The clock on St. Martin's Church struck eleven, but my sight could not penetrate through the dark veil that hung between its face and me. In fact, day had been completely turned into night; and the brilliant lights from the shop-windows almost persuaded me that another day had not appeared. A London fog cannot be described. To be appreciated, it must be seen, or, rather, felt, for it is altogether impossible to be clear and lucid on such a subject. It is the only thing which gives you an idea of what Milton meant when he talked of darkness visible. There is a kind of light, to be sure; but it only serves as a medium for a series of optical illusions; and, for all useful purposes of vision, the deepest darkness that ever fell from the heavens is infinitely preferable. A man perceives a coach a dozen yards off, and a single stride brings him among the horses' feet; he sees a gas-light faintly glimmering (as he thinks) at a distance, but scarcely has he advanced a step or two towards it, when he becomes convinced of its actual station by finding his head rattling against the post; and as for attempting, if you get once mystified, to distinguish one street from another, it is ridiculous to think of such a thing.

Turning, I retraced my steps, and was soon passing through the massive gates of Temple Bar, wending my way to the city, when a beggar-boy at my heels accosted me for a half-penny to buy bread. I had scarcely served the boy, when I observed near by, and standing close to a lamp-post, a colored man, and from his general appearance I was satisfied that he was an American. He eyed me attentively as I passed him, and seemed anxious to speak. When I had got some distance from him I looked back, and his eyes were still upon me. No longer able to resist the temptation to speak with him, I returned, and, commencing conversation with him, learned a little of his history, which was as follows: He had, he said, escaped from slavery in Maryland, and reached New York; but not feeling himself secure there, he had, through the kindness of the captain of an English ship, made his way to Liverpool; and not being able to get employment there, he had come up to London. Here he had met with no better success, and having been employed in the growing of tobacco, and being unaccustomed to any other work, he could not get labor in England. I told him he had better try to get to the West Indies; but he informed me that he had not a single penny, and that he had had nothing to eat that day.

By this man's story I was moved to tears, and, going to a neighboring shop, I took from my purse my last shilling, changed it, and gave this poor brother fugitive one half. The poor man burst into tears as I placed the sixpence in his hand, and said, "You are the first friend I have met in London." I bade him farewell, and left him with a feeling of regret that I could not place him beyond the reach of want. I went on my way to the city, and while going through Cheapside a streak of light appeared in the east, that reminded me that it was not night. In vain I wandered from street to street, with the hope that I might meet some one who would lend me money enough to get to Worcester. Hungry and fatigued I was returning to my lodgings, when the great clock of St. Paul's Church, under whose shadow I was then passing, struck four. A stroll through Fleet-street and the Strand, and I was again pacing my room. On my return, I found a letter from Worcester had arrived in my absence, informing me that a party of gentlemen would meet me the next day on my reaching that place, and saying, "Bring plenty of books, as you will doubtless sell a large number." The last sixpence had been spent for postage-stamps, in order to send off some letters to other places, and I could not even stamp a letter in answer to the one last from Worcester. The only vestige of money about me was a smooth farthing that a little girl had given to me at the meeting at Croydon, saying, "This is for the slaves." I was three thousand miles from home, with but a single farthing in my pocket! Where on earth is a man without money more destitute? The cold hills of the Arctic regions have not a more inhospitable appearance than London to the stranger with an empty pocket. But whilst I felt depressed at being in such a sad condition, I was conscious that I had done right in remitting the last ten pounds to America. It was for the support of those whom God had committed to my care, and whom I love as I can no others. I had no friend in London to whom I could apply for temporary aid. My friend, Mr. T——, was out of town, and I did not know his address.

The dark day was rapidly passing away,—the clock in the hall had struck six. I had given up all hopes of reaching Worcester the next day, and had just rung the bell for the servant to bring me some tea, when a gentle tap at the door was heard; the servant entered, and informed me that a gentleman below was wishing to see me. I bade her fetch a light and ask him up. The stranger was my young friend, Frederick Stevenson, son of the excellent minister of the Borough-Road Chapel. I had lectured in this chapel a few days previous; and this young gentleman, with more than ordinary zeal and enthusiasm for the cause of bleeding humanity, and respect for me, had gone amongst his father's congregation and sold a number of copies of my book, and had come to bring me the money. I wiped the silent tear from my eyes as the young man placed the thirteen half-crowns in my hand. I did not let him know under what obligation I was to him for this disinterested act of kindness. He does not know to this day what aid he has rendered to a stranger in a strange land, and I feel that I am but discharging in a trifling degree my debt of gratitude to this young gentleman, in acknowledging my obligation to him. As the man who called for bread and cheese, when feeling in his pocket for the last threepence to pay for it, found a sovereign that he was not aware he possessed, countermanded the order for the lunch, and bade them bring him the best dinner they could get; so I told the servant, when she brought the tea, that I had changed my mind, and should go out to dine. With the means in my pocket of reaching Worcester the next day, I sat down to dinner at the Adelphi, with a good cut of roast beef before me, and felt myself once more at home. Thus ended a dark day in London.

CHAPTER X.

"When I behold, with deepe astonishment,
  To famous Westminster how there resorte,
Living in brass or stoney monument,
  The princes and the worthies of all sorte;
Doe not I see reformde nobilitie,
  Without contempt, or pride, or ostentation,
And looke upon offenselesse majesty,
  Naked of pomp or earthly domination?
And how a play-game of a painted stone
  Contents the quiet now and silent sprites,
Whome all the world which late they stood upon
  Could not content nor quench their appetites.
Life is a frost of cold felicitie,
And death the thaw of all our vanitie."

For some days past the sun has not shown his face; clouds have obscured the sky, and the rain has fallen in torrents, which has contributed much to the general gloom. However, I have spent the time in as agreeable a manner as I well could. Yesterday I fulfilled an engagement to dine with a gentleman at the Whittington Club. One who is unacquainted with the club system as carried on in London can scarcely imagine the conveniences they present. Every member appears to be at home, and all seem to own a share in the club. There is a free-and-easy way with those who frequent clubs, and a license given there, that is unknown in the drawing-room of the private mansion. I met the gentleman at the club at the appointed hour, and after his writing my name in the visitors' book, we proceeded to the dining-room, where we partook of a good dinner.

We had been in the room but a short time, when a small man, dressed in black, with his coat buttoned up to the chin, entered the saloon, and took a seat at the table hard by. My friend, in a low whisper, informed me that this person was one of the French refugees. He was apparently not more than thirty years of age, and exceedingly good-looking,—his person being slight, his feet and hands very small and well-shaped, especially his hands, which were covered with kid gloves, so tightly drawn on that the points of the finger-nails were visible through them. His face was mild and almost womanly in its beauty, his eyes soft and full, his brow open and ample, his features well defined, and approaching to the ideal Greek in contour; the lines about his mouth were exquisitely sweet, and yet resolute in expression; his hair was short—his having no moustache gave him nothing of the look of a Frenchman; and I was not a little surprised when informed that the person before me was Louis Blanc. I could scarcely be persuaded to believe that one so small, so child-like in stature, had taken a prominent part in the revolution of 1848. He held in his hand a copy of *La Presse*, and as soon as he was seated opened it and began to devour its contents. The gentleman with whom I was dining was not acquainted with him, but at the close of our dinner he procured me an introduction through another gentleman.

As we were returning to our lodgings, we saw in Exeter-street, Strand, one of those exhibitions that can be seen in almost any of the streets in the suburbs of the metropolis, but which is something of a novelty to those from the other side of the Atlantic. This was an exhibition of "Punch and Judy." Everything was in full operation when we reached the spot. A puppet appeared, eight or ten inches from the waist upwards, with an enormous face, huge nose, mouth widely grinning, projecting chin, cheeks covered with grog-blossoms, a large protuberance on his back, another on his chest; yet with these deformities he appeared uncommonly happy. This was Mr. Punch. He held in his right hand a tremendous bludgeon, with which he amused himself by rapping on the head every one who came within his reach. This exhibition seems very absurd, yet not less than one hundred were present—children, boys, old men, and even gentlemen and ladies, were standing by, and occasionally greeting the performer with the smile of approbation. Mr. Punch, however, was not to have it all his own way, for another and better sort of Punch-like exhibition appeared a few yards off, that took away Mr. Punch's audience, to the great dissatisfaction of that gentleman. This was an exhibition called the Fantoccini, and far superior to any of the street performances which I have yet seen. The curtain rose and displayed a beautiful theatre in miniature, and most gorgeously painted. The organ which accompanied it struck up a hornpipe, and a sailor, dressed in his blue jacket, made his appearance, and commenced keeping time with the utmost correctness. This figure was not so long as Mr. Punch, but much better looking. At the close of the hornpipe the little sailor made a bow, and tripped off, apparently conscious of having deserved the undivided applause of the bystanders. The curtain dropped; but in two or three minutes it was again up, and a rope was discovered extended on two cross pieces for dancing upon. The tune was changed to an air in which the time was marked; a graceful figure appeared, jumped upon the rope with its balance-pole, and displayed all the manœuvres of an expert performer on the tight-rope. Many who would turn away in disgust from Mr. Punch will stand for hours and look at the performances of the Fantoccini. If people, like the Vicar of Wakefield, will sometimes "allow themselves to be happy," they can hardly fail to have a hearty laugh at the drolleries of the Fantoccini. There may be degrees of absurdity in the manner of wasting our time, but there is an evident affectation in decrying these humble and innocent exhibitions, by those who will sit till two or three in the morning to witness a pantomime at a theatre royal.

* * *

An autumn sun shone brightly through a remarkably transparent atmosphere this morning, which was a most striking contrast to the weather we had had during the past three days; and I again set out to see some of the lions of the city, commencing with the Tower of London. Every American, on returning home from a visit to the Old World, speaks with pride of the places he saw while in Europe; and of the many resorts of interest he has read of, few have made a more lasting impression upon his memory than the Tower of London. The stories of the imprisoning of kings and queens, the murdering of princes, the torturing of men and women, without regard to birth, education or station, and of the burning and rebuilding of the old pile, have all sunk deep into his heart. A walk of twenty minutes, after being set down at the bank by an omnibus, brought me to the gate of the Tower. A party of friends who were to meet me there had not arrived; so I had an opportunity of inspecting the grounds, and taking a good view of the external appearance of the old and celebrated building. The Tower is surrounded by a high wall, and around this a deep ditch partly filled with stagnated water. The wall encloses twelve acres of ground, on which stand the several towers, occupying, with their walks and avenues, the whole space. The most ancient part of the building is called the "White Tower," so as to distinguish it from the parts more recently built. Its walls are seventeen feet in thickness, and ninety-two in height, exclusive of the turrets, of which there are four. My company arrived, and we entered the Tower through four massive gates, the innermost one being pointed out as the "Water, or Traitors' Gate," so called from the fact that it opened to the river, and through it the criminals were usually brought to the prison within. But this passage is now closed up. We visited the various apartments in the old building. The room in the Bloody Tower where the infant princes were put to death by the command of their uncle, Richard III., also the recess behind the gate where the bones of the young princes were concealed, were shown to us. The warden of the prison, who showed us through, seemed to have little or no veneration for Henry VIII.; for he often cracked a joke or told a story at the expense of the murderer of Anne Boleyn. The old man wiped the tear from his eye as he pointed out the grave of Lady Jane Grey. This was doubtless one of the best as well as most innocent of those who lost their lives in the Tower; young, virtuous and handsome, she became a victim to the ambition of her own and her husband's relations. I tried to count the names on the wall in "Beauchamp's Tower," but they were too numerous. Anne Boleyn was imprisoned here. The room in the "Brick Tower" where Lady Jane Grey was imprisoned was pointed out as a place of interest. We were next shown into the "White Tower." We passed through a long room filled with many things having a warlike appearance; and among them a number of equestrian figures, as large as life, and clothed in armor and trappings of the various reigns from Edward I. to James II., or from 1272 to 1685. Elisabeth, or the "Maiden Queen," as the warden called her, was the most imposing of the group; she was on a cream-colored charger. We left the Maiden Queen, to examine the cloak upon which General Wolf died at the storming of Quebec. In this room Sir Walter Raleigh was imprisoned, and here was written his "History of the World." In his own hand, upon the wall, is written, "Be thou faithful unto death, and I will give thee a crown of life." His Bible is still shown, with these memorable lines written in it by himself a short time before his death:

> "Even such is Time, that takes on trust,
> Our youth, our joy, our all we have,
> And pays us but with age and dust;
> Who in the dark and silent grave,
> When we have wandered all our ways,
> Shuts up the story of our days."

Spears, battle-axes, pikes, helmets, targets, bows and arrows, and many instruments of torture, whose names I did not learn, grace the walls of this room. The block on which the Earl of Essex and Anne Boleyn were beheaded was shown among other objects of interest. A view of the "Queen's Jewels" closed our visit to the Tower. The gold staff of St. Edward, and the Baptismal Font used at the royal christenings, made of solid silver, and more than four feet high, were among the jewels here exhibited. The Sword of Justice was there, as if to watch the rest of the valuables. However, this was not the sword that Peter used. Our acquaintance with De Foe, Sir Walter Raleigh and Chaucer, through their writings, and the knowledge that they had been incarcerated within the walls of the bastile that we were just leaving, caused us to look back again and again upon its dark-gray turrets.

I closed the day with a look at the interior of St. Paul's Cathedral. A service was just over, and we met a crowd coming out as we entered the great building. "Service is over, and tuppence for all that wants to stay," was the first sound that caught our ears. In the Burlesque of "Esmeralda," a man is met in the belfry of the Notre Dame at Paris, and, being asked for money by one of the vergers, says,

> "I paid three pence at the door,
> And since I came in a great deal more;
> Upon my honor, you have emptied my purse,—
> St. Paul's Cathedral could not do worse."

I felt inclined to join in this sentiment before I left the

church. A fine statue of "Surly Sam" Johnson was one of the first things that caught our eyes on looking around. A statue of Sir Edward Packenham, who fell at the battle of New Orleans, was on the opposite side of the great hall. As we had walked over the ground where the general fell, we viewed his statue with more than ordinary interest. We were taken from one scene of interest to another, until we found ourselves in the "Whispering Gallery." From the dome we had a splendid view of the metropolis of the world. A scaffold was erected up here to enable an artist to take sketches, from which a panorama of London was painted. The artist was three years at work. The painting is now exhibited at the Colosseum; but the brain of the artist was turned, and he died insane. Indeed, one can scarcely conceive how it could be otherwise. You in America have no idea of the immensity of this building. Pile together half a dozen of the largest churches in New York or Boston, and you will have but a faint representation of St. Paul's Cathedral.

* * *

I have just returned from a stroll of two hours through Westminster Abbey. We entered the building at a door near Poet's Corner, and, naturally enough, looked around for the monuments of the men whose imaginative powers have contributed so much to instruct and amuse mankind. I was not a little disappointed in the few I saw. In almost any church-yard you may see monuments and tombs far superior to anything in Poets' Corner. A few only have monuments. Shakspeare, who wrote of man to man, and for man to the end of time, is honored with one. Addison's monument is also there; but the greater number have nothing more erected to their memories than busts or medallions. Poets' Corner is not splendid in appearance, yet I observed visitors lingering about it, as if they were tied to the spot by love and veneration for some departed friend. All seemed to regard it as classic ground. No sound louder than a whisper was heard during the whole time, except the verger treading over the marble floor with a light step. There is great pleasure in sauntering about the tombs of those with whom we are familiar through their writings; and we tear ourselves from their ashes, as we would from those of a bosom friend. The genius of these men spreads itself over the whole panorama of nature, giving us one vast and varied picture, the color of which will endure to the end of time. None can portray like the poet the passions of the human soul. The statue of Addison, clad in his dressing-gown, is not far from that of Shakspeare. He looks as if he had just left the study, after finishing some chosen paper for the *Spectator*. This memento of a great man was the work of the British public. Such a mark of national respect was but justice to the one who had contributed more to purify and raise the standard of English literature than any man of his day. We next visited the other end of the same transept, near the northern door. Here lie Mansfield, Chatham, Fox, the second William Pitt, Grattan, Wilberforce and a few other statesmen. But, above all, is the stately monument of the Earl of Chatham. In no other place so small do so many great men lie together. To these men, whose graves strangers from all parts of the world wish to view, the British public are in a great measure indebted for England's fame. The high preëminence which England has so long enjoyed and maintained in the scale of empire has constantly been the boast and pride of the English people. The warm panegyrics that have been lavished on her constitution and laws, the songs chanted to celebrate her glory, the lustre of her arms, as the glowing theme of her warriors, the thunder of her artillery in proclaiming her moral prowess, her flag being unfurled to every breeze and ocean, rolling to her shores the tribute of a thousand realms, show England to be the greatest nation in the world, and speak volumes for the great departed, as well as for those of the living present. One requires no company, no amusements, no books, in such a place as this. Time and death have placed within those walls sufficient to occupy the mind, if one should stay here a week.

On my return, I spent an hour very pleasantly in the Royal Academy, in the same building as the National Gallery. Many of the paintings here are of a fine order. Oliver Cromwell looking upon the headless corpse of King Charles I. appeared to draw the greatest number of spectators. A scene from "As You Like It" was one of the best executed pieces we saw. This was "Rosalind, Celia and Orlando." The artist did himself and the subject great credit. Kemble, in Hamlet, with that ever-memorable skull in his hand, was one of the pieces which we viewed with no little interest. It is strange that Hamlet is always represented as a thin, lean man, when the Hamlet of Shakspeare was a fat, John Bull kind of a man.

But the best piece in the gallery was "Dante meditating the episode of Francesca da Rimini and Paolo Malatesta, S'Inferno, Canto V." Our first interest for the great Italian poet was created by reading Lord Byron's poem, "The Lament of Dante." From that hour we felt like examining everything connected with the poet. The history of poets, as well as painters, is written in their works. The best written life of Goldsmith is to be found in his poem of "The Traveller," and his novel of "The Vicar of Wakefield." Boswell could not have written a better life of himself than he has done in giving the Biography of Dr. Johnson. It seems clear that no one can be a great poet without having been sometime during life a lover, and having lost the object of his affection in some mysterious way. Burns had his Highland Mary, Byron his Mary, and Dante was not without his Beatrice. Whether there ever lived such a person as Beatrice seems to be a question upon which neither of his biographers has thrown much light. However, a Beatrice existed in the poet's mind, if not on earth. His attachment to Beatrice Portinari, and the linking of her name with the immortality of his great poem, left an indelible impression upon his future character. The marriage of the object of his affections to another, and her subsequent death, and the poet's exile from his beloved Florence, together with his death amongst strangers, all give an interest to the poet's writings which could not be heightened by romance itself. When exiled and in poverty, Dante found a friend in the father of Francesca. And here, under the roof of his protector, he wrote his great poem. The time the painter has chosen is evening. Day and night meet in mid-air: one star is alone visible. Sailing in vacancy are the shadows of the lovers. The countenance of Francesca is expressive of hopeless agony. The delineations are sublime, the conception is of the highest order, and the execution admirable. Dante is seated in a marble vestibule, in a meditating attitude, the face partly concealed by the right hand upon which it is resting. On the whole, it is an excellently painted piece, and causes one to go back with a fresh relish to the Italian's celebrated poem.

In coming out we stopped a short while in the upper room of the gallery, and spent a few minutes over a painting representing Mrs. Siddons in one of Shakspeare's characters. This is by Sir Joshua Reynolds, and is only one of the many pieces that we have seen of this great artist. His genius was vast and powerful in its grasp, his fancy fertile, and his inventive faculty inexhaustible in its resources. He displayed the very highest powers of genius by the thorough originality of his conceptions, and by the entirely new path that he struck out in art. Well may Englishmen be proud of his name. And as time shall step between his day and those that follow after him, the more will his works be appreciated. We have since visited his grave, and stood over his monument in St. Paul's.

CHAPTER XI.

To give implicit credence to each tale
  Of monkish legends,—relics to order;
To think God honored by the cowl or veil,
  Regardless who, or what, the emblem wore,
Indeed is mockery, mummery, nothing more:
  But if cold Scepticism usurp the place
That Superstition held in days of yore,
  We may not be in much more hopeful case
Than if we still implored the Virgin Mary's grace.

BARTON.

SOME days since, I left the metropolis to fulfil a few engagements to visit provincial towns; and after a ride of nearly eight hours, we were in sight of the ancient city of York. It was night, the moon was in her zenith, and there seemed nothing between her and the earth but glittering cold. The moon, the stars, and the innumerable gas-lights, gave the city a panoramic appearance. Like a mountain starting out of a plain, there stood the cathedral in its glory, looking down upon the surrounding buildings, with all the appearance of a Gulliver standing over the Lilliputians. Night gave us no opportunity to view the minster. However, we were up the next morning before the sun, and walking round the cathedral with a degree of curiosity seldom excited within us. It is thought that a building of the same dimensions would take fifty years to complete it at the present time, even with all the improvements of the nineteenth century, and would cost no less than the enormous sum of two millions of pounds sterling. From what I had heard of this famous cathedral, my expectations were raised to the highest point; but it surpassed all the idea that I had formed of it. On entering the building, we lost all thought of the external appearance by the matchless beauty of the interior. The echo produced by the tread of our feet upon the floor as we entered, resounding through the aisles, seemed to say, "Put off your shoes, for the place whereon you tread is holy ground." We stood with hat in hand, and gazed with wonder and astonishment down the incomparable vista of more than five hundred feet. The organ, which stands near the centre of the building, is said to be one of the finest in the world. A wall, in front of which is a screen of the most gorgeous and florid architecture, and executed in solid stone, separates the nave from the service choir. The beautiful workmanship of this makes it appear so perfect, as almost to produce the belief that it is tracery-work of wood. We ascended the rough stone steps through a winding stair to the turrets, where we had such a view of the surrounding country as can be obtained from no other place. On the top of the centre and highest turret is a grotesque figure of a fiddler; rather a strange-looking object, we thought, to occupy the most elevated pinnacle on the house of God. All dwellings in the neighborhood appear like so many dwarfs crouching at the feet of the minster; while its own vastness and beauty impress the observer with feelings of awe and sublimity. As we stood upon the top of this stupendous mountain of ecclesiastical architecture, and surveyed the picturesque hills and valleys around, imagination recalled the tumult of the sanguinary battles fought in sight of the edifice. The rebellion of Octavius near three thousand years ago, his defeat and flight to the Scots, his return and triumph over the Romans, and being crowned king of all Britain; the assassination of Oswald, King of the Northumbrians; the flaying alive of Osbert; the crowning of Richard III.; the siege by William the Conqueror; the siege by Cromwell, and the pomp and splendor with which the different monarchs had been received in York, all appeared to be vividly before me. While we were thus calling to our aid our knowledge of history, a sweet peal from the lungs of the ponderous organ below cut short our stay among the turrets, and we descended to have our organ of tune gratified, as well as to finish the inspection of the interior.

I have heard the sublime melodies of Handel, Haydn and Mozart, performed by the most skilful musicians; I have listened with delight and awe to the soul-moving compositions of those masters, as they have been chanted in the most magnificent churches; but never did I hear such music, and played upon such an instrument, as that sent forth by the great organ in the Cathedral of York. The verger took much delight in showing us the horn that was once mounted with gold, but is now garnished with brass. We viewed the monuments and tombs of the departed, and then spent an hour before the great north window. The design on the painted glass, which tradition states was given to the church by five virgin sisters, is the finest thing of the kind in Great Britain. I felt a relief on once more coming into the open air, and again beholding Nature's own sunlight. The splendid ruin of St. Mary's Abbey, with its eight beautiful light Gothic windows, next attracted our attention. A visit to the castle finished our stay in York; and as we were leaving the old city we almost imagined that we heard the chiming of the bells for the celebration of the first Christian Sabbath, with Prince Arthur as the presiding genius.

* * *

England stands preeminently the first government in the world for freedom of speech and of the press. Not even in our own beloved America can the man who feels himself oppressed speak as he can in Great Britain. In some parts of England, however, the freedom of thought is tolerated to a greater extent than in others; and of the places favorable to reforms of all kinds, calculated to elevate and benefit mankind, Newcastle-on-Tyne doubtless takes the lead. Surrounded by innumerable coal-mines, it furnishes employment for a large laboring population, many of whom take a deep interest in the passing events of the day, and, consequently, are a reading class. The public debater or speaker, no matter what may be his subject, who fails to get an audience in other towns, is sure of a gathering in the Music Hall, or Lecture Room, in Newcastle.

Here I first had an opportunity of coming in contact with a portion of the laboring people of Britain. I have addressed large and influential meetings in Newcastle and the neighboring towns, and the more I see and learn of the condition of the working-classes of England, the more I am satisfied of the utter fallacy of the statements often made that their condition approximates to that of the slaves of America. Whatever may be the disadvantages that the British peasant labors under, he is free; and if he is not satisfied with his employer, he can make choice of another. He also has the right to educate his children; and he is the equal of the most wealthy person before an English court of justice. But how is it with the American slave? He has no right to himself; no right to protect his wife, his child, or his own person. He is nothing more than a living tool. Beyond his field or workshop he knows nothing. There is no amount of ignorance he is not capable of. He has not the least idea of the face of this earth, nor of the history or constitution of the country in which he dwells. To him the literature, science and art, the progressive history and the accumulated discoveries of by-gone ages, are as if they had never been. The past is to him as yesterday, and the future scarcely more than to-morrow. Ancestral monuments he has none; written documents, fraught with cogitations of other times, he has none; and any instrumentality calculated to awaken and expound the intellectual activity and comprehension of a present or approaching generation, he has none. His condition is that of the leopard of his own native Africa. It lives, it propagates its kind; but never does it indicate a movement towards that all but angelic intelligence of man. The slave eats, drinks and sleeps, all for the benefit of the man who claims his body as his property. Before the tribunals of his country he has no voice. He has no higher appeal than the mere will of his owner. He knows nothing of the inspired Apostles through their writings. He has no Sabbath, no church, no Bible, no means of grace,—and yet we are told that he is as well off as the laboring classes of England. It is not enough that the people of my country should point to their Declaration of Independence, which declares that "all men are created equal." It is not enough that they should laud to the skies a constitution containing boasting declarations in favor of freedom. It is not enough that they should extol the genius of Washington, the patriotism of Henry, or the enthusiasm of Otis. The time has come when nations are judged by the acts of the present, instead of the past. And so it must be with America. In no place in the United Kingdom has the American slave warmer friends than in Newcastle.

* * *

I am now in Sheffield, and have just returned from a visit to James Montgomery, the poet. In company with James Wall, Esq., I proceeded to the Mount, the residence of Mr. Montgomery; and our names being sent in, we were soon in the presence of the "Christian poet." He held in his left hand the

Eclectic Review for the month, and with the right gave me a hearty shake, and bade me "Welcome to Old England." He was anything but like the portraits I had seen of him, and the man I had in my mind's eye. I had just been reading his "Pelican Island," and I eyed the poet with no little interest. He is under the middle size; his forehead high and well formed, the top of which was a little bald; his hair of a yellowish color, his eyes rather small and deep-set, the nose long and slightly acquiline, his mouth rather small, and not at all pretty. He was dressed in black, and a large white cravat entirely hid his neck and chin; his having been afflicted from childhood with salt-rheum was doubtless the cause of his chin being so completely buried in the neckcloth. Upon the whole, he looked more like one of our American Methodist parsons than any one I have seen in this country. He entered freely into conversation with us. He said he should be glad to attend my lecture that evening, but that he had long since quit going out at night. He mentioned having heard William Lloyd Garrison some years before, and with whom he was well pleased. He said it had long been a puzzle to him how Americans could hold slaves and still retain their membership in the churches. When we rose to leave, the old man took my hand between his two, and with tears in his eyes said, "Go on your Christian mission, and may the Lord protect and prosper you! Your enslaved countrymen have my sympathy, and shall have my prayers." Thus ended our visit to the bard of Sheffield. Long after I had quitted the presence of the poet, the following lines of his were ringing in my ears:

"Wanderer, whither dost thou roam?
Weary wanderer, old and gray,
Wherefore hast thou left thine home,
In the sunset of thy day?
Welcome, wanderer, as thou art,
All my blessings to partake;
Yet thrice welcome to my heart,
For thine injured people's sake.
Wanderer, whither wouldst thou roam?
To what region far away?
Bend thy steps to find a home,

In the twilight of thy day,
Where a tyrant never trod,
Where a slave was never known—
But where Nature worships God
In the wilderness alone."

Mr. Montgomery seems to have thrown his entire soul into his meditations on the wrongs of Switzerland. The poem which we have just quoted is unquestionably one of his best productions, and contains more of the fire of enthusiasm than all his other works. We feel a reverence almost amounting to superstition for the poet who deals with nature. And who is more capable of understanding the human heart than the poet? Who has better known the human feelings than Shakspeare; better painted than Milton the grandeur of virtue; better sighed than Byron over the subtle weaknesses of Hope? Who ever had a sounder taste, a more exact intellect, than Dante? or who has ever tuned his harp more in favor of freedom than our own Whittier?

CHAPTER XII.

"How changed, alas! from that revered abode,
Graced by proud majesty in ancient days,
When monks recluse these sacred pavements trod,
And taught the unlettered world its Maker's praise!"
KEATS.

IN passing through Yorkshire, we could not resist the temptation it offered to pay a visit to the extensive and interesting ruin of Kirkstall Abbey, which lies embosomed in a beautiful recess of Airedale, about three miles from Leeds. A pleasant drive over a smooth road brought us abruptly in sight of the Abbey. The tranquil and pensive beauty of the desolate monastery, as it reposes in the lap of pastoral luxuriance, and amidst the touching associations of seven centuries, is almost beyond description, when viewed from where we first beheld it. After arriving at its base, we stood for some moments under the mighty arches that lead into the great hall, gazing at its old gray walls frowning with age. At the distance of a small field, the Aire is seen gliding past the foot of the lawn on which the ruin stands, after it has left those precincts, sparkling over a weir with a pleasing murmur. We could fully enter into the feelings of the poet when he says:

"Beautiful fabric! even in decay
And desolation, beauty still is thine;
As the rich sunset of an autumn day,
When gorgeous clouds in glorious hues combine
To render homage to its slow decline,
Is more majestic in its parting hour:
Even so thy mouldering venerable shrine
Possesses now a more subduing power
Than in thine earlier sway, with pomp and pride thy dower."

The tale of "Mary, the Maid of the Inn," is supposed, and not without foundation, to be connected with this abbey. "Hark to Rover," the name of the house where the key is kept, was, a century ago, a retired inn or pot-house, and the haunt of many a desperate highwayman and poacher. The anecdote is so well known that it is scarcely necessary to relate it. It, however, is briefly this:

"One stormy night, as two travellers sat at the inn, each having exhausted his news, the conversation was directed to the abbey, the boisterous night, and Mary's heroism; when a bet was at last made by one of them, that she would not go and bring back from the nave a slip of the alder-tree growing there. Mary, however, did go; but, having nearly reached the tree, she heard a low, indistinct dialogue; at the same time, something black fell and rolled towards her, which afterwards proved to be a hat. Directing her attention to the place whence the conversation proceeded, she saw, from behind a pillar, two men carrying a murdered body: they passed near the place where she stood, a heavy cloud was swept from off the face of the moon, and Mary fell senseless—one of the murderers was her intended husband! She was awakened from her swoon, but—her reason had fled forever." Mr. Southey wrote a beautiful poem founded on this story, which will be found in his published works. We spent nearly three hours in wandering through these splendid ruins. It is both curious and interesting to trace the early history of these old piles, which become the resort of thousands, nine tenths of whom are unaware either of the classic ground on which they tread, or of the peculiar interest thrown around the spot by the deeds of remote ages.

During our stay in Leeds, we had the good fortune to become acquainted with Wilson Armistead, Esq. This gentleman is well known as an able writer against slavery. His most elaborate work is "A Tribute for the Negro." This is a volume of five hundred and sixty pages, and is replete with facts refuting the charges of inferiority brought against the negro race. Few English gentlemen have done more to hasten the day of the slave's liberation than Wilson Armistead.

A few days after, I paid a visit to Newstead Abbey, the far-famed residence of Lord Byron. I posted from Hucknall over to Newstead one pleasant morning, and, being provided with a letter of introduction to Colonel Wildman, I lost no time in presenting myself at the door of the abbey. But, unfortunately for me, the colonel was at Mansfield, in attendance at the Assizes—he being one of the county magistrates. I did not, however, lose the object of my visit, as every attention was paid in showing me about the premises. I felt as every one must who gazes for the first time upon these walls, and remembers that it was here, even amid the comparative ruins of a building once dedicated to the sacred cause of Religion and her twin sister, Charity, that the genius of Byron was first developed; here that he paced with youthful melancholy the halls of his illustrious ancestors, and trode the walks of the long-banished monks. The housekeeper—a remarkably good-looking and polite woman—showed us through the different apartments, and explained in the most minute manner every object of interest connected with the interior of the building. We first visited the Monk's Parlor, which seemed to contain nothing of note, except a very fine-stained window—one of the figures representing St. Paul, surmounted by a cross. We passed through Lord Byron's Bed-room, the Haunted Chamber, the Library and the Eastern Corridor, and halted in the Tapestry Bed-room, which is truly a magnificent apartment, formed by the Byrons for the use of King Charles II. The ceiling is richly decorated with the Byron arms. We next visited the grand Drawing-room, probably the finest in the building. This saloon contains a large number of splendid portraits, among which is the celebrated portrait of Lord Byron, by Phillips. In this room we took into our hand the skull-cup, of which so much has been written, and that has on it:

"Start not—nor deem my spirit fled;
In me behold the only skull
From which, unlike a living head,
Whatever flows is never dull.

"I lived, I loved, I quaffed like thee;
I died—let earth my bones resign:
Fill up—thou canst not injure me;
The worm hath fouler lips than thine.

"Better to hold the sparkling grape,
Than nurse the earth-worm's slimy brood;
And circle in the goblet's shape
The drink of gods, than reptile's food.

"Where once my wit, perchance, hath shone,
In aid of others let me shine;

And when, alas! our brains are gone,
What nobler substitute than wine?

"Quaff while thou canst—another race,
When thou and thine like thee are sped,
May rescue thee from earth's embrace,
And rhyme and revel with the dead.

"Why not? since through life's little day
Our heads such sad effects produce;
Redeemed from worms and wasting clay,
This chance is theirs, to be of use."

Leaving this noble room, we descended by a few polished oak steps into the West Corridor, from which we entered the grand Dining Hall, and through several other rooms, until we reached the Chapel. Here we were shown a stone coffin which had been found near the high altar, when the workmen were excavating the vault intended by Lord Byron for himself and his dog. The coffin contained the skeleton of an abbot, and also the identical skull from which the cup of which I have made mention was made. We then left the building, and took a stroll through the grounds. After passing a pond of cold crystal water, we came to a dark wood, in which are two leaden statues of Pan, and a female satyr—very fine specimens as works of art. We here inspected the tree whereon Byron carved his own name and that of his sister, with the date, all of which are still legible. However, the tree is now dead, and we were informed that Colonel Wildman intended to have it cut down, so as to preserve the part containing the inscription. After crossing an interesting and picturesque part of the gardens, we arrived within the precincts of the ancient chapel, near which we observed a neat marble monument, and which we supposed to have been erected to the memory of some of the Byrons; but, on drawing near to it, we read the following inscription:

"Near this spot are deposited the Remains of one who possessed Beauty without Vanity, Strength without Insolence, Courage without Ferocity, and all the Virtues of Man without his Vices. This Praise, which would be unmeaning Flattery if inscribed over human ashes, is but a just tribute to the Memory of BOATSWAIN, a Dog, who was born at Newfoundland, May, 1803, and died at Newstead Abbey, Nov. 18, 1808.

"When some proud son of man returns to earth,
Unknown to glory, but upheld by birth,
The sculptured art exhausts the pomp of woe,
And storied urns record who rests below;
When all is done, upon the tomb is seen
Not what he was, but what he should have been.
But the poor dog, in life the firmest friend,
The first to welcome, foremost to defend,
Whose honest heart is still his master's own,
Who labors, fights, lives, breathes for him alone,
Unhonored falls, unnoticed all his worth,
Denied in heaven the soul he held on earth;
While man, vain insect! hopes to be forgiven,
And claims himself a sole, exclusive heaven.
O, man! thou feeble tenant of an hour,
Debased by slavery, or corrupt by power,
Who knows thee well must quit thee with disgust,
Degraded mass of animated dust;
Thy love is lust, thy friendship all a cheat,
Thy smiles hypocrisy, thy words deceit!
By nature vile, ennobled but by name,
Each kindred brute might bid thee blush for shame.
Ye, who perchance behold this simple urn,
Pass on—it honors none you wish to mourn:
To mark a friend's remains these stones arise;
I never knew but one,—and here he lies."

By a will which his lordship executed in 1811, he directed that his own body should be buried in a vault in the garden, near his faithful dog. This feeling of affection to his dumb and faithful follower, commendable in itself, seems here to have been carried beyond the bounds of reason and propriety.

In another part of the grounds we saw the oak-tree planted by the poet himself. It has now attained a goodly size, considering the growth of the oak, and bids fair to become a lasting memento to the noble bard, and to be a shrine to which thousands of pilgrims will resort in future ages, to do homage to his mighty genius. This tree promises to share in after times the celebrity of Shakspeare's mulberry, and Pope's willow. Near by, and in the tall trees, the rooks were keeping up a tremendous noise. After seeing everything of interest connected with the great poet, we entered our chaise, and left the premises. As we were leaving, I turned to take a farewell look at the abbey, standing in solemn grandeur, the long ivy clinging fondly to the rich tracery of a former age. Proceeding to the little town of Hucknall, we entered the old gray parish church, which has for ages been the last resting-place of the Byrons, and where repose the ashes of the poet, marked by a neat marble slab, bearing the following inscription:

In the vault beneath,
where many of his Ancestors and his Mother are
Buried,
lie the remains of
GEORGE GORDON NOEL BYRON,
Lord Byron, of Rochdale,
in the County of Lancaster,
the author of "Childe Harold's Pilgrimage."
He was born in London, on the
22nd of January, 1788.
He died at Missolonghi, in Western Greece, on the
19th of April, 1824,
Engaged in the glorious attempt to restore that
country to her ancient grandeur and renown.

His Sister, the Honorable
Augusta Maria Leigh,
placed this Tablet to his Memory.

From an Album that is kept for visitors to register their names in, I copied the following lines, composed by William Howitt, immediately after the interment:

"Rest in thy tomb, young heir of glory, rest!
Rest in thy rustic tomb, which thou shalt make
A spot of light upon thy country's breast,
Known, honored, haunted ever for thy sake.
Thither romantic pilgrims shall betake
Themselves from distant lands. When we are still
In centuries of sleep, thy fame shall wake,

And thy great memory with deep feelings fill
These scenes which thou hast trod, and hallow every hill."

This closed my visit to the interesting scenes associated with Byron's strange and eventful history—scenes that ever acquire a growing charm as the lapse of years softens the errors of the man, and confirms the genius of the poet.

The following lines, written by Byron in early life, were realized in his death in a foreign land:

"When Time or soon or late shall bring
The dreamless sleep that lulls the dead,
Oblivion! may thy languid limb
Wave gently o'er my dying bed!

"No band of friends or heirs be there,
To weep, or wish the coming blow:
No maiden, with dishevelled hair,
To feel, or feign, decorous woe.

"But silent let me sink to Earth,
With no officious mourners near;
I would not mar one hour of mirth,
Nor startle friendship with a tear."

CHAPTER XIII.

"Now, this once gorgeous edifice, if reared
By piety, which sought with honest aim
The glory of the Lord, should be revered
Even for that cause, by those who seek the same.
Perchance the builders erred; but who shall blame
Error, nor feel that they partake it too?
Then judge with charity, whate'er thy name,
Be thou a Pagan, Protestant, or Jew;
Nor with a scornful glance these Papal reliques view."

BARTON.

IT was on a lovely morning that I found myself on board the little steamer *Wye*, passing out of Bristol harbor. In going down the river, we saw on our right the stupendous rocks of St. Vincent towering some four or five hundred feet above our heads. By the swiftness of our fairy steamer, we were soon abreast of Cook's Folly, a singular tower, built by a man from whom it takes its name, and of which the following romantic story is told: "Some years since a gentleman, of the name of Cook, erected this tower, which has since gone by the name of 'Cook's Folly.' A son having been born, he was desirous of ascertaining, by means of astrology, if he would live to enjoy his property. Being himself a firm believer, like the poet Dryden, that certain information might be obtained from the above science, he caused the child's horoscope to be drawn, and found, to his dismay, that in his third, sixteenth, or twenty-first year, he would be in danger of meeting with some fearful calamity or sudden death, to avert which he caused the turret to be constructed, and the child placed therein. Secure, as he vainly thought, there he lived, attended by a faithful servant, their food and fuel being conveyed to them by means of a pulley-basket, until he was old enough to wait upon himself. On the eve of his twenty-first year his parent's hopes rose high, and great were the rejoicings prepared to welcome the young heir to his home. But, alas! no human skill could avert the dark fate which clung to him. The last night he had to pass alone in the turret, a bundle of fagots was conveyed to him as usual, in which lay concealed a viper, which clung to his hand. The bite was fatal; and, instead of being borne in triumph, the dead body of his only son was the sad spectacle which met the sight of his father."

We crossed the channel, and soon entered the mouth of that most picturesque of rivers, the Wye. As we neared the town of Chepstow the old castle made its appearance, and a fine old ruin it is. Being previously provided with a letter of introduction to a gentleman in Chepstow, I lost no time in finding him out. This gentleman gave me a cordial reception, and did what Englishmen seldom ever do, lent me his saddle-horse to ride to the abbey. While lunch was in preparation I took a stroll through the castle which stood near by. We entered the castle through the great doorway, and were soon treading the walls that had once sustained the cannon and the sentinel, but were now covered with weeds and wild-flowers. The drum and fife had once been heard within these walls—the only music now is the cawing of the rook and daw. We paid a hasty visit to the various apartments, remaining longest in those of most interest. The room in which Martin the Regicide was imprisoned nearly twenty years was pointed out to us. The Castle of Chepstow is still a magnificent pile, towering upon the brink of a stupendous cliff, on reaching the top of which, we had a splendid view of the surrounding country. Time, however, compelled us to retrace our steps, and, after partaking of a lunch, we mounted a horse for the first time in ten years, and started for Tintern Abbey. The distance from Chepstow to the abbey is about five miles, and the road lies along the banks of the river. The river is walled in on either side by hills of much beauty, clothed from base to summit with the richest verdure. I can conceive of nothing more striking than the first appearance of the abbey. As we rounded a hill, all at once we saw the old ruin standing before us in all its splendor. This celebrated ecclesiastical relic of the olden time is doubtless the finest ruin of its kind in Europe. Embosomed amongst hills, and situated on the banks of the most fairy-like river in the world, its beauty can scarcely be surpassed. We halted at the "Beaufort Arms," left our horse, and sallied forth to view the abbey. The sun was pouring a flood of light upon the old gray walls, lighting up its dark recesses, as if to give us a better opportunity of viewing it. I gazed with astonishment and admiration at its many beauties, and especially at the superb Gothic windows over the entrance-door. The beautiful Gothic pillars, with here and there a representation of a praying priest, and mailed knights, with saints and Christian martyrs, and the hundreds of Scriptural representations, all indicate that this was a place of considerable importance in its palmy days. The once stone floor had disappeared, and we found ourselves standing on a floor of unbroken green grass, swelling back to the old walls, and looking so verdant and silken that it seemed the very floor of fancy. There are more romantic and wilder places than this in the world, but none more beautiful. The preservation of these old abbeys should claim the attention of those under whose charge they are, and we felt like joining with the poet, and saying—

> "O ye who dwell
> Around yon ruins, guard the precious charge
> From hands profane! O save the sacred pile—
> O'er which the wing of centuries has flown
> Darkly and silently, deep-shadowing all
> Its pristine honors—from the ruthless grasp
> Of future violation!"

In contemplating these ruins more closely, the mind insensibly reverts to the period of feudal and regal oppression, when structures like that of Tintern Abbey necessarily became the scenes of stirring and highly-important events. How altered is the scene! Where were formerly magnificence and splendor, the glittering array of priestly prowess, the crowded halls of haughty bigots, and the prison of religious offenders, there is now but a heap of mouldering ruins. The oppressed and the oppressor have long since lain down together in the peaceful grave. The ruin, generally speaking, is unusually perfect, and the sculpture still beautifully sharp. The outward walls are nearly entire, and are thickly clad with ivy. Many of the windows are also in a good state of preservation; but the roof has long since fallen in. The feathered songsters were fluttering about, and pouring forth their artless lays as a tribute of joy; while the lowing of the herds, the bleating of flocks, and the hum of bees upon the farm near by, all burst upon the ear, and gave the scene a picturesque sublimity that can be easier imagined than described. Most assuredly Shakspeare had such ruins in view when he exclaimed,

> "The cloud-capped towers, the gorgeous palaces,
> The solemn temples, the great globe itself,
> Yes, all which it inherit, shall dissolve,
> And, like the baseless fabric of a vision,
> Leave not a wreck behind."

In the afternoon we returned to Bristol, and I spent the greater part of the next day in examining the interior of Redcliffe Church. Few places in the west of England have greater claims upon the topographer and historian than the church of St. Mary's, Redcliffe. Its antiquity, the beauty of its architecture, and, above all, the interesting circumstances connected with its history, entitle it to peculiar notice. It is also associated with the enterprise of genius; for its name has been blended with the reputation of Rowley, of Canynge, and of Chatterton, and no lover of poetry and admirer of art can visit it without a degree of enthusiasm. And, when the old building shall have mouldered into ruins, even these will be trodden with veneration, as sacred to the recollection of genius of the highest order. Ascending a winding stair, we were shown into the treasury room. The room forms an irregular octagon, admitting light through narrow, unglazed apertures, upon the broken and scattered fragments of the famous Rowleian chests, that, with the rubble and dust of centuries, cover the floor. It is here creative fancy pictures forth the sad image of the spirit of the spot—the ardent boy, flushed and fed by hope, musing on the brilliant deception he had conceived, whose daring attempt has left his name unto the intellectual world as a marvel and a mystery.

That a boy under twelve years of age should write a series of poems, imitating the style of the fifteenth century, and palm these poems off upon the world as the work of a monk, is indeed strange; and that these should become the object of interesting contemplation to the literary world, and should awaken inquiries, and exercise the talents of a Southey, a Bryant, a Miller, a Mathias, and others, savors more of romance than reality. I had visited the room in a garret in High Holborn where this poor boy died; I had stood over a grave in the burial-ground of

Shoe-Lane Work-house, which was pointed out to me as the last resting-place of Chatterton; and now I was in the room where, it was alleged, he obtained the manuscripts that gave him such notoriety. We descended and viewed other portions of the church. The effect of the chancel, as seen behind the pictures, is very singular, and suggestive of many swelling thoughts. We look at the great east window—it is unadorned with its wonted painted glass; we look at the altar-screen beneath, on which the light of day again falls, and behold the injuries it has received at the hands of time. There is a dreary mournfulness in the scene which fastens on the mind, and is in unison with the time-worn mouldering fragments that are seen all around us. And this dreariness is not removed by our tracing the destiny of man on the storied pavements or on the graven brass, that still bears upon its surface the names of those who obtained the world's regard years back. This old pile is not only an ornament to the city, but it stands a living monument to the genius of its founder. Bristol has long sustained a high position, as a place from which the American abolitionists have received substantial encouragement in their arduous labors for the emancipation of the slaves of that land; and the writer of this received the best evidence that in this respect the character of the people had not been exaggerated, especially as regards the "Clifton Ladies' Anti-Slavery Society." From Bristol I paid a hasty visit to the Scotch capital.

Edinburgh is the most picturesque of all the towns which I have visited since my arrival in the father-land. Its situation has been compared to that of Athens; but it is said that the modern Athens is superior to the ancient. I was deeply impressed with the idea that I had seen the most beautiful of cities, after beholding those fashionable resorts, Paris and Versailles. I have seen nothing in the way of public grounds to compare with the gardens of Versailles, or the Champs Elysees, at Paris; and as for statuary, the latter place is said to take the lead of the rest of the world.

The general appearance of Edinburgh prepossesses one in its favor. The town, being built upon the brows of a large terrace, presents the most wonderful perspective. Its first appearance to a stranger, and the first impression, can scarcely be but favorable. In my first walk through the town I was struck with the difference in the appearance of the people from the English. But the difference between the Scotch and the Americans is very great. The cheerfulness depicted in the countenances of the people here, and their free-and-easy appearance, is very striking to a stranger. He who taught the sun to shine, the flowers to bloom, the birds to sing, and blesses us with rain, never intended that his creatures should look sad. There is a wide difference between the Americans and any other people which I have seen. The Scotch are healthy and robust, unlike the long-faced, sickly-looking Americans.

While on our journey from London to Paris, to attend the Peace Congress, I could not but observe the marked difference between the English and American delegates. The former looked as if their pockets had been filled with sandwiches, made of good bread and roast beef; while the latter appeared as if their pockets had been filled with Holloway's pills and Mrs. Kidder's cordial.

I breakfasted this morning in a room in which the poet Burns, as I was informed, had often sat. The conversation here turned upon Burns. The lady of the house pointed to a scrap of poetry which was in a frame hanging on the wall, written, as she said, by the poet, on hearing the people rejoicing in a church over the intelligence of a victory. I copied it, and will give it to you:

"Ye hypocrites! are these your pranks,
To murder men and give God thanks?
For shame! give o'er, proceed no further;
God won't accept your thanks for murder."

The fact that I was in the room where Scotland's great national poet had been a visitor caused me to feel that I was on classic, if not hallowed ground. On returning from our morning visit, we met a gentleman with a colored lady on each arm. C—— remarked, in a very dry manner, "If they were in Georgia, the slaveholders would make them walk in a more hurried gait than they do." I said to my friend that, if he meant the pro-slavery prejudice would not suffer them to walk peaceably through the streets, they need go no further than the pro-slavery cities of New York and Philadelphia. When walking through the streets, I amused myself by watching C——'s countenance; and, in doing so, imagined I saw the changes experienced by every fugitive slave in his first month's residence in this country. A sixteen months' residence has not yet familiarized me with the change.

* * *

I remained in Edinburgh a day or two, which gave me an opportunity of seeing some of the lions in the way of public buildings, &c., in company with our friend C——. I paid a visit to the Royal Institute, and inspected the very fine collection of paintings, statues, and other productions of art. The collection in the Institute is not to be compared to the British Museum at London, or the Louvre at Paris, but is probably the best in Scotland. Paintings from the hands of many of the masters, such as Sir A. Vandyke, Tiziano Vercellio and Van Dellen, were hanging on the wall, and even the names of Rubens and Titian were attached to some of the finer specimens. Many of these represent some of the nobles and distinguished families of Rome, Athens, Greece, &c. A beautiful one, representing a group of the Lomellini family of Genoa, seemed to attract the attention of most of the visitors.

In visiting this place, we passed close by the monument of Sir Walter Scott. This is the most exquisite thing of the kind that I have seen since coming to this country. It is said to be the finest monument in Europe. There sits the author of "Waverley," with a book and pencil in hand, taking notes. A beautiful dog is seated by his side. Whether this is meant to represent his favorite dog, Camp, at whose death the poet shed so many tears, we were not informed; but I was of opinion that it might be the faithful Percy, whose monument stands in the grounds at Abbotsford. Scott was an admirer of the canine tribe. One may form a good idea of the appearance of this distinguished writer when living, by viewing this remarkable statue. The statue is very beautiful, but not equal to the one of Lord Byron, which was executed to be placed by the side of Johnson, Milton and Addison, in Poets' Corner, Westminster Abbey; but the vestry not allowing it a place there, it now stands in one of the colleges at Cambridge. While viewing the statue of Byron, I thought he, too, should have been represented with a dog by his side; for he, like Scott, was remarkably fond of dogs; so much so that he intended to have his favorite, Boatswain, interred by his side.

We paid a short visit to the monuments of Burns and Allan Ramsay, and the renowned old Edinburgh Castle. The castle is now used as a barrack for infantry. It is accessible only from the High Street, and must have been impregnable before the discovery of gunpowder. In the wars with the English, it was twice taken by stratagem: once in a very daring manner, by climbing up the most inaccessible part of the rock upon which it stands, and where a foe was least expected, and putting the guard to death; and at another time, by a party of soldiers disguising themselves as merchants, and obtaining admission inside the castle gates. They succeeded in preventing the gates from being closed until reinforced by a party of men under Sir Wm. Douglas, who soon overpowered the occupants of the castle.

We could not resist the temptation held out to see the palace of Holyrood. It was in this place that the beautiful but unfortunate Mary Queen of Scots resided for a number of years. On reaching the palace, we were met at the door by an elderly-looking woman, with a red face, garnished with a pair of second-hand curls, the whole covered with a cap having the widest border that I had seen for years. She was very kind in showing us about the premises, especially as we were foreigners, no doubt expecting an extra fee for politeness. The most interesting of the many rooms in this ancient castle is the one which was occupied by the queen, and where her Italian favorite, Rizzio, was murdered.

But by far the most interesting object which we visited while in Edinburgh was the house where the celebrated Reformer, John Knox, resided. It is a queer-looking old building, with a pulpit on the outside, and above the door are the nearly obliterated remains of the following inscription: "Lufe. God. Above. Al. And. your. Nichbour. As you. Self." This was probably traced under the immediate direction of the great Reformer. Such an inscription put upon a house of worship at the present day would be laughed at. I have given it to you, punctuation and all, just as it stands.

The general architecture of Edinburgh is very imposing, whether we regard the picturesque disorder of the buildings in the Old Town, or the symmetrical proportions of the streets and squares in the New. But on viewing this city, which has the reputation of being the finest in Europe, I was surprised to find that it had none of those sumptuous structures which, like St. Paul's, or Westminster Abbey, York Minster, and some other of the English provincial cathedrals, astonish the beholder alike by their magnitude and their architectural splendor. But in no city which I have visited in the kingdom is the general standard of excellence better maintained than in Edinburgh.

CHAPTER XIV.

> "I was a traveller then upon the moor;
> I saw the hare that raced about with joy;
> I heard the woods and distant waters roar,
> Or heard them not, as happy as a boy."
>
> WORDSWORTH.

I AM glad once more to breathe an atmosphere uncontaminated by the fumes and smoke of a city with its population of three hundred thousand inhabitants. In company with my friend C——, I left Glasgow on the afternoon of the 23d inst., for Dundee, a beautiful town situated on the banks of the river Tay. One like myself, who has spent the best part of an eventful life in cities, and who prefers, as I do, a country to a town life, feels a greater degree of freedom when surrounded by forest trees, or country dwellings, and looking upon a clear sky, than when walking through the thronged thoroughfares of a city, with its dense population, meeting every moment a new or strange face, which one has never seen before, and never expects to see again.

Although I had met with one of the warmest public receptions with which I have been greeted since my arrival in the country, and had had an opportunity of shaking hands with many noble friends of the slave, whose names I had often seen in print, yet I felt glad to see the tall chimneys and smoke of Glasgow receding in the distance, as our "iron-horse" was taking us with almost lightning speed from the commercial capital of Scotland.

The distance from Glasgow to Dundee is some seventy or eighty miles, and we passed through the finest country which I have seen in this portion of the queen's dominions. We passed through the old town of Stirling, which lies about thirty miles distant from Glasgow, and is a place much frequented by those who travel for pleasure. It is built on the brow of a hill, and the castle from which it most probably derived its name may be seen from a distance. Had it not been for a "professional" engagement the same evening at Dundee, I would most assuredly have halted to take a look at the old building.

The castle is situated or built on an isolated rock, which

seems as if nature had thrown it there for that purpose. It was once the retreat of the Scottish kings, and famous for its historical associations. Here the "Lady of the Lake," with the magic ring, sought the monarch to intercede for her father; here James II. murdered the Earl of Douglas; here the beautiful but unfortunate Mary was made queen; and here John Knox, the Reformer, preached the coronation sermon of James VI. The Castle Hill rises from the valley of the Forth, and makes an imposing and picturesque appearance. The windings of the noble river, till lost in the distance, present pleasing contrasts, scarcely to be surpassed.

The speed of our train, after passing Stirling, brought before us, in quick succession, a number of fine villas and farm-houses. Every spot seemed to have been arrayed by nature for the reception of the cottage of some happy family. During this ride we passed many sites where the lawns were made, the terraces defined and levelled, the groves tastefully clumped, the ancient trees, though small when compared to our great forest oaks, were beautifully sprinkled here and there, and in everything the labor of art seemed to have been anticipated by nature. Cincinnatus could not have selected a prettier situation for a farm than some which presented themselves during this delightful journey. At last we arrived at the place of our destination, where our friends were in waiting for us.

As I have already forwarded to you a paper containing an account of the Dundee meeting, I shall leave you to judge from these reports the character of the demonstration. Yet I must mention a fact or two connected with our first evening's visit to this town. A few hours after our arrival in the place, we were called upon by a gentleman whose name is known wherever the English language is spoken—one whose name is on the tongue of every student and school-boy in this country and America, and what lives upon their lips will live and be loved forever.

We were seated over a cup of strong tea, to revive our spirits for the evening, when our friend entered the room, accompanied by a gentleman, small in stature, and apparently seventy-five years of age, yet he appeared as active as one half that age. Feeling half drowsy from riding in the cold, and then the sudden change to a warm fire, I was rather inclined not to move on the entrance of the stranger. But the name of Thomas Dick, LL.D., roused me in a moment from my lethargy; I could scarcely believe that I was in the presence of the "Christian Philosopher." Dr. Dick is one of the men to whom the age is indebted. I never find myself in the presence of one to whom the world owes so much, without feeling a thrilling emotion, as if I were in the land of spirits. Dr. Dick had come to our lodgings to see and congratulate William and Ellen Craft upon their escape from the republican Christians of the United States; and as he pressed the hand of the "white slave," and bid her "welcome to British soil," I saw the silent tear stealing down the cheek of this man of genius. How I wished that the many slaveholders and pro-slavery professed Christians of America, who have read and pondered the philosophy of this man, could have been present! Thomas Dick is an abolitionist—one who is willing that the world should know that he hates the "peculiar institution." At the meeting that evening, Dr. Dick was among the most prominent. But this was not the only distinguished man who took part on that occasion.

Another great mind was on the platform, and entered his solemn protest in a manner long to be remembered by those present. This was the Rev. George Gilfillan, well known as the author of the "Portraits of Literary Men." Mr. Gilfillan is an energetic speaker, and would have been the lion of the evening, even if many others who are more distinguished as platform orators had been present. I think it was Napoleon who said that the enthusiasm of others abated his own. At any rate, the spirit with which each speaker entered upon his duty for the evening abated my own enthusiasm for the time being. The last day of our stay in Dundee, I paid a visit, by invitation, to Dr. Dick, at his residence in the little village of Broughty Ferry. We found the great astronomer in his parlor waiting for us. From the parlor we went to the new study, and here I felt more at ease, for I went to see the philosopher in his study, and not in his drawing-room. But even this room had too much the look of nicety to be an author's *sanctum*; and I inquired and was soon informed by Mrs. Dick, that I should have a look at the "*old study*."

During a sojourn of eighteen months in Great Britain, I have had the good fortune to meet with several distinguished literary characters, and have always managed, while at their places of abode, to see the table and favorite chair. William and Ellen Craft were seeing what they could see through a microscope, when Mrs. Dick returned to the room, and intimated that we could now see the old literary workshop. I followed, and was soon in a room about fifteen feet square, with but one window, which occupied one side of the room. The walls of the other three sides were lined with books, and many of these looked the very personification of age. I took my seat in the "*old arm-chair*;" and here, thought I, is the place and the seat in which this distinguished man sat while weaving the radiant wreath of renown which now, in his old age, surrounds him, and whose labors will be more appreciated by future ages than the present.

I took a farewell of the author of the "Solar System," but not until I had taken a look through the great telescope in the observatory. This instrument, through which I tried to see the heavens, was not the one invented by Galileo, but an improvement upon the original. On leaving this learned man, he shook hands with us, and bade us "God speed" in our mission; and I left the philosopher, feeling I had not passed an hour more agreeably with a literary character since the hour which I spent with the poet Montgomery a few months since. And, by-the-by, there is a resemblance between the poet and the philosopher. In becoming acquainted with great men I have become a convert to the opinion that a big nose is an almost necessary appendage to the form of a man with a giant intellect. If those whom I have seen be a criterion, such is certainly the case. But I have spun out this too long, and must close.

CHAPTER XV.

"Proud relic of the mighty dead!
Be mine with shuddering awe to tread
Thy roofless weedy hall,
And mark, with fancy's kindling eye,
The steel-clad ages, gliding by,
Thy feudal pomp recall."

KEATS.

I CLOSED my last in the ancient town of Melrose, on the banks of the Tweed, and within a stone's throw of the celebrated ruins from which the town derives its name. The valley in which Melrose is situated, and the surrounding hills, together with the monastery, have so often been made a theme for the Scottish bards, that this has become the most interesting part of Scotland. Of the many gifted writers who have taken up the pen, none have done more to bring the Eildon Hills and Melrose Abbey into note than the author of "Waverley." But who can read his writings without a regret that he should have so woven fact and fiction together that it is almost impossible to discriminate between the one and the other?

We arrived at Melrose in the evening, and proceeded to the chapel where our meeting was to be held, and where our friends, the Crafts, were warmly greeted. On returning from the meeting we passed close by the ruins of Melrose, and, very fortunately, it was a moonlight night. There is considerable difference of opinion among the inhabitants of the place as regards the best time to view the abbey. The author of the "Lay of the Last Minstrel" says:

"If thou wouldst view fair Melrose aright,
Go visit it by the pale moonlight:
For the gay beams of lightsome day
Gild but to flout the ruins gray."

In consequence of this admonition, I was informed that many persons remain in town to see the ruins by moonlight. Aware that the moon did not send its rays upon the old building every night in the year, I asked the keeper what he did on dark nights. He replied that he had a large lantern, which he put upon the end of a long pole, and with this he succeeded in lighting up the ruins. This good man labored hard to convince me that his invention was nearly, if not quite as good, as nature's own moon. But having no need of an application of his invention to the abbey, I had no opportunity of judging of its effect. I thought, however, that he had made a moon to some purpose, when he informed me that some nights, with his pole and lantern, he earned his four or five shillings. Not being content with a view by "moonlight alone," I was up the next morning before the sun, and paid my respects to the abbey. I was too early for the keeper, and he handed me the key through the window, and I entered the ruins alone. It is one labyrinth of gigantic arches and dilapidated halls, the ivy growing and clinging wherever it can fasten its roots, and the whole as fine a picture of decay as imagination could create. This was the favorite resort of Sir Walter Scott, and furnished him much matter for the "Lay of the Last Minstrel." He could not have selected a more fitting place for solitary thought than this ancient abode of monks and priests. In passing through the cloisters I could not but remark the carvings of leaves and flowers, wrought in stone in the most exquisite manner, looking as fresh as if they were just from the hands of the artist. The lapse of centuries seems not to have made any impression upon them, or changed their appearance in the least. I sat down among the ruins of the abbey. The ground about was piled up with magnificent fragments of stone, representing various texts of Scripture, and the quaint ideas of the priests and monks of that age. Scene after scene swept through my fancy as I looked upon the surrounding objects. I could almost imagine I saw the bearded monks going from hall to hall, and from cell to cell. In visiting these dark cells, the mind becomes oppressed by a sense of the utter helplessness of the victims who once passed over the thresholds and entered these religious prisons. There was no help or hope but in the will that ordered their fate. How painful it is to gaze upon these walls, and to think how many tears were shed by their inmates, when this old monastery was in its glory! I ascended to the top of the ruin by a circuitous stairway, whose stone steps were worn deep from use by many who, like myself, had visited them to gratify a curiosity. From the top of the abbey I had a splendid view of the surrounding hills and the beautiful valley through which flow the Gala Water and Tweed. This is unquestionably the most splendid specimen of Gothic architectural ruin in Scotland. But any description of mine conveys but a poor idea to the fancy. To be realized, it must be seen.

During the day, we paid a visit to Abbotsford, the splendid mansion of the late Sir Walter Scott, Bart. This beautiful seat is situated on the banks of the Tweed, just below its junction with the Gala Water. It is a dreary-looking spot, and the house from the opposite side of the river has the appearance of a small, low castle. In a single day's ride through England one may see half a dozen cottages larger than Abbotsford house. I was much disappointed in finding the premises undergoing repairs and alterations, and that all the trees between the house and the river had been cut down. This is to be regretted the more, because they were planted, nearly every one of them, by the same hand that waved its wand of enchantment over the world. The fountain had been removed from where it had been placed by the hands of the poet to the centre of the yard; and even a small stone that had been placed over the favorite dog "Percy" had been taken up and thrown among some loose stones. One visits Abbotsford because of the genius of the man that once presided over it. Everything connected with the great poet is of interest to his admirers, and anything altered or removed tends to diminish that interest. We entered the house, and were conducted through the great hall, which is hung all round with massive armor of all descriptions, and other memorials of ancient times. The floor is of white and black marble. In passing through the hall, we entered a narrow arched room, stretching quite across the building, having a window at each end. This little or rather narrow room is filled with all kinds of armor, which is arranged with great taste. We were next shown into the dining-room, whose roof is of black oak, richly carved. In this room is a painting of the head of Queen Mary, in a charger, taken the day after the execution. Many other interesting portraits grace the walls of this room. But by far the finest apartment in the building is the drawing-room, with a lofty ceiling, and furnished with antique ebony furniture. After passing through the library, with its twenty thousand volumes, we found ourselves in the study, and I sat down in the same chair where once sat the poet: while before me was the table upon which were written the "Lady of the Lake," "Waverley," and other productions of this gifted writer. The clothes last worn by the poet were shown to us. There was the broad-skirted blue coat, with its large buttons, the plaid trousers, the heavy shoes, the black vest and white hat. These were all in a glass case, and all looked the poet and novelist. But the inside of the buildings had undergone alterations, as well as the outside. In passing through the library, we saw a granddaughter of the poet. She was from London, and was only on a visit of a few days. She looked pale and dejected, and seemed as if she longed to leave this secluded spot and return to the metropolis. She looked for all the world like a hot-house plant. I don't think the Scotch could do better than to purchase Abbotsford, while it has some imprint of the great magician, and secure its preservation; for I am sure that, a hundred years hence, no place will be more frequently visited in Scotland than the home of the late Sir Walter Scott. After sauntering three hours about the premises, I left, but not without feeling that I had been well paid for my trouble in visiting Abbotsford.

In the afternoon of the same day, in company with the Crafts, I took a drive to Dryburgh Abbey. It is a ruin of little interest, except as being the burial-place of Scott. The poet lies buried in St. Mary's Aisle. His grave is in the left transept of the cross, and close to where the high altar formerly stood. Sir Walter Scott chose his own grave, and he could not have selected a sunnier spot if he had roamed the wide world over. A shaded window breaks the sun as it falls upon his grave. The ivy is creeping and clinging wherever it can, as if it would shelter the poet's grave from the weather. The author lies between his wife and eldest son, and there is only room enough for one grave more, and the son's wife has the choice of being buried here.

The four o'clock train took us to Hawick; and after a pleasant visit in this place, and the people registering their names against American slavery, and the Fugitive Bill in particular, we set out for Carlisle, passing through the antique town of Langholm. After leaving the latter place, we had to travel by coach. But no matter how one travels here, he travels at a more rapid rate than in America. The distance from Langholm to Carlisle, twenty miles, occupied only two and a half hours in the journey. It was a cold day, and I had to ride on the outside, as the inside had been taken up. We changed horses and took in and put out passengers with a rapidity which seems almost incredible. The road was as smooth as could be imagined.

We bid farewell to Scotland, as we reached the little town of Gretna Green. This town, being on the line between England and Scotland, is noted as the place where a little cross-eyed, red-faced blacksmith, by the name of Priestly, first set up his own altar to Hymen, and married all who came to him, without regard to rank or station, and at prices to suit all. It was worth a ride through this part of the country, if for no other purpose than to see the town where more clandestine marriages have taken place than in any other part of the world. A ride of eight or nine miles brought us in sight of the Eden, winding its way slowly through a beautiful valley, with farms on either side, covered with sheep and cattle. Four very tall chimneys, sending forth dense columns of black smoke, announced to us that we were near Carlisle. I was really glad of this, for Ulysses was never more tired of the shores of Ilion than I of the top of that coach.

We remained over night at Carlisle, partaking of the hospitality of the prince of bakers, and left the next day for the lakes, where we had a standing invitation to pay a visit to a distinguished literary lady. A cold ride of about fifty miles brought us to the foot of Lake Windermere, a beautiful sheet of water, surrounded by mountains that seemed to vie with each other which should approach nearest the sky. The margin of the lake is carved out and built up into terrace above terrace, until the slopes and windings are lost in the snow-capped peaks of the mountains. It is not surprising that such men as Southey, Coleridge, Wordsworth, and others, resorted to this region for inspiration. After a coach ride of five miles (passing on our journey the "Dove's Nest," home of the late Mrs. Hemans), we were put down at the door of the Salutation Hotel, Ambleside, and a few minutes after found ourselves under the roof of the authoress of "Society in America." I know not how it is with others, but, for my own part, I always form an opinion of the appearance of an author whose writings I am at all familiar with, or a statesman whose speeches I have read. I had pictured in my own mind a tall, stately-looking lady of about sixty years, as the authoress of "Travels in the East;" and for once I was right, with the single exception that I had added on too many years by twelve. The evening was spent in talking about the United States; and William Craft had to go through the narrative of his escape from slavery. When I retired for the night, I found it almost impossible to sleep. The idea that I was under the roof of the authoress of "The Hour and the Man," and that I was on the banks of the sweetest lake in Great Britain, within half a mile of the residence of the late poet Wordsworth, drove sleep from my pillow. But I must leave an account of my visit to the Lakes for a future chapter.

When I look around and see the happiness here, even among the poorer classes, and that too in a country where the soil is not at all to be compared with our own, I mourn for our down-trodden countrymen, who are plundered, oppressed and made chattels of, to enable an ostentatious aristocracy to vie with each other in splendid extravagance.

CHAPTER XVI.

"Why weeps the Muse for England? What appears
In England's case to move the Muse to tears?
From side to side of her delightful isle
Is she not clothed with a perpetual smile?
Can nature add a charm, or art confer
A new-found luxury, not seen in her?"

COWPER.

MY last left me under the hospitable roof of Harriet Martineau. I had long had an invitation to visit this distinguished friend of our race, and as the invitation was renewed during my tour through the north, I did not feel disposed to decline it, and thereby lose so favorable an opportunity of meeting with one who had written so much in behalf of the oppressed of our land. About a mile from the head of Lake Windermere, and immediately under Wonsfell, and encircled by mountains on all sides except the south-west, lies the picturesque little town of Ambleside; and the brightest spot in the place is "The Knoll," the residence of Miss Martineau.

We reached "The Knoll" a little after nightfall, and a cordial shake of the hand by Miss M., who was waiting for us, trumpet in hand, soon assured us that we had met with a warm friend.

It is not my intention to lay open the scenes of domestic life at "The Knoll," nor to describe the social parties of which my friends and I were partakers during our sojourn within the hospitable walls of this distinguished writer; but the name of Miss M. is so intimately connected with the Anti-slavery movement by her early writings, and those have been so much admired by the friends of the slave in the United States, that I deem it not at all out of place for me to give my readers some idea of the authoress of "Political Economy," "Travels in the East," "The Hour and the Man," &c.

The dwelling is a cottage of moderate size, built after Miss M.'s own plan, upon a rise of land, from which it derives the name of "The Knoll." The library is the largest room in the building, and upon the walls of it were hung some beautiful engravings and a continental map. On a long table, which occupied the centre of the room, were the busts of Shakspeare, Newton, Milton, and a few other literary characters of the past. One side of the room was taken up with a large case, filled with a choice collection of books; and everything indicated that it was the home of genius and of taste.

The room usually occupied by Miss M., and where we found her on the evening of our arrival, is rather small, and lighted by two large windows. The walls of this room were also decorated with prints and pictures, and on the mantel-shelf were some models in terra cotta of Italian groups. On a circular table lay casts, medallions, and some very choice water-color drawings. Under the south window stood a small table covered with newly-opened letters, a portfolio, and several new books, with here and there a page turned down, and one with a paper-knife between its leaves, as if it had only been half read. I took up the last-mentioned, and it proved to be the "Life and Poetry of Hartley Coleridge," son of S. T. Coleridge. It was just from the press, and had, a day or two before, been forwarded to her by the publisher. Miss M. is very deaf, and always carries in her left hand a trumpet; and I was not a little surprised on learning from her that she had never enjoyed the sense of smell, and only on one occasion the sense of taste, and that for a single moment. Miss M. is loved with a sort of idolatry by the people of Ambleside, and especially the poor, to whom she gives a course of lectures every winter gratuitously. She finished her last course the day before our arrival. She was much pleased with Ellen Craft, and appeared delighted with the story of herself and husband's escape from slavery, as related by the latter, during the recital of which I several times saw the silent tear stealing down her cheek, and which she tried in vain to hide from us.

When Craft had finished, she exclaimed, "I would that every woman in the British empire could hear that tale as I have, so that they might know how their own sex was treated in that boasted land of liberty." It seems strange to the people of this country, that one so white and so ladylike as Mrs. Craft should have been a slave, and forced to leave the land of her nativity and seek an asylum in a foreign country.

The morning after our arrival I took a stroll by a circuitous pathway to the top of Loughrigg Fell. At the foot of the mount I met a peasant, who very kindly offered to lend me his donkey, upon which to ascend the mountain. Never having been upon the back of one of these long-eared animals, I felt some hesitation about trusting myself upon so diminutive looking a creature. But, being assured that if I would only resign myself to his care, and let him have his own way, I would be perfectly safe, I mounted, and off we set. We had, however, scarcely gone fifty rods, when, in passing over a narrow part of the path and overlooking a deep chasm, one of the hind feet of the donkey slipped, and with an involuntary shudder I shut my eyes to meet my expected doom; but, fortunately, the little fellow gained his foothold, and in all probability saved us both from a premature death. After we had passed over this dangerous place I dismounted; and, as soon as my feet had once more gained terra firma, I resolved that I would never again yield my own judgment to that of any one, not even to a donkey.

It seems as if nature had amused herself in throwing these mountains together. From the top of Loughrigg Fell the eye loses its power in gazing upon the objects below. On our left lay Rydal Mount, the beautiful seat of the late poet Wordsworth; while to the right, and away in the dim distance, almost hidden by the native trees, was the cottage where once resided Mrs. Hemans. And below us lay Windermere, looking more like a river than a lake, and which, if placed by the side of our own Ontario, Erie or Huron, would be lost in the fog. But here it looks beautiful in the extreme, surrounded as it is by a range of mountains that have no parallel in the United States for beauty. Amid a sun of uncommon splendor, dazzling the eye with the reflection upon the water below, we descended into the valley, and I was soon again seated by the fireside of our hospitable hostess. In the afternoon of the same day we took a drive to the "Dove's Nest," the home of the late Mrs. Hemans.

We did not see the inside of the house, on account of its being occupied by a very eccentric man, who will not permit a woman to enter the house; and it is said that he has been known to run when a female had unconsciously intruded herself upon his premises. As our company was in part composed of ladies, we had to share their fate, and therefore were prevented from seeing the interior of the "Dove's Nest." The exhibitor of such a man would be almost sure of a prize at the Great Exhibition.

At the head of Grassmere Lake, and surrounded by a few cottages, stands an old, gray, antique-looking parish church, venerable with the lapse of centuries, and the walls partly covered with ivy, and in the rear of which is the parish burial-ground. After leaving the "Dove's Nest," and having a pleasant ride over the hills and between the mountains, and just as the sun was disappearing behind them, we arrived at the gate of Grassmere Church; and, alighting and following Miss M., we soon found ourselves standing over a grave, marked by a single stone, and that, too, very plain, with a name deeply cut. This announced to us that we were standing over the grave of William Wordsworth. He chose his own grave, and often visited the spot before his death. He lies in the most sequestered spot in the whole grounds; and the simplicity and beauty of the place were enough to make one in love with it, to be laid so far from the bustle of the world, and in so sweet a place. The more one becomes acquainted with the literature of the Old World, the more he must love her poets. Among the teachers of men, none are more worthy of study than the poets; and, as teachers, they should receive far more credit than is yielded to them. No one can look back upon the lives of Dante, Shakspeare, Milton, Goethe, Cowper, and many others that we might name, without being reminded of the sacrifices which they made for mankind, and which were not appreciated until long after their deaths. We need look no further than our own country to find men and women wielding the pen practically and powerfully for the right. It is acknowledged on all hands, in this country, that England has the greatest dead poets, and America the greatest living ones. The poet and the true Christian have alike a hidden life. Worship is the vital element of each. Poetry has in it that kind of utility which good men find in their Bible, rather than such convenience as bad men often profess to draw from it. It ennobles the sentiments, enlarges the affections, kindles the imagination, and gives to us the enjoyment of a life in the past, and in the future, as well as in the present. Under its light and warmth, we wake from our torpidity and coldness, to a sense of our capabilities. This impulse once given, a great object is gained. Schiller has truly said, "Poetry can be to a man what love is to a hero. It can neither counsel him, nor smite him, nor perform any labor for him;

but it can bring him up to be a hero, can summon him to deeds, and arm him with strength for all he ought to be." I have often read with pleasure the sweet poetry of our own Whitfield, of Buffalo, which has appeared from time to time in the columns of the newspapers. I have always felt ashamed of the fact that he should be compelled to wield the razor instead of the pen for a living. Meaner poets than James M. Whitfield are now living by their compositions; and were he a white man he would occupy a different position.

Near the grave of Wordsworth is that of Hartley Coleridge. This name must be lifted up as a beacon, with all its pleasant and interesting associations; it must be added to the list in which some names of brighter fame are written—Burns, Byron, Campbell, and others their compeers. They had all the rich endowment of genius, and might, in achieving fame for themselves, have gained glory for God, and great good for man. But they looked "upon the wine when it was red," and gave life and fame, and their precious gifts, and God's blessing, for its false and ruinous joys. We would not drag forth their names that we may gloat over their infirmities. We pity them for their sad fall. We acknowledge the strength of their temptations, and, walking backwards, would throw a mantle over their frailties. But these men are needed, also, as warnings. The moral world must have its light-houses. Thousands of young men are running down upon the same rocks on which they were cast away. If the light of their genius has made them conspicuous, let us then use their conspicuity, and throw a ray from them, as from a beacon, far out upon the dim and perilous sea.

Hartley Coleridge was the eldest son of Samuel Taylor Coleridge, poet and metaphysician. He had some of his father's gifts, particularly his captivating conversational power, and his propensity for novel and profound speculation. He had also his father's infirmity of purpose. In the case of the son, the reason, as the world is now informed in a biography written by his brother, was that he early became the slave of intemperate habits, from which no aspirations of his own heart, no struggles with the enslaving appetite, and no efforts of sympathizing and sorrowful friends, could ever deliver him. He gained a fellowship in Oriel College, Oxford, and forfeited it in consequence of these habits. He then cast himself, as a literary adventurer, into the wild vortex of London life; failed sadly in all his projects; drank deep of the treacherous wine-cup, often to his own shame and the chagrin of his friends, from whom he would sometimes hide himself in places where restraint was unknown and shame forgotten, that he might be delivered from their reproachful pity. In the end, he betook himself to a cottage near Grassmere, and where, on the 6th of January, 1849, he died, not, we trust, without penitence and faith in the Redeemer of guilty and wretched men.

Hartley Coleridge tells us, in one of his confessions, that his first resort to wine was for the purpose of seeking relief from the sting of defeated ambition. This temptation was necessarily brief in its duration; for time would gradually extract this sting from his sensitive mind and heart. This, therefore, was not the doorway of the path which led him down to the gulf. The "wine parties" of Oxford were the scenes in which Hartley Coleridge was betrayed and lost. We have but a momentary glimpse of these things in the biography; but that glimpse is sufficient. It reveals to us what in popular language is called a gay scene, but which to us, and in reality, is sombre as death. In the midst of it there sits a bright-eyed, enthusiastic, impetuous young man, heated with repeated draughts of wine, urged by his fellow-revellers to drink deeper, yielding readily to their solicitations, and pouring forth all the while a stream of continuous and sparkling discourse, which fascinated his companions by its wit, its facility and its beauty. Alas! how many of those companions, it may be, are with him in graves where men can only weep and be silent!

It has often been said, and with much truth, that there is no more dangerous gift for a young man than to be able to sing a good song. It is equally dangerous, we think, to be known as a good talker. The gift of rapid, brilliant, mirth-moving speech, is a perilous possession. The dullards, for whose amusement this gift is so often invoked, know well that to ply its possessor with wine is the readiest way to bring out its power. But in the end the wine destroys the intellect, and the man of wit degenerates into a buffoon, and dies a drunkard. Such is the brief life and history of many a young man, who, behind the stained-glass windows of the fashionable *restaurant*, or in the mirrored and cushioned rooms of the club-house, was hailed as the "prince of good fellows," and the rarest of wits. The laughing applauders pass on, each in his own way, and he who made them sport is left to struggle in solitude with the enemy they have helped to fasten upon him. Let every young man who longs for these gifts, and envies their possessors, remember "poor Hartley Coleridge." Let them be warned by the fate of one who was caught in the toils they are weaving around themselves, and perished therein, leaving behind him the record of a life of unfulfilled purposes, and of great departures from the path of duty and peace.

After remaining a short time, and reading the epitaphs of the departed, we again returned to "The Knoll." Nothing can be more imposing than the beauty of English park scenery, and especially in the vicinity of the Lakes. Magnificent lawns that extend like sheets of vivid green, with here and there a sprinkling of fine trees, heaping up rich piles of foliage, and then the forest with the hare, the deer, and the rabbit, "bounding away to the covert, or the pheasant suddenly bursting upon the wing—the artificial stream, the brook taught to wind in natural meanderings, or expand into the glassy lake, with the yellow leaf sleeping upon its bright waters, and occasionally a rustic temple or sylvan statue grown green and dark with age," give an air of sanctity and picturesque beauty to English scenery that is unknown in the United States. The very laborer with his thatched cottage and narrow slip of ground-plot before the door, the little flower-bed, the woodbine trimmed against the wall, and hanging its blossoms about the windows, and the peasant seen trudging home at nightfall with the avails of the toil of the day upon his back—all this tells us of the happiness both of rich and poor in this country. And yet there are those who would have the world believe that the laborer of England is in a far worse condition than the slaves of America. Such persons know nothing of the real condition of the working class of this country. At any rate, the poor here, as well as the rich, are upon a level, as far as the laws of the country are concerned. The more one becomes acquainted with the English people, the more one has to admire them. They are so different from the people of our own country. Hospitality, frankness and good humor, are always to be found in an Englishman. After a ramble of three days about the Lakes, we mounted the coach, bidding Miss Martineau farewell, and quitted the lake district.

CHAPTER XVII.

"And there are dresses splendid but fantastical,
Masks of all times and nations, Turks and Jews,
And Harlequins and Clowns with feats gymnastical;
Greeks, Romans, Yankee-doodles, and Hindoos."

PRESUMING that you will expect from me some account of the great World's Fair, I take my pen to give you my own impressions, although I am afraid that anything which I may say about this "lion of the day" will fall far short of a description. On Monday last, I quitted my lodgings at an early hour, and started for the Crystal Palace. The day was fine, such as we seldom experience in London, with a clear sky, and invigorating air, whose vitality was as rousing to the spirits as a blast from the "horn of Astolpho." Although it was not yet ten o'clock when I entered Piccadilly, every omnibus was full, inside and out, and the street was lined with one living stream, as far as the eye could reach, all wending their way to the "Glass House." No metropolis in the world presents such facilities as London for the reception of the Great Exhibition now collected within its walls. Throughout its myriads of veins the stream of industry and toil pulses with sleepless energy. Every one seems to feel that this great capital of the world is the fittest place wherein they might offer homage to the dignity of toil. I had already begun to feel fatigued by my pedestrian excursions as I passed "Apsley House," the residence of the Duke of Wellington, and emerged into Hyde Park.

I had hoped that on getting into the Park I would be out of the crowd that seemed to press so heavily in the street. But in this I was mistaken. I here found myself surrounded by and moving with an overwhelming mass, such as I had never before witnessed. And, away in the distance, I beheld a dense crowd, and above every other object was seen the lofty summit of the Crystal Palace. The drive in the Park was lined with princely-looking vehicles of every description. The drivers in their bright red and gold uniforms, the pages and footmen in their blue trousers and white silk stockings, and the horses dressed up in their neat, silver-mounted harness, made the scene altogether one of great splendor. I was soon at the door, paid my shilling, and entered the building at the south end of the transept. For the first ten or twenty minutes, I was so lost in astonishment, and absorbed in pleasing wonder, that I could do nothing but gaze up and down the vista of the noble building. The Crystal Palace resembles in some respects the interior of the cathedrals of this country. One long avenue from east to west is intercepted by a transept, which divides the building into two nearly equal parts. This is the greatest building the world ever saw, before which the Pyramids of Egypt, and the Colossus of Rhodes must hide their diminished heads. The palace was not full at any time during the day, there being only sixty-four thousand persons present. Those who love to study the human countenance in all its infinite varieties can find ample scope for the indulgence of their taste, by a visit to the World's Fair. All countries are there represented—Europeans, Asiatics, Americans and Africans, with their numerous subdivisions. Even the exclusive Chinese, with his hair braided, and hanging down his back, has left the land of his nativity, and is seen making long strides through the Crystal Palace, in his wooden-bottomed shoes. Of all places of curious costumes and different fashions, none has ever yet presented such a variety as this Exhibition. No dress is too absurd to be worn in this place.

There is a great deal of freedom in the Exhibition. The servant who walks behind his mistress through the Park feels that he can crowd against her in the Exhibition. The queen and the day laborer, the prince and the merchant, the peer and the pauper, the Celt and the Saxon, the Greek and the Frank, the Hebrew and the Russ, all meet here upon terms of perfect equality. This amalgamation of rank, this kindly blending of interests, and forgetfulness of the cold formalities of ranks and grades, cannot but be attended with the very best results. I was pleased to see such a goodly sprinkling of my own countrymen in the Exhibition—I mean colored men and women—well-dressed, and moving about with their fairer brethren. This, some of our pro-slavery Americans did not seem to relish very well. There was no help for it. As I walked through the American part of the Crystal Palace some of our Virginia neighbors eyed me closely and with jealous looks, especially as an English lady was leaning on my arm. But their sneering looks did not disturb me in the least. I remained the longer in their department, and criticized the bad appearance of their goods the more. Indeed, the Americans, as far as appearance goes, are behind every other country in the Exhibition. The "Greek Slave" is the only production of art which the United States has sent. And it would have been more to their credit had they kept that at home. In so vast a place as the Great Exhibition one scarcely knows what to visit first, or what to look upon last. After wandering about through the building for five hours, I sat down in one of the galleries and looked at the fine marble statue of Virginius, with the knife in his hand and about to take the life of his beloved and beautiful daughter, to save her from the hands of Appius Claudius. The admirer of genius will linger for hours among the great variety of statues in the long avenue. Large statues of Lords Eldon and Stowell, carved out of solid marble, each weighing above twenty tons, are among the most gigantic in the building.

I was sitting with my four hundred paged guide-book before me, and looking down upon the moving mass, when my attention was called to a small group of gentlemen standing near the statue of Shakspeare, one of whom wore a white coat and hat, and had flaxen hair, and trousers rather short in the legs. The lady by my side, and who had called my attention to the group, asked if I could tell what country this odd-looking gentleman was from. Not wishing to run the risk of a mistake, I was about declining to venture an opinion, when the reflection of the sun against a mirror, on the opposite side, threw a brilliant light upon the group, and especially on the face of the gentleman in the white coat, and I immediately recognized under the brim of the white hat the features of Horace Greeley, Esq., of the New York *Tribune*. His general appearance was as much out of the English style as that of the Turk whom I had seen but a moment before, in his bag-like trousers, shuffling along in his slippers. But oddness in dress is one of the characteristics of the Great Exhibition.

Among the many things in the Crystal Palace, there are some which receive greater attention than others, around which may always be seen large groups of the visitors. The first of these is the Koh-i-noor, the "Mountain of Light." This is the largest and most valuable diamond in the world, said to be worth two million pounds sterling. It is indeed a great source of attraction to those who go to the Exhibition for the first time, but it is doubtful whether it obtains such admiration afterwards. We saw more than one spectator turn away with the idea that, after all, it was only a piece of glass. After some jamming, I got a look at the precious jewel; and although in a brass-grated cage, strong enough to hold a lion, I found it to be no larger than the third of a hen's egg. Two policemen remain by its side day and night.

The finest thing in the Exhibition is the "Veiled Vestal," a statue of a woman carved in marble, with a veil over her face, and so neatly done that it looks as if it had been thrown over after it was finished. The Exhibition presents many things which appeal to the eye and touch the heart, and altogether it is so decorated and furnished as to excite the dullest mind, and satisfy the most fastidious.

England has contributed the most useful and substantial articles; France, the most beautiful; while Russia, Turkey and the West Indies, seem to vie with each other in richness. China and Persia are not behind. Austria has also contributed a rich and beautiful stock. Sweden, Norway, Denmark, and the smaller states of Europe, have all tried to outdo themselves in sending goods to the World's Fair. In machinery, England has no competitor. In art, France is almost alone in the Exhibition, setting aside England.

In natural productions and provisions, America stands alone in her glory. There lies her pile of canvassed hams; whether they were wood or real, we could not tell. There are her barrels of salt beef and pork, her beautiful white lard, her Indian-corn and corn-meal, her rice and tobacco, her beef-tongues, dried peas, and a few bags of cotton. The contributors from the United States seemed to have forgotten that this was an exhibition of art, or they most certainly would not have sent provisions. But the United States takes the lead in the contributions, as no other country has sent in provisions. The finest thing contributed by our countrymen is a large piece of silk with an eagle painted upon it, surrounded by stars and stripes.

After remaining more than five hours in the great temple, I turned my back upon the richly-laden stalls, and left the Crystal Palace. On my return home I was more fortunate than in the morning, inasmuch as I found a seat for my friend and myself in an omnibus. And even my ride in the close omnibus was not without interest. For I had scarcely taken my seat, when my friend, who was seated opposite me, with looks and gesture informed me that we were in the presence of some distinguished person. I eyed the countenances of the different persons, but in vain, to see if I could find any one who by his appearance showed signs of superiority over his fellow-passengers. I had given up the hope of selecting the person of note, when another look from my friend directed my attention to a gentleman seated in the corner of the omnibus. He was a tall man, with strongly-marked features, hair dark and coarse. There was a slight stoop of the shoulder—that bend which is almost always a characteristic of studious men. But he wore upon his countenance a forbidding and disdainful frown, that seemed to tell one that he thought himself better than those about him. His dress did not indicate a man of high rank; and had we been in America, I would have taken him for an Ohio farmer.

While I was scanning the features and general appearance of the gentleman, the omnibus stopped and put down three or four of the passengers, which gave me an opportunity of getting a seat by the side of my friend, who, in a low whisper, informed me that the gentleman whom I had been eying so closely was no less a person than Thomas Carlyle. I had read his "Hero-worship," and "Past and Present," and had formed a high opinion of his literary abilities. But his recent attack upon the emancipated people of the West Indies, and his laborious article in favor of the reëstablishment of the lash and slavery, had created in my mind a dislike for the man, and I almost regretted that we were in the same omnibus. In some things Mr. Carlyle is right: but in many he is entirely wrong. As a writer, Mr. Carlyle is often monotonous and extravagant. He does not exhibit a new view of nature, or raise insignificant objects into importance; but generally takes commonplace thoughts and events, and tries to express them in stronger and statelier language than others. He holds no communion with his kind, but stands alone, without mate or fellow. He is like a solitary peak, all access to which is cut off. He exists not by sympathy, but by antipathy. Mr. Carlyle seems chiefly to try how he shall display his own powers, and astonish mankind, by starting new trains of speculation, or by expressing old ones so as not to be understood. He cares little what he says, so as he can say it differently from others. To read his works, is one thing; to understand them, is another. If any one thinks that I exaggerate, let him sit for an hour over "Sartor Resartus," and if he does not rise from its pages, place his three or four dictionaries on the shelf, and say I am right, I promise never again to say a word against Thomas Carlyle. He writes one page in favor of reform, and ten against it. He would hang all prisoners to get rid of them; yet the inmates of the prisons and "workhouses are better off than the poor." His heart is with the poor; yet the blacks of the West Indies should be taught that if they will not raise sugar and cotton by their own free will, "Quashy should have the whip applied to him." He frowns upon the reformatory speakers upon the boards of Exeter Hall; yet he is the prince of reformers. He hates heroes and assassins; yet Cromwell was an angel, and Charlotte Corday a saint. He scorns everything, and seems to be tired of what he is by nature, and tries to be what he is not.

CHAPTER XVIII.

"The time shall come, when, free as seas or wind,
Unbounded Thames shall flow for all mankind
Whole nations enter with each swelling tide,
And seas but join the regions they divide;
Earth's distant ends our glories shall behold,
And the New World launch forth to meet the Old."

POPE.

THE past six weeks have been of a stirring nature in this great metropolis. It commenced with the Peace Congress, the proceedings of which have long since reached you. And although that event has passed off, it may not be out of place here to venture a remark or two upon its deliberations.

A meeting upon the subject of peace, with the support of the monied and influential men who rally around the peace standard, could scarcely have been held in Exeter Hall without creating some sensation. From all parts of the world flocked delegates to this practical protest against war. And among those who took part in the proceedings were many men whose names alone would, even on ordinary occasions, have filled the great hall. The speakers were chosen from among the representatives of the various countries, without regard to dialect or complexion; and the only fault which seemed to be found with the committee's arrangement was, that in their desire to get foreigners and Londoners, they forgot the country delegates, so that none of the large provincial towns were at all represented in the Congress, so far as speaking was concerned. Manchester, Leeds, Newcastle, and all the important towns in Scotland and Ireland, were silenced in the great meeting. I need not say that this was an oversight of the committee, and one, too, that has done some injury. Such men as the able chairman of the late Anti-Corn-Law League cannot be forgotten in such a meeting, without giving offence to those who sent him, especially when the committee brought forward, day after day, the same speakers, chosen from amongst the metropolitan delegation. However, the meeting was a glorious one, and will long be remembered with delight as a step onward in the cause of peace. Burritt's Brotherhood Bazaar followed close upon the heels of the Peace Congress; and this had scarcely closed, when that ever-memorable meeting of the American fugitive slaves took place in the Hall of Commerce.

The temperance people made the next reformatory move. This meeting took place in Exeter Hall, and was made up of delegates from the various towns in the kingdom. They had come from the North, East, West and South. There was the quick-spoken son of the Emerald Isle, with his pledge suspended from his neck; there, too, the Scot, speaking his broad dialect; also the representatives from the provincial towns of England and Wales, who seemed to speak anything but good English.

The day after the meeting had closed in Exeter Hall, the country societies, together with those of the metropolis, assembled in Hyde Park, and then walked to the Crystal Palace. Their number while going to the Exhibition was variously estimated at from fifteen thousand to twenty thousand, and was said to have been the largest gathering of teetotallers ever assembled in London. They consisted chiefly of the working classes, their wives and children—clean, well-dressed and apparently happy: their looks indicating in every way those orderly habits which, beyond question, distinguish the devotees of that cause above the common laborers of this country. On arriving at the Exhibition, they soon distributed themselves among the departments, to revel in its various wonders, eating their own lunch, and drinking from the Crystal Fountain.

And, now I am at the world's wonder, I will remain here until I finish this sheet. I have spent fifteen days in the Exhibition, and have conversed with those who have spent double that number amongst its beauties, and the general opinion appears to be that six months would not be too long to remain within its walls to enable one to examine its laden stalls. Many persons make the Crystal Palace their home, with the exception of night. I have seen them come in the morning, visit the dressing-room, then go to the refreshment-room, and sit down to breakfast as if they had been at their hotel. Dinner and tea would be taken in turn.

The Crystal Fountain is the great place of meeting in the Exhibition. There you may see husbands looking for lost wives, wives for stolen husbands, mothers for their lost children, and towns-people for their country friends; and, unless you have an appointment at a certain place at an hour, you might as well prowl through the streets of London to find a friend as in the Great Exhibition. There is great beauty in the "Glass House." Here, in the transept, with the glorious sunlight coming through that wonderful glass roof, may the taste be cultivated and improved, the mind edified, and the feelings chastened. Here, surrounded by noble creations in marble and bronze, and in the midst of an admiring throng, one may gaze at statuary which might fitly decorate the house of the proudest prince in Christendom.

He who takes his station in the gallery, at either end, and looks upon that wondrous nave, or who surveys the matchless panorama around him from the intersection of the nave and transept, may be said, without presumption or exaggeration, to see all the kingdoms of this world and the glory of them. He sees not only a greater collection of fine articles, but also a greater as well as more various assemblage of the human race, than ever before was gathered under one roof.

One of the beauties of this great international gathering is, that it is not confined to rank or grade. The million toilers from mine, and factory, and workshop, and loom, and office, and field, share with their more wealthy neighbors the feast of reason and imagination spread out in the Crystal Palace.

It is strange, indeed, to see so many nations assembled and represented on one spot of British ground. In short, it is one great theatre, with thousands of performers, each playing his own part. England is there, with her mighty engines toiling and whirring, indefatigable in her enterprises to shorten labor. India spreads her glitter and paint. France, refined and fastidious, is there every day, giving the last touch to her picturesque group; and the other countries, each in its turn doing what it can to show off. The distant hum of thousands of good-humored people, with occasionally a national anthem from some gigantic organ, together with the noise of the machinery, seems to send life into every part of the Crystal Palace.

When you get tired of walking you can sit down and write your impressions, and there is the "post" to receive your letter; or, if it be Friday or Saturday, you may, if you choose, rest yourself by hearing a lecture from Professor Anstead; and then, before leaving, take your last look, and see something that you have not before seen. Everything which is old in cities, new in colonial life, splendid in courts, useful in industry, beautiful in nature, or ingenious in invention, is there represented. In one place we have the Bible translated into one hundred and fifty languages; in another, we have saints and archbishops painted on glass; in another, old palaces, and the altars of a John Knox, a Baxter, or some other divines of olden time. In the old Temple of Delphi we read that every state of the civilized world had its separate treasury, where Herodotus, born two thousand years before his time, saw and observed all kinds of prodigies in gold and silver, brass and iron, and even in linen. The nations all met there on one common ground, and the peace of the earth was not a little promoted by their common interest in the sanctity and splendor of that shrine. As long as the Exhibition lasts, and its memory endures, we hope and trust that it may shed the same influence. With this hasty scrap I take leave of the Great Exhibition.

CHAPTER XIX.

"And gray walls moulder round, on which dull time
Feeds, like slow fire upon a hoary brand;
And one keen pyramid, with wedge sublime,
Stands o'er the dust of him who planned."

SHELLEY.

I HAVE just finished a short visit to the far-famed city of Oxford, which has not unaptly been styled the City of Palaces. Aside from this being one of the principal seats of learning in the world, it is distinguished alike for its religious and political changes in times past. At one time it was the seat of Popery; at another, the uncompromising enemy of Rome. Here the tyrant Richard the Third held his court; and when James the First and his son Charles the First found their capital too hot to hold them, they removed to their loyal city of Oxford. The writings of the great republicans were here committed to the flames. At one time Popery sent Protestants to the stake and fagot; at another, a Papist king found no favor with the people. A noble monument now stands where Cranmer, Ridley and Latimer, proclaimed their sentiments and faith, and sealed them with their blood. And now we read upon the town treasurer's book—"For three loads of wood, one load of fagots, one post, two chains and staples, to burn Ridley and Latimer, £1 5*s.* 1*d.*" Such is the information one gets by looking over the records of books written three centuries ago.

It was a beautiful day on which I arrived at Oxford, and, instead of remaining in my hotel, I sallied forth to take a survey of the beauties of the city. I strolled into Christ Church Meadows, and there spent the evening in viewing the numerous halls of learning which surround that splendid promenade. And fine old buildings they are: centuries have rolled over many of them, hallowing the old walls, and making them gray with age. They have been for ages the chosen homes of piety and philosophy. Heroes and scholars have gone forth from their studies here into the great field of the world, to seek their fortunes, and to conquer and be conquered. As I surveyed the exterior of the different colleges, I could here and there see the reflection of the light from the window of some student, who was busy at his studies, or throwing away his time over some trashy novel, too many of which find their way into the trunks or carpet-bags of the young men on setting out for college. As I looked upon the walls of these buildings I thought, as the rough stone is taken from the quarry to the finisher, there to be made into an ornament, so was the young mind brought here to be cultivated and developed. Many a poor, unobtrusive young man, with the appearance of little or no ability, is here moulded into a hero, a scholar, a tyrant, or a friend of humanity. I never look upon these monuments of education without a feeling of regret that so few of our own race can find a place within their walls. And, this being the fact, I see more and more the need of our people being encouraged to turn their attention more seriously to self-education, and thus to take a respectable position before the world, by virtue of their own cultivated minds and moral standing.

Education, though obtained by a little at a time, and that, too, over the midnight lamp, will place its owner in a position to be respected by all, even though he be black. I know that the obstacles which the laws of the land and of society place between the colored man and education in the United States are very great, yet if *one* can break through these barriers more can; and if our people would only place the right appreciation upon education, they would find these obstacles are easier to be overcome than at first sight appears. A young man once asked Carlyle what was the secret of success. His reply was, "Energy; whatever you undertake, do it with all your might." Had it not been for the possession of energy, I might now have been working as a servant for some brainless fellow who might be able to command my labor with his money, or I might have been yet toiling in chains and slavery. But thanks to energy, not only for my being to-day in a land of freedom, but also for my dear girls being in one of the best seminaries in France, instead of being in an American school, where the finger of scorn would be pointed at them by those whose superiority rests entirely upon their having a whiter skin.

Oxford is, indeed, one of the finest located places in the kingdom, and every inch of ground about it seems hallowed by interesting associations. The university, founded by the good King Alfred, still throws its shadow upon the side-walk;

and the lapse of ten centuries seems to have made but little impression upon it. Other seats of learning may be entitled to our admiration, but Oxford claims our veneration. Although the lateness of the night compelled me, yet I felt an unwillingness to tear myself from the scene of such surpassing interest. Few places in any country as noted as Oxford is are without some distinguished person residing within their precincts; and, knowing that the city of palaces was not an exception to this rule, I resolved to see some of its lions. Here, of course, is the head-quarters of the Bishop of Oxford, a son of the late William Wilberforce, Africa's noble champion. I should have been glad to have seen this distinguished pillar of the church; but I soon learned that the bishop's residence was out of town, and that he seldom visited the city, except on business. I then determined to see one who, although a lesser dignitary in the church, is, nevertheless, scarcely less known than the Bishop of Oxford. This was the Rev. Dr. Pusey, a divine whose name is known wherever the religion of Jesus is known and taught, and the acknowledged head of the Puseyites. On the second morning of my visit I proceeded to Christ Church Chapel, where the reverend gentleman officiates. Fortunately I had an opportunity of seeing the doctor, and following close in his footsteps to the church. His personal appearance is anything but that of one who is the leader of a growing and powerful party in the church. He is rather under the middle size, and is round-shouldered, or rather stoops. His profile is more striking than his front face, the nose being very large and prominent. As a matter of course, I expected to see a large nose, for all great men have them. He has a thoughtful and somewhat sullen brow, a firm and somewhat pensive mouth, a cheek pale, thin, and deeply furrowed. A monk fresh from the cloisters of Tinterran Abbey, in its proudest days, could scarcely have made a more ascetic and solemn appearance than did Dr. Pusey on this occasion. He is not apparently above forty-five, or, at most, fifty years of age, and his whole aspect renders him an admirable study for an artist. Dr. Pusey's style of preaching is cold and tame, and one looking at him would scarcely believe that such an apparently uninteresting man could cause such an eruption in the church as he has. I was glad to find that a colored young man was among the students at Oxford.

A few months since, I paid a visit to our countryman, Alexander Crummel, who is still pursuing his studies at Cambridge, —a place which, though inferior to Oxford as far as appearance is concerned, is yet said to be greatly its superior as a place of learning. In an hour's walk through the Strand, Regent-street or Piccadilly, in London, one may meet half a dozen colored men, who are inmates of the various colleges in the metropolis. These are all signs of progress in the cause of the sons of Africa. Then let our people take courage, and with that courage let them apply themselves to learning. A determination to excel is the sure road to greatness, and that is as open to the black man as the white. It is that which has accomplished the mightiest and noblest triumphs in the intellectual and physical world. It is that which has made such rapid strides towards civilization, and broken the chains of ignorance and superstition which have so long fettered the human intellect. It was determination which raised so many worthy individuals from the humble walks of society, and from poverty, and placed them in positions of trust and renown. It is no slight barrier that can effectually oppose the determination of the will;—success must ultimately crown its efforts. "The world shall hear of me," was the exclamation of one whose name has become as familiar as household words. A Toussaint once labored in the sugar-field with his spelling-book in his pocket, amid the combined efforts of a nation to keep him in ignorance. His name is now recorded among the list of statesmen of the past. A Soulouque was once a slave, and knew not how to read. He now sits upon the throne of an empire.

In our own country there are men who once held the plough, and that too without any compensation, who are now presiding at the editor's table. It was determination that brought out the genius of a Franklin, and a Fulton, and that has distinguished many of the American statesmen, who, but for their energy and determination, would never have had a name beyond the precincts of their own homes.

It is not always those who have the best advantages, or the greatest talents, that eventually succeed in their undertakings: but it is those who strive with untiring diligence to remove all obstacles to success, and who, with unconquerable resolution, labor on until the rich reward of perseverance is within their grasp. Then again let me say to our young men, Take courage. "There is a good time coming." The darkness of the night appears greatest just before the dawn of day.

CHAPTER XX.

> "Blush ye not
> To boast your equal laws, your just restraints,
> Your rights defined, your liberties secured;
> Whilst, with an iron hand, ye crush to earth
> The helpless African, and bid him drink
> That cup of sorrow which yourselves have dashed,
> Indignant, from Oppression's fainting grasp?"
>
> WILLIAM ROSCOE.

THE love of freedom is one of those natural impulses of the human breast which cannot be extinguished. Even the brute animals of the creation feel and show sorrow and affection when deprived of their liberty. Therefore is a distinguished writer justified in saying, "Man is free, even were he born in chains." The Americans boast, and justly too, that Washington was the hero and model patriot of the American Revolution,—the man whose fame, unequalled in his own day and country, will descend to the end of time, the pride and honor of humanity. The American speaks with pride of the battles of Lexington and Bunker Hill; and, when standing in Faneuil Hall, he points to the portraits of Otis, Adams, Hancock, Quincy, Warren and Franklin, and tells you that their names will go down to posterity among the world's most devoted and patriotic friends of human liberty.

It was on the first of August, 1851, that a number of men, fugitives from that boasted land of freedom, assembled at the Hall of Commerce in the city of London, for the purpose of laying their wrongs before the British nation, and, at the same time, to give thanks to the God of freedom for the liberation of their West India brethren on the first of August, 1834. Little notice had been given of the intended meeting, yet it seemed to be known in all parts of the city. At the hour of half-past seven, for which the meeting had been called, the spacious hall was well filled, and the fugitives, followed by some of the most noted English Abolitionists, entered the hall, amid the most deafening applause, and took their seats on the platform. The appearance of the great hall at this juncture was most splendid. Besides the committee of fugitives, on the platform there were a number of the oldest and most devoted of the slaves' friends.

On the left of the chair sat Geo. Thompson, Esq., M.P.; near him was the Rev. Jabez Burns, D.D., and by his side the Rev. John Stevenson, M.A., Wm. Farmer, Esq., R. Smith, Esq.; while on the other side were Joseph Hume, Esq., M.P., John Lee, LL.D., Sir J. Walmsley, M.P., the Rev. Edward Matthews, John Cunliff, Esq., Andrew Paton, Esq., J. P. Edwards, Esq., and a number of colored gentlemen from the West Indies. The body of the hall was not without its distinguished guests. The Chapmans and Westons of Boston, U. S., were there. The Estlins and Tribes had come all the way from Bristol to attend the great meeting. The Patons, of Glasgow, had delayed their departure, so as to be present. The Massies had come in from Upper Clapton. Not far from the platform sat Sir Francis Knowles, Bart.; still further back was Samuel Bowly, Esq., while near the door were to be seen the greatest critic of the age, and England's best living poet. Macaulay had laid aside the pen, entered the hall, and was standing near the central door, while not far from the historian stood the newly-appointed Poet Laureate. The author of "In Memoriam" had been swept in by the crowd, and was standing with his arms folded, and beholding for the first time (and probably the last) so large a number of colored men in one room. In different parts of the hall were men and women from nearly all parts of the kingdom, besides a large number who, drawn to London by the Exhibition, had come in to see and hear these oppressed people plead their own cause.

The writer of this sketch was chosen chairman of the meeting, and commenced its proceedings by delivering the following address, which we cut from the columns of the *Morning Advertiser*:

"The chairman, in opening the proceedings, remarked that, although the metropolis had of late been inundated with meetings of various characters, having reference to almost every variety of subjects, yet that the subject they were called upon that evening to discuss differed from them all. Many of those by whom he was surrounded, like himself, had been victims to the inhuman institution of slavery, and were in consequence exiled from the land of their birth. They were fugitives from their native land, but not fugitives from justice; and they had not fled from a monarchical, but from a so-called republican government. They came from amongst a people who declared, as part of their creed, that all men were born free; but who, while they did so, made slaves of every sixth man, woman and child, in the country. (Hear, hear.) He must not, however, forget that one of the purposes for which they were met that night was to commemorate the emancipation of their brothers and sisters in the isles of the sea. That act of the British Parliament, and he might add in this case, with peculiar emphasis, of the British nation, passed on the twelfth day of August, 1833, to take effect on the first day of August, 1834, and which enfranchised eight hundred thousand West Indian slaves, was an event sublime in its nature, comprehensive and mighty in its immediate influences and remote consequences, precious beyond expression to the cause of freedom, and encouraging beyond the measure of any government on earth to the hearts of all enlightened and just men. This act was the result of a long course of philanthropic and Christian efforts on the part of some of the best men that the world ever produced. It was not his intention to go into a discussion or a calculation of the rise and fall of property, or whether sugar was worth more or less by the act of emancipation. But the abolition of slavery in the West Indies was a blow struck in the right direction, at that most inhuman of all traffics, the slave-trade—a trade which would never cease so long as slavery existed; for where there was a market there would be merchandise; where there was demand there would be a supply; where there were carcasses there would be vultures; and they might as well attempt to turn the water, and make it run up the Niagara river, as to change this law.

"It was often said by the Americans that England was responsible for the existence of slavery there, because it was introduced into that country while the colonies were under the British crown. If that were the case, they must come to the conclusion that, as England abolished slavery in the West Indies, she would have done the same for the American States if she had had the power to do it; and if that was so, they might safely say that the separation of the United States from the mother country was (to say the least) a great misfortune to one sixth of the population of that land. England had set a noble example to America, and he would to heaven his countrymen would follow the example. The Americans boasted of their superior knowledge; but they needed not to boast of their superior guilt, for that was set upon a hill-top, and that, too, so high, that it required not the lantern of Diogenes to find it out. Every breeze from the western world brought upon its wings the groans and cries of the victims of this guilt. Nearly all countries had fixed the seal of disapprobation on slavery; and when, at some future age, this stain on the page of history shall be pointed at, posterity will blush at the discrepancy between American profession and American practice. What was to be thought of a people boasting of their liberty, their humanity, their Christianity, their love of justice, and at the same time keeping in slavery nearly four millions of God's children, and shutting out from them the light of the Gospel, by denying the Bible to the slave! (Hear, hear.) No education, no marriage, everything done to keep the mind of the slave in darkness. There was a wish on the part of the people of the Northern States to shield themselves from the charge of slaveholding; but, as they shared in the guilt, he was not satisfied with letting them off without their share in the odium.

"And now a word about the Fugitive Slave Bill. That measure was in every respect an unconstitutional measure. It set aside the right formerly enjoyed by the fugitive of trial by jury; it afforded to him no protection, no opportunity of proving his right to be free; and it placed every free colored person at the mercy of any unprincipled individual who might wish to lay claim to him. (Hear.) That law is opposed to the principles of Christianity—foreign alike to the laws of God and man. It had converted the whole population of the Free States into a band of slave-catchers, and every rood of territory is but so much hunting-ground, over which they might chase the fugitive. But while they were speaking of slavery in the United States, they must not omit to mention that there was a strong feeling in that land, not only against the Fugitive Slave Law, but also against the existence of slavery in any form. There was a band of fearless men and women in the United States, whose labors for the slave had resulted in good beyond calculation. This noble and heroic class had created an agitation in the whole country, until their principles have taken root in almost every association in the land, and which, with God's blessing, will, in due time, cause the Americans to put into practice what they have so long professed. (Hear, hear.) He wished it to be continually held up before the country, that the Northern States are as deeply implicated in the guilt of slavery as the South. The North had a population of 13,553,328 freemen; the South had a population of only 6,393,756 freemen; the North has 152 representatives in the House, the South only 81; and it would be seen by this that the balance of power was with the Free States. Looking, therefore, at the question in all its aspects, he was sure that there was no one in this country but who would find out that the slavery of the United States of America was a system the most abandoned and the most tyrannical. (Hear, hear.)"

At the close of this address, the Rev. Edward Matthews, from Bristol, but who had recently returned from the United States, where he had been maltreated on account of his fidelity to the cause of freedom, was introduced, and made a most interesting speech. The next speaker was George Thompson, Esq., M.P.; and we need only say that his eloquence, which has seldom if ever been equalled, and never surpassed, exceeded, on this occasion, the most sanguine expectations of his friends. All who sat under the thundering anathemas which he hurled against slavery seemed instructed, delighted, and animated. Scarcely any one could have remained unmoved by the pensive sympathies that pervaded the entire assembly. There were many in the meeting who had never seen a fugitive slave before, and when any of the speakers would refer to those on the platform the whole audience seemed moved to tears. No meeting of the kind held in London for years created a greater sensation than this gathering of refugees from the "Land of the free, and the home of the brave."

The Rev. J. Burns, D.D., next made an eloquent speech, and was followed by J. P. Edwards, Esq.

CHAPTER XXI.

"For 't is the mind that makes the body rich;
And as the sun breaks through the darkest clouds,
So Honor peereth in the meanest habit."

SHAKSPEARE.

AFTER strolling, for more than two hours, through the beautiful town of Lemington, in which I had that morning arrived, a gentleman, to whom I had a letter of introduction, asked me if I was not going to visit Shakspeare's House. It was only then that I called to mind the fact that I was within a few miles of the birthplace of the world's greatest literary genius. A horse and chaise was soon procured, and I on my way to Stratford. A quick and pleasant ride brought me to the banks of the Avon, and, a short time after, to the little but picturesque town of Stratford. I gave the horse in charge of the man-of-all-work at the inn, and then started for the much-talked-of and celebrated cottage. I found it to be a small, mean-looking house of wood and plaster, the walls of which are covered with names, inscriptions and hieroglyphics, in every language, by people of all nations, ranks and conditions, from the highest to the lowest, who have made their pilgrimage there. The old shattered and worn-out stock of the gun with which Shakspeare shot Sir Thomas Lucy's deer was shown to us. The old-fashioned tobacco-box was also there. The identical sword with which he played Hamlet, the lantern with which Romeo and Juliet were discovered, lay on the table. A plentiful supply of Shakspeare's mulberry-tree was there, and we were asked if we did not want to purchase; but, fearing that it was not the genuine article, we declined. In one of the most gloomy and dilapidated rooms is the old chair in which the poet used to sit. After viewing everything of interest, and paying the elderly young woman (old maid) her accustomed fee, we left the poet's birthplace to visit his grave. We were soon standing in the chancel of the parish church, a large and venerable edifice, mouldering with age, but finely ornamented within, and the ivy clinging around without. It stands in a beautiful situation on the banks of the Avon. Garrick has most truthfully said:

"Thou soft-flowing Avon, by thy silver stream
Of things more than mortal sweet Shakspeare would dream;

The fairies by moonlight dance round his green bed,
For hallowed the turf is which pillowed his head."

The picturesque little stream runs murmuring at the foot of the church-yard, disturbed only by the branches of the large elms that stand on the banks, and whose limbs droop down. A flat stone is the only thing that marks the place where the poet lies buried. I copied the following verse from the stone, and which is said to have been written by the bard himself:

"Good friend, for Jesus' sake, forbeare
To dig the dust enclosed here:
Blessed be he that spares these stones,
And cursed be he that moves my bones."

Above the grave, in a niche in the wall, is a bust of the poet, placed there not long after his death, and which is supposed to bear some resemblance. Shakspeare's wife and daughter lie near him. After beholding everything of any possible interest, we stepped into our chaise and were soon again in Lemington; which, by the by, is the most beautiful town in all Great Britain, not excepting Cheltenham. In the evening I returned to Coventry, and was partaking of the hospitality of my excellent friend, Joseph Cash, Esq., of Sherburne House, and had stretched myself out on a sofa, with Carlyle's Life of Stirling in my hands, when I was informed that the younger members of the family were preparing to attend a lecture at the Mechanics' Institution. I did not feel inclined to stir from my easy position, after the fatigues of the day; but, learning that the lecturer was George Dawson, Esq., I resolved to join the company.

The hall was nearly filled when we reached it, which was only a few minutes before the commencement of the lecture. The stamping of feet and clapping of hands—which is the best evidence of an Englishman's impatience—brought before us a thin-faced, spare-made, wiry-looking man, with rather a dark complexion for an Englishman, but with prepossessing features. I must confess that I entered the room with some little prejudice against the speaker, caused by an unfavorable criticism from the pen of George Gilfillan, the essayist. However, I was happily disappointed. His style is witty, keen and gentle, with the language of the drawing-room. His smiling countenance, piercing glance and musical voice, captivated his audience. Mr. Dawson's subject was "The Rise and Spread of the Anglo-Saxon Race," and he showed that he understood his task. During his discourse he said:

"The Greeks and Romans sent out colonies; but no nation but England ever before gave a nation birth. The Americans are a nation, with no language, no creed, no grave-yards. Their names are a derivation; and it is laughable to see the pains an American takes to appear national. He will soon explain to you that he is not an Englishman, but a free-born citizen of the U-nited States, with a pretty considerable contempt for them British-ers. These notions make an Englishman smile; the Americans are a nation without being a nation; they are impressed with an idea that they have characteristics,—they are odd, not national, and remind one of a long, slender youth, somewhat sallow, who has just had a new watch, consequently blasphemes the old one; and as for the watch his father used, what is it?—a turnip; by this means he assumes the independent. The American *is* independent; he flaunts it in your face, and surprises you with his galvanic attempts at showing off his nationality. They have, in fact, no literature; we don't want them to have any, as long as they can draw from the old country; the feeling is kindly, and should be cherished; it is like the boy at Christmas coming home to spend the holidays. Long may they draw inspiration from Shakspeare and Milton, and come again and again to the old well. Walking down Broadway is like looking at a page of the Polyglot Bible. America was founded in a great thought, peopled through liberty; and long may that country be the noblest thing that England has to boast of.

"Some people think that we, as a nation, are going down; that we have passed the millennium; but there is no reason yet. We have work to do,—gold mines to dig, railways to construct, &c. &c. When all the work is done, then, and not till then, will the Saxon folk have finished their destiny. We have continents to fill yet; our work is not done till Europe is free. When Emerson visited us, he said that England was not an old country, but had the two-fold character of youth and age; he saw new cities, new docks; a good day's work yet to be done, and many vast undertakings only just begun. The coal, the iron and the gold, are ours; we have noble days in store, but we must labor more than we have yet done. Talk of going down!—we have hardly arrived at our meridian. We have our faults; any Frenchman or German may point them out. We have our duties, and often waste our precious moments by indulging in one eternal grumble at what we do, compared to what we ought to do. A little praise is good sometimes,—we walk the taller for it, and work the better. Only as we know our work here, and do it as our fathers did, shall we promote good; working heartily, and not faltering until the object is gained. The more we add to the happiness of a people, the more we shall be worthy of the good gifts of God."

As an orator, Mr. Dawson stands deservedly high; and was on several occasions applauded to the echo. He was educated for the ministry in the Orthodox persuasion, but left it and became a Unitarian, and has since gone a step further. Mr. Dawson resides in Birmingham, where he has a fine chapel, and a most intellectual congregation, and is considered the Theodore Parker of England.

It is indeed strange, the impression which a mind well cultivated can make upon those about it; and in this we see more clearly the need of education. In whatever light we view education, it cannot fail to appear the most important subject that can engage the attention of mankind. When we contrast the ignorance, the rudeness and the helplessness of the savage, with the knowledge, the refinement and the resources of civilized man, the difference between them appears so wide, that they can scarcely be regarded as of the same species; yet compare the infant of the savage with that of the educated and enlightened philosopher, and you will find them in all respects the same. The same *high, capacious powers* of the mind lie folded up in both, and in both the organs of sensation adapted to these mental powers are exactly similar. All the difference which is afterwards to distinguish them depends entirely upon their education, energy and self-culture.

CHAPTER XXII.

"Proud pile! that rearest thy hoary head,
In ruin vast, in silence dread,
O'er Teme's luxuriant vale,
Thy moss-grown halls, thy precincts drear,
To musing Fancy's pensive ear
Unfold a varied tale."

IT WAS in the latter part of December, and on one of the coldest nights that I have experienced, that I found myself seated before the fire, and alone, in the principal hotel in the town of Ludlow, and within a few minutes' walk of the famous old castle from which the town derives its name. A ride of one hundred and fifty miles by rail, in such uncomfortable carriages as no country except Great Britain furnishes for the weary traveller, and twenty miles on the top of a coach, in a drenching rain, caused me to remain by the fire's side to a later hour than I otherwise would have done. "Did you ring, sir?" asked the waiter, as the clock struck twelve. "No," I replied; but I felt that this was the servant's mode of informing me that it was time for me to retire to bed, and consequently I asked for a candle, and was shown to my chamber, and was soon in bed. From the weight of the covering on the bed, I felt sure that the extra blanket which I had requested to be put on was there; yet I was shivering with cold. As the sheets began to get warm, I discovered, to my astonishment, that they were damp; indeed, wet. My first thought was to ring the bell for the chambermaid, and have them changed; but, after a moment's consideration, I resolved to adopt a different course. I got out of bed, pulled the sheets off, rolled them up, raised the window, and threw them into the street. After disposing of the wet sheets, I returned to bed and got in between the blankets, and lay there trembling with cold till Morpheus came to my relief. The next morning I said nothing about the uncomfortable night I had experienced, and determined to leave it until they discovered the loss of the sheets. As soon as I had breakfasted, I went out to view the castle. For many years this was one of the strongest baronial fortifications in England. It was from Ludlow Castle that Edward, Prince of Wales, and his brother, were taken to London and put to death in the Tower, by order of their uncle, Richard III., before that villain seized upon the crown. The family of Mortimer for centuries held the castle, and, consequently, ruled Herefordshire. The castle rises from the point of a headland, and its foundations are ingrafted into a bare gray rock. The front consists of square towers, with high connecting walls. The castle is a complete ruin, and has been for centuries; large trees are still growing in the midst of the old pile, which give it a picturesque appearance. It was here that the exquisite effusion of the youthful genius of Milton—The Masque of Comus—was composed, and performed before His Majesty Charles I., in 1631. Little did the king think that the poet would one day be secretary to the man who should put him to death and rule his kingdom. Although a ruin, this fact is enough to excite interest, and to cause one to venerate the old building, and to do homage to the memory of the divine poet who hallowed it with his immortal strains. From a visitor's book that is kept at the gate-house, I copied the following verses:

"Here Milton sung; what needs a greater spell
To lure thee, stranger, to these far-famed walls?
Though chroniclers of other ages tell
That princes oft have graced fair Ludlow's halls,
Their honors glide along oblivion's stream,
And o'er the wreck a tide of ruin drives;
Faint and more faint the rays of glory beam
That gild their course—the bard alone survives.
And, when the rude, unceasing shocks of Time
In one vast heap shall whelm this lofty pile,
Still shall his genius, towering and sublime,
Triumphant o'er the spoils of grandeur smile;
Still in these haunts, true to a nation's tongue,
Echo shall love to dwell, and say, Here Milton sung."

I lingered long in the room pointed out to me as the one in which Milton wrote his "Comus." The castle was not only visited by the author of "Paradise Lost," but here, amidst the noise and bustle of civil dissensions, Samuel Butler, the satirical author of "Hudibras," found an asylum. The part of the tower in which it is said he composed his "Hudibras" was shown to us. In looking over the different apartments, we passed through a cell with only one small window through which the light found its way. On a stone, chiselled with great beauty, was a figure in a weeping position, and underneath it some one had written with pencil, in a legible hand:

"The Muse, too, weeps; in hallowed hour
Here sacred Milton owned her power,
And woke to nobler song."

The weather was exceedingly cold, and made more so by the stone walls partly covered with snow and frost around us; and I returned to the inn. It being near the time for me to leave by the coach for Hereford, I called for my bill. The servant went out of the room; but soon returned, and began stirring up the fire with the poker. I again told him that the coach would shortly be up, and that I wanted my bill. "Yes, sir, in a moment," he replied, and left in haste. Ten or fifteen minutes passed away, and the servant once more came in, walked to the window, pulled up the blinds, and then went out. I saw that something was in the wind; and it occurred to me that they had discovered the loss of the sheets. The waiter soon returned again, and, in rather an agitated manner, said, "I beg your pardon, sir, but the landlady is in the hall, and would like to speak to you." Out I went, and found the finest specimen of an English landlady that I had seen for many a day. There she stood, nearly as thick as she was high, with a red face, garnished around with curls, that seemed to say, "I have just been brushed and oiled." A neat apron covered a black alpacca dress that swept the ground with modesty, and a bunch of keys hung at her side. O, that smile! such a smile as none but a woman who had often been before a mirror could put on. However, I had studied human nature too successfully not to know that thunder and lightning were concealed under that smile; and I nerved myself up for the occasion. "I am sorry to have to name it, sir," said she, "but the sheets are missing off your bed." "O, yes," I replied; "I took them off last night." "Indeed!" exclaimed she; "and pray what have you done with them?" "I threw them out of the window," said I. "What! into the street?" "Yes, into the street," I said. "What did you do that for?" "They were wet; and I was afraid that if I left them in the room they would be put on at night, and give somebody else a cold." And here I coughed with all my might, to remind her that I had suffered from the negligence of her chambermaid. The heaving of the chest and panting for breath which the lady was experiencing at this juncture told me plainly that an explosion was at hand; and the piercing glance of those wicked-looking black eyes, and the rapid changes that came over that never-to-be-forgotten face, were enough to cause the most love-sick man in the world to give up all ideas of matrimony, and to be contented with being his own master. "Then, sir," said the landlady, "you will have to pay for the sheets." "O, yes," replied I; "I will pay for them; put them in the bill, and I will send the bill to *The Times*, and have it published, and let the travelling public know how much you charge for wet sheets!" and I turned upon my heel and walked into the room.

A few minutes after, the servant came in and laid before me the bill. I looked, but in vain, to see how much I had been charged for my hasty indiscretion the previous night. No mention was made of the sheets; and I paid the bill as it stood. The blowing of the coachman's horn warned me that I must get ready; and I put on my top coat. As I was passing through the hall, there stood the landlady just where I had left her, looking as if she had not stirred a single peg. And that smile, that had often cheered or carried consternation to many a poor heart, was still to be seen. I would rather have gone without my dinner than to have looked her in the face, such is my timidity. But common courtesy demanded that I should at least nod as I passed by; and therefore I was thrown back upon my manners, and unconsciously found myself giving her one of my best bows. Whether this bow was the result of my early training while in slavery, the domestic discipline that I afterwards experienced in freedom, or the terror with which every nerve was shaken on first meeting the landlady, I am still unaware. However, the bow was made and the ice broken, and the landlady smilingly said, "You do not know, sir, how much I am grieved at your being put to so much trouble last night, with those wet sheets; it was all the fault of the chambermaid, and I have given her warning, and shall dismiss her a month from to-day. And I do hope, sir, that if you should ever mention this circumstance you will not name the house in which it occurred." How could I do otherwise than to acquiesce in her wishes? Yes, I promised that I would never name the inn at which I had caught the rheumatism; and, therefore, reader, you may ask me, but in vain,—I will not tell you. One more bow, and out I went, and mounted the coach. As the driver was pulling up his reins, and raising his whip in the air, I turned to take a farewell glance of the inn, when, to my surprise, I beheld the landlady at the door with a white handkerchief in her hand, and a countenance beaming with smiles that I still see in my mind's eye. I raised my hat, she nodded, and away went the coach. Although the ride was a cold and dreary one, I often caught myself smiling over the fright in which I had put the landlady by threatening to publish her house.

After a fatiguing stage twenty miles or more, over a bad road, we reached Hereford, a small city, situated in a fertile plain, bounded on all sides with orchards, and watered by the translucent Wye. I spent the greater part of the next day in seeing the lions of the little city. I first visited, what most strangers do, the cathedral; a building partly Gothic and partly Saxon in its architecture, the interior of which is handsome, and contains an excellent organ, a piece of furniture that often calls more hearers to a place of worship than the preacher. In passing through the cathedral I stood a moment or two over the grave of the poet Phillips, the author of the "Splendid Shilling," "Cider," etc. While in the library the verger showed me a manuscript Bible of Wickliffe's, the first in use, written on vellum in the old black letter, full of abbreviations. He also pointed out some Latin manuscripts, in various parts beautifully illuminated with most ingenious penmanship, the coloring of the figures very bright. After all, there is a degree of pleasure in handling these old and laid-aside books. Hereford is noted for having been the birthplace of several distinguished persons. I was shown the house in which David Garrick was born. From Hereford he was removed to Litchfield and became the pupil of Dr. Johnson, and eventually both master and pupil went to London in search of bread; one became famous as an actor, the other noted as *surly Sam Johnson*. An obscure cottage in Pipe-lane was pointed out as the birthplace of the celebrated Nell Gwynne, who first appeared in London in the pit of Drury-lane Theatre as an apple-girl, and afterwards became an actress, in which position she was seen by King Charles II., who took her to his bed and board, and created her Duchess of St. Albans. However, she had many crooked paths to tread, after becoming an actress, before she captivated the heart of the *Merry Monarch.* The following story of her life, told by herself, is too good to be lost; so I insert it here.

"When I was a poor girl," said the Duchess of St. Albans, "working very hard for my thirty shillings a week, I went down to Liverpool during the holidays, where I was always well received. I was to perform in a new piece, something like those pretty little affecting dramas they get up now at our minor theatres; and in my character I represented a poor, friendless orphan-girl, reduced to the most wretched poverty. A heartless tradesman prosecutes the sad heroine for a heavy debt, and insists on putting her in prison, unless some one will be bail for her. The girl replies, 'Then I have no hope; I have not a friend in the world.' 'What! will no one be bail for you, to save you from going to prison?' asks the stern creditor. 'I have told you I have not a friend on earth,' was the reply. But just as I was uttering the words, I saw a sailor in the upper gallery springing over the railing, letting himself down from one tier to another, until he bounded clear over the orchestra and footlights, and placed himself beside me in a moment. 'Yes, you shall have *one* friend at least, my poor young woman,' said he, with the greatest expression in his honest, sunburnt countenance; 'I will go bail for you to any amount. And as for *you*,' turning to the frightened actor, 'if you don't bear a hand and shift your moorings, you lubber, it will be worse for you when I come athwart your bows!' Every creature in the house rose; the uproar was indescribable—peals of laughter, screams of terror, cheers from his tawny messmates in the gallery, preparatory scrapings of violins from the orchestra; and, amidst the universal din, there stood the unconscious cause of it, sheltering me, 'the poor, distressed young woman,' and breathing defiance and destruction against my mimic persecutor. He was only persuaded to relinquish his care of me, by the manager pretending to arrive and rescue me, with a profusion of theatrical bank-notes."

Hereford was also the birthplace of Mrs. Siddons, the unequalled tragic actress. The views around Hereford are very sylvan, and from some points, where the Welsh mountains are discernible, present something of the magnificent. All this part of the country still shows unmistakable evidence that war has had its day here. In those times the arts and education received no encouragement. The destructive exploits of conquerors may dazzle for a while, but the silent labors of the student and the artist, of the architect and the husbandman, which embellish the earth, and convert it into a terrestrial paradise, although they do not shine with so conspicuous a glare, diversify the picture with milder colors and more beautiful shades.

CHAPTER XXIII.

"To him no author was unknown,
Yet what he writ was all his own;
Horace's wit, and Virgil's state,
He did not steal, but emulate;
And when he would like them appear,
Their form, but not their clothes, did wear."

DENHAM.

IF there be an individual living who has read the "Essay on Man," or "The Rape of the Lock," without a wish to become more acquainted with the writings of the gifted poet that penned those exquisite poems, I confess that such an one is made of different materials from myself.

It is possible that I am too great a devotee to authors, and especially poets; yet such is my reverence for departed writers, that I would rather walk five miles to see a poet's grave than to spend an evening at the finest entertainment that could be got up.

It was on a pleasant afternoon in September, that I had gone into Surrey to dine with Lord C——, that I found myself one of a party of nine, and seated at a table loaded with everything that the heart could wish. Four men-servants, in livery, with white gloves, waited upon the company.

After the different courses had been changed, the wine occupied the most conspicuous place on the table, and all seemed to drink with a relish unappreciated except by those who move in the higher walks of life. My glass was the only one on the table in which the juice of the grape had not been poured. It takes more nerve than most men possess to cause one to decline taking a glass of wine with a lady; and in English society they don't appear to understand how human beings can live and enjoy health without taking at least a little wine. By my continued refusal to drink with first one and then another of the company, I had become rather an object of pity than otherwise.

A lady of the party, and in company with whom I had dined on a previous occasion, and who knew me to be an abstainer, resolved to relieve me from the awkward position in which my principles had placed me, and therefore caused a decanter of raspberry vinegar to be adulterated and brought on the table. A note in pencil from the lady informed me of the contents of the new bottle. I am partial to this kind of beverage, and felt glad when it made its appearance. No one of the party, except the lady, knew of the fraud; and I was able, during the remainder of the time, to drink with any of the company. The waiters, as a matter of course, were in the secret; for they had to make the change while passing the wine from me to the person with whom I drank.

After a while, as is usual, the ladies all rose and left the room. The retiring of the fair sex left the gentlemen in a more free-and-easy position, and consequently the topics of conversation were materially changed, but not for the better. The presence of women is always a restraint in the right direction. An hour after the ladies had gone, the gentlemen were requested to retire to the drawing-room, where we found tea ready to be served up. I was glad when the time came to leave the dining-room, for I felt it a great bore to be compelled to remain at the table *three hours.* Tea over, the wine again brought on, and the company took a stroll through the grounds at the back of the villa. It was a bright moonlight night, and the stars were out, and the air came laden with the perfume of sweet flowers, and there were no sounds to be heard, except the musical splashing of the little cascade at the end of the garden, and the song of the nightingale, that seemed to be in one of the trees near by. How pleasant everything looked, with the flowers creeping about the summer-house, and the windows opening to the velvet lawn, with its modest front, neat trellis-work, and meandering vine! The small smooth fish-pond, and the life-like statues standing or kneeling in different parts of the grounds, gave it the appearance of a very paradise.

"There," said his lordship, "is where Cowley used to sit, under that tree, and read."

This reminded me that I was near Chertsey, where the poet spent his last days; and, as I was invited to spend the night within a short ride of that place, I resolved to visit it the next day. We returned to the drawing-room, and a few moments after the party separated, at ten o'clock.

After breakfast the following morning, I drove over to Chertsey, a pretty little town, with but two streets of any note. In the principal street, and not far from the railway station, stands a low building of wood and plaster, known as the *Porch*

House. It was in this cottage that Abraham Cowley, the poet, resided, and died in 1667, in the forty-ninth year of his age. It being the residence of a gentleman who was from home, I did not have an opportunity of seeing the interior of the building, which I much regretted. Having visited Cowley's house, I at once determined to do what I had long promised myself; that was, to see Pope's villa, at Twickenham; and I returned to London, took the Richmond boat, and was soon gliding up the Thames.

I have seldom had a pleasanter ride by water than from London Bridge to Richmond; the beautiful panoramic view which unfolds itself on either side of the river can scarcely be surpassed by the scenery in any country. In the centre of Twickenham stands the house made celebrated from its having been the residence of Alexander Pope. The house is not large, but occupies a beautiful site, and is to be seen to best advantage from the river. The garden and grounds have undergone some change since the death of the poet. The grotto leading from the villa to the Thames is in a sad condition.

The following lines, written by Pope soon after finishing this idol of his fancy, show in what estimate he held it, and should at least have preserved it from decay:

"Thou who shalt stop where *Thames*' translucent wave
Shines a broad mirror through the shadowy cave;
Where lingering drops from mineral roofs distill,
And pointed crystals break the sparkling rill;
Unpolished gems no ray on pride bestow,
And latent metals innocently glow—
Approach! Great nature studiously behold!
And eye the mine without a wish for gold.
Approach—but awful! Lo! the Ægerian grot,
Where, nobly pensive, St. John sate and thought;
Where *British* sighs from dying Wyndham stole,
And the bright flame was shot through Marchmont's soul.
Let such—such only—tread this sacred floor,
Who dare to love their country and be poor."

It is strange that there are some at the present day who deny that Pope was a poet; but it seems to me that such either show a want of appreciation of poetry, or themselves no judge of what constitutes poetry. Where can be found a finer effusion than the "Essay on Man"? Johnson, in his admirable Life of Pope, in drawing a comparison between him and Dryden, says, "If the flights of Dryden are higher, Pope continues longer on the wing; if of Dryden's fire the blaze is brighter, of Pope is the heat more regular and constant. Dryden often surpasses expectation, and Pope never falls below it; Dryden is read with frequent astonishment, and Pope with perpetual delight." In speaking of the "Rape of the Lock," the same great critic remarks that it "stands forward in the classes of literature, as the most exquisite example of ludicrous poetry." Another poet and critic of no mean authority calls him "The sweetest and most elegant of English poets, the severest chastiser of vice, and the most persuasive teacher of wisdom." Lord Byron terms him "the most perfect and harmonious of poets." How many have quoted the following lines without knowing that they were Pope's!

> "To look through Nature up to Nature's God."
> "An honest man's the noblest work of God."
> "Just as the twig is bent, the tree 's inclined."
> "If to her share some female errors fall,
> Look on her face, and you 'll forget them all."
> "For modes of faith let graceless zealots fight,
> His can't be wrong whose life is in the right."

Pope was certainly the most independent writer of his time; a poet who never sold himself, and never lent his pen to the upholding of wrong. And although a severe critic, the following verse will show that he did not wish to bestow his chastisement in a wrong direction:

> "Curst be the verse, how well soe'er it flow,
> That tends to make one honest man my foe,
> Give Virtue scandal, Innocence a fear,
> Or from the soft-eyed virgin steal a tear!"

No poet's pen was ever more thoroughly used to suppress vice than Pope's; and what he did was done conscientiously, as the following lines will show:

> "Ask you what provocation I have had?
> The strong antipathy of good to bad.

When Truth or Virtue an affront endures,
The affront is mine, my friend, and should be yours."

Pope is not only a poet of a high order, but as yet he is the unsurpassed translator of Homer.

My visit to Pope's villa was a short one, but it was attended with many pleasing incidents. I have derived much pleasure from reading his Iliad and other translations. The verse from the pen of Lord Denham, that heads this chapter, conveys but a faint idea of my estimate of Pope's genius and talents.

CHAPTER XXIV.

"This modest stone, what few vain marbles can,
May truly say, here lies an honest man:
A poet, blest beyond the poet's fate,
Whom heaven kept sacred from the proud and great."

POPE.

WHILE on a recent visit to Dumfries, I lodged in the same house with Robert Burns, the eldest son of the Scottish bard, who is now about sixty-five years old. I also visited the grave of the poet, which is in the church-yard at the lower end of the town. A few days afterwards I arrived at Ayr, and being within three miles of the birthplace of Burns, and having so lately stood over his grave, I felt no little interest in seeing the cottage in which he was born, and the monument erected to his memory; and therefore, after inquiring the road, I started on my pilgrimage. In going up the High Street, we passed the Wallace Tower, a Gothic building, with a statue of the renowned chief, cut by Thom, the famed sculptor of "Tam O'Shanter and Souter Johnny," occupying the highest niche. The Scottish hero is represented not in warlike attitude, but in a thoughtful mood, as if musing over the wrongs of his country. We were soon out of the town, and on the high road to the "Land of Burns." On the west side of the road, and about two miles from Ayr, stands the cottage in which the poet was born; it is now used as an ale-house or inn. This cottage was no doubt the fancied scene of that splendid poem, "The Cottar's Saturday Night." A little further on, and we were near the old kirk, in the yard of which is the grave of Burns' father, marked by a plain tombstone, on which is engraved the following epitaph, from the pen of the poet:

"O ye whose cheek the tear of pity stains,
Draw near with pious reverence and attend;
Here lie the loving husband's dear remains,
The tender father, and the generous friend.
The pitying heart that felt for human woe,
The dauntless heart that feared no human pride,
The friend of man—to vice alone a foe;
'For e'en his failings leant to Virtue's side.'"

A short distance beyond the church, we caught a sight of the "Auld Brig" crossing the Doon's classic stream, along which Tam O'Shanter was pursued by the witches, his "Gray Mare Meg" losing her tail in the struggle on the keystone. On the banks of the Doon stands the beautiful monument, surrounded by a little plat of ground very tastefully laid out. The edifice is of the composite order, blending the finest models of Grecian and Roman architecture. It is about sixty feet high; on the ground floor there is a circular room lighted by a cupola of stained glass, in the centre of which stands a table with relics, and editions of Burns' writings. Amongst these relics is the Bible given by the poet to his Highland Mary. It is bound in two volumes, which are enclosed in a neat oaken box with a glass lid. In both volumes is written "Robert Burns, Mossgiel," in the bard's own hand-writing. In the same room are the original far-famed figures of "Tam O'Shanter and Souter Johnny," chiselled out of solid blocks of freestone, by the self-taught sculptor, Thom. No one can look at these statues without feeling that the poet has not more graphically described than the sculptor has delineated the jolly couple. Immediately on the banks of the river stands the Shell Palace. This most beautiful of little edifices is scarcely less to be admired than the monument itself.

Like its great prototype, the Shell Palace, to be judged of, must be seen. It is not easy to describe even this miniature. Lying in the heart of the Monument scenery, it forms a fitting spot for something dazzlingly beautiful; and it realizes the aspiration. It is a palace of which rare and beautiful shells, gathered in many climes, form the entire surface, internal and external. The erection is twenty feet long, by fourteen and a half feet broad, and fourteen feet high in the roof. It is in form an irregular or oblong octagon—the two sides long, and the three sections at each end, of course, narrow, thus giving, by the cross reflections of no fewer than nineteen mirrors, an infinite multiplicity of its internal treasures. Of these the shells are the leading feature, and many thousands of the rarest sorts go to make up this conchological wonder. The floor is covered with a very rich carpet, and rugs to match front two unique dwarf grates. The seats, set on imitation granite props, are covered with rich crimson velvet. Opposite the stained-glass entrance-door, in a recess, is a beautiful fountain, surrounded by large ornamental shells, playing from a delightful spring, the jet rising from a rich green vase, in tasteful contrast with the "winking gold-fish," now sporting and now lazily floating round its base. The side walls are inlaid in the most regular and artistic manner with shells, which vary in size, the roof being studded with large ornamental shells, the upward unseen points of which, being bored, act as ventilators, while in the centre of the roof some of the very choicest middle-sized shells are grouped together in the form of flowers, with a very rich and beautiful effect, seldom attained in the choicest bouquets. With so much of the beautiful so very attractively arranged, the mirrors work wonders. The large mirrors at either end show a line of table as far as the eye can carry, and multiply the visitors accordingly—green vases and golden fish presenting themselves anew at every turn. The Doon ran silently past as we entered; but here it meanders round us on every side, and our fairy palace seems the centre of some enchanted island. It is, indeed, a beautiful grotto, and all who have not seen it will, we dare say, on visiting it, not begrudge it the title of the "Shell Palace."

We next visited Newark Castle, about a mile from the monument. It is remarkable for its antiquity, and for the splendid view obtained from the balcony on its summit. While standing on this celebrated spot, we saw at one glance the Frith of Clyde and Bay of Ayr; in the immediate foreground the cradle-land of Burns, and the winding Doon; and in the distance the eye wanders over a vast tract of richly-wooded country, embracing a panoramic view of portions of at least seven counties, and the much-admired and celebrated rock, Ailsacraig. While in the neighborhood, we could not forego the temptation which presented itself of visiting the scene of Burns' tender parting with Mary Campbell. It is near the junction of the water of Fail with the river Ayr, where the poet met his Mary on a Sunday in the month of May, and, laying their hands in the stream, vowed, over Mary's Bible, love while the woods of Montgomery grew and its waters ran. The death of the girl before the appointed time of marriage caused the composition of the following poem, one of Burns' sweetest pieces.

HIGHLAND MARY.

"Ye banks, and braes, and streams around
  The castle o' Montgomery,
Green be your woods, and fair your flowers,
  Your waters never drumlie!
There Simmer first unfaulds her robes,
  And there they langest tarry;
For there I took the last fareweel
  O' my sweet Highland Mary.

"How sweetly bloomed the gay green birk,
  How rich the hawthorn's blossom,
As underneath their fragrant shade
  I clasped her to my bosom!
The golden hours, on angel wings,
  Flew o'er me and my dearie:
For dear to me as light and life
  Was my sweet Highland Mary.

"Wi' mony a vow, and locked embrace,
  Our parting was fu' tender;
And, pledging aft to meet again,
  We tore oursels asunder;
But, O! fell Death's untimely frost,
  That nipt my flower sae early!
Now green 's the sod, and cauld 's the clay,
  That wraps my Highland Mary!

"O pale, pale now, those rosy lips,
  I aft hae kissed sae fondly!
And closed for aye the sparkling glance
  That dwalt on me sae kindly!
And mouldering now in silent dust
  That heart that lo'ed me dearly!
But still within my bosom's core
  Shall live my Highland Mary."

It was indeed pleasant to walk over the ground once pressed

by the feet of the Scottish bard, and to look upon the scenes that inspired his youthful breast, and gave animation to that blaze of genius that burst upon the world. The classic Doon, the ruins of the old kirk Alloway, the cottage in which the poet first drew breath, and other places made celebrated by his pen, all filled us with a degree of enthusiasm we have seldom experienced. In every region where the English language is known the songs of Burns give rapture; and from every land, and from climes the most remote, comes the praise of Burns as a poet. In song-writing he surpassed Sir Walter Scott and Lord Byron; for in that department he was above "all Greek, above all Roman fame;" a more than Simonides in pathos, as in his "Highland Mary;" a more than Tyrtæus in fire, as in his "Scots wha ha'e wi' Wallace bled;" and a softer than Sappho in love, as in his—

"Had we never loved so kindly,
Had we never loved so blindly,
Never met or never parted,
We had ne'er been broken-hearted."

CHAPTER XXV.

"If thou art worn and hard beset
With sorrows, that thou wouldst forget;
If thou wouldst read a lesson, that would keep
Thy heart from fainting and thy soul from sleep,—
Go to the Colosseum."

LONGFELLOW.

IT was in the middle of May, when London is usually inundated with strangers from the country, who come up to attend the anniversaries, that a party of friends called on me with a request that I would accompany them to some of the lions of the metropolis. We started for the Thames Tunnel, one of the wonders of London. The idea of making a thoroughfare under the largest river in England was a project that could scarcely have been carried out by any except a most enterprising people. We faintly heard the clock on St. Paul's striking eleven, as the Woolwich boat put us down at the Tunnel; which we entered, after paying the admission fee of one penny. After descending one hundred steps, we found ourselves under the river, and looking towards the faint glimmer of light that showed itself on the Surrey side. There are two arches, one of which is closed up, with here and there a stall, loaded with old maps, books, and views of the Tunnel. Lamps, some six or eight yards apart, light up the otherwise dark and dismal place. Signs of frequent repairs show that they must ever be on the watch to keep the water out. An hour spent in the Tunnel satisfied us all, and we left in the direction of the Tower, a description of which will be found in another chapter. Some of our party seemed bent on going next to the Colosseum, and to the Colosseum we went. On arriving at the doors, and entering a long, capacious passage, our eyes became quite dazzled by the gleams of colored light which shone upon them, both directly and reflectedly. The effect was heightened by the beautiful designs which figured on the walls, and by the graceful forms of the many statues which lined the path. In fact, the strength of the sense of sight became much greater, because the ear, which, all the day before, had listened to the busy hum of bustle and activity, now ceased to hear aught but a silent whisper or a wondering

"O,"—no echo had even the foot-fall from the luxuriant softness of the carpeting.

Following up this fairy viaduct, we merged into a spacious circularly-formed apartment, on the downy couches of which reclined many an enraptured group; while nimble fingers and enticing lips caused sweet harmonious strains to chase each other from niche to niche, and among marbled figures within that charming temple.

Ascending a narrow flight of stairs, we landed on a balcony, from which we viewed the principal spectacle exhibited—and, O, it was a grand one! We found ourselves, as it were, upon the summit of some high building in the centre of the French metropolis, and there, all brilliant with gas-lights, and favored by the shining moon, Paris lay spread far out beneath us, though the canvas on which the scene was painted was but half a dozen feet from where we gazed in wonder. The moon herself seemed actually in the heavens. Nay, bets were laid that she had risen since we entered. Nothing can surpass the uniformity of appearance which every spire, and house, and wood, and river—yea, which every shop-window, ornamented, presented. All seemed natural, from the twinkling of the stars above us, to the monkey of the organ-man in the market-place below. Reader, if ever thou hast occasion to go to London, leave it not till thou hast seen the Colosseum.

Mustering our forces to return together, the cry was raised "A man a-wanting!" It seems there is an apparatus constructed in an apartment leading from the balcony, by which parties may, with a great degree of suddenness, be raised or lowered from or to the music-room. Our friend, at all times anxious to make the most of a shilling, followed some parties into the "ascension-room," as it is called, and took his seat beside them, expecting that on the withdrawal of a curtain he should witness something which his companions would miss. A bell sounded, and suddenly our expectant found himself some twenty feet lower, and obliged to follow the example of his co-descendants still further, by furnishing the attendant with such a gratuity as became an imitator of the Queen Elizabeth.

To another, but extremely different, of nature's imitations, we now turned our steps. After traversing one or two passages, the lights of which became more dim as we advanced, we reached a cavern's mouth. Here our progress was arrested by an iron grating. Our inquisitive friend, however, soon discovered that this obstacle could be removed,—it being, in fact, similar to those revolving barriers (we forget the name given in the "trade") placed at the entrance to the Great Exhibition. Like them, too, they checked all egress, and, to the further astonishment of the man of prying propensity, we were soon called upon for so many extra sixpences, indicated by this telltale gateway as being the number of persons who had entered since the keeper left.

The damp and dripping stones, with their coat of foggy green, —the exclusion of every sound from without,—the stunted measure of our speech,—the sharp clank of our footsteps,— and the frowning gloom of every corner of this retreat, soon gave evidence of the excellence of the design and entire structure, in the impression which it raised that, in reality, we were in some secluded rendezvous of smugglers, or of outlaws. Yea, the question was put by one who had seldom crossed the Cree, Was Meg Merrilies' one like this? while a party who had explored Ben Lomond and its neighborhood was asked if from it there could not be formed some notion of that which bears the name of the chief, Rob Roy.

Relieved alike from depressing atmosphere and cloudy thoughts, we retired to a projecting window, from which to view the "Swiss cottage," as it is called. Upon the verge of a tremendous precipice is seen a lonely cot. All communication with it is cut off, save by the rugged trunk of a withered tree which spans an opposite projection. Under this unstable bridge gush torrents of foaming water, lashed down from the heights beyond. Yet morn and eve does an industrious peasant leave and return to his romantic home across this dangerous way. See now, as he returns from his toil, he paces cautiously along; and yonder, at the further end, stand wife and little ones waiting to greet him when he crosses. O! happy man, to live where thus thou 'rt called to venture much and oft for those thou lovest, and be as oft rewarded by renewed tokens of their affection and most tender attachment!

Through openings in the walls we witnessed, also, the representation of mines and manufactures in full operation; and then, as we withdrew, we passed through artificial walks adorned with every kind of fantastical structure, and at some points of which, from the position of reflecting-glasses, we viewed in them hundreds of the very objects of which we could, with the unaided eye, see but one.

> "Passing we looked, and, looking, grieved to pass
> From the fair (?) figures smiling in the glass."

CHAPTER XXVI.

> "The treasures of the deep are not so precious
> As are the concealed comforts of a man
> Locked up in woman's love. I scent the air
> Of blessings, when I come but near the house.
> What a delicious breath marriage sends forth! . . .
> The violet bed 's not sweeter."
>
> MIDDLETON.

DURING a sojourn of five years in Europe, I have spent many pleasant hours in strolling through old church-yards, and reading the epitaphs upon the tombstones of the dead. Part of the pleasure was derived from a wish for solitude; and no place offers as quiet walks as a village burial-ground. And the curious epitaphs that are to be seen in a church-yard six or eight hundred years old are enough to cause a smile, even in so solemn a place as a grave-yard. While walking through Horsleydown church, in Cumberland, a short time since, I read an inscription over a tomb which I copied, and shall give in this chapter, although at the risk of bringing down upon my devoted head the indignation of the fair sex. Domestic enjoyment is often blasted by an intermixture of foibles with virtues of a superior kind; and if the following shall prove a warning to wives, I shall be fully compensated for my trouble.

Here lie the bodies of
THOMAS BOND, and MARY his wife.
She was temperate, chaste and charitable;
But
She was proud, peevish and passionate.
She was an affectionate wife and a tender mother;
But
Her husband and child, whom she loved, seldom saw her countenance without a disgusting frown,
Whilst she received visitors, whom she despised, with an endearing smile.
Her behavior was discreet toward strangers;
But
imprudent in her family.
Abroad, her conduct was influenced by good-breeding;

But
at home, by ill-temper.
She was a professed enemy to flattery, and was
Seldom known to praise or commend;
But
the talents in which she principally excelled were
difference of opinion, and discovering
flaws and imperfections.
She was an admirable economist,
and, without prodigality,
dispensed plenty to every person in her family;
But
would sacrifice their eyes to a farthing candle.
She sometimes made her husband happy with her good
qualities;
But
Much more frequently miserable with her many failings;
Insomuch, that, in thirty years' cohabitation, he often
lamented that, maugre her virtues,
He had not, in the whole, enjoyed two years
of matrimonial comfort.
At length,
finding that she had lost the affections of her
husband, as well as the regard of her neighbors, family
disputes having been divulged by servants,
She died of vexation, July 20, 1768,
Aged 48 years.
Her worn-out husband survived her four months
and two days, and departed this life November 28, 1768,
in the 54th year of his age.
William Bond, brother to the deceased, erected
this stone,
a *weekly monitor* to the surviving wives of this
parish, that they may avoid the infamy
of having their memories handed down to posterity
with a *patch-work* character.

CHAPTER XXVII.

"To where the broken landscape, by degrees
Ascending, roughens into rigid hills;
O'er which the Cambrian mountains, like far clouds
That skirt the blue horizon, dusky rise."

THOMSON.

I HAVE visited few places where I found warmer friends, or felt myself more at home, than in Aberdeen. The dwellings, being built mostly of granite, remind one of Boston, especially in a walk down Union-street, which is thought to be one of the finest promenades in Europe. The town is situated on a neck of land between the rivers Dee and Don, and is the most important commercial place in the north of Scotland.

During our stay in the city we visited, among other places, the old bridge of Don, which is not only resorted to owing to its antique celebrity and peculiar appearance, but also for the notoriety that it has gained by Lord Byron's poem for the "Bridge of Don." His lordship spent several years here during his minority, and this old bridge was a favorite resort of his. In one of his notes he alludes to how he used to hang over its one arch, and the deep black salmon stream below, with a mixture of childish terror and delight. While we stood upon the melancholy bridge, and although the scene around was severely grand and terrific,—the river swollen, the wind howling amongst the leafless trees, the sea in the distance,—and although the walk where Hall and Mackintosh were wont to melt down hours to moments in high converse was in sight, it was, somehow or other, the figure of the mild lame boy leaning over the parapet that filled our fancy; and the chief fascination of the spot seemed to breathe from the genius of the author of "Childe Harold."

To Anthony Cruikshank, Esq., whose hospitality we shared in Aberdeen, we are indebted for showing us the different places of interest in the town and vicinity. An engagement, however, to be in Edinburgh, cut short our stay in the north. The very mild state of the weather, and a wish to see something of the coast between Aberdeen and Edinburgh, induced us to make the journey by water. Consequently, after delivering a lecture before the Mechanics' Institute, with His Honor the Provost in the chair, on the evening of February 15th, we went on board the steamer bound for Edinburgh. On reaching the vessel we found the drawing-saloon almost entirely at our service, and, prejudice against color being unknown, we had no difficulty in obtaining the best accommodation that the steamer afforded. This was so unlike the pro-slavery, negro-hating spirit of America, that my colored friends who were with me were almost bewildered by the transition. The night was a glorious one. The sky was cloudless, and the clear, bracing air had a buoyancy I have seldom seen. The moon was in its zenith; the steamer and surrounding objects were beautiful in the extreme. The boat left her moorings at half-past twelve, and we were soon out at sea. The "Queen" is a splendid craft, and, without the aid of sails, was able to make fifteen miles within the hour. I was up the next morning extremely early,—indeed, before any of my fellow-passengers,—and found the sea, as on the previous night, as calm and as smooth as a mirror.

"There was no sound upon the deep,
The breeze lay cradled there;
The motionless waters sank to sleep
Beneath the sultry air;
Out of the cooling brine to leap
The dolphin scarce would dare."

It was a delightful morning, more like April than February; and the sun, as it rose, seemed to fire every peak of the surrounding hills. On our left lay the Island of May, while to the right was to be seen the small fishing-town of Anstruther, twenty miles distant from Edinburgh. Beyond these, on either side, was a range of undulating blue mountains, swelling, as they retired, into a bolder outline and a loftier altitude, until they terminated some twenty-five or thirty miles in the dim distance. A friend at my side pointed out a place on the right, where the remains of an old castle or lookout house, used in the time of the border wars, once stood, and which reminded us of the barbarism of the past.

But these signs are fast disappearing. The plough and roller have passed over many of these foundations, and the time will soon come when the antiquarian will look in vain for those places that history has pointed out to him as connected with the political and religious struggles of the past. The steward of the vessel came round to see who of the passengers wished for breakfast; and as the keen air of the morning had given me an appetite, and there being no prejudice on the score of color, I took my seat at the table, and gave ample evidence that I was not an invalid. On our return to the deck again, I found that we had entered the Frith of Forth, and that "Modern Athens" was in sight; and far above every other object, with its turrets almost lost in the clouds, could be seen Edinburgh Castle.

After landing, and a pleasant ride over one of the finest roads in Scotland, with a sprinkling of beautiful villas on either side, we were once more at Cannon's Hotel. While in the city, on this occasion, we went on the Calton Hill, from which we had a delightful view of the place and surrounding country.

I had an opportunity, during my stay in Edinburgh, of visiting the Infirmary; and was pleased to see among the two or three hundred students three colored young men, seated upon the same benches with those of a fairer complexion, and yet there appeared no feeling on the part of the whites towards their colored associates, except of companionship and respect. One of the cardinal truths, both of religion and freedom, is the equality and brotherhood of man. In the sight of God and all just institutions, the whites can claim no precedence or privilege on account of their being white; and if colored men are not treated as they should be in the educational institutions in America, it is a pleasure to know that all distinction ceases by crossing the broad Atlantic. I had scarcely left the lecture-room of the Institute and reached the street, when I met a large number of the students on their way to the college, and here again were seen colored men arm in arm with whites. The proud American who finds himself in the splendid streets of Edinburgh, and witnesses such scenes as these, can but behold in them the degradation of his own country, whose laws would make slaves of these same young men, should they appear in the streets of Charleston or New Orleans.

During my stay in Edinburgh I accepted an invitation to breakfast with George Combe, Esq., the distinguished philosophical phrenologist, and author of "The Constitution of Man." Although not far from seventy years of age, I found him apparently as active and as energetic as many men of half that number of years. Mr. Combe feels a deep interest in the cause of the American slave. I have since become more intimately acquainted with him, and am proud to reckon him amongst the warmest of my friends. In all of Mr. Combe's philanthropic exertions he is ably seconded by his wife, a lady of rare endowments, of an attractive person and engaging manners, and whose greatest delight is in doing good. She took much interest in Ellen Craft, who formed one of the breakfast party; and was often moved to tears on the recital of the thrilling narrative of her escape from slavery.

CHAPTER XXVIII.

"Look here, upon this picture, and on this."
HAMLET.

NO one accustomed to pass through Cheapside could fail to have noticed a good-looking man, neither black nor white, engaged in distributing bills to the thousands who throng that part of the city of London. While strolling through Cheapside, one morning, I saw, for the fiftieth time, Joseph Jenkins, the subject of this chapter, handing out his bills to all who would take them as he thrust them into their hands. I confess that I was not a little amused, and stood for some moments watching and admiring his energy in distributing his papers. A few days after, I saw the same individual in Chelsea, sweeping a crossing; here, too, he was equally as energetic as when I met him in the city. Some days later, while going through Kensington, I heard rather a sweet, musical voice singing a familiar psalm, and on looking round was not a little surprised to find that it was the Cheapside bill-distributor and Chelsea crossing-sweeper. He was now singing hymns, and selling religious tracts. I am fond of patronizing genius, and therefore took one of his tracts and paid him for a dozen.

During the following week, I saw, while going up the city road, that Shakspeare's tragedy of Othello was to be performed at the Eagle Saloon that night, and that the character of the Moor was to be taken by "*Selim, an African prince.*" Having no engagement that evening, I resolved at once to attend, to witness the performance of the "African Roscius," as he was termed on the bills. It was the same interest that had induced me to go to the Italian opera to see Madames Sontag and Grisi in Norma, and to visit Drury Lane to see Macready take leave of the stage. My expectations were screwed up to the highest point. The excitement caused by the publication of "Uncle Tom's Cabin" had prepared the public for anything in the African line, and I felt that the *prince* would be sure of a good audience; and in this I was not disappointed, for, as I took my seat in one of the boxes near the stage, I saw that the house was crammed with an orderly company. The curtain was already up when I entered, and Iago and Roderigo were on the stage. After a while Othello came in, and was greeted with thunders of applause, which he very gracefully acknowledged. Just black enough to take his part without coloring his face, and being tall, with a good figure and an easy carriage, a fine, full and musical voice, he was well adapted to the character of Othello. I immediately recognized in the countenance of the Moor a face that I had seen before, but could not at the moment tell where. Who could this "prince" be, thought I. He was too black for Douglass, not black enough for Ward, not tall enough for Garnet, too calm for Delany, figure, though fine, not genteel enough for Remond. However, I was soon satisfied as to who the *star* was. Reader, would you think it? it was no less a person than Mr. Jenkins, the bill-distributor from Cheapside, and crossing-sweeper from Chelsea! For my own part, I was overwhelmed with amazement, and it was some time before I could realize the fact. He soon showed that he possessed great dramatic power and skill; and his description to the senate of how he won the affections of the gentle Desdemona stamped him at once as an actor of merit. "What a pity," said a lady near me to a gentleman that was by her side, "that a prince of the royal blood of Africa should have to go upon the stage for a living! It is indeed a shame!" When he came to the scene,

> "O, cursed, cursed slave!—whip me, ye devils,
> From the possession of this heavenly sight!
> Blow me about in winds, roast me in sulphur!
> Wash me in steep-down gulfs of liquid fire!
> O, Desdemona! Desdemona! dead?
> Dead? O! O! O!"

the effect was indeed grand. When the curtain fell, the prince was called upon the stage, where he was received with deafening shouts of approbation, and a number of *bouquets* thrown at his feet, which he picked up, bowed, and retired. I went into Cheapside the next morning, at an early hour, to see if the prince had given up his old trade for what I supposed to be a more lucrative one; but I found the hero of the previous night at his post, and giving out his bills as energetically as when I had last seen him. Having to go to the provinces for some months, I lost sight of Mr. Jenkins, and on my return to town did not trouble myself to look him up. More than a year after I had witnessed the representation of Othello at the Eagle, I was walking, one pleasant Sabbath evening, through one of the small streets in the borough, when I found myself in front of a little chapel, where a number of persons were going in. As I was passing on slowly, an elderly man said to me, "I suppose you have come to hear your colored brother preach." "No," I answered; "I was not aware that one was to be here." "Yes," said he; "and a clever man he is, too." As the old man offered to find me a seat, I concluded to go in and hear this son of Africa. The room, which was not large, was already full. I had to wait but a short time before the reverend gentleman made his appearance. He was nearly black, and dressed in a black suit, with high shirt-collar, and an intellectual-looking cravat, that nearly hid his chin. A pair of spectacles covered his eyes. The preacher commenced by reading a portion of Scripture; and then announced that they would sing the twenty-eighth hymn in "the arrangement." O, that voice! I felt sure that I had heard that musical voice before; but where, I could not tell. I was not aware that any of my countrymen were in London; but felt that, whoever he was, he was no discredit to the race; for he was a most eloquent and accomplished orator. His sermon was against the sale and use of intoxicating drinks, and the bad habits of the working classes, of whom his audience was composed.

Although the subject was intensely interesting, I was impatient for it to come to a close, for I wanted to speak to the preacher. But, the evening being warm, and the room heated, the reverend gentleman, on wiping the perspiration from his face (which, by the way, ran very freely), took off his spectacles on one occasion, so that I immediately recognized him, and saved me from going up to the pulpit at the end of the service. Yes; it was the bill-distributor of Cheapside, the crossing-sweeper of Chelsea, the tract-seller and psalm-singer of Kensington, and the Othello of the Eagle Saloon. I could scarcely keep from laughing right out when I discovered this to be the man that I had seen in so many characters. As I was about leaving my seat at the close of the services, the old man who showed me into the chapel asked me if I would not like to be introduced to the minister, and I immediately replied that I would. We proceeded up the aisle, and met the clergyman as he was descending. On seeing me, he did not wait for a formal introduction, but put out his hand and said, "I have seen you so often, sir, that I seem to know you." "Yes," I replied; "we have met several times, and under different circumstances." Without saying more, he invited me to walk with him towards his home, which was in the direction of my own residence. We proceeded; and, during the walk, Mr. Jenkins gave me some little account of his early history. "You think me rather an odd fish, I presume," said he. "Yes," I replied. "You are not the only one who thinks so," continued he. "Although I am not as black as some of my countrymen, I am a native of Africa. Surrounded by some beautiful mountain scenery, and situated between Darfour and Abyssinia, two thousand miles in the interior of Africa, is a small valley going by the name of Tegla. To that valley I stretch forth my affections, giving it the endearing appellation of my native home and fatherland. It was there that I was born, it was there that I received the fond looks of a loving mother, and it was there that I set my feet, for the first time, upon a world full of cares, trials, difficulties and dangers. My father being a farmer, I used to be sent out to take care of his goats. This service I did when I was between seven and eight years of age. As I was the eldest of the boys, my pride was raised in no small degree when I beheld my father preparing a farm for me. This event filled my mind with the grand anticipation of leaving the care of the goats to my brother, who was then beginning to work a little. While my father was making these preparations, I had the constant charge of the goats; and, being accompanied by two other boys, who resided near my father's house, we wandered many miles from home, by which means we acquired a knowledge of the different districts of our country.

"It was while in these rambles with my companions that I became the victim of the slave-trader. We were tied with cords, and taken to Tegla, and thence to Kordofan, which is under the jurisdiction of the Pacha of Egypt. From Kordofan I was brought down to Dongola and Korti, in Nubia, and from thence down the Nile to Cairo; and, after being sold nine times, I became the property of an English gentleman, who brought me to this country and put me into school. But he died before

I finished my education, and his family feeling no interest in me, I had to seek a living as best I could. I have been employed for some years in distributing hand-bills for a barber in Cheapside in the morning, go to Chelsea and sweep a crossing in the afternoon, and sing psalms and sell religious tracts in the evening. Sometimes I have an engagement to perform at some of the small theatres, as I had when you saw me at the Eagle. I preach for this little congregation over here, and charge them nothing; for I want that the poor should have the Gospel without money and without price. I have now given up distributing bills; I have settled my son in that office. My eldest daughter was married about three months ago; and I have presented her husband with the Chelsea crossing, as my daughter's wedding portion." "Can he make a living at it?" I eagerly inquired. "O, yes! that crossing at Chelsea is worth thirty shillings a week, if it is well swept," said he. "But what do you do for a living for yourself?" I asked. "I am the leader of a band," he continued; "and we play for balls and parties, and three times a week at the Holborn Casino."

By this time we had reached a point where we had to part; and I left Joseph Jenkins, impressed with the idea that he was the greatest genius that I had met in Europe.

CHAPTER XXIX.

"Farewell! we did not know thy worth;
But thou art gone, and now 't is prized.
So angels walked unknown on earth,
But when they flew were recognized."
THOMAS HOOD.

IT was on Tuesday, July 18, 1854, that I set out for Kensall Green Cemetery, to attend the inauguration of the monument erected to the memory of Thomas Hood, the poet. It was the first pleasant day we had had for some time, and the weather was exceedingly fine. The company was large, and many literary characters were present. Near the monument sat Eliza Cook, author of the "Old Arm Chair," with her hair cut short and parted on one side like a man's. She is short in stature, and thick-set, with fair complexion, and bright eyes. Not far from Miss Cook was Mrs. Balfour, author of the "Working Women of the Last Half-century," "Morning Dew Drops," etc. etc. Mrs. Balfour is both taller and stouter than Miss Cook; and both are about the same age,—not far from forty. Murdo Young, Esq., of *The Sun*, and George Cruikshank, stood near the monument. Horace Mayhew, author of "London Labor and London Poor," was by the side of Cruikshank. The Hon. Mrs. Milnes sat near Eliza Cook. As the ceremony was about to commence, a short, stout man, with dark complexion, and black hair, took his stand on a tomb near by; this was R. Monckton Milnes, Esq., author of "Poetry for the People," and M.P. for Pontefract. He was the orator of the occasion.

The monument, which has been ably executed by Mr. Matthew Noble, consists of a bronze bust of the poet elevated on a pedestal of highly-polished red granite, the whole being twelve feet high. In front of the bust are placed wreaths in bronze, formed of the laurel, the myrtle, and the *immortelle*; and on a slab beneath the bust appears that well-known line of the poet, which he desired should be used as his epitaph:

"He sang the Song of the Shirt."

Upon the front of the pedestal is carved this inscription:

"In memory of Thomas Hood, born 23d May, 1798; died 3d May, 1845. Erected by public subscription, A. D. 1854."

At the base of the pedestal a lyre and comic mask in bronze are thrown together, suggesting the mingled character of Hood's writings; whilst on the sides of the pedestal are bronze medallions illustrating the poems of "The Bridge of Sighs" and "The Dream of Eugene Aram." The whole design is worthy of the poet and the sculptor, and it is much to the honor of the latter that his sympathy with the object has entirely destroyed all hope of profit from the work.

Mr. Milnes was an intimate friend of the poet, and his selection as orator was in good taste. He spoke with great delicacy and kindness of Hood's personal characteristics, and with much taste upon the artistic value of the dead humorist's works. He touched with great felicity and subtlety upon the value of humor. He defined its province, and showed how closely it was connected with the highest forms in which genius manifests itself. Mr. Milnes spoke, however, more as a friend than as a critic, and his genial utterances excited emotions in the hearts of his hearers which told how deep was their sympathy both with the orator and the subject of his eulogium. There were not many dry eyes amongst his hearers when he quoted one or two exquisite portions of Hood's poems. It was evident that the greater part of the audience were well acquainted with the works of the poet, and were delighted to hear the quotations from poems which had afforded them exquisite gratification in the perusal.

Hood was not a merely ephemeral writer. He did not address himself to the feelings which mere passing events generated in the minds of his readers. He smote deep down into the hearts of his admirers. Had he been nothing more than a literary man, the ceremony on this occasion would have been an impertinence. The nation cannot afford to have its time taken up by eulogiums on every citizen who does his work well in his own particular line. Nevertheless, when a man not only does his own work well, but acts powerfully on the national mind, then his fame is a national possession, and may be with all propriety made the subject of public commemoration. A great author is distinguished from the merely professional scribe by the fact of adding something to the stock of national ideas. Who can tell how much of the national character is due to the operation of the works of Shakspeare? The flood of ideas with which the great dramatist inundated the national mind has enriched it and fertilized it. We are most of us wiser and better by the fact of Shakspeare having lived and written. It would not be difficult to find in most modern works traces of the influence which Shakspeare has exercised over the writers. A great author, such as Shakspeare, is, then, a great public educator. The national mind is enlarged and enriched by the treasures which he pours into it. There is, therefore, a great propriety in making such a writer the subject of public eulogium.

Hood was one of those who not only enriched the national literature, but instructed the national mind. His conceptions, it is true, were not vast. His labors were not, like those of Shakspeare, colossal. But he has produced as permanent an effect on the nation as many of its legislators.

Englishmen are wiser and better because Hood has lived. In one of his own poems, "The Death-Bed," how sweetly he sang:

"We watched her breathing through the night,
Her breathing soft and low,
As in her breast the wave of life
Kept heaving to and fro.

"So silently we seemed to speak,
So slowly moved about,
As we had lent her half our powers
To eke her living out.

"Our very hopes belied our fears,
Our fears our hopes belied;
We thought her dying when she slept,
And sleeping when she died.

"For when the morn came dim and sad,
And chill with early showers,
Her quiet eyelids closed—she had
Another morn than ours."

Thomas Hood has another morn; may that morn have

brightened into perfect day! It is well known that the poet died almost on the verge of starvation. Being seized, long before his death, with a malady that kept him confined to his bed the greater part of the time, he became much embarrassed. Still, in defiance of anguish and weakness, he toiled on, until nature could endure no more. Many of Hood's humorous pieces were written upon a sick bed, and taken out and sold to the publishers, that his family might have bread. Little did those who laughed over these comical sayings think of the pain that it cost the poet to write them. And, now that he is gone, we often hear some one say, "*Poor Hood!*" But peace to his ashes! He now lies in the finest cemetery in the world, and in one of its greenest spots. At the close of the inauguration, a rush was made to get a view of Eliza Cook, as being the next great novelty after the monument, if not its equal.

CHAPTER XXX.

> "Dull rogues affect the politician's part,
> And learn to nod, and smile, and shrug, with art;
> Who nothing has to lose, the war bewails;
> And he who nothing pays, at taxes rails."
>
> CONGREVE.

THE Abbey clock was striking nine, as we entered the House of Commons, and, giving up our ticket, were conducted to the strangers' gallery. We immediately recognized many of the members, whom we had met in private circles or public meetings. Just imagine, reader, that we are now seated in the strangers' gallery, looking down upon the representatives of the people of the British empire.

There, in the centre of the room, shines the fine, open, glossy brow and speaking face of Alexander Hastie, a Glasgow merchant, a mild and amiable man, of modest deportment, liberal principles, and religious profession. He has been twice elected for the city of Glasgow, in which he resides. He once presided at a meeting for us in his own city.

On the right of the hall, from where we sit, you see that small man, with fair complexion, brown hair, gray eyes, and a most intellectual countenance. It is Layard, with whom we spent a pleasant day at Hartwell Park, the princely residence of John Lee, Esq., LL.D. He was employed as consul at Bagdad, in Turkey. While there he explored the ruins of ancient Nineveh, and sent to England the Assyrian relics now in the British Museum. He is member for Aylesbury. He takes a deep interest in the Eastern question, and censures the government for their want of energy in the present war.

Not far from Layard you see the large frame and dusky visage of Joseph Hume. He was the son of a poor woman who sold apples in the streets of London. Mr. Hume spent his younger days in India, where he made a fortune; and then returned to England, and was elected a member of the House of Commons, where he has been ever since, with the exception of five or six years. He began political life as a tory, but soon went over to radicalism. He is a great financial reformer, and has originated many of the best measures of a practical character that have been passed in Parliament during the last thirty years. He is seventy-five years old, but still full of life and activity—capable of great endurance and incessant labor. No man enjoys to an equal extent the respect and confidence of the legislature. Though his opinions are called extreme, he contents himself with realizing, for the present, the good that is attainable. He is emphatically a progressive reformer; and the father of the House of Commons.

To the left of Mr. Hume you see a slim, thin-faced man, with spectacles, an anxious countenance, his hat on another seat before him, and in it a large paper rolled up. That is Edward Miall. He was educated for the Baptist ministry, and was called when very young to be a pastor. He relinquished his charge to become the conductor of a paper devoted to the abolition of the state church, and the complete political enfranchisement of the people. He made several unsuccessful attempts to go into Parliament, and at last succeeded Thomas Crawford in the representation of Rochdale, where in 1852 he was elected free of expense. He is one of the most democratic members of the legislature. Miall is an able writer and speaker—a very close and correct reasoner. He stands at the very head of the Nonconformist party in Great Britain; and *The Nonconformist*, of which he is editor, is the most radical journal in the United Kingdom.

Look at that short, thick-set man, with his hair parted on the crown of his head, a high and expansive forehead, and an uncommon bright eye. That is William Johnson Fox. He was a working weaver at Norwich; then went to Holton College, London, to be educated for the Orthodox Congregational ministry; afterwards embraced Unitarian views. He was invited to Finsbury Chapel, where for many years he lectured weekly upon a wide range of subjects, embracing literature, political science, theology, government and social economy. He is the writer of the articles signed "Publicola" in the *Weekly Dispatch*, a democratic newspaper. He has retired from his pulpit occupations, and supports himself exclusively by his pen, in connection with the liberal journals of the metropolis. Mr. Fox is a witty and vigorous writer, an animated and brilliant orator.

Yonder, on the right of us, sits Richard Cobden. Look at his thin, pale face, and spare-made frame. He started as a commercial traveller; was afterwards a calico-printer and merchant in Manchester. He was the expounder, in the Manchester Chamber of Commerce and in the town council, of the principles of free trade. In the council of the Anti-Corn-Law League, he was the leader, and principal agitator of the question in public meetings throughout the kingdom. He was first elected for Stockport. When Sir Robert Peel's administration abolished the corn-laws, the prime minister avowed in the House of Commons that the great measure was in most part achieved by the unadorned eloquence of Richard Cobden. He is the representative of the non-intervention or political peace party; holding the right and duty of national defence, but opposing all alliances which are calculated to embroil the country in the affairs of other nations. His age is about fifty. He represents the largest constituency in the kingdom—the western division of Yorkshire, which contains thirty-seven thousand voters. Mr. Cobden has a reflective cast of mind; and is severely logical in his style, and very lucid in the treatment of his subjects. He may be termed the leader of the radical party in the House.

Three seats from Cobden you see that short, stout person, with his high head, large, round face, good-sized eyes. It is Macaulay, the poet, critic, historian and statesman. If you have not read his Essay on Milton, you should do so immediately; it is the finest thing of the kind in the language. Then there is his criticism on the Rev. R. Montgomery. Macaulay will never be forgiven by the divine for that onslaught upon his poetical reputation. That review did more to keep the reverend poet's works on the publisher's shelves than all other criticisms combined. Macaulay represents the city of Edinburgh.

Look at that tall man, apparently near seventy, with front teeth gone. That is Joseph Brotherton, the member for Salford. He has represented that constituency ever since 1832. He has always been a consistent liberal, and is a man of business. He is no orator, and seldom speaks, unless in favor of the adjournment of the House when the hour of midnight has arrived. At the commencement of every new session of Parliament he prepares a resolution that no business shall be entered upon after the hour of twelve at night, but has never been able to carry it. He is a teetotaller and a vegetarian, a member of the Peace Society, and a preacher in the small religious society to which he belongs.

In a seat behind Brotherton you see a young-looking man, with neat figure, white vest, frilled shirt, with gold studs, gold breast-pin, a gold chain round the neck, white kid glove on the right hand, the left bare with the exception of two gold rings. It is Samuel Morton Peto. He is of humble origin—has made a vast fortune as a builder and contractor for docks and railways. He is a Baptist, and contributes very largely to his own and other dissenting denominations. He has built several Baptist chapels in London and elsewhere. His appearance is that of a gentleman; and his style of speaking, though not elegant, yet pleasing.

Over on the same side with the liberals sits John Bright, the Quaker statesman, and leader of the Manchester school. He is the son of a Rochdale manufacturer, and first distinguished himself as an agitator in favor of the repeal of the corn-laws. He represents the city of Manchester, and has risen very rapidly. Mr. Cobden and he invariably act together, and will, doubtless, sooner or later, come into power together. Look at his robust and powerful frame, round and pleasing face. He is but little more than forty; an earnest and eloquent speaker, and commands the fixed attention of his audience.

See that exceedingly good-looking man just taking his seat. It is William Ewart Gladstone. He is the son of a Liverpool merchant, and represents the University of Oxford. He came into Parliament in 1832, under the auspices of the tory Duke of Newcastle. He was a disciple of the first Sir R. Peel, and was by that statesman introduced into official life. He has been Vice-president and President of the Board of Trade, and is now Chancellor of the Exchequer. Mr. Gladstone is only forty-four. When not engaged in speaking he is of rather unprepossessing appearance. His forehead appears low, but his eye is bright and penetrating. He is one of the ablest debaters in the House, and is master of a style of eloquence in which he is quite unapproached. As a reasoner he is subtle, and occasionally jesuitical; but, with a good cause and a conviction of the right, he rises to a lofty pitch of oratory, and may be termed the Wendell Phillips of the House of Commons.

There sits Disraeli, amongst the tories. Look at that Jewish face, those dark ringlets hanging round that marble brow. When on his feet he has a cat-like, stealthy step; always looks on the ground when walking. He is the son of the well-known author of the "Curiosities of Literature." His ancestors were Venetian Jews. He was himself born a Jew, and was initiated into the Hebrew faith. Subsequently he embraced Christianity. His literary works are numerous, consisting entirely of novels, with the exception of a biography of the late Lord George Bentinck, the leader of the protectionist party, to whose post Mr. Disraeli succeeded on the death of his friend and political chief. Mr. Disraeli has been all round the compass in politics. He is now professedly a conservative, but is believed to be willing to support any measures, however sweeping and democratical, if by so doing he could gratify his ambition—which is for office and power. He was the great thorn in the side of the late Sir R. Peel, and was never so much at home as when he could find a flaw in that distinguished statesman's political acts. He is an able debater and a finished orator, and in his speeches wrings applause even from his political opponents.

Cast your eyes to the opposite side of the House, and take a good view of that venerable man, full of years, just rising from his seat. See how erect he stands; he is above seventy years of age, and yet he does not seem to be forty. That is Lord Palmerston. Next to Joseph Hume, he is the oldest member in the House. He has been longer in office than any other living man. All parties have, by turns, claimed him, and he has belonged to all kinds of administrations; tory, conservative, whig, and coalition. He is a ready debater, and is a general favorite, as a speaker, for his wit and adroitness, but little trusted by any party as a statesman. His talents have secured him office, as he is useful as a minister, and dangerous as an opponent.

That is Lord Dudley Cutts Stuart speaking to Mr. Ewart. His lordship represents the populous and wealthy division of the district of Marylebone. He is a radical, the warm friend of the cause of Poland, Hungary and Turkey. He speaks often, but always with a degree of hesitation which makes it painful to listen to him. His solid frame, strongly-marked features, and unmercifully long eye-brows are in strange contrast to the delicate face of Mr. Ewart.

The latter is the representative for Dumfries, a Scotch

borough. He belongs to a wealthy family, that has made its fortune by commerce. Mr. Ewart is a radical, a stanch advocate of the abolition of capital punishment, and a strenuous supporter of all measures for the intellectual improvement of the people.

Ah! we shall now have a speech. See that little man rising from his seat; look at his thin black hair, how it seems to stand up; hear that weak, but distinct voice. O, how he repeats the ends of his sentences! It is Lord John Russell, the leader of the present administration. He is now asking for three million pounds sterling to carry on the war. He is a terse and perspicuous speaker, but avoids prolixity. He is much respected on both sides of the House. Though favorable to reform measures generally, he is nevertheless an upholder of aristocracy, and stands at the head and firmly by his order. He is brother to the present Duke of Bedford, and has twice been Premier; and, though on the sunny side of sixty, he has been in office, at different times, more than thirty years. He is a constitutional whig and conservative reformer. See how earnestly he speaks, and keeps his eyes on Disraeli! He is afraid of the Jew. Now he scratches the bald place on his head, and then opens that huge roll of paper, and looks over towards Lord Palmerston.

That full-faced, well-built man, with handsome countenance, just behind him, is Sir Joshua Walmesley. He is about the same age of Lord John; and is the representative for Leicester. He is a native of Liverpool, where for some years he was a poor teacher, but afterwards became wealthy in the corn trade. When mayor of his native town, he was knighted. He is a radical reformer, and always votes on the right side.

Lord John Russell has finished and taken his seat. Joseph Hume is up. He goes into figures; he is the arithmetician of the House of Commons. Mr. Hume is in the Commons what James N. Buffum is in our Anti-Slavery meetings, the *man of facts*. Watch the old man's eye as he looks over his papers. He is of no religious faith, and said, a short time since, that the world would be better off if all creeds were swept into the Thames. His motto is that of Pope:

> "For modes of faith let graceless zealots fight:
> His can't be wrong whose life is in the right."

Mr. Hume has not been tedious; he is done. Now for Disraeli. He is going to pick Lord John's speech to pieces, and he can do it better than any other man in the House. See how his ringlets shake as he gesticulates! and that sarcastic smile! He thinks the government has not been vigorous enough in its prosecution of the war. He finds fault with the inactivity of the Baltic fleet; the allied army has made no movement to suit him. The Jew looks over towards Lord John, and then makes a good hit. Lord John shakes his head; Disraeli has touched a tender point, and he smiles as the minister turns on his seat. The Jew is delighted beyond measure. "The Noble Lord shakes his head; am I to understand that he did not say what I have just repeated?" Lord John: "The Right Hon. Gentleman is mistaken; I did not say what he has attributed to me." Disraeli: "I am glad that the Noble Lord has denied what I thought he had said." An attack is made on another part of the minister's speech. Lord John shakes his head again. "Does the Noble Lord deny that, too?" Lord John: "No, I don't, but your criticism is unjust." Disraeli smiles again: he has the minister in his hands, and he shakes him well before he lets him go. What cares he for justice? Criticism is his forte; it was that that made him what he is in the House. The Jew concludes his speech amid considerable applause.

All eyes are turned towards the seat of the Chancellor of the Exchequer: a pause of a moment's duration, and the orator of the House rises to his feet. Those who have been reading *The Times* lay it down; all whispering stops, and the attention of the members is directed to Gladstone, as he begins. Disraeli rests his chin upon his hat, which lies upon his knee: he too is chained to his seat by the fascinating eloquence of the man of letters. Thunders of applause follow, in which all join but the Jew. Disraeli changes his position on his seat, first one leg crossed, and then the other, but he never smiles while his opponent is speaking. He sits like one of those marble figures in the British Museum. Disraeli has furnished more fun for *Punch* than any other man in the empire. When it was resolved to have a portrait of the late Sir R. Peel painted for the government, Mr. Gladstone ordered it to be taken from one that appeared in *Punch* during the lifetime of that great statesman. This was indeed a compliment to the sheet of fun. But now look at the Chancellor of the Exchequer. He is in the midst of his masterly speech, and silence reigns throughout the House.

> "His words of learned length and thundering sound
> Amazed the gazing rustics ranged around;
> And still they gazed, and still the wonder grew
> That one small head could carry all he knew."

Let us turn for a moment to the gallery in which we are seated. It is now near the hour of twelve at night. The question before the House is an interesting one, and has called together many distinguished persons as visitors. There sits the Hon. and Rev. Baptist W. Noel. He is one of the first of the Nonconformist ministers in the kingdom. He is about fifty years of age; very tall, and stands erect; has a fine figure, complexion fair, face long and rather pale, eyes blue and deeply set. He looks every inch the gentleman. Near by Mr. Noel you see the Rev. John Cumming, D.D. We stood more than an hour last Sunday in his chapel in Crown-court to hear him preach; and such a sermon we have seldom ever heard. Dr. Cumming does not look old. He has rather a bronzed complexion, with dark hair, eyes covered with spectacles. He is an eloquent man, and seems to be on good terms with himself. He is the most ultra Protestant we have ever heard, and hates Rome with a perfect vengeance. Few men are more popular in an Exeter Hall meeting than Dr. Cumming. He is a most prolific writer; scarce a month passes by without something from his pen. But they are mostly works of a sectarian character, and cannot be of long or of lasting reputation.

Further along sits a man still more eloquent than Dr. Cumming. He is of dark complexion, black hair, light blue eyes, an intellectual countenance, and when standing looks tall. It is the Rev. Henry Melville. He is considered the finest preacher in the Church of England. There, too, is Washington Wilks, Esq., author of "The Half-century." His face is so covered with beard that I will not attempt a description; it may, however, be said that he has literally entered into the *Beard Movement*.

Come, it is time for us to leave the House of Commons. Stop a moment! Ah! there is one that I have not pointed out to you. Yonder he sits amongst the tories. It is Sir Edward Bulwer Lytton, the renowned novelist. Look at his trim, neat figure; his hair done up in the most approved manner; his clothes cut in the latest fashion. He has been in Parliament twenty-five years. Until the abolition of the corn-laws, he was a liberal; but as a land-owner he was opposed to free trade, and joined the protectionists. He has two country-seats, and lives in a style of oriental magnificence that is not equalled by any other man in the kingdom; and often gathers around him the brightest spirits of the age, and presses them into the service of his private theatre, of which he is very fond. In the House of Commons he is seldom heard, but is always listened to with profound attention when he rises to speak. He labors under the disadvantage of partial deafness. He is undoubtedly a man of refined taste, and pays a greater attention to the art of dress than any other public character I have ever seen. He has a splendid fortune, and his income from the labors of his pen is very great. His title was given to him by the queen, and his rank as a baronet he owes to his high literary attainments. Now take a farewell view of this assembly of senators. You may go to other climes, and look upon the representatives of other nations, but you will never see the like again.

CHAPTER XXXI.

> "Take the spade of Perseverance,
> Dig the field of Progress wide;
> Every bar to true instruction
> Carry out and cast aside."

THE anniversary of West India emancipation was celebrated here on Monday last. But little notice of the intended meeting had been given, yet the capacious lecture-room of St. Martin's Hall was filled at an early hour with a most respectable audience, who appeared to have assembled for the sake of the cause.

Our old and well-tried friend, Geo. Thompson, Esq., was unanimously called to preside, and he opened the proceedings with one of his characteristic speeches. The meeting was then addressed by the Rev. Wm. Douglass, a colored clergyman of Philadelphia, in a most eloquent and feeling manner. Mr. Douglass is a man of fine native talent.

Francis W. Kellogg, of the United States, was the next speaker. Mr. Kellogg is an advocate of temperance, of some note, I believe, in his own country, and has been lecturing with considerable success in Great Britain. He is one of the most peculiar speakers I have ever heard. Born in Massachusetts, and brought up in the West, he has the intelligence of the one and the roughness of the other. He has the retentive memory of Wendell Phillips, the overpowering voice of Frederick Douglass, and the too rapid gestures of Dr. Delany. He speaks faster than any man I ever heard, except C. C. Burleigh. His speech, which lasted more than an hour, was one stream of fervid eloquence. He gave the audience a better idea of a real American stump orator than they ever had before. Altogether, he is the best specimen of the rough material out of which great public speakers are manufactured that I have yet seen. Mr. Kellogg's denunciations of Clay and Webster (the dead lion and the living dog) reminded us of Wendell Phillips; his pictures of slavery called to memory Frederick Douglass in his palmiest days; and his rebuke of his own countrymen for their unchristian prejudice against color brought before us the favorite topic and best speeches of C. L. Remond. It was his maiden speech on the subject of slavery, yet it was the speech of the evening.

Hatred to oppression is so instilled into the minds of the people in Great Britain, that it needs but little to arouse their enthusiasm to its highest point; yet they can scarcely comprehend the real condition of the slaves of the United States. They have heard of the buying and selling of men, women and children, without any regard to the tenderest ties of nature; of the passage and execution of the infamous Fugitive Slave Law; and, as we walk through the streets of London, they occasionally meet an American slave, who reminds them of the fact that while their countrymen are boasting of their liberty, and offering an asylum to the exiled of other countries, they refuse it to their own citizens.

Much regret has been expressed on this side of the Atlantic that Kossuth should have kept so silent on the slavery question while in America; and this act alone has, to a great extent, neutralized his further operations in this country. He certainly is not the man now that he was before his visit to the New World.

I seldom pass through the Strand, or other great thoroughfares of the metropolis, without meeting countrymen of mine. I encountered one, a short time since, under peculiar circumstances. It was one of those days commonly experienced in London, of half cloud and half sunshine, with just fog enough to give everything a gray appearance, that I was loitering through Drury Lane, and came upon a crowd of poor people and street beggars, who were being edified by an exhibition of Punch and Judy, on the one hand, and an organ-grinder, with a well-dressed and intelligent-looking monkey, on the other. Punch looked happy, and was performing with great alacrity, while the organ-grinder, with his loud-toned instrument, was furnishing music for the million. Pushing my way through the crowd, and taking the middle of the street for convenience' sake, I was leaving the infected district in greater haste than I entered it. I had scarcely taken my eyes off the motley group, when I observed a figure approaching me from the opposite direction, and walking with a somewhat hasty step. I have seen so much oddity in dress, and the general appearance of members of the human family, that my attention is seldom ever attracted by the uncivilized look of any one. But this being whom I was meeting, and whose appearance was such as I had not seen before, threw the monkey and his companions entirely in the shade. In fact, all that I had beheld in the Great Exhibition, of a ludicrous nature, dwindled away into utter insignificance when compared to this Robinson Crusoe looking man; for, after all, it turned out to be a man. He was of small stature, and, although not a cold day, his person was enveloped in a heavy over-coat, which looked as if it had seen some service, and had passed through the hands of some of the second-hand gentlemen of Brattle-street, Boston. The trousers I did not see, as they were benevolently covered by the long skirts of the above garment. A pair of patent-leather boots covered a small foot. The face was entirely hidden by a huge beard, apparently from ten to fifteen inches in length, and of a reddish color. Long, dark hair joined the beard, and upon the head was thrown, in a careless manner, one of those hats known in America as the wide-awake, but here as the billy-cock. A pair of bright eyes were entirely hid by the hair around the face. I was not more attracted by his appearance than astonished at the man's stopping before me, as if he knew me. I now observed something like smoke emanating from the long beard round the mouth. I was immediately seized by the individual by his right hand, while the left hand took from his mouth a pipe about three inches in length, stem included, and, in a sharp, shrill voice, sounding as if it came from the interior of a hogshead or from a sepulchre, he called me by my name. I stood for a moment and eyed the figure from head to foot, "from top to toe," to see if I could discover the resemblance of any one I had ever seen before. After satisfying myself that the object was new, I said, "Sir, you have the advantage of me." "Don't you know me?" he exclaimed, in a still louder voice. I looked again, and shook my head. "Why," said he, "it is C——." I stepped back a few feet, and viewed him once more from top to bottom, and replied, "You don't mean to say that this is H. C——?" "Yes, it is he, and nobody else." After taking another look, I said, "An't you mistaken, sir, about this being H. C——?" "No," said he, "I am sure I know myself." So I very reluctantly had to admit that I was standing in presence of the ex-editor of the "L. P. and H. of F." Indeed, one meets with strange faces in a walk through the streets of London. But I must turn again to the question of slavery.

Some months since a lady, apparently not more than fifty years of age, entered a small dwelling on the estate of the Earl of Lovelace, situated in the county of Surrey. After ascending a flight of stairs, and passing through a narrow passage, she found herself in a small but neat room, with plain furniture. On the table lay copies of the *Liberator* and *Frederick Douglass' Paper*. Near the window sat a young woman, busily engaged in sewing, with a spelling-book laying open on her lap. The light step of the stranger had not broken the silence enough to announce the approach of any one, and the young woman still sat at her task, unconscious that any one was near. A moment or two, and the lady was observed, when the diligent student hastily rose, and apologized for her apparent inattention. The stranger was soon seated, and in conversation with the young woman. The lady had often heard the word "slave," and knew something of its application, but had never before seen one of her own sex who had actually been born and brought up in a state of chattel slavery; and the one in whose company she now was was so white, and had so much the appearance of an educated and well-bred lady, that she could scarcely realize that she was in the presence of an American slave. For more than an hour the illustrious lady and the poor exile sat and carried on a most familiar conversation. The thrilling story of the fugitive often brought tears to the eyes of the stranger. O, how I would that every half-bred, aristocratic, slave-holding, woman-whipping, negro-hating woman of America could have been present and heard what passed between the two distinguished persons! They would, for once, have seen one who, though moving in the most elevated and aristocratic society in Europe, felt it an honor to enter the small cottage and take a seat by the side of a poor, hunted and exiled American fugitive slave. Let it be rung in the ears of the thin-skinned aristocracy of the United States, who would rather receive a flogging from the cat-o'-nine-tails than to sit at the table of a negro, that Lady Noel Byron, widow of the great poet, felt it a peculiar pleasure to sit at the table and take tea with Ellen Craft. It must, indeed, be an interesting fact to the reader, and especially to those who are acquainted with the facts connected with the life and escape of William and Ellen Craft, to know that they are industrious students in a school, and attracting the attention of persons occupying the most influential positions in society. The wonderful escape of William and Ellen Craft is still fresh in the minds of all who take an interest in the cause of humanity; and their eluding the pursuit of the slave-hunters at Boston, and final escape from the Athens of the New World, will not be soon forgotten.

Every American should feel a degree of humiliation when the thought occurs to him that there is not a foot of soil over which the *Stars and Stripes* wave upon which Ellen Craft can stand and be protected by the constitution or laws of the country. Yet Ellen Craft is as white as most white women. Had she escaped from Austrian tyranny, and landed on the shores of America, her reception would have been scarcely less enthusiastic than that which greeted the arrival of Jenny Lind. But Ellen Craft had the misfortune to be born in one of the Slave States of the American Union, and that was enough to cause her to be driven into *exile* for daring to escape from American despotism.

CHAPTER XXXII.

"——when I left the shore,
  The distant shore, which gave me birth,
I hardly thought to grieve once more,
  To quit another spot on earth."

BYRON.

WHAT a change five years make in one's history! The summer of 1849 found me a stranger in a foreign land, unknown to its inhabitants; its laws, customs and history, were a blank to me. But how different the summer of 1854! During my sojourn I had travelled over nearly every railroad in England and Scotland, and had visited Ireland and Wales, besides spending some weeks on the continent. I had become so well acquainted with the British people and their history, that I had begun to fancy myself an Englishman by habit, if not by birth. The treatment which I had experienced at their hands had endeared them to me, and caused me to feel myself at home wherever I went. Under such circumstances, it was not strange that I commenced with palpitating heart the preparation to return to my *native land*. Native land! How harshly that word sounds to my ears! True, America was the land of my birth; my grandfather had taken part in her Revolution, had enriched the soil with his blood, yet upon this soil I had been worked as a slave. I seem still to hear the sound of the auctioneer's rough voice, as I stood on the block in the slave-market at St. Louis. I shall never forget the savage grin with which he welcomed a higher bid, when he thought that he had received the last offer. I had seen a mother sold and taken to the cotton-fields of the far South; three brothers had been bartered to the soul-driver in my presence; a dear sister had been sold to the negro-dealer, and driven away by him; I had seen the rusty chains fastened upon her delicate wrists; the whip had been applied to my own person, and the marks of the brutal driver's lash were still on my body. Yet this was my native land, and to this land was I about to embark.

In Edinburgh, I had become acquainted with the Wighams; in Glasgow, the Patons and Smeals; in Manchester, the Langdons; in Newcastle, the Mawsons and Richardsons. To Miss

Ellen Richardson, of this place, I was mainly indebted for the redemption of my body from slavery, and the privilege of again returning to my native country. I had also met, and become acquainted with, John Bishop Estlin, Esq., of Bristol, and his kind-hearted and accomplished daughter. Of the hundreds of British Abolitionists with whom I had the pleasure of shaking hands while abroad, I know of none whose hearts beat more fervently for the emancipation of the American slave than Mr. Estlin's. He is indeed a model Christian. His house, his heart and his purse, were always open to the needy, without any regard to sect, color or country. When those distinguished fugitive slaves, William and Ellen Craft, arrived in England, unknown and without friends, Mr. Estlin wrote to me and said, "If the Crafts are in want, send to me. If you cannot find a home for them, let them come to Bristol, and I will keep them, at my expense, until something better turns up." And nobly did he keep his word. He put the two fugitives in school, and saw that they did not want for the means of support. I have known him to keep concealed what he had given to benevolent objects. To Mr. Estlin I am indebted for many acts of kindness; and now that the broad Atlantic lies between us, and in all probability we shall never again meet on earth, it is with heartfelt gratitude and pleasure that I make this mention of him.

And last, though not the least, I had become intimate with that most generous-hearted philanthropist, George Thompson, who never feels so well as when giving a welcome to an American fugitive slave. I had spent hours at the hospitable firesides of Harriet Martineau, R. D. Webb, and other distinguished authors. You will not, reader, think it strange that my heart became sad at the thought of leaving all these dear friends, to return to a country in which I had spent some of the best days of my life as a slave, and where I knew that prejudice would greet me on my arrival.

Most of the time I had resided in London. Its streets, parks, public buildings and its fog, had become "as familiar as household words." I had heard the deep, bass voice of the Bishop of London, in St. Paul's Cathedral. I had sat in Westminster Abbey, until I had lost all interest in the services, and then wandered about amongst the monuments, reading the epitaphs placed over the dead. Like others, I had been locked in the Temple Church, and compelled to wait till service was over, whether I liked it or not. I had spent days in the British Museum and National Gallery, and in all these I had been treated as a man. The "negro pew," which I had seen in the churches of America, was not to be found in the churches of London. There, too, were my daughters. They who had been denied education upon equal terms with children of a fairer complexion, in the United States, had been received in the London schools upon terms of perfect equality. They had accompanied me to most of the noted places in the metropolis. We had strolled through Regent-street, the Strand, Piccadilly and Oxford-street, so often, that sorrow came over me as the thought occurred to me that I should never behold them again.

Then the English manner of calling on friends before one's departure. I can meet an enemy with pleasure, but it is with regret that I part with a friend. As the time for me to leave drew near, I felt more clearly my identity with the English people. By and by the last hour arrived that I was to spend in London. The cab stood at the door, with my trunks on its top; and, bidding the household "good-by," I entered the vehicle, the driver raised his whip, and I looked for the last time on my old home in Cecil-street. As we turned into the Strand, Nelson's monument, in Trafalgar-square, greeted me on the left, and Somerset House on the right. I took a farewell look at Covent Garden Market, through whose walks I had often passed, and where I had spent many pleasant hours. My youngest daughter was in France, but the eldest met me at the dépôt, and after a few moments the bell rang, and away we went.

As the train was leaving the great metropolis of the world behind, I caught a last view of the dome of St. Paul's, and the old pile of Westminster Abbey.

In every town through which we passed on our way to Liverpool I could call to mind the name of some one whose acquaintance I had made, and whose hospitality I had shared. The steamer City of Manchester had her fires kindled when we arrived, and we went immediately on board. We found one hundred and seventy-five passengers in the cabin, and above five hundred in the steerage. After some delay, the ship weighed anchor, the machinery was put in motion, and, bidding Liverpool a long farewell, the vessel moved down the Mersey, and was in a short time out at sea. The steam tender accompanied the ship about thirty miles, during which time search was made throughout the Manchester to see that no "stow-aways" were on board. No vessel ever leaves an English port without some one trying to get his passage out without pay. When the crew are at work, or not on the watch, these persons come on board, hide themselves under the berths in the steerage cabin, or amongst the freight, until the vessel is out to sea, and then they come out. As they are always poor persons, without either baggage or money, they succeed in getting their passage without giving anything in return. As the tender was about quitting us to return to Liverpool, it came along-side to take on board those who had come with the vessel to see their friends off. Any number of white napkins were called into requisition, as friends were shaking hands with each other, and renewing their promises to write by the first post. One young man had come out to spend a few more hours with a handsome Scotch lass, with whom he, no doubt, had a matrimonial engagement. Another, an English lady, seemed much affected when the last bell of the tender rung, and the captain cried "All on board." Having no one to look after, I found time to survey others. The tender let go her cables amid three hearty cheers, and a deafening salute from the two-pounder on board the City of Manchester. A moment more, and the two steamers were leaving each other with rapid speed. The two young ladies of whom I have already made mention, together with many others, had their faces buried in their handkerchiefs, and appeared to be dying with grief. However, all of them seemed to get over it very soon. On the second day out at sea I saw the young English lady walking the quarter-deck with a fine-looking gentleman, and holding as tightly to his arm as if she had left no one behind; and as for the Scotch lass, she was seated on a settee with a countryman of hers, who had made her acquaintance on board, and, from all appearance, had entirely forgotten her first love. Such is the waywardness of man and woman, and the unfaithfulness of the human heart.

In the latter part of the second day a storm overtook us, and for the ten succeeding days we scarcely knew whether we were on our heads or our heels. The severest part of the gale was on the eighth and ninth nights out. On one of those evenings a fellow-roommate came in and said, "If you wish to see a little fun, go into the forward steerage." It was about eight o'clock, and most of the passengers were either in bed, or preparing for the night's rest, such as is to be had on board a ship in a gale of wind. This cabin contained about two hundred and fifty persons; some Germans, some Irish, and twenty-five or thirty Gypsies. Forty or fifty of these were on their knees in their berths, engaged in prayer. No camp-meeting ever presented a more noisy spectacle than did this cabin. The ship was rolling, and the sea running mountains high, and many of these passengers had given up all hope of ever seeing land again. The Gypsies were foremost amongst those who were praying; indeed, they seemed to fancy themselves in a camp-meeting, for many of them shouted at the top of their voices. One of them, known as the "Queen of the Gypsies," came to me and said, "O, Master! do get down and help us to ask God to stop the wind! You are a black man; may be he'll pay more attention to what you say. Now do, master, do! and when the storm is over I will tell your fortune for nothing." At this juncture one of the chests which had been fastened to the floor broke away from its moorings, and came sliding across the cabin at the rate of about twenty miles per hour; soon another got loose, and these two locomotives broke up the prayer-meeting. Trunk after trunk became unfastened, until some eight or ten were crossing the cabin every time the vessel went over. At last the loose boxes upset the tables, on which were some of the passengers' eatables, and in a short time the whole cabin was in splendid confusion. The lamps, one after another, were knocked down and extinguished, so that the cabin was in total darkness. As I turned to retrace my steps, I heard the company joining in the prayer, and I was informed the next day that it was kept up during most of the night.

With all the watchfulness on the day of sailing, several persons succeeded in stowing themselves away. First one came out, and then another, until not less than five made their appearance on deck. As fast as these men were discovered they were put to work; so that labor, if not money, might be obtained for their passage. On the sixth day out I missed a small leather trunk, and search was immediately made in every direction, but no tidings of it could be found. However, after its being lost two days, I offered a reward for its recovery, and it was soon found, hid away in the forecastle. It had been broken open, and a few things, together with a little money, had been taken. The ships Chieftain and Harmony were the only vessels we met during the first ten days. An iceberg made its appearance while we were on the banks, but it was some distance to the larboard.

After a long passage of twenty days we arrived at the mouth of the Delaware, and took a pilot on board. The passengers were now all life; the Irish were basking in the sun, the Germans were singing, and the Gypsies were dancing. Some fifteen miles below Philadelphia, the officers came on board, to see that no sickness was on the vessel; and, after being passed by the doctors, each person began to get his luggage on deck, and prepare to go on shore. About four o'clock, on the twenty-sixth day of September, 1854, the City of Manchester hauled alongside the Philadelphia wharf, and the passengers all on the move; the Scotch lass clinging to the arm of her new Highland laddie, and the young English lady in company with her "fresh" lover. It is a dangerous thing to allow the Atlantic Ocean to separate one from his or her "affectionate friend." The City of Manchester, though not a fast steamer, is, nevertheless, a safe one. Her officers are men of experience and activity. Captain Wyly was always at his post; the first officer was an able seaman, and Mr. John Mirehouse, the second officer, was a most gentlemanly and obliging, as well as experienced officer. To this gentleman I am much indebted for kind attention shown me on the voyage. I had met him on a former occasion at Whitehaven. He is a stanch friend of humanity.

At Philadelphia I met with a most cordial reception at the hands of the Motts, J. M. M'Kim, the Stills, the Fortens, and that distinguished gentleman and friend of the slave, Robert Purvis, Esq. There is no colored man in this country to whom the Anti-slavery cause is more indebted than to Mr. Purvis. Endowed with a capacious and reflective mind, he is ever in search after truth; and, consequently, all reforms find in him an able and devoted advocate. Inheriting a large fortune, he has had the means, as well as the will, to do good. Few men in this country, either colored or white, possess the rare accomplishments of Robert Purvis. In no city in the Free States does the Anti-slavery movement have more bitter opponents than in Philadelphia. Close to two of our Southern States, and connected as it is in a commercial point of view, it could scarcely be otherwise. Colorphobia is more rampant there than in the pro-slavery, negro-hating city of New York. I was not destined to escape this unnatural and anti-christian prejudice. While walking through Chestnut-street, in company with two of my fellow-passengers, we hailed an omnibus going in the direction which we wished to go. It immediately stopped, and the white men were furnished with seats, but I was told that "We don't allow niggers to ride in here." It so happened that these two persons had rode in the same car with me from London to Liverpool. We had put up at the same hotel at the latter place, and had crossed the Atlantic in the same steamer. But as soon as we touch the soil of America we can no longer ride in the same conveyance, no longer eat at the same table, or be regarded with equal justice, by our thin-skinned democracy. During five years' residence in monarchical Europe I had enjoyed the rights allowed to all foreigners in the countries through which I passed; but on returning to my NATIVE LAND the influence of slavery meets me the first day that I am in the country. Had I been an escaped felon, like John Mitchell, no one would have questioned my right to a seat in a Philadelphia omnibus. Neither of the foreigners who were allowed to ride in this carriage had ever visited our country before. The constitution of these United States was as a blank to them; the Declaration of Independence, in all probability, they had never seen,—much less, read. But what mattered it? They were white, and that was enough. The fact of my being an American by birth could not be denied; that I had read and understood the constitution and laws, the most pro-slavery, negro-hating professor of Christianity would admit; but I was colored, and that was enough. I had partaken of the hospitality of noblemen in England, had sat at the table of the French Minister of Foreign Affairs; I had looked from the strangers' gallery down upon the great legislators of England, as they sat in the House of Commons; I had stood in the House of Lords, when Her Britannic Majesty prorogued her Parliament; I had eaten at the same table with Sir Edward Bulwer Lytton, Charles Dickens, Eliza Cook, Alfred Tennyson, and the son-in-law of Sir Walter Scott; the omnibuses of Paris, Edinburgh, Glasgow and Liverpool, had stopped to take me up; I had often entered the "Caledonia," "Bayswater," "Hammersmith," "Chelsea," "Bluebell," and other omnibuses that rattle over the pavements of Regent-street, Cheapside, and the west end of London,—but what mattered that? My face was not white, my hair was not straight; and, therefore, I must be excluded from a seat in a third-rate American omnibus. Slavery demanded that it should be so. I charge this prejudice to the pro-slavery pulpits of our land, which first set the example of proscription by erecting in their churches the "negro pew." I charge it to that hypocritical profession of democracy which will welcome fugitives from other countries, and drive its own into exile. I charge it to the recreant sons of the men who carried on the American revolutionary war, and who come together every fourth of July to boast of what their fathers did, while they, their sons, have become associated with bloodhounds, to be put at any moment on the track of the fugitive slave.

But I had returned to the country for the express purpose of joining in the glorious battle against slavery, of which this Negrophobia is a legitimate offspring. And why not meet it in its stronghold? I might have remained in a country where my manhood was never denied; I might have remained in ease in other climes; but what was ease and comfort abroad, while more than three millions of my countrymen were groaning in the prison-house of slavery in the Southern States? Yes, I came back to the land of my nativity, not to be a spectator, but a soldier—a soldier in this moral warfare against the most cruel system of oppression that ever blackened the character or hardened the heart of man. And the smiles of my old associates, and the approval of my course while abroad by my colored fellow-citizens, has amply compensated me for the twenty days' rough passage on my return.

THE
ESCAPE;
OR,
A LEAP FOR FREEDOM.

A Drama,

IN FIVE ACTS.

"Look on this picture, and on this."—HAMLET.

AUTHOR'S PREFACE.

THIS play was written for my own amusement, and not with the remotest thought that it would ever be seen by the public eye. I read it privately, however, to a circle of my friends, and through them was invited to read it before a Literary Society. Since then, the Drama has been given in various parts of the country. By the earnest solicitation of some in whose judgment I have the greatest confidence, I now present it in a printed form to the public. As I never aspired to be a dramatist, I ask no favor for it, and have little or no solicitude for its fate. If it is not readable, no word of mine can make it so; if it is, to ask favor for it would be needless.

The main features in the Drama are true. GLEN and MELINDA are actual characters, and still reside in Canada. Many of the incidents were drawn from my own experience of eighteen years at the South. The marriage ceremony, as performed in the second act, is still adhered to in many of the Southern States, especially in the farming districts.

The ignorance of the slave, as seen in the case of "BIG SALLY," is common wherever chattel slavery exists. The difficulties created in the domestic circle by the presence of beautiful slave women, as found in DR. GAINES'S family, is well understood by all who have ever visited the valley of the Mississippi.

The play, no doubt, abounds in defects, but as I was born in slavery, and never had a day's schooling in my life, I owe the public no apology for errors.

W. W. B.

CHARACTERS REPRESENTED.

DR. GAINES, *proprietor of the farm at Muddy Creek.*
REV. JOHN PINCHEN, *a clergyman.*
DICK WALKER, *a slave speculator.*
MR. WILDMARSH, *neighbor to Dr. Gaines.*
MAJOR MOORE, *a friend of Dr. Gaines.*
MR. WHITE, *a citizen of Massachusetts.*
BILL JENNINGS, *a slave speculator.*
JACOB SCRAGG, *overseer to Dr. Gaines.*
MRS. GAINES, *wife of Dr. Gaines.*
MR. and MRS. NEAL, and DAUGHTER, *Quakers, in Ohio.*
THOMAS, *Mr. Neal's hired man.*
GLEN, *slave of Mr. Hamilton, brother-in-law of Dr. Gaines.*
CATO, SAM, SAMPEY, MELINDA, DOLLY, SUSAN, and BIG SALLY, *slaves of Dr. Gaines.*
PETE, NED, and BILL, *slaves.*
OFFICERS, LOUNGERS, BARKEEPER, &c.

THE ESCAPE.

ACT I.

Scene I.—A SITTING-ROOM.

MRS. GAINES, *looking at some drawings*—SAMPEY, *a white slave, stands behind the lady's chair.*

Enter DR. GAINES, R.

Dr. Gaines. Well, my dear, my practice is steadily increasing. I forgot to tell you that neighbor Wyman engaged me yesterday as his family physician; and I hope that the fever and ague, which is now taking hold of the people, will give me more patients. I see by the New Orleans papers that the yellow fever is raging there to a fearful extent. Men of my profession are reaping a harvest in that section this year. I would that we could have a touch of the yellow fever here, for I think I could invent a medicine that would cure it. But the yellow fever is a luxury that we medical men in this climate can't expect to enjoy; yet we may hope for the cholera.

Mrs. Gaines. Yes, I would be glad to see it more sickly here, so that your business might prosper. But we are always unfortunate. Every body here seems to be in good health, and I am afraid that they'll keep so. However, we must hope for the best. We must trust in the Lord. Providence may possibly send some disease amongst us for our benefit.

Enter CATO, R.

Cato. Mr. Campbell is at de door, massa.

Dr. G. Ask him in, Cato.

Enter MR. CAMPBELL, R.

Dr. G. Good morning, Mr. Campbell. Be seated.

Mr. Campbell. Good morning, doctor. The same to you, Mrs. Gaines. Fine morning, this.

Mrs. G. Yes, sir; beautiful day.

Mr. C. Well, doctor, I've come to engage you for my family physician. I am tired of Dr. Jones. I've lost another very valuable nigger under his treatment; and, as my old mother used to say, "change of pastures makes fat calves."

Dr. G. I shall be most happy to become your doctor. Of course, you want me to attend to your niggers, as well as to your family?

Mr. C. Certainly, sir. I have twenty-three servants. What will you charge me by the year?

Dr. G. Of course, you'll do as my other patients do, send your servants to me when they are sick, if able to walk?

Mr. C. Oh, yes; I always do that.

Dr. G. Then I suppose I'll have to lump it, and say $500 per annum.

Mr. C. Well, then, we'll consider that matter settled; and as two of the boys are sick, I'll send them over. So I'll bid you good day, doctor. I would be glad if you would come over some time, and bring Mrs. Gaines with you.

Dr. G. Yes, I will; and shall be glad if you will pay us a visit, and bring with you Mrs. Campbell. Come over and spend the day.

Mr. C. I will. Good morning, doctor. [*Exit* MR. CAMPBELL, R.

Dr. G. There, my dear, what do you think of that? Five hundred dollars more added to our income. That's patronage worth having! And I am glad to get all the negroes I can to doctor, for Cato is becoming very useful to me in the shop. He can bleed, pull teeth, and do almost any thing that the blacks require. He can put up medicine as well as any one. A valuable boy, Cato!

Mrs. G. But why did you ask Mr. Campbell to visit you, and to bring his wife? I am sure I could never consent to associate with her, for I understand that she was the daughter of a tanner. You must remember, my dear, that I was born with a silver spoon in my mouth. The blood of the Wyleys runs in my veins. I am surprised that you should ask him to visit you at all; you should have known better.

Dr. G. Oh, I did not mean for him to visit me. I only invited him for the sake of compliments, and I think he so understood it; for I should be far from wishing you to associate with Mrs. Campbell. I don't forget, my dear, the family you were raised in, nor do I overlook my own family. My father, you know, fought by the side of Washington, and I hope some day to have a handle to my own name. I am certain Providence intended me for something higher than a medical man. Ah! by-the-by, I had forgotten that I have a couple of patients to visit this morning. I must go at once. [*Exit* DR. GAINES, R.

Enter HANNAH, L.

Mrs. G. Go, Hannah, and tell Dolly to kill a couple of fat pullets, and to put the biscuit to rise. I expect brother Pinchen here this afternoon, and I want every thing in order. Hannah, Hannah, tell Melinda to come here. [*Exit* HANNAH, L.

We mistresses do have a hard time in this world; I don't see why the Lord should have imposed such heavy duties on us poor mortals. Well, it can't last always. I long to leave this wicked world, and go home to glory.

Enter MELINDA.

I am to have company this afternoon, Melinda. I expect brother Pinchen here, and I want every thing in order. Go and get one of my new caps, with the lace border, and get out my scolloped-bottomed dimity petticoat, and when you go out, tell Hannah to clean the white-handled knives, and see that not a speck is on them; for I want every thing as it should be while brother Pinchen is here. [*Exit* MRS. GAINES, L, HANNAH, R.

Scene 2.—DOCTOR'S SHOP—CATO MAKING PILLS.

Enter DR. GAINES, L.

Dr. G. Well, Cato, have you made the batch of ointment that I ordered?

Cato. Yes, massa; I dun made de intment, an' now I is making the bread pills. De tater pills is up on the top shelf.

Dr. G. I am going out to see some patients. If any gentlemen call, tell them I shall be in this afternoon. If any servants come, you attend to them. I expect two of Mr. Campbell's boys over. You see to them. Feel their pulse, look at their tongues, bleed them, and give them each a dose of calomel. Tell them to drink no cold water, and to take nothing but water gruel.

Cato. Yes, massa; I'll tend to 'em. [*Exit* DR. GAINES, L.

Cato. I allers knowed I was a doctor, an' now de ole boss has put me at it, I muss change my coat. Ef any niggers comes in, I wants to look suspectable. Dis jacket don't suit a doctor; I'll change it. [*Exit* CATO—*immediately returning in a long coat.*] Ah! now I looks like a doctor. Now I can bleed, pull teef, or cut off a leg. Oh! well, well, ef I aint put de pill stuff an' de intment stuff togedder. By golly, dat ole cuss will be mad when he finds it out, won't he? Nebber mind, I'll make it up in pills, and when de flour is on dem, he won't know what's in 'em; an' I'll make some new intment. Ah! yonder comes Mr. Campbell's Pete an' Ned; dems de ones massa sed was comin'. I'll see ef I looks right. [*Goes to the looking-glass and views himself.*] I em some punkins, ain't I? [*Knock at the door.*] Come in.

Enter PETE *and* NED, R.

Pete. Whar is de doctor?

Cato. Here I is; don't you see me?

Pete. But whar is de ole boss?

Cato. Dat's none you business. I dun tole you dat I is de doctor, an dat's enuff.

Ned. Oh! do tell us whar de doctor is. I is almos dead. Oh me! oh dear me! I is so sick. [*Horrible faces.*]

Pete. Yes, do tell us; we don't want to stan here foolin'.

Cato. I tells you again dat I is de doctor. I larn de trade under massa.

Ned. Oh! well, den, give me somethin' to stop dis pain. Oh dear me! I shall die. [*He tries to vomit, but can't—ugly faces.*]

Cato. Let me feel your pulse. Now put out your tongue. You is berry sick. Ef you don't mine, you'll die. Come out in de shed, an' I'll bleed you. [*Exit all—re-enter.*

Cato. Dar, now take dese pills, two in de mornin' and two at night, and ef you don't feel better, double de dose. Now, Mr. Pete, what's de matter wid you?

Pete. I is got de cole chills, an' has a fever in de night.

Cato. Come out, an' I'll bleed you. [*Exit all—re-enter.*

Now take dese pills, two in de mornin' and two at night, an' ef dey don't help you, double de dose. Ah! I like to forget to feel your pulse and look at your tongue. Put out your tongue. [*Feels his pulse.*] Yes, I tells by de feel ob your pulse dat I is gib you de right pills.

Enter MR. *Parker's* BILL, L.

Cato. What you come in dat door widout knockin' for?

Bill. My toof ache so, I didn't tink to knock. Oh, my toof! my toof! Whar is de doctor?

Cato. Here I is; don't you see me?

Bill. What! you de doctor, you brack cuss! You looks like a doctor! Oh, my toof! my toof! Whar is de doctor?

Cato. I tells you I is de doctor. Ef you don't believe me, ax dese men. I can pull your toof in a minnit.

Bill. Well, den, pull it out. Oh, my toof! how it aches! Oh, my toof! [*Cato gets the rusty turnkeys.*]

Cato. Now lay down on your back.

Bill. What for?

Cato. Dat's de way massa does.

Bill. Oh, my toof! Well, den, come on. [*Lies down, Cato gets astraddle of Bill's breast, puts the turnkeys on the wrong tooth, and pulls—Bill kicks, and cries out*]—Oh, do stop! Oh! oh! oh! [*Cato pulls the wrong tooth—Bill jumps up.*]

Cato. Dar, now, I tole you I could pull your toof for you.

Bill. Oh, dear me! Oh, it aches yet! Oh me! Oh, Lor-e-massy! You dun pull de wrong toof. Drat your skin! ef I don't pay you for this, you brack cuss! [*They fight, and turn over table, chairs and bench—Pete and Ned look on.*]

Enter DR. GAINES, R.

Dr. G. Why, dear me, what's the matter? What's all this about? I'll teach you a lesson, that I will. [*The doctor goes at them with his cane.*]

Cato. Oh, massa! he's to blame, sir. He's to blame. He struck me fuss.

Bill. No, sir; he's to blame; he pull de wrong toof. Oh, my toof! oh, my toof!

Dr. G. Let me see your tooth. Open your mouth. As I live, you've taken out the wrong tooth. I am amazed. I'll whip you for this; I'll whip you well. You're a pretty doctor. Now lie down, Bill, and let him take out the right tooth; and if he makes a mistake this time, I'll cowhide him well. Lie down, Bill. [*Bill lies down, and Cato pulls the tooth.*] There now, why didn't you do that in the first place?

Cato. He wouldn't hole still, sir.

Bill. He lies, sir. I did hole still.

Dr. G. Now go home, boys; go home. [*Exit* PETE, NED *and* BILL, L.

Dr. G. You've made a pretty muss of it, in my absence. Look at the table! Never mind, Cato; I'll whip you well for this conduct of yours to-day. Go to work now, and clear up the office. [*Exit* DR. GAINES, R.

Cato. Confound dat nigger! I wish he was in Ginny. He bite my finger and scratch my face. But didn't I give it to him? Well, den, I reckon I did. [*He goes to the mirror, and discovers that his coat is torn—weeps.*] Oh, dear me! Oh, my coat—my coat is tore! Dat nigger has tore my coat. [*He gets angry, and rushes about the room frantic.*] Cuss dat nigger! Ef I could lay my hands on him, I'd tare him all to pieces,—dat I would. An' de ole boss hit me wid his cane after dat nigger tore my coat. By golly, I wants to fight somebody. Ef ole massa should come in now, I'd fight him. [*Rolls up his sleeves.*] Let 'em come now, ef dey dare—ole massa, or any body else; I'm ready for 'em.

Enter DR. GAINES, R.

Dr. G. What's all this noise here?

Cato. Nuffin', sir; only jess I is puttin' things to rights, as you tole me. I didn't hear any noise except de rats.

Dr. G. Make haste, and come in; I want you to go to town. [*Exit* DR. GAINES, R.

Cato. By golly, de ole boss like to cotch me dat time, didn't he? But wasn't I mad? When I is mad, nobody can do nuffin' wid me. But here's my coat, tore to pieces. Cuss dat nigger! [*Weeps.*] Oh, my coat! oh, my coat! I rudder he had broke my head den to tore my coat. Drat dat nigger! Ef he ever comes here agin, I'll pull out every toof he's got in his head—dat I will. [*Exit*, R.

Scene 3.—A ROOM IN THE QUARTERS.

Enter GLEN, L.

Glen. How slowly the time passes away. I've been waiting here two hours, and Melinda has not yet come. What keeps her, I cannot tell. I waited long and late for her last night, and when she approached, I sprang to my feet, caught her in my arms, pressed her to my heart, and kissed away the tears from her moistened cheeks. She placed her trembling hand in mine, and said, "Glen, I am yours; I will never be the wife of another." I clasped her to my bosom, and called God to witness that I would ever regard her as my wife. Old Uncle Joseph joined us in holy wedlock by moonlight; that was the only marriage ceremony. I look upon the vow as ever binding on me, for I am sure that a just God will sanction our union in heaven. Still, this man, who claims Melinda as his property, is unwilling for me to marry the woman of my choice, because he wants her himself. But he shall not have her. What he will say when he finds that we are married, I cannot tell; but I am determined to protect my wife or die. Ah! here comes Melinda.

Enter MELINDA, R.

I am glad to see you, Melinda. I've been waiting long and feared you would not come. Ah! in tears again?

Melinda. Glen, you are always thinking I am in tears. But what did master say to-day?

Glen. He again forbade our union.

Melinda. Indeed! Can he be so cruel?

Glen. Yes, he can be just so cruel.

Melinda. Alas! alas! how unfeeling and heartless! But did you appeal to his generosity?

Glen. Yes, I did; I used all the persuasive powers that I was master of, but to no purpose; he was inflexible. He even offered me a new suit of clothes, if I would give you up; and when I told him that I could not, he said he would flog me to death if I ever spoke to you again.

Melinda. And what did you say to him?

Glen. I answered, that, while I loved life better than death, even life itself could not tempt me to consent to a separation that would make life an unchanging curse. Oh, I would kill myself, Melinda, if I thought that, for the sake of life, I could consent to your degradation. No, Melinda, I can die, but shall never live to see you the mistress of another man. But, my dear girl, I have a secret to tell you, and no one must know it but you. I will go out and see that no person is within hearing. I will be back soon. [*Exit* GLEN, L.

Melinda. It is often said that the darkest hour of the night precedes the dawn. It is ever thus with the vicissitudes of human suffering. After the soul has reached the lowest depths of despair, and can no deeper plunge amid its rolling, fœtid shades, then the reactionary forces of man's nature begin to operate, resolution takes the place of despondency, energy succeeds instead of apathy, and an upward tendency is felt and exhibited. Men then hope against power, and smile in defiance of despair. I shall never forget when first I saw Glen. It is now more than a year since he came here with his master, Mr. Hamilton. It was a glorious moonlight night in autumn. The wide and fruitful face of nature was silent and buried in repose. The tall trees on the borders of Muddy Creek waved their leafy branches in the breeze, which was wafted from afar, refreshing over hill and vale, over the rippling water, and the waving corn and wheat fields. The starry sky was studded over with a few light, flitting clouds, while the moon, as if rejoicing to witness the meeting of two hearts that should be cemented by the purest love, sailed triumphantly along among the shifting vapors.

Oh, how happy I have been in my acquaintance with Glen! That he loves me, I do well believe it; that I love him, it is most true. Oh, how I would that those who think the slave incapable of the finer feelings, could only see our hearts, and learn our thoughts,—thoughts that we dare not utter in the presence of our masters! But I fear that Glen will be separated from me, for there is nothing too base and mean for master to do, for the purpose of getting me entirely in his power. But, thanks to Heaven, he does not own Glen, and therefore cannot sell him. Yet he might purchase him from his brother-in-law, so as to send him out of the way. But here comes my husband.

Enter GLEN, L.

Glen. I've been as far as the overseer's house, and all is quiet. Now, Melinda, as you are my wife, I will confide to you a secret. I've long been thinking of making my escape to Canada, and taking you with me. It is true that I don't belong to your master, but he might buy me from Hamilton, and then sell me out of the neighborhood.

Melinda. But we could never succeed in the attempt to escape.

Glen. We will make the trial, and show that we at least deserve success. There is a slave trader expected here next week, and Dr. Gaines would sell you at once if he knew that we were married. We must get ready and start, and if we can pass the Ohio river, we'll be safe on the road to Canada. [*Exit*, R.

Scene 4.—DINING-ROOM.

REV. MR. PINCHEN *giving* MRS. GAINES *an account of his experience as a minister*—HANNAH *clearing away the breakfast table*—SAMPEY *standing behind* MRS. GAINES' *chair*.

Mrs. Gaines. Now, do give me more of your experience, brother Pinchen. It always does my soul good to hear religious experience. It draws me nearer and nearer to the Lord's side. I do love to hear good news from God's people.

Mr. Pinchen. Well, sister Gaines, I've had great opportunities in my time to study the heart of man. I've attended a great many camp-meetings, revival meetings, protracted meetings, and death-bed scenes, and I am satisfied, sister Gaines, that the heart of man is full of sin, and desperately wicked. This is a wicked world, sister Gaines, a wicked world.

Mrs. G. Were you ever in Arkansas, brother Pinchen? I've been told that the people out there are very ungodly.

Mr. P. Oh, yes, sister Gaines. I once spent a year at Little Rock, and preached in all the towns round about there; and I found some hard cases out there, I can tell you. I was once spending a week in a district where there were a great many horse thieves, and one night, somebody stole my pony. Well, I knowed it was no use to make a fuss, so I told brother Tarbox to say nothing about it, and I'd get my horse by preaching God's everlasting gospel; for I had faith in the truth, and knowed that my Savior would not let me lose my pony. So the next Sunday I preached on horse-stealing, and told the brethren to come up in the evenin' with their hearts filled with the grace of God. So that night the house was crammed brim full with anxious souls, panting for the bread of life. Brother Bingham opened with prayer, and brother Tarbox followed, and I saw right off that we were gwine to have a blessed time. After I got 'em pretty well warmed up, I jumped on to one of the seats, stretched out my hands, and said, "I know who stole my pony; I've found out; and you are in here tryin' to make people believe that you've got religion; but you ain't got it. And if you don't take my horse back to brother Tarbox's pasture this very night, I'll tell your name right out in meetin' to-morrow night. Take my pony back, you vile and wretched sinner, and come up here and give your heart to God." So the next mornin', I went out to brother Tarbox's pasture, and sure enough, there was my bob-tail pony. Yes, sister Gaines, there he was, safe and sound. Ha, ha, ha.

Mrs. G. Oh, how interesting, and how fortunate for you to get your pony! And what power there is in the gospel! God's children are very lucky. Oh, it is so sweet to sit here and listen to such good news from God's people! You Hannah, what are you standing there listening for, and neglecting your work? Never mind, my lady, I'll whip you well when I am done here. Go at your work this moment, you lazy huzzy! Never mind, I'll whip you well. [*Aside.*] Come, do go on, brother Pinchen, with your godly conversation. It is so sweet! It draws me nearer and nearer to the Lord's side.

Mr. P. Well, sister Gaines, I've had some mighty queer dreams in my time, that I have. You see, one night I dreamed that I was dead and in heaven, and such a place I never saw before. As soon as I entered the gates of the celestial empire, I saw many old and familiar faces that I had seen before. The first person that I saw was good old Elder Pike, the preacher that first called my attention to religion. The next person I saw was Deacon Billings, my first wife's father, and then I saw a host of godly faces. Why, sister Gaines, you knowed Elder Goosbee, didn't you?

Mrs. G. Why, yes; did you see him there? He married me to my first husband.

Mr. P. Oh, yes, sister Gaines, I saw the old Elder, and he looked for all the world as if he had just come out of a revival meetin'.

Mrs. G. Did you see my first husband there, brother Pinchen?

Mr. P. No, sister Gaines, I didn't see brother Pepper there; but I've no doubt but that brother Pepper was there.

Mrs. G. Well, I don't know; I have my doubts. He was not the happiest man in the world. He was always borrowing trouble about something or another. Still, I saw some happy moments with Mr. Pepper. I was happy when I made his acquaintance, happy during our courtship, happy a while after our marriage, and happy when he died. [*Weeps.*]

Hannah. Massa Pinchen, did you see my ole man Ben up dar in hebben?

Mr. P. No, Hannah; I didn't go amongst the niggers.

Mrs. G. No, of course brother Pinchen didn't go among the blacks. What are you asking questions for? Never mind, my lady, I'll whip you well when I'm done here. I'll skin you from head to foot. [*Aside.*] Do go on with your heavenly conversation, brother Pinchen; it does my very soul good. This is indeed a precious moment for me. I do love to hear of Christ and Him crucified.

Mr. P. Well, sister Gaines, I promised sister Daniels that I'd come over and see her this morning, and have a little season of prayer with her, and I suppose I must go. I'll tell you more of my religious experience when I return.

Mrs. G. If you must go, then I'll have to let you; but before you do, I wish to get your advice upon a little matter that concerns Hannah. Last week, Hannah stole a goose, killed it, cooked it, and she and her man Sam had a fine time eating the goose; and her master and I would never have known a word about it, if it had not been for Cato, a faithful servant, who told his master. And then, you see, Hannah had to be severely whipped before she'd confess that she stole the goose. Next

Sabbath is sacrament day, and I want to know if you think that Hannah is fit to go to the Lord's supper after stealing the goose.

Mr. P. Well, sister Gaines, that depends on circumstances. If Hannah has confessed that she stole the goose, and has been sufficiently whipped, and has begged her master's pardon, and begged your pardon, and thinks she'll never do the like again, why then I suppose she can go to the Lord's supper; for

"While the lamp holds out to burn,
The vilest sinner may return."

But she must be sure that she has repented, and won't steal any more.

Mrs. G. Now, Hannah, do you hear that? For my own part, I don't think she's fit to go to the Lord's supper, for she had no occasion to steal the goose. We give our niggers plenty of good wholesome food. They have a full run to the meal tub, meat once a fortnight, and all the sour milk about the place, and I'm sure that's enough for any one. I do think that our niggers are the most ungrateful creatures in the world, that I do. They aggravate my life out of me.

Hannah. I know, missis, dat I steal de goose, and massa whip me for it, and I confess it, and I is sorry for it. But, missis, I is gwine to de Lord's supper, next Sunday, kase I ain't agwine to turn my back on my bressed Lord an' Massa for no old tough goose, dat I ain't. [*Weeps.*]

Mr. P. Well, sister Gaines, I suppose I must go over and see sister Daniels; she'll be waiting for me. [*Exit* MR. PINCHEN, M. D.

Mrs. G. Now, Hannah, brother Pinchen is gone, do you get the cowhide and follow me to the cellar, and I'll whip you well for aggravating me as you have to-day. It seems as if I can never sit down to take a little comfort with the Lord, without you crossing me. The devil always puts it into your head to disturb me, just when I am trying to serve the Lord. I've no doubt but that I'll miss going to heaven on your account. But I'll whip you well before I leave this world, that I will. Get the cowhide and follow me to the cellar. [*Exit* MRS. GAINES *and* HANNAH, R.]

ACT II.

Scene I.—PARLOR.

DR. GAINES *at a table, letters and papers before him.*

Enter SAMPEY, L.

Sampey. Dar's a gemman at de doe, massa, dat wants to see you, seer.

Dr. Gaines. Ask him to walk in, Sampey. [*Exit* SAMPEY, L.

Enter WALKER.

Walker. Why, how do you do, Dr. Gaines? I em glad to see you, I'll swear.

Dr. G. How do you do, Mr. Walker? I did not expect to see you up here so soon. What has hurried you?

Walk. Well, you see, doctor, I comes when I em not expected. The price of niggers is up, and I em gwine to take advantage of the times. Now, doctor, ef you've got any niggers that you wants to sell, I em your man. I am paying the highest price of any body in the market. I pay cash down, and no grumblin'.

Dr. G. I don't know that I want to sell any of my people now. Still, I've got to make up a little money next month, to pay in bank; and another thing, the doctors say that we are likely to have a touch of the cholera this summer, and if that's the case, I suppose I had better turn as many of my slaves into cash as I can.

Walk. Yes, doctor, that is very true. The cholera is death on slaves, and a thousand dollars in your pocket is a great deal better than a nigger in the field, with cholera at his heels. Why, who is that coming up the lane? It's Mr. Wildmarsh, as I live! Jest the very man I wants to see.

Enter MR. WILDMARSH.

Why, how do you do, Squire? I was jest a thinkin' about you.

Wildmarsh. How are you, Mr. Walker? and how are you, doctor? I am glad to see you both looking so well. You seem in remarkably good health, doctor?

Dr. G. Yes, Squire, I was never in the enjoyment of better health. I hope you left all well at Licking?

Wild. Yes, I thank you. And now, Mr. Walker, how goes times with you?

Walk. Well, you see, Squire, I em in good spirits. The price of niggers is up in the market, and I am lookin' out for bargains; and I was jest intendin' to come over to Lickin' to see you, to see if you had any niggers to sell. But it seems as ef the Lord knowed that I wanted to see you, and directed your steps over here. Now, Squire, ef you've got any niggers you wants to sell, I em your man. I am payin' the highest cash price of any body in the market. Now's your time, Squire.

Wild. No, I don't think I want to sell any of my slaves now. I sold a very valuable gal to Mr. Haskins last week. I tell you, she was a smart one. I got eighteen hundred dollars for her.

Walk. Why, Squire, how you do talk! Eighteen hundred dollars for one gal? She must have been a screamer to bring that price. What sort of a lookin' critter was she? I should like to have bought her.

Wild. She was a little of the smartest gal I've ever raised; that she was.

Walk. Then she was your own raising, was she?

Wild. Oh, yes; she was raised on my place, and if I could have kept her three or four years longer, and taken her to the market myself, I am sure I could have sold her for three thousand dollars. But you see, Mr. Walker, my wife got a little jealous, and you know jealousy sets the women's heads a teetering, and so I had to sell the gal. She's got straight hair, blue eyes, prominent features, and is almost white. Haskins will make a spec, and no mistake.

Walk. Why, Squire, was she that pretty little gal that I saw on your knee the day that your wife was gone, when I was at your place three years ago?

Wild. Yes, the same.

Walk. Well, now, Squire, I thought that was your daughter; she looked mightily like you. She was your daughter, wasn't she? You need not be ashamed to own it to me, for I am mum upon such matters.

Wild. You know, Mr. Walker, that people will talk, and when they talk, they say a great deal; and people did talk, and many said the gal was my daughter; and you know we can't help people's talking. But here comes the Rev. Mr. Pinchen; I didn't know that he was in the neighborhood.

Walk. It is Mr. Pinchen, as I live; jest the very man I wants to see.

Enter MR. PINCHEN, R.

Why, how do you do, Mr. Pinchen? What in the name of Jehu brings you down here to Muddy Creek? Any camp-meetins, revival meetins, death-bed scenes, or any thing else in your line going on down here? How is religion prosperin' now, Mr. Pinchen? I always like to hear about religion.

Mr. Pin. Well, Mr. Walker, the Lord's work is in good condition every where now. I tell you, Mr. Walker, I've been in the gospel ministry these thirteen years, and I am satisfied that the heart of man is full of sin and desperately wicked. This is a wicked world, Mr. Walker, a wicked world, and we ought all of us to have religion. Religion is a good thing to live by, and we all want it when we die. Yes, sir, when the great trumpet blows, we ought to be ready. And a man in your business of buying and selling slaves needs religion more than any body else, for it makes you treat your people as you should. Now, there is Mr. Haskins,—he is a slave-trader, like yourself. Well, I converted him. Before he got religion, he was one of the worst men to his niggers I ever saw; his heart was as hard as stone. But religion has made his heart as soft as a piece of cotton. Before I converted him, he would sell husbands from their wives, and seem to take delight in it; but now he won't sell a man from his wife, if he can get any one to buy both of them together. I tell you, sir, religion has done a wonderful work for him.

Walk. I know, Mr. Pinchen, that I ought to have religion, and I feel that I am a great sinner; and whenever I get with good pious people like you and the doctor, and Mr. Wildmarsh, it always makes me feel that I am a desperate sinner. I feel it the more, because I've got a religious turn of mind. I know that I would be happier with religion, and the first spare time I get, I am going to try to get it. I'll go to a protracted meeting, and I won't stop till I get religion. Yes, I'll scuffle with the Lord till I gets forgiven. But it always makes me feel bad to talk about religion, so I'll change the subject. Now, doctor, what about them thar niggers you thought you could sell me?

Dr. Gaines. I'll see my wife, Mr. Walker, and if she is willing to part with Hannah, I'll sell you Sam and his wife, Hannah. Ah! here comes my wife; I'll mention it.

Enter MRS. GAINES, L.

Ah! my dear, I am glad you've come. I was just telling Mr. Walker, that if you were willing to part with Hannah, I'd sell him Sam and Hannah.

Mrs. G. Now, Dr. Gaines, I am astonished and surprised that you should think of such a thing. You know what trouble I've had in training up Hannah for a house servant, and now that I've got her so that she knows my ways, you want to sell her. Hav n't you niggers enough on the plantation to sell, without selling the servants from under my very nose?

Dr. G. Oh, yes, my dear; but I can spare Sam, and I don't like to separate him from his wife; and I thought if you could let Hannah go, I'd sell them both. I don't like to separate husbands from their wives.

Mrs. G. Now, gentlemen, that's just the way with my husband. He thinks more about the welfare and comfort of his slaves, than he does of himself or his family. I am sure you need not feel so bad at the thought of separating Sam from Hannah. They've only been married eight months, and their attachment can't be very strong in that short time. Indeed, I shall be glad if you do sell Sam, for then I'll make Hannah *jump the broomstick* with Cato, and I'll have them both here under my eye. I never will again let one of my house servants marry a field hand—never! For when night comes on, the servants are off to the quarters, and I have to holler and holler enough to split my throat before I can make them hear. And another thing: I want you to sell Melinda. I don't intend to keep that mulatto wench about the house any longer.

Dr. Gaines. My dear, I'll sell any servant from the place to suit you, except Melinda. I can't think of selling her—I can't think of it.

Mrs. G. I tell you that Melinda shall leave this house, or I'll go. There, now you have it. I've had my life tormented out of me by the presence of that yellow wench, and I'll stand it no longer. I know you love her more than you do me, and I'll—I'll—I'll write—write to my father. [*Weeps.*] [*Exit* MRS. GAINES, L.

Walk. Why, doctor, your wife's a screamer, ain't she? Ha, ha, ha. Why, doctor, she's got a tongue of her own, ain't she? Why, doctor, it was only last week that I thought of getting a wife myself; but your wife has skeered the idea out of my head. Now, doctor, if you wants to sell the gal, I'll buy her. Husband and wife ought to be on good terms, and your wife won't feel well till the gal is gone. Now, I'll pay you all she's worth, if you wants to sell.

Dr. G. No, Mr. Walker; the girl my wife spoke of is not for sale. My wife does not mean what she says; she's only a little jealous. I'll get brother Pinchen to talk to her, and get her mind turned upon religious matters, and then she'll forget it. She's only a little jealous.

Walk. I tell you what, doctor, ef you call that a little jealous, I'd like to know what's a heap. I tell you, it will take something more than religion to set your wife right. You had better sell me the gal; I'll pay you cash down, and no grumblin'.

Dr. G. The girl is not for sale, Mr. Walker; but if you want two good, able-bodied servants, I'll sell you Sam and Big Sally. Sam is trustworthy, and Sally is worth her weight in gold for rough usage.

Walk. Well, doctor, I'll go out and take a look at 'em, for I never buys slaves without examining them well, because they are sometimes injured by over-work or under-feedin'. I don't say that is the case with yours, for I don't believe it is; but as I sell on honor, I must buy on honor.

Dr. G. Walk out, sir, and you can examine them to your heart's content. Walk right out, sir.

Scene 2.—VIEW IN FRONT OF THE GREAT HOUSE.

Examination of SAM *and* BIG SALLY.—DR. GAINES, WILDMARSH, MR. PINCHEN *and* WALKER *present.*

Walk. Well, my boy, what's your name?

Sam. Sam, sir, is my name.

Walk. How old are you, Sam?

Sam. Ef I live to see next corn plantin' time, I'll be 27, or 30, or 35, or 40—I don't know which, sir.

Walk. Ha, ha, ha. Well, doctor, this is rather a green boy. Well, mer feller, are you sound?

Sam. Yes, sir, I spec I is.

Walk. Open your mouth and let me see your teeth. I allers judge a nigger's age by his teeth, same as I dose a hoss. Ah! pretty good set of grinders. Have you got a good appetite?

Sam. Yes, sir.

Walk. Can you eat your allowance?

Sam. Yes, sir, when I can get it.

Walk. Get out on the floor and dance; I want to see if you are supple.

Sam. I don't like to dance; I is got religion.

Walk. Oh, ho! you've got religion, have you? That's so much the better. I likes to deal in the gospel. I think he'll suit me. Now, mer gal, what's your name?

Sally. I is Big Sally, sir.

Walk. How old are you, Sally?

Sally. I don't know, sir; but I heard once dat I was born at sweet pertater diggin' time.

Walk. Ha, ha, ha. Don't know how old you are! Do you know who made you?

Sally. I hev heard who it was in de Bible dat made me, but I dun forget de gentman's name.

Walk. Ha, ha, ha. Well, doctor, this is the greenest lot of niggers I've seen for some time. Well, what do you ask for them?

Dr. Gaines. You may have Sam for $1000, and Sally for $900. They are worth all I ask for them. You know I never banter, Mr. Walker. There they are; you can take them at that price, or let them alone, just as you please.

Walk. Well, doctor, I reckon I'll take 'em; but it's all they are worth. I'll put the handcuffs on 'em, and then I'll pay you. I likes to go accordin' to Scripter. Scripter says ef eatin' meat will offend your brother, you must quit it; and I say, ef leavin' your slaves without the handcuffs will make 'em run away, you must put the handcuffs on 'em. Now, Sam, don't you and Sally cry. I am of a tender heart, and it allers makes me feel bad to see people cryin'. Don't cry, and the first place I get to, I'll buy each of you a great big *ginger cake*,—that I will. Now, Mr. Pinchen, I wish you were going down the river. I'd like to have your company; for I allers likes the company of preachers.

Mr. Pinchen. Well, Mr. Walker, I would be much pleased to go down the river with you, but it's too early for me. I expect to go to Natchez in four or five weeks, to attend a camp-meetin', and if you were going down then, I'd like it. What kind of niggers sells best in the Orleans market, Mr. Walker?

Walk. Why, field hands. Did you think of goin' in the trade?

Mr. P. Oh, no; only it's a long ways down to Natchez, and I thought I'd just buy five or six niggers, and take 'em down and sell 'em to pay my travellin' expenses. I only want to clear my way.

Scene 3.—SITTING-ROOM—TABLE AND ROCKING-CHAIR.

Enter MRS. GAINES, R, *followed by* SAMPEY.

Mrs. Gaines. I do wish your master would come; I want supper. Run to the gate, Sampey, and see if he is coming. [*Exit* SAMPEY, L.

That man is enough to break my heart. The patience of an angel could not stand it.

Enter SAMPEY, L.

Samp. Yes, missis, master is coming.

Enter DR. GAINES, L.

[*The Doctor walks about with his hands under his coat, seeming very much elated.*]

Mrs. Gaines. Why, doctor, what is the matter?

Dr. Gaines. My dear, don't call me *doctor.*

Mrs. G. What should I call you?

Dr. G. Call me Colonel, my dear—Colonel. I have been elected Colonel of the Militia, and I want you to call me by my right name. I always felt that Providence had designed me for something great, and He has just begun to shower His blessings upon me.

Mrs. G. Dear me, I could never get to calling you Colonel; I've called you Doctor for the last twenty years.

Dr. G. Now, Sarah, if you will call me Colonel, other people will, and I want you to set the example. Come, my darling, call me Colonel, and I'll give you any thing you wish for.

Mrs. G. Well, as I want a new gold watch and bracelets, I'll commence now. Come, Colonel, we'll go to supper. Ah! now for my new shawl. [*Aside.*] Mrs. Lemme was here to-day, Colonel, and she had on, Colonel, one of the prettiest shawls, Colonel, I think, Colonel, that I ever saw, Colonel, in my life, Colonel. And there is only one, Colonel, in Mr. Watson's store, Colonel; and that, Colonel, will do, Colonel, for a Colonel's wife.

Dr. G. Ah! my dear, you never looked so much the lady since I've known you. Go, my darling, get the watch, bracelets and shawl, and tell them to charge them to Colonel Gaines; and when you say "Colonel," always emphasize the word.

Mrs. G. Come, Colonel, let's go to supper.

Dr. G. My dear, you're a jewel,—you are! [*Exit,* R.

Enter CATO, L.

Cato. Why, whar is massa and missis? I tought dey was here. Ah! by golly, yonder comes a mulatter gal. Yes, it's Mrs. Jones's Tapioca. I'll set up to dat gal, dat I will.

Enter TAPIOCA, R.

Good ebenin', Miss Tappy. How is your folks?

Tapioca. Pretty well, I tank you.

Cato. Miss Tappy, dis wanderin' heart of mine is yours. Come, take a seat! Please to squze my manners; love discommodes me. Take a seat. Now, Miss Tappy, I loves you; an ef you will jess marry me, I'll make you a happy husband, dat I will. Come, take me as I is.

Tap. But what will Big Jim say?

Cato. Big Jim! Why, let dat nigger go to Ginny. I want to know, now, if you is tinkin' about dat common nigger? Why, Miss Tappy, I is surstonished dat you should tink 'bout frowin' yousef away wid a common, ugly lookin' cuss like Big Jim, when you can get a fine lookin', suspectable man like me. Come, Miss Tappy, choose dis day who you have. Afore I go any furder, give me one kiss. Come, give me one kiss. Come, let me kiss you.

Tap. No you shan't—dare now! You shan't kiss me widout you is stronger den I is; and I know you is dat. [*He kisses her.*]

Enter DR. GAINES, R, *and hides.*

Cato. Did you know, Miss Tappy, dat I is de head doctor 'bout dis house? I beats de ole boss all to pieces.

Tap. I hev hearn dat you bleeds and pulls teef.

Cato. Yes, Miss Tappy; massa could not get along widout me, for massa was made a doctor by books; but I is a natral doctor. I was born a doctor, jess as Lorenzo Dow was born a preacher. So you see I can't be nuffin' but a doctor, while massa is a bunglin' ole cuss at de bissness.

Dr. Gaines, (in a low voice.) Never mind; I'll teach you a lesson, that I will.

Cato. You see, Miss Tappy, I was gwine to say—Ah! but afore I forget, jess give me anudder kiss, jess to keep company wid de one dat you give me jess now,—dat's all. [*Kisses her.*] Now, Miss Tappy, duse you know de fuss time dat I seed you?

Tap. No, Mr. Cato, I don't.

Cato. Well, it was at de camp-meetin'. Oh, Miss Tappy, dat pretty red calliker dress you had on dat time did de work for me. It made my heart flutter—

Dr. G. (low voice.) Yes, and I'll make your black hide flutter.

Cato. Didn't I hear some noise? By golly, dar is teves in dis house, and I'll drive 'em out. [*Takes a chair and runs at the Doctor, and knocks him down. The Doctor chases Cato round the table.*

Cato. Oh, massa, I didn't know 'twas you!

Dr. G. You scoundrel! I'll whip you well. Stop! I tell you. [*Curtain falls.*

ACT III.

Scene 1.—SITTING-ROOM.

MRS. GAINES, *seated in an arm chair, reading a letter.*

Enter HANNAH, L.

Mrs. Gaines. You need not tell me, Hannah, that you don't want another husband, I know better. Your master has sold Sam, and he's gone down the river, and you'll never see him again. So, go and put on your calico dress, and meet me in the kitchen. I intend for you to *jump the broomstick* with Cato. You need not tell me that you don't want another man. I know that there's no woman living that can be happy and satisfied without a husband.

Hannah. Oh, missis, I don't want to jump de broomstick wid Cato. I don't love Cato; I can't love him.

Mrs. G. Shut up, this moment! What do you know about love? I didn't love your master when I married him, and people don't marry for love now. So go and put on your calico dress, and meet me in the kitchen. [*Exit* HANNAH, L.

I am glad that the Colonel has sold Sam; now I'll make Hannah marry Cato, and I have them both here under my eye. And I am also glad that the Colonel has parted with Melinda. Still, I'm afraid that he is trying to deceive me. He took the hussy away yesterday, and says he sold her to a trader; but I don't believe it. At any rate, if she's in the neighborhood, I'll find her, that I will. No man ever fools me. [*Exit* MRS. GAINES, L.

Scene 2.—THE KITCHEN—SLAVES AT WORK.

Enter HANNAH, R.

Hannah. Oh, Cato, do go and tell missis dat you don't want to jump de broomstick wid me,—dat's a good man! Do, Cato; kase I nebber can love you. It was only las week dat massa sold my Sammy, and I don't want any udder man. Do go tell missis dat you don't want me.

Cato. No, Hannah, I ain't a gwine to tell missis no such thing, kase I dose want you, and I ain't a-gwine to tell a lie for you ner nobody else. Dar, now you's got it! I don't see why you need to make so much fuss. I is better lookin' den Sam; an' I is a house servant, an' Sam was only a fiel hand; so you ought to feel proud of a change. So go and do as missis tells you. [*Exit* HANNAH, L.

Hannah needn't try to get me to tell a lie; I ain't a-gwine to do it, kase I dose want her, an' I is bin wantin' her dis long time, an' soon as massa sold Sam, I knowed I would get her. By golly, I is gwine to be a married man. Won't I be happy! Now, ef I could only jess run away from ole massa, an' get to Canada wid Hannah, den I'd show 'em who I was. Ah! dat reminds me of my song 'bout ole massa and Canada, an' I'll sing it fer yer. Dis is my moriginal hyme. It comed into my head one night when I was fass asleep under an apple tree, looking up at de moon. Now for my song:—

AIR—"*Dandy Jim.*"

Come all ye bondmen far and near,
Let's put a song in massa's ear,
It is a song for our poor race,
Who're whipped and trampled with disgrace.

CHORUS.

My old massa tells me, Oh,
This is a land of freedom, Oh;
Let's look about and see if it's so,
Just as massa tells me, Oh.

He tells us of that glorious one,
I think his name was Washington,
How he did fight for liberty,
To save a threepence tax on tea. [*Chorus.*]

But now we look about and see
That we poor blacks are not so free;

We're whipped and thrashed about like fools,
And have no chance at common schools. [*Chorus.*]

They take our wives, insult and mock,
And sell our children on the block,
They choke us if we say a word,
And say that "niggers" shan't be heard. [*Chorus.*]

Our preachers, too, with whip and cord,
Command obedience in the Lord;
They say they learn it from the big book,
But for ourselves, we dare not look. [*Chorus.*]

There is a country far away,
I think they call it Canada,
And if we reach Victoria's shore,
They say that we are slaves no more.

Now haste, all bondmen, let us go,
And leave this *Christian* country, Oh;
Haste to the land of the British Queen,
Where whips for negroes are not seen.

Now, if we go, we must take the night,
And never let them come in sight;
The bloodhounds will be on our track,
And wo to us if they fetch us back.

Now haste all bondmen, let us go,
And leave this *Christian* country, Oh;
God help us to Victoria's shore,
Where we are free and slaves no more!

Enter MRS. GAINES, L.

Mrs. Gaines. Ah! Cato, you're ready, are you? Where is Hannah?

Cato. Yes, missis; I is bin waitin' dis long time. Hannah has bin here tryin' to swade me to tell you dat I do n't want her; but I telled her dat you sed I must jump de broomstick wid her, an' I is gwine to mind you.

Mrs. G. That's right, Cato; servants should always mind their masters and mistresses, without asking a question.

Cato. Yes, missis, I allers dose what you and massa tells me, an' axes nobody.

Enter HANNAH, R.

Mrs. Gaines. Ah! Hannah; come, we are waiting for you. Nothing can be done till you come.

Hannah. Oh, missis, I do n't want to jump de broomstick wid Cato; I can't love him.

Mrs. G. Shut up, this moment. Dolly, get the broom. Susan, you take hold of the other end. There, now hold it a little lower—there, a little higher. There, now, that'll do. Now Hannah, take hold of Cato's hand. Let Cato take hold of your hand.

Hannah. Oh, missis, do spare me. I do n't want to jump de broomstick wid Cato.

Mrs. G. Get the cowhide, and follow me to the cellar, and I'll whip you well. I'll let you know how to disobey my orders. Get the cowhide, and follow me to the cellar. [*Exit* MRS. GAINES *and* HANNAH, R.

Dolly. Oh, Cato, do go an' tell missis dat you do n't want Hannah. Do n't you hear how she's whippin' her in de cellar? Do go an' tell missis dat you do n't want Hannah, and den she'll stop whippin' her.

Cato. No, Dolly, I ain't a-gwine to do no such a thing, kase ef I tell missis dat I do n't want Hannah, den missis will whip me; an' I ain't a-gwine to be whipped fer you, ner Hannah, ner nobody else. No, I'll jump de broomstick wid every woman on de place, ef missis wants me to, before I'll be whipped.

Dolly. Cato, ef I was in Hannah's place, I'd see you in de bottomless pit before I'd live wid you, you great big wall-eyed, empty-headed, knock-kneed fool. You're as mean as your devilish old missis.

Cato. Ef you do n't quit dat busin' me, Dolly, I'll tell missis as soon as she comes in, an' she'll whip you, you know she will.

Enter MRS. GAINES *and* HANNAH, R.

[*Mrs. G. fans herself with her handkerchief, and appears fatigued.*]

Mrs. G. You ought to be ashamed of yourself, Hannah, to make me fatigue myself in this way, to make you do your duty. It's very naughty in you, Hannah. Now, Dolly, you and Susan get the broom, and get out in the middle of the room. There, hold it a little lower—a little higher; there, that'll do. Now, remember that this is a solemn occasion; you are going to jump into matrimony. Now, Cato, take hold of Hannah's hand. There, now, why couldn't you let Cato take hold of your hand before? Now get ready, and when I count three, do you jump. Eyes on the *broom-stick!* All ready. One, two, three, and over you go. There, now you're husband and wife, and if you do n't live happy together, it's your own fault; for I am sure there's nothing to hinder it. Now, Hannah, come up to the house, and I'll give you some whiskey, and you can make some apple toddy, and you and Cato can have a fine time. [*Exit* MRS. GAINES *and* HANNAH, L.

Dolly. I tell you what, Susan, when I get married, I is gwine to have a preacher to marry me. I ain't a-gwine to jump de broomstick. Dat will do for fiel' hands, but house servants ought to be 'bove dat.

Susan. Well, chile, you can't speck any ting else from ole missis. She come from down in Carlina, from 'mong de poor white trash. She don't know any better. You can't speck nothin' more dan a jump from a frog. Missis says she is one of de akastocacy; but she ain't no more of an akastocacy dan I is. Missis says she was born wid a silver spoon in her mouf; ef she was, I wish it had a-choked her, dat's what I wish. Missis wanted to make Linda jump de broomstick wid Glen, but massa ain't a-gwine to let Linda jump de broomstick wid anybody. He's gwine to keep Linda fer heself.

Dolly. You know massa took Linda 'way las' night, an' tell missis dat he has sold her and sent her down de river; but I do n't b'lieve he has sold her at all. He went ober towards de poplar farm, an' I tink Linda is ober dar now. Ef she is dar, missis'll find it out, fer she tell'd massa las' night, dat ef Linda was in de neighborhood, she'd find her. [*Exit* DOLLY *and* SUSAN.

Scene 3.—SITTING ROOM—CHAIRS AND TABLE.

Enter HANNAH, R.

Hannah. I do n't keer what missis says; I do n't like Cato, an' I won't live wid him. I always love my Sammy, an' I loves him now. [*Knock at the door—goes to the door.*

Enter MAJ. MOORE, M. D.

Walk in, sir; take a seat. I'll call missis, sir; massa is gone away. [*Exit* HANNAH, R.

Maj. Moore. So I am here at last, and the Colonel is not at home. I hope his wife is a good-looking woman. I rather like fine-looking women, especially when their husbands are from home. Well, I've studied human nature to some purpose. If you wish to get the good will of a man, do n't praise his wife, and if you wish to gain the favor of a woman, praise her children, and swear that they are the picture of their father, whether they are or not. Ah! here comes the lady.

Enter MRS. GAINES, R.

Mrs. G. Good morning, sir!

Maj. M. Good morning, madam! I am Maj. Moore, of Jefferson. The Colonel and I had seats near each other in the last Legislature.

Mrs. G. Be seated, sir. I think I've heard the Colonel speak of you. He's away, now; but I expect him every moment. You're a stranger here, I presume?

Maj. M. Yes, madam, I am. I rather like the Colonel's situation here.

Mrs. G. It is thought to be a fine location.

Enter SAMPEY, R.

Hand me my fan, will you, Sampey? [*Sampey gets the fan and passes near the Major, who mistakes the boy for the Colonel's son. He reaches out his hand.*

Maj. M. How do you do, bub? Madam, I should have known that this was the Colonel's son, if I had met him in California; for he looks so much like his papa.

Mrs. G. [*To the boy.*] Get out of here this minute. Go to the kitchen. [*Exit* SAMPEY, R.

That is one of the niggers, sir.

Maj. M. I beg your pardon, madam; I beg your pardon.

Mrs. G. No offence, sir; mistakes will be made. Ah! here comes the Colonel.

Enter DR. GAINES, M. D.

Dr. Gaines. Bless my soul, how are you, Major? I'm exceedingly pleased to see you. Be seated, be seated, Major.

Mrs. G. Please excuse me, gentlemen; I must go and look after dinner, for I've no doubt that the Major will have an appetite for dinner, by the time it is ready. [*Exit* MRS. GAINES, R.

Maj. M. Colonel, I'm afraid I've played the devil here to-day.

Dr. G. Why, what have you done?

Maj. M. You see, Colonel, I always make it a point, wherever I go, to praise the children, if there are any, and so to-day, seeing one of your little servants come in, and taking him to be your son, I spoke to your wife of the marked resemblance between you and the boy. I am afraid I've insulted madam.

Dr. G. Oh! do n't let that trouble you. Ha, ha, ha. If you did call him my son, you did n't miss it much. Ha, ha, ha. Come, we'll take a walk, and talk over matters about old times. [*Exit*, L.

Scene 4.—FOREST SCENERY.

Enter GLEN, L.

Glen. Oh, how I want to see Melinda! My heart pants and my soul is moved whenever I hear her voice. Human tongue cannot tell how my heart yearns toward her. Oh, God! thou who gavest me life, and implanted in my bosom the love of liberty, and gave me a heart to love, Oh, pity the poor outraged slave! Thou, who canst rend the veil of centuries, speak, Oh, speak, and put a stop to this persecution! What is death, compared to slavery? Oh; heavy curse, to have thoughts, reason, taste, judgment, conscience and passions like another man, and not have equal liberty to use them! Why was I born with a wish to be free, and still be a slave? Why should I call another man master? And my poor Melinda, she is taken away from me, and I dare not ask the tyrant where she is. It is childish to stand here weeping. Why should my eyes be filled with tears, when my brain is on fire? I will find my wife—I will; and wo to him who shall try to keep me from her!

Scene 5.—ROOM IN A SMALL COTTAGE ON THE POPLAR FARM, (*Ten miles from Muddy Creek, and owned by Dr. Gaines.*)

Enter MELINDA, R.

Melinda. Here I am, watched, and kept a prisoner in this place. Oh, I would that I could escape, and once more get with Glen. Poor Glen! He does not know where I am. Master took the opportunity, when Glen was in the city with his master, to bring me here to this lonely place, and fearing that mistress would know where I was, he brought me here at night. Oh, how I wish I could rush into the arms of sleep!—that sweet sleep, which visits all alike, descending, like the dews of heaven, upon the bond as well as the free. It would drive from my troubled brain the agonies of this terrible night.

Enter DR. GAINES, L.

Dr. Gaines. Good evening, Melinda! Are you not glad to see me?

Melinda. Sir, how can I be glad to see one who has made life a burden, and turned my sweetest moments into bitterness?

Dr. G. Come, Melinda, no more reproaches! You know that I love you, and I have told you, and I tell you again, that if you will give up all idea of having Glen for a husband, I will set you free, let you live in this cottage, and be your own mistress, and I'll dress you like a lady. Come, now, be reasonable!

Melinda. Sir, I am your slave; you can do as you please with the avails of my labor, but you shall never tempt me to swerve from the path of virtue.

Dr. G. Now, Melinda, that black scoundrel Glen has been putting these notions into your head. I'll let you know that you are my property, and I'll do as I please with you. I'll teach you that there is no limit to my power.

Melinda. Sir, let me warn you that if you compass my ruin, a woman's bitterest curse will be laid upon your head, with all the crushing, withering weight that my soul can impart to it; a curse that shall cling to you throughout the remainder of your wretched life; a curse that shall haunt you like a spectre in your dreams by night, and attend upon you by day; a curse, too, that shall embody itself in the ghastly form of the woman whose chastity you will have outraged. Command me to bury myself in yonder stream, and I will obey you. Bid me do any thing else, but I beseech you not to commit a double crime,—outrage a woman, and make her false to her husband.

Dr. G. You got a husband! Who is your husband, and when were you married?

Melinda. Glen is my husband, and I've been married four weeks. Old Uncle Joseph married us one night by moonlight. I see you are angry; I pray you not to injure my husband.

Dr. G. Melinda, you shall never see Glen again. I have bought him from Hamilton, and I will return to Muddy Creek, and roast him at the stake. A black villain, to get into my way in that manner! Here I've come ten miles to-night to see you, and this is the way you receive me!

Melinda. Oh, master, I beg you not to injure my husband! Kill me, but spare him! Do! do! he is my husband!

Dr. G. You shall never see that black imp again, so good night, my lady! When I come again, you'll give me a more cordial reception. Good night! [*Exit* DR. GAINES, L.

Melinda. I shall go distracted. I cannot remain here and know that Glen is being tortured on my account. I must escape from this place,—I must,—I must!

Enter CATO, R.

Cato. No, you ain't a-gwine to 'scape, nudder. Massa tells me to keep dese eyes on you, an' I is gwine to do it.

Melinda. Oh, Cato, do let me get away! I beg you, do!

Cato. No; I tells you massa telled me to keep you safe; an' ef I let you go, massa will whip me. [*Exit* CATO, L.

Enter MRS. GAINES, R.

Mrs. G. Ah, you trollop! here you are! Your master told me that he had sold you and sent you down the river, but I knew better; I knew it was a lie. And when he left home this evening, he said he was going to the city on business, and I knew that was a lie too, and determined to follow him, and see what he was up to. I rode all the way over here to-night. My side-saddle was lent out, and I had to ride ten miles bare-back, and I can scarcely walk; and your master has just left here. Now deny that, if you dare.

Melinda. Madam, I will deny nothing which is true. Your husband has just gone from here, but God knows that I am innocent of any thing wrong with him.

Mrs. G. It's a lie! I know better. If you are innocent, what are you doing here, cooped up in this cottage by yourself? Tell me that!

Melinda. God knows that I was brought here against my will, and I beg that you will take me away.

Mrs. G. Yes, Melinda, I will see that you are taken away, but it shall be after a fashion that you won't like. I know that your master loves you, and I intend to put a stop to it. Here, drink the contents of this vial,—drink it!

Melinda. Oh, you will not take my life,—you will not!

Mrs. G. Drink the poison this moment!

Melinda. I cannot drink it.

Mrs. G. I tell you to drink this poison at once. Drink it, or I will thrust this knife to your heart! The poison or the dagger, this instant! [*She draws a dagger; Melinda retreats to the back of the room, and seizes a broom.*

Melinda. I will not drink the poison! [*They fight;* MELINDA *sweeps off* MRS. GAINES,—*cap, combs and curls. Curtain falls.*

ACT IV.

Scene I.—INTERIOR OF A DUNGEON—GLEN IN CHAINS.

Glen. When I think of my unmerited sufferings, it almost drives me mad. I struck the doctor, and for that, I must remain here loaded with chains. But why did he strike me? He takes my wife from me, sends her off, and then comes and beats me over the head with his cane. I did right to strike him back again. I would I had killed him. Oh! there is a volcano pent up in the hearts of the slaves of these Southern States that will burst forth ere long. When that day comes, wo to those whom its unpitying fury may devour! I would be willing to die, if I could smite down with these chains every man who attempts to enslave his fellow-man.

Enter SAMPEY, R.

Sampey. Glen, I jess bin hear massa call de oberseer, and I spec somebody is gwine to be whipped. Anudder ting: I know whar massa took Linda to. He took her to de poplar farm, an' he went away las' night, an missis she follow after massa, an' she ain't come back yet. I tell you, Glen, de debil will be to pay on dis place, but don't you tell any body dat I tole you. [*Exit* SAMPEY, R.

Scene 2.—PARLOR.

DR. GAINES, *alone.*

Dr. Gaines. Yes, I will have the black rascal well whipped, and then I'll sell him. It was most fortunate for me that Hamilton was willing to sell him to me.

Enter MR. SCRAGG, L.

I have sent for you, Mr. Scragg. I want you to take Glen out of the dungeon, take him into the tobacco house, fasten him down upon the stretcher, and give him five hundred lashes upon his bare back; and when you have whipped him, feel his pulse, and report to me how it stands, and if he can bear more, I'll have you give him an additional hundred or two, as the case may be.

Scragg. I tell you, doctor, that suits me to a charm. I've long wanted to whip that nigger. When your brother-in-law came here to board, and brought that boy with him, I felt bad to see a nigger dressed up in such fine clothes, and I wanted to whip him right off. I tell you, doctor, I had rather whip that nigger than go to heaven, any day,—that I had!

Dr. G. Go, Mr. Scragg, and do your duty. Don't spare the whip!

Scragg. I will, sir; I'll do it in order. [*Exit* SCRAGG, L.

Dr. G. Every thing works well now, and when I get Glen out of the way, I'll pay Melinda another visit, and she'll give me a different reception. But I wonder where my wife is? She left word that she was going to see her brother, but I am afraid that she has got on my track. That woman is the pest of my life. If there's any place in heaven for her, I'd be glad if the Lord would take her home, for I've had her too long already. But what noise is that? What can that be? What is the matter?

Enter SCRAGG, L., *with face bloody.*

Scragg. Oh, dear me! oh, my head! That nigger broke away from me, and struck me over the head with a stick. Oh, dear me! Oh!

Dr. G. Where is he, Mr. Scragg?

Scragg. Oh! sir, he jumped out of the window; he's gone. Oh! my head; he's cracked my skull. Oh, dear me, I'm kilt! Oh! oh! oh!

Enter SLAVES, R.

Dr. G. Go, Dolly, and wash Mr. Scragg's head with some whiskey, and bind it up. Go at once. And Bob, you run over to Mr. Hall, and tell him to come with his hounds; we must go after the rascal. [*Exit all except the* DOCTOR, R.

This will never do. When I catch the scoundrel, I'll make an example of him; I'll whip him to death. Ah! here comes my wife. I wonder what she comes now for? I must put on a sober face, for she looks angry.

Enter MRS. GAINES, L.

Ah! my dear, I am glad you've come, I've been so lonesome without you. Oh! Sarah, I do n't know what I should do if the

Lord should take you home to heaven. I do n't think that I should be able to live without you.

Mrs. G. Dr. Gaines, you ought to be ashamed to sit there and talk in that way. You know very well that if the Lord should call me home to glory to-night, you'd jump for joy. But you need not think that I am going to leave this world before you. No; with the help of the Lord, I'll stay here to foil you in your meanness. I've been on your track, and a dirty track it is, too. You ought to be ashamed of yourself. See what promises you made me before we were married; and this is the way you keep your word. When I married you, every body said that it was a pity that a woman of my sweet temper should be linked to such a man as you. [*She weeps and wrings her hands.*

Dr. G. Come, my dear, do n't make a fool of yourself. Come, let's go to supper, and a strong cup of tea will help your head.

Mrs. G. Tea help my head! tea won't help my head. You're a brute of a man; I always knew I was a fool for marrying you. There was Mr. Comstock, he wanted me, and he loved me, and he said I was an angel, so he did; and he loved me, and he was rich; and mother always said that he loved me more than you, for when he used to kiss me, he always squeezed my hand. You never did such a thing in your life. [*She weeps and wrings her hands.*

Dr. G. Come, my dear, do n't act so foolish.

Mrs. G. Yes; every thing I do is foolish. You're a brute of a man; I won't live with you any longer. I'll leave you—that I will. I'll go and see a lawyer, and get a divorce from you—so I will.

Dr. G. Well, Sarah, if you want a divorce, you had better engage Mr. Barker. He's the best lawyer in town; and if you want some money to facilitate the business, I'll draw a check for you.

Mrs. G. So you want me to get a divorce, do you? Well, I won't have a divorce; no, I'll never leave you, as long as the Lord spares me. [*Exit* MRS. GAINES, R.

Scene 3.—FOREST AT NIGHT—LARGE TREE.

Enter MELINDA, L.

Melinda. This is indeed a dark night to be out and alone on this road. But I must find my husband, I must. Poor Glen! if he only knew that I was here, and could get to me, he would. What a curse slavery is! It separates husbands from their wives, and tears mothers from their helpless offspring, and blights all our hopes for this world. I must try to reach Muddy Creek before daylight, and seek out my husband. What's that I hear?—footsteps? I'll get behind this tree.

Enter GLEN, R.

Glen. It is so dark, I'm afraid I've missed the road. Still, this must be the right way to the poplar farm. And if Bob told me the truth, when he said that Melinda was at the poplar farm, I will soon be with her; and if I once get her in my arms, it will be a strong man that shall take her from me. Aye, a dozen strong men shall not be able to wrest her from my arms. [*Melinda rushes from behind the tree.*

Melinda. Oh, Glen! It is my husband,—it is!

Glen. Melinda! Melinda! it is, it is. Oh God! I thank Thee for this manifestation of Thy kindness. Come, come, Melinda, we must go at once to Canada. I escaped from the overseer, whom Dr. Gaines sent to flog me. Yes, I struck him over the head with his own club, and I made the wine flow freely; yes, I pounded his old skillet well for him, and then jumped out of the window. It was a leap for freedom. Yes, Melinda, it was a leap for freedom. I've said "master" for the last time. I am free; I'm bound for Canada. Come, let's be off, at once, for the negro dogs will be put upon our track. Let us once get beyond the Ohio river, and all will be right. [*Exit* R.

ACT V.

Scene I.—BAR-ROOM IN THE AMERICAN HOTEL—TRAVELLERS LOUNGING IN CHAIRS, AND AT THE BAR.

Enter BILL JENNINGS, R.

Barkeeper. Why, Jennings, how do you do?

Jennings. Say Mr. Jennings, if you please.

Barkeeper. Well, Mr. Jennings, if that suits you better. How are times? We've been expecting you, for some days.

Jennings. Well, before I talk about the times, I want my horses put up, and want you to tell me where my niggers are to stay to-night. Sheds, stables, barns, and every thing else here, seems pretty full, if I am a judge.

Barkeeper. Oh! I'll see to your plunder.

1*st Lounger.* I say, Barkeeper, make me a brandy cocktail, strong. Why, how do you do, Mr. Jennings?

Jennings. Pretty well, Mr. Peters. Cold evening, this.

1*st. Loun.* Yes, this is cold. I heard you speak of your niggers. Have you got a pretty large gang?

Jennings. No, only thirty-three. But they are the best that the country can afford. I shall clear a few dimes, this trip. I hear that the price is up.

Enter MR. WHITE, R.

White. Can I be accommodated here to-night, landlord?

Barkeeper. Yes, sir; we've bed for man and beast. Go, Dick, and take the gentleman's coat and hat. [*To the waiter.*] You're a stranger in these parts, I rec'on.

White. Yes, I am a stranger here.

2*d Loun.* Where mout you come from, ef it's a far question?

White. I am from Massachusetts.

3*d Loun.* I say, cuss Massachusetts!

1*st Loun.* I say so too. There is where the fanatics live; cussed traitors. The President ought to hang 'em all.

White. I say, landlord, if this is the language that I am to hear, I would like to go into a private room.

Barkeeper. We ain't got no private room empty.

1*st Loun.* Maybe you're mad 'bout what I said 'bout your State. Ef you is, I've only to say that this is a free country, and people talks what they please; an' ef you do n't like it, you can better yourself.

White. Sir, if this is a free country, why do you have slaves here? I saw a gang at the door, as I came in.

2*d Loun.* He did n't mean that this was a free country for niggers. He meant that it's free for white people. And another thing, ef you get to talking 'bout freedom for niggers, you'll catch what you won't like, mister. It's right for niggers to be slaves.

White. But I saw some white slaves.

1*st Loun*. Well, they're white niggers.

White. Well, sir, I am from a free State, and I thank God for it; for the worst act that a man can commit upon his fellow-man, is to make him a slave. Conceive of a mind, a living soul, with the germs of faculties which infinity cannot exhaust, as it first beams upon you in its glad morning of existence, quivering with life and joy, exulting in the glorious sense of its developing energies, beautiful, and brave, and generous, and joyous, and free,—the clear pure spirit bathed in the auroral light of its unconscious immortality,—and then follow it in its dark and dreary passage through slavery, until oppression stifles and kills, one by one, every inspiration and aspiration of its being, until it becomes a dead soul entombed in a living frame!

3*d Loun*. Stop that; stop that, I say. That's treason to the country; that's downright rebellion.

Barkeeper. Yes, it is. And another thing,—this is not a meeting-house.

1*st Loun*. Yes, if you talk such stuff as that, you'll get a chunk of cold lead in you, that you will.

Enter DR. GAINES *and* SCRAGG, *followed by* CATO, R.

Dr. G. Gentlemen, I am in pursuit of two valuable slaves, and I will pay five hundred dollars for their arrest. [*Exit* MR. WHITE, L.

1*st Loun*. I'll bet a picayune that your niggers have been stolen by that cussed feller from Massachusetts. Don't you see he's gone?

Dr. G. Where is the man? If I can lay my hands on him, he'll never steal another nigger. Where is the scoundrel?

1*st Loun*. Let's go after the feller. I'll go with you. Come, foller me. [*Exit all*, L., *except* CATO *and the waiter*.

Cato. Why don't you bring in massa's saddle-bags? What de debil you standin' dar for? You common country niggers do n't know nuffin', no how. Go an' get massa's saddle-bags, and bring 'em in. [*Exit* SERVANT, R.

By golly! ebry body's gone, an' de bar-keeper too. I'll tend de bar myself now; an' de fuss gemman I waits on will be dis gemman of color. [*Goes behind the counter, and drinks.*] Ah, dis is de stuff fer me; it makes my head swim; it makes me happy right off. I'll take a little more.

Enter BARKEEPER, L.

Barkeeper. What are you doing behind that bar, you black cuss?

Cato. I is lookin' for massa's saddle-bags, sir. Is dey here?

Barkeeper. But what were you drinking there?

Cato. Me drinkin'! Why, massa, you muss be mistaken. I ain't drink nuffin'.

Barkeeper. You infernal whelp, to stand there and lie in that way!

Cato. Oh, yes, seer, I did tase dat coffee in dat bottle; dat's all I did.

Enter MR. WHITE, L., *excited.*

Mr. White. I say, sir, is there no place of concealment in your house? They are after me, and my life is in danger. Say, sir, can't you hide me away?

Barkeeper. Well, you ought to hold your tongue when you come into our State.

Mr. White. But, sir, the Constitution gives me the right to speak my sentiments, at all times and in all places.

Barkeeper. We don't care for Constitutions nor nothin' else. We made the Constitution, and we'll break it. But you had better hide away; they are coming, and they'll lynch you, that they will. Come with me; I'll hide you in the cellar. Foller me. [*Exit* BARKEEPER *and* WHITE, L.

Enter the MOB, R.

Dr. Gaines. If I can once lay my hands on that scoundrel, I'll blow a hole through his head.

Jennings. Yes, I say so too; for no one knows whose niggers are safe, now-a-days. I must look after my niggers. Who is that I see in the distance? I believe it's that cussed Massachusetts feller. Come, let's go after him. [*Exit the* MOB, R.

Scene 2.—FOREST AT NIGHT.

Enter GLEN *and* MELINDA, R.

Melinda. I am so tired and hungry, that I cannot go further. It is so cloudy that we cannot see the North Star, and therefore cannot tell whether we are going to Canada, or further South. Let's sit down here.

Glen. I know that we cannot see the North Star, Melinda, and I fear we've lost our way. But, see! the clouds are passing away, and it'll soon be clear. See! yonder is a star; yonder is another and another. Ah! yonder is the North Star, and we are safe!

"Star of the North! though night winds drift
  The fleecy drapery of the sky
Between thy lamp and me, I lift,
  Yea, lift with hope my sleepless eye,
To the blue heights wherein thou dwellest,
And of a land of freedom tellest.

"Star of the North! while blazing day
  Pours round me its full tide of light,
And hides thy pale but faithful ray,
  I, too, lie hid, and long for night:
For night: I dare not walk at noon,
Nor dare I trust the faithless moon—

"Nor faithless man, whose burning lust
  For gold hath riveted my chain,—
Nor other leader can I trust
  But thee, of even the starry train;
For all the host around thee burning,
Like faithless man, keep turning, turning.

"I may not follow where they go:—
  Star of the North! I look to thee
While on I press; for well I know,
  Thy light and truth shall set me free:—
Thy light, that no poor slave deceiveth;
Thy truth, that all my soul believeth.

"Thy beam is on the glassy breast
  Of the still spring, upon whose brink

I lay my weary limbs to rest,
And bow my parching lips to drink.
Guide of the friendless negro's way,
I bless thee for this quiet ray!

"In the dark top of southern pines
I nestled, when the Driver's horn
Called to the field, in lengthening lines,
My fellows, at the break of morn.
And there I lay till thy sweet face
Looked in upon "my hiding place."

"The tangled cane-brake, where I crept
For shelter from the heat of noon,
And where, while others toiled, I slept,
Till wakened by the rising moon,
As its stalks felt the night wind free,
Gave me to catch a glimpse of thee.

"Star of the North! in bright array
The constellations round thee sweep,
Each holding on its nightly way,
Rising, or sinking in the deep,
And, as it hangs in mid heaven flaming,
The homage of some nation claiming.

"*This* nation to the Eagle cowers;
Fit ensign! she's a bird of spoil:—
Like worships like! for each devours
The earnings of another's toil.
I've felt her talons and her beak,
And now the gentler Lion seek.

"The Lion, at the Monarch's feet
Crouches, and lays his mighty paw
Into her lap!—an emblem meet
Of England's Queen, and English law:
Queen, that hath made her Islands free!
Law, that holds out its shield to me!

"Star of the North! upon that shield
Thou shinest,—Oh, for ever shine!
The negro, from the cotton field

Shall, then, beneath its orb recline,
And feed the Lion, couched before it,
Nor heed the Eagle, screaming o'er it!"

With the thoughts of servitude behind us, and the North Star before us, we will go forward with cheerful hearts. Come, Melinda, let's go on. [*Exit*, L.

Scene 3.—A STREET.

Enter MR. WHITE, R.

Mr. White. I am glad to be once more in a free State. If I am caught again south of Mason and Dixon's line, I'll give them leave to lynch me. I came near losing my life. This is the way our constitutional rights are trampled upon. But what care these men about Constitutions, or any thing else that does not suit them? But I must hasten on. [*Exit*, L.

Enter CATO, *in disguise*, R.

Cato. I wonder ef dis is me? By golly, I is free as a frog. But maybe I is mistaken; maybe dis ain't me. Cato, is dis you? Yes, seer. Well, now it is me, an' I em a free man. But, stop! I muss change my name, kase ole massa might foller me, and somebody might tell him dat dey seed Cato; so I'll change my name, and den he won't know me ef he sees me. Now, what shall I call myself? I'm now in a suspectable part of de country, an' I muss have a suspectable name. Ah! I'll call myself Alexander Washington Napoleon Pompey Cæsar. Dar, now, dat's a good long, suspectable name, and every body will suspect me. Let me see; I wonder ef I can't make up a song on my escape? I'll try.

AIR—"*Dearest Mae.*"

Now, freemen, listen to my song, a story I'll relate,
It happened in de valley of de ole Kentucky State:
Dey marched me out into de fiel', at every break of day,
And work me dar till late sunset, widout a cent of pay.

Chorus.—Dey work me all de day,
Widout a bit of pay,

And thought, because dey fed me well,
I would not run away.

Massa gave me his ole coat, an' thought I'd happy be,
But I had my eye on de North Star, an' thought of liberty;
Ole massa lock de door, an' den he went to sleep,
I dress myself in his bess clothes, an' jump into de street.

Chorus.—Dey work me all de day,
Widout a bit of pay,
So I took my flight, in the middle of de night,
When de sun was gone away.

Sed I, dis chile's a freeman now, he'll be a slave no more;
I travell'd faster all dat night, dan I ever did before.
I came up to a farmer's house, jest at de break of day,
And saw a white man standin' dar, sed he, "You are a runaway."

Chorus.—Dey work me all de day, &c.

I tole him I had left de whip, an' bayin' of de hound,
To find a place where man is man, ef sich dar can be found;
Dat I had heard, in Canada, dat all mankind are free,
An' dat I was going dar in search of liberty.

Chorus.—Dey work me all de day, &c.

I've not committed any crime, why should I run away?
Oh! shame upon your laws, dat drive me off to Canada.
You loudly boast of liberty, an' say your State is free,
But ef I tarry in your midst, will you protect me?

Chorus.—Dey work me all de day, &c. [*Exit*, L.

Scene 4.—DINING-ROOM.—TABLE SPREAD.

MRS. NEAL *and* CHARLOTTE.

Mrs. Neal. Thee may put the tea to draw, Charlotte. Thy father will be in soon, and we must have breakfast.

Enter MR. NEAL, L.

I think, Simeon, it is time those people were called. Thee knows that they may be pursued, and we ought not to detain them long here.

Mr. Neal. Yes, Ruth, thou art right. Go, Charlotte, and knock on their chamber door, and tell them that breakfast is ready. [*Exit* CHARLOTTE, R.

Mrs. N. Poor creatures! I hope they'll reach Canada in safety. They seem to be worthy persons.

Enter CHARLOTTE, R.

Charlotte. I've called them, mother, and they'll soon be down. I'll put the breakfast on the table.

Enter NEIGHBOR JONES, L.

Mr. N. Good morning, James. Thee has heard, I presume, that we have two very interesting persons in the house?

Jones. Yes, I heard that you had two fugitives by the Underground road, last night; and I've come over to fight for them, if any persons come to take them back.

Enter THOMAS, R.

Mr. N. Go, Thomas, and harness up the horses and put them to the covered wagon, and be ready to take these people on, as soon as they get their breakfast. Go, Thomas, and hurry thyself. [*Exit* THOMAS, R.

And so thee wants to fight, this morning, James?

Jones. Yes; as you belongs to a society that don't believe in fighting, and I does believe in that sort of thing, I thought I'd come and relieve you of that work, if there is any to be done.

Enter GLEN *and* MELINDA, R.

Mr. N. Good morning, friends. I hope thee rested well, last night.

Mrs. N. Yes, I hope thee had a good night's rest.

Glen. I thank you, madam, we did.

Mr. N. I'll introduce thee to our neighbor, James Jones. He's a staunch friend of thy people.

Jones. I am glad to see you. I've come over to render assistance, if any is needed.

Mrs. N. Come, friends, take seats at the table. Thee'll take seats there. [*To* GLEN *and* MELINDA.] [*All take seats at the table.*] Does thee take sugar and milk in thy tea?

Melinda. I thank you, we do.

Jones. I'll look at your *Tribune*, Uncle Simeon, while you're eating.

Mr. N. Thee'll find it on the table.

Mrs. N. I presume thee's anxious to get to thy journey's end?

Glen. Yes, madam, we are. I am told that we are not safe in any of the free States.

Mr. N. I am sorry to tell thee, that that is too true. Thee will not be safe until thee gets on British soil. I wonder what keeps Thomas; he should have been here with the team.

Enter THOMAS, L.

Thomas. All's ready; and I've written the prettiest song that was ever sung. I call it "The Underground Railroad."

Mr. N. Thomas, thee can eat thy breakfast far better than thee can write a song, as thee calls it. Thee must hurry thyself, when I send thee for the horses, Thomas. Here lately, thee takes thy time.

Thomas. Well, you see I've been writing poetry; that's the reason I've been so long. If you wish it, I'll sing it to you.

Jones. Do let us hear the song.

Mrs. Neal. Yes, if Thomas has written a ditty, do let us hear it.

Mr. Neal. Well, Thomas, if thee has a ditty, thee may recite it to us.

Thomas. Well, I'll give it to you. Remember that I call it, "The Underground Railroad."

AIR—"*Wait for the Wagon.*"

Oh, where is the invention
  Of this growing age,
Claiming the attention

Of statesman, priest, or sage,
In the many railways
Through the nation found,
Equal to the Yankees'
Railway under-ground?

Chorus.—No one hears the whistle,
Or rolling of the cars,
While negroes ride to freedom
Beyond the stripes and stars.

On the Southern borders
Are the Railway stations,
Negroes get free orders
While on the plantations;
For all, of ev'ry color,
First-class cars are found,
While they ride to freedom
By Railway under-ground.

Chorus.—No one hears the whistle, &c.

Masters in the morning
Furiously rage,
Cursing the inventions
Of this knowing age;
Order out the bloodhounds,
Swear they'll bring them back,
Dogs return exhausted,
Cannot find the track.

Chorus.—No one hears the whistle, &c.

Travel is increasing,
Build a double track,
Cars and engines wanted,
They'll come, we have no lack.
Clear the track of loafers,
See that crowded car!
Thousands passing yearly,
Stock is more than par.

Chorus.—No one hears the whistle, &c.

Jones. Well done! That's a good song. I'd like to have a copy of them verses. [*Knock at the door. Charlotte goes to the door, and returns.*

Enter CATO, L., *still in disguise.*

Mr. Neal. Who is this we have? Another of the outcasts, I presume?

Cato. Yes, seer; I is gwine to Canada, an' I met a man, an' he tole me dat you would give me some wittals an' help me on de way. By golly! ef dar ain't Glen an' Melinda. Dey do n't know me in dese fine clothes. [*Goes up to them.*] Ah, chillen! I is one wid you. I golly, I is here too! [*They shake hands.*]

Glen. Why, it is Cato, as I live!

Melinda. Oh, Cato, I am so glad to see you! But how did you get here?

Cato. Ah, chile, I come wid ole massa to hunt you; an' you see I get tired huntin' you, an' I am now huntin' for Canada. I leff de ole boss in de bed at de hotel; an' you see I thought, afore I left massa, I'd jess change clothes wid him; so, you see, I is fixed up,—ha, ha, ha. Ah, chillen! I is gwine wid you.

Mrs. Neal. Come, sit thee down, and have some breakfast.

Cato. Tank you, madam, I'll do dat. [*Sits down and eats.*

Mr. Neal. This is pleasant for thee to meet one of thy friends.

Glen. Yes, sir, it is; I would be glad if we could meet more of them. I have a mother and sister still in slavery, and I would give worlds, if I possessed them, if by so doing I could release them from their bondage.

Thomas. We are all ready, sir, and the wagon is waiting.

Mrs. Neal. Yes, thee had better start.

Cato. Ef any body tries to take me back to ole massa, I'll pull ebry toof out of dar heads, dat I will! As soon as I get to Canada, I'll set up a doctor shop, an' won't I be poplar? Den I rec'on I will. I'll pull teef fer all de people in Canada. Oh, how I wish I had Hannah wid me! It makes me feel bad when I tink I ain't a-gwine to see my wife no more. But, come, chillen, let's be makin' tracks. Dey say we is most to de British side.

Mr. Neal. Yes, a few miles further, and you'll be safe beyond the reach of the Fugitive-Slave Law.

Cato. Ah, dat's de talk fer dis chile. [*Exit*, M. D.

Scene 5.—THE NIAGARA RIVER—A FERRY.

FERRYMAN, *fastening his small boat.*

Ferryman, [*advancing, takes out his watch.*] I swan, if it ain't one o'clock. I thought it was dinner time. Now there's no one here, I'll go to dinner, and if any body comes, they can wait until I return. I'll go at once. [*Exit*, L.

Enter MR. WHITE, R., *with an umbrella.*

Mr. White. I wonder where that ferryman is? I want to cross to Canada. It seems a little showery, or else the mist from the Falls is growing thicker. [*Takes out his sketch-book and pencils,—sketches.*

Enter CANE PEDLAR, R.

Pedlar. Want a good cane to-day, sir? Here's one from Goat Island,—very good, sir,—straight and neat,—only one dollar. I've a wife and nine small children,—youngest is nursing, and the oldest only three years old. Here's a cane from Table Rock, sir. Please buy one! I've had no breakfast to-day. My wife's got the rheumatics, and the children's got the measles. Come, sir, do buy a cane! I've a lame shoulder, and can't work.

Mr. White. Will you stop your confounded talk, and let me alone? Don't you see that I am sketching? You've spoiled a beautiful scene for me, with your nonsense.

Enter 2*d* PEDLAR, R.

2*d Pedlar.* Want any bead bags, or money purses? These are all real Ingen bags, made by the Black Hawk Ingens. Here's a pretty bag, sir, only 75 cents. Here's a money purse, 50 cents. Please, sir, buy something! My wife's got the fever and ague, and the house is full of children, and they're all sick. Come, sir, do help a worthy man!

Mr. White. Will you hold your tongue? You've spoiled some of the finest pictures in the world. Don't you see that I am sketching? [*Exit* PEDLARS, R., *grumbling.* I am glad those fellows have gone; now I'll go a little further up the shore, and see if I can find another boat. I want to get over. [*Exit,* L.

Enter DR. GAINES, SCRAGG, *and an* OFFICER.

Officer. I do n't think that your slaves have crossed yet, and my officers will watch the shore below here, while we stroll up the river. If I once get my hands on them, all the Abolitionists in the State shall not take them from me.

Dr. G. I hope they have not got over, for I would not lose them for two thousand dollars, especially the gal.

Enter 1*st* PEDLAR.

Pedlar. Wish to get a good cane, sir? This stick was cut on the very spot where Sam Patch jumped over the falls. Only fifty cents. I have a sick wife and thirteen children. Please buy a cane; I ain't had no dinner.

Officer. Get out of the way! Gentlemen, we'll go up the shore. [*Exit,* L.

Enter CATO, R.

Cato. I is loss fum de cumpny, but dis is de ferry, and I spec dey'll soon come. But did n't we have a good time las' night in Buffalo? Dem dar Buffalo gals make my heart flutter, dat dey did. But, tanks be to de Lord, I is got religion. I got it las' night in de meetin.' Before I got religion, I was a great sinner; I got drunk, an' took de name of de Lord in vain. But now I is a conwerted man; I is bound for hebben; I toats de witness in my bosom; I feel dat my name is rote in de book of life. But dem niggers in de Vine Street Church las' night shout an' make sich a fuss, dey give me de headache. But, tank de Lord, I is got religion, an' now I'll be a preacher, and den dey'll call me de Rev. Alexander Washington Napoleon Pompey Cæsar. Now I'll preach and pull teef, bofe at de same time. Oh, how I wish I had Hannah wid me! Cuss ole massa, fer ef it warn't for him, I could have my wife wid me. Ef I had n't religion, I'd say "Damn ole massa!" but as I is a religious man, an' belongs to de church, I won't say no sich a thing. But who is dat I see comin'? Oh, it's a whole heap of people. Good Lord! what is de matter?

Enter GLEN *and* MELINDA, L., *followed by* OFFICERS.

Glen. Let them come; I am ready for them. He that lays hands on me or my wife shall feel the weight of this club.

Melinda. Oh, Glen, let's die here, rather than again go into slavery.

Officer. I am the United States Marshal. I have a warrant from the Commissioner to take you, and bring you before him. I command assistance.

Enter DR. GAINES, SCRAGG, *and* OFFICER, R.

Dr. Gaines. Here they are. Down with the villain! down with him! but do n't hurt the gal!

Enter MR. WHITE, R.

Mr. White. Why, bless me! these are the slaveholding fellows. I'll fight for freedom! [*Takes hold of his umbrella with both hands.—The fight commences, in which* GLEN, CATO, DR. GAINES, SCRAGG, WHITE, *and the* OFFICERS, *take part.—*FERRYMAN *enters, and runs to his boat.—*DR. GAINES, SCRAGG *and the* OFFICERS *are knocked down,* GLEN, MELINDA *and* CATO *jump into the boat, and as it leaves the shore and floats away,* GLEN *and* CATO *wave their hats, and shout loudly for freedom.—Curtain falls.*

THE END.

ENGRAVING BY J. W. WATTS FROM A PHOTOGRAPH
BY GRICE BROS. PORT AU PRINCE.

THE BLACK MAN,

HIS ANTECEDENTS, HIS GENIUS, AND HIS ACHIEVEMENTS.

TO

THE ADVOCATES AND FRIENDS

OF

NEGRO FREEDOM AND EQUALITY,

WHEREVER FOUND,

This Volume is Respectfully Dedicated,

BY THE AUTHOR.

PREFACE.

THE calumniators and traducers of the Negro are to be found, mainly, among two classes. The first and most relentless are those who have done them the greatest injury, by being instrumental in their enslavement and consequent degradation. They delight to descant upon the "natural inferiority" of the blacks, and claim that we were destined only for a servile condition, entitled neither to liberty nor the legitimate pursuit of happiness. The second class are those who are ignorant of the characteristics of the race, and are the mere echoes of the first. To meet and refute these misrepresentations, and to supply a deficiency, long felt in the community, of a work containing sketches of individuals who, by their own genius, capacity, and intellectual development, have surmounted the many obstacles which slavery and prejudice have thrown in their way, and raised themselves to positions of honor and influence, this volume was written. The characters represented in most of these biographies are for the first time put in print. The author's long sojourn in Europe, his opportunity of research amid the archives of England and France, and his visit to the West Indies, have given him the advantage of information respecting the blacks seldom acquired.

If this work shall aid in vindicating the Negro's character, and show that he is endowed with those intellectual and amiable qualities which adorn and dignify human nature, it will meet the most sanguine hopes of the writer.

CAMBRIDGEPORT, MASS., 1863.

CONTENTS

THE BLACK MAN

AND

HIS ANTECEDENTS.

OF the great family of man, the negro has, during the last half century, been more prominently before the world than any other race. He did not seek this notoriety. Isolated away in his own land, he would have remained there, had it not been for the avarice of other races, who sought him out as a victim of slavery. Two and a half centuries of the negro's enslavement have created, in many minds, the opinion that he is intellectually inferior to the rest of mankind; and now that the blacks seem in a fair way to get their freedom in this country, it has been asserted, and from high authority in the government, that the natural inferiority of the negro makes it impossible for him to live on this continent with the white man, unless in a state of bondage.

In his interview with a committee of the colored citizens of the District of Columbia, on the 14th of August last, the President of the United States intimated that the whites and the blacks could not live together in peace, on account of one race being superior intellectually to the other. Mr. Postmaster General Blair, in his letter to the Union mass meeting held at the Cooper Institute, in New York, in March last, takes this ground. The Boston "Post" and "Courier" both take the same position.

I admit that the condition of my race, whether considered in a mental, moral, or intellectual point of view, at the present time cannot compare favorably with the Anglo-Saxon. But it does not become the whites to point the finger of scorn at the blacks, when they have so long been degrading them. The negro has not always been considered the inferior race. The time was when he stood at the head of science and literature. Let us see.

It is the generally received opinion of the most eminent

historians and ethnologists, that the Ethiopians were really negroes, although in them the physical characteristics of the race were exhibited in a less marked manner than in those dwelling on the coast of Guinea, from whence the stock of American slaves has been chiefly derived. That, in the earliest periods of history, the Ethiopians had attained a high degree of civilization, there is every reason to believe; and that to the learning and science derived from them we must ascribe those wonderful monuments which still exist to attest the power and skill of the ancient Egyptians.

Among those who favor this opinion is our own distinguished countryman, Alexander H. Everett, and upon this evidence I base my argument. Volney assumes it as a settled point that the Egyptians were black. Herodotus, who travelled extensively through that interesting land, set them down as black, with curled hair, and having the negro features. The sacred writers were aware of their complexion: hence the question, "Can the Ethiopian change his skin?" The image of the negro is engraved upon the monuments of Egypt, not as a bondman, but as the master of art. The Sphinx, one of the wonders of the world, surviving the wreck of centuries, exhibits these same features at the present day. Minerva, the goddess of wisdom, was supposed to have been an African princess. Atlas, whose shoulders sustained the globe, and even the great Jupiter Ammon himself, were located by the mythologists in Africa. Though there may not be much in these fables, they teach us, nevertheless, who were then considered the nobles of the human race. Tertullian and St. Augustin were Ethiopians. Terence, the most refined and accomplished scholar of his time, was of the same race. Hanno, the father of Hamilcar, and grandfather of Hannibal, was a negro. These are the antecedents of the enslaved blacks on this continent.

From whence sprang the Anglo-Saxon? For, mark you, it is he that denies the equality of the negro. "When the Britons first became known to the Tyrian mariners," says Macaulay, "they were little superior to the Sandwich Islanders."

Hume says they were a rude and barbarous people, divided into numerous tribes, dressed in the skins of wild beasts. Druidism was their religion, and they were very superstitious. Such is the first account we have of the Britons. When the Romans invaded that country, they reduced the people to a state of vassalage as degrading as that of slavery in the Southern States. Their king, Caractacus, was captured and sent a slave to Rome. Still later, Hengist and Horsa, the Saxon generals, presented another yoke, which the Britons were compelled to wear. But the last dregs of the bitter cup of humiliation were drunk when William of Normandy met Harold at Hastings, and, with a single blow, completely annihilated the nationality of the Britons. Thousands of the conquered people were then sent to the slave markets of Rome, where they were sold very cheap on account of their inaptitude to learn.

This is not very flattering to the President's ancestors, but it is just. Cæsar, in writing home, said of the Britons, "They are the most ignorant people I ever conquered. They cannot be taught music." Cicero, writing to his friend Atticus, advised him not to buy slaves from England, "because," said he, "they cannot be taught to read, and are the ugliest and most stupid race I ever saw." I am sorry that Mr. Lincoln came from such a low origin; but he is not to blame. I only find fault with him for making mouths at me.

> "You should not the ignorant negro despise;
> Just such your sires appeared in Cæsar's eyes."

The Britons lost their nationality, became amalgamated with the Romans, Saxons, and Normans, and out of this conglomeration sprang the proud Anglo-Saxon of to-day. I once stood upon the walls of an English city, built by enslaved Britons when Julius Cæsar was their master. The image of the ancestors of President Lincoln and Montgomery Blair, as represented in Britain, was carved upon the monuments of Rome, where they may still be seen in their chains. Ancestry is something which the white American should not speak of, unless with his lips to the dust.

"Nothing," says Macaulay, "in the early existence of Britain, indicated the greatness which she was destined to attain." Britain has risen, while proud Rome, once the mistress of the world, has fallen; but the image of the early Englishman in his chains, as carved twenty centuries ago, is still to be seen upon her broken monuments. So has Egypt fallen; and her sable sons and daughters have been scattered into nearly every land where the white man has introduced slavery and disgraced the soil with his footprint. As I gazed upon the beautiful and classic obelisk of Luxor, removed from Thebes, where it had stood four thousand years, and transplanted to the Place de la Concorde, at Paris, and contemplated its hieroglyphic inscription of the noble daring of Sesostris, the African general, who drew kings at his chariot wheels, and left monumental inscriptions from Ethiopia to India, I felt proud of my antecedents, proud of the glorious past, which no amount of hate and prejudice could wipe from history's page, while I had to mourn over the fall and the degradation of my race. But I do not despair; for the negro has that intellectual genius which God has planted in the mind of man, that distinguishes him from the rest of creation, and which needs only cultivation to make it bring forth fruit. No nation has ever been found, which, by its own unaided efforts, by some powerful inward impulse, has arisen from barbarism and degradation to civilization and respectability. There is nothing in race or blood, in color or features, that imparts susceptibility of improvement to one race over another. The mind left to itself from infancy, without culture, remains a blank. Knowledge is not innate. Development makes the man. As the Greeks, and Romans, and Jews drew knowledge from the Egyptians three thousand years ago, and the Europeans received it from the Romans, so must the blacks of this land rise in the same way. As one man learns from another, so nation learns from nation. Civilization is handed from one people to another, its great fountain and source being God our Father. No one, in the days of Cicero and Tacitus, could have predicted that the barbarism and savage wildness of the Germans would give place to the learning, refinement, and culture which that people now exhibit. Already the blacks on this continent, though kept down under the heel of the white man, are fast rising in the scale of intellectual development, and proving their equality with the brotherhood of man.

In his address before the Colonization Society, at Washington, on the 18th of January, 1853, Hon. Edward Everett said, "When I lived in Cambridge, a few years ago, I used to attend, as one of the board of visitors, the examinations of a classical school, in which was a colored boy, the son of a slave in Mississippi, I think. He appeared to me to be of pure African blood.

There were at the same time two youths from Georgia, and one of my own sons, attending the same school. I must say that this poor negro boy, Beverly Williams, was one of the best scholars at the school, and in the Latin language he was the best scholar in his class. There are others, I am told, which show still more conclusively the aptitude of the colored race for *every kind of intellectual culture*."

Mr. Everett cited several other instances which had fallen under his notice, and utterly scouted the idea that there was any general inferiority of the African race. He said, "They have done as well as persons of European or Anglo-American origin would have done, after three thousand years of similar depression and hardship. The question has been asked, 'Does not the negro labor under some incurable, natural inferiority?' *In this, for myself, I have no belief.*"

I think that this is ample refutation of the charge of the natural inferiority of the negro. President Lincoln, in the interview to which I have already referred, said, "But for your race among us there would not be a war." This reminds me of an incident that occurred while travelling in the State of Ohio, in 1844. Taking the stage coach at a small village, one of the passengers (a white man) objected to my being allowed a seat inside, on account of my color. I persisted, however, in claiming the right which my ticket gave me, and got in. The objector at once took a seat on a trunk on the top of the coach. The wire netting round the top of the stage not being strong, the white passenger, trunks and all, slid off as we were going down a steep hill. The top passenger's shoulder was dislocated, and in his pain he cried out, "If you had not been black, I should not have left my seat inside."

The "New York Herald," the "Boston Post," the "Boston Courier," and the "New York Journal of Commerce," take the lead in misrepresenting the effect which emancipation in the West Indies had upon the welfare of those islands. It is asserted that general ruin followed the black man's liberation. As to the British colonies, the fact is well established that slavery had impoverished the soil, demoralized the people, bond and free, brought the planters to a state of bankruptcy, and all the islands to ruin, long before Parliament had passed the act of emancipation. All the colonies, including Jamaica, had petitioned the home government for assistance, ten years prior to the liberation of their slaves. It is a noticeable fact, that the free blacks were the least embarrassed, in a pecuniary point of view, and that they appeared in more comfortable circumstances than the whites. There was a large proportion of free blacks in each of the colonies, Jamaica alone having fifty-five thousand before the day of emancipation. A large majority of the West India estates were owned by persons residing in Europe, and who had never seen the colonies. These plantations were carried on by agents, overseers, and clerks, whose mismanagement, together with the blighting influence which chattel slavery takes with it wherever it goes, brought the islands under impending ruin, and many of the estates were mortgaged in Europe for more than their value. One man alone, Neil Malcomb, of London, had forty plantations to fall upon his hands for money advanced on them before the abolition of slavery. These European proprietors, despairing of getting any returns from the West Indies, gladly pocketed their share of the twenty million pounds sterling, which the home government gave them, and abandoned their estates to their ruin. Other proprietors residing in the colonies formed combinations to make the emancipated people labor for scarcely enough to purchase food for them. If found idle, the tread-wheel, the chain-gang, the dungeon, with black bread, and water from the moat, and other modes of legalized torture, were inflicted upon the negroes. Through the determined and combined efforts of the land owners, the condition of the freed people was as bad, if not worse, for the first three years after their liberation, than it was before. Never was an experiment more severely tested than that of emancipation in the West Indies.

Nevertheless, the principles of freedom triumphed; not a drop of blood was shed by the enfranchised blacks; the colonies have arisen from the blight which they labored under in the time of slavery; the land has increased in value; and, above all, that which is more valuable than cotton, sugar, or rice—the moral and intellectual condition of both blacks and whites is in a better state now than ever before. Sir William Colebrook, governor of Antigua, said, six years after the islands were freed, "At the lowest computation, the land, without a single slave upon it, is fully as valuable now as it was, including all the slaves, before emancipation." In a report made to the British Parliament, in 1859, it was stated that three fifths of the cultivated land of Jamaica was the *bona fide* property of the blacks. The land is in a better state of cultivation now than it was while slavery existed, and both imports and exports show a great increase. Every thing demonstrates that emancipation in the West India islands has resulted in the most satisfactory manner, and fulfilled the expectation of the friends of freedom throughout the world.

Rev. Mr. Underhill, secretary of the English Baptist Missionary Society, who has visited Jamaica, and carefully studied its condition, said, in a recent speech in London, that the late slaves in that island had built some two hundred and twenty chapels. The churches that worship in them number fifty-three thousand communicants, amounting to one eighth of the total population. The average attendance, in other than the state churches, is ninety-one thousand—a fourth of the population. One third of the children—twenty-two thousand—are in the schools. The blacks voluntarily contribute twenty-two thousand pounds (one hundred and ten thousand dollars) annually for religious purposes. Their landed property exceeds five million dollars. Valuing their cottages at only fifty dollars each, these amount to three million dollars. They have nearly three hundred thousand dollars deposited in the savings banks. The sum total of their property is much above eleven million dollars. All this has been accumulated since their emancipation.

Thus it is seen that all parties have been benefited by the abolition of negro slavery in the British possessions. Now we turn to our own land. Among the many obstacles which have been brought to bear against emancipation, one of the most formidable has been the series of objections urged against it upon what has been supposed to be the slave's want of appreciation of liberty, and his ability to provide for himself in a state of freedom; and now that slavery seems to be near its end, these objections are multiplying, and the cry is heard all over the land, "What shall be done with the slave if freed?"

It has been clearly demonstrated, I think, that the enslaved of the south are as capable of self-support as any other class of people in the country. It is well known that, throughout the entire south, a large class of slaves have been for years accustomed to hire their time from their owners. Many of these have paid very high prices for the privilege. Some able mechanics have been known to pay as high as six hundred dollars per annum, besides providing themselves with food and clothing; and this class of slaves, by their industry, have taken care of themselves so well, and their appearance has been so respectable, that many of the states have passed laws prohibiting masters from letting their slaves out to themselves, because, as it was said, it made the other slaves dissatisfied to see so many of their fellows well provided, and accumulating something for themselves in the way of pocket money.

The Rev. Dr. Nehemiah Adams, whose antecedents have not been such as to lead to the suspicion that he favors the free colored men, or the idea of giving to the slaves their liberty, in his "South-Side View," unconsciously and unintentionally gives a very valuable statement upon this particular point. Dr. Adams says, "A slave woman having had three hundred dollars stolen from her by a white man, her master was questioned in court as to the probability of her having had so much money. The master said that he not unfrequently had borrowed fifty and a hundred dollars from her himself, and added that she was always very strict as to his promised time of payment." There was a slave woman who had not only kept every agreement with her master—paying him every cent she had promised—but had accumulated three hundred dollars towards purchasing her liberty; and it was stolen from her, not by a black man, but, as Dr. Adams says, by a white man.

But one of the clearest demonstrations of the ability of the slave to provide for himself in a state of freedom is to be found in the prosperous condition of the large free colored population of the Southern States. Maryland has eighty thousand, Virginia seventy thousand, and the other slave states have a large number. These free people have all been slaves, or they are the descendants of those who were once slaves; what they have gained has been acquired in spite of the public opinion and laws of the south, in spite of prejudice, and every thing. They have acquired a large amount of property; and it is this industry, this sobriety, this intelligence, and this wealth of the free colored people of the south, that has created so much prejudice on the part of slaveholders against them. They have felt that the very presence of a colored man, looking so genteelly and in such a prosperous condition, made the slaves unhappy and discontented. In the Southern Rights Convention which assembled at Baltimore, June 8, 1860, a resolution was adopted, calling on the legislature to pass a law driving the free colored people out of the state. Nearly every speaker took the ground that the free colored people must be driven out to make the slave's obedience more secure. Judge Mason, in his speech, said, "It is the thrifty and well-to-do free negroes, that are seen by our slaves, that make them dissatisfied." A similar appeal was made to the legislature of Tennessee. Judge Catron, of the Supreme Court of the United States, in a long and able letter to the Nashville "Union," opposed the driving out of the colored people. He said they were among the best mechanics, the best artisans, and the most industrious laborers in the state, and that to drive them out would be an injury to the state itself. This is certainly good evidence in their behalf.

The New Orleans "True Delta" opposed the passage of a similar law by the State of Louisiana. Among other things it said, "There are a large free colored population here, correct in their general deportment, honorable in their intercourse with society, and free from reproach so far as the laws are concerned, not surpassed in the inoffensiveness of their lives by any equal number of persons in any place, north or south."

A movement was made in the legislature of South Carolina to expel the free blacks from that state, and a committee was appointed to investigate the matter. In their report the committee said, "We find that the free blacks of this state are among our most industrious people; in this city (Charleston) we find that they own over two and a half millions of dollars worth of property; that they pay two thousand seven hundred dollars tax to the city."

Dr. Nehemiah Adams, whom I have already quoted, also testifies to the good character of the free colored people; but he does it unintentionally; it was not a part of the programme; how it slipped in I cannot tell. Here it is, however, from page 41 of his "South-Side View:"—

"A prosecuting officer, who had six or eight counties in his district, told me that, during eight years service, he had made out about two thousand bills of indictment, of which not more than twelve were against colored persons."

Hatred of the free colored people, and abuse of them, have always been popular with the pro-slavery people of this country; yet, an American senator from one of the Western States—a man who never lost an opportunity to vilify and traduce the colored man, and who, in his last canvass for a seat in the United States Senate, argued that the slaves were better off in slavery than they would be if set free, and declared that the blacks were unable to take care of themselves while enjoying liberty—died, a short time since, twelve thousand dollars in debt to a black man, who was the descendant of a slave.

There is a Latin phrase—*De mortuis nil nisi bonum.* It is not saying any thing against the reputation of Hon. Stephen A. Douglas to tell the fact that he had borrowed money from a negro. I only find fault with him that he should traduce the class that befriended him in the time of need. James Gordon Bennett, of the New York Herald, in a time of great pecuniary distress, soon after establishing his paper, borrowed three hundred dollars of a black man; and now he is one of our most relentless enemies. Thus it is that those who fattened upon us often turn round and traduce us. Reputation is, indeed, dear to every nation and race; but to us, the colored people of this country, who have so many obstacles to surmount, it is doubly dear:—

> "Who steals my purse steals trash;
> 'Twas mine, 'tis his, and has been slave to thousands;
> But he who filches from me my good name,
> Robs me of that which not enriches him,
> And makes me poor indeed."

You know we were told by the slaveholders, just before the breaking out of the rebellion, that if we got into any difficulty with the south, their slaves would take up arms and fight to a man for them. Mr. Toombs, I believe, threatened that he would arm his slaves, and other men in Congress from the slave states made the same threat. They were going to arm the slaves and turn them against the north. They said they could be trusted; and many people here at the north really believed that the slave did not want his liberty, would not have it if he could, and that the slave population was a very dangerous element against the north; but at once, on the approach of our soldiers, the slaves are seen, with their bundles and baskets, and hats and coats, and without bundles or baskets, and without hats or coats, rushing to our lines; demonstrating what we have so often said, that all the slave was waiting for was the opportunity to get his liberty. Why should you not have believed this? Why should you have supposed for a moment, that, because a man's color differs a little from yours, he is better contented to remain a slave than you would be, or that he has no inclination, no wish, to escape from the thraldom that holds him so tight? What is it that does not wish to be free?

> "Go, let a cage with grates of gold,
> And pearly roof, the eagle hold;
> Let dainty viands be its fare,
> And give the captive tenderest care;
> But say, in luxury's limits pent,
> Find you the king of birds content?
> No; oft he'll sound the startling shriek,
> And dash the cage with angry beak:
> Precarious freedom's far more dear
> Than all the prison's pampering cheer."

As with the eagle, so with man. He loves to look upon the bright day and the stormy night; to gaze upon the broad, free ocean, its eternal surging tides, its mountain billows, and its foam-crested waves; to tread the steep mountain side; to sail upon the placid river; to wander along the gurgling stream; to trace the sunny slope, the beautiful landscape, the majestic forest, the flowery meadow; to listen to the howling of the winds and the music of the birds. These are the aspirations of man, without regard to country, clime, or color.

"What shall we do with the slave of the south? Expatriate him," say the haters of the negro. Expatriate him for what? He has cleared up the swamps of the south, and has put the soil under cultivation; he has built up her towns, and cities, and villages; he has enriched the north and Europe with his cotton, and sugar, and rice; and for this you would drive him out of the country! "What shall be done with the slaves if they are freed?" You had better ask, "What shall we do with the slaveholders if the slaves are freed?" The slave has shown himself better fitted to take care of himself than the slaveholder. He is the bone and sinew of the south; he is the producer, while the master is nothing but a consumer, and a very poor consumer at that. The slave is the producer, and he alone can be relied upon. He has the sinew, the determination, and the will; and if you will take the free colored people of the south as the criterion, take their past history as a sample of what the colored people are capable of doing, every one must be satisfied that the slaves can take care of themselves. Some say, "Let them alone; they are well cared for, and that is enough."

> "O, tell us not they're clothed and fed—
> 'Tis insult, stuff, and a' that;
> With freedom gone, all joy is fled,
> For Heaven's best gift is a' that."

But it is said, "The two races cannot live together in a state of freedom." Why, that is the cry that rung all over England thirty years ago: "If you liberate the slaves of the West Indies, they can't live with the whites in a state of freedom." Thirty years have shown the contrary. The blacks and the whites live together in Jamaica; they are all prosperous, and the island in a better condition than it ever was before the act of emancipation was passed.

But they tell us, "If the slaves are emancipated, we won't receive them upon an equality." Why, every man must make equality for himself. No society, no government, can make this equality. I do not expect the slave of the south to jump into equality; all I claim for him is, that he may be allowed to jump into liberty, and let him make equality for himself. I have some white neighbors around me in Cambridge; they are not very intellectual; they don't associate with my family; but whenever they shall improve themselves, and bring themselves up by their own intellectual and moral worth, I shall not object to their coming into my society—all things being equal.

Now, this talk about not letting a man come to this place or that, and that we won't do this for him, or won't do that for him, is all idle. The anti-slavery agitators have never demanded that you shall take the colored man, any more than that you shall take the uncultivated and uncouth white man, and place him in a certain position in society. All I demand for the black man is, that the white people shall take their heels off his neck, and let him have a chance to rise by his own efforts.

The idea of colonizing the slaves in some other country, outside of the United States, seems the height of folly. Whatever may be the mineral wealth of a country, or the producing capabilities of the soil, neither can be made available without the laborer. Four millions of strong hands cannot be spared from the Southern States. All time has shown that the negro is the best laborer in the tropics.

The slaves once emancipated and left on the lands, four millions of new consumers will spring into existence. Heretofore, the bondmen have consumed nothing scarcely from the north. The cost of keeping a slave was only about nineteen dollars per annum, including food, clothing, and doctors' bills. Negro cloth, negro shoes, and negro whips were all that were sent south by northern manufacturers. Let slavery be abolished, and stores will be opened and a new trade take place with the blacks south. Northern manufacturers will have to run on extra time till this new demand will have been supplied. The slave owner, having no longer an inducement to be idle, will go to work, and will not have time to concoct treason against the *stars and stripes.* I cannot close this appeal without a word about the free blacks in the non-slaveholding states.

The majority of the colored people in the Northern States descended from slaves: many of them were slaves themselves. In education, in morals, and in the development of mechanical genius, the free blacks of the Northern States will compare favorably with any laboring class in the world. And considering the fact that we have been shut out, by a cruel prejudice, from nearly all the mechanical branches, and all the professions, it is marvellous that we have attained the position we now occupy. Notwithstanding these bars, our young men have learned trades, become artists, gone into the professions, although bitter prejudice may prevent their having a great deal of practice. When it is considered that they have mostly come out of bondage, and that their calling has been the lowest kind in every community, it is still more strange that the colored people have amassed so much wealth in every state in the Union. If this is not an exhibition of capacity, I don't understand the meaning of the term. And if true patriotism and devotion to the cause of freedom be tests of loyalty, and should establish one's claim to all the privileges that the government can confer, then surely the black man can demand his rights with a good grace. From the fall of Attucks, the first martyr of the American revolution in 1770, down to the present day, the colored people have shown themselves worthy of any confidence that the nation can place in its citizens in the time that tries men's souls. At the battle of Bunker Hill, on the heights of Groton, at the ever-memorable battle of Red Bank, the sable sons of our country stood side by side with their white brethren. On Lakes Erie and Champlain, on the Hudson, and down in the valley of the Mississippi, they established their valor and their invincibility. Whenever the rights of the nation have been assailed, the negro has always responded to his country's call, at once, and with every pulsation of his heart beating for freedom. And no class of Americans have manifested more solicitude for the success of the federal arms in the present struggle with rebellion, than the colored people. At the north, they were among the earliest to respond to the president's first proclamation, calling for troops. At the south, they have ever shown a preference for the *stars and stripes.* In his official despatch to Minister Adams, Mr. Secretary Seward said,—

"Every where the American general receives his most useful and reliable information from the negro, *who hails his coming as the harbinger of freedom.*"

THE BLACK MAN,

HIS GENIUS AND HIS ACHIEVEMENTS.

BENJAMIN BANNEKER.

THE services rendered to science, to liberty, and to the intellectual character of the negro by Banneker, are too great for us to allow his name to sleep and his genius and merits to remain hidden from the world. BENJAMIN BANNEKER was born in the State of Maryland, in the year 1732, of pure African parentage; their blood never having been corrupted by the introduction of a drop of Anglo-Saxon. His father was a slave, and of course could do nothing towards the education of the child. The mother, however, being free, succeeded in purchasing the freedom of her husband, and they, with their son, settled on a few acres of land, where Benjamin remained during the lifetime of his parents. His entire schooling was gained from an obscure country school, established for the education of the children of free negroes; and these advantages were poor, for the boy appears to have finished studying before he arrived at his fifteenth year. Although out of school, Banneker was still a student, and read with great care and attention such books as he could get. Mr. George Ellicott, a gentleman of fortune and considerable literary taste, and who resided near to Benjamin, became interested in him, and lent him books from his large library. Among these books were Mayer's Tables, Fergusson's Astronomy, and Leadbeater's Lunar Tables. A few old and imperfect astronomical instruments also found their way into the boy's hands, all of which he used with great benefit to his own mind.

Banneker took delight in the study of the languages, and soon mastered the Latin, Greek, and German. He was also proficient in the French. The classics were not neglected by him, and the general literary knowledge which he possessed caused Mr. Ellicott to regard him as the most learned man in the town, and he never failed to introduce Banneker to his most distinguished guests. About this time Benjamin turned his attention particularly to astronomy, and determined on making calculations for an almanac, and completed a set for the whole year. Encouraged by this attempt, he entered upon calculations for subsequent years, which, as well as the former, he began and finished without the least assistance from any person or books than those already mentioned; so that whatever merit is attached to his performance is exclusively his own. He published an almanac in Philadelphia for the years 1792, '3, '4, and '5, which contained his calculations, exhibiting the different aspects of the planets, a table of the motions of the sun and moon, their risings and settings, and the courses of the bodies of the planetary system. By this time Banneker's acquirements had become generally known, and the best scholars in the country opened correspondence with him. Goddard & Angell, the well-known Baltimore publishers, engaged his pen for their establishment, and became the publishers of his almanacs. A copy of his first production was sent to Thomas Jefferson, together with a letter intended to interest the great statesman in the cause of negro emancipation and the elevation of the race, in which he says,—

"It is a truth too well attested to need a proof here, that we are a race of beings who have long labored under the abuse and censure of the world; that we have long been looked upon with an eye of contempt, and considered rather as brutish than human, and scarcely capable of mental endowments. I hope I may safely admit, in consequence of the report which has reached me, that you are a man far less inflexible in sentiments of this nature than many others; that you are measurably friendly and well disposed towards us, and that you are willing to lend your aid and assistance for our relief from those many distresses and numerous calamities to which we are reduced. If this is founded in truth, I apprehend you will embrace every opportunity to eradicate that train of absurd and false ideas and opinions which so generally prevail with respect to us, and that your sentiments are concurrent with mine, which are, that one universal Father hath given being to us all; that he hath not only made us all of one flesh, but that he hath also, without partiality, afforded us all the same sensations, and endowed us all with the same faculties; and that, however variable we may be in society or religion, however diversified in situation or in color, we are all of the same family, and stand in the same relation to him. If these are sentiments of which you are fully persuaded, you cannot but acknowledge that it is the indispensable duty of those who maintain the rights of human nature, and who profess the obligations of Christianity, to extend their power and influence to the relief of every part of the human race from whatever burden or oppression they may unjustly labor under; and this, I apprehend, a full conviction of the truth and obligation of these principles should lead all to. I have long been convinced that if your love for yourselves, and for those inestimable laws which preserved to you the rights of human nature, was founded on sincerity, you could not but be solicitous that every individual, of whatever rank or distinction, might with you equally enjoy the blessings thereof; neither could you rest satisfied short of the most active effusion of your exertions, in order to effect their promotion from any state of degradation to which the unjustifiable cruelty and barbarism of men may have reduced them.

"I freely and cheerfully acknowledge that I am one of the African race, and in that color which is natural to them, of the deepest dye; and it is under a sense of the most profound gratitude to the Supreme Ruler of the universe, that I now confess to you that I am not under that state of tyrannical thraldom and inhuman captivity to which too many of my brethren are doomed; but that I have abundantly tasted of the fruition of those blessings which proceed from that free and unequalled liberty with which you are favored, and which I hope you will willingly allow you have mercifully received from the immediate hand of that Being from whom proceedeth every good and perfect gift.

"Your knowledge of the situation of my brethren is too extensive to need a recital here; neither shall I presume to prescribe methods by which they may be relieved, otherwise than by recommending to you and to others to wean yourselves from those narrow prejudices which you have imbibed with respect to them, and, as Job proposed to his friends, 'put your soul in their souls' stead.' Thus shall your hearts be enlarged with kindness and benevolence towards them; and thus shall you need neither the direction of myself or others in what manner to proceed herein. . . . The calculation for this almanac is the production of my arduous study in my advanced stage of life; for having long had unbounded desires to become acquainted with the secrets of nature, I have had to gratify my curiosity herein through my own assiduous application to astronomical study, in which I need not recount to you the many difficulties and disadvantages which I have had to encounter."

Mr. Jefferson at once replied as follows:—

"PHILADELPHIA, *August* 30, 1791.

"SIR: I thank you sincerely for your letter and the almanac it contained. Nobody wishes more than I do to see such proofs as you exhibit, that nature has given to our black brethren talents equal to those of the other colors of men, and that the appearance of the want of them is owing merely to the degraded condition of their existence, both in Africa and America. I can add with truth, that nobody wishes more ardently to see a good system commenced for raising their condition, both of their body and their mind, to what it ought to be, as far as the imbecility of their present existence, and other circumstances, which cannot be neglected, will admit. I have taken the liberty of sending your almanac to Monsieur de Condorcet, secretary of the Academy of Sciences at Paris, and a member of the Philanthropic Society, because I consider it as a document to which your whole color have a right for their justification against the doubts which have been entertained of them.

"I am, with great esteem,

"Dear sir, your obedient, &c.,

"THOMAS JEFFERSON.

"TO MR. B. BANNEKER."

The letter from Banneker, together with the almanac, created in the heart of Mr. Jefferson a fresh feeling of enthusiasm in behalf of freedom, and especially for the negro, which ceased only with his life. The American statesman wrote to Brissot, the celebrated French writer, in which he made enthusiastic mention of the "Negro Philosopher." At the formation of the "Society of the Friends of the Blacks," at Paris, by Lafayette, Brissot, Barnave, Condorcet, and Gregoire, the name of Banneker was again and again referred to to prove the equality of the races. Indeed, the genius of the "Negro Philosopher" did much towards giving liberty to the people of St. Domingo.

In the British House of Commons, Pitt, Wilberforce, and Buxton often alluded to Banneker by name, as a man fit to fill any position in society. At the setting off of the District of Columbia for the capital of the federal government, Banneker was invited by the Maryland commissioners, and took an honorable part in the settlement of the territory. But throughout all his intercourse with men of influence, he never lost sight of the condition of his race, and ever urged the emancipation and elevation of the slave. He well knew that every thing that was founded upon the admitted inferiority of natural right in the African was calculated to degrade him and bring him nearer to the foot of the oppressor, and he therefore never failed to allude to the equality of the races when with those whites whom he could influence. He always urged self-elevation upon the colored people whom he met. He felt that to deprive the black man of the inspiration of ambition, of hope, of health, of standing among his brethren of the earth, was to take from him all incentives to mental improvement. What husbandman incurs the toil of seed time and culture, except with a view to the subsequent enjoyment of a golden harvest? Banneker was endowed by nature with all those excellent qualifications which are necessary previous to the accomplishment of a great man. His memory was large and tenacious, yet, by a curious felicity, chiefly susceptible of the finest impressions it received from the best authors he read, which he always preserved in their primitive strength and amiable order. He had a quickness of apprehension and a vivacity of understanding which easily took in and surmounted the most subtile and knotty parts of mathematics and metaphysics. He possessed in a large degree that genius which constitutes a man of letters; that quality without which judgment is cold and knowledge is inert; that energy which collects, combines, amplifies, and animates.

He knew every branch of history, both natural and civil; he had read all the original historians of England, France, and Germany, and was a great antiquarian. Criticism, metaphysics, morals, politics, voyages and travels, were all studied and well digested by him. With such a fund of knowledge his conversation was equally interesting, instructive, and entertaining. Banneker was so favorably appreciated by the first families in

Virginia, that in 1803 he was invited by Mr. Jefferson, then President of the United States, to visit him at Monticello, where the statesman had gone for recreation. But he was too infirm to undertake the journey. He died the following year, aged seventy-two. Like the golden sun that has sunk beneath the western horizon, but still throws upon the world, which he sustained and enlightened in his career, the reflected beams of his departed genius, his name can only perish with his language.

Banneker believed in the divinity of reason, and in the omnipotence of the human understanding with Liberty for its handmaid. The intellect impregnated by science and multiplied by time, it appeared to him, must triumph necessarily over all the resistance of matter. He had faith in liberty, truth, and virtue. His remains still rest in the slave state where he lived and died, with no stone to mark the spot or tell that it is the grave of Benjamin Banneker.

He labored incessantly, lived irreproachably, and died in the literary harness, universally esteemed and regretted.

NAT TURNER.

Biography is individual history, as distinguished from that of communities, of nations, and of worlds. Eulogy is that deserved applause which springs from the virtues and attaches itself to the characters of men. This is not intended either as a biography or a eulogy, but simply a sketch of one whose history has hitherto been neglected, and to the memory of whom the American people are not prepared to do justice.

On one of the oldest and largest plantations in Southampton county, Virginia, owned by Benjamin Turner, Esq., Nat was born a slave, on the 2d of October, 1800. His parents were of unmixed African descent. Surrounded as he was by the superstition of the slave quarters, and being taught by his mother that he was born for a prophet, a preacher, and a deliverer of his race, it was not strange that the child should have imbibed the principles which were afterwards developed in his career. Early impressed with the belief that he had seen visions, and received communications direct from God, he, like Napoleon, regarded himself as a being of destiny. In his childhood Nat was of an amiable disposition; but circumstances in which he was placed as a slave, brought out incidents that created a change in his disposition, and turned his kind and docile feeling into the most intense hatred to the white race.

Being absent one night from his master's plantation without a pass, he was caught by Whitlock and Mull, the two district patrolers, and severely flogged. This act of cruelty inflamed the young slave, and he resolved upon having revenge. Getting two of the boys of a neighboring plantation to join him, Nat obtained a long rope, went out at night on the road through which the officers had their beat, and stationing his companions, one on each side of the road, he stretched the rope across, fastening each end to a tree, and drawing it tight. His rope thus fixed, and his accomplices instructed how to act their part, Nat started off up the road. The night being dark, and the rope only six or eight inches from the ground, the slave felt sure that he would give his enemies a "high fall."

Nat hearing them, he called out in a disguised voice, "Is dat you, Jim?" To this Whitlock replied, "Yes, dis is me." Waiting until the white men were near him, Nat started off upon a run, followed by the officers. The boy had placed a sheet of white paper in the road, so that he might know at what point to jump the rope, so as not to be caught in his own trap. Arriving at the signal he sprung over the rope, and went down the road like an antelope. But not so with the white men, for both were caught by the legs and thrown so hard upon the ground that Mull had his shoulder put out of joint, and his face terribly lacerated by the fall; while Whitlock's left wrist was broken, and his head bruised in a shocking manner. Nat hastened home, while his companions did the same, not forgetting to take with them the clothes line which had been so serviceable in the conflict. The patrolers were left on the field of battle, crying, swearing, and calling for help.

Snow seldom falls as far south as the southern part of Virginia; but when it does, the boys usually have a good time snow-balling, and on such occasions the slaves, old and young, women and men, are generally pelted without mercy, and with no right to retaliate. It was only a few months after his affair with the patrolers, that Nat was attacked by a gang of boys, who chased him some distance, snow-balling with all their power. The slave boy knew the lads, and determined upon revenge. Waiting till night, he filled his pockets with rocks, and went into the street. Very soon the same gang of boys were at his heels, and pelting him. Concealing his face so as not to be known, Nat discharged his rocks in every direction, until his enemies had all taken to their heels.

The ill treatment he experienced at the hands of the whites, and the visions he claimed to have seen, caused Nat to avoid, as far as he could, all intercourse with his fellow-slaves, and threw around him a gloom and melancholy that disappeared only with his life.

Both the young slave and his friends averred that a full knowledge of the alphabet came to him in a single night. Impressed with the belief that his mission was a religious one, and this impression strengthened by the advice of his grandmother, a pious but ignorant woman, Nat commenced preaching when about twenty-five of age, but never went beyond his own master's locality. In stature he was under the middle size, long armed, round-shouldered, and strongly marked with the African features. A gloomy fire burned in his looks, and he had a melancholy expression of countenance. He never tasted a drop of ardent spirits in his life, and was never known to smile. In the year 1828 new visions appeared to Nat, and he claimed to have direct communication with God. Unlike most of those born under the influence of slavery, he had no faith in conjuring, fortune-telling, or dreams, and always spoke with contempt of such things. Being hired out to cruel masters, he ran away, and remained in the woods thirty days, and could have easily escaped to the free states, as did his father some years before; but he received, as he says in his confession a communication from the spirit, which said, "Return to your earthly master, for he who knoweth his Master's will, and doeth it not, shall be beaten with many stripes." It was not the will of his earthly, but his heavenly Master that he felt bound to do, and therefore Nat returned. His fellow-slaves were greatly incensed at him for coming back, for they knew well his ability to reach Canada, or some other land of freedom, if he was so inclined. He says further, "About this time I had a vision, and saw white spirits and black spirits engaged in battle, and the sun was darkened, the thunder rolled in the heavens, and blood flowed in streams; and I heard a voice saying, 'Such is your luck; such are you called on to see; and let it come, rough or smooth, you must surely bear it.'" Some time after this, Nat had, as he says, another vision, in which the spirit appeared and said, "The serpent is loosened, and Christ has laid down the yoke he has borne for the sins of men, and you must take it up, and fight against the serpent, for the time is fast approaching when the first shall be last, and the last shall be first." There is no doubt but that this last sentence filled Nat with enthusiastic feeling in favor of the liberty of his race, that he had so long dreamed of. "The last shall be first, and the first shall be last," seemed to him to mean something. He saw in it the overthrow of the whites, and the establishing of the blacks in their stead, and to this end he bent the energies of his mind. In February, 1831, Nat received his last communication, and beheld his last vision. He said, "I was told I should arise and prepare myself, and slay my enemies with their own weapons."

The plan of an insurrection was now formed in his own mind, and the time had arrived for him to take others into the secret; and he at once communicated his ideas to four of his friends, in whom he had implicit confidence. Hark Travis, Nelson Williams, Sam Edwards, and Henry Porter were slaves like himself, and like him had taken their names from their masters. A meeting must be held with these, and it must take place in some secluded place, where the whites would not disturb them; and a meeting was appointed. The spot where they assembled was as wild and romantic as were the visions that had been impressed upon the mind of their leader.

Three miles from where Nat lived was a dark swamp filled with reptiles, in the middle of which was a dry spot, reached by a narrow, winding path, and upon which human feet seldom trod, on account of its having been the place where a slave had been tortured to death by a slow fire, for the crime of having flogged his cruel and inhuman master. The night for the meeting arrived, and they came together. Hark brought a pig; Sam, bread; Nelson, sweet potatoes; and Henry, brandy; and the gathering was turned into a feast. Others were taken in, and joined the conspiracy. All partook heartily of the food and drank freely, except Nat. He fasted and prayed. It was agreed that the revolt should commence that night, and in their own master's households, and that each slave should give his oppressor the death blow. Before they left the swamp Nat made a speech, in which he said, "Friends and brothers: We are to commence a great work to-night. Our race is to be delivered from slavery, and God has appointed us as the men to do his bidding, and let us be worthy of our calling. I am told to slay all the whites we encounter, without regard to age or sex. We have no arms or ammunition, but we will find these in the houses of our oppressors, and as we go on others can join us. Remember that we do not go forth for the sake of blood and carnage, but it is necessary that in the commencement of this revolution all the whites we meet should die, until we shall have an army strong enough to carry on the war upon a Christian basis. Remember that ours is not a war for robbery and to satisfy our passions; it is a struggle for freedom. Ours must be deeds, and not words. Then let's away to the scene of action."

Among those who had joined the conspirators was Will, a slave, who scorned the idea of taking his master's name. Though his soul longed to be free, he evidently became one of the party, as much to satisfy revenge, as for the liberty that he saw in the dim distance. Will had seen a dear and beloved wife sold to the negro trader and taken away, never to be beheld by him again in this life. His own back was covered with scars, from his shoulders to his feet. A large scar, running from his right eye down to his chin, showed that he had lived with a cruel master. Nearly six feet in height, and one of the strongest and most athletic of his race, he proved to be the most unfeeling of all the insurrectionists. His only weapon was a broad-axe, sharp and heavy.

Nat and his accomplices at once started for the plantation of Joseph Travis, with whom the four lived, and there the first blow was struck. In his confession, just before his execution, Nat said,—

"On returning to the house, Hark went to the door with an axe, for the purpose of breaking it open, as we knew we were strong enough to murder the family should they be awakened by the noise; but reflecting that it might create an alarm in the neighborhood, we determined to enter the house secretly, and murder them whilst sleeping. Hark got a ladder and set it against the chimney, on which I ascended, and hoisting a window, entered and came down stairs, unbarred the doors, and removed the guns from their places. It was then observed that I must spill the first blood. On which, armed with a hatchet, and accompanied by Will, I entered my master's chamber. It being dark, I could not give a death blow. The hatchet glanced from his head; he sprang from the bed and called his wife. It was his last word; Will laid him dead with a blow of his axe, and Mrs. Travis shared the same fate, as she lay in bed. The murder of this family, five in number, was the work of a moment; not one of them awoke. There was a little infant sleeping in a cradle, that was forgotten until we had left the house and gone some distance, when Henry and Will returned and killed it. We got here four guns that would shoot, and several old muskets, with a pound or two of powder. We remained for some time at the barn, where we paraded; I formed them in line as soldiers, and after carrying them through all the manœuvres I was master of, marched them off to Mr. Salathiel Francis's, about six hundred yards distant.

"Sam and Will went to the door and knocked. Mr. Francis asked who was there; Sam replied it was he, and he had a letter for him; on this he got up and came to the door; they immediately seized him and dragging him out a little from the door, he was despatched by repeated blows on the head. There was no other white person in the family. We started from there to Mrs. Reese's, maintaining the most perfect silence on our march, where, finding the door unlocked, we entered and murdered Mrs. Reese in her bed while sleeping; her son awoke, but only to sleep the sleep of death; he had only time to say, 'Who is that?' and he was no more. From Mrs. Reese's we went to Mrs. Turner's, a mile distant, which we reached about sunrise, on Monday morning. Henry, Austin, and Sam, went to the still, where, finding Mr. Peebles, Austin shot him; the rest of us went to the house. As we approached, the family discovered us and shut the door. Vain hope! Will, with one stroke of his axe, opened it, and we entered, and found Mrs. Turner and Mrs. Newsome in the middle of a room, almost frightened to death. Will immediately killed Mrs. Turner with one blow of his axe. I took Mrs. Newsome by the hand, and with the sword I had when apprehended, I struck her several blows over the head, but was not able to kill her, as the sword was dull. Will, turning round and discovering it, despatched her also. A general destruction of property, and search for money and ammunition, always succeeded the murders.

"By this time, my company amounted to fifteen, nine men mounted, who started for Mrs. Whitehead's, (the other six were to go through a by-way to Mr. Bryant's, and rejoin us at Mrs. Whitehead's.) As we approached the house we discovered Mr. Richard Whitehead standing in the cotton patch, near the lane fence; we called him over into the lane, and Will, the executioner, was near at hand, with his fatal axe, to send him to an untimely grave. As we pushed on to the house, I discovered some one running round the garden, and thinking it was some of the white family, I pursued, but finding it was a servant girl belonging to the house, I returned to commence the work of death; but they whom I left had not been idle: all the family were already murdered but Mrs. Whitehead and her daughter Margaret. As I came round to the door I saw Will pulling Mrs. Whitehead out of the house, and at the step he nearly severed her head from her body with his broadaxe. Miss Margaret, when I discovered her, had concealed herself in the corner formed by the projection of the cellar cap from the house; on my approach she fled, but was soon overtaken, and after repeated blows with a sword, I killed her by a blow over the head with a fence rail. By this time the six who had gone by Mr. Bryant's rejoined us, and informed me they had done the work of death assigned them. We again divided, part going to Mr. Richard Porter's, and from thence to Nathaniel Francis's, the others to Mr. Howell Harris's and Mr. T. Doyles's. On my reaching Mr. Porter's, he had escaped with his family. I understood there that the alarm had already spread, and I immediately returned to bring up those sent to Mr. Doyles's and Mr. Howell Harris's; the party I left going on to Mr. Francis's, having told them I would join them in that neighborhood. I met those sent to Mr. Doyles's and Mr. Howell Harris's returning, having met Mr. Doyles on the road and killed him. Learning from some who joined them, that Mr. Harris was from home, I immediately pursued the course taken by the party gone on before; but knowing that they would complete the work of death and pillage at Mr. Francis's before I could get there, I went to Mr. Peter Edwards's, expecting to find them there; but they had been there already. I then went to Mr. John T. Barrow's; they had been there and murdered him. I pursued on their track to Captain Newitt Harris's. I found the greater part mounted and ready to start; the men, now amounting to about forty, shouted and hurrahed as I rode up; some were in the yard loading their guns, others drinking. They said Captain Harris and his family had escaped; the property in the house they destroyed, robbing him of money and other valuables. I ordered them to mount and march instantly; this was about nine or ten o'clock, Monday morning. I proceeded to Mr. Levi Waller's, two or three miles distant. I took my station in the rear, and as it was my object to carry terror and devastation wherever we went, I placed fifteen or twenty of the best mounted and most to be relied on in front, who generally approached the houses as fast as their horses could run; this was for two purposes, to prevent their escape and strike terror to the inhabitants—on this account I never got to the houses, after leaving Mrs. Whitehead's, until the murders were committed, except in one case. I sometimes got in sight in time to see the work of death completed, viewed the mangled bodies as they lay, in silent satisfaction, and immediately started in quest of other victims. Having murdered Mrs. Waller and ten children, we started for Mr. William Williams's. We killed him and two little boys that were there: while engaged in this, Mrs. Williams fled, and got some distance from the house; but she was pursued, overtaken, and compelled to get up behind one of the company, who brought her back, and after showing her the mangled body of her lifeless husband, she was told to get down and lie by his side, where she was shot dead. I then started for Mr. Jacob Williams's, where the family were murdered. Here we found a young man named Drury, who had come on business with Mr. Williams; he was pursued, overtaken, and shot. Mrs. Vaughan's was the next place we visited; and after murdering the family here, I determined on starting for Jerusalem. Our number amounted now to fifty or sixty, all mounted and armed with guns, axes, swords, and clubs. On reaching Mr. James W. Parker's gate, immediately on the road leading to Jerusalem, and about three miles distant, it was proposed to me to call there; but I objected, as I knew he was gone to Jerusalem, and my object was to reach there as soon as possible; but some of the men having relations at Mr. Parker's, it was agreed that they might call and get his people. I remained at the gate on the road, with seven or eight, the others going across the field to the house, about half a mile off. After waiting some time for them, I became impatient, and started to the house for them, and on our return we were met by a party of white men, who had pursued our blood-stained track, and who had fired on those at the gate, and dispersed them, which I knew nothing of, not having been at that time rejoined by any of them. Immediately on discovering the whites, I ordered my men to halt and form, as they appeared to be alarmed. The white men, eighteen in number, approached us in about one hundred yards, when one of them fired, and I discovered about half of them, retreating. I then ordered my men to fire and rush on them; the few remaining stood their ground until we approached within fifty yards, when they fired and retreated. We pursued and overtook some of them, whom we thought we left dead; after pursuing them about two hundred yards, and rising a little hill, I discovered they were met by another party, and had halted, and were reloading their guns, thinking that those who retreated first, and the party who fired on us at fifty or sixty yards distant, had only fallen back to meet others with ammunition. As I saw them reloading their guns, and more coming up than I saw at first, and several of my bravest men being wounded, the others became panic-struck and scattered over the field; the white men pursued and fired on us several times. Hark had his horse shot under him, and I caught another for him that was running by me; five or six of my men were wounded, but none left on the field. Finding myself defeated here, I instantly determined to go through a private way, and cross the Nottoway River at the Cypress Bridge, three miles below Jerusalem, and attack that place in the rear, as I expected they would look for me on the other road, and I had a great desire to get there to procure arms and ammunition."

Reënforcements came to the whites, and the blacks were overpowered and defeated by the superior numbers of their enemy. In this battle many were slain on both sides. Will, the bloodthirsty and revengeful slave, fell with his broadaxe uplifted, after having laid three of the whites dead at his feet with his own strong arm and his terrible weapon. His last words were, "Bury my axe with me." For he religiously believed that in the next world the blacks would have a contest with the whites, and that he would need his axe. Nat Turner, after fighting to the last with his short sword, escaped with some others to the woods near by, and was not captured for nearly two months. When brought to trial he pleaded "not guilty;" feeling, as he said, that it was always right for one to strike for his own liberty. After going through a mere form of trial, he was convicted and executed at Jerusalem, the county seat for Southampton county, Virginia. Not a limb trembled or a muscle was observed to move. Thus died Nat Turner, at the early age of thirty-one years—a martyr to the freedom of his race, and a victim to his own fanaticism. He meditated upon the wrongs of his oppressed and injured people, till the idea of their deliverance excluded all other ideas from his mind, and he devoted his life to its realization. Every thing appeared to him a vision, and all favorable omens were signs from God. That he was sincere in all that he professed, there is not the slightest doubt. After being defeated he might have escaped to the free states, but the hope of raising a new band kept him from doing so.

He impressed his image upon the minds of those who once beheld him. His looks, his sermons, his acts, and his heroism live in the hearts of his race, on every cotton, sugar, and rice plantation at the south. The present generation of slaves have a superstitious veneration for his name, and believe that in another insurrection Nat Turner will appear and take command. He foretold that at his death the sun would refuse to shine, and that there would be signs of disapprobation given from heaven. And it is true that the sun was darkened, a storm gathered, and more boisterous weather had never appeared in Southampton county than on the day of Nat's execution. The sheriff, warned by the prisoner, refused to cut the cord that held the trap. No black man would touch the rope. A poor old white man, long besotted by drink, was brought forty miles to be the executioner. And even the planters, with all their prejudice and hatred, believed him honest and sincere;

for Mr. Gray, who had known Nat from boyhood, and to whom he made his confession, says of him,—

"It has been said that he was ignorant and cowardly, and that his object was to murder and rob, for the purpose of obtaining money to make his escape. It is notorious that he was never known to have a dollar in his life, to swear an oath, or drink a drop of spirits. As to his ignorance, he certainly never had the advantages of education; but he can read and write, and for natural intelligence and quickness of apprehension, is surpassed by few men I have ever seen. As to his being a coward, his reason, as given, for not resisting Mr. Phipps, shows the decision of his character. When he saw Mr. Phipps present his gun, he said he knew it was impossible for him to escape, as the woods were full of men; he therefore thought it was better for him to surrender, and trust to fortune for his escape. He is a complete fanatic, or plays his part most admirably. On other subjects he possesses an uncommon share of intelligence, with a mind capable of attaining any thing, but warped and perverted by the influence of early impressions. He is below the ordinary stature, though strong and active; having the true negro face, every feature of which is strongly marked. I shall not attempt to describe the effect of his narrative, as told and commented on by himself, in the condemned hole of the prison; the calm, deliberate composure with which he spoke of his late deeds and intentions; the expressions of his fiend-like face, when excited by enthusiasm—still bearing the stains of the blood of helpless innocence about him, clothed with rags and covered with chains, yet daring to raise his manacled hands to heaven, with a spirit soaring above the attributes of man; I looked on him, and the blood curdled in my veins."

Well might he feel the blood curdle in his veins, when he remembered that in every southern household there may be a Nat Turner, in whose soul God has lighted a torch of liberty that cannot be extinguished by the hand of man. The slaveholder should understand that he lives upon a volcano, which may burst forth at any moment, and give freedom to his victim.

"Great God, hasten on the glad jubilee,
When my brother in bonds shall arise and be free,

And our blotted escutcheon be washed from its stains,
Now the scorn of the world—four millions in chains!
O, then shall Columbia's proud flag be unfurled,
The glory of freemen, and pride of the world,
While earth's strolling millions point hither in glee,
'To the land of the brave and the home of the free!'"

Fifty-five whites and seventy-three blacks lost their lives in the Southampton rebellion. On the fatal night when Nat and his companions were dealing death to all they found, Captain Harris, a wealthy planter, had his life saved by the devotion and timely warning of his slave Jim, said to have been half-brother to his master. After the revolt had been put down, and parties of whites were out hunting the suspected blacks, Captain Harris, with his faithful slave, went into the woods in search of the negroes. In saving his master's life, Jim felt that he had done his duty, and could not consent to become a betrayer of his race, and, on reaching the woods, he handed his pistol to his master, and said, "I cannot help you hunt down these men; they, like myself, want to be free. Sir, I am tired of the life of a slave; please give me my freedom, or shoot me on the spot." Captain Harris took the weapon and pointed it at the slave. Jim, putting his right hand upon his heart, said, "This is the spot; aim here." The captain fired, and the slave fell dead at his feet.

From this insurrection, and other manifestations of insubordination by the slave population, the southern people, if they are wise, should learn a grave lesson; for the experience of the past might give them some clew to the future.

Thirty years' free discussion has materially changed public opinion in the non-slaveholding states, and a negro insurrection, in the present excited state of the nation, would not receive the condemnation that it did in 1831. The right of man to the enjoyment of freedom is a settled point; and where he is deprived of this, without any criminal act of his own, it is his duty to regain his liberty at every cost.

If the oppressor is struck down in the contest, his fall will be a just one, and all the world will applaud the act.

This is a new era, and we are in the midst of the most important crisis that our country has yet witnessed. And in the crisis the negro is an important item. Every eye is now turned towards the south, looking for another Nat Turner.

MADISON WASHINGTON.

Among the great number of fugitive slaves who arrived in Canada towards the close of the year 1840, was one whose tall figure, firm step, and piercing eye attracted at once the attention of all who beheld him. Nature had treated him as a favorite. His expressive countenance painted and reflected every emotion of his soul. There was a fascination in the gaze of his finely-cut eyes that no one could withstand. Born of African parentage, with no mixture in his blood, he was one of the handsomest of his race. His dignified, calm, and unaffected features announced at a glance that he was one endowed with genius, and created to guide his fellow-men. He called himself Madison Washington, and said that his birthplace was in the "Old Dominion." He might have seen twenty-five years; but very few slaves have any correct idea of their age. Madison was not poorly dressed, and had some money at the end of his journey, which showed that he was not from among the worst used slaves of the south. He immediately sought employment at a neighboring farm, where he remained some months. A strong, able-bodied man, and a good worker, and apparently satisfied with his situation, his employer felt that he had a servant who would stay with him a long while. The farmer would occasionally raise a conversation, and try to draw from Madison some account of his former life; but in this he failed, for the fugitive was a man of few words, and kept his own secrets. His leisure hours were spent in learning to read and write, and in this he seemed to take the utmost interest. He appeared to take no interest in the sports and amusements that occupied the attention of others. Six months had not passed ere Madison began to show signs of discontent. In vain his employer tried to discover the cause.

"Do I not pay you enough, and treat you in a becoming

manner?" asked Mr. Dickson one day when the fugitive seemed in a very desponding mood.

"Yes, sir," replied Madison.

"Then why do you appear so much dissatisfied, of late?"

"Well, sir," said the fugitive, "since you have treated me with such kindness, and seem to take so much interest in me, I will tell you the reason why I have changed, and appear to you to be dissatisfied. I was born in slavery, in the State of Virginia. From my earliest recollections I hated slavery and determined to be free. I have never yet called any man master, though I have been held by three different men who claimed me as their property. The birds in the trees and the wild beasts of the forest made me feel that I, like them, ought to be free. My feelings were all thus centred in the one idea of liberty, of which I thought by day and dreamed by night. I had scarcely reached my twentieth year when I became acquainted with the angelic being who has since become my wife. It was my intention to have escaped with her before we were married, but circumstances prevented.

"I took her to my bosom as my wife, and then resolved to make the attempt. But unfortunately my plans were discovered, and to save myself from being caught and sold off to the far south I escaped to the woods, where I remained during many weary months. As I could not bring my wife away, I would not come without her. Another reason for remaining was, that I hoped to get up an insurrection of the slaves, and thereby be the means of their liberation. In this, too, I failed. At last it was agreed between my wife and me that I should escape to Canada, get employment, save my money, and with it purchase her freedom. With the hope of attaining this end I came into your service. I am now satisfied that, with the wages I can command here, it will take me not less than five years to obtain by my labor the amount sufficient to purchase the liberty of my dear Susan. Five years will be too long for me to wait, for she may die or be sold away ere I can raise the money. This, sir, makes me feel low-spirited, and I have come to the rash determination to return to Virginia for my wife."

The recital of the story had already brought tears to the eyes of the farmer, ere the fugitive had concluded. In vain did Mr.

Dickson try to persuade Madison to give up the idea of going back into the very grasp of the tyrant, and risking the loss of his own freedom without securing that of his wife. The heroic man had made up his mind, and nothing could move him. Receiving the amount of wages due him from his employer, Madison turned his face once more towards the south. Supplied with papers purporting to have been made out in Virginia, and certifying to his being a freeman, the fugitive had no difficulty in reaching the neighborhood of his wife. But these "free papers" were only calculated to serve him where he was not known. Madison had also provided himself with files, saws, and other implements with which to cut his way out of any prison into which he might be cast. These instruments were so small as to be easily concealed in the lining of his clothing; and armed with them the fugitive felt sure he should escape again were he ever captured. On his return, Madison met, in the State of Ohio, many of those whom he had seen on his journey to Canada, and all tried to prevail upon him to give up the rash attempt. But to every one he would reply, "Liberty is worth nothing to me while my wife is a slave." When near his former home, and unable to travel in open day without being detected, Madison betook himself to the woods during the day, and travelled by night. At last he arrived at the old farm at night, and hid away in the nearest forest. Here he remained several days, filled with hope and fear, without being able to obtain any information about his wife. One evening, during this suspense, Madison heard the singing of a company of slaves, the sound of which appeared nearer and nearer, until he became convinced that it was a gang going to a corn-shucking, and the fugitive resolved that he would join it, and see if he could get any intelligence of his wife.

In Virginia, as well as in most of the other corn-raising slave states, there is a custom of having what is termed "a corn-shucking," to which slaves from the neighboring plantations, with the consent of their masters, are invited. At the conclusion of the shucking a supper is provided by the owner of the corn; and thus, together with the bad whiskey which is freely circulated on such occasions, the slaves are made to feel very happy. Four or five companies of men may be heard in different directions and at the same time approaching the place of rendezvous, slaves joining the gangs along the roads as they pass their masters' farms. Madison came out upon the highway, and as the company came along singing, he fell into the ranks and joined in the song. Through the darkness of the night he was able to keep from being recognized by the remainder of the company, while he learned from the general conversation the most important news of the day.

Although hungry and thirsty, the fugitive dared not go to the supper table for fear of recognition. However, before he left the company that night, he gained information enough to satisfy him that his wife was still with her old master, and he hoped to see her, if possible, on the following night. The sun had scarcely set the next evening, ere Madison was wending his way out of the forest and going towards the home of his loved one, if the slave can be said to have a home. Susan, the object of his affections, was indeed a woman every way worthy of his love. Madison knew well where to find the room usually occupied by his wife, and to that spot he made his way on arriving at the plantation. But in his zeal and enthusiasm, and his being too confident of success, he committed a blunder which nearly cost him his life. Fearful that if he waited until a late hour Susan would be asleep, and in awakening her she would in her fright alarm the household, Madison ventured to her room too early in the evening, before the whites in the "great house" had retired. Observed by the overseer, a sufficient number of whites were called in, and the fugitive secured ere he could escape with his wife; but the heroic slave did not yield until he with a club had laid three of his assailants upon the ground with his manly blows; and not then until weakened by loss of blood. Madison was at once taken to Richmond, and sold to a slave trader, then making up a gang of slaves for the New Orleans market.

The brig Creole, owned by Johnson & Eperson, of Richmond, and commanded by Captain Enson, lay at the Richmond dock waiting for her cargo, which usually consisted of tobacco, hemp, flax, and slaves. There were two cabins for the slaves, one for the men, the other for the women. The men were generally kept in chains while on the voyage; but the women were usually unchained, and allowed to roam at pleasure in their own cabin. On the 27th of October, 1841, the

Creole sailed from Hampton Roads, bound for New Orleans, with her full load of freight, one hundred and thirty-five slaves, and three passengers, besides the crew. Forty of the slaves were owned by Thomas McCargo, nine belonged to Henry Hewell, and the remainder were held by Johnson & Eperson. Hewell had once been an overseer for McCargo, and on this occasion was acting as his agent.

Among the slaves owned by Johnson & Eperson was Madison Washington. He was heavily ironed, and chained down to the floor of the cabin occupied by the men, which was in the forward hold. As it was known by Madison's purchasers that he had once escaped and had been in Canada, they kept a watchful eye over him. The two cabins were separated, so that the men and women had no communication whatever during the passage.

Although rather gloomy at times, Madison on this occasion seemed very cheerful, and his owners thought that he had repented of the experience he had undergone as a runaway, and in the future would prove a more easily governed chattel. But from the first hour that he had entered the cabin of the Creole, Madison had been busily engaged in the selection of men who were to act parts in the great drama. He picked out each one as if by intuition. Every thing was done at night and in the dark, as far as the preparation was concerned. The miniature saws and files were faithfully used when the whites were asleep.

In the other cabin, among the slave women, was one whose beauty at once attracted attention. Though not tall, she yet had a majestic figure. Her well-moulded shoulders, prominent bust, black hair which hung in ringlets, mild blue eyes, finely-chiselled mouth, with a splendid set of teeth, a turned and well-rounded chin, skin marbled with the animation of life, and veined by blood given to her by her master, she stood as the representative of two races. With only one eighth of African, she was what is called at the south an "octoroon." It was said that her grandfather had served his country in the revolutionary war, as well as in both houses of Congress. This was Susan, the wife of Madison. Few slaves, even among the best used house servants, had so good an opportunity to gain general information as she. Accustomed to travel with her mistress, Susan had often been to Richmond, Norfolk, White Sulphur

Springs, and other places of resort for the aristocracy of the Old Dominion. Her language was far more correct than most slaves in her position. Susan was as devoted to Madison as she was beautiful and accomplished.

After the arrest of her husband, and his confinement in Richmond jail, it was suspected that Susan had long been in possession of the knowledge of his whereabouts when in Canada, and knew of his being in the neighborhood; and for this crime it was resolved that she should be sold and sent off to a southern plantation, where all hope of escape would be at an end. Each was not aware that the other was on board the Creole, for Madison and Susan were taken to their respective cabins at different times. On the ninth day out, the Creole encountered a rough sea, and most of the slaves were sick, and therefore were not watched with that vigilance that they had been since she first sailed. This was the time for Madison and his accomplices to work, and nobly did they perform their duty. Night came on; the first watch had just been summoned, the wind blowing high, when Madison succeeded in reaching the quarter deck, followed by eighteen others, all of whom sprang to different parts of the vessel, seizing whatever they could wield as weapons. The crew were nearly all on deck. Captain Enson and Mr. Merritt, the first mate, were standing together, while Hewell was seated on the companion smoking a cigar. The appearance of the slaves all at once, and the loud voice and commanding attitude of their leader, so completely surprised the whites, that—

> "They spake not a word;
> But, like dumb statues, or breathless stones,
> Stared at each other, and looked deadly pale."

The officers were all armed; but so swift were the motions of Madison that they had nearly lost command of the vessel before they attempted to use their weapons.

Hewell, the greater part of whose life had been spent on the plantation in the capacity of a negro-driver, and who knew that the defiant looks of these men meant something, was the first to start. Drawing his old horse pistol from under his coat, he fired at one of the blacks and killed him. The next moment Hewell lay dead upon the deck, for Madison had struck him with a capstan bar. The fight now became general, the white passengers, as well as all the crew, taking part. The battle was Madison's element, and he plunged into it without any care for his own preservation or safety. He was an instrument of enthusiasm, whose value and whose place was in his inspiration. "If the fire of heaven was in my hands, I would throw it at these cowardly whites," said he to his companions, before leaving their cabin. But in this he did not mean revenge, only the possession of his freedom and that of his fellow-slaves. Merritt and Gifford, the first and second mates of the vessel, both attacked the heroic slave at the same time. Both were stretched out upon the deck with a single blow each, but were merely wounded; they were disabled, and that was all that Madison cared for for the time being. The sailors ran up the rigging for safety, and a moment more he that had worn the fetters an hour before was master of the brig Creole. His commanding attitude and daring orders, now that he was free, and his perfect preparation for the grand alternative of liberty or death which stood before him, are splendid exemplifications of the truly heroic. After his accomplices had covered the slaver's deck, Madison forbade the shedding of more blood, and ordered the sailors to come down, which they did, and with his own hands he dressed their wounds. A guard was placed over all except Merritt, who was retained to navigate the vessel. With a musket doubly charged, and pointed at Merritt's breast, the slave made him swear that he would faithfully take the brig into a British port. All things now secure, and the white men in chains or under guard, Madison ordered that the fetters should be severed from the limbs of those slaves who still wore them. The next morning "Captain Washington" (for such was the name he now bore) ordered the cook to provide the best breakfast that the store room could furnish, intending to surprise his fellow-slaves, and especially the females, whom he had not yet seen. But little did he think that the woman for whom he had risked his liberty and life would meet him at the breakfast table. The meeting of the hero and his beautiful and accomplished wife, the tears of joy shed, and the hurrahs that followed from the men, can better be imagined than described. Madison's cup of joy was filled to the brim. He had not only gained his own liberty and that of one hundred and thirty-four others, but his dear Susan was safe. Only one man, Hewell, had been killed. Captain Enson and others, who were wounded, soon recovered; and were kindly treated by Madison; but they nevertheless proved ungrateful; for on the second night, Captain Enson, Mr. Gifford, and Merritt took advantage of the absence of Madison from the deck, and attempted to retake the vessel. The slaves, exasperated at this treachery, fell upon the whites with deadly weapons. The captain and his men fled to the cabin, pursued by the blacks. Nothing but the heroism of the negro leader saved the lives of the white men on this occasion, for as the slaves were rushing into the cabin, Madison threw himself between them and their victims, exclaiming, "Stop! no more blood. My life, that was perilled for your liberty, I will lay down for the protection of these men. They have proved themselves unworthy of life, which we granted them; still let us be magnanimous." By the kind heart and noble bearing of Madison, the vile slave-traders were again permitted to go unwhipped of justice. This act of humanity raised the uncouth son of Africa far above his Anglo-Saxon oppressors.

The next morning the Creole landed at Nassau, New Providence, where the noble and heroic slaves were warmly greeted by the inhabitants, who at once offered protection, and extended their hospitality to them. Not many months since, an American ship went ashore at Nassau, and among the first to render assistance to the crew was Madison Washington.

HENRY BIBB.

HENRY BIBB, like most fugitive slaves, did not know who his father was; that his mother was a slave was sufficient to decide his lot, and to send him, under fear of the lash, while yet a mere infant, to labor on his master's farm: when sufficiently old to be of much use to any one, he was hired out to one person and another for the space of eight or ten years, the proceeds of his labor going, we are told, to defray the expense of educating his owner's daughters. The year of Henry Bibb's birth was a memorable one—1815; little, however, knew he of

European struggles; he had a great battle of his own to fight against tremendous odds, and he seems to have fought it bravely. He formed the determination to be free at a very early age, and nothing could shake it; starvation, imprisonment, scourging, lacerating, punishments of every kind, and of every degree of severity short of actual death, were tried in vain; they could not subdue his indomitable spirit.

His first attempt to escape was made when he was about ten years of age, and from that time to 1840 his life was a constant series of flights and recaptures, the narrative of which makes one thrill and shudder at the sufferings endured and the barbarities inflicted. Securing his freedom by his own good legs, Henry Bibb at once began seeking an education; and in this he succeeded far beyond many white men who have had all the avenues to learning open to them. In personal appearance he was tall and slim, a pleasing countenance, half white, hair brown, eyes gray, and possessed a musical voice, and a wonderful power of delivery. No one who heard Mr. Bibb, in the years 1847, '8, and '9, can forget the deep impression that he left behind him. His natural eloquence and his songs enchained an audience as long as the speaker wanted them. In 1849, we believe, he went to Canada, and started a weekly paper called *The Voice of the Fugitives*, at Windsor. His journal was well conducted, and was long regarded as indispensable in every fugitive's house. His first wife being left in slavery, and no hope of her escaping, Mr. Bibb married for his second wife the well-educated and highly-cultivated Mary E. Miles, of Boston. After being in Canada a while, the two opened a school for their escaped brothers and sisters, which proved a lasting benefit to that much-injured class. His efforts to purchase a tract of land, and to deal it out in lots to the fugitives at a reasonable price, was only one of the many kind acts of this good man. There are few characters more worthy of the student's study and imitation than that of Henry Bibb. From an ignorant slave, he became an educated free man, by his own powers, and left a name that will not soon fade away.

In one of Cassimir de la Vigne's dramas, we met with an expression which struck us forcibly. It was said of Don John, who was ignorant of his birth, that perhaps he was a nobody; to which he replied, "That a man of good character and honorable conduct could never be a nobody." We consider this an admirable reply, and have endeavored to prove this truth by the foregoing example. If it is gratifying and noble to bear with honor the name of one's father, it is surely more noble to make a name for one's self; and our heart tells us that among our young readers there is more than one who will exclaim with ardor, and with a firm resolution to fulfil his promise, *I, too, shall make a name.*

PLACIDO.

In the year 1830, there was a young man in Havana, son of a woman who had been brought, when a child, from the coast of Africa, and sold as a slave. Being with a comparatively kind master, he soon found opportunity to begin developing the genius which at a later period showed itself. The young slave was called Placido. He took an especial interest in poetry, and often wrote poems that were set to music and sung in the drawing rooms of the most refined companies which assembled in the city. His young master paying his addresses to a rich heiress, the slave was requested to write a poem embodying the master's passion for the young lady. Placido acquitted himself to the entire satisfaction of the lover, who copied the epistle in his own hand, and sent it on its mission. The slave's compositions were so much admired that they found their way into the newspaper; but no one knew the negro as the author. In 1838, these poems, together with a number which had never appeared in print, were intrusted to a white man, who sent them to England, where they were published and much praised for the talent and scholarly attainment which they developed. A number of young whites, who were well acquainted with Placido and his genius, resolved to purchase him and present him his freedom, which they did in the year 1842. But a new field had opened itself to the freed black, and he began to tread in its paths. Freedom for himself was only the beginning; he sighed to make others free. The imaginative brain of the poet produced verses which the slaves sung in their own rude way, and which kindled in their hearts a more intense desire for liberty. Placido planned an insurrection of the slaves, in which he was to be their leader and deliverer; but the scheme failed. After a hasty trial, he was convicted and sentenced to death. The fatal day came; he walked to the place of execution with as much calmness as if it had been to an ordinary resort of pleasure. His manly and heroic bearing excited the sympathy and admiration of all who saw him. As he arrived at the fatal spot he began reciting the following hymn, which he had written in his cell the previous night:—

TO GOD—A PRAYER.

"Almighty God! whose goodness knows no bound,
To thee I flee in my severe distress;
O let thy potent arm my wrongs redress,
And rend the odious veil by slander wound
About my brow. The base world's arm confound,
Who on my front would now the seal of shame impress.

God of my sires, to whom all kings must yield,
Be thou alone my shield; protect me now:
All power is His, to whom the sea doth owe
His countless stores; who clothed with light heaven's field,
And made the sun, and air, and polar seas congealed;
All plants with life endowed, and made the rivers flow.

All power is thine: 'twas thy creative might
This goodly frame of things from chaos brought,
Which unsustained by thee would still be nought,
As erst it lay deep in the womb of night,
Ere thy dread word first called it into light;
Obedient to thy call, it lived, and moved, and thought.

Thou know'st my heart, O God, supremely wise;
Thine eye, all-seeing, cannot be deceived;
By thee mine inmost soul is clear perceived,
As objects gross are through transparent skies
By mortal ken. Thy mercy exercise,
Lest slander foul exult o'er innocence aggrieved.

But if 'tis fixed, by thy decree divine,
That I must bear the pain of guilt and shame,

And that my foes this cold and senseless frame
Shall rudely treat with scorn and shouts malign,
Give thou the word, and I my breath resign,
Obedient to thy will. Blest be thy holy name!"

When all preparation for the execution had been finished, Placido asked the privilege of giving the signal, and it was granted. With his face wearing an expression of almost superhuman courage, he said in Spanish, "Adieu, O world; there is no justice or pity for me here. Soldiers, fire!" Five balls entered his body, but did not deprive him of life. Still unsubdued, he again spoke, and placing his hand on his breast, said, "Fire here." Two balls from the reserve entered his heart, and he fell dead.

Thus died Placido, the slave's poet of freedom. His songs are still sung in the bondman's hut, and his name is a household word to all. As the *Marseillaise* was sung by the revolutionists of France, and inspired the people with a hatred to oppressors, so will the slaves of Cuba, at a future day, sing the songs of their poet-martyr, and their cry will be, "Placido and Liberty."

JEREMIAH B. SANDERSON.

NEW BEDFORD has produced a number of highly-intelligent men of the "doomed race;" men who, by their own efforts, have attained positions, intellectually, which, if they had been of the more favored class, would have introduced them into the halls of Congress. One of these is J. B. Sanderson. An industrious student, and an ardent lover of literature, he has read more than almost any one of his years within our circle of acquaintance. History, theology, and the classics, he is master of. We first met him while he was on a tour through the west, as a lecturer on slavery, and the impression then made on our mind became still stronger as we knew more of him. Although not at the time an ordained minister Mr. Sanderson, in 1848, preached for one of the religious societies of New Bedford, on Sunday, and attended to his vocation (hair dresser) during the week. Some of the best educated of the whites were always in attendance on these occasions. His sermons were generally beyond the comprehension of his hearers, except those well read. Emerson, Carlyle, and Theodore Parker, were represented in his discourses, which were always replete with historical incidents. Mr. Sanderson has been several years in California, where he now preaches to an intelligent congregation and is considered one of the ablest religious teachers in the Pacific state.

> "Honor and fame from no condition rise:
> Act well your part—there all the honor lies."
>
> "Who does the best his circumstance allows,
> Does well, acts nobly: angels could no more."

In stature Mr. Sanderson is somewhat above the medium height, finely formed, well-developed head, and a pleasing face; an excellent voice, which he knows how to use. His gestures are correct without being studied, and his sentences always tell upon his audience. Few speakers are more happy in their delivery than he. In one of those outbursts of true eloquence for which he is so noted, we still remember the impression made upon his hearers, when, on one occasion, he exclaimed, "Neither men nor governments have a right to sell those of their species; men and their liberty are neither purchasable nor salable. This is the law of nature, which is obligatory on all men, at all times, and in all places."

All accounts from California speak of J. B. Sanderson as doing more for the enfranchisement and elevation of his race than any one who has gone from the Atlantic states.

TOUSSAINT L'OUVERTURE.

At the commencement of the French revolution, in 1789, there were nine hundred thousand inhabitants on the Island of St. Domingo. Of these, seven hundred thousand were Africans, sixty thousand mixed blood, and the remainder were whites and Caribbeans. Like the involuntary servitude in our own Southern States, slavery in St. Domingo kept morality at a low stand. Owing to the amalgamation between masters and slaves, there arose the mulatto population, which eventually proved to be the worst enemies of their fathers.

Many of the planters sent their mulatto sons to France to be educated. When these young men returned to the island, they were greatly dissatisfied at the proscription which met them wherever they appeared. White enough to make them hopeful and aspiring, many of the mulattoes possessed wealth enough to make them influential. Aware, by their education, of the principles of freedom that were being advocated in Europe and the United States, they were ever on the watch to seize opportunities to better their social and political condition. In the French part of the island alone, twenty thousand whites lived in the midst of thirty thousand free mulattoes and five hundred thousand slaves. In the Spanish portion, the odds were still greater in favor of the slaves. Thus the advantage of numbers and physical strength was on the side of the oppressed. Right is the most dangerous of weapons—woe to him who leaves it to his enemies!

The efforts of Wilberforce, Sharp, Buxton, and Clarkson to abolish the African slave trade, and their advocacy of the equality of the races, were well understood by the men of color. They had also learned their own strength in the island, and that they had the sympathy of all Europe with them. The news of the oath of the Tennis Court and the taking of the Bastile at Paris was received with the wildest enthusiasm by the people of St. Domingo.

The announcement of these events was hailed with delight by both the white planters and the mulattoes; the former, because they hoped that a revolution in the mother country would secure to them the independence of the colony; the latter, because they viewed it as a movement that would give them equal rights with the whites; and even the slaves regarded it as a precursor to their own emancipation. But the excitement which the outbreak at Paris had created amongst the free men of color and the slaves, at once convinced the planters that a separation from France would be the death-knell of slavery in St. Domingo.

Although emancipated by law from the dominion of

individuals, the mulattoes had no rights: shut out from society by their color, deprived of religious and political privileges, they felt their degradation even more keenly than the bond slaves. The mulatto son was not allowed to dine at his father's table, kneel with him in his devotions, bear his name, inherit his property, nor even to lie in his father's graveyard. Laboring as they were under the sense of their personal social wrongs, the mulattoes tolerated, if they did not encourage, low and vindictive passions. They were haughty and disdainful to the blacks, whom they scorned, and jealous and turbulent to the whites, whom they hated and feared.

The mulattoes at once despatched one of their number to Paris, to lay before the Constitutional Assembly their claim to equal rights with the whites. Vincent Ogé, their deputy, was well received at Paris by Lafayette, Brissot, Barnave, and Gregoire, and was admitted to a seat in the Assembly, where he eloquently portrayed the wrongs of his race. In urging his claims, he said, if equality was withheld from the mulattoes, they would appeal to force. This was seconded by Lafayette and Barnave, who said, "*Perish the colonies rather than a principle*."

The Assembly passed a decree granting the demands of the men of color, and Ogé was made bearer of the news to his brethren. The planters armed themselves, met the young deputy on his return to the island, and a battle ensued. The free colored men rallied around Ogé, but they were defeated and taken, with their brave leader, were first tortured, and then broken alive on the wheel.

The prospect of freedom was put down for the time, but the blood of Ogé and his companions bubbled silently in the hearts of the African race; they swore to avenge them.

The announcement of the death of Ogé in the halls of the Assembly at Paris created considerable excitement, and became the topic of conversation in the clubs and on the Boulevards. Gregoire defended the course of the colored men, and said, "If Liberty was right in France, it was right in St. Domingo." He well knew that the crime for which Ogé had suffered in the West Indies, had constituted the glory of Mirabeau and Lafayette at Paris, and Washington and Hancock in the United

States. The planters in the island trembled at their own oppressive acts, and terror urged them on to greater violence. The blood of Ogé and his accomplices had sown every where despair and conspiracy. The French sent an army to St. Domingo to enforce the laws.

The planters repelled with force the troops sent out by France, denying its prerogatives and refusing the civic oath. In the midst of these thickening troubles, the planters who resided in France were invited to return and assist in vindicating the civil independence of the island. Then was it that the mulattoes earnestly appealed to the slaves, and the result was appalling. The slaves awoke as from an ominous dream, and demanded their rights with sword in hand. Gaining immediate success, and finding that their liberty would not be granted by the planters, they rapidly increased in numbers; and in less than a week from its commencement, the storm had swept over the whole plain of the north, from east to west, and from the mountains to the sea. The splendid villas and rich factories yielded to the furies of the devouring flames; so that the mountains, covered with smoke and burning cinders, borne upwards by the wind, looked like volcanoes; and the atmosphere, as if on fire, resembled a furnace.

Such were the outraged feelings of a people whose ancestors had been ruthlessly torn from their native land, and sold in the shambles of St. Domingo. To terrify the blacks and convince them that they could never be free, the planters were murdering them on every hand by thousands.

The struggle in St. Domingo was watched with intense interest by the friends of the blacks, both in Paris and in London, and all appeared to look with hope to the rising up of a black chief, who should prove himself adequate to the emergency. Nor did they look in vain. In the midst of the disorders that threatened on all sides, the negro chief made his appearance in the person of a slave, named Toussaint. This man was the grandson of the King of Ardra, one of the most powerful and wealthy monarchs on the west coast of Africa. By his own energy and perseverance, Toussaint had learned to read and write, and was held in high consideration by the surrounding planters as well as their slaves.

His private virtues were many, and he had a deep and pervading sense of religion, and in the camp carried it even as far as Oliver Cromwell. Toussaint was born on the island, and was fifty years of age when called into the field. One of his chief characteristics was his humanity.

Before taking any part in the revolution, he aided his master's family to escape from the impending danger. After seeing them beyond the reach of the revolutionary movement, he entered the army as an inferior officer, but was soon made aid-de-camp to General Bissou. Disorder and bloodshed reigned throughout the island, and every day brought fresh intelligence of depredations committed by whites, mulattoes, and blacks.

Such was the condition of affairs when a decree was passed by the Colonial Assembly giving equal rights to the mulattoes, and asking their aid in restoring order and reducing the slaves again to their chains. Overcome by this decree, and having gained all they wished, the free colored men joined the planters in a murderous crusade against the slaves. This union of the whites and mulattoes to prevent the bondman getting his freedom, created an ill feeling between the two proscribed classes which seventy years have not been able to efface. The French government sent a second army to St. Domingo, to enforce the laws giving freedom to the slaves; and Toussaint joined it on its arrival in the island, and fought bravely against the planters.

While the people of St. Domingo were thus fighting amongst themselves, the revolutionary movement in France had fallen into the hands of Robespierre and Danton, and the guillotine was beheading its thousands daily. When the news of the death of Louis XVI. reached St. Domingo, Toussaint and his companions left the French, and joined the Spanish army in the eastern part of the island, and fought for the king of Spain. Here Toussaint was made brigadier general, and appeared in the field as the most determined foe of the French planters.

The two armies met; a battle was fought in the streets, and many thousands were slain on both sides; the planters, however, were defeated. During the conflict the city was set on fire, and on every side presented shocking evidence of slaughter, conflagration, and pillage. The strifes of political and religious partisanship, which had raged in the clubs and streets of Paris, were transplanted to St. Domingo, where they raged with all the heat of a tropical clime and the animosities of a civil war. Truly did the flames of the French revolution at Paris, and the ignorance and self-will of the planters, set the island of St. Domingo on fire. The commissioners, with their retinue, retired from the burning city into the neighboring highlands, where a camp was formed to protect the ruined town from the opposing party. Having no confidence in the planters, and fearing a reaction, the commissioners proclaimed a general emancipation to the slave population, and invited the blacks who had joined the Spaniards to return. Toussaint and his followers accepted the invitation, returned, and were enrolled in the army under the commissioners. Fresh troops arrived from France, who were no sooner in the island than they separated—some siding with the planters, and others with the commissioners. The white republicans of the mother country arrayed themselves against the white republicans of St. Domingo, whom they were sent out to assist; the blacks and the mulattoes were at war with each other; old and young, of both sexes and of all colors, were put to the sword, while the fury of the flames swept from plantation to plantation and from town to town.

During these sad commotions, Toussaint, by his superior knowledge of the character of his race, his humanity, generosity, and courage, had gained the confidence of all whom he had under his command. The rapidity with which he travelled from post to post astonished every one. By his genius and surpassing activity, Toussaint levied fresh forces, raised the reputation of the army, and drove the English and Spanish from the island.

With the termination of this struggle every vestige of slavery and all obstacles to freedom disappeared. Toussaint exerted every nerve to make Hayti what it had formerly been. He did every thing in his power to promote agriculture; and in this he succeeded beyond the most sanguine expectations of the friends of freedom, both in England and France. Even the planters who had remained on the island acknowledged the prosperity of Hayti under the governorship of the man whose best days had been spent in slavery.

The peace of Amiens left Bonaparte without a rival on the continent, and with a large and experienced army, which he feared to keep idle; and he determined to send a part of it to St. Domingo.

The army for the expedition to St. Domingo was fitted out, and no pains or expense spared to make it an imposing one. Fifty-six ships of war, with twenty-five thousand men, left France for Hayti. It was, indeed, the most valiant fleet that had ever sailed from the French dominions. The Alps, the Nile, the Rhine, and all Italy, had resounded with the exploits of the men who were now leaving their country for the purpose of placing the chains again on the limbs of the heroic people of St. Domingo. There were men in that army that had followed Bonaparte from the siege of Toulon to the battle under the shades of the pyramids of Egypt—men who had grown gray in the camp.

News of the intended invasion reached St. Domingo some days before the squadron had sailed from Brest; and therefore the blacks had time to prepare to meet their enemies. Toussaint had concentrated his forces at such points as he expected would be first attacked. Christophe was sent to defend Cape City, and Port-au-Prince was left in the hands of Dessalines.

With no navy, and but little means of defence, the Haytians determined to destroy their towns rather than they should fall into the hands of the enemy. Late in the evening the French ships were seen to change their position, and Christophe, satisfied that they were about to effect a landing, set fire to his own house, which was the signal for the burning of the town. The French general wept as he beheld the ocean of flames rising from the tops of the houses in the finest city in St. Domingo. Another part of the fleet landed in Samana, where Toussaint, with an experienced wing of the army, was ready to meet them. On seeing the ships enter the harbor, the heroic chief said, "Here come the enslavers of our race. All France is coming to St. Domingo, to try again to put the fetters upon our limbs; but not France, with all her troops of the Rhine, the Alps, the Nile, the Tiber, nor all Europe to help her, can extinguish the soul of Africa. That soul, when once the soul of a man, and no longer that of a slave, can overthrow the pyramids and the Alps themselves, sooner than again be crushed down into slavery." The French, however, effected a landing, but they found nothing but smouldering ruins, where once stood splendid cities. Toussaint and his generals at once abandoned the towns, and betook themselves to the mountains, those citadels of freedom in St. Domingo, where the blacks have always proved too much for the whites.

Toussaint put forth a proclamation to the colored people, in which he said, "You are now to meet and fight enemies who have neither faith, law, nor religion. Let us resolve that these French troops shall never leave our shores alive." The war commenced, and the blacks were victorious in nearly all the battles. Where the French gained a victory, they put their prisoners to the most excruciating tortures; in many instances burning them in pits, and throwing them into boiling caldrons. This example of cruelty set by the whites was followed by the blacks. Then it was that Dessalines, the ferocious chief, satisfied his long pent-up revenge against the white planters and French soldiers that he made prisoners. The French general saw that he could gain nothing from the blacks on the field of battle, and he determined upon a stratagem, in which he succeeded too well.

A correspondence was opened with Toussaint, in which the captain-general promised to acknowledge the liberty of the blacks and the equality of all, if he would yield. Overcome by the persuasions of his generals and the blacks who surrounded him, and who were sick and tired of the shedding of blood, Toussaint gave in his adhesion to the French authorities. This was the great error of his life.

Vincent, in his "*Reflections on the Present State of the Colony of St. Domingo*," says, "Toussaint, at the head of his army, is the most active and indefatigable man of whom we can form an idea; we may say, with truth, that he is found wherever instructions or danger render his presence necessary. The particular care which he employs in his march, of always deceiving the men of whom he has need, and who think they enjoy a confidence he gives to none, has such an effect that he is daily expected in all the chief places of the colony. His great sobriety, the faculty, which none but he possesses, of never reposing, the facility with which he resumes the affairs of the cabinet after the most tiresome excursions, of answering daily a hundred letters, and of habitually tiring five secretaries, render him so superior to all those around him, that their respect and submission are in most individuals carried even to fanaticism. It is certain that no man, in the present times, has possessed such an influence over a mass of people as General Toussaint possesses over his brethren in St. Domingo."

The above is the opinion of an enemy—one who regarded the negro chief as a dangerous man to his interest.

Invited by the captain-general of the island to attend a council, the black hero was treacherously seized and sent on board the ship of war Hero, which set sail at once for France. On the arrival of the illustrious prisoner at Brest, he was taken in a close carriage and transferred to the castle of Joux, in the Lower Pyrenees. The gelid atmosphere of the mountain region, the cold, damp dungeon in which he was placed, with the water dripping upon the floor day and night, did not hasten the death of Toussaint fast enough. By Napoleon's directions the prisoner's servant was taken from him, sufficient clothing and bedding to keep him warm were denied, his food curtailed, and his keeper, after an absence of four days, returned and found the hero of St. Domingo dead in his cell. Thus terminated the career of a self-made man.

Toussaint was of prepossessing appearance, of middle stature, and possessed an iron frame. His dignified, calm, and unaffected features, and broad and well-developed forehead, would cause him to be selected, in any company of men, as one born for a leader. Endowed by nature with high qualities of mind, he owed his elevation to his own energies and his devotion to the welfare and freedom of his race. His habits were thoughtful; and like most men of energetic temperaments, he crowded much into what he said. So profound and original were his opinions, that they have been successively drawn upon by all the chiefs of St. Domingo since his era, and still without loss of adaptation to the circumstances of the country. The policy of his successors has been but a repetition of his plans, and his maxims are still the guidance of the rulers of Hayti. His thoughts were copious and full of vigor, and what he could express well in his native *patois* he found tame and unsatisfactory in the French language, which he was obliged to employ in the details of his official business. He would never sign what he did not fully understand, obliging two or three secretaries to re-word the document, until they had succeeded in furnishing the particular phrase expressive of his meaning. While at the height of his power, and when all around him were furnished with every comfort, and his officers living in splendor, Toussaint himself lived with an austere sobriety which bordered on abstemiousness. He was entirely master of his own passions and appetites. It was his custom to set off in his carriage with the professed object of going to some particular point of the island, and when he had passed over several miles of the journey, to quit the carriage, which continued its route under the same escort of guards, while Toussaint, mounted on horseback and followed by his officers, made rapid excursions across the country, to places where he was least expected. It was upon one of these occasions that he owed his life to his singular mode of travelling. He had just left his carriage when an ambuscade of mulattoes, concealed in the thickets of Boucassin, fired upon the guard, and several balls pierced the carriage, and one of them killed an old domestic who occupied the seat of his master. No person knew better than he the art of governing the people under his jurisdiction. The greater part of the population loved him to idolatry. Veneration for Toussaint was not confined to the boundaries of St. Domingo; it ran through Europe; and in France his name was frequently pronounced in the senate with the eulogy of polished eloquence. No one can look back upon his career without feeling that Toussaint was a remarkable man. Without being bred to the science of arms, he became a valiant soldier, and baffled the skill of the most experienced generals that had followed Napoleon. Without military knowledge he fought like one born in the camp. Without means he carried on the war. He beat his enemies in battle, and turned their own weapons against them. He laid the foundation for the emancipation of his race and the independence of the island. From ignorance he became educated by his own exertions. From a slave he rose to be a soldier, a general, and a governor, and might have been king of St. Domingo. He possessed splendid traits of genius, which was developed in the private circle, in the council chamber, and on the field of battle. His very name became a tower of strength to his friends and a terror to his foes. Toussaint's career as a Christian, a statesman, and a general, will lose nothing by a comparison with that of Washington. Each was the leader of an oppressed and outraged people, each had a powerful enemy to contend with, and each succeeded in founding a government in the new world. Toussaint's government made liberty its watchword, incorporated it in its constitution, abolished the slave trade, and made freedom universal amongst the people. Washington's government incorporated slavery and the slave trade, and enacted laws by which chains were fastened upon the limbs of millions of people. Toussaint liberated his countrymen; Washington enslaved a portion of his. When impartial history shall do justice to the St. Domingo revolution, the name of Toussaint L'Ouverture will be placed high upon the roll of fame.

CRISPUS ATTUCKS.

THE principle that taxation and representation were inseparable was in accordance with the theory, the genius, and the precedents of British legislation; and this principle was now, for the first time, intentionally invaded. The American colonies were not represented in Parliament; yet an act was passed by that body, the tendency of which was to invalidate all right and title to their property. This was the "Stamp Act," of March 23, 1765, which ordained that no sale, bond, note of hand, or other instrument of writing should be valid unless executed on paper bearing the stamp prescribed by the home government. The intelligence of the passage of the stamp act at once roused the indignation of the liberty-loving portion of the people of the colonies, and meetings were held at various points to protest against this high-handed measure. Massachusetts was the first to take a stand in opposition to the mother country. The merchants and traders of Boston, New York, and Philadelphia entered into non-importation agreements, with a view of obtaining a repeal of the obnoxious law. Under the pressure of public sentiment, the stamp act officers gave in their resignations. The eloquence of William Pitt and the sagacity of Lord Camden brought about a repeal of the stamp act in the British

Parliament. A new ministry, in 1767, succeeded in getting through the House of Commons a bill to tax the tea imported into the American colonies, and it received the royal assent. Massachusetts again took the lead in opposing the execution of this last act, and Boston began planning to take the most conspicuous part in the great drama. The agitation in the colonies provoked the home government, and power was given to the governor of Massachusetts to take notice of all persons who might offer any treasonable objections to these oppressive enactments, that the same might be sent home to England to be tried there. Lord North was now at the head of affairs, and no leniency was to be shown to the colonies. The concentration of British troops in large numbers at Boston convinced the people that their liberties were at stake, and they began to rally. A crowded and enthusiastic meeting, held in Boston in the latter part of the year 1769, was addressed by the ablest talent that the progressive element could produce. Standing in the back part of the hall, eagerly listening to the speakers, was a dark mulatto man, very tall, rather good looking, and apparently about fifty years of age. This was Crispus Attucks. Though taking no part in the meeting, he was nevertheless destined to be conspicuous in the first struggle in throwing off the British yoke. Twenty years previous to this, Attucks was the slave of William Brouno, Esq., of Framingham, Mass.; but his was a heart beating for freedom, and not to be kept in the chains of mental or bodily servitude.

From the Boston Gazette of Tuesday, November 20, 1750, now in the possession of William C. Nell, Esq., I copy the following advertisement:—

"Ran away from his master William Brouno Framingham, on the 30th of Sept., last, a Molatto Fellow, about 27 years of Age named Crispus, well set, six feet 2 inches high, short curl'd Hair, knees nearer together than common; had on a light coloured Bearskin Coat, brown Fustian jacket, new Buckskin Breeches, blew yarn Stockins and Checkered Shirt. Whoever shall take up said Run-away, and convey him to his above said Master at Framingham, shall have Ten Pounds, old Tenor Reward and all necessary Charges paid."

The above is a verbatim et literatim advertisement for a runaway slave one hundred and twelve years ago. Whether Mr.

Brouno succeeded in recapturing Crispus or not, we are left in the dark.

Ill-feeling between the mother country and her colonial subjects had been gaining ground, while British troops were concentrating at Boston. On the 5th of March, 1770, the people were seen early congregating at the corners of the principal streets, at Dock Square, and near the custom house. Captain Preston, with a body of redcoats, started out for the purpose of keeping order in the disaffected town, and was hissed at by the crowds in nearly every place where he appeared. The day passed off without any outward manifestation of disturbance, but all seemed to feel that something would take place after nightfall. The doubling of the guard in and about the custom house showed that the authorities felt an insecurity that they did not care to express. The lamps in Dock Square threw their light in the angry faces of a large crowd who appeared to be waiting for the crisis, in whatever form it should come. A part of Captain Preston's company was making its way from the custom house, when they were met by the crowd from Dock Square, headed by the black man Attucks, who was urging them to meet the redcoats, and drive them from the streets. "These rebels have no business here," said he; "let's drive them away." The people became enthusiastic, their brave leader grew more daring in his language and attitude, while the soldiers under Captain Preston appeared to give way. "Come on! don't be afraid!" cried Attucks. "They dare not shoot; and if they dare, let them do it." Stones and sticks, with which the populace was armed, were freely used, to the great discomfiture of the English soldiers. "Don't hesitate! come on! We'll drive these rebels out of Boston," were the last words heard from the lips of the colored man, for the sharp crack of muskets silenced his voice, and he fell weltering in his blood. Two balls had pierced his sable breast. Thus died Crispus Attucks, the first martyr to American liberty, and the inaugurator of the revolution that was destined to take from the crown of George the Third its brightest star. An immense concourse of citizens followed the remains of the hero to its last resting place, and his name was honorably mentioned in the best circles. The last words, the daring, and the death of Attucks gave spirit and enthusiasm to the revolution, and his heroism was imitated by both whites and blacks. His name was a rallying cry for the brave colored men who fought at the battle of Bunker's Hill. In the gallant defence of Redbank, where four hundred blacks met and defeated fifteen hundred Hessians headed by Count Donop, the thought of Attucks filled them with ardor. When Colonel Greene fell at Groton, surrounded by his black troops who perished with him, they went into the battle feeling proud of the opportunity of imitating the first martyr of the American revolution.

No monument has yet been erected to him. An effort was made in the legislature of Massachusetts a few years since, but without success. Five generations of accumulated prejudice against the negro had excluded from the American mind all inclination to do justice to one of her bravest sons. When negro slavery shall be abolished in our land, then we may hope to see a monument raised to commemorate the heroism of Crispus Attucks.

DESSALINES.

JEAN JACQUES DESSALINES was a native of Africa. Brought to St. Domingo at the age of sixteen, he was sold to a black man named Dessalines, from whom he took his own. His master was a tiler or house-shingler, and the slave learned that trade, at which he worked until the breaking out of the revolution of 1789, when he entered the army as a common soldier, under Toussaint. By his activity and singular fierceness on the field of battle, Dessalines attracted the attention of his general, who placed him among his guides and personal attendants; and he was subsequently rapidly advanced through several intermediate grades to the dignity of being the third in command. He was entirely ignorant of learning, as the utmost extent that he ever acquired was to sign his name. Dessalines was short in stature, but stout and muscular. His complexion was a dingy black; his eyes were prominent and scowling, and the lines of his features expressed the untamed ferocity of his character.

He had a haughty and disdainful look. Hunger, thirst, fatigue, and loss of sleep he seemed made to endure as if by peculiarity of constitution. He bore upon his arms and breast the marks of his tribe. Inured by exposure and toil to a hard life, his frame possessed a wonderful power of endurance. He was a bold and turbulent spirit, whose barbarous eloquence lay in expressive signs rather than in words. What is most strange in the history of Dessalines is, that he was a savage, a slave, a soldier, a general, and died, when an emperor, under the dagger of a Brutus.

A more courageous man than he never lived. Fearing that his men, during the attack upon the fort at Crete-a-Pierrot, would surrender it, he seized a torch, held it to the door of the magazine, and threatened to blow up the fort, and himself with it, if they did not defend it. Nearly all historians have set him down as a bloodthirsty monster, who delighted in the sufferings of his fellow-creatures. They do not rightly consider the circumstances that surrounded him, and the foe that he had to deal with.

Rochambeau, the commanding general, from the landing of Napoleon's expedition to the entire expulsion of the French, was a hard-hearted slaveholder, many of whose years had been spent in St. Domingo, and who, from the moment that he landed with his forces, treated the colored men as the worst of barbarians and wild beasts. He imported bloodhounds from Cuba to hunt them down in the mountains. When caught, he had them thrown into burning pits and boiling caldrons. When he took prisoners, he put them to the most excruciating tortures and the most horrible deaths. His ferocious and sanguinary spirit was too much for the kind heart of Toussaint, or the gentlemanly bearing of Christophe. His only match was Dessalines.

In a battle near Cape François, Rochambeau took five hundred black prisoners, and put them all to death the same day. Dessalines, hearing of this, brought five hundred white prisoners in sight of the French, and hung them up, so that the cruel monster could see the result of his own barbarous example.

Although Toussaint was away from the island, the war seemed to rage with greater fury than at any former period. The blacks grew wild as they looked upon the flames; they became conscious of their power and success; gaining confidence and increasing their numbers, all the pent-up feelings and hatred of years burst forth, and they pushed forward upon defenceless men, women, and children. The proud, haughty, and self-sufficient planter, who had been permitted, under the mild rule of Toussaint, to return and establish himself on his former estate, had to give way again to the terrible realities which came upon him.

The fertile plains that were in the highest state of cultivation, the lively green of the sugar-cane that filled the landscape through boundless fields, and the plantations of indigo and coffee, with all their beautiful hues of vegetation, were destroyed by the flames and smoke which spread every where. Dessalines was the commander-in-chief in fact, though he shared the name with Christophe and Clervaux. Forty thousand French troops had already perished by yellow fever and the sword. Leclerc, the captain-general of the island, lay sick, the hospitals were filled, and the blacks had possession of nearly all the towns.

Twenty thousand fresh troops arrived from France, but they were not destined to see Leclerc, for the yellow fever had taken him off. In the mountains were many barbarous and wild blacks, who had escaped from slavery soon after being brought from the coast of Africa. One of these bands of savages was commanded by Lamour de Rance, an adroit, stern, savage man, half naked, with epaulets tied to his bare shoulders for his only token of authority. This man had been brought from the coast of Africa, and sold as a slave in Port au Prince. On being ordered one day to saddle his master's horse, he did so, then mounted the animal, fled to the mountains, and ever after made those fearful regions his home. Lamour passed from mountain to mountain with something of the ease of the birds of his own native land. Toussaint, Christophe, and Dessalines, had each in their turn pursued him, but in vain. His mode of fighting was in keeping with his dress. This savage united with others like himself, and became complete master of the wilds of St. Domingo. They came forth from their mountain homes, and made war on the whites wherever they found them. Rochambeau, surrounded on all sides, drew his army together for defence rather than aggression. Reduced to the last extremity by starvation, the French general sued for peace, and promised that he would immediately leave the island. It was accepted by the blacks, and Rochambeau prepared to return to France. The French embarked in their vessels of war, and the standard of the blacks once more waved over Cape City, the capital of St. Domingo. As the French sailed from the island, they saw the tops of the mountains lighted up. It was not a blaze kindled for war, but for freedom. Every heart beat for liberty, and every voice shouted for joy. From the ocean to the mountains, and from town to town, the cry was, Freedom! Freedom! Thus ended Napoleon's expedition to St. Domingo. In less than two years the French lost more than fifty thousand persons. After the retirement of the whites, the men of color put forth a Declaration of Independence, in which they said, "We have sworn to show no mercy to those who may dare to speak to us of slavery."

The bravery and military skill which Dessalines had exhibited after the capture of Toussaint, the bold, resolute manner in which he had expelled the whites from the island, naturally pointed him out as the future ruler of St. Domingo. After serving a short time as president, Dessalines assumed the dignity of emperor, and changed the name of the island to that of Hayti.

The population of Hayti had been very much thinned by the ravages of war, and Dessalines, for the purpose of aiding those of his race, who had been taken away by force, to return, offered large rewards to captains of vessels for any that they might bring back as passengers.

One of the charges against Dessalines is based upon the fact that he changed his government from a republic to an empire. But we must consider that the people of Hayti had always lived under a monarchy, and were wedded to that kind of government. Had Toussaint allowed himself to be made a king, his power would have been recognized by Great Britain, and he would never have yielded to the solicitations of Leclerc, when that general's fleet landed on the island. Napoleon had just been crowned emperor of France, and it was not at all surprising that Dessalines should feel inclined to imitate the conqueror of Egypt.

The empire of Hayti was composed of six military divisions, each to be under the command of a general officer, who was independent of his associates who governed in other districts, as he was responsible to the head of the state alone. The supreme power was formally conferred upon Jean Jacques Dessalines, the avenger and liberator of his countrymen, who was to take the title of Emperor and Commander-in-chief of the Army, and to be addressed by the appellation of His Majesty—a dignity which was also conferred upon the empress, his wife, and the persons of both were declared inviolable. The crown was elective, but the power was conferred upon the reigning emperor to select and appoint his successor, by a nomination which required the sanction of the people to give it validity. The emperor was empowered to make the laws to govern the empire, and to promulgate them under his seal; to appoint all the functionaries of the state, and remove them at his will; to hold the purse of the nation; to make peace and war, and in all things to exercise the rights and privileges of an absolute sovereign. The monarch was assisted in wielding this mighty authority by a council of state, composed of generals of division and brigade. No peculiar faith in religion was established by law, and toleration was extended to the doctrines and worship of all sects. Surrounded by all the luxuries that wealth could procure, he was distinguished for the Roman virtues of abstinence and energy. Scorning effeminacy, he seemed ambitious to inure himself to the most laborious exercise and to the simplest mode of living. Dessalines was well schooled in the toils and labors of the camp. As his life was made up of extremes, so in his habits and personal endurances were seen great contrasts. Impetuosity and rapid movement were among his chief characteristics. He prided himself on his being able to surprise his enemies and taking them unprepared. Indeed, this was a leading trait in his military character, and places him alongside of Napoleon, or any other general, ancient or modern. As time smooths over his footsteps, and wears out the blood that marked his course, the circumstances attending it will, no doubt, be made to extenuate some of his many faults, and magnify his virtues as a general, a ruler, and a man.

The empress was a woman of rare beauty, and had some education, talent, and refinement. Her humanity caused her to restrain her husband, upon many occasions, from acts of cruelty. Though uneducated, Dessalines was not ignorant even of the classics, for he kept three secretaries, who, by turns, read to him.

As soon as he came into power, the emperor exerted every nerve to fortify the island, and to make it strong in the time of need. Much has been said of the cruelty of this man, and far be it from me to apologize for his acts. Yet, to judge rightly of him, we must remember that he had an ignorant people to govern, on the one hand, and the former planters to watch and control on the other. This latter class was scattered all over Europe and the United States, and they lost no opportunity to poison the minds of the whites against Dessalines and his government. He discovered many plots of the old white planters to assassinate him, and this drew out the ferociousness of his disposition, and made him cruel in the extreme. That he caused the death of innocent persons, there is not the slightest doubt; but that such a man as he was needed at the time, all must admit. Had Dessalines been in the place of Toussaint, he would never have been transferred from Hayti to France. Unlimited power, conferred upon him, together with the opposition of the whites in all countries, made him cruel even to his own race, and they looked forward with a degree of hope to his removal. The mulattoes, against whom he had never ceased to war, were ever watchful for an opportunity to take his life. A secret conspiracy was accordingly planned by this class, and on the 17th of October, 1806, while Dessalines was on a journey from St. Marks to Port au Prince, a party in ambuscade fired at him, and he fell dead.

Hayti had much improved under his management, especially in agriculture. The towns, many of them, had been rebuilt, commerce extended, and the arts patronized. Military talents have been ascribed to Dessalines even superior to Toussaint. He certainly had great courage, but upon the battle field it seemed to be the headlong fury of the tiger rather than the calm deliberation of L'Ouverture. Of all the heroic men which the boiling caldron of the St. Domingo revolution threw upon its surface, for the purpose of meeting the tyrannical whites, of bringing down upon them terrible retribution for their long and cruel reign, and of vindicating the rights of the oppressed in that unfortunate island, the foremost place belongs to the

African, the savage, the soldier, the general, the president, and lastly the emperor Jean Jacques Dessalines.

IRA ALDRIDGE.

On looking over the columns of *The Times*, one morning, I saw it announced under the head of "Amusements," that "Ira Aldridge, the African Roscius," was to appear in the character of Othello, in Shakspeare's celebrated tragedy of that name, and, having long wished to see my sable countryman, I resolved at once to attend. Though the doors had been open but a short time when I reached the Royal Haymarket, the theatre where the performance was to take place, the house was well filled, and among the audience I recognized the faces of several distinguished persons of the nobility, the most noted of whom was Sir Edward Bulwer Lytton, the renowned novelist—his figure neat, trim, hair done up in the latest fashion—looking as if he had just come out of a band-box. He is a great lover of the drama, and has a private theatre at one of his country seats, to which he often invites his friends, and presses them into the different characters.

As the time approached for the curtain to rise, it was evident that the house was to be "jammed." Stuart, the best Iago since the days of Young, in company with Roderigo, came upon the stage as soon as the green curtain went up. Iago looked the villain, and acted it to the highest conception of the character. The scene is changed, all eyes are turned to the right door, and thunders of applause greet the appearance of Othello. Mr. Aldridge is of the middle size, and appeared to be about three quarters African; has a pleasant countenance, frame well knit, and seemed to me the best Othello that I had ever seen. As Iago began to work upon his feelings, the Moor's eyes flashed fire, and, further on in the play, he looked the very demon of despair. When he seized the deceiver by the throat, and exclaimed, "Villain! be sure thou prove my love false: be sure of it—give me the ocular proof—or, by the worth of my eternal soul, thou hadst better have been born a dog, Iago, than answer my waked wrath," the audience, with one impulse, rose to their feet amid the wildest enthusiasm. At the end of the third act, Othello was called before the curtain, and received the applause of the delighted multitude. I watched the countenance and every motion of Bulwer Lytton with almost as much interest as I did that of the Moor of Venice, and saw that none appeared to be better pleased than he. The following evening I went to witness his Hamlet, and was surprised to find him as perfect in that as he had been in Othello; for I had been led to believe that the latter was his greatest character. The whole court of Denmark was before us; but till the words, "'Tis not alone my inky cloak, good mother," fell from the lips of Mr. Aldridge, was the general ear charmed, or the general tongue arrested. The voice was so low, and sad, and sweet, the modulation so tender, the dignity so natural, the grace so consummate, that all yielded themselves silently to the delicious enchantment. When Horatio told him that he had come to see his father's funeral, the deep melancholy that took possession of his face showed the great dramatic power of Mr. Aldridge. "I pray thee do not mock me, fellow-student," seemed to come from his inmost soul. The animation with which his countenance was lighted up, during Horatio's recital of the visits that the ghost had paid him and his companions, was beyond description. "Angels and ministers of grace defend us," as the ghost appeared in the fourth scene, sent a thrill through the whole assembly. His rendering of the "Soliloquy on Death," which Edmund Kean, Charles Kemble, and William C. Macready have reaped such unfading laurels from, was one of his best efforts. He read it infinitely better than Charles Kean, whom I had heard at the "Princess," but a few nights previous. The vigorous starts of thought, which in the midst of his personal sorrows rise with such beautiful and striking suddenness from the ever-wakeful mind of the humanitarian philosopher, are delivered with that varying emphasis that characterizes the truthful delineator, when he exclaims, "Frailty, thy name is woman!" In the second scene of the second act, when revealing to Guildenstern the melancholy which preys upon his mind, the beautiful and powerful words in which Hamlet explains his feelings are made very effective in Mr. Aldridge's rendering: "This most excellent canopy, the air, the brave o'erhanging firmament, this majestical roof fretted with golden fire. . . . What a piece of work is a man! How noble in reason! how infinite in faculties! in form and moving how express and admirable! in action how like an angel! in apprehension how like a God!" In the last scene of the second act, when Hamlet's imagination, influenced by the interview with the actors, suggests to his rich mind so many eloquent reflections, Mr. Aldridge enters fully into the spirit of the scene, warms up, and when he exclaims, "He would drown the stage with tears, and cleave the general ear with horrid speech,—make mad the guilty, and appall the free," he is very effective; and when this warmth mounts into a paroxysm of rage, and he calls the King "Bloody, bawdy villain! Remorseless, treacherous, lecherous, kindless villain!" he sweeps the audience with him, and brings down deserved applause. The fervent soul and restless imagination, which are ever stirring at the bottom of the fountain, and sending bright bubbles to the top, find a glowing reflection on the animated surface of Mr. Aldridge's colored face. I thought Hamlet one of his best characters, though I saw him afterwards in several others.

Mr. Aldridge is a native of Senegal, in Africa. His forefathers were princes of the Foulah tribe, whose dominions were in Senegal, on the banks of the river of that name, on the west coast of Africa. To this shore one of our early missionaries found his way, and took charge of Ira's father, Daniel Aldridge, in order to qualify him for the work of civilizing and evangelizing his countrymen. Daniel's father, the reigning prince, was more enlightened than his subjects, probably through the instruction of the missionary, and proposed that his prisoners taken in battle should be exchanged, and not, as was the custom, sold as slaves. This wish interfered with the notions and perquisites of his tribe, especially his principal chiefs; and a civil war raged among the people. During these differences, Daniel, then a promising youth, was brought to the United States by the missionary, and sent to Schenectady College to receive the advantages of a Christian education. Three days after his departure, the revolutionary storm, which was brewing, broke out openly, and the reigning prince, the advocate of humanity, was killed.

Daniel Aldridge remained in America till the death of the rebellious chief, who had headed the conspiracy, and reigned instead of the murdered prince. During the interval, Daniel had become a minister of the gospel, and was regarded by all classes as a man of uncommon abilities. He was, however, desirous to establish himself at the head of his tribe, possess himself of his birthright, and advance the cause of Christianity among his countrymen. For this purpose he returned to his native country, taking with him a young wife, one of his own color, whom he had but just married in America. Daniel no sooner appeared among the people of his slaughtered father, than old disagreements revived, civil war broke out, the enlightened African was defeated, barely escaping from the scene of strife with his life, and for some time unable to quit the country, which was watched by numerous enemies anxious for his capture. Nine years elapsed before the proscribed family escaped to America, during the whole of which time they were concealed in the neighborhood of their foes, enduring vicissitudes and hardships that can well be imagined, but need not be described.

Ira Aldridge was born soon after his father's arrival in Senegal, and on their return to America, was intended by the latter for the church. Many a white parent has "chalked out" in vain for his son a similar calling, and the best intentions have been thwarted by an early predilection quite in an opposite direction. We can well account for the father's choice in this instance, as in keeping with his own aspirations; and we can easily imagine his disappointment upon abandoning all hope of seeing one of his blood and color following specially in the service of his great Master. The son, however, began betimes to show his early preference and ultimate passion. At school he was awarded prizes for declamation, in which he excelled; and there his curiosity was excited by what he heard of theatrical representations, which he was told *embodied* all the fine ideas *shadowed forth* in the language he read and committed to memory. It became the wish of his heart to witness one of these performances, and that wish he soon contrived to gratify, and finally he became a candidate for histrionic fame.

Notwithstanding the progress Ira had made in learning, no

qualities of the mind could compensate, in the eyes of the Americans, for the dark hue of his skin. The prevailing prejudice, so strong among all classes, was against him. This induced his removal to England, where he entered at the Glasgow University, and, under Professor Sandford, obtained several premiums, and the medal for Latin composition.

On leaving college, Mr. Aldridge at once commenced preparing for the stage, and shortly after appeared in a number of Shaksperian characters, in Edinburgh, Glasgow, Manchester, and other provincial cities, and soon after appeared on the boards of Drury Lane and Covent Garden, where he was stamped the "African Roscius." The *London Weekly Times* said of him, "Mr. Ira Aldridge is a dark mulatto, with woolly hair. His features are capable of great expression, his action is unrestrained and picturesque, and his voice clear, full, and resonant. His powers of energetic declamation are very marked, and the whole of his acting appears impulsed by a current of feeling of no inconsiderable weight and vigor, yet controlled and guided in a manner that clearly shows the actor to be a person of much study and great stage ability." The *Morning Chronicle* recorded his "Shylock" as among the "finest pieces of acting that a London audience had witnessed since the days of the elder Kean."

JOSEPH CINQUE.

In the month of August, 1839, there appeared in the newspapers a shocking story—that a schooner, going coastwise from Havana to Neuvitas, in the island of Cuba, early in July, with about twenty white passengers, and a large number of slaves, had been seized by the slaves in the night time, and the passengers and crew all murdered except two, who made their escape to land in an open boat. About the 20th of the same month, a strange craft was seen repeatedly on our coast, which was believed to be the captured Spanish coaster, in the possession of the negroes. She was spoken by several pilot-boats and other vessels, and partially supplied with water, of which she was very much in want. It was also said that the blacks appeared to have a great deal of money. The custom-house department and the officers of the navy were instantly roused to go in pursuit of the "pirates," as the unknown possessors of the schooner were spontaneously called. The United States steamer Fulton, and several revenue cutters were despatched, and notice given to the collectors at the various seaports. On the 10th of August, the "mysterious schooner" was near the shore at Culloden Point, on the east end of Long Island, where a part of the crew came on shore for water and fresh provisions, for which they paid with undiscriminating profuseness. Here they were met by Captain Green and another gentleman, who stated that they had in their possession a large box filled with gold. Shortly after, on the 26th, the vessel was espied by Captain Gedney, U. S. N., in command of the brig Washington, employed on the coast survey, who despatched an officer to board her. The officer found a large number of negroes, and two Spaniards, Pedro Montez and Jose Ruiz, one of whom immediately announced himself as the owner of the negroes, and claimed his protection. The schooner was thereupon taken possession of by Captain Gedney.

The leader of the blacks was pointed out by the Spaniards, and his name given as Joseph Cinque. He was a native of Africa, and one of the finest specimens of his race ever seen in this country. As soon as he saw that the vessel was in the hands of others, and all hope of his taking himself and countrymen back to their home land at an end, he leaped overboard with the agility of an antelope. The small boat was immediately sent after him, and for two hours did the sailors strive to capture him before they succeeded. Cinque swam and dived like an otter, first upon his back, then upon his breast, sometimes his head out of water, and sometimes his heels out. His countrymen on board the captured schooner seemed much amused at the chase, for they knew Cinque well, and felt proud of the untamableness of his nature. After baffling them for a time, he swam towards the vessel, was taken on board, and secured with the rest of the blacks, and they were taken into New London, Connecticut.

The schooner proved to be the "Amistad," Captain Ramon Ferrer, from Havana, bound to Principe, about one hundred leagues distant, with fifty-four negroes held as slaves, and *two* passengers instead of twenty. The Spaniards said that, after being out four days, the negroes rose in the night, and killed the captain and a mulatto cook; that the helmsman and another sailor took to the boat and went on shore; that the only two whites remaining were the said passengers, Montez and Ruiz, who were confined below until morning; that Montez, the elder, who had been a sea captain, was required to steer the ship for Africa; that he steered eastwardly in the day time, because the negroes could tell his course by the sun, but put the vessel about in the night. They boxed about some days in the Bahama Channel, and were several times near the islands, but the negroes would not allow her to enter any port. Once they were near Long Island, but then put out to sea again, the Spaniards all the while hoping they might fall in with some ship of war that would rescue them from their awkward situation. One of the Spaniards testified that, when the rising took place, he was awaked by the noise, and that he heard the captain order the cabin boy to get some bread and throw to the negroes, in hope to pacify them. Cinque, however, the leader of the revolt, leaped on deck, seized a capstan bar, and attacked the captain, whom he killed at a single blow, and took charge of the vessel; his authority being acknowledged by his companions, who knew him as a prince in his native land.

The captives were taken before the Circuit Court of the United States for the District of Connecticut, Hon. Andrew T. Judson presiding. This was only the commencement in the courts, for the trial ran through several months. During this time, the Africans were provided with competent teachers by the abolitionists, and their minds were undergoing a rapid change, and civilization was taking the place of ignorance and barbarism.

Cinque, all this while, did nothing to change the high opinion first formed of him, and all those who came into his presence felt themselves before a superior man. After he and his countrymen had embraced Christianity, and were being questioned by a peace man as to the part that they had taken in the death of the men on board the Amistad, when asked if they did not think it wrong to take human life, one of the Africans replied that, if it was to be acted over again, he would pray for them instead of killing them. Cinque, hearing this, smiled and shook his head, whereupon he was asked if he would not pray for them also. To this he said, "Yes, I would pray for 'em, an' kill 'em too."

By the sagacity and daring of this man, he and his companions, fifty-four in number, were rescued from a life-long bondage of the worst character that ever afflicted the human family.

Cinque was a man of great intelligence and natural ability; he was a powerful orator, and although speaking in a tongue foreign to his audience, by the grace and energy of his motions and attitudes, the changeful expression of his features, and the intonations of his voice, made them understand the main incidents of his narrative, and swayed their minds in an extraordinary manner. Alluding to that point of his history at which Cinque described how, when on board the Spanish vessel, he, with the help of a nail, first relieved himself of his manacles, then assisted his countrymen to get rid of theirs, and then led them to the attack of the Spaniards, Lewis Tappan, in the account of the whole proceedings connected with the Amistad captives, which he published, says, "It is not in my power to give an adequate description of Cinque when he showed how he did this, and led his comrades to the conflict, and achieved their freedom. In my younger years I have seen Kemble and Siddons, and the representation of 'Othello,' at Covent Garden; but no acting that I have ever witnessed came near that to which I allude."

ALEXANDRE DUMAS.

I HAD been in Paris a week without seeing Dumas, for my letter of introduction from Louis Blanc, who was then in exile in England, to M. Eugene Sue, had availed me nothing as regarded a sight of the great colored author. Sue had promised me that I should have an interview with Dumas before I quitted the French capital; but I had begun to suspect that the latter felt that it would be too much of a condescension to give audience to an American slave, and I began to grow indifferent myself upon the matter. Invited by a friend to attend the opera, to witness the performances of Grisi and Mario, in Norma, I gladly accepted, and in company with my friend started for the place of amusement. Our seats were "reserved," and I took my place in the immense saloon before raising my eyes to view the vast audience which had already assembled. The splendid chandeliers, the hundreds of brilliant gas lights, the highly-colored drapery that hung its rich folds about the boxes and stalls, were in keeping with the magnificent diamonds, laces, and jewelry, that adorned the persons of the finest assembly that I had ever seen. In a double box nearly opposite to me, containing a party of six or eight, I noticed a light-complexioned mulatto, apparently about fifty years of age,—curly hair, full face, dressed in a black coat, white vest, white kids,—who seemed to be the centre of attraction, not only in his own circle, but in others. Those in the pit looked up, those in the gallery looked down, while curtains were drawn aside at other boxes and stalls to get a sight at the colored man. So recently from America, where caste was so injurious to my race, I began to think that it was his woolly head that attracted attention, when I was informed that the mulatto before me was no less a person than Alexandre Dumas. Every move, look, and gesture of the celebrated romancer were watched in the closest manner by the audience. Even Mario appeared to feel that his part on the stage was of less importance than that of the colored man in the royal box. M. Dumas' grandfather was the Marquis de la Pailleterie, a wealthy planter of St. Domingo, while his grandmother was a negress from Congo. Rainsford makes honorable mention of the father of Dumas, in his *Black Empire*, as having served in the army in his own native island. Dumas' father served under Napoleon during the whole of his campaigns, and rose to high distinction. Once, when near Lisle, Dumas, with four men, attacked a post of fifty Austrians, killed six, and made sixteen prisoners. For a long time he commanded a legion of horse composed of blacks and mulattoes, who were the terror of their enemies. General Dumas was with the army which Napoleon sent over the Alps; Napoleon crossed it in June, Marshal Macdonald in December. The latter sent Dumas to say it was impossible to pass in the winter, when great avalanches of snow were falling down, threatening to destroy the army. Napoleon's reply to the messenger was, "Go and tell Marshal Macdonald, where one man can pass over, an army can pass over in single file. The order is not to be countermanded." The order was obeyed, though at the cost of many lives. One of the generals that made the pass was the black General Dumas, who ascended the St. Bernard, which was defended by a number of fortifications, took possession of the cannon, and immediately directed them against the enemy. At the conclusion of the wars, the father returned to his island home, and after his death, the son went to France destitute, where he obtained a situation as a writer. Here he cultivated his literary taste. His imaginative mind and unsurpassed energies began to develop themselves, which soon placed the young man in easy circumstances. Dumas is now sixty-three years of age, and has been a writer for the press thirty-eight years. During this time he has published more novels, plays, travels, and historical sketches than any other man that ever lived. It is well understood that he is not the author of all the works that appear under his name, but that young writers gain a living by working out the plots and situations that his fecund brain suggests. When the novel or the play is complete, Dumas gives it a revision, touches up the dialogue, dashes in here and there a spirited scene of his own, and then receives from the publisher an enormous sum. Undeniably a man of great genius, endowed with true fertility of imagination, and masterly power of expression, his influence has been great.

Such is the vivacity of his descriptions, such the *entrainement* of his narrative, such the boldness of his invention, such the point of his dialogue, and the rapidity of his incidents, so matchless often the felicity and skill of particular passages, that he always inflames the interest of the reader to the end. You may be angry with him, but you will confess that he is the opposite of tedious. Certainly no writer fills a more prominent place in the literature of his country; and none has exercised a more potent influence upon its recent development than this son of the negro general, Dumas. His novels are every where, and the enthusiasm with which his dramatic pieces were received has been of the most flattering character.

HENRI CHRISTOPHE.

HENRI CHRISTOPHE was a native of the island of New Grenada, where he was born a slave. He went to St. Domingo at the age of eighteen, and was employed as *maître d'hôtel* in the principal *café* at Cape François. From strength of natural genius, as well as from his occupying a station in life above the ordinary condition of his race, he acquired considerable knowledge of the prevailing manners and customs of the society of which he was a daily spectator. He was master of the French, English, and Spanish languages, and was thought to be the most polished gentleman of all of Toussaint's generals. Being six feet three inches in height, Christophe made an imposing appearance on horseback, on the field of battle, in his uniform. He had a majestic carriage, and an eye full of fire; and a braver man never lived. Though far inferior to Toussaint in vigor and originality of mind, he was much his superior in acquaintance with the customs and habits of the world, and appeared more dignified in his intercourse with society.

After the breaking out of the revolution, Christophe joined the army under Toussaint, who soon discovered his good qualities, and made him his lieutenant; from which position he was soon advanced to second in command. It has been asserted that he was an abler military man than either Toussaint or Dessalines. When Napoleon's expedition invaded St. Domingo, Leclerc, with the largest part of the squadron, came to anchor off Cape City, and summoned the place to surrender. The reply which he received from Christophe was such as to teach the captain-general what he had to expect in the subjugation of St. Domingo. "Go, tell your general that the French shall march here only over ashes, and that the ground shall burn beneath their feet," was the answer that Leclerc obtained in return to his command. The French general sent another messenger to Christophe, urging him to surrender, and promising the black chief a commission of high rank in the French army. But he found he had a man, and not a slave, to deal with. The exasperated Christophe sent back the heroic reply, "The decision of arms can admit you only into a city in ashes, and even on these ashes will I fight still."

After Toussaint had been captured and sent to France, and

Leclerc was disarming the colored population, and the decree of the 30th of April for maintaining slavery in St. Domingo had been put forth, Christophe followed the example of Clervaux, and went over to the insurgents, and met and defeated Rochambeau in one of the hardest fought battles of the campaign. He soon after shut the French commander up in Cape François, where the latter remained like a tiger driven to his den.

During the reign of Dessalines, Christophe lived partly retired, "biding his time;" for although the former had been made emperor, the latter was most beloved by all classes. The death of the emperor at once opened a way for Christophe, for a provisional government was then constituted, and the latter was proclaimed the head of the state. This was a virtual revolution, and Christophe regarded himself, by the provisional appointment, as the chief of the army, to govern ad interim, until a new government could be formed. But the mulattoes, who had long been in obscurity, rallied, got a majority in the convention, and elected Petion president of the republic of Hayti. Christophe collected together his adherents, and determined to take by conquest what he thought he had a right to by succession, and, as he thought, by merit. Failing in this, he set up another government in the north, with Cape François as its capital. Christophe felt that his assumption of power was but a usurpation, and that, so long as his government remained in operation without the formal sanction of the people, his rival at Port au Prince possessed immense advantage over him, inasmuch as he had been made the constituted head of the country by an observance of the forms of the constitution. To remedy this palpable defect, which weakened his authority, he resolved to frame another constitution, which would confirm him in the power he had taken, and furnish him with a legal excuse for maintaining his present attitude. In accordance with this policy, he convoked another assembly at Cape François, composed of the generals of his army and the principal citizens of that province, and after a short session the legislators terminated their labors by adopting another constitution, dated upon the 17th of February, 1809. This new enactment declared all persons residing upon the territory of Hayti free citizens, and that the government was to be administered by a supreme magistrate, who was to take the title of president of the state and general-in-chief of the land and naval forces. Thus firmly seated, Christophe felt himself more powerful, and more secure from outbreaks. Nevertheless, he was not destined to hold peaceable possession of all the territory in his district, for the inhabitants of many of the towns in the vicinity of Cape François openly threw off their allegiance, and proclaimed their preference for the more legitimate government of Petion. The two presidents prepared for war, and Christophe opened the campaign by marching an immense army against Gonaives, which, in the month of June, 1807, he invested. Petion's troops were defeated, and, to save themselves from capture, escaped by sea to Port au Prince. The war continued three years, when a new competitor appeared in the person of Rigaud, the other mulatto general. Christophe now ceased for a while; but when he felt that the time had arrived he again renewed the war, and, in 1810, captured the Mole St. Nicholas, the strongest fort on the island. Becoming ambitious to be a monarch, Christophe called his council together, and on the 20th of March, 1811, the session closed by adopting a new frame of government. The imperial constitution of 1805 was modified to form an hereditary monarchy in the north, and to place the crown of Hayti upon Christophe under the title of Henry the First. When he entered upon the kingly station that had been conferred upon him, his first act was to promulgate an edict creating an hereditary nobility, as a natural support of his government. These dignitaries of the kingdom were taken mostly from the army, the chiefs who had fought under him in the struggle against the French, and consisted of two princes, seven dukes, twenty-two counts, thirty-five barons, and fourteen chevaliers. His coronation was the most magnificent display ever witnessed out of Europe. To furnish himself with all the appointments correspondent to his royal dignity, he now began the erection of a palace, situated a few miles from the cape, upon which he had bestowed the historical name of Sans Souci. This palace has the reputation of being the most splendid edifice in the West Indies. The rugged, mountainous region in the vicinity of his royal residence was changed from its original condition to form the gardens of the palace. Hills were levelled with the plain, deep ravines were filled up, and roads and passages were opened, leading in all directions from the royal dwelling. The halls and saloons of the palace were wrought with mahogany, the floors were laid with rich marble, and numerous jets-d'eau furnished coolness and a supply of pure water to the different apartments. Christophe held a levee on the Thursday evening of each week, which was attended by the most fashionable of all classes, including the foreign ambassadors and consuls. The ceremonial observances were modelled after the drawing rooms at St. Cloud and St. James. Though of pure African blood, Christophe was not a jet black, his complexion being rather a dusky brown. His person had grown slightly corpulent, and his address was cold, polished, and graceful. He possessed a certain air of native dignity that corresponded well with his high official situation. The whites of all countries, and especially the English, formed a high opinion of his character. That part of the island which came within his rule had been well cultivated, his government out of debt, and commerce was in a flourishing condition.

The removal of Napoleon from the throne of France once more gave to the French planters residing in the mother country hope of again possessing their estates. A move was made in the court of Louis XVIII. to send another expedition to Hayti, to bring the colony back to her allegiance. On learning this, Christophe issued a proclamation, in which he said, "If we love the blessings of peace, we fear not the fatigues and horrors of war. Let our implacable enemies, the French colonists, who for twenty years have never ceased from their projects for the reëstablishment of slavery, and who have filled all the governments of the earth with their importunities,—let them put themselves at the head of armies, and direct themselves against our country. They will be the first victims of our vengeance, and the soil of liberty will eagerly drink the blood of our oppressors. We will show to the nations of the earth what a warlike people can accomplish, who are in arms for the best of causes—the defence of their homes, their wives, their children, their liberty, and their independence."

A despatch was next sent to Christophe, in which he was threatened with an invasion by all the forces of combined Europe in case of his refusal to submit himself to the will of France. This last threat, however, had no influence over the black monarch, for he felt that no European power would invade Hayti after the failure of the sixty thousand men sent out by Napoleon. Nothing was attempted by the French, and the king of Hayti was left in possession of his government. In the month of August, 1820, Christophe was attacked, while at mass, with a paralytic disease, and was immediately conveyed to Sans Souci, where he remained an invalid until a revolt occurred among his subjects. He ordered his war-horse, his sword was brought, and he attempted to mount his charger; but in vain. He gave up the attempt, retired to his chamber, locked the door, and the report of a pistol alarmed his attendants. They rushed in, but it was too late; Henri Christophe was no more.

Christophe's aims were great, and many of them good. He was not only the patron of the arts, but of industry; and it gave him pleasure to see his country recovering the ground lost in the revolution and the civil wars, and advancing in name and wealth. He promoted industry on the principles laid down by his predecessor, Toussaint. A busy population covered the land with marks of its labors. Rich crops of the most coveted produce of nature annually rewarded the toil of the husbandman. Christophe was also the patron of education; and there are still on the island schools that were founded by him when king. In one respect he excelled Charlemagne,—he could write his own name; but that was all. He dictated letters and despatches, and was an admirable judge of the fitness and relevancy of words. He kept up a correspondence with Wilberforce and Clarkson, the English philanthropists, and both of these distinguished men had a high opinion of him as a man, and a friend of his race.

PHILLIS WHEATLEY.

In the year 1761, when Boston had her slave market, and the descendants of the Pilgrims appeared to be the most pious and God-fearing people in the world, Mrs. John Wheatley went into the market one day, for the purpose of selecting and purchasing a girl for her own use. Among the group of children just imported from the African coast was a delicately built, rather good-looking child of seven or eight years, apparently suffering from the recent sea voyage and change of climate. Mrs. Wheatley's heart was touched at the interesting countenance and humble modesty of this little stranger. The lady bought the child, and she was named Phillis. Struck with the slave's uncommon brightness, the mistress determined to teach her to read, which she did with no difficulty. The child soon mastered the English language, with which she was totally unacquainted when she landed upon the American shores. Her school lessons were all perfect, and she drank in the scriptural teachings as if by intuition. At the age of twelve, she could write letters and keep up a correspondence that would have done honor to one double her years. Mrs. Wheatley, seeing her superior genius, no longer regarded Phillis as a servant, but took her as a companion. It was not surprising that the slave girl should be an object of attraction, astonishment, and attention with the refined and highly cultivated society that weekly assembled in the drawing room of the Wheatleys. As Phillis grew up to womanhood, her progress and attainments kept pace with the promise of her earlier years. She drew around her the best educated of the white ladies, and attracted the attention and notice of the literary characters of Boston, who supplied her with books and encouraged the ripening of her intellectual powers. She studied the Latin tongue, and translated one of Ovid's tales, which was no sooner put in print in America, than it was republished in London, with eloquent commendations from the reviews. In 1773, a small volume of her poems, containing thirty-nine pieces, was published in London, and dedicated to the Countess of Huntingdon. The genuineness of this work was established in the first page of the volume, by a document signed by the governor of Massachusetts, the lieutenant-governor, her master, and fifteen of the most respectable and influential citizens of Boston, who were acquainted with her talents and the circumstances of her life. Her constitution being naturally fragile, she was advised by her physician to take a sea voyage as the means of restoring her declining health.

Phillis was emancipated by her master at the age of twenty-one years, and sailed for England. On her arrival, she was received and admired in the first circles of London society; and it was at that time that her poems were collected and published in a volume, with a portrait and memoir of the authoress. Phillis returned to America, and married Dr. Peters, a man of her own color, and of considerable talents. Her health began rapidly to decline, and she died at the age of twenty-six years, in 1780. Fortunately rescued from the fate that awaits the victims of the slave trade, this injured daughter of Africa had an opportunity of developing the genius that God had given her, and of showing to the world the great wrong done to her race. The limited place allowed for this sketch will not permit of our giving more than one short poem from the pen of the gifted Phillis Wheatley.

ON THE DEATH OF A YOUNG GIRL.

From dark abodes to fair ethereal light,
The enraptured innocent has winged her flight;
On the kind bosom of eternal love
She finds unknown beatitudes above.
This know, ye parents, nor her loss deplore—
She feels the iron hand of pain no more;
The dispensations of unerring grace
Should turn your sorrows into grateful praise;
Let, then, no tears for her henceforward flow
Nor suffer grief in this dark vale below.

Her morning sun, which rose divinely bright,
Was quickly mantled with the gloom of night;
But hear, in heaven's best bowers, your child so fair,
And learn to imitate her language there.
Thou, Lord, whom I behold with glory crowned,
By what sweet name, and in what tuneful sound,
Wilt thou be praised? Seraphic powers are faint
Infinite love and majesty to paint.
To thee let all their grateful voices raise,
And saints and angels join their songs of praise

Perfect in bliss, now from her heavenly home
She looks, and, smiling, beckons you to come;
Why then, fond parents, why these fruitless groans?

Restrain your tears, and cease your plaintive moans.
Freed from a world of sin, and snares, and pain,
Why would ye wish your fair one back again?
Nay, bow resigned; let hope your grief control,
And check the rising tumult of the soul.
Calm in the prosperous and the adverse day,
Adore the God who gives and takes away;

See him in all, his holy name revere,
Upright your actions, and your hearts sincere,
Till, having sailed through life's tempestuous sea,
And from its rocks and boisterous billows free,
Yourselves, safe landed on the blissful shore,
Shall join your happy child to part no more.

DENMARK VESEY.

No class of persons in the world, who have the name of being free, are more sorely oppressed than the free colored people of the Southern States. Each state has its code of black laws, which are rigorously enforced, and the victim made to feel his degradation at all times and in all places. An undeveloped discontent pervades the entire black population, bond and free, in all the slave states. Human bondage is ever fruitful of insurrection, wherever it exists, and under whatever circumstances it may be found. Every community the other side of "Dixon's Line" feels that it lives upon a volcano that is liable to burst out at any moment; and all are watchful, and fearfully in earnest, in looking after the colored man's affairs, and inventing sterner enactments to keep him in subjection. The most oppressive of all the states is South Carolina. In Charleston, free colored ladies are not allowed to wear veils about their faces in the streets, or in any public places. A violation of this law is visited with "*thirty-nine lashes upon the bare back.*" The same is inflicted upon any free colored man who shall be seen upon the streets with a cigar in his mouth, or a walking stick in his hand. Both, when walking the streets, are forbidden to take the inside of the pavement. Punishment of fine and imprisonment is laid upon any found out after the hour of nine at night. An extra tax is placed upon every member of a free colored family. While all these odious edicts were silently borne by the free colored people of Charleston in 1822 there was a suppressed feeling of indignation, mortification, and discontent, that was only appreciated by a few. Among the most dissatisfied of the free blacks was Denmark Vesey, a man who had purchased his freedom in the year 1800, and since that time had earned his living by his trade, being a carpenter and joiner. Having been employed on shipboard by his master, Captain Vesey, Denmark had seen a great deal of the world, and had acquired a large fund of information, and was regarded as a leading man among the blacks. He had studied the Scriptures, and never lost an opportunity of showing that they were opposed to chattel-slavery. He spoke freely with the slaves upon the subject, and often with whites, where he found he could do so without risk to his own liberty. After resolving to incite the slaves to rebellion, he began taking into his confidence such persons as he could trust, and instructing them to gain adherents from among the more reliable of both bond and free. Peter Poyas, a slave of more than ordinary foresight and ability, was selected by Vesey as his lieutenant; and to him was committed the arduous duty of arranging the mode of attack, and of acting as the military leader.

"His plans showed some natural generalship; he arranged the night attack; he planned the enrolment of a mounted troop to scour the streets; and he had a list of all the shops where arms and ammunition were kept for sale. He voluntarily undertook the management of the most difficult part of the enterprise,—the capture of the main guard-house,—and had pledged himself to advance alone and surprise the sentinel. He was said to have a magnetism in his eye, of which his confederates stood in great awe; if he once got his eye upon a man, there was no resisting it."

Gullah Jack, Tom Russell, and Ned Bennett. The last two were not less valuable than Peter Poyas; for Tom was an ingenious mechanic, and made battle-axes, pikes, and other instruments of death, with which to carry on the war. All of the above were to be generals of brigades, and were let into all the secrets of the intended rising. It has long been the custom in

Charleston for the country slaves to visit the city in great numbers on Sunday, and return to their homes in time to commence work on the following morning. It was therefore determined by Denmark to have the rising take place on Sunday. The slaves of nearly every plantation in the vicinity were enlisted, and were to take part.

"The details of the plan, however, were not rashly committed to the mass of the confederates; they were known only to a few, and were finally to have been announced after the evening prayer-meeting on the appointed Sunday. But each leader had his own company enlisted, and his own work marked out. When the clock struck twelve, all were to move. Peter Poyas was to lead a party ordered to assemble at South Bay, and to be joined by a force from James's Island; he was then to march up and seize the arsenal and guard-house opposite St. Michael's Church, and detach a sufficient number to cut off all white citizens who should appear at the alarm posts. A second body of negroes, from the country and the Neck, headed by Ned Bennett, was to assemble on the Neck and seize the arsenal there. A third was to meet at Governor Bennett's Mills, under command of Rolla, another leader, and, after putting the governor and intendant to death, to march through the city, or be posted at Cannon's Bridge, thus preventing the inhabitants of Cannonsborough from entering the city. A fourth, partly from the country and partly from the neighboring localities in the city, was to rendezvous on Gadsden's Wharf and attack the upper guard-house. A fifth, composed of country and Neck negroes, was to assemble at Bulkley's farm, two miles and a half from the city, seize the upper powder magazine, and then march down; and a sixth was to assemble at Denmark Vesey's and obey his orders. A seventh detachment, under Gullah Jack, was to assemble in Boundary Street, at the head of King Street, to capture the arms of the Neck company of militia, and to take an additional supply from Mr. Duquercron's shop. The naval stores on Mey's Wharf were also to be attacked. Meanwhile a horse company, consisting of many draymen, hostlers, and butcher boys, was to meet at Lightwood's Alley, and then scour the streets to prevent the whites from assembling. Every white man coming out of his own door was to be killed, and, if necessary, the city was to be fired in several places—slow match for this purpose having been purloined from the public arsenal and placed in an accessible position."

The secret and plan of attack, however, were incautiously divulged to a slave named Devany, belonging to Colonel Prioleau, and he at once informed his master's family. The mayor, on getting possession of the facts, called the city council together for consultation. The investigation elicited nothing new, for the slaves persisted in their ignorance of the matter, and the authorities began to feel that they had been imposed upon by Devany and his informant, when another of the conspirators, being bribed, revealed what he knew. Arrests after arrests were made, and the Mayor's Court held daily examinations for weeks. After several weeks of incarceration, the accused, one hundred and twenty in number, were brought to trial: thirty-four were sentenced to transportation, twenty-seven acquitted by the court, twenty-five discharged without trial, and thirty-five condemned to death. With but two or three exceptions, all of the conspirators went to the gallows feeling that they had acted right, and died like men giving their lives for the cause of freedom. A report of the trial, written soon after, says of Denmark Vesey,—

"For several years before he disclosed his intentions to any one, he appears to have been constantly and assiduously engaged in endeavoring to embitter the minds of the colored population against the white. He rendered himself perfectly familiar with all those parts of the Scriptures which he thought he could pervert to his purpose, and would readily quote them to prove that slavery was contrary to the laws of God,—that slaves were bound to attempt their emancipation, however shocking and bloody might be the consequences,—and that such efforts would not only be pleasing to the Almighty, but were absolutely enjoined, and their success predicted, in the Scriptures. His favorite texts, when he addressed those of his own color, were Zechariah xiv. 1–3, and Joshua vi. 21; and in all his conversations he identified their situation with that of the Israelites. The number of inflammatory pamphlets on slavery brought into Charleston from some of our sister states within the last four years, (and once from Sierra Leone,) and distributed amongst the colored population of the city, for which there was a great facility, in consequence of the unrestricted intercourse allowed to persons of color between the different states in the Union, and the speeches in Congress of those opposed to the admission of Missouri into the Union, perhaps garbled and misrepresented, furnished him with ample means for inflaming the minds of the colored population of this state; and by distorting certain parts of those speeches, or selecting from them particular passages, he persuaded but too many that Congress had actually declared them free, and that they were held in bondage contrary to the laws of the land. Even whilst walking through the streets in company with another, he was not idle; for if his companion bowed to a white person, he would rebuke him, and observe that all men were born equal, and that he was surprised that any one would degrade himself by such conduct,—that he would never cringe to the whites, nor ought any one who had the feelings of a man. When answered, 'We are slaves,' he would sarcastically and indignantly reply, 'You deserve to remain slaves;' and if he were further asked, 'What can we do?' he would remark, 'Go and buy a spelling-book and read the fable of Hercules and the Wagoner,' which he would then repeat, and apply it to their situation. He also sought every opportunity of entering into conversation with white persons, when they could be overheard by negroes near by, especially in grog shops; during which conversation, he would artfully introduce some bold remark on slavery; and sometimes, when, from the character he was conversing with, he found he might be still bolder, he would go so far, that, had not his declarations in such situations been clearly proved, they would scarcely have been credited. He continued this course until some time after the commencement of the last winter; by which time he had not only obtained incredible influence amongst persons of color, but many feared him more than their owners, and, one of them declared, even more than his God."

The excitement which the revelations of the trial occasioned, and the continual fanning of the flame by the newspapers, were beyond description. Double guard in the city, the country patrol on horseback and on foot, the watchfulness that was observed on all plantations, showed the deep feeling of fear pervading the hearts of the slaveholders, not only in South

Carolina, but the fever extended to the other Southern States, and all seemed to feel that a great crisis had been passed. And indeed, their fears seem not to have been without ground, for a more complicated plan for an insurrection could scarcely have been conceived. And many were of opinion that, the rising once begun, they would have taken the city and held it, and might have sealed the fate of slavery in the south. The best account of this whole matter is to be found in an able article in the Atlantic Monthly for June, 1861, from the pen of that eloquent friend of freedom T. W. Higginson, and to which I am indebted for the extracts contained in this memoir of Denmark Vesey.

HENRY HIGHLAND GARNETT.

THOUGH born a slave in the State of Maryland, Henry Highland Garnett is the son of an African chief, stolen from the coast of his native land. His father's family were all held as slaves till 1822, when they escaped to the north. In 1835, he became a member of Canaan Academy, New Hampshire. Three months after entering the school, it was broken up by a mob, who destroyed the building. Mr. Garnett afterwards entered Oneida Institute, New York, under the charge of that noble-hearted friend of man, Beriah Green, where he was treated with equality by the professors and his fellow-students. There he gained the reputation of a courteous and accomplished man, an able and eloquent debater, and a good writer. His first appearance as a public speaker was in 1837, in the city of New York, where his speech at once secured for him a standing among first-class orators. Mr. Garnett is in every sense of the term a progressive man. He is a strenuous advocate of freedom, temperance, education, and the religious, moral, and social elevation of his race. He is an acceptable preacher, evangelical in his profession. His discourses, though showing much thought and careful study, are delivered extemporaneously, and with good effect. Having complete command of his voice, he uses it with skill, never failing to fill the largest hall. One of the most noted addresses ever given by a colored man in this country was delivered by Mr. Garnett at the National Convention of Colored Americans, at Buffalo, New York, in 1843. None but those who heard that speech have the slightest idea of the tremendous influence which he exercised over the assembly. He spent some years over a church at Troy, and another at Geneva, New York, and in 1850 visited England, where he remained, lecturing, in different sections of the United Kingdom, upon American slavery, until 1852, we believe, when, being joined by his family, he went as a missionary to Jamaica. After spending three years among the people of that island, he returned to the United States, and is now settled over Shiloh Church, New York city. Mr. Garnett is about forty-five years of age, unadulterated in race, tall and commanding in appearance, has an eye that looks through you, and a clear, ringing voice. He has written considerably, and has edited one or two journals at different times, devoted to the elevation of his race. The following from his pen will give but a faint idea of Mr. Garnett's powers as a writer:—

"The woful volume of our history, as it now lies open to the world, is written with tears and bound with blood. As I trace it, my eyes ache and my heart is filled with grief. No other people have suffered so much, and none have been more innocent. If I might apostrophize that bleeding country, I would say, O Africa, thou hast bled, freely bled, at every pore. Thy sorrow has been mocked, and thy grief has not been heeded. Thy children are scattered over the whole earth, and the great nations have been enriched by them. The wild beasts of thy forests are treated with more mercy than they. The Libyan lion and the fierce tiger are caged, to gratify the curiosity of men, and the keeper's hands are not laid heavily upon them. But thy children are tortured, taunted, and hurried out of life by unprecedented cruelty. Brave men, formed in the divinest mould, are bartered, sold, and mortgaged. Stripped of every sacred right, they are scourged if they affirm that they belong to God. Women, sustaining the dear relation of mothers, are yoked with the horned cattle to till the soil, and their heart-strings are torn to pieces by cruel separations from their children. Our sisters, ever manifesting the purest kindness, whether in the wilderness of their fatherland, or amid the sorrows of the middle passage, or in crowded cities, are unprotected from the lust of tyrants. They have a regard for virtue, and they possess a sense of honor; but there is no respect paid to these jewels of noble character. Driven into unwilling concubinage, their offspring are sold by their Anglo-Saxon fathers. To them the marriage institution is but a name, for their despoilers break down the hymeneal altar, and scatter its sacred ashes on the winds.

"Our young men are brutalized in intellect, and their manly energies are chilled by the frosts of slavery. Sometimes they are called to witness the agonies of the mothers who bore them, writhing under the lash; and as if to fill to overflowing the already full cup of demonism, they are sometimes compelled to apply the lash with their own hands. Hell itself cannot overmatch a deed like this; and dark damnation shudders as it sinks into its bosom, and seeks to hide itself from the indignant eye of God."

Mr. Garnett paid a second visit to England a few months since, for the purpose of creating an interest there in behalf of emigration to Central Africa.

JAMES M. WHITFIELD.

THERE has long resided in Buffalo, New York, a barber, noted for his scholarly attainments and gentlemanly deportment. Men of the most polished refinement visit his saloon, and, while being shaved, take pleasure in conversing with him; and all who know him feel that he was intended by nature for a higher position in life. This is James M. Whitfield. He is a native of Massachusetts, and removed west some years since. We give a single extract from one of his poems.

"How long, O gracious God, how long
Shall power lord it over right?
The feeble, trampled by the strong,
Remain in slavery's gloomy night?
In every region of the earth
Oppression rules with iron power;
And every man of sterling worth,
Whose soul disdains to cringe or cower

Beneath a haughty tyrant's nod,
And, supplicating, kiss the rod
That, wielded by oppression's might,
Smites to the earth his dearest right,—
The right to speak, and think, and feel,
  And spread his uttered thoughts abroad,
To labor for the common weal,
  Responsible to none but God,—
Is threatened with the dungeon's gloom,
The felon's cell, the traitor's doom,
And treacherous politicians league
  With hireling priests to crush and ban
All who expose their vain intrigue,
  And vindicate the rights of man.
How long shall Afric raise to thee
  Her fettered hand, O Lord, in vain,
And plead in fearful agony
  For vengeance for her children slain?
I see the Gambia's swelling flood,
  And Niger's darkly-rolling wave,
Bear on their bosoms, stained with blood,
  The bound and lacerated slave;
While numerous tribes spread near and far
Fierce, devastating, barbarous war,
Earth's fairest scenes in ruin laid,
To furnish victims for that trade
Which breeds on earth such deeds of shame,
As fiends might blush to hear or name."

Mr. Whitfield has written several long poems, all of them in good taste and excellent language.

ANDRE RIGAUD.

Slavery, in St. Domingo, created three classes—the white planters, the free mulattoes, and the slaves, the latter being all black. The revolution brought out several valiant chiefs among the mulattoes, their first being Vincent Ogé. This man was not calculated for a leader of rebellion. His mother having been enabled to support him in France as a gentleman, he had cherished a delicacy of sentiment very incompatible with the ferocity of revolt. But Andre Rigaud, their next and greatest chief, was a far different man. A native of Aux Cayes, educated at Bourdeaux, and afterwards spending some time at Paris, maturing his mind amid scenes of science and literature, Rigaud's position among his followers was an exalted one. His father was white and his mother black. He was tall and slim, with features beautifully defined. Nature had been profligate in bestowing her gifts upon him.

While at the Military School at Paris, besides being introduced into good society, he became acquainted with Lafayette, Condorcet, Gregoire, and other distinguished statesmen, and his manners were polished and his language elegant. In religion he was the very opposite of Toussaint. An admirer of Voltaire and Rousseau, he had made their works his study. A long residence in the French metropolis had enabled him to become acquainted with the followers of these two distinguished philosophers. He had seen two hundred thousand persons following the bones of Voltaire, when removed to the Pantheon, and, in his admiration for the great author, had confounded liberty with infidelity. In Asia, he would have governed an empire; in St. Domingo, he was scarcely more than an outlawed chief; but he had in his soul the elements of a great man. In military science, horsemanship, and activity, Rigaud was the first man on the island, of any color. Toussaint bears the following testimony to the great skill of the mulatto general: "I know Rigaud well. He leaps from his horse when at full gallop, and he puts all his force in his arm when he strikes a blow." He was high-tempered, irritable, and haughty. The charmed power that he held over the men of his color can scarcely be described. At the breaking out of the revolution, he headed the mulattoes in his native town, and soon drew around him a formidable body of men.

After driving the English and Spaniards from the island, and subduing the French planters, Toussaint and Rigaud made war upon each other. As the mulattoes were less than fifty thousand in number, and the blacks more than five hundred thousand, Rigaud was always outnumbered on the field of battle; but his forces, fighting under the eyes of the general whom they adored, defended their territory with vigor, if not with success. Reduced in his means of defence by the loss of so many brave men in his recent battles, Rigaud had the misfortune to see his towns fall, one after another, into the power of Toussaint, until he was driven to the last citadel of his strength—the town of Aux Cayes. As he thus yielded foot by foot, every thing was given to desolation before it was abandoned, and the land, which under his active government had just before been so adorned with cultivation, was made such a waste of desolation, that, according almost to the very letter of his orders, "the trees were turned with their roots in the air." The genius and activity of Toussaint were completely at fault in his attempt to force the mulatto general from his intrenchments.

The government of France was too much engaged at home with her own revolution to pay any attention to St. Domingo. The republicans in Paris, after getting rid of their enemies, turned upon each other. The revolution, like Saturn, devoured its own children; priest and people were murdered upon the thresholds of justice. Marat died at the hands of Charlotte Corday. Louis XVI. and Marie Antoinette were guillotined, Robespierre had gone to the scaffold, and Bonaparte was master of France.

The conqueror of Egypt now turned his attention to St. Domingo. It was too important an island to be lost to France or destroyed by civil war, and, through the mediation of Bonaparte, the war between Toussaint and Rigaud was brought to a close.

Petion and several other generals followed Rigaud, when, at the conclusion of his war with Toussaint, he embarked for France. When Napoleon's ill-fated expedition came to St. Domingo, Rigaud returned, made his appearance at Aux Cayes, and, under his influence, the south soon rallied in arms against Toussaint. He fought bravely for France until the subjugation of the blacks and the transportation of their chief to the mother country, when Napoleon felt that Rigaud, too, was as dangerous to the peace of St. Domingo as Toussaint, and he was once more forced to return to France. Here he was imprisoned—not for any thing that he had done against the government of Bonaparte, but for fear that the mulatto chief would return to his native island, take up arms, and assist his race, who were already in rebellion against Leclerc.

Although the whites and the free colored men were linked together by the tender ties of nature, there was, nevertheless, a hatred to each other, even stronger than between the whites and the blacks. In the earlier stages of the revolution, before the blacks under Toussaint got the ascendency, several attempts had been made to get rid of the leaders of the mulattoes, and especially Rigaud. He was hated by the whites in the same degree as they feared his all-powerful influence with his race, and the unyielding nature of his character, which gave firmness and consistency to his policy while controlling the interests of his brethren. Intrigue and craftiness could avail nothing against the designs of one who was ever upon the watch, and who had the means of counteracting all secret attempts against him; and open force, in the field, could not be successful in destroying a chieftain whose power was often felt, but whose person was seldom seen. Thus, to accomplish a design which had long been in meditation, the whites of Aux Cayes were now secretly preparing a mine for Rigaud, which, though it was covered with roses, and to be sprung by professed friends, it was thought would prove a sure and efficacious method of ridding them of such an opponent, and destroying the pretensions of the mulattoes forever. It was proposed that the anniversary of the destruction of the Bastile should be celebrated in the town by both whites and mulattoes, in union and gratitude. A civic procession marched to the church, where Te Deum was chanted and an oration pronounced. The *Place d'Armes* was crowded with tables of refreshments, at which both whites and mulattoes seated themselves. But beneath this seeming patriotism and friendship, a dark and fatal conspiracy lurked, plotting treachery and death. It had been resolved that, at a preconcerted signal, every white at the table should plunge his knife into the bosom of the mulatto who was seated nearest to him. Cannon had been planted around the place of festivity, that no fugitive from the massacre should have the means of escaping; and that Rigaud should not fail to be secured, as the first victim of a conspiracy prepared especially against his life, the commander-in-chief of the National Guard had been placed at his side, and his murder of the mulatto chieftain was to be the signal for a general onset upon all his followers. The officer to whom had been intrusted the assassination of Rigaud, found it no small matter to screw his courage up to the sticking point, and the expected signal, which he was to display in blood to his associates, was so long delayed, that secret messengers began to throng to him from all parts of the tables, demanding why execution was not done on Rigaud. Urged on by these successive appeals, the white general at last applied himself to the fatal task which had been allotted him; but instead of silently plunging his dagger into the bosom of the mulatto chief, he sprung upon him with a pistol in his hand, and, with a loud execration, fired it at his intended victim. But Rigaud remained unharmed, and, in the scuffle which ensued, the white assassin was disarmed and put to flight. The astonishment of the mulattoes soon gave way to tumult and indignation, and this produced a drawn battle, in which both whites and mulattoes, exasperated as they were to the utmost, fought man to man. The struggle continued fiercely until the whites were driven from the town, having lost one hundred and fifty of their number, and slain many of their opponents.

Tidings of this conspiracy flew rapidly in all directions; and such was the indignation of the mulattoes at this attack upon their chief, whose death had even been announced in several places as certain, that they seized upon all the whites within their reach; and their immediate massacre was only prevented by the arrival of intelligence that Rigaud was still alive. Such were the persecutions which the leader of the mulattoes, now in exile, had experienced in his own land. Napoleon kept him confined in the prison of the Temple first, and then at the castle of Joux, where Toussaint had ended his life.

During this time, St. Domingo was undergoing a great change. Leclerc had died, Rochambeau and his forces had been driven from the island, Dessalines had reigned and passed away, and Christophe was master of the north, and Petion of the south. These two generals were at war with each other, when they were both very much surprised at the arrival of Rigaud from France. He had escaped from his prison, made his way to England, and thence to the island by way of the United States. Petion, the president of the republic in the south, regarded Rigaud as a more formidable enemy than Christophe. The great mulatto general was welcomed with enthusiasm by his old adherents; they showed the most sincere respect and attachment for him, and he journeyed in triumph to Port au Prince. Though Petion disliked these demonstrations in favor of a rival, he dared not attempt to interfere, for he well knew that a single word from Rigaud could raise a revolt among the mulattoes. Petion, himself a mulatto, had served under the former in the first stages of the revolution. The people of Aux Cayes welcomed their chief to his home, and he drew around him all hearts, and in a short time Rigaud was in full possession of his ancient power. The government of Petion was divided to make room for the former chief, and, though the two leaders for a while flew to arms against each other, they, nevertheless, were driven to an alliance on account of the encroachments of Christophe.

After a reign that was fraught only with tumult to himself and followers, Rigaud abdicated his province, retired to his farm, and in a few weeks died. Thus ended the career of the most distinguished mulatto general of which St. Domingo could boast.

FRANCES ELLEN WATKINS.

Miss Watkins is a native of Baltimore, where she received her education. She has been before the public some years as an author and public lecturer. Her "Poems on Miscellaneous Subjects," published in a small volume, show a reflective mind and no ordinary culture. Her "Essay on Christianity" is a beautiful composition. Many of her poems are soul-stirring, and all are characterized by chaste language and much thought. The following is entitled

THE SLAVE MOTHER.

'Heard you that shriek? It rose
So wildly on the air,

It seemed as if a burdened heart
  Was breaking in despair.

Saw you those hands so sadly clasped,
  The bowed and feeble head,
The shuddering of that fragile form,
  That look of grief and dread?

Saw you the sad, imploring eye?
  Its every glance was pain,
As if a storm of agony
  Were sweeping through the brain.

She is a mother pale with fear;
  Her boy clings to her side,
And in her kirtle vainly tries
  His trembling form to hide.

He is not hers, although she bore
  For him a mother's pains;
He is not hers, although her blood
  Is coursing through his veins.

He is not hers, for cruel hands
  May rudely tear apart
The only wreath of household love
  That binds her breaking heart.

His love has been a joyous light
  That o'er her pathway smiled,
A fountain, gushing ever new,
  Amid life's desert wild.

His lightest word has been a tone
  Of music round her heart;
Their lives a streamlet blent in one—
  O Father, must they part?

They tear him from her circling arms,
  Her last and fond embrace;
O, never more may her sad eyes
  Gaze on his mournful face.

No marvel, then, these bitter shrieks
  Disturb the listening air;

She is a mother, and her heart
Is breaking in despair.

Miss Watkins's advice to her own sex on the selection of a husband should be appreciated by all.

Nay, do not blush! I only heard
You had a mind to marry;
I thought I'd speak a friendly word;
So just one moment tarry.

Wed not a man whose merit lies
In things of outward show,
In raven hair or flashing eyes,
That please your fancy so.

But marry one who's good and kind,
And free from all pretence;
Who, if without a gifted mind,
At least has common sense.

Miss Watkins is about thirty years of age, of a fragile form, rather nervous, keen and witty in conversation, outspoken in her opinions, and yet appears in all the simplicity of a child.

EX-PRESIDENT ROBERTS.

J. J. Roberts, ex-president of the Republic of Liberia, is a native of the Old Dominion, and emigrated to his adopted country about twenty-five years ago. In stature he is tall, slim, and has a commanding appearance, sharp features, pleasant countenance, and is what the ladies would call "good looking." Mr. Roberts has much the bearing of an "English gentleman." He has fine abilities, and his state papers will compare favorably with the public documents of any of the presidents of the United States. He is thoroughly devoted to the interest of the rising republic, and has visited Europe several times in her behalf.

The following extract from the inaugural address of President Roberts to the legislature of Liberia, in 1848, on the colonists taking the entire responsibility of the government, is eloquent and pointed:—

"It must afford the most heartfelt pleasure and satisfaction to every friend of Liberia, and real lover of liberty, to observe by what a fortunate train of circumstances and incidents the people of these colonies have arrived at absolute freedom and independence. When we look abroad and see by what slow and painful steps, marked with blood and ills of every kind, other states of the world have advanced to liberty and independence, we cannot but admire and praise that all-gracious Providence, who, by his unerring ways, has, with so few sufferings on our part, compared with other states, led us to this happy stage in our progress towards those great and important objects. That it is the will of Heaven that mankind should be free, is clearly evidenced by the wealth, vigor, virtue, and consequent happiness of all free states. But the idea that Providence will establish such governments as he shall deem most fit for his creatures, and will give them wealth, influence, and happiness without their efforts, is palpably absurd. God's moral government of the earth is always performed by the intervention of second causes. Therefore, fellow-citizens, while with pious gratitude we survey the frequent interpositions of Heaven in our behalf, we ought to remember, that as the disbelief of an overruling Providence is atheism, so an absolute confidence of having our government relieved from every embarrassment, and its citizens made respectable and happy by the immediate hand of God, without our own exertions, is the most culpable presumption. Nor have we any reason to expect, that he will miraculously make Liberia a paradise, and deliver us, in a moment of time, from all the ills and inconveniences consequent upon the peculiar circumstances under which we are placed, merely to convince us that he favors our cause and government.

"Sufficient indications of his will are always given, and those who will not then believe, neither would they believe though one should rise from the dead to inform them. Who can trace the progress of these colonies, and mark the incidents of the wars in which they have been engaged, without seeing evident tokens of providential favor. Let us, therefore, inflexibly persevere in exerting our most strenuous efforts in a humble and rational dependence on the great Governor of all the world, and we have the fairest prospects of surmounting all the difficulties which may be thrown in our way. That we may expect, and that we shall have, difficulties, sore difficulties, yet to contend against in our progress to maturity, is certain; and, as the political happiness or wretchedness of ourselves and our children, and of generations yet unborn, is in our hands,—nay, more, the redemption of Africa from the deep degradation, superstition, and idolatry in which she has so long been involved,—it becomes us to lay our shoulders to the wheel, and manfully resist every obstacle which may oppose our progress in the great work which lies before us."

Mr. Roberts, we believe, is extensively engaged in commerce and agriculture, and, though out of office, makes himself useful in the moral, social, and intellectual elevation of his brethren. No one is more respected, or stands higher, in Liberia than he.

ALEXANDER CRUMMELL.

AMONG the many bright examples of the black man which we present, one of the foremost is Alexander Crummell. Blood unadulterated, a tall and manly figure, commanding in appearance, a full and musical voice, fluent in speech, a graduate of Cambridge University, England, a mind stored with the richness of English literature, competently acquainted with the classical authors of Greece and Rome, from the grave Thucydides to the rhapsodical Lycophron, gentlemanly in all his movements, language chaste and refined, Mr. Crummell may well be put forward as one of the best and most favorable representatives of his race. He is a clergyman of the Episcopal denomination, and deeply versed in theology. His sermons are always written, but he reads them as few persons can. In 1848 Mr. Crummell visited England, and delivered a well-conceived address before the Anti-Slavery Society in London, where his eloquence and splendid abilities were at once acknowledged and appreciated. The year before his departure for the old world, he delivered a "Eulogy on the Life and Character of Thomas Clarkson," from which we make the following extract, which is full of meaning and eloquence:—

"Let us not be unmindful of the prerogatives and obligations arising from the fact, that the exhibition of the greatest talent, and the development of the most enlarged philanthropy, in the nineteenth century, have been bestowed upon our race. The names of the great lights of the age,—statesmen, poets, and divines,—in all the great countries of Europe, and in this country too, are inseparably connected with the cause and destiny of the African race. This has been the theme whence most of them have reaped honor and immortality. This cause has produced the development of the most noble character of modern times—has given the world a Wilberforce and a Clarkson. Lowly and depressed as we have been, and as we now are, yet *our* interests and *our* welfare have agitated the chief countries of the world, and are now before all other questions, shaking this nation to its very centre. The providences of God have placed the negro race before Europe and America in the most commanding position. From the sight of us no nation, no statesman, no ecclesiastic, and no ecclesiastical institution, can escape. And by us and our cause the character and greatness of individuals and of nations in this day and generation of the world are to be decided, either for good or evil; and so, in all coming times, the memory and the fame of the chief actors now on the stage will be decided by their relation to our cause. The discoveries of science, the unfoldings of literature, the dazzlings of genius, all fade before the demands of this cause. This is the age of BROTHERHOOD AND HUMANITY, and the negro race is its most distinguished test and criterion.

"And for what are all these providences? For nothing? He who thinks so must be blinded—must be demented. In these facts are wound up a most distinct significance, and with them are connected most clear and emphatic obligations and responsibilities. The clear-minded and thoughtful colored men of America must mark the significance of these facts, and begin to feel their weight. For more than two centuries we have been working our way from the deep and dire degradation into which slavery had plunged us. We have made considerable headway. By the vigorous use of the opportunities of our partial freedom we have been enabled, with the divine blessing, to reach a position of respectability and character. We have pressed somewhat into the golden avenues of science, intelligence, and learning. We have made impressions there; and some few of our footprints have we left behind. The mild light of religion has illumined our pathway, and superstition and error have fled apace. The greatest paradoxes are evinced by us. Amid the decay of nations, a rekindled light starts up in us. Burdens under which others expire seem to have lost their influence upon us; and while *they* are 'driven to the wall,' destruction keeps far from *us* its blasting hand. We live in the region of death, yet seem hardly mortal. We cling to life in the midst of all reverses; and our nerveful grasp thereon cannot easily be relaxed. History reverses its mandates in our behalf: our dotage is in the past. 'Time writes not its wrinkles on our brow;' our juvenescence is in the future. All this, and the kindly nature which is acknowledgedly ours,—with gifts of freedom vouchsafed us by the Almighty in this land, in part, and in the West Indies; with the intellectual desire every where manifesting itself, and the exceeding interest exhibited for Africa by her own children, and by the Christian nations of the world, are indications from which we may not gather a trivial meaning, nor a narrow significance.

"The teaching of God in all these things is, undoubtedly, that ours is a great destiny, and that we should open our eyes to it. God is telling us all that, whereas the past has been dark, grim, and repulsive, the future shall be glorious; that the horrid traffic shall yet be entirely stopped; that the whips and brands, the shackles and fetters, of slavery shall be cast down to oblivion; that the shades of ignorance and superstition that have so long settled down upon the mind of Africa shall be dispelled; and that all her sons on her own broad continent, in the Western Isles, and in this Republic, shall yet stand erect beneath the heavens, 'with freedom chartered on their manly brows;' their bosoms swelling with its noblest raptures—treading the face of earth in the links of brotherhood and equality."

We have had a number of our public men to represent us in Europe within the past twenty-five years; and none have done it more honorably or with better success to the character and cause of the black man, than Alexander Crummell. We met him there again and again, and followed in his track wherever he preached or spoke before public assemblies, and we know whereof we affirm. In 1852, we believe, he went to Liberia, where he now resides. At present he and his family are on a visit to "the States," partly for his health and partly for the purpose of promoting emigration to Africa. Mr. C. has recently published a valuable work on Africa, which is highly spoken of by the press; indeed, it may be regarded as the only finished account of *our mother* land. Devotedly attached to the interest of the colored man, and having the moral, social, and intellectual elevation of the natives of Africa at heart, we do not regret that he considers it his duty to labor in his *father* land. Warmly interested in the Republic, and so capable of filling the highest position that he can be called to, we shall not be surprised, some day, to hear that Alexander Crummell is president of Liberia.

ALEXANDRE PETION.

THE ambitious and haughty mulattoes had long been dissatisfied with the obscure condition into which they had been thrown by the reign of Dessalines, and at the death of that ruler they determined to put forward their claim. Their great chief, Rigaud, was still in prison in France, where he had been placed by Napoleon. Christophe had succeeded to power at the close of the empire, and was at St. Marks when he heard that Alexandre Petion had been elected president of the Republic of Hayti, through the instrumentality of the mulattoes. Christophe at once began to prepare for war. Petion was a quadroon, the successor of Rigaud and Clervaux to the confidence of the mulattoes. He was a man of education and refined manners. He had been educated at the Military School of Paris, and had ever been characterized for his mildness of temper and the insinuating grace of his address. He was a skilful engineer, and at the time of his elevation to power he passed for the most scientific officer and the most erudite individual among the people of Hayti. Attached to the fortunes of Rigaud, he had acted as his lieutenant against Toussaint, and had accompanied him to France. Here he remained until the departure of the expedition under Leclerc, when he embarked in that disastrous enterprise, to employ his talents in again restoring his country to the dominion of France. Petion joined Dessalines, Christophe, and Clervaux, when they revolted and turned against the French, and aided in gaining the final independence of the island. Christophe, therefore, as soon as he heard that he had a rival in Petion, rallied his forces, and started for Port au Prince, to meet his enemy. The former was already in the field, and the two armies met; a battle ensued, and Petion, being defeated, and hotly pursued in his flight, found it necessary, in order to save his life, to exchange his uniform with a laborer, and to bury himself up to his neck in a marsh until his fierce pursuers had disappeared. Petion escaped, and reached his capital before the arrival of the troops under Christophe. The latter, after this signal success, pressed forward to Port au Prince, and laid siege to the town, in hope of an easy triumph over his rival. But Petion was in his appropriate sphere of action, and Christophe soon discovered that, in contending with an experienced engineer in a fortified town, success was of more difficult attainment than while encountering the same enemy in the open field, where his science could not be brought into action. Christophe could make no impression on the town, and feeling ill assured of the steadfastness of his own proper government at Cape François, he withdrew his forces from the investment of Port au Prince, resolved to establish in the north a separate government of his own, and to defer to some more favorable opportunity the attempt to subdue his rival at Port au Prince. In September, 1808, Petion commenced another campaign against Christophe, by sending an army to besiege Port de Paix, which it did; but after a while it was driven back to Port au Prince by the victorious legions of the president of the north. Christophe in turn attempted to take the Mole St. Nicholas from Lamarre, one of Petion's generals, but did not succeed. The struggle between the two presidents of Hayti had now continued three years, when a new competitor appeared in the field, by the arrival of Rigaud from France. This was an unexpected event, which awakened deep solicitude in the bosom of Petion, who could not avoid regarding that distinguished general as a more formidable rival than Christophe. He well knew the attachment of the people to the great mulatto chief, and he feared his superior talents. The enthusiasm with which Rigaud was received wherever he appeared, raised the jealousy of Petion to such a pitch, that he for a time forgot his black rival. Partisans flew to the standard of Rigaud, and a resort to arms seemed imminent between him and Petion. A meeting, however, was held by the two mulatto generals, at the bridge of Miragoane, where a treaty was signed, by which the south was to be governed by the former, and the west, and as much as could be wrested from Christophe, by the latter. But peace between these two was not destined to be of long duration. A war took place, and Rigaud's troops proved too much for Petion, and he was defeated with great loss, and his entire army almost annihilated. But the victorious general did not follow up his successes; and although he had gained a signal victory, he felt that much of his power over his followers was passing away. The death of Rigaud once more gave the field to Christophe and Petion, and they again commenced war upon each other. The latter was superior to the former in education, and in the refinement given him by a cultivated understanding and an extensive intercourse with European society; but he was greatly inferior to Christophe in boldness and decision of character. Petion was subtle, cautious, and desponding. He aspired to be the Washington, as Christophe was deemed the Bonaparte, of Hayti. By insinuating the doctrines of equality and republicanism, Petion succeeded in governing, with but ten thousand mulattoes, a population of more than two hundred thousand blacks. Assuming no pretensions to personal or official dignity, and totally rejecting all the ceremonial of a court, it was Petion's ambition to maintain the exterior of a plain republican magistrate. Clad in the white linen undress of the country, and with a Madras handkerchief tied about his head, he mixed freely and promiscuously with his fellow-citizens, or seated himself in the piazza of the government house, accessible to all. He professed to hold himself at the disposal of the people, and to be ready at any moment to submit to their will, whether it was to guide the power of the state, or yield his head to the executioner.

A republican officer one day called on Petion at the government house, and while they were alone, the former drew out a pistol and fired at the president, without injuring him, however; the latter immediately seized his visitor, disarmed him, and when the guard rushed in, he found the president and the officer walking the room locked in each other's arms. This man was ever after the warm friend of Petion. At the downfall of Napoleon, and the elevation of Louis XVIII., another effort was made to regain possession of the island by France. But the latter did not resort to arms. Having no confidence in the French, and fearing a warlike demonstration, both Petion and Christophe prepared for defence. Petion had long been despondent for the permanence of the republic, and this feeling had by degrees grown into a settled despair; and amidst these perplexities and embarrassments he fell sick, in the month of March, 1818, and after an illness which continued only eight days, he died, and was succeeded by General Boyer.

The administration of Petion was mild, and he did all that he could for the elevation of the people whom he ruled. He was the patron of education and the arts, and scientific men, for years after his death, spoke his name with reverence. He was highly respected by the representatives of foreign powers, and strangers visiting his republic always mentioned his name in connection with the best cultivated and most gentlemanly of the people of Hayti. Lightly lie the earth on the bones of Petion, and let every cloud pass away from his memory.

MARTIN R. DELANY, M.D.

DR. DELANY has long been before the public. His first appearance, we believe, was in connection with *The Mystery*, a weekly newspaper published at Pittsburg, and of which he was editor. His journal was faithful in its advocacy of the rights of man, and had the reputation of being a well-conducted sheet. The doctor afterwards was associated with Frederick Douglass in the editorial management of his paper at Rochester, N. Y. From the latter place he removed to Canada, and has since resided in Chatham, where he is looked upon as one of its leading citizens.

Dr. M. R. Delany, though regarded as a man high in his profession, is better and more widely known as a traveller, discoverer, and lecturer. His association with Professor Campbell in the "Niger Valley Exploring Expedition" has brought the doctor very prominently before the world, and especially that portion of it which takes an interest in the civilization of Africa. The official report of that expedition shows that he did not visit that country with his eyes shut. His observations and suggestions about the climate, soil, diseases, and natural productions of Africa, are interesting, and give evidence that the doctor was in earnest. The published report, of which he is the author, will repay a perusal.

On his return home, Dr. Delany spent some time in England, and lectured in the British metropolis and the provincial cities, with considerable success, on Africa and its resources. As a member of the International Statistical Congress, he acquitted himself with credit to his position and honor to his race. The foolish manner in which the Hon. Mr. Dallas, our minister to the court of St. James, acted on meeting Dr. Delany in that august assembly, and the criticisms of the press of Europe and America, will not soon be forgotten.

He is short, compactly built, has a quick, wiry walk, and is decided and energetic in conversation, unadulterated in race, and proud of his complexion. Though somewhat violent in his gestures, and paying but little regard to the strict rules of oratory, Dr. Delany is, nevertheless, an interesting, eloquent speaker. Devotedly attached to his fatherland, he goes for a "Negro Nationality." Whatever he undertakes, he executes it with all the powers that God has given him; and what would appear as an obstacle in the way of other men, would be brushed aside by Martin R. Delany.

ROBERT SMALL.

At the breaking out of the rebellion, Robert Small was a slave in Charleston, S. C. He stood amid a group of his fellow-slaves, as the soldiers were getting ready to make the assault upon Fort Sumter, and he said to his associates, "This, boys, is the dawn of freedom for our race." Robert, at this time, was employed as pilot on board the steamboat "Planter," owned at Charleston, and then lying at her dock. The following day, the steamer commenced undergoing alterations necessary to fit her for a gunboat. Robert, when within hearing of the whites, was loud in his talk of what "we'll do with the Yankees, when this boat is ready for sea." The Planter was soon transmogrified into a rebel man-of-war, to be used in and about the rivers and bays near Charleston, and Robert Small was her acknowledged pilot. One of Robert's brothers was second engineer, and a cousin to him was the second mate; the remainder of the crew were all slaves, except the white officers. It was the custom of the captain, chief mate, and chief engineer to spend the night with their families in the city, when the steamer was in port, the vessel being left in charge of Robert. The following is the account of the capture of the boat by her black crew, as given by the Port Royal correspondent of the *New York Commercial Advertiser*:—

"The steamer Planter, which was run away from the rebels by her pilot, Robert Small, is a new tug boat employed about Charleston harbor, which was seized by the Confederate government and converted into a gunboat, mounting a rifled gun forward and a siege gun aft. She has been in the habit of running out to sea to reconnoitre, and was, therefore, no unusual appearance near the forts guarding the entrance. Small, the helmsman and pilot, conceived the idea of running away, and plotted with several friends, slaves like him, to take them off.

"On the evening of May 11, her officers left the ship, then at the wharf in Charleston, and went to their homes. Small then took the firemen and assistant engineers, all of whom were slaves, in his confidence, had the fires banked up, and every thing made ready to start by daylight."

"At quarter to four on Saturday morning, the lines which fastened the vessel to the dock were cast off, and the ship quietly glided into the stream. Here the harbor guard hailed the vessel, but Small promptly gave the countersign, and was allowed to pass.

"The vessel now called at a dock a distance below, where the families of the crew came on board.

"When off Fort Sumter, the sentry on the ramparts hailed the boat, and Small sounded the countersign with the whistle—three shrill sounds and one hissing sound. The vessel being known to the officers of the day, no objection was raised, the sentry only singing out, 'Blow the d——d Yankees to hell, or bring one of them in.' 'Ay, ay,' was the answer, and every possible effort was made to get below.

"Hardly was the vessel out of range, when Small ran up a white flag, and went to the United States fleet, where he surrendered the vessel. She had on board seven heavy guns for Fort Ripley, a fort now building in Charleston harbor, which were to be taken thither the next morning.

"Small, with the crew and their families,—sixteen persons,—were sent to the flagship at Port Royal, and an officer placed on board the Planter, who took her also to Commodore Dupont's vessel. Small is a middle-aged negro, and his features betray nothing of the firmness of character he displayed. He is said to be one of the most skilful pilots of Charleston, and to have a thorough knowledge of all the ports and inlets on the coast of South Carolina."

We give below the official account of the taking and surrender of the boat to the naval authorities.

U.S. STEAMSHIP AUGUSTA,
OFF CHARLESTON, May 13, 1862.

SIR: I have the honor to inform you that the rebel armed steamer Planter was brought out to us this morning from Charleston by eight contrabands, and delivered up to the squadron. Five colored women and three children are also on board. She carried one 32-pounder and one 24-pounder howitzer, and has also on board four large guns, which she was engaged in transporting. I send her to Port Royal at once, in order to take advantage of the present good weather. I send Charleston papers of the 12th, and the very intelligent contraband who was in charge will give you the information which he has brought off. I have the honor to request that you will send back, as soon as convenient, the officer and crew sent on board.

Commander Dupont, in forwarding the despatch, says, in relation to the steamer Planter,—

She was the armed despatch and transportation steamer attached to the engineer department at Charleston, under Brigadier General Ripley, whose bark, a short time since, was brought to the blockading fleet by several contrabands. The bringing out of this steamer, under all the circumstances, would have done credit to any one. At four in the morning, in the absence of the captain, who was on shore, she left her wharf close to the government office and headquarters, with the Palmetto and "Confederate" flags flying, and passed the successive forts, saluting, as usual, by blowing the steam whistle. After getting beyond the range of the last gun, they hauled down the rebel flags, and hoisted a white one. The Onward was the inside ship of the blockading squadron in the main channel, and was preparing to fire when her commander made out the white flag. The armament of the steamer is a 32-pounder, or pivot, and a fine 24-pound howitzer. She has besides, on her deck, four other guns, one seven inch rifled, which were to be taken, on the morning of the escape, to the new fort on the middle ground. One of the four belonged to Fort Sumter, and had been struck, in the rebel attack, on the muzzle. Robert Small, the intelligent slave, and pilot of the boat, who performed this bold feat so skilfully, informed me of this fact, presuming it would be a matter of interest to us to have possession of this gun. This man, Robert Small, is superior to any who have come into our lines, intelligent as many of them have been. His information has been most interesting, and portions of it of the utmost importance. The steamer is quite a valuable acquisition to the squadron by her good machinery and very light draught. The officer in charge brought her through St. Helena Sound, and by the inland passage down Beaufort River, arriving here at ten last night. On board the steamer, when she left Charleston, were eight men, five women, and three children. I shall continue to employ Small as pilot on board the Planter, for inland waters, with which he appears to be very familiar.

I do not know whether, in the view of the government, the vessel will be considered a prize; but if so, I respectfully submit to the Department the claims of the man Small and his associates.

Very respectfully, your obedient servant,

S. F. DUPONT,

Flag Officer, Commanding, &c.

A bill was at once introduced in Congress to consider the Planter a prize, and to award the prize-money to her crew. The *New York Tribune* had the following editorial on the subject:—

"The House of Representatives at Washington, it is to be hoped, will be more just to their own sense of right, and to their more generous impulses, than to put aside again the

Senate bill giving the prize-money they have so well earned to the pilot and crew of the steamer Planter. Neither House would have done an act unworthy of their dignity had they promptly passed a vote of thanks to Robert Small and his fellows for the cool courage with which they planned and executed their escape from rebel bondage, and the unswerving loyalty which prompted them, at the same time, to bring away such spoils from the enemy as would make a welcome addition to the blockading squadron.

"If we must still remember with humiliation that the Confederate flag yet waves where our national colors were first struck, we should be all the more prompt to recognize the merit that has put into our possession the first trophy from Fort Sumter. And the country should feel doubly humbled if there is not magnanimity enough to acknowledge a gallant action, because it was the head of a black man that conceived, and the hand of a black man that executed it. It would better, indeed, become us to remember that no small share of the naval glory of the war belongs to the race which we have forbidden to fight for us; that one negro has recaptured a vessel from a southern privateer, and another has brought away from under the very guns of the enemy, where no fleet of ours has yet dared to venture, a prize whose possession a commodore thinks worthy to be announced in a special despatch."

The bill was taken up and passed, and the brave Small and his companions received justice at the hands of the government.

FREDERICK DOUGLASS.

THE career of the distinguished individual whose name heads this page is more widely known than that of any other living colored man, except, perhaps, Alexandre Dumas. The narrative of his life, published in 1845, gave a new impetus to the black man's literature. All other stories of fugitive slaves faded away before the beautifully written, highly descriptive, and thrilling memoir of Frederick Douglass. Other narratives had only brought before the public a few heart-rending scenes connected with the person described. But Mr. Douglass, in his book, brought not only his old master's farm and its occupants before the reader, but the entire country around him, including Baltimore and its ship yard. The manner in which he obtained his education, and especially his learning to write, has been read and re-read by thousands in both hemispheres. His escape from slavery is too well understood to need a recapitulation here. He took up his residence in New Bedford, where he still continued the assiduous student—mastering the different branches of education which the accursed institution had deprived him of in early life.

His advent as a lecturer was a remarkable one. White men and black men had talked against slavery, but none had ever spoken like Frederick Douglass. Throughout the north the newspapers were filled with the sayings of the "eloquent fugitive." He often travelled with others, but they were all lost sight of in the eagerness to hear Douglass. His travelling companions would sometimes get angry, and would speak first at the meetings; then they would take the last turn; but it was all the same—the fugitive's impression was the one left upon the mind. He made more persons angry, and pleased more, than any other man. He was praised, and he was censured. He made them laugh, he made them weep, and he made them swear. His "Slaveholder's Sermon" was always a trump card. He awakened an interest in the hearts of thousands who before were dead to the slave and his condition. Many kept away from his lectures, fearing lest they should be converted against their will. Young men and women, in those days of pro-slavery hatred, would return to their fathers' roofs filled with admiration for the "runaway slave," and would be rebuked by hearing the old ones grumble out, "You'd better stay at home and study your lessons, and not be running after the nigger meetings."

In 1841, he was induced to accept an agency as a lecturer for the Anti-slavery Society, and at once became one of the most valuable of its advocates. He visited England in 1845. There he was kindly received, and heartily welcomed; and after going through the length and breadth of the land, and addressing public meetings out of number on behalf of his countrymen in chains, with a power of eloquence which captivated his auditors, and brought the cause which he pleaded home to their hearts, he returned home and commenced the publication of the *North Star*, a weekly newspaper devoted to the advocacy of the cause of freedom.

Mr. Douglass is tall and well made. His vast and fully-developed forehead shows at once that he is a superior man intellectually. He is polished in his language, and gentlemanly in his manners. His voice is full and sonorous. His attitude is dignified, and his gesticulation is full of noble simplicity. He is a man of lofty reason; natural, and without pretension; always master of himself; brilliant in the art of exposing and abstracting. Few persons can handle a subject, with which they are familiar, better than he. There is a kind of eloquence issuing from the depth of the soul as from a spring, rolling along its copious floods, sweeping all before it, overwhelming by its very force, carrying, upsetting, ingulfing its adversaries, and more dazzling and more thundering than the bolt which leaps from crag to crag. This is the eloquence of Frederick Douglass. One of the best mimics of the age, and possessing great dramatic powers, had he taken up the sock and buskin, instead of becoming a lecturer, he would have made as fine a Coriolanus as ever trod the stage.

In his splendidly conceived comparison of Mr. Douglass to S. R. Ward, written for the "Autographs for Freedom," Professor William J. Wilson says of the former, "In his very look, his gesture, his whole manner, there is so much of genuine, earnest eloquence, that they leave no time for reflection. Now you are reminded of one rushing down some fearful steep, bidding you follow; now on some delightful stream, still beckoning you onward. In either case, no matter what your prepossessions or oppositions, you, for the moment at least, forget the justness or unjustness of his cause, and obey the summons, and loath, if at all, you return to your former post. Not always, however, is he successful in retaining you. Giddy as you may be with the descent you have made, delighted as you are with the pleasure afforded, with the Elysium to which he has wafted you, you return too often dissatisfied with his and your own impetuosity and want of firmness. You feel that you had only a dream, a pastime,—not a reality.

"This great power of momentary captivation consists in his eloquence of manners, his just appreciation of words. In listening to him, your whole soul is fired, every nerve strung, every passion inflated, and every faculty you possess ready to perform at a moment's bidding. You stop not to ask why or wherefore. 'Tis a unison of mighty yet harmonious sounds that play upon your imagination; and you give yourself up, for a time, to their irresistible charm. At last, the *cataract* which roared around you is hushed, the *tornado* is passed, and you find yourself sitting upon a bank, (at whose base roll but tranquil waters,) quietly asking yourself why, amid such a display of power, no greater effect had really been produced. After all, it must be admitted there is a power in Mr. Douglass rarely to be found in any other man."

As a speaker, Frederick Douglass has had more imitators than almost any other American, save, perhaps, Wendell Phillips. Unlike most great speakers, he is a superior writer also. Some of his articles, in point of ability, will rank with any thing ever written for the American press. He has taken lessons from the best of teachers, amid the homeliest realities of life; hence the perpetual freshness of his delineations, which are never over-colored, never strained, never aiming at difficult or impossible effects, but which always read like living transcripts of experience. The following from his pen, on "What shall be done with the slaves, if emancipated?" is characteristic of his style.

"What shall be done with the four million slaves, if they are emancipated? This question has been answered, and can be answered in many ways. Primarily, it is a question less for man than for God—less for human intellect than for the laws of nature to solve. It assumes that nature has erred; that the law of liberty is a mistake; that freedom, though a natural want of the human soul, can only be enjoyed at the expense of human welfare, and that men are better off in slavery than they would or could be in freedom; that slavery is the natural order of human relations, and that liberty is an experiment. What shall be done with them?

"Our answer is, Do nothing with them; mind your business, and let them mind theirs. Your *doing* with them is their greatest misfortune. They have been undone by your doings, and all they now ask, and really have need of at your hands, is just to let them alone. They suffer by every interference, and succeed best by being let alone. The negro should have been let alone in Africa—let alone when the pirates and robbers offered him for sale in our Christian slave markets (more cruel and inhuman than the Mohammedan slave markets)—let alone by courts, judges, politicians, legislators, and slave-drivers—let alone altogether, and assured that they were thus to be let alone forever, and that they must now make their own way in the world, just the same as any and every other variety of the human family. As colored men, we only ask to be allowed to *do* with ourselves, subject only to the same great laws for the welfare of human society which apply to other men—Jews, Gentiles, Barbarian, Scythian. Let us stand upon our own legs, work with our own hands, and eat bread in the sweat of our own brows. When you, our white fellow-countrymen, have attempted to do any thing for us, it has generally been to deprive us of some right, power, or privilege, which you yourselves would die before you would submit to have taken from you. When the planters of the West Indies used to attempt to puzzle the pure-minded Wilberforce with the question, 'How shall we get rid of slavery?' his simple answer was, 'Quit stealing.' In like manner we answer those who are perpetually puzzling their brains with questions as to what shall be done with the negro, 'Let him alone, and mind your own business.' If you see him ploughing in the open field, levelling the forest, at work with a spade, a rake, a hoe, a pickaxe, or a bill—let him alone; he has a right to work. If you see him on his way to school, with spelling-book, geography, and arithmetic in his hands—let him alone. Don't shut the door in his face, nor bolt your gates against him; he has a right to learn—let him alone. Don't pass laws to degrade him. If he has a ballot in his hand; and is on his way to the ballot-box to deposit his vote for the man who, he thinks, will most justly and wisely administer the government which has the power of life and death over him, as well as others—let him ALONE; his right of choice as much deserves respect and protection as your own. If you see him on his way to church, exercising religious liberty in accordance with this or that religious persuasion—let him alone. Don't meddle with him, nor trouble yourselves with any questions as to what shall be done with him.

"What shall be done with the negro, if emancipated? Deal justly with him. He is a human being, capable of judging between good and evil, right and wrong, liberty and slavery, and is as much a subject of law as any other man; therefore, deal justly with him. He is, like other men, sensible of the motives of reward and punishment. Give him wages for his work, and let hunger pinch him if he don't work. He knows the difference between fulness and famine, plenty and scarcity. 'But will he work?' Why should he not? He is used to it, and is not afraid of it. His hands are already hardened by toil, and he has no dreams of ever getting a living by any other means than by hard work. 'But would you turn them all loose?' Certainly! We are no better than our Creator. He has turned them loose, and why should not we? 'But would you let them all stay here?' Why not? What better is *here* than *there*? Will they occupy more room as freemen than as slaves? Is the presence of a black freeman less agreeable than that of a black slave? Is an object of your injustice and cruelty a more ungrateful sight than one of your justice and benevolence? You have borne the one more than two hundred years—can't you bear the other long enough to try the experiment?"

CHARLES L. REASON.

Professor C. L. Reason has for many years been connected with the educational institutions of New York and Philadelphia. In 1849, he was called to the professorship of Mathematics and Belles Lettres in New York Central College. This situation he held during his own pleasure, with honor to himself and benefit to the students. A man of fine education, superior intelligence, gentlemanly in every sense of the term, of excellent discrimination, one of the best of students, Professor Reason holds a power over those under him seldom attained by men of his profession. Were I a sculptor, and looking for a model of a perfect man in personal appearance, my selection would be Charles L. Reason. As a writer of both prose and poetry he need not be ashamed of his ability. Extremely diffident, he seldom furnishes any thing for the public eye. In a well-written essay on the propriety of establishing an industrial college, and the probable influence of the free colored people upon the emancipated blacks, he says, "Whenever emancipation shall take place, immediate though it be, the subjects of it, like many who now make up the so-called free population, will be, in what geologists call, the 'transition state.' The prejudice now felt against them for bearing on their persons the brand of slaves, cannot die out immediately. Severe trials will still be their portion: the curse of a 'taunted race,' must be expiated by almost miraculous proofs of advancement; and some of these miracles must be antecedent to the great day of jubilee. To fight the battle upon the bare ground of abstract principles will fail to give us complete victory. The subterfuges of pro-slavery selfishness must *now* be dragged to light, and the last weak argument, that the negro can never contribute any thing to advance the national character, 'nailed to the counter as base coin.' To the conquering of the difficulties heaped up in the path of his industry, the free colored man of the north has pledged himself. Already he sees, springing into growth, from out his foster *work-school*, intelligent young laborers, competent to enrich the world with necessary products; industrious citizens, contributing their proportion to aid on the advancing civilization of the country; self-providing artisans, vindicating their people from the never-ceasing charge of fitness for servile positions." In the "Autographs for Freedom," from which the above extract is taken, Professor Reason has a beautiful poem, entitled "Hope and Confidence," which, in point of originality and nicety of composition, will give it a place with the best productions of Wordsworth.

A poem signifies design, method, harmony, and therefore consistency of parts. A man may be gifted with the most vividly ideal nature; he may shoot from his brain some blazing poetic thought or imagery, which may arouse wonder and admiration, as a comet does; and yet he may have no constructiveness, without which the materials of poetry are only so many glittering fractions. A poem can never be tested by its length or brevity, but by the adaptation of its parts. A complete poem is the architecture of thought and language. It requires artistic skill to chisel rough blocks of marble into as many individual forms of beauty; but not only skill, but genius, is needed to arrange and harmonize those forms into the completeness of a Parthenon. A grave popular error, and one destructive of personal usefulness, and obstructive to literary progress, is the free-and-easy belief that because a man has the faculty of investing common things with uncommon ideas, therefore he can write a poem.

The idea of poetry is to give pleasurable emotions, and the world listens to a poet's voice as it listens to the singing of a summer bird; that which is the most suggestive of freedom and eloquence being the most admired. Professor Reason has both the genius and the artistic skill. We regret that we are able to give only the last two verses of "Hope and Confidence."

"There's nothing so lovely and bright below,
As the shapes of the purified mind;
Nought surer to which the weak heart can grow,
On which it can rest as it onward doth go,
Than that Truth which its own tendrils bind.

"Yes, Truth opes within a pure sun-tide of bliss,
And shows in its ever calm flood
A transcript of regions where no darkness is,
Where Hope its conceptions may realize,
And Confidence sleep in the good."

CHARLOTTE L. FORTEN.

In the autumn of 1854, a young colored lady of seventeen summers, unable to obtain admission into the schools of her native city (Philadelphia) on account of her complexion, removed to Salem, Massachusetts, where she at once entered the Higginson Grammar School. Here she soon secured the respect and esteem of the teachers and her fellow-pupils. Near the end of the last term, the principal of the establishment invited the scholars to write a poem each, to be sung at the last day's examination, and at the same time expressing the desire that the authors should conceal their names. As might have been expected, this drew out all the poetical genius of the young aspirants. Fifty or more manuscripts were sent in, and one selected, printed on a neat sheet, and circulated through the vast audience who were present. The following is the piece:—

A PARTING HYMN.

When Winter's royal robes of white
  From hill and vale are gone,
And the glad voices of the spring
  Upon the air are borne,
Friends, who have met with us before,
Within these walls shall meet no more.

Forth to a noble work they go:
  O, may their hearts keep pure,
And hopeful zeal and strength be theirs
  To labor and endure,
That they an earnest faith may prove
By words of truth and deeds of love.

May those, whose holy task it is
  To guide impulsive youth,
Fail not to cherish in their souls
  A reverence for truth;
For teachings which the lips impart
Must have their source within the heart.

May all who suffer share their love—
  The poor and the oppressed;
So shall the blessing of our God
  Upon their labors rest.
And may we meet again where all
Are blest and freed from every thrall.

The announcement that the successful competitor would be called out at the close of the singing, created no little sensation amongst the visitors, to say nothing of the pupils.

The principal of the school, after all parties had taken their seats, mounted the platform, and said, "Ladies and gentlemen, the beautiful hymn just sung is the composition of one of the students of this school, but who the talented person is I am unaware. Will the author step forward?" A moment's silence, and every eye was turned in the direction of the principal, who, seeing no one stir, looked around with a degree of amazement. Again he repeated, "Will the author of the hymn step forward?" A movement now among the female pupils showed that the last call had been successful. The buzzing and whispering throughout the large hall indicated the intense interest felt by all. "Sit down; keep your seats," exclaimed the principal, as the crowd rose to their feet, or bent forward to catch a glimpse of the young lady, who had now reached the front of the platform. Thunders of applause greeted the announcement that the distinguished authoress then before them was Miss Charlotte L. Forten. Her finely-chiselled features, well-developed forehead, countenance beaming with intelligence, and her dark complexion, showing her identity with an oppressed and injured race, all conspired to make the scene an exciting one. The audience was made up in part of some of the most aristocratic people in one of the most aristocratic towns in America. The impression left upon their minds was great in behalf of the race thus so nobly represented by the granddaughter of the noble-hearted, brave, generous, and venerable James Forten, whose whole life was a vindication of the character of his race.

> "'Tis the mind that makes the body rich;
> And as the sun breaks through the darkest clouds,
> So honor peereth in the meanest habit."

For several days after the close of the school, the name of Charlotte L. Forten was mentioned in all the private circles of Salem; and to imitate her was the highest aspiration of the fairest daughters of that wealthy and influential city. Miss Forten afterwards entered the State Normal School, where, in the language of the *Salem Register*, "she graduated with decided eclat." She was then appointed by the school committee to be a teacher in the Epes Grammar School, where she "was graciously received," says the same journal, "by parents of the district, and soon endeared herself to the pupils under her charge." These pupils were all white. Aside from having a finished education, Miss Forten possesses genius of a high order. An excellent student and a lover of books, she has a finely-cultivated mind, well stored with incidents drawn from the classics. She evinces talent, as a writer, for both prose and poetry. The following extracts from her "Glimpses of New England," published in the *National Anti-Slavery Standard*, are characteristic of her prose. "The Old Witch House," at Salem, is thus described:—

"This street has also some interesting associations. It contains a very great attraction for all lovers of the olden time. This is an ancient, dingy, yellow frame house, known as 'The Old Witch House.' Our readers must know that Salem was, two hundred years ago, the headquarters of the witches. And this is the veritable old Court House where the so-called witches were tried and condemned. It is wonderful with what force this singular delusion possessed the minds, not only of the poor and ignorant, but of the wisest and gravest of the magistrates appointed by his majesty's government.

"Those were dark days for Salem. Woe to the housewife or the household over whose door latch the protecting horseshoe was not carefully placed; and far greater woe to the unlucky dame who chanced to be suspected of such fanciful freaks as riding through the air on a broomstick, or muttering mystic incantations wherewith to undo her innocent neighbors. Hers was a summary and terrible punishment. Well, it is very pleasant to think how times have changed, and to say with Whittier,—

> 'Our witches are no longer old
> And wrinkled beldams, Satan-sold,
> But young, and gay, and laughing creatures,
> With the heart's sunshine on their features.'

Troops of *such* witches now pass the old house every day. I grieve to say that the 'Old Witch House' has recently been defaced and desecrated by the erection of an apothecary's shop in front of one of its wings. People say that the new shop is very handsome; but to a few of us, lovers of antiquity, it seems a profanation, and we can see no beauty in it."

The hills in the vicinity of Salem are beautifully pictured. "The pure, bracing air, the open sky," and the sheet of water in the distance, are all brought in with their lights and shades. Along with the brilliancy of style and warmth of imagination which characterize her writings, we find here and there gravity of thought and earnestness of purpose, befitting her literary taste. Of Marblehead Beach she writes,—

"The beach, which is at some distance from the town, is delightful. It was here that I first saw the sea, and stood 'entranced in silent awe,' gazing upon the waves as they marched, in one mass of the richest green, to the shore, then suddenly broke into foam, white and beautiful as the winter snow. I remember one pleasant afternoon which I spent with a friend, gathering shells and seaweed on the beach, or sitting on the rocks, listening to the wild music of the waves, and watching the clouds of spray as they sprang high up in the air, then fell again in snowy wreaths at our feet. We lingered there until the sun had sunk into his ocean bed. On our homeward walk we passed Forest River, a winding, picturesque little stream, dotted with rocky islands. Over the river, and along our quiet way, the moon shed her soft and silvery light. And as we approached Salem, the lights, gleaming from every window of the large factory, gave us a cheerful welcome."

She "looks on nature with a poet's eye." The visit to Lynn is thus given:—

"Its chief attraction to me was 'High Rock,' on whose summit the pretty little dwelling of the Hutchinsons is perched like an eagle's eyrie. In the distance this rock looks so high and steep that one marvels how a house could ever have been built upon it. At its foot there once lived a famous fortune-teller of the olden time—'Moll Pitcher.' She at first resided in Salem, but afterwards removed to Lynn, where her fame spread over the adjoining country far and near. Whittier has made her the subject of a poem, which every one should read, not only for its account of the fortune-teller, but for its beautiful descriptions of the scenery around Lynn, especially of the bold promontory of Nahant, whose fine beach, invigorating sea air, and, more than all, its grand, rugged old rocks,—the grandest I have ever seen,—washed by the waves of old Ocean, make it the most delightful of summer resorts."

The gifts of nature are of no rank or color; they come unbidden and unsought: as the wind awakes the chords of the Æolian harp, so the spirit breathes upon the soul, and brings to life all the melody of its being. The following poem recalls to recollection some of the beautiful yet solemn strains of Miss Landon, the gifted "L. E. L.," whose untimely death at Cape Coast Castle, some years since, carried sorrow to so many English hearts:—

THE ANGEL'S VISIT.

'Twas on a glorious summer eve,—
A lovely eve in June,—
Serenely from her home above
Looked down the gentle moon;
And lovingly she smiled on me,
And softly soothed the pain—
The aching, heavy pain that lay
Upon my heart and brain.

And gently 'mid the murmuring leaves,
Scarce by its light wings stirred,
Like spirit voices soft and clear,
The night wind's song was heard;
In strains of music sweet and low
It sang to me of peace;
It bade my weary, troubled soul
Her sad complainings cease.

For bitter thoughts had filled my breast,
And sad, and sick at heart,
I longed to lay me down and rest,
From all the world apart.
"Outcast, oppressed on earth," I cried,
"O Father, take me home;
O, take me to that peaceful land
Beyond the moon-lit dome.

"On such a night as this," methought,
"Angelic forms are near;
In beauty unrevealed to us
They hover in the air.
O mother, loved and lost," I cried,
"Methinks thou'rt near me now;
Methinks I feel thy cooling touch
Upon my burning brow.

"O, guide and soothe thy sorrowing child;
And if 'tis not His will
That thou shouldst take me home with thee,
Protect and bless me still;
For dark and drear had been my life
Without thy tender smile,
Without a mother's loving care,
Each sorrow to beguile."

I ceased: then o'er my senses stole
A soothing, dreamy spell,
And gently to my ear were borne
The tones I loved so well;
A sudden flood of rosy light
Filled all the dusky wood,
And, clad in shining robes of white,
My angel mother stood.

She gently drew me to her side,
She pressed her lips to mine,
And softly said, "Grieve not, my child;
A mother's love is thine.
I know the cruel wrongs that crush
The young and ardent heart;
But falter not; keep bravely on,
And nobly bear thy part.

"For thee a brighter day's in store;
And every earnest soul
That presses on, with purpose high,
Shall gain the wished-for goal.
And thou, beloved, faint not beneath
The weary weight of care;
Daily before our Father's throne
I breathe for thee a prayer.

"I pray that pure and holy thoughts
May bless and guard thy way;
A noble and unselfish life
For thee, my child, I pray."
She paused, and fondly bent on me
One lingering look of love,

Then softly said,—and passed away,—
"Farewell! we'll meet above."

I woke, and still the silver moon
In quiet beauty shone;
And still I heard amid the leaves
The night wind's murmuring tone;
But from my heart the weary pain
Forevermore had flown;
I knew a mother's prayer for me
Was breathed before the throne.

Nothing can be more touching than Miss Forten's allusion to her sainted mother. In some of her other poems she is more light and airy, and her muse delights occasionally to catch the sunshine on its aspiring wings. Miss Forten is still young, yet on the sunny side of twenty-five, and has a splendid future before her. Those who know her best consider her on the road to fame. Were she white, America would recognize her as one of its brightest gems.

WILLIAM H. SIMPSON.

It is a compliment to a picture to say that it produces the impression of the actual scene. Taste has, frequently, for its object works of art. Nature, many suppose, may be studied with propriety, but art they reject as entirely superficial. But what is the fact? In the highest sense, art is the child of nature, and is most admired when it preserves the likeness of its parent. In Venice, the paintings of Titian, and of the Venetian artists generally, exact from the traveller a yet higher tribute, for the hues and forms around him constantly remind him of their works. Many of the citizens of Boston are often called to mention the names of their absent or departed friends, by looking upon their features, as transferred to canvas by the pencil and brush of William H. Simpson, the young colored artist. He has evidently taken Titian, Murillo, and Raphael for his masters. The Venetian painters were diligent students of the nature that was around them. The subject of our sketch seems to have imbibed their energy, as well as learned to copy the noble example they left behind. The history of painters, as well as poets, is written in their works. The best life of Goldsmith is to be found in his poem of "The Traveller" and his novel of "The Vicar of Wakefield." No one views the beautiful portrait of J. P. Kemble, in the National Gallery in London, in the character of Hamlet, without thinking of Sir Thomas Lawrence, who executed it. The organ of color is prominent in the cranium of Mr. Simpson, and it is well developed. His portraits are admired for their life-like appearance, as well as for the fine delineation which characterizes them all. It is very easy to transcribe the emotions which paintings awaken, but it is no easy matter to say why a picture is so painted as that it must awaken certain emotions. Many persons feel art, some understand it, but few both feel and understand it. Mr. Simpson is rich in depth of feeling and spiritual beauty. His portrait of John T. Hilton, which was presented to the Masonic Lodge a few months since, is a splendid piece of art. The longer you look on the features, the more the picture looks like real life. The taste displayed in the coloring of the regalia, and the admirable perspective of each badge of honor, shows great skill. No higher praise is needed than to say that a gentleman of Boston, distinguished for his good judgment in the picture gallery, wishing to secure a likeness of Hon. Charles Sumner, induced the senator to sit to Mr. Simpson for the portrait; and in this instance the artist has been signally successful.

His likenesses have been so correct, that he has often been employed to paint whole families, where only one had been bargained for in the commencement. He is considered unapproachable in taking juvenile faces. Mr. Simpson does not aspire to any thing in his art beyond portrait painting. Nevertheless, a beautiful fancy sketch, hanging in his studio, representing summer, exhibits marked ability and consummate genius. The wreath upon the head, with different kinds of grain interwoven, and the nicety of coloring in each particular kind, causes those who view it to regard him as master of his profession. Portraits of his execution are scattered over most of the Northern States and the Canadas. Some have gone to Liberia, Hayti, and California.

Mr. Simpson is a native of Buffalo, New York, where he received a liberal education. But even in school, his early inclination to draw likenesses materially interfered with his studies. The propensity to use his slate and pencil in scratching down his schoolmates, instead of doing his sums in arithmetic, often gained him severe punishment. After leaving school, he was employed as errand boy by Matthew Wilson, Esq., the distinguished artist, who soon discovered young Simpson's genius, and took him as an apprentice. In 1854, they removed to Boston, where Mr. Simpson labored diligently to acquire a thorough knowledge of the profession. Mr. Wilson stated to the writer, that he never had a man who was more attentive or more trustworthy than William H. Simpson. The colored artist has been working in his own studio nearly three years, and has his share of public patronage. Of course he has many obstacles thrown in his path by the prejudice against him as a colored man; but he long since resolved that he would reach the highest round in the ladder. His career may well be imitated.

"Would you wrest the wreath of fame
   From the hand of Fate;
Would you write a deathless name
   With the good and great;
Would you bless your fellow-men,
   Heart and soul imbue
With the holy task,—why, then
   Paddle your own canoe."

Mr. Simpson is of small figure, unmixed in blood, has a rather mild and womanly countenance, firm and resolute eye, is gentlemanly in appearance, and intelligent in conversation.

JEAN PIERRE BOYER.

JEAN PIERRE BOYER was born at Port au Prince on the 2d of February, 1776; received in Paris the advantages of European culture; fought under Rigaud against Toussaint; and in consequence of the success of the latter, quitted the island. Boyer returned to Hayti in Leclerc's expedition: he, however, separated from the French general-in-chief, placed himself at the head of his own color, and aided in vindicating the claims of his race to freedom in the last struggle with the French. On the death of Dessalines, Christophe, already master of the north, sought to take the south out of the hands of Petion. Boyer assisted his fellow-mulatto in driving off the black general. This act endeared him to the former. Gratitude, as well as regard to the common interest, gave Boyer the president's chair, on the death of Petion. Raised to that dignity, he employed his power and his energies to complete those economical and administrative reforms with which he had already been connected under his predecessor. To labor for the public good was the end of his life. In this worthy enterprise he was greatly assisted, no less by his knowledge than his moderation. Well acquainted with the character of the people that he was called to govern, conversant with all the interests of the state, he had it in his power to effect his purpose by mild as well as judicious measures. Yet were the wounds deep which he had to heal; and he could accomplish in a brief period only a small part of that which it will require generations to carry to perfection. At the death of Christophe, in 1820, Boyer was proclaimed president of the north and south. In 1822, the Spanish part of the island, with its own accord, joined the republic; and thus, from Cape Tiburn to Cape Engano, Hayti was peacefully settled under one government, with Boyer at its head. At length, in 1825, after the recognition of Hayti by others, the French, under Charles X., sold to its inhabitants the rights which they had won by their swords, for the sum of one hundred and fifty millions of francs, to be paid as an indemnity to the old planters. The peace with France created a more fraternal feeling between the two countries, and Hayti now began to regain her ancient commercial advantages, and every thing seemed prosperous. In the year 1843, a party opposed to the president made its appearance, which formed itself into a conspiracy to overthrow the government. Seeing that he could not make head against it, Boyer, in disgust, took leave of the people in a dignified manner, and retired to Jamaica, where, a few years since, he died.

Though called a mulatto, Boyer was nearly black, and his long residence in Europe gave him a polish in manners foreign to the island. He was a brave man, a good soldier, and proved himself a statesman of no ordinary ability. When he came into power, the mountains were filled with Maroons, headed by a celebrated chief named Gomar. Rigaud and Pétion had tried in vain to rid the country of these brigands. Boyer soon broke up their strongholds, dispersed them, and finally destroyed or brought them all under subjection. By his good judgment, management, and humanity, he succeeded in uniting the whole island under one government, and gained the possession of what Christophe had exhausted himself with efforts to obtain, and what Petion had sighed for, without daring to cherish a single hope that its attainment could be accomplished. Boyer was blameless in his private life.

JAMES M'CUNE SMITH, M.D.

UNABLE to get justice done him in the educational institutions of his native country, James M'Cune Smith turned his face towards a foreign land. He graduated with distinguished honors at the University of Glasgow, Scotland, where he received his diploma of M. D. For the last twenty-five years he has been a practitioner in the city of New York, where he stands at the head of his profession. On his return from Europe, the doctor was warmly welcomed by his fellow-citizens, who were anxious to pay due deference to his talents; since which time, he has justly been esteemed among the leading men of his race on the American continent. When the natural ability of the negro was assailed, some years ago, in New York, Dr. Smith came forward as the representative of the black man, and his essays on the comparative anatomy and physiology of the races, read in the discussion, completely vindicated the character of the negro, and placed the author among the most logical and scientific writers in the country.

The doctor has contributed many valuable papers to the different journals published by colored men during the last quarter of a century. The New York dailies have also received aid from him during the same period. History, antiquity, bibliography, translation, criticism, political economy, statistics,—almost every department of knowledge,—receive emblazon from his able, ready, versatile, and unwearied pen. The emancipation of the slave, and the elevation of the free colored people, has claimed the greatest share of his time as a writer. The following, from the doctor, will give but a poor idea of his style:—

"FREEDOM—LIBERTY."

> "Freedom and liberty are not synonyms. Freedom is an essence; liberty, an accident. Freedom is born within man; liberty may be conferred on him. Freedom is progressive; liberty is circumscribed. Freedom is the gift of God; liberty, the creature of society. Liberty may be taken away from man; but on whatsoever soul freedom may alight, the course of that soul is thenceforth onward and upward; society, customs, laws, armies, are but as withes in its giant grasp, if they oppose—instruments to work its will, if they assent. Human kind welcome the birth of a free soul with reverence and shoutings, rejoicing in the advent of a fresh offshoot of the divine whole, of which this is but a part."

His article in the *Anglo-African Magazine*, on "Citizenship," is one of the most logical arguments ever written in this country upon that subject. In the same journal, Dr. Smith has an essay on "The Fourteenth Query of Thomas Jefferson's Notes on Virginia," not surpassed by any thing which we have seen. These are the result of choice study, of nice observation, of fine feeling, of exquisite fancy, of consummate art, and the graceful tact of the scholar. Space will not allow us to select the many choice bits that we could cull from the writings of James M'Cune Smith.

The law of labor is equally binding on genius and mediocrity. The mind and body rarely visit this earth of ours so exactly fitted to each other, and so perfectly harmonizing together, as to rise without effort, and command in the affairs of men. It is not in the power of every one to become great. No great approximation, even toward that which is easiest attained, can ever be accomplished without the exercise of much thought and vigor of action; and thus is demonstrated the supremacy of that law which gives excellence only when earned, and assigns to labor its unfailing reward.

It is this energy of character, industry, and labor, combined with great intellectual powers, which has given Dr. Smith so much influence in New York. As a speaker, he is eloquent, and, at times, brilliant, but always clear and to the point. In stature, the doctor is not tall, but thick, and somewhat inclined to corpulency. He has a fine and well-developed head, broad and lofty brow, round, full face, firm mouth, and an eye that dazzles. In blood, he appears to be rather more Anglo-Saxon than African.

BISHOP PAYNE.

TEACHER of a small school at Charleston, South Carolina, in the year 1834, Daniel A. Payne felt the oppressive hand of slavery too severely upon him, and he quitted the southern Sodom and came north. After going through a regular course of theological studies at Gettysburg Seminary, he took up his residence at Baltimore, where he soon distinguished himself as a preacher in the African Methodist denomination. He was several years since elected bishop, and is now located in the State of Ohio.

Bishop Payne is a scholar and a poet; having published, in 1850, a volume of his productions, which created considerable interest for the work, and gave the author a standing among literary men. His writings are characterized by sound reasoning and logical conclusions, and show that he is well read. The bishop is devotedly attached to his down-trodden race, and is constantly urging upon them self-elevation. After President Lincoln's interview with the committee of colored men at Washington, and the colonization scheme recommended to them, and the appearance of Mr. Pomeroy's address to the free blacks, Bishop Payne issued the following note of advice, which was published in the *Weekly Anglo-African*:—

To the Colored People of the United States.

"MEN, BRETHREN, SISTERS: A crisis is upon us which no one can enable us to meet, conquer, and convert into blessings for all concerned, but that God who builds up one nation and breaks down another.

For more than one generation, associations of white men, entitled Colonization Societies, have been engaged in plans and efforts for our expatriation; these have been met sometimes by denunciations, sometimes by ridicule, often by argument; but now the American government has assumed the work and responsibility of colonizing us in some foreign land within the torrid zone, and is now maturing measures to consummate this scheme of expatriation.

But let us never forget that there is a vast difference between voluntary associations of men and the legally constituted authorities of a country; while the former may be held in utter contempt, the latter must always be respected. To do so is a moral and religious, as well as a political duty.

The opinions of the government are based upon the ideas, that *white men and colored men cannot live together as equals in the same country*; and that unless a voluntary and peaceable separation is effected *now*, the time *must come when there will be a war of extermination* between the two races.

Now, in view of these opinions and purposes of the government, what shall we do? My humble advice is, before all, and first of all,—even before we say *yea* or *nay*,—let us seek from the mouth of God. Let every heart be humbled, and every knee bent in prayer before him. Throughout all this land of our captivity, in all this house of our bondage, let our cries ascend perpetually to Heaven for aid and direction.

To your knees, I say, O ye oppressed and enslaved ones of this Christian republic, to your knees, *and be there.*

Before the throne of God, if nowhere else, the black man can meet his white brother as an equal, and be heard.

It has been said that he is the God of the white man, and not of the black. This is horrible blasphemy—a *lie* from the pit that is bottomless—believe it not—no—never. Murmur not against the Lord on account of the cruelty and injustice of man. His almighty arm is already stretched out against slavery—against every man, every constitution, and every union that upholds it. His avenging chariot is now moving over the bloody fields of the doomed south, crushing beneath its massive wheels the very foundations of the blasphemous system. Soon slavery shall sink like Pharaoh—even like that brazen-hearted tyrant, it shall sink to rise no more forever.

Haste ye, then, O, hasten to your God; pour the sorrows of your crushed and bleeding hearts into his sympathizing bosom. It is true that 'on the side of the oppressor there is power'—the power of the purse and the power of the sword. That is terrible. But listen to what is still *more terrible*: on the side of the oppressed there is the *strong arm* of the Lord, the Almighty God of Abraham, and Isaac, and Jacob—before his redeeming power the two contending armies, hostile to each other, and hostile to you, are like chaff before the whirlwind.

Fear not, but believe. He who is for you is more than they who are against you. Trust in him—hang upon his arm—go, hide beneath the shadow of his wings.

O God! Jehovah-jireh! wilt thou not hear us? We are poor, helpless, unarmed, despised. Is it not time for thee to hear the cry of the needy—to judge the poor of the people—to break in pieces the oppressor.

Be, O, be unto us what thou wast unto Israel in the land of Egypt, our Counsellor and Guide—our Shield and Buckler—*our Great Deliverer—our Pillar of cloud by day—our Pillar of fire by night*!

Stand between us and our enemies, O thou angel of the Lord! Be unto us a shining light—to our enemies, confusion and impenetrable darkness. Stand between us till this Red Sea be crossed, and thy redeemed, *now* sighing, bleeding, weeping, shall shout and sing, for joy, the bold anthem of the free."

A deep vein of genuine piety pervades nearly all the productions of Bishop Payne. As a pulpit orator, he stands deservedly high. In stature, he is rather under the medium size, about three fourths African, rather sharper features than the average of his race, and appears to be about fifty years of age. He is very popular, both as a writer and a speaker, with his own color. The moral, social, and political standard of the black man has been much elevated by the influence of Bishop Payne.

WILLIAM STILL.

THE long connection of Mr. Still with the anti-slavery office, in a city through which fugitive slaves had to pass in their flight from bondage, and the deep interest felt by him for the freedom and general welfare of his race, have brought him prominently before the public. It would not be good policy to say how many persons passed through his hands while on their way to the north or the British dominions, even if we knew. But it is safe to say that no man has been truer to the fleeing slave than he. In the first town where I stopped in Canada, while on a visit there a year since, I took a walk through the market one Saturday morning, and saw a large sprinkling of men and women who had escaped from the south. As soon as it was understood that I was from "the States," I was surrounded and overwhelmed with inquiries about places and persons. A short, stout, full-faced, energetically talking woman, looking me fairly in the eyes, said, "Were you ever in Philadelphia, sonny?" I answered that I had been there. "Did you know Mr. Still?" "Yes," said I: "do you know him?" "God love your heart! I reckon I does. He put me fru dat city on a swingin' limb, dat he did. Ah! he's a man dat can be depended on." This was only the opening; for as soon as it was known that I was well acquainted with William Still, the conversation turned entirely upon him, and I was surprised to see so many before me whom he had assisted. And though there were some present who complained of other Underground Railroad conductors, not a single word was uttered against Mr. Still; but all united in the strongest praise of him. In every town that I visited during a stay of ten weeks in Canada, I met persons who made feeling inquiries after him, and I was glad to find that all regarded him as a benefactor. Mr. Still is well educated, has good talents, and has cultivated them. He is an interesting and forcible writer, and some of the stories of escaped slaves, which he has contributed to the press, will challenge criticism. A correspondent of one of the public journals sent the following account to his paper of an interview which he had with Mr. Still the day previous:—

"We sat down to talk. The ultimate destiny of the black man was discussed, our host opening that his struggle for a habitation and a name must be in America. He said that his people were attached to the republic, notwithstanding many disadvantages imposed upon them, their hope being strong that patience and good citizenship would eventually soften the prejudices of the whites. Tempered as they were to our habits and climate, it would be cruel to place them on a strand but dimly known, where, surrounded by savages, they might become savage themselves.

"There was to us a sincere pleasure in our host's discourse. He is one of the leading public men among his people, and has much of the ease and polish peculiar to the well-bred Caucasian. He laughed at times, but never boisterously, and in profounder moments threw a telling solemnity into his tone and expression. When the head was averted, we heard, in well-modulated speech, such vigorous sentences and thoughtful remarks, that the identity of the speaker with the proscribed race was half forgotten; but the biased eyesight revealed only a dusky son of Ham. On a 'whatnot' table were clustered a number of books. Most of them were anti-slavery publications, although there were several volumes of sermons, and a few philosophical and historical books. We turned the conversation to literature. He was well acquainted with the authors he had read, and ventured some criticisms, indicative of study. From the earnestness of the man, it seemed that the interests of his race were very dear to him.

"It is but just to say, that he has passed many years in constant companionship with Caucasians."

Mr. Still is somewhat tall, neat in figure and person, has a smiling face, is unadulterated in blood, and gentlemanly in his intercourse with society. He is now extensively engaged in the stove and fuel trade, keeps five or six men employed, and has the patronage of some of the first families of Philadelphia. He has the entire confidence of all who know and appreciate his moral worth and business talents.

EDWIN M. BANNISTER.

EDWIN M. BANNISTER was born in the town of St. Andrew, New Brunswick, and lost his father when only six years old. He attended the grammar school in his native place, and received a better education than persons generally in his position. From early childhood he seems to have had a fancy for painting, which showed itself in the school room and at home. He often drew portraits of his school-fellows, and the master not unfrequently found himself upon the slate, where Edwin's success was so manifest that the likeness would call forth merriment from the boys, and create laughter at the expense of the teacher. At the death of his mother, when still in his minority, he was put out to live with the Hon. Harris Hatch, a wealthy lawyer, the proprietor of a fine farm some little distance in the country. In his new home Edwin did not lose sight of his drawing propensities, and though the family had nothing in the way of models except two faded portraits, kept more as relics than for their intrinsic value, he nevertheless practised upon them, and often made the copy look more life-like than the original. On the barn doors, fences, and every place where drawings could be made, the two ancient faces were to be seen pictured. When the family were away on the Sabbath at church, the young artist would take possession of the old Bible, and copy its crude engravings, then replace it upon the dusty shelf, feeling an inward gratification, that, instead of satisfying the inclination, only gave him fresh zeal to hunt for new models. By the great variety of drawings which he had made on paper, and the correct sketches taken, young Bannister gained considerable reputation in the lawyer's family, as well as in the neighborhood. Often, after the household had retired at night, the dim glimmer from the lean tallow candle was seen through the attic chamber window. It was there that the genius of the embryo artist was struggling for development. Nearly every wall in the dwelling had designs or faces pencilled upon it, and many were the complaints that the women made against the lad. At last he turned his steps towards Boston, with the hope that he might get a situation with a painter, never dreaming that his color would be a barrier to the accomplishment of such an object. Weeks were spent by the friendless, homeless, and penniless young man, and every artist had seen his face and heard his wish to become a painter. But visiting these establishments brought nothing to sustain nature, and Mr. Bannister took up the business of a hair-dresser, merely as a means of getting bread, but determined to leave it as soon as an opening presented itself with an artist. The canvas, the paint, the easel, and the pallet were brought in, and the hair-dressing saloon was turned into a studio.

There is a great diversity of opinion with regard to genius, many mistaking talent for genius. Talent is strength and subtilty of mind; genius is mental inspiration and delicacy of feeling. Talent possesses vigor and acuteness of penetration, but is surpassed by the vivid intellectual conceptions of genius. The former is skilful and bold, the latter aspiring and gentle. But talent excels in practical sagacity; and hence those striking contrasts so often witnessed in the world—the triumph of talent through its adroit and active energies, and the adversities of genius in the midst of its boundless but unattainable aspirations.

Mr. Bannister possesses genius, which is now showing itself in his studio in Boston; for he has long since thrown aside the scissors and the comb, and transfers the face to the canvas, instead of taking the hair from the head. His portraits are correct representations of the originals, and he is daily gaining admirers of his talent and taste. He has painted several pictures from his own designs, which exhibit his genius. "Wall Street at Home," represents the old gent, seated in his easy chair, boots off and slippers on, and intently reading the last news. The carpet with its variegated colors, the hat upon the table, the cloak thrown carelessly across a chair, and the pictures hanging on the walls, are all brought out with their lights and shades. A beautiful landscape, representing summer, with the blue mountains in the distance, the heated sky, and the foliage to match, is another of his pieces. It is indeed commendable in Mr. Bannister, that he has thus far overcome the many obstacles thrown in his way by his color, and made himself an honor to his race.

Mr. Bannister is spare-made, slim, with an interesting cast of countenance, quick in his walk, and easy in his manners. He is a lover of poetry and the classics, and is always hunting up some new model for his gifted pencil and brush. He has a picture representing "Cleopatra waiting to receive Marc Antony," which I regret that I did not see. I am informed, however, that it is a beautifully-executed picture. Mr. Bannister has a good education, is often called upon to act as secretary to public meetings, and is not by any means a bad speaker, when on the platform. Still young, enterprising, and spirited, we shall be mistaken if Edwin M. Bannister does not yet create a sensation in our country as an artist.

LEONARD A. GRIMES.

LEONARD A. GRIMES is a native of Leesburg, Loudon county, Va., and was born in 1815. He went to Washington when a boy, and was first employed in a butcher's shop, and afterwards in an apothecary's establishment. He subsequently hired himself out to a slaveholder, whose confidence he soon gained. Accompanying his employer in some of his travels in the remote Southern States, young Grimes had an opportunity of seeing the different phases of slave life; and its cruelty created in his mind an early hatred to the institution which has never abated. He could not resist the appeals of the bondmen for aid in making their escape to a land of freedom, and consequently was among the first to take stock in the Underground Railroad. After saving money enough by his earnings, he purchased a hack and horses, and became a hackman in the city of Washington. In his new vocation, Mr. Grimes met with success, and increased his business until he was the owner of a number of carriages and horses, and was considered one of the foremost men in his line. During all this time he never lost sight of the slave, and there is no telling how many he put on the road to Canada. A poor woman and her seven children were about being carried away to the far south by the slave-trader. Her husband, a free black, sought out Leonard A. Grimes, and appealed to his humanity, and not in vain; for in less than forty-eight hours, the hackman penetrated thirty miles into Virginia, and, under cover of night, brought out the family. The husband, wife, and little ones, a few days after, breathed the free air of Canada. Mr. Grimes was soon suspected, arrested, tried, and sentenced to two years in the state prison, at Richmond. Here he remained; and the close, dank air, the gloom, the high, dull, cold, stone walls, the heavy fetters upon his limbs, the entire lack of any thing external to distract his thoughts from his situation, all together, produced a feeling of depression he had never known before. It was at this time that Mr. Grimes "felt," as he says, "that great spiritual change which makes all things new for the soul." From that hour he became a preacher to his keepers, and, as far as he was allowed, to his fellow-prisoners. This change lightened his confinement, and caused him to feel that he was sent there to do his Master's will.

At the expiration of his imprisonment, Mr. Grimes returned to Washington, and employed himself in driving a furniture car, and jobbing about the city. Feeling himself called to preach, he underwent the required examination, received a license, and, without quitting his employment, preached as occasion offered. Not long after this, he removed to New Bedford, Mass., where he resided two years. There was in Boston a small congregation, worshipping in a little room, but without a regular preacher. An invitation was extended to Mr. Grimes to become their pastor. He accepted, came to Boston, and, under his ministration, the society increased so rapidly that a larger house was soon needed. A lot was purchased, the edifice begun, and now they have a beautiful church, capable of seating six or seven hundred persons. The cost of the building, including the land, was $13,000; all of which, except $2,000, has been paid. We need not say that this was accomplished through the untiring exertions of Mr. Grimes. Besides his labors in the society, he was often engaged in aiding fugitive slaves in the redemption of their relations from the servitude of the south. During his fourteen years' residence in Boston, he has had $6,000 pass through his hands, for the benefit of that class of persons. In action he is always—

> "Upward, onward, pressing forward
>   Till each bondman's chains shall fall,
> Till the flag that floats above us
>   Liberty proclaims to all."

In 1854, Mr. Grimes became conspicuously connected with the fugitive slave Anthony Burns. Mainly through his efforts the latter gained his freedom. The pastor of the Twelfth Baptist Church is, emphatically, a practical man. Nearly all public meetings are held either in his church or vestry, he taking a suitable part in every thing that tends to the welfare of his race. "Brother" Grimes is above the middle size, good looking, has a full face, a countenance which has the appearance of one who has seen no trouble, and rather more Anglo-Saxon than African. He is polite in his manners, and genteel in his personal appearance. As a preacher, he is considered sound, and well versed in theology. He is regarded as one of the ablest men in prayer in Boston. His sermons are characterized by deep feeling and good sense. No man in the city has fewer enemies or more friends than Leonard A. Grimes.

PRESIDENT GEFFRARD.

Fabre Geffrard, born at Cayes, in the year 1806, was the son of a general who had shown himself humane under Dessalines, and had been with Petion, one of the chief promoters of the constitution of 1806. Left early an orphan, young Geffrard entered the army at the age of fifteen, and only after twenty-two years' service obtained his captain's commission. He took part—unwisely, as events proved—in the revolution of 1843, which overturned the able but indolent Boyer, and distinguished himself at the head of a small body of troops against the government forces, deceiving them as to his numbers by the rapidity of his movements, and as to his resources by supplying provisions to his famished enemies at a time when he himself was short of rations. When the revolution, which had originated with the most impatient of the mulattoes, led in turn to a rising of that portion of the blacks who represented absolute barbarism, and whose axiom was that every mulatto should be exterminated, Geffrard marched against and defeated the black leader, Arceau; but, true to that humanity which seems the very basis of his character, we find him in turn defending the middle classes from the blacks, and the insurgent blacks, when taken prisoners, from the National Guard. He became lieutenant-general during these movements; but General Riche, who was made president in 1846, and who bore Geffrard a grudge for having on a former occasion made him a prisoner, sent him before a court martial, which, in Hayti, means sending one to death. Through the adroitness, however, of Riche's minister of war, the general was acquitted. The president of the court martial was Soulouque, who seems to have imbibed, on this occasion, a strange friendship for the man whose life he had been the means of preserving, and who thus spared him, in an otherwise unaccountable manner, during his subsequent rule, and even forced on him the title of duke, which Geffrard did not care to assume. In two disastrous wars which he undertook, in 1849 and in 1855–6, against the Dominican republic, Geffrard alone won credit. In the former he was wounded at the head of the division; in both, by his courage, his activity, his cheerfulness, and above all, by his anxious care for the welfare of his soldiers, he exhibited the most striking contrast to Soulouque's imbecile generalship and brutal indifference to the safety of others.

In 1858, Soulouque, seeing that Geffrard's popularity was becoming great, sought an opportunity to have him arrested. Spies were placed near him. The general, however, was warned of his danger, and he knew that nothing was to be hoped for from Soulouque's ferocity when once aroused by jealousy. Just then, the emissaries of a conspiracy, formed in the valley of the Artibonite, beyond the mountain chain which forms the backbone of the island, were in Port au Prince in search of a leader. They addressed themselves to Geffrard. The cup of Soulouque's tyranny was full. Geffrard listened to their solicitations, but was barely able, by the aid of a friend, to escape in an open boat, on the very night when he was to have been arrested. He succeeded in reaching St. Mark, but found that the people were not ready for a revolution. He repaired to Gonaives, where the inhabitants were thoroughly ripe for a change of rulers. Thus six men coming by sea, met by three on land, were sufficient to carry the place without the shedding of a drop of blood. On the 22d of December, he issued two proclamations, the one abolishing the empire, the other establishing a republic. From thence he proceeded to St. Mark, where he was enthusiastically welcomed by all classes, the army joining him to a man. With two thousand men he started for Port au Prince, the capital. Soulouque, in the mean time, gathered his forces, amounting to six thousand well-drilled troops, and set out to meet his rival, but soon found that his army could not be relied on, and he returned amid the hootings of the people. The emperor was permitted to take refuge in the French consulate, and from thence took passage in an English steamer for Jamaica. Geffrard entered Port au Prince in triumph; the constitution of 1846 was adopted, and an election held which chose Geffrard president for life, with the privilege of nominating his successor. All agree that he is a good man. His great aim appears to be the moral, social, and intellectual improvement of the people.

Most of the army have been disbanded; and those retained are better fed, better paid, and clothed in a more suitable manner. New firearms have been introduced, reforms instituted both in the government and the army, agriculture and commerce encouraged, old roads repaired and new ones built. His state papers show him to be a man of superior natural abilities, and we believe that he is destined to do more for Hayti and her people than any ruler since the days of Toussaint L'Ouverture. Geffrard is a grief in color (nearly black), of middle height, slim in figure, a pleasing countenance, sparkling eye, gray hair, fifty-six years of age, limbs supple by bodily exercise, a splendid horseman, and liberal to the arts, even to extravagance. Possessing a polished education, he is gentlemanly in his conversation and manners. His democratic ideas induce him to dress without ornaments of any kind. Soon after assuming the presidency, he resolved to encourage immigration, and issued an address to the colored Americans, filled with patriotic and sympathetic feeling for his race.

GEORGE B. VASHON.

PASSING through the schools of Pittsburg, his native place, and graduating at Oberlin College with the degree of Master of Arts, George B. Vashon started in life with the advantage of a good education. He studied law with Hon. Walter Forward, and was admitted to the bar in 1847. He soon after visited Hayti, where he remained nearly three years, returning home in 1850. Called to a professorship in New York Central College, Mr. Vashon discharged the duties of the office with signal ability. A gentleman—a graduate of that institution, now a captain in the federal army—told the writer that he and several of his companions, who had to recite to Professor Vashon, made it a practice for some length of time to search Greek, Latin, and Hebrew, for phrases and historical incidents, and would then question the professor, with the hope of "running him on a snag." "But," said he, "we never caught him once, and we came to the conclusion that he was the best-read man in the college." Literature has a history, and few histories can compare with it in importance, significance, and moral grandeur. There is, therefore, a great price to pay for literary attainments, which will have an inspiring and liberalizing influence—a price not in silver and gold, but in thorough mental training. This training will give breadth of view, develop strength of character and a comprehensive spirit, by which the ever-living expressions of truth and principle in the past may be connected with those of a like character in the present.

Mr. Vashon seems to have taken this view of what constitutes the thorough scholar, and has put his theory into practice. All of the productions of his pen show the student and man of literature. But he is not indebted alone to culture, for he possesses genius of no mean order—poetic genius, far superior to many who have written and published volumes. As Dryden said of Shakspeare, "he needed not the spectacles of books to read Nature; he looked inward, and found her there." The same excellence appertains to his poetical description of the beautiful scenery and climate of Hayti, in his "Vincent Ogé." His allusion to Columbus's first visit to the island is full of solemn grandeur:—

> "The waves dash brightly on thy shore,
> Fair island of the southern seas,
> As bright in joy as when, of yore,
> They gladly hailed the Genoese—
> That daring soul who gave to Spain
> A world-last trophy of her reign."

Our limited space will not permit our giving more of this, or other poems of Mr. Vashon. The following extract from his admirable essay in the *Anglo-African Magazine*, entitled, "The Successive Advances of Astronomy," is characteristic of his prose:—

"The next important step recorded in the annals of astronomy was the effort to reform the calendar by means of the bissextile year. This effort was made at the time when Julius Cæsar was chief pontiff at Rome. It is noteworthy, as being the only valuable contribution made to astronomical science by the Romans; and, even in this matter, Cæsar acted under the guidance of the Grecian astronomer Sosigenes. We are not to suppose, however, that the Romans were totally indifferent to the subject of astronomy. We are informed by Cicero, in his elegant treatise concerning 'Old Age,' that Gaius Gallus was accustomed to spend whole days and nights in making observations upon the heavenly bodies, and that he took pleasure in predicting to his friends the eclipses of the sun and moon a long time before they occurred. Besides, in the 'Scipio's Dream' of the same author, we find, in the course of an admirable dissertation upon the immortality of the soul, an account of a terrestrial system, according to which our earth was the central body, around which the concave sphere of the starry heavens revolved; while, in the space between, the Moon, Venus, Mercury, the Sun, Mars, Jupiter, and Saturn moved with retrograde courses, in the order here mentioned. In fact, this system was the one which was afterwards adopted, elaborated, and zealously maintained by the famous Ptolemy of Alexandria, and which has ever since borne his name. To Ptolemy, then, who flourished about the commencement of the second century, the world is indebted for the first complete system of astronomy that secured the approbation of all the learned. This it was enabled to do by the ingenious, although not perfect, explanation which it gave of the planetary movements, by supposing these bodies to move in circles whose centres had an easterly motion along an imaginary circle. Thus these epicycles, as the circles were called, moving along the imaginary circle, or deferent, cause the planets to have, at times, an apparent easterly direction, at other times a westerly one, and at other times, again, to appear stationary. Thus recommended, the Ptolemaic system continued to gain adherents, until the irruptions of the Huns under Alaric and Attila, and the destruction of the celebrated library at Alexandria by the fanatical and turbulent Christians of that city, laid waste the fair domains of science. Being thus driven from the places where Learning had fixed her favorite seats, it took refuge with the Arabs, who preserved it with watchful care, until happier times restored it to Europe. It returned with the conquering Moors who established themselves in Spain, was brought again under the notice of the Christian states in the thirteenth century, through the patronage of the emperor Frederic II. of Germany, and Alphonso X. of Castile, and flourished more than two hundred years longer, without any rival to dispute its claims to correctness."

Mr. Vashon is of mixed blood, in stature of medium size, rather round face, with a somewhat solemn countenance,—a man of few words,—needs to be drawn out to be appreciated. While visiting a distinguished colored gentleman at Rochester, N. Y., some years ago, the host, who happened to be a wit as well as an orator, invited in "Professor T."—a man ignorant of education, but filled with big talk and high-sounding words without understanding their meaning—to entertain Mr. Vashon, intending it as a joke. "Professor T." used all the language that he was master of, but to no purpose: the man of letters sat still, listened, gazed at the former, but did not dispute any point raised. The uneducated professor, feeling that he had been imposed upon, called Mr. D. one side, and in a whisper said, "Are you sure that this is an educated man? I fear that he is an impostor; for I tried, but could not call him out."

ROBERT MORRIS.

About the year 1837, Ellis Gray Loring, Esq., took into his office, as an errand boy, a colored lad of fifteen years of age. The youngster had a better education than those generally of his age, which showed that he had been attentive at school. He was not long in his new situation ere he began to exhibit a liking for the contents of the sheepskin-covered books that stood around on the shelves, and lay upon the baize-covered tables. Mr. Loring, seeing the aptitude of the lad, inquired if he wanted to become a lawyer, and was answered in the affirmative. From that moment the errand boy became the student, and studied with an earnestness not often equalled. At scarcely twenty-one years of age he was admitted to the Boston bar. This was Robert Morris. With all the prejudice before him, he kept steadily on, resolving that he would overcome the negro-hate which stood in the way of his efforts to prosecute his profession. Gradually he grew in practice, until most of his fellow-members forgot his color in the admiration of his eloquence and business talent. Mr. Morris is of unmixed blood, but not black. Small in stature, a neat figure, smiling face, always dressed with the greatest care, gentlemanly in manner and conversation, his influence has been felt in behalf of his race. He is an interesting speaker, quick in his gestures, ardent in his feelings, and enthusiastic in what he undertakes. He rather inclines to a military life, and has, on more than one occasion, attempted the organization of an independent company.

At the presentation of the portrait of John T. Hilton to the Prince Hall Grand Lodge of Boston, Mr. Morris made a speech, of which the following is an extract:—

"I wish we could point to well-executed likenesses of those old colored heroes of revolutionary memory, who so nobly, patriotically, and willingly, side by side with their white brethren, fought, bled, and died to secure freedom and independence to America.

"It would be a source of continual pleasure could we have in some public room pictures true to life of those intrepid heroes, Denmark Veazie and Nat Turner, whose very names were a terror to oppressors; who, conceiving the sublime idea of freedom for themselves and their race, animated by a love of liberty of which they had been ruthlessly deprived, made an attempt to sever their bonds; and though, in such attempts to open the prison doors of slavery and let the oppressed go free, they were unsuccessful, their efforts and determination were none the less noble and heroic. In the future history of our country, their names to us will shine as brightly as that of the glorious old hero, who, with his colored and white followers, so strategically captured Harper's Ferry, and touched a chord in the life of our country that will vibrate throughout the land, and will not cease until the last fetter has been struck from the limbs of the last bondman in the nation; and though the bodies of these heroes lie mouldering in the clay, their souls are 'marching on.'

"I never visit our 'Cradle of Liberty,' and look at the portraits that grace its walls, without thinking that the selection is sadly incomplete, because the picture of the massacred Crispus Attucks is not there. He was the first martyr in the Boston massacre of March 5, 1770, when the British soldiers were drawn up in line on King (now State) Street, to intimidate the Boston populace. On that eventful day, a band of patriots, led by Attucks, marched from Dock Square to drive the redcoats from the vicinity of the old State House. Emboldened by the courageous conduct of this colored hero, the band pressed forward, and in attempting to wrest a musket from one of the British soldiers, Attucks was shot. His was the first blood that crimsoned the pavement of King Street, and by the sacrifice of his life, he awoke that fiery hatred of British oppression which culminated in the declaration of American independence. At this late day a portrait of this hero cannot be had; but our children will live to see the day when the people of this commonwealth, mindful of their deep and lasting obligation, will, through their legislature, appropriate a sufficient sum wherewith to erect a suitable monument to preserve the memory of Attucks, and mark the spot where he fell."

Mr. Morris deserves great credit for having fought his way up to his present position. Rumor says that his profession has paid him well, and that he is now a man of property. If so, we are glad; for the poet writes, "If thou wouldst have influence, put money in thy purse."

WILLIAM J. WILSON.

In the columns of Frederick Douglass's paper, the *Anglo-African Magazine*, and the *Weekly Anglo-African*, has appeared at times, over the signature of "Ethiop," some of the raciest and most amusing essays to be found in the public journals of this country. As a sketch writer of historical scenes and historical characters,—choosing his own subjects, suggested by his own taste or sympathies,—few men are capable of greater or more successful efforts than William J. Wilson. In his imaginary visit to the "Afric-American Picture Gallery," he gives the following sketch of the head of Phillis Wheatley.

"This picture hangs in the north-east corner of the gallery, and in good light, and is so decidedly one of the finest in the collection, whether viewed in an artistic light or in point of fact, that it is both a constant charm and study for me. The features, though indicative of a delicate organization, are of the most pleasing cast. The facial angle contains full ninety degrees; the forehead is finely formed, and the brain large; the nose is long, and the nostrils thin, while the eyes, though not large, are well set. To this may be added a small mouth, with lips prettily turned, and a chin—that perfection of beauty in the female face—delicately tapered from a throat and neck that are of themselves perfection. The whole make-up of this face is an index of healthy intellectual powers, combined with an active temperament, over which has fallen a slight tinge of religious pensiveness. Thus hangs Phillis Wheatley before you in the Afric-American Picture Gallery; and if we scrutinize her more closely through her career and her *works*, we shall find her truly an extraordinary person. Stolen at the tender age of seven years from the fond embraces of a mother, whose image never once faded from her memory, and ferried over in the *vile slave ship* from Afric's sunny clime to the cold shores of America, and sold under the hammer to a Boston merchant—a delicate child, a girl, alone, desolate; a chilly, dreary world before her, a chain on her feet, and a thorn in her bosom, and an iron mask on her head, what chance, what opportunity was there for her to make physical, moral, or mental progress? In these respects, how get up to, or keep pace with, other and more favored people?—how get in the advance?—how ascend, at last, without a single competitor, the highest scale of human eminence? Phillis Wheatley did all, and more than this. A sold thing, a bought chattel at seven years, she mastered, notwithstanding, the English language in sixteen months. She carried on with her friends and acquaintances an extensive and elegant epistolary correspondence at *twelve* years of age, composed her first poem at *fourteen*, became a proficient Latin scholar at *seventeen*, and published in England her book of poems, dedicated to the Countess of Huntington, at *nineteen*; and with the mantle of just fame upon her shoulders, sailed from America to England to receive the meed due to her learning, her talents, and her virtues, at *twenty-two*. What one of America's paler daughters, contemporary with her, with all the advantages that home, fortune, friends, and favor bring,—what one ascended so far up the hill of just fame at any age? I have searched in vain to find the name upon the literary page of our country's record.

"O Wheatley!
What degrading hand, what slavish chain,
What earthly power, could link thy nobler soul
To baser things, and check its eagle flight?
Angel of purity, child of beauteous song,
Thy harp still hangs within our sight,
To cheer, though thou art gone."

The succeeding extract from his poem "The Coming Man" is very suggestive, especially at this time.

"I break the chains that have been clanging
Down through the dim vault of ages;
I gird up my strength,—mind and arm,—
And prepare for the terrible conflict.
I am to war with principalities, powers, wrongs
With oppressions,—with all that curse humanity.
I am resolved. 'Tis more than half my task;
'Twas the great need of all my past existence.
The glooms that have so long shrouded me,
Recede as vapor from the new presence,
And the light-gleam—it must be life—
So brightens and spreads its pure rays before,
That I read my mission as 'twere a book.
It is life; life in which none but *men*—
Not those who only wear the form—can live
To give this life to the *World*; to make men
Out of the thews and sinews of oppressed slaves."

Mr. Wilson is a teacher, and whether the following is drawn from his own experience, or not, we are left to conjecture.

THE TEACHER AND HIS PUPIL.

SCENE.—School Room. School in session.

Dramatis Personæ.
TEACHER. A bachelor rising thirty.
PUPIL. A beautiful girl of sixteen.

I see that curling and high-archéd brow.
    "Scold thee?" Ay, that I will.
    Pouting I see thee still;
Thou jade! I know that thou art laughing now!

Silence! hush! nor dare one word to mutter!
    If it were e'er so gentle,
    (I speak in tone parental,)
Do not thy very softest whisper utter.

I know that startled trembling all a hoax,
    Thou pert and saucy thing!
    I'll make thy fine ears ring;
I'll pretermit thy silly, taunting jokes.

"Whip thee?" Ay, that I will, and whip thee well;
    Thy chattering tongue now hold!
    There, there; I will no further scold.
How down those lovely cheeks the hot tears fell!

How quickly changed! Nay, nay; come hither, child.
    'Tis with kindness I would rule;
    Severity's the erring fool,
Who harms the tender or excites the wild.

What! trembling yet, and shy? Nay, do not fear;
    Sure, sure I'll harm thee not;
    My gentlest, thine's a better lot;
So raise those azure eyes with radiant cheer.

Cheer up, then; there, now thou canst go. Retain,
    I pray, within thy heart,
    Not the unpleasant part
That's past. The other let remain.

To possess genius, the offspring of which ennobles the sentiments, enlarges the affections, kindles the imagination, and gives to us a view of the past, the present, and the future, is one of the highest gifts that the Creator bestows upon man. With acute powers of conception, a sparkling and lively fancy, and a quaintly curious felicity of diction, Mr. Wilson wakes us from our torpidity and coldness to a sense of our capabilities. In personal appearance he is under the middle size; his profile is more striking than his front face; he has a rather pleasing countenance, and is unmixed in race; has fine conversational powers, is genteel in his manners, and is a pleasant speaker upon the platform.

JOHN MERCER LANGSTON.

ONE of the most promising young men of the west is John M. Langston, a native of Chillicothe, Ohio, and a graduate of Oberlin College. He studied theology and law, and, preferring the latter, was admitted to the bar, and is now successfully practising his profession.

The end of all eloquence is to sway men. It is, therefore, bound by no arbitrary rules of diction or style, formed on no specific models, and governed by no edicts of self-elected judges. It is true, there are degrees of eloquence, and equal success does not imply equal excellence. That which is adapted to sway the strongest minds of an enlightened age ought to be esteemed the most perfect, and, doubtless, should be the criterion by which to test the abstract excellence of all oratory. Mr. Langston represents the highest idea of the orator, as exemplified in the power and discourses of Sheridan in the English House of Commons, and Vergniaud in the Assembly of the Girondists. He is not fragmentary in his speeches; but, a deep, majestic stream, he moves steadily onward, pouring forth his rich and harmonious sentences in strains of impassioned eloquence. His style is bold and energetic—full of spirit. He is profound without being hollow, and ingenious without being subtile.

Being at Oberlin a few years since, and learning that a suit was to be tried before a justice of the peace, in which Langston was counsel for the defence, I attended. Two white lawyers—one from Elyria, the other residing at Oberlin—were for the plaintiff. One day was consumed in the examination and cross-questioning of witnesses, in which the colored lawyer showed himself more than a match for his antagonists. The plaintiff's counsel moved an adjournment to the next day. The following morning the court room was full before the arrival of the presiding justice, and much interest was manifested on both sides.

Langston's oratory was a model for the students at the college, and all who could leave their studies or recitations were present. When the trial commenced, it was observed that the plaintiffs had introduced a third lawyer on their side. This was an exhibition of weakness on their part, and proved the power of the "black lawyer," who stood single-handed and alone. The pleading commenced, and consumed the forenoon; the plaintiff only being heard. An adjournment for an hour occurred, and then began one of the most powerful addresses that I had heard for a long time. In vigor of thought, in imagery of style, in logical connection, in vehemence, in depth, in point, and in beauty of language, Langston surpassed his opponents, won the admiration of the jury and the audience, and, what is still better for his credit, he gained the suit. Mr. Langston's practice extends to Columbus, the capital of the state, and in the county towns, within fifty miles of his home, he is considered the most successful man at the bar.

An accomplished scholar and a good student, he displays in his speeches an amount of literary acquirements not often found in the mere business lawyer. When pleading he speaks like a man under oath, though without any starched formality of expression. The test of his success is the permanent impression which his speeches leave on the memory. They do not pass away with the excitement of the moment, but remain in the mind, with the lively colors and true proportions of the scenes which they represent. Mr. Langston is of medium size and of good figure, high and well-formed forehead, eyes full, but not prominent, mild and amiable countenance, modest deportment, strong, musical voice, and wears the air of a gentleman. He is highly respected by men of the legal profession throughout the state. He is a vigorous writer, and in the political campaigns, contributes both with speech and pen to the liberal cause. Few men in the south-west have held the black man's standard higher than John Mercer Langston.

WILLIAM C. NELL.

No man in New England has performed more uncompensated labor for humanity, and especially for his own race, than William

C. Nell. Almost from the commencement of the *Liberator*, and the opening of an anti-slavery office in Boston, he has been connected in some way with the cause of freedom. In 1840, Mr. Nell, in company with William Lloyd Garrison, Wendell Phillips, and Francis Jackson, signed a petition to the city government, asking it to grant equal school rights to the colored children. From that time till 1855, Mr. Nell lost no opportunity to press this question. During all this while he had to meet the frowns of the whites, who were instigated by that mean and relentless prejudice which slavery had implanted in their minds; but he went steadily on, resolving that he would not cease till equality was acknowledged in the Boston schools. In 1855 the obnoxious rule was abolished, and the colored youths admitted to the schools, without regard to complexion. On the evening of December 17 of the same year, Mr. Nell was publicly presented with a testimonial by his fellow-citizens. This consisted of a valuable gold watch. Master Frederick Lewis, on behalf of the children, addressed Mr. Nell as follows:—

"Champion of equal school rights, we hail thee. With unbounded gratitude we bow before thee. Our youthful hearts bless thee for thy incessant labors and untiring zeal in our behalf. We would fain assist in swelling thy praise, which flows from every lip; but this were a tribute far too small. Noble friend: thou hast opened for us the gate that leadeth to rich treasures; and as we pass through, Ambition lendeth us a hand—ay, she quickeneth our pace; and as, obeying her, we look through the vista of future years, we recognize bright Fame in a field of literary glory, her right hand extended with laurels of honor, to crown those who shall be most fortunate in gaining the platform whereon she standeth; while before her is spread the banquet, with viands rich and rare, that our literary hunger may be satiated. To this we aspire. To gain this we will be punctual to school, diligent in study, and well-behaved; and may we be enabled to reach the goal, that, in thy declining years, thy heart may be gladdened by what thine eye beholdeth, and it shall be like a crown of gold encircling thy head, and like a rich mantle thrown around thee, studded with jewels and precious stones.

"Kind benefactor: accept, we entreat thee, this simple token, emblem of the bright, gladsome years of youthful innocence and purity; and as thou hast befriended us, so may we ever prove faithful friends to thee. May the blessings of Heaven attend thee through life's ever-changing scenes and intricate windings, is our prayer."

Mrs. Georgiana O. Smith then presented to Mr. Nell the watch, bearing this inscription:—

"A Tribute to
WILLIAM C. NELL,
FROM THE COLORED CITIZENS OF BOSTON,
For his untiring efforts in behalf of
EQUAL SCHOOL RIGHTS,
Dec. 17, 1855."

Mrs. Smith's address was well conceived, and delivered in an eloquent and feeling manner, which seemed to touch every heart and quicken every pulse. Mr. Nell responded in an able speech, recounting many of the scenes that they had passed through. William Lloyd Garrison and Wendell Phillips were both present, and addressed the meeting, showing their deep interest in the black man's rights. Besides contributing occasionally to the columns of the *Liberator*, Frederick Douglass's paper, the *Anglo-African*, and other journals, Mr. Nell is the author of the "Colored Patriots of the American Revolution," a book filled with interesting incidents connected with the history of the blacks of this country, past and present. He has also written several smaller works, all of which are humanitarian in their character. He has taken a leading part in most of the conventions and public gatherings of the colored citizens, held within the past twenty-five years. From 1835 to 1850, no public meeting was complete without William C. Nell as secretary.

Deeply interested in the intellectual development and cultivation of his race, he aided in the organization of the "Adelphic Union Association," which did much good in its day. Later still, he brought into existence the "Histrionic Club," a society that encouraged reading, recitation, and social conversation. In this he drew the finest talent that Boston could produce. They gave a public representation a few years since, which was considered one of the most classic performances which has ever been witnessed. Mr. Nell is of medium height, slim, genteel figure, quick step, elastic movement, a thoughtful yet pleasant brow, thin face, and chaste in his conversation. Born in Boston, passing through her public schools, a good student, and a lover of literature, he has a cultivated understanding, and has collected together more facts, on the race with whom he is identified, than any other man of our acquaintance. An ardent admirer of Wendell Phillips, he seems as much attached to that distinguished orator as Boswell was to Johnson. Mr. Nell's devotion to his race is not surpassed by any man living.

JOHN SELLA MARTIN.

J. SELLA MARTIN is a native of Charlotte, North Carolina, and was born on the 27th of September, 1832. His mother was a slave, and by the laws of the state the child follows the condition of the mother. Young Martin sustained the double but incongruous relation to his owner of master and son. At the tender age of six years, the boy, together with his mother and an only sister, was taken from the old homestead at midnight, and carried to Columbus, Georgia, where they were exposed for sale. Here they were separated, the mother and daughter being purchased by one man, and Sella by another. The latter had the good fortune, however, to fall into the hands of an old bachelor, with whom he lived, in the capacity of *valet de chambre*, until he was eighteen years old. His opportunities, while with him, for acquiring a knowledge of books and the world generally, were far better than usually fall to the lot of the most favored house servants. Both master and slave boarded at the principal hotel in the place; and the latter, associating with other servants, and occasionally meeting travellers from the free states, obtained much valuable information respecting the north and Canada, and his owner was not a little surprised one day when a complaint came to him that his servant had been furnishing passes for slaves in the neighborhood to visit their wives. Sella was called before the master, and threatened with severe punishment if he ever wrote another pass for a slave. About two years after this, the owner partially lost his sight, and the servant became first the reader of the morning paper, and subsequently the amanuensis in the transaction of all the master's business. An intimacy sprang up between the two, and it being for the white man's interest that his chattel should read and write correctly, the latter became in fact the pupil of the former, which accelerated his education. At the age of eighteen his owner died, and Sella was left free. But the influence of the heirs at law was sufficient to set the will aside, and the free young man, together with other slaves of the estate, was sold on the auction block, and the new owner took Sella to Mobile, where he resided till 1852, when he was again sold and taken to New Orleans. Here the subject of our sketch hired his own time, became a dealer in fruit and oysters, and succeeded in saving a little money for himself, with which he made his escape on a Mississippi steamer in December, 1855, and arrived at Chicago on the 6th of January, 1856. The great hope of his younger days had been attained, and he was now free. But Mr. Martin had seen too much of slavery to feel satisfied with merely getting his own freedom, and he therefore began the inquiry to see what he could do for those whom he had left in the prison house of bondage. While at Chicago, he made the acquaintance of Mr. H. Ford Douglass, who was just about to visit the interior of the state, to deliver a course of lectures. The latter observed by his conversation with Mr. Martin, that he possessed the elements of a good speaker, and persuaded him to join and take part in the meetings. It is said that Mr. Martin's first attempt in public was an entire failure. He often alludes to it himself, and says that the humiliation which he experienced reminded him of the time when he was sold on the auction block—only that the former seemed the cheaper sale of the two. He was advised never to try the platform again. But his want of success on the first occasion stimulated him to new exertion, and we are told that he wrote out a speech, committed it to memory, and delivered it two days after to the satisfaction of all present. Mr. Douglass himself characterizes it as a remarkable effort. But there was too much monotony in the delivery of one or two lectures over and over, and his natural aversion to committed speeches induced Mr. Martin to quit the lecturing field. He now resolved to resume his studies, and for this purpose he removed to Detroit, Michigan, where he commenced under the tutorage of an able Baptist minister. Feeling that he was called to preach, soon after this he began the study of theology, and remained the student until his education was so far finished that he felt justified in his own mind to commence lecturing and preaching. About this time he made the tour of the State of Michigan, and lectured with great success. In the beautiful and flourishing town of Coldwater, he addressed a large and influential meeting, and the effect upon the audience was such as to raise the speaker high in their estimation. The weekly paper said of this lecture,—

"Our citizens filled the court house to hear J. S. Martin speak for his own race and in behalf of the oppressed. The citizens admired and were even astonished at his success as a public speaker. He is a natural orator, and, considering his opportunities, is one of the most interesting and forcible speakers of his age, and of *the* age. Indeed, he is a prodigy. It would seem impossible that one kept in 'chains and slavery,' and in total ignorance till within a few months, could so soon attain so vast a knowledge of the English language, and so clear and comprehensive a view of general subjects. Nature has made him a great man. His propositions and his arguments, his deductions and illustrations, are new and original; his voice and manner are at his command and prepossessing; his efforts are unstudied and effectual. The spirit which manifests itself is one broken loose from bondage and stimulated with freedom."

Shortly after this, Mr. Martin was ordained and settled over the Michigan Street Baptist Church, Buffalo, New York, where he labored with signal success till April, 1859, when he removed east. During the same summer he was introduced to the Boston public by Mr. Kalloch, the popular preacher at the Tremont Temple. The latter, pleased with Mr. Martin, secured his services while away on his annual vacation, which occupied six or eight weeks. No place of religious worship was more thronged than the Temple during the time that he filled its pulpit. At the termination of his engagement at the Temple, Mr. Martin was invited by Dr. Eddy to preach for him a few weeks, which he did with credit to himself and satisfaction to the society. The first Baptist Church at Lawrence being without a pastor, Mr. Martin was engaged to supply the pulpit, and was there seven or eight months, and might have remained longer; but during this time he received a call from the Joy Street Church, Boston, and feeling that his labor was more needed with his own color, he accepted the latter. He has now been at the Joy Street Church about three years, where his preaching has met with marked success. That society had long been in a declining state; but the church is now as well filled on Sundays as any place in the city. In the summer of 1861, Mr. Martin visited England, and remained abroad six months, where he did good service for the cause of freedom. On his return home he was warmly welcomed by his church and congregation. Soon after, he secured the freedom of his only sister and her two children, whom he settled at the west. In person, Mr. Martin is somewhat taller than the medium height; firm, dignified walk; not what would be termed handsome, but has a pleasing countenance; in race, half and half; eyes clear and bright; forehead well developed; gentlemanly in his deportment; has a popularity not surpassed by any of the preachers of Boston.

He has written considerably for the press, both prose and poetry. Some of the latter is much admired. His poem "The Hero and the Slave" has been read in public entertainments, and received with applause.

CHARLES LENOX REMOND.

CHARLES L. REMOND is a native of Salem, Mass. He has the honor, we believe, of being the first colored man to take the field as a lecturer against slavery. He has been, more or less, in the employ of the Anti-Slavery Society for the past twenty-eight or thirty years. In 1840, he visited England as a delegate to the first "World's Anti-Slavery Convention," held in London. He remained abroad nearly two years, lecturing in the various towns and cities of Great Britain and Ireland. The following lines, addressed to him, appeared in one of the public journals, after the delivery of one of his thrilling speeches, in Belfast, and will give some idea of the estimation in which he was held as a platform speaker.

TO C. L. REMOND.

Go forth and fear not! Glorious is the cause
Which thou dost advocate; and nobly, too,

Hast thou fulfilled thy mission—nobly raised
Thy voice against oppression, and the woes
Of injured millions; and, if they are men,
Who can deny for them a Saviour died?
Nor will it e'er be asked, in that dread day
When black and white shall stand before the throne
Of Him their common Parent, "Unto which
Partition of the human race didst thou
Belong on earth?" Enough for thee to fill
The lot assigned thee, as ordained by Heaven.
I would not praise thee, Remond,—thou hast gifts
Bestowed upon thee for a noble end;
And for the use of which account must be
Returned to Him who lent them. May this thought
Preserve thee in his fear, and may the praise
Be given only to his mighty name.
And if, returning to thy native land,
By thee beloved, though dark with crimes that stain
Her boasted freedom, thou art called to prove
Thy true allegiance, even then go forth
Resigned to suffer,—trust thy all to Him
Who can support thee, whilst a still, small voice,
Within thy breast, shall whisper, "All is well."

Mr. Remond was welcomed on his return home, and again resumed his vocation as a lecturer. In stature he is small, spare made, neat, wiry build, and genteel in his personal appearance. He has a good voice, and is considered one of the best declaimers in New England. Faultless in his dress, and an excellent horseman, Mr. Remond has long been regarded the Count D'Orsay of the anti-slavery movement. He has written little or nothing for the press, and his notoriety is confined solely to the platform. Sensitive to a fault, and feeling sorely the prejudice against color which exists throughout the United States, his addresses have been mainly on that subject, on which he is always interesting. He is a good writer who embodies in his works the soul and spirit of the times in which he lives,—provided they are worth embodying,—and the common sympathy of the great mass is sounder criticism by far than the rules of mere scholars, who, buried up in their formulas, cannot speak so as to arrest the attention or move the heart. Adaptation without degeneracy is the great law to be followed. What is true of the writer is also true of the speaker. No man can put more real meaning in fewer words than Mr. Remond, and no one can give them greater force. The following extract from a speech of Mr. Remond, delivered before the New England Anti-Slavery Convention, at its anniversary in May, 1859, is characteristic of his style.

"If I had but one reason, why I consented to appear here, it was because, at this moment, I believe it belongs to the colored man in this country to say that his lot is a common one with every white man north of the Potomac River; and if you ask me who are my clients, I think I may answer, 'Every man north of Mason and Dixon's line, without reference to his complexion.' I have read in the newspapers that one or two distinguished men of this city propose to spend the coming summer in Europe. Born in Boston, educated at Harvard, having been dandled in the lap of Massachusetts favor and Massachusetts popularity, they are about to travel in Europe, among despotisms, monarchies, aristocracies, and oligarchies; and I trust in God they may learn, as they travel in those countries, that it is an everlasting disgrace that on the soil on which they were born, no man of color can stand and be considered free. If they shall learn no more than this, I will wish them a pleasant and prosperous tour; and unless they shall learn this, I hope they will come back and have the same padlock put upon their lips that is put upon men south of Mason and Dixon's line.

"I want to ask this large audience, Mr. Chairman, through you, supposing the citizens of Boston should call a meeting to-morrow, and resolve that, in the event of a southern man, with southern principles, being elected to the presidential office, this state will secede, how would the State of Mississippi receive it? Now, I am here to ask that the non-slaveholding states shall dare to do, and write, and publish, and resolve, in behalf of freedom, as the slaveholders dare to act and resolve in behalf of slavery.

The time has been, Mr. Chairman, when a colored man could scarcely look a white man in the face without trembling, owing to his education and experience. I am not here to boast;

but I may say, in view of what I have seen and heard during the last five years, as I said in the Representatives' Hall a few months ago, that our lot is a common one, and the sooner we shall so regard it, and buckle on our knapsacks and shoulder our muskets, and resolve that we will be free, the better for you as well as for me. The disgrace that once rested upon the head of the black man, now hovers over the head of every man and woman whom I have the honor to address this evening, just in proportion as they shall dare to stand erect before the oligarchy of slaveholders in the southern portion of our country; and God hasten forward the day when not only Music Hall, but every other hall in the city of Boston, the Athens of America, shall be made eloquent with tones that shall speak, as man has never before spoken in this country, for the cause of universal freedom. If the result of that speaking must be bloodshed, be it so! If it must be the dissolution of the Union, be it so! If it must be that we must walk over or through the American church, be it so! The time has come when, if you value your own freedom, James Buchanan must be hung in effigy, and such men as Dr. Nehemiah Adams must be put in the pillory of public disgrace and contempt; and then Massachusetts will cease to be a hissing and a by-word in every other country."

GEORGE T. DOWNING.

THE tall, fine figure, manly walk, striking profile, and piercing eye of George T. Downing would attract attention in any community, even where he is unknown. Possessing remarkable talents, finely educated, a keen observer, and devoted to the freedom and elevation of his race, he has long been looked upon as a representative man. A good debater, quick to take advantage of the weak points of an opponent, forcible in speech, and a natural orator, Mr. Downing is always admired as a speaker. Chosen president of the convention of colored citizens which assembled in Boston on the first of August, 1859, he delivered an impressive and eloquent opening address, of which we regret that we can give only an extract. He said,—

"The great consideration that presses upon me is, what may we do to make ourselves of more importance in community—necessary, indispensable? To sustain such a relation as this to community, (and it is possible,) is to secure, beyond a question, all the respect, to make sure the enjoyment of all the rights, that the most deferred to of the land enjoy. Society is deferential; it defers to power. Learning, and wealth, and power are most potent in society. It is not necessary that many men and women of us be wealthy and learned before we can force respect as a class; but it is necessary that we exhibit a proportionate representative character for learning and wealth, to be respected. It is not numbers alone, it is not universal wealth, it is not general learning, that secures to those, known by a distinction in society as whites—that gains them power; for they are not generally wealthy, not commonly learned. The number of these among them, as in all communities, is limited; but that number forms a representative character, some of whom excel; hence they have power—the class enjoy a name.

"There is another sense of power in community, which, though silent, has its weight—it should be most potent: that power is moral character. This also, like the other powers of which I have spoken, need not be universal to have an effect favorable to a class. I think that I am not claiming too much for the colored people in asserting that we have a decent representation in this respect—a most remarkable one, considering all the depressing influences which the present and preceding generations have had to struggle up under. Happily, this power on community is not growing less; it is on the increase. An illustration of the correctness of my position as to the power of a representative character for wealth and learning in commanding respect, is forcibly exhibited in the Celts in our midst, who came among us poor and ignorant, and who, consequently, fill menial, dependent positions. They are the least respected of all immigrants. In speaking thus, I am simply dealing with facts, not intending to be invidious. The German element, mingling with the general element which comes among us, representing a higher intelligence, more wealth, with great practical industry, is silently stealing a hold, a power in the nation, because of these possessions, at which native America will yet start. Now, gentlemen, if these be facts, is it not well for us, as sensible men here assembled, to consider our best interest—to have in view these sources of power? Would it not be well to consider these—to fall upon some plan by which we may possess or excite to the possession of them—rather than devote much of our time in a discussion as to the injustice of our fellow-countrymen in their relation to us? Of this *they* know full well, and *we* too bitterly.

"The ballot is a power in this country which should not be lost sight of by us. Were it more generally exercised by the colored people, the effect would be very perceptible. Those of them residents of the states that deny them the privilege of the elective franchise, should earnestly strive to have the right and the power secured to them; those who have it should never let an occasion pass, when they may consistently exercise it, without doing so. We know that the government and the states have acted most unfairly in their relation to us; but that government and the states, in doing so, have clearly disregarded justice, as well as perverted the legal interpretation of the supreme law of the land, as set forth in its constitution; which facts alone require that we exercise the right to vote, whenever we can, towards correcting this injustice. Were it known on election day that any colored man would deposit a vote, that there would be a concert of action in doing so, the effect would be irresistible. Cannot such a vote be cast at the approaching presidential election? Will the Republican party (a party which is entitled to credit for the service it has rendered to the cause of freedom) put in nomination, in 1860, a man for whom we can, with some degree of consistency, cast our ballots? It has such men in its ranks—prominent men of the party—men who are available.

"I would have it noted, that we cannot vote for a man who subscribes to the doctrine that, in struggling for freedom in a presidential or any other election, he ignores the rights of the colored man.

"There is an increased as well as an increasing respect for us in community. This is not simply because we have friends (all praise to them) who speak out boldly and uncompromisingly for the right,—in fact, the most of their efforts have been directed towards relieving the country of the blight and of the injustice of slavery,—but it is because our character, as a class, is better understood."

Mr. Downing is a native of New York, but spends his summers at Newport, where he has an excellent retreat for those seeking that fashionable watering-place, and where he stands high with the better class of the community.

ROBERT PURVIS.

Few private gentlemen are better known than Robert Purvis. Born in Charleston, S. C., a son of the late venerable William Purvis, Esq., educated in New England, and early associated with William Lloyd Garrison, Francis Jackson, and Wendell Phillips, he has always been understood as belonging to the most ultra wing of the radical abolitionists. Residing in Philadelphia when it was unsafe to avow one's self a friend of the slave, Mr. Purvis never was known to deny his hatred to the "peculiar institution." A writer for one of the public journals, seeking out distinguished colored persons as subjects for his pen, paid him a visit, of which the following is his account:—

"The stage put us down at his gate, and we were warned to be ready to return in an hour and a half. His dwelling stands some distance back from the turnpike. It is approached by a broad lawn, and shaded with ancient trees. In the rear stands a fine series of barns. There are magnificent orchards connected with his farm, and his live stock is of the most approved breeds. We understand that he receives numbers of premiums annually from agricultural societies. In this fine old mansion Mr. Purvis has resided many years.

"We were ushered, upon our visit, into a pleasant dining room, hung with a number of paintings. Upon one side of an old-fashioned mantel was a large portrait of a fine-looking white man; on the other side, a portrait of a swarthy negro. Above these old John Brown looked gloomily down, like a bearded patriarch.

"In a few minutes Mr. Purvis came in. We had anticipated a stubborn-looking negro, with a swagger, and a tone of bravado. In place of such, we saw a tall, beautifully knit gentleman, almost white, and handsomely dressed. His foot and hand were symmetrical, and, although his hair was gray with years, every limb was full, and every movement supple and easy. He saluted us with decorous dignity, and began to converse.

"It was difficult to forget that the man before us was not of our own race. The topics upon which he spoke were chiefly personal. He related some very amusing anecdotes of his relations with southern gentlemen. On one occasion he applied for a passage to Liverpool in a Philadelphia packet. Some southern gentlemen, unacquainted with Purvis, save as a man of negro blood, protested that he should not be received. Among these was a Mr. Hayne, a near relative of Hayne the orator.

"Purvis accordingly went to Liverpool by another vessel. He met Hayne and the southerners as they were about returning home, and took passage with them, passing for a white man. He gained their esteem, was cordially invited by each to visit him in the south, and no entertainment was complete without his joke and his presence. At a final dinner, given to the party by the captain of the vessel, Mr. Hayne, who had all along spoken violently of the negro race, publicly toasted Mr. Purvis, as the finest type of the Caucasian race he had ever met.

"Mr. Purvis rose to reply. 'I am not a Caucasian,' said he; 'I belong to the degraded tribe of Africans.'

"The feelings of the South Carolinians need not be described.

"Mr. Purvis has written a number of anti-slavery pamphlets, and is regarded, by rumor, as the president of the Underground Railroad. He has figured in many slave-rescue cases, some of which he relates with graphic manner of description.

"He is the heaviest tax-payer in the township, and owns two very valuable farms. By his influence the public schools of the township have been thrown open to colored children. He has also built, at his own expense, a hall for free debate. We left him with feelings of higher regard than we have yet felt for any of his people. It is proper to remark, that Purvis is the grandchild of a blackamoor, who was taken a slave to South Carolina."

Although disdaining all profession of a public character, Mr. Purvis is, nevertheless, often invited to address public gatherings. As a speaker he is energetic, eloquent, and sarcastic. He spares neither friend nor foe in his argument; uses choice language, and appears to feel that nature and humanity are the everlasting proprietors of truth, and that truth should be spoken at all times. Mr. Purvis is an able writer, and whatever he says comes directly from the heart. His letter to Hon. S. C. Pomeroy, on colonization, is characteristic of him. We regret that space will not allow us to give the whole of this timely and manly production.

"There are some aspects of this project which surely its advocates cannot have duly considered. You purpose to exile hundreds and thousands of your laborers. The wealth of a country consists mainly in its labor. With what law of economy, political or social, can you reconcile this project to banish from your shores the men that plough your fields, drive your teams, and help build your houses? Already the farmers around me begin to feel the pinching want of labor; how will it be after this enormous draft? I confess the project seems to me one of insanity. What will foreign nations, on whose good or ill will so much is supposed now to depend, think of this project? These nations have none of this vulgar prejudice against complexion. What, then, will they think of the wisdom of a people who, to gratify a low-born prejudice, deliberately plan to drive out hundreds and thousands of the most peaceful, industrious, and competent laborers? Mr. Roebuck said in a late speech at Sheffield, as an argument for intervention, 'that the feeling against the black was stronger at the north than in the south.' Mr. Roebuck can now repeat that assertion, and point to this governmental project in corroboration of its truth. A 'Slaveholders' Convention' was held a few years since in Maryland to consider whether it would not be best either to re-enslave the free blacks of that state, or banish them from its borders. The question was discussed, and a committee, the chairman of which was United States Senator Pearce, was appointed to report upon it. That committee reported 'that to enslave men now free would be inhuman, and to banish them from the state would be to inflict a deadly blow upon the material interests of the commonwealth; that their labor was indispensable to the welfare of the state.' Sir, your government proposes to do that which the Slaveholders' Convention of Maryland, with all their hate of the free blacks, declared to be inconsistent with the public interest.

"But it is said this is a question of prejudice, of national antipathy, and not to be reasoned about. The president has said, 'whether it is right or wrong I need not now discuss.'

"Great God! Is justice nothing? Is honor nothing? Is even pecuniary interest to be sacrificed to this insane and vulgar hate? But it is said this is the 'white man's country.' Not so, sir. This is the red man's country by natural right, and the black man's by virtue of his sufferings and toil. Your fathers by violence drove the red man out, and forced the black man in. The children of the black man have enriched the soil by their tears, and sweat, and blood. Sir, we were born here, and here we choose to remain. For twenty years we were goaded and harassed by systematic efforts to make us colonize. We were coaxed and mobbed, and mobbed and coaxed, but we refused to budge. We planted ourselves upon our inalienable rights, and were proof against all the efforts that were made to expatriate us. For the last fifteen years we have enjoyed comparative quiet. Now again the malign project is broached, and again, as before, in the name of humanity are we invited to leave.

"In God's name, what good do you expect to accomplish by such a course? If you will not let our brethren in bonds go free, if you will not let us, as did our fathers, share in the privileges of the government, if you will not let us even help fight the battles of the country, in Heaven's name, at least, *let us alone.* Is that too great a boon to ask of your magnanimity?

"I elect to stay on the soil on which I was born, and on the plot of ground which I have fairly bought and honestly paid for. Don't advise me to leave, and don't add insult to injury by telling me it's for my own good; of that I am to be the judge. It is in vain that you talk to me about the 'two races,' and their 'mutual antagonism.' In the matter of rights there is but one race, and that is the *human* race. 'God has made of one blood all nations to dwell on all the face of the earth.' And it is not true that there is a mutual antagonism between the white and colored people of this community. You may antagonize us, but we do not antagonize you. You may hate us, but we do not hate you. It may argue a want of spirit to cling to those who seek to banish us, but such is, nevertheless, the fact.

"Sir, this is our country as much as it is yours, *and we will not leave it.* Your ships may be at the door, but we choose to remain. A few may go, as a few went to Hayti, and a few to

Liberia; but the colored people as a mass will not leave the land of their birth. Of course, I can only speak by authority for myself; but I know the people with whom I am identified, and I feel confident that I only express their sentiment as a body when I say that your project of colonizing them in Central America, or any where else, with or without their consent, will never succeed. They will migrate, as do other people, when left to themselves, and when the motive is sufficient; but they will neither be 'compelled to volunteer,' nor *constrained* to go of their 'own accord.'"

JOSEPH JENKINS.

"Look here, upon this picture, and on this."—HAMLET.

No one accustomed to pass through Cheapside could fail to have noticed a good-looking man, neither black nor white, engaged in distributing bills to the thousands who throng that part of the city of London. While strolling through Cheapside, one morning, I saw, for the fiftieth time, Joseph Jenkins, the subject of this article, handing out his bills to all who would take them as he thrust them into their hands. I confess that I was not a little amused, and stood for some moments watching and admiring his energy in distributing his papers. A few days after, I saw the same individual in Chelsea, sweeping a crossing; here, too, he was equally as energetic as when I met him in the city. Some days later, while going through Kensington, I heard rather a sweet, musical voice singing a familiar psalm, and on looking round was not a little surprised to find that it was the Cheapside bill-distributor and Chelsea crossing-sweeper. He was now singing hymns, and selling religious tracts. I am fond of patronizing genius, and therefore took one of his tracts and paid him for a dozen.

During the following week, I saw, while going up the City Road, that Shakspeare's tragedy of Othello was to be performed at the Eagle Saloon that night, and that the character of the Moor was to be taken by "*Selim, an African prince.*" Having no engagement that evening, I resolved at once to attend, to witness the performance of the "African Talma," as he was called. It was the same interest that had induced me to go to the Italian opera to see Mesdames Sontag and Grisi in Norma, and to visit Drury Lane to see Macready take leave of the stage. My expectations were screwed up to the highest point. The excitement caused by the publication of "Uncle Tom's Cabin" had prepared the public for any thing in the African line, and I felt that the *prince* would be sure of a good audience; and in this I was not disappointed, for, as I took my seat in one of the boxes near the stage, I saw that the house was crammed with an orderly company. The curtain was already up when I entered, and Iago and Roderigo were on the stage. After a while Othello came in, and was greeted with thunders of applause, which he very gracefully acknowledged. Just black enough to take his part without coloring his face, and being tall, with a good figure and an easy carriage, a fine, full, and musical voice, he was well adapted to the character of Othello. I immediately recognized in the countenance of the Moor a face that I had seen before, but could not at the moment tell where. Who could this "prince" be? thought I. He was too black for Douglass, not black enough for Ward, not tall enough for Garnet, too calm for Delany, figure, though fine, not genteel enough for Remond. However, I was soon satisfied as to who the *star* was. Reader, would you think it? it was no less a person than Mr. Jenkins, the bill-distributor from Cheapside, and crossing-sweeper from Chelsea! For my own part, I was overwhelmed with amazement, and it was some time before I could realize the fact. He soon showed that he possessed great dramatic power and skill; and his description to the senate of how he won the affections of the gentle Desdemona stamped him at once as an actor of merit. "What a pity," said a lady near me to a gentleman that was by her side, "that a prince of the royal blood of Africa should have to go upon the stage for a living! It is indeed a shame!" When he came to the scene,—

"O, cursed, cursed slave!—whip me, ye devils,
From the possession of this heavenly sight!
Blow me about in winds, roast me in sulphur!
Wash me in steep-down gulfs of liquid fire!

O, Desdemona! Desdemona! dead?
Dead? O! O! O!"—

the effect was indeed grand. When the curtain fell, the prince was called upon the stage, where he was received with deafening shouts of approbation, and a number of *bouquets* thrown at his feet, which he picked up, bowed, and retired. I went into Cheapside the next morning, at an early hour, to see if the prince had given up his old trade for what I supposed to be a more lucrative one; but I found the hero of the previous night at his post, and giving out his bills as energetically as when I had last seen him. Having to go to the provinces for some months, I lost sight of Mr. Jenkins, and on my return to town did not trouble myself to look him up. More than a year after I had witnessed the representation of Othello at the Eagle, I was walking, one pleasant Sabbath evening, through one of the small streets in the borough, when I found myself in front of a little chapel, where a number of persons were going in. As I was passing on slowly, an elderly man said to me, "I suppose you have come to hear your colored brother preach." "No," I answered; "I was not aware that one was to be here." "Yes," said he; "and a clever man he is, too." As the old man offered to find me a seat, I concluded to go in and hear this son of Africa. The room, which was not large, was already full. I had to wait but a short time before the reverend gentleman made his appearance. He was nearly black, and dressed in a black suit, with high shirt-collar, and an intellectual-looking cravat, that nearly hid his chin. A pair of spectacles covered his eyes. The preacher commenced by reading a portion of Scripture, and then announced that they would sing the twenty-eighth hymn in "the arrangement." O, that voice! I felt sure that I had heard that musical voice before; but where, I could not tell. I was not aware that any of my countrymen were in London, but felt that, whoever he was, he was no discredit to the race; for he was a most eloquent and accomplished orator. His sermon was against the sale and use of intoxicating drinks, and the bad habits of the working classes, of whom his audience was composed.

Although the subject was intensely interesting, I was impatient for it to come to a close, for I wanted to speak to the preacher. But the evening being warm, and the room heated, the reverend gentleman, on wiping the perspiration from his face, (which, by the way, ran very freely,) took off his spectacles on one occasion, so that I immediately recognized him, which saved me from going up to the pulpit at the end of the service. Yes; it was the bill-distributor of Cheapside, the crossing-sweeper of Chelsea, the tract-seller and psalm-singer of Kensington, and the Othello of the Eagle Saloon. I could scarcely keep from laughing outright when I discovered this to be the man that I had seen in so many characters. As I was about leaving my seat at the close of the services, the old man who showed me into the chapel asked me if I would not like to be introduced to the minister; and I immediately replied that I would. We proceeded up the aisle, and met the clergyman as he was descending. On seeing me, he did not wait for a formal introduction, but put out his hand and said, "I have seen you so often, sir, that I seem to know you." "Yes," I replied; "we have met several times, and under different circumstances." Without saying more, he invited me to walk with him towards his home, which was in the direction of my own residence. We proceeded; and, during the walk, Mr. Jenkins gave me some little account of his early history. "You think me rather an odd fish, I presume," said he. "Yes," I replied. "You are not the only one who thinks so," continued he. "Although I am not as black as some of my countrymen, I am a native of Africa. Surrounded by some beautiful mountain scenery, and situated between Darfour and Abyssinia, two thousand miles in the interior of Africa, is a small valley going by the name of *Tegla*. To that valley I stretch forth my affections, giving it the endearing appellation of my native home and fatherland. It was there that I was born, it was there that I received the fond looks of a loving mother, and it was there that I set my feet, for the first time, upon a world full of cares, trials, difficulties, and dangers. My father being a farmer, I used to be sent out to take care of his goats. This service I did when I was between seven and eight years of age. As I was the eldest of the boys, my pride was raised in no small degree when I beheld my father preparing a farm for me. This event filled my mind with the grand anticipation of leaving the care of the goats to my brother, who was then beginning to work a little. While my father was making these preparations, I had the constant charge of the goats; and being accompanied by two other boys, who resided near my father's house, we wandered many miles from home, by which means we acquired a knowledge of the different districts of our country.

"It was while in these rambles with my companions that I became the victim of the slave-trader. We were tied with cords and taken to Tegla, and thence to Kordofan, which is under the jurisdiction of the Pacha of Egypt. From Kordofan I was brought down to Dongola and Korti, in Nubia, and from thence down the Nile to Cairo; and, after being sold nine times, I became the property of an English gentleman, who brought me to this country and put me into school. But he died before I finished my education, and his family feeling no interest in me, I had to seek a living as best I could. I have been employed for some years to distribute handbills for a barber in Cheapside in the morning, go to Chelsea and sweep a crossing in the afternoon, and sing psalms and sell religious tracts in the evening. Sometimes I have an engagement to perform at some of the small theatres, as I had when you saw me at the Eagle. I preach for this little congregation over here, and charge them nothing; for I want that the poor should have the gospel without money and without price. I have now given up distributing bills; I have settled my son in that office. My eldest daughter was married about three months ago; and I have presented her husband with the Chelsea crossing, as my daughter's wedding portion." "Can he make a living at it?" I eagerly inquired. "O, yes; that crossing at Chelsea is worth thirty shillings a week, if it is well swept," said he. "But what do you do for a living for yourself?" I asked. "I am the leader of a band," he continued; "and we play for balls and parties, and three times a week at the Holborn Casino." "You are determined to rise," said I. "Yes," he replied,—

'Upward, onward, is my watchword;
Though the winds blow good or ill,
Though the sky be fair or stormy,
This shall be my watchword still.'"

By this time we had reached a point where we had to part; and I left Joseph Jenkins, impressed with the idea that he was the greatest genius that I had met in Europe.

JOHN S. ROCK.

THE subject of this sketch was born in Salem, N. J., in 1825. When quite a child, he became passionately attached to his book, and, unlike most children, seldom indulged in amusements of any kind. His parents, anxious to make the most of his talents, kept him at school until he was eighteen years of age, at which time he was examined and approved as a teacher of public schools. He taught school from 1844 to 1848. Mr. David Allen writes, "His was certainly the most orderly, and the best conducted, school I ever visited, although myself a teacher for nearly twenty years." During the time Mr. Rock was teaching, Drs. Sharp and Gibbon opened their libraries to him, and he commenced the study of physic,—teaching six hours, studying eight, and giving private lessons two hours every day. After completing his medical studies, he found it impossible to get into a medical college; so he abandoned his idea of becoming a physician, and went with Dr. Harbert and studied dentistry. He finished his studies in the summer of 1849. In January, 1850, he went to Philadelphia to practise his profession. In 1851, he received a silver medal for artificial teeth. In the same year, he took a silver medal for a prize essay on temperance. After the Apprentices' High School had been established in Philadelphia, and while it was still an evening school, Mr. Rock took charge of it, and kept it until it was merged into a day school, under the direction of Professor Reason. He attended lectures in the American Medical College, and graduated in 1852.

In 1853, Dr. Rock came to Boston, where he now resides. On leaving the city of Philadelphia, the professors of the Dental College gave him letters bearing testimony to his high professional skill and integrity. Professor Townsend writes, "Dr. Rock is a graduate of a medical school in this city, and is favorably known, and much respected, by the profession. Having seen him operate, it gives me great pleasure to bear my testimony to his superior abilities." Professor J. F. B. Flagg writes, "I have seen his operations, and have been much pleased with them. As a scientific man, I shall miss the intercourse which I have so long enjoyed in his acquaintance." After Mr. R. graduated in medicine, he practised both of his professions. In 1856, he accepted an invitation to deliver a lecture on the "Unity of the Human Races," before the

Massachusetts legislature. In 1857, he delivered the oration on the occasion of the dedication of the new Masonic Temple in Eleventh Street, Philadelphia. His intense application to study and to business had so undermined his health that, in the summer of 1856, he was obliged to give up all business. After several unsuccessful surgical operations here, and when nearly all hope for the restoration of his health was gone, he determined to go to France. When he was ready to go, he applied to the government for a passport. This was refused, Mr. Cass, then secretary of state, saying in reply, that "a passport had never been granted to a colored man since the foundation of the government." Mr. Rock went to France, however, and underwent a severe surgical operation at the hands of the celebrated Nélaton. Professor Nélaton advised him to give up dentistry altogether; and as his shattered constitution forbade the exposure necessary for the practice of medicine, he gave up both, and bent all his energies to the study of law. In 1860, he accepted an invitation, and delivered a lecture on the "Character and Writings of Madame De Staël," before the Massachusetts legislature, which he did "with credit to himself and satisfaction to the very large audience in attendance." *Der Pionier*, a German newspaper, in Boston, said, when commenting on his criticism of De Staël's "Germany," "This thinking, educated German and French speaking negro proved himself as learned in German as he is in French literature." On the 14th of September, 1861, on motion of T. K. Lothrop, Esq., Dr. Rock was examined in the Superior Court, before Judge Russell, and admitted to practice as an attorney and counsellor at law in all the courts of Massachusetts. On the 21st of the same month Mr. Rock received a commission from the governor and council as a justice of the peace for seven years for the city of Boston and county of Suffolk.

We annex an extract from a speech made by him before the last anniversary of the Massachusetts Anti-Slavery Society.

"Other countries are held out as homes for us. Why is this? Why is it that the people from all other countries are invited to come here, and we are asked to go away? Is it to make room for the refuse population of Europe? Or why is it that the white people of this country desire to get rid of us? Does any one pretend to deny that this is *our* country? or that much of its wealth and prosperity is the result of the labor of *our* hands? or that our blood and bones have crimsoned and whitened every battle-field from Maine to Louisiana? Why this desire to get rid of us? Can it be possible that because the nation has robbed us for more than two centuries, and now finds that she can do it no longer and preserve a good character among the nations, she, out of hatred, wishes to banish, because she cannot continue to rob, us? Or why is it? I will tell you. The free people of color have succeeded in spite of every thing; and we are to-day a living refutation of that shameless assertion that we cannot take care of ourselves. Abject as our condition has been, our whole lives prove us to be superior to the influences that have been brought to bear upon us to crush us. This cannot be said of your race when it was oppressed and enslaved. Another reason is, this nation has wronged us; therefore many hate us. The Spanish proverb is, 'Since I have wronged you I have never liked you.' This is true of every class of people. When a man wrongs another, he not only hates him, but tries to make others dislike him. Unnatural as this may appear, it is nevertheless true. You may help a man during his lifetime, and he will speak well of you; but your first refusal will incur his displeasure, and show you his ingratitude. When he has got all he can from you, he has no further use for you. When the orange is squeezed, we throw it aside. The black man is a good fellow while he is a slave, and toils for nothing; but the moment he claims his own flesh and blood and bones, he is a most obnoxious creature, and there is a proposition to get rid of him. He is happy while he remains a poor, degraded, ignorant slave, without even the right to his own offspring. While in this condition the master can ride in the same carriage, sleep in the same bed, and nurse from the same bosom. But give this slave the right to use his own legs, his hands, his body, and his mind, and this happy and desirable creature is instantly transformed into a most loathsome wretch, fit only to be colonized somewhere near the mountains of the moon, or eternally banished from civilized beings! You must not lose sight of the fact it is the emancipated slave and the free colored man that it is proposed to remove—not the slave. This country is perfectly adapted to negro slavery; it is the free blacks that the air is not good for! What an idea! a country good for slavery and not good for freedom! This monstrous idea would be scorned by even a Fejee Islander."

As a public speaker Mr. Rock stands deservedly high; his discourses being generally of an elevated tone, and logically put together. As a member of the Boston bar, he has thus far succeeded well, and bids fair to obtain his share of public patronage. In personal appearance Mr. Rock is tall and of good figure, with a thoughtful countenance, and a look that indicates the student. In color he is what is termed a *grief*, about one remove from the negro. By his own color he has long been regarded as a representative man.

WILLIAM DOUGLASS.

WILLIAM DOUGLASS was a clergyman of the Protestant Episcopal denomination, and for a number of years was rector of St. Thomas Church, Philadelphia. We met Mr. Douglass in England in 1852, and became impressed with the belief that he was no ordinary man. He had a finished education, being well versed in Latin, Greek, and Hebrew. He possessed large and philanthropic views, but was extremely diffident, which gave one the opinion that he was a man of small ability. Being in Philadelphia in the spring of 1860, we attended the morning service at his church. When the preacher made his appearance, all eyes were turned to the pulpit. His figure was prepossessing—a great thing in a public speaker. Weak, stunted, deformed-looking men labor under much disadvantage. Mr. Douglass had a commanding look, a clear, musical voice, and was a splendid reader. He was no dull drone when the service was over and the sermon had commenced. With downcast eye he read no moral essay that touched no conscience and fired no heart. On the contrary, he was spirited in the pulpit. He looked his congregation in the face; he directed his discourse to them. He took care that not a single word should lose its aim. No one fell asleep while he was speaking, but all seemed intensely interested in the subject in hand. Mr. Douglass was a general favorite with the people of his own city, and especially the members of his society. He was a talented writer, and published, a few years ago, a volume of sermons, which are filled with gems of thought and original ideas. A feeling of deep piety and humanity runs through the entire book. Mr. Douglass was of unmixed blood, gentlemanly in his manners, chaste in conversation, and social in private life. Though not active in public affairs, he was, nevertheless, interested in all that concerned the freedom and elevation of his race. He visited England and the West Indies some years ago, and had an extensive acquaintance beyond the limits of his own country. Mr. Douglass was respected and esteemed by the white clergy of Philadelphia, who were forced to acknowledge his splendid abilities.

ELYMAS PAYSON ROGERS.

E. P. Rogers, a clergyman of the Presbyterian order, and pastor of a church at Newark, New Jersey, was a man of education, research, and literary ability. He was not a fluent and easy speaker, but he was logical, and spoke with a degree of refinement seldom met with. He possessed poetical genius of no mean order, and his poem on the "Missouri Compromise," which he read in many of the New England cities and towns in 1856, contains brilliant thoughts and amusing suggestions. The following on *Truth* is not without point:—

"When Truth is girded for the fight,
And draws her weapons keen and bright,
And lifts aloft her burnished shield,
Her godlike influence to wield,
If victory in that self-same hour
Is not accomplished by her power,
She'll not retreat nor flee away,
But win the field another day.
She will with majesty arise,
Seize her traducers by surprise,
And by her overwhelming might
Will put her deadly foes to flight."

The allusion to the threat of the south against the north is a happy one, in connection with the rebellion.

"I'll show my power the country through,
And will the factious north subdue;
And Massachusetts shall obey,
And yield to my increasing sway.

She counts her patriotic deeds,
But scatters her disunion seeds;
She proudly tells us of the tea
Sunk by her worthies in the sea,
And then she talks more proudly still
Of Lexington and Bunker Hill;
But on that hill, o'er patriots' graves,
I'll yet enroll my negro slaves.
I may have trouble, it is true,
But still I'll put the rebels through,
And make her statesmen bow the knee,
Yield to my claims, and honor me.
And though among them I shall find
The learned, the brilliant, and refined,
If on me they shall e'er reflect,
No senate chamber shall protect
Their guilty pates and heated brains,
From hideous gutta percha canes."

The election of N. P. Banks, as speaker of the House of Representatives, is mentioned in the succeeding lines:—

"But recently the north drove back
The southern tyrants from the track,
And put to flight their boasting ranks,
And gave the speaker's chair to Banks."

Mr. Rogers was of unmixed race, genteel in appearance, forehead large and well developed, fine figure, and pleasing in his manners. Anxious to benefit his race, he visited Africa in 1861, was attacked with the fever, and died in a few days. No man was more respected by all classes than he. His genial influence did much to soften down the pro-slavery feeling which existed in the city where he resided.

J. THEODORE HOLLY.

If there is any man living who is more devoted to the idea of a "Negro Nationality" than Dr. Delany, that man is J. Theodore

Holly. Possessing a good education, a retentive memory, and being of studious habits, Mr. Holly has brought himself up to a point of culture not often attained by men even in the higher walks of life. Unadulterated in race, devotedly attached to Africa and her descendants, he has made a "Negro Nationality" a matter of much thought and study. He paid a visit to Hayti in 1858 or 1859, returned home, and afterwards preached, lectured, and wrote in favor of Haytian emigration. In concluding a long essay on this subject, in the *Anglo-African Magazine*, he says,—

"From these thoughts it will be seen that whatsoever is to be the future destiny of the descendants of Africa, Hayti certainly holds the most important relation to that destiny. And if we were to be reduced to the dread alternative of having her historic fame blotted out of existence, or that celebrity which may have been acquired elsewhere by all the rest of our race combined, we should say, Preserve the name, the fame, and the sovereign existence of Hayti, though every thing else shall perish. Yes, let Britain and France undermine, if they will, the enfranchisement which they gave to their West Indian slaves, by their present apprenticeship system; let the lone star of Liberia, placed in the firmament of nationalities by a questionable system of American philanthropy, go out in darkness; let the opening resources of Central Africa be again shut up in their wonted seclusion; let the names and deeds of our Nat Turners, Denmark Veseys, Penningtons, Delanys, Douglasses, and Smiths be forgotten forever; but never let the self-emancipating deeds of the Haytian people be effaced; never let her heroically achieved nationality be brought low; no, never let the names of her Toussaint, her Dessalines, her Rigaud, her Christophe, and her Petion be forgotten, or blotted out from the historic pages of the world's history."

Mr. Holly is a clergyman of the Protestant Episcopal order, and for several years was pastor of a church at New Haven, Connecticut, where he sustained the reputation of being an interesting and eloquent preacher. His reading is at times rapid, yet clear and emphatic. He seems to aim more at what he says than how he says it; and if you listen, you will find food for thought in every phrase. As a writer he is forcible and argumentative, but never dull. In person, Mr. Holly is of the ordinary size, has a bright eye, agreeable countenance, form erect, voice clear and mellow. He uses good language, is precise in his manners, and wears the air of a gentleman. Infatuated with the idea of a home in Hayti, he raised a colony and sailed for Port au Prince in the spring of 1861. He was unfortunate in the selection of a location, and the most of those who went out with him, including his own family, died during their first six months on the island. Mr. Holly has recently returned to the United States. Whether he intends to remain or not, we are not informed.

JAMES W. C. PENNINGTON.

DR. PENNINGTON was born a slave on the farm of Colonel Gordon, in the State of Maryland. His early life was not unlike the common lot of the bondmen of the Middle States. He was by trade a blacksmith, which increased his value to his owner. He had no opportunities for learning, and was ignorant of letters when he made his escape to the north. Through intense application to books, he gained, as far as it was possible, what slavery had deprived him of in his younger days. But he always felt the early blight upon his soul.

Dr. Pennington had not been free long ere he turned his attention to theology, and became an efficient preacher in the Presbyterian denomination. He was several years settled over a church at Hartford, Conn. He has been in Europe three times, his second visit being the most important, as he remained there three or four years, preaching and lecturing, during which time he attended the Peace Congresses held at Paris, Brussels, and London. While in Germany, the degree of Doctor of Divinity was conferred upon him by the University of Heidelberg. On his return to the United States he received a call, and was settled as pastor over Shiloh Church, New York city.

The doctor has been a good student, is a ripe scholar, and is deeply versed in theology. While at Paris, in 1849, we, with the American and English delegates to the Peace Congress, attended divine service at the Protestant Church, where Dr.

Pennington had been invited to preach. His sermon on that occasion was an eloquent production, made a marked impression on his hearers, and created upon the minds of all a more elevated idea of the abilities of the negro. In past years he has labored zealously and successfully for the education and moral, social, and religious elevation of his race. The doctor is unadulterated in blood, with strongly-marked African features; in stature he is of the common size, slightly inclined to corpulency, with an athletic frame and a good constitution. The fact that Dr. Pennington is considered a good Greek, Latin, and German scholar, although his early life was spent in slavery, is not more strange than that Henry Diaz, the black commander in Brazil, is extolled in all the histories of that country as one of the most sagacious and talented men and experienced officers of whom they could boast; nor that Hannibal, an African, gained by his own exertion a good education, and rose to be a lieutenant-general and director of artillery under Peter the Great; nor that Don Juan Latino, a negro, became teacher of the Latin language at Seville; nor that Anthony William Amo, a native of Guinea, took the degree of Doctor of Philosophy at the University of Wittemburg; nor that James J. Capetein, fresh from the coast of Africa, became master of the Latin, Greek, Hebrew, and Chaldaic languages; nor that James Derham, an imported negro, should, by his own genius and energy, be considered one of the ablest physicians in New Orleans, and of whom Dr. Rush says, "I found him very learned. I thought I could give him information concerning the treatment of diseases; but I learned more from him than he could expect from me." We might easily extend the catalogue, for we have abundant materials. Blumenbach boldly affirms of the negro, "There is no savage people who have distinguished themselves by such examples of perfectibility and capacity for scientific cultivation."

A MAN WITHOUT A NAME.

It was in the month of December, 1852, while Colonel Rice and family were seated around a bright wood fire, whose blaze lighted up the large dining room in their old mansion, situated ten miles from Dayton, in the State of Ohio, that they heard a knock at the door, which was answered by the familiar "Come in" that always greets the stranger in the Western States. Squire Loomis walked in and took a seat on one of the three rocking-chairs, which had been made vacant by the young folks, who rose to give place to their highly influential and wealthy neighbor. It was a beautiful night; the sky was clear, the wind had hushed its deep moanings, the most brilliant of the starry throng stood out in bold relief, despite the superior light of the moon. "I see some one standing at the gate," said Mrs. Rice, as she left the window and came nearer the fire. "I'll go out and see who it is," exclaimed George, as he quitted his chair and started for the door. The latter soon returned and whispered to his father, and both left the room, evincing that something unusual was at hand. Not many minutes elapsed, however, before the father and son entered, accompanied by a young man, whose complexion showed plainly that other than Anglo-Saxon blood coursed through his veins. The whole company rose, and the stranger was invited to draw near to the fire. Question after question was now pressed upon the new-comer by the colonel and the squire, but without eliciting satisfactory replies.

"You need not be afraid, my friend," said the host, as he looked intently in the colored man's face, "to tell where you are from and to what place you are going. If you are a fugitive, as I suspect, give us your story, and we will protect and defend you to the last."

Taking courage from these kind remarks, the mulatto said, "I was born, sir, in the State of Kentucky, and raised in Missouri. My master was my father; my mother was his slave. That, sir, accounts for the fairness of my complexion. As soon as I was old enough to labor I was taken into my master's dwelling as a servant, to attend upon the family. My mistress, aware of my near relationship to her husband, felt humiliated, and often in her anger would punish me severely for no cause whatever. My near approach to the Anglo-Saxon aroused the jealousy and hatred of the overseer, and he flogged me, as he said, to make me know my place. My fellow-slaves hated me because I was whiter than themselves. Thus my complexion was construed into a crime, and I was made to curse my father for the Anglo-Saxon blood that courses through my veins.

"My master raised slaves to supply the southern market, and every year some of my companions were sold to the slave-traders and taken farther south. Husbands were separated from their wives, and children torn from the arms of their agonizing mothers. These outrages were committed by the man whom nature compelled me to look upon as my father. My mother and brothers were sold and taken away from me; still I bore all, and made no attempt to escape, for I yet had near me an only sister, whom I dearly loved. At last, the negro driver attempted to rob my sister of her virtue. She appealed to me for protection. Her innocence, beauty, and tears were enough to stir the stoutest heart. My own, filled with grief and indignation, swelled within me as though it would burst or leap from my bosom. My tears refused to flow: the fever in my brain dried them up. I could stand it no longer. I seized the wretch by the throat, and hurled him to the ground; and with this strong arm I paid him for old and new. The next day I was tried by a jury of slaveholders for the crime of having within me the heart of a man, and protecting my sister from the licentious embrace of a libertine. And—would you believe it, sir?—that jury of enlightened Americans,—yes, sir, Christian Americans,—after *grave* deliberation, decided that I had broken the laws, and sentenced me to receive five hundred lashes upon my bare back. But, sir, I escaped from them the night before I was to have been flogged.

"Afraid of being arrested and taken back, I remained the following day hid away in a secluded spot on the banks of the Mississippi River, protected from the gaze of man by the large trees and thick cane-brakes that sheltered me. I waited for the coming of another night. All was silence around me, save the sweet chant of the feathered songsters in the forest, or the musical ripple of the eddying waters at my feet. I watched the majestic bluffs as they gradually faded away, through the gray twilight, from the face of day into the darker shades of night. I then turned to the rising moon as it peered above, ascending the deep blue ether, high in the heavens, casting its mellow rays over the surrounding landscape, and gilding the smooth surface of the noble river with its silvery hue. I viewed with interest the stars as they appeared, one after another, in the firmament. It was then and there that I studied nature in its lonely grandeur, and saw in it the goodness of God, and felt that He who created so much beauty, and permitted the fowls of the air and the beasts of the field to roam at large and be free, never intended that man should be the slave of his fellow-man. I resolved that I would be a bondman no longer; and, taking for my guide the *north star*, I started for Canada, the negro's land of liberty. For many weeks I travelled by night, and lay by during the day. O, how often, while hid away in the forest, waiting for nightfall, have I thought of the beautiful lines I once heard a stranger recite:—

'O, hail Columbia! happy land!
The cradle land of liberty!
Where none but negroes bear the brand,
Or feel the lash of slavery.

'Then let the glorious anthem peal,
And drown "Britannia rules the waves:"
Strike up the song that men can feel—
"Columbia rules four million slaves!"'

"At last I arrived at a depot of the Underground Railroad, took the *express train*, and here I am."

"You are welcome," said Colonel Rice, as he rose from his chair, walked to the window and looked out, as if apprehensive that the fugitive's pursuers were near by. "You are welcome," continued he; "and I will aid you on your way to Canada, for you are not safe here."

"Are you not afraid of breaking the laws by assisting this man to escape?" remarked Squire Loomis.

"I care not for laws when they stand in the way of humanity," replied the colonel.

"If you aid him in reaching Canada, and we should ever have a war with England, may be he'll take up arms and fight against his own country," said the squire.

The fugitive eyed the law-abiding man attentively for a moment, and then exclaimed, "Take up arms against my country? What country, sir, have I? The Supreme Court of the United States, and the laws of the south, doom me to be the slave of another. There is not a foot of soil over which the *stars and stripes* wave, where I can stand and be protected by law. I've seen my mother sold in the cattle market. I looked upon my brothers as they were driven away in chains by the slave speculator. The heavy negro whip has been applied to my own shoulders until its biting lash sunk deep into my quivering flesh. Still, sir, you call this my country. True, true, I was born in this land. My grandfather fought in the revolutionary war; my own father was in the war of 1812. Still, sir, I am a slave, a chattel, a thing, a piece of property. I've been sold in the market with horses and swine; the initials of my master's name are branded deep in this arm. Still, sir, you call this my country. And, now that I am making my escape, you feel afraid, if I reach Canada, and there should be war with England, that I will take up arms against my own country. Sir, I have no country but the grave; and I'll seek freedom there before I will again be taken back to slavery. There is no justice for me at the south; every right of my race is trampled in the dust, until humanity bleeds at every pore. I am bound for Canada, and woe to him that shall attempt to arrest me. If it comes to the worst, I will die fighting for freedom."

"I honor you for your courage," exclaimed Squire Loomis, as he sprang from his seat, and walked rapidly to and fro through the room. "It is too bad," continued he, "that such men should be enslaved in a land whose Declaration of Independence proclaims all men to be free and equal. I will aid you in any thing that I can. What is your name?"

"I have no name," said the fugitive. "I once had a name,—it was William,—but my master's nephew came to live with him, and as I was a house servant, and the young master and I would, at times, get confused in the same name, orders were given for me to change mine. From that moment, I resolved that, as slavery had robbed me of my liberty and my name, I would not attempt to have another till I was free. So, sir, for once you have a man standing before you without a name."

SAMUEL R. WARD.

Few public speakers exercised greater influence in the pulpit and on the platform, in behalf of human freedom, than did

Samuel R. Ward, in the early days of abolition agitation. From 1840 up to the passage of the Fugitive Slave Law, in 1850, he either preached or lectured in every church, hall, or school house in Western and Central New York. Endowed with superior mental powers, and having, through the aid of Hon. Gerrit Smith, obtained a good education, and being a close student, Mr. Ward's intellectual faculties are well developed. He was, for several years, settled over a white congregation, of the Presbyterian order, at South Butler, N. Y., where he preached with great acceptance, and was highly respected. As a speaker, he was justly held up as one of the ablest men, white or black, in the United States. The first time we ever heard him, (in 1842,) he was announced in the advertisement as "the black Daniel Webster." Standing above six feet in height, possessing a strong voice, and energetic in his gestures, Mr. Ward always impressed his highly finished and logical speeches upon his hearers. No detractor of the negro's abilities ever attributed his talents to his having Anglo-Saxon blood in his veins. As a black man, Mr. Ward was never ashamed of his complexion, but rather appeared to feel proud of it. When Captain Rynders and his followers took possession of the platform of the American Anti-Slavery Society, at their anniversary, in New York, in the spring of 1852, Frederick Douglass rose to defend the rights of the Association and the liberty of speech. Rynders objected to the speaker upon the ground that he was not a negro, but half white. Ward, being present, came forward, amid great applause, and the rowdy leader had to "knock under," and confess that genuine eloquence was not confined to the white man. William J. Wilson says of Ward, "Ideas form the basis of all Mr. Ward utters. If words and ideas are not inseparable, then, as mortar is to the stones that compose the building, so are his words to his ideas. In this, I judge, lies Mr. Ward's greatest strength. Concise without abruptness; without extraordinary stress, always clear and forcible; if sparing of ornament, never inelegant,—in all, there appears a consciousness of strength, developed by close study and deep reflection, and only put forth because the occasion demands it. His appeals are directed rather to the understanding than the imagination; but so forcibly do they take possession of it, that the heart unhesitatingly yields."

Mr. Ward visited England in 1852, where he was regarded as

an eloquent advocate of the rights of his race. He now resides at Kingston, Jamaica.

SIR EDWARD JORDAN.

Edward Jordan was born in Kingston, Jamaica, in the year 1798. After quitting school he entered a clothing store as a clerk; but his deep hatred to slavery, and the political and social outrages committed upon the free colored men, preyed upon his mind to such an extent that, in 1826, he associated himself with Robert Osborn, in the publication of *The Watchman*, a weekly newspaper devoted to the freedom and enfranchisement of the people of color. His journal was conducted with marked ability, and Mr. Jordan soon began to wield a tremendous influence against the slave power. While absent from his editorial duties, in 1830, an article appeared in *The Watchman*, upon which its editor was indicted for constructive treason. He was at once arrested, placed in the dock, and arraigned for trial. He pleaded "not guilty," and asked for time to prepare for his defence. The plea was allowed, and the case was traversed to the next court. The trial came on at the appointed time; the jury was packed, for the pro-slavery element had determined on the conviction of the distinguished advocate of liberty. The whole city appeared to be lost to every thing but the proceedings of the assize. It was feared, that, if convicted, a riot would be the result, and the authorities prepared for this. A vessel of war was brought up abreast of the city, the guns of which were pointed up one of the principal streets, and at almost every avenue leading to the sea, a merchant vessel was moored, armed at least with one great gun, pointing in a similar direction, to rake the streets from bottom to top. A detachment of soldiers was kept under arms, with orders to be ready for action at a moment's warning. The officers of the court, including the judge, entered upon their duties, armed with pistols; and the sheriff was instructed to shoot the prisoner in the dock if a rescue was attempted. If convicted, Mr. Jordan's punishment was to be death. Happily for all, the verdict was "not guilty." The acquittal of the editor of *The*

Watchman carried disappointment and dismay into the ranks of the slave oligarchy, while it gave a new impetus to the anti-slavery cause, both in Jamaica and in Great Britain, and which culminated in the abolition of slavery on the 1st of August, 1834. The following year, Mr. Jordan was elected member of the Assembly for the city of Kingston, which he still represents. About this time, *The Watchman* was converted into a daily paper, under the title of *The Morning Journal*, still in existence, and owned by Jordan and Osborn. In 1853, Mr. Jordan was elected mayor of his native city without opposition, which office he still holds. He was recently chosen premier of the island and president of the privy council.

No man is more respected in the Assembly than Mr. Jordan, and reform measures offered by him are often carried through the house, owing to the respect the members have for the introducer. In the year 1860, the honorable gentleman was elevated to the dignity of knighthood by the Queen. Sir Edward Jordan has ever been regarded as an honest, upright, and temperate man. In a literary point of view, he is considered one of the first men in Jamaica.

It is indeed a cheering sign for the negro to look at one of his race, who, a few years ago, was tried for his life in a city in which he is now the chief magistrate, inspector of the prison in which he was once incarcerated, and occupying a seat in the legislature by the side of the white man who ejected him from his position as a clerk, on account of his color. To those who say that the two races cannot live in peace together, we point to the Jamaica Assembly, with more than half of its members colored; and to all who think that the negro is only fit for servitude, we reply by saying, Look at Sir Edward Jordan.

JOSEPH CARTER.

THE subject of this sketch is a native of the city of Bridgetown, Barbadoes, where he was born on the 16th of February, 1831. At the early age of eleven years, he was apprenticed to William Howell, a cabinet-maker of his native place. The boy showed so much genius and skill even at this tender age, that he excited an interest in his behalf, which culminated in his becoming the ward of Miss Hayes, a talented lady, of English origin, whose guardianship of young Carter did much to pave the way for the development of his hidden powers. In his seventeenth year, Joseph came to the States in company with his guardian, and settled in the city of Philadelphia, where he now resides. Buoyant with hopes, knowing his own capacity, and aspiring in his nature, the young man went forth in search of employment, little dreaming of the insurmountable prejudice which every man of his color has to meet in this country, and more especially in cities in the border states. In vain he went from shop to shop, appealing for simple justice, feeling confident that if once in employment, he could keep his situation by his ability as a workman. Wherever he appeared before a manufacturer, the reply was, "I would hire you if my hands, who are white, would not leave me." This calls to mind an incident that was related to me by a master gilder in Sixth Street, Philadelphia, a few years since. I had stepped into his place to purchase a picture frame, when, on learning that I was from Boston, he inquired if I was acquainted with Jacob R. Andrews. I replied that I was. "Then," said he, "do you see that bench there?" "Yes." "There was where he learned his trade." "Was he apprenticed to you?" I inquired. "No," said he; "he came to me, wishing to learn the business: my men refused to work in the same room with him, although he was as white as most of them. So, rather than turn him away, I put up a table there, and set him to work. In a short time he was able to turn out as good a job as any man in the establishment. He worked for me several years, and I must say that I never had a better workman, or a more reliable man in every respect, than he. Andrews often waited on my customers in my absence, and, whether at the bench at work or behind the counter, he was always the gentleman." I was pleased to hear so favorable an account of Mr. Andrews, for I had formed a high opinion of him, both as a man of integrity and a mechanic. He is now a flourishing manufacturer himself, in Beach Street, Boston, where he can count among his patrons some of the first families in the city. Mr. Carter, therefore, had energy similar to Mr. Andrews, and kept applying till he obtained work. A writer, to whom I am indebted for the early history of my subject, says, "Two years after his arrival we find Carter in business, manufacturing all sorts of furniture, from a pine table to the rarest cabinet. In 1859 we find him building organs for churches. One of the principal churches in this city (Philadelphia) has an organ manufactured by him. The whole work is done by his own hands; the rough stuff enters his establishment, and leaves it a perfect specimen of art and ingenuity, pure and mellow in tone, and polished, and carved, and elegantly finished. Unlike those extensive manufactories having branches and departments for fashioning the various portions of such instruments, his has none. You know it is said of the ancient Egyptians that their sculpture had an odd and awkward appearance, because their sculptors never chiselled out an entire figure. Some made the arms, some the legs, some the body, some the head. Perhaps Mr. Carter has the advantage of more extensive manufacturers by giving uniqueness and symmetry to his instruments. He is now making a very large one to order, having nine stops and pedals. The one he proposes to send to the Art Exhibition is an elaborately finished one of five stops and pedals, of walnut, carved, gothic style, and of exceeding richness of tone. This business he has taken up without ever receiving an hour's instruction. He was imperceptibly drawn into it through a fondness for music. He purchased a melodeon for his own use and amusement, and feeling the want of more stops and pedals, set about the work; and this attempt not being satisfactory, he built an organ which proved to be a very excellent one."

JAMES LAWSON.

JAMES LAWSON was born in slavery in the State of Virginia, where, for many years, he was the chief man on his master's plantation; and when the rebellion broke out, the rebel owner felt sure, from James's former fidelity, that he would stand by him in that contest. So confident was he of this, that he sent the chattel to an important military station with the following recommendation: "You may trust Jim in any way that you can use him, for he has been my slave fourteen years, and I never knew him to deceive me or any member of my family. Indeed, I have more respect, esteem, and good feeling for him, and more confidence in his integrity, than any white man of my acquaintance. He is able to undertake any affair, of either great or small importance."

When the history of the "Slaveholders' Rebellion" shall be impartially written, it will be found that no class has done more good service to the Union cause, and were more reliable in every respect, than those who had formerly been slaves. A correspondent of the "New York Times," writing from the head-quarters of the army of the Potomac, July 29, 1862, says, "Some of the most valuable information McClellan has received in regard to the position, movements and plans of the enemy, the topography of the country, and the inclination of certain inhabitants, has been obtained through contrabands. Even spies and traitors have been detected, and brought before the proper authorities, upon evidence furnished by this much-abused, but generally loyal class of people."

Probably no ten men have done so much in the way of giving information and performing daring acts in the enemy's immediate locality, as James Lawson. At one time we find him mounted on horseback, riding with the commanding general and his staff, piloting the Union forces through the enemy's country, and at another heading a scouting party, and saving them all from capture, by his superior knowledge of the district through which they travelled. After doing considerable service for the army, "Jim," as he was generally called, shipped on board the flag gunboat Freeborn, Lieutenant Samuel Magaw commanding. An officer from that vessel says of Jim, "He furnished Captain Magaw with much valuable intelligence concerning the rebel movements, and, from his quiet, every-day behavior, soon won the esteem of the commanding officer.

"Captain Magaw, shortly after Jim's arrival on board the Freeborn, sent him upon a scouting tour through the rebel fortifications, more to test his reliability than any thing else; and the mission, although fraught with great danger, was executed by Jim in the most faithful manner. Again Jim was sent into Virginia, landing at the White House, below Mount Vernon, and going into the interior for several miles, encountering the fire of picket guards and posted sentries, returned in safety to the shore, and was brought off in the captain's gig, under the fire of the rebel musketry.

"Jim had a wife and four children at that time still in Virginia. They belonged to the same man as Jim did. He was anxious to get them; yet it seemed impossible. One day in January Jim came to the captain's room and asked for permission to be landed that evening on the Virginia side, as he wished to bring off his family. 'Why, Jim,' said Captain Magaw, 'how will you be able to pass the pickets?'

"'I want to try, captain. I think I can get 'em over safely,' meekly replied Jim.

"'Well, you have my permission;' and Captain Magaw ordered one of the gunboats to land Jim that night on whatever part of the shore Jim designated, and return for him the following evening.

"True to his appointment, Jim was at the spot with his wife and family, and were taken on board the gunboat, and brought over to Liverpool Point, where Colonel Graham had given them a log house to live in, just back of his own quarters. Jim ran the gantlet of the sentries unharmed, never taking to the roads, but keeping in the woods, every foot-path of which, and almost every tree, he knew from his boyhood up.

"Several weeks afterwards, another reconnoissance was planned, and Jim sent on it. He returned in safety, and was highly complimented by Generals Hooker, Sickles, and the entire flotilla.

"On Thursday, a week ago, it became necessary to obtain correct information of the enemy's movements. Since then, batteries at Shipping and Cockpit Points had been evacuated, and their troops moved to Fredericksburg. Jim was the man picked out for the occasion by General Sickles and Captain Magaw. The general came down to Colonel Graham's quarters about nine in the evening, and sent for Jim. There were present the general, Colonel Graham, and myself. Jim came into the colonel's.

"'Jim,' said the general, 'I want you to go over to Virginia to-night and find out what forces they have at Aquia Creek and Fredericksburg. If you want any men to accompany you, pick them out.'

"'I know two men that would like to go,' Jim answered.

"'Well, get them and be back as soon as possible.'

"Away went Jim over to the contraband camp, and returning almost immediately, brought into our presence two very intelligent looking men.

"'Are you all ready?' inquired the general.

"'All ready, sir,' the trio responded.

"'Well, here, Jim, you take my pistol,' said General Sickles, unbuckling it from his belt, 'and if you are successful, I will give you a hundred dollars.'

"Jim hoped he would be, and bidding us good by, started off for the gunboat Satellite, Captain Foster, who landed them a short distance below the Potomac Creek Batteries. They were to return early in the morning, but were unable, from the great distance they went in the interior. Long before daylight on Saturday morning the gunboat was lying off the appointed place.

"As the day dawned, Captain Foster discovered a mounted picket guard near the beach, and almost at the same instant saw Jim to the left of them, in the woods, sighting his gun at the rebel cavalry. He ordered the 'gig' to be manned and rowed to the shore. The rebels moved along slowly, thinking to intercept the boat, when Foster gave them a shell, which scattered them. Jim, with only one of his original companions, and two fresh contrabands, came on board. Jim had *lost the other*. He had been challenged by a picket when some distance in advance of Jim, and the negro, instead of answering the summons, fired the contents of Sickles's revolver at the picket. It was an unfortunate occurrence, for at that time the entire picket guard rushed out of a small house near the spot, and fired the contents of their muskets at Jim's companion, killing him instantly. Jim and the other three hid themselves in a hollow, near a fence, and after the pickets gave up pursuit, crept through the woods to the shore. From the close proximity of the rebel pickets, Jim could not display a light, which was the signal for Foster to send a boat.

"Captain Foster, after hearing Jim's story of the shooting of his companion, determined to avenge his death; so, steaming his vessel close in to the shore, he sighted his guns for a barn, which the rebel cavalry were hiding behind. He fired two shells: one went right through the barn, killing four of the rebels and seven of their horses. Captain Foster, seeing the effect of his shots, said to Jim, who stood by, 'Well, Jim, I've avenged the death of poor Cornelius' (the name of Jim's lost companion).

"General Hooker has transmitted to the war department an account of Jim's reconnoissance to Fredericksburg, and unites with the army and navy stationed on the left wing of the Potomac, in the hope that the government will present Jim with a fitting recompense for his gallant services."

The gunboat soon after was ordered to Newbern, N. C., where James Lawson was again to be the centre of attraction, but in a new character. Anxious that his fellow-slaves (many of whom had shipped in the same vessel) should excel as oarsmen, he was frequently out practising with them, until a race was agreed upon, in which the blacks were to pull against the whites. A correspondent of the "New York Times" gives the following as the result:—

"One of the two boats entered was manned by six contraband seamen, beautifully attired in man-of-war costume, and the other was manned by eight white seamen, who were considered the crack crew of these waters. Distance was offered the contraband crew, who had only been seamen some three months; but their captain refused to accept of any advantage whatever, and insisted on giving the white seamen the advantage of two men. Every thing being in readiness, the word was given, and off went the boats, throwing the crowd, white and black, into the most intense excitement. Judge of the astonishment of all, when the boat containing the contrabands was seen to turn the mile post first; and great was the excitement and deafening were the cheers as they came in some three rods in advance of the white crew, who were dripping with perspiration, and thoroughly mortified at the unexpected result. They were inclined to think the contest an unfair one, until the captain of the contrabands offered to renew the race by having the crews exchange boats, which proposition was not accepted by the white seamen for fear of a like result. The captain said his contrabands could not only pull a small boat faster and with more steadiness than the same number of white seamen, but that they, with others he had on board, could man his big guns with more agility and skill in time of action than any white seamen he had ever seen."

Mr. Lawson, at last accounts, was holding a prominent office in General Foster's command.

CAPTAIN CALLIOUX.

"In war was never lion's rage so fierce;
In peace was never gentle lamb more mild."
SHAKSPEARE.

REVOLUTIONS are occasioned by the growth of society beyond the growth of government, and they will be peaceful or violent just in proportion as the people and government shall be wise and virtuous or vicious and ignorant. Such revolutions or reforms are generally of a peaceful nature in communities in which the government has made provision for the gradual expansion of its institutions, to suit the onward march of society. No government is wise in overlooking, whatever may be the strength of its own traditions, or however glorious its history, that human institutions will outlive their time; that those institutions which have been adapted for a barbarous state of society, will cease to be adapted for more civilized and intelligent times; and unless government make a provision for the gradual expansion, nothing can prevent a storm, either of an intellectual or a physical nature.

The great American rebellion, therefore, is a legitimate revolution growing out of the incongruity of freedom and slavery; and the first gun fired at Sumter was hailed by every true friend of freedom, and especially the negro, as the dawn of a brighter day for the black man. But it was evident, from the commencement of the clash of arms, that the despised race was to take no part in their exercise, unless the Federal authorities were forced into it by the magnitude of the rebellion. His services refused by the Federal government, all classes declaring that they would not "*fight by the side of a nigger*," the black man had nothing to do but to fold his arms and bide his time. Defeat after defeat appeared to make no change in the pro-slavery public mind, for the nation seemed determined to perish rather than receive help from a black hand. The rout at Bull Run, the sad affair at Ball's Bluff, the unfortunate mistake at Big Bethel, the loss of 100,000 brave men during the first fifteen months of the rebellion, and the display of Copperhead feeling in the Northern States, caused the far-seeing ones to feel that the ship of state was fast drifting to sea without a rudder. The announcement that a proclamation of emancipation would be issued on the 1st of January, 1863, brought forth a howl of denunciation from those who despised the negro more than they did the rebels. Still the cry rose from the majority, "Let the republic perish rather than see the nigger in uniform."

All this time, the black man was silently, yet steadily, creating an under-current, which was, at a later day, to carry him to the battle field. The heroic act of Tillman on the high seas, the "*strategy*" of Captain Small in taking the Planter past the guns of Sumter, and the reliable intelligence conveyed to the Union army by "intelligent contrabands,"—all tended to soften the negro hate, and to pave the way for justice. All honor to the "New York Tribune," for its noble defence of my race, and its advocacy of the black man's right to bear arms. The organization of negro regiments once begun by General Hunter, soon found favor with the more liberal portion of the northern people.

By and by, that brave, generous, and highly cultivated scholar, gentleman, and Christian, Thomas Wentworth Higginson, lent the influence of his name, and accepted an office in the first South Carolina regiment, made an excursion into the heart of slavery, met the rebels and defeated them with his negro soldiers, and reported through the public journals what he had witnessed of the black man's ability on the field of battle. Then the tide begun to turn.

The announcement that a regiment of colored soldiers was to be raised in Massachusetts, created another sensation among the Copperheads, and no means were left unused to deter them from enlisting. An early prejudice was brought against the movement, owing to the fact that the commissioned officers were white, and no door was to be opened to the black man's elevation. Would colored men enlist under such restrictions? was a question asked in every circle. All admitted that they had no inducement, save that of a wish to aid in freeing their brethren of the south.

Disfranchised in a majority of the free states, laboring under an inhuman and withering prejudice, shut out of the political, religious, and social associations of the nation, the black man's case was a hard one. In the past, every weapon that genius or ignorance could invent or command had been turned against him. Missiles had been hurled at his devoted head from every quarter.

The pulpit, the platform, and the press, had all united against him. The statesman in the councils of the nation had lowered his standard in his attempts to dehumanize the negro; the scholar had forgotten his calling while turning aside to coin epithets against the race. All of this he would have to forget before he could accept the musket and the knapsack. Yet he did forget all, and in a few short days the Massachusetts fifty-fourth regiment stood before the country as another evidence of the black man's fidelity and patriotism. It is but simple justice to say of this regiment, that the adjutant general, on its departure for the seat of war, paid it the high compliment of being the most sober and well behaved, and of having cost less for its organization, than any regiment that had left the commonwealth, and that it was better drilled than all, except the twelfth. While the fifty-fourth, by its military skill and good order, was softening the hard hearts of the people north, the negro regiments of Louisiana were attracting attention by the boldness of their request to General Banks to be sent to the field of active duty, and to be put in the front of the fight.

When New Orleans was captured by General Butler, he found there a regiment of colored men bearing the name of the "Native Guard." These men had been compelled to serve under the rebels; but when the latter left the city, the former refused to follow, and embraced the earliest opportunity to offer their services to the Union cause. They were at once accepted by General Butler, under the title of the first Louisiana regiment.

The census of 1860 placed the number of the inhabitants of the city of New Orleans at 175,000. Of these, 15,000 were free colored, 10,000 were slaves, and the remainder were whites. The free colored men were taxed for an average of $1000 to each person, while the white were taxed for only $732 to each person. The first Louisiana regiment was composed principally of this class of the free black population. The professions, the mercantile, and the trades were well represented, while not a few were men of extreme wealth. Nearly all were liberally educated; some were scholars of a high order. The brave, the enthusiastic, and the patriotic found full scope for the development of their powers in this regiment. One of the most efficient of the officers was Captain Callioux, a man whose identity with his race could never be mistaken, for he prided himself on being the blackest individual in the Crescent City. Whether in the drawing-room or on the parade, he was ever the centre of attraction. Finely educated, polished in his manners, a splendid horseman, a good boxer, bold, athletic, and daring, he never lacked admirers. His men were ready at any time to follow him to the cannon's mouth; and he was as ready to lead them. General Banks granted their request, and the regiment was brought before the rifle pits and heavy guns of Port Hudson on the 26th of May, 1863. Night fell—the lovely southern night, with its silvery moonshine on the gleaming waters of the Mississippi, that passed directly by the intrenched town. The glistening stars appeared suspended in the upper air as globes of liquid light, with its fresh, soft breeze, bearing such sweet scents from the odoriferous trees and plants, that a poet might have fancied angelic spirits were abroad, making the atmosphere luminous with their pure presence, and every breeze fragrant with their luscious breath. The deep-red sun that rose on the next morning indicated that the day would be warm, and, as it advanced, the heat became intense. The earth had been long parched, and the hitherto green verdure had begun to turn yellow. Clouds of dust followed every step and movement of the troops. The air was filled with dust; clouds gathered, frowned upon the earth, and hastened away. The weatherwise watched the red masses of the morning, and still hoped for a shower to cool the air and lay the dust, before the work of death commenced; but none came, and the very atmosphere seemed as if it was from an over-heated oven. The laying aside of all unnecessary accoutrements, and the preparation that showed itself on every side, told all present that the conflict was near at hand. General Dwight was the officer in command over the colored brigade, and his antecedents with regard to the rights and the ability of the negro were not of the most favorable character, and busy rumor, that knows every thing, had whispered it about, that the valor of the black man was to be put to the severest test that day.

The black forces consisted of the first Louisiana, under

Lieutenant-Colonel Bassett, and the third Louisiana, under Colonel Nelson. These officers were white, but the line officers of the first Louisiana were colored. The number of the colored troops was 1080 strong, and formed into four lines, Lieutenant-Colonel Bassett, first Louisiana, forming the first line, and the others forming the second line. As the moment of attack drew near, the greatest suppressed excitement existed, but all were eager for the fight. Captain Callioux walked proudly up and down the line, and smilingly greeted the familiar faces of his company. Colonel Nelson being called to act as brigadier-general, Lieutenant-Colonel Finnegas took his place. The third Louisiana was composed mostly of freed men, whose backs still bore the marks of the lash, and whose brave, stout hearts beat high at the thought that the hour had come when they were to meet their proud and unfeeling oppressors. New England officers and privates looked on, and asked each other what they thought would be the result. Would these blacks stand fire? Was not the test by which they were to be tried too severe?

The enemy, in his stronghold, felt his power, and bade defiance to the expected attack. At last, the welcome word was given, and our men started. The enemy opened a blistering fire of shell, canister, grape, and musketry. The first shell thrown by the enemy killed and wounded a number of the blacks; but on they went. "Charge" was the word—

> "'Charge!' Trump and drum awoke;
> Onward the bondmen broke;
> Bayonet and sabre-stroke
> Vainly opposed their rush."

At every pace the column was thinned by the falling dead and wounded. The negroes closed up steadily as their comrades fell, and advanced within fifty paces of where the rebels were working a masked battery, situated on a bluff where the guns could sweep the whole field over which the troops must charge. This battery was on the left of the charging line. Another battery of three or four guns commanded the front, and six heavy pieces raked the right of the line as it formed, and enfiladed its flank and rear as it charged on the bluff. It was ascertained that a bayou ran under the bluff where the guns lay—a bayou deeper than a man could ford. This charge was repulsed with severe loss.

Lieutenant-Colonel Finnegas was then ordered to charge, and in a well-dressed, steady line his men went on the double quick down over the field of death. No matter how gallantly the men behaved—no matter how bravely they were led—it was not in the course of things that this gallant brigade should take these works by charge. Yet charge after charge was ordered, and carried out, under all these disasters, with Spartan firmness. Six charges in all were made. Colonel Nelson reported to General Dwight the fearful odds he had to contend with. Says General Dwight, in reply, "Tell Colonel Nelson I shall consider that he has accomplished nothing unless he takes those guns." Thus the last few charges were made under the spur of desperation.

The ground was already strewn with the dead and wounded, and many of the brave officers had fallen early in the engagement. Among them was the gallant and highly-cultivated Anselms. He was a standard-bearer, and hugged the Stars and Stripes to his heart as he fell forward upon them, pierced by five balls. Two corporals near by struggled between themselves as to who should have the honor of again raising those blood-stained emblems to the breeze. Each was eager for the honor, and during the struggle a missile from the enemy wounded one of them, and the other corporal shouldered the dear old flag in triumph, and bore it through the charge in the front of the advancing line.

Shells from the rebel guns cut down trees three feet in diameter, and they fell at one time burying a whole company beneath their branches.

Thus they charged bravely on certain destruction, till the ground was slippery with the gore of the slaughtered, and cumbered with the bodies of the maimed. The last charge was made about one o'clock.

At this juncture, Captain Callioux was seen with his left arm dangling by his side,—for a ball had broken it above the elbow,—while his right hand held his unsheathed sword gleaming in the rays of the sun, and his hoarse, faint voice was heard cheering on his men. A moment more and the brave and generous Callioux was struck by a shell, and fell far in advance of his company. The fall of this officer so exasperated his men, that they appeared to be filled with new enthusiasm, and they rushed forward with a recklessness that probably never has been equalled. Seeing it to be a hopeless effort, the taking of these batteries, order was given to change the programme, and the troops were called off. But had they accomplished any thing more than the loss of many of their brave men? Yes, they had. The self-forgetfulness, the undaunted heroism, and the great endurance of the negro, as exhibited that day, created a new chapter in American history for the black man. No negro hater will ever again dare to urge the withholding of our rights upon the plea that we will not fight.

The stale and stereotyped falsehood that the blacks are wanting in patriotism, was nailed to the counter as base coin, on the banks of the Mississippi. Many Persians were slain at the battle of Thermopylæ, but history records only the fall of Leonidas and his four hundred companions. So, in the future, when we shall have passed away from the stage, and rising generations shall speak of the conflict at Port Hudson, and the celebrated charge of the Negro Brigade, they will forget all others, in their admiration for Captain Callioux and his black associates. I should have said, the expedition against this strongly fortified place was Major-General Banks's, under whom the other officers acted. The commander, in his official report of the engagement, bears the following testimony to the bravery of the colored troops. He says,—

"On the extreme right of our lines I posted the first and third regiments of negro troops. The first regiment of Louisiana engineers, composed exclusively of colored men, excepting the officers, was also engaged in the operations of the day. The position occupied by these troops was one of importance, and called for the utmost steadiness and bravery in those to whom it was confided.

"It gives me pleasure to report that they answered every expectation. In many respects their conduct was heroic; no troops could be more determined or more daring. They made, during the day, three charges upon the batteries of the enemy, suffering very heavy losses, and holding their position at nightfall with the other troops on the right of our lines. The highest commendation is bestowed upon them by all the officers in command on the right.

"Whatever doubt may have existed heretofore as to the efficiency of organizations of this character, the history of this day proves conclusively to those who were in condition to observe the conduct of these regiments, that the government will find in this class of troops effective supporters and defenders. The severe test to which they were subjected, and the determined manner in which they encountered the enemy, leaves upon my mind no doubt of their ultimate success."

The Hon. B. F. Flanders, writing from New Orleans, under date of June 2, 1863, pays the following tribute to the bravery of those invincible men:—

"The unanimous report of all those who were in the recent severe fight at Port Hudson, in regard to the negroes, is, that they fought like devils. They have completely conquered the prejudice of the army against them. Never was there before such an extraordinary revolution of sentiment as that of this army in respect to the negroes as soldiers."

CAPTAIN JOSEPH HOWARD.

"Freemen, now's your day for doing—
Great the issues in your hand;
Risk them not by faint pursuing,
Peal the watchword through the land:
On for Freedom,
God, our Country, and the Right!"

AMONG the colored troops which Major-General Butler found at New Orleans, when that place was evacuated by the rebels, was the Second Louisiana Native Guards. When General Banks superseded General Butler, and took command, the Second Louisiana was stationed at Baton Rouge. This was considered one of the finest regiments in that section. The line officers were all colored, and the best discipline prevailed throughout the ranks. Nevertheless, the white officers of the New England troops, either through jealousy, or hatred to the colored men on account of their complexion, demanded that the latter should be turned out of office, and that their places be filled by whites, from the ranks of the other regiments. And to the everlasting shame of General Banks, and the disgrace of the Union cause, the gallant men who had got up the Second Louisiana regiment were dismissed. The order for this change had scarcely been promulgated ere the retiring officers found themselves the object of so much obloquy and abuse that they were forced to quit Baton Rouge and return to New Orleans. The colored soldiers were deeply pained at seeing the officers of their choice taken from them, for they were much attached to their commanders, some of whom were special favorites with the whole regiment. Among these were First Lieutenant Joseph Howard, of Company I, and Second Lieutenant Joseph G. Parker, of Company C. These gentlemen were both possessed of ample wealth, and had entered the army, not as a matter of speculation, as too many have done, but from a love of military life. Their hatred of oppression, and attachment to the Union cause, kept them from following the rebels in their hasty flight.

Lieutenant Howard was a man of more than ordinary ability in military tactics, and a braver or more daring officer could not be found in the valley of the Mississippi. He was well educated, speaking the English, French, and Spanish languages fluently, and was considered a scholar of rare literary attainments. He, with his friend, felt sorely the deep humiliation attending their dismissal, and they seldom showed themselves on the streets of their native city.

When the news reached New Orleans of the heroic charge made by the first Louisiana regiment, at Port Hudson, on the 27th of May, Howard at once called on his friend Parker, and they were so fired with the intelligence that they determined to proceed to Port Hudson, and to join their old regiment as *privates*. That night they took passage, and the next day found them with their former friends in arms. The regiment was still in position, close to the enemy's works, and the appearance of the two lieutenants was hailed with demonstrations of joy. Instead of being placed as privates in the ranks, they were both immediately assigned the command of a company each, not from any compliment to them, but sheer necessity, because the *white officers* of these companies, feeling that the colored soldiers were put in the front of the battle owing to their complexion, were not willing to risk their lives, and had thrown up their commissions. On the 20th of June, these two officers were put to the test, and nobly did they maintain their former reputation for bravery. Captain Howard leading the way, they charged upon the enemy's rifle pits—drove them out and took possession, and held them for three hours, in the face of a raking fire of artillery. Several times the blacks were so completely hidden from view by the smoke of their own guns and the enemy's heavy cannon, that they could not be seen. It was at this time that Captain Howard exhibited his splendid powers as a commander. The negroes never hesitated, never flinched, but gallantly did their duty.

Amid the roar of artillery and the rattling of musketry, the groans of the wounded and the ghastly appearance of the dead, the heroic and the intrepid Howard was the same. He never said to his men, "Go," but always, "Follow me." At last, when many of their men were killed, and the severe fire of the enemy's artillery seemed to mow down every thing before it, these brave men were compelled to fall back from the pits which they had so triumphantly taken.

At nightfall, General Banks paid the negro officers a high compliment, shaking the hand of Captain Howard, and congratulating him on his return, and telling his aids that this man was worthy of a more elevated place. Great amount of prejudice was conquered that day by the intrepid Howard and his companions.

MY SOUTHERN HOME:

OR,

THE SOUTH AND ITS PEOPLE.

"Go, little book, from this thy solitude!
  I cast thee on the waters—go thy ways!
And if, as I believe, thy vein be good,
  The world will find thee after many days."
—SOUTHEY.

PREFACE.

No attempt has been made to create heroes or heroines, or to appeal to the imagination or the heart.

The earlier incidents were written out from the author's recollections. The later sketches here given, are the results of recent visits to the South, where the incidents were jotted down at the time of their occurrence, or as they fell from the lips of the narrators, and in their own unadorned dialect.

BOSTON, May, 1880.

CONTENTS

CHAPTER XVII.

CHAPTER XVIII.

CHAPTER XIX.

CHAPTER XX.

CHAPTER XXI.

CHAPTER XXII.

CHAPTER XXIII.

CHAPTER XXIV.

MY SOUTHERN HOME.

CHAPTER I.

TEN miles north of the city of St. Louis, in the State of Missouri, forty years ago, on a pleasant plain, sloping off toward a murmuring stream, stood a large frame-house, two stories high; in front was a beautiful lake, and, in the rear, an old orchard filled with apple, peach, pear, and plum trees, with boughs untrimmed, all bearing indifferent fruit. The mansion was surrounded with piazzas, covered with grape-vines, clematis, and passion flowers; the Pride of China mixed its oriental-looking foliage with the majestic magnolia, and the air was redolent with the fragrance of buds peeping out of every nook, and nodding upon you with a most unexpected welcome.

The tasteful hand of art, which shows itself in the grounds of European and New-England villas, was not seen there, but the lavish beauty and harmonious disorder of nature was permitted to take its own course, and exhibited a want of taste so commonly witnessed in the sunny South.

The killing effects of the tobacco plant upon the lands of "Poplar Farm," was to be seen in the rank growth of the brier, the thistle, the burdock, and the jimpson weed, showing themselves wherever the strong arm of the bondman had not kept them down.

Dr. Gaines, the proprietor of "Poplar Farm," was a good-humored, sunny-sided old gentleman, who, always feeling happy himself, wanted everybody to enjoy the same blessing. Unfortunately for him, the Doctor had been born and brought up in Virginia, raised in a family claiming to be of the "F. F. V.'s," but, in reality, was comparatively poor. Marrying Mrs. Sarah Scott Pepper, an accomplished widow lady of medium fortune, Dr. Gaines emigrated to Missouri, where he became a leading man in his locality.

Deeply imbued with religious feeling of the Calvinistic school, well-versed in the Scriptures, and having an abiding

GREAT HOUSE AT POPLAR FARM.

faith in the power of the Gospel to regenerate the world, the Doctor took great pleasure in presenting his views wherever his duties called him.

As a physician, he did not rank very high, for it was currently reported, and generally believed, that the father, finding his son unfit for mercantile business, or the law, determined to make him either a clergyman or a physician. Mr. Gaines, Senior, being somewhat superstitious, resolved not to settle the question too rashly in regard to the son's profession, therefore, it is said, flipped a cent, feeling that "heads or tails" would be a better omen than his own judgment in the matter. Fortunately for the cause of religion, the head turned up in favor of the medical profession. Nevertheless, the son often said that he believed God had destined him for the *sacred calling*, and devoted much of his time in exhorting his neighbors to seek repentance.

Most planters in our section cared but little about the religious training of their slaves, regarding them as they did their cattle,—an investment, the return of which was only to be considered in dollars and cents. Not so, however, with Dr. John Gaines, for he took special pride in looking after the spiritual welfare of his slaves, having them all in the "great house," at family worship, night and morning.

On Sabbath mornings, reading of the Scriptures, and explaining the same, generally occupied from one to two hours, and often till half of the negroes present were fast asleep. The white members of the family did not take as kindly to the religious teaching of the doctor, as did the blacks.

For his Christian zeal, I had the greatest respect, for I always regarded him as a truly pious and conscientious man, willing at all times to give of his means the needful in spreading the Gospel.

Mrs. Sarah Gaines was a lady of considerable merit, well-educated, and of undoubted piety. If she did not join heartily in her husband's religious enthusiasm, it was not for want of deep and genuine Christian feeling, but from the idea that he was of more humble origin than herself, and, therefore, was not a capable instructor.

This difference in birth, this difference in antecedents does much in the South to disturb family relations wherever it exists, and Mrs. Gaines, when wishing to show her contempt for the Doctor's opinions, would allude to her own parentage and birth in comparison to her husband's. Thus, once, when they were having a "family jar," she, with tears streaming down her cheeks, and wringing her hands, said,—

"My mother told me that I was a fool to marry a man so much beneath me,—one so much my inferior in society. And now you show it by hectoring and aggravating me all you can. But, never mind; I thank the Lord that He has given me religion and grace to stand it. Never mind, one of these days the Lord will make up His jewels,—take me home to glory, out of your sight,—and then I'll be devilish glad of it!"

These scenes of unpleasantness, however, were not of everyday occurrence, and, therefore, the great house at the "Poplar Farm," may be considered as having a happy family.

Slave children, with almost an alabaster complexion, straight hair, and blue eyes, whose mothers were jet black, or brown, were often a great source of annoyance in the Southern household, and especially to the mistress of the mansion.

Billy, a quadroon of eight or nine years, was amongst the young slaves, in the Doctor's house, then being trained up for a servant. Any one taking a hasty glance at the lad would never suspect that a drop of negro blood coursed through his blue veins. A gentleman, whose acquaintance Dr. Gaines had made, but who knew nothing of the latter's family relations, called at the house in the Doctor's absence. Mrs. Gaines received the stranger, and asked him to be seated, and remain till the host's return. While thus waiting, the boy, Billy, had occasion to pass through the room. The stranger, presuming the lad to be a son of the Doctor, exclaimed, "How do you do?" and turning to the lady, said, "how much he looks like his father; I should have known it was the Doctor's son, if I had met him in Mexico!"

With flushed countenance and excited voice, Mrs. Gaines informed the gentleman that the little fellow was "only a slave and nothing more." After the stranger's departure, Billy was seen pulling up grass in the garden, with bare head, neck and shoulders, while the rays of the burning sun appeared to melt the child.

This process was repeated every few days for the purpose of

giving the slave the color that nature had refused it. And yet, Mrs. Gaines was not considered a cruel woman,—indeed she was regarded as a kind-feeling mistress. Billy, however, a few days later, experienced a roasting far more severe than the one he had got in the sun.

The morning was cool, and the breakfast table was spread near the fireplace, where a newly-built fire was blazing up. Mrs. Gaines, being seated near enough to feel very sensibly the increasing flames, ordered Billy to stand before her.

The lad at once complied. His thin clothing giving him but little protection from the fire, the boy soon began to make up faces and to twist and move about, showing evident signs of suffering.

"What are you riggling about for?" asked the mistress. "It burns me," replied the lad; "turn round, then," said the mistress; and the slave commenced turning around, keeping it up till the lady arose from the table.

Billy, however, was not entirely without his crumbs of comfort. It was his duty to bring the hot biscuit from the kitchen to the great house table while the whites were at meal. The boy would often watch his opportunity, take a "cake" from the plate, and conceal it in his pocket till breakfast was over, and then enjoy his stolen gain. One morning Mrs. Gaines, observing that the boy kept moving about the room, after bringing in the "cakes," and also seeing the little fellow's pocket sticking out rather largely, and presuming that there was something hot there, said, "Come here." The lad came up; she pressed her hand against the hot pocket, which caused the boy to jump back. Again the mistress repeated, "Come here," and with the same result.

This, of course, set the whole room, servants and all, in a roar. Again and again the boy was ordered to "come up," which he did, each time jumping back, until the heat of the biscuit was exhausted, and then he was made to take it out and throw it into the yard, where the geese seized it and held a carnival over it. Billy was heartily laughed at by his companions in the kitchen and the quarters, and the large blister, caused by the hot biscuit, created merriment among the slaves, rather than sympathy for the lad.

Mrs. Gaines, being absent from home one day, and the rest

of the family out of the house, Billy commenced playing with the shot-gun, which stood in the corner of the room, and which the boy supposed was unloaded; upon a corner shelf, just above the gun, stood a band-box, in which was neatly laid away all of Mrs. Gaines' caps and cuffs, which, in those days, were in great use.

The gun having the flint lock, the boy amused himself with bringing down the hammer and striking fire. By this action powder was jarred into the pan, and the gun, which was heavily charged with shot, was discharged, the contents passing through the band-box of caps, cutting them literally to pieces and scattering them over the floor.

Billy gathered up the fragments, put them in the box and placed it upon the shelf,—he alone aware of the accident.

A few days later, and Mrs. Gaines was expecting company; she called to Hannah to get her a clean cap. The servant, in attempting to take down the box, exclaimed: "Lor, misses, ef de rats ain't bin at dees caps an' cut 'em all to pieces, jes look here." With a degree of amazement not easily described the mistress beheld the fragments as they were emptied out upon the floor.

Just then a new idea struck Hannah, and she said: "I lay anything dat gun has been shootin' off."

"Where is Billy? Where is Billy?" exclaimed the mistress; "Where is Billy?" echoed Hannah; fearing that the lady would go into convulsions, I hastened out to look for the boy, but he was nowhere to be found; I returned only to find her weeping and wringing her hands, exclaiming, "O, I am ruined, I am ruined; the company's coming and not a clean cap about the house; O, what shall I do, what shall I do?"

I tried to comfort her by suggesting that the servants might get one ready in time; Billy soon made his appearance, and looked on with wonderment; and, when asked how he came to shoot off the gun, declared that he knew nothing about it; and "ef de gun went off, it was of its own accord." However, the boy admitted the snapping of the lock or trigger. A light whipping was all that he got, and for which he was well repaid by having an opportunity of telling how the "caps flew about the room when de gun went off."

Relating the event some time after in the quarters he said: "I golly, you had aughty seen dem caps fly, and de dust and smok' in de room. I thought de judgment day had come, sure nuff." On the arrival of the company, Mrs. Gaines made a very presentable appearance, although the caps and laces had been destroyed. One of the visitors on this occasion was a young Mr. Sarpee, of St. Louis, who, although above twenty-one years of age, had never seen anything of country life, and, therefore, was very anxious to remain over night, and go on a coon hunt. Dr. Gaines, being lame, could not accompany the gentleman, but sent Ike, Cato, and Sam; three of the most expert coon-hunters on the farm. Night came, and off went the young man and the boys on the coon hunt. The dogs scented game, after being about half an hour in the woods, to the great delight of Mr. Sarpee, who was armed with a double barrel pistol, which, he said, he carried both to "protect himself, and to shoot the coon."

The halting of the boys and the quick, sharp bark of the dogs announced that the game was "treed," and the gentleman from the city pressed forward with fond expectation of seeing the coon, and using his pistol. However, the boys soon raised the cry of "polecat, polecat; get out de way"; and at the same time, retreating as if they were afraid of an attack from the animal. Not so with Mr. Sarpee; he stood his ground, with pistol in hand, waiting to get a sight of the game. He was not long in suspense, for the white and black spotted creature soon made its appearance, at which the city gentleman opened fire upon the skunk, which attack was immediately answered by the animal, and in a manner that caused the young man to wish that he, too, had retreated with the boys. Such an odor, he had never before inhaled; and, what was worse, his face, head, hands and clothing was covered with the cause of the smell, and the gentleman, at once, said: "Come, let's go home; I've got enough of coon-hunting." But, didn't the boys enjoy the fun.

The return of the party home was the signal for a hearty laugh, and all at the expense of the city gentleman. So great and disagreeable was the smell, that the young man had to go to the barn, where his clothing was removed, and he submitted to the process of washing by the servants. Soap, scrubbing brushes, towels, indeed, everything was brought into requisition, but all to no purpose. The skunk smell was there, and was likely to remain. Both family and visitors were at the breakfast table, the next morning, except Mr. Sarpee. He was still in the barn, where he had slept the previous night. Nor did there seem to be any hope that he would be able to visit the house, for the smell was intolerable. The substitution of a suit of the Doctor's clothes for his own failed to remedy the odor.

Dinkie, the conjurer, was called in. He looked the young man over, shook his head in a knowing manner, and said it was a big job. Mr. Sarpee took out a Mexican silver dollar, handed it to the old negro, and told him to do his best. Dinkie smiled, and he thought that he could remove the smell.

His remedy was to dig a pit in the ground large enough to hold the man, put him in it, and cover him over with fresh earth; consequently, Mr. Sarpee was, after removing his entire clothing, buried, all except his head, while his clothing was served in the same manner. A servant held an umbrella over the unhappy man, and fanned him during the eight hours that he was there.

Taken out of the pit at six o'clock in the evening, all joined with Dinkie in the belief that Mr. Sarpee "smelt sweeter," than when interred in the morning; still the smell of the "polecat" was there. Five hours longer in the pit, the following day, with a rub down by Dinkie, with his "Goopher," fitted the young man for a return home to the city.

I never heard that Mr. Sarpee ever again joined in a "coon hunt."

No description of mine, however, can give anything like a correct idea of the great merriment of the entire slave population on "Poplar Farm," caused by the "coon hunt." Even Uncle Ned, the old superannuated slave, who seldom went beyond the confines of his own cabin, hobbled out, on this occasion, to take a look at "de gentleman fum de city," while buried in the pit.

At night, in the quarters, the slaves had a merry time over the "coon hunt."

"I golly, but didn't de polecat give him a big dose?" said Ike.

"But how Mr. Sarpee did talk French to hissef when de ole coon peppered him," remarked Cato.

"He won't go coon huntin' agin, soon, I bet you," said Sam.

"De coon hunt," and "de gemmen fum de city," was the talk for many days.

CHAPTER II.

I HAVE already said that Dr. Gaines was a man of deep religious feeling, and this interest was not confined to the whites, for he felt that it was the Christian duty to help to save all mankind, white and black. He would often say, "I regard our negroes as given to us by an All Wise Providence, for their especial benefit, and we should impart to them Christian civilization." And to this end, he labored most faithfully.

No matter how driving the work on the plantation, whether seed-time or harvest, whether threatened with rain or frost, nothing could prevent his having the slaves all in at family prayers, night and morning. Moreover, the older servants were often invited to take part in the exercises. They always led the singing, and, on Sabbath mornings, were permitted to ask questions eliciting Scriptural explanations. Of course, some of the questions and some of the prayers were rather crude, and the effect, to an educated person, was rather to call forth laughter than solemnity.

Leaving home one morning, for a visit to the city, the Doctor ordered Jim, an old servant, to do some mowing in the rye-field; on his return, finding the rye-field as he had left it in the morning, he called Jim up, and severely flogged him without giving the man an opportunity of telling why the work had been neglected. On relating the circumstance at the supper-table, the wife said,—

"I am very sorry that you whipped Jim, for I took him to do some work in the garden, amongst my flower-beds."

To this the Doctor replied, "Never mind, I'll make it all right with Jim."

And sure enough he did, for that night, at prayers, he said, "I am sorry, Jim, that I corrected you, to-day, as your mistress tells me that she set you to work in the flower-garden. Now,

TROPICAL LUXURIANCE.

Jim," continued he, in a most feeling manner, "I always want to do justice to my servants, and you know that I never abuse any of you intentionally, and now, to-night, I will let you lead in prayer."

Jim thankfully acknowledged the apology, and, with grateful tears, and an overflowing heart, accepted the situation; for Jim aspired to be a preacher, like most colored men, and highly appreciated an opportunity to show his persuasive powers; and that night the old man made splendid use of the liberty granted to him. After praying for everything generally, and telling the Lord what a great sinner he himself was, he said,—

"Now, Lord, I would specially ax you to try to save marster. You knows dat marster thinks he's mighty good; you knows dat marster says he's gwine to heaven; but Lord, I have my doubts; an' yet I want marster saved. Please to convert him over agin; take him, dear Lord, by de nap of de neck, and shake him over hell and show him his condition. But, Lord, don't let him fall into hell, jes let him see whar he ought to go to, but don't let him go dar. An' now, Lord, ef you jes save marster, I will give you de glory."

The indignation expressed by the doctor, at the close of Jim's prayer, told the old negro that for once he had overstepped the mark. "What do you mean, Jim, by insulting me in that manner? Asking the Lord to convert me over again. And praying that I might be shaken over hell. I have a great mind to tie you up, and give you a good correcting. If you ever make another such a prayer, I'll whip you well, that I will."

Dr. Gaines felt so intensely the duty of masters to their slaves that he, with some of his neighbors, inaugurated a religious movement, whereby the blacks at the Corners could have preaching once a fortnight, and that, too, by an educated white man. Rev. John Mason, the man selected for this work, was a heavy-set, fleshy, lazy man who, when entering a house, sought the nearest chair, taking possession of it, and holding it to the last.

He had been employed many years as a colporteur or missionary, sometimes preaching to the poor whites, and, at other times, to the slaves, for which service he was compensated either by planters, or by the dominant religious denomination in the section where he labored. Mr. Mason had carefully studied the character of the people to whom he was called to preach, and took every opportunity to shirk his duties, and to throw them upon some of the slaves, a large number of whom were always ready and willing to exhort when called upon.

We shall never forget his first sermon, and the profound sensation that it created both amongst masters and slaves, and especially the latter. After taking for his text, "He that knoweth his master's will, and doeth it not, shall be beaten with many stripes," he spoke substantially as follows:—

"Now when *correction* is given you, you either deserve it, or you do not deserve it. But whether you really deserve it or not, it is your duty, and Almighty God requires that you bear it patiently. You may, perhaps, think that this is hard doctrine, but if you consider it right you must needs think otherwise of it. Suppose then, that you deserve correction, you cannot but say that it is just and right you should meet with it. Suppose you do not, or at least you do not deserve so much, or so severe a correction for the fault you have committed, you, perhaps, have escaped a great many more, and are at last paid for all. Or suppose you are quite innocent of what is laid to your charge, and suffer wrongfully in that particular thing, is it not possible you may have done some other bad thing which was never discovered, and that Almighty God, who saw you doing it, would not let you escape without punishment one time or another? And ought you not, in such a case, to give glory to Him, and be thankful that he would rather punish you in this life for your wickedness, than destroy your souls for it in the next life? But suppose that even this was not the case (a case hardly to be imagined), and that you have by no means, known or unknown, deserved the correction you suffered, there is this great comfort in it, that if you bear it patiently, and leave your cause in the hands of God, he will reward you for it in heaven, and the punishment you suffer unjustly here, shall turn to your exceeding great glory, hereafter."

At this point, the preacher hesitated a moment, and then continued, "I am now going to give you a description of hell, that awful place, that you will surely go to, if you don't be good and faithful servants.

"Hell is a great pit, more than two hundred feet deep, and is walled up with stone, having a strong, iron grating at the top.

The fire is built of pitch pine knots, tar barrels, lard kegs, and butter firkins. One of the devil's imps appears twice a day, and throws about half a bushel of brimstone on the fire, which is never allowed to cease burning. As sinners die they are pitched headlong into the pit, and are at once taken up upon the pitchforks by the devil's imps, who stand, with glaring eyes and smiling countenances, ready to do their master's work."

Here the speaker was disturbed by the "Amens," "Bless God, I'll keep out of hell," "Dat's my sentiments," which plainly told him that he had struck the right key.

"Now," continued the preacher, "I will tell you where heaven is, and how you are to obtain a place there. Heaven is above the skies; its streets are paved with gold; seraphs and angels will furnish you with music which never ceases. You will all be permitted to join in the singing and you will be fed on manna and honey, and you will drink from fountains, and will ride in golden chariots."

"I am bound for hebben," ejaculated one.

"Yes, blessed God, hebben will be my happy home," said another.

These outbursts of feeling were followed, while the man of God stood with folded arms, enjoying the sensation that his eloquence had created.

After pausing a moment or two, the reverend man continued, "Are there any of you here who would rather burn in hell than rest in heaven? Remember that once in hell you can never get out. If you attempt to escape little devils are stationed at the top of the pit, who will, with their pitchforks, toss you back into the pit, *curchunk*, where you must remain forever. But once in heaven, you will be free the balance of your days." Here the wildest enthusiasm showed itself, amidst which the preacher took his seat.

A rather humorous incident now occurred which created no little merriment amongst the blacks, and to the somewhat discomfiture of Dr. Gaines,—who occupied a seat with the whites who were present.

Looking about the room, being unacquainted with the negroes, and presuming that all or nearly so were experimentally interested in religion, Mr. Mason called on Ike to close with prayer. The very announcement of Ike's name in such a connection called forth a broad grin from the larger portion of the audience.

Now, it so happened that Ike not only made no profession of religion, but was in reality the farthest off from the church of any of the servants at "Poplar Farm"; yet Ike was equal to the occasion, and at once responded, to the great amazement of his fellow slaves.

Ike had been, from early boyhood, an attendant upon whites, and he had learned to speak correctly for an uneducated person. He was pretty well versed in Scripture and had learned the principal prayer that his master was accustomed to make, and would often get his fellow-servants together at the barn on a rainy day and give them the prayer, with such additions and improvements as the occasion might suggest. Therefore, when called upon by Mr. Mason, Ike at once said, "Let us pray."

After floundering about for a while, as if feeling his way, the new beginner struck out on the well-committed prayer, and soon elicited a loud "amen," and "bless God for that," from Mr. Mason, and to the great amusement of the blacks. In his eagerness, however, to make a grand impression, Ike attempted to weave into his prayer some poetry on "Cock Robin," which he had learned, and which nearly spoiled his maiden prayer.

After the close of the meeting, the Doctor invited the preacher to remain over night, and accepting the invitation, we in the great house had an opportunity of learning more of the reverend man's religious views.

When comfortably seated in the parlor, the Doctor said, "I was well pleased with your discourse, I think the tendency will be good upon the servants."

"Yes," responded the minister, "The negro is eminently a religious being, more so, I think, than the white race. He is emotional, loves music, is wonderfully gifted with gab; the organ of alimentativeness largely developed, and is fond of approbation. I therefore try always to satisfy their vanity; call upon them to speak, sing, and pray, and sometimes to preach. That suits for this world. Then I give them a heaven with music in it, and with something to eat. Heaven without singing and food would be no place for the negro. In the cities, where many of them are free, and have control of their own time, they are always late to church meetings, lectures, or almost anything else. But let there be a festival or supper announced and they are all there on time."

"But did you know," said Dr. Gaines, "that the prayer that Ike made to-day he learned from me?"

"Indeed?" responded the minister.

"Yes, that boy has the imitative power of his race in a larger degree than most negroes that I have seen. He remembers nearly everything that he hears, is full of wit, and has most excellent judgment. However, his dovetailing the Cock Robin poetry into my prayer was too much, and I had to laugh at his adroitness."

The Doctor was much pleased with the minister, but Mrs. Gaines was not. She had great contempt for professional men who sprung from the lower class, and she regarded Mr. Mason as one to be endured but not encouraged. The Rev. Henry Pinchen was her highest idea of a clergyman. This gentleman was then expected in the neighborhood, and she made special reference to the fact, to her husband, when speaking of the "negro missionary," as she was wont to call the new-comer.

The preparation made, a few days later, for the reception of Mrs. Gaines' favorite spiritual adviser, showed plainly that a religious feast was near at hand, and in which the lady was to play a conspicuous part; and whether her husband was prepared to enter into the enjoyment or not, he would have to tolerate considerable noise and bustle for a week.

"Go, Hannah," said Mrs. Gaines, "and tell Dolly to kill a couple of fat pullets, and to put the biscuit to rise. I expect Brother Pinchen here this afternoon, and I want everything in order. Hannah, Hannah, tell Melinda to come here. We mistresses do have a hard time in this world; I don't see why the Lord should have imposed such heavy duties on us poor mortals. Well, it can't last always. I long to leave this wicked world, and go home to glory."

At the hurried appearance of the waiting maid the mistress said: "I am to have company this afternoon, Melinda. I expect Brother Pinchen here, and I want everything in order. Go and get one of my new caps, with the lace border, and get out my scolloped-bottomed dimity petticoat, and when you go out, tell Hannah to clean the white-handled knives, and see that not a speck is on them; for I want everything as it should be while Brother Pinchen is here."

Mr. Pinchen was possessed with a large share of the superstition that prevails throughout the South, not only with the ignorant negro, who brought it with him from his native land, but also by a great number of well educated and influential whites.

On the first afternoon of the reverend gentleman's visit, I listened with great interest to the following conversation between Mrs. Gaines and her ministerial friend.

"Now, Brother Pinchen, do give me some of your experience since you were last here. It always does my soul good to hear religious experience. It draws me nearer and nearer to the Lord's side. I do love to hear good news from God's people."

"Well, Sister Gaines," said the preacher, "I've had great opportunities in my time to study the heart of man. I've attended a great many camp-meetings, revival meetings, protracted meetings, and death-bed scenes, and I am satisfied, Sister Gaines, that the heart of man is full of sin, and desperately wicked. This is a wicked world, Sister Gaines, a wicked world."

"Were you ever in Arkansas, Brother Pinchen?" inquired Mrs. Gaines; "I've been told that the people out there are very ungodly."

Mr. P. "Oh, yes, Sister Gaines. I once spent a year at Little Rock, and preached in all the towns round about there; and I found some hard cases out there, I can tell you. I was once spending a week in a district where there were a great many horse thieves, and, one night, somebody stole my pony. Well, I knowed it was no use to make a fuss, so I told Brother Tarbox to say nothing about it, and I'd get my horse by preaching God's everlasting gospel; for I had faith in the truth, and knowed that my Saviour would not let me lose my pony. So the next Sunday I preached on horse-stealing, and told the brethren to come up in the evenin' with their hearts filled with the grace of God. So that night the house was crammed brimfull with anxious souls, panting for the bread of life. Brother Bingham opened with prayer, and Brother Tarbox followed, and I saw right off that we were gwine to have a blessed time. After I got 'em pretty well warmed up, I jumped on to one of the seats, stretched out my hands, and said: 'I know who stole my pony; I've found out; and you are in here tryin' to make people believe that you've got religion; but you ain't got it. And if you don't take my horse back to Brother Tarbox's pasture this very night, I'll tell your name right out in meetin' to-morrow night. Take my pony back, you vile and wretched sinner, and come up here and give your heart to God.' So the next mornin', I went out to Brother Tarbox's pasture, and sure enough, there was my bob-tail pony. Yes, Sister Gaines, there he was, safe and sound. Ha, ha, ha!"

Mrs. G. "Oh, how interesting, and how fortunate for you to get your pony! And what power there is in the gospel! God's children are very lucky. Oh, it is so sweet to sit here and listen to such good news from God's people! [*Aside.*] 'You Hannah, what are you standing there listening for, and neglecting your work? Never mind, my lady, I'll whip you well when I am done here. Go at your work this moment, you lazy huzzy! Never mind, I'll whip you well.' Come, do go on, Brother Pinchen, with your godly conversation. It is so sweet! It draws me nearer and nearer to the Lord's side."

Mr. P. "Well, Sister Gaines, I've had some mighty queer dreams in my time, that I have. You see, one night I dreamed that I was dead and in heaven, and such a place I never saw before. As soon as I entered the gates of the celestial empire, I saw many old and familiar faces that I had seen before. The first person that I saw was good old Elder Pike, the preacher that first called my attention to religion. The next person I saw was Deacon Billings, my first wife's father, and then I saw a host of godly faces. Why, Sister Gaines, you knowed Elder Goosbee, didn't you?"

Mrs. G. "Why, yes; did you see him there? He married me to my first husband."

Mr. P. "Oh, yes, Sister Gaines, I saw the old Elder, and he looked for all the world as if he had just come out of a revival meetin'."

Mrs. G. "Did you see my first husband there, Brother Pinchen?"

Mr. P. "No, Sister Gaines, I didn't see Brother Pepper there; but I've no doubt but that Brother Pepper was there."

Mrs. G. "Well, I don't know; I have my doubts. He was not the happiest man in the world. He was always borrowing trouble about something or another. Still, I saw some happy moments with Mr. Pepper. I was happy when I made his acquaintance, happy during our courtship, happy a while after our marriage, and happy when he died." [*Weeps.*]

Hannah. "Massa Pinchen, did you see my ole man Ben up dar in hebben?"

Mr. P. "No, Hannah, I didn't go amongst the niggers."

Mrs. G. "No, of course Brother Pinchen didn't go among the blacks. What are you asking questions for? [*Aside.*] 'Never mind, my lady, I'll whip you well when I'm done here. I'll skin you from head to foot.' Do go on with your heavenly conversation, Brother Pinchen; it does my very soul good. This is indeed a precious moment for me. I do love to hear of Christ and Him crucified."

Mr. P. "Well, Sister Gaines, I promised Sister Daniels that I'd come over and see her a few moments this evening, and have a little season of prayer with her, and I suppose I must go."

Mrs. G. "If you must go, then I'll have to let you; but before you do, I wish to get your advice upon a little matter that concerns Hannah. Last week Hannah stole a goose, killed it, cooked it, and she and her man Sam had a fine time eating the goose; and her master and I would never have known anything about it if it had not been for Cato, a faithful servant, who told his master all about it. And then, you see, Hannah had to be severely whipped before she'd confess that she stole the goose. Next Sabbath is sacrament day, and I want to know if you think that Hannah is fit to go to the Lord's Supper, after stealing the goose."

"Well, Sister Gaines," responded the minister, "that depends on circumstances. If Hannah has confessed that she stole the goose, and has been sufficiently whipped, and has begged her master's pardon, and begged your pardon, and thinks she will not do the like again, why then I suppose she can go to the Lord's Supper; for—

> 'While the lamp holds out to burn,
> The vilest sinner may return.'

But she must be sure that she has repented, and won't steal any more."

"Do you hear that, Hannah?" said the mistress. "For my

part," continued she, "I don't think she's fit to go to the Lord's Supper; for she had no cause to steal the goose. We give our servants plenty of good food. They have a full run to the meal-tub, meat once a fortnight, and all the sour milk on the place, and I am sure that's enough for any one. I do think that our negroes are the most ungrateful creatures in the world. They aggravate my life out of me."

During this talk on the part of the mistress, the servant stood listening with careful attention, and at its close Hannah said:—

"I know, missis, dat I stole de goose, an' massa whip me for it, an' I confess it, an' I is sorry for it. But, missis, I is gwine to de Lord's Supper, next Sunday, kase I ain't agwine to turn my back on my bressed Lord an' Massa for no old tough goose, dat I ain't." And here the servant wept as if she would break her heart.

Mr. Pinchen, who seemed moved by Hannah's words, gave a sympathizing look at the negress, and said, "Well, Sister Gaines, I suppose I must go over and see Sister Daniels; she'll be waiting for me."

After seeing the divine out, Mrs. Gaines said, "Now, Hannah, Brother Pinchen is gone, do you get the cowhide and follow me to the cellar, and I'll whip you well for aggravating me as you have to-day. It seems as if I can never sit down to take a little comfort with the Lord, without you crossing me. The devil always puts it into your head to disturb me, just when I am trying to serve the Lord. I've no doubt but that I'll miss going to heaven on your account. But I'll whip you well before I leave this world, that I will. Get the cowhide and follow me to the cellar."

In a few minutes the lady returned to the parlor, followed by the servant whom she had been correcting, and she was in a high state of perspiration, and, on taking a seat, said, "Get the fan, Hannah, and fan me; you ought to be ashamed of yourself to put me into such a passion, and cause me to heat myself up in this way, whipping you. You know that it is a great deal harder for me than it is for you. I have to exert myself, and it puts me all in a fever; while you have only to stand and take it."

On the following Sabbath,—it being Communion,—Mr. Pinchen officiated. The church being at the Corners, a mile or so from "Poplar Farm," the Communion wine, which was kept at the Doctor's, was sent over by the boy, Billy. It happened to be in the month of April, when the maple trees had been tapped, and the sap freely running.

Billy, while passing through the "sugar camp," or sap bush, stopped to take a drink of the sap, which looked inviting in the newly-made troughs. All at once it occurred to the lad that he could take a drink of the wine, and fill it up with sap. So, acting upon this thought, the youngster put the decanter to his mouth, and drank freely, lowering the beverage considerably in the bottle.

But filling the bottle with the sap was much more easily contemplated than done. For, at every attempt, the water would fall over the sides, none going in. However, the boy, with the fertile imagination of his race, soon conceived the idea of sucking his mouth full of the sap, and then squirting it into the bottle. This plan succeeded admirably, and the slave boy sat in the church gallery that day, and wondered if the communicants would have partaken so freely of the wine, if they had known that his mouth had been the funnel through which a portion of it had passed.

Slavery has had the effect of brightening the mental powers of the negro to a certain extent, especially those brought into close contact with the whites.

It is also a fact, that these blacks felt that when they could get the advantage of their owners, they had a perfect right to do so; and the boy, Billy, no doubt, entertained a consciousness that he had done a very cunning thing in thus drinking the wine entrusted to his care.

CHAPTER III.

Dr. Gaines' practice being confined to the planters and their negroes, in the neighborhood of "Poplar Farm," caused his income to be very limited from that source, and consequently he looked more to the products of his plantation for support. True, the new store at the Corners, together with McWilliams'

Tannery and Simpson's Distillery, promised an increase of population, and, therefore, more work for the physician. This was demonstrated very clearly by the Doctor's coming in one morning somewhat elated, and exclaiming: "Well, my dear, my practice is steadily increasing. I forgot to tell you that neighbor Wyman engaged me yesterday as his family physician; and I hope that the fever and ague, which is now taking hold of the people, will give me more patients. I see by the New Orleans papers that the yellow fever is raging there to a fearful extent. Men of my profession are reaping a harvest in that section this year. I would that we could have a touch of the yellow fever here, for I think I could invent a medicine that would cure it. But the yellow fever is a luxury that we medical men in this climate can't expect to enjoy; yet we may hope for the cholera."

"Yes," replied Mrs. Gaines, "I would be glad to see it more sickly, so that your business might prosper. But we are always unfortunate. Everybody here seems to be in good health, and I am afraid they'll keep so. However, we must hope for the best. We must trust in the Lord. Providence may possibly send some disease amongst us for our benefit."

On going to the office the Doctor found the faithful servant hard at work, and saluting him in his usual kind and indulgent manner, asked, "Well, Cato, have you made the batch of ointment that I ordered?"

Cato. "Yes, massa; I dun made de intment, an' now I is making the bread pills. De tater pills is up on the top shelf."

Dr. G. "I am going out to see some patients. If any gentlemen call, tell them I shall be in this afternoon. If any servants come, you attend to them. I expect two of Mr. Campbell's boys over. You see to them. Feel their pulse, look at their tongues, bleed them, and give them each a dose of calomel. Tell them to drink no cold water, and to take nothing but water gruel."

Cato. "Yes, massa; I'll tend to 'em."

The negro now said, "I allers knowed I was a doctor, an' now de ole boss has put me at it; I must change my coat. Ef any niggers comes in, I wants to look suspectable. Dis jacket don't suit a doctor; I'll change it."

Cato's vanity seemed at this point to be at its height, and having changed his coat, he walked up and down before the mirror, and viewed himself to his heart's content, and saying to himself, "Ah! now I looks like a doctor. Now I can bleed, pull teef, or cut off a leg. Oh, well, well! ef I ain't put de pill stuff an' de intment stuff togedder. By golly, dat ole cuss will be mad when he finds it out, won't he? Nebber mind, I'll make it up in pills, and when de flour is on dem, he won't know what's in 'em; an' I'll make some new intment. Ah! yonder comes Mr. Campbell's Pete an' Ned; dem's de ones massa sed was comin'. I'll see ef I looks right. [*Goes to the looking-glass and views himself.*] I 'em some punkins, ain't I? [*Knock at the door.*] Come in." *Enter* PETE *and* NED.

Pete. "Whar is de Doctor?"

Cato. "Here I is; don't you see me?"

Pete. "But whar is de ole boss?"

Cato. "Dat's none you business. I dun tole you dat I is de doctor, an' dat's enuff."

Ned. "Oh, do tell us whar de Doctor is. I is almos' dead. Oh, me! oh, dear me! I is so sick." [*Horrible faces.*]

Pete. "Yes, do tell us; we don't want to stan' here foolin."

Cato. "I tells you again dat I is de doctor. I larn de trade under massa."

Ned. "Oh! well den; give me somethin' to stop dis pain. Oh, dear me! I shall die."

Cato. "Let me feel your pulse. Now, put out your tongue. You is berry sick. Ef you don't mine, you'll die. Come out in de shed, an' I'll bleed you. [*Taking them out and bleeding them.*] "Dar, now, take dese pills, two in de mornin', and two at night, and ef you don't feel better, double de dose. Now, Mr. Pete, what's de matter wid you?"

Pete. "I is got de cole chills, an' has a fever in de night."

"Come out in de shed, an' I'll bleed you," said Cato, at the same time viewing himself in the mirror, as he passed out. After taking a quart of blood, which caused the patient to faint, they returned, the black doctor saying, "Now, take dese pills, two in de mornin', and two at night, an' ef dey don't help you, double de dose. Ah! I like to forget to feel your pulse, and look at your tongue. Put out your tongue. [*Feels his pulse.*] Yes, I tells by de feel ob your pulse dat I is gib you de right pills?"

Just then, Mr. Parker's negro boy Bill, with his hand up to his mouth, and evidently in great pain, entered the office without giving the usual knock at the door, and which gave great offence to the new physician.

"What you come in dat door widout knockin' for?" exclaimed Cato.

Bill. "My toof ache so, I didn't tink to knock. Oh, my toof! my toof! Whar is de Doctor?"

Cato. "Here I is; don't you see me?"

Bill. "What! you de Doctor, you brack cuss! You looks like a doctor! Oh, my toof! my toof! Whar is de Doctor?"

Cato. "I tells you I is de doctor. Ef you don't believe me, ax dese men. I can pull your toof in a minnit."

Bill. "Well, den, pull it out. Oh, my toof! how it aches! Oh, my toof!" [*Cato gets the rusty turnkeys.*]

Cato. "Now lay down on your back."

Bill. "What for?"

Cato. "Dat's de way massa does."

Bill. "Oh, my toof! Well, den, come on." [*Lies down. Cato gets astraddle of Bill's breast, puts the turnkeys on the wrong tooth, and pulls—Bill kicks, and cries out*]—Oh, do stop! Oh, oh, oh! [*Cato pulls the wrong tooth—Bill jumps up.*]

Cato. "Dar, now, I tole you I could pull your toof for you."

Bill. Oh, dear me! Oh, it aches yet! Oh, me! Oh, Lor-e-massy! You dun pull de wrong toof. Drat your skin! ef I don't pay you for this, you brack cuss! [*They fight, and turn over table, chairs, and bench—Pete and Ned look on.*]

During the *melée*, Dr. Gaines entered the office, and unceremoniously went at them with his cane, giving both a sound drubbing before any explanation could be offered. As soon as he could get an opportunity, Cato said, "Oh, massa! he's to blame, sir, he's to blame. He struck me fuss."

Bill. "No, sir; he's to blame; he pull de wrong toof. Oh, my toof! oh, my toof!"

Dr. G. "Let me see your tooth. Open your mouth. As I live, you've taken out the wrong tooth. I am amazed. I'll whip you for this; I'll whip you well. You're a pretty doctor. Now, lie down, Bill, and let him take out the right tooth; and if he makes a mistake this time, I'll cowhide him well. Lie down, Bill." [*Bill lies down, and Cato pulls the tooth.*] "There, now, why didn't you do that in the first place?"

Cato. "He wouldn't hole still, sir."

NEGRO DENTISTRY.

Bill. "I did hole still."

Dr. G. "Now go home, boys; go home."

"You've made a pretty muss of it, in my absence," said the Doctor. "Look at the table! Never mind, Cato; I'll whip you well for this conduct of yours to-day. Go to work now, and clear up the office."

As the office door closed behind the master, the irritated negro, once more left to himself, exclaimed, "Confound dat nigger! I wish he was in Ginny. He bite my finger, and scratch my face. But didn't I give it to him? Well, den, I reckon I did. [*He goes to the mirror, and discovers that his coat is torn—weeps.*] Oh, dear me! Oh, my coat—my coat is tore! Dat nigger has tore my coat. [*He gets angry, and rushes about the room frantic.*] Cuss dat nigger! Ef I could lay my hands on him, I'd tare him all to pieces,—dat I would. An' de old boss hit me wid his cane after dat nigger tore my coat. By golly, I wants to fight somebody. Ef ole massa should come in now, I'd fight him. [*Rolls up his sleeves.*] Let 'em come now, ef dey dare—ole massa, or anybody else; I'm ready for 'em."

Just then the Doctor returned and asked, "What's all this noise here?"

Cato. "Nuffin', sir; only jess I is puttin' things to rights, as you tole me. I didn't hear any noise, except de rats."

Dr. G. "Make haste, and come in; I want you to go to town."

Once more left alone, the witty black said, "By golly, de ole boss like to cotch me dat time, didn't he? But wasn't I mad? When I is mad, nobody can do nuffin' wid me. But here's my coat tore to pieces. Cuss dat nigger! [*Weeps.*] Oh, my coat! oh, my coat! I rudder he had broke my head, den to tore my coat. Drat dat nigger! Ef he ever comes here agin, I'll pull out every toof he's got in his head—dat I will."

CHAPTER IV.

During the palmy days of the South, forty years ago, if there was one class more thoroughly despised than another, by the high-born, well-educated Southerner, it was the slave-trader who made his money by dealing in human cattle. A large number of the slave-traders were men of the North or free States, generally from the lower order, who, getting a little money by their own hard toil, invested it in slaves purchased in Virginia, Maryland, or Kentucky, and sold them in the cotton, sugar, or rice-growing States. And yet the high-bred planter, through mismanagement, or other causes, was compelled to sell his slaves, or some of them, at auction, or to let the "soul-buyer" have them.

Dr. Gaines' financial affairs being in an unfavorable condition, he yielded to the offers of a noted St. Louis trader by the name of Walker. This man was the terror of the whole Southwest amongst the black population, bond and free,—for it was not unfrequently that even free colored persons were kidnapped and carried to the far South and sold. Walker had no conscientious scruples, for money was his God, and he worshipped at no other altar.

An uncouth, ill-bred, hard-hearted man, with no education, Walker had started at St. Louis as a dray-driver, and ended as a wealthy slave-trader. The day was set for this man to come and purchase his stock, on which occasion, Mrs. Gaines absented herself from the place; and even the Doctor, although alone, felt deeply the humiliation. For myself, I sat and bit my lips with anger, as the vulgar trader said to the faithful man,—

"Well, my boy, what's your name?"

Sam. "Sam, sir, is my name."

Walk. "How old are you, Sam?"

Sam. "Ef I live to see next corn plantin' time I'll be twenty-seven, or thirty, or thirty-five,—I don't know which, sir."

Walk. "Ha, ha, ha! Well, Doctor, this is rather a green boy. Well, mer feller, are you sound?"

Sam. "Yes, sir, I spec I is."

Walk. "Open your mouth and let me see your teeth. I allers judge a nigger's age by his teeth, same as I dose a hoss. Ah! pretty good set of grinders. Have you got a good appetite?"

Sam. "Yes, sir."

Walk. "Can you eat your allowance?"

Sam. "Yes, sir, when I can get it."

Walk. "Get out on the floor and dance; I want to see if you are supple."

Sam. "I don't like to dance; I is got religion."

Walk. "Oh, ho! you've got religion, have you? That's so much the better. I likes to deal in the gospel. I think he'll suit me. Now, mer gal, what's your name?"

Sally. "I is Big Sally, sir."

Walk. "How old are you, Sally?"

Sally. "I don't know, sir; but I heard once dat I was born at sweet pertater diggin' time."

Walk. "Ha, ha, ha! Don't you know how old you are? Do you know who made you?"

Sally. "I hev heard who it was in de Bible dat made me, but I dun forget de gentman's name."

Walk. "Ha, ha, ha! Well, Doctor, this is the greenest lot of niggers I've seen for some time."

The last remark struck the Doctor deeply, for he had just taken Sally for debt, and, therefore, he was not responsible for her ignorance. And he frankly told him so.

"This is an unpleasant business for me, Mr. Walker," said the Doctor, "but you may have Sam for $1,000, and Sally for $900. They are worth all I ask for them. I never banter, Mr. Walker. There they are; you can take them at that price, or let them alone, just as you please."

Walk. "Well, Doctor, I reckon I'll take 'em; but it's all they are worth. I'll put the handcuffs on 'em, and then I'll pay you. I likes to go accordin' to Scripter. Scripter says ef eatin' meat will offend your brother, you must quit it; and I say ef leavin' your slaves without the handcuffs will make 'em run away, you must put the handcuffs on 'em. Now, Sam, don't you and Sally cry. I am of a tender heart, and it allers makes me feel bad to see people cryin'. Don't cry, and the first place I get to, I'll buy each of you a great big *ginger cake*,—that I will."

And with the last remark the trader took from a small satchel two pairs of handcuffs, putting them on, and with a laugh said: "Now, you look better with the ornaments on."

Just then, the Doctor remarked,—"There comes Mr. Pinchen." Walker, looking out and seeing the man of God, said: "It is Mr. Pinchen, as I live; jest the very man I wants to see." And as the reverend gentleman entered, the trader grasped his hand, saying: "Why, how do you do, Mr. Pinchen? What in the name of Jehu brings you down here to Muddy Creek? Any camp-meetins, revival meetins, death-bed scenes, or anything else in your line going on down here? How is religion prosperin' now, Mr. Pinchen? I always like to hear about religion.

Mr. Pin. "Well, Mr. Walker, the Lord's work is in good condition everywhere now. I tell you, Mr. Walker, I've been in the gospel ministry these thirteen years, and I am satisfied that the heart of man is full of sin and desperately wicked. This is a wicked world, Mr. Walker, a wicked world, and we ought all of us to have religion. Religion is a good thing to live by, and we all want it when we die. Yes, sir, when the great trumpet blows, we ought to be ready. And a man in your business of buying and selling slaves needs religion more than anybody else, for it makes you treat your people as you should. Now, there is Mr. Haskins,—he is a slave-trader, like yourself. Well, I converted him. Before he got religion, he was one of the worst men to his niggers I ever saw; his heart was as hard as stone. But religion has made his heart as soft as a piece of cotton. Before I converted him he would sell husbands from their wives, and seem to take delight in it; but now he won't sell a man from his wife, if he can get any one to buy both of them together. I tell you, sir, religion has done a wonderful work for him."

Walk. "I know, Mr. Pinchen, that I ought to have religion, and I feel that I am a great sinner; and whenever I get with good pious people like you and the Doctor, it always makes me feel that I am a desperate sinner. I feel it the more, because I've got a religious turn of mind. I know that I would be happier with religion, and the first spare time I get, I am going to try to get it. I'll go to a protracted meeting, and I won't stop till I get religion."

The departure of the trader with his property left a sadness even amongst the white members of the family, and special sympathy was felt for Hannah for the loss of her husband by the sale. However, Mrs. Gaines took it coolly, for as Sam was a field hand, she had often said she wanted her to have one of the house servants, and as Cato was without a wife, this seemed to favor her plans. Therefore, a week later, as Hannah entered the sitting-room one evening, she said to her:—"You need not tell me, Hannah, that you don't want another husband, I know

REV. HENRY PINCHEN.

better. Your master has sold Sam, and he's gone down the river, and you'll never see him again. So go and put on your calico dress, and meet me in the kitchen. I intend for you to *jump the broomstick* with Cato. You need not tell me you don't want another man. I know there's no woman living that can be happy and satisfied without a husband."

Hannah said: "Oh, missis, I don't want to jump de broomstick wid Cato. I don't love Cato; I can't love him."

Mrs. G. "Shut up, this moment! What do you know about love? I didn't love your master when I married him, and people don't marry for love now. So go and put on your calico dress, and meet me in the kitchen."

As the servant left for the kitchen, the mistress remarked: "I am glad that the Doctor has sold Sam, for now I'll have her marry Cato, and I'll have them both in the house under my eyes."

As Hannah entered the kitchen, she said: "Oh, Cato, do go and tell missis dat you don't want to jump de broomstick wid me,—dat's a good man. Do, Cato; kase I nebber can love you. It was only las week dat massa sold my Sammy, and I don't want any udder man. Do go tell missis dat you don't want me."

To which Cato replied: "No, Hannah, I ain't a-gwine to tell missis no such thing, kase I does want you, and I ain't a-gwine to tell a lie for you ner nobody else. Dar, now you's got it! I don't see why you need to make so much fuss. I is better lookin' den Sam; an' I is a house servant, an' Sam was only a fiel hand; so you ought to feel proud of a change. So go and do as missis tells you."

As the woman retired, the man continued: "Hannah needn't try to get me to tell a lie; I ain't a-gwine to do it, kase I dose want her, an' I is bin wantin' her dis long time, an' soon as massa sold Sam, I knowed I would get her. By golly, I is gwine to be a married man. Won't I be happy? Now, ef I could only jess run away from ole massa, an' get to Canada wid Hannah, den I'd show 'em who I was. Ah! dat reminds me of my song 'bout ole massa and Canada, an' I'll sing it. Dis is my moriginal hyme. It comed into my head one night when I was fass asleep under an apple tree, looking up at de moon."

While Hannah was getting ready for the nuptials, Cato amused himself by singing—

De happiest day I ever did see,
I'm bound fer my heavenly home,
When missis give Hannah to me,
Through heaven dis chile will roam.
CHORUS.—Go away, Sam, you can't come a-nigh me,
Gwine to meet my friens in hebben,
Hannah is gwine along;
Missis ses Hannah is mine,
So Hannah is gwine along.
CHORUS, *repeated.*
Father Gabriel, blow your horn,
I'll take wings and fly away,
Take Hannah up in the early morn,
An' I'll be in hebben by de break of day.
CHORUS.—Go away, Sam, you can't come a-nigh me,
Gwine to meet my friens in hebben,
Hannah is gwine along;
Missis ses Hannah is mine,
So Hannah is gwine along.

Mrs. Gaines, as she approached the kitchen, heard the servant's musical voice and knew that he was in high glee; entering, she said, "Ah! Cato, you're ready, are you? Where is Hannah?"

Cato. "Yes, missis; I is bin waitin' dis long time. Hannah has bin here tryin' to swade me to tell you dat I don't want her; but I telled her dat you sed I must jump de broomstick wid her, an' I is gwine to mind you."

Mrs. G. "That's right, Cato; servants should always mind their masters and mistresses, without asking a question."

Cato. "Yes, missis, I allers dose what you and massa tells me, an' axes nobody."

While the mistress went in search of Hannah, Dolly came in saying, "Oh, Cato, do go an' tell missis dat you don't want Hannah. Don't yer hear how she's whippin' her in de cellar? Do go an' tell missis dat you don't want Hannah, and den she'll stop whippin' her."

Cato. "No, Dolly, I ain't a gwine to do no such a thing, kase ef I tell missis dat I don't want Hannah, den missis will whip me; an' I ain't a-gwine to be whipped fer you, ner Hannah, ner nobody else. No, I'll jump the broomstick wid every woman on de place, ef missis wants me to, before I'll be whipped."

Dolly. "Cato, ef I was in Hannah's place, I'd see you in de bottomless pit before I'd live wid you, you great, big, wall-eyed, empty-headed, knock-kneed fool. You're as mean as your devilish old missis."

Cato. "Ef you don't quit dat busin' me, Dolly, I'll tell missis as soon as she comes in, an' she'll whip you, you know she will."

As Mrs. Gaines entered she said, "You ought to be ashamed of yourself, Hannah, to make me fatigue myself in this way, to make you do your duty. It's very naughty in you, Hannah. Now, Dolly, you and Susan get the broom, and get out in the middle of the room. There, hold it a little lower—a little higher; there, that'll do. Now, remember that this is a solemn occasion; you are going to jump into matrimony. Now, Cato, take hold of Hannah's hand. There, now, why could n't you let Cato take hold of your hand before? Now, get ready, and when I count three, do you jump. Eyes on the *broomstick*! All ready. One, two, three, and over you go. There, now you're husband and wife, and if you don't live happy together, it's your own fault; for I am sure there's nothing to hinder it. Now, Hannah, come up to the house, and I'll give you some whiskey, and you can make some apple-toddy, and you and Cato can have a fine time. Now, I'll go back to the parlor."

Dolly. "I tell you what, Susan, when I get married, I is gwine to have a preacher to marry me. I ain't a-gwine to jump de broomstick. Dat will do for fiel' hands, but house servants ought to be 'bove dat."

Susan. "Well, chile, you can't spect any ting else from ole missis. She come from down in Carlina, from 'mong de poor white trash. She don't know any better. You can't speck nothin' more dan a jump from a frog. Missis says she is one ob de akastocacy; but she ain't no more of an akastocacy dan I is. Missis says she was born wid a silver spoon in her mouf; ef she was, I wish it had a-choked her, dat' what I wish."

The mode of jumping the broomstick was the general custom in the rural districts of the South, forty years ago; and, as there was no law whatever in regard to the marriage of slaves, this custom had as binding force with the negroes, as if they had been joined by a clergyman; the difference being the one was not so high-toned as the other. Yet, it must be admitted that the blacks always preferred being married by a clergyman.

CHAPTER V.

DR. GAINES and wife having spent the heated season at the North, travelling for pleasure and seeking information upon the mode of agriculture practised in the free States, returned home filled with new ideas which they were anxious to put into immediate execution, and, therefore, a radical change was at once commenced.

Two of the most interesting changes proposed, were the introduction of a plow, which was to take the place of the heavy, unwieldy one then in use, and a washing-machine, instead of the hard hand-rubbing then practised. The first called forth much criticism amongst the men in the field, where it was christened the "Yankee Dodger," and during the first half a day of its use, it was followed by a large number of the negroes, men and women wondering at its superiority over the old plow, and wanting to know where it was from.

But the excitement in the kitchen, amongst the women, over the washing-machine, threw the novelty of the plow entirely in the shade.

"An' so dat tub wid its wheels an' fixin' is to do de washin', while we's to set down an' look at it," said Dolly, as ten or a dozen servants stood around the new comer, laughing and making fun at its ungainly appearance.

"I don't see why massa didn't buy a woman, out dar whar de ting was made, an' fotch 'em along, so she could learn us how to wash wid it," remarked Hannah, as her mistress came into the kitchen to give orders about the mode of using the "washer."

"Now, Dolly," said the mistress, "we are to have new rules, hereafter, about the work. While at the North, I found that the women got up at four o'clock, on Monday mornings, and commenced the washing, which was all finished, and out on the lines, by nine o'clock. Now, remember that, hereafter, there is to be no more washing on Fridays, and ironing on Saturdays, as you used to do. And instead of six of you great, big women to do the washing, two of you with the 'washer,' can do the work." And out she went, leaving the negroes to the contemplation of the future.

"I wish missis had stayed at home, 'stead of goin' round de world, bringin' home new rules. Who she tinks gwine to get out of bed at four o'clock in de mornin', kase she fotch home dis wash-box," said Dolly, as she gave a knowing look at the other servants.

"De Lord knows dat dis chile ain't a-gwine to git out of her sweet bed at four o'clock in de mornin', for no body; you hears dat, don't you?" remarked Winnie, as she gave a loud laugh, and danced out of the room.

Before the end of the week, Peter had run the new plow against a stump, and had broken it beyond the possibility of repair.

When the lady arose on Monday morning, at half-past nine, her usual time, instead of finding the washing out on the lines, she saw, to her great disappointment, the inside works of the "washer" taken out, and Dolly, the chief laundress, washing away with all her power, in the old way, rubbing with her hands, the perspiration pouring down her black face.

"What have you been doing, Dolly, with the 'washer?'" exclaimed the mistress, as she threw up her hands in astonishment.

"Well, you see, missis," said the servant, "dat merchine won't work no way. I tried it one way, den I tried it an udder way, an' still it would not work. So, you see, I got de screwdriver an' I took it to pieces. Dat's de reason I ain't got along faster wid de work."

Mrs. Gaines returned to the parlor, sat down, and had a good cry, declaring her belief that "negroes could not be made white folks, no matter what you should do with them."

Although the "patent plow" and the "washer" had failed, Dr. and Mrs. Gaines had the satisfaction of knowing that one of their new ideas was to be put into successful execution in a few days.

While at the North, they had eaten at a farm-house, some new cheese, just from the press, and on speaking of it, she was told by old Aunt Nancy, the black *mamma* of the place, that she understood all about making cheese. This piece of information gave general satisfaction, and a cheese-press was at once ordered from St. Louis.

The arrival of the cheese-press, the following week, was the signal for the new sensation. Nancy was at once summoned to the great house for the purpose of superintending the making of the cheese. A prouder person than the old negress could scarcely have been found. Her early days had been spent on the eastern shores of Maryland, where the blacks have an idea that they are, by nature, superior to their race in any other part of the habitable globe. Nancy had always spoken of the Kentucky and Missouri negroes as "low brack trash," and now, that all were to be passed over, and the only Marylander on the place called in upon this "great occasion," her cup of happiness was filled to the brim.

"What do you need, besides the cheese-press, to make the cheese with, Nancy?" inquired Mrs. Gaines, as the old servant stood before her, with her hands resting upon her hips, and looking at the half-dozen slaves who loitered around, listening to what was being said.

"Well, missis," replied Nancy, "I mus' have a runnet."

"What's a runnet?" inquired Mrs. Gaines.

"Why, you see, missis, you's got to have a sheep killed, and get out of it de maw, an' dat's what's called de runnet. An' I puts dat in de milk, an' it curdles the milk so it makes cheese."

"Then I'll have a sheep killed at once," said the mistress, and orders were given to Jim to kill the sheep. Soon after the sheep's carcass was distributed amongst the negroes, and "de runnet," in the hands of old Nancy.

That night there was fun and plenty of cheap talk in the negro quarters and in the kitchen, for it had been discovered amongst them that a calf's runnet, and not a sheep's, was the article used to curdle the milk for making cheese.

The laugh was then turned upon Nancy, who, after listening to all sorts of remarks in regard to her knowledge of cheese-making, said, in a triumphant tone, suiting the action to the words,—

"You niggers tink you knows a heap, but you don't know as much as you tink. When de sheep is killed, I knows dat you niggers would git de meat to eat. I knows dat."

With this remark Nancy silenced the entire group. Then putting her hand a-kimbo, the old woman sarcastically exclaimed: "To-morrow you'll all have calf's meat for dinner, den what will you have to say 'bout old Nancy?" Hearing no reply, she said: "Whar is you smart niggers now? Whar is you, I ax you?"

"Well, den, ef Ant Nancy ain't some punkins, dis chile knows nuffin," remarked Ike, as he stood up at full length, viewing the situation, as if he had caught a new idea. "I allers tole yer dat Ant Nancy had moo in her head dan what yer catch out wid a fine-toof comb," exclaimed Peter.

"But how is you going to tell missis 'bout killin' de sheep?" asked Jim.

Nancy turned to the head man and replied: "De same mudder wit dat tole me to get some sheep fer you niggers will tell me what to do. De Lord always guides me through my troubles an' trials. Befoe I open my mouf, He always fills it."

The following day Nancy presented herself at the great house door, and sent in for her mistress. On the lady's appearing, the servant, putting on a knowing look, said: "Missis, when de moon is cold an' de water runs high in it, den I have to put calf's runnet in de milk, instead of sheep's. So, lass night, I see dat de moon is cold an' de water is runnin' high."

"Well, Nancy," said the mistress, "I'll have a calf killed at once, for I can't wait for a warm moon. Go and tell Jim to kill a calf immediately, for I must not be kept out of cheese much longer." On Nancy's return to the quarters, old Ned, who was past work, and who never did anything but eat, sleep and talk, heard the woman's explanation, and clapping his wrinkled hands exclaimed: "Well den, Nancy, you is wof moo den all de niggers on dis place, fer you gives us fresh meat ebbry day."

After getting the right runnet, and two weeks' work on the new cheese, a little, soft, sour, hard-looking thing, appearing like anything but a cheese, was exhibited at "Poplar Farm," to the great amusement of the blacks, and the disappointment of the whites, and especially Mrs. Gaines, who had frequently remarked that her "mouth was watering for the new cheese."

No attempt was ever made afterwards to renew the cheese-making, and the press was laid under the shed, by the side of the washing machine and the patent plow. While we had three or four trustworthy and faithful servants, it must be admitted that most of the negroes on "Poplar Farm" were always glad to shirk labor, and thought that to deceive the whites was a religious duty.

Wit and religion has ever been the negro's forte while in slavery. Wit with which to please his master, or to soften his anger when displeased, and religion to enable him to endure punishment when inflicted.

Both Dr. and Mrs. Gaines were easily deceived by their servants. Indeed, I often thought that Mrs. Gaines took peculiar pleasure in being misled by them; and even the Doctor, with his long experience and shrewdness, would allow himself to be carried off upon almost any pretext. For instance, when he retired at night, Ike, his body servant, would take his master's clothes out of the room, brush them off and return them in time for the Doctor to dress for breakfast. There was nothing in this out of the way; but the master would often remark that he thought Ike brushed his clothes too much, for they appeared to wear out a great deal faster than they had formerly. Ike, however, attributed the wear to the fact that the goods were wanting in soundness. Thus the master, at the advice of his servant, changed his tailor.

About the same time the Doctor's watch stopped at night, and when taken to be repaired, the watchmaker found it badly damaged, which he pronounced had been done by a fall. As the Doctor was always very careful with his time-piece, he could in no way account for the stoppage. Ike was questioned as to his handling of it, but he could throw no light upon the subject. At last, one night about twelve o'clock, a message came for the Doctor to visit a patient who had a sudden attack of cholera morbus. The faithful Ike was nowhere to be found, nor could any traces of the Doctor's clothes be discovered. Not even the watch, which was always laid upon the mantle-shelf, could be seen anywhere.

It seemed clear that Ike had run away with his master's daily wearing apparel, watch and all. Yes, and further search showed that the boots, with one heel four inches higher than the other, had also disappeared. But go, the Doctor must; and Mrs. Gaines and all of us went to work to get the Doctor ready.

MRS. SARAH PEPPER GAINES.

While Cato was hunting up the old boots, and Hannah was in the attic getting the old hat, Jim returned from the barn and informed his master that the sorrel horse, which he had ordered to be saddled, was nowhere to be found; and that he had got out the bay mare, and as there was no saddle on the place, Ike having taken the only one, he, Jim, had put the buffalo robe on the mare.

It was a bright moonlight night, and to see the Doctor on horseback without a saddle, dressed in his castaway suit, was, indeed, ridiculous in the extreme. However, he made the visit, saved the patient's life, came home and went snugly to bed. The following morning, to the Doctor's great surprise, in walked Ike, at his usual time, with the clothes in one hand and the boots nicely blacked in the other. The faithful slave had not seen any of the other servants, and consequently did not know of the master's discomfiture on the previous night.

"Were any of the servants off the place last night?" inquired the Doctor, as Ike laid the clothes carefully on a chair, and was setting down the boots.

"No, I speck not," answered Ike.

"Were you off anywhere last night?" asked the master.

"No, sir," replied the servant.

"What! not off the place at all?" inquired the Doctor sharply. Ike looked confused and evidently began to "smell a mice."

"Well, massa, I was not away only to step over to de prayer-meetin' at de Corners, a little while, dat's all," said Ike.

"Where's my watch?" asked the Doctor.

"I speck it's on de mantleshelf dar, whar I put it lass night, sir," replied Ike, and at the same time reached to the time-piece, where he had laid it a moment before, and holding it up triumphantly, "Here it is, sir, right where I left it lass night."

Ike was told to go, which he was glad to do. "What shall I do with that fellow?" said the Doctor to his wife, as the servant quitted the room.

Ike had scarcely reached the back yard when he met Cato, who told him of his absence on the previous night being known to his master. When Ike had heard all, he exclaimed, "Well, den ef de ole boss knows it, dis nigger is kotched sure as you is born."

"I would not be in your shoes, Ike, fer a heap, dis mornin'," said Cato.

"Well," replied Ike, "I thank de Lord dat I is got religion to stand it."

Dr. Gaines, as he dressed himself, found nothing out of the way until he came to look at the boots. The Doctor was lame from birth. Here he saw unmistakable evidence that the high heel had been taken off, and had been replaced by a screw put through the inside, and the seam waxed over. Dr. Gaines had often thought, when putting his boots on in the morning, that they appeared a little loose, and on speaking of it to his servant, the negro would attribute it to the blacking, which he said "made de lether stretch."

That morning when breakfast was over, and the negroes called in for family prayers, all eyes were upon Ike.

It has always appeared strange that the negroes should seemingly take such delight in seeing their fellow-servants in a "bad fix." But it is nevertheless true, and Ike's "bad luck" appeared to furnish sport for old and young of his own race. At the conclusion of prayers, the Doctor said, "Now, Ike, I want you to tell me the truth, and nothing but the truth, of your whereabouts last night, and why you wore away my clothes?"

"Well, massa," said Ike, "I'm gwine to tell you God's truth."

"That's what I want, Ike," remarked the master.

"Now," continued the negro, "I ware de clothes to de dance, kase you see, massa, I knowed dat you didn't want your body servant to go to de ball looking poorer dressed den udder gentmen's boys. So you see I had no clothes myself, so I takes yours. I had to knock the heel off de lame leg boot, so dat I could ware it. An' den I took 'ole Sorrel,' kase he paces so fass an' so easy. No udder hoss could get me to de city in time fer de ball, ceptin' 'ole Sorrel.' You see, massa, ten miles is a good ways to go after you is gone to bed. Now, massa, I hope you'll forgive me dis time, an' I'll never do so any moo."

During Ike's telling his story, his master kept his eyes rivetted upon him, and at its conclusion said: "You first told me that you were at the prayer-meeting at the Corners; what did you do that for?"

"Well, massa," replied Ike, "I knowed dat I ought to had gone to de prar-meetin', an' dat's de reason I said I was dar."

"And you're a pretty Christian, going to a dance, instead of your prayer-meeting. This is the fifth time you've fallen from grace," said the master.

"Oh, no," quickly responded Ike; "dis is only de fourf time dat I is back slid."

"But this is not the first time that you have taken my clothes and worn them. And there's my watch, you could not tell the time, what did you want with that?" said the Doctor.

"Yes, massa," replied Ike, "I'll tell de truth; I wore de clothes afore dis time, an' I take de watch too, an' I let it fall, an' dat's de reason it stop dat time. An' I know I could not tell de time by de watch, but I guessed at it, an' dat made de niggers star at me, to see me have a watch."

The announcement that Col. Lemmy was at the door cut short the further investigation of Ike's case. The Colonel was the very opposite to Dr. Gaines, believing that there was no good in the negro, except to toil, and feeling that all religious efforts to better the condition of the race was time thrown away.

The Colonel laughed heartily as the Doctor told how Ike had worn his clothes. He quickly inquired if the servant had been punished, and when informed that he had not, he said: "The lash is worth more than all the religion in the world. Your boy, Ike, with the rest of the niggers around here, will go to a prayer meetin' and will tell how good they feel or how bad they feel, just as it may suit the case. They'll cry, groan, clap their hands, pat their feet, worry themselves into a lather of sweat, sing,

I'm a-gwine to keep a-climbin' high,
  See de hebbenly land;
Till I meet dem er angels in a de sky
  See de hebbenly lan'.

Dem pooty angels I shall see,
  See de hebbenly lan';
Why don't de debbil let a-me be,
  See de hebbenly lan'.

"Yes, Doctor; these niggers will pray till twelve o'clock at night; break up their meeting and go home shouting and singing, 'Glory hallelujah!' and every darned one of them will steal a chicken, turkey, or pig, and cry out 'Come down, sweet chariot, an' carry me home to hebben!' yes, and still continue to sing till they go to sleep. You may give your slaves religion, and I'll give mine the whip, an' I'll bet that I'll get the most tobacco and hemp out of the same number of hands."

"I hardly think," said the Doctor, after listening attentively to his neighbor, "that I can let Ike pass without some punishment. Yet I differ with you in regard to the good effects of religion upon all classes, more especially our negroes, for the African is preeminently a religious being; with them, I admit, there is considerable superstition. They have a permanent belief in good and bad luck, ghosts, fortune-telling, and the like; but we whites are not entirely free from such notions."

At the last sentence or two, the Colonel's eyes sparkled, and he began to turn pale, for it was well known that he was a firm believer in ghosts and fortune-telling.

"Now, Doctor," said Col. Lemmy, "every sensible man must admit the fact that ghosts exist, and that there is nothing in the world truer than that the future can be told. Look at Mrs. McWilliams' lawsuit with Major Todd. She went to old Frank, the nigger fortune-teller, and asked him which lawyer she should employ. The old man gazed at her for a moment or two, and said, 'missis, you's got your mind on two lawyers,—a big man and a little man. Ef you takes de big man, you loses de case; ef you takes de little man, you wins de case.' Sure enough, she had in contemplation the employment of either McGuyer or Darby. The first is a large man; the latter was, as you know, a small man. So, taking the old negro's advice, she obtained the services of John F. Darby, and gained the suit."

"Yes," responded the Doctor, "I have always heard that the Widow McWilliams gained her case by consulting old Frank."

"Why, Doctor," continued the Colonel, in an animated manner, "When the races were at St. Louis, three years ago, I went to old Betty, the blind fortune-teller, to see which horse was going to win; and she said, 'Massa, bet your money on de gray mare.' Well, you see, everybody thought that Johnson's black horse would win, and piles of money was bet on him. However, I bet one hundred dollars on the gray mare, and, to the utter surprise of all, she won. When the race was over, I was asked how I come to bet on the mare, when everybody was putting their funds on the horse. I then told them that I never risked my money on any horse, till I found out which was going to win.

"Now, with regard to ghosts, just let me say to you, Doctor, that I saw the ghost of the peddler that was murdered over on the old road, just as sure as you are born."

"Do you think so?" asked the Doctor.

"Think so! Why, I know it, just as well as I know that I see you now. He had his pack on his back; and it was in the day-time, no night-work about it. He looked at me, and I watched him till he got out of sight. But wasn't I frightened; it made the hair stand up on my head, I tell you,"

"Did he speak to you?" asked the Doctor.

"Oh, no! he didn't speak, but he had a sorrowful look, and, as he was getting out of sight, he turned and looked over his shoulder at me."

Most of the superstition amongst the whites, in our section, was the result of their close connection with the blacks; for the servants told the most foolish stories to the children in the nurseries, and they learned more, as they grew older, from the slaves in the quarters, or out on the premises.

CHAPTER VI.

PROFITABLE and interesting amusements were always needed at the Corners, the nearest place to the "Poplar Farm." At the tavern, post-office, and the store, all the neighborhood assembled to read the news, compare notes, and to talk politics.

Shows seldom ventured to stop there, for want of sufficient patronage. Once in three months, however, they had a "Gander Snatching," which never failed to draw together large numbers of ladies as well as gentlemen, the *elite*, as well as the common. The getter-up of this entertainment would procure a gander of the wild goose species. This bird had a long neck, which was large as it rose above the breast, but tapered gradually, for more than half the length, until it became small and serpent-like in form, terminating in a long, slim head, and peaked bill. The head and neck of the gander was well-greased; the legs were tied together with a strong cord, and the bird was then fastened by its legs, to a swinging limb of a tree. The *Snatchers* were to be on horseback, and were to start fifteen or twenty rods from the gander, riding at full speed, and, as they passed along under the bird, they had the right to pull his head off if they could. To accelerate the speed of the horses, a man was stationed a few feet from the gander, with orders to give every horse a cut with his whip, as he went by.

Sometimes the bird's head would be caught by ten or a dozen before they would succeed in pulling it off, which was necessary; often by the sudden jump of the animal, or the rider having taken a little too much wine, he would fall from his horse, which event would give additional interest to the "Snatching."

The poor gander would frequently show far more sagacity than its torturers. After having its head caught once or twice, the gander would draw up its head, or dodge out of the way. Sometimes the snatcher would have in his hand a bit of sandpaper, which would enable him to make a tighter grasp. But this mode was generally considered unfair, and, on one occasion, caused a duel in which both parties were severely wounded.

But the most costly and injurious amusement that the people in our section entered into was that of card-playing, a species of gambling too much indulged in throughout the entire South. This amusement causes much sadness, for it often occurs that gentlemen lose large sums at the gambling-table, frequently seriously embarrassing themselves, sometimes bringing ruin upon whole families.

Mr. Oscar Smith, residing near "Poplar Farm," took a trip to St. Louis, thence to New Orleans and back. On the steamer he was beguiled into gaming.

"Go call my boy, steward," said Mr. Smith, as he took his cards one by one from the table.

In a few moments a fine-looking, bright-eyed mulatto boy, apparently about fifteen years of age, was standing by his master's side at the table.

"I will see you and five hundred dollars better," said Smith, as his servant Jerry approached the table.

"What price do you set on that boy?" asked Johnson, as he took a roll of bills from his pocket.

"He will bring a thousand dollars, any day, in the New Orleans market," replied Smith.

"Then you bet the whole of the boy, do you?"

"Yes."

"I call you, then," said Johnson, at the same time spreading his cards out upon the table.

"You have beat me," said Smith, as soon as he saw the cards.

Jerry, who was standing on top of the table, with the bank-notes and silver dollars round his feet, was now ordered to descend from the table.

"You will not forget that you belong to me," said Johnson, as the young slave was stepping from the table to a chair.

"No, sir," replied the chattel.

"Now go back to your bed, and be up in time to-morrow morning to brush my clothes and clean my boots, do you hear?"

"Yes, sir," responded Jerry, as he wiped the tears from his eyes.

As Mr. Smith left the gaming-table, he said: "I claim the right of redeeming that boy, Mr. Johnson. My father gave him to me when I came of age, and I promised not to part with him."

"Most certainly, sir, the boy shall be yours whenever you hand me over a cool thousand," replied Johnson.

The next morning, as the passengers were assembling in the breakfast saloons, and upon the guards of the vessel, and the servants were seen running about waiting upon or looking for their masters, poor Jerry was entering his new master's state-room with his boots.

The genuine wit of the negro is often a marvel to the whites, and this wit or humor, as it may be called, is brought out in various ways. Not unfrequently is it exhibited by the black, when he really means to be very solemn.

Thus our Sampey met Davidson's Joe, on the road to the Corners, and called out to him several times without getting an answer. At last, Joe, appearing much annoyed, stopped, looked at Sampey in an attitude of surprise, and exclaimed: "Ain't you got no manners? Whare's your eyes? Don't you see I is a funeral?"

GAMBLING FOR A SLAVE.

It was not till then that Sampey saw that Joe had a box in his arms, resembling a coffin, in which was a deceased negro child. The negro would often show his wit to the disadvantage of his master or mistress.

When visitors were at "Poplar Farm," Dr. Gaines would frequently call in Cato to sing a song or crack a joke, for the amusement of the company. On one occasion, requesting the servant to give a toast, at the same time handing the negro a glass of wine, the latter took the glass, held it up, looked at it, began to show his ivory, and said:

"De big bee flies high,
De little bee makes de honey,
De black man raise de cotton,
An' de white man gets de money."

The same servant going to meeting one Sabbath, was met on the road by Major Ben. O'Fallon, who was riding on horseback, with a hoisted umbrella to keep the rain off. The Major, seeing the negro trudging along bareheaded and with something under his coat, supposing he had stolen some article which he was attempting to hide, said, "What's that you've got under your coat, boy?"

"Nothin', sir, but my hat," replied the slave, and at the same time drawing forth a second-hand beaver.

"Is it yours?" inquired the Major.

"Yes, sir," was the quick response of the negro.

"Well," continued the Major, "if it is yours, why don't you wear it and save your head from the rain?"

"Oh!" replied the servant, with a smile of seeming satisfaction, "de head belongs to massa an' de hat belongs to me. Let massa take care of his property, an' I'll take care of mine."

Dr. Gaines, while taking a neighbor out to the pig sty, to show him some choice hogs that he intended for the next winter's bacon, said to Dolly who was feeding the pigs: "How much lard do you think you can get out of that big hog, Dolly?"

The old negress scratched her wooly head, put on a thoughtful look, and replied, "I specks I can get a pail full, ef de pail aint too big."

"I reckon you can," responded the master.

The ladies are not without their recreation, the most common of which is snuff-dipping. A snuff-box or bottle is carried, and with it a very small stick or cane, which has been chewed at the end until it forms a small mop. The little dippers or sticks are sold in bundles for the use of the ladies, and can be bought simply cut in the requisite lengths or chewed ready for use. This the dipper moistens with saliva, and dips into the snuff-box, and then lifts the mop thus loaded inside the lips. In some parts they courteously hand round the snuff and dipper, or place a plentiful supply of snuff on the table, into which all the company may dip.

Amongst even the better classes of whites, the ladies would often assemble in considerable numbers, especially during revival meeting times, place a wash-dish in the middle of the room, all gather around it, commence snuff-dipping, and all using the wash-dish as a common spittoon.

Every well bred lady carries her own snuff-box and dipper. Generally during church service, where the clergyman is a little prosy, snuff-dipping is indispensible.

CHAPTER VII.

FORTY years ago, in the Southern States, superstition held an exalted place with all classes, but more especially with the blacks and uneducated, or poor, whites. This was shown more clearly in their belief in witchcraft in general, and the devil in particular. To both of these classes, the devil was a real being, sporting a club-foot, horns, tail, and a hump on his back.

The influence of the devil was far greater than that of the Lord. If one of these votaries had stolen a pig, and the fear of the Lord came over him, he would most likely ask the Lord to forgive him, but still cling to the pig. But if the fear of the devil came upon him; in all probability he would drop the pig and take to his heels.

In those days the city of St. Louis had a large number who had implicit faith in Voudooism. I once attended one of their midnight meetings. In the pale rays of the moon the dark outlines of a large assemblage was visible, gathered about a small fire, conversing in different tongues. They were negroes of all ages,—women, children, and men. Finally, the noise was hushed, and the assembled group assumed an attitude of respect. They made way for their queen, and a short, black, old negress came upon the scene, followed by two assistants, one of whom bore a cauldron, and the other, a box.

The cauldron was placed over the dying embers, the queen drew forth, from the folds of her gown, a magic wand, and the crowd formed a ring around her. Her first act was to throw some substance on the fire, the flames shot up with a lurid glare—now it writhed in serpent coils, now it darted upward in forked tongues, and then it gradually transformed itself into a veil of dusky vapors. At this stage, after a certain amount of gibberish and wild gesticulation from the queen, the box was opened, and frogs, lizards, snakes, dog liver, and beef hearts drawn forth and thrown into the cauldron. Then followed more gibberish and gesticulation, when the congregation joined hands, and began the wildest dance imaginable, keeping it up until the men and women sank to the ground from mere exhaustion.

In the ignorant days of slavery, there was a general belief that a horse-shoe hung over the door would insure good luck. I have seen negroes, otherwise comparatively intelligent, refuse to pick up a pin, needle, or other such object, dropped by a negro, because, as they alleged, if the person who dropped the articles had a spite against them, to touch anything they dropped would voudou them, and make them seriously ill.

Nearly every large plantation, with any considerable number of negroes, had at least one, who laid claim to be a fortune-teller, and who was regarded with more than common respect by his fellow-slaves. Dinkie, a full-blooded African, large in frame, coarse featured, and claiming to be a descendant of a king in his native land, was the oracle on the "Poplar Farm." At the time of which I write, Dinkie was about fifty years of age, and had lost an eye, and was, to say the least, a very ugly-looking man.

No one in that section was considered so deeply immersed in voudooism, goopherism, and fortune-telling, as he. Although he had been many years in the Gaines family, no one could remember the time when Dinkie was called upon to perform manual labor. He was not sick, yet he never worked. No one interfered with him. If he felt like feeding the chickens, pigs, or cattle, he did so. Dinkie hunted, slept, was at the table at meal time, roamed through the woods, went to the city, and returned when he pleased, with no one to object, or to ask a question. Everybody treated him with respect. The whites, throughout the neighborhood, tipped their hats to the old one-eyed negro, while the policemen, or patrollers, permitted him to pass without a challenge. The negroes, everywhere, stood in mortal fear of "Uncle Dinkie." The blacks who saw him every day, were always thrown upon their good behavior, when in his presence. I once asked a negro why they appeared to be afraid of Dinkie. He looked at me, shrugged his shoulders, smiled, shook his head and said,—

"I ain't afraid of de debble, but I ain't ready to go to him jess yet." He then took a look around and behind, as if he feared some one would hear what he was saying, and then continued: "Dinkie's got de power, ser; he knows things seen and unseen, an' dat's what makes him his own massa."

It was literally true, this man was his own master. He wore a snake's skin around his neck, carried a petrified frog in one pocket, and a dried lizard in the other.

A slave speculator once came along and offered to purchase Dinkie. Dr. Gaines, no doubt, thought it a good opportunity to get the elephant off his hands, and accepted the money. A day later, the trader returned the old negro, with a threat of a suit at law for damages.

A new overseer was employed, by Dr. Gaines, to take charge of "Poplar Farm." His name was Grove Cook, and he was widely known as a man of ability in managing plantations, and in raising a large quantity of produce from a given number of hands. Cook was called a "hard overseer." The negroes dreaded his coming, and, for weeks before his arrival, the overseer's name was on every slave's tongue.

Cook came, he called the negroes up, men and women; counted them, looked them over as a purchaser would a drove of cattle that he intended to buy. As he was about to dismiss them he saw Dinkie come out of his cabin. The sharp eye of the overseer was at once on him.

"Who is that nigger?" inquired Cook.

"That is Dinkie," replied Dr. Gaines.

"What is his place?" continued the overseer.

"Oh, Dinkie is a gentleman at large!" was the response.

"Have you any objection to his working?"

"None, whatever."

"Well, sir," said Cook, "Ill put him to work to-morrow morning."

Dinkie was called up and counted in.

At the roll call, the following morning, all answered except the conjurer; he was not there.

The overseer inquired for Dinkie, and was informed that he was still asleep.

"I will bring him out of his bed in a hurry," said Cook, as he started towards the negro's cabin. Dinkie appeared at his door, just as the overseer was approaching.

"Follow me to the barn," said the impatient driver to the negro. "I make it a point always to whip a nigger, the first day that I take charge of a farm, so as to let the hands know who I am. And, now, Mr. Dinkie, they tell me that you have not had your back tanned for many years; and, that being the case, I shall give you a flogging that you will never forget. Follow me to the barn." Cook started for the barn, but turned and went into his house to get his whip.

At this juncture, Dinkie gave a knowing look to the other slaves, who were standing by, and said, "Ef he lays the weight ob his finger on me, you'll see de top of dat barn come off."

The reappearance of the overseer, with the large negro whip in one hand, and a club in the other, with the significant demand of "follow me," caused a deep feeling in the breast of every negro present.

Dr. Gaines, expecting a difficulty between his new driver and the conjurer, had arisen early, and was standing at his bedroom window looking on.

The news that Dinkie was to be whipped, spread far and near over the place, and had called forth men, women, and children. Even Uncle Ned, the old negro of ninety years, had crawled out of his straw, and was at his cabin door. As the barn doors closed behind the overseer and Dinkie, a death-like silence pervaded the entire group, who, instead of going to their labor, as ordered by the driver, were standing as if paralyzed, gazing intently at the barn, expecting every moment to see the roof lifted.

Not a word was spoken by anyone, except Uncle Ned, who smiled, shook his head, put on a knowing countenance, and said, "My word fer it, de oberseer ain't agwine to whip Dinkie."

Five minutes, ten minutes, fifteen minutes passed, and the usual sound of "Oh, pray, massa! Oh, pray, massa!" heard on the occasion of a slave being punished, had not yet proceeded from the barn.

Many of the older negroes gathered around Uncle Ned, for he and Dinkie occupied the same cabin, and the old, superannuated slave knew more about the affairs of the conjurer, than anyone else. Ned told of how, on the previous night, Dinkie had slept but little, had closely inspected the snake's skin around his neck, the petrified frog and dried lizard, in his pockets, and had rubbed himself all over with goopher; and when he had finished, he knelt, and exclaimed,—

"Now, good and lovely devil, for more than twenty years, I have served you faithfully. Before I got into your service, de white folks bought an' sold me an' my old wife an' chillen, an' whip me, and half starve me. Dey did treat me mighty bad, dat you knows. Den I use to pray to de Lord, but dat did no good, kase de white folks don't fear de Lord. But dey fears you, an' ever since I got into your service, I is able to do as I please. No white dares to lay his hand on me; and dis is all owing to de power dat you give me. Oh, good and lovely devil! please to continer dat power. A new oberseer is to come here to-morrow, an' he wants to get me in his hands. But, dear devil, I axe you to stand by me in dis my trial hour, an' I will neber desert you as long as I live. Continer dis power; make me strong in your cause; make me to be more faithful to you, an' let me still be able to conquer my enemies, an' I will give you all de glory, and will try to deserve a seat at your right hand."

With bated breath, everyone listened to Uncle Ned. All had the utmost confidence in Dinkie's "power." None believed that he would be punished, while a large number expected to see the roof of the barn burst off at any moment. At last the suspense was broken. The barn door flew open; the overseer and the conjurer came out together, walking side by side, and separated when half-way up the walk. As they parted, Cook went to the field, and Dinkie to his cabin.

The slaves all shook their heads significantly. The fact that the old negro had received no punishment, was evidence of his victory over the slave driver. But how the feat had been accomplished, was a mystery. No one dared to ask Dinkie, for he was always silent, except when he had something to communicate. Everyone was afraid to inquire of the overseer.

There was, however, one faint chance of getting an inkling of what had occurred in the barn, and that was through Uncle Ned. This fact made the old, superannuated slave the hero and centre of attraction, for several days. Many were the applications made to Ned for information, but the old man did not know, or wished to exaggerate the importance of what he had learned.

"I tell you," said Dolly, "Dinkie is a power."

"He's nobody's fool," responded Hannah.

"I would not make him mad wid me, fer dis whole world," ejaculated Jim.

Just then, Nancy, the cook, came in brim full of news. She had given Uncle Ned some "cracklin bread," which had pleased the old man so much that he had opened his bosom, and told her all that he got from Dinkie. This piece of information flew quickly from cabin to cabin, and brought the slaves hastily into the kitchen.

It was night. Nancy sat down, looked around, and told Billy to shut the door. This heightened the interest, so that the fall of a pin could have been heard. All eyes were upon Nancy, and she felt keenly the importance of her position. Her voice was generally loud, with a sharp ring, which could be heard for a long distance, especially in the stillness of the night. But now, Nancy spoke in a whisper, occasionally putting her finger to her mouth, indicating a desire for silence, even when the breathing of those present could be distinctly heard.

"When dey got in de barn, de oberseer said to Dinkie, 'Strip yourself; I don't want to tear your clothes with my whip. I'm going to tear your black skin.'

"Den, you see, Dinkie tole de oberseer to look in de east corner ob de barn. He looked, an' he saw hell, wid all de torments, an' de debble, wid his cloven foot, a-struttin' about dar, jes as ef he was cock ob de walk. An' Dinkie tole Cook, dat ef he lay his finger on him, he'd call de debble up to take him away."

"An' what did Cook say to dat?" asked Jim.

"Let me 'lone; I didn't tell you all," said Nancy. "Den you see de oberseer turn pale in de face, an' he say to Dinkie, 'Let me go dis time, an' I'll nebber trouble you any more.'"

This concluded Nancy's story, as related to her by old Ned, and religiously believed by all present. Whatever caused the overseer to change his mind in regard to the flogging of Dinkie, it was certain that he was most thoroughly satisfied to let the old negro off without the threatened punishment; and, although he remained at "Poplar Farm," as overseer, for five years, he never interfered with the conjurer again.

It is not strange that ignorant people should believe in characters of Dinkie's stamp; but it is really marvellous that well-educated men and women should give any countenance whatever, to such delusions as were practised by the oracle of "Poplar Farm."

The following illustration may be taken as a fair sample of the easy manner in which Dinkie carried on his trade.

Miss Martha Lemmy, being on a visit to Mrs. Gaines, took occasion during the day to call upon Dinkie. The conjurer knew the antecedents of his visitor, and was ready to give complete satisfaction in his particular line. When the young lady entered the old man's cabin, he met her, bade her be welcome, and tell what she had come for. She took a seat on one stool, and he on another. Taking the lady's right hand in his, Dinkie spit into its palm, rubbed it, looked at it, shut his one eye, opened it, and said: "I sees a young gentman, an' he's rich, an' owns plenty of land an' a heap o' niggers; an', lo! Miss Marfa, he loves you."

The lady drew a long breath of seeming satisfaction, and asked, "Are you sure that he loves me, Uncle Dinkie?"

"Oh! Miss Marfa, I knows it like a book."

"Have you ever seen the gentleman?" the lady inquired.

The conjurer began rubbing the palm of the snow-white hand, talked to himself in an undertone, smiled, then laughed out, and saying: "Why, Miss Marfa, as I lives it's Mr. Scott, an' he's thinkin' 'bout you now; yes, he's got his mind on you dis bressed minute. But how he's changed sense I seed him de lass time. Now he's got side whiskers an' a mustacher on his chin. But, let me see. Here is somethin' strange. De web looks a little smoky, an' when I gets to dat spot, I can't get along till a little silver is given to me."

Here the lady drew forth her purse and gave the old man a half dollar piece that made his one eye fairly twinkle.

He resumed: "Ah! now de fog is cleared away, an' I see dat Mr. Scott is settin in a rockin-cheer, wid boff feet on de table, an' smokin' a segar."

"Do you think Mr. Scott loves me?" inquired the lady.

"O! yes," responded Dinkie; "he jess sets his whole heart on you. Indeed, Miss Marfa, he's almos' dyin' 'bout you."

"He never told me that he loved me," remarked the lady.

"But den, you see, he's backward, he ain't got his eye-teef cut yet in love matters. But he'll git a little bolder ebbry time he sees you," replied the negro.

"Do you think he'll ever ask me to marry him?"

"O! yes, Miss Marfa, he's sure to do dat. As he sets dar in his rockin-cheer, he looks mighty solem-colly—looks like he wanted to ax you to haf him now."

"Do you think that Mr. Scott likes any other lady, Uncle Dinkie?" asked Miss Lemmy.

"Well, Miss Marfa, I'll jess consult de web an' see." And here the conjurer shut his one eye, opened it, shut it again, talked to himself in an undertone, opened his eye, looked into the lady's hand, and exclaimed: "Ah! Miss Marfa, I see a lady in de way, an' she's got riches; but de web is smoky, an' it needs a little silver to clear it up."

With tears in her eyes, and almost breathless, Miss Lemmy hastily took from her pocket her purse, and handed the old man another piece of money, saying: "Please go on."

Dinkie smiled, shook his head, got up and shut his cabin door, sat down, and again took the lady's hand in his.

"Yes, I see," said he, "I see it's a lady; but bless you soul, Miss Marfa, it's a likeness of you dat Mr. Scott is lookin' at; dat's all."

This morsel of news gave great relief, and Miss Lemmy dried her eyes with joy.

Dinkie then took down the old rusty horseshoe from over

RUNNING DOWN SLAVES WITH DOGS.

his cabin door, held it up, and said: "Dis horseshoe neffer lies." Here he took out of his pocket a bag made of the skin of the rattlesnake, and took from it some goopher, sprinkled it over the horseshoe, saying: "Dis is de stuff, Miss Marfa, dat's gwine to make you Mr. Scott's conqueror. Long as you keeps dis goopher 'bout you he can't get away from you: he'll ax you fer a kiss, de berry next time he meets you, an' he can't help hisself fum doin' it. No woman can get him fum you so long as you keep dis goopher 'bout you."

Here Dinkie lighted a tallow candle, looked at it, smiled, shook his head,—"You's gwine to marry Mr. Scott in 'bout one year, an' you's gwine to haf thirteen children—sebben boys an' six gals, an' you's gwine to haf a heap of riches."

Just then, Dinkie's interesting revelations were cut short by Ike and Cato bringing along Peter, who, it was said, had been killed by the old bell sheep.

It appears that Peter had a way of playing with the old ram, who was always ready to butt at any one who got in his way. When seeing the ram coming, Peter would get down on his hands and knees and pretend that he was going to have a butting match with the sheep. And when the latter would come full tilt at him, Peter would dodge his head so as to miss the ram, and the latter would jump over the boy, turn around angrily, shake his head and start for another butt at Peter.

This kind of play was repeated sometimes for an hour or more, to the great amusement of both whites and blacks. But, on this occasion, Peter was completely caught. As he was on his hands and knees, the ram started on his usual run for the boy; the latter, in dodging his head, run his face against a stout stub of dry rye stalk, which caused him to quickly jerk up his head, just in time for the sheep to give him a fair butt squarely in the forehead, which knocked Peter senseless. The ram, elated with his victory, began to back himself for another lick at Peter, when the men, seeing what had happened to the poor boy, took him up and brought him to Dinkie's cabin to be resuscitated, or "brought to," as they termed it.

Nearly an hour passed in rubbing the boy, before he began to show signs of consciousness. He "come to," but he never again accepted a butting match with the ram.

CHAPTER VIII.

Cruelty to negroes was not practised in our section. It is true there were some exceptional cases, and some individuals did not take the care of their servants at all times, that economy seemed to demand. Yet a certain degree of punishment was actually needed to insure respect to the master, and good government to the slave population. If a servant disobeyed orders, it was necessary that he should be flogged, to deter others from following the bad example. If a servant ran away, he must be caught and brought back, to let the others see that the same fate awaited them if they made similar attempts.

While the keeping of bloodhounds, for running down and catching negroes, was not common, yet a few were kept by Mr. Tabor, an inferior white man, near the Corners, who hired them out, or hunted the runaway, charging so much per day, or a round sum for the *catch.*

Jerome, a slave owned by the Rev. Mr. Wilson, when about to be punished by his master, ran away. Tabor and his dogs were sent for. The slave-catcher came, and at once set his dogs upon the trail. The parson and some of the neighbors went along for the fun that was in store.

These dogs will attack a negro, at their master's bidding, and cling to him as a bull-dog will cling to a beast. Many are the speculations as to whether the negro will be secured alive or dead, when these dogs get on his track. However, on this occasion, there was not much danger of ill-treatment, for Mr. Wilson was a clergyman, and was of a humane turn, and bargained with Tabor not to injure the slave if he could help it.

The hunters had been in the wood a short time, ere they got on the track of two slaves, one of whom was Jerome. The negroes immediately bent their steps toward the swamp, with the hope that the dogs would, when put upon the scent, be unable to follow them through the water. Nearer and nearer the whimpering pack pressed on; their delusion began to dispel.

All at once the truth flashed upon the minds of the fugitives like a glare of light,—that it was Tabor with his dogs! They at last reached the river, and in the negroes plunged, followed by the catch-dog. Jerome was finally caught, and once more in

TABOR'S CATCH-DOG, "GROWLER."

the hands of his master; while the other man found a watery grave. They returned, and the preacher sent his slave to the city jail for safe-keeping.

While the planters would employ Tabor, without hesitation, to hunt down their negroes, they would not receive him into their houses as a visitor any sooner than they would one of their own slaves. Tabor was, however, considered one of the better class of poor whites, a number of whom had a religious society in that neighborhood. The pastor of the poor whites was the Rev. Martin Louder, somewhat of a genius in his own way. The following sermon, preached by him, about the time of which I write, will well illustrate the character of the people for whom he labored.

More than two long, weary hours had now elapsed since the audience had been convened, and the people began to exhibit slight signs of fatigue. Some few scrapings and rasping of cow-hide boots on the floor, an audible yawn or two, a little twisting and turning on the narrow, uncomfortable seats, while, in one or two instances, a somnolent soul or two snored outright. These palpable signs were not lost upon our old friend Louder. He cast an eye (emphatically, an eye) over the assemblage, and then—he spoke:—

"My dear breethering, and beloved sistering! You've ben a long time a settin' on your seats. You're tired, I know, an' I don't expect you want to hear the ole daddy preach. Ef you don't want to hear the ole man, jist give him the least bit of a sign. Cough. Hold up your hand. Ennything, an' Louder'll sit rite down. He'll dry up in a minit."

At this juncture of affairs, Louder paused for a reply. He glanced furtively over the audience, in search of the individual who might be "tired of settin' on his seat," but no sign was made: no such malcontent came within the visual range.

"Go on, Brother Louder!" said a sonorous voice in the "amen corner" of the house. Thus encouraged, the speaker proceeded in his remarks:—

"Well, then, breethering, sense you say so, Louder'll perceed; but he don't intend to preach a reg'lar sermon, for it's a gittin' late, and our sect which hit don't believe in eatin' cold vittles on the Lord's day. My breethering, ef the ole Louder gits outen the rite track, I want you to call him back. He don't want to teach you any error. He don't want to preach nuthin' but what's found between the leds of this blessed Book."

"My dear breethering, the Lord raised up his servant, Moses, that he should fetch his people Isrel up outen that wicked land—ah. Then Moses, he went out from the face of the Lord, and departed hence unto the courts of the old tyranickle king—ah. An' what sez you, Moses? Ah, sez he, Moses sez, sez he to that wicked old Faro: Thus sez the Lord God of hosts, sez he: Let my Isrel go—ah. An' what sez the ole, hard-hearted king—ah? Ah! sez Faro, sez he, who is the Lord God of hosts, sez he, that I should obey his voice—ah? An' now what sez you, Moses—ah. Ah, Moses sez, sez he: Thus saith the Lord God of Isrel, let my people go, that they mought worship me, sez the Lord, in the wilderness—ah. But—ah! my beloved breethering an' my harden', impenitent frien's—ah, did the ole, hard-hearted king harken to the words of Moses, and let my people go—ah? Nary time."

This last remark, made in an ordinary, conversational tone of voice, was so sudden and unexpected that the change, the transition from the singing state was electrical.

"An' then, my beloved breethering an' sistering, what next—ah? What sez you, Moses, to Faro—that contrary ole king—ah? Ah, Moses sez to Faro, sez he, Moses sez, sez he: Thus seth the Lord God of Isrel: Let my people go, sez the Lord, leest I come, sez he, and smite you with a cuss—ah! An' what sez Faro, the ole tyranickle king—ah? Ah, sez he, sez ole Faro, Let

REV. MR. WILSON AND HIS CAPTURED SLAVE.

their tasks be doubled, and leest they mought grumble, sez he, those bricks shall be made without straw—ah! [Vox naturale.] Made 'em pluck up grass an' stubble outen the fields, breethering, to mix with their mud. Mity hard on the pore critters; warn't it, Brother Flood Gate?" [The individual thus interrogated replied, "Jess so;" and "ole Louder" moved along.]

"An' what next—ah? Did the ole king let my people Isrel go—ah? No, my dear breethering, he retched out his pizen hand, and he hilt 'em fash—ah. Then the Lord was wroth with that wicked ole king—ah. An' the Lord, he sed to Moses, sez he: Moses, stretch forth now thy rod over the rivers an' the ponds of this wicked land—ah; an' behold, sez he, when thou stretch out thy rod, sez the Lord, all the waters shall be turned into blood—ah! Then Moses, he tuck his rod, an' he done as the Lord God of Isrel had commanded his servant Moses to do—ah. An' what then, say you, my breethering—ah? Why, lo an' behold! the rivers of that wicked land was all turned into blood—ah; an' all the fish an' all the frogs in them streams an' waters died—ah!"

"Yes!" said the speaker, lowering his voice to a natural tone, and glancing out of the open window at the dry and dusty road, for we were at the time suffering from a protracted drouth: "An' I believe the frogs will all die now, unless we get some rain purty soon. What do you think about it, Brother Waters?" [This interrogatory was addressed to a fine, portly-looking old man in the congregation. Brother W. nodded assent, and old Louder resumed the thread of his discourse.] "Ah, my beloved breethering, that was a hard time on old Faro an' his wicked crowd—ah. For the waters was loathsome to the people, an' it smelt so bad none of 'em cood drink it; an' what next—ah? Did the ole king obey the voice of the Lord, and let my people Isrel go—ah? Ah, no, my breethering, not by a long sight—ah. For he hilt out agin the Lord, and obeyed not his voice—ah. Then the Lord sent a gang of bull-frogs into that wicked land—ah. An' they went hoppin' an' lopin' about all over the country, into the vittles, an' everywhere else—ah. My breethering, the old Louder thinks that was a des'prit time—ah. But all woodent do—ah. Ole Faro was as stubborn as one of Louder's mules—ah, an' he woodent let the chosen seed go up outen the land of bondage—ah. Then the Lord sent a mighty hail, an', arter that, his devourin' locuses—ah! An' they et up blamed nigh everything on the face of the eth—ah."

"Let not yore harts be trubbled, for the truth is mitay and must prevale—ah. Brother Creek, you don't seem to be doin' much of ennything, suppose you raise a tune!"

This remark was addressed to a tall, lank, hollow-jawed old man, in the congregation, with a great shock of "grizzled gray" hair.

"Wait a minit, Brother Louder, till I git on my glasses!" was the reply of Brother Creek, who proceeded to draw from his pocket an oblong tin case, which opened and shut with a tremendous snap, from which he drew a pair of iron-rimmed spectacles. These he carefully "dusted" with his handkerchief, and then turned to the hymn which the preacher had selected and read out to the congregation. After considerable deliberation, and some clearing of the throat, hawking, spitting, etc., and other preliminaries, Brother Creek, in a quavering, split sort of voice, opened out on the tune.

Louder seemed uneasy. It was evident that he feared a failure on the part of the worthy brother. At the end of the first line, he exclaimed:—

"'Pears to me, Brother Creek, you hain't got the right miter."

Brother Creek suspended operations a moment, and replied, "I am purty kerrect, ginerally, Brother Louder, an' I'm confident she'll come out all right!"

"Well," said Louder, "we'll try her agin," and the choral strain, under the supervision of Brother Creek, was resumed in the following words:—

"When I was a mourner just like you,
  Washed in the blood of the Lamb,
I fasted and prayed till I got through,
  Washed in the blood of the Lamb.

CHORUS.—"Come along, sinner, and go with us;
  If you don't you will be cussed.

"Religion's like a blooming rose,
  Washed in the blood of the Lamb,

As none but those that feel it knows,
Washed in the blood of the Lamb."—*Cho.*

The singing, joined in by all present, brought the enthusiasm of the assembly up to white heat, and the shouting, with the loud "Amen," "God save the sinner," "Sing it, brother, sing it," made the welkin ring.

CHAPTER IX.

WHILE the "peculiar institution" was a great injury to both master and slaves, yet there was considerable truth in the oft-repeated saying that the slave "was happy." It was indeed, a low kind of happiness, existing only where masters were disposed to treat their servants kindly, and where the proverbial light-heartedness of the latter prevailed. History shows that of all races, the African was best adapted to be the "hewers of wood, and drawers of water."

Sympathetic in his nature, thoughtless in his feelings, both alimentativeness and amativeness large, the negro is better adapted to follow than to lead. His wants easily supplied, generous to a fault, large fund of humor, brimful of music, he has ever been found the best and most accommodating of servants. The slave would often get rid of punishment by his wit; and even when being flogged, the master's heart has been moved to pity, by the humorous appeals of his victim. House servants in the cities and villages, and even on plantations, were considered privileged classes. Nevertheless, the field hands were not without their happy hours.

An old-fashioned corn-shucking took place once a year, on "Poplar Farm," which afforded pleasant amusement for the out-door negroes for miles around. On these occasions, the servants, on all plantations, were allowed to attend by mere invitation of the blacks where the corn was to be shucked.

As the grain was brought in from the field, it was left in a pile near the corn-cribs. The night appointed, and invitations sent out, slaves from plantations five or six miles away, would assemble and join on the road, and in large bodies march along, singing their melodious plantation songs.

To hear three or four of these gangs coming from different directions, their leaders giving out the words, and the whole company joining in the chorus, would indeed surpass anything ever produced by "Haverly's Ministrels," and many of their jokes and witticisms were never equalled by Sam Lucas or Billy Kersands.

A supper was always supplied by the planter on whose farm the shucking was to take place. Often when approaching the place, the singers would speculate on what they were going to have for supper. The following song was frequently sung:—

"All dem puty gals will be dar,
Shuck dat corn before you eat.
Dey will fix it for us rare,
Shuck dat corn before you eat.
I know dat supper will be big,
Shuck dat corn before you eat.
I think I smell a fine roast pig,
Shuck dat corn before you eat.
A supper is provided, so dey said,
Shuck dat corn before you eat.
I hope dey'll have some nice wheat bread,
Shuck dat corn before you eat.
I hope dey'll have some coffee dar,
Shuck dat corn before you eat.
I hope dey'll have some whisky dar,
Shuck dat corn before you eat.
I think I'll fill my pockets full,
Shuck dat corn before you eat.
Stuff dat coon an' bake him down,
Shuck dat corn before you eat.
I speck some niggers dar from town,
Shuck dat corn before you eat.
Please cook dat turkey nice an' brown.
Shuck dat corn before you eat.
By de side of dat turkey I'll be foun,
Shuck dat corn before you eat.

I smell de supper, dat I do,
Shuck dat corn before you eat.
On de table will be a stew,
Shuck dat corn, ete."

Burning pine knots, held by some of the boys, usually furnished light for the occasion. Two hours is generally sufficient time to finish up a large shucking; where five hundred bushels of corn is thrown into the cribs as the shuck is taken off. The work is made comparatively light by the singing, which never ceases till they go to the supper table. Something like the following is sung during the evening:

"De possum meat am good to eat,
Carve him to de heart;
You'll always find him good and sweet,
Carve him to de heart;
My dog did bark, and I went to see,
Carve him to de heart;
And dar was a possum up dat tree,
Carve him to de heart.

CHORUS.—"Carve dat possum, carve dat possum children,
Carve dat possum, carve him to de heart;
Oh, carve dat possum, carve dat possum children,
Carve dat possum, carve him to de heart.

"I reached up for to pull him in,
Carve him to de heart;
De possum he began to grin,
Carve him to de heart;
I carried him home and dressed him off,
Carve him to de heart;
I hung him dat night, in de frost,
Carve him to de heart.
CHORUS.—"Carve dat possum, etc.

"De way to cook de possum sound,
Carve him to de heart;
Fust par-bile him, den bake him brown,
Carve him to de heart;

Lay sweet potatoes in de pan,
Carve him to de heart;
De sweetest eatin' in de lan,'
Carve him to de heart.
CHORUS.—"Carve dat possum, etc."

Should a poor supper be furnished, on such an occasion, you would hear remarks from all parts of the table,—

"Take dat rose pig 'way from dis table."

"What rose pig? you see any rose pig here?"

"Ha, ha, ha! Dis ain't de place to see rose pig."

"Pass up some dat turkey wid clam sauce."

"Don't talk about dat turkey; he was gone afore we come."

"Dis is de las' time I shucks corn at dis farm."

"Dis is a cheap farm, cheap owner, an' a cheap supper."

"He's talkin' it, ain't he?"

"Dis is de tuffest meat dat I is been called upon to eat fer many a day; you's got to have teeth sharp as a saw to eat dis meat."

"Spose you ain't got no teef, den what you gwine to do?"

"Why, ef you ain't got no teef you muss *gum it!*"

"Ha, ha, ha!" from the whole company, was heard.

On leaving the corn-shucking farm, each gang of men, headed by their leader, would sing during the entire journey home. Some few, however, having their dogs with them, would start on the trail of a coon, possum, or some other game, which might keep them out till nearly morning.

To the Christmas holidays, the slaves were greatly indebted for winter recreation; for long custom had given to them the whole week from Christmas day to the coming in of the New Year.

On "Poplar Farm," the hands drew their share of clothing on Christmas day for the year. The clothing for both men and women was made up by women kept for general sewing and housework. One pair of pants, and two shirts, made the entire stock for a male field hand.

The women's garments were manufactured from the same goods that the men received. Many of the men worked at night for themselves, making splint and corn brooms, baskets, shuck mats, and axe-handles, which they would sell in the city during Christmas week. Each slave was furnished with a pass, something like the following:—

"*Please let my boy, Jim, pass anywhere in this county, until Jan.* 1, 1834, *and oblige* *Respectfully,*
"JOHN GAINES, M.D.
"'*Poplar Farm,' St. Louis County, Mo.*"

With the above precious document in his pocket, a load of baskets, brooms, mats, and axe-handles on his back, a bag hanging across his shoulders, with a jug in each end,—one for the whiskey, and the other for the molasses,—the slaves trudged off to town at night, singing,—

"Hurra, for good ole massa,
He give me de pass to go to de city.
Hurra, for good ole missis,
She bile de pot, and giv me de licker.
Hurra, I'm goin to de city."

"When de sun rise in de mornin',
Jes' above de yaller corn,
You'll fin' dis nigger has take warnin',
An's gone when de driver blows his horn.

"Hurra, for good ole massa,
He giv me de pass to go to de city.
Hurra for good ole missis,
She bile de pot, and give me de licker.
Hurra, I'm goin to de city."

Both the Methodists and Baptists,—the religious denominations to which the blacks generally belong,—never fail to be in the midst of a revival meeting during the holidays, and most of the slaves from the country hasten to these gatherings. Some, however, spend their time at the dances, raffles, cockfights, foot-races, and other amusements that present themselves.

CHAPTER X

A YOUNG and beautiful lady, closely veiled and attired in black, arrived one morning at "Poplar Farm," and was shown immediately into a room in the eastern wing, where she remained, attended only by old Nancy. That the lady belonged to the better class was evident from her dress, refined manners, and the inviolable secrecy of her stay at the residence of Dr. Gaines. At last the lady gave birth to a child, which was placed under the care of Isabella, a quadroon servant, who had recently lost a baby of her own.

The lady left the premises as mysteriously as she had come, and nothing more was ever seen or heard of her, certainly not by the negroes. The child, which was evidently of pure Anglo-Saxon blood, was called Lola, and grew up amongst the negro children of the place, to be a bright, pretty girl, to whom her adopted mother seemed very much attached. At the time of which I write, Lola was eight years old, and her presence on the plantation began to annoy the white members of Dr. Gaines' family, especially when strangers visited the place.

The appearance of Mr. Walker, the noted slave speculator, on the plantation, and whom it was said, had been sent for, created no little excitement amongst the slaves; and great was the surprise to the blacks, when they saw the trader taking Isabella and Lola with him at his departure. Unable to sell the little white girl at any price, Mr. Walker gave her to Mr. George Savage, who having no children of his own adopted the child.

Isabella was sold to a gentleman, who took her to Washington. The grief of the quadroon at being separated from her adopted child was intense, and greatly annoyed her new master, who determined to sell her on his arrival home. Isabella was sold to the slave-trader, Jennings, who placed the woman in one of the private slave-pens, or prisons, a number of which then disgraced the national capital.

Jennings intended to send Isabella to the New Orleans market, as soon as he purchased a sufficient number. At the dusk of the evening, previous to the day she was to be sent off, as the old prison was being closed for the night, Isabella suddenly darted past the keeper, and ran for her life. It was not a great distance from the prison to the long bridge which passes from the lower part of the city, across the Potomac to the extensive forests and woodlands of the celebrated Arlington Heights, then occupied by that distinguished relative and descendant of the immortal Washington, Mr. Geo. W. Custis.

Thither the poor fugitive directed her flight. So unexpected was her escape, that she had gained several rods the start before the keeper had secured the other prisoners, and rallied his assistants to aid in the pursuit. It was at an hour, and in a part of the city where horses could not easily be obtained for the chase; no bloodhounds were at hand to run down the flying woman, and for once it seemed as if there was to be a fair trial of speed and endurance between the slave and the slave-catchers.

The keeper and his force raised the hue-and-cry on her path as they followed close behind; but so rapid was the flight along the wide avenue, that the astonished citizens, as they poured forth from their dwellings to learn the cause of alarm, were only able to comprehend the nature of the case in time to fall in with the motley throng in pursuit, or raise an anxious prayer to heaven, as they refused to join in the chase (as many a one did that night), that the panting fugitive might escape, and the merciless soul-dealer for once be disappointed of his prey. And now, with the speed of an arrow, having passed the avenue, with the distance between her and her pursuers constantly increasing, this poor, hunted female gained the "Long Bridge," as it is called, where interruption seemed improbable. Already her heart began to beat high with the hope of success. She had only to pass three-quarters of a mile across the bridge, when she could bury herself in a vast forest, just at the time when the curtain of night would close around her, and protect her from the pursuit of her enemies.

But God, by His providence, had otherwise determined. He had ordained that an appalling tragedy should be enacted that night within plain sight of the President's house, and the Capitol of the Union, which would be an evidence, wherever it should be known, of the unconquerable love of liberty which the human heart may inherit, as well as a fresh admonition to the slave-dealer of the cruelty and enormity of his crimes.

Just as the pursuers passed the high draw, soon after entering upon the bridge, they beheld three men slowly approaching from the Virginia side. They immediately called to them to arrest the fugitive, proclaiming her a runaway slave. True to their Virginia instincts, as she came near, they formed a line across the narrow bridge to intercept her. Seeing that escape was impossible in that quarter, she stopped suddenly, and turned upon her pursuers.

On came the profane and ribald gang, faster than ever, already exulting in her capture, and threatening punishment for her flight. For a moment, she looked wildly and anxiously around to see if there was no hope of escape, on either hand; far down below, rolled the deep, foaming waters of the Potomac, and before and behind were the rapidly approaching steps and noisy voices of her pursuers.

Seeing how vain would be any further effort to escape, her resolution was instantly taken. She clasped her hands convulsively together, raised her tearful and imploring eyes towards heaven, and begged for the mercy and compassion there, which was unjustly denied her on earth; then, with a single bound, vaulted over the railing of the bridge, and sank forever beneath the angry and foaming waters of the river.

In the meantime Mr. and Mrs. Savage were becoming more and more interested in the child, Lola, whom they had adopted, and who was fast developing into an intellectual and beautiful girl, whose bright, sparkling hazel eyes, snow-white teeth and alabaster complexion caused her to be admired by all. In time, Lola became highly educated, and was duly introduced into the best society.

The cholera of 1832, in its ravages, swept off many of St. Louis' most valued citizens, and among them, Mr. George Savage. Mrs. Savage, who was then in ill-health, regarded Lola with even greater solicitude, than during the lifetime of her late husband. Lola had been amply provided for by Mr. Savage, in his will. She was being courted by Mr. Martin Phelps, previous to the death of her adopted father, and the failing health of Mrs. Savage hastened the nuptials.

The marriage of Mr. Phelps and Miss Savage partook more of a private than of a public affair, owing to the recent death of Mr. Savage. Mr. Phelps' residence was at the outskirts of the city, in the vicinity of what was known as the "Mound," and was a lovely spot. The lady had brought considerable property to her husband.

One morning in the month of December, and only about three months after the marriage of the Phelps's, two men alighted from a carriage, at Mr. Phelps' door, rang the bell, and were admitted by the servant. Mr. Phelps hastened from the breakfast-table, as the servant informed him of the presence of the strangers.

On entering the sitting-room, the host recognized one of the men as Officer Mull, while the other announced himself as James Walker, and said,—

"I have come, Mr. Phelps, on rather an unpleasant errand. You've got a slave in your house that belongs to me."

"I think you are mistaken, sir," replied Mr. Phelps; "my servants are all hired from Major Ben. O'Fallon."

Walker put on a sinister smile, and blandly continued, "I see, sir, that you don't understand me. Ten years ago I bought a slave child from Dr. Gaines, and lent her to Mr. George Savage, and I understand she's in your employ, and I've come to get her," and here the slave speculator took from his side pocket a large sheepskin pocket book, and drew forth the identical bill of sale of Lola, given to him by Dr. Gaines at the time of the selling of Isabella and the child.

"Good heavens!" exclaimed Mr. Phelps, "that paper, if it means anything, it means my wife."

"I can't help what it means," remarked Walker; "here's the bill of sale, and here's the officer to get me my nigger."

"There must be a mistake here. It is true that my wife was the adopted daughter of the late Mr. George Savage, but there is not a drop of negro blood in her veins; and I doubt, sir, if you have ever seen her."

"Well, sir," said Walker, "jest bring her in the room, and I guess she'll know me."

Feeling confident that the bill of sale had no reference to his wife, Mr. Phelps rang the bell, and told the boy that answered it to ask his mistress to come in. A moment or two later, and the lady entered the room.

"My dear," said Mr. Phelps, "are you acquainted with either of these gentlemen?"

The lady looked, hesitated, and replied, "I think not."

Then Walker arose, stepped towards the window, where he could be seen to better advantage, and said, "Why, Lola, have you forgotten me, its only about ten years since I brought you from 'Poplar Farm,' and lent you to Mr. Savage. Ha, ha, ha!"

This coarse laugh of the rough, uneducated negro-trader had not ceased, when Lola gave a heart-rending shriek, and fell fainting upon the floor.

"I thought she'd know me when I jogged her memory," said Walker, as he re-seated himself.

Mr. Phelps sprang to his wife, and lifted her from the floor, and placed her upon the sofa.

"Throw a little of Adam's ale in her face, and that'll bring her to. I've seen 'em faint afore; but they allers come to," said the trader.

"I thank you, sir, but I will attend to my own affairs," said Mr. Phelps, in a rather petulant tone.

"Yes," replied Walker; "but she's mine, and I want to see that she comes to."

As soon as she revived, Mr. Phelps led his wife from the room. A conference of an hour took place on the return of Mr. Phelps to the parlor, which closed with the understanding that a legal examination of the papers should settle the whole question the next day.

At the appointed time, on the following morning, one of the ablest lawyers in the city, Col. Strawther, pronounced the bill of sale genuine, for it had been drawn up by Justice McGuyer, and witnessed by George Kennelly and Wilson P. Hunt.

For this claim, Walker expressed a willingness to sell the woman for two thousand dollars. The payment of the money would have been a small matter, if it had not carried with it the proof that Lola was a slave, which was undeniable evidence that she had negro blood in her veins.

Yet such was the result, for Dr. Gaines had been dead these three years, and whoever Lola's mother was, even if living, she would not come forth to vindicate the free birth of her child.

Mr. Phelps was a man of fine sensibility and was affectionately attached to his wife. However, it was a grave question to be settled in his mind, whether his honor as a Southern gentleman, and his standing in society would allow him to acknowledge a woman as his wife, in whose veins coursed the accursed blood of the negro slave.

Long was the struggle between love and duty, but the shame of public gaze and the ostracism of society decided the matter in favor of duty, and the young and lovely wife was informed

LEAP OF THE FUGITIVE SLAVE.

by the husband that they must separate, never to meet again. Indescribable were the feelings of Lola, as she begged him, upon her knees, not to leave her. The room was horrible in its darkness,—her mind lost its reasoning powers for a time. At last consciousness returned, but only to awaken in her the loneliness of her condition, and the unfriendliness of that law and society that dooms one to everlasting disgrace for a blood taint, which the victim did not have.

Ten days after the proving of the bill of sale, the innocent Lola died of a broken heart, and was interred in the negro burial ground, with not a white face to follow the corpse to its last resting-place. Such is American race prejudice.

CHAPTER XI.

THE invention of the Whitney cotton gin, nearly fifty years ago, created a wonderful rise in the price of slaves in the cotton States. The value of able-bodied men, fit for field-hands, advanced from five hundred to twelve hundred dollars, in the short space of five years. In 1850, a prime field-hand was worth two thousand dollars. The price of women rose in proportion; they being valued at about three hundred dollars less each than the men. This change in the price of slaves caused a lucrative business to spring up, both in the breeding of slaves and the sending of them to the States needing their services. Virginia, Kentucky, Missouri, Tennessee, and North Carolina became the slave-raising sections; Virginia, however, was always considered the banner State. To the traffic in human beings, more than to any other of its evils, is the institution indebted for its overthrow.

From the picture on the heading of *The Liberator*, down to the smallest tract printed against slavery, the separation of families was the chief object of those exposing the great American sin. The tearing asunder of husbands and wives, of parents and children, and the gangs of men and women chained together, *en route* for the New-Orleans' market, furnished newspaper correspondents with items that never wanted readers. These newspaper paragraphs were not unfrequently made stronger by the fact that many of the slaves were as white as those who offered them for sale, and the close resemblance of the victim to the trader, often reminded the purchaser that the same blood coursed through the veins of both.

The removal of Dr. Gaines from "Poplar Farm" to St. Louis, gave me an opportunity of seeing the worst features of the internal slave-trade. For many years Missouri drove a brisk business in the selling of her sons and daughters, the greater number of whom passed through the city of St. Louis. For a long time, James Walker was the principal speculator in this species of property. The early life of this man had been spent as a drayman, first working for others, then for himself, and eventually purchasing men who worked with him. At last, disposing of his horses and drays, he took his faithful men to the Louisiana market and sold them. This was the commencement of a career of cruelty, that, in all probability, had no equal in the annals of the American slave trade.

A more repulsive-looking person could scarcely be found in any community of bad-looking men than Walker. Tall, lean, and lank, with high cheek-bones, face much pitted with the small-pox, gray eyes, with red eyebrows, and sandy whiskers, he indeed stood alone without mate or fellow in looks. He prided himself upon what he called his goodness of heart, and was always speaking of his humanity.

Walker often boasted that he never separated families if he could "persuade the purchaser to take the whole lot." He would always advertise in the New Orleans' papers that he would be there with a prime lot of able-bodied slaves, men and women, fit for field-service, with a few extra ones calculated for house servants,—all between the ages of fifteen and twenty-five years; but like most men who make a business of speculating in human beings, he often bought many who were far advanced in years, and would try to pass them off for five or six years younger than they were. Few persons can arrive at anything approaching the real age of the negro, by mere observation, unless they are well acquainted with the race. Therefore, the slave-trader frequently carried out the deception with perfect impunity.

As soon as the steamer would leave the wharf, and was fairly on the bosom of the broad Mississippi, the speculator would call his servant Pompey to him, and instruct him as to getting the slaves ready for the market. If any of the blacks looked as if they were older than they were advertised to be, it was Pompey's business to fit them for the day of sale.

Pomp, as he was usually called by the trader, was of real negro blood, and would often say, when alluding to himself, "Dis nigger am no counterfeit, he is de ginuine artikle. Dis chile is none of your haf-and-haf, dere is no bogus about him."

Pompey was of low stature, round face, and, like most of his race, had a set of teeth, which, for whiteness and beauty, could not be surpassed; his eyes were large, lips thick, and hair short and woolly. Pomp had been with Walker so long, and seen so much of buying and selling of his fellow-creatures, that he appeared perfectly indifferent to the heart-rending scenes which daily occurred in his presence. Such is the force of habit:—

> "Vice is a monster of such frightful mien,
> That to be hated, needs but to be seen;
> But seen too oft, familiar with its face,
> We first endure, then pity, then embrace."

Before reaching the place of destination, Pompey would pick out the older portion and say, "I is de chap dat is to get you ready for de Orleans market, so dat you will bring marser a good price. How old is you?" addressing himself to a man that showed some age.

"Ef I live to see next corn-plantin' time, I'll be forty."

"Dat may be," replied Pompey, "but now you is only thirty years old; dat's what marser says you is to be."

"I know I is mo' dan dat," responded the man.

"I can't help nuffin' 'bout dat," returned Pompey; "but when you get in de market, an' any one ax you how old you is, an' you tell um you is forty, massa will tie you up, an' when he is done whippin' you, you'll be glad to say you's only thirty."

"Well den, I reckon I is only thirty," said the slave.

"What is your name?" asked Pompey of another man in the group.

"Jeems," was the response.

"Oh! Uncle Jim, is it?"

"Yes."

"Den you muss' hab all dem gray whiskers shaved off, and dem gray hairs plucked out of your head. De fack is, you's got ole too quick." This was all said by Pompey in a manner which showed that he knew his business.

"How ole is you?" asked Pompey of a tall, strong-looking man.

"I am twenty-nine, nex' Christmas Eve," said the man.

"What's your name?"

"My name is Tobias," replied the slave.

"Tobias!" ejaculated Pompey, with a sneer, that told that he was ready to show his brief authority. "Now you's puttin' on airs. Your name is Toby, an' why can't you tell the truf? Remember, now, dat you is twenty-three years ole; an' afore you goes in de market your face muss' be greased; fer I see you's one of dem kind o' ashy niggers, an' a little grease will make your face look black an' slick, an' make you look younger."

Pompey reported to his master the condition of affairs, when the latter said, "Be sure that the niggers don't forget what you have taught them, for our luck depends a great deal upon the appearance of our stock."

With this lot of slaves was a beautiful quadroon, a girl of twenty years, fair as most white women, with hair a little wavy, large black eyes, and a countenance that betokened intelligence beyond the common house servant. Her name was Marion, and the jealousy of the mistress, so common in those days, was the cause of her being sold.

Not far from Canal Street, in the city of New Orleans, in the old days of slavery, stood a two-story, flat building, surrounded by a stone wall, some twelve feet high, the top of which was covered with bits of glass, and so constructed as to prevent even the possibility of any one's passing over it without sustaining great injury. Many of the rooms in this building resembled the cells of a prison, and in a small apartment, near the "office," were to be seen any number of iron collars, hobbles, hand-cuffs, thumb-screws, cowhides, chains, gags, and yokes.

A back-yard, enclosed by a high wall, looked like the playground attached to one of our large New England schools, in which were rows of benches and swings. Attached to the back premises was a good-sized kitchen, where, at the time of which we write, two old negresses were at work, stewing, boiling, and baking, and occasionally wiping the perspiration from their furrowed and swarthy brows.

The slave-trader, Walker, on his arrival at New Orleans, took up his quarters here, with his gang of human cattle, and the morning after, at ten o'clock, they were exhibited for sale. First of all, came the beautiful Marion, whose pale countenance and dejected look, told how many sad hours she had passed since parting with her mother. There, too, was a poor woman, who had been separated from her husband, and another woman, whose looks and manners were expressive of deep anguish, sat by her side. There was "Uncle Jeems," with his whiskers off, his face shaven clean, and the gray hairs plucked out, ready to be sold for ten years younger than he was. Toby was also there, with his face shaven and greased, ready for inspection.

The examination commenced, and was carried on in such a manner as to shock the feelings of any one not entirely devoid of the milk of human kindness.

"What are you wiping your eyes for?" inquired a fat, red-faced man, with a white hat set on one side of his head and a cigar in his mouth, of a woman who sat on one of the benches.

"Because I left my man behind."

"Oh, if I buy you, I will furnish you with a better man than you left. I've got lots of young bucks on my farm," responded the man.

"I don't want and never will have another man," replied the woman.

"What's your name?" asked a man, in a straw hat, of a tall negro, who stood with his arms folded across his breast, leaning against the wall.

"My name is Aaron, sar."

"How old are you?"

"Twenty-five."

"Where were you raised?"

"In ole Virginny, sar."

"How many men have owned you?"

"Four."

"Do you enjoy good health?"

"Yes, sar."

"How long did you live with your first owner?"

"Twenty years."
"Did you ever run away?"
"No, sar."
"Did you ever strike your master?"
"No sar."
"Were you ever whipped much?"
"No, sar; I spose I didn't desarve it, sar."
"How long did you live with your second master?"
"Ten years, sar."
"Have you a good appetite?"
"Yes, sar."
"Can you eat your allowance?"
"Yes, sar,—when I can get it."
"Where were you employed in Virginia?"
"I worked in de tobacker fiel'."
"In the tobacco field, eh?"
"Yes, sar."
"How old did you say you was?"
"Twenty-five, sar, nex' sweet-'tater-diggin' time."

"I am a cotton-planter, and if I buy you, you will have to work in the cotton field. My men pick one hundred and fifty pounds a day, and the women one hundred and forty pounds; and those who fail to perform their task receive five stripes for each pound that is wanting. Now do you think you could keep up with the rest of the hands?"

"I don't know, sar, but I reckon I'd have to."
"How long did you live with your third master?"
"Three years, sar," replied the slave.

"Why, that makes you thirty-three; I thought you told me you were only twenty-five."

Aaron now looked first at the planter, then at the trader, and seemed perfectly bewildered. He had forgotten the lesson given him by Pompey, relative to his age; and the planter's circuitous questions—doubtless to find out the slave's real age—had thrown the negro off his guard.

"I must see your back, so as to know how much you have been whipped, before I think of buying."

Pompey, who had been standing by during the examination, thought that his services were now required, and, stepping forth with a degree of officiousness, said to Aaron:—"Don't you hear de gemman tell you he wants to zamin you? Cum, unharness yo-seff, ole boy, an' don't be standin' dar."

Aaron was examined, and pronounced "sound"; yet the conflicting statement about his age was not satisfactory.

On the following trip down the river, Walker halted at Vicksburg, with a "prime lot of slaves," and a circumstance occurred which shows what the slaves in those days would resort to, to save themselves from flogging, while, at the same time, it exhibits the quick wit of the race.

While entertaining some of his purchasers at the hotel, Walker ordered Pompey to hand the wine around to his guests. In doing this, the servant upset a glass of wine upon a gentleman's lap. For this mishap, the trader determined to have his servant punished. He, therefore, gave Pompey a sealed note, and ordered him to take it to the slave prison. The servant, suspecting that all was not right, hastened to open the note before the wafer had dried; and passing the steamboat landing, he got a sailor to read the note, which proved to be, as Pompey had suspected, an order to have him receive "thirty-nine stripes upon the bare back."

Walker had given the man a silver dollar, with orders to deliver it, with the note, to the jailor, for it was common in those days for persons who wanted their servants punished and did not wish to do it themselves, to send them to the "slave pen," and have it done; the price for which was one dollar.

How to escape the flogging, and yet bring back to his master the evidence of having been punished, perplexed the fertile brain of Pompey. However, the servant was equal to the occasion. Standing in front of the "slave pen," the negro saw another well dressed colored man coming up the street, and he determined to inquire in regard to how they did the whipping there.

"How de do, sar," said Pompey, addressing the colored brother. "Do you live here?"

"Oh! no," replied the stranger, "I am a free man, and belong in Pittsburgh, Pa."

"Ah! ha, den you don't live here," said Pompey.

"No, I left my boat here last week, and I have been trying every day to get something to do. I'm pretty well out of money, and I'd do almost anything just now."

WALKER, THE SLAVE TRADER.

A thought flashed upon Pompey's mind—this was his occasion.

"Well," said the slave, "ef you want a job, whar you can make some money quick, I specks I can help you."

"If you will," replied the free man, "you'll do me a great favor."

"Here, then," said Pompey, " take dis note, an' go in to dat prison, dar, an' dey will give you a trunk, bring it out, an' I'll tell you where to carry it to, an' here's a dollar; dat will pay you, won't it?"

"Yes," replied the man, with many thanks; and taking the note and the shining coin, with smiles, he went to the "Bell Gate," and gave the bell a loud ring. The gate flew open, and in he went.

The man had scarcely disappeared, ere Pompey had crossed the street, and was standing at the gate, listening to the conversation then going on between the jailor and the free colored man.

"Where is the dollar that you got with this note?" asked the "*whipper*," as he finished reading the epistle.

"Here it is, sir; he gave it to me," said the man, with no little surprise.

"Hand it here," responded the jailor, in a rough voice. "There, now; take this nigger, Pete, and strap him down upon the stretcher, and get him ready for business."

"What are you going to do to me!" cried the horrified man, at the jailor's announcement.

"You'll know, damn quick!" was the response.

The resistance of the innocent man caused the "whipper" to call in three other sturdy blacks, and, in a few minutes, the victim was fastened upon the stretcher, face downwards, his clothing removed, and the strong-armed white negro-whipper standing over him with uplifted whip.

The cries and groans of the poor man, as the heavy instrument of torture fell upon his bare back, aroused Pompey, who retreated across the street, stood awaiting the result, and wondering if he could obtain, from the injured man, the receipt which the jailor always gives the slave to take back to his master as evidence of his having been punished.

As the gate opened, and the colored brother made his appearance, looking wildly about for Pompey, the latter called out, "Here I is, sar!"

Maddened by the pain from the excoriation of his bleeding back, and the surprise and astonishment at the quickness with which the whole thing had been accomplished, the man ran across the street, upbraiding in the most furious manner his deceiver, who also appeared amazed at the epithets bestowed upon him.

"What have I done to you?" asked Pompey, with a seriousness that was indeed amusing.

"What hain't you done!" said the man, the tears streaming down his face. "You've got my back cut all to pieces," continued the victim.

"What did you let 'em whip you for?" said Pompey, with a concealed smile.

"You knew that note was to get somebody whipped, and you put it on me. And here is a piece of paper that he gave me, and told me to give it to my master. Just as if I had a master."

"Well," responded Pompey, "I have a half a dollar, an' I'll give that to you, ef you'll give me the paper."

Seeing that he could make no better bargain, the man gave up the receipt, taking in exchange the silver coin.

"Now," said Pompey, "I'm mighty sorry for ye, an' ef ye'll go down to de house, I'll pray for ye. I'm powerful in prayer, dat I is." However the free man declined Pompey's offer.

"I reckon you'll behave yourself and not spill the wine over gentlemen again," said Walker, as Pompey handed him the note from the jailor. "The next time you commit such a blunder, you'll not get off so easy," continued the speculator.

Pompey often spoke of the appearance of "my fren'," as he called the colored brother, and would enjoy a hearty laugh, saying, "He was a free man, an' could afford to go to bed, an' lay dar till he got well."

Strangers to the institution of slavery, and its effects upon its victims, would frequently speak with astonishment of the pride that slaves would show in regard to their own value in the market. This was especially so, at auction sales where town or city servants were sold.

"What did your marser pay for you?" would often be asked by one slave of another.

"Eight hundred dollars."

"Eight hundred dollars! Ha, ha! Well, ef I didn't sell for mo' dan eight hundred dollars, I'd neber show my head agin 'mong 'spectable people."

"You got so much to say 'bout me sellin' cheap, now I want to know how much your boss paid fer you?"

"My boss paid fifteen hundred dollars cash, for me; an' it was a rainy day, an' not many out to de auction, or he'd had to pay a heap mo', let me tell you. I'm none of your cheap niggers, I ain't."

"Hy, uncle! Did dey sell you, 'isterday? I see you down dar to de market."

"Yes, dey sole me."

"How much did you fetch?"

"Eighteen hundred dollars."

"Dat was putty smart fer man like you, ain't it?"

"Well, I dunno; it's no mo' dan I is wuf; fer you muss' 'member, I was raised by de Christy's. I'm none of yer common niggers, sellin' fer a picayune. I tink my new boss got me mighty cheap."

"An' so you sole, las' Sataday, fer nine hundred dollars; so I herd."

"Well, what on it?"

"All I got to say is, ef I was sole, to-morrow, an' did'nt bring more dan nine hundred dollars, I'd never look a decent man in de face agin."

These, and other sayings of the kind, were often heard in any company of colored men, in our Southern towns.

CHAPTER XII.

THROUGHOUT the Southern States, there are still to be found remnants of the old time Africans, who were stolen from their native land and sold in the Savannah, Mobile, and New Orleans markets, in defiance of all law. The last-named city, however, and its vicinity, had a larger portion of these people than any other section. New Orleans was their centre, and where their meetings were not uninteresting.

Congo Square takes its name, as is well known, from the Congo negroes who used to perform their dance on its sward every Sunday. They were a curious people, and brought over with them this remnant of their African jungles. In Louisiana there were six different tribes of negroes, named after the section of the country from which they came, and their representatives could be seen on the square, their teeth filed, and their cheeks still bearing tattoo marks. The majority of our city negroes came from the Kraels, a numerous tribe who dwell in stockades. We had here the Minahs, a proud, dignified, warlike race; the Congos, a treacherous, shrewd, relentless people; the Mandringas, a branch of the Congos; the Gangas, named after the river of that name, from which they had been taken; the Hiboas, called by the missionaries the "Owls," a sullen, intractable tribe, and the Foulas, the highest type of the African, with but few representatives here.

These were the people that one would meet on the square many years ago. It was a gala occasion, these Sundays in those years, and not less than two or three thousand people would congregate there to see the dusky dancers. A low fence enclosed the square, and on each street there was a little gate and turnstile. There were no trees then, and the ground was worn bare by the feet of the people. About three o'clock the negroes began to gather, each nation taking their places in different parts of the square. The Minahs would not dance near the Congos, nor the Mandringas near the Gangas. Presently the music would strike up, and the parties would prepare for the sport. Each set had its own orchestra. The instruments were a peculiar kind of banjo, made of a Louisiana gourd, several drums made of a gum stump dug out, with a sheepskin head, and beaten with the fingers, and two jaw-bones of a horse, which when shaken would rattle the loose teeth, keeping time with the drums. About eight negroes, four male and four female, would make a set, and generally they were but scantily clad.

It took some little time before the tapping of the drums would arouse the dull and sluggish dancers, but when the point of excitement came, nothing can faithfully portray the wild and frenzied motions they go through. Backward and forward, this way and that, now together and now apart, every motion intended to convey the most sensual ideas. As the dance progressed, the drums were thrummed faster, the contortions became more grotesque, until sometimes, in frenzy, the women and men would fall fainting to the ground. All this was going on with a dense crowd looking on, and with a hot sun pouring its torrid rays on the infatuated actors of this curious ballet. After one set had become fatigued, they would drop out to be replaced by others, and then stroll off to the groups of some other tribe in a different portion of the square. Then it was that trouble would commence, and a regular set-to with short sticks followed, between the men, and broken heads ended the day's entertainment.

On the sidewalks, around the square, the old negresses, with their spruce-beer and peanuts, cocoa-nuts and pop-corn, did a thriving trade, and now and then, beneath petticoats, bottles of tafia, a kind of Louisiana rum, peeped out, of which the *gendarmes* were oblivious. When the sun went down, a stream of people poured out of the turn-stiles, and the *gendarmes*, walking through the square, would order the dispersion of the negroes, and by gun-fire, at nine o'clock, the place was well-nigh deserted. These dances were kept up until within the memory of men still living, and many who believe in them, and who would gladly revive them, may be found in every State in the Union.

The early traditions, brought down through the imported Africans, have done much to keep alive the belief that the devil is a personal being, with hoofs, horns, and having powers equal with God. These ideas give influence to the conjurer, goopher doctor, and fortune-teller.

While visiting one of the upper parishes, not long since, I was stopping with a gentleman who was accustomed to make weekly visits to a neighboring cemetery, sitting for hours amongst the graves, at which occurrence the wife felt very sad.

I inquired of her the object of her husband's strange freak.

"Oh!" said she, "he's influenced out there by angels."

"Has he gone to the cemetery now?" I asked.

"Yes," was the reply.

"I think I can cure him of it, if you will promise to keep the whole thing a secret."

"I will," was the reply.

"Let me have a sheet, and unloose your dog, and I will put the cure in motion," I said. Rolla, the big Newfoundland dog, was unfastened, the sheet was well fitted around his neck, tightly sewed, and the pet told to go hunt his master.

Taking the trail, the dog at once made for the cemetery. Screams of "Help, help! God save me!" coming from the direction of the tombs, aroused the neighborhood. The cries of the man frightened the dog, and he returned home in haste; the sheet, half torn, was removed, and Rolla again fastened in his house.

Very soon Mr. Martin was led in by two friends, who picked him up from the sidewalk, with his face considerably bruised. His story was, that "The devil had chased him out of the cemetery, tripped him up on the sidewalk, and hence the flow of blood from the wound on his face."

The above is a fair index to most of the ghost stories.

CHAPTER XIII.

FORTY years ago, the escapes of slaves from the South, although numerous, were nevertheless difficult, owing to the large rewards offered for their apprehension, and the easy mode of extradition from the Northern States. Little or no difficulty was experienced in capturing and returning a slave from Ohio, Indiana, Illinois, or Pennsylvania, the four States through which the fugitives had to pass in their flight to Canada. The Quaker element in all of the above States showed itself in the furnishing of food to the flying bondman, concealing him for days, and even weeks, and at last conveying him to a place of safety, or carrying him to the Queen's dominions.

Instinct seemed to tell the negro that a drab coat and a broad-brimmed hat covered a benevolent heart, and we have no record of his ever having been deceived. It is possible that the few Friends scattered over the slave States, and the fact that they were never known to own a slave, gave the blacks a favorable impression of this sect, before the victim of oppression left his sunny birth-place.

A brave and manly slave resolved to escape from Natchez, Miss. This slave, whose name was Jerome, was of pure African origin, was perfectly black, very fine-looking, tall, slim, and erect as any one could possibly be. His features were not bad, lips thin, nose prominent, hands and feet small. His brilliant black eyes lighted up his whole countenance. His hair, which was nearly straight, hung in curls upon his lofty brow. George Combe or Fowler would have selected his head for a model. He was brave and daring, strong in person, fiery in spirit, yet kind and true in his affections, earnest in whatever he undertook.

To reach the free States or Canada, by travelling by night and lying by during the day, from a State so far south as Mississippi, no one would think for a moment of attempting to escape. To remain in the city would be a suicidal step. The deep sound of the escape of steam from a boat, which was at that moment ascending the river, broke upon the ears of the slave. "If that boat is going up the river," said he, "why not I conceal myself on board, and try to escape?" He went at once to the steamboat landing, where the boat was just coming in.

"Bound for Louisville," said the captain, to one who was making inquiries. As the passengers were rushing on board, Jerome followed them, and proceeding to where some of the hands were stowing away bales of goods, he took hold and aided them.

"Jump down into the hold, there, and help the men," said the mate to the fugitive, supposing that, like many persons, he was working his way up the river. Once in the hull, among the boxes, the slave concealed himself. Weary hours, and at last days, passed without either water or food with the hidden slave. More than once did he resolve to let his case be known; but the knowledge that he would be sent back to Natchez, kept him from doing so. At last, with his lips parched and fevered to a crisp, the poor man crawled out into the freight-room, and began wandering about. The hatches were on, and the room dark. There happened to be on board, a wedding-party; and a box, containing some of the bridal cake, with several bottles of port wine, was near Jerome. He found the box, opened it, and helped himself. In eight days, the boat tied up at the wharf at the place of her destination. It was late at night; the boat's crew, with the single exception of the man on watch, were on shore. The hatches were off, and the fugitive quietly made his way on deck and jumped on shore. The man saw the fugitive, but too late to seize him.

Still in a slave State, Jerome was at a loss to know how he should proceed. He had with him a few dollars, enough to pay his way to Canada, if he could find a conveyance. The fugitive procured such food as he wanted from one of the many eating-houses, and then, following the direction of the North Star, he passed out of the city, and took the road leading to Covington. Keeping near the Ohio River, Jerome soon found an opportunity to pass over into the State of Indiana. But liberty was a mere name in the latter State, and the fugitive learned, from some colored persons that he met, that it was not safe to travel by daylight. While making his way one night, with nothing to cheer him but the prospect of freedom in the future, he was pounced upon by three men who were lying in wait for another fugitive, an advertisement of whom they had received through the mail. In vain did Jerome tell them that he was not a slave. True, they had not caught the man they expected; but, if they could make this slave tell from what place he had escaped, they knew that a good price would be paid them for the slave's arrest.

Tortured by the slave-catchers, to make him reveal the name of his owner and the place from whence he had escaped, Jerome gave them a fictitious name in Virginia, and said that his master would give a large reward, and manifested a willingness to return to his "old boss."

By this misrepresentation, the fugitive hoped to have another chance of getting away.

Allured with the prospect of a large sum of the needful the slave-catchers started back with their victim. Stopping on the second night at an inn, on the banks of the Ohio River, the kidnappers, in lieu of a suitable place in which to confine their prize during the night, chained him to the bed-post of their sleeping chamber.

The white men were late in retiring to rest, after an evening spent in drinking. At dead of night, when all was still, the slave arose from the floor, upon which he had been lying, looked around and saw that Morpheus had possession of his captors. "For once," thought he, "the brandy bottle has done a noble work." With palpitating heart and trembling limbs, he viewed his position. The door was fast, but the warm weather had compelled them to leave the window open. If he could but get the chains off, he might escape through the window to the piazza. The sleepers' clothes hung upon chairs by the bedside. The slave thought of the padlock key, examined the pockets, and found it. The chains were soon off, and the negro stealthily making his way to the window. He stopped, and said to himself, "These men are villains, they are enemies to all who, like me, are trying to be free. Then why not teach them a lesson?" He then dressed himself in the best suit, hung his own worn-out and tattered garments on the same chair, and silently passed through the window to the piazza, and let himself down by one of the pillars, and started once more for Canada.

Daylight came upon him before he had selected a hiding-place for the day, and he was walking at a rapid rate, in hopes of soon reaching some woodland or forest. The sun had just begun to show itself, when Jerome was astonished at seeing behind him, in the distance, two men upon horseback. Taking a road to the right he saw before him a farmhouse, and so near was he to it that he observed two men in front of him looking at him. It was too late to turn back. The kidnappers were behind—strange men before. Those in the rear he knew to be enemies, while he had no idea of what principles were the farmers. The latter also saw the white men coming, and called to the fugitive to come that way.

The broad-brimmed hats that the farmers wore told the slaves that they were Quakers.

Jerome had seen some of these people passing up and down the river, when employed on a steamer between Natchez and New Orleans, and had heard that they disliked slavery. He, therefore, hastened toward the drab-coated men who, on his approach, opened the barn-door, and told him to "run in."

When Jerome entered the barn, the two farmers closed the door, remaining outside themselves, to confront the slave-catchers, who now came up and demanded admission, feeling that they had their prey secure.

"Thee can't enter my premises," said one of the Friends, in rather a musical voice.

The negro-catchers urged their claim to the slave, and intimated that, unless they were allowed to secure him, they would force their way in. By this time, several other Quakers had gathered around the barn-door. Unfortunately for the kidnappers, and most fortunately for the fugitive, the Friends had just been holding a quarterly meeting in the neighborhood, and a number of them had not yet returned to their homes.

After some talk, the men in drab promised to admit the hunters, provided they procured an officer and a search-warrant from a justice of the peace. One of the slave-catchers was left to see that the fugitive did not get away, while the other went in pursuit of an officer. In the mean time, the owner of the barn sent for a hammer and nails, and began nailing up the barn-door.

After an hour in search of the man of the law, they returned with an officer and a warrant. The Quaker demanded to see the paper, and, after looking at it for some time, called to his son to go into the house for his glasses. It was a long time before Aunt Ruth found the leather case, and when she did, the glasses wanted wiping before they could be used. After comfortably adjusting them on his nose, he read the warrant over leisurely.

"Come, Mr. Dugdale, we can't wait all day," said the officer.

"Well, will thee read it for me?" returned the Quaker.

The officer complied, and the man in drab said,—"Yes, thee may go in, now. I am inclined to throw no obstacles in the way of the execution of the law of the land."

On approaching the door, the men found some forty or fifty nails in it, in the way of their progress.

"Lend me your hammer and a chisel, if you please, Mr. Dugdale," said the officer.

"Please read that paper over again, will thee?" asked the Quaker.

The officer once more read the warrant.

"I see nothing there which says I must furnish thee with tools to open my door. If thee wants a hammer, thee must go elsewhere for it; I tell thee plainly, thee can't have mine."

The implements for opening the door are at length obtained, and, after another half hour, the slave-catchers are in the barn. Three hours is a long time for a slave to be in the hands of Quakers. The hay is turned over, and the barn is visited in every part; but still the runaway is not found. Uncle Joseph has a glow upon his countenance; Ephraim shakes his head knowingly; little Elijah is a perfect know-nothing, and if you look toward the house you will see Aunt Ruth's smiling face ready to announce that breakfast is ready.

"The nigger is not in this barn," said the officer.

"I know he is not," quietly remarked the Quaker.

"What were you nailing up your door for, then, as if you were afraid we would enter?" inquired one of the kidnappers.

"I can do what I please with my own door, can't I?" said the Friend.

The secret was out; the fugitive had gone in at the front door, and out at the back; and the reading of the warrant, nailing up of the door, and other preliminaries of the Quaker, was to give the fugitive time and opportunity to escape.

It was now late in the morning, and the slave-catchers were a long way from home, and the horses were jaded by the rapid manner in which they had travelled. The Friends, in high glee, returned to the house for breakfast; the officer and the kidnappers made a thorough examination of the barn and premises, and satisfied that Jerome had gone into the barn, but had not come out, and equally satisfied that he was out of their reach, the owner said, "He's gone down into the earth, and has taken an underground railroad."

And thus was christened that famous highway over which so many of the oppressed sons and daughters of African descent were destined to travel, and an account of which has been published by one of its most faithful agents, Mr. William Still, of Philadelphia.

At a later period, Cato, servant of Dr. Gaines, was sold to Captain Enoch Price, of St. Louis. The Captain took his slave with him on board the steamer *Chester*, just about sailing for New Orleans. At the latter place, the boat obtained a cargo for Cincinnati, Ohio. The master, aware that the slave might give him the slip, while in a free State, determined to leave the chattel at Louisville, Ky., till his downward return. However, Mrs. Price, anxious to have the servant's services on the boat, questioned him with regard to the contemplated visit to Cincinnati.

"I don't want to go to a free State," said Cato; "fer I knowed a servant dat went up dar, once, an' dey kept beggin' him to run away; so I druther not go dar; kase I is satisfied wid my marser, an' don't want to go off, whar I'd have to take keer of mysef."

This was said in such an earnest and off-hand manner, that it removed all of the lady's suspicions in regard to his attempting to escape; and she urged her husband to take him to Ohio.

Cato wanted his freedom, but he well knew that if he expressed a wish to go to a free State, he would never be permitted to do so. In due season, the *Chester* arrived at Cincinnati, where she remained four days, discharging her cargo, and reloading for the return trip. During the time, Cato remained at his post, attending faithfully to his duties; no one dreaming that he had the slightest idea of leaving the boat. However, on the day previous to the *Chester's* leaving Cincinnati, Cato divulged the question to Charley, another slave, whom he wished to accompany him.

Charley heard the proposition with surprise; and although

he wanted his freedom, his timid disposition would not allow him to make the trial.

"My master is a pretty good man, and treats me comparatively well; and should I be caught and taken back, he would no doubt sell me to a cotton or sugar-planter," said Charley to Cato's invitation. "But," continued he, "Captain Price is a mean man; I shall not blame you, Cato, for running away and leaving him. By the by, I am engaged to go to a surprise-party, to-night, and I reckon we'll have a good time. I've got a new pair of pumps to dance in, and I've got Jim, the cook, to bake me a pie, and I'll have some sandwiches, and I'm going with a pretty gal."

"So you won't go away with me, to-night?" said Cato to Charley.

"No," was the reply.

"It is true," remarked Cato, "your marser is a better man, an' treats you a heap better den Captain Price does me, but, den, he may get to gambling, an' get broke, and den he'll have to sell you."

"I know that," replied Charley; "none of us are safe as long as we are slaves."

It was seven o'clock at night, Cato was in the pantry, washing the supper dishes, and contemplating his flight, the beginning of which was soon to take place. Charley had gone up to the steward's hall, to get ready for the surprise, and had been away some time, which caused uneasiness to Cato, and he determined to go up into the cabin, and see that everything was right. Entering the cabin from the Social Hall, Cato, in going down and passing the Captain's room, heard a conversation which attracted his attention, and caused him to halt at his master's room door.

He was not long, although the conversation was in a low tone, in learning that the parties were his master and his fellow-servant Charley.

"And so he is going to run away, to-night, is he?" said the Captain.

"Yes, sir," replied Charley; "he's been trying to get me to go with him, and I thought it my duty to tell you."

"Very well; I'll take him over to Covington, Ky., put him

in jail, for the night, and when I get back to New Orleans, I will sell the ungrateful nigger. Where is he now?" asked the Captain.

"Cato is in the pantry, sir, washing up the tea-things," was the reply.

The moving of the chairs in the room, and what he had last heard, satisfied Cato that the talk between his master and the treacherous Charley was at an end, and he at once returned to the pantry undetermined what course to pursue. He had not long been there, ere he heard the well-known squeak of the Captain's boots coming down the stairs. Just then Dick, the cook's boy, came out of the kitchen and threw a pan full of cold meat overboard. This incident seemed to furnish Cato with words, and he at once took advantage of the situation.

"What is dat you throw overboard dar?"

"None your business," replied Dick, as he slammed the door behind him and returned to the kitchen.

"You free niggers will waste everything dar is on dis boat," continued Cato. "It's my duty to watch dees niggers an' see dat dey don't destroy marser's property. Now, let me see, I'll go right off an' tell marser 'bout Charley, I won't keep his secrets any longer." And here Cato threw aside his dish towel and started for the cabin.

Captain Price, who, during Cato's soliloquy, was hid behind a large box of goods, returned in haste to his room, where he was soon joined by his dutiful servant.

In answer to the rap on the door, the Captain said "Come in."

Cato, with downcast look, and in an obsequious manner, entered the room, and said, "Marser, I is come to tell you somethin' dat hangs heavy on my mine, somethin' dat I had ought to tole you afore dis."

"Well," said the master, "what is it, Cato?"

"Now, marser, you hires Charley, don't you?"

"Yes."

"Well, den, ser, ef Charley runs away you'll have to pay fer him, won't you?"

"I think it very probable, as I brought him into a free State,—and thereby giving him an opportunity to escape. Why, is he thinking of running away?"

"Yes, ser," answered Cato, "he's gwine to start to-night, an' he's bin pesterin' me all day to go wid him."

"Do you mean to say that Charley has been trying to persuade you to run away from me?" asked the Captain, rather sharply.

"Yes, ser, dats jess what he's bin a doin' all day. I axed him whar he's gwine to, an' he sed he's gwine to Canada, an' he call you some mighty mean names, an' dat made me mad."

"Why, Charley has just been here telling me that you were going to run away to-night."

With apparent surprise, and opening his large eyes, Cato exclaimed, "Well, well, well, ef dat nigger don't beat de debble!" And here the negro raised his hands, and looking upward said, "Afoe God, marser, I would'nt leave you fer dis worl'. Now, ser, jess let me tell you how you can find out who tells de trufe. Charley has got ebry ting ready an' is a gwine right off. He's got two pies, some sweet-cake, some sandwiches, bread an' butter, an' he's got a pair of pumps to dance in when he gets to Canada. An' ef you want to kotch him in de ack of runnin' away, you jess wait out on de dock an' you'll kotch him."

This was said in such an earnest manner, and with such protestations of innocence, that Captain Price determined to follow Cato's advice and watch for Charley.

"Go see if you can find where Charley is, and come back and let me know," said the Captain.

Away went Cato, on his tip-toes, in the direction of the steward's room, where, by looking through the key-hole, he saw the treacherous fellow-servant getting ready for the surprise party that he had engaged the night previous to attend.

Cato returned almost breathless, and in a whisper said, "I foun' him ser, he's gittin' ready to start. He's got a bundle of provisions tied up all ready, ser; you'll be shur to kotch him as he's gwine away, ef you go on de dock."

Throwing his camlet cloak over his shoulders, the Captain passed out upon the wharf, took a position behind a pile of wood, and awaited the coming of the negro; nor did he remain long in suspense.

With lighted cigar, dressed in his best apparel, and his eatables tied up in a towel, Charley was soon seen hastily leaving the boat.

Stepping out from his hiding-place, the Captain seized the negro by the collar and led him back to the steamer, exclaiming, "Where are you going, what's that you've got in that bundle?"

"Only some washin' I is takin' out to get done," replied the surprised and frightened negro.

As they reached the lighted deck, "Open that bundle," said the Captain.

Charley began to obey the command, and at the same time to give an explanation.

"Shut your mouth, you scoundrel," vociferously shouted the Captain.

As the man slowly undid the parcel, and the contents began to be seen, "There," said the Captain, "there's the pies, cake, sandwiches, bread and butter that Cato told me you had put up to eat while running away. Yes, there's the pumps, too, that you got to dance in when you reached Canada."

Here the frightened Charley attempted again to explain, "I was jess gwine to—"

"Shut your mouth, you villain; you were going to escape to Canada."

"No, Marser Price, afoe God I was only—"

"Shut your mouth, you black rascal; you told me you were taking some clothes to be washed, you lying scamp."

During this scene, Cato was inside the pantry, with the door ajar, looking out upon his master and Charley with unfeigned satisfaction.

Still holding the negro by the collar, and leading him to the opposite side of the boat, the Captain called to Mr. Roberts, the second mate, to bring up the small boat to take him and the "runaway" over the river.

A few moments more, and the Captain, with Charley seated by his side, was being rowed to Covington, where the negro was safely locked up for the night.

"A little longer," said the Captain to the second officer, as he returned to the boat, "a little longer and I'd a lost fifteen hundred dollars by that boy's running away."

"Indeed," responded the officer.

"Yes," continued the Commander, "my servant Cato told me, just in time to catch the rascal in the very act of running off."

One of the sailors who was rowing, and who had been attentively listening to the Captain, said, "I overheard Cato today, trying to persuade Charley to go somewhere with him to-night, and the latter said he was going to a 'surprise party.'"

"The devil you did," exclaimed the Captain. "Hasten up there," continued he, "for these niggers are a slippery set."

As the yawl came alongside of the steamer, Captain Price leaped on deck and went directly in search of Cato, who could nowhere be found. And even Charley's bundle, which he left where he had been opening it, was gone. All search for the tricky man was in vain.

On the following morning, Charley was brought back to the boat, saying, as they were crossing the river, "I tole de boss dat Cato was gwine to run away, but he did'nt bleve me. Now he sees Cato's gone."

After the Captain had learned all that he could from Charley, the latter's account of his imprisonment in the lock-up caused great merriment amongst the boat's crew.

"But I tell you dar was de biggest rats in dat jail, eber I seed in my life. Dey run aroun' dar an' make so much fuss dat I was 'fraid to set down or lay down. I had to stan' up all night."

The *Chester* was detained until in the latter part of the day, during which time every effort was made to hunt up Cato, but without success.

When upbraided by the black servants on the boat for his treachery to Cato, Charley's only plea was, "I 'speck it was de debble dat made me do it."

Dressing himself in his warmest and best clothes, and getting some provisions that he had prepared during the day, and also taking with him Charley's pies, cakes, sandwiches, and pumps, Cato left the boat and made good his escape before his master returned from Covington.

It was during the cold winter of 1834, that the fugitive travelled by night and laid by in the woods in the day. After a week's journey, his food gave out, and then came the severest of his trials, cold coupled with hunger.

Often Cato would resolve to go to some of the farm-houses and apply for food and shelter, but the fear of being captured and again returned prevented him from following his inclinations. One night a pelting rain that froze as fast as it fell, drove the fugitive into a barn, where, creeping under the hay, he remained, sleeping sweetly while his garments were drying upon his person.

Sounds of the voices of the farmer and his men feeding the cattle and doing the chores, awakened the man from his slumbers, who, seeing that it was daylight, feared he would be arrested. However, the day passed, and the fugitive coming out at nightfall, started once more on his weary journey, taking for his guide the North Star, and after travelling the entire night, he again lay by, but this time in the forest.

Three days of fasting had now forced hunger upon Cato, so that he once more determined to seek food. Waiting till night, he came upon the highway, and soon approached a farmhouse, of the olden style, built of logs. The sweet savor of the supper attracted the hungry man's attention as he neared the dwelling. For once there was no dog to herald his coming, and he had an opportunity of viewing the interior of the house, through the apertures that a log cabin generally presents.

As the fugitive stood with one eye gazing through the *crack*, looking at the table, already set, and snuffing in the delicious odor from a boiling pot, he heard the mother say,—"Take off the chicken, Sally Ann, I guess the dumplings are done. Your father will be home in half an hour; if he should catch that nigger and bring him along, we'll feed him on the cold meat and potatoes."

With palpitating heart, Cato listened to the last sentences that fell from the woman's lips. Who could the "nigger" be, thought he.

Finding only the woman and her daughter in the house, the black man had been debating in his own mind whether or not to go in and demand a part of the contents of the kettle. However, the talk about "catching a nigger," settled the question at once with him.

Seizing a sheet that hung upon the clothes-line, Cato covered himself with it; leaving open only enough to enable him to see, he rushed in, crying at the top of his voice,—"Come to judgment! Come to judgment."

Both women sprang from their seats, and, screaming, passed out of the room, upsetting the table as they went. Cato seized the pot of chicken with one hand, and a loaf of bread, that had fallen from the table, with the other; hastily leaving the house and taking to the road, he continued on his journey.

The fugitive, however, had gone but a short distance when he heard the tramp of horses and the voices of men; and, fearing to meet them, he took to the woods till they had passed by.

As he hid behind a large tree by the roadside, Cato heard distinctly:

"And what is your master's name?"

"Peter Johnson, ser," was the reply.

"How much do you think he will give to have you brought back?"

"Dunno, ser," responded a voice which Cato recognized by the language to be a negro.

It was evident that a fugitive slave had been captured, and was about to be returned for the reward. And it was equally evident to Cato that the slave had been caught by the owner of the pot of stewed chicken that he then held in his hand, and he felt a thrill of gladness as he returned to the road and pursued his journey.

CHAPTER XIV.

In the year 1850, there were fifty thousand free colored people in the slave States, the greater number residing in Louisiana, Maryland, Virginia, Tennessee, and South Carolina. In all the States these people were allowed but few privileges not given to the slaves; and in many their condition was thought to be even worse than that of the bondmen. Laws, the most odious, commonly known as the "Black Code," were enacted and enforced in every State. These provided for the punishment of the free colored people—punishment which was not mentioned in the common law for white persons; for binding out minors, a species of slavery, and naming thirty-two offences more for blacks than had been enacted for the whites, and eight of which made it capital punishment for the offences committed.

Public opinion, which is often stronger than law, was severe in the extreme. In many of the Southern cities, including Charleston, S. C., a colored lady, free, and owning the fine house in which she lived, was not allowed to wear a veil in the public streets.

In passing through the thoroughfares, blacks of both sexes were compelled to take the outside, on pain of being kicked into the street, or sent to the lock-up and whipped.

As late as 1858, a movement was made in several of the Southern States to put an exorbitant tax upon them, and in lieu of which they were to be sold into life-long slavery. Maryland led off with a bill being introduced into the Legislature by Mr. Hover, of Frederick County, for levying a tax of two dollars per annum on all colored male inhabitants of the State over twenty-one years of age, and under fifty-five, and of one dollar on every female over eighteen and under forty-five, to be collected by the collectors of the State taxes, and *devoted to the use of the Colonization Society.* In case of the refusal to pay of a property-holder or housekeeper, his or her goods were to be seized and sold; if not a property-holder, the body of the non-paying person was to be seized, and hired out to the lowest bidder who would agree to pay the tax; and in case of not being able to hire said delinquents out, they were to be sold to any person who would pay the amount of tax and costs for the lowest period of service!

Tennessee followed in the same strain. The annexed protest of one of her noblest sons,—Judge Catron, appeared at the time. He said:

"My objection to the bill is, *that it proposes to commit an outrage, to perpetrate an oppression and cruelty.* This is the plain truth, and it is idle to mince words to soften the fact. Let us look the proposition boldly in the face. This depressed and helpless portion of our population is designed to be driven out, or to be enslaved for life, and their property forfeited, as no slave can hold property. The mothers are to be sold, or driven away from their children, many of them infants. The children are to be bound out until they are twenty-one years of age, and then to leave the State or be sold; which means that they are to be made slaves for life, in fact. Now, of these women and children, there is hardly one in ten that is of unmixed negro blood. Some are half-white; many have half-white mothers and white fathers, making a cast of 87 1-2–100ths of white blood; many have a third cross, in whom the negro blood is almost extinct; such is the unfortunate truth. This description of people, who were born free, and lived as free persons, are to be introduced as slaves into our families, or into our negro quarters, there to be under an overseer, or they are to be sold to the negro-trader and sent South, there to be whipped by overseers—*and to preach rebellion* in the negro quarters—as they will *preach* rebellion everywhere that they may be driven to by this unjust law, whether it be amongst us here in Tennessee or south of us on the cotton and sugar plantations, or in the abolition meetings in the free States. Nor will the women be the least effective in preaching a crusade, when begging money in the North, to relieve their children, left behind in this State, in bondage.

"We are told that this 'free-negro bill' is a politic, popular measure. Where is it popular? *In what nook or corner of the State are principles of humanity so deplorably deficient that a majority of the whole inhabitants would commit an outrage not committed in a Christian country of which history gives any account?* In what country is it, this side of Africa, that the majority have enslaved the minority, sold the weak to the strong, and applied the proceeds of the sale to educate the children of the stronger side, as this bill proposes? It is an open assertion that 'might makes right.' It is re-opening the African slave trade. In that trade the strong capture the weak, and sell them; and so it will be here, if this policy is carried out."

In some of the States the law was enacted and the people driven out or sold. Those who were able to pay their way out, came away; those who could not raise the means, were doomed to languish in bondage till released by the Rebellion.

About the same time, in Georgia, Florida, and South Carolina, strong efforts were being made to re-open the African slave trade. At the Democratic State Convention, held in the city of Charleston, S. C., May 1, 1860, Mr. Gaulden made the following speech:—

"MR. PRESIDENT, AND FELLOW DEMOCRATS:—As I stated to you a few moments ago, I have been confined to my room by severe indisposition, but learning of the commotion and the intense excitement which were existing upon the questions before this body, I felt it to be my duty, feeble as I was, to drag myself out to the meeting of my delegation, and when there I was surprised to find a large majority of that delegation voting to secede at once from this body. I disagree with those gentlemen. I regret to disagree with my brethren from the South upon any of the great questions which interest our common country. I am a Southern States' Rights man; I am an African slave-trader. I believe I am one of those Southern men who believe that slavery is right, morally, religiously, socially, and politically. (Applause.) I believe that the institution of slavery has done more for this country, more for civilization, than all other interests put together. I believe if it were in the power of this country to strike down the institution of slavery, it would put civilization back two hundred years. I tell you, fellow Democrats, that the African slave-trader is the true Union man. (Cheers and laughter.) I tell you that the slave-trading of Virginia is more immoral, more un-Christian in every possible point of view, than that African slave-trade which goes to Africa and brings a heathen and worthless man here, makes him a useful man, Christianizes him, and sends him and his posterity down the stream of time to join in the blessings of civilization. (Cheers and laughter.) Now, fellow-democrats, so far as any public expression of opinion of the State of Virginia—the great slave-trading State of Virginia—has been given, they are all opposed to the African slave-trade."

DR. REED, of Indiana.—I am from Indiana, and I am in favor of it.

MR. GAULDEN.—Now, gentlemen, we are told, upon high authority, that there is a certain class of men who strain at a gnat and swallow a camel. Now, Virginia, which authorizes the buying of Christian men, separating them from their wives and children, from all the relations and associations amid whom they have lived for years, rolls up her eyes in holy horror when I would go to Africa, buy a savage, and introduce him to the blessings of civilization and Christianity. (Cheers and laughter.)

MR. RYNDERS, of New York.—You can get one or two recruits from New York to join with you.

THE PRESIDENT.—The time of the gentleman has expired. (Cries of "Go on! go on!")

The President stated that if it was the unanimous wish of the Convention, the gentleman could proceed.

MR. GAULDEN.—Now, fellow Democrats, the slave-trade in

Virginia forms a mighty and powerful reason for its opposition to the African slave-trade, and in this remark I do not intend any disrespect to my friends from Virginia. Virginia, the Mother of States and of statesmen, the Mother of Presidents, I apprehend, may err as well as other mortals. I am afraid that her error in this regard lies in the promptings of the almighty dollar. It has been my fortune to go into that noble old State to buy a few darkies, and I have had to pay from one thousand to two thousand dollars a head, when I could go to Africa and buy better negroes for fifty dollars a-piece. (Great laughter.) Now, unquestionably, it is to the interests of Virginia to break down the African slave-trade when she can sell her negroes at two thousand dollars. She knows that the African slave-trade would break up her monopoly, and hence her objection to it. If any of you Northern Democrats—for I have more faith in you than I have in the Carpet Knight Democracy of the South—will go home with me to my plantation in Georgia, but a little way from here, I will show you some darkies that I bought in Maryland, some that I bought in Virginia, some in Delaware, some in Florida, some in North Carolina, and I will also show you the pure African, the noblest Roman of them all. (Great laughter.) Now, fellow Democrats, my feeble health and failing voice admonish me to bring the few remarks I have to make to a close. (Cries of "Go on! go on!") I am only sorry that I am not in better condition than I am to vindicate before you to-day the words of truth, of honesty, and of right, and to show you the gross inconsistencies of the South in this regard. I came from the First Congressional District of the State of Georgia. I represent the African slave-trade interests of that section. (Applause.) I am proud of the position I occupy in that respect. I believe that the African slave-trader is a true missionary, and a true Christian. (Applause.)

Such was the feeling in a large part of the South, with regard to the enslavement of the negro.

CHAPTER XV.

THE success of the slave-holders in controlling the affairs of the National Government for a long series of years, furnishing a large majority of the Presidents, Speakers of the House of Representatives, Foreign Ministers, and moulding the entire policy of the nation in favor of slave-holding, and the admitted fact that none could secure an office in the national Government who were known to be opposed to the *peculiar* institution, made the Southerners feel themselves superior to the people of the free States. This feeling was often manifested by an outburst of intemperate language, which frequently showed itself in the pulpit, on the rostrum, and in the drawing-room. On all such occasions the placing of the institution of slavery above liberty, seemed to be the aim of its advocates.

"The principle of slavery is in itself right, and *does not depend on difference of complexion*,"—said the Richmond (Va.) *Enquirer*.

A distinguished Southern statesman exclaimed,—

"Make the laboring man the slave of *one* man, instead of the slave of society, and he would be far better off." "Slavery, *black or white*, is right and necessary." "*Nature has made the weak in mind or body for slaves.*"

Another said:—

"*Free* society! We sicken of the name. What is it but a conglomeration of *greasy mechanics*, *filthy operators*, *small-fisted farmers*, and moonstruck theorists? All the Northern States, and especially the New England States, are *devoid of society filled for well-bred gentlemen*. The prevailing class one meets with is that of mechanics struggling to be genteel, and small farmers, who do their own drudgery; and yet who are hardly fit for association with a gentleman's body servant [slave]. This is your free society."

The insults offered to John P. Hale and Charles Sumner in the United States Senate, and to Joshua R. Giddings and Owen Lovejoy in the House of Representatives, were such as no legislative body in the world would have allowed, except one controlled by slave-drivers. I give the following, which may be taken as a fair specimen of the *bulldozing* of those days.

In the National House of Representatives Hon. O. Lovejoy, member from Illinois, was speaking against the further extension of slavery in the territories, when he was interrupted by Mr. Barksdale, of Mississippi—

"Order that black-hearted scoundrel and nigger-stealing thief to take his seat."

By Mr. Boyce, of South Carolina, addressing Mr. Lovejoy—

"Then behave yourself."

By Mr. Gartrell, of Georgia, (in his seat)—

"The man is crazy."

By Mr. Barksdale, of Mississippi, again—

"No, sir; you stand there to-day, an infamous, perjured villain."

By Mr. Ashmore, of South Carolina—

"Yes; he is a perjured villain, and he perjures himself every hour he occupies a seat on this floor."

By Mr. Singleton, of Mississippi—

"And a negro thief into the bargain."

By Mr. Barksdale, of Mississippi, again—

"I hope my colleague will hold no parley with that perjured negro thief."

By Mr. Singleton, of Mississippi, again—

"No sir; any gentleman shall have time, but not such a mean, despicable wretch as that."

By Mr. Martin, of Virginia—

"And if you come among us, we will do with you as we did with John Brown—hang you as high as Haman. I say that as a Virginian."

Hon. Robert Toombs, of Georgia, made a violent speech in the Senate, January, 1860, in which he said:—

"*Never permit this Federal Government to pass into the traitorous hands of the Black Republican party.* It has already declared war against you and your institutions. It every day commits acts of war against you; it has already compelled you to arm for your defence. Listen to 'no vain babblings,' to no treacherous jargon about 'overt acts;' they have already been committed. Defend yourselves; the enemy is at your door; wait not to meet him at the hearthstone,—meet him at the door-sill, and drive him from the temple of liberty, or pull down its pillars and involve him in a common ruin."

Such and similar sentiments expressed at the South, and even by Southerners when sojourning in the free States, did much to widen the breach, and to bring on the conflict of arms that soon followed.

CHAPTER XVI.

THE night was dark, the rain descended in torrents from the black and overhanging clouds, and the thunder, accompanied with vivid flashes of lightning, resounded fearfully, as I entered a negro cabin in South Carolina. The room was filled with blacks, a group of whom surrounded a rough board table, and at it sat an old man holding in his hand a watch, at which all were intently gazing. A stout negro boy held a torch which lighted up the cabin, and near him stood a Yankee soldier, in the Union blue, reading the President's Proclamation of Freedom.

As it neared the hour of twelve, a dead silence prevailed, and the holder of the time-piece said,—"By de time I counts ten, it will be midnight an' de lan' will be free. One, two, three, four, five, six, seven, eight, nine,—" just then a loud strain of music came from the banjo, hanging upon the wall, and at its sound the whole company, as if by previous arrangement, threw themselves upon their knees, and the old man exclaimed,—"O, God, de watch was a minit' too slow, but dy promises an' dy mercy is allers in time; dou did promise dat one of dy angels should come an' give us de sign, an' shore 'nuff de sign did come. We's grateful, O, we's grateful, O, Lord, send dy angel once moe to give dat sweet sound."

At this point another strain from the banjo was heard, and a sharp flash of lightning was followed by a clap of thunder, such as is only heard in the tropics. The negroes simultaneously rose to their feet and began singing; finishing only one verse, they all fell on their knees, and Uncle Ben, the old white-haired man, again led in prayer, and such a prayer as but few outside of this injured race could have given. Rising to their feet, the leader commenced singing:—

"Oh! breth-er-en, my way, my way's cloudy, my way,
    Go send dem angels down.
Oh! breth-er-en, my way, my way's cloudy, my way,
    Go send dem angels down.
There's fire in de east an' fire in de west,
    Send dem angels down.
An' fire among de Methodist,
    O, send dem angels down.

Ole Sa-tan's mad, an' I am glad,
Send dem angels down.
He missed the soul he thought he had,
O, send dem angels down.
I'll tell you now as I tole afore,
Send dem angels down.
To de promised lan' I'm bound to go,
O, send dem angels down.
Dis is de year of Jubilee,
Send dem angels down.
De Lord has come to set us free,
O, send dem angels down."

One more short prayer from Uncle Ben, and they arose, clasped each other around the neck, kissed, and commenced shouting, "Glory to God, we's free."

Another sweet strain from the musical instrument was followed by breathless silence, and then Uncle Ben said, "De angels of de Lord is wid us still, an' dey is watching ober us, fer ole Sandy tole us moe dan a mont ago dat dey would."

I was satisfied when the first musical strain came, that it was merely a vibration of the strings, caused by the rushing wind through the aperture between the logs behind the banjo. Fearing that the blacks would ascribe the music to some mysterious Providence, I plainly told them of the cause.

"Oh, no ser," said Uncle Ben, quickly, his eyes brightening as he spoke, "dat come fum de angels. We been specken it all de time. We know the angels struck the strings of de banjo."

The news of the music from the instrument without the touch of human hands soon spread through the entire neighborhood, and in a short time the cabin was jammed with visitors, who at once turned their attention to the banjo upon the wall.

All sorts of stories were soon introduced to prove that angelic visits were common, especially to those who were fortunate enough to carry "de witness."

"De speret of de Lord come to me lass night in my sleep an' tole me dat I were gwine to be free, an' sed dat de Lord would sen' one of His angels down to give me de warnin'. An' when de banjo sounded, I knowed dat my bressed Marster were a' keepin' His word," said Uncle Ben.

An elderly woman amongst the visitors, drew a long breath, and declared that she had been lifted out of her bed three times on the previous night; "I knowed," she continued, "dat de angelic hoss was hoverin' round about us."

"I dropped a fork to-day," said another, "an' it stuck up in de floo', right afore my face, an' dat is allers good luck fer me."

"De mule kicked at me three times dis mornin' an' he never did dat afore in his life," said another, "an' I knowed good luck would come fum dat."

"A rabbit run across my path twice as I come fum de branch lass Saturday, an' I felt shor' dat somethin' mighty was gwine to happen," remarked Uncle Ben's wife.

"I had a sign that showed me plainly that all of you would be free," said the Yankee soldier, who had been silent since reading the proclamation. All eyes were instantly turned to the white man from the North, and half a dozen voices cried out simultaneously, "O, Mr. Solger, what was it? what was it? what was it?"

"Well," said the man in blue, "I saw something on a large white sheet—"

"Was it a goos?" cried Uncle Ben, before the sentence was finished by the soldier. Uncle Ben's question about a ghost, started quite a number to their feet, and many trembled as they looked each other in the face, and upon the soldier, who appeared to feel the importance of his position.

Ned, the boy who was holding the torch, began to tell a ghost story, but he was at once stopped by Uncle Ben, who said, "Shet your mouf, don't you see de gentmun ain't told us what he see in de 'white sheet?'"

"Well," commenced the soldier, again, "I saw on a large sheet of paper, a printed Proclamation from President Lincoln, like the one I've just read, and that satisfied me that you'd all be free to-day."

Every one was disappointed at this, for all were prepared for a ghost story, from the first remark about the "white sheet" of paper. Uncle Ben smiled, looked a little wise, and said, "I speck dat's a Yankee trick you's given us, Mr. Solger."

The laugh of the man in blue was only stopped by Uncle Ben's striking up the following hymn, in which the whole company joined:—

"A storm am brewin' in de Souf,
A storm am brewin' now.
Oh! hearken den, and shut your mouf,
And I will tell you how:
And I will tell you how, ole boy,
De storm of fire will pour,
And make de black folks sing for joy,
As dey neber sing afore.

"So shut your mouf as close as deafh,
And all you niggas hole your breafh,
And do de white folks brown!

"De black folks at de Norf am ris,
And dey am comin' down—
And comin' down, I know dey is,
To do de white folks brown!
Dey'll turn ole Massa out to grass,
And set de niggas free,
And when dat day am come to pass
We'll all be dar to see!

"So shut your mouf as close as deafh,
And all you niggas hole your breafh,
And I will tell you how.

"Den all de week will be as gay
As am de Chris'mas time;
We'll dance all night and all de day,
And make de banjo chime,
And make de banjo chime, I tink,
And pass de time away,
Wid 'nuf to eat and 'nuf to drink,
And not a bit to pay!

"So shut your mouf as close as deafh,
And all you niggas hole your breafh,
And make de banjo chime."

However, there was in this company, a man some forty years old, who, like a large number of the slaves, had been separated in early life from his relatives, and was now following in the wake of the Union army, hoping to meet some of those dear ones.

This was Mark Myers. At the age of twenty he fled from Winchester, Va., and although pursued by bloodhounds, succeeded in making good his escape. The pursuers returned and reported that Mark had been killed. This story was believed by all.

Now the war had opened the way, Mark had come from Michigan, as a servant for one of the officers; Mark followed the army to Harper's Ferry, and then went up to Winchester. Twenty years had caused a vast change, and although born and brought up there, he found but few that could tell him anything about the old inhabitants.

"Go to an ole cabin at de edge of de town, an' darh you'll find ole Unkel Bob Smart, an' he know ebbrybody, man an boy, dat's lived here for forty years," said an old woman of whom he inquired. With haste Mark proceeded to the "ole cabin," and there he found "Unkel Bob."

"Yer say yer name is Mark Myers, an' yer mamma's name is Nancy," responded the old man to the inquiries put to him by Mark.

"Yes," was the reply.

"Well, sonney," continued Uncle Bob, "de Myers niggers was all sold to de traders 'bout de beginnin' ov de war, septin some ov de ole ones dat dey couldn't sell, an' I specks yer mamma is one ov dem dat de traders didn't want. Now, sonney, yer go over to de Redman place, an' it 'pers to me dat de oman yer's lookin' fer is over darh."

Thanking Uncle Bob, Mark started for the farm designated by the old man. Arriving there, he was told that "Aunt Nancy lived over yarnder on de wess road." Proceeding to the low log hut, he entered, and found the woman.

"Is this Aunt Nancy Myers?"

"Yes, sar, dis is me."

"Had you a son named Mark?"

"Yes, dat I did, an' a good boy he were, poor feller." And here the old woman wiped the tears away with the corner of her apron.

"I have come to bring you some good news about him."

"Good news 'bout who?" eagerly asked the woman.

"Good news about your son Mark."

"Oh! no; you can't bring me no good news 'bout my son, septin you bring it from hebben, fer I feel sartin dat he is darh, fer he suffered nuff when de dogs killed him, to go to hebben."

Mark had already recognized his mother, and being unable to longer conceal the fact, he seized her by the hand and said:

"Mother, don't you know me? I am your long-lost son Mark."

Amazed at the sudden news, the woman trembled like a leaf, the tears flowed freely, and she said:

"My son, Mark, had a deep gash across the bottom of his left foot, dat he will take wid him to his grave. Ef you is my son, show me de mark."

As quick almost as thought, Mark pulled off his boot, threw himself on the floor and held up the foot. The old woman wiped her glasses, put them on, saw the mark of the deep gash; then she fainted, and fell at her son's side.

Neighbors flocked in from the surrounding huts, and soon the cabin was filled with an eager crowd, who stood in breathless silence to catch every word that should be spoken. As the old woman revived, and opened her eyes, she tremblingly said:

"My son, it is you."

"Yes, mother," responded the son, "it is me. When I ran away, old master put the dogs upon my track, but I jumped into the creek, waded down for some distance, and by that means the dogs lost the scent, and I escaped from them."

"Well," said the old woman, "in my prayers I axed God to permit me to meet you in hebben, an' He promised me I should; but He's bin better den His promise."

"Now, mother, I have a home for you at the North, and I have come to take you to it."

The few goods worth bringing away from the slave hut were soon packed up, and ere the darkness had covered the land, mother and son were on their way to the North.

CHAPTER XVII.

DURING the Rebellion and at its close, there was one question that appeared to overshadow all others; this was Negro Equality. While the armies were on the field of battle, this was the great bugbear among many who warmly espoused the cause of the Government, and who approved all its measures, with this single exception. They sincerely wished the rebels to be despoiled of their property. They wished every means to be used to secure our success on the field, including Emancipation. But they would grow pale at the words Negro Equality; just as if the liberating of a race, and securing to them personal, political, social and religious rights, made it incumbent upon us to take these people into our houses, and give them seats in our social circle, beyond what we would accord to other total strangers. No advocate of Negro Equality ever demanded for the race that they should be made pets. Protect them in their natural, lawful, and acquired rights, is all they ask.

Social equality is a condition of society that must make itself. There are colored families residing in every Southern State, whose education and social position is far above a large portion of their neighboring whites. To compel them to associate with these whites would be a grievous wrong. Then, away with this talk, which is founded in hatred to an injured people. Give the colored race in the South equal protection before the law, and then we say to them—

> "Now, to gain the social prize,
> Paddle your own canoe."

But this hue and cry about Negro Equality generally emanates from a shoddy aristocracy, or an uneducated class, more afraid of the negro's ability and industry than of his color rubbing off against them,—men whose claims to equality are so frail that they must be fenced about, and protected by every possible guard; while the true nobleman fears not that his reputation will be compromised by any association he may choose to form. So it is with many of those men who fear negro competition. Conscious of their own inferiority to the mass of mankind, and recognizing the fact that they exist and thrive only by the aid of adventitious advantages, they look with jealousy on any new rivals and competitors, and use every means, fair and unfair, to keep them out of the market.

The same sort of opposition has been made to the introduction of female labor into any of the various branches of manufacture. Consequently, women have always been discriminated against. They have been restricted to a small range of employments; their wages have been kept down; and many who would be perfectly competent to perform the duties of clerks or accountants, or to earn good wages in some branch of manufacture, have been driven by their necessities either to suicide or prostitution.

But the nation, knowing the Southerners as they did, aware of the deep hatred to Northern whites, and still deeper hatred to their ex-slaves, who aided in blotting out the institution of slavery, it was the duty of the nation, having once clothed the colored man with the rights of citizenship and promised him in the Constitution full protection for those rights, to keep this promise most sacredly. The question, while it is invested with equities of the most sacred character, is not without its difficulties and embarrassments. Under the policy adopted by the Democrats in the late insurrectionary States, the colored citizen has been subjected to a reign of terror which has driven him from the enjoyment of his rights and leaves him as much a nonentity in politics, unless he obeys their behests, as he was when he was in slavery. Under this condition of things to-day, while he if properly protected in his rights would hold political supremacy in Mississippi, Georgia, South Carolina, Louisiana, Alabama, and Florida, he has little or no voice in either State or National Government.

Through fear, intimidation, assassination, and all the horrors that barbarism can invent, every right of the negro in the Southern States is to-day at an end. Complete submission to the whites is the only way for the colored man to live in peace.

KU-KLUX EMBLEMS.

Some time since there was considerable talk about a "War of Races," but the war was all on the side of the whites. The freedman has succumbed to brute force, and hence the war of races is suspended; but let him attempt to assert his rights of citizenship, as the white man does at the North, according to the dictates of his own conscience and sense of duty, and the bloody hands of the Ku-Klux and White Leaguer will appear in all their horrors once more—the "dream that has passed" would become a sad reality again.

CHAPTER XVIII.

IMMEDIATELY after the Rebellion ceased, the freedmen throughout the South, desiring no doubt to be fully satisfied that they were actually free and their own masters, and could go where they pleased, left their homes in the country and took up their abode in the cities and towns. This, as a matter of course, threw them out of business, and large numbers could be seen idly lolling about the steps of the court house, town hall, or other county buildings, or listlessly wandering through the streets. That they were able to do this seemed to them positive evidence that they were really free. It was not long, however, before they began to discover that they could not live without work, and that the only labor that they understood was in the country on the plantations. Consequently they returned to the farms, and in many instances to their former masters. Yet the old love for visiting the cities and towns remained, and they became habituated to leaving their work on Saturdays, and going to the place nearest to them. This caused Saturday to be called "nigger day," in most of the Southern States.

On these occasions they sell their cotton or other produce, do their trading, generally having two jugs, one for the molasses, the other for the whiskey, as indispensible to the visit. The store-keepers get ready on Saturday morning, putting their brightest and most gaudy-colored goods in the windows or on the front of their counters. Jew shops put their hawkers at their doors, and the drinking saloons, billiard saloons, and other places of entertainment, kept for their especial accommodation, either by men of their own race or by whites, are all got ready for an extra run.

Being on a visit to the State of Alabama, for a while, I had a fair opportunity of seeing the colored people in that section under various circumstances. It was in the autumn and I was at Huntsville. The principal business houses of the city are situated upon a square which surrounds the court house, and at an early hour in the morning this is filled with colored people of all classes and shades. On Saturdays there are often fully two thousand of them in the streets at one time. At noon the throng was greatest, and up to that time fresh wagon-loads of men, women, and children, were continually arriving. They came not only in wagons, but on horses, and mules, and on foot. Their dress and general appearance were very dissimilar. Some were dressed in a queer looking garment made of pieces of old army blankets, a few were apparelled in faded military overcoats, which were liberally supplied with patches of other material. The women, unlike their husbands and other male relations, were dressed in finery of every conceivable fashion. All of them were decked out with many-colored ribbons. They wore pinchbeck jewelry in large quantities. A few of the young girls displayed some little taste in the arrangement of their dress; and some of them wore expensive clothes. These, however, were "city niggers," and found but little favor in the eyes of the country girls. As the farmers arrived they hitched their tumble-down wagons and bony mules near the court house, and then proceeded to dispose of the cotton and other products which they had brought to town.

While the men are selling their effects, the women go about from store to store, looking at the many gaudy articles of wearing apparel which cunning shop-keepers have spread out to tempt their fancy. As soon as "the crop" is disposed of, and a negro farmer has money in his pocket, his first act is to pay the merchant from whom he obtained his supplies during the year. They are improvident and ignorant sometimes, but it must be said, to their credit, that as a class they always pay their debts, the moment they are in a position to do so. The country would not be so destitute if a larger number of white men followed their example in this respect. When they have settled up all their accounts, and arranged for future bills, they go and hunt up their wives, who are generally on the look-out. They then proceed to a dining saloon, call for an expensive meal, always finishing with pies, puddings, or preserves, and often with all three. When they have satisfied their appetites, they go first to the dry-goods stores. Here, as in other shops, they are met by obsequious white men, who conduct them at once to a back or side room, with which most of the stores are supplied. At first I could not fathom the mystery of this ceremony. After diligent inquiry, however, I discovered that, since the war, unprincipled store-keepers, some of them northern men, have established the custom of giving the country negroes, who come to buy, as much whiskey as they wish to drink. This is done in the back rooms I have mentioned, and when the unfortunate black men and women are deprived of half their wits by the vile stuff which is served out to them, they are induced to purchase all sorts of useless and expensive goods.

In their soberest moments average colored women have a passion for bright, colored dresses which amounts almost to madness, and, on such occasions as I have mentioned, they never stop buying until their money is exhausted. Their husbands have little or no control over them, and are obliged, whether they will or not, to see most of their hard earnings squandered upon an unserviceable jacket, or flimsy bonnet, or many-colored shawl. I saw one black woman spend upward of thirty dollars on millinery goods. As she received her bundle from the cringing clerk she said, with a laugh:

"I 'clare to the Lord I'se done gone busted my old man, sure."

"Never mind," said the clerk, "he can work for more."

"To be sure," answered the woman, and then flounced out of the store.

The men are but little better than the women in their extravagance. I saw a man on the square who had bargained for a mule, which he very much needed, and which he had been intending to purchase as soon as he sold his cotton. He agreed to pay fifty-seven dollars for the animal, and felt in his pocket for the money, but could find only sixteen dollars. Satisfying himself that he had no more, he said:

"Well, well, ef dis ain't de most stravagant nigger I ever see;

I sole two bales of cotton dis bressed day, an' got one hundred and twenty-two dollars, an' now I is got only dis." Here he gave a loud laugh and said:

"Ole mule, I want you mighty bad, but I'll have to let you slide dis time."

While the large dealers were selling their products and emptying their wagons, those with vegetables and fruits were vending them in different sections of the city. A man with a large basket upon his head came along through one of the principal streets shouting:

"Hellow, dar, in de cellar, I is got fresh aggs, jess fum de hen, lay 'em dis mornin' fer de 'casion; here dey is, big hen's aggs, cheap. Now's yer time. Dees aggs is fresh an' good, an' will make fuss-rate agg-nog. Now's yer time fer agg-nogg wid new aggs in it; all laid dis mornin'." Here he set down his basket as if to rest his head. Seeing a colored servant at one of the windows, he called out:

"Here, sister, here's de fresh aggs; here dey is, big aggs fum big hen, much as she could do to lay 'em. Now's yer time; don't be foolish an' miss dis chance."

Just then, a man with a wagon-load of stuff came along, and his voice completely shut out the man with "de fresh aggs."

"Here," cried he, "here's yer nice winter squash, taters,—Irish taters, sweet taters, Carliner taters. Big House, dar, Big House, look out de winder; here's yer nice cabbages, taters, sweet taters, squash. Now's yer time to get 'em cheap. To-morrow is Christmas, an' yer'll want 'em, shore."

The man with the basket of eggs on his head, and who had been silenced by the overpowering voice of the "tater" man, called out to the other, "Now, I reckon yer better go in anudder street. I's been totin' dees aggs all day, an' I don't get in nobody's way."

"I want to know, is dis your street?" asked the "tater" man.

"No; but I tank de Lord, I is got some manners 'bout me. But, den, I couldn't speck no more fum you, fer I knowed you afore de war; you was one of dem cheap niggers, clodhopper, never taste a bit of white bread till after de war, an' den didn't know 'twas bread."

"Well, den, ef you make so much fuss 'bout de street, I'll go out of it; it's nothin' but a second-handed street, no how," said the "tater" man, and drove off, crying, "taters, sweet taters, Irish taters, an' squash."

Passing into a street where the colored people are largely represented, I met another head peddler. This man had a tub on his head and with a musical voice was singing:—

"Here's yer chitlins, fresh an' sweet,
Who'll jine de Union?
Young hog's chitlins hard to beat,
Who'll jine de Union?
Methodist chitlins, jest been biled,
Who'll jine de Union?
Right fresh chitlins, dey ain't spiled,
Who'll jine de Union?
Baptist chitlins by de pound,
Who'll jine de Union?
As nice chitlins as ever was found,
Who'll jine de Union?

"Here's yer chitlins, out of good fat hog; jess as sweet chitlins as ever yer see. Dees chitlins will make yer mouf water jess to look at 'em. Come an' see 'em."

At this juncture the man took the tub from his head, sat it down, to answer a woman who had challenged his right to call them "Baptist chitlins."

"Duz you mean to say dat dem is Baptiss chitlins?"

"Yes, mum, I means to say dat dey is real Baptist chitlins, an' nuffin' else."

"Did dey come out of a Baptiss hog?" inquired the woman.

"Yes, mum, dem chitlins come out of a Baptist hog."

"How duz you make dat out?"

"Well, yer see, dat hog was raised by Mr. Roberson, a hard-shell Baptist, de corn dat de hog was fatted on was also raised by Baptists, he was killed and dressed by Geemes Boone, an' you all know dat he'e as big a Baptist as ever lived."

"Well," said the woman, as if perfectly satisfied, "lem-me have two poun's."

By the time the man had finished his explanation, and weighed out her lot, he was completely surrounded with women and men, nearly all of whom had their dishes to get the choice morsel in.

"Now," said a rather solid-looking man. "Now, I want some of de Meth-diss chitlins dat you's bin talking 'bout."

"Here dey is, ser."

"What," asked the purchaser, "you take 'em all out of de same tub?"

"Yes," quickly replied the vender.

"Can you tell 'em by lookin' at 'em?" inquired the chubby man.

"Yes, ser."

"How duz you tell 'em?"

"Well, ser, de Baptist chitlins has bin more in de water, you see, an' dey's a little whiter."

"But, how duz I know dat dey is Meth-diss?"

"Well, ser, dat hog was raised by Uncle Jake Bemis, one of de most shoutin' Methodist in de Zion connection. Well, you see, ser, de hog pen was right close to de house, an' dat hog was so knowin' dat when Uncle Jake went to prayers, ef dat hog was squeelin' he'd stop. Why, ser, you could hardly get a grunt out of dat hog till Uncle Jake was dun his prayer. Now, ser, ef dat don't make him a Methodist hog, what will?"

"Weigh me out four pounds, ser."

"Here's your fresh chitlins, Baptist chitlins, Methodist chitlins, all good an' sweet."

And in an hour's time the peddler, with his empty tub upon his head, was making his way out of the street, singing,—

"Methodist chitlins, Baptist chitlins,
Who'll jine de Union?"

Hearing the colored cotton-growers were to have a meeting that night, a few miles from the city, and being invited to attend, I embraced the opportunity. Some thirty persons were assembled, and as I entered the room, I heard them chanting—

Sing yo' praises! Bless de Lam!
  Getting plenty money!
Cotton's gwine up—'deed it am!
  People, ain't it funny?

CHORUS.—Rise, shine, give God the glory.
[*Repeat* glory.]

Don't you tink hit's gwine to rain?
  Maybe was, a little;
Maybe one ole hurricane
  'S bilin' in de kittle!—*Chorus.*

Craps done fail in Egypt lan'—
  Say so in de papers;
Maybe little slight o' hand
  'Mong de specerlaters.—*Chorus.*

Put no faith in solemn views;
  Keep yo' pot a smokin',
Stan' up squah in yo' own shoes—
  Keep de debble chokin'!—*Chorus.*

Fetch me 'roun' dat tater juice!
  Stop dat sassy grinnin'!
Turn dat stopper clean a-loose—
  Keep yo' eye a skinnin'!—*Chorus.*

Here's good luck to Egypt lan'!
  Hope she ain't a-failin'!
Hates to see my fellerman
  Straddle ob de pailin'!—*Chorus.*

The church filled up; the meeting was well conducted, and measures taken to protect cotton-raisers, showing that these people, newly-made free, and uneducated, were looking to their interests.

Paying a flying visit to Tennessee, I halted at Columbia, the capital of Maury County. At Redgerford Creek, five miles distant from Columbia, lives Joe Budge, a man with one hundred children. Never having met one with such a family, I resolved to make a call on the gentleman and satisfy my own curiosity.

This distinguished individual is seventy-one years old, large frame, of unadulterated blood, and spent his life in slavery up to the close of the war.

"How many children have you, Mr. Budge?" I asked.

"One hundred, ser," was the quick response.

"Are they all living?"

"No, ser."

"How many wives had you?"

"Thirteen, ser."

"Had you more than one wife living at any time?"

"O, yes, ser, nearly all of dem ware livin' when de war broke out."

"How was this, did the law allow you to have more than one wife at a time?"

"Well, yer see, boss, I waren't under de law, I ware under marser."

"Were you married to all of your wives by a minister?"

"No, ser, only five by de preacher."

"How did you marry the others?"

"Ober de broomstick an' under de blanket."

"How was that performed?"

"Well, yer see, ser, dey all 'sembles in de quarters, an' a man takes hold of one en' of de broom an' a 'oman takes hole of tudder en', an' dey holes up de broom, an' de man an' de 'oman dats gwine to get married jumps ober an' den slips under a blanket, dey put out de light an' all goes out an' leabs em dar."

"How near together were your wives?"

"Marser had fore plantations, an' dey live 'bout on 'em, dem dat warn't sold."

"Did your master sell some of your wives?"

"O! yes, ser, when dey got too ole to bare children. You see, marser raised slaves fer de market, an' my stock ware called mighty good, kase I ware very strong, an' could do a heap of work."

"Were your children sold away from you?"

"Yes, ser, I see three of 'em sole one day fer two thousand dollars a-piece; yer see dey ware men grown up."

"Did you select your wives?"

"Dunno what you mean by dat word."

"Did you pick out the women that you wanted?"

"O! no, ser, I had nuthin ter say 'bout dat. Marser allers get 'em, an' pick out strong, hearty young women. Dat's de reason dat de planters wanted to get my children, kase dey ware so helty."

"Did you never feel that it was wrong to get married in such a light manner?"

"No, ser, kase yer see I toted de witness wid me."

"What do you mean by that?"

"Why, ser, I had religion, an' dat made me feel dat all ware right."

"What was the witness that you spoke of?"

"De change of heart, ser, is de witness dat I totes in my bosom; an' when a man's got dat, he fears nuthin, not eben de debble himsef."

"Then you know that you've got the witness?"

"Yes, ser, I totes it right here." And at this point, Mr. Budge put his hand on his heart, and looked up to heaven.

"I presume your master made no profession of religion?"

"O! yes, ser, you bet he had religion. He ware de fustest man in de church, an' he ware called mighty powerful in prayer."

"Do any of your wives live near you now, except the one that you are living with?"

"Yes, ser, dar's five in dis county, but dey's all married now to udder men."

"Have you many grand-children?"

"Yes, ser, when my 'lations am all tergedder, dey numbers 'bout fore hundred, near as I ken get at it."

"Do you know of any other men that have got as many children as you?"

"No, ser, dey calls me de boss daddy in dis part of de State."

Having satisfied my curiosity, I bade Mr. Budge "good-day."

CHAPTER XIX.

SPENDING part of the winter of 1880 in Tennessee, I began the study of the character of the people and their institutions. I soon learned that there existed an intense hatred on the part of the whites, toward the colored population. Looking at the past, this was easily accounted for. The older whites, brought up in the lap of luxury, educated to believe themselves superior to the race under them, self-willed, arrogant, determined, skilled in the use of side-arms, wealthy—possessing the entire political control of the State—feeling themselves superior also to the citizens of the free States,—this people was called upon to subjugate themselves to an ignorant, superstitious, and poverty-stricken, race—a race without homes, or the means of obtaining them; to see the offices of State filled by men selected from this servile set made these whites feel themselves deeply degraded in the eyes of the world. Their power was gone, but their pride still remained. They submitted in silence, but "bided their time," and said: "Never mind; we'll yet make your hell a hot one."

The blacks felt their importance, saw their own power in national politics, were interviewed by obsequious and cringing white men from the North—men, many of them, far inferior, morally, to the negro. Two-faced, second-class white men of the South, few in number, it is true, hung like leeches upon the blacks. Among the latter was a respectable proportion of free men—free before the Rebellion; these were comparatively well educated; to these and to the better class of freedmen the country was to look for solid work. In the different State Legislatures, the great battle was to be fought, and to these the interest of the South centred. All of the Legislatures were composed mainly of colored men. The few whites that were there were not only no help to the blacks, but it would have been better for the character of the latter, and for the country at large, if most of them had been in some State prison.

Colored men went into the Legislatures somewhat as children go for the first time to a Sabbath school. They sat and waited to see "the show." Many had been elected by constituencies, of which not more than ten in a hundred could read the ballots they deposited; and a large number of these Representatives could not write their own names.

This was not their fault. Their want of education was attributable to the system of slavery through which they had passed, and the absence of the educated intelligent whites of the South, was not the fault of the colored men. This was a trying position for the recently-enfranchised blacks, but nobly did they rise above the circumstances. The speeches made by some of these men exhibited a depth of thought, flights of eloquence, and civilized statesmanship, that throw their former masters far in the back-ground. Yet, amongst the good done, bills were introduced and passed, giving State aid to unworthy objects, old, worn-out corporations re-galvanized, bills for outrageous new frauds drawn up by white men, and presented by blacks; votes of both colors bought up, bills passed, money granted, and these ignorant men congratulated as "Statesmen."

While this "Comedy of Errors" was being performed at the South, and loudly applauded at the North, these very Northern men, who had yelled their throats sore, would have fainted at the idea of a negro being elected a member of their own Legislature.

By and by came the reaction. The disfranchised whites of the South submitted, but complained. Northern men and women, the latter, always the most influential, sympathized with the dog underneath. As the tide was turning, the white adventurers returned from the South with piles of greenbacks, and said that they had been speculating in cotton; but their neighbors knew that it was stolen, for they had been members of Southern Legislatures.

While Northern carpet-baggers were scudding off to their kennels with their ill-gotten gains, the Southern colored politicians were driving fast horses, their wives in their fine carriages; and men, who, five years before were working in the cotton field under the lash, could now draw their checks for thousands.

This extravagance of black men, followed by the heavy taxes, reminded the old Southerners of their defeat in the Rebellion; it brought up thoughts of revenge; Northern sympathy emboldened them at the South, which resulted in the Ku-Klux organizations, and the reign of terror that has cursed the South ever since.

The restoring of the rebels to power and the surrendering the colored people to them, after using the latter in the war, and at the ballot box, creating an enmity between the races, is the most bare-faced ingratitude that history gives any account of.

After all, the ten years of negro Legislation in the South challenges the profoundest study of mankind. History does not record a similar instance. Five millions of uneducated, degraded people, without any preparation whatever, set at liberty in a single day, without shedding a drop of blood, burning a barn, or insulting a single female. They reconstructed the State Governments that their masters had destroyed; became Legislators, held State offices, and with all their blunders, surpassed the whites that had preceded them. Future generations will marvel at the calm forbearance, good sense, and Christian zeal of the American Negro of the nineteenth century.

Nothing has been left undone to cripple their energies, darken their minds, debase their moral sense, and obliterate all traces of their relationship to the rest of mankind; and yet how wonderfully they have sustained the mighty load of oppression under which they have groaned for thousands of years.

After looking at the past history of both races, I could easily see the cause of the great antipathy of the white man to the black, here in Tennessee. This feeling was most forcibly illustrated by an incident that occurred one day while I was standing in front of the Knoxville House, in Knoxville. A good-looking, well-dressed colored man approached a white man, in a business-like manner, and began talking to him, but ere he had finished the question, the white raised his walking stick, and with much force, knocked off the black man's hat, and with an oath said, "Don't you know better than to speak to a white man with your hat on, where's your manners?" The negro picked up his hat, held it in his hand, and resumed the conversation.

I inquired of the colored gentleman with whom I was talking, who the parties were; he replied,—"The white man is a real estate dealer, and the colored man is Hon. Mr. ——, ex-member of the General Assembly."

This race feeling is still more forcibly set forth in the dastardly attack of John Warren, of Huntingdon. The wife of this ruffian, while passing through one of the streets of that town, was accidentally run against by Miss Florence Hayes, who offered ample apology, and which would have been accepted by any well-bred lady. However, Mrs. Warren would not be satisfied with anything less than the punishment of the young lady. Therefore, the two-fisted, coarse, rough, uncouth ex-slave-holder, proceeded to Miss Hayes' residence, gained admission, and without a word of ceremony seized the young lady by the hair, and began beating her with his fist, and kicking her with his heavy boots.

Not until his victim lay prostrate and senseless at his feet, did this fiend cease his blows. Miss Hayes was teaching school at Huntingdon when this outrage was committed, and so severe was the barbarous attack, that she was compelled to return to her home at Nashville, where she was confined to her room for several weeks. Yet, neither law nor public opinion could reach this monster.

A few days after the assault, the following paragraph appeared in the Huntingdon *Vindicator*:

"The occurrences of the past two weeks in the town of Huntingdon should prove conclusively to the colored citizens that there is a certain line existing between themselves and the white people which they cannot cross with impunity. The incident which prompts us to write this article, is the thrashing which a white gentleman administered to a colored woman last week. With no wish to foster a spirit of lawlessness in this community, but actuated by a desire to see the negro keep in his proper place, we advise white men everywhere to *stand up for their rights*, and in no case yield an inch to the encroachment of an inferior race."

"Stand up for their rights," with this editor, means for the white ruffianly coward to knock down every colored lady that does not give up the entire sidewalk to him or his wife.

It was my good fortune to meet on several occasions Miss Florence T. Hayes, the young lady above alluded to, and I never came in contact with a more retiring, lady-like person in my life. She is a student of Tennessee Central College, where she bears an unstained reputation, and is regarded by all who know her to possess intellectual gifts far superior to the average white young women of Tennessee.

Spending a night in the country, we had just risen from the supper-table when mine host said:

"Listen, Mingo is telling how he re-converted his daughter; listen, you'll hear a rich story, and a true one." Mr. Mingo lived in the adjoining room.

"Yes, Mrs. Jones, my darter has bin home wissitin' me, an' I had a mighty trial wid her, I can tell yer."

"What was the matter, Mr. Mingo?" inquired the visitor.

"Well, yer see, Fanny's bin a-livin' in Philamadelfy, an' she's a mighty changed 'oman in her ways. When she come in de house, she run up to her mammy and say,—'O! mar, I'm exquisitely pleased to greet you.' Den she run ter me an' sed,—'O! par,' an' kiss me. Well, dat was all well enuff, but to see as much as two yards of her dress a-dragin' behind her on de floor, it was too much,—an' it were silk, too. It made my heart ache. Ses I,—'Fanny, you's very stravagant, dragin' all dat silk on de floor in dat way.' 'O!' sed she, 'that's the fashion, par.' Den, yer see, I were uneasy fer her. I were 'fraid she'd fall, fer she had on a pair of boots wid the highess heels I eber see in my life, which made her walk as ef she were walkin' on her toes. Den, she were covered all over wid ribbons and ruffles.

"When we set down to dinner, Fanny eat wid her fork, an' when she see her sister put de knife in her mouf, she ses,— 'Don't put your knife in your mouth; that's vulgar.' Nex' mornin', she took out of her pocket some seeds, an' put 'em in a tin cup, an' pour bilin' hot water on 'em. Ses I,—'Fanny, is yer sick, an' gwine to take some medicine?'

"'O! no, par, it's quince seed, to make some gum-stick-um.'

"'What is dat fer?' I axed.

"'Why, par, it's to make Grecian waves on my forehead. Some call them "scallopes." We ladies in the city make them. You see, par, we comb our hair down in little waves, and the gum makes them stick close to the forehead. All the white ladies in the city wear them; it's all the fashion.'

"Well, yer see, Mrs. Jones, I could stand all dat, but when we went to prayers I ax Fanny to lead in prayer; an' when dat gal got on her knees and took out of her pocket a gilt-edge book, and read a prayer, den I were done, I ax myself is it possible dat my darter is come to dat. So, when prayer were over, I sed: 'Fanny, what kind of religion is dat yer's got?' Sed she,— 'Why, par, I em a Piscopion.' 'What is dat?' I axed. 'That's the English Church service.' 'Den yer's no more a Methodist?' 'O! no', said she, 'to be a Piscopion is all the fashion.'"

"Stop, Mr. Mingo," sed Mrs. Jones; "what kind of religion is dat? Is it Baptiss?"

"No, no," replied the old man; "ef it were Baptiss, den I could a-stood dat, kase de Baptiss religion will do when yer can't get no better. Fer wid all dey faults, I believe de Baptiss ken get into hebben by a tight squeeze. Kase, yer see, Mrs. Jones, I is a Methodiss, an' I believes in ole-time religion, an' I wants my chillen to meet me in hebben. So, I jess went right down on my knees an' ax de Lord to show me my juty about Fanny, fer I wanted to win her back to de ole-time religion. Well, de Lord made it all plain to me, an' follerin' de Lord's message to me, I got right up an' went out into de woods an' cut some switches, an' put 'em in de barn. So I sed to Fanny: 'Come, my darter, out to de barn; I want to give yer a present to take back to Philamadelfy wid yer.'

"'Yes, par,' said she, fer she was a-fixin' de 'gum-stick-um' on her hair. So I went to de barn, an' very soon out come Fanny. I jess shut de door an' fasten it, and took down my switches, an' ax her,—'What kind of religion is dat yer's got?'

"'Piscopion, par.' Den I commence, an' I did give dat gal sech a whippen, and she cry out,—'O! par. O! par, please stop, par.' Den I ax her,—'What kind of religion yer's got?' 'Pis-co-copion,' sed she. So I give her some moo, an' I ax her again,—'What kind of religion is yer got?' She sed,—'O! par, O! par.' Sed I,—'Don't call me "par." Call me in de right way.' Den she said,—'O! daddy, O! daddy, I is a Methodiss. I is got ole-time religion; please stop an' I'll never be a Piscopion any more.'

"So, yer see, Mrs. Jones, I converted dat gal right back to de ole-time religion, which is de bess of all religion. Yes, de Lord answered my prayer dat time, wid de aid of de switches."

Whether Mingo's conversion of his daughter kept her from joining the Episcopalians, on her return to Philadelphia, or not, I have not learned.

CHAPTER XX.

THE moral and social degradation of the colored population of the Southern States, is attributable to two main causes, their mode of living, and their religion. In treating upon these causes, and especially the latter, I feel confident that I shall throw myself open to the criticism of a numerous, if not an intelligent class of the people upon whom I write. The entire absence of a knowledge of the laws of physiology, amongst the colored inhabitants of the South is proverbial. Their small unventilated houses, in poor streets and dark alleys, in cities and towns, and the poorly-built log huts in the country, are often not fit for horses. A room fifteen feet square, with two, and sometimes three beds, and three or four in a bed, is common in Tennessee.

No bathing conveniences whatever, and often not a wash dish about the house, is the rule. The most inveterate eaters in the world, yet these people have no idea of cooking outside of hog, hominy, corn bread, and coffee. Yes, there is one more dish, it is the negro's sun-flower in the South, cabbages.

It is usual to see a woman coming from the market about five o'clock in the evening, with a basket under her shawl, and in it a piece of pork, bacon, or half a hog's head, and one or two large heads of cabbage, and some sweet potatoes. These are put to cook at once, and the odor from the boiling pot may be snuffed in some distance off.

Generous to a fault, the host invites all who call in, to "stop to supper." They sit down to the table at about nine o'clock, spend fully an hour over the first course, then the apple dumplings, after that, the coffee and cake. Very few vegetables, except cabbages and sweet potatoes, are ever used by these people. Consequently they are not unfrequently ill from a want of the knowledge of the laws of health. The assembling of large numbers in the cities and towns has proved fatal.

Nearly all the statistics relating to the subject now accessible are those coming from the larger Southern cities, and these would seem to leave no doubt that in such centres of population the mortality of the colored greatly exceeds that of the white race. In Washington, for instance, where the negroes have enjoyed longer and more privileges than in most Southern cities, the death-rate per thousand in the year 1876 was for the whites 26.537; for the colored 49.294; and for the previous year it was a little worse for the blacks. In Baltimore, a very healthy city, the total death-rate for 1875 was 21.67 in one thousand, of which the whites showed 19.80, the colored 34.42. In a still healthier little city, Chattanooga, Tenn., the statistics of the last five years give the death-rate of the whites at 19.9; of the colored, 37. The very best showing for the latter, singularly enough, is made in Selma, Ala. It stands per one thousand, white, 14.28; colored, 18.88. In Mobile, in the same State, the mortality of the colored was just about double the rate among the whites. New Orleans for 1875 gives the record of 25.45 for the death-rate of the whites, to 39.69 for that of the colored.

Lecturers of their own race, male and female, upon the laws of health, is the first move needed.

After settling the question with his bacon and cabbage, the next dearest thing to a colored man, in the South, is his religion. I call it a "thing," because they always speak of getting religion as if they were going to market for it.

"You better go an' get religion, dat's what you better do, fer de devil will be arter you one of dees days, and den whar will yer be?" said an elderly Sister, who was on her way to the "Revival," at St. Paul's, in Nashville, last winter. The man to whom she addressed these words of advice stopped, raised his hat, and replied:

"Anty, I ain't quite ready to-night, but I em gwine to get it before the meetins close, kase when that getting-up day comes, I want to have the witness; that I do."

"Yes, yer better, fer ef yer don't, dar'll be a mighty stir 'mong de brimstone down dar, dat dey will, fer yer's bin bad nuff; I knows yer fum A to izzard," returned the old lady.

The church was already well filled, and the minister had taken his text. As the speaker warmed up in his subject, the Sisters began to swing their heads and reel to and fro, and eventually began a shout. Soon, five or six were fairly at it, which threw the house into a buzz. Seats were soon vacated near the shouters, to give them more room, because the women did not wish to have their hats smashed in by the frenzied Sisters. As a woman sprung up in her seat, throwing up her long arms, with a loud scream the lady on the adjoining seat quickly left, and did not stop till she got to a safe distance.

"Ah, ha!" exclaimed a woman near by, "'fraid of your new bonnet! Ain't got much religion, I reckon. Specks you'll have to come out of that if you want to save your soul."

"She thinks more of that hat now, than she does of a seat in heaven," said another.

"Never mind," said a third, "when she gets de witness, she'll drap dat hat an' shout herself out of breath."

The shouting now became general; a dozen or more entering into it most heartily. These demonstrations increased or abated, according to movements of the leaders, who were in and about the pulpit; for the minister had closed his discourse, and first one, and then another would engage in prayer. The meeting was kept up till a late hour, during which, four or five sisters becoming exhausted, had fallen upon the floor and lay there, or had been removed by their friends.

St. Paul is a fine structure, with its spire bathed in the clouds, and standing on the rising land in South Cherry Street, it is a building that the citizens may well be proud of.

In the evening I went to the First Baptist Church, in Spruce Street. This house is equal in size and finish to St. Paul. A large assembly was in attendance, and a young man from Cincinnati was introduced by the pastor as the preacher for the time being. He evidently felt that to set a congregation to shouting, was the highest point to be attained, and he was equal to the occasion. Failing to raise a good shout by a reasonable amount of exertion, he took from his pocket a letter, opened it, held it up and began, "When you reach the other world you'll be hunting for your mother, and the angel will read from this paper. Yes, the angel will read from this paper."

For fully ten minutes the preacher walked the pulpit, repeating in a loud, incoherent manner, "And the angel will read from this letter." This created the wildest excitement, and not less than ten or fifteen were shouting in different parts of the house, while four or five were going from seat to seat shaking hands with the occupants of the pews. "Let dat angel come right down now an' read dat letter," shouted a Sister, at the top of her voice. This was the signal for loud exclamations from various parts of the house. "Yes, yes, I want's to hear the letter." "Come, Jesus, come, or send an angel to read the letter." "Lord, send us the power." And other remarks filled the house. The pastor highly complimented the effort, as one of "great power," which the audience most cordially endorsed. At the close of the service the strange minister had hearty shakes of the hand from a large number of leading men and women of the church. And this was one of the most refined congregations in Nashville.

It will be difficult to erase from the mind of the negro of the South, the prevailing idea that outward demonstrations, such as, shouting, the loud "amen," and the most boisterous noise in prayer, are not necessary adjuncts to piety.

A young lady of good education and refinement, residing in East Tennessee, told me that she had joined the church about a year previous, and not until she had one shouting spell, did most of her Sisters believe that she had "the Witness."

"And did you really shout?" I inquired.

"Yes. I did it to stop their mouths, for at nearly every

meeting, one or more would say, 'Sister Smith, I hope to live to see you show that you've got the Witness, for where the grace of God is, there will be shouting, and the sooner you comes to that point the better it will be for you in the world to come.'"

To get religion, join a benevolent society that will pay them "sick dues" when they are ill, and to bury them when they die, appears to be the beginning, the aim, and the end of the desires of the colored people of the South. In Petersburg I was informed that there were thirty-two different secret societies in that city, and I met persons who held membership in four at the same time. While such associations are of great benefit to the improvident, they are, upon the whole, very injurious. They take away all stimulus to secure homes and to provide for the future.

As a man observed to me, "I b'longs ter four s'ieties, de 'Samaritans,' de 'Gallalean Fisherman,' de 'Sons of Moses,' an' de 'Wise Men of de East.' All of dees pays me two dollars a week when I is sick, an' twenty-five dollars ter bury me when I dies. Now ain't dat good?"

I replied that I thought it would be far better, if he put his money in a home and educated himself.

"Well," said he, "I is satisfied, kas, ef I put de money in a house, maybe when I got sick some udder man might be hangin' roun' wantin' me ter die, an' maybe de ole 'oman might want me gone too, an' not take good kere of me, an' let me die an' let de town bury me. But, now, yer see, de s'iety takes kere of me and burries me. So, now, I am all right fer dis worl' an' I is got de Witness, an' dat fixes me fer hebben."

This was all said in an earnest manner, showing that the brother had an eye to business.

The determination of late years to ape the whites in the erection of costly structures to worship in, is very injurious to our people. In Petersburg, Va., a Baptist society pulled down a noble building, which was of ample size, to give place to a more fashionable and expensive one, simply because a sister Church had surpassed them in putting up a house of worship. It is more consistent with piety and Godly sincerity to say that we don't believe there is any soul-saving and God-honoring element in such expensive and useless ornaments to houses in which to meet and humbly worship in simplicity and sincerity the true and living God, according to his revealed will. Poor, laboring people who are without homes of their own, and without (in many instances) steady remunerative employment, can ill afford to pay high for useless and showy things that neither instruct nor edify them. The manner, too, in which the money is raised, is none of the best, to say the least of it. For most of the money, both to build the churches and to pay the ministers, is the hard earnings of men in the fields, at service, or by our women over the wash-tub. When our people met and worshipped in less costly and ornamental houses, their piety and sincerity was equally as good as now, if not better. With more polish within and less ornament without, we would be more spiritually and less worldly-minded.

Revival meetings, and the lateness of the hours at which they close, are injurious to both health and morals. Many of the churches begin in October, and continue till the holidays; and commencing again the middle of January, they close in April. They often keep the meetings in till eleven o'clock; sometimes till twelve; and in some country places, they have gone on later. I was informed of a young woman who lost her situation—a very good one—because the family could not sit up till twelve o'clock every night to let her in, and she would not leave her meeting so as to return earlier. Another source of moral degradation lies in the fact that a very large number of men, calling themselves "missionaries," travel the length and breadth of the country, stopping longest where they are best treated. The "missionary" is usually armed with a recommendation from some minister in charge, or has a forged one, it makes but little difference which. He may be able to read enough to line a hymn, but that is about all.

His paper that he carries speaks of him as a man "gifted in revival efforts," and he at once sets about getting up a revival meeting. This tramp, for he cannot be called anything else, has with him generally a hymn-book, and an old faded, worn-out carpet-bag, with little or nothing in it. He remains in a place just as long as the people will keep him, which usually depends upon his ability to keep up an excitement. I met a swarm of these lazy fellows all over the South, the greatest number, however, in West Virginia.

The only remedy for this great evil lies in an educated ministry, which is being supplied to a limited extent. It is very difficult, however, to induce the uneducated, superstitious masses to receive and support an intelligent Christian clergyman.

The great interest felt in the South for education amongst the colored people often produce scenes of humor peculiar to the race. Enjoying the hospitality of a family in West Virginia, I was not a little amused at the preparation made for the reception of their eldest son, who had been absent six months at Wilberforce College. A dinner with a turkey, goose, pair of fowls, with a plentiful supply of side dishes, and apple dumplings for dessert, was on the table at the hour that the son was expected from the train.

An accident delayed the cars to such an extent that we were at the table and dinner half through, when suddenly the door flew open, and before us stood the hope of the family. The mother sprang up, raised her hands and exclaimed, "Well, well, ef dar ain't Peter, now. De Lord bress dat chile, eh, an' how college-like he seems. Jess look at him, don't he look edecated? Come right here dis minit an' kiss your mammy."

During this pleasant greeting, Peter stood near the door where he had entered; dressed in his college rig, small cap on his head, bag swung at his side, umbrella in the left hand, and a cigar in the right, with a smile on his countenance, he looked the very personification of the Harvard student. The father of the family, still holding his knife and fork, sat with a glow upon his face, while the two youngsters, taking advantage of the occasion, were helping themselves to the eatables.

At the bidding, "Come an' kiss your mammy," Peter came forward and did the nice thing to all except the youngest boy, who said, "I can't kiss yer now, Pete, wait till I eat dees dumplins, den I'll kiss yer."

Dinner over, and Peter gave us some humorous accounts of college life, to the great delight of his mother, who would occasionally exclaim, "Bress de chile, what a hard time he muss hab dar at de college. An' how dem boys wory's him. Well, people's got to undergo a heap to git book larnin', don't dey?"

At night the house was filled, to see the young man from college.

CHAPTER XXI.

In the olden time, ere a blow was struck in the Rebellion, the whites of the South did the thinking, and the blacks did the work; the master planned, and the slave executed. This unfitted both for the new dispensation that was fast coming, and left each helpless, without the other.

But the negro was the worst off of the two, for he had nothing but his hands, while the white man had his education, backed up by the lands that he owned. Who can wonder at the negro's improvidence and his shiftlessness, when he has never had any systematic training—never been compelled to meet the cares of life?

This was the black man's misfortune on gaining his freedom, and to learn to save, and to manage his own affairs, appeared to all to be his first duty.

The hope of every one, therefore, seemed to centre in the Freedman's Saving Bank. "This is our bank," said they; and to this institution the intelligent and the ignorant, the soldier fresh from the field of battle, the farmer, the day laborer, and the poor washerwoman, all alike brought their earnings and deposited them in the Freedman's Bank. This place of safety for their scanty store seemed to be the hope of the race for the future. It was a stimulus for a people who had never before been permitted to enter a moneyed institution, except at his master's heels, to bring or to take away the bag of silver that his owner was too proud or too lazy to "tote."

So great was the negro's wish to save, that the deposits in the Freedman's Bank increased from three hundred thousand dollars, in 1866, to thirty-one million dollars, in 1872, and to fifty-five million dollars, in 1874. This saving of earnings became infectious throughout the South, and the family that had no bank-book was considered poorly off. These deposits were the first instalments toward purchasing homes, or getting ready to begin some mercantile or mechanical business. The first announcement, therefore, of the closing of the Freedman's Saving Bank had a paralyzing effect upon the blacks everywhere.

Large numbers quit work; the greater portion sold their bank-books for a trifle, and general distrust prevailed throughout the community. Many who had purchased small farms, or cheap dwellings in cities and towns, and had paid part of the purchase money, now became discouraged, surrendered their claims, gave up the lands, and went about as if every hope was lost. It was their first and their last dealings with a bank.

These poor people received no sympathy whatever, from the whites of the South. Indeed, the latter felt to rejoice, for the negro obtained his liberty through the Republican party, and the Freedmen's Bank was a pet of that party.

The negro is an industrious creature, laziness is not his chief fault, and those who had left their work, returned to it. But the charm for saving was gone.

"No more Banks for me, I'll use my money as I get it, and then I'll know where it has gone to," said an intelligent and well-informed colored man to me.

This want of confidence in the saving institutions of the country, has caused a general spending of money as soon as obtained; and railroad excursions, steamboat rides, hiring of horses and buggies on Sabbath, and even on week days, have reaped large sums from colored people all over the South. Verily, the failure of the Freedman's Saving Bank was a National calamity, the influence of which will be felt for many years.

Not satisfied with robbing the deluded people out of the bulk of their hard earnings, commissioners were appointed soon after the failure, with "appropriate" salaries, to look after the interest of the depositors, and these leeches are eating up the remainder.

Whether truly or falsely, the freedmen were led to believe that the United States Government was responsible to them for the return of their money with interest. Common justice would seem to call for some action in the matter.

CHAPTER XXII.

THOSE who recollect the standing of Virginia in days gone by, will be disappointed in her at the present time. The people, both white and black, are poor and proud, all living on their reputation when the "Old Dominion" was considered the first State in the Union.

I viewed Richmond with much interest. The effect of the late Rebellion is still visible everywhere, and especially amongst those who were leaders in society thirty years ago. I walked through the market and observed several men with long, black cloth cloaks, beneath which was a basket. Into this they might be seen to deposit their marketing for the day.

I noticed an old black man bowing very gracefully to one of these individuals, and I inquired who he was. "Ah, massa," said the negro, "dat is Major ——, he was berry rich before de war, but de war fotch him right down, and now he ain't able to have servants, and he's too proud to show his basket, so he covers it up in his cloak." And then the black man smiled and shook his head significantly, and walked on. Standing here in the market place, one beholds many scenes which bring up the days of slavery as seen by the results. Here is a girl with a rich brown skin; after her comes one upon whose cheek a blush can just be distinguished; and I saw one or two young women whose cream-like complexion would have justly excited the envy of many a New York belle. The condition of the women of the latter class is most deplorable. Beautiful almost beyond description, many of them educated and refined, with the best white blood of the South in their veins, it is perhaps only natural that they should refuse to mate themselves with coarse and ignorant black men. Socially, they are not recognized by the whites; they are often without money enough to buy the barest necessaries of life; honorably they can never procure sufficient means to gratify their luxurious tastes; their mothers have taught them how to sin; their fathers they never knew; debauched white men are ever ready to take advantage of their destitution, and after living a short life of shame and dishonor they sink into early and unhallowed graves. Living, they were despised by whites and blacks alike; dead, they are mourned by none.

I went to hear the somewhat celebrated negro preacher, Rev. John Jasper. The occasion was one of considerable note, he having preached, and by request, a sermon to prove that the "Sun do move," and now he was to give it at the solicitation of forty-five members of the Legislature, who were present as hearers.

Those who wanted the sermon repeated were all whites, a number of whom did it for the fun that they expected to enjoy, while quite a respectable portion, old fogy in opinion, felt that the preacher was right.

On reaching the church, I found twelve carriages and two omnibuses, besides a number of smaller vehicles, lining the street, half an hour before the opening of the doors. However, the whites who had come in these conveyances had been admitted by the side doors, while the streets were crowded with blacks and a poorer class of whites.

By special favor I was permitted to enter before the throng came rushing in. Members of the Legislature were assigned the best seats, indeed, the entire centre of the house was occupied by whites, who, I was informed, were from amongst the F. F. Vs. The church seats one thousand, but it is safe to say that twelve hundred were present at that time.

Rev. John Jasper is a deep black, tall, and slim, with long arms and somewhat round-shouldered, and sixty-five years old. He has preached in Richmond for the last forty-five years, and is considered a very good man. He is a fluent speaker, well versed in Scriptures, and possesses a large amount of wit. The members of Jasper's church are mainly freedmen, a large number of whom are from the country, commonly called "cornfield niggers."

The more educated class of the colored people, I found, did not patronize Jasper. They consider him behind the times, and called him "old fogy." Jasper looked proudly upon his audience, and well he might, for he had before him some of the first men and women of Virginia's capital. But these people had not come to be instructed, they had really come for a good laugh and were not disappointed.

Jasper had prepared for the occasion, and in his opening service saved himself by calling on "Brother Scogin" to offer prayer. This venerable Brother evidently felt the weight of responsibility laid upon him, and discharged the duty, at least to the entire satisfaction of those who were there to be amused. After making a very sensible prayer, Scogin concluded as follows:—"O Lord, we's a mighty abused people, we's had a hard time in slavery, we's been all broken to pieces, we's bow-legged, knock-kneed, bandy-shanked, cross-eyed, and a great many of us is hump-backed. Now, Lord, we wants to be mendid up, an' we wants you to come an' do it. Don't send an angel, for dis is too big a job for an angel. You made us, O Lord, an' you know our wants, an' you can fix us up as nobody else can. Come right down yourself, and come quickly." At this sentence Jasper gave a loud groan, and Scogin ceased. After service was over I was informed that when Jasper finds any of his members a little too long-winded in prayer, singing, or speaking, he gives that significant groan, which they all well understand. It means "enough."

The church was now completely jammed, and it was said that two thousand people sought admission in vain. Jasper's text was "God is a God of War." The preacher, though wrong in his conclusions, was happy in his quotations, fresh in his memory, and eloquently impressed his views upon his hearers.

He said, "If the sun does not move, why did Joshua command it to 'stand still?' Was Joshua wrong? If so, I had rather be wrong with Joshua than to be right with the modern philosophers. If this earth moves, the chimneys would be falling, tumbling in upon the roofs of the houses, the mountains and hills would be changing and levelling down, the rivers would be emptying out. You and I would be standing on our heads. Look at that mountain standing out yonder; it stood there fifty years ago when I was a boy. Would it be standing there if the earth was running round as they tell us?"

"No, blessed God," cried a Sister. Then the laugh came, and Jasper stood a moment with his arms folded. He continued: "The sun rises in the east and sets in the west; do you think any one can make me believe that the earth can run around the world in a single day so as to give the sun a chance to set in the west?"

"No, siree, that doctrine don't go down with Jasper."

At this point the preacher paused for breath, and I heard an elderly white in an adjoining pew, say, in a somewhat solemn tone—"Jasper is right, the sun moves."

Taking up his bandanna, and wiping away the copious perspiration that flowed down his dusky cheeks, the preacher opened a note which had just been laid upon the desk, read it, and continued,—"A question is here asked me, and one that I am glad to answer, because a large number of my people, as well as others, can't see how the children of Israel were able to cross the Red Sea in safety, while Pharaoh and his hosts were drowned. I have told you again and again that everything was possible with God. But that don't seem to satisfy you.

"Those who doubt these things that you read in Holy Writ are like the infidel,—won't believe unless you can see the cause. Well, let me tell you. The infidel says that when the children of Israel crossed the Red Sea, it was in winter, and the sea was frozen over. This is a mistake, or an intentional misrepresentation." Here the preacher gave vivid accounts of the sufferings and flight of the children of Israel, whose case he likened to the colored people of the South. The preacher wound up with an eloquent appeal to his congregation not to be led astray by "these new-fangled notions."

Great excitement is just now taking hold of the people upon the seeming interest that the colored inhabitants are manifesting in the Catholic religion. The Cathedral in Richmond is thrown open every Sunday evening to the blacks, when the bishop himself preaches to them, and it is not strange that the eloquent and persuasive voice of Bishop Kean, who says to the negro, "My dear beloved brethren," should captivate these despised people. I attended a meeting at the large African Baptist Church, where the Rev. Moses D. Hoge, D. D., was to preach to the colored people against Catholicism. Dr. Hoge, though noted for his eloquence, and terribly in earnest, could not rise higher in his appeals to the blacks than to say "men and women" to them.

The contrast was noticeable to all. After hearing Dr. Hoge through I asked an intelligent colored man how he liked his sermon. His reply was: "If Dr. Hoge is in earnest, why don't he open his own church and invite us in and preach to us there? Before he can make any impression on us, he must go to the Catholic Church and learn the spirit of brotherly love."

One Sunday, Bishop Kean said to the colored congregation, numbering twelve hundred, who had come to hear him: "There are distinctions in the business and in the social world, but there are no distinctions in the spiritual. A soul is a soul before God, may it be a black or a white man's. God is no respecter of persons, the Christian Church cannot afford to be. The people who would not let you learn to read before the war, are the ones now that accuse me of trying to use you for political purposes.

"Now, my dear beloved brethren, when I attempt to tell you how to vote, you need not come to hear me preach any more."

The blacks have been so badly treated in the past that kind words and social recognition will do much to win them in the future, for success will not depend so much upon their matter as upon their manner; not so much upon their faith as upon the more potent direct influence of their practice. In this the Catholics of the South have the inside track, for the prejudice of the Protestants seems in a fair way to let the negro go anywhere except to heaven, if they have to go the same way.

CHAPTER XXIII.

NORFOLK is the place above all others, where the "old-Verginny-never-tire" colored people of the olden time may be found in their purity. Here nearly everybody lives out of doors in the warm weather. This is not confined to the blacks. On the sidewalks, in front of the best hotels, under the awnings at store-doors, on the door-sills of private houses, and on the curbstones in the streets, may be seen people of all classes. But the blacks especially give the inside of the house a wide berth in the summer.

I went to the market, for I always like to visit the markets on Saturday, for there you see "life among the lowly," as you see it nowhere else. Colored men and women have a respectable number of stalls in the Norfolk market, the management of which does them great credit.

But the costermongers, or street-venders, are the men of music. "Here's yer nice vegables—green corn, butter beans, taters, Irish taters, new, jess bin digged; come an' get 'em while dey is fresh. Now's yer time; squash, Calafony quash, bess in de worl'; come an' git 'em now; it'll be Sunday termorrer, an' I'll be gone to church. Big fat Mexican peas, marrer fat squash, Protestant squash, good Catholic vegables of all kinds."

Now's yer time to git snap-beans,
Okra, tomatoes, an' taters gwine by;
Don't be foolish virgins;

Hab de dinner ready
When de master he comes home,
Snap-beans gwine by.

Just then the vender broke forth in a most musical voice:

Oh! Hannah, boil dat cabbage down,
  Hannah, boil 'em down,
And turn dem buckwheats round and round,
  Hannah, boil 'em down.
It's almost time to blow de horn,
  Hannah, boil 'em down,
To call de boys dat hoe de corn,
  Hannah, boil 'em down.

Hannah, boil 'em down,
  De cabbage just pulled out de ground,
Boil 'em in de pot,
  And make him smoking hot.

* * *

Some like de cabbage made in krout,
  Hannah, boil 'em down,
Dey eat so much dey get de gout,
  Hannah, boil 'em down,
Dey chops 'em up and let dem spoil,
  Hannah, boil 'em down;
I'd rather hab my cabbage boiled,
  Hannah, boil 'em down.

Some say dat possum's in de pan,
  Hannah, boil 'em down,
Am de sweetest meat in all de land,
  Hannah, boil 'em down;
But dar is dat ole cabbage head,
  Hannah, boil 'em down,
I'll prize it, children, till I's dead,
  Hannah, boil 'em down.

This song, given in his inimitable manner, drew the women to the windows, and the crowd around the vegetable man in the street, and he soon disposed of the contents of his cart. Other venders who "toted" their commodities about in baskets on their heads, took advantage of the musical man's company to sell their own goods. A woman with some really fine strawberries, put forth her claims in a very interesting song; the interest, however, centered more upon the manner than the matter:—

"I live fore miles out of town,
    I am gwine to glory.
My strawberries are sweet an' soun',
    I am gwine to glory.
I fotch 'em fore miles on my head,
    I am gwine to glory.
My chile is sick, an' husban' dead,
    I am gwine to glory.
Now's de time to get 'em cheap,
    I am gwine to glory.
Eat 'em wid yer bread an' meat,
    I am gwine to glory.
Come sinner get down on your knees,
    I am gwine to glory.
Eat dees strawberries when you please,
    I am gwine to glory."

Upon the whole, the colored man of Virginia is a very favorable physical specimen of his race; and he has peculiarly fine, urbane manners. A stranger judging from the surface of life here, would undoubtedly say that they were a happy, well-to-do people. Perhaps, also, he might say: "Ah, I see. The negro is the same everywhere—a hewer of wood, a peddler of vegetables, a wearer of the waiter's white apron. Freedom has not altered his status."

Such a judgment would be a very hasty one. Nations are not educated in twenty years. There are certain white men who naturally gravitate also to these positions; and we must remember that it is only the present generation of negroes who have been able to appropriate any share of the nobler blessings of freedom. But the colored boys and girls of Virginia are to-day vastly different from what the colored boys and girls of fifteen or twenty years ago were. The advancement and improvement is so great that it is not unreasonable to predict from it a very satisfactory future.

The negro population here are greatly in the majority, and formerly sent a member of their own color to the State Senate, but through bribery and ballot-box stuffing, a white Senator is now in Richmond. One negro here at a late election sold his vote for a barrel of sugar. After he had voted and taken his sugar home, he found it to be a barrel of sand. I learn that his neighbors turned the laugh upon him, and made him treat the whole company, which cost him five dollars.

I would not have it supposed from what I have said about the general condition of the blacks in Virginia that there are none of a higher grade. Far from it, for some of the best mechanics in the State are colored men. In Richmond and Petersburg they have stores and carry on considerable trade, both with the whites and their own race. They are doing a great deal for education; many send their sons and daughters North and West for better advantages; and they are building some of the finest churches in this State. The Second Baptist Church here pulled down a comparatively new and fine structure, last year, to replace it with a more splendid place of worship, simply because a rival church of the same denomination had surpassed them. I viewed the new edifice, and feel confident it will compare favorably with any church on the Back Bay, Boston.

The new building will seat three thousand persons, and will cost, exclusive of the ground, one hundred thousand dollars, all the brick and wood work of which is being done by colored men.

CHAPTER XXIV.

THE education of the negro in the South is the most important matter that we have to deal with at present, and one that will claim precedence of all other questions for many years to come. When, soon after the breaking out of the Rebellion, schools for the freedmen were agitated in the North, and teachers dispatched from New England to go down to teach the "poor contrabands," I went before the proper authorities in Boston, and asked that a place be given to one of our best-educated colored young ladies, who wanted to devote herself to the education of her injured race, and the offer was rejected, upon the ground that the "time for sending colored teachers had not come." This happened nearly twenty years ago. From that moment to the present, I have watched with painful interest the little progress made by colored men and women to become instructors of their own race in the Southern States.

Under the spur of the excitement occasioned by the Proclamation of Freedom, and the great need of schools for the blacks, thousands of dollars were contributed at the North, and agents sent to Great Britain, where generosity had no bounds. Money came in from all quarters, and some of the noblest white young women gave themselves up to the work of teaching the freedmen.

During the first three or four years, this field for teachers was filled entirely by others than members of the colored race, and yet it was managed by the "New England Freedmen's Association," made up in part by some of our best men and women.

But many energetic, educated colored young women and men, volunteered, and, at their own expense, went South and began private schools, and literally forced their way into the work. This was followed by a few appointments, which in every case proved that colored teachers for colored people was the great thing needed. Upon the foundations laid by these small schools, some of the most splendid educational institutions in the South have sprung up. Fisk, Howard, Atlanta, Hampton, Tennessee Central, Virginia Central, and Straight, are some of the most prominent. These are all under the control and management of the whites, and are accordingly conducted upon the principle of whites for teachers and blacks for pupils. And yet each of the above institutions are indebted to the sympathy felt for the negro, for their very existence. Some of these colleges give more encouragement to the negro to become an instructor, than others; but, none however, have risen high enough to measure the black man independent of his color.

At Petersburg I found a large, fine building for public schools for colored youth; the principal, a white man, with six assistants, but not one colored teacher amongst them. Yet Petersburg has turned out some most excellent colored teachers, two of whom I met at Suffolk, with small schools. These young ladies had graduated with honors at one of our best institutions, and yet could not obtain a position as teacher in a public school, where the pupils were only their own race.

At Nashville, the School Board was still more unjust, for they employed teachers who would not allow their colored scholars to recognize them on the streets, and for doing which, the children were reprimanded, and the action of the teachers approved by the Board of Education.

It is generally known that all the white teachers in our colored public schools feel themselves above their work; and the fewest number have any communication whatever with their pupils outside the school-room. Upon receiving their appointments and taking charge of their schools some of them have been known to announce to their pupils that under no circumstances were they to recognize or speak to them on the streets. It is very evident that these people have no heart in the work they are doing, and simply from day to day go through the mechanical form of teaching our children for the pittance they receive as a salary. While teachers who have no interest in the children they instruct, except for the salary they get, are employed in the public schools and in the Freedman's Colleges, hundreds of colored men and women, who are able to stand the most rigid examination, are idle, or occupying places far beneath what they deserve.

It is to be expected that the public schools will, to a greater or less extent, be governed by the political predilections of the parties in power; but we ought to look for better things from Fisk, Hampton, Howard, Atlanta, Tennessee Central and Virginia Central, whose walls sprung up by money raised from appeals made for negro education.

There are, however, other educational institutions of which I have not made mention, and which deserve the patronage of the benevolent everywhere. These are: Wilberforce, Berea, Payne Institute, in South Carolina, Waco College, in Texas, and Storer College, at Harper's Ferry.

Wilberforce is well known, and is doing a grand work. It has turned out some of the best of our scholars,—men whose labors for the elevation of their race cannot be too highly commended.

Storer College, at Harper's Ferry, looks down upon the ruins of "John Brown's Fort." In the ages to come, Harper's Ferry will be sought out by the traveller from other lands. Here at the confluence of the Potomac and the Shenandoah Rivers, on a point just opposite the gap through which the united streams pass the Blue Ridge, on their course toward the ocean, stands the romantic town, and a little above it, on a beautiful eminence, is Storer, an institution, and of whose officers I cannot speak too highly.

I witnessed, with intense interest, the earnest efforts of these good men and women, in their glorious work of the elevation of my race. And while the benevolent of the North are giving of their abundance, I would earnestly beg them not to forget Storer College, at Harper's Ferry.

The other two, of which I have made mention, are less known, but their students are numerous and well trained. *Both these schools are in the South*, and both are owned and managed by colored men, free from the supposed necessity of having white men to do their *thinking*, and therein ought to receive the special countenance of all who believe in giving the colored people a chance to paddle their own canoe.

I failed, however, to find schools for another part of our people, which appear to be much needed. For many years in the olden time the South was noted for its beautiful Quadroon women. Bottles of ink, and reams of paper, have been used to portray the "finely-cut and well-moulded features," the "silken curls," the "dark and brilliant eyes," the "splendid forms," the "fascinating smiles," and "accomplished manners" of these impassioned and voluptuous daughters of the two races,—the unlawful product of the crime of human bondage. When we take into consideration the fact that no safeguard was ever thrown around virtue, and no inducement held out to slave-women to be pure and chaste, we will not be surprised when told that immorality pervaded the domestic circle in the cities and towns of the South to an extent unknown in the Northern States. Many a planter's wife has dragged out a miserable existence, with an aching heart, at seeing her place in the husband's affections usurped by the unadorned beauty and captivating smiles of her waiting-maid. Indeed, the greater portion of the colored women, in the days of slavery, had no greater aspiration than that of becoming the finely-dressed mistress of some white man. Although freedom has brought about a new order of things, and our colored women are making rapid strides to rise above the dark scenes of the past, yet the want of protection to our people since the old-time whites have regained power, places a large number of the colored young women of the cities and towns at the mercy of bad colored men, or worse white men. To save these from destruction, institutions ought to be established in every large city.

Mrs. Julia G. Thomas, a very worthy lady, deeply interested in the welfare of her sex, has a small institution for orphans and friendless girls, where they will have a home, schooling, and business training, to fit them to enter life with a prospect of success. Mrs. Thomas' address is 190 High Street, Nashville, Tennessee.

CHAPTER XXV.

Among the causes of that dissatisfaction of the colored people in the South which has produced the exodus therefrom, there is one that lies beneath the surface and is concealed from even an astute observer, if he is a stranger to that section. This cause consists in certain legislative enactments that have been passed in most of the cotton States, ostensibly for other purposes, but really for the purpose of establishing in those States a system of peonage similar to, if not worse than, that which prevails in Mexico. This is the object of a statute passed by the Legislature of Mississippi, in March, 1878. The title of the act, whether intentionally so or not, is certainly misleading. It is entitled "An act to reduce the judiciary expenses of the State." But how it can possibly have that effect is beyond human wisdom to perceive. It, however, does operate, and is used in such a way as to enslave a large number of negroes, who have not even been convicted of the slightest offence against the laws.

The act provides that "all persons convicted and committed to the jail of the county, except those committed to jail for contempt of court, and except those sentenced to imprisonment in the Penitentiary, shall be delivered to a contractor, to be by him kept and worked under the provisions of this act; and all persons committed to jail, except those not entitled to bail, may also, with their consent, be committed to said contractor and worked under this act before conviction." But Sect. 5, of the act provides ample and cogent machinery to produce the necessary consent on the part of the not yet convicted prisoner to work for the contractor. In that section it is provided "that if any person committed to jail for an offence that is bailable shall not consent to be committed to the safe keeping and custody of said contractor, and to work for said contractor, and to work for the same under this act, the prisoner shall be entitled to receive only six ounces of bacon, or ten ounces of beef, and one pound of bread and water."

This section also provides that any prisoner not consenting to work before his conviction for the contractor, and that too, without compensation, "If said prisoner shall afterward be convicted, he shall, nevertheless, work under said contractor a sufficient term to pay all cost of prosecution, including the regular jail fees for keeping and feeding him. The charge for feeding him, upon the meagre bill of fare above stated, is twenty cents a day." Now, it cannot be denied that the use made of this law is to deprive the negro of his natural right to choose his own employer; and in the following manner: Let us suppose a case, and such cases are constantly occurring. A is a cotton planter, owns three or four thousand acres of land, and has forty, fifty, or one hundred negro families on his plantation. At the expiration of the year, a negro proposes to leave the plantation of A, and try to better his condition by making a more advantageous bargain with B, or C, for another year. If A can prevent the negro from leaving him in no other way, this statute puts full power in his hands. A trumps up some petty charge against the negro, threatens to have him arrested and committed to jail. The negro knows how little it will take to commit him to jail, and that then he must half starve on a pound of bread and water and six ounces of bacon a day, or work for the contractor for nothing until he can be tried; and when tried he must run the risk of conviction, which is not slight, though he may be ever so innocent. Avarice—unscrupulous avarice—is pursuing him, and with little power to resist, there being no healthy public sentiment in favor of fair play to encourage him, he yields, and becomes the peon of his oppressor.

I found the whipping-post in full operation in Virginia, and heard of its being enforced in other States. I inquired of a black man what he thought of the revival of that mode of punishment. He replied, "Well, sar, I don't ker for it, kase dey treats us all alike; dey whips whites at de poss jess as dey do de blacks, an' dat's what I calls equality before de law."

A friend of mine meeting a man who was leaving Arkansas, on account of the revival of her old slave laws, the following conversation occurred, showing that the oppression of the blacks extends to all the States South.

"You come from Arkansas, I understand?"

"Yes."

"What wages do you generally get for your work?"

"Since about '68, we've been getting about two bits a day—that's twenty cents. Then there are some people that work by the month, and at the end of the month they are either put off or cheated out of their money entirely. Property and goods are worth nothing to a black man there. He can't get his price for them; he gets just what the white man chooses to give him. Some people who raise from ten to fifteen bales of cotton sometimes have hardly enough to cover their body and feet. This goes on while the white man gets the price he asks for his goods. This is unfair, and as long as we pay taxes we want justice, right, and equality before the people."

"What taxes do you pay?"

"A man that owns a house and lot has to pay about twenty-six dollars a year; and if he has a mule worth about one hundred and fifty dollars they tax him two dollars and a half extra. If they see you have money—say you made three thousand dollars—you'd soon see some bill about taxes, land lease and the other coming in for about two thousand of it. They charge a black man thirteen dollars where they would only charge a white man one or two. Now, there's a man," pointing to a portly old fellow, "who had to run away from his house, farm, and all. It is for this we leave Arkansas. We want freedom, and I say, 'Give me liberty or give me death.' We took up arms and fought for our country, so we ought to have our rights."

"How about the schooling you receive?"

"We can't vote, still we have to pay taxes to support schools for the others. I got my education in New Orleans and paid for it, too. I have six children, and though I pay taxes not one of them has any schooling from the public schools. The taxes and rent are so heavy that the children have to work when they are as young as ten years. That's the way it is down there."

"Did you have any teachers from the North?"

"There were some teachers from the North who came down there, but they were run out. They were paid so badly and treated so mean that they had to go."

"What county did you live in?"

"Phillips County."

"How many schools were in that county?"

"About five."

"When do they open?"

"About once every two years and keep open for two or three weeks. And then they have a certain kind of book for the children. Those that have dogs, cats, hogs, cows, horses, and all sorts of animals in them. They keep the children in these and never let them get out of them."

"Have you any colleges in the State for colored men?"

"No, they haven't got any colleges and don't allow any. The other day I asked a Republican how was it that so many thousands of dollars were taken for colleges and we didn't get any good of it? He said, 'The bill didn't pass, somehow.' And now I guess those fellows spent all that money."

"As a general thing, then, the people are very ignorant?"

"Yes, sir; the colored man that's got education is like some people that's got religion—he hides it under a bushel; if he didn't, and stood up for his rights as a citizen, he would soon become the game of some of the Ku-Klux clubs."

Having succeeded in getting possession of power in the South, and driving the black voters from the polls at elections, and also having them counted in National Representation, the ex-rebels will soon have a power which they never before enjoyed. Had the slaveholders in 1860 possessed the right of representing their slaves fully instead of partly in Congress and in the Electoral College, they would have ruled this country indefinitely in the interest of slavery. It was supposed that by the result of the war, freedom profited and the slaveholding class lost power forever. But the very act which conferred the full right of representation upon the three million freedmen, by the help of the policy, has placed an instrument in the hands of the rebel conspirators which they will use to pervert and defeat the objects of the Constitutional amendments. Through this policy the thirty-five additional electoral votes given to the freedmen have been "turned over to the Democratic party." Aye, more than that; they have been turned over to the ex-rebels, who will use them in the cause of oppression scarcely second in hatefulness to that of chattel slavery. In a contest with the solid South, therefore, the party of freedom and justice will have greater odds to overcome than it did in 1860, and the Southern oligarchs hold a position which is well nigh impregnable for whatever purpose they choose to use it.

Of the large number of massacres perpetrated upon the blacks in the South, since the ex-rebels have come into power, I give one instance, which will show the inhumanity of the whites. This outrage occurred in Gibson County, Tennessee. The report was first circulated that the blacks in great numbers were armed, and were going to commit murder upon the whites. This created the excitement that it was intended to, and the whites in large bodies, armed to the teeth, went through Gibson, and adjoining counties, disarming the blacks, taking from them their only means of defence, and arresting all objectionable blacks that they could find, taking them to Trenton and putting them in jail.

The following account of the wanton massacre, is from the *Memphis Appeal*:—

"About four hundred armed, disguised, mounted men entered this town at two o'clock this morning, proceeded to the jail, and demanded the keys of the jailor, Mr. Alexander. He refused to give up the keys. Sheriff Williams, hearing the noise, awoke and went to the jail, and refused to surrender the keys to the maskers, telling them that he did not have the keys. They cocked their pistols, and he refused again to give them the keys, whereupon the Captain of the company ordered the masked men to draw their pistols and cock them, swearing they would have the keys or shoot the jailor. The jailor dared them to shoot, and said they were too cowardly to shoot. They failed to do this. Then they threatened to tear down the jail or get the prisoners. The jailor told them that rather than they should tear down the jail he would give them the keys if they would go with him to his office. The jailor did this because he saw that the men were determined to break through. 'They were all disguised. Then they came,' says the Sheriff, 'and got the keys from my office, and giving three or four yells, went to the jail, unlocked it, took out the sixteen negroes who had been brought here from Pickettsville (Gibson), and, tying their hands, escorted them away. They proceeded on the Huntingdon road without saying a word, and in fifteen minutes I heard shots. In company with several citizens I proceeded down the road in the direction taken by the men and prisoners, and just beyond the river bridge, half a mile from town, I found four negroes dead, on the ground, their bodies riddled with bullets, and two wounded. We saw no masked men. Ten negroes yet remain unaccounted for. Leaving the dead bodies where we found them, we brought the two wounded negroes to town, and summoned medical aid. Justice J. M. Caldwell held an inquest on the bodies, the verdict being in accordance with the facts that death resulted from shots inflicted by guns in the hands of unknown parties. The inquest was held about eight o'clock this morning. These are all the facts relative to the shooting I can give you. I did my duty to prevent the rescue of the negroes, but found it useless to oppose the men, one of whom said there were four hundred in the band.'

"Night before last the guard that brought the prisoners from Pickettsville remained. No fears or intimations of the attempted rescue were then heard of or feared. This morning, learning that four or five hundred armed negroes, on the Jackson road, were marching into town to burn the buildings and kill the people, the citizens immediately organized, armed, and prepared for active defence, and went out to meet the negroes, scouted the whole country around but found no armed negroes. The citizens throughout the country commenced coming into town by hundreds. Men came from Union City, Kenton, Troy, Rutherford, Dyer Station, Skull Bone, and the whole country, but found no need of their services. The two wounded negroes will die. The bodies of the ten other negroes taken from the jail were found in the river bottom about a mile from town.

"We blush for our State, and with the shame of the bloody murder, the disgraceful defiance of law, of order, and of decency full upon us, are at a loss for language with which to characterize a deed that, if the work of Comanches or Modocs, would arouse every man in the Union for a speedy vengeance on the perpetrators. To-day, we must hold up to merited reprobation and condemnation the armed men who besieged the Trenton Jail, and wantonly as wickedly, without anything like justification, took thence the unarmed negroes there awaiting trial by the courts, and brutally shot them to death; and, too, with a show of barbarity altogether as unnecessary as the massacre was unjustifiable. To say that we are not, in any county in the State, strong enough to enforce the law, is to pronounce a libel upon the whole Commonwealth. We are as a thousand to one in moral and physical force to the negro; we are in possession of the State, of all the machinery of Government, and at a time more momentous than any we ever hope to see again have proved our capacity to sustain the law's executive officers and maintain the laws. Why, then, should we now, in time of profound peace, subvert the law and defy its administrators? Why should we put the Government of our own selection under our feet, and defy and set at naught the men whom we have elected to enforce the laws, and this ruthlessly and savagely, without any of the forms, even, that usually attend on the administration of the wild behests of Judge Lynch? And all without color of extenuation; for no sane man who has regard for the truth will pretend to say that because the unfortunate negroes were arrested as the ringleaders of a threatening and armed band that had fired upon two white men, they were, therefore, worthy of death, and without the forms of law, in a State controlled and governed by law-abiding men."

No one was ever punished, or even an attempt made to ferret out the perpetrators of this foul murder. And the infliction of the death punishment, by "Lynch Law," on colored persons for the slightest offence, proves that there is really no abatement in this hideous race prejudice that prevails throughout the South.

CHAPTER XXVI.

YEARS ago, when the natural capabilities of the races were more under discussion than now, the negro was always made to appear to greater disadvantage than the rest of mankind. The public mind is not yet free from this false theory, nor has the colored man done much of late years to change this opinion. Long years of training of any people to a particular calling, seems to fit them for that vocation more than for any other. Thus, the Jews, inured to centuries of money-lending and pawn-broking, they, as a race, stick to it as if they were created for that business alone.

The training of the Arabs for long excursions through wild deserts, makes them the master roamers of the world. The Gypsies, brought up to camping out and trading in horses, send forth the idea that they were born for it. The black man's position as a servant, for many generations, has not only made the other races believe that is his legitimate sphere, but he himself feels more at home in a white apron and a towel on his arm, than with a quill behind his ear and a ledger before him.

That a colored man takes to the dining-room and the kitchen, as a duck does to water, only proves that like other races, his education has entered into his blood. This is not theory, this is not poetry; but stern truth. Our people prefer to be servants.

This may be to some extent owing to the fact that the organ of alimentativeness is more prominently formed in the negro's make-up, than in that of almost any other people.

During several trips in the cars between Nashville and Columbia, I noticed that the boy who sold newspapers and supplied the passengers with fruit, had a basket filled with candy and cakes. The first time I was on his car he offered me the cakes, which I declined, but bought a paper. Watching him I observed that when colored persons entered the car, he would offer them the cakes which they seldom failed to purchase. One day as I took from him a newspaper, I inquired of him why he always offered cakes to the colored passengers. His reply was:—"Oh! they always buy something to eat."

"Do they purchase more cakes than white people?"

"Yes," was the response.

"Why do they buy your cakes and candy?" I asked.

"Well, sir, the colored people seem always to be hungry. Never see anything like it. They don't buy papers, but they are always eating."

Just then we stopped at Franklin, and three colored passengers came in. "Now," continued the cake boy, "you'll see how they'll take the cakes," and he started for them, but had to pass their seats to shut the door that had been left open. In going by, one of the men, impatient to get a cake, called, "Here, here, come here wid yer cakes."

The peddler looked at me and laughed. He sold each one a cake, and yet it was not ten o'clock in the morning.

Not long since, in Massachusetts, I succeeded in getting a young man pardoned from our State prison, where he had been confined for more than ten years, and where he had learned a good trade.

I had already secured him a situation where he was to receive three dollars per day to commence with, with a prospect of an advance of wages.

As we were going to his boarding place, and after I had spent some time in advising him to turn over a new leaf and to try and elevate himself, we passed one of our best hotels. My ward at once stopped, began snuffing as if he "smelt a mice." I looked at him, watched his countenance as it lighted up and his eyes sparkled; I inquired what was the matter. With a radiant smile he replied, "I smell good wittles; what place is that?"

"It is the Revere House," I said.

"Wonder if I could get a place to wait on table there?" he asked.

I thought it a sorry comment on my efforts to instil into him some self-respect. This young man had learned the shoemaking trade, and at a McKay machine, I understood that he could earn from three dollars and a half to five dollars per day.

A dozen years ago, two colored young men commenced the manufacture of one of the necessary commodities of the day. After running the establishment some six or eight months successfully, they sold out to white men, who now employ more than one hundred hands. Both of the colored men are at their legitimate callings; one is a waiter in a private house, the other is a porter on a sleeping car.

The failure of these young men to carry on a manufacturing business was mainly owing to a want of training, in a business point of view. No man is fit for a profession or a trade, unless he has learned it.

Extravagance in dress is a great and growing evil with our people. I am acquainted with a lady in Boston who wears a silk dress costing one hundred and thirty dollars. She lives in two rooms, and her husband is a hair-dresser.

Since the close of the war, a large number of freedmen settled in Massachusetts, where they became servants, the most of them. These people surpass in dress, the wealthiest merchants of the city.

A young man, now a servant in a private house, sports a sixty-dollar overcoat while he works for twenty dollars per month.

A woman who cooks for five dollars per week, in Arlington Street, swings along every Sunday in a hundred-dollar silk dress, and a thirty-dollar hat. She cannot read or write.

Go to our churches on the Sabbath, and see the silk, the satin, the velvet, and the costly feathers, and talk with the uneducated wearers, and you will see at once the main hindrance to self-elevation.

To elevate ourselves and our children, we must cultivate self-denial. Repress our appetites for luxuries and be content with clothing ourselves in garments becoming our means and our incomes. The adaptation and the deep inculcation of the principles of total abstinence from all intoxicants. The latter is a pre-requisite for success in all the relations of life.

Emerging from the influence of oppression, taught from early experience to have no confidence in the whites, we have little or none in our own race, or even in ourselves.

We need more self-reliance, more confidence in the ability of our own people; more manly independence, a higher standard of moral, social, and literary culture. Indeed, we need a union of effort to remove the dark shadow of ignorance that now covers the land. While the barriers of prejudice keep us morally and socially from educated white society, we must make a strong effort to raise ourselves from the common level where emancipation and the new order of things found us.

We possess the elements of successful development; but we need live men and women to make this development. The last great struggle for our rights; the battle for our own civilization, is entirely with ourselves, and the problem is to be solved by us.

We must use our spare time, day and night, to educate ourselves. Let us have night schools for the adults, and not be ashamed to attend them. Encourage our own literary men and women; subscribe for, and be sure and pay for papers published by colored men. Don't stop to inquire if the paper will live; but encourage it, and make it live.

With the exception of a few benevolent societies, we are separated as far from each other as the east is from the west.

CHAPTER XXVII.

Union is strength, has long since passed into a proverb. The colored people of the South should at once form associations, combine and make them strong, and live up to them by all hazards. All civilized races have risen by means of combination and co-operation. The Irishman, the German, the Frenchman, all come to this country poor, and they stay here but a short time before you see them succeeding in some branch of business. This success is not the result of individual effort—it is the result of combination and co-operation. Whatever an Irishman has to spend he puts in the till of one of his own countrymen, and that accounts for Irish success.

A German succeeds in this country because all his fellow-countrymen patronize him in whatever business he engages. A German will put himself to inconvenience, and go miles out of his way to spend money with one of his own race and nationality.

With all his fickleness, the Frenchman never forgets to find out and patronize one of his own people. Italians flock together and stand by each other, right or wrong. The Chinese are clannish, and stick by one another. The Caucasian race is the foremost in the world in everything that pertains to advanced civilization,—simply owing to the fact that an Englishman never passes the door of a countryman to patronize another race; and a Yankee is a Yankee all the days of his life, and will never desert his colors. But where is the Negro?

A gentlemanly and well-informed colored man came to me a few days since, wishing to impart to me some important information, and he commenced by saying; "Now, Doctor, what I am going to tell you, you may rely on its being true, because I got it from a white man—no nigger told me this."

On Duke Street, in Alexandria, Va., resides an Irishman, who began business in that place a dozen years ago, with two jugs, one filled with whiskey, the other with molasses, a little pork, some vegetables, sugar and salt. On the opposite side of the street was our good friend, Mr. A. S. Perpener. The latter had a respectable provision store, minus the whiskey. Colored people inhabited the greater part of the street. Did they patronize their own countryman? Not a bit of it. The Irishman's business increased rapidly; he soon enlarged his premises, adding wood and coal to his salables. Perpener did the same, but the blacks passed by and went over on the other side, gave their patronage to the son of Erin, who now has houses "to let," but he will not rent them to colored tenants.

The Jews, though scattered throughout the world, are still Jews. Their race and their religion they have maintained in all countries and all ages. They never forsake each other. If they fall out, over some trade, they make up in time to combine against the rest of mankind. Shylock says: "I will buy with you, sell with you, talk with you, walk with you, and so following; but I will not eat with you, drink with you, nor pray with you." Thus, the Jew, with all his love of money, will not throw off his religion to satisfy others, and for this we honor him.

It is the misfortune of our race that the impression prevails that "one nigger is as good as another." Now this is a great error; there are colored men in this country as far ahead of others of their own race as Webster and Sumner were superior to the average white man.

Then, again, we have no confidence in each other. We consider the goods from the store of a white man necessarily better than can be purchased from a colored man.

No man ever succeeded who lacked confidence in himself. No race ever did or ever will prosper or make a respectable history which has no confidence in its own nationality.

Those who do not appreciate their own people will not be appreciated by other people. If a white man will pat a colored man on the shoulder, bow to him, and call him "Mr.," he will go a mile out of his way to patronize him, if in doing so he passes a first-class dealer of his own race. I asked a colored man in Columbia if he patronized Mr. Frierson. He said, "No." I inquired, "Why?" "He never invited me to his house in his life," was the reply.

"Does the white man you deal with invite you?"

"No."

"Then, why do you expect Mr. Frierson to do it?"

"Oh! he's a nigger and I look for more from him than I do from a white man." So it is clear that this is the result of jealousy.

The recent case of the ill-treatment of Cadet Whittaker, at West Point, shows most clearly the unsuspecting character of the negro, when dealing with whites. Although Whittaker had been repeatedly warned that an attack was to be made upon him, and especially told to look out for the assault the very night that the crime was committed, he laid down with his room-door unfastened, went off into a sound sleep, with no weapon or means of defence near him. This was, for all the world, like a negro. A Yankee would have had a revolver with every chamber loaded; an Irishman would have slept with one eye open, and a stout shillalah in his right hand, and in all probability somebody would have had a nice funeral after the attack. But that want of courage and energy, so characteristic of the race, permitted one of the foulest crimes to be perpetrated which has come to light for years.

But the most disgraceful part in this whole transaction lies with the Court of Investigation, now being conducted at West Point under the supervision of United States officials. The unfeeling and unruly cadets that outraged Whittaker, no doubt, laid a deep plan to cover up their tracks, and this was to make it appear that their victim had inflicted upon himself his own injuries. And acting upon this theory, one of the young scamps, who had no doubt been rehearsing for the occasion, volunteered to show the Court how the negro could have practised the imposition.

And, strange to say, these sage *investigators* sat quietly and looked on while the young ruffian laid down upon the floor, tied himself, and explained how the thing was done.

If the victim had been a white man and his persecutors black, does any one believe for a moment that such a theory would have been listened to?

Generations of oppression have done their work too thoroughly to have its traces wiped away in a dozen years. The race must be educated out of the ignorance in which it at present dwells, and lifted to a level with other races. Colored lawyers, doctors, artisans and mechanics, starve for patronage, while the negro is begging the white man to do his work. Combinations have made other races what they are to-day.

The great achievements of scientific men could not have been made practical by individual effort. The great works of genius could never have benefited the world, had those who composed them been mean and selfish. All great and useful enterprises have succeeded through the influence and energy of numbers.

I would not have it thought that all colored men are to be bought by the white man's smiles, or to be frightened by intimidation. Far from it. In all the Southern States we have some of the noblest specimens of mankind,—men of genius, refinement, courage and liberality, ready to do and to die for the race.

CHAPTER XXVIII.

ADVICE upon the formation of Literary Associations, and total abstinence from all intoxications is needed, and I will give it to you in this chapter. The time for colored men and women to organize for self-improvement has arrived. Moral, social, and intellectual development, should be the main attainment of the negro race. Colored people have so long been in the habit of aping the whites, and often not the better class either, that I fear this characteristic in them, more than anything else. A large percentage of them being waiters, they see a great deal of drinking in white society of the "Upper Ten." Don't follow their bad example. Take warning by their degradation.

During the year 1879, Boston sent four hundred drunken women to the Sherborn prison; while two private asylums are full, many of them from Boston's first families. Therefore, I beseech you to never allow the intoxicant to enter your circles.

It is bad enough for men to lapse into habits of drunkenness. A drunken husband, a drunken father—only those patient, heart-broken, shame-faced wives and children on whom this great cross of suffering is laid, can estimate the misery which it brings.

But a drunken girl—a drunken wife—a drunken mother—is there for woman a deeper depth? Home made hideous—children disgraced, neglected, and maltreated.

Remember that all this comes from the first glass. The wine may be pleasant to the taste, and may for the time being, furnish happiness; but it must never be forgotten that whatever degree of exhiliration may be produced in a healthy person by the use of wine, it will most certainly be succeeded by a degree of nervous depression proportioned to the amount of previous excitement. Hence the immoderate use of wine, or its habitual indulgence, debilitates the brain and nervous system, paralyzes the intellectual powers, impairs the functions of the stomach, produces a perverted appetite for a renewal of the deleterious beverage, or a morbid imagination, which destroys man's usefulness.

The next important need with our people, is the cultivation of habits of business. We have been so long a dependent race, so long looking to the white as our leaders, and being content with doing the drudgery of life, that most who commence business for themselves are likely to fail, because of want of a knowledge of what we undertake. As the education of a large percentage of the colored people is of a fragmentary character, having been gained by little and little here and there, and must necessarily be limited to a certain degree, we should use our spare hours in study and form associations for moral, social, and literary culture. We must aim to enlighten ourselves and to influence others to higher associations.

Our work lies primarily with the inward culture, at the springs and sources of individual life and character, seeking everywhere to encourage, and assist to the fullest emancipation of the human mind from ignorance, inviting the largest liberty of thought, and the utmost possible exaltation of life into approximation to the loftier standard of cultivated character. Feeling that the literature of our age is the reflection of the existing manners and modes of thought, etherealized and refined in the alembic of genius, we should give our principal encouragement to literature, bringing before our associations the importance of original essays, selected readings, and the cultivation of the musical talent.

If we need any proof of the good that would accrue from such cultivation, we have only to look back and see the wonderful influence of Homer over the Greeks, of Virgil and Horace over the Romans, of Dante and Ariosto over the Italians, of Goethe and Schiller over the Germans, of Racine and Voltaire over the French, of Shakespeare and Milton over the English. The imaginative powers of these men, wrought into verse or prose, have been the theme of the king in his palace, the lover in his dreamy moods, the farmer in the harvest field, the mechanic in the work-shop, the sailor on the high seas, and the prisoner in his gloomy cell.

Indeed, authors possess the most gifted and fertile minds who combine all the graces of style with rare, fascinating powers of language, eloquence, wit, humor, pathos, genius and learning. And to draw knowledge from such sources should be one of the highest aims of man. The better elements of society can only be brought together by organizing societies and clubs.

The cultivation of the mind is the superstructure of the moral, social and religious character, which will follow us into our every-day life, and make us what God intended us to be—the noblest instruments of His creative power. Our efforts should be to imbue our minds with broader and better views of science, literature, and a nobleness of spirit that ignores petty aims of patriotism, glory, or mere personal aggrandizement. It is said, never a shadow falls that does not leave a permanent impress of its image, a monument of its passing presence. Every character is modified by association. Words, the image of the ideas, are more impressive than shadows; actions, embodied thoughts, more enduring than aught material. Believing these truths, then, I say, for every thought expressed, ennobling in its tendency and elevating to Christian dignity and manly honor, God will reward us. Permanent success depends upon intrinsic worth. The best way to have a public character is to have a private one.

The great struggle for our elevation is now with ourselves. We may talk of Hannibal, Euclid, Phyllis Wheatly, Benjamin Bannaker, and Toussaint L'Overture, but the world will ask us for our men and women of the day. We cannot live upon the past; we must hew out a reputation that will stand the test, one that we have a legitimate right to. To do this, we must imitate the best examples set us by the cultivated whites, and by so doing we will teach them that they can claim no superiority on account of race.

The efforts made by oppressed nations or communities to throw off their chains, entitles them to, and gains for them the respect of mankind. This, the blacks never made, or what they did, was so feeble as scarcely to call for comment. The planning of Denmark Vesey for an insurrection in South Carolina, was noble, and deserved a better fate; but he was betrayed by the race that he was attempting to serve.

Nat Turner's strike for liberty was the outburst of feelings of an insane man,—made so by slavery. True, the negro did good service at the battles of Wagner, Honey Hill, Port Hudson, Millikin's Bend, Poison Springs, Olustee and Petersburg. Yet it would have been far better if they had commenced earlier, or had been under leaders of their own color. The St. Domingo revolution brought forth men of courage. But the subsequent course of the people as a government, reflects little or no honor on the race. They have floated about like a ship without a rudder, ever since the expulsion of Rochambeau.

The fact is the world likes to see the exhibition of pluck on the part of an oppressed people, even though they fail in their object. It is these outbursts of the love of liberty that gains respect and sympathy for the enslaved. Therefore, I bid God speed to the men and women of the South, in their effort to break the long spell of lethargy that hangs over the race. Don't be too rash in starting, but prepare to go, and "don't stand upon the order of going, but go." By common right, the South is the negro's home. Born, and "raised" there, he cleared up the lands, built the cities, fed and clothed the whites, nursed their children, earned the money to educate their sons and daughters; by the negro's labor churches were built and clergymen paid.

For two hundred years the Southern whites lived a lazy life at the expense of the negro's liberty. When the rebellion came, the blacks, trusted and true to the last, protected the families and homes of white men while they were away fighting the Government. The South is the black man's home; yet if he cannot be protected in his rights he should leave. Where white men of liberal views can get no protection, the colored man must not look for it. Follow the example of other oppressed races, strike out for new territory. If suffering is the result, let it come; others have suffered before you. Look at the Irish, Germans, French, Italians, and other races, who have come to this country, gone to the West, and are now enjoying the blessings of liberty and plenty; while the negro is discussing the question of whether he should leave the South or not, simply because he was born there.

While they are thus debating the subject, their old oppressors, seeing that the negro has touched the right chord, forbid his leaving the country. Georgia has made it a penal offence to invite the blacks to emigrate, and one negro is already in prison for wishing to better the condition of his fellows. This is the same spirit that induced the people of that State to offer a reward of five thousand dollars, in 1835, for the head of Garrison. No people has borne oppression like the negro, and no race has been so much imposed upon. Go to his own land. Ask the Dutch boor whence comes his contempt and inward dislike to the negro, the Hottentot, and Caffre; ask him for his warrant to reduce these unhappy races to slavery; he will point to the fire-arms suspended over the mantle-piece—"There is my right."

Want of independence is the colored man's greatest fault. In the present condition of the Southern States, with the lands in the hands of a shoddy, ignorant, superstitious, rebellious, and negro-hating population, the blacks cannot be independent. Then emigrate to get away from the surroundings that keep you down where you are. All cannot go, even if it were desirable; but those who remain will have a better opportunity. The planters will then have to pursue a different policy. The right of the negroes to make the best terms they can, will have to be recognized, and what was before presumption that called for repression will now be tolerated as among the privileges of freedom. The ability of the negroes to change their location will also turn public sentiment against bull-dozing.

Two hundred years have demonstrated the fact that the negro is the manual laborer of that section, and without him agriculture will be at a stand-still.

The negro will for pay perform any service under heaven, no matter how repulsive or full of hardship. He will sing his old plantation melodies and walk about the cotton fields in July and August, when the toughest white man seeks an awning. Heat is his element. He fears no malaria in the rice swamps, where a white man's life is not worth sixpence.

Then, I say, leave the South and starve the whites into a realization of justice and common sense. Remember that tyrants never relinquish their grasp upon their victims until they are forced to.

Whether the blacks emigrate or not, I say to them, keep away from the cities and towns. Go into the country. Go to work on farms.

If you stop in the city, get a profession or a trade, but keep in mind that a good trade is better than a poor profession.

In Boston there are a large number of colored professionals, especially in the law, and a majority of whom are better fitted for farm service, mechanical branches, or for driving an ash cart.

Persons should not select professions for the name of being a "professional," nor because they think they will lead an easy life. An honorable, lucrative and faithfully-earned professional reputation, is a career of honesty, patience, sobriety, toil and Christian zeal.

No drone can fill such a position. Select the profession or trade that your education, inclination, strength of mind and body will support, and then give your time to the work that you have undertaken, and work, work.

Once more I say to those who cannot get remunerative employment at the South, emigrate.

Some say, "stay and fight it out, contend for your rights, don't let the old rebels drive you away, the country is as much yours as theirs." That kind of talk will do very well for men who have comfortable homes out of the South, and law to protect them; but for the negro, with no home, no food, no work, the land-owner offering him conditions whereby he can do but little better than starve, such talk is nonsense. Fight out what? Hunger? Poverty? Cold? Starvation? Black men, emigrate.

CHAPTER XXIX.

In America, the negro stands alone as a race. He is without mate or fellow in the great family of man. Whatever progress he makes, it must be mainly by his own efforts. This is an unfortunate fact, and for which there seems to be no remedy.

All history demonstrates the truth that amalgamation is the great civilizer of the races of men. Wherever a race, clan, or community have kept themselves together, prohibiting by law, usage, or common consent, inter-marriage with others, they have made little or no progress. The Jews, a distinct and isolated people, are good only at driving a bargain and getting rich. The Gipsies commence and stop with trading horses. The Irish, in their own country, are dull. The Coptic race form but a handful of what they were—those builders, unequalled in ancient or modern times. What has become of them? Where are the Romans? What races have they destroyed? What races have they supplanted? For fourteen centuries they lorded it over the semi-civilized world; and now they are of no more note than the ancient Scythians, or Mongols, Copts, or Tartars. An un-amalgamated, inactive people will decline. Thus it was with the Mexicans, when Cortes marched on Mexico, and the Peruvians, when Pizarro marched on Peru.

The Britons were a dull, lethargic people before their country was invaded, and the hot, romantic blood of Julius Cæsar and William of Normandy coursed through their veins.

Caractacus, king of the Britons, was captured and sent to Rome in chains. Still later, Hengist and Horsa, the Saxon generals, imposed the most humiliating conditions upon the Britons, to which they were compelled to submit. Then came William of Normandy, defeated Harold at Hastings, and the blood of the most renowned land-pirates and sea-robbers that ever disgraced humanity, mixed with the Briton and Saxon, and gave to the world the Anglo-Saxon race, with its physical ability, strong mind, brave and enterprising spirit. And, yet, all that this race is, it owes to its mixed blood. Civilization, or the social condition of man, is the result and test of the qualities of every race. The benefit of this blood mixture, the negro is never to enjoy on this continent. In the South where he is raised, in the North, East, or West, it is all the same, no new blood is to be infused into his sluggish veins.

His only hope is education, professions, trades, and copying the best examples, no matter from what source they come.

This antipathy to amalgamation with the negro, has shown itself in all of the States. Most of the Northern and Eastern State Legislatures have passed upon this question years ago. Since the coming in of the present year, Rhode Island's Senate refused to repeal the old law forbidding the intermarriage of whites and blacks. Thus the colored man is left to "paddle his own canoe" alone. Where there is no law against the mixture of the two races, there is a public sentiment which is often stronger than law itself. Even the wild blood of the red Indian refuses to mingle with the sluggish blood of the negro. This is no light matter, for race hate, prejudice and common malice all die away before the melting power of amalgamation. The beauty of the half-breeds of the South, the result of the crime of slavery, have long claimed the attention of writers, and why not a lawful mixture? And then this might help in

> "Making a race far more lovely and fair,
> Darker a little than white people are:
> Stronger, and nobler, and better in form,
> Hearts more voluptuous, kinder, and warm;
> Bosoms of beauty, that heave with a pride
> Nature had ever to white folks denied."

Emigration to other States, where the blacks will come in contact with educated and enterprising whites, will do them much good. This benefit by commercial intercourse is seen in the four thousand colored people who have come to Boston, where most of them are employed as servants. They are sought after as the best domestics in the city. Some of these people, who were in slavery before the war, are now engaged in mercantile pursuits, doing good business, and showing what contact will do. Many of them rank with the ablest whites in the same trades. Indeed, the various callings are well represented by Southern men, showing plainly the need of emigration. Although the colored man has been sadly at fault in not vindicating his right to liberty, he has, it is true, shown ability in other fields. Benjamin Banneker, a negro of Maryland, who lived a hundred years ago, exhibited splendid natural qualities. He had a quickness of apprehension, and a vivacity of understanding, which easily took in and surmounted the most subtile and knotty parts of mathematics and metaphysics. He possessed in a large degree that genius which constitutes a man of letters; that quality without which judgment is cold, and knowledge is inert; that energy which collects, combines, amplifies, and animates.

The rapid progress made in acquiring education and homesteads by the colored people of the South, in the face of adverse circumstances, commends the highest admiration from all classes.

The product of their native genius and industry, as exhibited at county and State Agricultural Fairs, speak well for the race.

At the National Fair, held at Raleigh, N. C., in the autumn of 1879, the exhibition did great credit to the colored citizens of the South, who had the matter in charge. Such manifestations of intellectual and mechanical enterprise will do much to stimulate the people to further development of their powers, and higher facilities.

The colored people of the United States are sadly in need of a National Scientific Association, to which may be brought yearly reports of such investigations as may be achieved in science, philosophy, art, philology, ethnology, jurisprudence, metaphysics, and whatever may tend to *unite* the race in their moral, social, intellectual and physical improvement.

We have negro artists of a high order, both in painting and sculpture; also, discoverers who hold patents, and yet the world knows little or nothing about them. The time for the negro to work out his destiny has arrived. Now let him show himself equal to the hour.

In this work I frequently used the word "Negro," and shall, no doubt, hear from it when the negro critics get a sight of the book. And why should I not use it? Is it not honorable? What is there in the word that does not sound as well as "English," "Irish," "German," "Italian," "French?"

"Don't call me a negro; I'm an American," said a black to me a few days since.

"Why not?" I asked.

"Well, sir, I was born in this country, and I don't want to be called out of my name."

Just then, an Irish-American came up, and shook hands with me. He had been a neighbor of mine in Cambridge. When the young man was gone, I inquired of the black man what countryman he thought the man was.

"Oh!" replied he, "he's an Irishman."

"What makes you think so?" I inquired.

"Why, his brogue is enough to tell it."

"Then," said I, "why is not your color enough to tell that you're a negro?"

"Arh!" said he, "that's a horse of another color," and left me with a "Ha, ha, ha!"

Black men, don't be ashamed to show your colors, and to own them.

SPEECHES & PUBLIC LETTERS

Letter from Wm. W. Brown—
A Methodist Deacon's Prayer

September 26, 1844

Brown conducted an antislavery lecture tour in 1844 across Ohio, a free state bitterly divided over slavery. At one meeting hosted at a Methodist church, an institution normally closed to antislavery gatherings, its deacon accepted Brown's offer to open the proceedings with a benediction. He went on to do more: he defended Senator Henry Clay, the state's adopted favorite son in his frequent runs for the presidency, against antislavery critics. In one of his earliest known writings, Brown retorted in the *National Anti-Slavery Standard* with this mock prayer.

A few evenings since, at one of my meetings, after the audience had assembled, a deacon of the Methodist Church arose, and asked if I wanted the meeting opened with prayer. I answered, that if there were any one in the house that felt himself called upon to pray, that an opportunity was then offered. The deacon then said, "Let us pray;" and he prayed as follows: "Lord! thou knowest that we depend upon thy aid. Without thy aid we can do nothing. Lord! we look to thee to aid us in selecting good rulers. Lord! let us have men that will rule over us with fear; let us have good rulers. Whatever thy servant, that is going to address us, may say, let it be said in love; let it be truth; give us the truth, let it cut where it will. But Lord! let nothing be said that will give dissatisfaction. Lord! let nothing be said that will hurt any one's feelings. Lord! may he say nothing about political parties. Lord! thou knowest that some of the Abolition lecturers do say hard things about our Southern brethren. Lord! thou knowest that some of them have attempted to villify Mr. Clay, and slander him by saying that he is a duellist, and calling him hard names. Lord! let nothing of the kind be said this evening. Lord! thou knowest that Mr. Clay is a good man, and if we do not elect him, we will get a worse one. Thou knowest that the Abolitionists are trying to keep out Mr. Clay, but let them not do it. Now, Lord! take charge of thy servant that is going to speak, and let him present nothing but the truth, and let him say nothing about politics, and the glory shall be thine forever, Amen."

I could scarcely keep from laughing out several times during the time that the deacon was praying. When he had concluded, I took the stand and commenced. My text was, the Farmer of Ashland. As you know, I am not a politician, but I was compelled that evening to go into political matters, or at least the merits and demerits of the two great political parties, and I occasionally looked at the deacon. I was told after the meeting that I had handled the hero of Ashland too roughly. At the close of the meeting, I called on the deacon to pray; but said he, "No, I thank you; I would rather you would get some one else." I do not make it a practice to call upon any one to pray in meeting, but I could not help calling upon the deacon.

Yours, in the cause of the slave,

WM. W. BROWN.

A Lecture Delivered before the Female Anti-Slavery Society of Salem at Lyceum Hall

November 14, 1847

Enjoying his new celebrity after the publication of his *Narrative* in July 1847, Brown accepted an offer to deliver a lyceum lecture in Salem, Massachusetts, to the local women's antislavery society. Whereas he generally spoke spontaneously, for this more formal occasion he delivered a prepared, polished lecture, whose text was recorded on the spot by a local stenographer, then printed and disseminated by the Massachusetts Anti-Slavery Society. It delivers one of his most rhetorically skillful attacks on the institution of slavery in clear, urgent language and in terms of direct address designed to move his audience to sympathy and action.

Mr. Chairman, and Ladies and Gentlemen:—In coming before you this evening to speak upon this all-important, this great and commanding subject of freedom, I do not appear without considerable embarrassment; nor am I embarrassed without a cause. I find myself standing before an audience whose opportunities for education may well be said to be without limit. I can scarcely walk through a street in your city, or through a city or a town in New England, but I see your common schools, your high schools, and your colleges. And when I recollect that but a few years since, I was upon a Southern plantation, that I was a Slave, a chattel, a thing, a piece of property,—when I recollect that at the age of twenty-one years I was entirely without education, this, every one will agree, is enough to embarrass me. But I do not come here for the purpose of making a grammatical speech, nor for the purpose of making a speech that shall receive the applause of my hearers. I did not accept the invitation to lecture before this association, with the expectation or the hope that I should be able to present anything new. I accepted the invitation because I felt that I owed a duty to the cause of humanity; I felt that I owed a duty to three millions of my brethren and sisters, with some of whom I am identified by the dearest ties of nature, and with most of whom I am identified by the scars which I carry upon my back. This, and this alone, induced me to accept the invitation to lecture here.

My subject for this evening is Slavery as it is, and its influence upon the morals and character of the American people.

I may try to represent to you Slavery as it is; another may follow me and try to represent the condition of the Slave; we may all represent it as we think it is; and yet we shall all fail to represent the real condition of the Slave. Your fastidiousness would not allow me to do it; and if it would, I, for one, should not be willing to do it;—at least to an audience. Were I about to tell you the evils of Slavery, to represent to you the Slave in his lowest degradation, I should wish to take you, one at a time, and whisper it to you.

Slavery has never been represented; Slavery never can be represented. What is a Slave? A Slave is one that is in the power of an owner. He is a chattel; he is a thing; he is a piece of property. A master can dispose of him, can dispose of his labor, can dispose of his wife, can dispose of his offspring, can dispose of everything that belongs to the Slave, and the Slave shall have no right to speak; he shall have nothing to say. The Slave cannot speak for himself; he cannot speak for his wife, or his children. He is a thing. He is a piece of property in the hands of a master, as much as is the horse that belongs to the individual that may ride him through your streets to-morrow. Where we find one man holding an unlimited power over another, I ask, what can we expect to find his condition? Give one man power *ad infinitum* over another, and he will abuse that power; no matter if there be law; no matter if there be public sentiment in favor of the oppressed.

The system of Slavery, that I, in part, represent here this evening, is a system that strikes at the foundation of society, that strikes at the foundation of civil and political institutions. It is a system that takes man down from that lofty position which his God designed that he should occupy; that drags him down, places him upon a level with the beasts of the field, and there keeps him, that it may rob him of his liberty. Slavery is a system that tears the husband from the wife, and the wife from the husband; that tears the child from the mother, and the sister from the brother; that tears asunder the tenderest ties of nature. Slavery is a system that has its blood-hounds, its chains, its negro-whips, its dungeons, and almost every instrument of cruelty that the human eye can look at; and all this for the purpose of keeping the Slave in subjection; all this for the purpose of obliterating the mind, of crushing the intellect, and of annihilating the soul.

I have read somewhere of an individual named Caspar Hauser, who made his appearance in Germany some time since, and represented that he had made his escape from certain persons who had been trying to obliterate his mind, and to annihilate his intellect. The representation of that single individual raised such an excitement in Germany, that law-makers took it in hand, examined it, and made a law covering that particular case and all cases that should occur of that kind; and they denominated it the "murder of the soul." Now, I ask, what is Slavery doing in one half of the States of this Union, at the present time? The souls of three millions of American citizens are being murdered every day, under the blighting influence of American Slavery. Twenty thousand have made their escape from the prison-house; some have taken refuge in the Canadas, and others are lurking behind the stumps in the Slave-States. They are telling their tales, and representing that Slavery is not only trying to murder their souls, but the souls of three million of their countrymen at the present day; and the excitement that one individual raised in monarchical Germany, three millions have failed to raise in democratic, Christian, republican America!

I ask, is not this a system that we should examine? Ought we not to look at it? Ought we not to see what the cause is that keeps the people asleep upon the great subject of American Slavery? When I get to talking about Slavery as it is,—when I think of the three millions that are in chains at the present time, I am carried back to the days when I was a Slave upon a Southern plantation; I am carried back to the time when I saw dear relatives, with whom I am identified by the tenderest ties of nature, abused and ill-treated. I am carried back to the time when I saw hundreds of Slaves driven from the Slave-growing to the Slave-consuming States. When I begin to talk of Slavery, the sighs and the groans of three millions of my countrymen come to me upon the wings of every wind; and it causes me to feel sad, even when I think I am making a successful effort in representing the condition of the Slave.

What is the protection from the masters which Slaves receive? Some say, law; others, public sentiment. But, I ask, Where is the law; where is the public sentiment? If it is there, it is not effectual; it will not protect the Slave. Has the case ever occurred where the Slaveholder has been sent to the State's Prison, or anything of the kind, for ill-treating, or for murdering a Slave? No such case is upon record; and it is because the Slave receives no protection and can expect no protection from the hands of the master. What has the brother not done, upon the Slave-plantation, for the purpose of protecting the chastity of a dearly beloved sister? What has the father not done to protect the chastity of his daughter? What has the husband not done to protect his wife from the hands of the tyrant? They have committed murders. The mother has taken the life of her child, to preserve that child from the hands of the Slave-trader. The brother has taken the life of his sister, to protect her chastity. As the noble Virginius seized the dagger, and thrust it to the heart of the gentle Virginia, to save her from the hands of Appius Claudius of Rome, so has the father seized the deadly knife, and taken the life of his daughter, to save her from the hands of the master or of the Negro-driver. And yet we are told that the Slave is protected; that there is law and public sentiment! It is all a dead letter to the Slave.

But why stand here and try to represent the condition of the Slave? My whole subject must necessarily represent his condition, and I will therefore pass to the second part,—the influence of Slavery upon the morals of the people; not only upon the morals of the Slave-holding South, or of the Slave, but upon the morals of the people of the United States of America. I am not willing to draw a line between the people of the North and the people of the South. So far as the people of the North are connected with Slaveholding, they necessarily become contaminated by the evils that follow in the train of Slavery.

Let me look at the influence which Slavery has over the morals of the people of the South. Three millions of Slaves unprotected! A million of females that have no right to marriage! Among the three millions of Slaves upon the Southern plantations, not a single lawful marriage can be found! They are out of the pale of the law. They are herded together, so far as the law is concerned, as so many beasts of burden are in the free States.

Talk about the influence of Slavery upon the morals of the people, when the Slave is sold in the Slave-holding States for the benefit of the church? when he is sold for the purpose of building churches? when he is sold for the benefit of the minister?

I have before me a few advertisements, taken from public journals and papers, published in the Slaveholding States of this Union. I have one or two that I will read to the audience, for I am satisfied that no evidence is so effectual for the purpose of convincing the people of the North of the great evils of Slavery as is the evidence of Slaveholders themselves. I do not present to you the assertion of the North; I do not bring before you the advertisement of the Abolitionists, or my own assertion; but I bring before you the testimony of the Slaveholders themselves,—and by their own testimony must they stand or fall.

The first is an advertisement from the columns of the New Orleans Picayune, one of the most reputable papers published in the State of Louisiana, and I may say one of the most reputable papers published South of Mason and Dixon's line. If you take up the Boston Courier, or any other reputable paper, you will probably find in it an extract from the New Orleans Picayune, whose editor is at the present time in Mexico, where our people are cutting the throats of their neighbors.

> COCK-PIT.—*Benefit of Fire Company No.* 1, *Lafayette.*—A cock-fight will take place on Sunday, the 17th inst., at the well-known house of the subscriber. As the entire proceeds are for the benefit of the Fire Company, a full attendance is respectfully solicited. ADAM ISRANG,
> *Corner of Josephine and Tchoupitolas Streets, Lafayette*
> [N. O. Pic. of Sunday, Dec. 17

> TURKEY SHOOTING.—This day, Dec. 17, from 10 o'clock, A. M., until 6 o'clock, P. M., and the following Sundays, at M'Donoughville, opposite the Second Municipality Ferry.
> [From the same paper

The next is an advertisement from the New Orleans Bee, an equally popular paper.

> A BULL FIGHT, between a ferocious bull and a number of dogs, will take place on Sunday next, at 11 o'clock, P. M., on the other side of the river, at Algiers, opposite Canal Street. After

the bull fight, a fight will take place between a bear and some dogs. The whole to conclude by a combat between an ass and several dogs.

Amateurs bringing dogs to participate in the fight will be admitted gratis. Admittance—Boxes, 50 cts; Pit, 30 cts. The spectacle will be repeated every Sunday, weather permitting.

PEPE LEULLA.

Now these are not strange advertisements to be found in a Southern journal. They only show what Slavery has been doing there to contaminate the morals of the people. Such advertisements can be found in numbers of the public journals that are published in the Slaveholding States of this Union. You would not find such an advertisement in a Boston or a Salem paper. Scarcely a paper in New England would admit such an advertisement; and why? Because you are not so closely connected with Slavery; you are not so much under its blighting influence as are the Slave-owners in the Slaveholding States of the Union.

I have another advertisement, taken from a Charleston paper, advertising the property of a deceased Doctor of Divinity, probably one of the most popular men of his denomination that ever resided in the United States of America. In that advertisement it says, that among the property are "twenty-seven Negroes, two mules, one horse, and an old wagon." That is the property of a Slave-holding Doctor of Divinity!*

I have another advertisement before me, taken from an Alabama paper, in which eight Slaves are advertised to be sold for the benefit of an Old School Theological Seminary for the purpose of making ministers. I have another, where ten Slaves are advertised to be sold for the benefit of Christ Church Parish. I have another, where four Slaves are advertised to be sold for the benefit of the Missionary cause,—a very benevolent cause indeed. I might go on and present to you advertisement after advertisement representing the system of American Slavery, and its contaminating influence upon the morals of the people. I have an account, very recent, that a Slave-trader,—one of the meanest and most degrading positions in which a man can be found upon God's footstool,—buying and selling the bodies and souls

*Dr. Furman, of South Carolina.

of his fellow-countrymen, has joined the church, and was, probably, hopefully converted. It is only an evidence that when Wickedness, with a purse of gold, knocks at the door of the Church, she seldom, if ever, is refused admission.

This is not the case here; for, some forty years since, the Church was found repudiating Slavery; she was found condemning Slavery as man-stealing, and a sin of the deepest dye. The Methodists, Presbyterians, and other denominations, and some of the first men in the country, bore their testimony against it. But Slavery has gone into all the ramifications of society; it has taken root in almost every part of society, and now Slavery is popular. Slavery has become popular, because it has power.

Speak of the blighting influence of Slavery upon the morals of the people! Go into the Slaveholding States, and there you can see the master going into the church, on the Sabbath, with his Slave following him into the church, and waiting upon him,—both belonging to the same church. And the day following, the master puts his Slave upon the auction-stand and sells him to the highest bidder. The Church does not condemn him; the law does not condemn him; public sentiment does not condemn him; but the Slaveholder walks through the community as much respected after he has sold a brother belonging to the same church with himself, as if he had not committed an offence against God.

Go into the Slaveholding States, and to-morrow you may see families of Slaves driven to the auction-stand, to be sold to the highest bidder; the husband to be sold in presence of the wife, the wife in presence of the husband, and the children in presence of them both. All this is done under the sanction of law and order; all is done under the sanction of public sentiment, whether that public sentiment be found in Church or in State.

Leaving the Slaveholding States, let me ask what is the influence that Slavery has over the minds of the Northern people? What is its contaminating influence over the great mass of the people of the North? It must have an influence, either good or bad. People of the North, being connected with the Slaveholding States, must necessarily become contaminated. Look all around, and you see benevolent associations formed for the purpose of carrying out the principles of Christianity; but what have they been doing for Humanity? What have they ever done for the Slave?

First, we see the great American Bible Society. It is sending bibles all over the world for the purpose of converting the heathen. Its agents are to be found in almost every country and climate. Yet three millions of Slaves have never received a single bible from the American Bible Society. A few years since, the American Anti-Slavery Society offered to the American Bible Society a donation of $5,000 if they would send bibles to the Slaves, or make an effort to do it, and the American Bible Society refused even to *attempt* to send the bible to the Slaves!

A Bible Society, auxiliary to the American Bible Society, held a meeting a short time since, at Cincinnati, in the State of Ohio. One of its members brought forward a resolution that the Society should do its best to put the bible into the hands of every poor person in the country. As soon as that was disposed of, another member brought forward a resolution that the Society should do its best to put the bible into the hands of every Slave in the country. That subject was discussed for two days, and at the end of that time they threw the resolution under the table, virtually resolving that they would not make an attempt to send bibles to the Slaves.

Leaving the American Bible Society, the next is the American Tract Society. What have you to say against the American Tract Society? you may ask. I have nothing to say against any association that is formed for a benevolent purpose, if it will only carry out the purpose for which it was formed. Has the American Tract Society ever published a single line against the sin of Slaveholding? You have all, probably, read tracts treating against licentiousness, against intemperance, against gambling, against Sabbath-breaking, against dancing, against almost every sin that you can think of; but not a single syllable has ever been published by the American Tract Society against the sin of Slaveholding. Only a short time since they offered a reward of $500 for the best treatise against the sin of dancing. A gentleman wrote the treatise, they awarded him the $500, and the tract is now in the course of publication, if it is not already published. Go into a nice room, with fine music, and good company, and they will publish a tract against your dancing; while three millions are dancing every day at the end of the master's cowhide, and they cannot notice it! Oh, no; it is too small fry for them! They cannot touch that, but they can spend their money in publishing tracts against your dancing here at the North, while the Slave at the South may dance until he dances into his grave, and they care nothing about him.

A friend of mine, residing at Amsterdam, N. Y., who had been accustomed every year to make a donation to the American Tract and Bible Societies, some two years since said to the Agent when he was called upon, "I will not give you anything now, but tell the Board at New York that if they will publish a tract against the sin of Slaveholding, they may draw on me for $50." The individual's name is Ellis Clisby, a member of the Presbyterian church, and a more reputable individual than he cannot be found. The next year when the Agent called upon him, he asked where was the tract. Said the Agent, "I laid it before the Committee and they said they dared not publish it. If they published it their Southern contributions would be cut off." So they were willing to sacrifice the right, the interest, and the welfare of the Slave for the "almighty dollar." They were ready to sacrifice humanity for the sake of receiving funds from the South. Has not Slavery an influence over the morals of the North?

I have before me an advertisement where some Slaves are advertised to be sold at the South for the benefit of merchants in the city of New York, and I will read it to you. It is taken from the Alabama Beacon.

> "PUBLIC SALE OF NEGROES.—By virtue of a deed of trust made to me by Charles Whelan, for the benefit of J. W. & R. Leavitt, and of Lewis B. Brown, all of the city of New York, which deed is on record in Greene County, I shall sell at public auction, for cash, on Main Street, in the town of Greensborough, on Saturday, the 22d day of December next, a Negro Woman, about 30 years old, and her child, eleven months old; a Negro Girl about 10 years old, and a Negro Girl about 8 years old.
>
> WM. TRAPP, *Trustee.*"

Now if I know anything about the history of this country, the 22d day of December is the anniversary of the landing of the Pilgrims; the anniversary of the day when those ambassadors, those leaders in religion, came to the American shore; when they landed within the encircling arms of Cape Cod and Cape Ann, fleeing from political and religious tyranny, seeking political and religious freedom in the New World. The anniversary of that day is selected for selling an American mother and her four children for the benefit of New York merchants.

I happen to know something of one of the parties. He is a member of Dr. Spring's church, and it is said that he gives more money to support that church than any other individual. And I should not wonder, when the bones, and muscles, and sinews, and hearts of human beings are put upon the auction-stand and sold for his benefit, if he could give a little to the church. I should not wonder if he could give a little to some institution that might throw a cloak over him, white-wash him, and make him appear reputable in the community. Has not Slavery an influence over the morals of the North, and of the whole community?

Now let us leave the morals of the American people and look at their character. When I speak of the character of the American people, I look at the nation. I place all together, and draw no mark between the people and the government. The government is the people, and the people are the government. You who are here, all who are to be found in New England, and throughout the United States of America, are the persons that make up the great American confederacy; and I ask, what is the influence that Slavery has had upon the character of the American people? But for the blighting influence of Slavery, the United States of America would have a character, would have a reputation, that would outshine the reputation of any other government that is to be found upon God's green earth.

Look at the struggle of the fathers of this country for liberty. What did they struggle for? What did they go upon the battle-field for, in 1776? They went there, it is said, for the purpose of obtaining liberty; for the purpose of instituting a democratic, republican government. What is Democracy? Solon, upon one occasion, while speaking to the Athenians said, "A democratic government is a government where an injury done to the least of its citizens is regarded as an insult and an injury to the whole commonwealth." That was the opinion of an old law-maker and statesman upon the subject of Democracy. But what says an American statesman? A South Carolina governor says that Slavery is the corner-stone of our Republic. Another eminent American statesman says that two hundred years have sanctioned and sanctified American Slavery, and that is property which the law declares to be property. Which shall we believe? One that is reared in republican America, or one that is brought up in the lap of aristocracy. Every one must admit that democracy is nothing more or less than genuine freedom and liberty, protecting every individual in the community.

I might carry the audience back to the time when your fathers were struggling for liberty in 1776. When they went forth upon the battle-field and laid down their bones, and moistened the soil with their blood, that their children might enjoy liberty. What was it for? Because a three-penny tax upon tea, a tax upon paper, or something else had been imposed upon them. We are not talking against such taxes upon the Slave. The Slave has no tea; he has no paper; he has not even himself; he has nothing at all.

When we examine the influence of Slavery upon the character of the American people, we are led to believe that if the American Government ever had a character, she has lost it. I know that upon the 4th of July, our 4th of July orators talk of Liberty, Democracy, and Republicanism. They talk of liberty, while three millions of their own countrymen are groaning in abject Slavery. This is called the "land of the free, and the home of the brave;" it is called the "Asylum of the oppressed;" and some have been foolish enough to call it the "Cradle of Liberty." If it is the "cradle of liberty," they have rocked the child to death. It is dead long since, and yet we talk about democracy and republicanism, while one-sixth of our countrymen are clanking their chains upon the very soil which our fathers moistened with their blood. They have such scenes even upon the holy Sabbath, and the American people are perfectly dead upon the subject. The cries, and shrieks, and groans of the Slave do not wake them.

It is deplorable to look at the character of the American people, the character that has been given to them by the institution of Slavery. The profession of the American people is far above the profession of the people of any other country. Here the people profess to carry out the principles of Christianity. The American people are a sympathizing people. They not only profess, but appear to be a sympathizing people to the inhabitants of the whole world. They sympathize with everything else but the American Slave. When the Greeks were struggling for liberty, meetings were held to express sympathy. Now they are sympathizing with the poor down-trodden serfs of Ireland, and are sending their sympathy across the ocean to them.

But what will the people of the Old World think? Will they not look upon the American people as hypocrites? Do they not look upon your professed sympathy as nothing more than hypocrisy? You may hold your meetings and send your words across the ocean; you may ask Nicholas of Russia to take the chains from his poor down-trodden serfs, but they look upon it all as nothing but hypocrisy. Look at our twenty thousand fugitive Slaves, running from under the stars and stripes, and taking refuge in the Canadas; *twenty thousand*, some leaving their wives, some their husbands, some leaving their children, some their brothers, and some their sisters,—fleeing to take refuge in the Canadas. Wherever the stars and stripes are seen flying in the United States of America, they point him out as a Slave.

If I wish to stand up and say, "I am a man," I must leave the land that gave me birth. If I wish to ask protection as a man, I must leave the American stars and stripes. Wherever the stars and stripes are seen flying upon American soil, I can receive no protection; I am a Slave, a chattel, a thing. I see your liberty-poles around in your cities. If to-morrow morning you are hoisting the stars and stripes upon one of your liberty-poles, and I should see the man following me who claims my body and soul as his property, I might climb to the very top of your liberty-pole, I might cut the cord that held your stars and stripes and bind myself with it as closely as I could to your liberty-pole, I might talk of law and the Constitution, but nothing could save me unless there be public sentiment enough in Salem. I could not appeal to law or the Constitution; I could only appeal to public sentiment; and if public sentiment would not protect me, I must be carried back to the plantations of the South, there to be lacerated, there to drag the chains that I left upon the Southern soil a few years since.

This is deplorable; and yet the American Slave *can* find a spot where he may be a man;—but it is not under the American flag. Fellow citizens, I am the last to eulogise any country where they oppress the poor. I have nothing to say in behalf of England or any other country, any further than as they extend protection to mankind. I say that I honor England for protecting the black man. I honor every country that shall receive the American Slave, that shall protect him, and that shall recognise him as a man.

I know that the United States will not do it; but I ask you to look at the efforts of other countries. Even the Bey of Tunis, a few years since, has decreed that there shall not be a Slave in his dominions; and we see that the subject of liberty is being discussed throughout the world. People are looking at it; they are examining it; and it seems as though every country, and every people, and every government were doing something, excepting the United States. But Christian, democratic, republican America is doing nothing at all. It seems as though she would be the last. It seems as though she was determined to be the last to knock the chain from the limbs of the Slave. Shall the American people be behind the people of the Old World? Shall they be behind those who are represented as almost living in the dark ages?

> "Shall every flap of England's flag
> Proclaim that all around are free,
> From farthest Ind to each blue crag
> That beetles o'er the western sea?
> And shall we scoff at Europe's kings,
> When Freedom's fire is dimmed with us;
> And round our country's altar clings
> The damning shade of Slavery's curse?"

Shall we, I ask, shall the American people be the last? I am here, not for the purpose of condemning the character of the American people, but for the purpose of trying to protect or vindicate their character. I would to God that there was some feature that I could vindicate. There is no liberty here for me; there is no liberty for those with whom I am associated; there is no liberty for the American Slave; and yet we hear a great deal about liberty! How do the people of the Old World regard the American people? Only a short time since, an American gentleman, in travelling through Germany, passed the window of a bookstore where he saw a number of pictures. One of them was a cut representing an American Slave on his knees, with chains upon his limbs. Over him stood a white man, with a long whip; and underneath was written, "the latest specimen of American democracy." I ask my audience, who placed that in the hands of those that drew it? It was the people of the United States. Slavery, as it is to be found in this country, has given the serfs of the Old World an opportunity of branding the American people as the most tyrannical people upon God's footstool.

Only a short time since an American man-of-war was anchored in the bay opposite Liverpool. The English came down by hundreds and thousands. The stars and stripes were flying; and there stood those poor persons that had never seen an American man-of-war, but had heard a great deal of American democracy. Some were eulogising the American people; some were calling it the "land of the free and the home of the brave." And while they stood there, one of their number rose up, and pointing his fingers to the American flag, said:

"United States, your banner wears
Two emblems,—one of fame;
Alas, the other that it bears,
Reminds us of your shame.
The white man's liberty entyped,
Stands blazoned by your stars;
But what's the meaning of your stripes?
They mean your Negro-scars."

What put that in the mouth of that individual? It was the system of American Slavery; it was the action of the American people; the inconsistency of the American people; their profession of liberty, and their practice in opposition to their profession.

I find that the time admonishes me that I am going on too far; but when I get upon this subject, and find myself surrounded by those who are willing to listen, and who seem to sympathise with my down-trodden countrymen, I feel that I have a great duty to discharge. No matter what the people may say upon this subject; no matter what they may say against the great Anti-Slavery movement of this country; I believe it is the Anti-Slavery movement that is calculated to redeem the character of the American people. Much as I have said against the character of the American people this evening, I believe that it is the Anti-Slavery movement of this country that is to redeem its character. Nothing can redeem it but the principles that are advocated by the friends of the Slave in this country.

I look upon this as one of the highest and noblest movements of the age. William Lloyd Garrison, a few years since, planted the tree of Liberty, and that tree has taken root in all branches of Government. That tree was not planted for a day, a week, a month, or a year; but to stand till the last chain should fall from the limbs of the last Slave in the United States of America, and in the world. It is a tree that will stand. Yes, it was planted of the very best plant that could be found among the great plants in the world.

"Our plant is of the cedar,
That knoweth not decay;
Its growth shall bless the mountains,
Till mountains pass away;
Its top shall greet the sunshine,
Its leaves shall drink the rain,
While on its lower branches
The Slave shall hang his chain."

Yes, it is a plant that will stand. The living tree shall grow up and shall not only liberate the Slave in this country, but shall redeem the character of the American people.

The efforts of the American people not only to keep the Slaves in Slavery, but to add new territory, and to spread the institution of Slavery all over Christendom,—their high professions and their inconsistency, have done more to sadden the hearts of the reformers in the Old World than anything else that could have been thought of. The reformers and lovers of liberty in the Old World look to the American Government, look to the lovers of liberty in America, to aid them in knocking the chains from their own limbs in Europe, to aid them in elevating themselves; but instead of their receiving cooperation from the Government of the United States, instead of their being cheered on by the people of the United States, the people and the Government have done all that they could to oppose liberty, to oppose democracy, and to oppose reform.

Go to the capital of our country, the city of Washington; the capital of the freest government upon the face of the world. Only a few days since, an American mother and her daughter were sold upon the auction-block in that city, and the money was put into the Treasury of the United States of America. Go there and you can scarcely stand an hour but you will see caufles of Slaves driven past the Capitol, and likely as not you will see the foremost one with the stars and stripes in his hand; and yet the American Legislators, the people of the North and of the South, the "assembled wisdom" of the nation, look on and see such things and hold their peace; they say not a single word against such oppression, or in favor of liberty.

In conclusion let me say, that the character of the American people and the influence of Slavery upon that character have been blighting and withering the efforts of all those that favor liberty, reform, and progression. But it has not quite accomplished it. There are those who are willing to stand by the Slave. I look upon the great Anti-Slavery platform as one upon which those who stand, occupy the same position,—I would say, a higher position, than those who put forth their Declaration in 1776, in behalf of American liberty. Yes, the American Abolitionists now occupy a higher and holier position than those who carried on the American Revolution. They do not want that the husband should be any longer sold from his wife. They want that the husband should have a right to protect his wife; that the brother should have a right to protect his sister. They are tired and sick at heart in seeing human beings placed upon the auction-block and sold to the highest bidder. They want that man should be protected. They want that a stop should be put to this system of iniquity and bloodshed; and they are laboring for its overthrow.

I would that every one here could go into the Slave-States, could go where I have been, and see the workings of Slavery upon the Slave. When I get to talking upon this subject I am carried back to the day when I saw a dear mother chained and carried off in a Southern steamboat to supply the cotton, sugar, or rice plantations of the South. I am carried back to the day when a dear sister was sold and carried off in my presence. I stood and looked at her. I could not protect her. I could not offer to protect her. I was a Slave, and the only testimony that I could give her that I sympathised with her, was to allow the tears to flow freely down my cheeks; and the tears flowing freely down her cheeks told me that my affection was reciprocated. I am carried back to the day when I saw three dear brothers sold, and carried off.

When I speak of Slavery I am carried back to the time when I saw, day after day, my own fellow-countrymen placed upon the auction-stand; when I saw the bodies, and sinews, and hearts, and the souls of men sold to the highest bidder. I have with me an account of a Slave recently sold upon the auction-stand. The auctioneer could only get a bid of $400, but as he was about to knock her off, the owner of the Slave made his way through those that surrounded him and whispered to the auctioneer. As soon as the owner left, the auctioneer said, "I have failed to tell you all the good qualities of this Slave. I have told you that she was strong, healthy, and hearty, and now I have the pleasure to announce to you that she is very pious. She has got religion." And although, before that, he could only get $400, as soon as they found that she had got religion they commenced bidding upon her, and the bidding went up to $700. The writer says that her body and mind were sold for $400, and her religion was sold for $300. My friends, I am aware that there are people at the North who would sell their religion for a $5 bill, and make money on it; and that those who purchased it would get very much cheated in the end. But the piety of the Slave differs from the piety of the people in the nominally free States. The piety of the Slave is to be a good servant.

This is a subject in which I ask your cöoperation. I hope that every individual here will take hold and help carry on the Anti-Slavery movement. We are not those who would ask the men to help us and leave the women at home. We want all to help us. A million of women are in Slavery, and as long as a single woman is in Slavery, every woman in the community should raise her voice against that sin, that crying evil that is degrading her sex. I look to the rising generation. I expect that the rising generation will liberate the Slave. I do not look to the older ones. I have sometimes thought that the sooner we got rid of the older ones the better it would be. The older ones have got their old prejudices, and their old associations, and they cling to them, and seem not to look at the Slave or to care anything about him.

Now, fellow-citizens, when you shall return home, and be scattered around your several firesides, and when you have an opportunity to make a remark about what I have said here this evening, all I ask of you is to give the cause, justice; to give what I have said, justice. Give it a fair investigation. If you have not liked my grammar, recollect that I was born and brought up under an institution, where, if an individual was found teaching me, he would have been sent to the State's Prison. Recollect that I was brought up where I had not the privilege of education. Recollect that you have come here to-night to hear a Slave, and not a man, according to the laws of the land; and if the Slave has failed to interest you, charge it not to the race, charge it not to the colored people, but charge it to the blighting influences of Slavery,—that institution that has made me property, and that is making property of three millions of my countrymen at the present day. Charge it upon that institution that is annihilating the minds of three millions of my countrymen. Charge it upon that institution, whether found in the political arena or in the American churches. Charge it upon that institution, cherished by the American people, and looked upon as the essence of Democracy,—upon AMERICAN SLAVERY.

Speech at the Royal Public Subscription Rooms, Exeter, England

May 5, 1851

During his five years' residence as a fugitive slave in England after the passage of the Fugitive Slave Law in 1850, Brown became an expert in addressing British sensibilities. One of the hundreds of lectures he gave was at the Royal Public Subscription Rooms in the southwestern city of Exeter in May 1851. Brown's remarks that day, as rendered by a local reporter, contrasted the exculpatory psychology of white Americans who allowed the Fugitive Slave Law to pass through a northern-dominated Congress with the fighting spirit—which he was inciting as he spoke—of freedom-loving Englishmen and -women.

Mr. WILLIAM WELLS BROWNE was received with loud cheers. He hoped that there would be but one feeling entertained by the audience, on the present occasion, and that a feeling of the most intense hatred against an institution that was at the present time perpetrating more wrong, more injustice, and more inhumanity upon one-sixth of the people of the United States, than could be found in any other part of the world—and on the people, not only of the present generation of the United States, but he feared on future generations—(hear, hear.) When the American colonies separated from the mother country in 1776, and adopted the constitution for themselves, and formed a government upon their own plan, they engrafted in the constitution of that country certain provisions, giving certain rights to the slave-holding people of the colonies—rights of property in their fellow man—the right of carrying on the African slave trade for a period of twenty years, the right of chasing a runaway slave, not only in the free states, and re-capturing him if they could find him, and taking him back to the prison house he had left, to fasten the chains upon his limbs; but it was required that they should bind themselves to put down any insurrection, any effort on the part of the blacks of the slave states to regain their liberties—by physical force. These were certain parts of the American constitution, which had become the law of the land. That spirit had grown with the growth of the country, and now they found the United States—the north, and the south—the free and slave states—combined to keep in degradation and slavery between three and four millions of the people of that country—(hear, hear). He knew the question had been asked in this country, how was it that the American Fugitive Slave Bill could be enacted by the people of the United States when it was well known that not only one-half of the States were free, or called so; but that above two-thirds of the free white population of that country resided in the free states. But it was through the connection of the people of the free states with the people of the slave states—a connection, commercial, social, political, and religious—it was through that connection and influence that the people of the slave states succeeded in carrying every measure through the United States Congress, upon which they depended, for the protection of that infernal system in that country—(hear, hear). The combination of the people of the free with the slave states was the very life-blood of the institution of American Slavery, and he wanted that they should understand this for many reasons—for they had not only slaveholders coming to this country and apologising for the institution of slavery, but they had men from the free states—from the north and the west,—men, who travelled through the country for pleasure and other purposes, and when spoken to on the subject, would try to get out of it by saying—"Oh, I reside in New York, or Massachusetts, or Ohio, where there is no slavery, and one state cannot interfere with another—it is a State Institution with which we have nothing to do." When they tried however to exculpate themselves by such arguments, and such sophistries, they must not believe them, for there was not a single citizen of a Free State in the American Union who had taken the oath of allegiance to the Constitution—but what was bound to put down any effort of the slave population towards regaining their liberties—not a single citizen, but what was bound to return the fugitive slave back again into slavery, if he would do his duty as an American citizen—(hear, hear). Many fugitive slaves had been dragged back again to slavery from the free states, under this infamous Fugitive Bill. Boston was called the Athens of America, because there were no slaves in that part of the country, and they would therefore imagine that there the bondsman would be protected when he escaped from the sugar, the cotton, or the rice plantations, and found himself under the shadow of Bunker Hill—(cheers). But the last steamer told them—the last post revealed to them the fact, that a poor slave, named Simms, was seized in the city of Boston, dragged on board a vessel, over which the American flag was floating, and was now probably in a rice plantation, or in a loathsome dungeon of the Slave States—(shame). Such was the fact as it regarded the Free States. When, therefore, these apologists came there, and said they had nothing to do with slavery, ask them who passed the Fugitive Law—the free or the slave states?—(hear, hear). The free states had a large majority in both houses of Congress—in the Senate as well as the House of Assembly, where they had a majority of twenty members. The Fugitive Slave Bill was brought forward and carried by men from the Free States—by such men as Daniel Webster, of Massachusetts, one of the greatest political jugglers that ever appeared on the stage—(cheers)—a man, who had turned his political coat, and got more holes in it, than any beggar to be found in the street—(laughter)—a man, who had sacrificed principle and everything, for the purpose of hoisting himself into the presidential chair, and who had been backed up by professing Christians, by ministers, professing to be the followers of the humble, meek, and lowly Saviour—by doctors of divinity, professors of theology—and he said this in the face of the old and the new countries, knowing it would be reported—that the Fugitive Slave Bill was carried through Congress by such men as these—by men of the northern free states, who professed to love liberty as much as any man in that room—(hear, and cheers). That Law was one of the most abominable laws ever enacted by any people under heaven. They might search Europe throughout—search all Christendom, and go beyond into heathen lands taking with them the lantern of Diogenes, and he would challenge them to find a parallel to this infamous Fugitive Slave Law—(loud cheers). Mr. Browne then proceeded at some length to comment upon the different provisions of the Bill, with considerable ability, relating several anecdotes illustrative of its cruel character. It was said by certain apologists of the bill that if it was annulled, it would be the signal for the dissolution of the American Union. All he could say to that was that if the American Union were dissolved, and the slaves emancipated, let it be so—(loud cheers). If it could not exist, unless at the expense of human liberty, and the lifeblood of one-sixth of the population, then let it go down—(cheers). When William Tell directed the aim that was to strike the fatal apple upon the head of his son, he exclaimed "Let my name and memory perish so that Switzerland be free." He would say "Let the American Union and Constitution perish, if it might be, that the slaves, shall have their liberty"—(loud cheers). Many slave-holders would come over to the Great Exhibition, and would probably travel through the country, with the money obtained by the sale of their slaves. Whilst eschewing the advocacy of physical force, still he believed that Old England should demonstrate its abhorrence of the system, by refusing to associate with them—for they would not do so with the man who stole their property, and ought they not to avoid men who were men-stealers?—(hear, hear). He concluded as follows—"I must thank you Mr. Chairman, and Ladies and Gentlemen, for the very warm reception you have given my friends and myself. I thank you because I feel that you sympathize with the bondsman in the United States. I thank you because you have expressed your feelings in favour of a class of people, with whom I am connected by the tenderest ties of nature, who are suffering under a system, which inflicted upon me the very scars I carry upon my person now. You have expressed your feelings against an institution that robbed my friends of their liberties—one of 31 years, and the other of 22—(hear, hear). I thank you, because you have expressed your abhorrence of an institution, which not only robbed me of my liberty until I was twenty years of age, but kept me from getting any education before that time, and is now keeping in chains my own kindred—a dear and affectionate sister, three dear brothers, a beloved and aged mother—all, if living, are clanking their chains upon a soil which we are told is consecrated to freedom—(shame). I thank you for your reception of us, because I am glad that my friends here to-night are not only receiving hospitality at your hands, but are standing upon soil that *is* really consecrated to freedom—(loud cheers)—standing upon soil where a slave-holder—no matter how many angry whips he might have in his pocket—no matter how many constitutions, or declarations of independence he might have in his hat—no matter how many prayers he has put up to his Creator—let him come here; and while you recognise *his* right to be free, you will not recognise his right to lay his hands upon us, and drag us back to slavery"—(loud and prolonged cheering).

The thanks of the meeting were unanimously accorded to the rev. chairman; and after Mr. Browne had sung an anti-slavery melody, of his own composition, in a voice of much sweetness and power, the meeting separated.

An Appeal to the People of Great Britain and the World

August 1, 1851

Brown organized a mass meeting at London's Hall of Commerce to celebrate Emancipation Day, the August 1, 1851, anniversary of Britain's 1833 abolition of slavery in most of its empire. He drafted the following address on the model of the Declaration of Independence, passed it through a committee of fellow fugitive slaves gathered in London, and persuaded one of them, Alexander Duval, to recite it at the meeting. Rarely noted or reprinted since 1851, it is one of Brown's most powerful assaults on the makers and chroniclers of American history, two categories merging in the ample target of Thomas Jefferson.

We consider it just, both to the people of the United States and to ourselves, in making an appeal to the inhabitants of other countries against the laws which have exiled us from our native land, to state the ground upon which we make our appeal, and the causes which impel us to do so. There are in the United States of America, at the present time, between three and four millions of persons who are held in a state of slavery which has no parallel in any other part of the world, and whose members have, within the past fifty years, increased to a fearful extent. These people are not only deprived of the rights to which the laws of Nature and of Nature's God entitle them, but every avenue to knowledge is closed against them, and the blessed teachings of the Savior denied them. The laws do not recognize the family relation of a slave, and extend to him no protection in the enjoyment of domestic endearments. Brothers and sisters, parents and children, husbands and wives, are torn asunder, and permitted to see each other no more. The shrieks and agonies of the slave are heard in the markets, at the seat of government, and within hearing of the American Congress, as well as on the cotton, sugar and rice plantations of the far South.

The history of the negroes in America is but a history of repeated injuries and acts of oppression committed upon them by the whites. It was amongst this oppressed class that we were born and brought up, and it was from under the laws which keep them in chains that we have escaped. It is not for ourselves that we make this appeal, but for those whom we have left behind.

In their Declaration of Independence, the Americans declare that 'all men are created equal; that they are endowed by their Creator with certain inalienable rights; that among these are life, liberty, and the pursuit of happiness.' Yet, one-sixth of the inhabitants of the great Republic are slaves. Thus they give the lie to their own professions. No one forfeits his or her character or standing in society by being engaged in holding, buying or selling a slave; the details of which, in all their horror, can scarcely be told.

Although the holding of slaves is confined to fifteen of the thirty-one States, yet we hold that the non-slaveholding States are equally guilty with the slaveholding. If any proof is needed on this point, it will be found in the passage of the inhuman Fugitive Slave Law, by Congress; a law which could never have been enacted without the votes of a portion of the representatives from the free States, and which is now being enforced, in many of the States, with the utmost alacrity. It was the passage of this law that exiled us from our native land, and it has driven thousands of our brothers and sisters from the free States, and compelled them to seek a refuge in the British possessions in North America. The Fugitive Slave Law has converted the entire country, North and South, into one vast hunting-ground. We would respectfully ask you to expostulate with the Americans, and let them know that you regard their treatment of the colored people of that country as a violation of every principle of human brotherhood, of natural right, of justice, of humanity, of Christianity, of love to God and to man.

It is needless that we should remind you that the religious sects of America, with but few exceptions, are connected with the sin of slavery—the churches North as well as South. We would have you tell the professed Christians of that land, that if they would be respected by you, they must separate themselves from the unholy alliance with men who are daily committing deeds which, if done in England, would cause the perpetrator to be sent to a felon's doom; that they must refuse the right hand of Christian fellowship, whether individually or collectively, to those implicated, in any way, in the guilt of slavery.

We do not ask for a forcible interference on your part, but only that you will use all lawful and peaceful means to restore to this much injured race their God-given rights. The moral and religious sentiment of mankind must be arrayed against slaveholding, to make it infamous, ere we can hope to see it abolished. We would ask you to set them the example, by excluding from your pulpits and from religious communion, the slaveholding and pro-slavery ministers who may happen to visit this country. We would even go further, and ask you to shut your doors against either ministers or laymen who are at all guilty of upholding and sustaining this monster sin. By the cries of the slave, which come from the fields and swamps of the far South, we ask you to do this! By that spirit of liberty and equality which you all admire, we would ask you to do this! And by that still nobler, higher and holier spirit of our beloved Savior, we would ask you to stamp upon the forehead of the slaveholders, with a brand deeper than that which marks the victim of his wrongs, the infamy of theft, adultery, man-stealing, piracy and murder, and, by the force of public opinion, compel him to 'unloose the heavy burden, and let the oppressed go free'!

Visit of a Fugitive Slave to the Grave of Wilberforce

Brown was still living as a fugitive slave in London when he sent this essay for inclusion in a volume of original antislavery writings, *Autographs for Freedom* (1854), edited by Julia Griffiths, a well-connected ally of Frederick Douglass who worked with him in Rochester, New York. It pays homage to one of the greatest figures in the British abolition movement, William Wilberforce, a longtime Member of Parliament who orchestrated the outlawing of the slave trade in the British Empire. Brown's account of this visit to his shrine in Westminster Abbey was presumably compiled from multiple visits to a site he had come to know intimately.

On a beautiful morning in the month of June, while strolling about Trafalgar Square, I was attracted to the base of the Nelson column, where a crowd was standing gazing at the bas-relief representations of some of the great naval exploits of the man whose statue stands on the top of the pillar. The death-wound which the hero received on board the Victory, and his being carried from the ship's deck by his companions, is executed with great skill. Being no admirer of warlike heroes, I was on the point of turning away, when I perceived among the figures (which were as large as life) a full-blooded African, with as white a set of teeth as ever I had seen, and all the other peculiarities of feature that distinguish that race from the rest of the human family, with musket in hand and a dejected countenance, which told that he had been in the heat of the battle, and shared with the other soldiers the pain in the loss of their commander. However, as soon as I saw my sable brother, I felt more at home, and remained longer than I had intended. Here was the Negro, as black a man as was ever imported from the coast of Africa, represented in his proper place by the side of Lord Nelson, on one of England's proudest monuments. How different, thought I, was the position assigned to the colored man on similar monuments in the United States. Some years since, while standing under the shade of the monument erected to the memory of the brave Americans who fell at the storming of Fort Griswold, Connecticut, I felt a degree of pride as I beheld the names of two Africans who had fallen in the fight, yet I was grieved but not surprised to find their names colonized off, and a line drawn between them and the whites. This was in keeping with American historical injustice to its colored heroes.

The conspicuous place assigned to this representative of an injured race, by the side of one of England's greatest heroes, brought vividly before my eye the wrongs of Africa and the philanthropic man of Great Britain, who had labored so long and so successfully for the abolition of the slave trade, and the emancipation of the slaves of the West Indies; and I at once resolved to pay a visit to the grave of Wilberforce.

A half an hour after, I entered Westminster Abbey, at Poets' Corner, and proceeded in search of the patriot's tomb; I had, however, gone but a few steps, when I found myself in front of the tablet erected to the memory of Granville Sharpe, by the African Institution of London, in 1816; upon the marble was a long inscription, recapitulating many of the deeds of this benevolent man, and from which I copied the following:—"He aimed to rescue his native country from the guilt and inconsistency of employing the arm of freedom to rivet the fetters of bondage, and establish for the negro race, in the person of Somerset, the long-disputed rights of human nature. Having in this glorious cause triumphed over the combined resistance of interest, prejudice, and pride, he took his post among the foremost of the honorable band associated to deliver Africa from the rapacity of Europe, by the abolition of the slave-trade; nor was death permitted to interrupt his career of usefulness, till he had witnessed that act of the British Parliament by which the abolition was decreed." After viewing minutely the profile of this able defender of the negro's rights, which was finely chiselled on the tablet, I took a hasty glance at Shakspeare, on the one side, and Dryden on the other, and then passed on, and was soon in the north aisle, looking upon the mementoes placed in honor of genius. There stood a grand and expressive monument to Sir Isaac Newton, which was in every way worthy of the great man to whose memory it was erected. A short distance from that was a statue to Addison, representing the great writer clad in his morning gown, looking as if he had just left the study, after finishing some chosen article for the *Spectator*. The stately monument to the Earl of Chatham is the most attractive in this part of the Abbey. Fox, Pitt, Grattan, and many others, are here represented by monuments. I had to stop at the splendid marble erected to the memory of Sir Fowell Buxton, Bart. A long inscription enumerates his many good qualities, and concludes by saying:—"This monument is erected by his friends and fellow-laborers, at home and abroad, assisted by the grateful contributions of many thousands of the African race." A few steps further and I was standing over the ashes of Wilberforce. In no other place so small do so many great men lie together. The following is the inscription on the monument erected to the memory of this devoted friend of the oppressed and degraded negro race:—

"To the memory of WILLIAM WILBERFORCE, born in Hull, August 24, 1759, died in London, July 29, 1833. For nearly half a century a member of the House of Commons, and for six parliaments during that period, one of the two representatives for Yorkshire. In an age and country fertile in great and good men, he was among the foremost of those who fixed the character of their times; because to high and various talents, to warm benevolence, and to universal candor, he added the abiding eloquence of a Christian life. Eminent as he was in every department of public labor, and a leader in every work of charity, whether to relieve the temporal or the spiritual wants of his fellow men, his name will ever be specially identified with those exertions which, by the blessings of God, removed from England the guilt of the African slave-trade, and prepared the way for the abolition of slavery in every colony of the empire. In the prosecution of these objects, he relied not in vain on God; but, in the progress, he was called to endure great obloquy and great opposition. He outlived, however, all enmity, and, in the evening of his days, withdrew from public life and public observation, to the bosom of his family. Yet he died not unnoticed or forgotten by his country; the Peers and Commons of England, with the Lord Chancellor and the Speaker at their head, in solemn procession from their respective houses, carried him to his fitting place among the mighty dead around, here to repose, till, through the merits of Jesus Christ his only Redeemer and Saviour, whom in his life and in his writings he had desired to glorify, he shall rise in the resurrection of the just."

The monument is a fine one; his figure is seated on a pedestal, very ingeniously done, and truly expressive of his age, and the pleasure he seemed to derive from his own thoughts. Either the orator or the poet have said or sung the praises of most of the great men who lie buried in Westminster Abbey, in enchanting strains. The statues of heroes, princes, and statesmen are there to proclaim their power, worth, or brilliant genius, to posterity. But as time shall step between them and the future, none will be sought after with more enthusiasm or greater pleasure than that of Wilberforce. No man's philosophy was ever moulded in a nobler cast than his; it was founded in the school of Christianity, which was, that all men are by nature equal; that they are wisely and justly endowed by their Creator with certain rights which are irrefragable, and no matter how human pride and avarice may depress and debase, still God is the author of good to man; and of evil, man is the artificer to himself and to his species. Unlike Plato and Socrates, his mind was free from the gloom that surrounded theirs. Let the name, the worth, the zeal, and other excellent qualifications of this noble man, ever live in our hearts, let his deeds ever be the theme of our praise, and let us teach our children to honor and love the name of William Wilberforce.

LONDON.

Speech at Town Hall, Manchester, England

August 1, 1854

Brown's freedom had recently been purchased thanks to a fundraising campaign by English supporters when he attended a mass Emancipation Day rally at Manchester's impressive Town Hall in August 1854. In his final antislavery appearance in Great Britain, he declared himself "almost an Englishman" as he took his leave among calls and warnings from comrades not to return to his native land. He made sure in this final speech to inspire the British public to continue to make the polemical war against antislavery a two-continent campaign.

Mr. Chairman, and ladies and gentlemen, I would much have preferred that my friend Mr. Pilsbury should have occupied the time that is intended for myself. As has been said, he is not only thoroughly acquainted with the working of slavery in the United States, but he is one of its oldest and best pioneers. He has had the advantage of early education, he has the advantage of me at the present time, and I feel confident could not only claim your attention, but could give you better information in a better manner than I could possibly hope to do. I stand here to-night without ever having had a day's schooling in my life. You have been called together to hear men speak to-night—I am here as a piece of property. I am a slave according to the laws of the United States at the present time. Something has been said this afternoon about my having been purchased by the liberality of the English people; I know not that such a purchase has taken place; I know it is in contemplation, and many suppose it may have been accomplished by this time, but I do not know that such is the case. I stand here, this evening, therefore, not only a slave, a piece of property according to the laws of the United States, but I am here without education or without having received a day's schooling in my life, and what education I have has been of my own seeking in my own way; and, therefore, I can hope to say but little that shall go to aid in making up the testimony that is intended by the holding of this conference. (Applause.) No one can read, Mr. Chairman, the declaration of the American independence, and compare that document with the history of the legislation of the federal government of the United States, without being struck with the marked inconsistency of the theory of the people and their acts; the one declaring that all men are created equally, endowed by their Creator with certain inalienable rights, among which are life, liberty, and the pursuit of happiness, and the other is the history of the encroachment of slavery upon liberty, or legislation in favour of slavery in that country against the cause of freedom. From the very hour that the convention that was held to form the constitution of the United States down to the present time, the acts of the government have been for the perpetuation and the spread of slavery in that land. As has been said, slavery was introduced into the constitution by allowing the African slave trade to be continued for twenty years, making it lawful and constitutional, which it had never been before; and then the slaveowner was allowed representation for this slave property, and every man that would go to the Coast of Africa, and steal five negroes and bring them to the United States, was allowed by the constitution, then, three votes for the five slaves. And it is carried down to the present time, as the American congress has more than twenty-five representatives based upon this slave representation. And that is one of the reasons why in the national congress the slaveowners have the power of carrying so many of their measures, and the twenty-five, I need not say, who are slaveowners themselves, do not represent, but misrepresent, their "property," and these slaveowners go for the purpose of spreading the system of slavery over the land. America is called a free and independent country, and yet there is not a single foot of soil over which the stars and the stripes wave upon which I could stand and be protected by law. (Sensation.) There is not a foot of soil in the United States upon which I could stand where the constitution would give me any protection; and let me return to the United States, I am liable to be seized at any moment and conveyed in chains to the southern states, and there handed over to a man who claims me as his property, and to be worked up as he may think fit. Such is true as regards even the early history of slavery. It is true that the congress of the United States, or the constitution, agreed to abolish slavery in 20 years, but the internal slave trade is carried on, and I aver that it is even worse—setting aside the middle passage—than anything connected with the foreign slave trade. In the old states, slaves are raised for the market; they have their family attachments, and they are probably, to some extent, more enlightened and not so much degraded by heathenism as the negroes upon the coast of Africa, and, as men become more enlightened, the separation of families, and the buying and selling of them to slavery, is so much the worse. They feel it the more, and therefore, I think that when we look and see that 100,000 slaves are annually taken from the slave-raising states, to supply the southern markets—the cotton, sugar, and rice plantations of the far south—we must be satisfied that the internal slave trade that is carried on by the people of the United States is as grievous in its effect as the African slave trade when carried on by the people of that country. I know that some suppose that the evils of slavery are exaggerated; I have been asked again and again if certain portions of "Uncle Tom's Cabin" were not exaggeration. Of the working of slavery, in my opinion, I don't think anything can exaggerate that infamous system. When we look and see that there are at the present time enslaved between three and four millions of God's children, who are put upon the auction stand and sold to the highest bidder, no language which we can use can exaggerate the workings or the evils of the system of slavery as it is carried on in that country. (Applause.) The fugitive slave law, that by many people here is considered a great evil, is at present the law in America, and it is the most atrocious law ever concocted by the human brain or human legislation—a law that sets every other statute in existence in the shade when we look at the barbarous enactments that it contains. By the fugitive slave law every coloured person in that country is liable to be arrested and carried off to the far south and made a slave of, no matter whether born in New York, Massachusetts, Vermont, or any free state. The gate of separation which has hitherto kept the inhabitants of the northern states from participating in slaveholding, is now thrown down; and every man who wishes to go into the slaveholding business, has now only to find some one who shall participate in the gain, and to swear that the coloured person whom he means to enslave, is the property of that man whom he has brought forward for that purpose, and so the poor coloured man is carried away to the south. In the state of Illinois, during the past few months, a coloured man was arrested under this fugitive slave law, who had lived in the same town some fifteen years, and had by his industry accumulated 1,000 or 2,000 dollars worth of property; and the man who came upon this man, and claimed and seized him as a slave, was not only a professing Christian, but was a minister of the gospel, and one who belonged to the same denomination as the man whom he claimed for his property. It was in vain this coloured man asserted that he was a free man, and had a right to be free; that no one had any right to take him away, that he was free born, and from the state of Ohio. The only respite he could obtain was, that he was allowed, as a favour, to go to prison, and to stay there for a while, until he could get his property and other affairs in the place disposed of; and in the meantime he was obliged to find security, and to pay an officer three dollars a day to watch him and see that he did not run away. He agreed to this, but after a while he had collected evidence by which he proved himself to be free, and was enabled to demand his release. But a debt had been accumulated during his detention, to the amount of some $3,000, so that, although he had thus escaped being sent into slavery, he was utterly ruined. This is the history of a free coloured man in the state of Illinois. There is a more atrocious case I can tell you. Within the last year, two villains from a southern state arrived in a certain town of Pennsylvania, and attempted to seize a coloured man, who was employed there as a waiter, in one of the inns. They approached him in a clandestine manner, and threw their chains upon his limbs; but the man, whom they would have made a slave, escaped from his pursuers; he ran out of the house, he ran to the nearest stream, and plunged into it, and there stood at bay, immersed up to his neck in the running water. The slave-hunters came up, and many people gathered around, sympathising with the hunted fugitive. He exclaimed to his persecutors, "If any of you come near me here, I will drown him in this water that flows about me." The slave-hunters answered him, "If you don't come out of the river, and surrender, we will shoot you where you are." And then, suddenly, to the horror and astonishment of all the bystanders, one of the slave-hunters raised his gun or pistol, aimed it at the fugitive, and fired at him. We are told how the water then ran red with the blood of the slave; and how a crowd of four or five hundred people, who stood by and saw this thing done, did nothing more than cry "Shame" upon those who had done it, because it was the law. Sir, I do feel confident, that if in this country such a law existed, and if any two persons came into a town of England, and dared openly to ill-treat a human being in that way, there would not be three or four hundred Englishmen standing by so cold to the feelings of humanity as to let such a thing be done in their presence, and content themselves with crying "Shame!" I feel certain, that, in England, the villains who should do such an outrage would instantly be compelled to fly the spot. (Cheers.)

Mr. PILLSBURY: My friend will allow me to interrupt his narrative with the addition of one or two circumstances which he has forgotten to mention. While that poor fellow stood up to his neck in water, they fired three rifle balls at him, two of which took effect upon him, and dyed the river with his blood. He escaped across the river, however, but fainted and fell, from the wounds he had received, the moment he reached the opposite shore. Some of his friends assisted him, and he was delivered; but those ruffians who shot him were arrested and tried, and were acquitted of having committed any crime in what they had done.

Mr. WELLS BROWN (continued): Well, now, you will recollect that all this was perpetrated in the state of Pennsylvania, in one of those which are called the free states. We hear people speak of free and slave states; but I hold that there is no such distinction; for now there are no free states in the United States of America. There are none of them free, because that cannot be a free state which cannot protect the freedom of its inhabitants; and there is no state in the union now which can give liberty, or even secure his liberty, to the coloured man. His rights are nothing if the slaveholder pursues him. The courts of justice in some of those "free states" have been converted into prisons, in which the fugitive slaves of the southerners have been kept for them; and very recently, in Boston, a slave was arrested, and confined for six or seven days in the court house, which was guarded by muskets and cannon to prevent his rescue; thence he was put on board a vessel in the harbour and carried away to the far south, to a life of slavery. The boast of the "free states," that people there enjoy perfect freedom is most untrue; for under the fugitive slave law, the slaveowners of the south are empowered to enter those "free states," and employ not only the marshals of the union, in arresting any of the coloured people whom they choose to claim, but compel the inhabitants of the place, under severe penalties, to abet the seizure of the slave. I cannot exaggerate, sir, the effect of this fugitive slave law, and indeed, of everything else that is connected with slavery in the United States. If you had been, as I have been, for twenty years of your life in the southern states of America, and had seen there, as I have seen, the workings of slavery, the trading in human beings, the buying and selling of them, the whipping and abusing of them, as I have seen all that carried on there,—and if you had seen the dear ones torn from you, and taken to be sold at the auction block, and handed over to the highest bidder, as I have seen my dear ones taken, never to see them again,—if you had seen all this, you could not think anything, in the statements made at this conference, or in the publications you may have read, was at all exaggerated. (Cheers.) I know you read, with palpitating hearts, the history of the Bloody Assize in this country; you loathe the name of Judge Jeffries, when you remember that Reign of Terror in England. Now, go to the United States, and you will see, that acts as cruel as ever were done in England, in that age, are done in America now,—done every day in the southern states, and done almost every week in the northern states; you will see there judges who sit on the bench, giving their sentence in favour of slavery, and condemning freedom; judges who knew, too, that the persons whom their sentence orders thus to be seized and carried back into the southern states, will be cruelly tortured there. It was asserted not long since in Boston, by Theodore Parker, that one of those slaves, who had been seized in the north, and carried back to slavery, had been flogged to death, or nearly to death; and such will be the fate of many of them. Then, ought not facts like those to be known throughout this country? I am glad these meetings are held, and that this association has been formed. I hope it will do something to instruct the people here, and to maintain anti-slavery principles, so that Englishmen, when they visit the United States, may not do henceforth, as many of their countrymen have done, give their influence to the side of the oppressor, instead of the oppressed. (Cheers.) That is now most important to the cause; for thousands of persons, emigrants and others, are going to the United States every year, and they ought to understand this matter. If nothing else could be accomplished yet, meetings like these and lecturing would be worthy objects of the efforts of this association. It is true, there is already in England an anti-slavery society established. But I must say, and with great respect for the excellent persons who belong to it, that society is so inactive, it scarcely does anything throughout the year but hold an anniversary meeting; and it is a fact, sir, that speeches like those which were made in the conference to-day, or to-night upon this platform, would not be tolerated on the platform of the British and Foreign Anti-Slavery Society in London. (Cheers.) It may be said of us, that we have used very strong language. Why, sir, has not the time come for strong language? Those who want milk and water, let them go to London at anniversary time, and they will get it there, in homœopathic doses. (A laugh.) Probably, the fact of my having once been a slave, and of my feeling upon this subject so intensely, having relations of my own, still dragging out the life of slavery, has made me feel, that something strong should be uttered. (Cheers.) People want something strong,—they are willing to hear it; then I say, why not give it them? There is need I think, of an association in this country, which shall expose to the British nation the working of slavery in America and the fact as it is; which shall give a true representation also, and not merely a partial account, of what the abolitionists in America are doing. (Cheers.) I am identified, as you may well believe, with the most ultra of the abolitionists, who are, I consider, speaking the truth more effectually than any other party or association in the United States; and I consider also, that the greatest of the champions of human liberty there is the present leader of the anti-slavery movement in the United States,—William Lloyd Garrison. (Great cheering.) I know there are some who would be afraid to utter that sentiment, because they would be afraid of losing caste. I, sir, have nothing to lose, but everything to gain. (Cheers.) I have now been five years in this country. I have travelled through Great Britain, and am almost an Englishman. I think I know something of the public sentiment here; and I say, the people want to know the truth, and to know what they can do for us. I tell them, that those ultra abolitionists in America, to whom I have referred, are those who in America are considered to be the greatest foes of the fugitive slave law, and of all the acts of the pro-slavery party; *those* are the persons of whom slaveowners speak with most malignity, and who are more vilified by the American pro-slavery press than all other parties and associations put together. This may be, unless I can comply with an invitation to speak on Thursday (and I am afraid that I cannot do so), my last opportunity of speaking publicly in this country; but I shall return to the United States, after being five years in England, conscious that I may safely give to the free coloured people of the north, and to the abolitionists of the United States, the assurance that something is being done here for their cause, and that the English people only want to know what they can do, and they will set about it and do it. (Cheers.) We do not ask you to take up arms; we do not ask you to do any act, or utter any language, unbecoming Christians; but we ask you to learn the facts and the truth of this matter, and honestly and strongly to speak out upon it. (Mr. Brown resumed his seat amidst very cordial cheers.)

Speech at Brick Wesley Church, Philadelphia

October 17, 1854

Weeks after a rough return passage to the United States in September 1854, Brown was a featured speaker before the black congregation of Brick Wesley Church in Philadelphia. Summoning them as co-passengers on "an experimental voyage" to an eventual freedom, he reviewed with them the workings of "the monster slavery," which segregated churches around the country and had territorial ambitions on Haiti, the Americas' sole beacon of black freedom. Loyal to his friend William Lloyd Garrison, who was also honored that night, he encouraged the congregation to give its support to Garrison's American Anti-Slavery Society and its official newspapers in the fight against slavery.

Mr. CHAIRMAN, LADIES AND GENTLEMEN: On my return from Europe, a few weeks since, we encountered very rough weather for the season of the year. For several days the clouds obscured the sky, the wind blew, and the waves run mountains high, so that the Captain was unable to ascertain the latitude in which he was, or the distance he had run. However, one morning the clouds cleared away, the sun appeared, and the waves ceased. The Captain then came on deck, with glass in hand, to take the sun, and find out the longitude, and the distance. We, the coloured people of this country, have been put upon an experimental voyage, and for more than two centuries we have been surrounded by the most boisterous weather, with clouds obscuring from our gaze the sun of freedom, and our bark in a leaky condition, seeking a safe harbour. Let us, my friends, stop and take the sun, and see where we are. Our fathers, torn from their native country, and brought to this, were made the "hewers of wood and drawers of water." We, their children, are following in their footsteps. It was said, seventy years ago, that Christianity would cause slavery to cease. The Gospel, it was said, would wipe out the stain from the escutcheon of the country; but behold the result. This nation started with half a million of slaves, and to-day there are more than three millions, and this increase, too, under the preaching of the American Gospel. My friends, how could it be otherwise? Look at the tendency of this Gospel, and the cause is obvious. From Andover down to the man who teaches Theology on his "own hook," the world has been taught that slavery is God-ordained. Moses Stuart was for more than forty years preparing men to preach this most infamous doctrine. Go to the fashionable churches in our cities, and you will see that those who worship there believe what has been taught them, by the "Negro pew," or the isolated gallery that you will there find. "Slavery is the corner stone of our Republican Institutions," said a church member. "Two hundred years have sanctioned and sanctified Negro Slavery," says another; and to-day, the cardinal principle of American religion is to teach man to enslave his fellow-man. In politics as well as religion, we are denied our equality. What Court of Justice in the United States ever thinks of selecting coloured men as jurors? In Great Britain, if a foreigner is to be tried for an offence, one-half of his jury is drawn from amongst his own countrymen. Here, we are tried by men who are taught to hate us, and who never entertain the idea that we should have justice. The churches, schools, social circle, and all places where we should seek improvement, are shut against us. One thing is certain, and that is, our own education and elevation is to be one of the main levers to overthrow the institution of slavery in these United States. Then let us be true to ourselves and to the cause of our enslaved countrymen. By all means let us prove that we are worthy cooperators with the noble band who are advocating our rights. I am glad, my friends, that you have given such an enthusiastic welcome to our staunch friend, Mr. Garrison, to-night. We need union in this contest with the monster slavery, especially when we see it not content with keeping the ground it formerly occupied, but now seeking to spread itself over soil heretofore consecrated to freedom. The eye of the viper is now on Hayti, that government of people who have shown themselves such worthy recipients of liberty. If the Dominican Republic attempts to give the American Government a foothold in St. Domingo, let us hope that the Emperor of Hayti will put a stop to it. And if he gets into a war with them, and this nation interferes, let not only our prayers, but our sympathy, and, if needs be, let our arms speak for the Haytians. Your Vigilance Committee was formed for a high and grand purpose. What can be nobler than to help men and women who are escaping from the oppression of the Southern States of this confederacy? Then give of your abundance, that this association may be able to assist those that need their aid. You, no doubt, expect to hear from me something about Europe. (And here Mr. Brown narrated some of his experience abroad; showing that prejudice was unknown in Europe, and that every man was treated according to his merits and not according to his complexion.) I might have remained abroad, said Mr. Brown, and kept out of the danger of the Fugitive Slave Law, for no coloured person is safe, even though he may have been purchased, but I wanted to be here in the contest; I felt that duty called me home, and here I am. For the invitation which you extended to me, and the hearty welcome that you have given me, I am truly thankful to you. Before we separate to-night, let us renew our determination to devote our lives and our energies to the cause of human freedom. Let us ask ourselves what we are doing. How many of us take anti-slavery papers? Who of us takes the *Anti-Slavery Standard* or the *Liberator*? Friends, let us remember those in bonds as bound with them.

Speech at Horticultural Hall, West Chester, Pennsylvania

October 23, 1854

Brown was the guest of honor at the annual convention of the Pennsylvania Anti-Slavery Society five nights after addressing the Brick Wesley Church in Philadelphia. Shifting into rhetoric appropriate for a primarily white assembly, he paraded the racial history of the United States before his audience's eyes and led them to the dilemma of the present moment: they could not be free citizens of the United States as long as he and his fellow African Americans were denied equal status.

Mr. Chairman and Ladies and Gentlemen: The short time that I shall occupy your attention will be devoted more particularly to considering the condition and past treatment of the slaves and free people of colour in this country. With all the boasted philanthropy and Christianity of the people of this Republic, the coloured race has received at their hands treatment scarcely equalled by that of any people the world has ever known. Introduced into the colonies more than two centuries ago, bought and sold from generation to generation, they have indeed become the "hewers of wood and drawers of water." You have all heard of the horrors of the African slave trade. I do not know that I had a just idea of its horror until I heard them depicted in the House of Commons in England, and I am sure that no countryman of mine would have been willing to have been identified on that occasion as a dealer in human beings. A great mistake was made by the fathers of this country when they incorporated the slave trade in the Constitution of the country, allowed the slave representation in Congress, and gave to the slaveholder the right to hunt his victims in the free States. It was believed that Christianity and Republicanism would wipe out the foul blot, but such has not been the result. On the contrary, the number of slaves has increased from a little more than half a million to three and a half millions. The African slave trade was abolished after a certain time, but a worse than the African slave trade continued to exist. The internal slave trade, it is true, has not the middle passage and the drowning of its victims; but the black race has, to some extent, become refined by intercourse and commingling of blood with the Anglo-Saxon, so that they feel more sensitively the separations of families, sundering of ties and other cruelties which are inseparable from the system. A hundred thousand slaves are taken from the slave-raising to the slave-consuming States every year. What a tale to tell future generations about the people of this country! Professors of Christianity, members of the popular religious denominations engaged in raising, selling, buying and whipping men and women on their plantations! Go into a southern market and see men and women sold in lots to suit purchasers, and then place yourselves in their condition, if you would feel for them as you ought. Place your wife, daughter or child in their position, to be struck off to the highest bidder, if you would realize their wrongs and sufferings. Indifference from our own friends and relations is sad; it is terrible indeed to the sensitive bosom. Then think of the slave mother who sees her child placed in the market and knows that that child is sold by its own father. This is no fancy picture; we know that such scenes do take place every day. Why do I stand before you, Mr. Chairman, to-night, not an African nor an Anglo-Saxon, but of mixed blood? It is attributable to the infernal system of American slavery. My father is a slave-owner, and at his instance was I sold on a southern plantation.

They tell us that the slave is contented and happy. I heard a gentleman travelling between New York and Philadelphia remark about his old slaves being cared for and watched over. It reminded me of what I saw in the Isle of Wight—a donkey enjoying a degree of liberty that no other animal was allowed to enjoy. For thirty years that donkey had drawn water from a very deep well and was now a pensioner. He was allowed his penny loaf of bread every day and full range of the premises, and he was strutting around like a duke; but, alas, his limbs were so stiff that he could scarcely move; his best days had been spent in a tread mill, drawing water, and he was hobbling about in his decrepitude. And so it is with the human donkeys in the South; if one poor slave lives to be so old and infirm that he is unfit to labour he is pensioned off like this superannuated donkey. Should that fact weigh a single moment upon the minds of intelligent persons in favour of enslaving a race because they happen to have skins not coloured like your own?

We cannot tell the evils that exist in the southern States. Like the painter who stands idle by the side of his picture, waiting for the crowd to go out before lifting the screen from the canvas, for fear of frightening his visitors with the unfinished work, so we must wait and let the future historian complete the picture. I know that, after having spent twenty years as a slave, one would suppose that I might relate the evils that I witnessed. And so I might. I might stand here for hours and tell you what I saw, and felt, and know, but now is not the time. The time has passed for devoting ourselves to such a purpose. We need not go out of the free States to see its cruelties. They are all about us. Look at the coloured people of the free States, thrown out of your schools, your churches and your social circles, deprived of their political rights and debarred from those avenues of employment that are necessary to a proper maintenance of themselves and families. We find the degrading influences of slavery all about us. Pennsylvania deprives the black man of the elective franchise, and so does New York, except with a property qualification. In most of the northern States, he is looked upon as something to be knocked and kicked about as they see fit. There were two passengers on board the Atlantic when I returned from Europe, who had rode with me on the same car from London to Liverpool, and we enjoyed the same privileges on board the steamer. They were foreigners and I an American; and when they landed in this country, they were boasting that they had arrived at a land of liberty where they could enjoy religious and political freedom. I, too, might have rejoiced had I not been a coloured man, at my return to my native land; but I knew what treatment to expect from my countrymen—that it would not be even such as was meted out to those foreigners, and I rejoiced only to meet my anti-slavery friends. We all started to walk up the streets of Philadelphia together; we hailed an omnibus; the two foreigners got in; I was told that "niggers" were not allowed to ride. Foreigners, mere adventurers, perhaps, in this country, are treated as equals, while I, an American born, whose grandfather fought in the revolution, am not permitted to ride in one of your fourth-rate omnibuses. The foreigner has a right, after five years' residence, to say who shall be President, as far as his vote goes, even though he cannot read your Constitution or write his name, while 600,000 free coloured people are disfranchised. And then you talk about equality and liberty, the land of the free and the home of the brave, the asylum of the oppressed, the cradle of liberty! You have the cradle, but you have rocked the child to death.

I think I have a right to speak of the shortcomings of the people of this country. I stand here as the representative of the slave to speak for those who cannot speak for themselves, and I stand here as the representative of the free coloured man who cannot come up to this convention. I saw not long since in one of your papers a statement that a coloured American had applied to an American Consul in a foreign land for a passport and it was denied him; the Consul would not admit that he was a citizen of the United States, and he was obliged to go without a passport. When I wished to leave this country, through the aid of my eloquent friend, Wendell Phillips, I secured a paper from the State of Massachusetts showing that I was a citizen of this country. I went to Mr. Davis, the Secretary of Abbott Lawrence, and asked for my passport. I was told that I was not an American citizen. I produced my paper and said that if he refused me a passport I would get one from the English government and would sail under foreign colours. I knew I could get one from the English government, because I had been offered it. The Secretary was ashamed and turned round and made out my passport. He was afraid I would go before the English public, where the anti-slavery feeling was so strong, and make the fact known that the American Minister in England refused to recognise my citizenship.

There is no parallel in history to the treatment of the coloured people in this country; certainly none in the present. Tell me of any nation treating any portion of their subjects as we are treated. We are told by the colonizationists that we must be sent out of the country—that we are not citizens of it. If I am not a citizen of the United States, pray, are you? Did your father not come from another country? We were brought here by force, it is true (I speak not now as an Anglo-Saxon, as I have a right to speak, but as an African), but that fact does not alter our birthright. And you are willing to acknowledge the citizenship of the foreigner no matter how ignorant or degraded; but because I am a shade darker than you, you disfranchise me. I am ashamed when I hear men talking about the national honour of this country being insulted by the Spaniards, or Cubans, just as if we had any national honour to be insulted! A nation that enslaves and scourges one-sixth part of its people talking about national honour! Go to the South and see Methodist carting Methodist to the market and selling him, Baptist whipping Baptist, and Presbyterian purchasing Presbyterian, and Episcopalian tying chains upon the limbs of Episcopalian, and then talk about national character and honour! I know these are hard sayings, but they are true and must be told, and they are the best friends of their country who sound the alarm. You need not be startled at our motto, "No Union with Slaveholders"; this nation has within it the elements of disunion. And are you not, after all, as much in favour of disunion as I am? Where are your rights, guaranteed by the Constitution to every citizen? Where is the right of free locomotion in the slave States? Go into the southern States an avowed enemy of slaveholding, and are you free? I point you to the murdered Lovejoy; to Burr, Work and Thompson spending four or five years in a Missouri prison; to Torrey pining away in a southern prison; to Fairbank now in a Kentucky penitentiary; to Delia Webster persecuted and imprisoned in the same State; to Mrs. Douglass shut up in a Virginia jail, and all because they did not think as slaveholders think. Can you be as free in South Carolina as the South Carolinian can be in Pennsylvania? He can walk the streets of Philadelphia or New York and say what he pleases, and he is protected, while a southern Senator threatens a northern man with hanging upon the tallest tree if he shows himself in Mississippi, simply because he speaks his thoughts on the subject of freedom. And when you send a man to the South to test by law this very right of the citizens of any State to all the immunities of the citizens of the several States under the Constitution, to bring it before one of the Courts of the United States in the South to be adjudicated, he is expelled from the State by mob violence.

I thank God, Mr. Chairman, that this question of American slavery is no longer a question between the black man and the slave-owner, but a question between the people of the North and South. You have allowed them to enslave the black man, to extend the institution and to make the whole North a hunting ground for their slaves, until the people of the free States can endure it no longer, and the North is now fairly pitted against the South. Look at your political parties torn asunder by the slavery issue—and I am glad of it. Look at your religious denominations divided on the same question—and I am glad of it. The great issue is beginning to be between the North and South. The people of the South have always looked upon the people of the North as their pliant tools, and I am glad to see the North becoming aware of it. You welcome the fugitive from European oppression, and, after shaking hands with him and congratulating him for his escape, you turn to catch the fugitive from American oppression and return him to his chains. And when you could find no better man to welcome, you welcomed John Mitchel, who is ready to join in the chase with you. Four hundred thousand foreigners come here every year, and you welcome them, while you drive the coloured American from your very doors.

But the people of the North are beginning to be aroused, and the cry of "disunion," which they have heretofore hated so much to hear, is practically becoming their watchword. The North is arrayed against the South, and you know it, and you are become practically co-workers with us. If you do not go as far as we do, you follow in the wake, and are coming up. Men that were Democrats and Whigs ten years ago are disunionists to-day, and Democrats and Whigs of to-day will be disunionists before the next ten years roll round. You have fostered slavery until you find yourselves enslaved. It was the sentiment of a distinguished writer that no man could put a chain upon the limbs of another without fastening a chain upon his own. You have helped the slaveholder put chains upon his slave until he has fettered your own limbs, and you are now beginning to see it.

I stand here to-night a freeman only by the act of British philanthropists. I left this country a slave; I returned a freeman. I am not indebted to my birth, or to your Constitution, or to your Christianity, or to your philanthropy for it. Am I then indeed an American citizen, or am I a foreigner? Call me what you please, I am nevertheless a freeman; and yet I feel scarcely more free than I did twenty years ago when I was working on Price's plantation. I felt then that I had as good a right to my freedom as the man who claimed me as his property, and, acting under that conviction, I started for the North. I could not help thinking, while abroad, of the treatment I had received in this country at the hands of the American people, and I asked myself, why is it that I can put up at one of the best hotels in Liverpool, or London, or Paris, or Rotterdam, and not in Philadelphia? Why is it that I can ride in the coach, or omnibus, or railcar, or steamboat, in Great Britain or on the continent, and enjoy the same privileges that any man enjoys, while I cannot do it here? It is not because of the colour of my skin, but because of the influence of slavery. My daughters were kept out of school in the State of New York, and would have been brought up in ignorance in this country, and so I resolved to take them away from this liberty-loving country and educate them under a monarchical government and institutions. They go abroad and they are received and treated according to their merits and not according to their colour, and to-day one of them, the daughter of an American slave, teaches a school of Anglo-Saxons, and the other is preparing herself, under another monarchical government, France, to follow the same employment. You talk about the despotism of Napoleon III. and yet your own countrymen escaping from American despotism can find protection under his throne. I could walk free and protected in any part of the Kingdom of Great Britain, but I dared not set foot on American soil until some southern scoundrel first received $300 for me. You have not a single foot of soil in all this republic on which I could have stood a year ago and said I was a freeman, though born and brought up here, and descended from ancestors who fought in the American revolution for American liberty. I know there is oppression abroad; I am not blind to the fact, that in all the governments of Europe there is more or less oppression, but before we talk of the oppression of other countries, let us look at our own; before you put out your hands to welcome the victims of foreign oppression, wash them clean so that the blood of the slave may not contaminate the hand of the foreigner. Before you boast of your freedom and Christianity, do your duty to your fellow-man.

Letter from the West

The life of an antislavery reformer was a life spent frequently on the road. Brown accumulated weeks or even months each year traveling the country, spreading the antislavery message, and laying the foundation for further activism. The work was challenging and occasionally even dangerous, as he casually remarked in this March 1855 letter to the *National Anti-Slavery Standard* describing a train wreck he survived in the Berkshires en route to a speaking tour of Ohio. That same night, he delivered his talk as scheduled, in Albany, and, continuing west, within a few days he was giving nightly talks in cities and towns from Cleveland to central and southern Ohio.

SALEM, Ohio, March 19th.

MESSRS. EDITORS: After a fatiguing journey of three days, I find myself in the town of Salem, somewhat noted for being the centre of radical anti-slavery in the Buckeye State. I left Springfield on the morning of the 10th inst., and came very near getting my neck broken before I had arrived at Albany. When within ten miles of Pittsfield, the train run off the track, smashing and otherwise damaging several of the cars, but without injuring any of the passengers. The jolting of the car in which I was seated, until the classic Dante that I was reading was fairly shaken out of my hand, was the first intimation I had of the approaching catastrophe. The next moment, my head was unceremoniously introduced to the top of the car—which, but for its hardness and its being insured, would have been seriously damaged. As our car plunged head first into the snow-bank, an indescribable scene occurred. A tall man, and of otherwise large dimensions, was thrown forward and succeeded in breaking to pieces four seats, before he found himself on all fours. Eight or ten other persons were emptied out of their seats, while the stove was upset. When it was ascertained that all was over, a rush was made for the doors, by those who were not too frightened to run, or could regain their self-possession. But those who attempted to escape found that the doors could not be opened. At this juncture, a scene of rather an amusing character took place. A Frenchman, who spoke very bad English, in trying to get out by one of the windows, became fastened, so that he could neither get in nor out. The tall man that had broken down so many seats, in his exploring expedition, instead of getting up, cried out, "Let's have a word of prayer," and immediately commenced repeating the Lord's Prayer. As I was trying to set the stove right, I heard the cry, "water, water—a lady has fainted," and saw a number of persons crowding to a seat occupied by the only lady in our car. As the doors could not be moved, neither water nor snow could be procured; and, there being no other women present, of course camphor bottles were scarce. However, an admirable substitute was introduced by the big Scotchman, who, by this time, had finished his prayers. Seeing that neither water, camphor or anything else could be obtained, the Highlander took from his pocket his box of snuff, and at once put a pinch to the lady's nose, which, by the bye, had the desired effect. A moment more, and the lady, with open eyes, exclaimed, "Don't crush my new bonnet." As the engine had not run off the track, it started for Pittsfield for a new set of cars. The day was one of the coldest we have had this winter. The windows of the cars were covered with frost, while the pelting snow was driving in through the ventilators. The trees, with their branches covered with snow and ice, looked like so many chandeliers hung in the forest, and the reflection of the sun upon them, and the snow-birds twittering in their tops, gave them a splendid appearance. The return of the engine with other cars relieved us from our unpleasant position, and enabled us to reach Albany a few hours after the time. Our friends gave me a large and attentive audience at Albany. The next night I spent at Buffalo, where I met some old and attached friends, who would only allow me to go through without a meeting upon condition that I should give them more than one lecture on my return in May. I was met at Cleveland by William H. Day, one of the most promising and intelligent coloured young men in the West, and one who, at some future day, will fill an important position among his oppressed race. You will, no doubt, remember that Mr. Day was editor of the *Aliened American*, published at Cleveland. Last winter, he was, by a vote of the Legislature of the State, excluded from it as a reporter. He is now the Librarian of the Cleveland Association. Mr. Day is about twenty-five years of age, has a fine forehead, expressive eyes, and a mouth beautifully cut, and indicative of decision and energy. Having gone through a regular course of studies at Oberlin, he has a polished education, and is qualified to fill, with credit to himself, the highest place to which he may be called.

Wm. H. Day is one of the few coloured men of this country who are capable of appreciating the anti-slavery cause. Indeed, the movement is too vast to be comprehended by the majority of whites, with all their education. In Ohio, Spring has fairly set in. Yesterday was a dreary, wet and uncomfortable day, with melting snow and high wind. I cannot give a better idea of the state of the roads here than to assure you that, while I write, a horse with an empty cart is sticking in the mud before my door. But remember I am in a town.

Yours, very truly, W. W. B.

Letter from W. W. Brown

Brown described to the public in this April 1855 letter to the *National Anti-Slavery Standard* his first return to Cincinnati since he had escaped from his master's steamboat when it docked at the Public Landing in January 1834. Full of memories, he visited the harbor to locate the spot of his escape, as well as the marsh where he hid while waiting for dark before beginning his trek north toward freedom. With a little free time in his schedule, he took a steamboat up the Ohio River to travel a short distance to New Richmond, where he was the guest of an abolitionist family. From a perch in their house overlooking the Ohio River, Brown could see slaves working the fields opposite him in Kentucky, the state in which he was born a slave.

NEW RICHMOND, Ohio, April 10, 1855.

After lecturing, in most instances to large audiences, in a number of towns between New Lisbon and Massillon, I came on to Cincinnati, by way of Crestline and Dayton, over a new and rather ricketty railroad, which made me feel that although my head was insured, it was not entirely out of danger. The long journey was made pleasant by the fine weather and the sun pouring its effulgent beams of warmth and radiance over the fertile country through which we passed. When I inform you that it was at Cincinnati that I escaped from my old master, twenty-one years ago, you will believe me when I tell you that no language which I am master of can adequately describe the strange feelings with which I entered the Queen City of the West. How different the scene now! Twenty-one years ago, Cincinnati had only a population of about 35,000 or 40,000, now it numbers nearly 200,000 souls; then, many of its streets run through swamps and low lands; now, they are beautifully paved and will compare, in point of splendour, with some of our Eastern cities. In company with our friend W. W. Watson, I took a walk to the wharf, to view, once more, the spot where my old master's steamer lay when I leaped on shore, with an empty pocket but a full heart. A few buildings, still standing, enabled me to point out the identical place. The long string of steamers lying, apparently, as I saw them, when, with a throbbing heart and trembling limbs, I started for the land of *freedom*, carried me back to the days when I was a victim to the hydra-headed system that pollutes our moral atmosphere, and stigmatizes the national character, and proves ruinous to all that it touches. The lowness of the river brought me more to the Kentucky side, and the mean looking buildings in Covington, and its deserted streets, told too well the want of enterprise which slavery has entailed upon its inhabitants. In the afternoon of the same day, I strolled through the back part of the city, to see if I could recognise the place which was a marshy wood-land when I escaped, and in which I hid on the memorable day, until night-fall; but the swamp had disappeared, and where trees then stood, now are to be seen the beautiful brick dwellings with their green painted window-blinds. When I escaped, there was no Underground Railroad. The North Star was, in many instances, the only friend that the weary and foot-sore fugitive found on his pilgrimage to his new home amongst strangers, and, consequently, the means of getting away from slavery was not as easy then as now. During my first day at Cincinnati, the Rosetta slave-case was before the Court and, although I did not see the girl, I saw her claimant, the Rev. H. M. Dennison, and the distinguished lawyers engaged in the suit on both sides. I was pleased with the appearance as well as the speech of ex-Senator Chase. Mr. Chase's successor (George Pugh, Esq.) was Dennison's counsel, and the Reverend slaveholder could not have secured a more devoted tool to the Slave Power than this newly-elected Senator from the State of Ohio. Mr. Pugh is of small stature, with a thin face and a receding forehead; hair, dark brown; nose, long; and eyes rather deeply set. He is a good lawyer, an eloquent speaker, but said to be a most unprincipled man. What a fall Ohio took when she elected this man to take the place of S. P. Chase. I met the Donaldsons, Blackwells and a few others of the slave's devoted friends there, and with whom I was much pleased. It was not intended for me to speak at Cincinnati until the Convention. But our coloured friends would not let me off, so I lectured in the Baker street Baptist church, Bishop Paine in the chair. The following day, Monday, I came to New

Richmond, on board the steamboat Bostona, and lost my dinner, or rather failed to get it, because I would not eat with the *servants*. However, I enjoyed the trip, although hungry. One can scarcely pass through a more picturesque part of the country than when on a steamer gliding up or down the Ohio river. The beautiful valleys have been made to bloom, new arteries of commerce are filling up every avenue made vacant by the disappearance of the injured red men of the forest. Splendid mansions now sit where the Indian once roamed. The glorious scenery on both sides of the river, the soft and lovely valleys through which the waters of the Ohio linger, with a thousand coquettish wanderings, as if unwilling to leave, and upon whose bosom is here and there a splendid steamer with its steam and smoke curling towards the clouds, gives the whole an indescribable appearance.

A large meeting welcomed me to New Richmond, from which place I visited Laurel, Filicity and Bethel. You will remember that the latter town was the birth-place and residence of Thomas Morris, who first "bearded the lion in his den" at Washington, in his reply to Henry Clay. Mr. Morris lies buried in a sweet spot about a quarter of a mile from the town, where a beautiful monument, with a fitting inscription, points out his grave, and where, like watchful sentinels, the lofty trees stand around.

I have just had the pleasure of shaking the hand of another passenger by the Underground Railroad. He was a young man of fine appearance, and had with him an only child of eight months. The poor man's wife had been given to her young mistress, who was just married, and the young lady wanting the waiting-maid without the "incumbrance," as they say in Britain, the child and disconsolate husband were left behind; and the injured man was told to select another wife. However, he thought the surest way to guard against such another outrage, was to escape. But the determination not to leave his child behind, shows a degree of attachment that cannot be surpassed by the most refined and educated whites. His trembling voice, and eyes filled with the deepest emotion, while he related the story of his wrongs, was an index to a heart filled with the keenest grief. We cannot conceive of deeper, deadlier wrongs than these. There is but little doubt that this poor fugitive, ere this, is safe on the other side of Jordan. The anti-slavery feeling here, so near the slave territory, seems to be more favourable to Free Soil than Free Men. From the window where I am seated, I see the slave toiling on the Kentucky side of Mason and Dixon's Line. Nature could scarcely throw together more picturesque scenery than that which surrounds Frandon, the home of the Donaldsons, from which this is written. Situated in this lovely valley, with the murmuring Ohio running at the foot of the garden, I see the rafts and flat-bottomed boats floating down the river, with the children playing and "*roosters*" crowing on the tops. From present appearance, the coming Convention at Cincinnati, on the 25th, 26th and 27th of this month, will be well attended. The late slave-case has, no doubt, created a feeling in the Queen City of the West that will give additional interest to the cause at the approaching meeting.

Yours very truly, W. W. B.

Speech at Anniversary of the New York Anti-Slavery Society

May 8, 1856

How does an initiated individual possibly represent the barbarism of "the great Sodom" of the American South to an uninitiated, squeamish public? One of Brown's most distinctive strategies was to disarm his audience, as in these remarks delivered to an antislavery convention in New York City in May 1856, with a combination of humorous anecdotes and hard-hitting commentary designed to appeal to their moral sentiments.

Mr. Chairman, Ladies and Gentlemen: Those of you who have been here during yesterday and to-day will bear witness that the several speakers have hesitated not to declare the truth as it regards the iniquity of slavery. It can scarcely be expected, however, that those of us who understand the workings of slavery in the Southern States will bring before you the wrongs of the slave as we could wish. Language will not allow us; and if we had the language, the fastidiousness of the people would not permit our portraying them. Slavery has justly been termed the crime of crimes. Man cannot inflict upon his fellow-man a greater crime than to enslave him, for by so doing he not only injures his fellow-man, but himself. It is not possible for one part of mankind to enslave another portion without injuring themselves. That may be seen in the workings of slavery in this country.

Every one who speaks of the condition of the slave will tell you of his ignorance and degradation. This ignorance and debasement necessarily affect the master. The master may get education and refinement, but his relation to the slave is such that he is contaminated. Those of us who have lived in slavery could tell you privately what we cannot tell you publicly of the degradation in the domestic circle of the master. We could tell you of the ignorance of the white people as well as the black. The white children are brought up with the black children; it is not possible to separate them; hence the ignorance and degradation that is found among the slave population communicates itself to them. The child grows up to the age of ten or twelve years: then the master discovers that that son or daughter must be removed to a part of the country where the rough edges that intercourse with the slave children has imparted may be rubbed off. The young man is sent off to the North to get an education; and in coming to your Northern seminaries of learning, among your own sons, he must necessarily rub off those rough edges upon them. And the same is true with regard to the slaveowner's daughter. Thus your children partake of this degradation, vice and ignorance. This is one of the results of your toleration of such a system. A distinguished writer has justly said that no one can fasten a chain upon the limbs of his neighbour without afterwards inevitably fastening the other end upon his own neck. This is exemplified not only in the slaveholder at the South, but in the people of the North, who have folded their arms and permitted this iniquity to live.

You have, no doubt, all of you, read of the riot that occurred, some three months since, among the students of Columbia College, South Carolina, in which the students drove the police back to their stations, and at length demanded the chief of the police, that they might sacrifice him to their ferocity; and when the mayor had called out the militia, they could do nothing, and the chief of the police was murdered, with two other policemen. That was a legitimate fruit of slavery. The young white boy is brought up with these ferocious passions. He has been accustomed to kick and drive the black slave about; and when he meets with white persons, he considers them his inferiors, and his passions break forth on the slightest provocation. Northern men complain that they send men to Congress and they exhibit no backbone—that they don't face the music in the halls of Congress. To send your Northern men to Congress, there to meet the bully, the duellist, the woman-scourger, the gambler, the murderer, is like taking your little son from the country and sending him to the city, where he finds a thousand rude boys who insult and abuse him. Men in the South who are accustomed to flog old men and young women, and to sell children from the mother's breast, are more than a match for your Northern man when it comes to bullying and threats. To talk about a good slaveholder is a contradiction. A good slaveholder is a bad man, a Christian slaveholder an infidel, a just slaveholder a thief, for to rob a man of himself is the greatest theft that a human being can commit. The South is the great Sodom of this country. I hold in my hand an advertisement, taken from the New Orleans *Picayune*, by which you may see the evidence of what I assert, coming from the slaveholder himself.

> "$20 REWARD—Ran away from the plantation of the undersigned the negro man SHADRACK, a preacher, five feet nine inches high, about forty years old, and stamped N. E. upon the breast and having both small toes cut off. He has a very dark complexion, with eyes small but bright, and a look quite insolent."

The slaveowner has the audacity to say that his slave has a look quite insolent. I rather think if the Rev. Dr. Nehemiah Adams, who has just been reelected as a member of the Board of Directors of the Tract Society, and who thinks the slaves are so happy, contented and always look so smiling, should happen to be sold down South, be stamped with the letters "N. E.," and have his toes cut off—I rather think he would look quite as insolent as that "very dark-complexioned" man mentioned in this advertisement (laughter and applause).

I saw in a newspaper published in my town, St. Louis—for I happen to have come from among the "border ruffians" (laughter)—an editorial announcement that a man who owned a slave there, a short time since, had caused that slave to be branded upon the right cheek with the words "slave for life," and the editor spends a great deal of invective and indignation upon this owner of the slave, saying that the slave was a good servant and had committed no offence to merit such treatment. The crime of this victim was, being born with a white skin, for the editor tells us that he had straight hair and would pass for a white man. Being white, it was easy for him to escape, and hence the necessity of branding these words on his cheek, so as to prevent his running away. Perhaps, too, he had too much Anglo-Saxon blood in him to be a submissive slave, as Theodore Parker would say.

Such are the workings of slavery. A slave must always be made to know his place; if it were not so, he could not be kept in his chains. We see the effects of slavery everywhere throughout the North. I saw an illustration of it to-day in your own city. A very nice-looking coloured lady, a stranger in this city, no doubt, who was not aware that on the Sixth Avenue they have cars expressly for coloured people, entered a car that stopped to take in some other ladies. She was rudely thrust from the platform by the conductor and told that that was not the car for her to ride in. She was considerably lighter in complexion than myself, and perhaps as white as some that were seated in the car.

Some year and a half ago, I landed in this city from a British steamer, having just left England, after having been abroad in different countries in Europe for a number of years, where I was once never reminded that I was a coloured person, so that I had quite forgotten the distinction of caste that existed in democratic America. I walked into an eating-house. I had scarcely got my hat off when the proprietor told me I could not eat there. Said I, "I have got a good appetite, and if you will give me a trial, I rather think I will convince you that I can." "But," said he, "it is not allowable." I did not know what to make of it; I had been away five years, and had forgotten the great power of slavery over the North. I felt insulted. I walked into another eating-house. The proprietor asked me what I wanted. I said I wanted my dinner. "You can't get it here; we don't accommodate niggers." That was twice I was insulted. I went into a third, with a like result. I then went and stood by a lamp post for some five minutes. I thought of the nineteen years I had worked as a slave; I thought of the glorious Declaration of Independence; I looked around me and saw no less than seven steeples of churches; and I resolved I would have my dinner in the city of New York (applause). I went to another restaurant. I made up my mind what I would do. I saw a vacant plate at a table; I took aim at it. I pulled back the chair, and sat down, turned over the plate, and stuck my knife in something. I was agitated, and did not know what it was, until I got it on my plate, when I found it was a big pickle (laughter). At any rate I went to work at it. The waiter stared at me. Said I, "Boy, get me something to eat." He stared again, walked to the proprietor, and said something to him, came back and helped me. When I got through my dinner, I went up to the bar, and handed the proprietor a dollar. He took it, and then said, "You have got the greatest impudence of any nigger I have seen for a great while (laughter); and if it had n't been that I did n't want to disturb my people sitting at the table, I would have taken you up from that table a little the quickest." "Well, sir," said I, "if you had, you would have taken the table cloth, dishes and all with me. Now, sir, look at me; whenever I come into your dining saloon, the best thing you can do is to let me have what I want to eat quietly. You keep house for the accommodation of the public; I claim to be one of that public."

Some twenty days after that, I was about to start for Boston; I had n't time to go to that saloon, so I went to a confectionary establishment, and thought I would do with a little pastry. I walked in; a young woman, who attended, came up and said she, "Can't accommodate you, sir." I paid no attention to her, but picked up a knife, and pitched into a piece of pie. Said she, "We can't accommodate you, sir." Said I, "This is very good pastry" (laughter). Then said she, "We don't accommodate niggers." Said I, "Did you make this?" (Laughter.) I finished my piece of pie, and then a second piece. By and by another lady came to me, and said, "Sir, we don't accommodate niggers." Said I, "You give very good accommodations; I shall always patronize you." I finished my third piece of pie, and asked for a glass of soda water. Says she, "Just leave my place, and I will charge you nothing." Said I, "Madam, I expect to pay wherever I get accommodation, but I can't pay for this until you give me a glass of soda water." So I took a chair and sat down, saying I was in no hurry; for I concluded to wait and go on the next train. As soon as she saw I was determined to stay, she said, "You may have your soda water." I drank it and walked out. Now that grated very hard on my feelings, after being away so long, and forgetting almost everything about the way coloured people were treated in this country.

Such are the workings of slavery, and yet, with all your boasted benevolence and religion, there is scarce a pulpit in New York that has a word to say against these wrongs (applause). Still, such is the compromising character of the American people that the time will probably come when colourphobia will become the subject of compromise, even with this religious sentiment. Not long since, a coloured man, of great wealth, came to visit a merchant in one of our eastern cities, who, by a business connection with this coloured man, had acquired a considerable fortune. The merchant knew he must treat him kindly, and so he invited him to his house, and on Sunday he asked him to go to his church. It was one of the fine churches where a coloured face is never seen inside, except, perhaps, to do some menial work. The pew was near the pulpit. When the merchant, with his black friend, entered the pew, the congregation stared. There was no mistake about its being a black man. The minister entered his pulpit and commenced the services. He did n't discover the black man until he got into the midst of his sermon. It disconcerted him, and he could not go on. He lost his place in his sermon, hesitated, and at length had to slip secondly, and go to thirdly. He made a botch of it and concluded. As soon as service was over, a neighbour of the merchant came to him, and asked him what he meant by bringing a nigger into the church. "Why, it is my pew," said the merchant. "Is that any reason why you must insult the whole congregation?" said the man. "Yes, but he is an educated man," the merchant replied. "What of that?" said the man, "he is black." "But, sir, he is a correspondent of mine, and is worth a million of dollars." "Worth what!" "A million of dollars." "I beg pardon, introduce me to him" (laughter and applause).

Ladies and gentlemen, you may think lightly of these insults and annoyances which the coloured people have to endure, but they are felt keenly by us. And if there were nothing else for the people of the North to do, they have got enough to revolutionize the public sentiment in this respect. You see nothing of this hatred abroad. A black man is treated in Europe according as he behaves, and not according to his colour. This feeling is one of the great hindrances to the abolition movement. The Colonization Society fosters this hatred and makes itself one of the great props of slavery. There are churches that refuse to open their doors for a meeting in behalf of the slave, but throw them wide open to the Colonization Society, and yet pretend that they are opposed to slavery and in favour of elevating the black man.

The American Anti-Slavery Society is the only one, of all the various societies, of whatsoever name, that meet this week in this city, that goes for the abolition of slavery. Our work is to look after humanity and try to lift it up in the person of the down-trodden slave. I feel that if those in the Southern States with whom I am identified by complexion could only know of the sentiment and feeling which animates those who take part in this great cause, they would put up their prayer to God for our success (applause).

I speak not for the purpose of making any display of eloquence or rhetoric. Whenever I come before a cultivated audience like this, I remember that I was nineteen years a slave, and never had a day's schooling in my life, and yet that it is a duty I owe to my enslaved countrymen, to those who are bound to me by tenderest ties, to my God and to my country, to labour in the cause of humanity and remember those in bonds as bound with them. And if I can be the means of helping to remove a single obstacle out of the way of the anti-slavery cause, I shall feel well paid (applause).

John Brown and the Fugitive Slave Law

William Wells Brown shared in the John Brown mania that swept the antislavery movement following the raid on the federal arsenal at Harpers Ferry in October 1859. He led anniversary celebrations for Brown's raid in Boston after the Civil War and on at least one occasion even made the acquaintance of Brown's widow. The following story of heroic resistance, however, was wholly or partially made up, since William Wells Brown was still living in England when the long arm of the Fugitive Slave Law reached up to Boston, nabbed Anthony Burns, and returned him forcibly to slavery. For unknown reasons, Brown did not publish this piece until March 1870.

When the Fugitive Slave Act of 1851 became the law of the land, it found a large number of escaped slaves in the Northern States, who, on their flight from the South, had temporarily taken up their abode in towns through which they were passing, instead of going to Canada, as they had at first intended. Many of these had been years from slavery, had accumulated property, raised up families, and were considered a part of the resident population. In some places they had churches of their own, where a sufficient number warranted a separate organization. The announcement of the passage of the law created a profound sensation throughout the country, both amongst the whites and blacks; and especially the latter. So great was their feeling and the fear of recapture that large numbers fled to Canada, without waiting to dispose of their property; others sold out at an enormous sacrifice; while many laborers and domestics left without stopping to settle with employers. Thus families were suddenly broken up, and every railroad train toward the British Provinces was a bearer of these people. In one town in the State of New York the whole of the members of a Methodist church, with their pastor, fled to Canada. In Springfield, Mass., where a large number of fugitives had taken up their residence, the excitement appeared intense. The blacks left their employment, and were seeking more secluded hiding-places in the surrounding towns, or preparing to leave the country. At this period John Brown, who had formerly resided at Springfield, hearing of the state of affairs, returned, called the fugitives together, organized them into a body for mutual defense, inspired them with hope and self-reliance, and thus saved these frightened and helpless people from suffering and poverty.

The advice, agreement, and code of laws that bound this little band together was written out by John Brown, and is now for the first time put in print, and is as follows:

WORDS OF ADVICE.

Branch of the United States League of Gileadites. Adopted January 15th, 1851. As written and recommended by John Brown.

UNION IS STRENGTH.

Nothing so charms the American people as personal bravery. The trial for life of one bold and to some extent successful man, for defending his rights in good earnest, would arouse more sympathy throughout the nation than the accumulated wrongs and sufferings of more than three millions of our submissive colored population. We need not mention the Greeks struggling against the oppressive Turks, the Poles against Russia, nor the Hungarians against Austria and Russia combined, to prove this. No jury can be found in the Northern States that would convict a man for defending his rights to the last extremity. This is well understood by Southern congressmen, who insisted that the right of trial by jury should not be granted to the fugitive. Colored people have more fast friends amongst the whites than they suppose, and would have ten times the number they now have were they but half as much in earnest to secure their dearest rights as they are to ape the follies and extravagances of their white neighbors, and to indulge in idle show, in ease, and in luxury. Just think of the money expended by individuals in your behalf in the past twenty years. Think of the number who have been mobbed and imprisoned on your account. Have any of you seen the Branded Hand? Do you remember the names of Lovejoy and Torrey? Should one of your number be arrested, you must collect together as quickly as possible, so as to outnumber your adversaries who are taking an active part against you. Let no able-bodied man appear on the ground unequipped, or with his weapons exposed to view; let that be understood beforehand. Your plans must be known only to yourself, and with the understanding that all traitors must die, wherever caught and proven to be guilty. 'Whosoever is fearful or afraid, let him return and depart early from Mount Gilead.'—Judges, vii. chap., 3 verse; Deut., xx. chap, 6 verse. Give all cowards an opportunity to show it on condition of holding their peace. Do not delay one moment after you are ready; you will lose all your resolution if you do. Let the first blow be the signal for all to engage, and when engaged do not do your work by halves; but make clean work with your enemies, and be sure you meddle not with any others. By going about your business quietly, you will get the job disposed of before the number that an uproar would bring together can collect; and you will have the advantage of those who come out against you, for they will be wholly unprepared with either equipments or matured plans—all with them will be confusion and terror. Your enemies will be slow to attack you after you have once done up the work nicely; and, if they should, they will have to encounter your white friends as well as you, for you may safely calculate on a division of the whites, and may by that means get to an honorable parley.

Be firm, determined, and cool; but let it be understood that you are not to be driven to desperation without making it an awful dear job to others as well as to you. Give them to know distinctly that those who live in wooden houses should not throw fire, and that you are just as able to suffer as your white neighbors. After effecting a rescue, if you are assailed, go into the houses of your most prominent and influential white friends with your wives, and that will effectually fasten upon them the suspicion of being connected with you, and will compel them to make a common cause with you, whether they would otherwise live up to their professions or not. This would leave them no choice in the matter. Some would, doubtless, prove themselves true of their own choice; others would flinch. That would be taking them at their own words. You may make a tumult in the court-room where a trial is going on by burning gunpowder freely in paper packages, if you cannot think of any better way to create a momentary alarm, and might possibly give one or more of your enemies a hoist. But in such case the prisoner will need to take the hint at once and bestir himself; and so should his friends improve the opportunity for a general rush.

A lasso might possibly be applied to a slave-catcher for once with good effect. Hold on to your weapons, and never be persuaded to leave them, part with them, or have them far away

> from you. Stand by one another, and by your friends, while a drop of blood remains; and be hanged, if you must, but tell no tales out of school. Make no confession.

This closes John Brown's advice to the fugitives, as written out. Then comes the

> AGREEMENT.
>
> As citizens of the United States of America, trusting in a Just and Merciful God, whose spirit and all-powerful aid we humbly implore, we will ever be true to the Flag of our beloved Country, always acting under it. We whose names are hereunto affixed do constitute ourselves a Branch of the United States League of Gileadites. That we will provide ourselves at once with suitable implements, and will aid those who do not possess the means, if any such are disposed to join us. We invite every colored person whose heart is engaged for the performance of our business, whether male or female, old or young. The duty of the aged, infirm, and young members of the League shall be to give instant notice to all members in case of an attack upon any of our people.
>
> We agree to have no officers except a Treasurer and Secretary *pro tem.*, until after some trial of courage and talent of ablebodied members shall enable us to elect officers from those who shall have rendered the most important services. Nothing but wisdom and undaunted courage, efficiency, and general good conduct shall in any way influence us in electing our officers.

Following this are the names of forty-four men and women, all in the handwriting of John Brown, who seems to have presided over the meeting as well as to have been its master spirit.

A code of laws which we found in the MS., and which we omit, followed this agreement. During the week following the rendition of Anthony Burns the writer was passing through Springfield, and learned that the colored people of the place were in a state of great excitement, owing to the report that the slave-hunters were there and intended to arrest some of the fugitives and return them to the South. As night drew near, the excitement among the blacks became more intense; and a feeling of despair and revenge seemed depicted upon the countenances of the colored people, which feeling was shared by many of the whites, who deeply sympathized with the intended victims. With a friend, we visited the locality where most of the colored people resided, a little after eight o'clock in the evening, and when the excitement was at its hight. The clear moonlight enabled us to see the black sentinels stationed at the corners of the streets and alleys approaching the dusky neighborhood, in the midst of which stood a large two-story house, occupied exclusively by colored families. After submitting to an examination that satisfied the outposts that we were of the right stripe, we were permitted to pass, and one of their number was sent in advance of us to prevent our being disturbed. By special invitation, we were conducted to the "hot room," as it was called, of the large building. On entering, we found this to be a room of about thirty by forty feet square, in the center of which stood an old-fashioned cook-stove, the top of which seemed filled with boilers, and all steaming away, completely filling the place with a dense fog. Two lamps, with dingy chimneys, and the light from the fire, which shone brightly through the broken doors of the stove, lighted up the room. Eight athletic black women, looking for all the world as if they had just returned from a Virginia cornfield, weary and hungry, stood around the room.

Each of these Amazons was armed with a tin dipper, apparently new, which had no doubt been purchased for the occasion. A woman of exceedingly large proportions—tall, long-armed, with a deep scar down the side of her face, and with a half grin, half smile—was the commander-in-chief of the "hot room." This woman stood by the stove, dipper in hand, and occasionally taking the top from the large wash-boiler, which we learned was filled with boiling water, soap, and ashes.

In case of an attack, this boiler was to be the "King of Pain." As we saw the perspiration streaming down the faces of these women, we ventured a few questions. "Do you expect an attack?" we asked. "Dunno, honey; but we's ready ef dey comes," was the reply from the aunty near the stove. "Were you ever in slavery?" we continued. "Yes; ain't bin from dar but little while." "What state?" "Bread and born in ole Virginny, down on de Pertomuc." "Have you any of your relations in Virginia now?" "Yes; got six chilens down dar somewhar, an' two husbuns—all sole to de speclaturs afore I run away." "Did you come off alone?" "No; my las ole man bring me way." "You don't mean to be taken back by the slave-catchers, in peace?"

"No; I'll die fuss." "How will you manage if they attempt to come into this room?" "We'll all fling hot water on 'em, an scall dar very harts out." "Can you all throw water without injuring each other?" "Oh, yes, honey; we's bin practicin all day." And here the whole company joined in a hearty laugh, which made the old building ring.

The intense heat drove us from the room. As we descended the steps and passed the guards, we remarked to one of them: "The women seem to be prepared for battle." "Yes," he replied; "dem wimmens got de debil in em to-night, an' no mistake. Dey'll make dat a hot hell in dar fur somebody, ef de slave-catchers comes here to-night; dat dey will." And here the guards broke forth in a hearty laugh, which was caught up and joined in by the women in the house, which showed very clearly that these blacks felt themselves masters of the situation. Returning to the depot to take the train for Boston, we found there some ten or fifteen blacks, all armed to the teeth and swearing vengeance upon the heads of any who should attempt to take them.

True, the slave-catchers had been there. But the authorities, foreseeing a serious outbreak, advised them to leave the city; and, feeling alarmed for their personal safety, these disturbers of the peace had left in the evening train for New York. No fugitive slave was ever afterward disturbed at Springfield.

Speech at Annual Meeting of the American Anti-Slavery Society

May 9, 1860

Brown gave this address at the 1860 annual convention of the American Anti-Slavery Society in New York City. Although he typically prepared his remarks with special care for this major event on the antislavery calendar, he was well-known for mixing humorous anecdotes of sometimes questionable authenticity with serious commentary on the state of the racial union. In this instance, he went even further by poking fun at his own mixed-race heritage, which by association also reflected back onto his presumed aristocratic white cousins "Fanny" and "Bob" in their native Kentucky.

MR. CHAIRMAN, LADIES AND GENTLEMEN: The colored man in this country may well exclaim, "Suffering is the badge of all our race." Go into the Southern States and there he need not utter such an exclamation; it is seen on the surface of society; it is seen all through the slave States. The slave at the South, to-day is enduring a bondage such as no other country has ever yet inflicted upon a people. We look in vain to all lands to find a parallel to the system of chattel slavery in Louisiana, Mississippi and the Carolinas. Slavery in the West Indies never came up to what it is in the Southern States. In Cuba, to-day, there are many circumstances surrounding the slave that make his servitude far preferable to slavery in the States. In Cuba, if a slave, by some meritorious act, or by industry, shall secure the sum of $300, his master is compelled to set him free, on his making the claim and presenting the money. In the South, the slave may have ten times that amount given to him, perhaps for some act of heroism in saving the life of a white person, and yet the law declares that all the slave may possess shall be the property of the master. That is slavery in the South. The slave can own nothing; he is not allowed to protect himself, his wife, his children; he toils for another, and his offspring are put upon the auction-block and sold to the highest bidder. The slave is not permitted to get education; he is not permitted to worship God according to the dictates of his own conscience. If half a dozen slaves are found together in the States where I was born and brought up, they are punished by the police, or by the person finding them, unless some white person is there to vouch for them.

The new importations into the South, the high prices paid for slaves, all show that the system is going forward as it has never gone forward before. The price of an able-bodied man, when I ran away from the South, was not more than seven or eight hundred dollars; to-day, a slave of the same description will bring double that sum in the New Orleans market. The cotton raised by the slave twenty years ago brought the master only about one-half what it brings to-day. The sugar, the cotton and the rice plantations all yield a better profit than formerly, and the slaveholder makes a business of driving cotton, sugar and rice out of his slaves, and the overseer who can raise the most of either of those articles, out of a given number of hands, claims a greater salary at the hands of the master.

Mr. Chairman, looking at the South and seeing the spirit of slavery, seeing how it has taken hold upon the people, seeing the importance that it has acquired, I am not surprised that the slaveholders are to-day trying to reduce the free colored people to bondage. That shows the demoralizing effects of the system upon the white people in the slave States. Some half dozen or more slave States, during the last two years, have introduced resolutions or bills in their different legislative bodies for reducing the free colored people to slavery, or driving them out of the State. Look at the free colored people driven from Arkansas within the last eight or nine months! Men, women and children driven out—driven away from what little property they had, without regard to age or sex—under penalty of being reduced to bondage! I saw the announcement recently, in a Tennessee paper, that a free colored woman who had left the State and returned, had been taken and sold to the highest bidder, bringing the sum of $1,200. The money, it was said, was given over to the school fund! A free colored woman in Alabama, a short time since, having gone into the State ignorantly in one of the steamers, was arrested, taken to the public square, and flogged thirty-nine lashes, and ordered to leave the State in ten days. That shows the meanness of the slaveholders.

Now, in regard to the free people of color, the slaveholders blow hot and blow cold when talking upon the subject. Some declare that the free colored people of the South are a nuisance and ought to be driven out; another, when it suits him, declares that they are a very orderly class of people, and among the best mechanics and artisans of the State, as Judge Catron said in a letter to the Legislature of his State, a short time since. I say they blow hot and blow cold. They are ready to use the free colored man when they can, they are ready to drive him out of the State when they want to get rid of him.

There is no justice at all for the free colored people in the slave States, and there seems to be but little justice for the colored people in the free States. They have no justice for us. We cannot have justice anywhere at the hands of this slaveholding nation. History has thrown the colored man out. You look in vain to Bancroft and the other historians for justice to the colored people. Although it is admitted that they fought in the war of the Revolution and in the last war, the historian passes it by. Go to the few monuments that have been erected to those who fell for liberty, and you will see that the colored man has been excluded, or, if he be found there at all, he is found, as in the monument at Fort Griswold, cut off from his white fellow-patriots by a broad line. On that monument, the names of the white men who fell in the Revolution are given first, and then a long line is drawn and the colored men put down—only the first name—Caesar, Jumbo, Pompey, Dick, Tom. The colored man is colonized off from the white man, or mentioned in a sort of appendix (laughter). Mr. Chairman, you, and all who have walked through the streets of London, and especially through Trafalgar Square, and have looked upon that noble monument there, in commemoration of the great deeds of Nelson, and his death in battle, have seen, as I saw there, a black man—as black a man as was ever imported from the coast of Africa—among the white soldiers, his musket in his hand, and his countenance showing that he was in the battle. He is there as large as life, as large as the white man; no mark is drawn between him and the white man. It seems that every country is willing to give the colored man justice, or something like justice, except the people of the United States.

I say that this is characteristic of this nation. It seems that we can have no justice whatever—nothing at all like justice. Citizenship is denied us. The Supreme Court of the United States declares that we are not citizens, and have no rights that white men are bound to respect. A colored man writes to Gen. Cass, your Secretary of State, and asks for a passport. He, like the whole American nation, is ready to utter a falsehood, and says that the colored man has never been recognized as a citizen, is not a citizen, and never has received a passport as a citizen from the government. Now, this is as gross a falsehood as could be uttered. It is well known that colored men have received passports. I have one in my pocket that I received at the hands of the Hon. Abbott Lawrence, in London, in exchange for a passport that I had carried from this country, certifying that I was a citizen of the United States. [Mr. Brown read the passport, which is in the usual form.] My friend Robert Purvis, who spoke so eloquently from this platform yesterday, also received a passport as a citizen of the United States; and another colored friend of mine, as black as black can be, received a passport, direct from Washington, certifying that he was a citizen of the United States.

I say we are going backward. This nation is determined not only to keep the colored man in slavery, but to reduce the free colored people to slavery, and blot out, so far as they can, everything that tends to show that the colored man is a man, and at all worthy of respect as a citizen of this country. But, Mr. Chairman, I rejoice at one thing—that while they are imposing upon black men in the slave States, they are also imposing upon white men. The Reign of Terror that has existed at the South since the John Brown invasion has brought the white man down to a level with the black man. As I have read in the newspapers of white men being chased out of the Carolinas, Virginia, Kentucky, and other States, I have rejoiced at it, because it shows that slavery is no respecter of persons; it cares no more for the rights of the white man than for those of the black man.

Mr. Brown then told the story of a miscreant who, by making love to a young girl of sixteen, free and white, induced her to elope with him, under promise of marriage, when he took her to Alabama, and sold her for $900. Then he came back, and, by representing to the brother of the girl that she was doing well in her new home, and desired to see him, induced him, too, to go with him to the South, where he also was sold for $700. At length the girl found means to inform her mother of her condition, who immediately went after her. She was brought before a court of justice upon a warrant, and the man who had purchased her, a clergyman, appeared and stated that he bought her in good faith, and that she had been very well treated, for she had been allowed to attend prayers with the white portion of the family every morning. The result was that the girl, who appeared in court with a young babe in her arms, was delivered up to her mother.

Now, continued Mr. Brown, I say that there is no justice for the colored man in this country. Every particle of pity is for the white man. Talk with a man about the slave or the abolition of slavery, and he begins to pity the white man; he has no pity for the black man. If he prays, he does it as Dr. Blagden did in Boston, at a Union meeting. He prayed, "Oh Lord, bless our country, our whole country, and especially the Southern half of our country" (laughter). It reminded me of an anecdote that I heard when I was in the South. Two men owned an old and blind black man, whom they kept in a shop turning out table-legs, bedstead-legs, &c. One of the men was pious, the other a great sinner. Well, the cholera came along, and the pious man wanted to sell out his half of the slave to the other, but he would not buy, and he asked more for his half than the pious man would give; so he determined he would put up a prayer to Heaven, and he prayed, "Oh Lord, protect my family and house from the cholera; protect my neighbors, all my relations, and especially my half of Sam!" (Much merriment.)

Now, Mr. Chairman, just as the condition of the colored man in this country begins to improve, and his prospects to look more encouraging, the white people are trying to get rid of him. Mr. Wade, a Republican, says he is tired of hearing so much said about the equality of the negro. Another Republican says he wants the colored people sent off to South America, New Mexico, or somewhere else. Another gets up and says that he is willing to give his vote for money to send the negroes out of the country to Africa. Now, my friends, let me say, on behalf of the colored people, that we are not going to Africa—we are not going to leave this country at all (applause). The slaveholders have mixed the Anglo-Saxon blood with ours, so that even in the pro-slavery cities of New York and Philadelphia colored men and women ride in the cars and omnibuses, and are so light that they are mistaken for white people, while the white man is so dark that he is sometimes taken for a negro (laughter). In 1844, Henry Clay, in one of his letters, said that slavery was to be abolished by the inevitable law of population. Some one asked him what he meant, and he said, "amalgamation, as carried on in the slave States." It is fearful to think of or look at; but it is doing a work at the South at the present time, and we throw upon the slavocracy of the South the responsibility of the whole system of illegitimate amalgamation that exists in this country.

I say the black people are not going to leave the United States. We are connected with the South by the tenderest ties of nature. The free colored people of the North are connected with the slaves of the South. Many of the free colored people of the North, especially the fugitive slaves, are connected with the slaveholders of the South. They look into the Southern States, and they see there their white relatives as slaveholders. I met a good friend of mine yesterday, who came from the South about the time I did, and one of the first questions he asked me was, how my white relatives in Lexington prospered since I came away (laughter); and I asked after his white relatives. He wanted to know how my cousin William was, who is our Minister Plenipotentiary to the Court of Spain. The Hon. William Preston married my cousin Fanny (laughter). If you had been there, and heard us talking about our relatives, you would have thought that I was just from the United States Senate, for he knew very well that my relatives were among the first in the State of Kentucky. My cousin Bob Wickliffe—the Wickliffe family is a very aristocratic family in Kentucky—died a few months since, worth, it is said, five millions. My cousin Charles A. Wickliffe was Postmaster-General under John Tyler (laughter). Probably many of you don't know anything about John Tyler, he filled such a small niche in our country's history, but certainly you must have heard of my cousin Charles (great merriment).

Now, Mr. Chairman, and ladies and gentlemen, I do not look upon these white relatives of mine with as much pleasure as you would think, perhaps; but still, they are my relatives (laughter). Sometimes, you know, we find ourselves related to some people that we don't care much about (renewed laughter). But I say, here we are. We are connected with the slaves and the slaveholders by the tenderest ties of nature; and if this country wants me to run away and leave my white relatives, I can't do it (great merriment). If they want to drive me away from my black relatives, I shall stay here and labor for their emancipation (loud applause).

I speak thus, friends, because there is a great deal said now about colored emigration—about trying to coax the colored people out of the country, getting them to go off to some wilderness or some place they know nothing about. I have no objection to the black men entering into commercial enterprises, and going to California, Australia, or Africa, or anywhere else—I have no objection to their leaving the country and going where they think they can better their condition; but I am entirely opposed to the colored people becoming the victims of the Colonization Society, or any other scheme of expatriation. So far as I can, I shall say to our colored people, "Stay here! Educate yourselves! Attain to as high a point of culture as you possibly can, and remain here until you get your rights, so that you may labor the more effectually for the abolition of slavery in the Southern States!" (Applause.)

Mr. Chairman, I have sat here during these two days, and listened with interest to the speeches which have been made in the cause of freedom. I rejoiced yesterday in my heart that Dr. Cheever came here and made his speech, though I did not agree with him in every particular. Still, I am willing to welcome any one upon the platform of freedom who will come forward and speak for the slave, though he may not speak in my dialect. Let him come and speak rightly and speak truly; if he will only be honest and true, I, for one, will bid him Godspeed in the cause of freedom. But I was speaking of the colored people of this country. They are determined to labor on, to work on. They have faith in the great cause of freedom, faith in the Anti-Slavery movement, that it will eventually abolish slavery in this land. Progress is written all over the land. Although the slavocracy are trying to wipe out every landmark we have in this country, still everything indicates that the cause of freedom is advancing, on the one hand, while slavery is making progress on the other. Every one must have noted how the Southern States have tried and are trying to wipe out everything that points to freedom. The Declaration of Independence, if it is read at all on the 4th of July in the Southern States, is not commented upon as it was twenty or thirty years ago. The Fourth of July orator dare not speak in the Southern States unless he qualifies the expression. In the pulpit, if a minister speak of freedom, it must be with a qualification. Everything is done in order to wipe out the old landmarks. It was my pleasure and privilege to visit Paris in 1849, where I saw the motto of the Republic upon the public buildings and at the corners of the streets—"Liberty, Equality, Fraternity"; and up and down the Boulevards, and on the Champ Elysses, were planted the Liberty-trees. This went on very well for a time, but by-and-by comes Louis Napoleon. He has in his mind's eye an empire, with himself as emperor, and he commences blotting out these landmarks of the Republicans. The Liberty-trees are cut down by the soldiery and painters are ordered to blot out the words, "Liberty, Equality, Fraternity," upon the public buildings. It was only preparing the nation to receive its master. Now, Slavery is determined to triumph and rule in this country. The Supreme Court has been converted into an instrument of falsehood; the United States Senate has been converted into an instrument of torture, and an American citizen is carried there, and, if he is unwilling to answer questions that he conscientiously believes he is not bound to answer, he is thrown into prison; and Slavery, with a lie upon its lips, sends its officers to Massachusetts, and seeks to kidnap a free citizen of that State, and drag him to Washington. That shows the iniquity of the whole system of slavery in the Southern States, and the iniquity of this government, as it is administered by the slavocracy of the land. I say to my colored friends, if a white man is kidnapped from the free States, if a white man is unjustly imprisoned in Washington, if a white woman is sold as a slave in the Southern States, what justice can the colored people expect at the hands of this nation? They can expect none at all.

But I say the cause of freedom is going forward. We have the truth on our side, and that shall make us free. The tree of Liberty has been planted; it is growing, its branches are spreading all over the land, and the spirit of freedom is entering the hearts and consciences of the people; and with the poet we may well say,

> "Our plant is of the cedar,
> That knoweth not decay;
> Its growth shall bless the mountains,
> Till mountains pass away;
> Its top shall greet the sunshine,
> Its leaves shall drink the rain,
> While on its lower branches
> The slave shall hang his chain"

(Prolonged cheering.)

Review of Mr. Yancey's Speech

October 26, 1860

Brown was the featured speaker before the African American congregation of Boston's Joy Street Church ten days before the fateful 1860 presidential election. He took the podium that evening to respond to the provocatively racist, proslavery speech former Alabama congressman William L. Yancey had given the previous week in the heart of Yankeedom at Faneuil Hall. Indicating Yancey had declined his cheeky invitation to debate him that evening at the church, Brown proceeded to give an alternative view of race history in both Africa and the United States in order to challenge the standard view Yancey was advocating of Anglo-Saxon superiority.

FELLOW-CITIZENS: This is an interesting crisis in the political history of our country, and especially as it regards the Anglo-African race. For the last forty years, there has been a great struggle between Freedom and Slavery in the United States, and the Slave Power has spared no pains and no amount of money to carry its unholy cause. While the advocates of freedom have not been permitted to go South and agitate the subject, slaveholders have been freely admitted to the free States, and permitted to speak as they pleased; and, on Friday evening last, many of us who are here to-night went to Faneuil Hall, to listen to one of the fire-eaters of the South, Hon. W. L. Yancey, of Alabama. He is no doubt one of the ablest as well as one of the most eloquent men of which the Slave Power can boast. And it is for the purpose of listening to a criticism upon that gentleman's speech, that you have assembled here this evening. I wrote Mr. Yancey on Saturday, inviting him to be present to-night, promising that he should have an opportunity of replying to me, if he wished. If he is not here, the fault is his, and not mine. Although the honorable gentleman on Friday evening averred that he would treat the subject fairly and candidly, he nevertheless entirely ignored conscientiousness and morality. He made a long argument, and brought forward many figures to prove that slave labor was more beneficial to the country than free; all of which I will pass over by putting 'Helper's Impending Crisis' against him. It has been shown that the product of the hay crop alone in the Free States is worth more than the entire products of the South. So I will turn Mr. Yancey out to grass. (Applause.) He said that the Declaration of Independence meant that white men were created equal, and did not include the negro. 'It was never intended,' said he, 'that the blacks should be citizens.'

Upon this point, Mr. Yancey shows his ignorance of history, and proves that with all his smartness, he has been a very dull student. What says the history of our country on this question of negro citizenship? We were regarded as citizens by those who drew up the articles of Confederation between the States in 1778. The fourth of said articles contains the following language: 'The free inhabitants of each of these States, paupers, vagabonds, and fugitives from justice excepted, shall be entitled to all the privileges and immunities of free citizens in the several States.' That we were not excluded under the phrase 'paupers, vagabonds, and fugitives from justice,' any more than the whites, is plain from the debates that preceded the adoption of the article; for, on the 25th of June, 1778, 'the delegates from South Carolina moved the following in behalf of their State: In article fourth, between the words *free* inhabitants insert the word *white*. Decided in the negative, ayes, two States; nays, eight States; one State divided.' Such was the decision of the Revolutionary Congress, upon the citizenship of the negro.

At the ratification of the articles of Confederation, all the free native-born inhabitants of the States of New Hampshire, Massachusetts, New York, New Jersey and North Carolina, though descended from African slaves, were not only recognized and considered citizens of those States, but such of them as had the necessary qualification possessed the elective franchise on equal terms with the other citizens. Judge Gaston, of the Supreme Court of North Carolina, in the case of the State vs. Manuel, clearly defines the law on this point. Says he, 'The Constitution of the State extended the elective franchise to every freeman who had arrived at the age of 21 years, and paid a public tax; and under it, free persons, without regard to color, claimed and exercised the franchise until it was taken away from free men of color, a few years since, by our amended

Constitution.' And, as late as the year 1859, Judge Catron, of the Supreme Court of the United States, in a letter to the Nashville *Union and American*, in which he opposes the forcible expulsion of the free colored people from Tennessee, says, 'Under our Constitution of 1796, the free colored men voted at the polls. That the old Constitution extended to them, and protected their rights, is free from doubt. They were considered citizens.'

Thus it will be seen that several of the States, including at least two of the slave States, regarded free colored persons as citizens. Yet Mr. Yancey has not read the history of his country enough to find it out. (Applause.)

And why should the black man not be considered in the light of citizenship? Did not the Negro contribute his proportion towards securing the liberty and the independence of the country? If we go back to the foundation of the Republic, we shall find colored men in all the scenes of the great American drama. In times of peril has our aid been called for, and our services as promptly given. When the country, its interests, its best and most cherished rights and institutions have been assailed, not unavailingly have we been looked to. When the people of the Colonies, aroused by the injustice of British policy, arose as one man, for the maintenance of natural and imprescriptable rights, the colored man stood by the side of his white fellow-citizen. During that memorable conflict, in severe and trying service, did they contend for those principles of liberty set forth in the Declaration of Independence, which are not for *white men alone*, but which pertain alike to every being possessed of those high and exalted endowments that distinguish humanity. The Negro's blood mingled with the soil of every battle-field, made glorious by revolutionary reminiscence; and their bones have enriched the most productive lands of the country. But, what cares Mr. Yancey about history or facts? He goes for slavery, without any regard to complexion. He would as soon have his plantation stocked with men taken from the audience which he addressed on Friday night, as to have them from the coast of Africa. As I listened to the loud applause which was given to the speaker by the hard-fisted laboring men of Boston, and knowing how the working man is looked upon in the South, I felt a degree of mingled shame, pity and contempt for them. Who has forgotten that impudent speech of Mr. Senator Hammond of South Carolina, a year or two since, in which he said—

> 'In all social systems, there must be a class to do the menial duties, to perform the drudgery of life; a class requiring but a low order of intellect and little skill. It constitutes the *mud-sill* of society and of political government. . . . Your whole class of manual hireling laborers at the North, and your "operatives," as you call them, are essentially slaves.'

And who will ever forget the contemptuous remarks of the editor of the Muscogee *Herald*, published in Mr. Yancey's own State, and by one of his nearest neighbors? Hear what he thinks of such men as the honorable (?) gentleman spoke to in Faneuil Hall:—

> '*Free* society! We sicken at the name. What is it but a conglomeration of *greasy mechanics, filthy operatives, small-fisted farmers*, and moon-struck theorists? All the Northern States, and especially the New England States, are devoid of society fitted for well-bred gentlemen. The prevailing class one meets with is that of mechanics struggling to be genteel, and small farmers who do their own drudgery; and yet who are hardly fit for association with a gentleman's body servant. That is your free society!'

And in a political Convention held in Alabama, in 1856, at which Mr. Yancey made a speech, a resolution was unanimously adopted, in which the following was embodied:—

> 'The great evil of Northern society is, that it is burdened with *a servile class of mechanics and laborers, unfit for self-government*, and yet clothed with the attributes and powers of citizens. Master and slave is a relation in society as necessary as that of parent and child, and *the Northern States will yet have to introduce it.* The theory of free government is a delusion. *Slavery is the natural and normal condition of the laboring man, white or black.*'

But I leave the Alabama Senator in the hands of the sunburnt and hard-working men who applauded him so enthusiastically on Friday evening, and the Democratic Committee that imported him to Boston, to settle with them for this contempt of honest labor.

In his remarks, Mr. Yancey contended that the North should go for the increase of slave States and slaves, because slaveholders purchased shoes and clothing for their negroes from Northern manufacturers. 'No,' said he, 'the nigger won't work if free.' Now, if Mr. Yancey had wished, he could have told his audience that there were 16,000 free colored people in Alabama, and the census of 1850 shows that among the citizens of Montgomery there are five free men of color set down as worth $20,000 each, and one of these was a slave till thirty years old. It is well known that there are nearly seventy thousand free colored inhabitants in Maryland, some of whom are worth more than $100,000. It was only during the last session of the Virginia Legislature, that a bill was introduced to enact a law driving the free blacks from the State. The only reason given for this expulsion was, that 'the free negroes were getting too wealthy and too influential in the State.' Judge Catron, of whom I have already spoken, says of the free blacks in Tennessee, 'They are industrious, useful, and among them are some of the best mechanics and artizans in the State, and to drive them out would be great injury to ourselves.' A St. Louis paper of a recent date has the following paragraph:—

> 'In the foundry of Gaty, M'Cune & Co., in this city, among its two hundred and seventy operatives are two negroes, who began life at the establishment, in 1849, as slaves. By dint of unflagging industry, in due course of time one of them bought himself, wife and five children, paying for himself $1400, and on an average for his wife and children $800 each. This negro is now supposed to be worth, in his own right, more than $5000 in real estate in that city. Another negro entered the factory about the same time, amassed sufficient money by his attention to duty to purchase himself at the price of $1500, his wife at $500, and four children at $400, and is now worth $6000 in real estate. These negroes were bought from their masters by Mr. Gray, with the understanding that they should work themselves free, and out of his own pocket he gave two per cent. interest on the deferred payments.'

Yet Mr. Yancey is of opinion that 'the nigger won't work, if free'!

The *Alabama Beacon* of March 6, 1858, tells its readers that 'there are free negroes of too much wealth in the State, and that they ought to be driven out.'

Let me turn to another phase of the subject. 'You say,' said the speaker, 'that our institution demoralizes the whites and the blacks. I say you are mistaken.' And here the gentleman undertook to prove that raising cotton was the highest idea of morality. Cotton—cotton—cotton—was the burden of his song. It reminded me, fellow-citizens, of the servant girl, not long from the Emerald Isle, who wanted her employer, an old gentleman, to read a letter from her lover; and not wishing him to know its contents, she came with the letter in one hand and some cotton in the other, and said, 'Please, Mr. Maine, will you be kind enough to read this letter for me? and as you won't want to know what is in it, I brought this cotton, that you might put it in your ears, so that you might not hear what was in the letter.' (Loud applause.)

But let us try the moral character of slavery in Alabama by the testimony of her own citizens. Mr. John Balch, a resident of Tuscaloosa, in that State, advertises his runaway woman in the following manner:—

> 'Ranaway from me, a negro woman, named Fanny. *She is as white as most white women; with straight light hair, and blue eyes, and can pass herself off for a white woman.* She is *very intelligent*; can read and write, and so forge passes for herself. She is *very pious*, prays a great deal, and was, as supposed, *contented and happy*. I will give $500 for her delivery to me.'

Mr. John Peck, of Mobile, Ala., has lost his man Sam, and says: 'He has *light sandy hair*, *blue eyes*, *ruddy complexion*, and will no doubt try to pass himself for a *free white man*.' Whether Fanny and Sam got their 'blue eyes, straight hair, and *white complexion*,' as such slaves generally do, from their masters, or not, I will leave Mr. Yancey to say. The Hon. C. C. Clay, who once occupied the seat in the United States Senate, now held by the orator of Friday night last, said, in a speech in his own State, 'Slavery corrupts the morals of the whites as well as the blacks. The evils of the system cannot be enumerated. They glare upon us at every step.' Yet Mr. Yancey thinks that there is nothing immoral in the institution! (Applause.)

The speaker was asked if men from the North could go South. He replied, 'Yes, if you don't go there to steal our niggers.' If the person who made this inquiry had kept pace with the insolence of the Slave Power, he could have found an answer to his own question in the expulsion of the bookseller from Mobile, three years ago, for obtaining a copy of Frederick Douglass's Narrative for a customer. During the present year, a book agent was arrested in Alabama for soliciting subscribers to 'Fleetwood's Life of Christ,' published by a Northern publisher. The Methodist Conference was in session at that time, and the case was noticed on the floor of that body. The members advocated the unfortunate agent's immediate expulsion from the place, on the ground that his continued presence would be dangerous to the existence of Southern institutions! A paper was drawn up, adopted, and published in the newspapers, setting forth the ground of their action, substantially as follows:

> 'We have examined this man's case. We find no evidence to convict him of tampering with slaves, but as he is from the North, and engaged in selling a book published at the North, we have a right to suspect him of being an Abolitionist, and we therefore recommend, in order to guard ourselves against possible danger, that he be immediately conducted by the military out of this county into the next adjoining.'

Here is a poor simple book agent escorted out of the town by the military, to save him from a mob of Mr. Yancey's friends and constituents! The Hon. gentleman knew very well that no Northern man is safe at the South, if it is suspected that his opinions are against oppression.

'The superior ought to govern the inferior; the blacks were intended for slaves, owing to their inferiority,' said the Alabama Senator. What opportunity has he ever given his slaves to show their intellectual endowments? The whole South is aware that the blacks would rise from their present degraded condition, if they had the chance (loud applause); therefore the slave is forbidden to have a book or to learn to read. Genius may always rise, as it often has done, from the cottage to the mansion, from manual labor to mental occupation, from the hard lot of the many to the privileges of the few, to occupy positions of power in the State, or of eminence in the republic of letters. But intellect must have the opportunity of free development; it must not be placed in the hands of such men as Mr. Yancey, whose highest boast was, that he gave his slaves two pairs of coarse shoes every year.

'The nigger can't be any thing,' exclaimed the speaker; and in the next breath he said, 'You have nigger lawyers here in Boston; we don't have such in our State.' The gentleman stopped short at this point, for he saw that if men could be lawyers in Boston, they could be in Alabama, if they were permitted. He stands with his feet upon the neck of the negro, and exclaims, 'He's inferior, because he don't rise!' And who is this man that claims a superiority over the black man? Will his antecedents bear a critical examination? Let us see. 'When the Britons first became known to the Tyrian mariners,' says Macaulay, 'they were little superior to the Sandwich Islanders.' Hume says, 'They were a rude and barbarous people, divided into numerous tribes, dressed in the skins of wild beasts. Druidism was their religion, and they were filled with superstition.' When the Romans invaded Britain, the people were reduced to a state of slavery or vassalage, as degrading as the slavery on Mr. Yancey's plantation. Their king, Caractacas, was captured, and sent a slave to Rome. Still later, Henghist and Horsa, the Saxon generals, presented another yoke to the Britons, which they were compelled to wear. But the last dregs of the cup of humiliation were drunk when William of Normandy met Harold at Hastings, and with a single blow, completely annihilated the nationality of the Britons. Out of this conglomeration of Britons, Romans, Normans and Saxons sprang the proud Anglo-Saxon of to-day. During the time that the Anglo-Saxon was passing through this crucible of refinement, his condition was scarcely less humiliating than that of the slave on the banks of the Mississippi. And it is the descendant of such a race who claims a superiority over us! (Loud applause.)

But, fellow-citizens, this is not all. It is an historical fact, that when the Stuarts were on the English throne, it was the custom to transport their convicts to the West Indies and to the American Colonies. Many of these criminals were sent to the Colony of Virginia, and afterwards rose from their servile condition, spread over the Southern States, and their antecedents lost in the increase of population. Now, as it is a physiological fact, that the parent transmits his propensities to the child, it is reasonable to suppose that the convict blood of 1640 courses through the veins of the proud sons of the South of the present time. And instead of that blood becoming purer by the removal, it has become still more corrupt by its course through the veins of nine generations of woman-whippers, slave-traders and fillibusters. (Loud applause.)

Now let me look at the antecedents of the negro, three thousand years ago, when in the period of their greatness and glory, when they held the foremost rank in the march of civilization; when they constituted, in fact, the whole civilized world of their time. Euclid, Homer and Plato were Ethiopians; Terence, the most refined and accomplished scholar of his time was of the same race; Hanno, the father of Hamilcar and grandfather of Hannibal, was a negro. Herodotus, the father of history, says that the Ethiopians were black, and had curled hair. The Romans, Saxons and Normans, who swallowed up the Britons and gave them a name and a language, received their civilization from Egypt and Ethiopia. When Mr. Yancey's ancestors were bending their necks to the yoke of William the Conqueror, the ancestors of his slaves were revelling in the halls of science and learning. If the Hon. Senator from Alabama wants antecedents, he shall have them; and upon such, I claim a superiority for the negro. (Loud applause.)

But an editorial from the *Montgomery Mail*, Mr. Yancey's own paper, tells us the reason why he spoke as he did on Friday evening. It says:—

> 'The Democrats of the South, in the present canvass, cannot rely on the old grounds of defence and excuse for slavery; for they seek not merely to retain it where it is, but *to extend it into regions where it is unknown*. Much less can they rely on the mere constitutional guarantees of slavery; for such reliance is pregnant with the admission that slavery is wrong, and, *but for the Constitution*, should be abolished. If we stop there, we weaken our cause; for *we propose to introduce into new territory human beings whom we assert to be unfit for liberty, self-government and equal association with other men*. We must go a step further. We must show that African slavery is a moral, religious, natural, and probably, in the general, a necessary institution of society. This is the only line of argument that will enable Southern Democrats to maintain the doctrines of State equality and *slavery extension*.' . . . 'Northern Democrats

need not go thus far. They do not seek to extend slavery, but only to *agree to its extension*, as a matter of right on our part.'

Thus it will be seen that the whole drift of Mr. Yancey's speech was settled before he left his State.

Now, fellow-citizens, I have done with the Alabama Senator; but I must confess that I felt ashamed of the intelligence of that portion of the working men of Boston, who applauded so loudly on Friday evening, when, if they should go South, Mr. Yancey would not shake hands with them with a pair of tongs ten feet long. (Laughter and loud applause.)

Speech at Annual Meeting of the American Anti-Slavery Society

May 6, 1862

As the raging Civil War upset existing social and political relations, Brown came to the 1862 annual meeting of the American Anti-Slavery Society to answer a question with a question. Employing a favorite rhetorical device, he shifted the presumed burden of the conflict from enslaved African Americans—"What shall be done with the slaves, if freed?"—to southern whites—"What shall you do with the slaveholders?"

MR. PRESIDENT AND LADIES AND GENTLEMEN: For the last thirty years, the colored people have taken the greatest interest in the agitation of the abolition question, as carried on by this Society. We have watched with hope and fear as impediment after impediment has been thrown in the way of its progress. Among the many obstacles which have been brought to bear against emancipation, one of the most formidable has been the series of objections urged against it upon what has been supposed to be the slave's want of appreciation of liberty, and his ability to provide for himself in a state of freedom; and now that slavery seems to be near its end, these objections are multiplying, and the cry is heard all over the land, "What shall be done with the slave, if freed?" I propose to use the short time allowed me this morning in examining these phases of the question.

It has been clearly demonstrated, I think, that the enslaved of the South are as capable of self-support as any other class of people in the country. It is well known, that throughout the entire South, a large class of slaves have been for years accustomed to hire their time from their owners. Many of these have paid very high prices for the privilege. Some able mechanics have been known to pay as high as $600 per annum, besides providing themselves with food and clothing; and this class of slaves, by their industry, have taken care of themselves so well, and their appearance has been so respectable, that many of the States have passed laws, prohibiting masters from letting their slaves out to themselves, because, as it was said, it made the slaves dissatisfied to see so many of their fellows well-provided, and accumulating something for themselves in the way of pocket-money. The Rev. Dr. Nehemiah Adams, whose antecedents have not been such as to lead to the suspicion that he favors the free colored men, or the idea of giving to the slaves their liberty, in his "Southside View," unconsciously and unintentionally gives a very valuable statement upon this particular point. Dr. Adams says:—

> "A slave woman having had $300 stolen from her by a white man, her master was questioned in court as to the probability of her having had so much money. The master said that he not unfrequently had borrowed fifty and a hundred dollars from her himself, and added that she was always very strict as to his promised time of payment."

There was a slave woman who had not only kept every agreement with her master—paying him every cent she had promised—but had accumulated $300 toward purchasing her liberty, and it was stolen from her, not by a black man, but, as Dr. Adams says, by a white man.

But one of the clearest demonstrations of the ability of the slave to provide for himself in a state of freedom is to be found in the prosperous condition of the large free colored population of the Southern States. Maryland has 80,000, Virginia 70,000, and the other slave States have a large number. These free people have all been slaves, or they are the descendants of those who were once slaves; what they have gained has been required in spite of the public opinion and laws of the South, in spite of prejudice, and everything. They have acquired a large amount of property; and it is this industry, this sobriety, this intelligence, and this wealth of the free colored people of the South, that has created so much prejudice on the part of slaveholders against them. They have felt that the very presence of a colored man, looking so genteelly and in such a prosperous condition, made the slaves unhappy and discontented. In the Southern Rights Convention which assembled at Baltimore, June 8th, 1860, a resolution was adopted, calling on the Legislature to pass a law driving the free colored people out of the State. Nearly every speaker, Mr. President, took the ground that the free colored people must be driven out to make the slave's obedience more secure. Judge Mason, in his speech, said, "It is the thrifty and well-to-do free negroes, that are seen by our slaves, that make them dissatisfied." A similar appeal was made to the Legislature of Tennessee. Judge Catron, of the Supreme Court of the United States, in a long and able letter to the Nashville *Union*, opposed the driving out of the colored people. He said they were among the best mechanics, the best artisans, and the most industrious laborers in the State, and that to drive them out would be an injury to the State itself. This is certainly good evidence in their behalf.

The State of Arkansas passed a law driving the free colored people out of the State, and they were driven out, three years ago. The Democratic press howled upon the heels of the free blacks until they had all been expatriated; but after they had been driven out, the Little Rock *Gazette*—a Democratic paper—made a candid acknowledgment with regard to the character of the free colored people. It said:—

> "Most of the exiled free negroes are industrious and respectable. One of them, Henry King, we have known from our boyhood, and take the greatest pleasure in testifying to his good character. The community in which he casts his lot will be blessed with that noblest work of God, an honest man."

Yet these free colored people were driven out of the State, and those who were unable to go, as many of the women and children were, were reduced to slavery, and there they are toiling in chains and slavery to-day.

The New Orleans *True Delta* opposed the passage of a similar law by the State of Louisiana. Among other things, it said:—

> "There are a large free colored population here, correct in their general deportment, honorable in their intercourse with society, and free from reproach so far as the laws are concerned, not surpassed in the inoffensiveness of their lives by any equal number of persons, in any place North or South."

That I consider testimony of real value. I produce this, Mr. Chairman, because there is nothing entitled to greater weight on this point than the testimony of the people of the slave States themselves.

Dr. Nehemiah Adams, whom I have already quoted, also testifies to the good character of the free colored people; but he does it unintentionally; it was not a part of the programme; how it slipped in I cannot tell. Here it is, however, from page 41 of his "Southside View":—

> "A prosecuting officer, who had six or eight counties in his district, told me that, during eight years of service, he had made out about two thousand bills of indictment, of which not more than twelve were against colored persons." (Applause.)

Hatred of the free colored people, and abuse of them, have always been popular with the pro-slavery people of this country; yet, an American Senator, from one of the Western States—a man who never lost an opportunity to villify and traduce the colored man, and who, in his last canvass for a seat in the United States Senate, argued that the slaves were better off in slavery than they would be if set free, and declared that the blacks were unable to take care of themselves, while enjoying liberty—died, a short time since, $12,000 in debt to a black man, who was the descendant of a slave. (Applause.) Thus, those who have fattened upon us, often turn round and traduce us. Reputation is, indeed, dear to every nation and race; but to us, the colored people of this country, who have so many obstacles to surmount, it is doubly dear.

> "Who steals my purse, steals trash;
> 'Twas mine, 'tis his, and has been slave to thousands;
> But he who filches from me my good name,
> Robs me of that which not enriches him,
> And make me poor indeed."

(Applause.)

In the District of Columbia, since the abolition of slavery, it is found that, according to their numbers, the larger proportion of the property-holders are among the negroes. Figures, though we are told that they very often lie, are sometimes found to tell the truth. The Tammany Hall Young Men's Democratic Committee of the city of New York, on the 18th of March, 1862, passed the following resolution:—

> "Resolved, That we are opposed to emancipating negro slaves, unless on some plan of colonization, in order that they may not come in contact with the white man's labor."

Now, Mr. President, this resolution is based upon the supposition that the slaves, if freed, will all flock to the North; and that is a very popular cry with the pro-slavery people of the free States, because they know that nothing would be so effective to the accomplishment of their ends as to make the laboring whites of the North believe that they will be overrun by the negroes, if slavery is abolished. Now, I hold to the right of the black man, whether liberated or not, to go where he pleases, to make himself a home in any part of the country he chooses; but I do not believe that, if slavery is abolished, the slaves will flock into the free States. I do not believe it, because I have a reason for not believing it. Look at the large free colored population in the slave States! See how odious are the laws they live under! See how cruelly they have been oppressed! Why, the State of Virginia long had a law on her statute-books, and has now, unless it has been very recently repealed, taxing the free colored people one dollar per head, over and above any other class in the community, by which the State of Virginia put into her treasury, in one year, $50,000, taken from the colored people. Maryland had a similar law. The Gulf States have been still more severe on this class of their population; and yet the free colored people have remained in the Southern States. Why did they not come North? Because they were unwilling to leave the congenial climate of the sunny South for the snowy hills of the rugged North; and, where you have found ten colored persons coming from the South to the North, nine out of the ten have been fugitive slaves, flying from the South because they could not enjoy liberty there; not the free colored people, who had the right to go off if they chose. Now, Mr. President, what has kept the free colored people in the Southern States will prevent the slaves coming here, if slavery is abolished.

But we are told that the contrabands are flocking, even now, into Pennsylvania, and the Pennsylvania Legislature has been petitioned, by the working people of Philadelphia and other cities, to pass a law prohibiting their settling in that State. Illinois has already passed such a law. Ohio either has, or is trying to do so. But you must expect that the slave, running away now, will seek to get beyond the Border Slave States. His liberty is in doubt; we have had Generals who have sent slaves back; and, after getting out of his master's hands, his first thought is to get further North, where his liberty is secure. If you were there, and in his position, you would take the same course the contraband takes now. He feels precisely as he did before the commencement of the rebellion; he wants to get out of the way. But if you want to stop the contraband from coming into the free States, if you want to stop the slave's running off from the South, give him his freedom upon the soil. (Loud applause.) The Tammany Hall Committee is opposed to abolition, unless expatriation shall follow it. The first Napoleon was waited upon by a Committee of the old planters of St. Domingo, urging him to send an army to Hayti to reduce the emancipated slaves again to chains. After the Committee had withdrawn, Napoleon turned to Gregoire, and asked him what he thought of the advice. The latter replied: "If those planters should change their color to-night, they would come back to-morrow, and give your Majesty different advice." So it would be, Mr. President, with the Young Men's Democratic Committee of New York. (Applause.)

Now, everything has shown that the slave can be trusted in slavery, except when he can get a chance to use his heels; for the slaveholders themselves have testified to his good character. You know we were told by the slaveholders, just before the breaking out of the rebellion, that if we got into any difficulty with the South, their slaves would take up arms, and fight to a man for them. Mr. Toombs, I believe, threatened that he would arm his slaves, and other men in Congress from the slave States made the same threat. They were going to arm the slaves, and turn them against the North. They said they could be trusted; and many people here at the North really believed that the slave did not want his liberty, would not have it if he could, and that the slave population was a very dangerous element against the North; but at once, Mr. President, on the approach of our soldiers, the slaves are seen, with their bundles and baskets, and hats and coats, and without bundles or baskets, and without hats or coats, rushing to our lines; demonstrating what we have so often said, that all the slave was waiting for was the opportunity to get his liberty. Why should you not have believed this? Why should you have supposed for a moment, that, because a man's color differs a little from yours, he is better contented to remain a slave than you would be, or that he has no inclination, no wish, to escape from the thraldom that holds him so tight? What is it that does not wish to be free?

> "Go, let a cage with grates of gold,
> And pearly roof, the eagle hold,
> Let dainty viands be its fare,
> And give the captive tenderest care;
> But say, in luxury's limits pent,
> Find you the king of birds content?
> No, oft he'll sound the startling shriek,
> And dash the cage with angry beak:
> Precarious freedom's far more dear
> Than all the prison's pampering cheer."

As with the eagle, so with man. He loves to look upon the bright day and the stormy night; to gaze upon the broad free ocean, its eternal surging tides, its mountain billows and its foam-crested waves; to tread the steep mountain side; to sail upon the placid river; to wander along the gurgling stream; to trace the sunny slope, the beautiful landscape, the majestic forest, the flowery meadow; to listen to the howling of the winds and the music of the birds. These are the aspirations of man, without regard to country, clime, or color. (Loud applause.)

What shall we do with the slave of the South? "Expatriate him," say the haters of the negro. Expatriate him for what? He has cleared up the swamps of the South, and has put the soil under cultivation; he has built up her towns and cities and villages; he has enriched the North and Europe with his cotton and sugar and rice; and for this, you would drive him out of the country! "What shall be done with the slaves, if they are freed?" You had better ask, "What shall we do with the slaveholders, if the slaves are freed?" (Applause.) The slave has shown himself better fitted to take care of himself than the slaveholder. (Renewed applause.) He is the bone and sinew of the South; he is the producer, while the master is nothing but a consumer, and a very poor consumer at that. (Laughter.) The slave is the producer, and he alone can be relied upon. He has the sinew, the determination, and the will; and if you will take the free colored people of the South as the criterion, take their past history as a sample of what the colored people are capable of doing, every one must be satisfied that the slaves can take care of themselves.

But it is said, "The two races cannot live together in a state of freedom." Why, that is the cry that rung all over England twenty years ago—"If you liberate the slaves of the West Indies, they can't live with the whites in a state of freedom." Twenty years have shown the contrary. The blacks and the whites live together in Jamaica; they are all prosperous, and the island in a better condition than it ever was before the act of emancipation was passed.

But they tell us, "If the slaves are emancipated, we won't receive them upon an equality." Why, every man must make equality for himself. No society, no government, can make this equality. I do not expect the slave of the South to jump into equality; all I claim for him is, that he may be allowed to jump into liberty, and let him make equality for himself. (Loud applause.) I have got some white neighbors around me; they are not very intellectual; they don't associate with my family (laughter and applause); but whenever they shall improve themselves, and bring themselves up by their own intellectual and moral worth, I shall not object to their coming into my society. (Renewed merriment.)

Now, Mr. Chairman, this talk about not letting a man come to this place or that, and that we won't do this for him, we won't do that for him, is all idle. The anti-slavery agitators have never demanded that you shall like the colored man, any more than that you shall like the uncultivated and uncouth white man, and place him in a certain position in society. All I demand for the black man is, that the white people shall take their heels off his neck, and let him have a chance to rise by his own efforts. (Applause.) One of the first things that I heard when I arrived in the free States—and it was the strangest thing to me that I heard—was, that the slaves cannot take care of themselves. I came off without any education. Society did not take me up; I took myself up. (Laughter.) I did not ask society to take me up. All I asked of the white people was, to get out of the way, and give me a chance to come from the South to the North. That was all I asked, and I went to work with my own hands. And that is all I demand for my brethren of the South to-day—that they shall have an opportunity to exercise their own physical and mental abilities. Give them that, and I will leave the slaves to take care of themselves, and be satisfied with the result.

Now, Mr. President, I think that the present contest has shown clearly that the fidelity of the black people of this country to the cause of freedom is enough to put to shame every white man in the land who would think of driving us out of the country, provided freedom should be proclaimed. I remember well, when Mr. Lincoln's proclamation went forth, calling for the first 75,000 men, that among the first to respond to that call were the colored men. A meeting was held in Boston, crowded as I never saw a meeting before; meetings were held in Rhode Island and Connecticut, in New York and Philadelphia, and throughout the West, responding to the President's call. Although the colored men in many of the free States were disfranchised, abused, taxed without representation, their children turned out of the schools; nevertheless, they went on, determined to try to discharge their duty to the country, and to save it from the tyrannical power of the slaveholders of the South. But the cry went forth—"We won't have the niggers; we won't have anything to do with them; we won't fight with them; we won't have them in the army, nor about us." Yet scarcely had you got into conflict with the South, when you were glad to receive the news that contrabands brought. (Applause.) The first telegram announcing any news from the disaffected district commences with—"A contraband just in from Maryland tells us" so much. The last telegram, in to-day's paper, announces that a contraband tells us so much about Jefferson Davis and Mrs. Davis and the little Davises. (Laughter.) The nation is glad to receive the news from the contraband. We have an old law with regard to the mails, that a negro shall not touch the mails at all; and for fifty years the black man has not had the privilege of touching the mails of the United States with his little finger; but we are glad enough now to have the negro bring the mail in his pocket! The first thing asked of a contraband is—"Have you got a newspaper?—what's the news?" And the news is greedily taken in, from the lowest officer or soldier in the army, up to the Secretary of War. They have tried to keep the negro out of the war, but they could not keep him out, and now they drag him in, with his news, and are glad to do so. Gen. Wool says the contrabands have brought the most reliable news. Other Generals say their information can be relied upon. The negro is taken as a pilot to guide the fleet of Gen. Burnside through the inlets of the South. (Applause.) The black man welcomes your armies and your fleets, takes care of your sick, is ready to do anything, from cooking up to shouldering a musket; and yet these would-be patriots and professed lovers of the land talk about driving the negro out!

Now, what shall you do with the slaveholders? That is the other question. The only recommendation I have to make in regard to that is, that you shall take the slave from the slave-holder, and let the slaveholder go to work and labor for him-self, and let him keep out of mischief. (Applause.) If the slaveholders had had the opportunity of laboring for them-selves, for the last forty years, we should never have had this rebellion. It is because they have had nothing to do but to drink and walk about and concoct mischief, while the black man was toiling for their support, that this rebellion has taken place.

Mr. President, I must bring my remarks to a close. This na-tion owes the colored people a great debt. You, the people of New York, owe us a great debt. You have kept us down, helped to degrade us by your odious laws—the fugitive slave enact-ments and others—you have loved to keep us in chains, while the slaveholders have deprived us of our liberty and everything; and now the time has come for you to do your duty in this matter. You see that this has affected you, as well as it has af-fected the black man, North and South; and now the world is looking on, expecting that your duty to the negro, to the cause of freedom, will be performed; and the moral sentiment of the world will hold the American people accountable, if this rebel-lion shall close, and the negro be still left weltering in his blood and chains. There is no mistake about it: the time has come for the nation to discharge its duty to the black man. Now is the time, and I hope the nation will have the moral courage to perform its duty. That the slave will have his liberty, I have not the slightest doubt. These black men in the slave States, whom Jefferson Davis and Beauregard have been teaching the science of arms on the one hand, and the contrabands at Port Royal and Fortress Monroe, to whom your men and women have been teaching the science of letters, on the other hand, have implanted in the black man's bosom in the Southern States that which will ultimately give him his liberty, if you do not give it to him. (Applause.) I am confident that the tree of Liberty has been planted. If it was not planted by this Society, Mr. President, it has been planted by the rebellion of the South, and it is growing—it is growing, and its branches are overshadowing the land; and, in the language of the poet, we may say:

"Our plant is of the cedar,
That knoweth not decay;
Its growth shall bless the mountain,
Till mountains pass away;
Its top shall greet the sunshine,
Its leaves shall drink the rain,
While on its lower branches
The slave shall hang his chain."

(Loud and prolonged applause.)

“The Black Man” and Its Critics

July 21, 1863

Brown’s pioneering history of African Americans, *The Black Man*, appeared in December 1862 during the tense hundred-day waiting period between the Preliminary Emancipation Proclamation, issued on September 22, 1862, and the Emancipation Proclamation, issued on January 1, 1863. A book so timely and novel drew extraordinary attention in both the black and the white press, though not precisely the kind of attention to satisfy a prickly author. Brown responded to his critics in this important early commentary on black writing, which took specific aim at the black community for failing to give due recognition not only to his book but also to black writing generally.

Sir: The first edition of “The Black Man” having been sold, and a second being now in the printer’s hands, and will be out in a few days, I shall be glad if you will allow me space enough to say a word in regard to the book and its critics. The Negro being forced before the country so prominently by the rebellion, his bravery, his cowardice, and his general usefulness became matters of discussion in every section of the land. Those who took part in canvassing the black man’s abilities were continually applying to Abolitionists for books and papers from which to post themselves upon the subject in hand. As there was no work containing anything like a history of our people, I was applied to from various quarters to get up a book to supply this deficiency. Feeling that there were others who could perform the task better, I waited more than a year, but in vain, for some one to take up the pen. Persuaded at last to commence the work, my first thought was, to collect together such biographies of distinguished persons as had appeared in print, and the most favorable facts concerning the race, that had been given to the public, and put them in a cheap form. This, however had been done in part by Mr. W. C. Nell, and well done. It then occurred to me that I might take ten or a dozen of our most celebrated men, and give to each fifteen or twenty pages, and by that means get out the best qualities of the Anglo-African. But in this, I feared that I would only be repeating what had been said again and again of our few great men, and I therefore resolved to give a short essay on the Negro's antecedents, and a series of still shorter sketches of persons of genius and ability, without regard to past celebrity or notoriety in any manner. I never intended that the book should be considered as a history of our people, or as containing sketches of all our distinguished men, but selected such characters as suited me best to make a book for the present crisis.

In the preface to the work, I distinctly say: "To meet and refute these misrepresentations (the charge of natural inferiority) and to supply a deficiency long felt in the community, of a work containing *sketches of individuals* who, by their own genius, capacity and intellectual development, have surmounted the many obstacles which slavery and prejudice have thrown in their way, and raised themselves to positions of honor and influence, this volume was written." Nothing can be plainer than the above. Any person perusing the book, unless it be those who do so to find fault with it, can see at a glance that it is intended only as an *argument*, not as a history. The great blunder committed by those who have taken upon themselves the office of the critic, lies in the fact that they could not, or would not, understand either the title or the preface. In each case they erected a man of straw, and then fired away at it. They criticized, not what was in it, but what was out of it. If they had read the work with the eye of a scholar and a critic, they could have found errors enough in it to have enabled them to have given it a decent cutting up: for being engaged in travelling while it was going through the press, I did not get a last reading of the proofs, and the stereotyper made mistakes which mortified me exceedingly when the book was printed. One of these is on page 33, where he makes me say, "Euclid, Homer and Plato were Ethiopians." In the MS. it was written, "Tertullian and St. Augustine were Ethiopians." The explanation given me was, that "the type-setter had two manuscripts before him while correcting the proofs," which, I think, was a very lame excuse, to say the least. There were other typographical errors; yet the critics, with all their smartness, did not discover these mistakes. The worst of these critical blunderers is Mr. William H. Yates, who writes in *The Pacific Appeal*, over the signature of "Amigo." In his article of May 30th he is really furious. He opens his battery as follows:

"This book comes far short of the truth, and is but a poor exhibit of the 'genius' of the black man. Indeed, a more *ex parte* or garbled statement in relation to our origin, progress, present position and future hopes could not well be imagined. According to Mr. Brown, there are at least *fifty-three* intelligent colored in the world (for he does not claim his host for America) that may, in some degree, be considered 'representative men.' If, out of a population of 6,000 in California, we cannot multiply his figures by 4, then we are more mistaken than we have ever been before."

There is not a word in the whole book about "our origin." This is one of his men of straw. If we are to judge Mr. Yates's estimate of intelligence by the scholarly attainment and literary ability exhibited in the composition of this criticism, then I'll admit that the "*fifty-three*" can be multiplied by four times four of Californians. He then names a number of men whom he thinks should have been in the work, not appearing to understand that the book contained only 288 pages, and that it was not possible to put in more, even if they were all actually worthy of a place, which I do not admit. Some of them should find a place in a collection of colored men when such a work is published; but as I have never attempted to write a volume of that kind, and don't think of doing so now, I will leave the task to Mr. Yates, or some other competent writer. Again he says:

"Mr. B. proves himself to have but a limited acquaintance with our people throughout the whole country, and certain it is that his knowledge is quite as imperfect in relation to California as to any other portion of the continent."

"We claim to have a fair representation of the industry, fidelity, progress and wealth of the black man in this State, and all that is required for its fair development is union. With a population of about 6,000, we represent nearly $3,000,000. We can go to the forest, fell the timbers, build a ship, officer, man and freight her with our own artisans and producers. Our mechanics are not to be surpassed, our orators are profuse; and then we have our distinguished poet, with never ceasing food for his inspiration."

Well, Mr. Yates, let us see. With your 6,000 population and $3,000,000 wealth, and what you "can" do. Have you Californians ever built a ship and officered her? With your *profuse* orators and distinguished poet, have you ever published a book advocating the right and freedom of the race? True, you have *The Pacific Appeal*, a paper well conducted and showing talent; but with all your wealth and boast, I venture the assertion that it *(The Appeal)* has not Five Hundred colored paying subscribers in California. One quotation more and I am done:

"But here we tire, and will refer only to his confused, disordered and unjust arrangement of his *fifty-three* characters, and, for the present, leave Mr. Brown with all the glory his gross misrepresentation of his people may entitle him to."

"At first glance, we thought his subjects were alphabetically arranged, if not, then according to date or merit—a very common practice with authors, and especially reviewers. If the latter, in Mr. Brown's introduction he has sought to acquaint parties that will never recognize each other."

If our critic had been as well posted in literary matters as he was in inclination to find fault, he would have known that sketches of individuals are seldom, if ever, put in alphabetical form; and as for date or merit, the first cannot always be found, and the latter must be decided by the reader. He is mistaken if he supposes that I "sought to acquaint parties that will never recognize each other." All I ask or care for is, that the whites "recognize" the genius and ability of the characters which I have grouped together. I do not expect that they will all be recognized by their own color. No black man's ability was ever "recognized" by his own people until it had been first discovered and acknowledged by the whites. This is owing to the fact that we have so long been under the whites, and looked up to them as the only class possessing talent, that we have no confidence in the ability of our own color. If we want advice, need a lawyer or a doctor, we go to the whites; if we wish for an agent to collect our rents in our absence, we employ a white man; if he cheats us, we try another. No colored man's talents have ever been rewarded by his own class. The narratives of a few escaped slaves have sold rapidly, but principally among the whites. No work written by a colored person in favor of the freedom and elevation of his race, and appealing to them directly, has ever received their support. Dr. Delany's book stopped with one edition; Mr. Nell's work has not reached a second edition; in point of numbers, our newspapers have been legion, yet nearly all have died of the same disease, *starvation*. The New York *Herald* has more subscribers and readers to-day, and gets a larger support from the colored people of California and the other States, than *Douglass's Monthly*, THE ANGLO-AFRICAN and *The Pacific Appeal* put together. "Will you subscribe for *Douglass's Monthly*?" I asked a lady in New Hampshire, a few weeks since. "No," was the reply. "Why?" I inquired. "Because Mr. Douglass, in his lectures, always calls colored people "negroes." "Will you subscribe for THE ANGLO-AFRICAN?" I asked. "No, for I am no negro and no Anglo-African." Yet she was one of the darkest in complexion that I had seen for months.

If a colored man publishes a book, every scribbler supposes himself a scholar and a critic, and commences an attack, feeling that his ability will not be seen unless he can disagree with the author. Most of the opposition to "The Black Man" arises from jealousy; and this jealousy is founded in ignorance.

Upon the supposition that the book was a history of all our great men, everyone who felt himself to be great considered that he had a right to a place within its pages. An old and well known friend of freedom in Philadelphia, in a note, says, "the greatest opposition comes from *those who are left out*." Not long after the work was published, I met an old and venerated friend, whom I had not seen for many months. We shook hands, and I remarked that I had just been thinking of him. He gave a long sigh and an unearthly groan, and said, "You say you were just thinking of me?" "Yes," I replied. Another groan and a heavier sigh followed. At this I looked him full in the face, for I really thought he had been attacked with a sick spell. His face was pale, and his countenance wore a dejected form. "Ah," said he, "you were thinking of me just now, but you could not think of me when you were writing your book." "But," said I, "the book was so small that I could not put in all that I wished." "Yes," replied he, "but you might have left some of the others out, and put me in." This, I confess, was a "knock-down" argument. Another good man said, "I don't care so much about myself, but I think you might have put my father in, for he was a good man."

"Cosmopolite," in *The Pacific Appeal* of June 13th, says:

"I am glad to see the strictures of G. L. R. and Amigo; it shows the works of our own authors are read and appreciated, for men do not usually condemn things which are beneath their notice. Mr. Brown's book will do good; it shows that we have men who have made their mark in almost every field of art and science, and are capable with equal opportunities of competing with any."

Our friend is much mistaken if he imagines for a moment that these attacks grow out of a reading interest, or a wish to see the productions of colored men circulated. I know of at least one critic who actually borrowed a copy of "The Black Man" for the purpose of reviewing it. And he done what most persons forget to do who borrow books—he returned it after writing the criticism. A letter before me from a colored gentleman says: "I would like a copy of your book if it had some other name. To call a book 'The Black Man' is a lasting disgrace to our people. I can't patronize you, sir."

But, Mr. Editor, let it not be presumed that I consider that my work is disliked by all colored men and women; for I don't believe anything of the kind. There are men of our own caste who appreciate the efforts of their brethren, let these efforts be ever so humble. But they are the better educated portion, and those who have labored in season, and out for the redemption of the race.

The following cheering words are from one of that class:

"Though Mr. Brown's book may stand alone upon its own merits and stand strong, yet while reading its interesting pages—abounding in fact and argument—replete with eloquence, logic and learning—clothed with simple yet eloquent language—it is hard to repress the inquiry. Whence has this man this knowledge? He seems to have read and remembered nearly everything which has been written or said respecting the ability of the negro, and has condensed and arranged the whole into an admirable argument, calculated both to interest and convince."—*Frederick Douglass*, in his *Monthly.*

The press generally throughout the country have been liberal in its comments on the book, all appearing to understand that it is only a leaf in behalf of the genius and the ability of the oppressed and injured Negro.

Some have found fault with the sketches on account of their shortness. But they should remember that we have no literature, no history, and that the injustice of the American people have, in the past, kept us out of sight. Let anyone attempt to write biographies of our "great men," and he will at once see how soon he will run ashore for material. Any fool can find fault with a book, but a dozen cannot write one.

Common justice would seem to demand that *The Pacific Appeal*, which published the most ferocious of these attacks on "The Black Man," should give this article an insertion.

Respectfully your obedient servant,

WILLIAM WELLS BROWN.

Cambridgeport, Mass., July 21.

Speech at Annual Meeting of the American Anti-Slavery Society

May 7, 1867

After more than three decades out of slavery, Brown received a visit—or so he claimed—from his "old master." In this anecdote with which he entertained the 1867 annual meeting of the American Anti-Slavery Society, he fabricated their encounter and its outcome: he outsmarted his old master in a battle of wits over ownership of a coat Brown supposedly had stolen when he ran away, but neither man mentions reparations over the family members, wages, and freedom stolen from Brown when a slave.

I shall speak but a moment at this late hour. I have watched with interest the movements of the Southern people, the movements of the old slaveholders towards their slaves; but I have very little confidence in the new propositions they are now making. While I am willing to recognize all the progress made, North and South, I am still of the opinion that a great many of the old planters at the South look forward to the day when they shall again be reinstated. Look at Hayti. After thirty years of freedom to the people of the island, the French were still hoping, still striving to reinstate themselves in power. In Jamaica, after more than thirty years of freedom and of peace, the feelings of the old planters and their sons still remained, so as to prevent their doing equal justice to the colored people of that country. Now, we cannot expect the American people, though they are accustomed to turn somersets and change their coats, to change their principles and become honest so soon.

While at the South not long ago, I had a very interesting interview with my old master. It was indeed very interesting to both of us. We had not met for thirty years. He congratulated me on my position, and I congratulated him on his. (Laughter.) We compared opinions and talked over all the ground. Every once in a while he would give a long sigh, especially when I spoke of the progress of freedom in the land. At last he said, "Well, it may be that this thing will last; but I don't know as it will." Then he went back to reckon up some old scores that stood between us. My English friends, some dozen years ago, had bought me for a small sum, in consideration of his giving up all claim to me; but he said that never covered even the interest of the money. (Laughter.) I saw that he was getting round to bring some kind of account against me, and I was not prepared for anything of the kind; and so I kept harping on justice. After he had given up all hope of getting anything out of me on that score, said he, "You remember when you ran away that you stole one of my coats." Well, I had to plead guilty to the coat; but said I, "You had two coats, and I had none; and you was not willing to apply the Scripture doctrine to the coat, and so I did." (Laughter.) Said he, "I have heard a great deal about your travelling in Europe and this country, and read a book you sent me, and bought another I saw advertised, and you said a good deal there about justice and all this kind of thing. Now, I think you ought to pay me for that coat." (Laughter.) "How much is the coat worth?" "It cost me thirty-five dollars." Said I, "Your memory is good on that subject, after thirty years." "Well," he said, "I remember it." Said I, "Are you poor?" "Well, no; still I want justice done. And I think you ought to pay me a little interest on the coat." I told him I could not do anything of the kind. "Well," said he, "you seem to have been among people who talk a good deal about justice and Christianity, and you must pay me for that coat. If you don't I will meet you at the day of judgment and demand pay for the coat." I looked at him. He seemed very serious. He had got into one of his religious moods, and he preached me a short sermon, closing by demanding pay for the coat. "Well," said I, "I shall have to say to you what the Irishman said to the priest. A woman in Ireland lost a pig, and she found out after some days who stole it. So she went to the priest and told him about it. The priest sent for the man, and said to him: 'Mrs. Malone says you have stolen her pig. Did you steal it?' 'Faith, and your reverence, I did.' 'You must give it up.' Now Pat had killed the pig and half devoured it. So he said, 'Faith, and what if I don't return the pig?' 'If you don't, you will have to answer for it in the day of judgment.' What will you say, then? 'And will Mrs. Malone be there?' 'Yes.' 'And will I be there?' 'Yes.' 'And will the pig be there?' 'Yes.' 'Then I'll tell Mrs. Malone to take her pig.' So I said to my old master, that if he was there, and I was there, and the coat was there, he might take his coat." (Laughter and applause.)

The meeting then adjourned untill the evening, after singing the Doxology.

Dr. Wells Brown on the Colour Question

November 1, 1876

In the 1870s Brown became an internationally known leader in combatting the growing segregation of temperance lodges in the South. He delivered this ferocious attack in North Adams, Massachusetts, at a session of the Grand Lodge of Massachusetts, of which he was a member, on the growth of Jim Crow in the supposedly Reconstructed South. His immediate target was the segregationist Colonel John J. Hickman from his native state of Kentucky, but Brown was also addressing the growing reactionary turn against racial progress throughout the Reconstruction South. The speech was printed in a leading temperance newspaper in London, England, whose host organization took sides in the racial controversy fracturing the movement on both sides of the Atlantic.

Grand Worthy Chief Templar.—We have listened for an hour-and-a-half to P.R.W.G. Templar Hastings, in his defence of the actions of the R.W.G.L. at its late session in Louisville, where that body practically re-affirmed its former policy of permitting the exclusion of coloured persons from our Order in the Southern States. He has tried to prove to you that the R.W.G.L. has always been on the side of giving justice to the negro; that it had never sanctioned the exclusion of the blacks from our Order in the South. Let us see how far his assertions are correct.

For ten years the coloured people have been excluded from our Order in the South. They are excluded *to-day*. Somebody has done it. Who is it?

As early as 1866 the G.L. of Kentucky put in her Constitution, that no person in that State would be admitted into the Order except those of "pure white blood;" a most ridiculous proposition since there is no such thing as "pure white blood," and if there is, Kentucky is about the last State in the American Union that should make such a claim, for it is a historical fact that during our colonial times England transported a large number of convicts to her American possessions, and landed them in Virginia and Maryland, and many of them afterwards emigrated to Kentucky. The blood of these transported convicts courses through the veins of the present white population of Kentucky. So much for the "pure blood."

This exclusion of the blacks by the Kentucky G.L. was well known to the R.W.G.L., and sanctioned by it. At the Madison Session, in 1872, this exclusion on account of colour came up, and here the Southerners declared that the negroes would not accept our Order; that they *would* not become Good Templars; and it was this positive assurance on the part of Southern Representatives that induced Joseph Malins to reluctantly consent to the blacks having the Temperance cause presented to them in another way than that of Good Templarism. And now the Southerners claim that Bro. Malins—whose amendment was *lost*—was the author of the "U.O. of True Reformers." A greater falsehood never was circulated.

In North Carolina the blacks had subordinate lodges before the whites, and yet when Col. Hickman, as R.W.G.Coun., went to North Carolina to organise a Grand Lodge he ignored the coloured lodges, and took in only the whites. And yet the P.R.W. Templar Hastings says the R.W.G.L. knew nothing of exclusion?

Among the decisions given in his report at the London Session in 1873, R.W.G. Templar Russell gave this:—

> "The action of the R.W.G. Lodge, at its late session, relating to Lodges of our Order among the coloured population of the Southern States, gives to all Grand Lodges now existing, or hereafter to be organised, full power over that question within their respective jurisdictions, even to the discontinuing of Subordinate Lodge Charters previously granted by this R.W.G. Lodge."

This shews most clearly that the American leaders of the R.W.G.L. not only knew that the blacks were excluded from our Order in the South, but that the R.W.G.T. committed them to the mercy of the Southern G.Lodges, even to the right of taking away their charters.

But in England the Representatives saw through this transparent veil, and demanded that something should be done for the negroes, and this demand caused the passage of the following:—

> "That all Subordinate Lodges, within the jurisdiction of any Grand Lodge, whose Charters have not been revoked or

suspended for a violation of the Constitution, Laws or Rules of the Order, are entitled to be recognised and receive quarterly Password, and that the refusal thereof, because of race, colour, or condition, will be a violation of duty and obligation."

This action of the London Session so exasperated the Good Templars of the Southern States that they at once began to arrange for withdrawing from the R.W.G.Lodge altogether.

But the majority of the R.W.G.L. Executive were *Conservative* men—men who were accustomed to bow to the behests of the old Slaveocracy, and down they went upon their knees. Hear what the then R.W.G. Templar Hastings said in his report to the Boston Session in 1874. I am glad he is present, so that if I misrepresent him he can correct me:—

THE ORDER AT THE SOUTH.

On my return from London in September last, I found an intense feeling of excitement prevailing in several of these States, growing out of misapprehension of the action of this body touching the question of lodges for the coloured people at the South. It was evident to my mind that unless something was done speedily to allay the excitement, several of the Southern Grand Lodges would be *lost to the Order*.

With the most efficient aid of our worthy brother, J. J. Hickman, P.R.W.G. Coun., who at his own expense went from one Grand Lodge Session to another, explaining the real situation of matters and urging moderation, the matter was finally understood, and perfect harmony and good feeling restored.

A Council to decide what action should be taken by the Southern Grand Lodges was convened at Atlanta, Ga., on the 12th November, 1873. Delegates were present from Kentucky, Tennessee, Alabama, and Georgia. The whole matter was laid before the Council in a most able and lucid report by Bro. Hickman, when the following resolutions were unanimously adopted:—

"After a careful examination of the explanation by the R.W.G.T. (S. D. Hastings) of the action taken by the R.W.G. Lodge, at its recent session in London, relative to the subject of negro lodges, we, as a Council of the Southern Grand Lodges, submit that the R.W.G. Lodge having disclaimed all intention to detract from the rights guaranteed to us, and that we have full protection under our charters and laws; therefore be it *Resolved*—That there exists no further cause for disagreement between the Southern Grand Lodges and R.W.G. Lodge.

> "*Resolved*—That we recommend to the several Grand Lodges represented by us that we *retain* our relationship with the R.W.G. Lodge as heretofore."

A gentleman who was present at a meeting in the South where Col. Hickman was pledging that the R.W.G.L. Executive would not enforce the London resolution, said he was ashamed that he was a Good Templar when he saw the depth of degradation to which the head of the Order had descended.

And yet Bro. Hastings tells us that the R.W.G.L. has always been on the side of justice to the negro! At the Boston Session I placed upon the journal the notice of a change in the Constitution so as to give the negro the Order by separate G.Lodges.

This was called up at the Bloomington Session in 1875, and we were again cheated.

Then came the Louisville Session of 1876, which is familiar to you all.

The demand of Representative Gladstone, of Scotland, was *just and reasonable*, and was the thing needed to settle the question.

But the Southern Representatives were determined in their opposition to the rights of the negro, and nothing but the continued exclusion of that race from the Order in the South would satisfy them.

The substitute offered by Dr. Oronhyatekha, filled as it was with a mess of high sounding phrases about human liberty, the well-understood fundamental principle of the Order, and the equality of all mankind without regard to race or colour, was ridiculous in the extreme when we take into consideration the fact that his was only a subterfuge to keep the blacks out of the Order. And this is clear enough when we come to the *conclusion* of Dr. O.'s substitute, which is a mere play upon words. Resolved—

> "That any provision in the Constitution or Bye-laws of any Grand Lodge that in any manner contravenes this well understood fundamental principle of the Order, is absolutely null and void, and this R.W.G. Lodge is prepared at any time to revoke the Charter of any Lodge that may persist in violating this or any other law of the Order."

This concoction reminds us of a town's meeting called in New Hampshire to consider the subject of building a new poor-house, and where the votes were about equally divided as to the propriety of going to the expense of erecting the new building. The committee reported as follows:—1st, *Resolved*—That we build a new poor-house. 2nd, *Resolved*—That we build the new house where the old one stands. 3rd, *Resolved*—That we keep the paupers in the old poor-house till the new one is built!!"

Before the adjournment of our opponents at the Louisville Session, they felt that it was a duty to take a little glorification to themselves, and to tickle Dr. O. and the Southern delegates, so the following deliverance was adopted:—

> "The substitute offered by the Representatives from Canada, a country that has always offered a refuge to the oppressed of all nations, be they bond or free, and accepted by the Representatives from the South, practically demonstrated that in this great humanitarian work, in this great moral work, this Order knows no North, no South, no East, no West, no nationality, no race—the world is our field, our subjects mankind."

The work was finished; the negro was still successfully kept out of the Order; the South was safe; and one of the Southern Representatives proposed that the R.W.G.L. have a season of prayer!! Thus they "steal the livery of the courts of Heaven to serve the devil in."

While it is true that Canada was the land of refuge for the slave during the existence of that institution here, we are not so much indebted to the people of Canada as to the *home* Government of Great Britain, which made "Freedom" the watchword in all her colonies.

The population of Canada is still made up largely of low French and Indians, and in parts of Canada prejudice against the negro is as rampant as in the Southern States.

And Dr. Oronhyatekha has that combination of instincts which have distinguished him for his hatred to the negro.

While at the Boston Session in 1874 an English Representative, who had for the first time seen a negro initiated into the R.W.G.L., thought that it would be a capital thing to carry back to his own country a picture of a white, a negro, and an Indian

Good Templar in a group. He therefore asked the Doctor if he would sit. His reply was to the effect that he did not object to be taken with a white man, but he would not be taken "WITH A NIGGER." Of the two races the negro is infinitely above the Indian in this country, and if either had cause to object it should have been myself, for I was the person referred to.

P.R.W. Templar Hastings finds great fault with the British Representatives for coming here with an ultimatum. Does Bro. Hastings forget that the Southerners have for the past ten years presented their ultimatums for the continued exclusion of the negro? This ultimatum they have passed at some session of the R.W.G.L., and when beaten at the London Session, the Kentucky Representatives withdrew the invitation extended the day previous for that body to hold its next session in Kentucky; while the Representative from Alabama, who had been elected to an office in the R.W.G.L., resigned his position; so that it was to meet a Southern ultimatum that the R.W.G. Templar, on his return to America, hastened to the South and assured them that the London enactment should not be enforced. Talk no more of the British ultimatums!

But SHAME upon the Northern Representatives, who remained silent while the black man's rights and the principles of the Independent Order of Good Templars had to be advocated by foreigners.

Then the motives of the British Representatives have been called in question by Bro. Hastings. He says that "Malins was ambitious and immovable, and that Gladstone would not accept any modification to his amendment; and that an alteration of four words would have satisfied the South." Yes; but the alteration of the four words which they proposed would have taken from the negro the justice that the English demanded.

For one, I thank God that He put it into the hearts of the English and Scotch people to send over here Joseph Malins, George Gladstone, and James Yeames—men with backbone, who to-day enjoy the respect and esteem of the liberty-loving people of this entire continent.

These men had been misled in 1872, cheated in 1873, deceived in 1874, and swindled in 1875. They prepared for 1876, and, thank God, they stood by their ultimatum.

P.R.W.G. Templar Hastings finds fault with the British

delegates for re-organising the R.W.G. Lodge. He says they are *not* a R.W.G.L. Let me tell Bro. Hastings here to his face that the R.W.G.L. of the World occupies a position to-day infinitely higher than Col. Hickman and his associates. The re-organised body is *in the right*; numerically it has two-thirds of the Order, and above all, it presents the Order to the coloured people, and has made glad hearts among the millions in our Southern States whom Col. Hickman has laboured so diligently to keep out of the Order.

And where stand Col. Hickman to-day and *his* "R.W.G.L."?

You have there on your table, Grand Worthy Chief Templar, a letter from Col. Hickman, asking this G.L. to endorse the act of the Louisville Session; and he insists that, should Massachusetts fail to endorse the doings at Louisville, it will very much impede his work in England; and he hopes this G.L. will give him a letter of introduction to the Good Templars of England.

Now I tell Bro. Hastings that this G.L. will *not* endorse the work done at the Louisville Session, nor will it give Col. Hickman a recommendation to the English, simply because he does not deserve it.

He and his Southern associates have torn this noble Order to pieces; driven out the good and brave men and women of this country, of Europe, of the West Indies, the East Indies, and wherever they can appreciate justice. He has pandered to these low, mean instincts of an unholy prejudice of colour which have cast a blight upon one of the greatest of reforms.

P.R.W. Templar Hastings says that "four hundred subordinate lodges in England have resolved to join us." Let me tell Bro. Hastings that I don't believe there are that number of fools in England. I regret that P.R.W.T. Hastings has come here to-day in such a bad cause.

He has begged this G.L. not to pass the vote of censure upon the ex-R.W.G.L.! He has almost shed tears in behalf of Col. Hickman and his Southern friends. But it is all of no avail.

Unfortunately for the cause of justice this semi-annual session of our G.L. is held in North Adams, nearly 200 miles from the capital of the State, which makes the attendance so small.

But for the respect I have for the large number of lodges which are not represented here to-day, I would move a resolution that our G.W. Secretary be at once instructed to send to England for her supplies.

I regret that this question must go over to our annual session. We want to shew where this G.L. stands upon this important subject. I know where I stand, and I know where I shall go, whether this G.L. goes or not.

Here, you see, I have a handful of letters from black men at the South, asking my opinion. I tell every one of them that the R.W.G.L. of the World is their only hope, and I advise them to apply at once for charters for subordinate and Grand Lodges.

CHRONOLOGY

NOTE ON THE TEXTS

NOTES

INDEX

Chronology

1814 — Born on a farm outside Mt. Sterling, Montgomery County, Kentucky, the son of Elizabeth, a slave woman owned by Dr. John Young, a successful entrepreneur who operated a medical practice and small-scale manufacturing interests in Mt. Sterling and owned farms supervised by overseers in the surrounding countryside. Named William, or a colloquial variant, at birth. His father is Young's first cousin, George W. Higgins, a white man of considerable property, including slaves, living nearby. Higgins shortly afterward marries a white woman and migrates to Tennessee. William is probably the youngest of his mother's seven children (his siblings are Solomon, Leander, Benjamin, Joseph, Milford, and Elizabeth), each one, he claimed, the offspring of a different father.

1817 — Young relocates with his wife and slaves to a large tract of land in the Missouri Territory near the old French pioneer settlement of Charrette, about sixty miles west of St. Louis and one mile north of the Missouri River, where he lays out a working farm for himself and auctions off lots for a settlement he names Marthasville. William's family survives intact through the move and through the eight years they reside on Young's farm in Marthasville.

1820–21 — Missouri enters the Union as a slave state in 1821. Sometime during this period William is renamed "Sandford" by Young to distinguish him from Young's nephew, William Moore Young, an act William never forgives.

1825 — Family moves with Young to St. Louis, where they are hired out to locally based employers.

1826–30 — William begins working outside the Young house and farm, including periods of service as a waiter and steward onboard Missouri and Mississippi river steamboats. He is also hired out by Young for a variety of odd jobs for employers in St. Louis, including stints working in a hotel, inn, and the printing shop of newspaper editor Elijah Lovejoy. Young begins to sell members of William's family to local slaveholders, including tinner and roofing contractor Isaac Mansfield.

1831–32 Spends a year contracted to William Walker, one of the most notorious slave traders on the Mississippi River. Accompanies Walker on three slave-trading circuits, assisting him in purchasing slaves in the interior of Missouri and then descending the Mississippi River to sell them at the markets of Vicksburg, Natchez, and New Orleans. Remembers the experience as "the longest year I ever lived."

1832 Isaac Mansfield sells William's sister Elizabeth to a buyer who takes her and other female slaves down to the market town of Natchez for sale. William responds by persuading his mother to join him in a joint escape. They cross the Mississippi in a rowboat and flee for ten days across Illinois until they are apprehended by mounted slave catchers, returned to St. Louis, and placed for safekeeping in jail. Mansfield summarily sells William's mother to a slave trader, who transports her to New Orleans; William never sees his sister or mother again. Dr. Young reclaims him and sells him to a St. Louis merchant tailor, Samuel Willi, who hires him out to various local men.

1833 William is sold by Willi in early October to a well-known Mississippi River steamboat owner and pilot, Enoch Price, who plans to employ him as a domestic servant. In late November Price takes William along to serve his family during a trip to New Orleans. After receiving William's assurance he will not take flight if they dock in free territory, Price alters his original plan to return straight to St. Louis and goes up the Ohio River to Cincinnati.

1834 William absconds as soon as the ship docks in Cincinnati on New Year's Day and travels by foot northeast toward Cleveland with the goal of crossing Lake Erie to slave-free Canada. Harsh wintry conditions force him to seek refuge with an elderly Quaker couple, who prepare him for the remainder of his journey. The man, Wells Brown, tells William that free men should have two names and offers his own. William Wells Brown finds passage to Canada blocked by winter ice and settles in Cleveland, where by spring he finds work on Lake Erie steamers and aids fugitive slaves in reaching freedom in Canada. He meets a teenaged woman named Elizabeth (Betsey) Schooner, of mixed African American and American Indian ancestry, and marries her within a matter of weeks. Functionally illiterate at the time of his escape, he begins the process of self-education with her help.

1836 Daughter Clarissa Brown born in Cleveland in spring. The family moves to Buffalo, New York, a city with a much larger African American community. Brown continues to work primarily as a sailor on Lake Erie steamers.

1839 Daughter Elizabeth Josephine Brown is born in either Detroit or Buffalo.

1842 Serves as president of a local temperance society in Buffalo. His first known published work is a letter to the *Northern Star and Freeman's Advocate*, a black weekly published in Albany, New York, on the recent meeting of his Union Total Abstinence Society. Daughter Henrietta Helen Brown is born in Buffalo in August.

1843 Takes part in the National Convention of Colored Men in Buffalo, at which he meets Frederick Douglass, Henry Highland Garnet (who recites his insurrectionary "An Address to the Slaves of the United States"), Charles Lenox Remond, and other black abolitionists. Joins Douglass and Remond in opposing Garnet's attempt to persuade the Convention to underwrite the publication of his Address. Soon afterward becomes a lecturer for the Western New York Anti-Slavery Society, a new branch of the Garrisonian American Anti-Slavery Society.

1844 Daughter Henrietta dies in Buffalo on May 6 while Brown is in New York City attending national convention of the American Anti-Slavery Society. His official lecturing itinerary takes him beyond western New York State back to Ohio, where he crisscrosses the eastern third of the state and gets dangerously close to slave territory. In December reports about his family's poverty lead officials of the Western New York Anti-Slavery Society to raise funds for their support.

1845 Marriage, undermined by his frequent absences, deteriorates further when he twice discovers Betsey with another man. To end the affair, he moves his family to the Quaker reform community of Farmington, New York, near Rochester. In September he corresponds with former governor William H. Seward about black suffrage in New York State but fails to make headway.

1847 Separates from Betsey in May and moves to Boston with their daughters, whom he boards with the respected black family of Polly and Nathan Johnson in New Bedford, Massachusetts. He soon finds employment as a lecturer with the Massachusetts Anti-Slavery Society, led by William Lloyd Garrison and Wendell Phillips, who will become lifelong friends and associates. *Narrative of William W. Brown*, published in July, proves so popular that three additional editions appear over the next two years. He also earns a reputation within the antislavery movement as a riveting lecturer.

1848 Publishes first edition of *The Anti-Slavery Harp*, a collection of antislavery hymns; three more U.S. printings follow during the next few years. During a speaking tour in Pennsylvania in December he meets and befriends the fugitive couple Ellen and William Craft, just escaped from slavery in Georgia in a feat of deception in which Ellen cross-dressed as a white man accompanied in his travels north by his servant. Brown escorts them to Boston and enlists them in a successful speaking tour that continues into the following spring.

1849 Plans a visit of indefinite duration to the United Kingdom. Days before embarking in July, reaches an agreement with the Irish printer Richard Webb for an Anglo-Irish edition of *Narrative of William W. Brown* and transports with him the stereotype plates. In September, attends the second International Peace Congress in Paris as a delegate of the U.S. Peace Society and makes strong impression as speaker on activists and journalists from the United Kingdom and the Continent. Establishes himself as a popular and successful antislavery lecturer in the United Kingdom, which he tours extensively for five years.

1850 Postpones indefinitely any plan to return home following passage of the Fugitive Slave Act on September 18. An English edition of *The Anti-Slavery Harp* appears in Newcastle, and additional printings of *Narrative of William W. Brown* are issued in London. During summer he commissions London artists to paint an antislavery panorama, which beginning in November he takes on tour across England, Scotland, and Wales. Forced to publicly defend his reputation when Betsey's charges of infidelity and abandonment are publicized in the *New York Tribune* and reprinted in other U.S. papers.

1851 Continues to travel widely across Great Britain, often alternating antislavery lectures with panorama presentations. Stages an informal protest in June against U.S. slavery at the Great Exhibition, at the Crystal Palace in London, which Enoch Price (still his legal owner) visits sometime in summer or fall when Brown is away. Brown organizes a mass meeting in London to commemorate West Indian Emancipation Day, August 1, at which a supporter reads his "An Appeal to the People of Great Britain and the World." Daughters Clarissa and Josephine arrive in London but stay with him only briefly before he sends them to boarding school in Calais.

1852 In September, publishes *Three Years in Europe*, to considerable acclaim, in London and Edinburgh. Clarissa and Josephine return to London after a year in Calais and attend the Home and Colonial Society Training School to prepare for careers as teachers or governesses. Betsey dies destitute in Buffalo.

1853 Publishes novel *Clotel* in London.

1854 Publishes "Visit of a Fugitive Slave to the Grave of Wilberforce" in *Autographs for Freedom*, anthology edited by British abolitionist Julia Griffiths. Supporters led by Ellen Richardson purchase Brown's manumission from Enoch Price (as Richardson had helped buy Frederick Douglass's freedom in 1846). Speaks at a mass meeting in Manchester held to celebrate West Indian Emancipation Day. When his daughters decide to remain in Europe, embarks alone from Liverpool on September 6, arriving in Philadelphia on September 26. Resumes lecturing for the Massachusetts Anti-Slavery Society from his home base in Boston. In December publishes *The American Fugitive in Europe*, an expanded version of his European travel book, as well as *St. Domingo: Its Revolution and its Patriots*, a lecture originally given in London.

1855 Returns to Cincinnati in early spring and visits the scene of his escape from Price's riverboat. Daughter Clarissa marries Fritz Alcide Humbert in London and decides to remain in England. Daughter Josephine, escorted across the Atlantic by Horace Greeley, returns home in August and joins Brown in Boston. They lecture together in New England, and in December Josephine publishes *Biography of an American Bondman*, a biography of her father, probably coauthored with Brown.

1856 Breaks off relations with Josephine over sexual improprieties. He completes but does not publish *Experience*, an antislavery play (the text is not known to have survived). Travels extensively across the Northeast and Midwest, giving one-man recitations of the play and also lecturing on slavery.

1857 Writes a second antislavery play, *The Escape*, which he performs widely on tour.

1858 Publishes *The Escape; or, A Leap for Freedom. A Drama in Five Acts*, the first play published by an African American, and continues to perform and lecture extensively.

1859 Publishes *Memoir of William Wells Brown, an American Bondman. Written by Himself*, an abbreviated version of his fugitive memoir.

1860 Marries Annie Elizabeth Gray, of a respected black family from Cambridge, Massachusetts, in April at the Twelfth Baptist Church in Boston, and moves into house in Cambridge, the family home until 1878. Supports no candidate in the presidential election, finding Lincoln no more trustworthy than Stephen Douglas as a foe of slavery. Serializes a condensed version of *Clotel*, retitled *Miralda; or, The Beautiful Quadroon. A Romance of American Slavery, Founded on Fact*, that runs December 6, 1860–March 16, 1861, in the *Weekly Anglo-African*.

1861 Takes skeptical view at the outbreak of the Civil War that the war is unlikely to end slavery. Instead of supporting it, he joins the Haitian Emigration Bureau as a promoter of voluntary migration of North American blacks to the Republic of Haiti and lectures on behalf of the movement in Ontario, New York, and New Jersey. William Wells Brown Jr. is born in February and dies of cholera on July 25.

1862 Publishes *The Black Man*, his first book on African American history, and lectures widely on the history of people of African descent, slavery, and the future of both blacks and whites in a post-slavery United States. Daughter Clotelle is born on May 8.

1863 Reads the Preliminary Emancipation Proclamation to the assembled black community of Boston at Tremont Temple on New Year's Day as it awaits confirmation that President Lincoln has signed the final Emancipation Proclamation.

Now an active supporter of the Union cause, recruits locally and in New York City for the Massachusetts 54th, the first black regiment formed in the North, and follows its progress (and that of other black regiments) in the field. He issues a second, expanded edition of *The Black Man*.

1864 Publishes third version of *Clotel*, retitled *Clotelle: A Tale of the Southern States*, in the Books for the Camp Fires series, for sale to Union troops in the field. Continues to lecture widely.

1865 Sponsors and presides over jubilee meeting at Tremont Temple celebrating congressional passage of the Thirteenth Amendment abolishing slavery. After years of reading medicine, advertises himself as a medical doctor operating out of an office in Boston and maintains a practice for the remainder of his life. Heads reception committee welcoming the Massachusetts 54th on their return to Boston following the Confederate surrender. Continues his activity as a reformer, shifting focus from emancipation to civil rights and temperance in both the North and the South.

1866 Elected first chief officer of the John Brown Division of the Sons of Temperance, one of many senior positions he will hold in the temperance movement during the last two decades of his life.

1867 Serves as general agent of the Freedmen's Memorial Monument, an African American association that plans to honor President Lincoln and commemorate emancipation with a public statue in Washington, D.C. During his first visit to Washington, tours Virginia and Maryland, meets with freedmen, and emerges with a more urgent sense of the need for political action on their behalf. Publishes *The Negro in the American Rebellion: His Heroism and His Fidelity*, which goes through multiple printings; also the fourth and final version of *Clotel*, now retitled *Clotelle; or, The Colored Heroine. A Tale of the Southern States.*

1868 Elected president of the National Association for the Organization of Night Schools and the Spread of Temperance among the Freed People of the South, and engages in fundraising to subsidize sending educational publications and temperance agents to the South.

1869 Goes on lecture tour in the West, stopping first in Chicago to debate his old antislavery touring comrade Susan B. Anthony on the relative importance of African American and women's suffrage, a debate intensified by recent congressional passage of the Fifteenth Amendment and its submission to the states for ratification. Continues to St. Louis for his first trip "home" since escaping from slavery thirty-five years earlier. Apparently meets his former master Enoch Price during the visit in a friendly encounter.

1870 Supports Prohibition Party in Massachusetts and attends convention that nominates Wendell Phillips for governor, who receives 14.5 percent of the vote running on Prohibition and Labor Reform tickets. On June 12 in New York City, Josephine Brown marries thirty-two-year-old George Dogans, a free black born in Alexandria, Virginia, who trained as a butcher in Washington, D.C. Daughter Clotelle dies suddenly on October 1 and is buried in her mother's family plot in Cambridge Cemetery.

1871 Presides over Emancipation Day observance at Tremont Temple attended by Sojourner Truth and Leonard Grimes. Sponsors essay contest won by twelve-year-old Pauline Hopkins, the future author, with an essay on "The Evils of Intemperance and Their Remedies." Successfully argues for seating of black delegates from Maryland at the Boston meeting of the National Division of the Sons of Temperance of North America. Returns to Kentucky for the first time since infancy and works to promote temperance, education, and general self-improvement among freedmen. On his way to give a talk in central Kentucky, he is abducted by the Ku Klux Klan and threatened with hanging but escapes, takes the train to Cincinnati, and tells his story to the press. Daughter Clarissa Brown Humbert, widowed by 1861, marries George Wainwright Sylvestre in Yorkshire.

1872 Commends Massachusetts senator Charles Sumner's sponsorship of civil rights bill prohibiting discrimination in public accommodation (passed 1875, overturned by Supreme Court in 1883). Continues temperance activity, mostly on the local level.

1873 Completes *The Rising Son; or, the Antecedents and Advancement of the Colored Race*, his third and most comprehensive study of African, African Caribbean, and African American history. When the plan for commercial publication is thwarted at the last moment by the financial panic of 1873, he and Annie publish it under the imprint of A. G. Brown and Company.

1874 Josephine Brown, now known as Campbell, dies in Cambridge of tuberculosis and is buried in the same plot in Cambridge Cemetery with her half sister Clotelle Brown, whom she never met. On April 14 and May 17, Brown eulogizes Senator Charles Sumner at commemorative meetings in Boston and, on May 30, his friend and fellow historian William C. Nell. In spring Clarissa Brown Sylvestre dies in Leeds, England.

1876 Takes outspoken position within the national and international temperance movement against attempts to segregate lodges by race. In North Adams, Massachusetts, at meeting of the Grand Lodge of Massachusetts, delivers a denunciation of segregation in the southern temperance movement as promulgated in his native Kentucky, sarcastically dismissing the notion of "pure white blood" in Kentucky as "a most ridiculous proposition." Runs for Massachusetts Senate from Middlesex County (Cambridge) on Prohibition ticket and comes in third.

1877 Makes highly publicized return visit to England and Scotland to take part in the international meeting of the Right Worthy Grand Lodge of the World of the Independent Order of Good Templars, an international temperance organization, in Glasgow. The most famous black figure in the organization, he tours the United Kingdom for three months, gives more than thirty talks on the "Negro Question" then dividing the international temperance movement, and sees old acquaintances.

1878 Moves home and medical office to Decatur Street in the South End of Boston.

1879 Spends much of year on field trips through West Virginia, Tennessee, and Virginia to promote black temperance and education for the Right Worthy Grand Lodge of the World. Informs his English contacts that weeks of discrimination in transportation and accommodation make him "feel rather blue in the South." Attends the funeral service for William Lloyd Garrison in Boston in May before resuming missionary work in the South in fall.

1880 Returns in February from final trip to the South. In spring, publishes *My Southern Home*, which A. G. Brown and

Company sells nationally by subscription, along with copies of *The Negro in the American Rebellion* and *The Rising Son* by mail order. Moves his home and office to 28 East Canton Street in the South End of Boston.

1882 Moves office to 35 Hanover Street, East End.

1883 Moves home from East Canton to 89 Beacon Street in Chelsea, a fast-growing community with a mixed population across the Mystic River from Boston.

1884 Eulogizes Wendell Phillips at Faneuil Hall on February 8. Gravely ill himself, makes his last public appearance at the Revere House on October 31 at event celebrating the seventy-fifth birthday of former Massachusetts state legislator and antislavery activist F. W. Bird. Dies on November 6 of bladder cancer at home in Chelsea and is buried three days later in the Gray family plot in Cambridge Cemetery.

Note on the Texts

This volume contains six works by William Wells Brown: *Narrative of William W. Brown, A Fugitive Slave. Written by Himself* (1847); *Clotel; or, The President's Daughter* (1853); *The American Fugitive in Europe: Sketches of Places and People Abroad* (1855); *The Escape; or, A Leap for Freedom* (1858); *The Black Man, His Antecedents, His Genius, and His Achievements* (1862); and *My Southern Home: or, The South and Its People* (1880). Also included are eighteen speeches and public letters published from 1844 to 1876.

Brown's works often appeared in multiple editions in his lifetime, and he frequently revised and rewrote them extensively. His novel *Clotel*, to cite the most extreme example of this practice, was published in four versions, each under a different title and with a different publisher: the first in London with a trade house in 1853, the second as a heavily revised serial fiction in the New York *Weekly Anglo-African* in 1860–61, the third in Boston as a dime novel in James Redpath's Books for the Camp Fires series in 1864, and the fourth in Boston in 1867 as a hardbound novel. He adapted each edition to a specific audience: the first, with its light-complexioned fugitive slaves taking refuge in Europe, was a polemical work addressed principally to a British audience; the second edition, with its principal African American male character darkened and more committed to black solidarity, aimed at an African American readership; the third, an abridged romance, designed chiefly to recruit Union soldiers to the cause of black freedom; and the fourth, with four chapters added at the end to extend the plot beyond the Civil War, serving to deliver a message about communal elevation to a post-emancipatory audience.

Brown's first published book, *Narrative of William W. Brown, A Fugitive Slave. Written by Himself*, was published in Boston in 1847 by the Massachusetts Anti-Slavery Society, the only fugitive slave narrative to receive its imprimatur other than the 1845 *Narrative of the Life of Frederick Douglass*. The first printing, issued in both paper and cloth covers, sold out within six months. Brown had three additional printings made during 1848–49, adding illustrations and content but making few alterations to the core narrative. Brown owned the stereotype plates, which he took with him to Ireland in 1849 for use in issuing the first in a series of Anglo-Irish printings, which appeared from 1849 to 1852. The text in the present volume follows the 1847 first printing.

Clotel; or, The President's Daughter: A Narrative of Slave Life in the United States, the first novel written by an African American, was published in London in 1853 by the firm of Partridge and Oakey. It sold poorly, with few copies crossing the Atlantic, and was not reprinted in this form for more than a century, though Brown (as described above) brought out several revised versions. The present volume reprints the first published edition.

The American Fugitive in Europe: Sketches of Places and People Abroad is an expanded version of the first travelogue by an African American, *Three Years in Europe; or, Places I Have Seen and People I Have Met*, which Brown had published in London and Edinburgh in 1852. Brown published *The American Fugitive* in 1855 with the Boston-based firm of John P. Jewett and Company, the leading antislavery publisher in the country. Although widely reviewed and praised, it was not reprinted in the nineteenth century. The 1855 version is the text printed in the present volume.

The Escape; or, A Leap for Freedom. A Drama in Five Acts, the first play published by an African American, was issued in Boston by Robert Wallcut in 1858 as a cheap softcover pamphlet. Sales figures are unknown, but it apparently required only a single edition. Brown had completed the play eighteen months before its publication, and often performed it across the northern states in one-person recitations that continued up to the Civil War. The text in the present volume is that of the 1858 pamphlet.

The Black Man, His Antecedents, His Genius, and His Achievements was first published jointly by Thomas Hamilton in New York and Robert Wallcut in Boston in late 1862 (though the copyright date is 1863), just a month before the issuance of the Emancipation Proclamation. It sold well, and a new, slightly expanded version came out the next year, with further printings and editions to follow, the last, bearing an 1865 Savannah, Georgia, imprint, published shortly after the Union Army occupied the city. The present volume prints the text of the 1863 expanded edition published in Boston by James Redpath.

My Southern Home: or, The South and Its People was self-published in Boston in 1880 by Brown and his wife Annie Gray Brown under the imprint A. G. Brown and Company and sold by subscription. It proved popular and required multiple printings, with sales continuing at least until Brown's death in 1884. The first printing of 1880 provides the text used here.

The following is a list of the speeches and public letters included in this volume, in the order of their appearance, giving the source of each text.

"Letter from Wm. W. Brown—A Methodist Deacon's Prayer," *National Anti-Slavery Standard* 5 (September 26, 1844), 66.

A Lecture Delivered before the Female Anti-Slavery Society of Salem at Lyceum Hall, Nov. 14, 1847 (Boston: Massachusetts Anti-Slavery Society, 1847).

"Speech at the Royal Public Subscription Rooms, Exeter, England, May 5, 1851," [Exeter] *Western Times*, May 10, 1851.

"An Appeal to the People of Great Britain and the World," *Liberator* 21 (September 5, 1851), 142.

"Visit of a Fugitive Slave to the Grave of Wilberforce," Julia Griffiths, ed. *Autographs for Freedom*, 2nd series (Auburn, NY: Alden, Beardsley, and Co., 1854), 70–76.

"Speech at Town Hall, Manchester, England, August 1, 1854," *Manchester Examiner and Times*, August 5, 1854.

"Speech at Brick Wesley Church, Philadelphia, October 17, 1854," *National Anti-Slavery Standard* 15 (October 28, 1854), 2–3.

"Speech at Horticultural Hall, West Chester, Pennsylvania, October 23, 1854," *National Anti-Slavery Standard* 15 (November 4, 1854), 1.

"Letter from the West," *National Anti-Slavery Standard* 15 (March 31, 1855), 3.

"Letter from W. W. Brown," *National Anti-Slavery Standard* 15 (April 21, 1855), 3.

"Speech at Anniversary of New York Anti-Slavery Society, May 8, 1856," *National Anti-Slavery Standard* 16 (May 16, 1856), 2.

"John Brown and the Fugitive Slave Law," *The Independent* 22 (March 10, 1870), 6.

"Speech at Annual Meeting of the American Anti-Slavery Society, May 9, 1860," *National Anti-Slavery Standard* 21 (May 26, 1860), 4.

"Review of Mr. Yancey's Speech," *Liberator* 30 (October 26, 1860), 172.

"Speech at Annual Meeting of the American Anti-Slavery Society, May 6, 1862," *Liberator* 32 (May 16, 1862), 77.

"'The Black Man' and Its Critics," *Anglo-African* 3 (August 8, 1863), 1.

"Speech at Annual Meeting of the American Anti-Slavery Society, May 7, 1867," *National Anti-Slavery Standard* 28 (May 18, 1867), 3.

"Dr. Wells Brown on the Colour Question," *The Good Templars' Watchword* 3 (November 1, 1876), 724–25.

This volume presents the texts of the printings chosen as sources here but does not attempt to reproduce features of their typographical design. The texts are printed without alteration except for the correction of typographical errors. Spelling, punctuation, and capitalization are often expressive features, and they are not otherwise altered, even when inconsistent or irregular. The following is a list of typographical errors corrected, cited by page and line number: 38.5, told

I; 62.5, master."; 85.14, master."; 86.5, examination,; 91.11, 'I think; 95.15, hazlenuts.; 97.14, Synder; 101.11, Mr J. C.; 110.11, "God; 110.16, murders;; 118.27, school'; 121.37, i'll; 125.1, or l ying; 131.38, slave,; 131.39, she"; 134.37–38, unthinkeing; 151.26, sleeper's; 173.19, I; I am; 173.26, use. 'No,'; 184.16, heard. and; 184.31, bitterand; 190.2, Curtis; 195.29, statesman,; 207.29, address,"; 207.30, Green?; 212.25, recal; 213.18, statment,; 268.32, "In; 268.35, it."; 305.20, to to; 310.13, Tiziano, Vercellio; 338.35, they been; 370.12, 'How; 383.22, It is; 420.38, *Cato*—; 422.28, somebody,; 443.9, fine looking-women,; 446.22, *Dr. G* You; 453.37, in. *Exit*; 465.1, Washinton; 482.32, them Mr.; 489.20, acknowldge; 492.28, in in; 529.7, Groton,; 562.21, Murat; 598.8, Regaud; 609.23, Arcaau;; 613.5, Caius; 623.29, C Nell; 696.40, hands'; 697.13, people?; 702.7, in' em;; 706.26, name.; 732.16, you, said; 741.19, a—h!"; 750.22, become; 763.5, offer."; 775.11, "With; 776.9, at the the; 777.7, "As; 781.15, bill"; 785.27, *party*."; 793.18, nonenity; 797.2, dis.'; 804.28, emnity; 812.22, himself."; 823.25, that that; 829.22, day. Now; 844.9, Phyllis, Wheatly,; 846.12, hardship,; 854.3, bethine; 854.3, severaltimes; 866.7, sympathising; 868.5, up n; 877.7, slavery—; 891.19, (Cheers. It; 914.26, Said, I; 920.37, depair; 924.34–35, bidder bringing; 928.12, amalgation; 938.11, wold; 939.18, degading; 940.15, Romans Saxons; 944.11, State and; 949.2, are doing,; 956.10, to.

Notes

In the notes below, the reference numbers denote page and line of this volume (the line count includes headings). No note is made for material included in standard desk-reference books. Quotations from Shakespeare are keyed to *The Riverside Shakespeare*, ed. G. Blakemore Evans (Boston: Houghton Mifflin, 1974). Biblical quotations are keyed to the King James Version. For references to other studies and further information than is included in the Chronology, see Ezra Greenspan, *William Wells Brown: An African American Life* (New York: W. W. Norton, 2014); *William Wells Brown: A Reader*, ed. Ezra Greenspan (Athens, GA: University of Georgia Press, 2008); *Clotel: or, The President's Daughter*, ed. Robert S. Levine. 2nd ed. (Boston: Bedford/St. Martin's, 2011); *The Escape; or, A Leap for Freedom*, ed. John Ernest (Knoxville, TN: The University of Tennessee Press, 2001); *My Southern Home: The South and Its People*, ed. John Ernest (Chapel Hill, NC: University of North Carolina Press, 2011).

The editor would like to thank Christopher Stampone for writing the notes for this volume.

NARRATIVE OF WILLIAM W. BROWN

1.11 COWPER] The quotation is actually from *Cato: A Tragedy* (1713) by Joseph Addison (1672–1719); Addison's fourth line reads: "Who owes his Greatness to his Country's Ruin?"

3.3–5 I was a . . . clothed me.] Cf. Matthew 25:35–36.

4.2 EDMUND QUINCY] Quincy (1808–1877) was corresponding secretary of the Massachusetts Anti-Slavery Society and an editor of the *National Anti-Slavery Standard* and the *Abolitionist.*

4.10 the admirable story of Mr. Douglass] *Narrative of the Life of Frederick Douglass, an American Slave* (1845).

4.19–20 "move . . . mutiny"] Cf. *Julius Caesar*, III.ii.229–30.

5.6–7 "Let me . . . laws;"] Andrew Fletcher, *An Account of a Conversation Concerning the Right to Regulation of Governments* (1703).

6.13–14 "clothed . . . heaven"] Cf. the Rev. Robert Pollok, *The Course of Time* (1827), Bk. 8, ll. 16–18 "He was a man / Who stole the livery of the court of Heaven / To serve the Devil in."

7.3–6 "Have ye . . . land?"] James Russell Lowell, "The Present Crisis" (1844).

7.25–26 "For he . . . tyranny."] James Russell Lowell, "L'Envoi" (1844).

7.33–34 "MEN-STEALERS—guilty . . . rank."] Article adopted by the General Assembly of the Presbyterian Church in 1794 as part of its rule of discipline for church members.

8.3–4 "The common . . . foul."] Robert Blair, *The Grave* (1743).

8.8–9 "When man . . . slave."] Cf. James Montgomery, "Inscription Under the Picture of an Aged Negro-Woman," in *The Pelican Island, and Other Poems* (1827). The original lines read: "Nor son nor daughter born within her empire, / Shall buy, or sell, or hold, or be a slave."

8.10 J. C. HATHAWAY] Joseph Comstock Hathaway (1810–1873), president of the Western New York Anti-Slavery Society.

10.18 It was not yet daylight.] In the revised version of the *Narrative* published in 1848, Brown replaced this sentence with the following: "Experience has taught me that nothing can be more heart-rending than for one to see a dear and beloved mother or sister tortured, and to hear their cries, and not to be able to render them assistance. But such is the position which an American slave occupies."

13.10 Major Benjamin O'Fallon.] A nephew of explorer William Clark, O'Fallon (1793–1842) was an Indian agent for the Upper Missouri region, 1819–26.

15.5–6 Lovejoy . . . Times."] Elijah Lovejoy (1802–1837), publisher and editor of the moderate *St. Louis Times*, 1829–32; later, from 1833 to 1836, publisher and editor of the *St. Louis Observer*, which received so many threats for its antislavery views that Lovejoy was forced to move his paper across the Mississippi River to Alton, Illinois, where he was murdered by a pro-slavery mob in 1837.

15.15–17 Col. Harney . . . death.] William S. Harney (1800–1889), U.S. cavalry officer during the Mexican-American War. On June 26, 1834, Harney fatally whipped his slave Hannah after accusing her of hiding his keys. He fled to Washington, D.C., but later returned to Missouri and was acquitted of murder on March 25, 1835.

15.17–19 Francis McIntosh . . . stake.] McIntosh was a porter and cook on the steamboat *Flora*, which docked in St. Louis on April 28, 1836. While out to visit a woman who worked on another boat, McIntosh was arrested for breach of the peace. After being told that he faced a lengthy prison sentence, McIntosh stabbed the two police officers, killing a deputy sheriff and seriously wounding a deputy constable, before being apprehended. A mob broke into the jail where he was being held, chained him to a tree, and burned him alive.

18.11 "sleep . . . eyelids."] Cf. Psalm 132:4, Proverbs 6:4.

26.11–34 "O, master . . . go."] From "The Slave and Her Babe," by English writer Charlotte Elizabeth Tonna (1790–1846), known as Charlotte Elizabeth. In the version of the *Narrative* published in London in 1849, Brown replaced this quotation with two paragraphs attacking the slave trade within the United States.

27.6–29 "See these poor . . . jubilee!"] This song was first printed in 1844 in *The Liberator*, the antislavery newspaper published by William Lloyd Garrison, under the title "The Plantation Song." It was also recorded by ex-slave Henry Bibb in the *National Anti-Slavery Standard* (August 8, 1844), described there as a song sung by slaves being sent to the Deep South.

30.31 "Slavery as it is."] *American Slavery As It Is: Testimony of a Thousand Witnesses* (1839), by Theodore Dwight Weld (1803–1895).

35.23 —the NORTH STAR.] At this point in the revised version of the *Narrative* published in 1848, Brown quotes twenty-one lines from "The Fugitive Slave's Apostrophe to the North Star" by John Pierpont (1785–1866).

40.4–7 the glory . . . my side."] Elizabeth Margaret Chandler, "The Bereaved Father" (1845).

40.13–14 "Gone . . . dank and lone!"] John Greenleaf Whittier, "The Farewell of a Virginia Slave Mother to Her Daughters Sold into Southern Bondage" (1838).

41.31 Thomas H. Benton] Thomas Hart Benton (1782–1858) was Missouri's leading statesman, serving in the U.S. Senate from 1821 to 1851.

42.4–5 "He that . . . many stripes!"] Cf. Luke 12:47.

42.15–18 "I would . . . despair."] Anonymous song, "I Am Monarch of Nought I Survey."

49.12–13 "Behind I left . . . plains!"] From "The Flying Slave," which appeared in Brown's *The Anti-Slavery Harp: A Collection of Songs for Anti-Slavery Meetings* (1848).

50.27 "Thompsonian"] A follower of the American herbalist Samuel Thomson (1769–1843).

53.24 "*Genius of Universal Emancipation*,"] Established in 1821 by Benjamin Lundy (1789–1839), a Quaker, in Mount Pleasant, Ohio, and later moved to Baltimore.

CLOTEL; OR, THE PRESIDENT'S DAUGHTER

57.5 introduction of slaves . . . 1620] It was in 1619 that a Dutch ship brought the first Africans to Jamestown, Virginia. Their exact status, as slaves or indentured servants, is unclear.

57.28–29 "honours the corruption, . . . head."] *Julius Caesar*, IV.iii.15–16.

61.6–9 "WHY stands she . . . weeping there?"] From "The Slave-Auction—A Fact," first published in Brown's *Anti-Slavery Harp* (1848).

61.26–30 the law says:— . . . whatsoever."] George McDowell Stroud, *A Sketch of the Laws relating Slavery in the Several States of the United States of America* (1827).

62.19–63.11 "Is a servant, . . . separation."] Both passages are from Brown's lecture partner, Parker Pillsbury, *The Church as It Is; Or, The Forlorn Hope of Slavery* (1847).

65.17–18 Thomas Jefferson, by whom she had two daughters] Largely discredited until the late twentieth century, the rumor that Thomas Jefferson had fathered children by his slave Sally Hemings (1773–1835) first captured the public's attention in 1802, when muckraking journalist James T. Callender, a former agent of Jefferson's who turned against the president when he refused to offer him a government sinecure, wrote in a Richmond newspaper, "It is well known that the man, whom it delighteth the people to honor, keeps, and for many years has kept, as his concubine, one of his slaves. Her name is SALLY." Hemings is recorded as having given birth to at least six children, four of whom survived to adulthood, and most historians now agree that a preponderance of evidence—genetic, circumstantial, and oral historical—suggests that Jefferson was in fact their father.

68.24–31 "O God! . . . and thee!"] From the anonymous poem "The Slave-Auction—A Fact" (1848).

69.3–8 "My country, . . . slaves."] From "Freedom's Banner" in Brown's *Anti-Slavery Harp* (1848).

78.8 Actæon and his dogs.] In Greek mythology, Actæon, a hunter, was transformed into a stag by Artemis and killed by his own dogs.

81.3–6 "How sweetly . . . blaze."] W. H. Burleigh, "Summer Morning in the Country" (1842).

82.35–36 "a change . . . his dreams."] Cf. Henry Glassford Bell, "The Stranger: A Tale" (1829).

84.3–6 "WHAT! mothers . . . *Whittier.*] John Greenleaf Whittier, "Expostulation" (1834).

86.27–32 "Where the slave-whip . . . air."] Whittier, "The Farewell of a Virginia Mother to Her Daughters Sold into Southern Bondage" (1838).

87.3–6 "WHAT! preach . . . *Whittier.*] Whittier, "Clerical Oppressors" (1837).

88.9 the sons of Ham] An influential line of interpretation adopted by defenders of slavery maintained that the "curse of Ham" (Genesis 9:25) justified the enslavement of blacks, because African peoples were listed among Ham's descendants in Genesis 10:6–20, or because, according to a view first put forth in the fifteenth century, the descendants of Canaan were black, while those of his uncles Shem and Japheth (Noah's other sons) were white.

89.3–4 constitution of our own Connecticut] Connecticut adopted its first state constitution in 1818, which began with a declaration of rights similar to the Bill of Rights in the U.S. Constitution.

90.37 'Thou shalt love thy neighbor as thyself.'] Mark 12:31.

92.7–8 'All things whatsoever . . . them;'] Matthew 7:12.

92.37–39 not with eye-service, . . . heart;] Ephesians 6:6.

95.19–20 "When I can . . . sky."] Isaac Watts, "When I Can Read My Title Clear" (1707).

95.24–96.13 "*Q.* What command . . . runaway?— *A.* 'No.'] Cf. "Duties of Servants" in *A Catechism, of Scripture Doctrine and Practice, for Families and Sabbath Schools. Designed Also for the Oral Instruction of Colored Persons* (1837) by Charles C. Jones. The rest of the catechism seems to be Brown's addition.

98.3–6 "NO seeming . . . *Parker.*] "Hope for Africa," a sermon delivered in Philadelphia on April 22, 1849, by Presbyterian minister Joel Parker (1799–1873).

98.36 lost sheep of the house of Israel.'] Cf. Matthew 15:24.

103.3–6 "IN many ways . . . show."] Samuel Taylor Coleridge, "In many ways does the full heart reveal" (1826).

106.21–24 "Tis ever . . . last."] From "The Wife," published anonymously in *The British Orator* (1849).

107.3–6 "My tongue . . . *Shakspeare.*] *Richard III*, I.ii.168–70.

109.3–6 "HERE we see . . . *Orleans.*] Theodore Clapp, *Slavery: A Sermon Delivered in the First Congregational Church in New Orleans, April 15, 1838.*

110.10–12 'God has created . . . earth.'] Acts 17:26.

110.30–32 'They all continued . . . women.'] Acts 1:14.

110.40–111.3 the blessing . . . earth?] Cf. Psalms 41:1–2.

111.3–4 'Inasmuch as ye . . . me,'] Matthew 25:40.

112.18–19 'He that stealeth . . . death;'] Exodus 21:16.

112.20–22 'Woe unto . . . work;'] Jeremiah 22:13.

112.24–27 'Behold the hire . . . Saboath.'] James 5:4.

112.27–32 'The law . . . persons.'] 1 Timothy 1:9–10.

113.36–40 'Therefore, thus saith . . . famine.'] Jeremiah 34:17.

114.9–10 'Well done . . . Lord.'"] Cf. Matthew 25:23.

116.13–19 "Some advantages . . . *community!*"] From an 1824 advertisement for the Medical School of South Carolina that appeared in *The New York Medical and Physical Journal.*

124.3–5 "'Tis too much . . . *Shakspeare.*] *Hamlet*, III.i.46–48.

126.38–127.10 "Send Bibles . . . read."] From "Missionary Hymn, For the South," published in *Voices of the True Hearted* (1846).

130.11 Salome] Sally Miller (c. 1813–?), a woman held in slavery in New Orleans, sued for her freedom in 1844, claiming that she was Salomé Müller, a white German immigrant and indentured servant who had been separated from her family as a child and sold into slavery. In *Sally Miller v. Louis Belmonti and John F. Miller* (1845), the Louisiana Supreme Court ruled in her favor.

133.3–6 "I promised . . . *Coleridge.*] Coleridge, "Introduction to the Tale of the Dark Ladie" (1848).

141.3–6 "I had . . . me."] Stephen Glover, "The Georgian Slave Ballad" (1852).

142.6–143.9 "The whole . . . struggle.] From *Notes on the State of Virginia* (1781), Query XVIII.

144.3–6 "We hold . . . *Independence.*] Brown added that all men are created "free" as well as equal.

146.17–33 "Soldiers!—When . . . ardour.'] Andrew Jackson, "Address to the Free People of Color" (December 18, 1814).

147.12 liberties awarded by Ali Pasha of Egypt] Muhammad Ali (1769–1849), pasha and viceroy of Egypt, notorious for his brutal rule.

149.15 General Wade Hampton] A veteran of the Revolutionary War and the War of 1812, Wade Hampton (1752–1835) was said to own as many as 3,000 slaves on plantations throughout the South.

150.3–6 "The fetters . . . play."] Elizur Wright Jr., "The Fugitive Slave to the Christian."

153.4–5 "I will assume . . . steamboat] The plan is based on the true story of Ellen Craft (1826–1891) and William Craft (1824–1900), married slaves from Macon, Georgia, who escaped to the North in December 1848 by train and steamboat with Ellen masquerading as a white gentleman and William as her slave. Brown befriended them shortly after their arrival in Philadelphia and enlisted them in the antislavery movement. In 1860 they published a narrative of their escape, apparently composed with Brown's assistance, *Running a Thousand Miles for Freedom; or the Escape of William and Ellen Craft from Slavery.*

153.38–39 John C. Calhoun] A leading southern statesman of his generation, Calhoun (1782–1850) had delivered a speech in the U.S. Senate in 1837, "Slavery a Positive Good," that signaled a major escalation in the sectional debate over slavery.

158.3 Thomas Corwin] Corwin (1794–1865), Ohio's fifteenth governor (1840–42), U.S. senator (1845–50), and member of the House of Representatives (1831–40, 1859–61).

159.34–160.8 "And it is . . . society."] From "Deed of Pew," published in Isaac Ridler Butts's *The Business Man's Assistant* (1847).

161.3–12 "WHO can . . . *Moore.*] Thomas Moore, "Epistle VI. To Lord Viscount Forbes from the City of Washington" (1823).

161.30–163.10 That government is despotism . . . and God abhor?"] This passage is taken from a speech made in the U.S. House of Representatives on February 20, 1850, by radical abolitionist Thaddeus Stevens (1792–1868), who served as a congressman from Pennsylvania, 1849–53 and 1859–68.

161.38–162.2 Athens . . . Three Thousand Tyrants.] The Thirty Tyrants were an oligarchy that controlled Athens after its defeat in the Peloponnesian War in 404 B.C.E. Under the Thirty, only three thousand Athenians were given the right to carry weapons or receive a trial by jury. The Four Hundred controlled Athens for a brief time after the Athenian Coup of 411 B.C.E.

163.1–2 butcher of Austria] General Julius Jacob von Haynau (1786–1853), Austrian general who brutally suppressed insurrections in Italy and Hungary in 1848.

163.12–26 The loss of . . . her classic fields.] From an oration delivered in Schenectady, New York, on July 4, 1803, by Milton Maxcy. (The passage was quoted in several nineteenth-century American books on rhetoric and elocution.)

165.3–4 "O WEEP, . . . sweep."] From "Your Brother is a Slave," in Brown's *Anti-Slavery Harp* (1848).

166.33–35 "pure religion . . . world."] James 1:27.

166.35–37 "Look not . . . others."] Philippians 2:4.

166.37–38 "Remember them . . . them."] Hebrews 13:3.

166.38–39 "Whatsoever ye would . . . them."] Matthew 7:12.

167.37–38 Colonization Society . . . people.] Headed by Robert Finley (1772–1817), the American Colonization Society was formed in 1816 to encourage and assist free blacks to establish settlements in Africa on the theory that they would never be accepted by white society.

168.19 speeches of Henry Clay] Clay served as president of the American Colonization Society from 1836 to 1849.

169.8 a lamp . . . path.] Cf. Psalms 119:105.

169.15–18 "'Twas midnight, . . . head."] Mary Leman Gillies, "Alone" (1847).

170.19–26 "Shall every . . . curse?"] John Greenleaf Whittier, "Our Countrymen in Chains!" (1837), first published as a broadside under the antislavery icon "Am I Not a Man and a Brother?"

171.34–36 Clay, Van Buren . . . Convention.] President Martin Van Buren was nominated for a second term by the 1840 Democratic National Convention, but was defeated by Whig William Henry Harrison in the election.

172.3 'Old Tip,'] A nickname for William Henry Harrison, whose national celebrity dated to the Battle of Tippecanoe (1811).

172.28 "Maine Law."] Maine became the first state to pass temperance legislation when it passed a law in 1851 prohibiting the manufacture and sale of alcohol except for medicinal or industrial purposes.

173.34–35 "Cold Water Army."'] Term for those who took a temperance pledge.

178.37–38 bulls of Bashan.] Cf. Psalms 22:12–13.

180.3–7 "Is the poor . . . *Byron.*] Byron, *Don Juan* (1821), Canto V, stanza 68.

185.3–7 "THE fearful . . . *Carter.*] J. G. Carter, "Ye Sons of Freemen," in Brown's *Anti-Slavery Harp* (1848).

190.2 Mr. George W. Custis.] George Washington Parke Custis (1781–1857), writer, agricultural reformer, and step-grandson of George Washington.

193.3–194.21 "Now, rest . . . hurrah!"] Sarah Jane Lippincott, "The Leap From the London Bridge." Lippincott published the poem under the pseudonym Grace Greenwood.

195.3–6 "NO refuge . . . brave!"] E. A. Atlee, "For the Signal of Liberty. New Version of the National Song—The Star Spangled Banner."

196.12 oppressed Poles] Poland had lost its national sovereignty when it was partitioned in 1795 by Russia, Prussia, and Austria. Repressive policies by the governing powers led to a series of failed uprisings by Polish nationalists in 1830, 1846, and 1848.

196.13 Grecian liberty] Greece declared independence from the Ottoman Empire in 1821, initiating a war of independence that ended in 1828 with the help of Russia, Great Britain, and France. It was recognized as an independent nation in 1832.

198.15–18 'O land . . . desolate.'] Cf. Matthew 23:37–38.

199.34–37 "Star of the . . . night."] John Pierpont, "The Fugitive Slave's Apostrophe to the North Star" (1840).

204.8 Roscoe's *Leo X.*] Biography of Pope Leo X (1475–1521) by the English historian William Roscoe (1753–1831).

206.3–4 "Man's love . . . *Byron.*] Byron, *Don Juan*, Canto I, stanza 194.

212.11–17 A celebrated writer . . . heart."] Washington Irving, "The Broken Heart," in *The Sketch Book of Geoffrey Crayon, Gent.* (1819–20).

213.12–14 To Mrs. Child, . . . story.] Brown borrowed extensively from Lydia Maria Child's work, especially the short story "The Quadroons" (1842).

214.6 the Year of Jubilee.] In the biblical book of Leviticus, the Year of Jubilee occurs every fiftieth year and occasions the release of slaves from bondage.

214.6–8 "earth indeed . . . Him."] Psalms 67:6–7.

THE AMERICAN FUGITIVE IN EUROPE

215.6–10 "Go, little book, . . . SOUTHEY.] Robert Southey, "L'Envoy" in *The Lay of the Laureate* (1816).

218.4 with a dozen or more additional chapters.] Brown significantly expanded, updated, and Americanized the English edition, adding chapters 9, 16–19, and 21–24.

223.2–10 "Adieu, adieu! . . . CHILDE HAROLD.] Byron, *Childe Harold's Pilgrimage* (1812), Canto I, stanza 13.

224.19 the President of the Oberlin Institute] Asa Mahan (1799–1889), a leading educator and moral philosopher.

224.27–34 "With thee, . . . good-night!"] Byron, *Childe Harold's Pilgrimage*, Canto I, stanza 13.

225.5–6 Curran, Emmet and O'Connell.] Irish nationalists John Philpot Curran (1750–1817), Robert Emmet (1778–1803), and Daniel O'Connell (1775–1847).

228.2–5 "It seems . . . sea."] John Dryden, "Annus Mirabilis: The Year of Wonders, 1666. An Historical Poem" (1667).

229.32–36 "Where is the slave . . . slowly?"] Thomas Moore, "Where is the Slave?"

233.3–4 Burke, Sheridan, Flood, Grattan, O'Connell, and Shiel] Edmund Burke (1729–1797), Richard Brinsley Sheridan (1751–1816), Henry Flood (1732–1791), Henry Grattan (1746–1820), and Richard Lalor Sheil (1791–1851). For O'Connell, see note 225.5–6.

233.6–7 the trial of Warren Hastings] Warren Hastings (1732–1818), governor-general of India, 1773–85, was accused of corruption and impeached, but acquitted of all charges in 1795.

234.2–5 "There is no . . . Liberty."] James Gates Percival, "No Land Like Ours."

234.30–31 "Hansom's Patent"] Horse carriage with a low center of gravity that was designed for increased safety and patented by Joseph Hansom (1803–1882).

234.34 Peace Congress.] The first International Peace Conference was held in London in 1843 and hosted by the London Peace Society. Subsequent conferences were held in Brussels (1848), Paris (1849), Frankfurt am Main (1850), London (1851), Manchester (1852), and Edinburgh (1853).

234.34–35 The Sturges . . . the Thomases] Leading families, mostly Quakers, involved in the British antislavery movement and its primary organization, the British and Foreign Anti-Slavery Society, founded by Joseph Sturge in 1839.

237.23 Elihu Burritt] Burritt (1810–1879), American all-purpose reformer who was an organizer of the 1849 Paris Peace Congress, which Brown attended.

237.31 "Ocean Penny Postage"] A proposal to reduce postal rates for ocean transit to a flat rate of one English penny, or two cents.

239.17–18 "*Notre Dame de Paris*"] *The Hunchback of Notre-Dame* (1831).

239.23–25 the President . . . Richard Cobden.] Auguste Visschers, the president of the International Peace Conference held in Brussels in 1848, a lawyer and knight of the Order of Léopold in Belgium; Henry Vincent (1813–1878), a member of the London Working Men's Association and a Chartist leader; Richard Cobden (1804–1865), a British reformer and member of Parliament, 1841–57 and 1859–65.

239.31–32 Mr. Ewart, M. P.] William Ewart (1798–1869), British reformer and member of Parliament, 1828–37 and 1839–68.

242.7 Mrs. C——] Maria Weston Chapman (1806–1885), an abolitionist from Massachusetts then living in France who assisted Brown and his daughters during their years in Europe.

242.28 M. Coquerel] Athanase Laurent Charles Coquerel (1795–1868), Calvinist minister who was a member of the Constituent Assembly, and subsequently of the Legislative Assembly, after the Revolution of 1848.

243.6–7 M. Emile de Girardin, the editor of *La Presse*] Girardin (1802–1881), liberal French journalist and politician, author of *Emile* (1827) and *Almanach de France* (1834).

245.7–8 Edward Miall, editor of the *Nonconformist*.] Miall (1809–1881), a Dissenting minister and later member of Parliament, 1852–57 and 1869–74, and founder of the *Nonconformist*, a newspaper advocating the disestablishment of the Church of England.

246.36 A French army had invaded Rome] On February 9, 1849, a constitutional assembly declared the end of papal temporal rule and the creation of a Roman Republic, under which all religions could be practiced freely. Louis Napoleon, recently elected president of France, sent an army to invade Rome that restored the government of Pope Pius IX in July 1849.

247.9–10 Wendell Phillips] Phillips (1811–1884), a radical abolitionist and lawyer noted for his oratorical skill.

248.2–6 "Man, on . . . COWPER.] William Cowper, *Truth* (1794).

248.23 Madame de Tocqueville] Marie de Tocqueville (1799–1864), born Mary Mottley, English-born wife of Alexis de Tocqueville.

248.30–31 "observed of all observers"] *Hamlet*, III.i.154.

248.33–34 the American Consul, Mr. Walsh.] Robert Walsh (1785–1859), Consul General of the United States in Paris, 1844–51.

250.12–13 the Rev. James Freeman Clarke.] Minister and abolitionist (1810–1888) who helped establish the Unitarian Church of the Disciples in 1841 in Boston.

253.2–6 "Types of . . . CAMPBELL.] Thomas Campbell, "Pledge to the Much Loved Land," originally titled "The Rose, Shamrock, and Thistle" (1809).

254.31 R. D. Webb, Esq.] Richard Davis Webb (1805–1872), Irish publisher and founding member of the Hibernian Anti-Slavery Society.

257.2 Lamartine] Alphonse Marie Louis de Prat de Lamartine (1790–1869).

260.2–10 "The moon . . . SIR WALTER SCOTT.] Walter Scott, *Lay of the Last Minstrel* (1805), Canto II, stanza 11.

260.22–23 Henry G. Chapman] Henry Grafton Chapman (1833–1883), son of Maria Weston Chapman.

260.37–38 Callot's painting of the battle of Marengo] *Allegory of the Battle of Marengo* by Antoine-François Callet (1741–1823).

260.39 Bouchat's of the 18th Brumaire] *Napoleon Bonaparte in the coup d'état of 18 Brumaire in Saint-Cloud* (1840) by François Bouchat (1800–1842).

262.9 Marshal Ney.] Marshal Michel Ney (1769–1815), French military commander during the French Revolution and Napoleonic Wars who joined Napoleon during the Hundred Days and fought at Waterloo; later executed for treason by the Bourbon regime.

263.29–30 M. Beranger, the poet;] Pierre-Jean de Béranger (1780–1857), French Romantic poet and chansonnier.

265.2–6 "There was . . . SOUTHEY.] Robert Southey, *Madoc* (1805).

266.4 John Lee, Esq., LL.D.] Lee (1783–1866), president of the Royal Meteorological Society, 1855–57, and the Royal Astronomical Society, 1861–63.

266.20–27 "United States, . . . Negro-scars"—] Thomas Campbell, "To the United States of America" (1838).

266.37 John Hampden the patriot] John Hampden (c. 1595–1643) died fighting for the parliamentary cause in the English Civil War and was widely celebrated in America, as witnessed by the many place-names in his honor.

269.26 Sir Peter Lely] Dutch painter (1618–1680) who spent most of his career as an English court portraitist.

270.11 the Right Hon. Henry Labouchere.] Henry Labouchere, 1st Baron

Taunton (1798–1869), president of the Board of Trade and Whig member of Parliament, 1826–59.

270.27–28 George Thompson, Esq., M. P.] Prominent abolitionist (1804–1878) and member of Parliament, 1847–52.

275.2–7 "We might . . . MISS MITFORD.] Mary Russell Mitford, "Weston Grove" (1812).

275.36 Baxter] Richard Baxter (1615–1691), English Puritan theologian.

276.16–17 "To be . . . known."] Alexander Pope, *An Essay On Man* (1733–34), Epistle IV, line 260.

278.26 Milton . . . darkness visible.] Cf. John Milton, *Paradise Lost*, I.61–64: "A Dungeon horrible, on all sides round / As one great Furnace flam'd, yet from those flames / No light, but rather darkness visible / Serv'd only to discover sights of woe."

282.2–15 "When I behold, . . . vanitie."] Thomas Bastard, *Chrestoleros: Seven Books of Epigrames* (1598).

283.8 Louis Blanc] French socialist and historian (1811–1882).

283.11 *La Presse*] Penny press newspaper started by Émile de Girardin. See note 243.6–7.

284.14–15 Vicar of Wakefield] Novel (1766) by Oliver Goldsmith (1730–1774).

286.2–3 "Be thou . . . life."] Revelation 2:10.

286.5–10 "Even such . . . days."] Sir Walter Raleigh, "Even Such is Time."

286.20–21 the sword that Peter used.] Cf. John 18:10–11.

287.3 Sir Edward Packenham] Pakenham (1778–1815), an Anglo-Irish army officer who served with his brother-in-law Wellington in the Peninsular War, was killed at the Battle of Orleans (1815), the last major battle of the War of 1812.

288.12–13 Mansfield . . . Wilberforce] William Murray, 1st Earl of Mansfield (1705–1793), Lord Chief Justice, best known for his ruling in *Somersett's Case* (1772) that would eventually result in de facto emancipation in Great Britain; William Pitt, 1st Earl of Chatham (1708–1778), de facto leader of the government, 1756–61, during much of the Seven Years War and prime minister, 1766–68; Charles James Fox (1749–1806), Whig member of Parliament, 1768–74 and 1780–1806, chief opponent of William Pitt the Younger and antislavery campaigner; William Pitt the Younger (1759–1806), prime minister, 1783–1801 and 1804–6, during the French Revolution and the Napoleonic Wars; William Wilberforce (1759–1833), member of Parliament, 1788–1825, instrumental in abolishing the British slave trade. For Grattan, see note 233.3–4.

288.39 Kemble] Charles Kemble (1775–1854), British Shakespearean actor.

289.4–6 "Dante meditating . . . Canto V."] By Scottish artist Sir Joseph Noel Paton (1821–1901).

290.3 Mrs. Siddons] Sarah Siddons (1755–1831), actress famous for her portrayal of Lady Macbeth; sister of Charles Kemble.

291.2–11 To give . . . BARTON.] Bernard Barton, "Leiston Abbey" (1820).

292.18–22 rebellion of Octavius . . . Osbert] Legendary figure Octavius (Eudah Hen), said to be the half brother of Constantine I, staged a rebellion after Constantine left Britain to become emperor. York was then the capital of Britannia Secunda, a province of Roman Britain, and so would have been the site of Octavius's coronation. Oswald (c. 604–642) and Osberht (d. 867) were kings of Northumbria, a medieval kingdom whose capital was York. A long-standing myth held that Richard III (1452–1485) was crowned at York; he was actually crowned at Westminster Abbey. William the Conqueror (1028–1087) marched on York in 1068 to deal with Anglo-Saxon resistance to his rule. York was besieged for three months in 1644 by a parliamentary army in which Oliver Cromwell (1599–1658) served as a cavalry commander.

295.11–12 salt-rheum] Term for skin eruptions such as eczema.

295.29–296.5 "Wanderer, whither . . . alone."] James Montgomery, *The Wanderer of Switzerland: A Poem, in Six Parts* (1806), Part I.

297.2–6 "How changed, . . . KEATS.] Actually from George Keate, *Natley Abbey: An Elegy* (1769).

297.23–31 "Beautiful fabric! . . . dower."] Bernard Barton, "Leiston Abbey" (1820).

298.36 Colonel Wildman] Colonel Thomas Wildman (1787–1859), an officer in the Napoleonic Wars who bought and saved Byron's Newstead Abbey.

299.25–300.10 "Start not— . . . use."] Byron, "Lines Inscribed Upon a Cup Formed From a Skull" (1808).

301.3–28 "When some . . . lies."] Byron, "Epitaph to a Dog" (1808).

303.9–20 "When Time . . . tear."] Byron, "Euthanasia" (1812).

304.2–11 "Now, this . . . BARTON.] Bernard Barton, "Leiston Abbey" (1820).

305.19 Martin the Regicide] Henry Marten (1602–1680), member of Parliament, 1640–43 and 1646–53, one of the fifty-nine commissioners at the trial that sentenced Charles I to death.

306.15–21 "O ye . . . violation!"] Nicholas Toms Carrington, *Dartmoor* (1826).

307.3–7 "The cloud-capped . . . behind."] *The Tempest*, IV.i.152–56.

307.16 Rowley, . . . Chatterton] Thomas Rowley was the pen name of poet Thomas Chatterton (1752–1770), whose uncle was the sexton of St. Mary

Radcliffe. William II Canynges (c. 1399–1474) was a wealthy British merchant who completed work on the interior of St. Mary and is buried there. His epitaph inspired Chatterton to write "The Storie of William Canynge."

309.16–17 Holloway's pills and Mrs. Kidder's cordial.] Patent medicines advertised as panaceas.

309.33 C——] William Craft. See note 153.4–5.

311.14–15 Sir Wm. Douglas] Sir William Douglas, Lord of Liddesdale (c. 1300–1353), military leader during the Second War of Scottish Independence.

313.2–6 "I was . . . WORDSWORTH.] William Wordsworth, "Resolution and Independence" (1807).

314.21–22 Cincinnatus . . . farm] After being chosen by the Roman Senate as dictator to fight a war against the Aequi, Cincinnatus was summoned to Rome by a group of senators who found him at his plow. He resigned his dictatorship at the end of the war and returned to his farm.

317.2–8 "Proud relic . . . KEATS.] The actual source is Lucy Aikin, *Epistles on Women* (1810).

317.27–32 The author . . . gray."] Walter Scott, "The Lay of the Last Minstrel," Canto II.

321.33 Mrs. Hemans] Felicia Hemans (1793–1835), English poet.

321.36 the authoress of "Society in America."] Harriet Martineau (1802–1876), progressive English writer on economics, social theory, and abolition.

323.2–8 "Why weeps . . . COWPER.] William Cowper, "Expostulation," *Poems* (1782).

327.4 Whitfield] James Monroe Whitfield (1822–1871), an African American poet known to Brown from Buffalo, New York, whose work appeared in Garrison's *Liberator* and Douglass's *North Star*.

327.17 looked "upon the wine when it was red,"] See Proverbs 23:31.

329.19 "bounding away . . . age,"] Washington Irving, "Rural Life in England," *The Sketch Book of Geoffrey Crayon, Gent.* (1819–20).

331.2–5 "And there . . . Hindoos."] Byron, "Beppo" (1817).

331.14 "horn of Astolpho."] In Ludovico Ariosto's *Orlando Furioso*, the blast of the warrior Astolpho's horn causes all enemies to flee.

333.5 "Greek Slave"] Sculpture (1844) by American artist Hiram Powers (1805–1873).

333.11–13 Virginius . . . Appius Claudius.] According to the Roman historian Livy, the centurion Virginius stabbed his daughter Virginia to death to protect her from the lust of the *decimvir* (magistrate) Appius Claudius, who had falsely declared her a slave. The painting described is *Virginius and His Daughter* by Irish artist Patrick MacDowell (1799–1870).

334.10 "Veiled Vestal,"] By Raffaelo Monti (1818–1881), an Italian sculptor who settled in London in 1848.

337.2–8 "The time . . . POPE.] Alexander Pope, "Windsor-Forest" (1713).

337.38 Burritt's Brotherhood Bazaar] Elihu Burritt's (see note 237.23) Free-Labor Bazaar raised funds for the League of Universal Brotherhood, a pacifist society.

341.2–6 "And gray . . . SHELLEY.] Percy Bysshe Shelley, *Adonais* (1821).

343.10 Bishop of Oxford] Samuel Wilberforce (1805–1873), third son of William Wilberforce (see note 288.12–13).

343.17 the Rev. Dr. Pusey] Edward Bouverie Pusey (1800–1882), for fifty years Regius Professor of Hebrew at Oxford and a leader of the Oxford Movement in which High Church Anglicans revived ancient Christian traditions and incorporated them into the Anglican liturgy.

344.26 Soulouque] Faustin-Élie Soulouque (1782–1867), general in the Haitian army who in 1847 was elected president of Haiti and in 1849 declared himself emperor. He was deposed in 1859 and lived in exile in Jamaica thereafter.

346.2–9 "Blush ye . . . ROSCOE.] *The Wrongs of Africa* (1787–88), Part I.

346.13–15 a distinguished . . . chains."] Friedrich Schiller, "The Words of Faith" (1797).

347.9 Chapmans and Westons] For Chapman, see note 242.7. Three of her younger sisters, Caroline, Anne, and Deborah Weston, were also involved in the antislavery movement.

347.9–10 Estlins] John Bishop Estlin (1785–1855), a noted eye surgeon, and his daughter Mary Anne Estlin (1820–1902), antislavery activists in Bristol, England.

347.18–19 newly-appointed Poet Laureate.] Alfred Tennyson (1809–1892).

350.7 Rev. Edward Matthews] Mathews (1812–?), a Baptist missionary, had nearly been lynched in Kentucky in 1850 for antislavery speeches. Harriet Beecher Stowe used him as the model for Father Dickson in her novel *Dred* (1856).

351.2–5 "For 't . . . SHAKSPEARE.] *The Taming of the Shrew*, IV.iii.172–74.

351.22 Sir Thomas Lucy's deer] According to popular legend, Shakespeare was prosecuted for poaching deer from the park of local knight Sir Thomas Lucy.

351.36–352.2 Garrick . . . head."] David Garrick, "Thou Soft-flowing Avon" (1769).

352.22 Carlyle's Life of Stirling] *The Life of John Sterling* (1851).

354.19 Theodore Parker] Parker (1810–1860), radical Unitarian minister, abolitionist, and Transcendentalist.

355.2–7 "Proud pile! . . . tale."] Lucy Aikin, "Ode to Ludlow Castle," *Epistles on Women* (1810).

356.37 Samuel Butler] English poet (1613–1680).

357.6–8 "The Muse, . . . song."] Lucy Aikin, "Ode to Ludlow Castle."

359.24 the poet Phillips] John Philips (1676–1709).

359.33 David Garrick] Garrick (1717–1779), English actor and manager of the Theatre Royal, Drury Lane.

362.2–8 "To him . . . DENHAM.] John Denham, "On Mr. Abraham Cowley his Death and Burial amongst the Ancient Poets" (1667).

362.9–10 "Essay on . . . Lock,"] Poems by Alexander Pope.

363.30 Cowley] Abraham Cowley (1618–1667), English poet.

364.22–35 "Thou who . . . poor."] Pope, "On His Grotto at Twickenham" (1740).

365.17–23 "To look . . . right."] Pope, *Essay on Man* (1732–34).

365.29–32 "Curst . . . tear!"] Pope, *Epistle to Dr. Arbuthnot* (1735).

365.36–366.2 "Ask you . . . yours."] Pope, *Epilogue to Satires* (1738).

367.2–6 "This modest . . . POPE.] From an epitaph Pope wrote on the wall of St. Michael and St. Mary Magdalene Church, Easthampstead, for English poet Elijah Fenton (1683–1730).

367.18–19 Thom . . . Johnny,"] Scottish sculptor James Thom (1802–1850).

372.2–7 "If thou . . . LONGFELLOW.] "Sunrise on the Hills" (1840).

374.20 Meg Merrilies] Gypsy woman in Walter Scott's novel *Guy Mannering* (1815) who leads one of the central characters to a smuggler's cave.

374.23 Rob Roy.] Rob Roy MacGregor (1671–1734), a folk hero and outlaw, and the subject of Walter Scott's novel *Rob Roy* (1817).

375.6–7 "Passing we . . . glass."] George Crabbe, *Posthumous Tales* (1834).

376.2–8 "The treasures . . . MIDDLETON.] Thomas Middleton, *Women Beware Women*, III.i.84–89 (1621).

378.2–6 "To where . . . THOMSON.] James Thomson, *Spring* (1728).

379.19–24 "There was . . . dare."] From an anonymously published poem, "The Slave Ship," sometimes attributed to Thomas Pringle (1789–1834).

380.38 George Combe, Esq.] Combe (1788–1858), founder of the Edinburgh Phrenological Society in 1820.

382.2–3 "Look here, . . . HAMLET.] *Hamlet*, III.iv.53.

382.27 "African Roscius,"] Ira Frederick Aldridge (1807–1867), African American actor known for his Shakespearean roles, especially Othello.

382.29 Madames Sontag and Grisi] Henriette, Countess Rossi (1806–1854), born Gertrude Walpurgis Sontag, and Giulia Grisi (1811–1869), opera singers.

382.30 Macready] William Charles Macready (1793–1873), English Shakespearean actor and manager of the Covent Garden (1837–39) and Drury Lane (1841–43) Theatres.

383.9–11 Ward, . . . Remond.] Samuel Ringgold Ward (1817–c. 1866), author of *Autobiography of a Fugitive Negro: his Anti-Slavery Labours in the United States, Canada and England* (1855); Henry Highland Garnet (1815–1882), African American minister and advocate of militant abolitionism; Martin Robison Delany (1812–1885), African American doctor, writer, African explorer, and major in the U.S. Army during the Civil War; Charles Lenox Remond (1810–1873), lecturer and recruiter for the 54th and 55th Massachusetts Infantry.

383.24–29 "O, cursed, . . . O! O! O!"—] *Othello*, V.ii.276–82.

387.2–6 "Farewell! . . . THOMAS HOOD.] Thomas Hood, "To an Absentee" (1822).

387.13 Eliza Cook] English poet (1818–1889) associated with the Chartist movement.

387.16 Mrs. Balfour] Clara Lucas Balfour (1808–1878), English author and temperance campaigner. Harriet Beecher Stowe wrote the preface to Balfour's *Morning Dew Drops* (1853).

387.19–23 Murdo Young, . . . Horace Mayhew] Murdo Young (1790–1870), editor and proprietor of London newspaper *The Sun*; George Cruikshank (1792–1878), British illustrator of Charles Dickens's works; Horace Mayhew (1816–1872), author of *London Labour and the London Poor* (1851).

387.25–26 R. Monckton Milnes, Esq.] Richard Monckton Milnes (1809–1885), poet and member of Parliament, 1837–63.

387.28–29 Mr. Matthew Noble] Matthew Noble (1818–1876), sculptor.

391.2–6 "Dull rogues . . . CONGREVE.] William Congreve, "Of Pleasing: An Epistle to Sir Richard Temple."

391.15 Alexander Hastie] Scottish antislavery activist (1805–1864), member of Parliament, 1847–57, and Lord Provost of Glasgow, 1846–48.

391.22 Layard] Sir Austen Henry Layard (1817–1894), English archaeologist who excavated the ancient Assyrian city of Nimrud.

391.31 Joseph Hume.] Scottish doctor (1777–1855) and member of Parliament, 1812 and 1818–55.

392.17–18 Thomas Crawford] William Sharman Crawford (1781–1861), member of Parliament for Dundalk, 1835–37, and for Rochdale, 1841–52.

392.27 William Johnson Fox.] Unitarian minister (1786–1864) and editor of *Monthly Repository.*

393.26 the Rev. R. Montgomery.] Robert Montgomery (1807–1855).

393.32 Joseph Brotherton] Brotherton (1783–1857) was a member of Parliament, 1832–57.

394.7 Samuel Morton Peto.] Civil engineer (1809–1889) responsible for the construction of the Houses of Parliament, and member of Parliament, 1847–54 and 1859–68.

394.14 John Bright] Bright (1811–1889) was a founder of the Anti-Corn Law League and a prominent reformer who was a member of Parliament, 1843–89.

395.32 Lord Dudley Cutts Stuart . . . Mr. Ewart.] Lord Dudley Coutts Stuart (1803–1854), member of Parliament, 1830–37 and 1847–54. For Ewart, see note 239.31–32.

396.24 Sir Joshua Walmesley.] Walmsley (1794–1871), Liberal member of Parliament, 1849–57, and founder of the National Reform Association.

396.33 James N. Buffum] Buffum (1807–1887), a Massachusetts abolitionist, accompanied Frederick Douglass on his tour of the British Isles in 1845.

396.38–39 "For modes . . . right."] Alexander Pope, *Essay on Man* (1733–34), Epistle III.

398.3–6 "His words . . . knew."] Oliver Goldsmith, "The Deserted Village" (1770).

398.16 Rev. John Cumming, D.D.] Cumming (1807–1881), Scottish clergyman.

398.32–33 Washington Wilks, Esq.] Wilks (c. 1825–1864), editor of the *London Star.*

400.2–5 "Take the spade . . . aside."] Charles Swain, "Perseverance."

400.18 Francis W. Kellogg] Kellogg (1810–1879), Republican congressman from Michigan, 1859–65, and from Alabama, 1868–69.

400.27 C. C. Burleigh.] Charles Calistus Burleigh (1810–1878), American journalist and abolitionist.

401.16 Kossuth] Lajos Kossuth (1802–1894), leader in the Hungarian Revolution in 1848, denounced by American abolitionists for his refusal to criticize slavery during his tour of the United States in 1851–52.

402.18–19 wide-awake . . . billy-cock.] A bowler.

402.37–40 H. C—? . . . "L. P. and H. of F."] Henry Clapp Jr. (1814–1875) of Massachusetts, editor of the *Lynn Pioneer* and *Herald of Freedom* in the 1840s.

405.2–6 "——when . . . BYRON.] Byron, "To Florence" (1809).

411.24 John Mitchell] Irish nationalist and political journalist John Mitchel (1815–1875) was arrested in 1848 and later found guilty of treason. He was transported to Van Dieman's Land (Tasmania), escaped in 1853, and settled in the United States, where he became an outspoken defender of slavery.

THE ESCAPE; OR, A LEAP FOR FREEDOM

413.7 "Look on . . . HAMLET.] *Hamlet*, III.iv.53.

419.33 bread pills. . . . tater pills] Placebos.

428.9–10 "While the lamp . . . return."] Isaac Watts, *Hymns and Spiritual Songs* (1707), Book I, Hymn 88.

437.20 Lorenzo Dow] American itinerant preacher (1777–1834).

439.22 AIR—"*Dandy Jim.*"] "A Song for Freedom," published in Brown's *Anti-Slavery Harp* (1848).

455.11–457.3 "Star of . . . o'er it!"] John Pierpont, "The Fugitive Slave's Apostrophe to the North Star" (1839).

457.27 AIR—"*Dearest Mae.*"] "The Slave's Song," published in Brown's *Anti-Slavery Harp* (1848).

464.18 Sam Patch] Patch (1799–1829), a daredevil who successfully jumped from a platform 118 feet about the Niagara River below the falls on October 17, 1829. He died later that year on November 13 jumping into the Genesee River gorge below the falls in Rochester, New York.

THE BLACK MAN

473.11–12 now that the blacks . . . country] *The Black Man* was published after Lincoln issued the Preliminary Emancipation Proclamation on September 22, 1862, but before he signed the final Proclamation on January 1, 1863.

473.21–23 Mr. Postmaster General Blair . . . March last] Montgomery Blair (1813–1883) served in Lincoln's cabinet from March 1861 to September 1864.

474.12 Alexander H. Everett] Everett (1792–1847), American author, politician, and U.S. minister to the Netherlands and Spain. In an address delivered to the Massachusetts Colonization Society in 1833, Everett said: "See what the blacks were and what they did three thousand years ago, in the period of their greatness and glory, when they occupied the forefront in the march of civilization—when they constituted in fact the whole civilized world of their time."

474.13 Volney] Constantin François de Chassebœuf, Comte de Volney

(1757–1820), French philosopher and historian, author of *The Ruins, or Meditations on the Revolutions of Empires* (1791).

474.18 "Can the Ethiopian change his skin?"] Jeremiah 13:23.

474.34–36 "When the Britons . . . Islanders."] See Thomas Macaulay, *The History of England from the Ascension of James the Second* (1848), volume 1, chapter 1.

474.37–38 Hume says . . . beasts.] In David Hume, *The History of England* (1754–61).

475.3 Caractacus] Tribal chieftain identified by Roman historians as a leader of resistance to Roman conquest in the first century C.E.

475.4 Hengist and Horsa] Legendary Anglo-Saxon conquerors of Britain in the fifth century C.E.

476.36 Hon. Edward Everett] Everett (1794–1865), American author, educator, and statesman.

477.39–40 Parliament had passed the act of emancipation.] The Slavery Abolition Act of 1833.

481.2–3 Southern Rights Convention] A convention of Maryland slaveholders met in Baltimore on June 8, 1859, to adopt measures aimed at the state's free black population. In 1860 the Democratic National Convention met in Baltimore on June 18. After it nominated Stephen A. Douglas for president, southern delegates held a second convention that met in Baltimore on June 28 and nominated John C. Breckinridge.

481.7–8 Judge Mason] John Thomson Mason (1815–1873), a former judge of the Maryland Court of Appeals and a delegate to the 1859 Baltimore slaveholders convention.

481.10–11 Judge Catron] John Catron (1786–1865), Supreme Court justice, 1837–65.

482.11 *De mortuis nil nisi bonum.*] Latin: literally, "of the dead, nothing unless good"; usually translated as "speak only good of the dead."

482.24–28 "Who steals . . . indeed."] *Othello*, III.iii.155–61.

482.32 Mr. Toombs] Robert Augustus Toombs (1810–1885), U.S. representative and senator from Georgia who later served the Confederacy as secretary of state and as a general.

484.10–13 "O, tell . . . that."] A. B., "A Parody on 'A Man's A Man For A' That'."

486.17–18 the president's first proclamation, calling for troops.] Lincoln called for 75,000 troops after the fall of Fort Sumter in April 1861, but blacks were not allowed to serve at that time.

487.24 Mayer's Tables, . . . Lunar Tables.] Eighteenth-century astronomical guides: the *Lunar Tables* of Tobias Mayer, *Astronomy Explained Upon Sir Isaac Newton's Principles* by James Ferguson, and Charles Leadbeaters's *Lunar Tables.*

489.37–38 as Job proposed . . . stead.'] Cf. Job 16:4.

490.21 Monsieur de Condorcet] Antoine Nicolas de Caritat, Marquis de Condorcet (1743–1794), French mathematician and philosopher, author of the political treatise *Historical Tableau of the Progress of the Human Spirit.*

490.36 "Society of the Friends of the Blacks,"] French abolitionist group led by Jacques-Pierre Brissot (1754–1793).

490.36–37 Barnave . . . Grégoire] Antoine Pierre Joseph Marie Barnave (1761–1793); Henri Grégoire.

491.2 Buxton] Sir Thomas Fowell Buxton (1786–1845), English antislavery parliamentarian.

494.33–35 he who knoweth . . . stripes."] Cf. Luke 12:47.

495.9–10 the first . . . first."] Cf. Matthew 19:30.

496.34 his confession] Published in Thomas R. Gray, *The Confessions of Nat Turner, The Leader of the Late Insurrection in Southampton, Va.* (1831).

502.38–503.6 "Great God, . . . free!'"] Frederick Douglass, "The Fugitive's Song," published in Brown's *Anti-Slavery Harp* (1848).

509.28–30 "They spake . . . pale."] *Richard III*, III.vii.24–26.

512.27 Mary E. Miles] Miles (1820–1877), teacher and antislavery activist who married Henry Bibb in June 1848.

512.37 one of Cassimir de la Vigne's dramas] Jean-François Casimir Delavigne (1793–1843), popular French dramatist; the play to which Brown alludes is *Don John of Austria* (1835).

516.10–13 "Honor and fame . . . no more."] Pope, *Essay on Man,* Epistle IV.

516.22–25 "Neither men . . . places."] George Wallace, *A System of the Principles of the Law of Scotland* (1760).

517.21 Sharp . . . Clarkson] Granville Sharp (1735–1813), advocate of black colonization in Sierra Leone; Thomas Clarkson (1760–1846), cofounder of the Society for Effecting the Abolition of the Slave Trade.

517.26 oath of the Tennis Court] On June 20, 1789, at Versailles, the deputies of the Third Estate, locked out of their regular meeting place after breaking with the Estates General and pronouncing themselves the National Assembly, convened on the Jeu de Paume, an indoor tennis court, in defiance of Louis

XVI's order to disperse. There they took an oath pledging not to disband until a new French constitution had been adopted.

518.13 Constitutional Assembly] The National Constituent Assembly was formed by the French National Assembly on July 9, 1789. It dissolved on September 30, 1791, and was replaced by the Legislative Assembly.

518.14 Vincent Ogé] Jacques Vincent Ogé (1755–1791), a wealthy free man of color, helped instigate a revolt in Saint-Domingue that lasted from October to December of 1790; he was executed at Cap-Français after the uprising failed.

522.1 peace of Amiens] Signed in March 1802, the Treaty of Amiens marked a temporary peace between France and Great Britain during the French Revolutionary and Napoleonic Wars; hostilities were resumed in May 1803.

522.14–15 siege of Toulon . . . Egypt] At the siege of Toulon, September–December 1793, a Republican army defeated the royalist forces holding the city. At the Battle of the Pyramids, July 21, 1798, the French army under Napoleon defeated Egyptian forces.

522.21 Christophe] Henri Christophe (1767–1820), former slave who was a leader of the Haitian Revolution (1791–1804); in 1811 he established a kingdom in northern Haiti, proclaiming himself Henry I.

522.22 Dessalines] Jean-Jacques Dessalines (1758–1806), leader of the Haitian Revolution who became first ruler of independent Haiti, proclaiming himself Emperor Jacques I in 1804.

526.35–36 Lord Camden] Charles Pratt, 1st Earl Camden (1714–1794).

527.28 William C. Nell, Esq.] Nell (1816–1874), a black activist and reformer from Boston, wrote for Garrison's *Liberator* and Douglass's *North Star*. His *The Colored Patriots of the American Revolution* (1855) was a pioneering work of African American history.

528.7–8 Captain Preston] Thomas Preston (1722–1798) stood trial for his role in the "Boston Massacre" but was acquitted.

529.4–7 Redbank . . . Colonel Greene fell at Groton] Christopher Greene (1737–1781) commanded white Rhode Island troops in the fighting against the Hessians at Fort Mercer on the Delaware River in November 1777. Greene then became the commander of the 1st Rhode Island, a regiment that contained a substantial number of black soldiers, and led it until he was killed in a Loyalist cavalry raid near the Croton River in Westchester County, New York, in May 1781, and not, as Brown states, in the Battle of Groton Heights in September 1781.

530.19 Rochambeau] Donatien-Marie-Joseph de Vimeur, Vicomte de Rochambeau (1755–1813), led the French expeditionary force to suppress the rebellion in Saint-Domingue; he was defeated, surrendering to Jean-Jacques Dessalines in November 1803.

535.33–536.1 "Villain! . . . wrath,"] *Othello*, III.iii.359–63.

536.11–12 "'Tis not . . . mother,"] *Hamlet*, I.ii.77.

536.20 "I pray . . . fellow-student,"] *Hamlet*, I.ii.177.

536.24 "Angels and . . . us,"] *Hamlet*, I.iv.39.

536.26–27 "Soliloquy on Death,"] The soliloquy beginning "To be or not to be," *Hamlet*, III.i.55–89. Modern editions place the speech in Act III, scene i, following the First Folio of 1616, but it seems likely from Brown's account that Aldridge's production placed the speech in Act II, scene ii, its placement in the Quarto 1 version of the play.

536.27 Edmund Kean] Edmund Kean (1787–1833), English Shakespearean actor.

536.29–30 Charles Kean] Son (1811–1868) of actor Edmund Kean.

536.36 "Frailty, thy name is woman!"] *Hamlet*, I.ii.146.

536.40–537.5 "This most . . . God!"] *Hamlet*, II.ii.299–307.

537.9–11 "He would . . . free,"] *Hamlet*, II.ii.562–64.

537.13–14 "Bloody, bawdy . . . villain!"] *Hamlet*, II.ii.580–81.

537.22 a native of Senegal] Aldridge was actually born in New York City. Brown was misled by claims Aldridge had made in an autobiographical sketch.

537.36 Schenectady College] Founded in 1790; now Union College.

539.5 Sandford] Sir Daniel Keyte Sandford (1798–1838), professor of Greek at the University of Glasgow, 1821–38.

540.15 Captain Gedney] U.S. Navy lieutenant Thomas R. Gedney (d. 1857).

542.20–21 Lewis Tappan, in the account] Tappan (1788–1873), a New York businessman and antislavery activist, was a cofounder with William Lloyd Garrison of the American Anti-Slavery Society. He helped secure funding and lawyers to aid the enslaved Africans of the *Amistad*.

542.32 M. Eugene Sue] Sue (1804–1857) was the author of many popular novels, including *The Mysteries of Paris* (1842–43) and *The Wandering Jew* (1844–45).

543.3–4 Mario, in Norma] Giovanni Matteo De Candia (1810–1883), known as Mario, Italian tenor. *Norma* (1831), opera by Vincenzo Bellini.

543.28 Marquis de la Pailleterie] Marquis Alexandre Antoine Davy de la Pailleterie (1714–1786).

543.30–31 Rainsford . . . *Black Empire*] Marcus Rainsford, *An Historical Account of the Black Empire of Hayti* (1805).

543.32 Dumas' father] Thomas-Alexandre Davy de la Pailleterie (1762–1806), also known as Thomas-Alexandre Dumas, was a military commander in the French Revolutionary War and under Napoleon.

543.40 Marshal Macdonald] Jacques MacDonald (1765–1840), a marshal of France under Napoleon.

544.20–22 he is not the author . . . situations] Auguste Maquet (1813–1888) played a major role in researching and plotting some of Dumas's historical novels.

546.19 Pétion] Alexandre Sabès Pétion (1770–1818), first president of the Republic of Haiti, from 1807 until his death.

547.14 Rigaud] Benoît Joseph André Rigaud (1761–1811), a military leader during the Haitian Revolution.

549.23–24 In one respect he excelled Charlemagne] According to his biographer Einhard, the great king had "tried to learn to write . . . but although he tried very hard, he had begun too late in life and made little progress."

549.34 Mrs. John Wheatley] Susanna Wheatley (d. 1774).

550.26 translated one of Ovid's tales] "Niobe in Distress for Her Children Slain by Apollo, from Ovid's Metamorphoses, Book VI and from a View of the Painting of Mr. Richard Wilson."

550.28–29 a small volume . . . was published] *Poems on Various Subjects, Religious and Moral* (1773).

550.30 Countess of Huntingdon.] Selina Hastings, Countess of Huntingdon (1707–1791), Methodist leader and literary patron.

551.4 Dr. Peters] Wheatley married John Peters, a free black grocer, on April 1, 1778.

554.20 Governor Bennett's] Thomas Bennett Jr. (1781–1865), governor of South Carolina, 1820–22.

556.20–21 Hercules and the Wagoner,'] Fable attributed to Aesop in which a farmer's cart falls into a ravine and he asks Hercules for help; Hercules appears and advises him to put his shoulder to the wheel first. The story is often associated with the proverb "God helps those who help themselves."

557.18 Canaan Academy] The Noyes Academy in Canaan, New Hampshire, was established in 1835 to provide education for both white and black students; within months of its opening it was demolished by a mob from Canaan and nearby towns.

557.21 Oneida Institute] Presbyterian school founded in 1827 in Whitestown, New York; under the presidency (1833–44) of abolitionist Beriah Green (1795–1874), its students included Henry Highland Garnet and Alexander Crummell.

558.11–12 Shiloh Church] Shiloh Presbyterian Church, founded by Samuel Cornish in 1822.

558.19–559.15 "The woful . . . God."] From *Past and the Present Condition, and the Destiny, of the Colored Race: A Discourse Delivered at the Fifteenth Anniversary of the Female Benevolent Society* (1848).

559.28–560.28 "How long, . . . name."] From "How Long," in *Autographs for Freedom* (1853).

562.19–20 like Saturn, devoured its own children] According to Roman mythology, Saturn devoured all his children at birth to avert his prophesied overthrow by one of them.

564.4 screw his courage up to the sticking-point] Cf. *Macbeth*, I.vii.60.

568.35–36 neither would . . . dead] Cf. Luke 16:31.

571.12 'Time writes not its wrinkles on our brow;'] From *God's Image in Ebony: Being a Series of Biographical Sketches, Facts, Anecdotes, etc.*, ed. H. G. Adams (1854).

575.13 General Boyer.] Jean-Pierre Boyer (c. 1776–1850), a leader in the Haitian Revolution, and president of Haiti, 1818–43.

575.30–31 Frederick Douglass . . . his paper] The *North Star*, founded by Douglass in Rochester, New York, in December 1847, ran until June 1851, when it merged with the Syracuse-based *Liberty Party Paper* to form *Frederick Douglass' Paper.*

575.36–576.1 Professor Campbell . . . Expedition"] Robert Campbell (b. 1829), African American teacher at the Institute of Colored Youth in Philadelphia and an abolitionist who advocated the emigration of free blacks to Africa, participated with Martin Delany in the Niger Valley Exploring Party (1859–60), which negotiated settlement rights with Egba tribesmen in Abeokuta (present-day Nigeria), although no settlements were ultimately established. He later settled in Lagos, where he founded and edited the *Anglo-African Weekly.*

576.13 International Statistical Congress] Nine international statistical congresses were held in various European cities from 1853 to 1876.

576.15 Hon. Mr. Dallas] George Mifflin Dallas (1792–1864), vice president of the United States, 1845–49, and U.S. minister to Great Britain, 1856–61. At the opening session of the International Statistical Congress in 1860 and in the presence of Prince Albert, Dallas pointedly snubbed Martin Delany when the latter, a participant in the congress, was pointed out to him by Lord Brougham. Delany was quoted as having responded: "I pray your Royal Highness will allow me to thank his lordship, who is always a most unflinching friend of the negro, for the observation he has made, and I assure your Royal Highness and his lordship that I also am a man."

578.11–12 Commodore Dupont's] Samuel Francis Du Pont (1803–1865), U.S. naval commander in the Mexican-American War and the Civil War.

578.37 Brigadier General Ripley] Roswell Sabine Ripley (1823–1887).

581.23 "Slaveholder's Sermon"] In his addresses of the 1840s and '50s Douglass often mocked pro-slavery sermons delivered by southern preachers. *The Liberator* remarked of one such oration (November 4, 1842): "He evinced great imitative powers, in an exhibition of their style of preaching to the slaves . . . His graphic mimicry of Southern priestly whining and sophistry was replete with humor and apparent truth."

589.11 Charlotte L. Forten] Charlotte Forten Grimké (1837–1914), poet, teacher, and antislavery activist.

589.20 James Forten] Forten (1766–1842), African American businessman and abolitionist allied with William Lloyd Garrison.

589.22–24 "'Tis the mind . . . habit."] *The Taming of the Shrew*, IV.iii. 169–171.

590.24–27 'Our witches . . . features.'] John Greenleaf Whittier, "Extract from 'A New England Legend'" (1833).

591.4–5 'entranced in silent awe,'] James Challen, "The Angels' Mission," *The Cave of Machpelach* (1854).

591.19 "looks on nature with a poet's eye."] Rufus Dawes, "The True Poet" (1842).

592.1–2 Miss Landon] Letitia Elizabeth Landon (1802–1838), author of *The Fate of Adelaide* (1821), *The Improvisatrice* (1824), and other works. She died, possibly a suicide, several months after marrying the governor of Cape Coast Castle in present-day Ghana.

595.6 J. P. Kemble] John Philip Kemble (1757–1823), English actor, brother of Sarah Siddons (see note 290.3) and Charles Kemble (see note 288.39).

595.17 John T. Hilton] Hilton (1801–1864) was an African American community leader from Boston who helped found the Massachusetts General Colored Association and became vice president of the Massachusetts Anti-Slavery Society in 1854.

595.25 Hon. Charles Sumner] Sumner (1811–1874), antislavery U.S. senator from Massachusetts, 1851–74. He was severely beaten on the Senate floor by Representative Preston Brooks of South Carolina on May 22, 1856.

596.19–26 "Would you . . . canoe."] Sarah Bolton, "Paddle Your Own Canoe" (1854).

600.31–33 President Lincoln's . . . Washington] The widely publicized meeting President Lincoln hosted at the White House with a group of black leaders from the District of Columbia on August 14, 1862, to enlist their support for colonizing blacks in Central America, infuriated Brown.

600.34–35 Mr. Pomeroy's address to the free blacks] Samuel Pomeroy's address to the "Free Colored People of the United States," printed on August 26, 1862, in which Pomeroy (1816–1891), a Republican senator from Kansas, tried to enlist one hundred black families for a planned settlement in Central America.

602.11 chaff before the whirlwind.] Cf. Isaiah 17:13.

608.25–28 "Upward, onward, . . . all."] John Howard Bryant, "Upward! Onward!"

608.30 Anthony Burns.] Burns (1834–1862), a fugitive slave from Virginia, was arrested in Boston on May 24, 1854. On May 26 a special guard hired by the U.S. marshal was killed when a crowd stormed the courthouse in an unsuccessful rescue attempt. Burns was subsequently taken on board a federal revenue cutter as 1,500 militiamen and marines stood guard. After his manumission was purchased by sympathizers in Boston, Burns attended Oberlin College and became a Baptist minister in Canada.

609.28 General Riche] Jean-Baptiste Riché (1780–1847), president of Haiti, 1846–47.

612.17–19 as Dryden said . . . there."] From *Of Dramatic Poesy: An Essay* (1668).

614.20 Ellis Gray Loring, Esq.] Loring (1803–1858), lawyer and an organizer of the New England Anti-Slavery Society in 1831.

615.27 the glorious old hero] John Brown (1800–1859), leader of the unsuccessful 1859 assault on the federal arsenal at Harpers Ferry for which he was speedily tried, convicted, and executed.

616.18–19 the poet writes, . . . purse."] *Othello*, I.iii.334–81.

616.21–22 the *Anglo-African Magazine*, and the *Weekly Anglo-African*] Black periodicals founded in New York City by Thomas Hamilton in 1859.

620.20–21 Sheridan . . . Vergniaud] Richard Brinsley Sheridan (1751–1816); Pierre Victurnien Vergniaud (1753–1793).

622.5 Francis Jackson] Jackson (1789–1861), Boston abolitionist leader and businessman, associated with the Massachusetts Anti-Slavery Society.

625.20 Mr. H. Ford Douglass] Douglas (1831–1865) escaped from slavery and became a proponent of black emigration in the 1850s. During the Civil War he raised and commanded a company of the 10th Louisiana Infantry (African Descent).

626.28 Mr. Kalloch] Isaac Smith Kalloch (1832–1887), Baptist preacher.

627.26 "World's Anti-Slavery Convention,"] Historic international convention, organized by the British and Foreign Anti-Slavery Society, took place June 12–23, 1840, in London. Its exclusion of women caused lasting animosity within the antislavery movement.

628.30 Count D'Orsay] Alfred d'Orsay (1801–1852).

630.20 Dr. Nehemiah Adams] Adams (1806–1878), Congregationalist minister in Boston who argued in *A South-Side View of Slavery* (1854) that slavery was beneficial to the religious character of African Americans.

630.22 a hissing and a by-word] Cf. Jeremiah 29:18.

634.10–11 Mr. Hayne . . . Hayne the orator.] The poet Paul Hamilton Hayne (1830–1886) was raised in the home of his uncle, Robert Young Hayne (1791–1834), South Carolina senator and governor.

635.3–4 Hon. S. C. Pomeroy] See note 600.34–35.

635.22 Mr. Roebuck] John Arthur Roebuck (1802–1879), a reformer and member of Parliament, 1832–37, 1841–47, 1849–68, and 1874–79.

636.31–32 'God has made . . . earth.'] See Acts 17:26.

637.12 "Look here, . . . HAMLET.] *Hamlet*, III.iv.53.

638.1 "African Talma,"] François Joseph Talma (1763–1826), French actor.

638.36–639.2 "O, cursed, . . . O! O! O!"—] *Othello*, V.ii.276–82.

641.33–36 'Upward, onward, . . . still.'"] Cf. John H. Bryant, "Upward! Onward!"

643.9 Mr. Cass] Lewis Cass (1782–1866).

643.13 Professor Nélaton] Auguste Nélaton (1807–1873).

647.18 gutta percha canes."] A cane made from gutta-percha was used by Preston Brooks in his attack on Charles Sumner in the Senate chamber in May 1856.

647.19 N. P. Banks] Nathaniel Prentice Banks (1816–1894) of Massachusetts was elected speaker in February 1856 by a coalition of antislavery congressmen from several parties.

648.26 Penningtons] James Pennington (1807–1870) escaped from slavery in Maryland to become a prominent Presbyterian minister and abolitionist; he served, along with Brown, in the U.S. delegation at the 1849 Paris Peace Congress. His memoir *The Fugitive Blacksmith* was published in 1849.

650.15 Hannibal] Abram Petrovich Gannibal (1696–1781), a kidnapped African who became a prominent military and political figure at the court of Peter the Great; his great-grandson Alexander Pushkin wrote an account of his life, *The Negro of Peter the Great* (1828).

650.19 Anthony William Amo] Anton Wilhelm Amo (1703–c. 1759), a native of Axim (present-day Ghana), received a doctorate from the University of Wittenberg in 1734; he became a professor of philosophy and published works, including *Treatise on the Art of Philosophizing Soberly and Accurately* (1738), before returning to Africa.

650.21 James J. Capetein] Jacobus Elisa Johannes Capitein (1717–1747), born in present-day Ghana, was ordained as a minister in the Dutch Reformed Church and returned to Africa as a missionary.

650.23 James Derham] Derham (c. 1757–c. 1802), born in slavery in Philadelphia, was taught medicine by one of his owners, purchased his freedom, and thereafter opened a medical practice.

650.26 Dr. Rush] Benjamin Rush (1746–1813) wrote in a letter to the Pennsylvania Abolition Society on November 14, 1788: "I have conversed with him upon most of the acute and epidemic diseases of the country where he lives, and was pleased to find him perfectly acquainted with the modern simple mode of practice in those diseases. I expected to have suggested some new medicines to him, but he suggested many more to me."

650.30 Blumenbach] Johann Friedrich Blumenbach (1752–1840), German scientist concerned with racial classification; his *On the Natural Variety of Mankind* was published in 1755.

650.34 A MAN WITHOUT A NAME.] Brown's fanciful account of his own escape.

653.12–19 'O, hail . . . slaves!'"] Richard Robert Madden, "Hail Columbia, Happy Land!" published in the Appendix of *A Twelvemonth's Residence in the West Indies* (1835).

655.5–6 Hon. Gerrit Smith] Smith (1797–1874), abolitionist, philanthropist, and U.S. congressman from New York State.

655.20 Captain Rynders] Isaiah Rynders (1804–1885), a New York gang leader who engaged in voter intimidation and election fraud on behalf of the Democratic Party.

656.9 Robert Osborn, . . . *The Watchman*] Osborn (1800–1878) founded the abolitionist paper *The Watchman and Jamaica Free Press* with Edward Jordan in 1829.

660.10 McClellan] George B. McClellan (1826–1885), commander of the Army of the Potomac from July 1861 until November 1862; he subsequently ran unsuccessfully against Lincoln on the Democratic ticket in the election of 1864.

660.13 contrabands] Term employed for slaves who escaped to safety across Union lines.

664.2–4 "In war . . . SHAKSPEARE.] *Richard II*, II.i.173–74.

665.8 Tillman] William Tillman, a black steward and cook who served aboard the merchant schooner *S.J. Waring*. When the ship was commandeered by Confederate privateer *Jeff Davis* off New Jersey in July 1861 and rerouted toward Charleston, Tillman led a successful rebellion that regained control from the Confederate crew and returned the ship to New York.

665.15 General Hunter] David Hunter (1802–1886), Union general who on his own authority issued a general order in May 1862 emancipating slaves in South Carolina, Georgia, and Florida; the order was immediately rescinded by Lincoln. Soon thereafter Hunter began recruiting ex-slaves as soldiers in South Carolina, until forced to desist by the War Department.

665.19–20 Thomas Wentworth Higginson] Higginson (1823–1911) was an abolitionist, minister, and writer who served as colonel of the first federally authorized black regiment in the Civil War, the 1st South Carolina Volunteers. His *Life in a Black Regiment* was published in 1870.

666.22 New Orleans . . . General Butler] Benjamin Franklin Butler (1818–1893), Union major general, established a precedent in 1861 by classifying slaves escaping to Union positions in Virginia as contrabands, or confiscated property (see note 660.13). In May 1862 he commanded the troops that occupied New Orleans and governed the city until December.

667.11 Port Hudson] From May 22 to July 9, 1863, the Union army besieged Confederate forces in Port Hudson, Louisiana.

667.33 General Dwight] William Dwight Jr. (1831–1888).

668.26–29 "'Charge!' Trump . . . rush."] George Henry Boker, "The Black Regiment" (1863).

671.11 B. F. Flanders] Louisiana Republican Benjamin Franklin Flanders (1816–1896), a special agent in the U.S. Treasury Department during the Civil War who later became a supervising agent in the Freedmen's Bureau for the Gulf region. He was appointed governor of Louisiana during military Reconstruction and served from June 1867 to January 1868.

671.21–26 "Freemen, now's . . . Right!"] William Augustus Muhlenberg, "On for Freedom: A Republican Hymn, written for the Presidential Election of 1860."

MY SOUTHERN HOME

675.4–8 "Go, little . . . *Southey*.] See note 215.6–10.

681.10 Pride of China] Better known as chinaberry (*Melia azedarach*), a spreading tree native to Asia, widely cultivated in the American South.

681.29 "F. F. V.' s,"] First Families of Virginia.

692.7–9 "He that knoweth . . . stripes,"] Cf. Luke 12:47.

694.34 organ of alimentativeness] In phrenology, the organ, located toward the ear, that dictates an appetite for food.

698.35–36 'While the lamp . . . return.'] Isaac Watts, "Life Is the Time to Serve the Lord" (1707).

701.31 calomel] Mercury chloride, used as a diuretic and laxative in the nineteenth century.

707.25–26 Scripter says . . . quit it] Cf. 1 Corinthians 8:9–11.

710.30 Father Gabriel, blow your horn] Cf. 1 Thessalonians 4:16–17.

720.28–35 I'm a gwine . . . lan'.] From the traditional plantation song "Gwine Up."

742.31–743.2 "When I was . . . *Cho.*] "O Redeemed," a spiritual.

743.14–15 "hewers of wood, and drawers of water."] Cf. Joshua 9:21.

743.17 amativeness] In phrenology, the faculty associated with sexual attraction and love.

744.6 "Haverly's Ministrels,"] J. H. Haverly's United Mastodon Minstrels, a popular minstrel troupe created in 1877.

744.7–8 Sam Lucas or Billy Kersands.] Lucas (1850–1916) was an African American performer who started his career as a blackface minstrel and later starred in dramatic roles, including Uncle Tom. Kersands (1842–1915) was an African American comedian and dancer best known for his work in blackface minstrelsy.

756.17–20 "Vice is . . . embrace."] Pope, *An Essay on Man*, Epistle II.

767. 27 Fowler] Orson Squire Fowler (1809–1887), publisher and editor of *The American Phrenological Journal* (1863–80).

769.20 Morpheus] A god of dreams in Ovid's *Metamorphoses.*

783.16 Carpet Knight] Someone who receives knighthood without earning it in war or tournament; figuratively, someone who spends time in idleness or luxury.

783.20–21 the noblest Roman of them all.] *Julius Caesar*, V.v.68.

784.30–32 The insults . . . Owen Lovejoy] John P. Hale (1806–1873) of New Hampshire, first elected to the Senate in 1847, was the most outspoken opponent of slavery in that body until he was joined by Salmon P. Chase in 1849 and Charles Sumner in 1851; Joshua Reed Giddings (1795–1864) of Ohio; Owen Lovejoy (1811–1864) of Illinois, brother of the martyred newspaper editor Elijah Lovejoy.

784.36–37 Hon. O. Lovejoy . . . was speaking] On April 5, 1860.

784.39 Mr. Barksdale, of Mississippi—] William Barksdale (1821–1863), U.S. congressman from Mississippi, 1853–61, and later a Confederate general; he was killed at Gettysburg.

785.3 Mr. Boyce] William Waters Boyce (1818–1890) U.S. congressman from South Carolina, 1853–60, and later a Confederate congressman.

785.5 Mr. Gartrell] Lucius Jeremiah Gartrell (1821–1891), U.S. congressman from Georgia, 1857–61, and later a Confederate general.

785.9 Mr. Ashmore] John Ashmore (1819–1871) was a U.S. congressman from South Carolina, 1859–60.

785.12 Mr. Singleton] Otho Robards Singleton (1814–1889), U.S. congressman from Mississippi (1853–55 and 1857–61) and later a Confederate congressman.

785.20 Mr. Martin] Elbert Sevier Martin (c. 1829–1876), U.S. congressman from Virginia, 1859–61, and later a Confederate army captain.

785.22 hang you as high as Haman.] Cf. Esther 7.

786.31–787.12 "Oh! breth-er-en, . . . down."] From the spiritual "My Way's Cloudy."

794.7 White Leaguer] Member of the Louisiana-based paramilitary group founded in 1874 that employed violence and intimidation to suppress the black vote and defeat Republican candidates.

815.17 Freedman's Saving Bank.] The Freedman's Saving and Trust Company was a U.S. government-chartered bank established in 1865 to help aid the economic development of newly emancipated African Americans after the Civil War. It collapsed in 1874.

817.36 Rev. John Jasper] Jasper (1812–1901) was a former slave who achieved fame as a fundamentalist preacher in antebellum Virginia; in 1867 he founded the Sixth Mount Zion Baptist Church in Richmond.

820.18 Bishop Kean] John Joseph Keane (1839–1918), Roman Catholic bishop of Richmond, 1878–88, and archbishop of Dubuque, 1900–11.

820.21 Rev. Moses D. Hoge, D. D.] Moses Drury Hoge (1818–1899), minister of Richmond's Second Presbyterian Church.

839.28–30 Shylock says: . . . you."] *The Merchant of Venice*, I.iii.35–9.

840.18 Cadet Whittaker] Johnson Chesnut Whittaker (1858–1931), one of the first African Americans to earn an appointment to the United States Military Academy at West Point. In 1880 he was assaulted by three fellow cadets and then accused of faking the attack. Whittaker was convicted by a court-martial whose verdict was later overturned, but in 1882 he was expelled for failing an exam. His name was not cleared until he was posthumously commissioned by President Bill Clinton in 1995.

842.6 Sherborn prison] The Massachusetts Reformatory for Women, which opened in 1877.

844.40–845.1 "don't stand . . . go."] *Macbeth*, III.iv.118–19.

SPEECHES & PUBLIC LETTERS

857.6 Caspar Hauser] Kaspar Hauser (c. 1812–1833) was a German youth of undetermined parentage who claimed to have grown up in isolation, confined to a dark cell.

860.39 Dr. Furman] Richard Furman (1755–1825), South Carolina Baptist leader.

867.24–31 "Shall every . . . curse?"] John Greenleaf Whittier, "Our Countrymen in Chains!" (1837).

868.22–29 "United States, . . . Negro-scars."] Thomas Campbell, "To the United States of America" (1838).

869.18–25 "Our plant . . . chain."] "The Liberty Party," published in the *Liberty and Anti-Slavery Song Book* (1842).

870.9 caufles] Coffles: groups of slaves chained together during transportation.

875.6 Simms] Thomas Sims (b. 1834?), fugitive slave from Georgia who was captured in Boston and returned to his master in the face of public protest in April 1851. He escaped again in 1863 and returned to Boston.

882.1 storming of Fort Griswold] Revolutionary War battle fought on September 6, 1781, at which a larger British force overwhelmed the American defenders.

885.12 Mr. Pilsbury] Parker Pillsbury (1809–1898), New Hampshire abolitionist associated with William Lloyd Garrison; a frequent lecture partner of Brown.

890.23–24 Bloody Assize . . . Jeffries] The "Bloody Assizes" were a series of trials conducted in England by Lord Chief Justice George Jeffreys in the wake of the Monmouth Rebellion in 1685 that resulted in about two hundred executions for treason.

893.30 "hewers of wood and drawers of water."] Cf. Joshua 9:21.

894.6 Moses Stuart] Stuart (1780–1852) was a religious scholar who in *Conscience and the Constitution* (1850) argued for biblical justification of slavery, but called for voluntary emancipation of slaves by their owners.

894.11–12 "Slavery is the corner stone . . . church member.] The South Carolina senator, congressman, and governor James Henry Hammond attributed to onetime governor George McDuffie the words "Slavery is the cornerstone of our republican edifice."

894.12–13 "Two hundred . . . another;] Henry Clay, "Petitions for the Abolition of Slavery," speech delivered in the Senate on February 7, 1839.

894.36–38 Dominican Republic . . . Emperor of Hayti] Faustin-Élie Soulouque (1782–1867), emperor of Haiti, 1849–59.

895.21–22 let us remember . . . them.] Cf. Hebrews 13:3.

899.20–21 Abbott Lawrence] Abbott Lawrence (1792–1855), U.S. minister to the United Kingdom, 1849–52.

900.21–25 Lovejoy; to Burr, . . . Mrs. Douglass] For Lovejoy, see note 15.5–6. Alanson Work, James E. Burr, and George Thompson were arrested and imprisoned in Missouri for attempting to help slaves escape. Charles Turner Torrey (1813–1846) was convicted of helping slaves escape from Maryland and died in prison of tuberculosis. Calvin Fairbank (1816–1898) was a Methodist minister who was imprisoned in Kentucky in 1845–49 and 1852–64 for helping slaves escape from the state. Delia Ann Webster (1817–1876) was briefly imprisoned in Kentucky for aiding Fairbank in rescuing slaves. Margaret Douglass, a former slaveholder, was jailed for a month in Virginia in 1854 for teaching free blacks to read and write in violation of state law.

904.34 William H. Day] Day (1825–1900), one of the first black graduates of Oberlin, worked for the Freedman's Bureau and was ordained as a minister in the African Methodist Episcopal Church in 1867.

907.22–24 the Rosetta slave-case . . . Rev. H. M. Dennison] In 1855 Rosetta Armstead, a sixteen-year-old slave, was travelling with her owner's agent from Kentucky to Virginia by way of Ohio when antislavery activists obtained a writ of habeas corpus from the probate court in Columbus. Henry Dennison, her owner and the son-in-law of former president John Tyler, had Armstead arrested and brought before the U.S. fugitive slave commissioner at Cincinnati for trial. Her attorneys, who included Salmon P. Chase and future president Rutherford B. Hayes, won a ruling in state court that the right of transit of slave property did not exist under Ohio law and that Armstead had been freed by being brought into the state. They then successfully argued before the federal commissioner that since she had been brought into Ohio by her owner's agent, she was not legally a fugitive.

907.26–27 ex-Senator Chase . . . George Pugh, Esq.)] Salmon Portland Chase (1808–1873), U.S. senator from Ohio, 1849–55; George Pugh, U.S. senator from Ohio, 1855–61.

908.19–20 Thomas Morris, . . . reply to Henry Clay.] Thomas Morris (1776–1844) was a U.S. senator from Ohio, 1833–39. His reply to an anti-abolitionist speech of Henry Clay was delivered in the Senate on February 9, 1839.

912.36–37 as Theodore Parker would say] See note 354.19. Parker came under criticism from abolitionists for his views on racial characteristics, as in an address delivered on May 12, 1854: "There are [in America] twenty-four millions of men; fifteen and a half millions with Anglo-Saxon blood in their veins—strong, real Anglo-Saxon blood; eight millions and a half more of other families and races, just enough to temper the Anglo-Saxon blood, to furnish a new composite tribe, far better, I trust, than the old."

918.34 the Branded Hand] Jonathan Walker (1799–1878), an abolitionist arrested in Florida while attempting to help slaves escape, had the letters "S.S." (Slave Stealer) branded on his hand in 1844.

925.16 Bancroft] George Bancroft's multivolume *History of the United States* was published from 1854 to 1878.

927.16 Dr. Blagden] George Washington Blagden (1802–1884), pastor at the Old South Church in Boston.

927.33 Mr. Wade] Benjamin Wade (1800–1878), a Republican senator from Ohio, argued in a speech opposing the expansion of slavery into the territories given on March 7, 1860, for colonization of free blacks in "some congenial clime, where they may be maintained, to the mutual benefit of all," concluding, "I hope, after that is done, to hear no more about negro equality or anything of that kind."

929.26–27 Dr. Cheever] George Barrell Cheever (1807–1890), pastor of the Church of Puritans in New York City.

931.4–11 "Our plant . . . chain"] See note 869.18–25.

932.23–24 Hon. W. L. Yancey] William Lowndes Yancey (1814–1863).

933.2 'Helper's Impending Crisis'] In *The Impending Crisis of the South* (1857), Hinton Rowan Helper of North Carolina argued that slavery damaged the southern economy and prevented the economic advancement of non-slaveholding whites.

933.33–35 Judge Gaston, . . . State vs. Manuel] William J. Gaston (1778–1844), North Carolina state supreme court judge, presided over the case of *State vs. Manuel* (1838), in which William Manuel, a freed slave, was ordered to work off a fine of $20 because he did not have the money to pay it. Gaston overruled the lower court's verdict, ruling that Manuel, as a citizen of the state, had a right to plead insolvency.

935.4–9 'In all social . . . slaves.'] From a March 4, 1858, speech before the U.S. Senate on the admission of Kansas.

937.30 The Hon. C. C. Clay] Clement Claiborne Clay Jr. (1816–1882), U.S. senator from Alabama, 1853–61, and Confederate senator, 1861–63. Brown was mistaken; Yancey was never elected to the U.S. Senate.

938.6 'Fleetwood's Life of Christ,'] The Reverend John Fleetwood, *The Life of Our Lord and Saviour Jesus Christ* (1778).

945.12 an American Senator] See note 482.32.

945.23–27 "Who steals . . . indeed."] *Othello*, III.iii.155–61.

951.1 Gen. Wool] John Ellis Wool (1784–1869).

952.11–18 "Our plant . . . chain."] See note 869.18–25.

956.38 Dr. Delany's book] Martin R. Delany's *The Condition, Elevation, Emigration and Destiny of the Colored People of the United States* (1852).

963.15 P.R.W.G. Templar Hastings] Past Right Worthy Good Templar Samuel Dexter Hastings (1816–1903), originally from Massachusetts, an antislavery and temperance activist who served a decade in the Wisconsin legislature.

963.16 R.W.G.L.] Right Worthy Grand Lodge.

964.10 Joseph Malins] Malins (1844–1926) led the English branch of a temperance organization, the International Order of Good Templars. He resisted segregation until 1887, when he compromised to allow the reunion of the American and English branches.

964.17 Col. Hickman, as R.W.G.Coun.] Right Worthy Grand Counsellor John J. Hickman (1839–1902), born in Lexington, Kentucky, leader of the segregationist faction of the I.O.G.T.

966.16 the Louisville Session of 1876] At this annual meeting of the I.O.G.T., the organization split over the issue of the segregation of southern lodges.

966.25 Dr. Oronhyatekha] Peter Martin Oronhyatekha (1841–1907), Canadian Mohawk physician, scholar, and temperance activist.

967.24–25 "steal the livery . . . devil in."] See note 6.13–14.

968.34 James Yeames—] English temperance activist (1834–1931), author of *Life in London Alley* (1877), *Told with a Purpose: Temperance Papers for the People* (1880), and many other books. Brown worked with him during his 1877 temperance tour of the British Isles; Yeames later moved to Boston, where he became a close friend of Brown and spoke at his funeral.

Index

This book is set in 10 point ITC Galliard Pro, a face designed for digital composition by Matthew Carter and based on the sixteenth-century face Granjon. The paper is acid-free lightweight opaque and meets the requirements for permanence of the American National Standards Institute. The binding material is Brillianta, a woven rayon cloth made by Van Heek–Scholco Textielfabrieken, Holland. Composition by Dedicated Book Services. Printing and binding by Edwards Brothers Malloy, Ann Arbor. Designed by Bruce Campbell.

THE LIBRARY OF AMERICA SERIES

The Library of America fosters appreciation and pride in America's literary heritage by publishing, and keeping permanently in print, authoritative editions of America's best and most significant writing. An independent nonprofit organization, it was founded in 1979 with seed funding from the National Endowment for the Humanities and the Ford Foundation.

1. Herman Melville: *Typee, Omoo, Mardi*
2. Nathaniel Hawthorne: *Tales and Sketches*
3. Walt Whitman: *Poetry and Prose*
4. Harriet Beecher Stowe: *Three Novels*
5. Mark Twain: *Mississippi Writings*
6. Jack London: *Novels and Stories*
7. Jack London: *Novels and Social Writings*
8. William Dean Howells: *Novels 1875–1886*
9. Herman Melville: *Redburn, White-Jacket, Moby-Dick*
10. Nathaniel Hawthorne: *Collected Novels*
11. Francis Parkman: *France and England in North America*, vol. I
12. Francis Parkman: *France and England in North America*, vol. II
13. Henry James: *Novels 1871–1880*
14. Henry Adams: *Novels, Mont Saint Michel, The Education*
15. Ralph Waldo Emerson: *Essays and Lectures*
16. Washington Irving: *History, Tales and Sketches*
17. Thomas Jefferson: *Writings*
18. Stephen Crane: *Prose and Poetry*
19. Edgar Allan Poe: *Poetry and Tales*
20. Edgar Allan Poe: *Essays and Reviews*
21. Mark Twain: *The Innocents Abroad, Roughing It*
22. Henry James: *Literary Criticism: Essays, American & English Writers*
23. Henry James: *Literary Criticism: European Writers & The Prefaces*
24. Herman Melville: *Pierre, Israel Potter, The Confidence-Man, Tales & Billy Budd*
25. William Faulkner: *Novels 1930–1935*
26. James Fenimore Cooper: *The Leatherstocking Tales*, vol. I
27. James Fenimore Cooper: *The Leatherstocking Tales*, vol. II
28. Henry David Thoreau: *A Week, Walden, The Maine Woods, Cape Cod*
29. Henry James: *Novels 1881–1886*
30. Edith Wharton: *Novels*
31. Henry Adams: *History of the U.S. during the Administrations of Jefferson*
32. Henry Adams: *History of the U.S. during the Administrations of Madison*
33. Frank Norris: *Novels and Essays*
34. W.E.B. Du Bois: *Writings*
35. Willa Cather: *Early Novels and Stories*
36. Theodore Dreiser: *Sister Carrie, Jennie Gerhardt, Twelve Men*

37a. Benjamin Franklin: *Silence Dogood, The Busy-Body, & Early Writings*

37b. Benjamin Franklin: *Autobiography, Poor Richard, & Later Writings*

38. William James: *Writings 1902–1910*
39. Flannery O'Connor: *Collected Works*
40. Eugene O'Neill: *Complete Plays 1913–1920*
41. Eugene O'Neill: *Complete Plays 1920–1931*
42. Eugene O'Neill: *Complete Plays 1932–1943*
43. Henry James: *Novels 1886–1890*
44. William Dean Howells: *Novels 1886–1888*
45. Abraham Lincoln: *Speeches and Writings 1832–1858*
46. Abraham Lincoln: *Speeches and Writings 1859–1865*
47. Edith Wharton: *Novellas and Other Writings*
48. William Faulkner: *Novels 1936–1940*
49. Willa Cather: *Later Novels*
50. Ulysses S. Grant: *Memoirs and Selected Letters*
51. William Tecumseh Sherman: *Memoirs*
52. Washington Irving: *Bracebridge Hall, Tales of a Traveller, The Alhambra*
53. Francis Parkman: *The Oregon Trail, The Conspiracy of Pontiac*
54. James Fenimore Cooper: *Sea Tales: The Pilot, The Red Rover*
55. Richard Wright: *Early Works*
56. Richard Wright: *Later Works*
57. Willa Cather: *Stories, Poems, and Other Writings*
58. William James: *Writings 1878–1899*
59. Sinclair Lewis: *Main Street & Babbitt*
60. Mark Twain: *Collected Tales, Sketches, Speeches, & Essays 1852–1890*
61. Mark Twain: *Collected Tales, Sketches, Speeches, & Essays 1891–1910*
62. *The Debate on the Constitution: Part One*
63. *The Debate on the Constitution: Part Two*
64. Henry James: *Collected Travel Writings: Great Britain & America*
65. Henry James: *Collected Travel Writings: The Continent*

66. *American Poetry: The Nineteenth Century*, Vol. 1
67. *American Poetry: The Nineteenth Century*, Vol. 2
68. Frederick Douglass: *Autobiographies*
69. Sarah Orne Jewett: *Novels and Stories*
70. Ralph Waldo Emerson: *Collected Poems and Translations*
71. Mark Twain: *Historical Romances*
72. John Steinbeck: *Novels and Stories 1932–1937*
73. William Faulkner: *Novels 1942–1954*
74. Zora Neale Hurston: *Novels and Stories*
75. Zora Neale Hurston: *Folklore, Memoirs, and Other Writings*
76. Thomas Paine: *Collected Writings*
77. *Reporting World War II: American Journalism 1938–1944*
78. *Reporting World War II: American Journalism 1944–1946*
79. Raymond Chandler: *Stories and Early Novels*
80. Raymond Chandler: *Later Novels and Other Writings*
81. Robert Frost: *Collected Poems, Prose, & Plays*
82. Henry James: *Complete Stories 1892–1898*
83. Henry James: *Complete Stories 1898–1910*
84. William Bartram: *Travels and Other Writings*
85. John Dos Passos: *U.S.A.*
86. John Steinbeck: *The Grapes of Wrath and Other Writings 1936–1941*
87. Vladimir Nabokov: *Novels and Memoirs 1941–1951*
88. Vladimir Nabokov: *Novels 1955–1962*
89. Vladimir Nabokov: *Novels 1969–1974*
90. James Thurber: *Writings and Drawings*
91. George Washington: *Writings*
92. John Muir: *Nature Writings*
93. Nathanael West: *Novels and Other Writings*
94. *Crime Novels: American Noir of the 1930s and 40s*
95. *Crime Novels: American Noir of the 1950s*
96. Wallace Stevens: *Collected Poetry and Prose*
97. James Baldwin: *Early Novels and Stories*
98. James Baldwin: *Collected Essays*
99. Gertrude Stein: *Writings 1903–1932*
100. Gertrude Stein: *Writings 1932–1946*
101. Eudora Welty: *Complete Novels*
102. Eudora Welty: *Stories, Essays, & Memoir*
103. Charles Brockden Brown: *Three Gothic Novels*
104. *Reporting Vietnam: American Journalism 1959–1969*
105. *Reporting Vietnam: American Journalism 1969–1975*
106. Henry James: *Complete Stories 1874–1884*
107. Henry James: *Complete Stories 1884–1891*
108. *American Sermons: The Pilgrims to Martin Luther King Jr.*
109. James Madison: *Writings*
110. Dashiell Hammett: *Complete Novels*
111. Henry James: *Complete Stories 1864–1874*
112. William Faulkner: *Novels 1957–1962*
113. John James Audubon: *Writings & Drawings*
114. *Slave Narratives*
115. *American Poetry: The Twentieth Century*, Vol. 1
116. *American Poetry: The Twentieth Century*, Vol. 2
117. F. Scott Fitzgerald: *Novels and Stories 1920–1922*
118. Henry Wadsworth Longfellow: *Poems and Other Writings*
119. Tennessee Williams: *Plays 1937–1955*
120. Tennessee Williams: *Plays 1957–1980*
121. Edith Wharton: *Collected Stories 1891–1910*
122. Edith Wharton: *Collected Stories 1911–1937*
123. *The American Revolution: Writings from the War of Independence*
124. Henry David Thoreau: *Collected Essays and Poems*
125. Dashiell Hammett: *Crime Stories and Other Writings*
126. Dawn Powell: *Novels 1930–1942*
127. Dawn Powell: *Novels 1944–1962*
128. Carson McCullers: *Complete Novels*
129. Alexander Hamilton: *Writings*
130. Mark Twain: *The Gilded Age and Later Novels*
131. Charles W. Chesnutt: *Stories, Novels, and Essays*
132. John Steinbeck: *Novels 1942–1952*
133. Sinclair Lewis: *Arrowsmith, Elmer Gantry, Dodsworth*
134. Paul Bowles: *The Sheltering Sky, Let It Come Down, The Spider's House*
135. Paul Bowles: *Collected Stories & Later Writings*
136. Kate Chopin: *Complete Novels & Stories*
137. *Reporting Civil Rights: American Journalism 1941–1963*
138. *Reporting Civil Rights: American Journalism 1963–1973*
139. Henry James: *Novels 1896–1899*
140. Theodore Dreiser: *An American Tragedy*
141. Saul Bellow: *Novels 1944–1953*
142. John Dos Passos: *Novels 1920–1925*

143. John Dos Passos: *Travel Books and Other Writings*
144. Ezra Pound: *Poems and Translations*
145. James Weldon Johnson: *Writings*
146. Washington Irving: *Three Western Narratives*
147. Alexis de Tocqueville: *Democracy in America*
148. James T. Farrell: *Studs Lonigan: A Trilogy*
149. Isaac Bashevis Singer: *Collected Stories I*
150. Isaac Bashevis Singer: *Collected Stories II*
151. Isaac Bashevis Singer: *Collected Stories III*
152. Kaufman & Co.: *Broadway Comedies*
153. Theodore Roosevelt: *The Rough Riders, An Autobiography*
154. Theodore Roosevelt: *Letters and Speeches*
155. H. P. Lovecraft: *Tales*
156. Louisa May Alcott: *Little Women, Little Men, Jo's Boys*
157. Philip Roth: *Novels & Stories 1959–1962*
158. Philip Roth: *Novels 1967–1972*
159. James Agee: *Let Us Now Praise Famous Men, A Death in the Family*
160. James Agee: *Film Writing & Selected Journalism*
161. Richard Henry Dana, Jr.: *Two Years Before the Mast & Other Voyages*
162. Henry James: *Novels 1901–1902*
163. Arthur Miller: *Collected Plays 1944–1961*
164. William Faulkner: *Novels 1926–1929*
165. Philip Roth: *Novels 1973–1977*
166. *American Speeches: Part One*
167. *American Speeches: Part Two*
168. Hart Crane: *Complete Poems & Selected Letters*
169. Saul Bellow: *Novels 1956–1964*
170. John Steinbeck: *Travels with Charley and Later Novels*
171. Capt. John Smith: *Writings with Other Narratives*
172. Thornton Wilder: *Collected Plays & Writings on Theater*
173. Philip K. Dick: *Four Novels of the 1960s*
174. Jack Kerouac: *Road Novels 1957–1960*
175. Philip Roth: *Zuckerman Bound*
176. Edmund Wilson: *Literary Essays & Reviews of the 1920s & 30s*
177. Edmund Wilson: *Literary Essays & Reviews of the 1930s & 40s*
178. *American Poetry: The 17th & 18th Centuries*
179. William Maxwell: *Early Novels & Stories*
180. Elizabeth Bishop: *Poems, Prose, & Letters*
181. A. J. Liebling: *World War II Writings*
182s. *American Earth: Environmental Writing Since Thoreau*
183. Philip K. Dick: *Five Novels of the 1960s & 70s*
184. William Maxwell: *Later Novels & Stories*
185. Philip Roth: *Novels & Other Narratives 1986–1991*
186. Katherine Anne Porter: *Collected Stories & Other Writings*
187. John Ashbery: *Collected Poems 1956–1987*
188. John Cheever: *Collected Stories & Other Writings*
189. John Cheever: *Complete Novels*
190. Lafcadio Hearn: *American Writings*
191. A. J. Liebling: *The Sweet Science & Other Writings*
192s. *The Lincoln Anthology: Great Writers on His Life and Legacy from 1860 to Now*
193. Philip K. Dick: *VALIS & Later Novels*
194. Thornton Wilder: *The Bridge of San Luis Rey and Other Novels 1926–1948*
195. Raymond Carver: *Collected Stories*
196. *American Fantastic Tales: Terror and the Uncanny from Poe to the Pulps*
197. *American Fantastic Tales: Terror and the Uncanny from the 1940s to Now*
198. John Marshall: *Writings*
199s. *The Mark Twain Anthology: Great Writers on His Life and Works*
200. Mark Twain: *A Tramp Abroad, Following the Equator, Other Travels*
201. Ralph Waldo Emerson: *Selected Journals 1820–1842*
202. Ralph Waldo Emerson: *Selected Journals 1841–1877*
203. *The American Stage: Writing on Theater from Washington Irving to Tony Kushner*
204. Shirley Jackson: *Novels & Stories*
205. Philip Roth: *Novels 1993–1995*
206. H. L. Mencken: *Prejudices: First, Second, and Third Series*
207. H. L. Mencken: *Prejudices: Fourth, Fifth, and Sixth Series*
208. John Kenneth Galbraith: *The Affluent Society and Other Writings 1952–1967*
209. Saul Bellow: *Novels 1970–1982*
210. Lynd Ward: *Gods' Man, Madman's Drum, Wild Pilgrimage*
211. Lynd Ward: *Prelude to a Million Years, Song Without Words, Vertigo*
212. *The Civil War: The First Year Told by Those Who Lived It*
213. John Adams: *Revolutionary Writings 1755–1775*
214. John Adams: *Revolutionary Writings 1775–1783*
215. Henry James: *Novels 1903–1911*
216. Kurt Vonnegut: *Novels & Stories 1963–1973*

217. *Harlem Renaissance: Five Novels of the 1920s*
218. *Harlem Renaissance: Four Novels of the 1930s*
219. Ambrose Bierce: *The Devil's Dictionary, Tales, & Memoirs*
220. Philip Roth: *The American Trilogy 1997–2000*
221. *The Civil War: The Second Year Told by Those Who Lived It*
222. Barbara W. Tuchman: *The Guns of August & The Proud Tower*
223. Arthur Miller: *Collected Plays 1964–1982*
224. Thornton Wilder: *The Eighth Day, Theophilus North, Autobiographical Writings*
225. David Goodis: *Five Noir Novels of the 1940s & 50s*
226. Kurt Vonnegut: *Novels & Stories 1950–1962*
227. *American Science Fiction: Four Classic Novels 1953–1956*
228. *American Science Fiction: Five Classic Novels 1956–1958*
229. Laura Ingalls Wilder: *The Little House Books, Volume One*
230. Laura Ingalls Wilder: *The Little House Books, Volume Two*
231. Jack Kerouac: *Collected Poems*
232. *The War of 1812: Writings from America's Second War of Independence*
233. *American Antislavery Writings: Colonial Beginnings to Emancipation*
234. *The Civil War: The Third Year Told by Those Who Lived It*
235. Sherwood Anderson: *Collected Stories*
236. Philip Roth: *Novels 2001–2007*
237. Philip Roth: *Nemeses*
238. Aldo Leopold: *A Sand County Almanac & Other Writings on Ecology and Conservation*
239. May Swenson: *Collected Poems*
240. W. S. Merwin: *Collected Poems 1952–1993*
241. W. S. Merwin: *Collected Poems 1996–2011*
242. John Updike: *Collected Early Stories*
243. John Updike: *Collected Later Stories*
244. Ring Lardner: *Stories & Other Writings*
245. Jonathan Edwards: *Writings from the Great Awakening*
246. Susan Sontag: *Essays of the 1960s & 70s*

To subscribe to the series or to order individual copies, please visit www.loa.org or call (800) 964.5778.

Book Return Policy - 7 days*
RECEIPT REQUIRED
*Coursebooks: 3 days
Studyguides: No Return

Harvard COOP
1400 Massachusetts Avenue
Cambridge, MA 02238
(617) 499-2000

HARVARD COOP 617-499-2000
thecoop.com

STORE:03000 REG:001 TRAN#:4129
CASHIER:EMILY B

William Wells Brow
TRADE
9781598532913 T
(1 @ 40.00)
PROMO 10% (4.00)
(1 @ 36.00) 36.00
Bernard Malamud: N
TRADE
9781598532920 T
(1 @ 35.00)
PROMO 10% (3.50)
(1 @ 31.50) 31.50

Subtotal 67.50
T1 Sales Tax (06.250%) 4.22
TOTAL 71.72
CHECK 71.72
Acct#: XXXXX4295
Chk#: 6149
Entry Method: Keyed

Amount Saved 7.50

1400 MASS AVE
CAMBRIDGE MA, 02138

V200.69 03/20/2014 01:03PM

CUSTOMER COPY

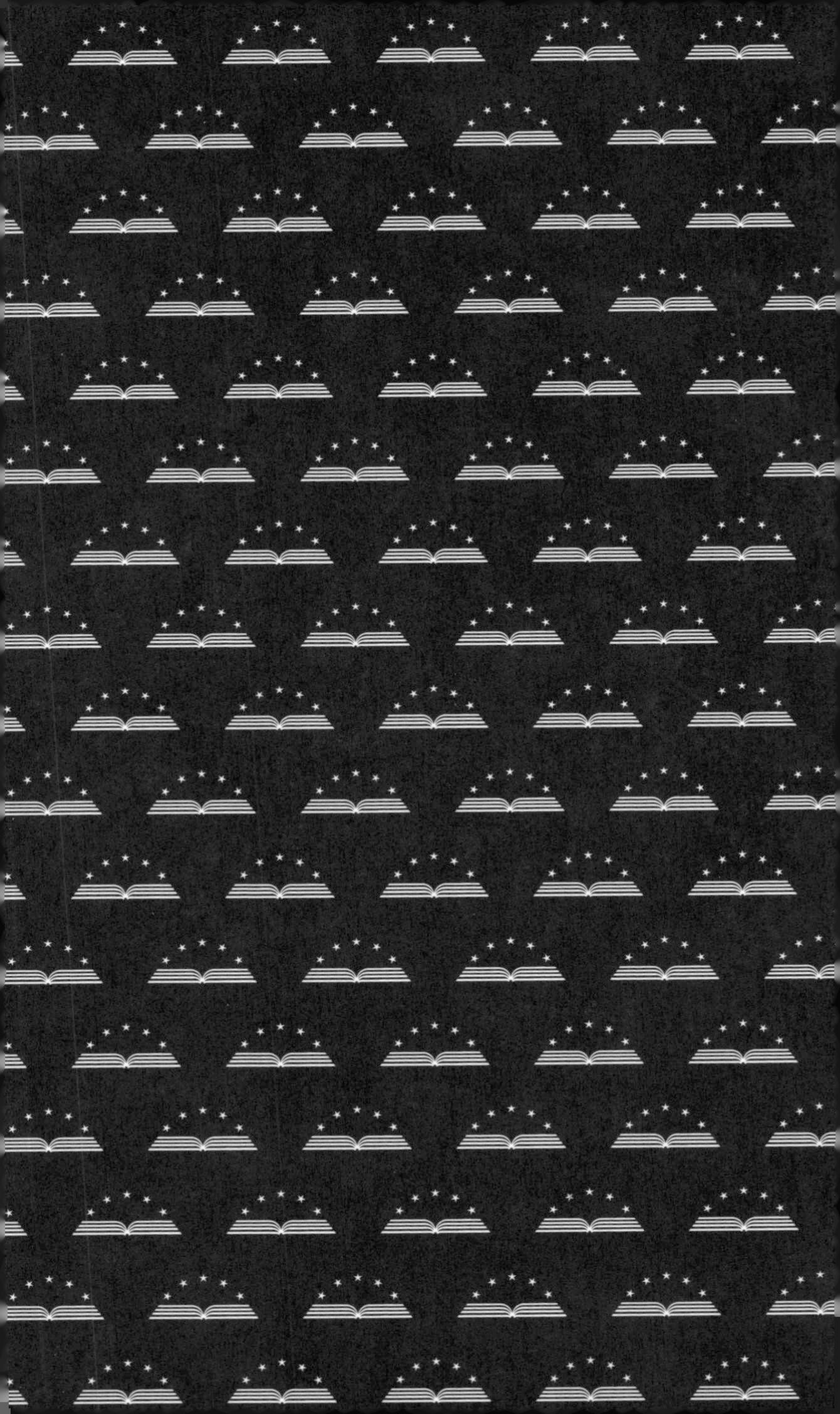